The Saxon Chronicle

Donated by

Michael Dearing
2008

The Saxon Chronicle

Volume I
The Capitalists

Jane Ellen Swan

VANTAGE PRESS
New York

Published by Vantage Press, Inc.
516 West 34th Street, New York, New York 10001

Manufactured in the United States of America
ISBN: 0-533-12859-5

Library of Congress Catalog Card No.: 98-90600

0 9 8 7 6 5 4 3 2 1

To NANNIE
Who started it all

In Memoriam

The Capitalists

Book I
The Opportunists

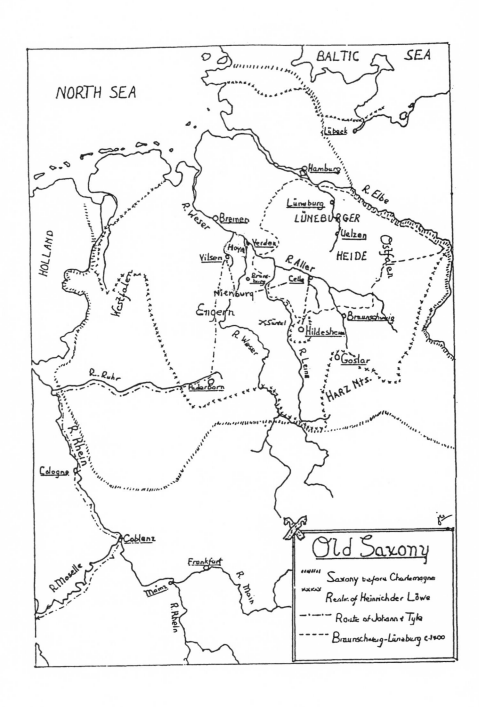

BALTIC SEA

NORTH SEA

Lübeck

Hamburg

R. Elbe

Lüneburg

LÜNEBURGER

Uelzen

HEIDE

Ostfalen

R. Weser

Bremen

Verden

Hoya

R. Aller

Vilsen

Celle

Braunschweig

Nienburg

Engern

Braunschweig

×Süntel

Hildesheim

HOLLAND

Westfalen

R. Weser

R. Leine

Goslar

R. Ruhr

HARZ Mts.

Paderborn

R. Rhein

Cologne

Coblenz

Frankfurt

R. Main

R. Moselle

Mainz

R. Rhein

Old Saxony

Saxony before Charlemagne

Realm of Heinrich der Löwe

Route of Johann & Tyle

Braunschweig-Lüneburg c.1400

1

AD 782

The lone rider moved leisurely along the path that followed the river's bank. At least he appeared to be riding leisurely, but his pace was steady and deliberate and his alert brown eyes scanned the countryside with caution. Horse and rider seemed to blend into one entity. The rider's short brown hair, only a few shades lighter than the glossy coat of his mount, his heavily padded leather jerkin and the leather thongs that bound his shoes and leggings matched the horse's coloring. Only the leggings themselves and what could be seen of his shirt under the leather armor were of a faded green wool. His heavy traveling cloak, which also served him as a sleeping mat and blanket when on the road, was securely rolled behind him.

He was a young man, perhaps about eighteen, with the build and demeanor of a warrior, which, indeed, he was. His straight nose and firm, clean-shaven chin bespoke noble blood, a future leader. His heavily muscled thighs and arms rippled in perfect synchronization with the horse's, indicating a lifetime in the saddle. He was heavily armed. A broad sword hung from one side of his wide leather belt and a heavy, razor-sharp battle-axe from the other. Slung across his back was a sturdy bow and a quiver full of arrows. But he did not seem to expect immediate battle because his iron-encased pointed leather helmet and wooden leather-covered iron-studded shield were perched on the horse's back, in front of him. His only adornment was an exquisitely wrought golden belt buckle set with several precious stones. However, so that no glint from this might betray him to unwanted eyes, his old leather purse hung over it. The purse contained some cheese and hard black bread, the remains of his lunch, which he just might need on the morrow.

The horse's hoofs barely whispered on the sandy, grassy path, betraying their approach to no one. On their right wide marshes spread between the firm ground and the river itself, wide, placid, beautiful, peacefully meandering this way and that through the flat green fertile countryside. On their left side was dense forest, fir, pine, oak, beech, the colors of which blended so perfectly with horse and rider that any observer on the far side of the river would be hard put to notice them.

The river was the Weser. It rose in the southern mountains, flowing north and fed by many tributaries, finally to empty into the North Sea near the town of Bremen. It was the main highway, travel in those days being far easier by water than by land, through the middle of Engern, which in itself was the rich heartland of Saxony. From here, only a few hundred years earlier, had sailed the Saxon tribes who gave the name of their homeland and of several of their towns as well to the great isle of the northwest, England. Their cousins who had remained behind were now fighting for their homeland, their freedom, for their very lives against the invading Franks.

The Franks were another Germanic tribe, who some centuries before, during the great migrations, had invaded and settled in Roman Gaul. Under the influence of the Gallo-Romans the Franks had become somewhat civilized and, more importantly, had gradually given up their old gods and had been converted to Christianity. They were now reasonably unified under an enthusiastic young ruler named Karl. He was not yet called "the Great" or, as the late medieval chroniclers handed his name down to future generations, Charlemagne. Karl had been educated by the brilliant Celtic and Saxon monks from the north of England. He had even learned to read Latin, although he never mastered the more difficult art of writing. Along with his education he was imbued by the monks with a dream of restoring the Roman Empire to its former glory. But the empire of his dreams was to be under the aegis of the Franks.

Encouraged by the popes in Rome, who had long chafed under the belittling quarrels with the still-extant eastern half of the Roman Empire, Karl undertook to be their protector and champion. But the papal blessing added a new dimension to his dreams of empire, that of religious fanaticism. He had long lusted after the rich Saxon lands, and the fact that they were still "heathen", never having been conquered by Rome, now gave him the excuse, legitimate in his own eyes and those of the Pope, to invade Saxony and attempt to add it to his empire

Although travel by the many waterways of the land was the quickest and safest, there were, in fact, a number of roads crisscrossing the country, some very old, even predating the Romans. These were the Volksweg—Folkways—known in ancient times as the famous Amber Roads. Several

4

of them led all the way from Rome, across the Alps, and north to the Baltic and North Seas. They had been used by peaceful traders since time immemorial. Another bisected them running east out of Colonia Agrippina (now increasingly being called Köln or Cologne) to the coastal towns of Bremen and Hamburg.

The lone rider was now approaching this road, and it was apparent that he was becoming more cautious and alert than before. His eyes scanned the countryside, the river, the woods and most especially the path that lay ahead of him, his ears straining to catch the slightest sound. But all was quiet on this beautiful early fall afternoon. The air was crisp and cool, but the sun shone warm upon his back. Scarcely a leaf moved in the woods and even the birds seemed unusually still.

Why? he mused. Because all the spirits of the woods and the river, even the great gods themselves, were holding their breath wondering what was going to happen next. Why, oh, why won't this Frankish king Karl leave us alone? What have we ever done to him to merit his wrath? All we want is to be left in peace to farm our farms and hunt in our forests and dig in our mines. And freedom, yes, especially freedom to worship our gods as we always have. He and his chief priest in Rome claim their god is better than ours. How so? If he is truly a god of peace, he wouldn't let them bring war and burning and pillage and unspeakable atrocities. I can't understand it. If Wotan says, go to war, or Donar hurls a thunderbolt in anger, or Frigga says, bring the young maidens to serve my priests so you will have a bountiful harvest, that I can understand. There is no hypocrisy. Ah, me.

He thought of the last farms he had passed an hour or so ago surrounding the pretty little village of Bücken, rich, fertile, so far unharmed. Milk-heavy cattle, fat pigs, bustling chickens, the superb horses for which Saxony was famous, and the fields of ripe grain just about ready to be harvested, in which nestled the neat little half-timbered, thatched-roof houses, each with the crossed Saxon horses at the gable peak and the eternal fire always burning on the round open hearth. How much longer would they stand? And then it suddenly dawned on him. Of course, this religion thing is just their excuse. What they really want is the wealth of our land, the richness of our farms and forests and mines. And the only way they can get it is to kill us all off — or make us slaves of their god.

He had ridden out that morning from the hidden fortress of Brunsburg on the other side of the Weser. It was his father Bruno's home castle, strong, well fortified with a high, double earthwork ring-wall, the inner

5

one topped by a sharp wooden palisade. Between the walls a deep moat ran that was fed by the nearby brook. Astride the only gate sat a strong wooden watch tower. The fortress stood a ways back from the Weser but guarded one of the many fords across the river. As yet, it had been undiscovered by the Franks.

He, as eldest son, was also named Bruno. The name was derived from the word brown but was also a nickname for the great god Wotan and meant in that sense "well-favored". Because brown hair and brown eyes were so rare among the blond, blue-eyed Saxons, those who had them were thought to be especially favored by the chief of the gods. His father was also brother to the charismatic Saxon leader Wittekind, who had so valiantly been leading the resistance against the Franks these many years.

For ten years now the Franks had been invading and trying to conquer Saxony, and for most of that time Wittekind had led the stubborn resistance. There had been a few breaks in the campaign when Karl had withdrawn his main army to drive the invading Saracens out of Frankland and back to Spain and when he had conquered the kingdom of the Lombards in Italy. But in the last few years he personally had led his huge army with a vengeance and the greatly outnumbered Saxons were gradually forced to give way. Because of the disparity in numbers, the Saxons tried to avoid pitched battles as often as possible, relying on guerrilla tactics and their knowledge of their woods and streams to fade away and renew the attack in another place, much to the superstitious consternation of the Frankish troops.

The greatest weakness of the Saxons lay not in their courage or even in their fewer numbers, but in the fact that after a battle they would simply go home to their farms and their leaders would raise another contingent of troops at the next neighborhood in danger of attack. The Franks would probably have done the same thing in their home territory, but being far from home and apparently somewhat better organized, they did not. In addition, they were driven by the cruel fanaticism of their king. As a result most of Westfalen, the western third of the land, and the southern half of Engern had already fallen to them. But suddenly, about ten days ago, the Saxon forces had rallied and won a resounding victory over the Franks at Süntel.

Bruno could still see in his mind's eye the great battle. It had been his first experience in a major encounter, and he admitted now to himself that he had been afraid. But when the great buffalo horns had rung out their clarion call to arms and the war cries of "for Wotan", "for Donar", "for the

6

homeland" stirred the blood, his courage had not been lacking. The Saxons had caught the Frankish army in a narrow valley. The Franks had not been expecting battle. Karl was moving a great army across Engern to Ostfalen ostensibly to "protect" the eastern part of Saxony from the inroads of the Slavs. The Saxons had swooped down from the hillsides and trapped the Franks. Bruno rode at his father's right hand swinging his mighty battle-axe, Hritha. He knew that more than one Frankish head had been separated from its body by Hritha's bite. The clang of steel on steel and the screams of the dying were deafening. Suddenly his great horse Siegfried had slipped in the gore and was down on his knees. Bruno leapt from Siegfried's back and cleared a swath around him with Hritha, then drew his sword and took on the nearest Frank in hand-to-hand combat. He knew he should not be worrying about the horse, but only about killing Franks, but he could not help thinking, stay away from my dear Siegfried, you bastards. If he is injured, I'll kill him myself, but you won't.

The momentary diverting of his attention had almost cost him his life. He was suddenly surrounded by three burly Franks. He swung out with sword and battle-axe at the same time, but the effort cost him the precision of his sword thrust and he was certain he would be on the way to Valhalla in the next few minutes. But he had drawn the press of battle away from Siegfried and the great horse was not injured, only down on his knees. He quickly recovered and when he saw his master in trouble he reared up and his great hoofs came crashing down on two of the Franks. The third was so surprised that Bruno was able to skewer him quickly with his sword before he knew what was happening. Even in the heat of battle Siegfried took a moment to nuzzle Bruno, as if to say, "Your time is not yet, young master."

Bruno was quickly remounted and back into the fray. He had lost track of his father and others of their clan, but kept slashing and battering at every Frank he met until suddenly there was no one in front of him. The Franks seemed to be disappearing down the valley. He paused for a moment and looked around. The carnage was appalling. The little brook ran red with blood. The ground was covered with bodies, both Frank and Saxon, and slippery with mud and gore. He hesitated, not sure whether to pursue the Franks. He looked about him for some direction, some leadership. Then behind him he heard the buffalo horns blowing the victory signal. He hadn't realized how far he had pushed from the main body of the Saxon troops. He was suddenly very tired, but as he turned his weary horse back to where the others were regrouping his heart sang, "We have won! We have won at last."

When he reached the other Saxons, he thanked the gods that his father still lived, but he had lost some cousins, for the death toll was very high on both sides. His uncle Wittekind personally commended him on his bravery and coolness in the battle, "A seasoned warrior could not have done better. I am very proud of you."

Bruno, slightly embarrassed at being singled out, stepped back into the ranks. A friend clapped him on the shoulder. "Well, we have beaten them soundly this time."

"Yes, Donar was with us," said another.

"Perhaps now we can live our lives in peace."

"I'm sure they have learned this day that they will never conquer us. Our gods are more powerful than theirs."

Bruno listened to his friends' joyous comments on the battle, but he wondered if they were not rejoicing too soon. Aloud he said, "But they have been trying for ten years. What makes you think they will stop now?"

"Ach, don't be a killjoy, Bruno Brunoson," replied his friend. "Never have we had such a decisive victory. They retreated, didn't they? They'll not come back here."

Bruno agreed, but in his heart he feared that his friends were over-confident. The men started to disperse. Wittekind called them to attention.

"I go now to Brunsburg to rest awhile and make plans to follow up this great victory. I shall not be satisfied until Karl and his hordes are driven out of Saxony and our homeland is at peace. You may go to your homes now. I shall send word."

A great cheer went up from the crowd. "Hail, Wittekind! Hail, Donar! Hail, Wotan! To the halls!"

"Ach, I can taste the mead already."

"And I can feel my woman's arms about me."

"I long for the hearthstone and peace."

Bruno sought his father, who was gathering the rest of the Bruns clan around him. Wittekind rode with them back to the Brunsburg. The journey took them two days, as they dared not push their weary horses. Men left the troop as they came to their various villages and homesteads.

When at last they approached the gates of the fortress, the women watchers on the walls sounded the buffalo horn to welcome their men and the great wooden gates opened wide. Ach, our wonderful Saxon women, thought Bruno. They were trained to the sword and the horse from childhood just like the young men. Often, indeed, they fought beside their men in battle, just as the Valkyrie did, and they had been trusted to defend the castle in the absence of their men.

Bruno sought one in particular. He was disappointed when he did not immediately see her. Suddenly a strong pair of arms came around him from behind. He turned and looked into shining blue eyes, bluer than the sky at midsummer. Her complexion was fair and clear, with apple red cheeks. Her thick blond braids bounced off her back as he picked her up and hugged her. Her luscious lips were inviting, and without thinking, he held her to him and kissed her deeply. She quickly backed away from him.

"Welcome home, my warrior," she said shyly.

"Ach, my Hildegard, I thought you had forgotten me while I was gone."

"I could never forget you, Bruno. Every day I have prayed to—to all the gods for your safe return." She had almost said to Frigga, the goddess of good marriages, to whom, indeed, she had fervently prayed, but she dared not let him know that, as he had not yet spoken for her. In fact, she should not have let him kiss her like that. She hoped he didn't think her too forward, but oh, it had made her feel so good.

"And, you see, your prayers have been answered, for here I am." He tried to make it sound like a joke, but he was deeply moved by her concern. She was fifteen now and almost ripe for marriage. Her breasts were firm and full and her hips just right for childbearing, though not so wide that she would turn into a sow after several babies. She was almost as tall as he, her posture erect, and she bore herself like a queen. And she was very intelligent, that he knew. Why, she could even read the runes, which he could not. And proud, ach, ja, she was a proud one, but he didn't think that would be a problem, as she was also sweet-tempered and kind. Sometimes he had even known her to nurse injured wild creatures, birds and foxes, back to health. Perhaps he should speak to her father soon. He had now proven himself in battle, so he felt reasonably sure his father would give him the bride price and a little piece of land. Yes, I shall speak to him very soon.

"Come to our house for a bit. I have made something special for you," she said.

"Ach, but, Hilde, I must see my mother first."

"Your mother is so busy welcoming your father and the other great lords she will not miss you for a few minutes."

"I suppose you're right," he admitted as Hilde took him by the hand

9

and led him away from the crowd thronging the courtyard before the great Hall. They slipped down the quiet lane that led between the little thatched houses that filled the great fortress.

Wittekind stayed at Brunsburg for two days, conferring with Bruno and the other leaders far into the night. At last he announced his plans. "I shall go to Paderborn in Westfalen and there raise another army. If we can drive the Franks back down the Ruhr valley, Saxony will be free again. All we need is one more great victory to drive them back across the Rhein to their own lands. Are you with me?" he asked his brother.

"You know I am always with you," replied the elder Bruno. "Let my men rest by their hearths a few days while you raise the troops in Westfalen. Then I shall gather them together and join you."

"Good. Until then." The brothers embraced and Wittekind rode off with just his personal elite guard.

Bruno's father had permitted him to attend some of the conferences with Wittekind and the other lords as an observer, but he had no right to speak his opinions as yet, being both landless and unmarried. He wondered how they could be so sure the Franks were retreating toward the Ruhr valley. Suppose they had gone in another direction. Wittekind could be trapped in Paderborn or, worse yet, ambushed en route before he could collect the new army. But Bruno could not speak up, and the others were so elated with their victory at Süntel that they were sure the Franks were slinking back to their own land with their tails between their legs.

After the others had left, Bruno voiced his fears to his father. "Ach, no," countered the elder Bruno, "my brother knows what he is doing. You will see him proven right."

"I sincerely hope so, but I saw the way those Franks fight—vicious, almost fanatical, like they didn't care about anything but killing us all. They won't stop till they do."

His father laughed. "Well, isn't that what war is all about? Remember, it was your first real battle. You may yet see worse. Perhaps that young god of theirs hanging from his cross pushes them a little harder, and certainly that fanatical king of theirs does, but our men fought just as well, for don't we all know that the quickest path to Valhalla is to die in battle. And we won, don't forget that.

"Come now, enjoy these few days of rest before we take up arms again. Your mother and the other women are preparing a special banquet for all my men-at-arms tonight. Go and polish your weapons, curry your horse, seek out your beautiful Hildegard. I haven't seen her all day—probably helping the others. But forget about the Franks. We shall see them soon enough."

Bruno acquiesced, but doubts still weighed heavily on his heart. He knew his father was teasing him about Hilde, trying to lighten his mood, but this was not the right time to speak to him about her. Perhaps when we are sure this endless war is really over, he thought, if any of us are still alive.

The very next day his worst fears were confirmed when a frantic rider approached the castle gates and demanded to see his father Bruno immediately. The horse was lathered and the man appeared breathless as he dashed into the great hall.

Bruno and many others followed him into his father's hall to hear the messenger's startling news.

"The Franks are marching northward from Süntel!"

"Northward?" exclaimed many in disbelief.

"Yes, northward. They are cutting a wide swath between the Weser and the Leine, burning and pillaging and destroying every homestead, every demesne, all the villages in their path. And worst of all, they are not really fighting, but capturing everyone. And not just fighting men, but everyone—women, children and old graybeards. No one can oppose them. Those few that do try to defend their homes and families are dragged off in chains, even though they may be grievously wounded."

"Oh, ye gods, that cannot be," exclaimed Bruno.

"It can and is," replied the messenger. "I saw it with my own eyes. I escaped only by the sheerest good luck of Wotan so that I could warn Wittekind." He paused a moment and looked around, suddenly realizing that Bruno was the only great lord present. "And where might be Wittekind?"

"He rode but yesterday toward Westfalen to raise another army to chase the Franks out of Saxony once and for all."

"Oh, by the gods, then we are lost," moaned the dismayed man, who seemed about to collapse from exhaustion. Someone quickly led him to a bench by the great hearth.

"Forgive me, I have been remiss," apologized Bruno upon seeing the poor man's white countenance. "Get him food and a draught of mead," he said to a servant. And to his herald, "Sound the call to arms." And to another he ordered, "Pass the rune-sticks to the men on the outlying farms."

The messenger took a long, refreshing drink from the flagon of mead and it seemed to revive him quickly. He once more became alert to what

11

was going on around him and held up his hand. "Lord Bruno, if I may be so bold," he said, "don't attempt to fight them yourself with none but your own men. They are too many and you are too few. You would only fall prey to them, and to what purpose? Gather your people here and defend your castle and hearth if it comes to that, but pray to Donar and Wotan that they will pass you by. They were already heading more to the northeast, towards the Aller, when I last saw them. With luck they may pass to the east of here. Send word to Wittekind that he may join you. To face them alone would be a needless, yea, a worthless, sacrifice."

"Aye, messenger, I see the truth in your words," sighed Bruno, "but what of all these prisoners you mention? Would they not rise up and help us if we were to attack the Franks?"

"My lord, I fear they would be slaughtered the moment the lookouts caught sight of you. All their weapons have been taken from them, even their eating knives and the women's scissors. Their hands are tied and then they are bound to one another in long lines like a string of trader's pack animals. The strongest men and the recalcitrant are chained hand and foot. And each group is surrounded by a strong guard. They already have captured hundreds and hundreds and it may well be thousands before they get wherever that cursed Karl intends to take them. He may even drive them into the North Sea. Only the gods know. 'Tis said he is so angered over our victory at Süntel that he wants to set an example by slaughtering the ringleaders of the Saxon rebellion. Those are his words, Lord, not mine."

"Rebellion!" exclaimed Bruno, aghast. "It is rebellion to defend our own homeland from invaders and foreign gods? And ring-leaders? Why, those people to the east of here have hardly been touched by the war. Few of them have as yet joined us in battle. And women and children and graybeards? What kind of a fool is the man to call those innocents ringleaders?"

"Not such a fool as you think, my Lord," replied the messenger. "He is vindictive and vicious, but no fool. Think you, Lord Bruno. Is it not easier to wreak vengeance on the unprepared, the defenseless, the innocent than on seasoned troops in battle armor? He seeks to break our spirit by taking these hostages. What he plans to do with them I know not, but I fear me it will not be pleasant."

"You are right, ach, ja, you are right. Oh, gods, what to do." Bruno closed his eyes for a moment, and it seemed as though he were praying. He slowly opened his eyes and shook his shaggy brown head. Once again he was the man of action.

"A messenger is already on his way to Wittekind," he told the gathered company. "But it may take days to find him and more days before he can return with an army. Within a few hours all my men and their families and livestock will be inside the castle gates and we can withstand a long, long siege. But we must know where the Franks are going and what they intend."

He thought a moment. "I shall send my most trusted warrior to spy on them and bring back a report. Bruno, my son, saddle your best horse. Arm yourself well, but with no excess, so that you can travel swiftly and circumspectly. The women will pack you enough food for a few days. Go up the left bank of the Weser so that you will not run afoul of them, but look you carefully, for they may have spies of their own or lookouts. If any of our own people question you, say only that you ride to Bremen on an errand for me. Bide in no house, but sleep carefully concealed in the woods off the road. Cross over the river again at Hoya, or if the heathens are already that far, then cross at the ford by Verden where the Aller joins the Weser. You must find out what their intentions are and where they are going so that Wittekind can meet them in battle."

"I understand, my lord father. I shall do as you command," murmured the astonished Bruno. Holy gods, he prayed quickly to himself, he has called me his most trusted warrior, make me worthy of the trust. "One question, my Lord. If I succeed in crossing the river ahead of them, shall I not warn the people?"

"That you may do if you are *far* enough ahead of them, but do not linger in the vicinity or let those people know who you are. You cannot take a chance on being caught. And remember, no fighting, no matter how tempting, except in self-defense. Your only duty is to gather information and return safely here with it. Is that clear?"

"Yes, my Lord."

"Good. Then go and make ready. I want you on the road before one more hour by the sun."

He made a hurried farewell with Hildegard, who promised to pray for him. "I'll even sacrifice a chicken for your safe return," she said.

"Not a goat?" he teased.

"Well," she apologized tearfully, "I don't think my mother would think it important enough for a goat."

He laughed. "Be of good cheer, my love. Just stay true to me, and I shall be back in two or three days."

13

In less than an hour he was back in his father's hall. His mother embraced him and gave him the leather bag of food. He knelt before his father.

"Your blessing, my Lord."

"You have it, my son. May Wotan ride at your back and Donar protect you. Return safely."

And he rode out of the gates of Brunsburg toward the ford in the river.

Now he was a great many miles from home, having passed through Bücken about noontime. The next village he would reach on this path was Hoya, where the Weser made a great bend. There was another small castle there on a spit sticking out into the river. At times there was also a wooden bridge, but it usually washed out during the spring floods and had to be rebuilt every year. He did not know if with the chaos created by the war it would be passable or not. He would probably have to take the ford. But long before he came to Hoya he would meet the Volksweg, and then he would have to be exceedingly careful, as it was always a well-travelled road.

Right now he knew he was passing, about a mile or so to his left, one of the holiest places in Engern. He could not see it because of the dense forest, but he was very aware of it because his heart leapt in awe. There were three hills, a rarity in this flat land. Two were on an east–west line and a lesser one directly to the north of the westernmost. In between them delightful little brooks of the coldest, clearest water ran through thickly wooded valleys. The first hill to the east had no name, but it was held in great awe by the people, as it was full of ancient graves. No one knew how old they were nor to what people they belonged. Some said they were the tombs of the giants and elves the gods had destroyed when they had conquered the earth. Whatever they were, he knew that no one in his right mind would go there if he could help it. The great hill to the west of it was called the Holy Mountain—Heiligenberg. On its flat top was a grove of oaks and firs sacred to Wotan. It was one of his most important shrines in all the northern world. There was no temple, for the Saxons believed that their gods were all around them in nature and could best be worshiped in the sacred groves and on the hilltops. There was a small altar, however, intricately carved with the sacred runes and other designs and inlaid with metal filigree and precious stones. It was here that once a year, and more often in times of national peril, a great white horse, sacred to Wotan, was sacrificed and the auguries read by the chief priest and his small band of assistants. Here the sacred fire was kept burning forever, and death by

14

hanging was the lot of any priest or acolyte that let it go out. Part way down the hill was the sacred spring that was the source of all the brooks in the vicinity, which flowed eventually into the great river. Heiligenberg was so secluded that an uninitiated passerby would never even suspect its existence, let alone its importance. Bruno prayed the Franks would never find it.

Before it on the third hill to the north was the Holy Town. This was not its real name, but it had come to be called that due to its proximity to Heiligenberg. Also a meadow at the foot of the hill was sacred to the twin gods of fertility, Freyr and Freya. And the surrounding farms were, indeed, some of the richest in that area. The charming town on the hill had been there since time immemorial. It was said that the ancient people of the hill graves had thrown up dikes and dammed the brooks to form a natural moat around the hills. The remains of some of these dams still stood in many places. The town had grown in importance as a market town due to the fact that the main east–west Volksweg passed right by the foot of the hill.

Siegfried suddenly nickered very softly and Bruno was instantly alert. He reached forward and patted the horse's neck to quiet him, at the same time reining him to a halt. Bruno strained his ears, and then he, too, heard it. The tramp of horses, the rattle of armor, the shouts of men who had nothing to conceal. Many men, many horses—and instinctively Bruno knew they were not friends. Quickly he led his great horse off the path into the deep woods. He donned his helmet and dismounted, the better to pass through the dense undergrowth. He quietly led the horse, angling off until he was parallel to the Volksweg. He followed it a ways, choosing his path carefully, until he came to a spot where he and his horse were well concealed but he was afforded a clear view of the road.

He did not have long to wait. Within moments there appeared the van of the Frankish army, or at least a good part of it. The men seemed to be in high spirits, laughing and joking, indulging in horseplay. In fact, it seemed to Bruno that many of them were intoxicated. There obviously was no discipline or attempt at secrecy or even order. Their clothes were disheveled and filthy—or were those bloodstains? Oh, Wotan! exclaimed Bruno to himself as a horrible thought occurred to him. But where are the hostages? There was not a Saxon face among them.

I must find out what has happened. He tethered Siegfried to a branch and patted his nose. He knew the horse would be quiet, as he was well trained. Bruno slithered on his belly through the underbrush to get as

15

close to the road as he dared. Finally, he was close enough to be able to discern what the men were saying. Frankish German was somewhat different from Saxon, having been corrupted over almost three centuries by Gallic and Latin, but it was close enough so that Bruno could understand most of it and piece together the rest.

"Well, I guess we've finally fixed these heathen Saxons this time. They won't be so quick to fight us again."

"Yes, they'll know now that our Karl means to be king of all this land right to the river Elbe, make no mistake."

"Aye, and perhaps beyond, if the truth were known. There'll be no stopping him now."

"And he'll teach these heathens to be Christians—with a sword at their throat. It's the only way they understand."

"Aye, provided we leave any for the monks to convert." They laughed uproariously at this.

A cold sweat was pouring off Bruno as he lay hidden in the underbrush listening to this, but he still was not sure what had really happened. The next group that passed made it horribly clear.

"Forty-five hundred in one day! What a master stroke!"

"Our Karl's a genius, that he is. To have picked that spot right at Verden where they used to vote in their *Allthing*. That should break the back of this whole rebellion."

"Well, they won't vote there anymore. That's for sure."

"Democracy, hah! No wonder they're so disorganized, letting women have a say in their government."

"Well, he gave them their choice, didn't he? The cross or the sword. They had their vote."

"But he really didn't give them much chance to decide. Heads were falling before most of them really knew what it was all about."

"I don't think he intended to give them a choice. He only let them think that. He wanted to set an example."

"And he surely did that. But why the women and children? That bothered me a little."

"Ah, my friend, don't you know that most of their women can fight as well as the men? And as long as they are alive they can bear more potential rebels—and children grow up."

"I suppose you're right, but then why the old people? Some of them were so feeble they could hardly walk. They would have died soon enough of the shock."

16

"But they are the very ones who keep alive the dreams and the stories of their old gods, and they stir up the young ones."

"Well, I for one thought it was pretty awful, herding them together like that—forty-five hundred of them all slaughtered. They were so helpless."

"What would you have done, you fool? Handed them swords and said, 'Let's have a fair fight'. No, that's not our Karl's way. He saw an opportunity to avenge Süntel and he took advantage of it. That's why he's a great king."

"I still think it was brutal. There was blood running everywhere. Look, we're still covered with it. I wish I could wash my clothes."

"Ach, you're too squeamish, young one," said an old veteran. "I rather enjoyed swinging this old battle-axe to the right and to the left with no opposition for a change."

Bruno felt the bile rise in his gorge. He almost vomited where he lay. Then, as the next group came abreast, he heard more.

"Too bad we had to sack and burn Verden. Kind of a pretty little place where the two rivers come together."

"But look at the loot we got. Some of the best yet."

"Ah, but you won't see any of that, my friend. Those beautiful white horses from that big stud farm, the King and his nobles will keep them, you can be sure."

Bruno was aghast. The sacred horses of Wotan! His rage was so great he almost betrayed his hiding place in his desire to throttle the speaker. But he was so weak from the shock of what he had heard that he could not move. All the hostages slaughtered in one day at Verden! Forty-five hundred, if these brutish yokels could be believed. And at the *Allthing*, the centuries-old parliamentary meeting place of the Saxon nation. Silently he cursed them and their fiendish king in the name of every god he knew. And then he laid his face in the leaves and wept.

After a while, his grief spent, he worked his way back from the road until he could safely stand erect. His great horse was still standing where he had left him. He threw his arm around the horse's neck and laid his head against him. "Siegfried, Siegfried, what are we to do now?" he whispered. The horse nuzzled him gently, and he was somewhat comforted. Gradually he calmed down and his brain started working again. A cold, calculating fury filled him. He vowed he would avenge this outrage if it took him the rest of his life. He did not yet know how, but he was sure that in time the gods would place the means in his hand.

17

Right now he must decide what to do next. He had enough information to report back to Brunsburg, but perhaps he could find out more of Karl's plans before he left the area. He knew they were heading toward the Holy Town, and he also knew it was too late to warn the people. He feared for their fate. O ye gods, O Wotan, he prayed, please don't let them find the Holy Mountain. He knew then that he must watch and see what happened, even though he was bitterly aware he could do nothing to prevent it.

He unloosed Siegfried and led him quietly through the woods parallel to the Volksweg. Soon the trees began to thin out and Bruno had to be extremely careful, although he noticed that the Franks had no lookouts posted and, in fact, were so boisterous and rowdy, he doubted they would notice him if he were to actually ride among them. Should he? The idea teased him, but then prudence reasserted itself and he thought better of it. His father had commanded him not to fight and, moreover, to return safely with information. An order was an order. So let me gather more information.

He crossed the sparkling brook that ran along the eastern limits of the town. Beyond the next small copse began the open fields of the farms. He dared go no farther. He moved a little to his left to a spot where he was still well secluded yet was afforded a clear view of the road and the town on the hill. The village had no fortifications. It had always been considered so holy, for as long as anyone could remember, that no one would have believed it could ever be desecrated. But the Frankish army was approaching.

"Ho, and what have we here? Another nest of vipers to be wiped out."

"But King Karl told us no more fighting unless we were attacked."

"Then let us tell him we were attacked. We'll not leave anyone to tell the tale."

"That would be lying and our Lord would know. Besides, Karl told us not to stop until we were back in Westfalen and to await him and the rest of the army there. Suppose he catches up to us while we are—are detained here?"

"He won't. He'll be in Verden a few more days. He is going to write out new laws for these heathens. Laws they will understand."

"I say let's at least see if there is any loot in this place."

"There can't be much. It isn't even defended."

"There must be women, though. That would satisfy me well enough."

"You're right. Karl wouldn't even let us touch those hostages. I'd have loved to shove my sword into one or two juicy ones before I lopped off their heads."

They were still intoxicated by the horrible bloodletting at Verden, and thirst for more blood drove them. But here and there a few sober ones tried to hold them back and keep them on the march. The Volksweg ran under the hill on the north side of the town, and for a short while Bruno let himself hope they might bypass it and continue on their way. But then they arrived at the meadow shrine of Freyr and Freya and all hell broke loose.

"Here is where they have their pagan orgies, where they train their whores."

"Ah, just what we're looking for. You know, all these so-called priestesses are nothing but prostitutes."

"How do you know that?"

"Hah, I've tasted a few in my day—while trying to convert them, of course."

"You better confess that to the next priest that comes along."

"Like hell, I will."

"But there's no one here."

"Well, they've all fled up into the town, of course. You don't think they were going to wait for us here with open arms. They know we mean business. Come on, boys, there's a bunch of souls to be saved up there."

That convinced even the reticent, and with true Christian fervor they swarmed up the hill.

Bruno could watch no more. Another two or three hundred martyrs. We can never call this place the Holy Town again. It has been defiled. And, in fact, from that time on it was called Villers-husen—the town of the bloody slaughter—or Vilsen.

He turned away, sick all over again. He led his horse to the brook and let him drink. He knelt down on the mossy bank and splashed cold water in his face. The icy shock made him feel better. I must go to Heiligenberg and warn the priests there. Perhaps the Frankish bloodlust would be sated here and they would not seek any further victims. He prayed that would be so, but he must hasten there and warn them anyway.

He mounted Siegfried and they followed the brook upstream until they were far from the town. However, before he left he could already hear the screams of terror and the clang of steel. Then he smelled the smoke. It chilled him to the bone. But soon he was far enough away and the peace

19

and quiet of the beautiful valley enveloped him.

"My beautiful, beautiful homeland," he sighed. "Why, oh why, all ye gods, are you letting this happen to us?" he cried out from the anguish in his soul. The only answer was the soughing of the breeze and the call of the cuckoo in the treetops.

Soon the brook made a sharp turn to the west and he left the water and sought the almost hidden path that led to Heiligenberg. At the foot of the hill he recrossed the brook at the bottom of a dancing waterfall, and from there the path zigzagged steeply up the hill. The forest grew thicker as he ascended, the oaks taller, the firs more majestic. Sometimes the soft needles of their lower branches brushed his face caressingly.

"Ach, it is so peaceful here," he murmured to himself. "No wonder the gods seem so close. One truly feels worshipful in this place."

When he reached the top, he paused for a moment to gaze upon the broad vista that opened before him. The top of the hill was flat and formed an almost perfect circle. On the far northern edge was a semicircle of neat little thatched houses, each with the crossed Saxon horses at the gable peak. These, he knew, were the homes of the acolytes and the peasants who farmed for the little community. Most of the middle of the circle consisted of fields of ripening grain, vegetable gardens and an orchard. On the south side stood a somewhat larger house off by itself. Here lived the priests of this sacred shrine of Wotan. Between where Bruno stood and this house lay a verdant meadow brilliant with wildflowers and lush grass. In the center of the meadow, slightly to the left on a line with the house, was the altar with its magic runes and precious stones sparkling in the late afternoon sunshine.

He was awestruck by the solemnity of the place and at the same time heavily burdened with the terrible tidings he was bearing. He murmured a quick prayer to Wotan for guidance and started toward the house. As he did so, an ancient man came out of the dwelling to meet him. His hair was long and pure white, his flowing white beard even longer. He wore a loose pure white robe and carried a heavy staff. But his bearing was erect and his step light. It appeared that the staff was more a symbol of authority than something to lean on.

As he neared Bruno, he raised his arm in greeting. "Hail, Bruno Brunoson. Wotan's blessings on you. Welcome to Heiligenberg."

"Hail, my lord priest Otto," replied Bruno. "I come in peace and my father sends his greetings. But I bear grave tidings."

"I know of the tidings you bring, but I would hear more from you."

"You know?" asked Bruno, disappointed that someone had been here before him. "Have aught been here already?"

"Nay, nay," replied the old man, "you are the first, but the ravens of Wotan are swifter than any man afoot or ahorse."

Bruno knew that these great priests all had the second sight, that often they could read men's minds and see scenes of far-off happenings. But ravens? Well, here in this holy place he could believe anything. "Then you know you must flee. I have come to warn you, to help you escape before the Franks come here."

"There is no hurry," said the priest, with unbelievable calm. "Come bide with us this night, " he invited.

"Nay, nay, I cannot. Nor can you, my Lord Otto. You and your people are in great danger." He felt like screaming at the old simpleton. Ravens indeed. Cuckoos more likely. "Even now the Franks are burning and pillaging the Holy Town, slaughtering the inhabitants and, yes, raping the womenfolk."

"Yes, but they will not come here," replied Otto, and then added sadly, "not this time anyway."

"You are sure?"

"I am sure, young one." He paused to let this sink in and then repeated his invitation. "Come and sup with us and tell me all you know. The day is far spent and you will be safe here tonight."

Faced with the man's utter and serene faith, Bruno let himself be persuaded. He was suddenly overwhelmingly tired. The nerve-wracking day had taken its toll, and the thought of sleep was very appealing. The ancient priest seemed to read his thoughts. He held out his hand and said, "Come. The kerl will take care of your horse."

Slowly, as if mesmerized, Bruno dismounted, and as if by magic a peasant appeared and led his horse toward the snug barn behind the house. He followed the old man into the house. Inside the door, before entering the hall itself, he deposited his shield, helmet and weapons, for it was discourteous to enter a friend's home, to say nothing of a high priest's hall, armed. Only his eating knife he kept at his belt.

He entered the great hall and looked around. The fire was burning merrily on the circular hearth and something savory was bubbling in the great black cauldron hung on a hook above it. The women were already busy preparing the evening meal and the men sat around on the benches quaffing mead, conversing as if they had not a care in the world.

Otto led him to the high seat and indicated a stool next to it. Bruno collapsed gratefully onto the stool and, as if out of nowhere, a drinking horn of mead was placed in his hand. He took several great gulps and felt himself relax.

"Now, tell me all that you have seen and heard this day," urged the old priest.

Slowly and thoughtfully Bruno told his tale, commencing with the arrival of the messenger at Brunsburg early that morning. He related all he had heard about the terrible massacre at Verden and what he knew of Karl's plans. He almost broke down when he described what had happened at the Holy Town before he left. "It has been defiled!" he cried.

The old priest patted his hand. "Aye, that it has, but the Holy Town will live again and this day's infamous deeds will always be in the people's memory, for the town will be known as Vilsen from now on."

Bruno sighed. "And did you really learn all I have just told you from the ravens, sir?"

"I knew of the treachery and massacre at Verden, but not all the details. You must know that many of us priests can communicate with certain birds and animals. The ravens and the wolves are Wotan's own. Who better to bring the message to me?"

"Forgive me, my Lord, I didn't doubt your word. It's just that I wondered how you do it."

"I am a priest—and not just an ordinary priest, but one chosen by Wotan to be a chief priest. There are many mysteries given to us that are beyond the understanding of lay folk. And those of us who have these talents are almost always chosen by one god or another to serve him as priests—or priestesses." The old man seemed to be staring into space, seeing things that no one else in the hall could see. After a moment he roused himself and asked, "Have you told me everything? Is there nothing you have omitted?"

"I can't think of anything, my Lord." Bruno tried to think back to all he had heard and seen that day. "Well, there is one thing. I did not think it of much importance, and all the horrible things put it out of my mind."

"Everything is important. What is it?"

"The Franks mentioned something about some new laws that Karl is going to impose on the Saxon lands. How can he make us obey laws when he is not our king? He has not conquered us yet and, the gods willing, he never will."

"Ah, my young friend," replied Otto sadly, "I grieve to tell you this, but it is only a matter of time. After this day's work he has, for all intents

22

and purposes, conquered us. I have cast the lots and thrown the rune-sticks, and they all spell out disaster and death."

"No, no, that cannot be. What of Wittekind? He is a brave and fearless prince. He will lead us to victory. I know he will," declared Bruno.

"Wittekind is a young hothead and an idealistic dreamer, for all that he is your uncle, and I apologize if I offend you," stated the old priest softly. "I know the people love him because he exemplifies everything that is fine and good in the Saxon people and he supports the old ways, but he is not the military leader that Karl is, nor the politician. All of Westfalen is fallen and more than a third of Engern. Most of the Saxon nobles there have already forsworn our gods and have accepted the Christian baptism in order to keep their castles. Many lives could be saved if Wittekind would do the same."

"Never," hissed Bruno, shocked. "How can you, a chief priest of Wotan, advise such a thing?"

"I have already seen it in the runes. They have predicted the same Twilight of the Gods that our gods themselves foretold thousands of years ago, but no one knew when it would happen. My son, it is happening now."

"But what of Saxony? It will cease to exist if we are absorbed into the Frankish Empire."

"Nay. There will always be a Saxony and a Saxon people, but in a different form. Karl cannot rule so great a territory alone. He needs the cooperation of the Saxon nobles, and he is beginning to get it. And he, in turn, is honoring his promise to them if they but worship his god Christ. They get to keep their castles and lands under his vassalage and rule in peace."

"Traitors, that's what they are, and they will be his slaves. I would rather be a free Saxon than a Frankish slave."

"And you would most likely be a dead Saxon and your country over-run by the Slavs. And let me tell you that is a far worse fate. Saxony cannot stand alone any longer. We are not a militaristic people, nor are we politicians. Someone stronger will always be coveting our rich land. At least Karl has learned a lot from the Romans. Why, he is even having his priests teach the people to read the runes. Soon there will be no more mystery in them for the priests to interpret."

"I cannot believe I am hearing this from you." Bruno put his head in his hands. It was almost too much for his young mind to absorb. Then it occurred to him. "My friend Hilde has learned to read the runes and she

23

has the sight, too, but she doesn't want to be a priestess," he whispered.

"There. You see," replied Otto gently. "That is progress. A sign of the new times. We cannot prevent it."

"But what of the gods? Will they not destroy us if we turn to foreign gods?"

"Is Wotan jealous because a man chooses to worship Donar? Is Donar jealous if a woman turns to Frigga when the hour of birthing comes? There are many gods, but most of them are the same with different names. The Christians, too, have their father god and their Christ god and their virgin mother goddess. It matters not what you call them. Don't you think that those nobles that accepted the baptism for political reasons don't still worship Wotan in their hearts? Many who now wear the cross amulet still regard it as Donar's hammer."

"But what of you? What of this Holy Mountain, if all this should come to pass?"

The old priest ignored the first question. "Heiligenberg will always be a holy place. I have seen a great Christian temple standing here for hundreds of years." He did not mention that he had seen that, too, destroyed in the dim distant future and something else, he knew not what, replace it.

Bruno shook his head as if to clear it. "But why are you telling me this, my lord priest? You know that I could turn you in to my father as a traitor."

"But you won't. I have only told you the truth that I have seen. The rune-sticks don't lie. Your father and his brother will continue this fruitless war for several years yet, and many lives will be wasted. But it is your generation, young Bruno, that will win, because you will learn to be politicians instead of warriors. Your sons and grandsons will rebuild Saxony under Saxon lords. That is why you will not tell your father what I have said. And I shall prophesy something else for you. The Bruns tribe will flourish and, especially in this part of Engern, there will be men bearing the Bruns name forever."

Bruno was overwhelmed. The sheer power of the old priest's speech made him believe every word of it, and he knew in his heart that he would never betray the man to his father. Bruno was speechless, and yet his mind was whirling with questions.

"Come now," said Otto gently, "we have talked far into the night and my poor servant is sleeping on his feet. You have a long ride tomorrow. He will show you where you can bed down."

"But, my lord," objected Bruno, "I have many questions. How does

24

one learn of this—this politics, since I obviously cannot learn it from my esteemed father?"

"Enough for tonight. I am weary. In a year or two—yes, better two—you will be more mature then. Come back to me and I shall endeavor to teach you."

"And—and, if you are not here?" queried the young man timidly.

"I shall find you." The ancient rose from the high seat with great dignity, bowed to the fire and left the hall.

Early the next morning, having broken his fast with mead and black bread, Bruno went out to the barn to seek his horse. Siegfried had been beautifully curried and well fed. As Bruno mounted, the old priest himself came out of the house and walked with him a ways. When they came to the edge of the clearing, he said, "Do not go back the way you came. The Franks are probably still around Vilsen."

"But I thought that was the only access to his holy place."

"No, there are several, but known to few men. When you come to the first turn in the path, there," he pointed, "bear slightly to the right instead of to the left. There is a path there, although it is not visible from here. It goes almost straight down the hill behind the Sacred Spring. It is quite steep, so you may have to lead the horse. These pine needles can be very slippery. When you reach the valley, turn to the right, keep going, and eventually you will come out of the forest into open farmland. You will be safe enough because it is very lonely country and the farmers have left many small woods. About three miles from here you will pass the great spring called Brüne, where, incidentally, your father was born. Shortly after that you will come to a crossroad. Take the left and it will lead you right into Bücken. From there you know the way."

"Thank you, my lord priest; you have been most helpful. And thank you, too, for your hospitality this past night. I shall always remember what you have told me, but I shall never betray it, rest assured of that."

"I know that," replied Otto. "And ponder carefully all I have revealed to you, Bruno Bruns, for it is you and your descendants who will be the new leaders of Saxony. Fare thee well."

Bruno followed the path as Otto had directed him, and by midafternoon he was approaching the gate of Brunsburg. He dreaded having to tell his father the terrible news but heartened, although saddened at the same time, by Otto's revelations he vowed to keep up his courage in the dark days ahead.

A few days later Bruno's father rode out of the Brunsburg with a large troop of his best warriors. His son had tried to dissuade him but could not offer too strong an argument for fear of betraying his friend Otto.

The elder Bruno said, "But Wittekind needs me more than ever now. I have been at his side in every major engagement. I cannot let him down now."

His son wondered how he could refuse to go without appearing to be a coward, but Wotan must have heard Otto's prayers, for his father suggested, "I know you will be disappointed, but this time I dare not leave the women to defend the castle alone. I should like to leave you in charge here if you don't mind. I shall leave several good men to watch with you."

Mind, thought Bruno, if only he knew. "I should be most honored to keep the castle and defend the folk in your absence, my lord father."

"Good. Then I shall have nothing to worry about here."

For weeks the people at the Brunsburg were isolated from the world. Then, bit by bit, news began to filter back to them, most of it bad. First they heard about Karl's new laws designed to stamp out their ancient religion. The death penalty was decreed for anyone who continued to worship the old gods, for anyone who swore against Christians or who mocked the Christian church, for anyone who worshipped or even gathered together by sacred springs, in sacred groves or meadows, and for anyone who cremated the dead, long a Saxon practice.

The people were horrified. He was destroying their very souls.

Then word came back of a terrible battle at Detmold in which the Saxons were badly defeated. Karl had immediately erected a Christian church there.

Then came the bitterest blow of all. He had uprooted 7000 Saxons from their homes—whole families, men, women and children—and transported them to the northern Frankish territory of Belgae and there made them slaves of the Frankish nobles and even of the peasants.

"Oh, ye gods," moaned the people, "that is worse than Verden. Will there be any of us left?"

Bruno could see the prophecies of Otto gradually coming true. He had long ceased to urge the people to fight. He did not yet understand what the old priest had meant by politics but was beginning to see that the only way to save any of the Saxon people and their land would be to compromise in some way with this vicious Frankish king. And Bruno could also see that the angrier Karl became, the less chance there would be for compromise.

Weeks merged into months and there was still no direct word from

Bruno's father. But rumors flew like the ravens. Rumors and more rumors. Almost all the fighting was in Westfalen again, much to the relief of the people waiting for word in the Brunsburg. Wittekind and his brothers Bruno and Abbio had fled to the north. They refused open battle, fighting only guerrilla warfare. Wittekind had removed his wife and children from his most important castle and had hidden them in a castle across the Elbe, out of Saxon territory.

Winter closed in on the land, and the primitive roads became almost impassable. The fighting should have been ended for the year, but still the Franks remained in the country. That was against the rules, but then nothing seemed to be according to the rules anymore. And Bruno's father and his men had still not returned.

The little group at the Brunsburg went about their daily tasks but there was no joy in it. Everyone was worried, but no one wanted to admit it to the others. The oxen and pigs had been slaughtered by the women with the help of the handful of men left behind. The ritual sacrifices had been made, but the auguries were not good, and now they were smoking and drying the meat for the winter. Fortunately, their fields had not been devastated and the harvest had been abundant. Their granaries and storehouses were full, but the great harvest festival had not been the joyous celebration of thanksgiving it normally was.

"Who is there to dance with?" the women asked one another dolefully. "The harpist plays to an empty hall. Who will warm our beds now that the nights grow cold?"

Bruno tried to comfort and console them, but they knew, perhaps better than he, what the portends were. He always believed that the Saxon women were especially prescient and intuitive. They could read signs in the flight of birds, in the way the leaves fell from the trees, how the snow drifted or an icicle formed. At the full of the moon their mystic talents seemed especially potent.

He often discussed it with Hilde, for the whole process mystified him, a mere male. She always gave the same reply, "I don't know how it works, but I know it to be true. It is a gift from the gods. I have it myself." But she was reluctant to fully use her knowledge because she was only partially trained and never would be completely unless she chose to become a priestess. And that she was hesitant about.

One evening after supper they were sitting together by the fire in the almost empty hall. A few of the men were off to one side drinking ale and conversing desultorily. The others were out keeping watch on the walls. It

27

had started to snow again and the wind was bitter.

"It doesn't seem fair. We are so cozy here and they are out in the cold," she murmured.

"But they are just doing their duty, as we all must," replied Bruno. "Even you have taken your turn on the walls. At least they are not fighting out in some strange woods with no bed to return to."

"I know. I don't mean to be maudlin when we here have so much to be thankful for. I guess I just feel a little sad tonight. It will pass."

Bruno put his arm around her and drew her to him. She nestled against his shoulder and they sat in companionable silence. As she stared into the fire, he noticed a dreamy look come over her lovely face. Her eyes were half-shut. Believing that she was falling asleep, he was about to suggest that he walk her home to her mother's cottage when she started talking. But it was obvious she was not talking to him. It was as though she were far away, and he had to listen carefully to distinguish her words.

"The ravens are falling, Oh Mother, they are falling out of the sky. It is Donar's hammer all ablaze. No . . . no, it's not Donar's hammer, but a great cross lighting up the sky. And a castle, a great castle built all out of stone, and there are pennants flying from the towers. I can't see whose emblem is on them. Yes, now I can see—it is two bear's claws. And the bear's claws are not afraid of the cross. They are reaching up and embracing it. They are not afraid, I tell you."

Hilde's head fell against Bruno's shoulder, and he held her tightly. He knew she had had a vision, and he was thunderstruck at her prophecy. And prophecy he knew it was, because it so closely paralleled what the old priest Otto had told him. But the bear's claws . . . bruin, bruno? No, it can't be. He held his breath for fear of waking her, but his heart was pounding and his brain was awhirl.

Suddenly Hilde shook her head. "Oh, I must have fallen asleep, and I think I had a terrible dream. I can't remember. Something about ravens and wolves running and running. I was very frightened." She paused and looked up at him. "But now, you know, I'm not at all frightened. I feel strangely at peace—almost as if a problem has been solved."

He put his other arm around her and held her close. "That is because you are safe here in my arms. I shall always protect you, my love." He kissed her ripe lips gently at first, then more passionately, and was thrilled when she responded in kind. He slipped his hand over her full breast and felt it grow taut under his touch. She arched her body toward him and he felt his desire going hard with wanting her.

28

Suddenly she backed away. "No, no, Bruno, not now. Not yet!" she cried.

"But I love you, my fair goddess. I want to marry you," he whispered, longing to undo her thick braids and bury his face in her golden hair.

"But you have not spoken for me yet."

"I shall. I shall."

"My father is not here, Bruno. You know that. Nor is yours. Frigga would never bless our marriage if we did any . . . anything before we were honorably betrothed."

"I know, my love. I am sorry. I did not intend to force you into anything dishonorable. It's just that I love you so and am so happy that you will marry me. Wait a minute, you haven't answered me yet. You will, won't you?"

She laughed. "Of course I will, you big bear, when the time is right."

"Then I am truly happy—at least for tonight. But, oh Donar, when are they coming back? You know, Hilde, I am really worried. I can't let the others know because I must keep up their courage, but I am very worried. It is long past time they should have returned."

"They will return," she stated, and that mystic look was once again in her eyes.

"You are sure?"

"I am sure," and she turned away from him, but not before he noticed tears running down her cheeks.

He took her gently by the shoulders. "Then why do you weep if you are so sure?" he asked.

"Because I feel great sadness in connection with their homecoming. Do not ask me more. I do not know aught else of it. Only sadness." She stood up and smoothed her gown. "Walk me home now, Bruno. I would go to my mother."

Afterward Bruno sat for a long time in the empty hall pondering Hilde's prophecy—prophecies, actually. He had not mentioned the first, more startling one to her as they walked the short distance to her cottage. He was dying to ask her about it but he was quite certain that she did not remember a thing about it and was afraid he would only upset her if he questioned her about the oracle. As for the second one, about his father's return, she had begged him to ask no more, so he had held his peace. After he had seen her home, he went up on the walls to check on the men keeping watch there. In truth, all four of them were gathered in the wooden watchtower over the gate, but he could not fault them, for the wind was

29

sharp although the snow had let up. A half-moon was trying to emerge from the clouds scudding across the sky. When it did, the snow covering the huge fir trees sparkled as though fairy lights were dancing on them. Then the moon would disappear again and the enchantment was gone. Everything seemed peaceful, and he realized his tension was not from fear of attack. He bid the men a good night and returned to the hall.

The cold, fresh air had cleared his mind, but it had also made him wide awake. The other men were sprawled on their accustomed sleeping benches along the sides of the hall, sound asleep. A few of the assorted dogs gave him a halfhearted wag of the tail and closed their eyes again. The servants had banked the great fire and departed. But Bruno could not sleep, and so he sat and thought—deep thoughts. Try as he would, he could not understand the symbolism of Hilde's first prophecy. It needed a priest to interpret it. He wished old Otto were there to talk to. One part Bruno was afraid he did understand too well. That the Christian cross would chase away the ravens and wolves of Wotan seemed more and more a distinct possibility. But what was the meaning of the castle—a stone castle, yet, when there were no such in all of Saxony? And the bear's claws? It was no one's emblem that he knew of. Or was it the beast of another god even stronger than the Christ god? No, that did not seem likely, since she had said that the bear's claws *embraced* the cross.

He finally gave up trying to figure it out and turned his thoughts to her second profound statement, that his father would return, but in sadness. That he could understand. They would probably bring wounded back with them, provided they could survive in this weather. Without a doubt some of them had gone to Valhalla. Those were the happy ones. Yes, she had said for sure they would be back, but when? She had not permitted him to ask.

The winter solstice will soon be upon us, he thought, and then the great weeklong festival of the Mothering Nights. It was one of the four great festivals of the year, although there were minor ones almost every month in between. The great ones marked the four most important points of the sun's journey through the year. There were the fertility rites of Freyr and Freya at the spring equinox, followed by the plowing and sowing of the fields, the great bonfires of Midsummer's Day after the first hay had been cut, and the harvest festival after the autumnal equinox, but all of these had work connected with them. Mothering Nights was the longest, the most fun-filled and relaxing, when everyone could sit around drinking ale and listening to the songs and stories of the minstrels and bards, could feast all day and dance and sing all night. Of course, the women had a lot of work to do with all that cooking and baking, but they enjoyed it. It was really their festival, theirs and the children's.

It was in honor of the great Mother goddess, who was older than any of the gods, who had been worshipped by men as long as there had been men to worship anything. It was said she had borne every living thing in the world, including the first gods themselves, in this darkest time of the year, having conceived of the sky at the vernal equinox. She was all alone in her agony, for even the sun had fled, but when he heard the birth cries and her rejoicing, he had returned.

Whatever, Bruno knew that the women enjoyed making everyone happy at this time of the year, especially the children. Even the truculent elves behaved themselves and often secretly helped with chores and always left gifts for the children in the wooden shoes that were carefully placed by the hearth. Bruno remembered his own excitement as a child on finding a beautifully carved wooden toy in his shoe.

What if the men don't come back in time? he wondered wistfully. Will the women even want to celebrate? Of course they will—for the children. His spirits rose. Yes, we must make the festival better than ever this year, so that the children will not miss their fathers too much, in case they are not back in time. Tomorrow I shall send some of the men out into the forest to start searching for the Yule log. It must be the biggest and best we've ever had. And the little fir tree must be perfectly shaped. The women and children would decorate it with dried fruit and nuts, with honey cakes and cookies, and his mother would place a real gold star on the top. And woe betide the child who stole a cookie from the tree before the last day of the festival. Closer to the time, he would send Hilde and some of the older girls out with the children to gather mistletoe and holly and evergreen boughs to decorate the hall. Yes, they would make the Mother goddess proud of them this year. With those happy thoughts he finally fell into a deep sleep.

True to Hilde's words, Bruno's father and his men did return, and in ample time for the festival, it being two days before the solstice. When the buffalo horn sounded, everyone ran to the top of the wall. As soon as Bruno recognized who was approaching, he ran down to the great gate to welcome them. The whole community was cheering and rejoicing, but then the sadness that Hilde had predicted became apparent. The men rode very slowly, as if their bones were stiff with the cold. Bruno's father had aged far beyond his years. He had lost weight and his gaunt face had

31

an unhealthy pallor. Then Bruno saw the litters—several litters slung between pairs of horses. Oh, ye gods, he thought, no wonder it took them so long. I wonder how many we have lost—and are still losing.

As they rode into the courtyard, his father raised his arm in greeting but spoke not a word. When finally all were within and the gates were shut, he dismounted. His squire had to help him, and he was obviously in great pain. He embraced and kissed his wife as if he wasn't sure she was real. Then he turned to his son. "Ah, Bruno, my son, I am glad to see that you are well and that you have kept my castle so well. I will talk to you later, when I have rested, for there is much to tell. Now see that the wounded are tended to. The women will know what to do. And I fear that some are gravely hurt." He turned to the gathered company. "Thank you for your welcome. I would have some time alone with my wife." He put his arm around her, and they entered the great hall alone.

Bruno turned to find Hilde. At first he could not see her in the crowd of the other women seeking their men. Then he saw her with her mother bending over one of the litters. "Her father!" he cried to himself. "Oh, no, it can't be." But it was. He hurried over to them. Both women were weeping, but quietly as befitted a warrior's kin. Bruno touched Hilde gently on the shoulder so as not to startle her. "Hilde, is it Arndt?" She turned her tear-streaked face to him and almost fell against him. He held her closely as she sobbed her grief against his broad chest. Great heaving sobs wracked her now as she gave in to her overwhelming sorrow. The depths of her anguish unnerved him. He had never seen her like this. She was always so strong, his Hilde. At last, when her shuddering subsided somewhat, he asked, "Is he so badly hurt then? Perhaps it is not so bad as it seems. What can I do to help?"

"He is dying, Bruno. My Papi is dying. Better he had gone straight to Valhalla from the battlefield than to be maimed like this. They brought him all the way home," her voice was becoming hysterical, "but he's going to die anyway."

"No, he is not," Bruno denied, trying to comfort her. "Arndt is a very brave man and a strong one, too. If he could make it all this way, surely he will recover with good care and comfort. Try to be brave yourself, my love; he would expect it from a Saxon maid."

"I know, Bruno," she murmured against his shirt. "I shall try. It's just—just that it's so shocking seeing him like this." She paused and took a deep breath. She straightened her back, and he could almost feel the determination pulsing through her. "I must help my mother."

Together they turned toward the man on the litter. His left arm was gone above the elbow. The stump was covered with soft leather sewed together. There did not appear to be any inflammation, yet his eyes looked feverish and his countenance was ghostly pale. He saw them then. "Ach, young Bruno," he whispered hoarsely, "is it not a sorry hero that comes home on his shield instead of carrying it?" He was trying to joke, but Bruno could see that every word cost him a tremendous effort.

"Fret yourself not, friend Arndt. These two lovely ladies will have you up and around in no time," Bruno replied as cheerfully as he could. He put his other arm around Irmengard.

"Ach, ja," said Irmengard irritably, "if we could but get him home. But these oafs don't seem to realize how serious it is, just standing around staring instead of moving out of the way."

Bruno remembered then that his father had ordered him to take charge of the wounded, but he had been too concerned about Hilde and her father. He felt like an oaf himself when he looked around and saw that there were others as bad, if not worse than Arndt. Immediately Bruno took command of the situation.

"You and you, help take these litters down from the horses. Gently now. And you, get these horses to the stables to make some room here. We'll have to carry the litters ourselves. Two horses with a litter between can never fit down the narrow lanes. Take the men who live at the Hall there—"

"But, Bruno," interrupted someone, "your father said he wanted to be alone."

"You fool." Bruno turned on the man. "My father and mother are in their private chamber by now. The Hall is empty, for everyone is out here in the court gawking. Lend a hand there before you count yourself among the maimed." He looked to some of the maids. "Inge, Eileke, take others and tend to those who live in the Hall, for they are yet bachelors and have no women to look after their needs." The women scurried off to do his bidding. "The rest of you who still have both your arms and legs, but I fear no brains, take a litter two-by-two and get the rest of these men to their homes. Hinrik, my friend, help me here with Arndt."

Together the men gently lifted the litter from between the patient horses and followed Hilde down the lane to her home. Irmengard followed, fussing all the while that they take care not to jar Arndt too much.

When they had carefully laid Arndt on his bed, Bruno said, "Hinrik, go to the Hall and there await my father's bidding. If he asks after me,

33

come and fetch me at once. I would bide here a bit."

"No, no," said Irmengard sharply. "Go, go. It is enough that you brought him here. We can manage."

"But Arndt is a heavy man," objected Bruno. He knew that Irmengard was a skilled healing woman and normally had a sunny disposition, always calm, even a bit of a stoic. That she was so sharp-tongued now betrayed the depth of her worry. "Let me help you as much as I can," he pleaded.

"Well, all right," she reluctantly agreed. "Get those filthy clothes off of him and wrap him in furs, while I make a poultice. Be very careful you don't jar the arm and start it bleeding again. But it is the chill—the chill that worries me," she mumbled half to herself as she turned away and went to her herb cabinet. Suddenly spying Hilde standing in the middle of the room she shouted, "Hildegard, do something! Don't just stand there. Help the man!"

"Yes, Mama, I was just waiting for you to tell me how I can be of help." She started to weep silently again as she turned to Bruno and her father.

Bruno put his arm gently around her again while her mother's back was turned. "Don't let her get to you," he whispered. "She is holding her grief in so tightly. Once she has done all she can for your father and lets go, she will feel better."

"I understand," she replied, "but I, too, am grieving. Oh, Papi, Papi." She knelt down beside the bed and took her father's good hand in hers. It felt very cold.

"Little one, little one," said Arndt. He weakly patted her golden head. "Don't worry. Be happy that I am home. It takes a lot to kill a tough old soldier like me. Your mother is the best healer in the Brunsburg. I trust her and the gods. You'll see; I'll be up and dancing in the Hall before the Mothering festival is half over."

But he was not.

Each day Bruno visited the tiny cottage, sometimes twice a day, if he could. Always he found Hilde sitting by her father's bed, gently placing cool cloths on his feverish brow, changing the poultice on his chest, sometimes just holding his hand while he dozed. Bruno tried to get her to go riding with him or even for a short walk, anything to get her out of the house for a while, but she always refused. He feared her grief was becoming morbid, but he could not penetrate the seemingly iron shell she had built around herself. She seemed devoid of any emotion and at times was not even very friendly toward him. If he could only talk to her, hold her in his arms, but the tiny cottage afforded no privacy. It consisted of one large room with the hearth in the center. The smoke went out a hole in the roof. Or it was supposed to, but often it did not, and at times the air in the room was stifling and fetid. Otherwise it was clean and spotless. On one side wall was the built-in cupboard bed where Arndt lay. A great, lavishly carved chest stood against the front wall. On the other side of the hearth stood a table with stools and benches nearby, and against the other wall Irmengard's cupboard. Sweet-smelling rushes lay on the earthen floor and oiled parchment covered the tiny windows. A ladder led to a split loft above. On either side of the smokehole under the eaves were the cozy nooks where the children slept. Hilde had only one brother, Hinrik, who was at present learning to be a squire and as such now slept with the single men up at the great Hall. Irmengard was now sleeping in his bed, so as not to disturb her husband.

One day Irmengard met Bruno at the door and took him aside. "I know you want to help her, and so do I. But she responds to nothing I say or do. She knows her father is dying, and it is very hard for her. They have always been so close."

Bruno quailed at hearing in Irmengard's voice what he had been fearing yet did not want to admit. "Is he really dying then? But how can this be? The arm seems to be healing cleanly."

"Yes, but it is the chill he caught all those many days lying on the litter without being able to move enough to keep his body warm. It has turned into the lung fever. I have tried every remedy I know, and nothing helps. His breast is filling with water and his lungs are too weak to expel it. It is like he is drowning." Her voice caught for a moment, and then she continued, "There is nothing more I can do for my man. It is Hilde we must try to help now. I think you should stay away for a few days."

Bruno was so shocked at this suggestion he simply stared at her. When he found his voice he exclaimed, "But Irme, how can I help her if I stay away? She will think ill of me."

"No, she won't, and perhaps she will begin to miss you. Do you see what I am saying? Tomorrow is the first Mothering Night. Perhaps I can make her go to the Hall for the festivities. But send her brother after her. We shall tell her you are too busy."

"But, Irme, it is not fair to make her jealous when she is already so troubled. I love her, Irme, I would marry her, but now I fear we shall have to wait so long. I have not even had the opportunity to speak to Arndt."

35

There, I have said it, he thought.

"Don't worry about that. He knows. We both know that you two have been in love since you were children. It will work out. Just be patient with her. And let us see if my plan works."

"Well—very well," he replied sadly, turning away. But then he stopped. "But promise you will send for me if anything—if anything—if she needs me," he finished lamely.

Bruno spent most of the next day in the Hall conversing with his father, who was telling him yet again about the disastrous campaign against the Franks and about Wittekind's plans for next season. But it was really a one-sided conversation, for Bruno was barely listening. He was watching the children and young people decorate the Hall with holly and evergreen boughs and, of course, the mischievous mistletoe. Will she come? he wondered. The giant Yule log had been brought in days ago and lay drying by the hearth, ready to brighten the feasting for a whole week. The women were putting the finishing touches on the beautiful little fir tree. The great boar had been turning on the spit over the hearth for hours. Every time the fat dripped, the flames flared up.

All Bruno could think of was a funeral pyre.

He interrupted his father. "Arndt is dying, you know."

The elder Bruno put his hand on his son's arm and said quietly, "Yes, I know. I have been trying to keep your mind off it with idle chatter, but I see you haven't heard a word of it."

"I am sorry, Father, it's just that—"

"I understand. Perhaps if we do talk about it, it will help you."

"It is not I who needs help, but Hilde. She is so changed, so different."

"No, I don't think she has changed. It is just that she is so young and has not seen much of death. And it is the first of her own loved ones. You must be patient, be strong and mature for both of you."

"But, Father, I love her so. I want to marry her, but now she hints that she is not interested in marriage but would rather be a priestess."

"I doubt that. It is just that she does not yet know how to handle grief. She mistakenly thinks that to be happy would offend the gods and they would take her father the more quickly. She also may fear that since her father did not die on the battlefield, he may have trouble getting to Valhalla. That is not true, of course. He is dying a warrior's death, and a very brave one, too."

"I know all that, Father, but how can I make her see it?"

"She will. She will. Give her time. And if it will make you feel better, let me tell you that Arndt has already spoken to me. You have his permission to marry her."

"Oh, Father," Bruno was deeply touched. "In all his pain and agony he thought of that. What a fine man. It's no wonder I love his daughter so much."

"Yes, he is. In fact, it was much on his mind. He spoke to me shortly after he was wounded, before we ever started home. We even discussed tentative terms for the marriage contract in case he should die before we got back."

Bruno felt much better having talked with his father. If only Arndt would live, that would solve everything. But he knew in his heart that would not be.

Hilde did not show up for the Mothering Night feast. Her brother came back and whispered to Bruno, "I tried every way I could outside of picking her up bodily and carrying her here. But she was adamant. All she would say was, 'Suppose Papi should die whilst I am dancing and feasting. I could not forgive myself for letting him die alone.'"

"I understand, Hinrik, you did your best. Thank you. Now enjoy yourself. We can't all sit around being sad on this night of all nights."

But Bruno's heart was not in the festivities either. The Great Hall was ablaze with light. Great pitch torches in sconces lined the walls and the very best candles brightened the great boards groaning with food and drink. The boar had been removed from the spit and was being carved, while the men heaved the great Yule log onto the fire and arranged it in just the proper way so that the gods would be pleased. When it finally caught and blazed brightly, a great cheer went up. Then, before anyone took a bite to eat, the women carried the ancient silver-bound drinking horns to the men. They were filled with a special mulled ale laced with precious spices, made especially for this night. They could not be put down until they were empty, as the bottoms were pointed. They had belonged to the tribe for hundreds of years. So, starting with the elder Bruno, the women took the horns to the men, moving up and down the lines, giving each a hearty sip until the last drop was drunk. Then the feasting began.

Bruno could barely swallow his food, tasty though it was. He found if he washed it down with ale, it helped, but soon he was drinking more than he was eating. During the feasting the bard strummed his harp and told the story of the great Mother Goddess. Then he told the saga of the Saxon

37

people from the time they left their original homeland to the north and settled in this beautiful, bounteous land. After that he recited to music the entire genealogy and great deeds of Wittekind and Bruno's forebears.

All of this took a long time, but there was a lot to eat and the people enjoyed it. Even though they had heard these stories all their lives and, indeed, most of them knew them by heart, it gave them a sense of pride in being Saxons and, above all, in being part of Bruno's tribal family. And Bruno Brunoson became lonelier the more he listened and the more he imbibed.

After the meal was cleared away, the boards were stacked against the walls and the Great Hall cleared for dancing. Then the minstrels took over from the bard, beginning to play the jolly, happy songs and carols of the midwinter season. Everyone joined in the singing, and the old folk dances were gay and carefree.

Bruno could not stand it any longer. He had already drunk far too much and was not too steady on his feet, but he managed to wend his way through the crowd and left the hall without anyone noticing. Oh, Hilde, Hilde, he thought, why couldn't you have come to be with me just this one night? When he stepped out into the courtyard, the bitter cold air made him stagger just a little. He turned toward the lane leading to her house, but when he lurched against a building he thought better of it. Ach, Donar, I am drunk. She would really be disgusted with me. Instead he went up on the wall.

It was very cold, but he did not feel it. There was no moon, but the stars were exceptionally bright. One very bright one seemed to burn right into his soul. He leaned against the palisade and stared at it for a long time, and a sort of peace seemed to come over him. Then he saw it. The great curtains of the gods in the northern sky—cold fire of blue and red, green and white—moving up to the zenith and back again. He could feel the pulsating power of it and he was deeply moved. Thus, they say, will be the Twilight of the Gods. But more than that, it always presaged some great event—usually happy, occasionally tragic, but always earthshaking.

What did it portend, that tremendous display of incandescence in the northern sky? He remembered the old priest Otto's prophecy that the great gods would be defeated by the Frankish god called Christ. Could it be coming soon? he wondered. He tried to imagine more prosaic things that could possibly happen. A happy one would be his marriage to Hilde; a tragic one would be Arndt's death. But, no, they were too personal, nothing of the magnitude that this hinted at. The dazzling waves of color moving up and down the heavens held him spellbound. Then suddenly in the midst of all this magnificence a shooting star sped across the sky and fell to earth in a shower of sparks.

Oh, Wotan! Bruno exclaimed to himself. He started shivering and was now thoroughly frightened, and quite sober. What next? What else? He wanted to leave the wall. The mysterious behavior of the heavenly bodies was too awe-inspiring for a mere human to comprehend, but he was mesmerized by its power. He felt enveloped by some magic beyond his control. He stood staring at it, leaning against the parapet until finally the spectral lights started to die down and gradually sink into the northern horizon. The silent, brilliant stars took over the sky once again.

He then became aware of the fact that he was trembling. It is just the cold, he thought. I have stayed out here too long without a jacket. But down deep he knew that he had been shaken to the depths of his soul by what he had seen. He started back to the Hall, but the sounds of music and laughter met his ears and he knew they would be going on most of the night. He turned instead to the stables and bedded down in the hay next to his warm horse.

The next morning Bruno awoke when the grooms came in to tend the animals. He had a fierce headache, and when he tried to get up he was sick. Disgusted with himself and also sorry for himself, he sat for a few minutes in the hay trying to focus his eyes and regain his equilibrium. He tried again and managed to stand up. He wanted to avoid the grooms who were cheerfully going about their work, discussing last night's wonderful feast. He didn't want to talk to anybody. He made his way out to the horse trough, broke the thin layer of ice that had formed on it during the night, and splashed the icy water on his face. It woke him up and he felt slightly better.

He entered the hall. Servants were busy cleaning up the mess. Many of the men were still snoring away on the benches that lined the walls. The great Yule log sputtered and crackled cheerfully. One of the servants noticed him and said, "Morning, young Bruno. Your father is looking for you. They have sent word from Arndt's house."

"Is he dead then?"

"I don't know," replied the man. "Your father is in his chamber."

Cursing himself for a drunken fool, Bruno hurried to seek his father. When he entered the private room, the elder Bruno was cheerfully giving another servant orders for continuing the feasting. Bruno waited, puzzled.

When the man left, his father greeted him merrily. "Well, that was a sumptuous feast last night, was it not? But you look somewhat the worse for the ale."

"Father, how can you be so cheerful when Arndt has died?" Bruno looked at his elder's smiling face. "Or so they tell me."

"Who told you that?" asked his father sharply.

"Well, one of the servants said they sent for me, so—so I just assumed . . . " His voice trailed off sheepishly.

"Arndt lives yet. In fact, they tell me he is somewhat better today. Actually sat up and tried to eat by himself. It was he himself who sent for you, not your sweetheart."

"He himself?" exclaimed Bruno delightedly. "Then I had best go at once."

"You had best not let them see you like that," chided his father. "Take a cup of mead. 'Twill settle your stomach. And then get you into the steam house. 'Tis the best cure for too much ale."

Bruno then realized that he not only felt rotten but looked it as well. The mead almost made him heave again but finally quelled the nausea. He sat in the steam house until he felt light-headed and giddy. Then he gasped as the serving wench doused him with buckets of ice water. But he felt immeasurably better. He ran naked to his own private quarters and wrapped himself in a large linen towel until his teeth stopped chattering. Then he carefully dressed in his best clothes, combed his thick hair, and set out for Hilde's house. He had to force himself to walk slowly and keep calm.

Irmengard met him at the door. "Ah, you have come at last. My man wishes to speak with you. He is much better today." Then she lowered her voice to a whisper, "But don't tire him overmuch. I tried to get her to go the Hall last night, but she wouldn't budge from his side."

Bruno merely nodded and walked over to where Arndt was sitting on the side of the bed, wrapped in furs although the room was stifling. Hilde was sitting on the same stool next to him, as if she had not moved since Bruno's last visit. Irmengard rushed up with another stool for him and placed it before her husband.

Arndt smiled and tried to raise his arm in greeting, but the effort was too much and he let it drop in his lap again. "Hail, Bruno Brunoson, greetings of the season." His voice was quivery, like an old man's. "I am glad you were able to come. I should have come to you, but . . . " He looked down at himself in dismay. "I would talk to you about this lovely, loyal daughter of mine, who would not even leave her poor father's bedside to go to the year's greatest feast."

40

"But, Papi, I told you . . ." Hilde started to protest, but shut her mouth at a flick of her father's hand.

"Enough of that," said Arndt. "I have heard all your excuses and I have told you what I intend to do and it shall be done." Arndt's voice grew stronger as he continued, "If the gods will that I give my life for the glory of the homeland, I can make no better sacrifice, and I shall go proudly. But I would settle things here first, while I am still master of this household."

Bruno was bewildered by this exchange between father and daughter but said nothing.

Arndt paused a moment to catch his breath and then went on, "Go, find something to help your mother with, whilst I talk to young Bruno."

Hilde bowed her head. "Yes, Father," she acquiesced and went to the far side of the room.

"Now, Bruno, I shall tell you what I have in mind. I hope it will gladden your heart as it will mine." He lowered his voice conspiratorially. "I wish your betrothal to my daughter to take place the day after tomorrow."

Bruno was astounded. He could hardly believe this wonderful piece of news. His mouth gaped open and he could not speak.

"Well?" urged Arndt. "Say something, or I shall think you are as foolish as my daughter."

"The day after tomorrow?" asked Bruno stupidly.

"What better time than during the Mothering Festival?"

"Of course," agreed Bruno, recovering from the surprise. "I only meant, is it not too soon, while you are yet so ill?"

Arndt lowered his voice to such a faint whisper that Bruno had to lean forward to hear him. "I am dying, Bruno. I know it. This is just a brief remission, and I pray it will last long enough for me to see this through. If we put it off and the Norns decide to snip the thread, she will never marry you—or anyone. She talks foolishness about becoming a priestess. Ah, yes, she has the gifts," he sighed, "but she is a woman in love, although she will not admit it right now, even to herself. She would be terribly unhappy—in fact, would ruin her life—if she denied her love for you. With that burden, she would not be a dedicated priestess either, although she doesn't realize this now. I insist we celebrate the betrothal immediately. That is the important thing. Once you are betrothed, the marriage can take place anytime, whether I am here or not. She cannot back out." He started gasping for breath.

Bruno quickly fetched a dipperful of water from the bucket that stood nearby. Putting his arm around the other man's shoulder, he held the dip-

41

per to his lips. He feared Arndt had overtaxed his failing strength. "Would you lie down again, my friend?" Arndt nodded and Bruno eased him back onto the plump feather pillow. "Arndt," he said, "you make me so happy I could cry. And I know you are right in insisting on the betrothal, but will she not hate me for forcing her?"

"Nay, nay, lad, she will come around in time. You shall have to have a tremendous amount of patience and give her a lot of love, especially if I am gone. But once the betrothal is an accomplished fact, she will marry you. She is a woman of honor and will not go back on her sworn word."

"Ach, Arndt, I hope you are right. I do love her so much. And I can never thank you enough for thinking of this. Does she know of your plan?"

"Ja, she knows and she will obey me. She is a good daughter."

"How well I know," replied Bruno, "and she will be a good wife, too. And now, my friend, you must rest and husband your strength for the big event."

"Don't worry," said Arndt, and a big grin lit up his features. "I shall have them carry me to the Hall. I would not miss this for the world."

"Then don't trouble yourself about a thing. I shall make all the arrangements. Later today, when you have rested a bit, I shall send my father to you to arrange the bride price."

"There is no need," replied Hilde's father. "We have already discussed it, and everything is all agreed upon."

Bruno shook his head in wonder at this remarkable man. And his daughter just like him, if she would only let herself be herself. "I shall go now to the Hall and start setting things up. And I myself shall come back to tell you all I have done."

"Just don't wake me if I am sleeping." Arndt winked at him.

Bruno laughed. "I shan't. And I thank you from the bottom of my heart."

He had turned to go when suddenly Arndt shouted, "Women! Come here."

Hilde and Irmengard scurried to his bedside. "Unpack all that wedding finery you made so long ago," he ordered, "and shake the moths out of it. The betrothal will take place day after tomorrow."

Bruno grinned at Hilde and ached to take her in his arms, but she only glared at him and turned to her mother and howled.

Bruno fairly flew to the Hall. His heart was pounding in his chest with joy. His father was not surprised at the news. He explained to Bruno what the bride price and his own inheritance was to be. It was far more

42

generous than he ever expected. He made the arrangements for the ceremony with the priestess of Frigga, Wotan's wife and goddess of good marriages, and offered the necessary sacrifices.

When all was set in motion for the betrothal to take place, Bruno was breathless and felt the need for solitude. He went to the stables and saddled Siegfried. He patted the great stallion's neck and said, "Come, old boy, you must share my joy." He rode out of the gate of the Brunsburg and wandered through the wintry woods for a long time. His heart was bursting with happiness so great it overshadowed any doubts he might have about Hilde's response to it all.

The day of the betrothal it started snowing again, a light, feathery snow that garlanded everything with white, as though to purify it for the happy event. The Great Hall was once again brightly lit and more crowded than before, for word had been sent out to kinsfolk as far away as Bücken and Vilsen. And most of them had come, bringing food for the feast and gifts for the bridal couple, for after all, it was only once a generation that the eldest son of their lord was betrothed. Cousins greeted cousins whom they had not seen in years. There was much talk of the war and particularly of the atrocious massacres and deportations. Many—far too many—were missing. An undercurrent of sadness and despair ran through the clan, although they welcomed a chance for a celebration in the midst of sorrow and all put on their best faces in anticipation of the imminent ceremony.

The elder Bruno sat in full princely regalia on the high seat, also known as the gift-chair. An unsheathed sword with a magnificent jeweled hilt lay across his lap. His son Bruno stood at his left side dressed in colorful new woolen hose and a jerkin of the softest leather richly embroidered and studded with jewels. Over his shoulders lay a rich fur cloak clasped at the neck with an heirloom gold and cloisonné brooch. Although he tried his best to look calm and dignified, his heart was pounding with excitement and little gestures of hands and feet betrayed his nervousness. At his father's right hand, truly calm and dignified, waited the priestess of Frigga in her long, flowing hooded white robes. She smiled reassuringly at Bruno. How often she had seen this before.

At last someone near the door shouted, "Make way! Make way! They are coming!" Two men bearing a litter entered. Not only was Arndt wrapped in furs, but someone had also constructed a little tent of furs over his head to shield him from the snow. Irmegard walked alongside. Bruno could see the effort she was making not to fuss over her man and give orders. They carried the litter to a specially prepared chair close to the high seat, lifted Arndt into it and carefully tucked the furs around him, even though the Hall was warm with the roaring fire and the packed humanity. Bruno thought, even Irmengard can't complain about that. Arndt's color seemed to be a little better and his eyes were bright. Once he was comfortably settled with his wife standing by his side, he turned to Bruno and gave him a broad wink. Bruno's heart soared.

Then all eyes turned to the door again as two buffalo horns sounded and his love entered on the arm of her brother Hinrik. Servants threw back her fur cloak and hood to reveal her magnificent wedding gown. It was of pure silk of the brightest red color imaginable. The silk had been bought years ago from the traders from the north, who had bought it from the Arab traders at Kiev, who in turn had brought it from the almost mythical land of Cathay. It was so heavily embroidered with gold and silver thread that it stood stiffly away from her body in panels. Pearls and garnets, adding to the splendor, were worked into the embroidery as well. The dress reached to just below her knees. Her underhose were bright yellow, of a wool so soft and fine it almost matched the silk in texture. Her shoes were of the softest, most supple leather, trimmed with gold, and the garters that wound crisscross up her calves were, instead of the usual leather thongs, red silken ribbons to match the dress. Bruno stared. He had rarely seen her in anything but homespun clothes and wooden klompen. Her headdress was worthy of a queen. Her thick blond braids were wound in circles over her ears like a Valkyrie's helmet, and strands of gold and rare colored glass beads ran through them and around the crown of her head. Around her neck was a thick gold torque, worthy of a nobleman's daughter.

Hilde walked slowly the length of the Hall with her eyes downcast. When they arrived before the high seat, Hinrik stepped back and went to stand beside his parents.

Then the elder Bruno called out in a loud voice, "Where is Bruno Brunoson?"

Bruno moved to stand beside Hilde, facing his father. "I am here, my Lord."

"I am told that you wish to take this woman to wife."

"I do, my Lord," replied Bruno

"Where is Hildegard Arndt's daughter?"

"I am here, my lord," whispered Hilde.

"I am told that you wish to take this man to husband."

Hilde gulped. "Ja."

"Speak up, child, they must hear you in the back of the Hall."

"I do, my Lord," she said.

"Then, since you will soon form a new household in my domain, I would have your oath of fealty."

The couple knelt before him, and each put their head on one of his knees. The bard stepped forward and recited the oath, which they repeated together after him. Then Bruno the elder took the sword and laid it across the back of their necks. "May Wotan accept your oath, as I do, and may this sword ever bind you to me and the clan of Bruns forever." He removed the sword. "Now, before this company of witnesses, we shall give from this gift-chair the wedding gift and the bride price. To you, Bruno, my son, I bestow five farms that surround the spring Brüne, together with all houses and barns thereon, all horses, cattle, swine and other livestock, and all the peasants thereof to work it for you and all income therefrom. One of these with all appurtenances, whichever you choose, for they are all rich, you shall give to Hildegard for her own income as bride price. I further give you, Bruno, this sword, which was my great-grandfather's. Use it wisely and with courage. I further give you, Hildegard, this purse of silver coins. Use it wisely and prudently."

Then Arndt spoke up from his chair. "I, too, would give gifts. To my son soon-to-be this sheath for the sword. Wear it with honor. To my daughter, this necklace, which was her great-grandmother's. And to them both, a milking cow and a sow soon to drop piglets."

Then the couple rose and the priestess of Frigga stepped forward and took the sword from Bruno the elder. She faced the couple and turned them slightly toward each other and placed the sword between them, the tip resting on the ground. Then she instructed them to place their hands on its hilt, first Hilde's, then Bruno's, then Hilde's, and then Bruno's.

She raised her arms and intoned, "I call on the power of Frigga, great goddess of good marriage and childbirth, beloved wife of great Wotan, to bless this couple, Bruno and Hildegard, who have stated before thee and this company that they wish to marry. Unite them in love and defend them in adversity; grant them many children, good health and a long life to honor thee with their substance." She lowered her arms and placed one hand on each shoulder. "Hildegard, plight your troth to Bruno."

"Bruno, I plight thee my troth," said Hilde in a quivering voice.

"Bruno, do you accept her troth and plight yours to Hildegard?"

"Hildegard, I accept thy troth and plight thee mine."

"On this sword of Wotan ye have sworn your oaths of love and loyalty. May it never stand between you again and only be raised in defense of one another. Frigga will bless you. Now seal your betrothal with a kiss."

With their hands still on the hilt of the sword, Bruno leaned forward and kissed Hilde, who had never once raised her eyes. The kiss was cool and chaste, but he was grateful even for that, for he noticed tears on her cheeks.

The priestess raised her arms once again in blessing. "Go in peace."

Bruno's father stood up and roared, "Let the feasting begin!" Pandemonium reigned. Everyone tried to crowd around the couple offering congratulations and gifts. Bruno's heart was filled with pride and joy. Hilde only wanted to be alone and weep, but she put on a brave face and turned a stiff little smile toward the assorted cousins and kin.

Although the marriage could have been consummated that very night, and often was, because the betrothal was the far more important ceremony of the two—in fact, sometimes the only one—Bruno did not even ask Hilde. He knew she needed time and, in any event, wanted to be with her father. So he was willing to wait until she came to him willingly and in love. But it was not easy for him. After the feasting he saw her and her parents home and went back to his lonely room in the Great Hall.

Arndt seemed to have expended the last of his meagre strength in the effort of going to the betrothal ceremony. The next day his fever was raging again and he had great difficulty breathing. When Bruno arrived at the cottage, he was met with a tirade from Hilde. "Well, I hope you are happy," she spat, with such vitriol in her voice that he was taken aback. "I am sure you are well satisfied. You have your bride gifts and your bride, just as you wanted, without a thought of what your selfish scheming would do to my father. He is truly dying now and it is all your fault."

"But, Hilde," stammered Bruno, "it was his wish as well as—nay, more than mine."

"I don't want to talk about it. You paid the bride price but will never have me the way you want me. I intend to remain virgin the rest of my life. Go back to your Great Hall and think on that."

"Hilde, Hilde," Arndt whispered weakly from the bed, but she ignored him. Bruno was deeply hurt, even though he realized how she was suffering. "It's time you grew up, Hilde," he lashed back at her. "You are a woman betrothed now and you act like a child. In good time you *will* be a wife to me in every way I demand. Right now I am ashamed of you." He turned on his heel and left without waiting for a reply.

Hilde put her face in her hands and wept. Arndt called her over to him. "Why are you weeping?" he asked gently. "You told him to go."

"But—but," she blubbered, "I did not expect that he would."

"Did you think he would stand there and listen to you screeching like an ice witch? No man will take that from a woman—or a child. He's right, you know. You are acting like a child—a spoiled child. I am disappointed. I thought I had taught you to be a true Saxon maid."

"But you did, Papi," she protested, somewhat calmer now. "I can ride and fight with the sword like any man."

"That does not make a woman—or a man either for that matter."

"And I can spin and weave and sew. I can cook and clean. I know all about herbs and medicine, which is more than many women know."

"And you are still a child."

"But it is true," she said as she tried to change the subject from herself, "that you are sicker today than before. You were doing so well, and then you were forced to go out in the cold to that—that—to my betrothal. It will be all his fault if you worsen and die."

"Hilde, my child, listen to me carefully, for my strength is failing. Was it Bruno who wielded the Frankish ax that took my arm?"

"No."

"Was it Bruno who gave me the chill on the long way home?"

"No, of course not."

"And you know it was my own idea to see you safely betrothed before I go. When I knew I was dying, I made the decision—not the other way around. Bruno was as surprised as you, you know."

"I suppose so."

"Now, let me explain something. No one can live on this earth forever. Death is a part of life. It is just a transition of the soul to Valhalla—or to Hel. Mature people understand that, and most welcome it. Only the gods are immortal, although 'tis said that even they one day will die. Do you understand?"

"I think I do."

"But there is one way men can be immortal—through their children. The Bruns clan is a great and noble one and, the gods willing, it will prosper for hundreds of years. But think, Hilde, if every woman acted like you think you want to and did not give herself in love to her man, how long do you think this clan would survive?"

"Not long, I guess."

"We Saxons are brought up to put duty before all else, as you well

47

know. That is your duty to me, to your husband and to the clan. But I had a duty as well. The world is rough and cruel. A woman alone has no protection. It was my duty, when I knew that you would soon be without my protection, to turn you over to the protection of a man I know and trust and love, even as he loves you. Although I would have preferred to die on the battlefield and go straight to Valhalla in the arms of a Valkyrie, I am grateful to the gods for giving me this time to see you are well cared for. I have done my duty and I am very happy. Now let me go in peace and do not upset me anymore with all this foolishness."

"Oh, Papi, I am grateful, too, it's just that . . . "

Arndt weakly flicked his hand. "Smile, daughter, smile. I want to know that you are happy, too." She smiled. "And promise that my funeral will be a happy occasion. When the flames of the pyre take my soul to Valhalla, I want you and everyone to rejoice with me."

"Yes, Papi, I promise."

"Now, go to Bruno and apologize and let me rest and prepare my soul for its journey."

Hilde stood up, reluctant to go. He flicked his hand again and she turned to fetch her cloak. Then, with a tiny burst of strength, Arndt added with his old grin, "And tell them not to sacrifice my horse on the pyre. I am not noble enough and he is too good a horse to waste on that. I want you to have him."

Hilde laughed in spite of her grief, and left the house to do Arndt's bidding. She felt better than she had since they brought him home. If he was happy to die, she would not spoil that happiness by indulging in her excessive grief. That much she could understand, and she would abide by his wishes. But apologizing to Bruno was another thing. She admitted that she was wrong and should not have blamed him for her father's illness, but she didn't want him to think she had stopped grieving.

It was a good excuse to hold him at bay for a while. Ach, ja, she knew all about what happened between men and women and how babies came to be conceived. Living in a one-room cottage in a close-knit community like the Brunsburg with scores of farm animals, to say nothing of innumerable dogs and cats, one could not help but know. But she just didn't feel right about it yet. She thought back to the evening in the Hall a few weeks ago, when Bruno had been so passionate. She had almost wanted it then. If they had been betrothed then — but they weren't, and so much has happened since . . . She let her thoughts drift off. What has changed? She had no answer.

As she approached the Hall, she lost her courage and decided not to seek him out. Not yet, she thought. If I should meet him by chance, well that was one thing. But she was not ready to face him—yet.

Several days after the end of the Mothering Festival, on a cold night in the first month of the year, Arndt finally succumbed to the dread pneumonia. Toward the end it was Irmengard, not Hilde, whom he wanted near him. They had eyes only for each other. She held his hand and kissed him a tender farewell.

How they love each other, thought Hilde, and yet she has never broken down as I did. She has remained calm and—yes, mature through it all. Hilde began to understand a bit more of what her father had been trying to tell her. Perhaps there is more to marriage than just rutting like animals, she mused. And she had still not seen Bruno.

"I shall take word to the Hall," she volunteered. Perhaps she would see him and she would explain why she had been so distraught. She hoped he would understand. But she was worried because he had not been near the house all these long days, not even to visit her father. But he loves me, she reassured herself.

She suddenly realized with amazement that Arndt's death was actually a relief. The long siege was over. And now, without consciously intending to, her thoughts turned to love and eventual marriage. Ach, her dear father had been so right and she so wrong.

But Bruno was not at the Hall, nor was his father. A sleepy man-at-arms heard her news. "Our master is already abed," he said, "but I shall wake him forthwith."

She hesitated. She had not realized it was so late. Should she ask him to wake Bruno the younger as well? Better not now. "Yes, if you would," she replied.

When she returned to the cottage, the Angel of Death was already there. The ancient crone had the unsavory job of preparing the dead of the entire community for the funeral. When she had left with her two burly assistants carrying Arndt's body, Hilde turned to her mother.

"You loved him very much, didn't you, Mama?" she asked.

"Ja, and I always will. But he died happy and so I am happy. He couldn't have lived like this. But in two days he will be in Valhalla and happier than even I could make him. He is a good man, your father."

"I know, Mama," and the two women clung together for a long time.

For two days men had been gathering wood from the forest and stacking it near the moat between the two walls of the fortress. It was an arduous task this time of year, when most of the wood was wet and frozen. They even made little fires to dry it, for it must not smolder but flame up quickly and fiercely. The higher the smoke rose, the quicker the deceased's soul would arrive at Valhalla. When the wood was piled high enough they set four long poles around it and on these they placed Arndt's armor, shield, sword and spear.

The day of the funeral was cold and overcast. Thick gray snow clouds hung low, but the snow itself held off. Every inhabitant of the Brunsburg as well as nearby kinfolk was gathered around the pyre. Hilde, though wrapped snugly in her hooded fur cloak, was numb from the cold. Perhaps her heart was numb as well, for she felt no grief, no emotion of any kind. Her brother stood beside her, for only their mother was allowed to accompany the corpse on its last journey. Even in the press of the crowd Hilde felt terribly alone. Her eyes searched the crowd for Bruno and finally found him standing with his father on the opposite side of the circle, but he was staring at the pyre and appeared not to see her.

The crowd grew restless and many were stomping their feet from the cold. At last the buffalo horn sounded and the funeral procession started out the gate led by the priest of Wotan, followed by the Angel of Death. Her two assistants carried Arndt's body on a flat wooden bier. He was dressed in his finest clothing. A gold and garnet brooch held his cloak across his chest. Behind her husband came Irmengard, also dressed in her best with a serene half-smile on her face. Then followed a man bearing a flaring torch and the priests and priestesses of all the other gods and goddesses who had altars at the Brunsburg.

When the party reached the waiting pyre, the priest of Wotan stepped aside and the Angel of Death climbed up onto the stacked wood and instructed her assistants how to place the body. They laid the bier down just so, with the head to the north and the feet to the south. They then erected a small cloth tent over the body. The assistants climbed down from the pyre, but the Angel of Death remained inside the tent with the dead man.

The priest of Wotan began intoning a long prayer that included a number of magic formulas to ensure the soul's quick release and safe journey to the Hall of Wotan himself. After that the priest of Donar had his say, for in accordance with Arndt's wishes they had not sacrificed his horse, but were going to offer a goat, the sacred animal of Donar. After the prayers, the priest led the goat up onto the pyre and turned it over to the Angel of Death, who took it inside the tent and quickly dis-

50

patched it with a deft slice across the throat. The goat was laid in the proper position at the deceased's feet.

When this was done, the priest of Wotan called out, "Are there any others who wish to sacrifice for love of this man?"

The priestess of Frigga stepped forward, a suckling pig in her arms. "My lord priest, Irmengard, wife to Arndt, wishes to honor our lady Frigga in thanksgiving for a blessed and fruitful marriage with this man." Hilde was surprised. She had not known her mother was planning this. Another facet of love was revealed to her. Unbidden tears came to her eyes as she watched the priestess mount the pyre and hand the little pig to the Angel of Death. The old crone quickly cut the piglet's throat and laid it gently at Arndt's head.

"Are there any other sacrifices?" asked the priest. There were none, so the Angel of Death made a last inspection to be sure all was in order.

"All is in readiness," she announced from the top of the pyre. "Let the journey of this soul begin."

As she climbed down from the top, men were quickly lighting torches from the first one and passing them around.

Then the priest of Wotan asked Irmengard, "Do you love this man, your lord?"

"I do," replied Irmengard.

The priest handed her a flaming torch. "Then release his soul to Wotan."

Irmengard took the torch and quickly shoved it into the dry kindling at the bottom of the pyre.

The priest was before Hinrik and Hilde. "Do you love this man, your father?"

"I do," each one answered, and they were handed torches. Hilde felt her knees shaking. She was not sure she could go through with this, but her brother urged her forward. And strangely, when she pushed her torch into the kindling and murmured the ritual words, "I do it for love of him," a sensation of peace and happiness came over her.

Then all the elders and kinfolk of the tribe, starting with Bruno the elder, took torches and added them to the fire and a great conflagration leapt up, the flames licking around the bier and the tent. The smoke rose straight to heaven, carrying Arndt's soul with it.

"He goes! He goes!" cried someone, and a great cheer went up, men beating on their shields with their swords and women ringing bells, everyone screaming. No one was cold now. They stood as long as

51

the flames roared, consuming everything.

When the fire started to die down, the people began to drift away. The Angel of Death would take care of the rest. After the ashes cooled she would carefully place the ashes, bones and jewelry in a specially prepared urn and bury it. That was simply an anticlimax. The funeral itself was over once the soul left the body.

Bruno the elder called out to the crowd, "To the Hall! To the Hall! Let the feasting begin!" He took Irmengard by the hand and led her thence.

"I don't think I can face it," said Hilde to her brother.

"You must," he replied. "You have Bruno now. Our Arndt saw to that. You are not alone."

Hilde was not so sure. At the Hall, she picked at the food while most of the others gorged themselves and got happily drunk. Her brother had left her to join the other young men, and she noticed Bruno laughing and joking with them. Her mother sat at the head table with the elder Bruno and his wife. The bard had composed a new song honoring Arndt and the accomplishments of his lifetime. It seemed to go on and on, and Hilde barely paid attention to it. The party swirled around her and she sank deeper into her self-imposed misery.

Vaguely she became aware that someone was standing close behind her. As she started to turn, a leg was slung over the bench and Bruno sat next to her. "Still so sad, my sweet maid?" he asked gently and took her hand in his.

"Oh, Bruno, it is so good to see you. You have stayed away so long. I—I have missed you," she admitted hesitantly.

"Have you, indeed?" In her joy at being near him again, she missed the sarcasm in his voice.

"Truly, I have."

"I asked if you were still sad."

"No, not really," she replied. "My father explained a lot of things before he—he died. About things like duty—and love."

"Did he now?"

"Yes, and I am truly sorry I was so—so discourteous to you. I was not myself."

"I understand, but do you understand—really?" he asked.

"I think so. I have been watching my mother these last days. She says very little, but her actions have taught me a lot."

"Like what?"

"About love. That there is much more to love between a man and a woman than just—just—than I thought," she finished lamely.

"But that is very important, too, when a couple loves one another."

Hilde said nothing. The truth was she didn't know what to say to that.

Bruno released her hand. "Hilde, I shall never force you to do anything you are not ready for. I had hoped that you truly missed me as much as you say. I shall wait until you come to me." He stood up, kissed her lightly on the forehead, and mingled with the crowd.

Her brief moment of hope shattered around her like shards of thin ice when a stone is tossed into the pond. She sank back into abject misery.

Not long after, Irmengard rose from the table and came to Hilde. "They will go on feasting all night and I appreciate the honor they do Arndt, but I, for one, have work to do. Come."

As they walked out into the court, Hilde could see the glowing embers of the funeral pyre beyond the wall reflected against the low-lying clouds. "Papi, Papi," she whispered, "what have I done wrong now? I apologized to him and he said he understood. Yet he is still so cold to me."

"What did you say?" asked Irmengard.

"Nothing. Nothing. I—I was just wondering where Papi is now," she dissembled.

"Safe from harm and happy."

When they had changed back into their workaday clothes, her mother handed her a bucket and together they went out to milk the cows and feed the pigs.

"Work is the best antidote for any kind of problem," said her wise mother, who understood more than Hilde realized. "Sometimes I think the animals are smarter than we. All they want is a full belly and a warm stall."

"Mama, I want to ask you something—about the pig."

"It was the least I could do. In the olden days, a woman who loved her man so much that she felt she could not live without him often sacrificed herself. Nowadays that is frowned upon," explained her mother.

"Really?" Hilde was aghast at this bit of information.

The winter wore on. Hilde was lonely. She missed her father, but she had to admit she missed Bruno's lighthearted companionship more. When she happened to meet him he was always courteous, but their old camaraderie was missing. She threw herself into her spinning and weaving with a vengeance, for there was not much else to be done in the inclement weather.

Wittekind had spent the winter with his family in the fortress beyond the Elbe. King Karl had sent his own personal herald with the message that he could have his freedom and rule Saxony in peace if he would but surrender and become a Christian. Wittekind refused. And the worst news of all was that the Franks had not gone home for the winter, as was customary, but had garrisoned the captured towns and fortresses in Westfalen and dug in.

At last the icicles on the southern eaves of the houses dripped longer and longer. The frozen river began to break up and the snow melted away wherever the sun could get at it. Every once in a while a hint of spring would come on a gentle breeze from the south.

Suddenly the first snowdrops pushed up through the forest floor, the meadow grass turned green and the buds began to swell on the trees. Hearts lifted and the blood ran quicker. Bruno took long rides around the countryside to ease the heat of his frustration. Didn't the girl realize why he had to stay away from her? He couldn't be near her without wanting to fondle and caress her, and that could only lead to one thing—which she obviously did not want. Oh, ye gods, what to do?

Bruno's father was impatiently awaiting word from his brother Wittekind as to his plans for the new season's campaign against the Frankish invaders. Where were they to meet and when?

"He'll no doubt wait until after the Spring Festival so that the men can plow the fields and plant the seed before they leave," he remarked to Bruno one day.

"I want to go with you this year, Father," said Bruno.

"No, no. I need you to stay here to hold the Brunsburg and defend the women. You did well last year."

"Please, my lord father, let someone else stay. I need to get away for a while. I want to fight to get some of this—this fire out of my blood," begged Bruno.

"There is only one thing that will quench that kind of fire, and I can't understand why you haven't done it ere now. What is the matter with that girl?"

"She still mourns for her father," replied Bruno.

"Ach, such foolishness. Arndt would be ashamed of her, as I am of you. Why in the olden days a man would have slung her over his shoulder and carried her to his bed—and no two ways about it."

"But, Father," Bruno objected, "I love her too much to force her."

54

"Ach, Donar, I don't know what this younger generation is coming to. I want a grandson in her belly before I leave," he roared, and then more softly, "I want to know that there will be an heir in case I don't come back. And that is why you must stay. We can't both be killed."

Bruno hung his head in shame. He had not thought of it in that light. "Yes, my lord. I'll try."

The vernal equinox arrived and with it the great Spring Festival, which would ensure the fertility of the fields and an abundant crop.

Meanwhile Bruno had been seeing more of Hilde, visiting the cottage often, trying to break through the shell she had built around herself. He had succeeded in getting her to take walks with him, but she would never come to the Hall on her own. Finally, a few weeks previously, on a beautiful day she had consented to go riding with him. As they passed through fields and woods burgeoning with new life, she felt a strange stirring in her own blood that she had never experienced before. It was as though she, too, wanted to be a part of this budding and blossoming—this creation of new life. However, instead of loosening her inhibitions, the sensation frightened her and she withdrew even more. And Bruno was even more perplexed.

"I feel strange riding my father's horse," she remarked.

"I am sure he deemed you worthy of him," replied Bruno, hoping to bolster her ego.

"I just don't know," she murmured, and they rode on in silence.

One day as the time for the Spring Festival drew nigh, Bruno was visiting Hilde and her mother. The little house was spotless, for they, like everyone, had been cleaning for days. This was an essential preparation for the festival. They should have been exhausted, but Irmengard seemed full of life, more so than her daughter.

Bruno gathered his courage and asked Hilde, "Will you dance with me at the festival?"

Hilde had been expecting the question and wanted so much to say yes, but she was still afraid. When she hesitated, Irmengard replied for her, "Of course she will. And I am going to, too."

"You, Mother?" Hilde was shocked.

"Yes, me. Do you think I am dead, too, just because your father has died?"

"And why not?" said Bruno with a grin. "Your mother is yet a young woman. Who is it, Irme?" he teased.

Irmengard laughed. "I'll not tell yet, but you will see."

55

"There, you see, Hilde," said Bruno. "Every woman worth her salt will dance with Freyr and Freya. And you will dance with me. After all, we are betrothed—and for too long a time already."

Hilde didn't know what to make of this revelation. If her mother was going to make a fool of herself, that was her business. But I can't, I'm a coward. No, I'm not, her inner voice told her. I really want Bruno to bed me, but the dance was so explicitly sexual she didn't know what to say. Oh, Freya, she inadvertently cried to the fertility goddess, queen of the festival, what should I do? Trust Bruno, do it, said the inner voice.

"Very well," she said meekly, "I shall dance with you, Bruno. But I— I am so—so—stupid. You must show me what to do."

"With pleasure, my love," agreed Bruno exultingly.

On the day of the first full moon after the equinox all the virgins of the clan went out to the sacred meadow of Freyr and Freya where the festivities would later take place. As dawn broke in the eastern sky, they sang hymns to Oster, the virgin goddess of dawn, of beauty and of spring. As the sun rose, they spread out to the fields and woods and gathered armfuls of flowers, which they carefully wove into head crowns and long garlands.

Shortly after noon the buffalo horns sounded and the long procession wound out of the gates of the Brunsburg toward the sacred meadow, led by the priest of Freyr and the priestess of Freya, the twin god and goddess of fertility, who were stark naked but garlanded with flowers. All the married and betrothed couples, and anyone else who wanted to, followed. Most of the men wore only loincloths, although a few were more sedately dressed. But they all wore the horns of some beast on their heads, the royal staghorn being reserved for Bruno the elder, and garlands of flowers around their necks. The women mostly wore loose strapless shifts simply wrapped around them with no fastenings. Each wore an exquisitely wrought crown of flowers in her hair. The men on one side of the procession, the women on the other, carried a long chain of flowers that stretched in one continuous length from beginning to end. The virgins were not compelled to take part in the festival, but many chose to know their first man on this night to honor Freyr and Freya.

When they reached the meadow they were met by several of the old people of the clan who were handing out cups of mead. There were two kinds, one plain and the other laced with a powerful aphrodisiac for the shy and timid, or impotent. You had your choice. After everyone took a cup of mead the dance began. Slowly, and sedately at first, the priest and priestess led them around the meadow until a huge circle was formed.

Every time they passed the old people they were handed another cup of mead. After a while you had no choice, you took whatever was handed to you, and soon no one cared. The dance became more spirited, and then at a signal they all stopped and the pattern was reversed, the men going in one direction, the women in the other. Still carrying the long floral chains, they wound in and out of each other, effectively braiding the flowers until when at last when each reached his own partner, they formed a continuous circle of flowers and humanity.

When Hilde reached Bruno once again she was gasping for breath and her eyes were sparkling.

"Happy, my love?" he asked.

"Oh, yes, Bruno. I am so glad I came. It is much more fun than I expected."

"It gets better yet," he promised.

At this point the dancing stopped and the interlocked men and women started swaying back and forth, chanting prayers and incantations to Freyr and Freya. The priest and priestess went to the center of the circle, the heart of the sacred meadow, and there performed an extremely erotic dance, at the climax of which they lay down in the meadow and joined in ecstasy, dedicating their seed to the god and goddess, that the fields might be fertile and the crops abundant.

Bruno stole a glance at Hilde. Her face was beet red, but her eyes never left the rhythmic sacrifice taking place before her. He put his arm around her and held her close and felt her arm slip around his waist.

The dancing began again, more frantic than before, and soon reached a pitch of erotic intensity. Before very long the circle was broken again and again by couples who fell to the ground and copulated where they lay. Bruno could hardly contain himself, but he knew instinctively that such crudity would spoil it for Hilde the first time. So, still dancing, he steered her over to the woods at the edge of the meadow. His manhood was standing up hard and straight, but she didn't seem to notice it. No one else noticed anything either as they left the crowd and entered the wood.

Still half dancing and half running, before she could ask any foolish questions, he quickly led her to a spot he had carefully selected in advance, a little grassy glen covered with a soft, thick carpet of pine needles. There he stopped and immediately started kissing her. To his great joy, she responded passionately.

He opened her mouth with his tongue and felt the searing warmth as her tongue met his. He kissed her eyelids and the pulse of her neck. His hand cupped one of her lovely breasts. He felt her stiffen slightly, but despite herself the nipple hardened under his touch.

Hilde felt an electric shock from his touch run down to the pit of her stomach and beyond. Her loins were suddenly on fire. Why, I don't want him to stop, she thought, amazed at this new, wonderful, melting sensation that overtook her.

Bruno reached beyond her and took his fur cloak from the crotch of a tree where he had hidden it that morning. He momentarily released her while he spread it on the ground.

"Oh, Bruno, don't stop!" she cried.

"I won't, my love. Come here." He took her hand and pulled her down beside him on the soft cloak. Once again he was kissing her passionately, as he loosened her shift and let it fall away from her body. He gazed at her loveliness and tore away his own loincloth.

"My beautiful love," he murmured and started kissing her breasts while his hand slid down to her golden triangle.

Hilde gasped at the fire that shot through her body. Her mind ceased functioning, and she was pure erotic sensation centered on that secret spot. Help me, help me, before I explode, she thought.

But he was holding himself in check in order to give her still greater pleasure. His flicking tongue slid across her belly and found the soft, moist recess between her thighs. Her ecstasy reached a pinnacle she could not have believed possible. She spread her legs to welcome him.

He positioned himself over her and gradually eased himself into her eager warmth. She felt a stab of pain and then he was moving inside her, slowly, in and out, then faster and faster. Pain was forgotten in a blinding starburst of light as they climaxed together.

He slowly raised himself on his elbows and gently kissed her mouth, her eyes, the top of her nose. He brushed back the stray hairs stuck to the sweat on her forehead. "My beautiful wife," he said. "I love you so much."

"I love you, too, Bruno. And I really am your wife now, aren't I?"

"At last," he teased.

"Why did I wait so long?" she asked. "I never dreamed it could be so wonderful."

"You weren't ready—until today." He reached out and drew the cloak around them, as it was growing chilly.

She looked at the cloak and said suddenly, "Bruno, you planned this. How did you know I would be ready today?"

"I only hoped," he replied. He kissed her again and they lay in each other's arms as the full moon rose in all its splendor.

After the fields had been plowed and the seed sown, Bruno's father and his warriors left the Brunsburg to meet Wittekind at Wildeshausen, where there was an ancient fortress built by their forefather Wigald and still in Saxon hands. Wittekind had negotiated an alliance with Surbold, king of the Frisians, and this did wonders for the spirit of the Saxon army. But their enthusiasm was short-lived. The combined armies met the Franks at Bokeloh and were completely overwhelmed. Surbold was killed and the Frisians went home to their island kingdom. The few remaining loyal Saxons fled with Wittekind to another of his fortresses where his family had taken refuge. The Franks followed and captured and burned the fortress. Wittekind and most of the others escaped except for one of his daughters, who had lingered too long to take some jewels with her and was brutally slain.

All this bad news filtered back to the inhabitants of the Brunsburg in agonizing bits and pieces. They were shocked, dismayed and discouraged. "What will become of us? How long before they come here and destroy our homes? Have the gods deserted Saxony?" they asked. Bruno tried to keep up their courage, but it was difficult in the face of the increasingly grave reports from Westfalen. He had had no direct word from his father and did not know if he yet lived or not.

One evening he and Hilde were sitting before the fire after supper. As he stared into the flames, he was reminded of Hilde's vision a year ago. He decided it was time to discuss it with her now.

"I don't remember it at all," she said, "but I am not surprised. I have had such things happen before."

He described it to her in detail. "What can it mean?" he asked.

Hilde glanced about the Hall before she answered. No one was near enough to hear their conversation. She lowered her voice, "The ravens and wolves fleeing can only mean that Wotan is deserting us—or, since I can't really believe he would do that to a people so loyal to him, perhaps there is a war in heaven just as there is here on earth and this Christ god is defeating our gods. Yes, I believe that is what is happening, for it certainly seems to be happening here on earth."

Bruno nodded. It was similar to Otto's prediction.

"And what of the stone castle and the bear's claws embracing the cross?" he asked.

"I don't know," she replied. "Perhaps whoever it is that has the bear's

59

claws emblem will embrace the Frankish religion. What the castle means, I can't guess. Perhaps we should ask one of the priestesses. They are experts at interpreting these things."

"No, I don't think we should. I don't think we dare. If it is as you think, they could even condemn us to death," he said. "Let us keep it our secret for now."

"Yes, you are right." She shuddered.

"Do you know of anyone whose emblem is the bear's claws?" he asked.

"No, I don't," she replied. Then she looked at him strangely. "Bruno! Could it refer to you — or your father?"

"My father, never," he denied.

"And you?" she asked, almost afraid of what his answer might be.

He hesitated a moment and then told her all that the ancient priest Otto of Heiligenberg had told him. "So you see," he finished, "he is convinced that the Twilight of the Gods is at hand, and that from a chief priest of Wotan. He said that many of the nobles in Westfalen have nominally accepted this Christian baptism, even though they still worship our gods in their hearts, in order to save their castles, their lands and their people."

"Hypocrites," she spat.

"Perhaps," he replied, "but he has almost convinced me that it is the better way. It would save many lives. He wants me to come to him and learn about this thing called politics."

"Hah," she said. "Politics is saving your own neck regardless of your beliefs and loyalties."

"Your words are harsh."

"But true."

"Maybe so, but I am responsible for many lives," he waved his arm around the Hall, "not just here in the Brunsburg but all the kinfolk roundabout who depend on us. Should I sacrifice them needlessly if the Franks and their god are going to win anyway? I saw what they did to the people, especially the women, in Vilsen. I could not live if that happened to you. Besides," he patted her still flat belly, "we have another to think of now. Otto said that we — you and I — are responsible for the future of the Bruns tribe and that there would be Bruns here forever. The rune-sticks told him."

Hilde smiled. She had only a few days ago told Bruno of the babe he had started inside her and he had been overjoyed. "Is that all you can think of, the Bruns that will be here a thousand years hence?" she teased.

"No, my love," he replied. "I am thinking about how I can keep you and our son safe right now so that he can grow up in a peaceful land."

"Bruno, are you really seriously thinking about surrendering to this Frankish king and his god?" she asked gravely.

"I don't know. I really don't," he said thoughtfully. "It seems such a terribly final step to take. And it is death to backsliders. In fact, all I have seen of this Christ god is cruelty and death. And yet, to save our lives and our lands, it might be worth it." He put his arm around Hilde and held her close while they watched the flames sputter and leap on the hearth. Then he seemed to come to a decision. "I need advice," he said, "good advice. I think I should seek Otto out before very long, before it's too late."

"Oh, Bruno," said Hilde, "the countryside is so dangerous now. I could not bear it if anything happened to you."

"Calm your fears, my love. I shall be very careful. It is only a day's journey. And he is so old. I should not wait any longer."

Two days later Bruno set out for Heiligenberg to confer with the old priest. Once again he took the forest paths and avoided the roads. He rode past his farms around the Brüne spring and they all looked well kept and prosperous. His heart swelled with pride. Yes, it would even be worth surrendering to the Christ god to keep these beautiful acres from being devastated. Have I already made up my mind then? he asked himself, shocked that the idea had come to him so readily. But he recalled his wife's sharp comment about hypocrisy and thought, no, no, not yet.

He wished he could stop and get to know his farmers but dared not take the time. He sought access to the Holy Mountain by the secret path Otto had shown him. When the way grew too steep, he dismounted and silently led Siegfried along the needle-carpeted path. An eerie feeling of disquietude came over him—not a premonition exactly, but a sense that all was not right. It was very quiet, almost too quiet. When he reached the top and cautiously entered the clearing he knew something was wrong. No peasant was working the fields, no acolyte or servant came out to meet him. There was no sign of fire or pillage. And then, as he approached closer, he saw it. The sacred altar of Wotan was overturned and smashed, the jewels all gone.

"Oh, Wotan! Oh, all ye gods! They have been here. I am too late!" Bruno exclaimed in anguish. He looked carefully around but could see no sign of the enemy. The silence was utter. He cautiously approached the priest's house, not daring to call out. He noticed the door was partially open. As he drew closer, he heard a faint whimpering sound. Something or someone still living, he thought. He pushed the door wider open without daring to enter. Suddenly a tiny ball of gray fur came hurtling toward him, whining, jumping, slavering. He reached down and sharp puppy teeth nipped his finger.

"So, it is you I heard crying. Is there no one else here?" he asked.

As if in answer, the puppy ran back into the interior of the house. When he saw Bruno made no move to follow, he ran back to him again, made a baby lunge at his knees and ran back into the hall, where he started whimpering again. This time Bruno followed.

"Oh, Wotan. Oh, gods." He rushed to Otto's side. The old priest lay on the floor near the hearth, his once white robe covered with blood. The puppy was licking his face. Bruno thought the old priest was dead, but when he placed his hand on his breast there was still some warmth, and he could feel a faint heartbeat and shallow breathing. He lifted Otto's head off the floor and said, "Otto, Otto, my lord priest, it is I, Bruno Brunoson."

The old man's eyes flickered and he whispered faintly, "Ah, you have come. I have been waiting for you."

"Thank the gods you live," said Bruno. "Let me bind your wounds and help you to lie in a bed. Then tell me what has happened here."

"Nay, nay," replied Otto. "There is no time. I am mortally wounded and have forced myself to stay alive until you got here—with the help of my little friend here." His rheumy eyes glanced toward the puppy.

"You knew I was coming?" asked Bruno in amazement.

"Of course. Did I not send a message to your soul?" replied the priest, as if this were an everyday occurrence. "But let me speak quickly, for I have little time left."

Bruno sat down on the floor and held the dying man's head on his lap. "Speak then, lord priest."

"Wittekind was captured but escaped. You will hear all the details eventually, so I won't waste my breath telling you. He fled to Ostfalen and Karl and his army followed. They were moving swiftly and apparently had strict orders to destroy nothing except our altars and holy places. They harmed no houses or fields. They killed no one except priests and our sacred animals."

"Oh, Otto, how awful."

The old man shook his head. "Nay, I knew it was coming. I am the last priest of our gods. You and your children must learn to live with the new god. There is no other way."

Bruno drew in his breath. "What shall I do, my lord?" he asked.

"Harken to me carefully, young Bruno." Otto's voice grew so faint that Bruno had to lean over him to hear his words. "When they come to you, and they will come within the year, go along with what they ask. Pretend, if you must, but tell them that you will worship their god. But harken well—you must strike a bargain with them. All the nobles in Westfalen have done it. There is no longer any shame. Tell them that in order to rule your lands properly they must build you a strong castle out of stone." Bruno gasped, but the old man paid no attention. "At Hoya, yes, I think Hoya is the best place. And if you are to be a great noble, they will want you to choose an emblem. They set great store by that. I want you to choose two raised bear's claws." Bruno couldn't believe what he was hearing, but the priest wasn't finished yet. "They will not give you all this in return for your conversion alone. You must promise them that you will convert your people as well. You will receive a sign, so that you will know when it is time to start preparing the people for this. They will hate you at first, but in the end they will be grateful that you have saved their lives and lands."

"But what if my father objects?" asked Bruno. "They are his people. I have no authority."

"Your father will die in the faith of our fathers. He will never know. It will be your responsibility."

"My lord, I need time to absorb all this."

"You will have time—not much, but enough. You are more than half prepared for it already."

"Ach, Otto," said Bruno, perplexed. "I came to you for advice and you have given me more than I bargained for."

"You can handle it," replied the old man gently. "You are a prince's son. Now go and let me go to my gods, while *they* yet live."

"But, my lord," objected Bruno, "let me bide with you awhile until— until—so that I can give you a proper funeral. It is the least I can do. You have done so much for me."

"Nay, nay, it is too dangerous for you. My soul goes gladly to Valhalla, and Wotan's ravens will take care of my poor old body." Bruno shuddered at the implication, but the priest went on calmly. "The peasants all ran away, but they will come creeping back soon and will take care of things."

"If you insist, my lord."

Otto inclined his head slightly and closed his eyes. Bruno felt the old body sag against him and thought he was gone. But Otto made one more effort to speak. "This little one," he indicated the puppy with his eyes, "is

63

the last whelp of Wotan's prized she-wolf. How he escaped them I don't know. He was the runt of the litter. Take him home with you and raise him with your son. He will guard him better than the new god."

"Gladly, my lord Otto," replied Bruno, "and thank you for your counsel."

"You can thank me by being wise, by saving our land for our people. Fare thee well."

Bruno laid the ancient head gently down on the floor, picked up the wolf puppy and tip-toed out of the house. He knew he had witnessed the passing of a very great man and was humbled by it.

His horse shied slightly at the scent of the wolf, but Bruno stroked his neck and calmed him, and when the great stallion saw how insignificant the tiny thing was, he made no further fuss. After descending the hill on foot, Bruno rode slowly and cautiously home. He had much to ponder and needed time to sort it all out before he told Hilde. The puppy, tucked inside his shirt, slept contentedly the whole way.

Hilde greeted him with obvious relief at his safe return. When he had dismounted and turned his horse over to a groom, he went to kiss her. She hugged him close to her and the puppy squealed and nipped Bruno's chest. He backed away quickly.

"What magic has that old man done to you that you cry like a baby at a little hug?" she exclaimed.

He roared with laughter at the puzzled look on her face. "No magic, but a very special gift from Otto for our son." He chuckled again. "'Twas indeed a baby that objected to your lusty hug." He opened his shirt and took out the now fully awake wolf cub.

"Ach, how adorable." She clapped her hands with pleasure and took the squirming ball of fur from him. "But how did Otto know we were to have a child—much less that it will be a son—when I myself only knew for sure these last few weeks?"

"He knows many things," replied Bruno. "Many things, and I have much to tell you. Come, let us go into the Hall and bid the servants to fetch us some supper, for I am famished. Also a bowl of milk for this little beast, who must be even hungrier than I."

"How did you come by him?" Hilde asked. "He is a wolf, is he not? And more important, how did you fare with Otto? Did he explain my vision? Ach, I have so many questions."

"In good time." He held up his hand. "I shall endeavor to answer them all and more besides, but what I have to say is for your ears alone, at least for now." Hilde raised her eyebrows as Bruno went on. "Yes, the puppy is a wolf, but we shall raise and train him as a dog and, when the time comes, shall breed him with our bravest, most intelligent bitch. Come, let us sup in the privacy of our own chamber, where none may hear, and when I have told you all, I shall seek your advice and counsel."

"My advice?" asked Hilde, bewildered.

"Yes, love, for are you not a wisewoman seeress?"

Hilde just squeezed his hand, for she did not know what to say.

After they had eaten, Bruno began to tell her all that had transpired at Heiligenberg. His story was interspersed with comments of amazement at the old priest's foreknowledge. "He was dying in agony," he said, "and yet he forced himself to stay alive because he knew I was coming. He said he sent a message to my soul. I don't recall any such message, Hilde."

"But the idea to go to him came to you like a bolt out of the blue, did it not?"

"You are right. It never occurred to me until we were discussing your vision, and then suddenly it seemed very urgent that I go, even though he had told me to wait two years."

"To the uninitiated," she explained patiently, "such things appear to be a bolt from Donar's hammer, when in reality they are a message from another soul."

"I see," he said thoughtfully, although he wasn't sure if he did. "And I didn't even have to ask him about your vision. He not only explained what it meant but told me exactly what to do about it." He told her the rest of the amazing story and Hilde listened very carefully. He knew her sharp mind was analyzing the whole thing.

When he finished, she was silent for a while. Finally she said, "It is very frightening, this thing. It will take a great deal of courage and wisdom on both our parts. The people will call us cowards and, yes, even traitors. I hope your Otto will send us more messages of guidance from wherever he is. I shall pray for his soul."

"You are right and I hope he does," replied Bruno. "We shall need all the guidance we can get. But he did make one thing quite clear. This politics thing is not always as selfish as you would have it. It means more a trading of one thing for another, much as we haggle with the traders who come from Rome or from the Northmen, except that in this case it means trading in power and privilege."

"Yes, I see. And you will be in a much stronger trading position if you can offer the Franks and their god the loyalty of all our people and not just yourself alone. Yes, I see, but it seems so callous trading people's beliefs for their lives. It's not like trading a jewel for a length of silk."

"But the way things are going with the war—and Otto says they will only get worse—we shall soon have no choice. If the people refuse to convert, the Franks put them to the sword. Then we would have no bargaining power left at all."

"Yes, I am afraid you are right," replied Hilde. "We shall start with the young people. The old ones are too set in their ways. They will only be forced to go along with it, grumbling all the way, when there is no other choice. But the young ones—yes, we can put it to them as progress. They, after all, are the ones who will have to live in this new world."

"Ach, my little Hilde, I told you you were a wisewoman," said Bruno proudly. "But we must wait. Otto said we would receive a sign."

"Yes, we must wait to approach them openly, for this is indeed a very radical—yes, traitorous—concept. However, there are some very subtle ways by which we can begin preparing them even now."

"And what ways are those?" Bruno asked.

"For example, when the news comes in about Wittekind's flight we shall emphasize all the bad, discouraging aspects and play down the good. And the same with whatever other news there is. That shouldn't be hard, as most of it is so bad lately anyway. That way they will begin to accept in their hearts Wittekind's defeat and Karl's victory, which seems to be almost a certainty. Then, when the sign comes, they will hear your suggestions much more willingly than if there were still hope of victory in their hearts."

"Only a woman would think of that," said Bruno, amazed at her astuteness.

Hilde smiled knowingly. "Now tell me about the wolf cub."

"That puppy is very special. He is the last whelp of Wotan's finest she-wolf. Although he didn't actually say it, I believe Otto wants us to perpetuate the line, just as he expects you and me to perpetuate the Bruns line."

"What a lovely thought," replied Hilde. "That way a part of Wotan will always be with us, even if we have to accept the Christian god. I shall take very special care of him and train him to guard our family. I think perhaps Wotan understands the problems we are facing more than we realize or he wouldn't have saved this little one from the Frankish swords just for us."

Once again Bruno marvelled at the way her woman's mind worked.

The next day a messenger came from Bruno's father and told them the story of Wittekind's capture and escape with the aid of a beggar. Their sadly diminished troop—it could hardly be called an army anymore—had fled with him. He had sought aid from the King of Denmark, his father-in-law, but that worthy had enough troubles of his own—he was fighting their own distant cousins in England—and had no desire to antagonize the vastly superior Frankish army. He closed the borders of Denmark and turned them away. Wittekind turned then to Ostfalen and tried to raise a new army there. This eastern third of Saxony had hardly been touched by the war up to now, and very few of the men had joined in any of the fighting in the west. It was then that Karl had led his army in a lightning dash across Engern and was now waiting in a huge encampment between the Aller and the Elbe to see what Wittekind would do next.

Bruno and Hilde pretended they had not heard any of this but, as they had agreed, used the discouraging news to plant the first seeds of discontent by pointing out very subtly the futility of further opposing the mighty Frankish king. Of course, they met with many responses like, "The men of Ostfalen haven't done any fighting yet. Just wait, with a fresh army Wittekind will drive the Franks out. Our gods will not desert us."

They carefully made no response or argument to any of these statements, because they realized that at least half of it was bravado to cover up niggling doubts and disappointment in their leader—and perhaps in their gods.

The summer passed quickly and the harvest was like an anticlimax, so disheartened were the people. All the news was bad. Karl had Wittekind blocked in Ostfalen. Most of the fighting amounted to nothing more than futile skirmishes. Moreover, very few men of Ostfalen joined Wittekind. They had so far been spared the long and vicious fighting that had subjugated Westfalen and most of Engern, and they had no desire at this point to incur the wrath of the Frankish king, especially when most of them were aware that they would be fighting a losing battle.

Bruno and Hilde made good use of this news to turn the clan toward their way of thinking. They themselves, after much soul-searching, had come to accept the fact that the days of an independent Saxon nation were at an end and with it would come the Twilight of their gods, foretold so long ago. What this new religion was all about they had no idea, but they hoped that their 'politics' would work.

Hilde grew heavy with their child. Once she remarked to Bruno, "I had hoped that the sign would come ere this, so that our son could be born in a peaceful land. But now I think I am glad he will still be part of the old ways." Her ambivalence was typical of the feeling of so many people.

67

Winter came and once again the Franks did not go away but stayed in their huge camp near the Elbe. It was rumored that Karl even had a church set up in a tent, so semi-permanent had the camp become. This year Bruno's father and the other men did not come home even for the Mothering Nights. No one knew where they were or even if they were alive or dead. It was a sad festival, indeed. And Hilde's baby was due at any moment.

On the very last day of the Mothering Festival and the last day of the year, Hilde's pains started. "Fetch the priestess and my mother," she instructed Bruno. He ran quickly to fetch both women, although Hilde assured him there was plenty of time. The priestess of Frigga, goddess of good marriages and childbirth, was a professional midwife, but Irmengard, as a wisewoman, was even more skilled in the healing arts. Bruno made sure his adorable wife would have the best care available.

When the women arrived, they asked a servant to help them and chased Bruno out of the room. He fidgeted and paced up and down the Hall. As the hours passed, nervousness turned into anxiety, anxiety to worry, worry to near-panic. The other men teased him, and when he snapped at them, they merely laughed. He wanted desperately to go for a long ride in the woods, but he dared not leave. He marvelled at how men ruled every facet of the clan's life but this female mystery, which reduced a man to a helpless fool. He chided himself for being an idiot, but he loved his wife so deeply and life was so fragile.

The other men went to sleep on their benches or went out to stand watch on the walls. Bruno continued to pace. He had hardly touched his supper. He dared not drink too much ale. Suddenly, just before midnight, a piercing scream echoed through the Hall. He rushed to the door of their chamber, but the servant blocked the way.

"I must go to my wife. What is happening?"

"Nay, nay, not yet," said the servant. "She is doing fine," and she shut the door in his face.

Another scream and Bruno was ready to knock the door in, although he knew he was behaving like a fool. While he hesitated, he heard one of the women say, "Push once again. Hard. Ah, that's it." Then silence. Bruno could hear his own heart pounding, and then came a tiny mewling sound, not unlike the puppy's, which quickly turned into a lusty wail. "Oh, ye gods, the babe lives, but let her be all right," he prayed.

A few moments later the servant came out with an armful of bloody linen and a pan of something disgusting. He could not look, but he asked, "How is my wife?"

"She is just fine," she replied, "and you have a healthy son. Don't go in yet. They will call you."

Bruno waited impatiently but was relieved at the news. How can women go through this year after year, he wondered. But his fears for Hilde allayed, he realized that the woman had said he had a son, an heir. So Otto was right. If only his dear father were here to share his joy.

At last the door opened and Irmengard beckoned to him, her face all smiles. She was holding a tiny bundle wrapped in linen and wool. "Your son, my lord Bruno," she said. He took a quick glance at the tiny human she held and rushed to Hilde's side. She was propped up against huge feather pillows and looked radiant. He couldn't believe it after the agonizing screams he had heard.

"My love," he said, "are you all right?" He was afraid to touch her.

"Of course, I am," she replied. "Just a little tired is all. And you can kiss me if you want."

As he was kissing and embracing her, the babe wailed again. "He is offended that you didn't greet him properly," she teased.

"But I was so worried about you," he said sheepishly.

"I am fine," she reiterated. "Now go and say hello to our son. I just know he will be strong, for was he not born on a Mothering Night after the sun had turned back to us?"

Bruno did as he was bid. Then the priestess blessed them all and took her leave. In forty days Hilde would go to her for the ritual purification and they would have the naming ceremony.

After the priestess left, Irmengard placed the babe in the beautifully carved, silver inlaid cradle by Hilde's side, took Bruno by the arm and urged him to the door. "Let her rest now. You will sleep in the Hall tonight. I shall bide the night here, so you shall have no worry."

Winter slowly gave way to spring, and the baby grew fat and strong. Naturally they named him Bruno, as it appeared that he would have the same brown eyes and hair as his father. At the Spring Festival Hilde joined eagerly in the dance and smiled at the hesitant young brides, remembering herself a year ago. She considered herself a very mature matron now.

Shortly after the festival a very strange story reached the ears of those waiting at the Brunsburg. Apparently the Franks, too, had some sort of religious festival associated with the full moon after the vernal equinox. But there was no similarity at all to the joyous, erotic fertility rite of the Saxons.

Most of it was very solemn and involved a lot of worship inside their churches. They would not even fight during this time. Wittekind had decided to take this opportunity to reconnoitre the Frankish camp for any weakness he might take advantage of. Rumor had it he was also curious about their strange religion. He disguised himself as a beggar and mingled with the other medicants that loitered about the camp. It was on the day of the week called Friggasdag.

"Why do the people go about looking so sad?" he asked one of the beggars.

"Because their god has died," was the reply.

Now we can defeat them for sure, thought Wittekind, overjoyed. He was about to rush back to his men to organize the attack when a powerful urge, more than mere curiosity, to know more about this strange turn of events held him where he was. He hung around the camp for two days, and on Sonnedag he heard the most joyous singing he had ever heard in his life coming from the tent-church where Karl and all his people were gathered. Wittekind waited outside with the other beggars, for they had told him it was Karl's custom to give out money at this festival. Then, to his amazement, he heard the shouts of joy coming from within the tent. A strange word that sounded like, "Alleluia!" Then, "He lives. He lives. He is risen from the dead!"

Wittekind did not know what to make of all this until his fellow beggar explained. "Every year it happens. This god of theirs, he dies and in three days rises from the dead, supposedly stronger than ever. I don't believe all that rubbish, but it's always good for a handout."

But Wittekind was deeply disturbed by it all. No wonder their god is undefeatable, he thought, perhaps I have been foolish to fight him so long.

When Karl emerged from the tent-church his face was radiant. Two servants accompanied him carrying bags of coins—one of copper coins, the other of silver. To most of the beggars he gave a copper coin. When he came to Wittekind, he looked straight into his eyes and Wittekind, knowing he was recognized, trembled, expecting to be cut down mercilessly. Instead Karl dipped into the other bag and placed a silver coin in Wittekind's hand. "Go in peace," he said. "The Lord is risen." Wittekind fled.

As soon as he got back to where the Saxons were hiding, he called his brothers Bruno and Abbio to him and described all that had happened and how deeply moved he had been by it all. After hours of discussion

70

Abbio seemed in favor of an honorable surrender, but Bruno was most vehemently against it.

"I shall die with my gods," he declared, "before I surrender to that fiend. He has put a magic spell on you, Wittekind, and if you give in to it, I shall no longer call you brother."

When this story reached the Brunsburg, the people were astounded that Wittekind and Abbio would even consider surrender. Many of them said, "Good for Bruno. He is a loyal Saxon." But some of the younger ones, whom young Bruno and Hilde had been gradually leading toward their way of thinking, came to them privately and said, "I think Wittekind has finally come to his senses. You were right, Bruno Brunoson."

"It is the sign," Bruno said to Hilde.

"No, I think not yet," she replied, "but soon, soon."

"Why do you say 'not yet'?" he asked. "What stronger sign could there be that Karl spared Wittekind and that Wittekind himself is perturbed by this god that dies and rises again from the dead?"

"Right now, it has incensed the people against Wittekind. You heard how many of them praised your father's stand against him. I say wait a bit. A stronger sign will come. Mark my words."

"You are the wisewoman," he said, "so I shall abide by what you say. But you admit we can't wait too much longer. Any day the Franks could be at the gates."

"It won't be too much longer," Hilde assured him with a knowing look.

The futile little skirmishes continued, accomplishing nothing but the loss of more men. Then came the surprising news that Karl was withdrawing his army from Ostfalen. The great host crossed southern Engern without harming a soul except in rear-guard actions against those Saxon warriors foolish enough to attack him. He gathered his army outside of Osnabrück, a long ago subjugated town in Westfalen, and settled down to wait. His last message to Wittekind had been that he would meet him halfway.

"What can this mean?" the people asked. Hilde and Bruno were as puzzled as anyone.

Then hard on the heels of this came the report of Bruno the elder's death in one of the useless attacks against Karl's rear guard. Wittekind sent the message himself with deep regrets that they had buried Bruno where he fell as they dared not light a funeral pyre for fear of giving away their

71

position to the enemy. Several loyal men from the Brunsburg had died with him.

Bruno grieved deeply. "If I had been there it wouldn't have happened," he berated himself. "I should have tried to talk him out of such foolishness."

But Hilde tried to console him. "Don't chastise yourself, Bruno. You could have done nothing. His brothers tried to talk him out of it, but he was too stubborn to listen. Do not grieve, my love, beyond normal honor for your father, for this is the sign we have been waiting for."

Bruno was shocked. "How can my father's death be the sign?"

"He wanted to die in the faith of our gods, while his brothers were leaning toward this new god. He vehemently opposed Wittekind and was struck down. This Christ god is stronger than our gods," she said, nodding her head as if she had never had any doubts. "That is why I am sure it is the sign. There is no opposition to him now, don't you see?"

"Perhaps," replied Bruno doubtfully.

"And now I think I understand what Karl meant by meeting Wittekind halfway," she said, and that strange, faraway look that Bruno recognized came over her face.

"And what is that?" he asked.

"This Christ god is stronger even than Karl," she said. "That is why he held Karl's hand from killing Wittekind when he had the opportunity. The god knew he had already planted the seed of curiosity about himself in Wittekind's heart and if he were dead he could not lead his people to this new god."

Bruno said nothing. Such profound thinking was almost beyond him.

"Yes," Hilde went on, "soon Wittekind will go to Karl and they will be like blood brothers."

"You jest," said Bruno.

"Nay, nay," she replied. "I can see it."

Bruno knew his wisewoman wife too well to doubt her word. But if old Otto had not forewarned Bruno, it would have been impossible for him to conceive of such a thing happening. Nevertheless, he began talking to his people more openly now about the apparent strength of this god of the Franks. Some would hear none of it, rather taking Karl's withdrawal as the sign that their gods were the stronger. Others allowed that he might be right but feared to trust the Franks, for which he couldn't blame them. And some agreed with him wholeheartedly and tried to help him convince the others. Night after night arguments and discussions filled the Hall, some loud and vociferous, obviously the result of too much ale and too little knowledge. Others were quiet and profound, and Bruno enjoyed those, as they helped everyone to see the problems more clearly. No one knew anything about the Frankish religion, but most agreed that peace was worth almost anything.

Hilde circulated her ideas among the women, and on the whole they were much easier to convince. Many had lost husbands, fathers and sons. Many had fatherless children. The consensus was that their gods were indeed losing their power, for all their prayers and sacrifices had achieved little or nothing. And things were only getting worse.

Then a few weeks later Hilde's prediction came true. Wittekind sent word to Karl that he wished to meet and confer with him under a flag of truce. Karl kept his word and literally met him halfway at a place called Exeter in southern Engern, not far from Wittekind's own ruined castle. Karl had somehow learned that in former, more peaceful times it had been Wittekind's favorite spot to retreat from the cares of the world. There was an ancient Saxon altar there, now desecrated. But the great stone part of it still stood.

When Wittekind and his men arrived at the clearing, he saw Karl standing alone on the other side of the stone, his right hand lying relaxed on top of it. He was unarmed and his nobles, priests and other men stood well back at the edge of the woods. Wittekind knew he could do no less. He dismounted from his great black stallion and left his men at the edge of the clearing. He walked alone toward the great stone. Karl smiled but never moved. Everyone held their breath at this duel of nerves between the two giants. When Wittekind reached the stone he hesitated only a moment, then reached out his right hand to Karl's. They shook hands and then Karl came around the stone and warmly embraced him.

"This day we are reconciled and shall be like brothers," said Karl. The men on both sides cheered.

"And this day I place myself, my nobles and all of Saxony in vassalage to you," said Wittekind.

"And I shall take you under my protection. Furthermore, I shall restore to you all of your castles and lands for you to rule as my duke, and the same for all of your nobles who take the oath of fealty to me."

Wittekind was more than gratified by this unexpected largesse. He would never have expected such generosity from this man who had been his bitter enemy, the man who had so wantonly destroyed so much of his

73

country. But recently some power had compelled him to trust him.

Karl had more to offer. "If you need help in restoring your towns, castles and homes, I shall assign as many men as you need to the task. Only you must let us build churches as well."

"Willingly, my lord," replied Wittekind. "Your generosity is far more than I expected, I who have been your sworn enemy for so long."

" 'Tis naught," said Karl with a wave of his hand. "This day you have saved many souls."

"I don't understand. What do you mean?" asked Wittekind.

"Let me answer your question with another question," said Karl. "What made you finally decide to become reconciled to me?"

Wittekind noticed that he had carefully avoided using the word 'surrender'. He told Karl how he had noticed the strange behavior of his people, so sad one day that their god had died and then so joyous that he had risen from the dead. "It was very puzzling to me," he admitted. "Yet I sensed something of the power this god must have." He omitted the fact that he had been trembling for fear of his life when Karl recognized him outside the tent-church.

Karl nodded. "And would you like to learn more about Him?" he asked.

"Yes, indeed, I should," replied Wittekind.

Karl then ordered a feast to be spread and there was much rejoicing. The men mingled freely, Saxon and Frank, and the old enmities were momentarily forgotten.

Afterward Wittekind, Abbio and the Saxon nobles were turned over to the several priests, who always accompanied Karl's army, to begin their instruction in the new religion. They learned that there was only one God, and that His Son, Jesus, with his death on the cross had made the only sacrifice ever necessary for all men, for all time. No more horses for Wotan, goats for Donar, boars for Freyr, and on and on. And that it was the Holy Spirit who had implanted the seed of curiosity in Wittekind's heart.

All of this was a very strange concept and not at all easy for the Saxons to assimilate. After a short while, Wittekind called a halt. He said to Karl, "We need time to digest all this, my lord. It is a wondrous concept and I would hear more of it, but before we go any further, I would ask your leave to send for my wife and family and one other that they, too, may learn about this Jesus."

"You have my leave," replied Karl, "and who is the other?"

"My nephew Bruno, son of my dearest brother. He is a fine, forward-thinking young man and heir to extensive lands along the Weser. I have already heard that he is interested in learning more about your god but dared not while my brother lived."

"Send for him then and as many of his people who would come." agreed Karl.

When the messenger from Wittekind reached the Brunsburg, Bruno was astounded at the news. He hurried to seek Hilde. "You were right. You were right, my wisewoman," he exclaimed, "and the news is more unbelievable than even you guessed! Wittekind has asked to be instructed in the Frankish religion and asks that I come to learn about this Christ god, too!"

"Ah, at last," she sighed happily. "I thought he would never come to his senses. What wonderful news. I shall have the servants start packing our saddlebags immediately so we can leave at first light tomorrow. I am glad the weather is so nice. The baby can ride in a sling on my back."

"The baby? You?"

"But of course. I can't leave him. Who would feed him?"

"But—but—I thought to go alone with perhaps just a few men who were sympathetic to the new ideas," he objected.

Hilde looked at him as if he were out of his mind. "And who predicted all this in the first place?" she asked.

"You did, I know, but—"

"And since when do women not worship the gods? In fact, if truth were known, are more sincere than most men."

"Yes, but—"

"And do not women have an equal vote in the *Allthing* and stand beside their men in all things?"

"You win," he admitted, laughing in spite of himself at her determination. "You and little Bruno may come."

"Thank you, my lord," she said with mock humility. "I shall go and spread the word."

"Wait, Hilde," he cautioned. "Not too many."

"Why not?" she asked. "There are many who would like to learn about this powerful Christ god and I think others who will be curious now that Wittekind has made the decision for them. Don't you see? The more of our people who accompany you, the more Karl is apt to go along with your 'politics'. Remember my vision and Otto's confirmation of it."

He did see then. He embraced her hungrily and murmured in her hair, "My wise wisewoman. Go and spread the word."

75

Early the next morning a great cortege of men, women and even several children left the Brunsburg. Only the very old people and the priests remained behind. Irmengard rode gaily behind Bruno and Hilde. "This is so exciting," she said. "I have heard that his god is a great healer. I would learn more of his methods."

Even the priestess of Frigga accompanied them. "I am very curious about this god who is said to have been born of an earthly mother," she admitted. "Only don't tell them that I am a priestess. I am sure that even these Christians have need of a midwife."

At the end of the second day they arrived at Exeter. To their surprise, they found that groups of people were arriving from many parts of Saxony. It was almost like a fair. Women were setting up cooking hearths, the men cutting pine and fir boughs to build temporary shelters.

Wittekind introduced Bruno and Hilde to Karl. Indicating the baby, he said, "And this is their heir, whom I myself am meeting for the first time."

Karl looked pleased and embraced Bruno in brotherhood as he had done earlier with his uncle. Bruno told him a part of Otto's prediction and Hilde's vision but did not mention the part about the stone castle or the bear's claws.

Karl looked wistful when he heard about Otto. "I should like to have met this man. Perhaps some of your priests are wiser than I gave them credit for."

"Your men killed him in cold blood," said Bruno.

"A regrettable incident," replied Karl, "but the men were acting on orders. We had no time to make a distinction between the wise ones and those who were inciting your people to rebellion. That is why I am glad your uncle finally decided to become reconciled to the inevitable. Many lives have been saved by it. Otherwise we should have had no choice but to destroy every one of your rebellious Saxons."

Bruno said nothing, but he could see that this man was still a ruthless killer, who could only be generous when he was getting his own way, regardless of this religion of love that his priests preached. He would be a hard master, but they were committed now. To turn back would mean certain death and the confiscation of their lands. Bruno hoped that the peace would be worth it. The need for very subtle politics became more and more apparent to him.

Karl called in more priests and monks to instruct the large group, and even some of the converted Saxons from the Westfalish towns who had been Christians for some years now. The priests were very thorough in their teaching but surprisingly patient nonetheless. They answered all the questions and allayed all the doubts. Some of the Saxons were totally bewildered, others grasped the ideas more quickly. A few became discouraged or lost interest and began drifting away. The Franks let them go, but Bruno observed that they took careful note of who they were and where they were from. Those poor people have just condemned themselves to death, he shivered at the thought. Better to put up a pretense of interest and wrestle with your conscience later. Why, I myself do not understand all of what they are saying, but I shall persevere because I do understand that it is the only way to save ourselves and our land.

A few weeks later, Wittekind announced that he was ready to accept the Christian baptism. A number of his people had become truly enthusiastic in their new faith, but the majority thought, as Bruno did, that it was the expedient thing to do. So that it came to pass in the year of their new Lord 785 the chief priest of the Franks, whom they called a bishop, Karl himself standing godfather, baptized the royal family of Saxony — first Wittekind, his wife Geva and their children, then Abbio and Bruno with Hilde and baby Bruno. Then the priests went up and down the kneeling rows of people, baptizing them in the name of the Christian god, Father, Son and Holy Ghost.

After the ceremony, Karl embraced Wittekind and said, "It is customary for the godparent to give the new Christian a gift at this time. I have observed how that black stallion of yours has always been a rallying point for your warriors and a symbol of the rebellion. I want to replace him with this white one as a symbol of the purity of Christ." A groom led forth a magnificent white horse. Wittekind gave his beloved black mount to his squire and graciously accepted the gift from Karl. What the king apparently did not know, but every Saxon present did, was that herein lay the perfect irony — to them, the white horse was most sacred to Wotan.

Then Wittekind announced that he would like to build a church in this spot to enshrine the stone of reconciliation, with Karl's help, of course, since the Saxons did not yet know too much about church building. Karl was overjoyed and enthusiastically offered the services of his master builders. Bruno thought sardonically, here again is the politics, par excellence.

Then, as if he could read his nephew's mind, Wittekind said to Karl, "Bruno was not present when you offered to restore my nobles' castles.

77

Might I ask a boon on his behalf?" Karl nodded. "The Brunsburg, his late father's fortress, is old and obsolete and no longer of much strategic value. Would you grant him leave to build a castle, with your help, of course, on the great bend of the Weser by the Hoya bridgehead? He is ever loyal to me and now to you, and I know he will defend your interests well from there."

Karl was a bit taken aback at the simple audacity of the request, but today he could deny Wittekind nothing, and besides, he could quickly see the military advantage of a castle at that spot. He turned to Bruno. "You have heard your uncle's request. Is that your desire as well?"

"It is, my lord," replied Bruno.

"And if I help you build this castle will you defend it well, and always in my interest before your own or any other?"

"I will, my lord," replied Bruno, unable to believe this was happening.

"Then kneel and pledge your fealty to me."

When Bruno had repeated the oath, Karl tapped him on the shoulder with the flat of his sword. "Arise, Lord Bruno, you are now the first Count of Hoya of the German Empire—for that is what I shall call my realm from now on, for this day the two greatest German tribes, the Franks and the Saxons, are united into one people under Christ our Lord." Bruno almost smiled at this illusion of grandeur, but forced himself to look serious. Karl went on, "Now, if you are to be a Count of the Realm, you must have an emblem for your coat of arms. Have you anything in mind?"

Bruno's answer was ready. "Yes, sire, I had thought of two raised bear's claws. It seems to me symbolic of our family name."

"Very good. An apt symbol. I know of no other who has such. I shall tell the herald to record it by your name."

And so the bear's claws would be the coat-of-arms of the Counts of Hoya for over eight hundred years, although many different families were to bear the title. Just so, Wittekind, as first Duke of Saxony, chose the white horse on a red field, symbol of the blood of the martyrs, which was to remain the arms of what was later known as Lower Saxony to this day.

Intermezzo

Charlemagne's hard-won empire outlasted his death in 814 by only one generation, but the Salic laws of the Franks, known as the Lex Saxorum as it applied to Saxony, were to have a devastating effect on Germany for over a thousand years, dividing and subdividing it ad infinitum. They also took away the rights of women to vote or to inherit either property or titles. His son Louis the Pious was more interested in founding monasteries and establishing bishoprics than in extending the territory, but even these were only secure in the major towns, such as Bremen, Verden and Hildesheim. Pockets of revolt and unrest and loyalty to the old gods continued everywhere in the rural areas for well over a hundred years. Meanwhile the Slavs and Magyars were constantly battering on the eastern border of the Elbe and the Northmen had begun their devastating raids down the rivers from the north and into France as well.

On the death of Louis in 840, the empire was divided among his three sons, for Salic law provided that all male heirs inherited equally, instead of only the eldest as in England, for example, and as it had been among the Saxons. The result was three countries: France, Burgundy and Germany.

The Bruns clan was prolific and gradually divided itself into two branches, the peasants and the nobility. The peasants remained attached to the ancestral lands around the spring of Brüne and gradually spread out from there. The nobility remained Dukes of Saxony and gradually moved into Ostfalen and later even beyond the Elbe as the center of power moved eastward. In 880 one Bruno and his brother Dankward (Tanquard) were given royal permission to found the town of Braunschweig on the site of a tiny trading post or *wik* on the old Volksweg (Bruns-wik). In 986 another Bruno was ordered to build a castle on the site of an old Saxon earthwork fort at a ford of the river Aller at a place called Celle. It was called Brunonenburg and became one of a string of fortresses extending north and south of Braunschweig in order to hold back the incursions of the Slavs.

Meanwhile, the undying hatred and bitter enmity between the Saxon nobles and their Frankish overlords continued unabated, always seething under the surface, occasionally breaking out into open rebellion. But the Frankish kings had to put up with the unhappy situation, for without the nobles' help there was no way they could control the people. The land was more or less Christianized by the end of the ninth century, but the people kept many of the old traditions, such as Christmas trees and Yule logs, midsummer bonfires and ghosts on the Eve of All Saints. The great Christian spring festival was given the name of the pure goddess of dawn, Oster, and rabbits and eggs took the place of the fertility rites. The Church was forced to compromise and did.

Bruno and Dankward of Braunschweig were killed fighting the Vikings, and their third brother, Otto, was left to rule as Duke. In 919 the last Salic king of Germany, Conrad, was dying without an heir. On his deathbed, he apparently realized the futility of trying to continue Frankish rule in a country where they were not wanted and never could rule in peace. So he named Heinrich, the son of his bitterest enemy Otto, as his heir. And thus the prophecy of the old priest of Wotan finally came true that through patience and politics the descendants of Wittekind and Bruno would once again rule their own land in peace and prosperity.

The Golden Age of peace and prosperity, commerce and education, of a more or less united Germany lasted almost 250 years, but gradually the old line of the Brunonen began dying out. By Salic law females could not inherit, but they could bring dowries of vast lands into marriage. The (Hohen)staufen family of Bavaria replaced the Brunonen as kings, and Gertrud, one of the last daughters of the ducal line, was married to Heinrich the Proud of another Bavarian family, the Welfs. Of this union was born in 1129 a son Heinrich, later to be known as the Lion.

2

AD 1165

"Hi-ho, Hans, methinks the sheep are watching you instead of you watching the sheep."

Hans started out of his daydreams and turned to see the shepherd striding across the moor toward him, crook in hand. The boy had felt the end of that staff as often as the sheep did, but he wasn't afraid. Fritz was a stern man but kindly nonetheless, and he well understood the tedium of the long lonely hours out on the moor.

"I was only looking at the road for a moment," Hans prevaricated. "The sheep are fine."

"But the wolves come from the woods, not the road," replied the shepherd phlegmatically, "and it only takes a moment. Especially this time of year, you know as well as I do, that we must be extra careful."

"I know that, Fritz," replied the boy. "I have just made the rounds of the woods and there are no signs of any wolves."

"All right. I'll take your word for it this time. But keep a sharp eye out and don't let the master catch you daydreaming or it will go hard with you." He tousled the boy's bright blond hair and strode off to check on the other boys.

It was early spring, for Hans the best time of the year. The world had a new, fresh brightness about it that he loved. Not only because the sun was higher in the sky and the days were longer or because everything was alive again with that special color of green, but also because something seemed to stir inside a person as well, which made one feel more alive than at any other time of year. He watched the little black lambs gamboling on their wobbly legs around their staid mothers and admitted to himself that this was really the only time of year that he loved his work. The rest of the year was something else. The boredom and monotony of the summer and fall almost drove him to distraction, for he was an intelligent lad. And the winter he positively hated, almost feared, for that was when the wolves were the most dangerous and the tiny shepherd's hut offered scant shelter from the winds that swept across the great moor. And in fact, the worse the weather the less time he was able to spend in the hut, for the sheep, never very smart animals to begin with, seemed stupider than ever when the snow lay heavy on the land. He had to keep them moving, for if they got stuck in the snow they would simply stand there and freeze to death or let themselves be easy prey for the hungry wolves.

Fortunately, this did not happen too often in this part of northeastern Saxony. Seldom was there really heavy snow, although the winters were cold, blustery and damp on the great moor called the Lüneburger Heide, a large plateau lying south of the fortress of Lüneburg with its famous salt mines. It was bounded by rivers on all four sides, the Ilmenau, on which stood the Lüneburg, on the north, the Elbe on the east, the Aller on the south, and the Weser on the west. In the late summer it was truly a glory to behold when the heather (*Heide*) for which it was named bloomed rampant in all shades of pink, mauve and purple. And the sheep of the Heide, called Heidenschnucken, were famous throughout Europe. They had long curving horns and were unusual in that the lambs were almost always black at birth, but when they were adults the long, almost silky wool became the normal grayish-white color.

Hans loved the lambs. For the past two years he had been allowed to help with the lambing, and he now felt very knowledgeable about the whole process. One had to be very careful because sometimes the clumsy ewes would step on their babies and break their backs or, if it was their first lamb, often refused to nurse them. Then Hans would have to milk the mother and feed the little one himself with a rag dipped in the milk wrapped around his finger. Often at night when the lambs, tired from playing all day, could not find their own mothers, their plaintive cry sounded just like "ma-ma".

Hans often wondered about his own Mama. He clearly remembered her thick blond braids and rosy cheeks, her peaches-and-cream complexion, and her ample bosom to which she would hold him when he was hurt or frightened. How long ago it seemed. He guessed he was about eleven years old now, so that he would have been about six when his father sold him to the Master. This was not an uncommon practice in the days when there were so often more children than a family could support and more kept coming. And strangely, it was a result of the new freedom of the peasants. What had been intended as a blessing sometimes was not. When the peasants were serfs, they belonged to their lord, but the lord was obliged to care for them. With the new freedom, they were free to move about the land, marry whom they chose and farm their land as they liked. In many cases the land became hereditary. The only obligations to the lord were the payment of rent and military service, when and as needed.

At first the annual payment of the rent continued in the old way as payment in kind and posed no problem. But when the lord's granaries or animal pens began to overflow with more produce or stock than he needed for his own household and he could not always trade it for the luxury goods he desired, he began to demand payment of the rents in money. This often created a hardship for the peasant, who had to take a part of his produce to the nearest market to sell. This bottom rung of the trade network was, of course, the greatest stimulant to the growth of commerce and even enabled the peasant's wife to buy a few tiny luxuries for her family and eventually led to the great trading empires of succeeding centuries, proving the truism that freedom is the parent of capitalism. But in its earliest stages, until the peasants learned to reserve a part of their efforts for cash crops as opposed to subsistence crops, the transition from serfdom to freedom left many floundering.

The right to inherit the land was also a mixed blessing. In Saxony under the Salic law of Charlemagne the inheritance must be equally divided amongst all the male heirs. In an era of many children this created problem enough among the duchies, counties and great estates of the minor nobility, but with the peasant's few acres it was quite self-defeating. The problem was addressed in various ways. The nobility usually sent excess sons into the church, but the illiterate peasants had no such option. In later years, as increasing commerce developed the towns, many younger sons went there to become craftsmen, artisans or just day laborers. But in the early days the "selling" of their children often made the difference between starvation and at least subsistence for both the peasant and his child. Often, in fact, the child ended up better off than the family he left behind, particularly when he was bought by a family without children of their own or who had a holding large enough to support and need the extra help. It was not like being sold into slavery, but more like an indenture. After the child had worked off the purchase price, he was supposed to be paid for his labors. It was always a pittance and subject to the whims of generosity or penuriousness of the master, but a payment nonetheless, and when he was of age, usually about twelve, he, having been born of free parents, was free to leave if he chose. Some did and many did not, and some even became the heirs of childless couples. Meanwhile the parents had had a relatively large amount of ready cash to pay their rents and one less mouth to feed.

Hans understood all this and accepted without question the practices of his times. He did not blame his parents for what they had done, but he often wondered about them and how they fared. He supposed there were several more babies by now. In the first few years he had missed his mother, although he hardly remembered his father. But the master's wife was a kindly woman who saw that Hans and the other two boys were well fed and clothed. Eventually he was glad about what had happened for it made him feel independent at an early age.

Hans knew that he was reasonably well treated, for although the master was very strict, sometimes harsh and not at all friendly, he had heard stories of the treatment of the children and even adult servants on other farms and should have been well satisfied with his lot. It could have been much worse. But he was too bright and intelligent a lad to be content with the monotony of caring for someone else's sheep. Besides, there was no future in it. The highest advancement he could aspire to was perhaps one day becoming the shepherd when Fritz died or moved on. But Fritz was still a young man and seemed well suited to the job.

Hence Hans' daydreams. His knowledge of the world was very limited and his experience of it even more so. Since coming to the sheep farm, the farthest he had ever been was to the tiny chapel—it was not even a proper church—in the nearest hamlet about three miles away. Once a month when a visiting priest came to celebrate Mass, the master on his horse with his wife and the servants walking behind made the journey. But for the boys it was not even a monthly trip, because someone always had to guard the sheep. Hans didn't mind when it came his turn to be left behind, because he didn't understand very much of what the priest was saying anyway. He would much rather sneak off to the old wisewoman who lived in the woods, who regaled him with stories of dragons, giants and fair maidens and of the old gods and heroes of his people. At least she spoke good Low German—as the Saxon language had come to be called—that he could understand. And besides, the tiny hamlet was so isolated it didn't even boast a market.

Hans remembered well the market in the village nearest his parents' home. His mother often took him along when she went to sell her butter and eggs. He was enthralled by all the sights and smells, the color and excitement. Sometimes on special feast days there were even jugglers and dancers. Very occasionally, if his mother had done exceptionally well, she would buy him a little honey cake at one of the stalls. Although she made perfectly good ones herself, honey cakes always tasted better to him at the market.

Hans also had an inquiring mind, and he carefully filed away in his memory tidbits of knowledge he picked up from visitors at his master's house. Although the farm was very isolated, as were most of them on the Heide, it did lie on the main north–south road between Lüneburg and Braunschweig, the capital of the Duchy of Saxony, and travelers often stopped at the farm for directions, occasionally for meals and sometimes for a place to spend the night. The master's wife earned a little extra money this way, for most of the guests reimbursed her generously. She would never charge the monks and priests who came by, because they in turn charged no one for hospitality at the guesthouses of their monasteries. The occasional pretentious "new" noble, as she called them, who demanded food and lodging as his right got the pot-scrapings and couldn't say a word because she did not officially operate an inn.

Although he couldn't possibly listen to, much less talk to, all these people, because he was usually up in the pasture with the sheep, Hans took advantage of every opportunity he could to mingle with their servants and ask all sorts of questions. Sometimes, if the master wasn't around, he boldly queried the guests themselves. From this he learned all sorts of interesting and exciting things about the geography, history and people of his country.

He learned that the next sizeable town to the north was Uelzen, which had grown up around a small monastery, then came Ebsdorf, a large and wealthy monastery, and at the end of the road Lüneburg, a relatively new town which had been founded by the present Duke Heinrich when he took over ownership of the famous salt mines from the owner of the ancient castle of the same name. Beyond Lüneburg there were other roads that led to Hamburg and Lübeck, great seaports on the North and East Seas. And from there one could even travel in great ships to far-off lands like Holland, England and France. The whole concept was mind-boggling to Hans, who had never even seen a small ship much less a great one.

He also learned that not far to the south of the farm ran the river Aller and the road forded it at a small town with an ancient castle called Celle and beyond that was the magnificent new capital of Saxony, Braunschweig. Duke Heinrich had turned it from a small market village into a great city. He had just built for himself a sumptuous palace-castle called Dankwarderode and was now completing a huge cathedral in the modern Gothic style. All of this was totally beyond Hans' comprehension, but the sheer grandeur of it all overawed him.

They also told him that Duke Heinrich was not a native Saxon but belonged to a family called the Welf, who came from far-off Bavaria and had inherited the duchy from his mother and grandmother, both Saxon princesses. This caused some hard feelings among a few of the minor nobles of ancient lineage, but the majority of the people loved him because he was a great warrior and a man of culture besides. A warrior Hans could understand, but when he asked what culture meant, he was told that the Duke sponsored education and schools, also the writing of books, poetry and music. This perplexed the young boy even more because he had never even seen a book, but he did know a little bit about music. Hadn't Fritz shown him how to make his very own shepherd's pipe out of hollow wood and reeds? And he had taught himself how to play it passably well.

Beyond Braunschweig, he learned, the road ran all the way to far-off Rome, where the Pope lived. Hans had no idea who the Pope was and this time was afraid to ask and show his ignorance, because it seemed as though this was a very august personage and apparently a controversial figure as well. Every time he was mentioned, people seemed to get into heated arguments either for or against him. Sometimes, although Hans couldn't be sure, it seemed as though there were two Popes. Hans decided the less he knew about that subject the better.

Hans didn't care about Rome or the Pope. For him the road ended in Braunschweig. And for that reason the road figured prominently in his daydreams. It not only led to the fabulous city but also represented freedom to him—the freedom not only to end the drudgery of being a shepherd boy but also to do something exciting, he knew not what, but which he felt very capable of doing.

He had often discussed his dreams with the old wisewoman in the woods. He dared tell no one else. She had encouraged his ambition, but cautioned him to wait until a propitious time. Besides, he was too young yet, she said. But Hans was growing impatient. He had all but made up his mind to leave right after the sheepshearing, for when the wool merchant's representatives paid the master, the boys received their annual wages. Hans had scrupulously saved two copper coins from the previous years. This would make three—a fortune to his young mind.

And so, Hans' favorite pastime was watching the road and dreaming about seeking his fortune in Braunschweig. Not that he was remiss in his duties. He loved the little black lambs too much for that, and he had a very well trained dog to help him guard them. He would really miss the dog when he left. He considered him a more trustworthy friend than any of the humans he knew. One of the bitches had had a litter of puppies not too long ago. He wondered if the master would let him take one with him. He doubted it, because good shepherd dogs were worth a lot, this breed particularly. It was said that they had been bred with wolves in the olden days and that was why they were so fearless and could guard so well, because they understood the wolves' habits. Anyway, it was nice to think about.

One day toward evening Hans, watching the road as usual, saw a company of travellers turn into the lane leading to the farmhouse. He thought it might be the merchant come for the shearing. He was due any day now. But no. They were too many and much more lavishly dressed than any merchants Hans had seen so far. It was soon time for the night boy to come and relieve him. He hoped the people would still be there when he got down to the house. His imagination went wild with excitement. Suppose it was the great Duke Heinrich himself. He'd better not get caught again watching the road or they would say he was neglecting the sheep and make him go without supper. Then he'd never even have a chance to talk to the strangers.

He was busy checking all the lambs when the older shepherd boy, who would watch for the night, arrived. "Hi, Hans," he greeted him cheerfully. "You'd best hurry and get your supper before these royal visitors eat all there is."

"Royal?" asked Hans astonished.

"Well, not quite royal," replied the other, "but 'tis said they are from the Duke's own household."

Hans needed no urging. He fairly flew toward the house. His wildest dreams were coming true. He just knew they were. He quickly washed his face and hands in the horse trough and entered the house. In the big common room were four of the most elegantly dressed gentlemen he had ever seen. All were fully armored in chain mail. Over the armor each wore a long surcoat beautifully embroidered with elaborate designs. Hans knew from the armor that they must be knights. One was a distinguished-looking gray-haired man, another middle-aged and somewhat portly, the other two younger and very handsome to Hans' eyes.

He sidled up to the round hearth as the master's wife was dishing out huge bowls of succulent mutton stew. His mouth watered. The woman noticed him and hissed, "Hans, get out of here before you disturb their Lordships."

This was so unusual from her that Hans almost wept. "But my supper . . . ," he managed to get out.

She seemed to relent a moment and spooned a tiny bit of stew into a small bowl, less than half his usual portion, and handed it to him. "Go," she said. "Eat it out in the courtyard."

Hans scurried away with his precious supper. Not even a crust of bread to spare to mop up the gravy, he thought. And she so nervous. They must be important indeed. Out in the courtyard things were not much better. The place was crowded with men and horses. Hans had always thought it a large courtyard, but the throng was so great he could not even find a corner to himself to sit and eat his meal. He accidentally bumped into a tall young man and only by careful juggling managed not to spill his stew on the man's fine clothes.

Hans mumbled an apology and the young man looked down at him. "Is that all the supper you've been given, lad? I should go back and complain, if I were you. Why, those varlets over there have already had two portions."

Hans gaped at the man. "I couldn't very well do that," he said. "You see, I only work here."

"Aha, I do see," replied the man, "and the goodwife is cheating her own servants in order to impress their noble lordships. Well, I can certainly go back for more. Here, take mine." Before Hans could protest, the man shoved the large bowl at him and went into the house.

Hans, now with two bowls to juggle, made his way even more carefully through the crowd to a corner of the courtyard and sat down on the ground. He poured the small portion into the larger one and started eating. He drank the gravy and picked out the pieces of succulent meat and tender vegetables with his fingers. It was more than he had ever had at one time in his whole life. He wasn't sure if he could eat it all, but he was determined to try.

While he was eating he saw the young man come back into the courtyard and look around. Finally he saw Hans sitting in the corner and came directly over to him. "Do you mind if I eat with you?" he asked.

Hans had never had anybody ask if he minded anything. "Of course not, sir," he replied, "but there is no place for you to sit."

"That ground looks just as good as any other I've sat on," he said and promptly sat down next to Hans.

"I thought gentlemen only supped on the board," Hans ventured, perplexed yet pleased at the friendliness and generosity of this young man, wanting to know him better.

"When we can we do, but on the road we eat wherever we can, and glad of it. Besides, I'm not yet a gentleman."

"But surely you're not a servant," said Hans, eyeing the man's fine clothes.

"Well, yes and no."

"Are you a knight then?" asked Hans, ever more curious now.

"Uh, yes and no."

"Why do you keep saying 'yes and no'? You either are something or you are not. What are you then?" Hans knew he was being impolite, but he somehow knew the man wouldn't mind.

The man laughed. "I am a squire."

"I am not sure what a squire is, sir."

"A squire is a 'neither-nor'. He is a servant, but not a servant. He is almost a knight, but not quite." He saw the puzzled look on Hans' face and decided it was not fair to tease him. "Forgive me. You are a bright boy and would really know of these things, methinks."

"Yes, I would indeed, sir," replied Hans eagerly.

"Let me explain then. Because there are often too many sons, the young boys of noble families are sent to the households of wealthier nobles for their education and to learn the knightly arts. They are called pages. When they have completed their education and are proficient in arms, they become squires, until such time as they are knighted. Both the pages and squires are servants of a sort. The pages serve in the household. They often wait on the ladies as well as the lords. A squire is attached to one particular older knight in order to gain practical experience in what he has learned. He tends to his lord's destrier and keeps his armor oiled and polished and so on."

"And when does he become a knight?" asked Hans, bright-eyed with wonder.

"When he or his father can afford to furnish him with his own horse and armor."

"And if he cannot?"

"Sometimes he is lucky enough to find another lord who will sponsor him, but sometimes he remains a squire all his life."

"I see," said Hans, not quite sure if he did or not, but thrilled at the knowledge he was accumulating. "Something of the same happened to me. There were too many children at home, so my father sold me to the master to be a shepherd's boy. But I am a free peasant and I am going to leave soon to seek my fortune." Hans was suddenly aghast that he had confided his secret to this stranger. Could he trust the man or not? Well, it was out now.

"Indeed?" said the squire, as it if were nothing unusual. "And where will you seek your fortune?"

"I should like to go to Braunschweig."

"Aha! A lovely city, an admirable choice. But why Braunschweig?"

"I want to see our Duke Heinrich and his new castle, and his new church, too." Hans thought he had better add the latter just in case the man doubted his piety. Besides, he couldn't resist showing off how much he knew about his dream city.

"Then you must come and see me when you come there. I am attached to the Duke's household. Perhaps I can help you."

Hans' mouth hung open. He couldn't believe his luck. "Could I — could I come with you now?" he asked timidly.

"No, no," replied the other, "not now. This is a special mission, and even the servants have been carefully selected. But come when you can and ask for me. I am Brandt von Eltze."

"And I am called Hans," he said to his new friend. "And I thank you for your offer." He lowered his voice. "I plan to leave right after the sheepshearing."

"And when is that?" asked Brandt.

"Very soon. In the next few weeks. We get paid then," he whispered.

"Good. I should be there. Some very exciting things will be happening soon. You will enjoy being part of it. It will be a good time for you to seek work at the castle. They will be needing extra help."

"And what is going to be happening?" asked Hans, hardly able to control his excitement.

"The Duke is getting married again."

"Married again? But I thought he had a wife."

"Nay. He divorced the dour Clementia three years ago. And now Henry of England has offered him the hand of his daughter Mathilde. We have even now come from England."

"Across the sea?" asked Hans in awe.

"Ja, across the sea, and a rough voyage it was. It is good to be almost home again. Our Heinrich sent yon archbishop to look over the lass."

"And did you see King Henry himself?"

"Only once, but it was Queen Eleanor we dealt with. Now there is a woman."

"How so?"

"She is perhaps the greatest queen in Christendom, but I wouldn't want her to wife."

"Why not?"

"She is not to be trusted, but she rules the roost, especially where her children are concerned."

"And how did you find the Princess Mathilde?"

"A likely lass. Quick-witted and intelligent like her mother, but of a much sweeter temperament than that awesome lady."

"You say 'lass'. Is she young then?"

"Only a child. She is but eight years old."

"Only eight years old!" exclaimed Hans. "How can she be married then?"

"Oh, the marriage will not take place for another three and a half years. She will be old enough then. But it was important for political reasons that the betrothal take place immediately. It was done by proxy while we were at Winchester."

Hans did not quite understand the mechanics of all this or what 'political reasons' meant. Why she is younger than I, he thought. It is not only peasants who get sold. "But isn't Duke Heinrich an old man?" he asked.

"He is only thirty-six," replied Brandt. "That is not so old." Hans thought it was ancient but refrained from saying so.

There was a stir in the courtyard as the Archbishop and the other lords came out of the house. The master's wife was fluttering around them.

"Won't you stay the night, my lord?" she asked. "It soon grows dark and the roads are not safe."

"My goodwife, you obviously do not have room for such a company," replied the Archbishop somewhat sarcastically, "and if the best knights in Saxony cannot protect me, I should be in a sorry state indeed. No, we shall press on to Celle this night. The castle there is old and mouldering, but at least it has beds."

Brandt rose to fetch his own horse and that of the lord he was squiring from the grooms. As he rode out of the courtyard, he waved. "Auf Wiedersehen, Hans."

91

Hans waved back. "Wiedersehen, Sir Brandt."

The goodwife, irate at the Archbishop's parting remark, took her fury out on Hans. "How dare you talk to those gentlemen?" And she boxed his ear. Hans didn't care. He was happier than he had ever been in his life.

A few weeks later Hans was standing by the bank of the Aller River trying to figure out how to get across the ford. He had left the sheep farm before dawn that morning and the sun was now high in the sky. It was not yet noon—he knew that—but he was hungry. The farmer's wife had given him some black bread and a chunk of cheese to bring along, but he was determined not to indulge his appetite until he was across the river. If he could beg some food in yon village, he would save his precious bread and cheese for another day, because he had no idea how long it would take him to get to Braunschweig. The sheep farmer had been very angry when Hans had announced that he was leaving, but his wife had been kind and understanding. She convinced the irate man that if he did not give his permission, the lad would probably run away anyway. She had even urged Hans to take the sheepskin cloak, which he was not sure really belonged to him. He certainly didn't need it in this weather, but she reminded him that winter would eventually come again and besides, it made a good bed. At the last moment he had decided to take one of the puppies. Even the goodwife didn't know about that, but he didn't think she would mind. The cloak and his lunch were in a woolen sack slung over his shoulder, his three copper pennies wrapped securely in it. Except for the clothes on his back, all he owned in the world was in that sack. But he felt rich, indeed, and very happy because he was starting out to seek his fortune.

The puppy was tucked inside his blouse. As soon as he was far enough from the farm, he had let him walk and he followed Hans readily. But soon his tender baby paws became raw from the road and the poor little thing fell farther and farther behind. So Hans decided to carry him. He had not yet decided what to name him.

Now standing by the riverbank, Hans surveyed the first obstacle to his journey. The road had descended a hill from the plateau of the Heide and led directly to the river, and he could see where it emerged on the other side. There was a little house of some sort there. The ford was not really deep, and the current was not very strong, especially for springtime. It looked about as high as a horse's belly or the bottom of a wagon, but he had neither horse nor wagon and he was not yet full-grown and he couldn't swim. Downstream a ways he could see rapids, and he briefly entertained the notion of hopping across on the rocks. But they looked slippery and jagged, and if he ever fell there where the current was swifter, that would be the end of his dream. He dismissed that idea.

"I shall just have to wait until someone comes along," he said to himself. He let the puppy run around a bit while he sat down on the bank. He did not have to wait long, for it was a well-travelled road.

He heard the sound of horses' hoofs and coming down the hill he saw a man riding a scrawny, half-starved horse and leading an even more decrepit beast almost buried beneath a huge pack. Hans recognized him for a pedlar and was almost afraid to ask for help, as he had been taught that many of the itinerant pedlars were not to be trusted. But then he feared that it might be a long while before someone else came by. So he tucked the puppy in his shirt and stood up with his sack.

"Hi, ho, sir," he called cheerfully. "Could I trouble you for a ride across to the other side?"

The man seemed annoyed. "Afraid of getting your feet wet?"

"No, sir," replied Hans, "but methinks it is my head that might get wet."

"You *are* a bit of a runt," observed the man. "What's in that sack?"

"Just an old, worn-out cloak that I am taking to my old grandmother," lied Hans.

"That's all?"

"Yes, that's all."

"Now why would you be taking a cloak to your grandmother?"

"Because she is very poor and suffers from the ague."

"You didn't steal it?"

"No. My master's wife gave it to me for her."

"And you're not a runaway?"

"No, sir. My master gave me leave to visit her."

"Where does she live?"

Instinctively Hans knew he shouldn't tell the man his real destination. He quickly thought of the town nearest his parents' home. "Near Sehnde," he replied.

"Ah, that's too bad. I'm going in the opposite direction—to Braunschweig." Hans held his breath. "Very well, climb up behind me. I haven't got all day."

"Thank you very much, sir." Hans could see that the man was not going to help him mount, and there was nothing to stand on. He threw his sack across the horse's back, stepped back, and with a flying leap slung himself across the horse's rump, grabbed onto the protruding hip bones

93

and hauled himself up. The puppy squealed.

"What in thunder is that?" exclaimed the pedlar.

"Just a puppy, sir. I'm afraid I squashed him a bit."

The man shook his head. "Well, keep him under control. I can't have the horses getting skittish in midstream."

Hans smiled to himself. He didn't think the poor horses had been skittish for many years. The man jogged the horse and they started across the ford.

About halfway across the broad stream, the man suddenly asked, "Can you pay the toll?"

"What is that?" asked Hans.

"Everyone who crosses the river at this ford must pay a toll at yon house."

"But I have no money," lied Hans. "Besides, I have no goods."

"Everyone must pay just for the privilege of using the ford, goods or no," retorted the man, "and I'm certainly not paying for some waif I've picked up as a favor."

Hans made no reply, afraid the man might dump him off the horse in the middle of the river. But while they had been talking, the old horse was plodding steadily along and they soon reached the other side. The pedlar halted the horses at the toll station. They dismounted. Hans decided the best way to solve this new problem was to keep walking, but the pedlar guessed his intent and collared him just as the toll-collector came out of the house.

"Good morning. Well, what have we here?" asked the official cheerily.

The pedlar became obsequious. "Good morning, sir tollman. This lad here is a runaway and probably a thief, too. I would turn him over to you to claim my reward."

"I am not!" cried Hans.

"We have no reports of any runaways," said the toll-collector. "Who is his master?"

"Why—why—I don't rightly know, but it's one of the farmers across the river," said the pedlar.

"Then you'll have to go back and find his master and bring him here to claim him."

"What! And pay your toll two more times? You people make it difficult enough for a man to earn an honest living. I don't have time to go back. Let his master come here, but I want my reward."

94

"In that case, leave the boy here. I'll take care of the matter."

"But my reward?" objected the pedlar.

"You can collect that next time you come by here, if the master claims him."

"But I'm not a runaway. I'm free," protested Hans vehemently.

The toll-collector turned to Hans then. "Come into the house, lad, and wait there." He gave Hans a broad wink. "We don't want to delay this busy man any more than necessary."

Hans realized then that the tollman knew the pedlar was lying and went willingly into the little house.

The toll-collector carefully checked the contents of the pedlar's pack, wrote something down in a big book that lay open on the table, collected the toll due, and sent the devious man on his way. When the toll-collector returned to the house, Hans was staring with fascination at the huge book.

"Well, son, have you had your noonday meal?" Hans shook his head. "I was just fixing mine. Come, join me. Give that rogue a chance to be well away from here before you set out again. Where are you going?"

"I'm not a runaway. I'm free," repeated Hans.

"I know that, but I had to get you away from yon rogue. You have to be wary of such. There are many honest pedlars, but one like him gives the whole lot a bad name. They steal children with all manner of fancy tales and then sell them two or three towns down the road."

"Really?" said Hans in disbelief.

"Really. You must be very careful or you won't be free for long. But things are much better than they used to be. Time was merchants had to travel in groups with an armed guard because the robber-barons would swoop out of their castles and rob them and murder them, sometimes torturing them first. But our Heinrich has cleaned out a lot of those wasps' nests and put a stop to that, but there are still bandits and other criminal types to attack a lone traveller. Now tell me where you are going."

Hans decided he could trust this man, so he told him the truth. "I am going to Braunschweig to seek my fortune. I have a friend there," he added.

"Indeed. Then I wish you the best of luck. With all the building going on there you should have no trouble finding work."

At that moment the puppy began to whimper. Hans took him out of his blouse and set him down. He promptly piddled on the floor.

"Oh, I am sorry, sir, and you have been so kind," apologized Hans.

"No matter," said the tollman. "He's going to be a fine looking dog.

95

And he's hungry, too. Here, give him a little of our food. There's plenty."

"Oh, thank you, sir." Hans couldn't believe the man's generosity. Giving a dog anything but inedible scraps was unheard of.

"What do you call him?"

"I haven't thought of a name yet," replied Hans.

"Well, you will. Now eat up and be on your way. You have a long journey ahead of you. When you get to Braunschweig, tell them that Wulfstan the Tollman at Celle helped you."

"I certainly shall, for you have been very kind, Sir Wulfstan, and I do thank you. Now can you show me which is the road to Braunschweig?"

They went outside and Wulfstan pointed to the road leading southeast. "Stay right on that road. It goes directly to Braunschweig. It is a long way and there is only one small village in between, but there are many farms where you could seek shelter."

Hans thanked him again and started down the road, the puppy tumbling along behind.

"I think I shall name you Wulfstan after that nice man," he said to the dog. "Then I can call you Wulf for short." Hans was very happy. He had a full belly and he was on the road to Braunschweig. He passed the castle in Celle that the Archbishop had derided and it looked quite grand to him. He whistled a merry tune as he strode along.

He had no further adventures. Once he accepted a ride in a farmer's wagon, and that helped ease his weary feet. But he assiduously avoided the pedlars. And on the third day the walls and towers of his dream city rose before him in the distance. He was so excited he almost broke into a run, but he was very tired and footsore. He was carrying the puppy again and the sack with the cloak weighed heavy on his shoulder. Instead he sat down for a moment on a tree stump and drank in the sight.

Hans had never seen a city before. To his inexperienced eyes Braunschweig seemed immense, and he was filled with awe. Duke Heinrich had enlarged and beautified the town when he made it his capital some twenty years before. Hans could see the new walls bristling with towers and in the center rose the bulk of the not yet completed cathedral. In a few minutes he was on his way again, for he knew that the gates would be shut at sunset and he didn't want to be left outside.

As he passed through the gate, the way under the thick wall seemed like a veritable tunnel to him. Country people, some on foot, a few driving carts, were leaving the town, heading home after a day at the market. All kinds of others, from finely accoutered knights to filthy beggars, were entering the town. He was swept along with the crowd, and suddenly there he was, in Braunschweig. He eased himself out of the stream of people and stood to one side for his first close look.

He had never seen such magnificent houses, and so tall, too. Why, some of them had three, even five storeys. Many of them had glass windows. Some were built out over the street in such a way that they almost met the house opposite, effectively blocking out most of the sunlight. The streets were narrow and twisting, but many of the larger ones were paved with stones and had gutters down the middle. But one thing that brightened the aspect some were the numerous flower boxes. How strange, thought Hans, that the houses are so crowded together there is no space for gardens. How sad that they must plant a few flowers in boxes. But he thought the effect pretty just the same. What he didn't know was that most of the houses had huge gardens and stalls for animals at the back, which could not be seen from the street.

He wondered where the castle was but decided to wander around a bit before he asked. As long as he was safely inside the gates, there was no hurry. He knew from his first glimpse of the town from the distance that the great new cathedral was near the center. He would go there first and try to orient himself. He headed down one of the larger streets and was immediately swallowed up by the dimness and the press of people. For a few minutes he felt almost claustrophobic with the houses so close on either side and the people bumping into him. He chided himself. If I am going to live here, I'll have to get over that. I'm just not used to it.

At last he came to a large square which he knew was the Market. He remembered those trips to Sehnde with his mother. But this place seemed immense in comparison. The entire square was paved, and although most of the stalls were already closed or closing, he was bewildered by the variety of foodstuffs for sale. All kinds of meat, fowl and fish, fruits and vegetables, even flowers. He didn't even know what some of them were. And then he noticed something else he had never seen before. Around the perimeter on three sides of the square were open-fronted shops, right in the ground floor of the houses. They were still doing a brisk business and, fascinated, he went to take a look. The goods were displayed on shelves in the front of the shop. The shopkeeper stood behind the shelf and at the sight of a prospective customer immediately started an eloquent sales pitch praising the quality of his wares. The cloth cutters' shops seemed to be the most numerous and there were a great variety of these—common and fine wool, plain old fustian and sheer linen, silk and cloth-of-gold.

97

The latter two he had heard of but never seen. He had thought they were the stuff of fairy tales. Farther on were gold- and silver-smiths, jewelers and workers in cloisonné. Then there were the specialized smiths who made fine swords and knives. He could see the fires of their forges far out in the back. I bet they don't shoe horses there, he thought.

When he came to the bakers, his mouth started watering from the delicious smells emanating therefrom. He was hungry, not having eaten since morning, and he was sorely tempted to spend one of his precious pennies. But no, he reasoned, not yet. I've been pretty lucky begging my meals. After I get work, I'll come here and treat myself. As he passed the wine merchants' the sweet-sour smell came out to him and he could see clouds of fruit flies around the huge barrels that were stacked to the ceiling. How can anyone drink that much? he wondered. For that matter, how can all these tradesmen sell enough to stay in business. Yet they were obviously all thriving. There must be hundreds of people living here. The numbers were mind-boggling. Even though Hans could not read or write, he had learned to count. Counting the sheep had been an important part of his job. But even so, the concept of hundreds of people living together in one place not much bigger than the whole sheep farm was almost beyond his comprehension.

On the fourth side of the Market Square was a very large half-timbered building. It was too large to be a private house. He wondered if it might be the castle. He ventured to ask one of the men standing in front of the wine merchant's enjoying a cup of wine.

The man laughed. "No, son, that building is more important to us than the castle. It is the Town Hall."

Hans didn't know how anything could be more important than the castle, but the man showed such obvious pride in the Town Hall that he didn't want to question him. So he asked, "Then can you direct me to the castle?"

The man was about to laugh again, wondering what business a young country bumpkin could possibly have at the castle, but the lad was so serious he thought better of it. Probably a nephew of one of the third maids, he decided. "You go out of the center of town, which is here," he directed, "down that street there, until you come to a big open square. On one side you will see the new church our Lion is building, and opposite it is the Dankwarderode."

"The Dankwarderode?" asked Hans, puzzled.

"Ja, that is the name our Lion has given his new castle. It used to be open farmland. Belonged to the Brunonen dukes. It was the farm of Dankward, who, with his brother Bruno, founded our lovely city a long time ago."

"I see," said Hans. "Thank you for the information." He waved and set off down the indicated street. He mused about the man's calling Duke Heinrich the Lion and wondered if the people really loved him as he had heard or if the man was just being facetious.

Very soon he came to the Castle Square. It was indeed large. It was immense, more than twice the size of the Market Square and completely paved with perfectly fitted stones. On one side stood the massive bulk of the new cathedral. The nave of the church was already completed. Only the towers were lacking and men were working on them from scaffolding that covered the building like a giant wooden cobweb. The stonemasons, carpenters and their helpers were just packing up their tools, ready to quit for the day. Huge piles of lumber and stones and the ingredients for mortar were all over the place. It looked chaotic. He was tempted to go into the church to make a prayer of thanksgiving for his safe arrival, but he was afraid a brick or something might fall on his head, so he murmured his prayer where he stood, crossed himself and looked across the square.

There it was. The castle of his dreams. The Dankwarderode. Its lines were much more beautiful and graceful than those of the cathedral, in his opinion, although they were both built in the same new Gothic style. It was not a fortress, as he had imagined, but really a palace. The next problem was how to get in and find his friend Sir Brandt. Butterflies started fluttering in his stomach and the palms of his hands grew damp. And, of course, just then the puppy started squirming. He set the dog down while he debated how to approach the gatekeeper. There was no question of just walking in here. The gates were open but heavily guarded.

Unexpectedly, it was Wulf who gained him entrée. As Hans approached the gatekeeper, the dog was busy sniffing all the interesting smells among the building materials stacked by the church. Other dogs, and cats, too, had been here before him. How exciting all these strange smells were!

"Good evening, sir," said Hans politely. "I wonder if you could tell me where I can find Sir Brandt von Eltze. I am a friend of his."

The man looked at Hans in disbelief. "And who might you be—Sir Lord Almighty?" he asked sarcastically.

"I am Hans," he replied simply. "And Sir Brandt told me to come here to visit him."

"Indeed?" said the man. "And you look just like you've come on a state visit with that pedlar's pack on your shoulder."

"I am not a pedlar," denied Hans. "I am—I was a shepherd boy and he really is my friend."

"A likely story," said the gatekeeper as the other guard ambled over. "Doesn't this just look like the kind of friend our uppity Brandt would have?" he asked his companion.

"Oh, sure," replied his friend. "Hasn't he just knighted you, *sir*, and our Brandt, too, *sir*? Why, he must be the Emperor Friedrich himself."

Hans knew they were making fun of him and didn't believe them at all. How could he get it through their thick skulls that Brandt really had invited him? If he couldn't get into the castle tonight, he would have to beg his supper and a place to sleep. And he somehow was beginning to realize that city people weren't as friendly as country folk.

"Sir," he began again and realized that he shouldn't have said that. "Won't you just tell Brandt that I am here? He will tell you that it's all right to let me in."

"Brandt can't be bothered with the likes of you," said the first man importantly.

"And we don't admit pedlars, beggars or waifs," said the other. "Be off with you, lad."

Hans felt tears of frustration fill his eyes. He knew he mustn't cry like a little boy. He was almost a man. But what to do?

Suddenly there was a commotion across the square. "Get out of here, you damned mutt!" someone shouted. "Peeing on the stones for our church!" Hans heard the puppy squeal, and suddenly a gray ball of fur flashed past the astounded guards and through the open gate of the castle.

"What was that?" And as the guards turned to look Hans sped by them after the dog.

"Wulf! Wulf!" he called.

"Hey, you can't go in there!" the guard called after him. But while they were debating whether to leave their post and follow him, Hans had reached the castle courtyard.

The puppy was nowhere to be seen. "Wulf, Wulf, come here!" Hans called again.

"What is going on here?" A tall, handsome man in a long flowing robe of magenta silk was approaching. He was clean-shaven, with a strong chin and straight nose. He had wavy reddish-gold hair cut just below the ear and piercing blue eyes. The aura of command hung about him. He was obviously someone in authority.

"Oh, sir," said Hans, his voice quivering, "my dog has run away and I can't find him. I fear he is hurt. He is only a small puppy."

The man raised his eyebrows. "I don't see any dog. And how come you to be in here in the first place?"

"I have come to visit Sir Brandt von Eltze."

"Indeed?" But it was not said unkindly.

Encouraged, the words spilled out of Hans. "Yes, he is my friend. I met him when he stopped at the farm a few weeks back. He was coming from far-off England on a mission for Duke Heinrich. He went there with the Archbishop and some other lords to look at the Princess Mathilde. We became friends and he told me to come here and he would help me to find work. I am a free peasant," he added, just in case.

"Indeed," said the man. "And did Brandt tell you how he found the Princess?"

"Oh, yes, he said she was intelligent and quick-witted but of a much sweeter nature than her mother, who is a great queen, but not to be trusted." The man roared with laughter at this. "But she is only a child," added Hans, "younger than I."

The man was still smiling. He put a hand on Hans' shoulder. "Methinks you speak the truth. Wait here a moment while I speak with the guards. They are ready to shut the gates. Then we shall find Brandt and see if he acknowledges your friendship."

Hans crossed his fingers and stood as he was bid. As soon as the man moved off, Wulf reappeared and lunged against Hans' legs. He picked the puppy up and could see he was not hurt, only frightened. "Wulf, I thank you," whispered Hans. "You have helped me meet someone evidently quite important, who I think will help us."

He could hear part of the conversation at the gate. "But, Your Grace," protested one man, "we thought he was just a beggar waif."

"Of course, I can understand, but you should at least have called Brandt to verify his story. He obviously has met him. He knows too much about the mission to England to have made it up."

"I am sorry, Your Grace."

"No problem. Good night."

Your Grace, thought Hans. Could this be the Duke himself? he wondered and the butterflies started again. As the man returned to where Hans was standing, the boy fell to his knees. "Your Grace," he mumbled, "forgive me for being so discourteous. I didn't know who you were."

"Of course you didn't," said the Duke kindly. "I see you have found your dog. Now come and let us see if we can find your friend."

Hans stumbled to his feet and followed Duke Heinrich into the great hall of the castle.

The hall was vast. Hans thought, why at least six of the farmhouses, attached stalls and all, would easily fit in here with room to spare, and I thought that was a big house compared to my parents' cottage. Heavy, fat square columns held up the vaulted arches of the ceiling. Mullioned windows in the Gothic style with real leaded glass lined one wall. And on the other side, instead of in its usual place in the center of the room, was a cavernous fireplace, lavishly decorated with grotesque carvings and with a real chimney. This was something else that Hans had never seen before, for chimneys were the newest architectural innovation of the century.

The hall was crowded with people, both men and women, all lavishly dressed. Most of the men wore the same type of flowing gown as the Duke's, in a variety of colors, although not all of such fine material. Some others were still in their chain mail, but most were rapidly shedding it with the help of their squires. These men wore tight hose and short tunics, the better to fit under the armor. The ladies were equally colorful. Their elaborate towering headdresses with wimples and flowing veils and their low-cut dresses made Hans' eyes bug out of his head.

Supper was about to be laid and the many servants were busy setting up the trestles and laying the boards which they took from stacks against the wall. Hans expected everyone to fall on their knees when the Duke entered, but no one paid him any attention at all.

Heinrich stopped a servant. "Do you know where our Brandt is? I don't see him," he asked.

"I believe he went out into the tiltyard with Sir Wigbert, Your Grace," replied the man. "They were discussing some point or other about today's exercises."

"Thank you, my goodman. Would you kindly go and call him in forthwith?"

"Certainly, Your Grace."

"Just like our Brandt," remarked the Duke to Hans, "ever arguing with his betters."

Hans marvelled that the Duke had actually thanked a servant. He had always heard that the word 'courtesy' derived from the elegant manners at court but until now had never understood the true meaning of the word. How different from the way my master ever treated me. Right then and there he made up his mind that he would learn to act like these high-born people even though he wasn't one himself.

A few moments later he saw Brandt enter through a door at the far end of the hall. As he came striding towards them, his face lit up. "Ah, my little friend Hans, the shepherd boy!" he exclaimed. "I didn't think you would really come"

"But I promised you I would, Sir Brandt," replied Hans.

"He is not 'Sir' yet," corrected Heinrich. "Very soon, but not yet."

"I am sorry, my lord—I mean, Your Grace," stammered Hans. "I didn't know. I thought all high-born people were called 'Sir'."

The two men laughed. "My fault entirely," said Brandt. "I didn't disabuse him of the idea."

"No, you wouldn't," commented the Duke. "But I am glad to see the lad was telling the truth."

"Ah, yes," said Brandt. "In fact, he has come to be a playmate for your bride."

"What?" exclaimed the Duke loudly, and Hans was afraid Brandt had gone too far. But Heinrich seemed to think it was hilarious. "You know, that might not be a bad idea at that. She will need someone her own age for a while. The lad seems intelligent enough, and we have plenty of time to train him before she comes." Heinrich pondered that for a moment. "Well, I have a few things to tend to before we sup. Take the boy to the kitchen and have the cook feed and bed him—and that hungry wolf he carries in his arms. I am sure we can use another pot-boy or some such."

Hans smiled his broadest grin. "Thank you so much, Your Grace."

When the Duke had left, he turned to Brandt. "And thank you so much, Sir—I mean, Brandt, for inviting me here. I promise I'll never disgrace you."

Brandt smiled and put his arm around Hans' shoulders. "Hans, my boy," he said, "I think your future is assured. Our Lion is pleased with you."

And so Hans settled into castle life. For the first few weeks he was set to the most menial tasks, most of which were as monotonous as watching sheep. He turned the spit in the huge fireplace until his arms ached and his face felt charred. He scraped and scrubbed pots and cauldrons and ached even more. But he had more leisure time than before and spent most of it thoroughly training Wulf. They were not allowed near the tilt-yard for fear of making the horses nervous, but he had the freedom of the open fields behind the castle and occasionally he took the dog for a long run outside the walls of the town.

After about a month Hans was promoted, through Brandt's good offices, he was sure, to waiting on table in the great hall. The head footman who trained him was persnickety and fussy, but Hans was eager and learned fast, so that the man could find few things with which to fault him. He soon realized that he was the only commoner among the pages. All the others were sons of noblemen, some rich, some impoverished, but all noble. And he had his first experience of being the object of jealousy and derision. He tried to ignore it, but it was difficult.

He seldom saw Brandt except at a distance. Hans longed to talk to him but knew he shouldn't bother him with what he might consider petty problems. He had heard that Brandt was to be knighted soon and would be deeply involved in the elaborate preparation for the ceremony. Aside from the problems with the other boys, Hans had another idea he wanted to discuss with the squire as well.

One day to his surprise, Brandt sought him out. He was just about to take Wulf out into the fields and was at the gate of the kitchen garden when he heard his name called.

"Where are you off to, Hans?" asked the young man.

"I was about to take my dog for a run in the fields," replied Hans.

"May I come with you?"

"Of course, Brandt. It is good to see you. I have been wanting to talk to you."

"And I with you."

"Indeed?" asked Hans, imitating his superiors to a tee.

"Yes," replied Brandt. "Ah, what a glorious day. Much too nice to be indoors."

"Yes, it is," agreed Hans, wondering if Brandt only wanted to discuss the weather. "I thought you were practicing in the tiltyard."

"Ach, ja. Much too warm to be smothered in armor." Brandt glanced back to the castle, satisfied now that they were well out of earshot. "I have often seen you watching us practice our feats of arms. Would you like to learn?"

"Oh, Brandt, I would like it very much!" exclaimed Hans, growing excited at the prospect. "I am quick and agile, and strong, too. I'm sure I can learn quickly. But," and his face fell, "would they let me?"

"I think I have thought of a way, but I first wanted to be sure you were interested."

104

"Oh, Brandt, I am truly," replied Hans. "Just tell me what I must do."

"Nothing you have to do just yet. But we must make up a little story for the world," said Brandt. "Where are you from?"

"Near Sehnde."

"Where is that?" asked Brandt.

"Just a little village—although I used to think it was a big town—west of here. About three days' walk, I would guess."

"And is there a lord there?"

"Yes, but it is a small, poor demesne."

"What is his name? What do you know about him?" asked Brandt eagerly.

Hans couldn't see where all this was leading, but he would humor Brandt as best he could. "I don't know his name. I was very small when I left, you know. But I do remember that he was a grouchy old man with no children. I think his wife was dead. My parents were free peasants, because he didn't want the tithe—couldn't use it all by himself. I'm sure he was poor—relatively, that is—because he wanted the money instead, which made it very hard for us."

"Perfect! Perfect!" exclaimed Brandt. "Couldn't be better."

Hans looked at him as if he were out of his mind.

"How good are you at telling stories and making people believe they are true?" Brandt asked him.

"Pretty good, I guess," said Hans doubtfully. "I once told a pedlar some lies, because I was afraid he would rob me. I don't know if he believed me or not."

"These will not be lies," said Brandt deliberately, "just something that you have only now learned about yourself."

"I don't understand," Hans replied, perplexed.

"Listen to me. In less than two weeks I shall be knighted and I would like to choose you for my squire."

"But, Brandt, how can I?"

"Hear me out. From now on your name will be 'Hans von Sehnden'."

"What!" exclaimed Hans.

Brandt held up his hand. "Let us say that the old lord's wife died in childbirth and he gave his son to your parents to bring up as their own, because he was so overcome with grief he didn't want to look at the child that caused his wife's death. It happens, you know. But your parents—or, we must now say, the peasant couple—didn't really know the child was his either. Now that he is old and filled with remorse at what he did, he has

105

traced you here but, finding you so well situated in the Duke's own house-hold, decided to let you stay until you are knighted."

"Knighted! Brandt, I think you are crazy," declared Hans. "You have made this all up."

"Of course I have, but only you and I will ever know that."

"What will His Grace say?"

"He will never know. When the old lord dies the estate will revert to the Duchy. Since you will already have the name, it is more than likely that, provided you are still in the Duke's favor by the time you are knighted, he will return the land to you."

"I can't believe all this," said Hans, shaking his head but beginning to enjoy the game. "Do you really think people will believe this?"

"That's up to you," said Brandt. "You've got to convince yourself first and then practice telling the story again and again until it becomes the truth."

"I'll try," said Hans enthusiastically. "I'll certainly try, but what if we're found out?"

"We'll worry about that if it should happen, but I doubt it. And in two weeks you'll be my squire. I can offer you some measure of protection."

The more Hans turned the idea over in his head, the more he liked it. The rewards were certainly worth the risk. Then he was reminded of the thing he wanted to discuss with Brandt. It would fit in perfectly with his new background.

"Brandt, can we add something else to it?" he asked hesitantly.

"Add anything you want, as long as it can't be too carefully checked."

"No, I meant something different. Brandt, I know there is a school for the boys here at the castle. Brandt, could I learn to read and write?"

Brandt looked surprised. He hadn't expected this. "You're not going to go clerky on me?"

"No, no," Hans assured him. "I'll practice very hard at all the feats of arms so that I will be a good squire to you, but I would so much like to learn to read and write," he pleaded.

"That's strange," mused Brandt. "Most of the boys have to be forced to it. They never had to before our Heinrich was duke, you know. I'm not too good at it myself. But if that's what you want, I'll see that it's part of your preparation."

"Oh, thank you, thank you, Brandt. When can I start?" he asked eagerly.

"Not until after you become my squire," replied Brandt. "I must go

106

back now or they will be looking for me." As he turned to go, he smiled. "We are equals now, Hans von Sehnden."

Hans called Wulf to him and tussled with the dog until they were both tired. Then he sat down in the grass and practiced his story on his best friend.

Hans was so busy with all the new things he had to learn that time passed very swiftly. Brandt and several other young men were knighted in an elaborate ceremony following a nightlong vigil in the new cathedral. Hans was not allowed to attend, but at the great banquet that followed he spent his last day as a page. There was a great deal of surprise and questioning looks when Brandt chose him for his squire, but Brandt told the company the story of Hans' 'birth' and subsequent 'rediscovery' by his 'father' with such aplomb that few thought to doubt its truth.

Hans was immediately plunged into the routine of a squire's training. He learned to ride, and because of his feel for animals, he amazed the master of horse with how quickly and naturally he took to it. He even trained the horse to let Wulf run alongside without getting nervous. He practiced fencing until he thought his arms would fall off. But he persevered and muscles started developing he didn't know he had. He was also growing rapidly with all the good food and exercise and showed promise of becoming a tall man. He kept Brandt's horse groomed, his clothes clean, and his armor and weapons shining.

However, what Hans loved best of all were the morning hours spent in the schoolroom. At first the other boys made fun of his stumbling efforts, not so much because they had a few years' head start, but because they were jealous that he was already a squire. But very soon his agile mind got the knack, and from then he made rapid progress in reading and soon began to tackle writing. The old priest who was his teacher was so pleased that he often let the boy return to the schoolroom in the evenings and practice his new found skills.

A year passed and the great cathedral was finally completed. An elaborate and solemn Mass of dedication and consecration was celebrated by the Bishop. Days of special Masses, feasting and tournaments followed. Then the Duke had a surprise for everyone. On a tall pedestal in the center of the Castle Square was placed a large, finely cast bronze lion.

After the Bishop dedicated the statue and blessed it, Heinrich declared, "There you have it—I, the Lion of Saxony. Now you will have your Lion forever even after I am gone."

The people went wild with cheering.

"Why does he like to call himself 'the Lion'?" asked Hans.

"Because there is no stopping him," replied Brandt. "He is the greatest duke we have ever had and he's not even a Saxon, but he has done a great deal for our country."

"He's not a Saxon?"

"Well, only partly. He is a Welf from Bavaria, but both his grandfather and father married Saxon princesses, so he's more than half, I should say. When his father died, he inherited both the ancestral Welf lands in Bavaria and also Saxony from his mother, Gertrud. He was only twelve and his mother and grandmother ruled as regents. I did not know them, but I have heard they were very astute ladies. He chose to make Braunschweig his new capital and immediately started enlarging and beautifying the city."

"Then he must be very happy today," remarked Hans.

"I'm sure he is, and we have every cause to be proud with him. He has united the original three parts of Saxony back together again as it was before Karl the Great. And then he proceeded to enlarge it by conquering much land beyond the Elbe. Besides all that, he has fought for years beside the Emperor Friedrich helping him conquer large portions of Italy for the Empire. Friedrich couldn't have done it without him. He is the most powerful duke in Germany."

"I see," said Hans, awed at such power, yet he knew the man could be kind and courteous.

"Watch it there now!" shouted the dockhand. "Those damned temperamental horses will end up in the harbor yet if you're not careful." He lowered his voice and mumbled to his companion, "High-strung beasts are just as spoiled as some of their masters."

Hans stood patiently waiting his turn to help load Brandt's destrier and palfrey and his own palfrey onto the ship. He was on the great wharf at Bremen, and they were making ready to leave for England. Hans couldn't believe that he was going to England—really going. Brandt had once more been chosen to accompany the mission as the Duke's emissary and, of course, Hans was to go along with him. This mission was far more important than the previous one, as they were going to fetch Heinrich's bride, the Princess Mathilde.

Hans tried to look very nonchalant and sophisticated as he waited, but inwardly he was seething with excitement. Since he had become Brandt's squire he had grown considerably, and not just in height and

108

breadth but in experience as well. He had become an excellent horseman and quite proficient in arms, although he knew he had a long ways to go before he was capable of entering a tournament, let alone a real battle. He was now a voracious reader and had even secretly written a few poems. Hans had learned a great deal about his country, having ridden to many different places with Brandt on errands for the Duke. Once Brandt had taken him to his father's castle at Eltze and there he had been welcomed as graciously and warmly as though he were part of the family. He had been deeply moved, never having known the warmth of a loving family relationship before.

But this was the first time ever he was to go out of the country to a foreign land—although perhaps it would not seem too foreign. Ever since he had learned he was going, he had read everything he could find in the Duke's library about England. Hans had learned that many centuries ago Saxons from this very part of the country had gone there to settle and that the language spoken by the common people was not too different from his own Low German. And then about a hundred years ago Duke William of Normandy had crossed the Channel and conquered the Saxons. The Normans were really descended from Vikings but now spoke French. The present King Henry II was the great-grandson of William and ruled over a vast territory consisting of not only the island kingdom but also Normandy from his father and the huge Duchy of Aquitaine from his wife, the indomitable Eleanor. They had several children—the eldest was Henry, whom his father had named as his heir, then Mathilde and Richard, who was supposed to be his mother's favorite, and some younger ones as well.

It took two days to load all the horses, equipment, baggage and food for the party. There were eight ships but some of them sailed almost empty, although they carried some trade goods, for it was expected that the princess would have a great deal of baggage and several ladies and servants. Hans had never been on anything larger than a river boat before and it was a strange sensation, indeed, to feel the deck moving beneath his feet. At first he enjoyed it as he stood by the rail watching the riverbanks slide by, the huge colorful square sail billowing over his head. All of a sudden as the river joined the great swells of the sea the pleasure turned to dismay. He clung to the rail fearful of falling overboard, and his stomach roiled. Before he knew what was happening he turned green and lost his breakfast over the side. He sat down on the deck and held his head, wishing he had never set foot on this ship. Brandt was laughing.

"It's not funny, Brandt," he moaned. "Why am I so sick? I felt perfectly well a few minutes ago."

"It happens to everyone the first time," explained Brandt. "It is the motion of the sea. In a day or two you will get used to it."

Hans just wanted to die. He would never get used to it. But by the next day he felt better and once again began to enjoy the trip. The workings of the ship fascinated him and he asked all sorts of questions of the captain and crew. Someday I should like to be rich enough to own a ship like this, he thought. Why, one could go all over the world and make money besides, for he knew that the captain had been paid handsomely for this voyage.

For three days they sailed west and then gradually turned toward the southwest. Occasionally Hans could see misty flat islands in the far distance off the larboard side, for the ships did not venture too far out of sight of land. On the afternoon of the sixth day they headed in toward land. After passing close by several large, sandy, windswept islands they entered a winding river. The surrounding countryside was low, flat and green, much like home.

"Is this England?" asked Hans.

"No, not yet," replied Brandt. "This is Flanders. We shall be stopping for a few days at Brugge to get fresh water and food and to unload some of the trade goods. England is another day and a half to two days' sail west of here, depending on the weather. The Channel can be very rough, although now in July it shouldn't be too bad. But sometimes sudden storms come out of nowhere."

"I can't wait to see England," said Hans.

"But you will enjoy visiting Brugge, too. It is a lovely city with canals running every which way through it. And in its harbor you will see ships from all over the world."

The Channel crossing was better than expected and everyone cheered when the sheer cliffs near Dover loomed on the horizon. "Why are they so white?" asked Hans.

"Because they consist of pure chalk," replied Brandt. "We actually have something like it near the little village of Hannover called the Calenberg, but you barely notice it riding by. These are much more extensive and seem so spectacular because they rise straight out of the sea."

When they landed, they were met by the lord of Dover Castle. He greeted the Archbishop and Lord Wigbert, who were the senior members of their party, in courtly French. Hans made another resolution. Someday he was going to study that universal language of the elite, so that he could converse directly with them. But he noticed that the German crews and the English dockhands had little difficulty in understanding one another.

"Why do the lords speak in French?" he asked. "It seems as though the common people have no problem understanding each other."

"Because all the nobility here are Norman," explained Brandt. "Most of them consider it beneath their dignity to learn Anglo-Saxon. Many of them cannot even communicate with their own peasants."

"How stupid," commented Hans. "So tell me what they are saying. Can you understand French?"

"Well enough. And you will pick it up quickly if we stay here long enough," said Brandt. "They are saying that they have brought horses for our use today, as they don't want to wait here while ours are off-loaded. Besides, the animals will be very disoriented for a while after the long voyage. Haven't you noticed your own legs are a bit wobbly?"

"I sure did," agreed Hans.

"It is the opposite of being seasick. Your body has to adjust again to terra firma," explained Brandt. "Now they are saying that we shall go up to Dover Castle and there await the Princess."

"Are we then not going to London?" asked Hans, disappointed.

"It appears not. But the Archbishop is arguing the point right now."

"Oh, I hope he convinces them to let us go. I so wanted to see London."

"He just may. He is a very strong-willed and persuasive man. The last time I heard him discussing a minor point of protocol with Queen Eleanor herself, they were like two bulls circling in a field."

"And did he win?" asked Hans.

"Yes, he did. So you may get to see London yet. It is big, crowded and indescribably filthy, but very interesting."

The Lord of Dover and the Archbishop apparently decided to continue their discussion in more comfortable circumstances, so they all mounted the horses provided for them and started the steep ascent up the winding path that led to the great and very old castle atop the cliff. Brandt pointed out that parts of it, including the famous lighthouse, had been built by the Romans.

For the first few days the Saxon delegation was feasted and feted at the King's expense, but then the celebratory atmosphere tapered off and the castle went back to its normal routine. They were just extra mouths to feed and extra horses to stable. July passed into August and the boredom of

111

waiting set in. There was nothing for them to do but take long rides out into the countryside or practice in the tiltyard. Hans learned to swim in the bone-chilling waters of the Channel, but he didn't like the salt water very much.

"Well, it looks like we'll not get to London this time," Brandt told him one day when they were out riding.

"Oh, I'm so disappointed," replied Hans. "Whyever not?"

"It is a very complicated political situation. I shall try to explain, although I am not sure I understand it all myself. Apparently King Henry is feuding with his own Archbishop of Canterbury, Thomas Becket, whom he has exiled to France. He is afraid that the very presence of our own Archbishop might stir up trouble. Thomas has excommunicated several of Henry's nobles, although not Henry himself, but the Bishop of London has chosen to ignore the excommunications. It is similar to our own Emperor Friedrich's feud with the Pope. He has refused to acknowledge Alexander and has invested his own Pope, Paschall III, in the tradition that ever since Charlemagne, the Emperor had the right to choose the pope. Our Heinrich, of course, has been helping Friedrich in his wars in Italy against Alexander."

"My God, it *is* complicated," agreed Hans. "How can people we are supposed to look up to manage to get things so tangled up?"

Brandt ignored the question. "It gets more complicated yet. King Henry is also feuding with his archenemy Louis VII of France, who has given Thomas asylum. They hate each other because Queen Eleanor was once married to Louis but divorced him to marry Henry and brought her huge Duchy of Aquitaine, almost a third of France, with her."

"Unbelievable." Hans shook his head.

"And so, I am afraid our little Duchess-to-be Mathilde is just a pawn in all this," continued Brandt. "By using her for a political union with our Heinrich, King Henry is literally thumbing his nose at Thomas and Pope Alexander. Moreover, he is assured of the political support of the Emperor against Louis. And our Heinrich gains an alliance with one of the largest kingdoms in Christendom, which is becoming more powerful every day, just in case he should have a falling out with Friedrich, for they do not always see eye to eye on this investiture thing."

"Poor little Mathilde," mused Hans.

"Yes," agreed Brandt, "you can well say 'poor little Mathilde'. But that is all royal women are good for. They often have less freedom of choice than our peasant women."

112

Hans thought deeply about this. "I am grateful that I have become a nobleman and I want very much to be knighted someday, but I think I should hate to be a king. I shall have to channel my ambitions in another direction."

Brandt laughed and clapped him on the shoulder. "Well spoken," he said, "and smart, too."

The days drifted lazily by from August into September. Goldenrod and Michaelmas daisies covered the fields with gold and purple splendor. It reminded Hans a little of the Heide. The nights were beginning to get cool but the days remained sunny and warm. At last in the middle of the month word reached Dover that the Princess' entourage was leaving London and that her mother, Queen Eleanor, would be accompanying her. Hans was as excited as everyone else, eager not only to see their future duchess at last but also to see the famous Queen as well. Besides, it meant they would soon be going home.

At last the royal retinue arrived at Dover. The size of the company was astonishing. It looked as though half the nobles and prelates in the kingdom, together with all their servants, were there to see the Princess off. Young Mathilde was quite pretty with reddish blonde hair and deep blue eyes, but her beauty faded in comparison with that of the Queen. Eleanor was truly a handsome and very regal lady.

The quantity of baggage that was to be sent with one small Princess was incredible. A good thing the Saxons had brought so many ships with them, thought Hans. There still might not be enough room for all of it. There were thirty-four packhorses alone to carry the stuff once they landed at Bremen, to say nothing of the personal mounts of the Princess and her attendants. Besides their normal equipment there were seven additional saddles gilded and covered with scarlet and twenty pairs of saddlebags. Twenty large chests held Mathilde's clothes and personal belongings as well as large pieces of cloth, tapestry and furs. Both Henry and Eleanor wanted the world to know that their eldest daughter came from a powerful kingdom. The fact that Henry had imposed a special tax on his barons and the towns in order to pay for it all was quickly pushed to the background.

To load all this on board the ships took several days. So Eleanor settled in at the castle and held her usual court, her world famous 'Court of Love' which was not usual at all.

Aside from the lavish feasting, there were jousts and tournaments held every day, with rich prizes for the winners. Sometimes the Saxon

113

knights won and sometimes they didn't. The English knights were very good. Some of the knights took it much to heart when they lost, especially if they were wearing a lady's favor, but Brandt didn't seem to care either way.

When Hans queried Brandt on this, he said, "It's only a game, after all. A good way to keep one's skills sharp for real war."

"But don't you want to win?" asked Hans.

"Of course," replied Brandt, "but I don't need the money. My father has a rich fief and it will all be mine one day. Some of these knights are younger sons who make their living by winning in these tourneys. That prize money can mean the difference for them between eating next week and not. And in some of the jousts the rules are that the loser must forfeit both his horse and his armor to the winner. I just do not have the heart to take that from someone to whom it means his livelihood."

Hans' respect for his beloved mentor went up several points.

In the evenings the 'Court of Love' shone in its true magnificence. Eleanor's famous troubadours from Provence entertained them with exquisite songs of unrequited love for the high-born ladies so far beyond their reach. Although it was rumored the love was often returned, everything was very discreet. And the heady atmosphere of pure, unprofane love was quite uplifting. The Queen also held contests for unknown singers and poets and Hans was tempted to enter one of them, but when he heard the exquisite, plaintive verses, he was glad he hadn't. He needed a lot more polish to even begin to compete with these courtly artists.

At last the ships were loaded and it was time to depart. The Lord of Dover escorted Mathilde and her ladies to the wharf. Eleanor must have had her private farewells with her daughter at the castle, for she had left for London early that morning. How like Eleanor to worship 'courtly love' in public but keep her own emotions very private. The girl's father had not even come to Dover to see her off. He was somewhere in Normandy. It was rumored that all was not well between Henry and his imperious wife. How sad, thought Hans. He had been greatly impressed by Eleanor.

Hans hoped he would be on the same ship as the princess and his luck held. He and Brandt were among the last to be squeezed on board the flagship, and it was very crowded. All the men, noble or otherwise, except the Archbishop, had to sleep on deck in order to allow the ladies the limited cabin space. In the crowded quarters of the ship it was easy for Hans to make the Princess' acquaintance.

One day she and some of her ladies were sitting on deck embroidering. Or at least the Princess was. Some of the others looked a bit peaked. It was a beautiful day, but the following wind was cool and strong. It filled the great square sail to the straining point, and as the ship raced through the waves, every so often a burst of spray would come over the side, drenching everything. Hans approached them.

"Wouldn't you be more comfortable in your cabin, Your Grace?" he suggested. "It's a bit wet out here."

"I am still Your Highness," she retorted, "and who are you?"

"I beg your pardon, Your Highness, I already think of you as our Duchess," apologized Hans suavely. "I am Hans von Sehnden."

"Well, Hans, you can't be much of a sailor if you think those stuffy cabins are more comfortable than out here in the fresh air. I love it. I have travelled back and forth across the Channel more times than I can remember, ever since I was a tiny child. And I have often sailed across the Biscay to Bordeaux. Now there you have storms that make even the ablest sailors fearful."

"I admit that this trip to England is my first sea voyage. I was even sea-sick the first day out of Bremen." He laughed at the recollection. "But I, too, love it now. And I have travelled widely throughout our land of Saxony and even to some other parts of Germany."

"Ha," she smirked, putting him in his place, "and I have travelled all over England, Normandy, Brittany, Anjou *and* Aquitaine, which are all my father's—and my mother's—realm. And I have been to Paris several times as well."

Hans was duly impressed. He couldn't think of what to say next. But Mathilde had her audience now and decided to make the most of it.

"Tell me about Duke Heinrich," she said.

"He is very tall and quite handsome."

"But old," she interrupted.

"Not really," said Hans, echoing Brandt's words to him so long ago. "He is thirty-nine but doesn't look it."

"What else?"

"He is a very great warrior and the most powerful duke in the Empire."

She waved her hand impatiently. "I have heard all that. Tell me what kind of a *man* he is."

"He is very kind, fair and just. Sometimes he gets a little impatient at laggards or stupidity and then he loses his temper, but not for long."

"Nothing could be so terrible as my father's rages. My poor mother," sighed the little princess wistfully.

Hans thought Queen Eleanor was hardly an object of pity, but he refrained from commenting. "He is also very intelligent," he went on, "and believes in education. He has founded many schools in different towns. He is also promoting trade and commerce. He made Lübeck into a great port from an insignificant fishing village, so that we can send ships across the East Sea to Sweden and Novgorod. His court is also brilliant and gay, perhaps not quite so magnificent as your mother's, but very similar. He encourages the writing of books and poetry and the Minnesänger."

"The what?" she asked.

"The Minnesänger are what you call troubadours. There, you have learned your first word in German," said Hans.

Mathilde turned the word over on her tongue. It was not difficult. "Will you teach me to speak German, Hans?" she asked.

"I should be most happy to," replied Hans. "Let us start with your name. In Saxony you will be called Mechthild."

"Oh, no, not my name," she objected. "I am already Mathilde in French and Matilda in English. I refuse to be called that horrible-sounding word."

So much for the German lesson, thought Hans. But in the course of the voyage they became good friends, and after they disembarked at Bremen he and Brandt rode by her side on the long journey to Braunschweig.

To the surprise of everyone except Hans, Duke Heinrich fell madly in love with his little bride, despite the disparity in their ages. Mathilde had inherited too much of both her parents' strong-willed character to remain quietly sequestered in the solar, sewing and embroidering with her ladies. She was quite mature for her age, undoubtedly a result of having been dragged from court to court both in England and on the Continent since she was one month old. Her influence upon the court at Dankwarderode was felt immediately. Yet she was entirely feminine and quite sweet-tempered. From her earliest childhood she had seen too much of her father's violent temper and her mother's conniving stubbornness not to realize that these traits were divisive and eventually had cost both her parents the loss of respect of the people. She had learned there were other, more subtle ways of imposing her desires.

She was tiny and doll-like, built like neither parent. Henry was short and heavyset, his wife tall and statuesque. Mathilde's face was rounded, more like Henry's than Eleanor's long oval, but there was no doubt that she had her mother's strong chin and the determination that went with it.

116

And Heinrich, the Lion of Saxony, melted like butter in her hands.

The Christmas Court that year was the most lavish anyone had ever seen. Although Heinrich had long been a patron of the arts and letters, the influence of Eleanor's Court of Love through her daughter was very much in evidence. Besides the usual tournaments, balls and other festivities of the season, there were elaborate performances of the Minnesänger and poets. New books were commissioned to be written. Everyone agreed that, aside from Eleanor's own, the ducal court of Saxony must be the most enlightened in Christendom — the very epitome of all that chivalry was beginning to stand for.

The wedding was scheduled for February of 1168. The bride would be twelve years old in June. In the meantime Mathilde was diligently studying German and eagerly learning about her new country. Although Hans no longer regularly attended classes at the castle school, he continued to frequent the library whenever his duties as Brandt's squire permitted. Mathilde chose him as her unofficial mentor and often sought him out to discuss a point of history or politics. He admitted he learned as much from her about the rest of Europe as she did from him about Germany.

The nuptial Mass at the new cathedral, now called St. Blasius, was magnificent. Both King Henry and Queen Eleanor sent personal representatives but neither attended. Hans wondered if Mathilde was disappointed at this. If she was, her royal demeanor betrayed no sign of it. Perhaps she knew her selfish, volatile parents too well. But the lack was more than filled by the attendance of almost all the dukes, counts and lesser nobility from all parts of Germany. All the crowned heads of Europe, with the notable exception of Louis of France, sent family members or nobles. It was a very grand affair.

Two joyful weeks of feasting and celebration followed. There were numerous tournaments and jousts. Some countries sent whole teams of knights, and this time Brandt made every effort to win. The honor of Saxony was at stake. But Hans noticed a new incentive. Brandt was now wearing a lady's favor on his sleeve.

"Who is it, Brandt?" Hans asked teasingly.

"Ach, just a neighbor girl I have known for years," replied Brandt offhandedly. "She and her family came to Braunschweig for the wedding. I sought to please her, that's all."

But Hans suspected there was more to it than that. Brandt had never shown much interest in any of the girls at court and he certainly could have had his pick.

117

Sure enough, a year later Brandt announced that he was getting married and, furthermore, that he wished to leave the Duke's active service and return to Eltze to learn how to run his father's estates. It was more than time he did.

"You are more than welcome to come with me, Hans," he said. "I shall always need a squire, and you are exemplary. I shall miss you very much, but the choice is yours."

Hans thought about it a long time. "I shall miss you, too, Brandt. But I just don't know."

Brandt sensed Hans' quandary. "No, it was selfish of me to suggest it. Your opportunity lies here at court. With me you will always be a squire. Here you have the chance to become a knight and maybe much more."

Hans agreed. "I really think I would rather stay here, if I can find someone else to take me into his service. But on the other hand, I hate to desert you. You have done so much for me."

"Ach, foolishness," said Brandt. "The best thing I can do for you is see that you are well settled before I leave."

A few weeks later Mathilde gave birth to her first child, a son and heir whom they named Heinrich after his father. There was tremendous rejoicing in Braunschweig and indeed throughout the whole duchy. The great bells of the cathedral pealed the entire day. Once again the usual elaborate feasting and celebrations took place. Hans decided to gather up his courage and enter one of his poems of courtly love—a Minnelied—in the contest. He could not sing very well, but he was willing to share the glory with one of the minstrels, who had agreed to set it to music for him. He had learned a lot about the art since Mathilde's advent, especially from the frequent visiting troubadours from Provence, where the songs of courtly love had originated. Besides, he was secretly half in love with his Duchess, so it was very easy to sing her praises in the most pure and chaste form.

To his surprise and great joy the song was well received. Although it did not win the prize, he received many compliments and was encouraged to continue writing songs. Mathilde was especially pleased. Even Heinrich called Hans to his side and said with a broad grin, "I see I shall have to keep an eye on you." Hans hoped he was teasing.

Shortly thereafter the Duke sent for Hans. He entered the private chamber with some trepidation, hoping Heinrich had not been upset by the song in honor of his wife.

"I am told that you will soon be a squire without a knight," said the

118

Duke, coming straight to the point.

"I am afraid so, Your Grace," replied Hans.

"You do not wish to remain with Sir Brandt?" asked Heinrich.

"I could go to Eltze with him," explained Hans, "but I much prefer to remain here, Your Grace—that is, if a place can be found for me."

"Why is that?"

"I do not wish to remain a squire all my life, Your Grace," replied Hans. "I feel I am capable of much more, and I am sure the opportunity to use my talents lies here."

"An honest answer," commented Heinrich, "even if you have a slightly inflated opinion of yourself."

"I am sorry, Your Grace, but you asked," said Hans humbly.

"Never apologize for telling the truth," said the Duke forcefully. "What talents do you believe you have that might be of use to me?"

"I am good at dealing with people, Your Grace. I seem to have a knack for convincing people of the right of things."

"A diplomat," said Heinrich.

Hans permitted himself a shy smile. "I don't fool myself, Your Grace, that I am old enough or sophisticated enough for that, but it is the sort of thing I like to do. I enjoyed very much going on all those missions with Brandt to other courts. I learned a lot from it. I should like to continue doing that, if you would permit it, Your Grace."

"Hmm, interesting," mused Heinrich. "We shall see. Meanwhile we need a title for you to enable you to stay here and at the same time free you to do whatever tasks I choose to set for you. Since you are yet too young to be knighted, it must be something that a squire can fill without arousing too much jealousy in others. My dear little wife, who also thinks highly of *some* of your talents, has made a brilliant suggestion. Your new duties will be as equerry to my son and heir, Sir Heinrich."

Hans looked at him astonished. "But, but, Your Grace, he is not even a month old."

"Exactly," said Heinrich. "It will be many years before he needs the services of any but a nursemaid. Therefore you will be free to be at my personal service for whatever special duties I shall name."

"Oh, thank you, Your Grace, I am most appreciative . . . "

Heinrich cut him short. "Remember, I expect to use those talents you speak of," he challenged.

"Indeed, Your Grace, I shall do my best," replied Hans.

"Go now to the court tailor. You shall need livery as befits your new rank." Heinrich dismissed him and turned to other matters.

In the next few years Hans had more than his share of travelling about the numerous courts of Germany. The dukes and nobles of the fragmented country were becoming ever more powerful. Alliances were made and broken, bargains sealed and then betrayed. The Emperor Friedrich, often called Redbeard (or Barbarossa by the Italians), needed their support in pursuing his dreams of re-creating the empire of Charlemagne. But in order to gain that support Friedrich had to grant them more and more privileges, and their power increased accordingly. And Heinrich of Saxony was the most powerful of all.

In his attempt to restore the Empire Friedrich collided head-on with the Pope. There were two reasons for this. Charlemagne had rescued a weak Papacy by conquering all of northern Italy and giving it better government than it had had since the fall of Imperial Rome. In return the Pope had given the Emperor the right of investing all prelates—archbishops, bishops, abbots—in his Empire, and under the ensuing feudal system these men owed fealty for their lands and other temporal power to the Emperor. But Charlemagne's empire had been broken up under his own obsolete Salic law. The popes had begun dabbling in politics and, especially since the first two crusades, the secular territory over which they ruled had become quite large, the rich heartland of central Italy. Friedrich felt, quite rightly, that the popes had no business being temporal rulers and in a series of wars from 1154 to 1161 reconquered most of this part of Italy for the Empire. Heinrich had supplied most of the troops and the brilliant leadership that had accomplished this.

The question of investiture was a stickier problem. Under the influence of powerful theologians such as Bernard and Peter Abelard, the weak French kings had gradually relinquished the right. The English kings had no respect for the Papacy but usually tolerated their appointees if it were politically expedient. If not, they took matters into their own hands, as in the case of Henry and Becket. Friedrich, however, clung stubbornly to the tradition handed down to him from the successors of Charlemagne that the Emperor had the right to make all clerical appointments in his territory. When Pope Alexander, who hated Friedrich anyway for divesting him of his rich Italian lands, refused and excommunicated him, the Emperor carried things a step further and appointed his own Pope, Victor IV. When the latter died in 1164, Friedrich appointed Paschal III as his successor.

By this time some of the German nobles were becoming ambivalent about the schism. A few were worried about the excommunication, particularly in the south which had been Christian since Roman times, far longer than the north. In the Saxon north the rule of Rome was generally resented and had been since earliest times. So Heinrich had been an ardent supporter of the Emperor and in return had been given his own right of investiture in all of Saxony. More importantly he had been permitted to conquer and add to Saxony large Slavish territories east of the Elbe all the way to the borders of the tiny Margravate of Brandenburg.

This volatile situation naturally demanded much and frequent diplomatic negotiation, as the great nobles switched sides for one reason or another. Out of this gradually evolved the system of Diets (occasional parliaments) and eventually the electoral system, which chose the emperors for almost eight hundred years thereafter.

Hans particularly enjoyed visiting the Imperial city of Goslar, when the Emperor's court was in residence and he accompanied Heinrich thence. The Empire had no official capital as such, although the Emperors were still crowned at Aachen, Charlemagne's old capital. But Aachen was too near the French border for comfort and too far out of the mainstream of German politics and the burgeoning trade routes. As the center of power shifted east and then south on the accession to the throne of the Staufen family, the Emperors ruled first from their own castles in the ancestral Staufen territory in Bavaria, which bordered on the ancient Welf lands. In fact, Friedrich and Heinrich were cousins. Gradually, as the need to keep a closer eye on the vast reaches of the Empire became apparent, a network of Imperial cities came into being. They were the first 'free cities'. Their citizens ruled their own internal affairs through a mayor and town council. The typical chain of feudal hierarchy—peasant, vassal, lord, count, duke, king—did not exist for them. They were beholden only and directly to the Emperor. The Emperor was constantly on the move, trailing his enormous court with him and each of these favored cities in turn became the 'capital' of the Empire during the time that the court was in residence there.

Goslar was Friedrich's favorite, as it had been the favorite of most of his predecessors. It lay well within the borders of Saxony in the southeast part of the Duchy, where the great alluvial plain of the north abruptly ended at the foot of the Harz Mountains. Goslar was of no strategic importance. It did not lie on a river or at a ford or on an important trade route. Its wealth was under the ground. Hanging over it like a dark brooding giant was the mountain called the Rammelsberg, deep in the bowels of which were the richest silver, copper and lead mines in Germany. Since the first two crusades had opened up trade with the Levant and the east, the whole of Europe had been gradually switching over to a money economy, and Goslar grew in importance with it. Faraway commercial cities like Venice and Genoa depended on its silver to conduct their trade, and the local peasants were increasingly expected to pay their tithes in pennies minted from its copper.

The palace was already over a hundred years old, having been built by one of the Brunonen emperors, Heinrich III. It was very large and ultramodern for its time. It sat in great dignity on a low hill under the Rammelsberg, but overlooking the charming town. Facing it at the foot of the hill was the huge cathedral, up to that time the largest in Germany. Behind it was the separate community of the miners' homes. The houses were of a unique style all their own with steeply pitched slate roofs, instead of the usual thatch. Farther on was a very rich monastery, said to have been founded by Charlemagne and now supported by the miners' tithes.

Goslar was a town rife with old legends. It was said that elves and trolls had mined the rich ore from the mountain for thousands of years but had jealously guarded their secret until one day about two hundred years ago a knight had done them a kindness and they showed him their silver palace under the mountain. Now it was early spring and Hans was watching for the famous witches of Goslar. He stood high on the battlements of the palace with several other squires, shivering from the cold and perhaps from anticipation as well. Spring came late in the mountains. It was already mild back home in Braunschweig. There was just a quarter-moon and dark clouds were scudding swiftly by. Suddenly a tremendous screeching and howling sound seemed to slide down the mountain and rush through the valley and into the town.

"There, there, I see one!" cried one of the young lads.

"That's just a cloud," said Hans.

"No, no. I can see her broom and her black cloak billowing out behind."

"There's another!" yelled someone else. "and I can see her cat, too!"

Hans looked this way and that as others claimed to see witches, but all he could see were clouds—dark and strangely shaped, but clouds nonetheless. He saw no witches that night, but he certainly could hear them. The weird sound rushing down the mountain was eerie and spine-chilling. He decided he'd had enough of screeching witches and cold wind. He went down to the great hall where it was warm and sought his pallet.

Hans enjoyed exploring the huge palace when he had free time. He was particularly intrigued by the octagonal royal chapel of St. Ulrich, which looked like it had been attached to a corner of the palace as an afterthought. In the middle of the tiny chapel, almost filling it, was a huge sarcophagus with an effigy of Emperor Heinrich III reposing on top of it. Within it was a silver casket containing the heart of the builder of the palace. Although a resident priest celebrated Mass there every morning, it was too small for official functions, which took place in the great cathedral opposite. For the rest of the day the chapel was usually deserted.

One rainy afternoon with nothing else to do Hans decided to continue his perusal of the frescoes in the chapel. He had never heard of St. Ulrich before and wanted to learn more about him. As Hans approached, he heard voices. He hesitated before entering, not wishing to disturb anyone at their prayers.

"He is getting too big for his breeches," said one man.

"I agree," said the other, "but what can be done about it? He is Friedrich's favorite."

Hans wondered whom they were talking about. He edged a little closer. The light in the chapel was always very dim and poor even on the brightest days. Today it was so dark he was unable to see the men clearly.

"I know what I would do," the first man went on. "A tournament without wooden-tipped lances, an unfortunate fall from a horse, a misguided arrow while out hunting . . ."

His companion sounded shocked. "You are suggesting assassination?"

"The quickest and surest way to rid ourselves of him."

"Sir, you go too far," said the other indignantly. "The Emperor would hang us all."

"It can be made to look like an accident."

"No, no, there must be another way. I agree with you that I am tired of lying down like a lamb while the Lion of Saxony steals all the glory, but assassination, no. I'll have no part of it."

Hans gasped. He realized then that they were talking about his beloved Duke Heinrich, plotting against him. He must find out who they were. He ducked behind the far side of the sarcophagus and crouched low in the shadows.

"What was that?"

123

Both men turned.

"There's no one."

"Are you sure? I thought I heard something."

"No one ever comes here this time of day. It was probably the wind in the branches of that great tree outside."

"Well, let's get on with it then. This place gives me the creeps. What would you suggest, if not a quick demise?"

"We could start rumors."

"Like what?"

"Perfidy. Simony. Nepotism. Perhaps adultery."

"Friedrich would never believe it. And if he did, he wouldn't care less. They are two of a kind. You've got to come up with something better than that."

The second man thought a moment. "Suppose we can convince Friedrich that he is a traitor—that he is trying to steal his own throne away from him."

"That would shake Friedrich up. But how would you go about it? We can't just go to him and tell him, 'The Welf wants to usurp your throne'. He would laugh at us. We have no basis for any accusations."

"Of course not. But we start rumors—very subtly. Plant seeds of distrust here and there. Let others carry the tale to him."

"That will take time."

"Naturally, but we must bide our time. It will be more sure in the end. Think ye, if you should arrange your so-called accident, so what? He has two infant sons who will inherit. If we can convince Friedrich to deprive him of his lands and titles, to disinherit him, what care we how many whelps he has? There'll be nothing for them to inherit."

"Yes, I see your point. Do you think we can convince the Emperor?"

"Eventually, yes. And Heinrich will play right into our hands. He grows more powerful every day. I shouldn't wonder that the Emperor might be worried already. And he has such a good opinion of himself, he won't think he could ever fall from grace. Him and his schools and his 'Court of Love'—he is getting soft—and complacent. We'll fix him."

"Good. Then let's get started. I've already thought of a juicy little tidbit. I'll tell my squire, and it will be all over court by tomorrow."

The men left the chapel.

Hans was aghast at what he had heard. He remained where he was, crouched in the shadows until he was sure the conspirators were well away. He knew who one of them was, the Count of Zähringen, an insignif-

124

icant little backwater of Bavaria. He was one of the least of the lesser nobles, but unfortunately, he was brother to Heinrich's first wife Clementia, whom he had divorced. The other Hans recognized as another petty noble, but he did not know his name. Hans knew he had to warn Heinrich of the dastardly plot against him as soon as possible, but he would have to seek an opportune moment.

What Hans didn't know was that at that moment Heinrich was closeted with the Emperor and they were discussing the very possibility of such a plot. Only it was Friedrich who was warning Heinrich.

"They are so jealous of you, cousin," said the Emperor, "that they may even go so far as to accuse you of treason."

"I care not a fig what they accuse me of," retorted Heinrich, "as long as *you* know that I am your loyalest servant."

"I trust you implicitly—yea, more than a brother," Friedrich assured him. "But they are circulating stories that you are beginning to favor Alexander over Paschal. If that were true, I should be most disconcerted."

"I care little for either Pope, if you want the truth," said Heinrich forthrightly. "Let them stick to their Masses and breviaries and let rulers rule."

The Emperor noted Heinrich did not say 'let *you* rule', but said nothing. "Just the same, I think it would be wise to put a stop to such rumors. I realize that it is just petty jealousy on their part. I know that you are the most progressive and forward-looking prince in the Empire and that my goal for a united Germany is yours also. But they are centuries behind you in outlook and cannot understand this—or don't want to. Until they begin to modernize their outlook, I have decided to make a pretense of restricting some of your privileges."

Heinrich waited, wondering what was coming next. His loyalty to his cousin did not include trusting him. He knew him too well.

"I have decided temporarily to rescind your right of investiture and take it back upon myself."

"What!" exclaimed Heinrich, disbelieving.

"As I said, it is only a temporary gesture," said Friedrich, "but it will silence any rumors that maintain that you might be appointing clerics who may favor Alexander."

"I see. And do you believe that I am doing that, sire?" asked Heinrich formally.

"No, no, of course not," the Emperor assured him. "It just seems expedient at the moment. And I would further suggest that you refrain from any further military expeditions—on your own, that is. Naturally, if I command you, I would expect you to obey."

"But, dear cousin," objected Heinrich, "I have not undertaken any military expeditions—except peacekeeping within my own lands, since my marriage."

"Ah, yes, the ideal husband and father," commented Friedrich, and Heinrich wasn't sure if he was being sarcastic or not. "That English alliance, in the eyes of some, makes you seem even more powerful than I."

"You know that is not so, sire. And you admit you share in the benefits of it."

"I understand that," replied Friedrich, "and I care not if you and Henry play games with that nincompoop Louis. But I do not want my other German princes shivering in their beds wondering who will be your next victim. Enough is enough. Their sovereignties are just as valid as yours, maybe more so in some cases." Friedrich let that veiled threat hang in the air a moment before he went on. "Many of them still remember the war between your father and my uncle. It *will* not happen again."

"I assure you it will not, sire," protested Heinrich. "My loyalty to you is unconditional, but methinks these unfounded rumors have undermined your trust in me. How can I prove it to you?"

"By sitting quietly in your Dankwarderode and playing at your Court of Love. Stop running around the country stirring things up and let me rule my Empire," replied the Emperor firmly.

"As you wish, sire." Heinrich thought a moment. "Perhaps it would be well if I left the country entirely for a while."

"And go where? Do what?" asked Friedrich suspiciously.

"I would go on a pilgrimage to Jerusalem," said Heinrich. "Yes, methinks it would greatly benefit my soul—and perhaps set yours at ease as well."

Friedrich was flabbergasted. This brilliant cousin of his was always one step ahead of him. Leave it to him to make the magnificent gesture, he thought. There was no way he could deny Heinrich's request, but somehow he suspected an ulterior motive.

Thus when Hans was seeking Heinrich out to tell him his news, the Duke was also seeking his squire.

"Let us go for a ride," he suggested. "I have sat too long in the royal presence. It gets stuffy after a while. I need some fresh air."

Hans had their horses saddled and they quickly left the town and headed up a deep valley. It was the same one where the witches had

126

swooped down. Later Hans was to wonder if that was significant.

Preparations for the pilgrimage moved rapidly apace. It was the year 1172. There temporarily was peace in the Holy Land and Jerusalem remained in Christian hands. Both Popes were granting indulgences to pilgrims, so it mattered not on which side of the papal schism one stood. One's soul benefitted regardless.

Heinrich was planning on taking a large party of knights with him, more befitting a king than a duke. But that was part of the Lion's glamour. Give oneself the image and soon people believed it. Besides his blood was every bit as good as his cousin's, the Emperor's. If Heinrich's father had not been killed in that war when he was ten, he might well be sitting at the pinnacle himself instead of Friedrich. But at other times Heinrich felt he was more content just ruling Saxony. At least no group of Electors could take it away from him.

Hans was eighteen that year and naturally was included in the party. He had half-hoped that Heinrich would consider knighting him before they left, but so far there was no indication that this would happen. Hans also realized he should be thinking about marriage, but aside from tumbling a few kitchen wenches, there was no one in whom he was particularly interested. The fact that he was still only a squire limited his possibilities. With the knighting he could raise his sights. He was determined to wait until that time. Besides, he was still secretly in love with Mathilde and he knew of no one who could measure up to her.

Mathilde was now posing a problem for Heinrich. She was determined to go on the pilgrimage with him. Her second son, who had been named Otto after the greatest Emperor ever, was already over a year old and in the care of nursemaids. Mathilde was not presently pregnant. So she could see no reason why she could not go.

When Heinrich objected, she said with a stamp of her tiny foot, "My mother went on a Crusade, which was far more dangerous than a mere pilgrimage in peacetime. What's more, my grandfather went on the very first Crusade. It is a tradition in our family. Do you consider me any less than they?"

"No, of course not, my sweet," replied her husband, "but it still could be very dangerous."

"I am not made of butter," she commented caustically. "I am every bit as seasoned a traveller as you."

The Lion of Saxony saw he could not win against this little termagant, so finally he acquiesced, but she must limit the baggage. Mathilde

127

paid no attention to this and the size of the party instantly doubled, for she must take certain of her ladies with her and, of course, maids. And all of these ladies naturally insisted that all their assorted husbands accompany them for protection.

Hans enjoyed listening to this reparte and admired his determined Duchess all the more. He was glad she would be going. It would brighten things up a lot on the long tedious journey. He was greatly excited about the prospect of seeing strange lands of which he was only vaguely aware. Outremer—the fabulous land beyond the sea that few of his generation had visited. He could hardly wait to get started.

At last all was in readiness. On a bright sunny day toward the end of May, after attending Mass at the Cathedral, with the bishop's blessing and with the bright red crosses sewn on their surcoats or tunics, they left Braunschweig and headed south. Heinrich's lion pennant flew proudly at their head. The sun glinted on the knights' highly polished armor, the bright colorful gowns of the ladies contrasted with the stark white of their close-fitting coifs and wimples. Everyone rode horses, beautifully groomed palfreys. The great destriers, used only in war or tournaments, were led by the squires. A few litters were brought along in case any of the ladies should become faint or ill. The servants trudged behind leading a long string of packhorses. Everyone was in a high good humor. The adventure had begun.

They made good time for the weather held fine and the size of the well-armed party discouraged brigands. Many of the frequent tolls for crossing bridges or fords or entering towns or counties were waived when it was learned they were pilgrims. And, of course, Heinrich's fame went before him. They were welcomed at castles, monasteries and towns. Their route took them through Würzburg, Nürnburg, and Augsburg, the wealthiest commercial city of southern Germany and capital of the ancestral Welf demesne. Hans saw so many fascinating things he had never seen before, he was afraid he would forget them, so he started writing them down in a journal. When they entered the mountains, he was awed by them and wondered how they would ever get across, but they were to get higher yet. They crossed the Danube at Donauwerth where it was still a small stream, but he was told that it later became a mighty river and flowed over a thousand miles to the east before it reached the sea. Many pilgrims went east by this route, but Heinrich evidently preferred another.

At Innsbrück they stopped for a few days. Up to this point their stops had been very brief, usually only overnight or at most, a day and two nights. Heinrich had vowed he would not get into political discussions with any of the various dignitaries within Germany, but sometimes courtesy demanded something more than just an overnight stay. Besides, he had written beforehand to certain merchants and shipowners in Venice more or less when to expect him. He would brook no unnecessary delays for fear that the superior ships he had arranged for would grow tired of waiting and leave without him. But at Innsbrück it was necessary to wait a few days while special preparations were made for transitting the treacherous Brenner Pass. Snow still lay heavy in the Alps and a special guide was hired to lead them through. His equipment included several huge dogs trained for the purpose of rescuing people stranded in the snow. Food supplies were checked and a goodly amount of the fine wine of the country was added to them. Fur-lined cloaks and boots were pulled out of the baggage and kept in readiness on each person's horse, for there would be times when the horses had to be led along narrow icy trails through deep snowdrifts.

It seemed as though they never stopped going up and up. The crystal clear air grew thin and some people got dizzy and had trouble breathing. Sun glaring off the snow was blinding. Most everyone donned cloaks and boots long before it was necessary to dismount. Hans had never seen so much snow and here it was June. He hugged the walls of the narrow ledges, wanting to look down but terrified that the fascination would lure him to his death. They spent the first night wrapped in their horse blankets huddled around pitiful fires in the courtyard of a small monastery. There were only enough guest rooms for the Duchess and a few of her ladies. The next morning they were on their way at first light. No one wanted to linger here. Now the guide warned them to be very quiet. Any sudden loud noise might set off an avalanche, which could bury them all. And this time of year was the most dangerous of all. Hans had never been so cold in his life. He never wanted to see another mountain. But there were many more to go.

At last they reached the pass. They spent that night at a large monastery where at least they were able to shelter in the hall and the servants in the stables. There was mulled wine for all and it helped take the chill out of their bones. Numbed hands and feet were thawed before a great fire. The worst must be past if they are breaking out the wine, thought Hans. And so it was, although it was not immediately apparent. There were still mountains and more mountains, but now the trail seemed to lead down more often than up. One day Heinrich and the guide stopped and pointed. Everyone gathered round and looked to see. There at their feet lay the lush plain of Lombardy. A great shout of joy arose and prayers of thanksgiving were offered. Some of the younger knights were all for racing down.

"Hold," called the Duke. "If you do that, you will be dizzier and just as short of breath as you were up in the heights. Your body needs time to adjust. We shall go down just as slowly as we went up."

Hans asked why they did not now dispense with the services of the guide.

Heinrich explained, "The pass is under control of the city of Verona, which lies yonder, still several leagues away. Our agreement with the guide is that he accompanies us thence and there we pay the toll to the city and the other half of his fee."

"It seems that Verona is rather far away to have control of the pass," commented Hans.

"Ah, but it lies on the only road that comes out of the mountains. One has no choice. There is not a crossroad until one arrives there. After that we shall head directly east to Venice. Now there is a city you will enjoy. It is quite unique."

But Hans was destined never to see the floating city. When the party reached Verona, they were met by several of the leading citizens, who advised them to avoid Venice and seek another way.

"Why do you suggest that?" asked Heinrich, suspecting a political gambit, for he knew the Italian cities had no love of him for his part in Friedrich's wars of conquest.

"Plague has broken out," they warned.

"Plague!" exclaimed Heinrich, turning pale. Hans had never seen the indomitable Lion afraid before, but he certainly was now. "Has this just happened? We had no word of it before we left."

"Just these past few weeks," replied the Veronese, "and what's more, the Doge has been murdered and the city is in a turmoil. It is not safe."

"My God," said Heinrich, incredulous. "We have been so isolated these past weeks crossing the mountains that no word of this disaster has reached us. Tell me everything that has happened."

"It is a long story."

"I would hear it all. I need to know all the facts so I can decide what to do. May we have the hospitality of your fair city until such time?" asked Heinrich in his best conciliatory manner. He did not trust the Italians, nor they him, but he needed their help at the moment.

"Since you come in peace as pilgrims, you may stay for a while, but I doubt we can feed such a large party for very long," said the man doubtfully.

"We shall be glad to pay."

The other's face brightened. "Very well then. And your knights will not molest our women?"

"They will behave," Heinrich assured them. "I shall take personal responsibility."

"Then come along to the palace," they invited. "Let us get your people settled and we shall tell you all we know of it."

When this had been done and the ladies were bathing and resting, they met with the Duke of Verona in his audience hall. Hans was at Heinrich's right hand. They were served little cakes and wine.

"Here, Hans, taste this wine for me," said Heinrich, handing him his cup.

Hans innocently did as he was bid. "Ah, it is very good, Your Grace," he commented.

Heinrich watched him for a moment and then took the cup back. He whispered, "Thank you, Hans, you are very brave. These Italians would as soon poison a man as look at him."

Hans was disgusted when he realized how he had been used. But then, he reflected, it meant the Duke trusted him, but he would not be so gullible in future. There were servants for that.

The Duke of Verona was not too friendly. He seemed to barely tolerate their presence and let his citizens do most of the talking. They related how the Byzantine Emperor Manuel Comnenus had accused the Venetians of burning a large Genoese settlement outside of Constantinople. The Venetians had denied any responsibility in the matter, but the Emperor had rounded up thousands of Venetian citizens living in the city and imprisoned them. Venice had promptly declared war and in a great naval battle was soundly defeated. While the remaining ships lay helpless and disabled, plague had broken out among the crews. The Doge had headed for home regardless and brought the dreaded plague with him. The people had been furious with the Doge for sacrificing the greater part of their fleet, which was their lifeblood. The plague on top of it had been the last straw. Mob rule had broken out, the Doge had fled for his life but had been caught on one of the bridges and stabbed to death.

"And so," concluded the Veronese, "they are a city without a ruler, without their fleet and very nearly bankrupt. We do not fear that the plague will spread, since they are so isolated in their lagoon, but no one dares go there either. The last we heard, it was in complete chaos."

Heinrich pondered all this information for a few moments. He showed no emotion, only annoyance at the delay it was causing him. Such were the tides of men. He shrugged. "Then I shall have to find another way."

"The most direct way to Outremer is to take ship at Bari, or better, from Messina in Sicily," suggested the Veronese.

Heinrich looked at the man as if he were crazy. "Surely you know, sir," he retorted indignantly, "that this is the last way I could go. I, of all people, would not be welcome in the Papal States, and as for Roger of Sicily, methinks the bottom of his dungeons would be the only place he would welcome me. Even with an army at my back, I know better than to antagonize him. And here I am, with but a handful of knights, a bunch of simpering women and more unarmed servants than I have need for. Do you take me for a fool?"

The Duke of Verona seemed amused by this outburst, but he said nothing. The first citizen replied suavely, "No, no, Your Grace. I merely meant that that was the way most pilgrims go. Perhaps at Genoa you may find ships that can take you."

"Yes, yes," agreed Heinrich, "that will have to be it. I shall send a messenger at once to make the necessary arrangements."

The group of Saxons settled down to wait in Verona. At first the warm Italian sun felt good after the rigors of the Alpine crossing, but soon the uncomfortable knights shed their armor and the women shed petticoats. Woolen underwear, both male and female, began to itch. But it was pleasant to stroll in the gardens of the castle and listen to the minstrels sing love songs in the evening. Hans learned to play chess from a young Italian gallant and was taught the not-so-subtle art of flirtation by the raven-haired young ladies of the Veronese court. But remembering the prohibition against molesting the women, he merely played the game and kept his distance. He was sure any one of them would have welcomed him in her bed, but Heinrich had warned him that they were to be trusted no more than the men. Besides, he was afraid of catching the pox.

After three weeks the messenger finally returned from Genoa with the information that the Genoese would be happy to supply ships for the Duke of Saxony, but at a steep price. They were well aware of the problem in Venice and intended to take full advantage of it. Also there might be some delay until enough ships reached port to accommodate so large a party. If the Duke would come thither as soon as possible, they would see what could be done.

Heinrich fumed and sputtered, called them thieves and pirates, but he knew he had no other alternative than recrossing the Alps and taking the arduous Danube route. Some of the older knights recalled that they had advised taking that way in the first place, but his mood was so foul, they dared not remind him of it. So everything was packed up again and they took leave of Verona and headed west to Genoa.

When they arrived at the gates of Genoa, they were refused entry. Heinrich's rage knew no bounds. Everyone stayed out of his way. Father Theodorich, his chaplain, reminded Heinrich that he was putting his soul in double jeopardy by ranting and raving so while on a pilgrimage.

"Let it be in triple jeopardy," shouted Heinrich. "Ah, if only I had my army with me. I would level this misbegotten town and string up those whoresons by their very balls."

"Your Grace!" said Father Theodorich, shocked. "Please be patient. I am sure there is an explanation for this."

"By God's teeth, they'd better have a good explanation."

"I am sure they are being extra cautious for fear of the plague," said the priest soothingly.

At last a delegation from the town fathers came out to meet them. They were most apologetic.

"We are most sorry you have been inconvenienced, Your Grace. You arrived sooner than we expected. The watch didn't realize who it was and they have strict orders to admit no large party with armed knights. You see, we—uh—had some problems during the Crusades."

"Well, you shall have more problems, I trow, if you don't admit us forthwith," replied Heinrich.

"I am afraid," continued the Genoese, "that our town is quite over-crowded and our accommodations are limited. There are but a few inns on the waterfront. There would perhaps be room for yourself and a few of the ladies. That is all. The rest will have to wait here until the ships are ready to depart."

Heinrich was on the verge of losing his temper again but quickly realized that they had the advantage. He felt like a beggar on the church steps. Humility did not set well with him, but before Father Theodorich could remind him that it was good for his soul, he made a decision. "Then we shall all wait here. Let your merchants and captains come here to deal with me."

133

"Very well, Your Grace, if that is your wish," replied the oily Genoese. "But does Your Grace not want to inspect the ships and suggest what supplies you might need? We should not want Your Grace to say they were worm-eaten or ill-found after they have been loaded." He paused a moment to let this sink in. "And then there is the matter of payment."

Heinrich gritted his teeth. No wonder these thieving rascals were so rich. "Have no fear about that," he said. "You shall have your payment at the proper time. And yes, I should like to inspect the ships. But I shall spend the night here with my people. I prefer the fresh air to your flea-ridden inns. Come along, Hans."

"If it please Your Grace," said the other man, "to leave your horses here and come on foot. The streets are very steep."

Hans expected another explosion, but it did not come. Heinrich merely shrugged and dismounted. He gave the order to set up the tents, which they had not expected to use until they reached the Holy Land, and followed the Genoese through the gate and into the town.

The streets were indeed steep, so much so that they had to take small steps to keep from slipping. The tall houses were jumbled almost on top of each other on the hillside so that in many cases the rooftop of one faced the ground floor of another in the next street up. At last they reached the waterfront and surveyed the beautiful harbor, sheltered by a huge breakwater. Hans had never seen so many ships of all descriptions, even in Bremen or Brugge. And the people. One could hardly walk without elbowing someone aside. It seemed as though the whole world were doing business here. There were Jews with their conical hats, swarthy turbaned Arabs from Alexandria, tall black men in flowing white robes from Africa. And the Genoese merchants themselves were dressed in robes richer than those of many northern kings.

The Genoese led them along the curving quay until they came to a large, richly embellished house that stood opposite the longest wharf. Hans noticed that the largest ships of all were tied up here. The man bade them enter. The room was luxuriously furnished but appeared to be an office rather than living quarters, judging by the number of parchments strewn on the table and filling numerous pigeonholes lining the wall. There were several small caskets and a few large chests, and a scale for weighing money stood on the table. There were even chairs with leather backs and gleaming tiles on the floor.

The man who sat behind the table wore a robe of a dark magenta cloth that seemed to shimmer as he moved. Hans had never seen silk before. Around the man's neck hung a large ruby on a golden chain and his fingers were bejewelled with two or three rings on each hand. He had a long face and sharp nose, olive complexion, dark wavy hair and jet-black eyes that seemed to see right through a person. He laid aside his quill pen as they entered, rose and gave a half-bow.

"My lord," said their escort, "this is His Grace, the Duke of Saxony, whom we were expecting. And this, Your Grace, is Signore Andrea Doria, who is the owner of the ships."

"My pleasure, Your Grace, welcome to Genoa," said Signore Doria graciously. "Won't you please make yourself comfortable." He indicated chairs.

Heinrich and Hans sat down and the other Genoese departed. Signore Doria clapped his hands and a servant appeared with wine and the usual little cakes. This time Hans was not asked to taste it first. Heinrich apparently trusted the man, or thought it would be just too obvious.

The merchant wasted no time getting down to business. While they were haggling over the number of ships needed, the type of supplies required and, above all, the price, Hans turned his attention to a large, colorfully detailed map hanging on the wall. He had seen maps before in the Duke's library, but none so large or accurate. It showed the entire Mediterranean basin and little pennants were flying on all the ports where the Genoese did business. Now Hans could really see how far away Outremer was and why it was called 'Over-the-Sea'. There were many other lands in between also, and he wondered how long it would take them to get there.

Suddenly he became aware that the merchant and the Duke were arguing heatedly, not just haggling.

"I refuse to pay for a fourth ship that we do not need," Heinrich was saying.

"But you do need it, Your Grace," argued Doria.

"I have sufficient armed knights along to protect us," affirmed Heinrich.

"A mere handful, who will be divided between two ships and who, moreover, are totally ignorant of naval warfare. I doubt many of them could fight at all without a horse under them."

"You insult the honor of my knights," snapped the Duke.

"No insult was intended, Your Grace," replied the merchant. "I am only being realistic. The corsairs out there are vicious, like a swarm of hornets. Even other Christians like the Pisans and Venetians attack our ships with no provocation, and I hate to think what would happen if you fell into the hands of the Saracens, who make a living from piracy."

"I have heard something of that," admitted Heinrich doubtfully.

"Why, I would never send any of my merchant ships out without an armed escort to protect their precious cargoes. Think you less of your dear little wife, Your Grace?" asked the wily Doria.

That convinced Heinrich and the deal was quickly concluded. Signore Doria then took them out to see the ships—great galleys with seemingly bottomless holds. Hans could easily see the difference between the lumbering merchant ships and the swift, sleek naval galleys with vicious-looking rams protruding under their bows.

After Heinrich had thoroughly inspected the ships and appeared to be satisfied, Signore Doria asked if they would care to join him for supper.

"No, sir, I thank you, but I think not," declined Heinrich. "I do not think it wise to leave the ladies alone after dark."

"I understand," replied the merchant, "and I am sure Your Grace realizes now that it is better for your party to remain where it is until it is time to sail. Even we, those of us who can afford it, have our homes up in the valleys outside the town. It is no place for ladies."

Heinrich agreed and they took their leave.

Several days later on a bright summer morning, they carefully made their way down the steep streets of Genoa and boarded the ships. There were two for the people and one just for the horses and their fodder, plus the armed escort ship. The company was divided between the two large ships in almost equal number of knights, ladies and servants to each ship. The lines were cast and the powerful rowers sped the ships across the harbor, past the two lighthouses on the breakwater. Once at sea the great square sail was raised and they were on their way.

Hans' first impression of the Holy Land was glare—glare off the sparkling water, off the white buildings, off the yellow-gray sand. Glare, and then heat. The pleasant warmth of Italy was as nothing compared to this white heat. He commented on it to Father Theodorich, who was standing beside him at the rail as they entered the harbor of Joppa.

"Ah, this is nothing," said the priest. "At least here you still have the sea breezes. Those who have been here tell me that away from the coast it is so hot and dusty, one can scarcely breathe, but that at night it gets very cold."

"How can that be?" wondered Hans.

"I don't know. I just know what I have been told."

The voyage had been generally uneventful. Four weeks, the captain told them, was excellent time. Hans had found the Mediterranean calm compared to the North Sea and English Channel, but a few people got seasick regardless. He suspected the cramped quarters had acerbated the problem. Once in the eastern Mediterranean they had had some severe storms, the dread 'summer storms' of the region, but the Genoese were superb seamen and they had come through unscathed. Occasionally there had been flat calms, but then the husky rowers took over and they kept moving. Twice they had sighted corsairs and the ladies went into a panic, but the armed escort ship had chased them off and everyone breathed a prayer of thanksgiving at Signore Doria's foresight in providing it for them. Only Hans knew how Heinrich had argued against it, but he said nothing. He wondered what Heinrich was thinking on those two occasions. They had made three stops, mostly for fresh water and food. At Messina in Sicily, Heinrich refused to let any Saxon go ashore, for their own safety. He did not trust Roger. But at Candia in Crete and at Famagusta in Cyprus they had time for a little sightseeing and marvelled at the ancient ruins.

Now the galleys were easing into the harbor of Joppa. Hans could see no wharves or quays, only sandy beach. He wondered how they were going to accomplish the unloading of the horses and the heavy baggage. He soon found out. The oarsmen pulled at almost full speed straight toward the shore. At the last possible moment they made a sharp turn that almost threw him off his feet. Father Theodorich staggered and Hans grabbed for him with one hand while holding onto the rail with the other. The ships stopped dead in the shallow water, parallel to the shore, canting at a dangerous angle. But then Hans realized they were resting on the sandy bottom. Crowds of people had been watching their approach from the shore. Now they produced long gangplanks and ran them out to the lowest part of the gunwale of each ship. Everyone was able to walk ashore dryshod.

Joppa was a small, dusty, dirty, malodorous town, but it was the port nearest to Jerusalem. Everyone's saddlebags with their personal belonging had been packed since dawn. So they trooped ashore and stood around the beach in groups, waiting for Heinrich to tell them what to do next. Mathilde beckoned to Hans.

"Well, Hans, we are here at last. What think you now of Outremer?" she asked.

"It is very strange, Your Grace," replied Hans, looking around, "and hot."

"Of course, I knew what to expect, but still I find it very exciting to be here."

"Ah, yes, your mother was here, was she not?"

"Indeed she was, during the Second Crusade, when she was married to her first husband, Louis VII of France. All of my life I have heard her stories of Outremer."

"And now at last you see it for yourself," said Hans. "I can well understand your excitement."

"Thank God, these are more peaceful times than then and Jerusalem is in Christian hands," remarked the Duchess. "I shouldn't care to have been here then."

"But wouldn't it have been even more exciting to fight gloriously to rescue the Holy City from the Infidel?" suggested Hans.

Mathilde shook her head gravely. "Not all my mother's stories were pleasant. Most were horrible. They suffered from thirst and starvation and disease. Many were so weakened by the long overland journey they could hardly fight. Only our Lord gave them the strength."

"Yes, I have heard that," replied Hans. " 'Tis said the Emperor's uncle Conrad returned a broken man."

"That is true," she replied. "He wanted Heinrich to go with him — he was just eighteen then — but he thought it was wiser to stay home and consolidate his inheritance. Some called him a coward, but I am glad he did not go. I might never have known him," she added wistfully.

"You are right, Your Grace," agreed Hans. " 'Tis said that over nine-tenths of Conrad's army were killed by the Turks before they ever got here. His Grace is a very wise man."

Mathilde smiled.

Meanwhile the Duke was pacing the beach, obviously very annoyed at something. At length the captain disembarked and joined him.

"A fine welcome, this," complained Heinrich. "We were to have been met by some Templars, who are to escort us to Jerusalem."

"Ai," moaned the captain, shrugging his shoulders, "they are a very uppity lot, the Templars. Think they own the place. They will not come to you, Your Grace. You must go to them."

"What!" exclaimed Heinrich.

"You have no choice, Your Grace. You are dependent upon them. The Frankish king in Jerusalem is a debauched reprobate that cares little

138

for pilgrims except for the revenues they bring him."

"I had heard that," said Heinrich, "but I had hoped it was not true. It's that bad then?"

"Worse. A desecration of the holy places." The Italian shrugged again and tactfully changed the subject. "It will take at least the rest of the day to unload your horses and gear, Your Grace. And the horses will be very unsteady on their legs for a while. I suggest you take the ladies to the Hospice of St. John and bide there the night. Tomorrow you can seek out the Templars."

"But I understand they hate each other. Why do we not go directly to the Templars?"

"It is no fit place for the ladies, Your Grace," warned the captain. "An abomination of too much piety mixed with hard drinking, of celibacy and sodomy."

Even Heinrich was shocked at this. "But are they then fit to be our escort?"

"They have the right and privilege of policing all the roads in the Holy Land, so you have no choice, Your Grace. And they are the bravest, most accomplished knights in Christendom."

"Very well, I shall take your advice then," said Heinrich. "Show us the way to the Hospitallars."

The captain detached a Genoese sailor to be their guide and they entered the town. Hans had been embarrassed that Mathilde had overheard this conversation and stayed close by her side.

She laughed at his distress. "Think you not, Hans, that I know not whereof they speak? My father's language would put them both to shame. I did not have a sheltered childhood."

Hans nodded. "Look you at the strange houses, Your Grace, they have flat roofs."

"And no windows," she observed.

"They are built around courtyards for privacy," explained Father Theodorich. "They have no gardens such as we do. And the roofs are flat to catch water, which is very precious in this dry land. Often they sleep there on hot nights as well."

"Sleep there? Without shelter?" asked Mathilde.

"Ah, like David and Bathsheba," put in Hans.

Father Theodorich laughed. "Our Hans knows his Scripture well."

"Indeed," agreed Mathilde, "better than I. Think you to be a monk, Hans?"

"No, no, indeed not, Your Grace," protested Hans.

"But I have never seen you courting any of my lovely ladies," she said.

"I am just waiting," he hesitated, "just waiting till I find the right one."

She smiled her lovely smile. "Forgive me for prying."

They arrived at the Hospice of St. John and there were ample guest rooms for all of them. Pilgrimage had become a booming business in the Holy Land and the Hospitallars were taking full advantage of it.

The next morning Heinrich sent two of the senior nobles to deal with the Templars. He refused to lower himself, he said. Once again there was haggling over the price. The Templars had learned well from their Moslem brethren. Legally they were obligated to protect all pilgrims free of charge, but they were a law unto themselves. The order had not become the wealthiest in Christendom by giving away their services. They apparently had a sliding scale of fees according to the rank of the person to be escorted. The Duke and Duchess of Saxony did not get away cheap.

The following morning they were ready to leave. A party of six knights, heavily armored, with their distinctive white mantles with the red cross emblazoned on them, appeared at the hospice. They refused to enter. A huge, burly young man was their leader. "I am Sir Geoffrey, Your Grace. If your people are ready, we shall leave immediately." And they set off on the desolate, dusty road to Jerusalem.

Their first glimpse of the Holy City came close to sunset, when the westering sun lit up the walls like fire. They were duly awestruck and made the customary stop on the heights known as the Pilgrims' Ladder and knelt down to offer prayers of thanksgiving for a safe journey and the privilege of gazing on the sacred place. Father Theodorich wanted to offer a Mass right there, but the Templars urged them on.

"Sorry, Father, there is no time," said Sir Geoffrey. "The gates will be closing in a half an hour and we have yet to cross yon valley. We must make haste."

One of their number rode ahead to advise the royal court of the arrival of their prestigious guest, but Sir Geoffrey warned Heinrich, "Do not expect too much of them, Your Grace. I expect nothing will have been prepared for you. You may bide with us this night. That will give them time to prepare a proper welcome for you. They are much too preoccupied with the pursuit of pleasure and gold to give much thought to pilgrims, however noble."

By this time Heinrich was learning to put up with these annoyances.

140

He shrugged and followed the Templars down into the valley and through the Joppa gate. Some of the party wanted to go immediately to the Holy Sepulchre, but Sir Geoffrey forbade them. "It will soon be dark and the streets are not at all safe at night. Even during the day hold tight to your purses and jewels, for there are cutthroats and pickpockets who deliberately prey on pilgrims, even sometimes when they are at Mass," he warned the entire company.

Early the next morning they all trooped to the Church of the Holy Sepulchre. Father Theodorich had asked and received permission to celebrate Mass for them. It was obviously the high point of his life. Everyone was deeply moved to be in this holiest place in that Holy City.

When they returned to their lodgings, a message was waiting for Heinrich from Amalric, King of the Latin Kingdom of Jerusalem. He would be happy to receive the ducal couple that afternoon. One attendant each was specified. No one else was invited. Some of the nobles were offended at this obvious slight. Heinrich tried to pacify them.

"Be thankful you don't have to go. You are in a state of grace now but I fear would not remain so long in this debauched court, from what I hear. I have no liking for it myself, but I am obligated to go. I won't stay long, I assure you."

Mathilde chose an older woman, Lady Catherine, for her attendant, and Hans accompanied Heinrich. The Latin Kingdom of Jerusalem had been set up during the First Crusade, some seventy years earlier, by Frankish nobles, one of whom, Godfrey of Bouillon, became the first 'Defender of the Holy Sepulchre'. His successors called themselves kings. Confronted with the riches and luxuries of the east, religious fervor had quickly been forgotten. The old feudal pastime of stealing one another's land and riches soon reasserted itself.

When they entered the luxurious audience chamber, the first thing that struck them was a sickeningly sweet, cloying smell, a combination of heavy oriental perfume and something else that resembled incense but was definitely not incense. They strode over deep-piled carpets to the elaborate throne. Heinrich made a perfunctory bow and Mathilde curtseyed, but Hans and Lady Catherine had to fall to their knees in a deep obeisance. Lady Catherine muttered to herself as Hans helped her up and then had to help her sit after they were led to low piles of cushions. The man on the throne, dressed in a long, flowing, colorful silken robe, looked more like an Oriental potentate than a Frankish knight. He was probably about forty but looked much older because of his obe-

141

sity and ravages of dissipation and pox on his face.

"Welcome to the Holiest City in the world, cousins," said King Amalric. At Heinrich's look of surprise at being so addressed, the King explained, "Ah, I long so for the sight of European faces that I call all visiting royalty my cousins."

Heinrich immediately detested the man but answered graciously, "We are most happy to be here, Your Majesty."

"And how does your dear mother fare, my lady?" he asked Mathilde.

"Very well, my lord," she replied. "She has often spoken of the kindness of your mother, Queen Melisende, and of your brother Baldwin, but I don't believe she met you."

"I was but a lad, but I remember her well. A very great lady, but very unhappy, I'm afraid. That overly pious husband of hers was a fool."

Mathilde said nothing. The conversation continued in this trivial vein for some time. Hans was more interested in his surroundings. Several beautiful women, obviously Saracens, dressed in almost nothing, lolled about on the plump cushions. There was no sign of a queen. Bowls of strange-looking fruit stood on low tables. Seeing his curiosity, one of the girls carried one of the bowls over to him, knelt before him and offered it to him. All thoughts of fruit left his brain as he stared at her lush breasts clearly visible through the flimsy garment. As she bent over he could see almost to her navel. He turned red to the roots of his blond hair. "Wh-what are these fruits?" he stammered. "They look strange to me."

"Those are oranges," snapped Lady Catherine, plainly disgusted. "We tried some in Italy."

"And those?" he asked.

"Those are dates, figs and pomegranates, my lord," replied the girl with a strange accent.

He selected a ripe fig, although he had lost all desire for fruit, as he felt other desire warm his loins. Since he could obviously do nothing about it here, he wished the girl would go away. She rose languidly and walked enticingly back to her cushions, while Hans' eyes followed her hungrily.

"Disgusting," said Lady Catherine, her tightly bound wimple quivering with indignation. Hans' ardor cooled rapidly.

Heinrich and Mathilde soon took their leave. When they were outside the palace, Heinrich wiped his brow and said, "God's teeth, I'm glad to be out of there."

Mathilde laughed. "The sensuous east too much for you, my love?"

"A den of iniquity is what," he replied, "and phony. I'd sooner trust a snake than trust that man. He tells me that apartments have been prepared for us at the Tower of David. Let us get the company out of the clutches of the Templars and moved into the royal hostel."

"I believe my mother stayed there, too," said Mathilde.

"Then we can be sure they are decent accommodations."

"Ah, but that was almost thirty years ago," she reminded him.

"You are right. Well, we shall soon see."

The apartments were still luxurious and surprisingly well kept. The Saxons quickly settled in, glad to be away from the astringent atmosphere of the Templars' headquarters. Every morning they attended Mass at the Holy Sepulchre, 'The Center of the World', or at some other famous church. They trod barefoot along the Via Dolorosa, Heinrich himself carrying the heavy cross, although he seemed glad to relinquish it to Hans, who played Simon of Cyrene at the fifth station. This was for Hans perhaps the most moving experience since they arrived in Jerusalem. He really felt the weight of his sins, but also that this pilgrimage would help expiate them. If only it hadn't been somewhat spoiled at the sixth station, where Veronica wiped Jesus' face, by the women selling cloths painted with His face. And they were obviously Jews or Moslems, not even Christians. Must they commercialize everything? Hans thought.

He was to find out that they did. The pilgrims visited all the famous shrines and holy places, even took day trips out to Bethlehem and Gethsemane. And everywhere it was the same. Men and women crowded around the pilgrims trying to sell them relics, which Hans suspected were fake, and souvenirs. They were offered everything from packets of white powder in Bethlehem, supposedly milk from the Virgin's own breasts, guaranteed to ensure fertility, to splinters of the True Cross at Golgotha. Monks and beggars competed for their alms.

Hans was getting disgusted. "Oh, dear Lord," he prayed fervently every day, "don't let me be disturbed by these vultures. Help me to keep a pure soul, that I may see only the holiness in the places Thou hast trod and the stones Thou mayest have touched. I truly thank Thee that Thou hast given me the opportunity to come to Thy Holy City with our Heinrich. Help me to make a worthy pilgrimage." And Hans sincerely meant every word of it, but the distractions were many.

He was not the only one who was dismayed by the blatant commercialization of the holy places. One day Mathilde announced, "I have had enough of praying and sightseeing. If these rapacious people are so anxious to sell us things, let us go to the bazaars and spend our money on something worthwhile. I have a fancy for some of that beautiful silken cloth and some golden jewelry."

Her ladies were immediately excited at the prospect. Heinrich gave his permission on the condition that Hans and another squire Dieter, well armed, would accompany them, that they would all stay together and be back to the hostel at least one hour before sunset. They all solemnly promised and set off joyfully on what, to them, was a far more interesting adventure than visiting holy shrines.

They wended their way through the narrow, crowded streets, up the steep steps and down again. All the stalls were open to the street, but huge awnings stretched across from one side to the other to shade the shoppers from the blazing sun. Aside from Mathilde, there were four of her ladies and two maids, seven in all, carefully shepherded by Hans and Dieter. In the press of humanity it was difficult to keep them all together. One would see a treasured piece of cloth, another a jewelled ring, another an intricately carved ivory box, and despite their promise, would go skittering off after the object of their desires. The stench was abominable. Offal, garbage and manure littered the alleys and the odor of sweat-soaked, unwashed bodies was overpowering. The noise, too, was deafening—the vendors shouting the virtue of their wares, the customers haggling with them, the competition screaming insults. Hans wondered if Lady Catherine were offended by it all, but she, like the others, was apparently too engrossed in her shopping to notice. There were goods from all over the east, valuable items intermingled indiscriminately with junk. And everywhere even more fraudulent souvenirs than at the shrines.

At one point Hans felt he could relax his vigilance for just a moment. The ladies, for once all herded together, were dickering with a silk merchant over various pieces of the exquisite stuff. He and Dieter lolled in the narrow street. His attention was drawn to some huge banners for sale at the stall opposite.

"Fine banners, my lord," said the wily Jew, rubbing his hands together. "Take home a remembrance of the valiant Crusaders who liberated our Holy City from the heavy hand of the Saracen."

Hans saw several banners with the eagles of the Empire and the lilies of France. Others with a red field had a yellow star and crescent. "How come you buy these?" he asked, curious.

"They were given to my father by the Crusader kings in gratitude for their victory."

"Your father?" questioned Hans.

"Ah, yes," sighed the merchant. "He was one of the noble Jews who welcomed the Crusaders to our beloved Jerusalem. But alas," he sighed again, "the family has fallen on hard times and we are forced to sell these precious mementos."

"But they look brand-new," said Hans. "I should think they would be tattered and ragged."

"Ah, but these were spares the kings had in their coffers. Never used. And my father kept them carefully packed away these forty years."

Hans knew then that the man was lying but led him on. "And these?" he asked, fingering a red and yellow one.

"Those are Turkish, captured from them by the valiant Crusaders."

"And in equally pristine condition?" said Hans sarcastically. "Sir, I make bold to say that you are a faker and a liar. I suggest you check on your history as well. The last Crusade was less than thirty years ago."

The Jew was about to reply, when Lady Catherine let out a scream. "My purse! My purse!"

The cry went up. "Thief! Thief!"

Hans turned and saw the thief zigzagging through the crowd and Dieter after him. Lady Catherine took off after them both.

"Lady Catherine, wait!" Hans called. "Lady Catherine, come back. You will get lost in the crowd." But she did not hear and soon all three were lost to sight. Hans debated for a moment whether to follow, but the other ladies were in various states of consternation and indignation. Mathilde was trying to comfort them. He decided it was best to stay with them and see that no more harm befell them. Dieter would take care of the thief.

Hans was about to suggest that they make their way slowly in the direction the others had gone in the hope of finding Lady Catherine, when a wall of fire rose in front of them. Evidently the thief in his haste had knocked over an oil lamp. In falling the oil had soaked into the gossamer cloth, creating an instant inferno.

Now the cries were, "Fire! Fire! Water! Water!"

"Quickly," Hans urged the ladies, "we must get out of here—out of the bazaar entirely. This way."

"But Lady Catherine," objected Mathilde. "We can't leave her."

"Dieter will take care of her. They are beyond the flames. We couldn't get through there, Your Grace. Hurry now," he urged.

The other ladies and their poor maids, heavily burdened with packages, were already fleeing toward the open end of the street. While

Mathilde hesitated, a flaming piece of awning fell behind her, and to his horror Hans saw tongues of flame licking up the back of her gown. Without thinking, Hans grabbed one of the fake Turkish banners and wrapped it around her, smothering the flames and nearly smothering her as well. He picked her up and carried her away from the fire. He had difficulty making his way along the narrow street with his burden as the crowd had panicked, leaving only the poor merchants and their slaves to fight the fire. Fortunately, they were all going in the same direction and he was swept along with them.

At last they reached the end of the bazaar where the narrow alley emptied into a wider street. He saw the other ladies huddled together in a corner. He thanked God they had had the sense to wait for him. They all chattered at once when they saw him with his burden. "The Duchess." "Your Grace, are you all right?" "Hans, is she hurt?"

From beneath the Turkish banner came a muffled voice, "Hans, put me down."

He set Mathilde down and carefully unwrapped the banner from around her. He was not sure if she had been injured or not. He prayed not.

"Ah, fresh air," she said as she breathed deeply. "Hans, you nearly suffocated me."

"I am sorry, Your Grace," he apologized. "Your gown was afire. I had to act quickly. Are you all right, Your Grace? You're not harmed?" She was dirty and disheveled but seemed to be unhurt. Thanks to several petticoats and a heavy woolen shift, the flames had not reached her delicate skin, but her gown was ruined. The ladies tittered as he removed the last of the banner.

"I am fine," she said, "but my gown seems uninhabitable. I am afraid you shall have to wrap me up again, but not over my head this time. What is that thing?"

"A Turkish banner captured by the Crusaders," he smiled, "or so the man claimed."

"Indeed?" she laughed. "Then to the victor go the spoils. A fitting garment for a pilgrim."

He draped the banner unwittingly upside down, with the star over her shoulders and the crescent outlining her derriere. She clutched the ends in front of her, unaware of the suggestive blazon on her back. Hans smiled but said nothing. He started to lead them back to the hostel.

Mathilde stopped him. "Hans, we cannot leave Lady Catherine. I am worried about her."

"Dieter will have found her, I'm sure," he reassured her with a confidence he did not himself feel. "We cannot go back in there. There are other ways out. Let's get out of this crowd before anything else happens. When I have seen you ladies safely home, I'll go back and look for them" He gently urged them along until they were away from the worst of the throngs.

When they could walk more freely, Mathilde laid her hand on his arm. "I am afraid I owe you an apology."

"Whatever for, Your Grace?"

"I owe you my life. If I had not been so stubborn back there, you wouldn't have had so much trouble—and I would still have a gown."

Hans smiled. "But now you have a 'real' Turkish banner for a souvenir."

She laughed, but there were tears in her eyes. "Captured by my brave squire," she said.

When they reached the apartments, Mathilde took him by the hand and led him directly to the Duke.

"What in the world are you wearing?" exclaimed Heinrich.

"My lord, don't jest. Hans has just saved my life." Nervous reaction set in and she started to cry.

"How so? What has happened?" asked Heinrich anxiously, immediately ready to do battle.

"'Twas nothing, Your Grace," replied Hans. "Anyone else would have done the same." And he told the Duke the story of what had happened. By the time he finished, Mathilde had regained her composure.

"I insist, my lord, that you reward him handsomely," she said.

"And indeed I shall," replied Heinrich. "For now, Hans, my heartfelt thanks. I need cool, sensible heads around me." He turned to Mathilde. "Now go and wash and rest, my dear, and get rid of that disreputable thing." Hans was a little disappointed. He had thought to keep the flag as a souvenir, but he could not gainsay his Duke's orders. "Now, Hans," continued Heinrich, "take two of my knights with you and see if you can find Lady Catherine. I am quite concerned about her. She is not so young anymore."

"Yes. I am very worried, too, Your Grace."

But before they could leave, they saw Dieter coming up the street with Lady Catherine on his arm. Her first concern was for the others. "Oh, Hans, are Her Grace and her ladies safe? I was so worried when we couldn't get back to you."

147

"They are all safely back and unharmed," Hans reassured her, "but how fare you, my lady?"

"I am quite well, thank you, a bit tired is all. But brave Dieter recovered my purse, and you should have seen what he did to that nasty thief. I had to stop him or he would have surely killed him. And he was only a young boy. I believe he has learned his lesson."

The next day Hans was summoned to the ducal apartment. The main room looked like an audience chamber. All the senior nobles of Saxony were there. Heinrich was in his full regalia, seated on a chair, draped to look like a throne, at the far end of the room. Mathilde, also wearing her crown, sat beside him. She did not smile but looked very serious. Hans wondered what he had done wrong. The nobles parted to let him pass. He suddenly was very nervous. What is going on here, he wondered.

"Present yourself to His Grace, the Duke of Saxony," said the herald formally.

Hans walked between the nobles, almost stumbling on the thick carpet, until he came face to face with Heinrich. He bowed formally.

"Hans von Sehnden, kneel before your lord and master," said Sir Wigbert.

Oh, Lord, what have I done, thought Hans as he knelt before the Duke with some trepidation.

The Duke stood up. "It is our privilege and prerogative on certain occasions to forego and dispense with the customary preparations and ritual of creating a knight." A knight? thought Hans, not sure he was hearing correctly. He listened carefully as the Duke continued. "This often happens on the field of battle as a reward for exceptional bravery or for protecting the person of the king or leader. There are betimes other occasions when a man has performed a deed above and beyond the call of duty and is deserving of a just reward. Therefore, as a token of my extreme personal gratitude in saving the life of my beloved wife, Her Grace the Duchess Mathilde, with this sword I knight thee Hans von Sehnden, in the name of the Father, the Son, and the Holy Ghost." He took his sword and dealt Hans such a blow on his shoulder with the flat of it that Hans almost reeled.

"Do you pledge your loyalty to me and to the Duke of Saxony?"

"I do so pledge, Your Grace," whispered the astounded Hans.

"Then repeat the oath of fealty for your person and your fief."

My fief—but I have no fief, thought Hans. But Sir Wigbert was already intoning the words of the feudal oath, and Hans quickly repeated them after him.

Then Heinrich said, "Arise, Sir Hans." Hans rose, bewildered and unsteady, and the Duke stepped forward and embraced him and kissed him on the cheek. "Receive your sword, Sir Hans." One of the knights buckled a brand-new sword around his waist. It had a beautiful black and silver cloisonné hilt. "Receive your spurs, Sir Hans." And Sir Wigbert himself knelt and fastened the golden spurs to his feet. Hans wondered where they had gotten all these things on such short notice. "Receive your coat-of-arms, Sir Hans." This time Mathilde herself came forward carrying something red. It was the Turkish banner made over into a handsome surcoat. She placed it over his head. He noticed the star was over the upside-down crescent, just as he had wrapped her in it, only the crescent was now silver.

"All ye company," announced Heinrich, "note well the new emblem of the noble house of von Sehnden." They all acknowledged it. "Welcome, Sir Hans, to the company of the noble knights of Saxony." Hans turned around and the knights cheered. Then one by one they came and embraced him and gave him the kiss of peace, many offering congratulations as well.

"Now leave us for a few minutes," said Heinrich. "I would speak privately to my new knight. We shall join you at Mass in about ten minutes. Afterward there will be a feast to celebrate this joyous occasion. I regret that we cannot have a tournament as well, but we shall make up for that once we are home. In fact, I think we shall soon quit ourselves of this Holy City, which I find is no longer very holy."

The knights smiled and left the room.

"Well, Sir Hans," boomed Heinrich heartily, "what think you of your reward?"

"Your Grace, I am overwhelmed," replied Hans. "I can never thank you enough."

"I had in mind to do it as soon as we returned home, but it was my lady's idea to do it now."

"Then I thank you, too, with all my heart, Your Grace," Hans said to Mathilde. He shook his head as if he still wasn't sure all this had happened to him. "I have many questions."

"Ask what you will. We have ten minutes."

"How did you get all these things so quickly?" He indicated the sword and spurs.

"Everything can be found ready-made in the bazaars of the east."

"And the surcoat?"

149

"That, too, was my lady's idea. You recognize it surely. She had her seamstress up half the night stitching it. We knew you had no family arms, but we had to make a few changes. It is customary only for Crusaders who have killed Turks in battle to take the crescent and star into their own arms. But I know of no rule that says you can't have it upside-down just as you draped it over Mathilde. There was a little fire damage where the crescent was, and the seamstress only had a piece of cloth-of-silver instead of gold to cover it. Do you like your new emblem?"

"Very much, Your Grace," replied Hans. "I had thought to ask for the flag as a souvenir, but this is far better than I could have dreamed. Now I have a coat-of-arms and no armor."

"Here, take this. It is my sponsor's gift for you." Heinrich handed Hans a heavy purse. "There is more than enough there to outfit yourself in a good suit of armor and to buy a good sturdy mount and some to spare to start you off in life. But I would advise your waiting until we get home or at least until we reach Constantinople. There is no time here to be fitted properly, although there are some excellent armorers after the Damascene style, but I fear they are also highway robbers. As for the horse, I would have you buy none but our good Saxon stock."

"Again I thank you, Your Grace, you are too kind," said Hans. "I have but one more question. You had me pledge fealty for a fief which I do not have."

"Aha, but you will shortly," said Heinrich, smiling. "Before we left Saxony, we learned that your erstwhile 'father' had died without an heir. The demesne reverted to us. I had planned to enfeoff you with it upon your knighting. We shall draw up the legal papers as soon as we arrive home, but I had you take the oath for it before all the nobles so that no one could dispute your claim, in case anything should happen to me before we get there."

"Oh, Your Grace!" exclaimed Hans, humbled by this good fortune. "Then you knew the story."

Heinrich winked.

"I had it from Sir Brandt before he left court, but I choose to forget where I heard it. You have earned it on your own merit. You have been an exemplary squire. Be now an honorable knight." Heinrich rose and stretched. "So now, let us go and give thanks to the Lord."

"Amen to that," agreed Hans.

Two days later they were heading north along the dusty roads of Outremer. Heinrich had had enough of Jerusalem, but he decided that before leaving the Holy Land he wished to pay his respects to some of the other places associated with Our Lord, such as Nazareth. Once again several Templars accompanied them. They were to take ship at Acre for the great metropolis of Constantinople.

The renowned capital of the Greek Byzantine Empire was the largest and wealthiest city in the world. Although they had recently lost large sections of Asia Minor to the Turks, Constantinople was still the formidable bastion that protected all of Christendom from being overrun by the Muslims from the east. It was also the primate city of the Greek rite of the Church, which had separated itself from Rome over one hundred years before, after years of bitter theological disputes.

They had been lucky to find passage on Byzantine ships at a much more reasonable rate than the Genoese would have charged. It was a pleasant voyage among the myriad Greek isles and through the Sea of Marmora. No one in the party had ever been there before, although everyone knew about it. Thus they all experienced the same emotions of awe and delight as the golden domes and spires of the city hove into sight. No one had ever seen so many different ships at one time as the forest of masts at anchor or docked in the Golden Horn, one of the finest, most sheltered harbors in the world. No one had seen so many or so large or such beautiful buildings. And the double-curtained city walls ran for miles.

The moment the ships docked, a messenger was sent to the Emperor, known as the Basileus, Manuel Comnenus, to advise him of the arrival of his illustrious guests. Within an hour a large welcoming party arrived at the dock to escort them to the palace. Each man wore an exquisite flowing robe of richest silk, the horses were elaborately caparisoned, colorful pennants flew everywhere. Two slaves unrolled a red carpet over the gangplank for Heinrich and Mathilde to walk on and immediately rolled it up again before the rest of the party disembarked. Since their horses were not yet unloaded, a magnificent, high-spirited stallion was provided for Heinrich and luxurious curtained litters for Mathilde and all her ladies.

When Mathilde was about to object, Heinrich silenced her. "You must follow the customs of the country, my dear. Here they consider it uncouth for a lady to ride a horse." So Mathilde succumbed and entered the litter, which was immediately hoisted onto the shoulders of four husky eunuchs. The others followed on foot.

The first thing that struck them was the cleanliness of the streets. No unpleasant odors assailed the nostrils, no garbage or manure offended the eye, no gutters ran down the middle of the street. At every square were

151

charming fountains gushing with pure, clear water. The next thing was the beauty of the buildings. Even ordinary houses were painted with flowers and butterflies. The more elaborate were faced with marble and mosaics, and the public buildings were truly grandiose with colonnades and statues.

When they reached the Blachernae Palace, they were so overwhelmed by the beauty of the exterior, they agreed nothing could be more magnificent. But they were wrong. The interior surpassed their wildest imaginings. Gold and elaborate mosaics covered the walls; marble of more colors than they knew existed paved the floors. They passed through courtyard after courtyard of fragrant formal gardens and tinkling fountains, each colonnaded in a different style. Massive oaken and elaborately carved bronze doors separated one section from another. Each was guarded by two giant eunuchs in colorful uniforms. It seemed they walked for miles before reaching the throne room.

At last they reached a pair of golden doors and here they were halted. The doors were flung open, trumpets blared, and the herald announced, "Their Royal Majesties, the King and Queen of Saxony." Even Heinrich seemed surprised at this, but with great aplomb he entered the room and walked sedately down the long carpet toward the throne, Mathilde at his side but one step behind, as she had been instructed by their escort. The others had to wait outside, but Hans caught a glimpse of the room. It was fully as large as the entire nave of the cathedral back home in Braunschweig.

After Heinrich had solemnly bowed and Mathilde curtseyed, the Basileus Manuel stepped forward, placed his hands on Heinrich's shoulders and gave him the kiss of peace. The Empress did likewise with Mathilde.

"Peace be with thee," said Manuel.

"And with thy spirit, my lord," replied Heinrich.

"Welcome to the city of Constantine."

"Thank you, my lord. I rejoice to be once again in so civilized a place after the rigors of Outremer."

Manuel smiled. "Now let us meet your company." The knights were announced one by one in order of seniority. Although Hans was the very last, his breast swelled with pride when the herald called out, "Sir Hans von Sehnden." Then came the ladies. And finally the squires and servants were allowed to enter and stand along the back wall.

While Manuel and Heinrich exchanged civilities, Hans glanced around the room. The men were grouped on one side, the women on the other. At least twenty of the Emperor's knights were in attendance. The contrast between them and the Saxons was startling. Their exquisite, colorful silken robes embroidered with gold and silver made them look like so many peacocks. It made the Saxons look like farmers. The women, too, in gowns ranging from gossamer to damask resembled beautiful butterflies. Hans noticed none wore the confining coifs and wimples, but had their hair arranged in elaborate coiffures, laced with jewels and ribbons. The Saxon ladies looked positively dowdy by comparison. He wondered what Mathilde was thinking.

There was nothing effeminate about the Greek knights, however, for all their dandified clothes. They were lithe and well built, although on the average, shorter than the Saxons. Most were typically swarthy-skinned, darkened still further by the sun, with curly black hair, most of them bearded. But there were two or three tall blond Nordic types, obviously not Greeks. Hans wondered about these. He turned his attention to the ladies opposite and noticed the same sort of mixture. Most of them were small-built, with smooth olive complexions and thick, dark hair. Their lips were reddened with something and their flashing black eyes were enhanced with kohl. But there were four ladies who stood out because they were taller and blond and blue-eyed. Except for the elaborate clothes and cosmetics, they looked just like anyone of his countrywomen. Two of them were quite young and looked as though they might be sisters, the eldest, he guessed, about sixteen. She was very beautiful in a silver-embroidered azure gown. Her blond hair was wound about with silver strands, and her deep blue eyes, too, were outlined with kohl, which surprisingly made them look bigger and more innocent, instead of seductive like the Greek ladies'. He was intrigued by her and wondered who she was.

At last the amenities were concluded and the visitors were ushered to their quarters. The entire company, even the servants, was easily accommodated under the palace roof with room to spare. The Duke and Duchess had the extensive apartment reserved for visiting royalty. Cubbyholes immediately adjoining were provided for all their personal servants, besides which a bevy of slaves was assigned to them to take care of the menial tasks, such as laundry, errands, or just to guide them around the intricate maze of the palace. The knights and ladies were given private or semiprivate rooms according to their rank. Hans and another young knight shared a commodious room with their squires. It was cool and immaculate, with comfortable beds covered with snow white linen. A far cry from sleeping in the Great Hall at Dankwarderode, thought Hans. Two slaves were assigned to them and these slept on cots outside the door so as to be at their beck and call day and night.

As they were leaving the audience chamber, Hans had tried to get near Mathilde. He wanted to enlist her aid, if possible, in finding out who the blond girl was. But everything was so formal here, he had no chance. There was to be a great banquet in a few hours. Perhaps then he might be able to make her acquaintance. So he washed and shaved carefully, combed his hair and put on his best clothes, which now looked very old-fashioned to him. He vowed the first opportunity he had to seek out a tailor and use part of Heinrich's gift to buy a new robe in the Byzantine style.

The banquet was another new and sometimes bewildering experience for the Saxons. There were innumerable courses, each consisting of an infinite variety of dishes, many of which were strange to them. Always hearty eaters, even they had trouble consuming just a small part of it. A different wine was served with every course and it seemed as though the crystal goblets were always full, so efficient were the slaves hovering over them like mother hens. They were served on individual solid gold plates, instead of sharing a wooden trencher or a pewter bowl with their partners, as at home. Even those below the salt had silver plates. And the strangest thing of all was a two-pronged knife, an implement they were expected to eat with, instead of spearing a piece of meat with their knives and eating with their fingers. Many of the men nearly stabbed their tongues with this thing. The ladies, eating more daintily, seemed to have less trouble. The usual finger bowls were passed between courses, but they were each handed individual towels instead of wiping their hands on the edge of the tablecloth. It was all very new and strange. Hans was beginning to realize that the hundreds and hundreds of more years of civilization that lay behind all this had created a wider gap between east and west than any of them had been led to believe.

The Duke and Duchess sat at the head table on a raised dais with the Basileus and the Empress, together with their chief advisers. Each of the Saxons was partnered with one of the Greeks, presumably that the two nations might get to know one another better. But in Hans' case it was not working out too well. His partner was an attractive, but painfully shy, young lady who spoke no German. As he had no Greek, they had to use Latin, the common language of Europe. His was far from fluent, but hers was extremely limited. So their conversation died entirely after a few stilted attempts. She did spare him the embarrassment of floundering with the new eating implement, by deftly demonstrating its use, and for that he was grateful. He noticed that Sir Wigbert, at the head table with Heinrich, had one of the older blond ladies for a partner. They seemed to be deep in conversation. She must be able to speak German, Hans thought, or could Wigbert's Latin be better than he suspected? He wondered where the young blond girl who had so attracted him might be. He finally spotted her far down the table, below the salt, coupled with one of the squires. A twinge of jealousy went through him and he immediately chided himself, Why, I don't even know her.

But it made him more determined than ever to find out who she was.

The nearest familiar face was that of Lady Catherine, seated diagonally opposite him. She, too, seemed to be having problems conversing, she who was normally so voluble, but to give her credit, she was making valiant attempts. Hans finally succeeded in catching her eye. If anyone knew all the gossip, she would.

"Lady Catherine," he whispered in German, "who are these blond people mixed with the Greeks? They have aroused my curiosity. Could they be Germans?"

"I believe they might be," she replied sotto voce. "Of the men, I am not sure. I have heard that some of them are descendants of Vikings who came down through the Rus-land to trade and stayed to become members of the Emperor's elite guard. The women are very likely to be German. You know the Emperor's first wife was German."

"I did not know that," replied Hans, surprised.

"Yes, just plain old Bertha of Sulzbach," imparted Lady Catherine. "She was sister-in-law to Emperor Conrad, our Friedrich's uncle. When she became Empress here she took on airs and changed her name to Irene. She wanted to become thoroughly Greek, she said, but we noticed that she kept herself surrounded by a large number of German ladies, so as not to get too homesick, I should imagine. These could be some that stayed after her death."

"When did she die?" asked Hans.

"Oh, some years ago," replied Lady Catherine. "Back in '58, I believe."

"Then they would be too young," said Hans, without thinking.

"No, they wouldn't," and then Lady Catherine's sharp nose scented a bit of intrigue. "Which one were you referring to?"

Hans knew he was trapped, but then he thought, why not, it's just the sort of little plot she would love to get involved in. "That pretty one, down there," he indicated.

Lady Catherine craned her neck to see and brightened immediately. "Aha, so our Hans has finally seen someone who interests him."

Hans turned crimson. "No, no, my lady," he protested. "I was just curious."

Lady Catherine was not fooled. "She *is* pretty," she agreed. "I shall make inquiries."

"Oh, my lady," objected Hans, "please don't make it too obvious."

"Have no fear, Sir Hans, I shall be very discreet." And she beamed at him.

The next day, true to her word, Lady Catherine sought him out. They were strolling in one of the many courtyards near their quarters, not yet familiar enough with the vast palace to go too far afield.

"Come, let us sit over here in the shade," she invited. "This sun is really unhealthy for the complexion."

He joined her on a marble bench surrounded by flowers.

"I have some information that might interest you," she went on. Hans waited expectantly. "She is indeed German, from Sulzbach, the same county the late Empress came from. Her name is Margarete. I don't know her father's name. The younger one is her sister Sophie. Their mother is Lady Anna, the one who was dining with Sir Wigbert. She was indeed one of the Empress Irene's ladies; the other one is her sister. The husband was evidently one of Conrad's knights who was much taken with the Lady Anna when they passed through here on the Crusade. When Conrad was so disastrously defeated by the Turks, he was gravely wounded but somehow made his way back here, rather than go on to Jerusalem. Whether he deserted or was given permission is of no importance. The Lady Anna nursed him back to health, they were married, and he offered his services to Manuel. Which came first, I'm not sure. Isn't that a romantic story?"

"It certainly is," agreed Hans. "But what of the girls? And which gentleman is their father?"

"Unfortunately, he was killed in one of Manuel's many wars with the Turks."

"How sad, after all that," sighed Hans. "Why, then, don't they go back to Germany?"

"I guess because they have nothing really to go back to," surmised Lady Catherine. "Lady Anna's sister, remember, is here. She is married to a Greek. The new Empress kindly kept them in her service and the girls are being groomed as ladies-in-waiting. They have known no other home."

Hans thought about all this. "Lady Catherine," he said, "you have learned more than I could have in a week. I am most grateful for the information. It is very interesting."

"And now you wonder how you can meet her," she said.

"Yes, I should like to very much, but—"

"Leave it to me," said Lady Catherine, relishing her little plot. "I shall speak to Her Grace. We shall think of something. The older women remember her mother, Queen Eleanor, very well. That could be useful."

"But, my lady, you go too fast for me. I don't wish to appear overly bold."

"Fear not. I said 'trust me'. Something very subtle—a chance meeting—will be arranged. The rest will be up to you. But remember," she warned, "we shall be here no more than about two weeks. Don't be overly timid either." She patted Hans' hand and strolled away, leaving him contemplating this new turn of events with both fear and anticipation.

Later that afternoon, after the long siesta that followed the noon meal, when the heat of the day had diminished somewhat, Hans was summoned to the Duchess' apartment.

"Sir Hans, my ladies and I would go shopping this afternoon," announced Mathilde. "Would you care to escort us?"

Hans knew the request was really an order, but he hesitated. One shopping trip with the ladies had been enough for him. "Well, Your Grace, I don't know . . ."

Mathilde interrupted, "Oh, I know now that you are a knight, you have better things to do than squire ladies about in trivial pursuits."

"It's not that, Your Grace," protested Hans. "You know that were I the first knight of the realm, I should always be your humble squire. But this city is so huge and I have not yet set foot outside the palace, I fear I would get us hopelessly lost."

"Have no fear of that. Her Majesty, the Empress, is providing us with several slaves who know their way about and will carry our purchases. Even some of her own ladies are coming along to show us the best shops and help us to haggle with the merchants. I hear they are even more unscrupulous here than in Jerusalem, and we don't speak the language. No, your responsibility will be my personal safety. You can't deny you are well qualified for that," she said with a smile.

"In that case, I am honored, Your Grace," replied Hans. "Shall I bring another?"

"Yes—better two, I think. I don't really trust all these gelded slaves either."

Hans went to fetch Dieter and another squire and was back in a quarter-hour. He had placed some silver coins from the Duke's gift in his purse, thinking he might as well take advantage of the opportunity and buy himself some clothes as well. The ladies were all a-twitter with excitement when the young men arrived.

Lady Catherine gave Hans a twinkling smile but said nothing to him. However, she patted Dieter's arm. "Here is my stalwart. Now I know we shall be safe."

A slave came to the door and beckoned to Mathilde indicating that they should follow him. In one of the courtyards they met the other ladies surrounded by a whole troop of slaves. A few were giants with wicked-looking curved swords tucked into their belts. I should not like to tangle with them, thought Hans. At first he could not see the women beyond them, and then suddenly it all became clear. Their shopping companions were the two German ladies and Margarete. Of course, he thought, I should have realized. They are the only ones who can speak both German and Greek. Oh, bless you, Lady Catherine.

When they reached one of the huge exterior courtyards, they found several large heavily curtained litters awaiting them with more slaves to carry them.

"Oh, no," objected Mathilde. "I should prefer to walk. We have as yet seen nothing of your fabulous city."

Lady Anna was shocked. "A lady *never* walks abroad in the streets of the city. It is unseemly and beneath her dignity."

"Then I shall pretend I am a peasant," argued Mathilde.

Lady Anna shook her head in disbelief. "Your Grace, it is not safe."

"We seem to have more than sufficient escort. My mother told me she rode her own horse about when she visited the Empress Irene. I would do the same."

"Your Grace, your mother was—uh—unique. Besides, she was staying at the Crusaders' camp outside the walls. It was a different situation entirely." Lady Anna forbore adding that the late Empress was embarrassed by Eleanor and had been glad to be rid of her. Is the daughter as bad, she wondered. She tried a different tack. "I am afraid, Your Grace, that the Basileus would be deeply offended if you refused the litters that he has so graciously put at your disposal."

"Very well, since you put it that way," acquiesced Mathilde with a sigh. "I have no desire to offend the Basileus, who has been so generous with his hospitality. But I insist on the curtains remaining open so that I may see the sights."

Lady Anna shook her head again. "As you wish, Your Grace. The Greek men are very jealous, but if you feel His Grace your husband would not object . . . "

Mathilde laughed. "He will not object."

And so the ladies entered the litters two and two. But when Mathilde found she was expected to travel alone since there was no one else of equal rank, she objected again. "I would have someone with me who can point out the sights I am hoping to see." She looked over the group. "Perhaps your daughter, Lady Anna," she suggested.

And so Margarete joined Mathilde in the open litter while the latter bade Hans walk beside them. "So that you, too, may learn about this great city," she said. Hans was sure then that the Duchess was also privy to Lady Catherine's plotting.

The ladies pronounced the shopping trip an unqualified success. They purchased ells and ells of precious silks, from sheerest gossamer to heaviest taffeta, and of the rare Egyptian cotton, only now beginning to be known in Europe, some fine enough for dainty undershifts, other heavy damask of intricate weaves. They purchased jewelry and expensive trinkets of mother-of-pearl, which many had never seen before.

But for Hans the excursion was far from a success. He felt no nearer his goal of getting to know the alluring blond girl than before. Of a truth, Mathilde had very graciously and courteously introduced Margarete to him, even including a few words of praise for his virtues, but after that the girl had totally ignored him. After her initial shyness, she seemed to warm to Mathilde's free and easy manner and chattered easily as she pointed out the passing sights to the Duchess. But Hans might as well not have been there. The few times Margarete looked out of the litter, she looked right past him, although most of the time she kept her eyes demurely downcast as though she were uneasy at the curtains being open.

When they returned to the palace, Mathilde graciously thanked Lady Anna and expressed her desire to see Sancta Sophia, the greatest church in Christendom, and some of the other famous historic sites. While arrangements for the sightseeing were made for the morrow, Hans approached Margarete.

"Thank you for making the afternoon so pleasant for Her Grace, Lady Margarete," he said in his best courtly manner. "Will you be with us again tomorrow?"

The girl blushed to the roots of her hair. Obviously flustered, she backed away from him. "Perhaps," she murmured shyly and fled to stand beside her mother. Then from the safety of this position, she surprised him with a wistful smile.

Hans was perplexed by her attitude. Is she afraid of me? he wondered. I can't think of anything I have done to offend her.

The little exchange and Hans' subsequent puzzlement did not go unnoticed by Lady Catherine. When the Saxon party took leave of the others and was being escorted back to their quarters in the palace, she walked beside Hans.

"She likes you," she whispered.

"How can you say that, Lady Catherine?" retorted Hans. "She wouldn't even speak to me. In fact, she ignored me all afternoon. And then just now, when I finally had a chance to address her, she almost ran away."

"Remember, Hans, these Greek ladies are raised more sequestered than some of our cloistered nuns," Lady Catherine reminded him. "She probably doesn't know how to handle a man's attentions. May even have been warned against them."

"But she's German, not Greek," protested Hans.

"Maybe so, but she was born and raised in the Imperial Court of Byzantium. Their attitude toward women is very different from ours. You heard what Lady Anna said." She lowered her voice to a whisper. "They were shocked by Queen Eleanor's—uh—forwardness. I've heard they were terrified she might corrupt their women."

"But then how am I to get to know her?" moaned Hans. "I appreciate your help and all that, but it doesn't seem to have done much good."

Lady Catherine patted his arm reassuringly. "It will. Just wait. Tomorrow you may have a better opportunity. I know she's interested in you."

"I don't see how you can know that."

"I am certain. Women can sense these things."

Hans hoped she was right.

The next morning the same group assembled in the outer courtyard and once again Margarete rode with Mathilde. This time Duke Heinrich and the older Saxon knights accompanied them. They, too, wanted to see some of the most famous shrines of Christendom with their equally famous relics. And horses were provided for the men. Hans' spirits lifted a bit. Perhaps that would increase his stature somewhat in Margarete's eyes. Even though he did not as yet have proper armor, he wore his dashing surcoat.

Heinrich rode on one side of Mathilde's litter and Hans, as often as the narrow streets permitted, on the other. Heinrich flirted openly with his duchess and they seemed to be sharing their own private jokes, which gave Hans an opportunity to speak to Margarete.

"I am pleased that you accompany us again this morning, my lady," he said.

She smiled but made no reply.

"Your city is very beautiful. I cannot help but notice how clean the streets are."

Again she smiled. Has she lost her tongue, he wondered, and tried again.

"Where do we go first on our tour?" he asked.

She could hardly avoid the direct question, and after a moment, during which it appeared as though she were praying, she murmured shyly, "We are going first to the old palace of the Emperor Constantine."

"Then the palace where we are staying was not built by him?"

"Oh, no," she replied, shocked at his ignorance. "We live in the most modern palace in the world, built not too long ago by His Majesty's grandfather. Constantine's is very old."

"Ah, yes, it would be about eight hundred years old now. Forgive my ignorance. I did not know there were two."

"Not two. There are several."

"I see. Then why do we go to see a mouldering old palace?"

"It is old but not mouldering," she replied indignantly, "and very holy."

"Oh? And why, pray tell, is it so holy—just because Constantine lived there?" he asked.

"No!" she exclaimed, exasperated. "You really are ignorant, aren't you?"

He was surprised at her sharpness but chose to ignore it. Anything to keep her talking to him. "I have studied a great deal, but an intelligent man is ever thirsty for more knowledge. If you would but teach me, my lady," he replied humbly.

Somewhat mollified, she explained, "The Great Palace is holy because of the relics in the chapel."

161

"Ah, so, and what relics are they?"

"The cross on which Our Lord was crucified and the nail that pierced His right hand, the crown of thorns and the spear of Longinus, and even the stone which lay before His tomb." She recited the litany with awe, as if such holy things should scarcely be spoken of by mere mortals.

"All those?" said Hans, duly impressed. "And how did Constantine come by them?"

"It was his mother, St. Helena, who found them. Our Lord came to her in a dream and told her where to look."

At last they reached the Great Palace and were met by the Greek monks who guarded the treasure. At the chapel a Greek priest led them to the relics, which could hardly be seen, buried as they were in dazzling bejeweled reliquaries. The entire company fell to their knees. After a suitable time for silent prayer, Father Theodorich asked if he might celebrate Mass for his people here in this holy place.

The Greek priest, who at the Emperor's command had been making an effort to be gracious to these Westerners whom he regarded as schismatics, suddenly turned cold. "I am afraid that is impossible at the moment, Father. We—uh—we are—we have temporarily run out of wine."

"Then may my people at least kiss the sacred relics?" asked Father Theodorich.

"No, we can no longer permit that," replied the priest. "They are too old and fragile."

Father Theodorich was becoming very annoyed. "But surely you would permit Their Graces the Duke and Duchess of Saxony, if no one else."

"I—uh—I should have to ask."

Heinrich nudged Father Theodorich to be quiet and spoke up himself. "Never mind Father, we who are also Christians, although you would not have it so, have no wish to embarrass you. We shall say our prayers and be gone."

The Greek priest, realizing he had gone too far but glad to have gotten out of his predicament so easily, was immediately conciliatory. "Yes, yes, there are prayers written especially for these holy relics." He signalled to a monk who handed him a long parchment. "If you would like to lead your people . . . " He handed the scroll to Father Theodorich.

The Saxon priest almost sputtered when he looked at it. "But this is all in Greek. I am afraid I cannot read Greek."

"Then I shall have to translate for you," said the Greek priest smugly, very visibly enjoying the put-down.

After they had left the Great Palace, Margarete said to Hans, who had never left her side, "That was terrible, terrible. He was not even courteous, and your Duke and Duchess guests of the Basileus. Why, even I have touched those relics many times."

Hans was so confused by the whole thing he didn't know what to say, but Heinrich overheard her and guffawed heartily. "I thought it all quite funny myself. I'd have enjoyed baiting him further, but the pompous fool had no sense of humor."

Margarete was amazed at his words. "His Grace is indeed gracious," she said to Hans, as if she were afraid to address the Duke directly. "If that priest had so insulted the Basileus, he would have been—been castrated, or worse."

Mathilde joined the fun. "Perhaps he already is."

And Heinrich roared again with laughter. "I assure you, my lady, if he had been one of mine, I should have hung him up by the balls, if he had any, after tearing out his insolent tongue. But then," he reflected, "none of mine would have acted so. They would have shown Christian charity and humility, which I would not expect from these apostate Greeks. Not only that, but I think all their fine relics are fakes."

Hans watched Margarete's face as she blushed at the Duke's crudities, then registered dismay at his comment on the Greeks and finally shock at his apparent blasphemy. "Your Grace, how can you say that?" she gasped, forgetting her reluctance in addressing Heinrich directly.

"Very easily," replied the Duke. "Our churches are full of pieces of the true cross, thorns and nails and I know not what else brought back in the saddlebags of thousands of crusaders." As if that settled the matter, he strode to his horse. "Come, let us see what other miracles these wily Greeks have to show us."

Margarete looked as though she were about to cry. Mathilde took her arm as they walked to their litter. "Be not dismayed, my lady. My husband is rather outspoken."

And Hans added, "But he speaks true and can be trusted. That is why we love him."

When they arrived at Sancta Sophia, Hans was once again at Margarete's side. In the great square before the cathedral they stopped to admire the heroic bronze equestrian statue of the Emperor Justinian.

"He built this church many years ago," Margarete told them.

163

"He must have been a great emperor indeed," said Hans.

"Oh, yes," she agreed, "second only to Constantine himself. Except, of course, our present Basileus—he is the greatest."

"Of course, always," said Hans with a touch of sarcasm. "Lady Margarete, are you afraid of him?"

"A little bit, I guess," she replied reluctantly. "He is so—so unapproachable. Not at all like your Duke. He is so human. I couldn't get over the way he spoke to us—as if we were friends."

"He is a friend, and a very good one," Hans told her. "He treats us all alike, even though I am the newest knight in his realm—and he is the most powerful duke in Germany."

"Ah, Germany," she sighed longingly. "I should love to see it someday. I am told it is very beautiful."

"It is that, especially Saxony. You have never been to your homeland, then?" he asked.

"No," she replied. "I do not even know which is my homeland. I was born of German parents, as you may know, and my mother suffered often from homesickness, especially after my father died. But I was born here and know no other home. I learned Greek at the same time as German, and I studied at the palace school, so I even learned to read and write in Greek. I do not know how to read and write in German, although my mother has tried to teach me a little of the alphabet. And I was raised in the Greek rite of the church. We are taught to hate the Pope, that he is an apostate. And now there are two popes. Which one should we hate? It is all very confusing."

Hans agreed that it was. He didn't know what else to say. He could see she was very intelligent as well as beautiful and that she was seriously concerned about these things. The more he learned about her, the more intrigued he became. He longed to tell her all about Germany, but now they entered the great church and the entire party was struck silent with awe at its sheer magnificence.

Thousands of candles made it bright as day, and their tens of thousands of reflections off the golden mosaics made the whole interior shimmer with celestial light. It was as though God permitted these humble mortals a foretaste of heaven. Marble of every color, green, pink, brown, yellow, white, lined the great pillars, the walls, the floor. And over all the great dome seemed to float in the air and led the eye to heaven.

Heinrich was the first to recover. "God's teeth!" he exclaimed, "It's huge. My poor little cathedral would be lost in one corner of this." He studied the architecture of the dome. "How did they do it?"

The Greek priest ignored his question. "Come this way, Your Grace, we have here one of the greatest miracles since Our Lord walked the earth." He led them to a statue of the Virgin that continuously wept copious tears. "See how Our Lady weeps for the sins of mankind. See how she weeps for her crucified Son."

Heinrich whispered to Mathilde, "Methinks another fake. In a city so full of fountains, what is one more?"

"Hush, he will hear you."

"What care I? These Greeks are of a kind with the Jews in the bazaars of Jerusalem. Nay, I think they are worse. At least the Jews were honest enough to call their relics souvenirs."

After a few prayers at the foot of the statue, the priest led them to the church's other famous relics — the three gifts of the Magi. The gold could well have been a genuine Roman coin, the myrrh appeared to be a black lump of tar and the frankincense was nothing but dust. After a cursory glance Heinrich turned to study the architecture of the great church. It seemed to fascinate him.

The priest, offended, tried to turn his attention back to the relics. "Would Your Grace not care to leave an offering for Our Lord as did the Wise Men?"

"Don't bother me with trivialities, priest. The real miracle in your church is how it is built. How did they do it?"

"God came to the Emperor Justinian in a dream and told him how to build it," answered the priest piously.

"Man, do you take me for an idiot?" snapped the Duke. "He must have had architects and engineers and plans. Who would know?"

"I don't know, Your Grace. I am but a humble servant of God. Perhaps the engineers at the Palace . . ." He let his voice trail off and turned his attention back to the few in the group who were reverently impressed by the Magis' gifts, confirmed in his opinion that these Westerners were truly uncouth, primitive clods.

Hans and Margarete could hardly keep from laughing at this exchange. "He's right, you know," whispered Hans. "I don't see how that great dome has stayed up there all these centuries."

"Yes," she agreed. "You know, in all the years I have been coming to Divine Worship here, I have never really realized that it is the building itself that is the miracle of this church."

When they returned to the Palace, Hans asked Margarete if he might meet her on the morrow in one of the courtyards. He longed to kiss her hand in the new courtly manner promulgated by Queen Eleanor, but he didn't dare. Although Margarete had relaxed in his company to some extent, she still reminded him of a deer in the forest, ready to flee at the slightest movement. "I should like to tell you more about Germany," he said.

"I should like that very much." She smiled her shy, fleeting smile. "But I don't know if I can. I shall ask." At his look of disappointment, she added, "I shall send word." And she slipped away.

The next day Heinrich summoned Hans. "I have made arrangements for you to procure your armor from the Emperor's own armorer. That way you can be sure it is of the best quality and you will not be cheated by the rogues in the city. He is even now awaiting you for the first fitting. This slave will show you the way."

"That is very kind of Your Grace," replied Hans, wondering what the cost would be.

"I have decided to return home by the overland route up the Danube valley. I am assured that now that the Hungarians have become Christians it is quite safe. Nevertheless, I want all my men fully armored and well mounted. Go now."

Hans was surprised at this news and had many questions, but the Duke seemed to be preoccupied with other matters, so he merely said, "Yes, Your Grace, thank you, Your Grace," and followed the slave.

Soon Hans was in another part of the Palace he had never seen. It was like a city unto itself. There were workshops of every kind. There were cutters of stone and marble, artisans working with the delicate mosaics, carpenters, and furniture makers. There were workers in copper and bronze, lead and iron. Five different blacksmiths specialized in each phase of the ironwork. Some shod horses and others made weapons. At last they arrived at the forge of the most skilled, the armorer.

The heat from the furnace was unbearable, but Hans had to wait patiently while the powerful little man meticulously measured every part of his body. He stood and sat and bent. He raised and lowered his arms, leaned this way and that. Then came the measuring of his head, which the armorer explained was the most important of all, for if the helm were too tight, it would give him headaches and perhaps even cause him to faint, and if it were too loose, it could fall off in battle. First the little man laid his hands on Hans' head as if memorizing the shape of it; then he measured his ears and eyes, his nose and mouth, his chin and neck. Hans

166

felt as if he were being roasted alive, but when he looked at the great lengths of chain-mail hanging from the wall, just waiting to be cut to his size, his pride took over and he suffered the heat gladly.

But at the back of his mind he kept worrying that Margarete might have sent word to him and no one would know that he was hidden in this inferno. At last the armorer was satisfied and let him go but told him to come back the next day for the first fitting.

"How many fittings will there be?" asked Hans.

"At least four or five," the man told him, "but you can assure your lord that it will be ready in a week."

Hans was amazed. Only a week. Back home it would have taken a month, but then he realized that the intricate, tedious work of weaving and fastening the tiny links of chain-mail together was already done here. It was just a matter of putting pieces of it together to fit him.

He hurried back to his quarters, but he needn't have. There was no word from Margarete. Disappointed, he paced his room and strolled through the courtyard but dared not go too far afield for fear she would send for him. But she never did.

That evening in the luxurious dining hall he was overjoyed to find that she was to be his supper partner. Someone had graciously rearranged the seating. He was a little farther down the table than previously, she a little further up. This evidently satisfied whatever protocol was involved in these things.

"What happened?" he asked. "I waited for you all day."

"I am sorry," she replied. "I told you I might not be able to meet you. My mother had—uh—other things for me to do." And he had to accept that.

Intimate conversation was difficult at the table with all the other talk and chatter going on around them in three languages. But he tried to tell her enough about his homeland to whet her appetite. He spoke of the peace and quiet, of the clean smell of pine and fir forests, of lush green fields, of the lovely meandering rivers.

"Braunschweig is very tiny compared to Constantinople, but very charming nonetheless. It is a new city, most of it built since our Heinrich became duke. He made it his capital. Before that Saxony was divided into three parts. He united it and even added more territory to the east when he and our Emperor drove the Magyars back into Hungary."

"Your Duke, then, is very warlike?" she asked.

"He is a great warrior but prefers peace. However, he has had to fight and conquer and chastise many of the independent robber-barons who were burning and pillaging the land, stealing the peasants' flocks and even their women, and robbing the peaceful traders."

"How terrible!" she exclaimed. "I don't think I should like that. Here no baron would dare rise up against the Basileus and our roads are safe for all travellers. Only the Turks give us trouble and they are ruthless barbarians."

"Oh, but it is not like that anymore," Hans quickly amended. "Heinrich has cleaned them all out of their nests and our roads are probably the safest in all the West. He does everything he can to encourage peaceful trade."

She pondered this a moment. "Then your Braunschweig has a bazaar where one can purchase fine cloth and jewels and such things?"

"Well, it is not exactly like the bazaars here, but it has a fine market and shops in the houses around the marketplace. The town is located on an ancient trading route that leads from Rome to the North Sea. So most of the things they sell here can be found there, only not so much of it." Hans hoped he was not promising too much, but then chances of her ever seeing Braunschweig and proving him a liar were slim indeed.

"Tell me about your home," she said, changing the subject.

"I live in the palace called Dankwarderode. The Duke only finished building it a few years ago. It is much smaller than this, of course, but quite comfortable in winter with huge modern fireplaces with great chimneys that keep out the snow. There also is a fine library."

"I have never seen a fireplace. Nor have I ever seen snow. What a strange land you live in," she mused. "But I meant for you to tell me about your family home, your demesne. I believe you have been just recently knighted."

"Yes, I have, but I must tell you true, my lady, I have not seen my fief since I was a tiny babe, so I have very little memory of it," he admitted. Then he told her the carefully concocted story of his background. He wished this once he could tell the truth, but he did not yet know her well enough and feared what her reaction might be. "As soon as we return, His Grace says I am to take possession of it and then I would be able to tell you more."

"How sad," she remarked wistfully. "Then you and I have much in common, for I, too, have no knowledge of the homeland my mother speaks of so fondly."

"How I wish," said Hans daringly, "that I could take you back with

168

me, so you could see it for yourself."

Her eyes opened wide and stared at him for a moment. Then she lowered her lashes demurely and fell silent. After a time she murmured, "I might as well wish that I could fly to the moon." And she said nothing more for the rest of the meal.

Hans was mentally kicking himself for being too forward and outspoken. He realized he was rushing her too fast. But that one instant when her beautiful blue eyes looked straight into his, he saw such longing there and perhaps a little love, that it gave him hope.

Every morning Hans went to the armorer for a fitting and every afternoon he waited for word from Margarete, but it never came. At supper she would apologize and say she was busy. But she still seemed to enjoy his company and asked him many questions about Germany. She wanted to know about Sulzbach, but he could tell her little, never having been there.

Finally he asked her outright, "What do you do with yourself all these days I have been waiting to meet you?"

"My mother and sister and I have been busy sewing new clothes."

"Is that all? Couldn't that wait until after we have gone?" He felt hurt that sewing should take precedence over his company.

"I think not," she replied cryptically and would discuss it no more. But her smile that evening had lost its shyness. Her eyes even had a flirtatious twinkle that endeared her to him even more.

The next day Hans decided it was time he had new clothes, too. He never did purchase anything on that first shopping trip. So taking with him the only slave assigned to him as guide and interpreter, he went out into the city to the great bazaar by himself. With the slave's help Hans purchased enough cloth to make two fine silk shirts and two of cotton, which he noticed was of a much finer weave than the linen he was used to. He purchased some serviceable material for a doublet and hose to be worn under his new armor, but on his gown he decided to be a little extravagant. He disdained the customary black wool that all the merchants and many nobles wore back home and chose instead a length of rich silken velvet in a dark forest green. Then the cloth merchant insisted that he must have a cloak as well if he were going to travel to the north and showed him a heavy deep brown velvet and a soft, silky fur of the same color.

"If you line one with the other," he explained, "you will always be warm and comfortable. When the weather is fine, but cold, you turn the fur to the inside. When it rains, you turn the fur to the outside and not a

169

drop will penetrate. That fur comes from far-off Rusland. It is called sable. The tailor next door can make it up for you in two days."

Hans let himself be convinced. He completed his purchases and let the tailor measure him for the cloak. "But only that," he said. "Her Grace has fine seamstresses who can make the shirts and other things for me.

As they left the tailor's, the slave reminded him, "My lord, you also need a cap and shoes to match your new clothes."

"Of course," said Hans. So they visited a hat maker and ordered a cap of the green velvet to be adorned with a jaunty peacock feather. At the shoemaker's he was measured for bright green shoes with long pointy toes of the softest kid. All would be ready in two days.

Satisfied with all the purchases, they were about to leave the bazaar when Hans spied a jewel merchant. He only intended to look. Perhaps he should order a signet ring, now that he had a coat-of-arms. Before he could even ask, the jeweler brought out a silver necklace set with blue stones Hans had never seen before. The center one seemed to encase a star set in a blue heaven.

"If your lady's eyes are as blue as yours, my lord, they will match perfectly," said the wily merchant.

Hans was beguiled. How could he know? he thought. Would she accept a parting gift from me? Do I dare be so bold as to offer it? He ended up purchasing not only the necklace, but also a ring to match. He forgot all about the signet ring.

When he returned to the Palace, a young page met him in the corridor. He was very excited. "Oh, Sir Hans!" he exclaimed. "Where have you been? Duke Heinrich sent me to fetch you over an hour ago and I could not find you. I fear he will be greatly wroth with me. His Grace commands your presence immediately."

"Fear not, young one," Hans reassured the lad. "I shall explain to him. I could not know he would have need of me." Hans instructed his slave to take the costly cloth to the Duchess' seamstresses and hurried to the ducal apartments.

When he arrived, Heinrich was busy discussing plans for their return journey with Sir Wigbert and the other senior knights. Mathilde and some of the ladies were also in attendance. They were so engrossed that no one seemed to notice Hans' entrance.

"I have discussed all the affairs of state with Manuel that I intend to," the Duke was saying. "There is no point in remaining here any longer. He treats me like royalty because he believes I am the strongest ruler in Germany. That is as may be, but I succumb not to his flattery, nor would I like Friedrich to hear of it. The power of Byzantium is waning rapidly before the onslaught of the Turks, but I did not fall into the trap of offering him an alliance. I merely agreed to advise Friedrich of his problems. Besides, he is weak and I don't trust the Greeks." He paused a moment to take a sip of wine. No one had any comment. "So, it is settled then," he continued. "We leave in one week on the eve of the Nones of October." His curious mixture of the old Saxon reckoning with the official Roman one confused no one. "I would be home by Christmas, the gods willing. We go by ship to the mouth of the Danube and there will be supplied with sufficient horses, wagons and victuals for the journey. Now leave us. I would speak with Sir Hans privately. Where have you been, you young puppy?" he roared, much to Han's embarrassment, "I have news for you and you are nowhere to be found."

Hans stepped forward as most of the others left. He noticed Sir Wigbert and Lady Catherine remained. "I am sorry, Your Grace," he began apologetically, "but you yourself suggested I buy some clothes here. I didn't think you would have need of me this day."

"In that case you are forgiven. You certainly need to replace those peasant rags you've been wearing. The more so when you hear our news."

"Thank you, Your Grace. I am most curious to hear your news."

"Only curious? You should be most anxious and enthusiastic."

"I am indeed, Your Grace. I thought only to be courtly and restrained."

"Stop teasing him, my lord," put in Mathilde. "He knows not whereof you speak."

"I was merely testing his manners," replied Heinrich, "and by God's teeth, I do not find him wanting. He is as courtly as a gentleman born, perhaps more so. Your mother could not have taught him better, my sweet."

Mathilde smiled.

"Tell me of this wench you are panting after," asked the Duke.

"What wench?" asked Hans, mystified. "I have lusted after no one, not even the slaves that were offered."

Mathilde decided to put an end to the teasing. "My lord is referring to the Lady Margarete, Hans."

"But she is no wench, Your Grace," protested Hans indignantly. "She is a lady born and raised."

"Hah," retorted Heinrich, "all women are wenches when you get them in bed. Wouldn't you like to bed her, friend Hans?"

171

Hans turned red to his ears. "I most certainly would, Your Grace. But—but—I have not had time to court her properly and now—now it looks as though I never shall."

"Oh, yes, you will, for she is yours. I have spoken to Manuel and he will right gladly give her to you."

"You mean—you mean—as a mistress, as a whore. Oh no, Your Grace, I could never," exclaimed Hans. "I love her too much for that. If I could not have her as my wedded wife, I would not so dishonor her."

"Enough of this," shouted Mathilde. "I think it is you, Heinrich, who have forgotten your courtly manners. Tell Hans the right of it from the beginning."

Heinrich roared with laughter. "You see, Hans, every woman is a wench, even my duchess." He leaned over and tweaked Mathilde's breast. "I but wanted to know the lad's true feelings for the girl. You tell him, sweet, lest I be too crude in my words."

"We know of your interest in the Lady Margarete, Hans," began Mathilde more calmly, "and it has gladdened our hearts. My lord has long despaired that you would show interest in any girl. Lady Catherine has been urging me to ask the Empress to release her to me as one of my ladies so that she could return with us. However, before I could, we learned two interesting things. The present Empress would like to be rid of all the German ladies—except, of course, Lady Anna's sister, who is married to a Greek. They apparently remind her too much of her predecessor. And the Lady Anna is very homesick. She annoys the Empress by refusing to become totally Greek. So both were hinting that my lord take them under his patronage. We were considering one, but three unwed ladies seemed a bit too much responsibility on a journey such as we shall be undertaking. But then came a surprise. Sir Wigbert, who as you know is long widowed, began paying court to the Lady Anna. He wishes to wed her and will take responsibility for the younger daughter, which leaves the Lady Margarete for you. My lord has made all the arrangements, but he was kind enough to consider your feelings. If you had not wanted her, we would have left her here with her aunt."

Hans was astounded at his good fortune, but before he could speak his gratitude, Heinrich said, "Mind you, there will be no wedding, or even betrothal, here. I despise the Greek rite. But Father Theodorich will draw up and bless the consent agreement privately before our witness."

"You make me very happy, Your Grace, and I am deeply grateful that you arranged this," said Hans, "but the Lady Margarete, does she know? Will she have me?"

"She has no choice. The Basileus and I have settled the matter. But I hope you are man enough to have some idea of the lady's feelings."

"I think she is willing," said Hans.

"How do you know?" asked Mathilde. "Has she said?"

"No," replied Hans, "but they have been sewing feverishly these last days."

"Aha!" said Mathilde, as if no other proof were required.

Hans' horse ambled slowly alongside the wagon in which rode Lady Anna and her daughters. In their sequestered upbringing at the Greek court the girls had never learned to ride and Lady Anna had long since forgotten. Hans was weary. The horse was weary. After weeks in the saddle he often wished they had taken the sea route home, but his discomfort was nothing compared to the misery he knew the women were suffering in the jolting wagon. Only the oxen seemed to have no feelings as they plodded steadily on.

They were passing through the Gorges of the Danube and the deeply rutted road wound up and down mountains, along the edge of precipices and under cliffs. Often they had to push huge boulders out of the way so that the wagons could pass. All the men were on constant alert, as the region was known to be rife with bandits and robber-barons. They more often than not had spent the night in their tents, for they found little welcome among the Greeks. Manuel's safe conduct and Heinrich's rank gave them a measure of safety but opened few doors. Some monasteries turned them away when they learned they were Westerners, and many a town with bitter memories of the Crusaders' depredations closed their gates to them. Occasionally a castle gave them food and lodging for the night, but so many were notorious highway robbers that the Duke, forewarned, avoided them. Those that did were usually primitive and filthy, offering shelter but no comfort and little warmth. The luxury of a bath was a distant memory.

The colorful foliage and crisp sunny days of October had given way to the leafless, gray drizzle of November. Everyone lucky enough to have furs pulled them closer and tighter as the wind whipped down the valleys and the rain pelted them. Everyone was bone-weary and miserable as one dreary day followed another. Only the knowledge that each step westward brought them nearer home kept their flagging spirits up. But for Lady

Anna and her daughters it was one more step away from the comfort and luxury they were accustomed to, one more step into the unknown.

One morning Hans stepped out of the tent he shared with five other men into a fog so dense he could barely discern the horses tethered nearby. Everything dripped and for once there was no wind at all. Yet despite the dismal prospect, something seemed to buoy his spirits. At first he could not pinpoint it. And then it came to him. The smell.

"It smells like spring!" he exclaimed aloud. "It almost smells like home!"

One of the older men, who had made the trip before, joined him. "Ah, lad, your nose tells you true. We shall be out of these blasted mountains soon and into the great plains of Hungary. The river turns north and the going will be easier. Even a bit warmer, too. That is what makes this fog."

"How can it be warmer if we travel north?" asked Hans, puzzled.

"Because it is like a huge bowl surrounded by mountains, but sheltered by them, too. It is a very rich, fertile land, though not much under cultivation yet. Great forests mostly. That is what you smell. But still a long ways from home."

"And the people? Is it safe? I have heard that the Magyars are greatly to be feared, wild barbarians who raid and pillage."

"Not so much anymore now that they have become Christians. Our great Otto had to fight them constantly but finally drove them out of Germany. Conrad and our Heinrich's father finally subdued them, and now, even though they have their own king, they are under fief to the Duke of Austria."

"So we should have no trouble?"

"I think not. The peasants, though still mostly nomads, are held under tight control by the bishops and nobles, and the great lords dare not offend Heinrich or Friedrich. They know reprisal would be swift and merciless."

Camp was quickly broken and they were once again on their way. Hans, as usual, rode beside Lady Anna's wagon. He was worried. All these weeks on the road had brought him no closer to Margarete. Conversation had been extremely limited due to the rigors of travel. They seemed to have lost what little intimacy and camaraderie they had had back in Constantinople. He feared she was regretting the decision to return to Germany and the prospect of marriage with him. What he had hoped would be a two or more month idyll before their betrothal had turned into an ordeal. He realized he would have to court her all over again once they reached home.

The river did, indeed, turn north and they descended into Hungary. The ancient Roman road, though long neglected, was in better condition. The horses and oxen no longer had to strain. Hans decided on a bold move.

"Lady Margarete, now that the road is easier, would you like to ride with me?" he asked.

She looked very doubtful. "I don't know how, kind sir."

"No need to know anything. I shall guide the horse and see that you don't fall off. It is more comfortable than the wagon, I assure you."

She was tempted. "Anything would be more comfortable than this horrible old wagon, but I am a little afraid."

Hans said, sharper than he meant to, "If you are to marry a Saxon, you must learn to ride, and that right soon."

"He is right," spoke up Lady Anna. "If you don't, Grete, I shall accept his offer myself. I rode quite well as a young girl and this wagon is virtually rattling my bones apart."

"Very well, I'll try," said Margarete, "but you must hold me very tight."

"With a glad heart, my lady," Hans assured her, for he was far more interested in holding her in his arms than in teaching her how to ride. They stopped the wagon and he helped her onto the saddle in front of him. He held her securely against him as they moved off. Soon he felt her relax against him and the warmth of her body aroused his desire. He forced himself to pay strict attention so that the horse would not wander.

"This is fun," she said at last, "and ever so much nicer than that rickety old wagon. Warmer, too." She giggled.

Hans held her tighter. "I heard your mother call you Grete. May I?"

"Why yes, Sir Hans. I suppose it is all right since you will soon be part of the family."

"Then I shall call you my Gretchen. And please no 'Sir'. I am just plain Hans to you."

"Hah, Hans and Gretchen. That sounds nice together, just like the fairy tale."

He laughed. "And I shall protect you well from the wicked witch."

"But we must not get lost in the woods."

"Not here, but wait till we get home," he teased. "And shall we live happily ever after?"

"I hope so," replied Gretchen and snuggled closer to him. He kissed her on the cheek and was happy at last.

After some days they arrived at the grim castle of Buda, brooding on its cliff high above the river. However, its menacing aspect was soon forgotten, for they received a royal welcome from King Stephan. Although his castle was a far cry from the palace at Constantinople, the king was doing his best to imitate some of the amenities of the west. The ladies, at least, were able to have baths, although all but Mathilde had to sleep on straw pallets. The food was good and plentiful, served with an excellent wine. And at last they felt secure knowing they were among Christians of the Roman rite. Heinrich stayed there three days to let both pilgrims and animals rest, and everyone's spirits rose.

One afternoon Hans and Gretchen were strolling on the ramparts known as the Fisherman's Bastion. They were well bundled in their furs, for a sharp wind blew down the river. On their left was a small but charming church, the first to have been built in Hungary. Beyond it the tiny town of Buda huddled close to the castle on its promontory. A steep path led down from it to a wooden bridge that crossed the river in two sections. On the island in the middle could still be seen the ruins of the original Roman settlement. On the other side was a strange collection of structures that could have been a village but looked more like a camp.

"What is that, I wonder?" asked Gretchen.

"I don't know," replied Hans. "Let us inquire of yon priest."

The priest willingly explained, "That is Pest. It is a village that has come into being solely to supply the many pilgrims that come this way."

"Those are houses?" questioned Hans. "They look more like tents to me."

"In a way they are. You see, our people are only very slowly beginning to give up the nomadic life and settle in one place. So they still build their houses—huts, really—as though they were tents. A few staves, covered with wattle and reed. Most of the roofs are still animal skins."

"And what do they do for the pilgrims?"

"Supply them with food and shelter, even horses. All for a price, of course. I do not approve of making money off of people's faith, but when our St. Stephan of blessed memory converted them to Christ and forbade them to raid and plunder, what were they to do? Some have developed lucrative businesses and could live in fine houses, but they won't."

"Do you think we could buy a good horse there?" asked Gretchen.

"Of a certain, my lady. The steppe ponies of the Magyars are among the swiftest and best-trained, yet the gentlest, anywhere. But have a care that you take someone with you who speaks the language. They are sharp traders in Pest." The priest strolled on.

Hans looked at Gretchen as if he weren't sure she was the same shy, quiet girl he had known. "A horse?" he queried. "What do you want to buy a horse for?"

"Why, to ride, of course," she replied. "Isn't that what most people do with them?"

"But I have a horse. I admit it's not my own, but His Grace specifically cautioned me to wait until we get home and buy one of our strong Saxon horses at the Verden horse fair."

"I mean for me, *Sir* Hans. I don't need a destrier, you know. I think one of these swift, but gentle, ponies would be just right for a beginner."

Hans was hurt. "You mean you don't want to ride with me anymore, Gretchen?"

She was immediately contrite. "I'm sorry, my Hans. I didn't mean that the way it sounded. Of course, I love riding with your arms around me. But I have heard that we have many more mountains to cross before we reach your home and I know it will be too much even for the strongest horse to be ridden double then. Hans, I can't bear to go back to that wagon. Besides, you have taught me so much, I am sure I can handle it. You told me I must become a real Saxon maid, and that right soon."

Hans' ego immediately took a great leap. He swept her into his arms and kissed her soundly. "And that's a real Saxon kiss. To hell with these courtly manners. A horse you shall have, my lady."

And so, together with the king's head groom, they crossed over to Pest. The squalor was distressing, but the groom warned, "Don't let that fool you. They prefer to keep it that way so the pilgrims will be more generous. Gullible is more like it. But they have some fine mounts."

Hans had seen enough in the East to know what haggling was all about, but he couldn't believe the performance put on by this supposedly shy little maid. Even the groom was amazed when they came away with a beautiful little mare at a remarkably low price.

"Even I could not have done that well, my lady," he said admiringly. "Yet you admitted you know nothing about horseflesh. How did you do it?"

Gretchen laughed. "It is true I know little about horses, although I sense that this little lady and I are going to be great friends. Females often have a sixth sense about each other. But I do know about traders. I have not lived all my life among the Greeks and not learned something of that from them."

By the time they got back to the castle, the horse was indeed nuzzling Gretchen and eating out of her hand. Hans kissed her again. "Methinks I have found me not only a sweet and loving wife but a very shrewd one, too. I fear for the poor merchants in Braunschweig."

A few weeks later the erstwhile pilgrims rode into Braunschweig, weary, saddle-sore and glad to be home. They were just in time for Christmas and Heinrich and Mathilde held the most lavish Christmas court the Saxons had ever seen. All the nobles, knights and bishops of the realm were commanded to attend, and most did, with large retinues. But there were some conspicuous absences.

The duchy had been reasonably well governed by the regents during Heinrich's absence and peace had been maintained. But only just, and all the news was bad. Several of Saxony's powerful neighbors to both east and west were poisoning the Emperor's ear again and stirring up trouble among some of the Duke's own nobles, particularly with those whom he had recently subdued and enfeoffed to himself.

Hans was happy to see his friend Brandt again at court. They embraced like brothers. "How good it is to see you again," Hans said. "You look as though marriage agrees with you."

"That it does," agreed Brandt, "and I hear that you are now *Sir* Hans. May I offer my congratulations? I want to hear about it from you. I have heard a strange story of the circumstances."

Hans laughed and told Brandt the story of his knighting. "It was silly, really, although lucky for me it worked out as it did. I think Heinrich was just looking for an excuse to do what he really wanted to do anyway."

Brandt roared hilariously at the tale but then sobered. "Our Lion doesn't need an excuse to do anything he has a mind to do. I believe he really was grateful. It is as well that he is a bit beholden to you. You may find that useful in future."

Hans introduced Gretchen and Brandt's wife immediately took her under her wing.

Their betrothal took place during the Christmas court, and after the banns had been read for three weeks they were married on the porch of the church as was the custom.

Gretchen looked glorious in a deep rose silk gown in the Greek style, lavishly embroidered with gold thread. It was the envy of all the noble ladies, many of whom had never seen silk of such fine quality. Some of them even considered it much too daring and heathenish. But the bride did give in to western custom and put up her hair as was considered proper for a married woman, but even there she surprised them. The coif was of such delicately woven gold netting that it seemed as though her head was sprinkled with stars.

Hans had given her the sapphire ring at the betrothal, and now for the morning gift he presented her with the exquisite necklace.

"Oh Hans, this is too beautiful," she exclaimed with delight. "You surely did not buy that here."

"No, my love, I admit I bought it in Constantinople. It was to have been a farewell gift for you."

"For me? You loved me that much even then? My beloved husband, now I know we shall be very happy," she sighed.

During this period the Duke's lawyers drew up all the required documents for transferring the tiny demesne of Sehnde to Hans. Nominally the property still belonged to the Duke but was designated a hereditary fief for Hans and his heirs forever, as long as they fulfilled their feudal obligations to their liege lord and his heirs. Heinrich then graciously released the newlyweds from these obligations for a period of two years so that they could rebuild and refurbish the old house and get at least two crops in. From the second harvest, the Duke would expect his just dues.

"Unless, of course, I have dire need of your personal services in the meantime," he added solemnly. "The times are unsettled and I do not know what my enemies may do. Nor am I even sure who are still my friends. And my dear cousin Friedrich I trust not at all. Therefore, get yourself that horse as soon as possible and keep your knightly skills well honed, for I may need every loyal man sooner than we think. Meanwhile, God's blessing on you."

The two years were good ones for Hans and Gretchen. The house was still sound, though it needed numerous repairs. Heinrich had given them another purse at the wedding, which he said was not a gift but their rightful share of the past year's rents of the fief. So they gave all the decrepit furnishings to the peasants and had all new things built by the village cabinetmaker. Hans' real father had long since died, so there was no need to explain to Gretchen the true story of his parentage. But his mother still lived and their reunion was a joyous mixture of tears and disbelief. He immediately installed her in the manor as his chief housekeeper. The crops were bountiful and the peasants worked for him willingly after the years of deprivation and cruelty under the old lord. Besides, it lifted their spirits and gave them hope for themselves that one of their own had been elevated to the knighthood.

Hans and Brandt kept in close touch over the years, for Sehnde and Eltze were less than a day's ride apart, and their wives became close friends. Hans' and Gretchen's first son was born shortly after the New Year of 1174, and she was well into her second pregnancy when he received the first call from the Duke. Hans set his eldest brother as overseer of the demesne and rode off on a handsome palfrey, his groom leading a magnificent destrier, both caparisoned with his new arms—the upside-down crescent and star. He wore his Byzantine armor and the surcoat Mathilde had given him. He led a troop of a dozen well-armed men.

Gretchen's heart swelled with pride as she watched him go and then she fell to weeping in her mother-in-law's arms, for it was their first time apart.

Friedrich once again was having trouble in Italy, with the now powerful Lombard League of cities. He foolishly refused to relinquish his dream of restoring Charlemagne's old empire. Moreover, he wished to keep the Pope from becoming too powerful. Heinrich realized it was an exercise in futility, so he refused his help, which was vital to Friedrich's success. More importantly Heinrich had troubles at home and dared not leave. Petty nobles were rebelling, some out of foolish spite, others at the instigation of powerful neighbors.

Heinrich had had a dream, too—that of forging the ancient tribal territory of the Saxons into one nation. But the combination of Friedrich's jealousy and fear of the Duke's power and the sheer ponderousness of the feudal system was to doom his efforts. The Emperor was well aware that he owed his election to Heinrich and for almost twenty years was content to let Heinrich rule in northern Germany while he, more or less, controlled the south. Furthermore, the Emperor could not even hold that securely without Heinrich's army and military genius. So he ended up buying favors and the dubious loyalty of the other powerful lords and bishops by granting them lands enfeoffed directly to himself, bypassing much of the usual feudal hierarchy. These shortsighted lords did pretty much as they pleased, paying little attention to either Emperor or Pope, and worked together only to oppose Heinrich's dream of a united north Germany, which threatened their personal power.

Thus for the next several years Heinrich was kept busy quelling minor revolts, subduing petty lords who had reverted to robber-barons and securing his own borders from powerful lords such as the Archbishop of Cologne on the west and Albert of Brandenburg on the east. Even within his borders the Archbishop of Magdeburg, whom he himself had invested, was trying for independence.

In 1176 Friedrich once again sought Heinrich's help in his campaign in Italy. The Duke agreed to help on condition he be given the Imperial city of Goslar together with its rich silver mines, which lay right within the boundaries of Saxony. Friedrich refused and as a result was severely defeated at the battle of Legnano in May of that year. He blamed his loss entirely on Heinrich, and their tenuous friendship came to an end. In 1177 a difficult peace with the Lombard League was concluded at Venice with the further humiliation that Friedrich had to acknowledge Alexander III as Pope with the kiss of peace on the steps of St. Mark's. In 1178 Friedrich returned to Germany in a furor, determined to break the power of and similarly humiliate his cousin Heinrich, whom he now regarded as his worst enemy. He found powerful and willing allies in the two Archbishops and the Margrave of Brandenburg.

Hans and Brandt sat at table with Heinrich in the great hall of Dankwarderode. They had never seen their liege lord so downcast, so dispirited. The year was 1180. The other nobles called for the meeting had left or gone to their beds. The three friends sat alone. The wall torches burned low in their sconces and even the dogs were quiet.

"So it has come to this," said Heinrich. "At least I know who my friends are. I appreciate your loyalty."

"I shall *always* be your loyal servant, Your Grace," protested Hans. "You have given me everything I have. How could I be otherwise?"

"And I, too, Your Grace," said Brandt. "But you must not give in so easily. We can still fight this. We have the men and the arms."

"No," sighed Heinrich, "not yet. Too much power and ill feeling is aligned against us. He has even taken away my beloved Lübeck, the jewel of the northeast. Doesn't the fool realize what wealth its trade with the Baltic lands has brought us? Of course, he does. He is jealous that he didn't think of it first, instead of wasting time and men fighting useless battles in Italy. I broke the Peace he claims. Hah, at least my fighting served a useful purpose."

A few days ago a messenger had come with the decision of the Imperial court at Gelnhausen. Under pressure from the great princes the Emperor had convened a court to try Heinrich on trumped up charges based on his altercations last year with the Bishop of Halberstadt. The

Duke had refused to go and defend himself, for he knew that the trial would be a farce. With him *in absentia* his enemies heaped up charge after charge. Friedrich, to give him credit, had tried to be fair and had dismissed many of the obvious lies, but by convening the court at all, he had given in to the demands of the princes, and now they were too powerful for him. The court found Heinrich guilty of having on numerous occasions from 1174 to 1180 broken the so-called Peace of the Empire, and the Emperor decreed that he be stripped of all lands and titles, except his hereditary one of Braunschweig-Lüneburg, and that he be sent into exile.

"He claims it is against the law to hold two duchies at the same time," continued Heinrich morosely. "Since when? I have never heard of such a law. He never heard of it either back in '56 when he finally gave me back title to the ancient Welf lands in Bavaria that I inherited from my father together with the Saxon lands from my mother. Methinks that law conveniently appeared now at Gelnhausen. I smell the stink of my ex-brother-in-law Zähringen's hand in that. He's always coveted Bavaria. But you wait and see, he won't get it either. It will go to some insignificant unknown."

"And as for that bear's cub of Brandenburg, he is trying to make the best of a bad bargain. That family has always been troublemakers since way back in the days of the Brunonen. His father Albert the Bear owes it to me that Friedrich made him Margraf there. He was more than willing to emigrate when the Emperor put out the call for colonists, if truth were known. I was glad to be rid of him. He thought to carve a great demesne out of those desolate eastern marches, but what does he have? A poor land with more Slavs than Saxons. So he eyes the new part of Saxony around the upper Elbe that I conquered and colonized. That is indeed a rich land. Ludwig of Thuringia would like to have it, too. I hope they cut each other's throats fighting over it."

Heinrich sighed bitterly. "But the most treacherous of all has been that blasted Phillip, the Archbishop of Cologne. For a man of God he acts more like the spawn of the devil. His predecessor Reinald was bad enough, tricky as Loki. He could twist words to mean anything he chose. You remember him?" The young men nodded. "He died right after that trip to England to fetch my dear wife. But this one—he tries to set himself up as pope of the north. It isn't enough that he holds all the Rheinland, he would add all of Westfalen and more to it.

"So what do I have left?" He spread his hands and sighed again. "Braunschweig-Lüneburg, they call it. Not even Ostfalen anymore, for that would remind people too much of how they've dismembered Saxony.

Why, neither one was anything—a tiny crossroads market and an old castle sitting on top of a salt mine—not even towns, before I built them up.

"Ach, God, what use is it to go on so? I am beginning to sound like an old man in his dotage. Forgive me, my friends, but I just had to get it out of my system. And I *am* getting old."

"We understand your grief, Your Grace," said Hans.

"Yes," added Brandt. "It is like losing beloved children."

"Ah, ja, that it is," signed Heinrich. "And remember, no more 'Your Grace'. They haven't decided yet whether to call me a count or—or—a nothing. From now on I am just plain Heinrich. But I am still the Lion of Saxony," he stated with a show of bravura. "The Lion may be sorely wounded but he is not dead yet. Now I must make plans."

"We are prepared to accompany you into exile," volunteered Brandt.

"Yes, nothing here will be the same without you," agreed Hans.

"No, no, I will not hear of it," protested Heinrich. "You both have young families and lands to oversee. Who knows how many years I shall be gone or if I shall even live long enough to return? I would not have you lose everything on my account. But look not so downcast, my friends. I have better plans for you both and a few others. It is your loyalty I value more than your company. Mathilde and I shall be leaving shortly to join her father's court in Normandy, and eventually to England. I shall, of course, seek Henry's help, but I don't expect much. He has enough trouble with France and now with his own sons as well. I shall be taking my two eldest sons, Heinrich and Otto, as well as my daughter with me. I shall also be taking those nobles I had rather keep an eye on than leave here. But," and he paused significantly, "I shall leave my son Lothar here, as Count—or lord—or whatever—of Braunschweig-Lüneburg. And that is where you come in, my friends. I can trust no others with this important undertaking. The lad is but eight years old. I shall appoint you Regents until I return. You will guard him and guide him. Nothing must happen to that boy. There will be others to attend to the day-to-day trivia of governing, but he will be your personal responsibility. I also charge you with guarding the treasure of the Welfs, which is considerable, as you know. Since you both can write your own hand, I expect frequent reports from you."

"Your Grace—I mean Heinrich—I am overwhelmed that you place such trust in me," said Hans. "I promise to serve you and your son with all my means, with my life and above all with my honor."

"Yes, Heinrich," agreed Brandt. "I willingly accept the responsibility, and I assure you your trust has not been misplaced. I am deeply honored."

"It is agreed then, and I am deeply grateful," replied Heinrich. "I promise you the Lion of Saxony and the Welf descendants will never forget that the houses of von Eltze and von Sehnden are our loyal friends."

Intermezzo

Heinrich and Mathilde remained in exile first in Normandy, later in England, at the court of her father Henry II from 1181 through 1185. In 1184, a few days after the crossing from Normandy, their youngest son Wilhelm was born in Winchester. Shortly thereafter Phillip, Archbishop of Cologne, had the gall to make a pilgrimage to the shrine of Thomas Becket at Canterbury. Phillip was sumptuously entertained at St. Paul's in London and by Henry at Westminster Palace. It is not known if the Archbishop met Heinrich at this time, but it is more than likely that the latter remained at Winchester with his wife and her mother Queen Eleanor. Meanwhile, Henry was trying everything in his power, short of armed warfare, to persuade Friedrich to restore his son-in-law's lands to him. Henry's efforts met with little success, but finally in 1185 Friedrich at least allowed Heinrich and Mathilde to return home. They left their son Otto behind to be raised at the English court.

Heinrich almost immediately began fighting again to regain his lost estates, but he had been gone too long and accomplished little besides antagonizing Friedrich and his other enemies again. In 1189 when the Pope issued the call for the Third Crusade, Friedrich ordered Heinrich to join him, but the latter refused and was once again exiled to England. His father-in-law died in July 1189 and his beloved Mathilde died in her mother's arms later the same year. In 1190 word came that Friedrich had drowned while attempting to cross the Saleph River on the way to the Holy Land and Heinrich immediately returned to Germany. Friedrich's son was elected Emperor Henry VI and for a while continued the fight against Heinrich, but they were soon reconciled at Fulda in July of the same year. Later, when Henry VI started a new campaign in Italy to continue his father's dream, Heinrich tried once more to reconquer his lost possessions.

Meanwhile, Richard of England on his way home from the Crusade in December 1192 had been captured in Vienna by everyone's enemy, the vicious Leopold of Austria. It was largely through Heinrich's efforts that his brother-in-law was turned over to Henry's jurisdiction in 1193 and imprisoned in the castle of Trifels. However, Henry VI demanded the outrageous ransom of 100,000 marks for Richard's release, for his treasury had been emptied by his father's wars and crusade. Then he shrewdly demanded an additional 50,000 marks unless Richard could persuade Heinrich to lay down his arms and both do homage to him for their respective lands. This was done. Richard was released and Heinrich and Henry VI were reconciled. Heinrich died after a fall from his horse on 6 August 1195 in Braunschweig.

Heinrich the Lion was a man far ahead of his time. His goal of a united north Germany collided head-on with Friedrich's dream of a Holy Roman Empire. The feudal system set up by Charlemagne ultimately defeated them both. The Salic laws further splintered the country. Bavaria was given to a complete unknown, Otto von Wittelsbach, whose descendants ruled there until modern times. The Archbishop of Cologne was given all Heinrich's ducal rights and titles and the new Duchy of Westphalia set up for him. But the rights of tolls, mints and fairs in all of Heinrich's former territory were retained by the Emperor himself. Ironically, the name of Saxony as a connotation for the ancient tribal lands disappeared from the map until 1945, when it reappeared as Niedersachsen. The newly colonized eastern marches around the upper Elbe, given to Bernhard of Anhalt, son of Albert the Bear, were henceforth and to this day erroneously known as Saxony. The old territory of Saxony was subdivided each generation by the Salic laws until by the end of the Middle Ages it contained no fewer than seventy-five separate entities.

Heinrich's most lasting contribution was the stimulus of trade and education. Under his powerful protection roads, rivers and harbors were safe for merchants and many stifling tolls were eliminated. He founded or developed towns that were to be the glory of commerce in the later Middle Ages. From Lübeck he sent his merchants as far as Sweden and Novgorod and the seeds of the later Hanseatic League were sown. He freed all the serfs. He founded schools and colleges everywhere and instilled in his people a love of education and an awareness of its value long before it was perceived elsewhere, and which they still have. He commissioned not only Minnelieder and books, but the first encyclopedia ever, in the vernacular, Low German. And, largely due to his dream, the common people never lost the memory of their Saxon culture regardless of who their overlord was at the moment.

The year before Heinrich's death, his eldest son Heinrich married

Agnes, the only daughter of Conrad, Count of the Palatine, and niece of Friedrich. It was a love match, rare in those days, and over five hundred years later one of their descendants was to sit on the throne of England. Henry VI died in 1197 and ironically Heinrich's second son, who had been raised at the English court, was elected his successor as Otto IV. The Electors were led by the new Archbishop of Cologne with heavy financial backing by Richard of England. Thus his youngest son Wilhelm inherited Braunschweig-Lüneburg.

Finally, in 1235, Wilhelm's son known as Otto the Child officially turned his realm over to the Emperor Friedrich II at a Diet at Mainz and received his lands back as a fief, thereby satisfying feudal protocol. His title, rights and privileges as a duke were restored, and more importantly he was once again an Elector of the Empire. The territory was divided into two halves, Braunschweig and Lüneburg under his sons Albert and Johann. Over the centuries under the Salic law there were further subdivisions and reunitings through inheritance, wars, and even purchases. But although there might be several dukes ruling different parts simultaneously, there was only *one* Duchy, as an Imperial fief and only one Elector. This privilege was most often held by the Lüneburg line. Johann died in 1277 and his son Otto the Strong inherited.

3

The bells in the cathedral tower were ringing tierce. Johann looked up from the book he was studying in dismay. *The morning half gone already and there is so much more I want to review.* He looked about the library. The monks were already hurrying out and many of the students followed. But some remained deep in their studies, ignoring the bells. Johann debated for a moment whether to skip the office and continue his studies. The book he was using was in great demand and might not be available when he returned. But then he thought better of it. His last examination, in geometry, was scheduled at dawn tomorrow, right after prime, and he had been studying in the precious transcription of Boethius' Geometry commissioned by the great Bishop Bernward over two hundred years ago. But it was not this examination that worried Johann. He loved all forms of mathematics and knew he was good at it.

AD 1292

However, before he could take part in the commencement, all the students of his class had to undergo a moral examination, which had been the downfall of many students in the past. Not that Johann had any major sins on his conscience, but one never knew to what extent the examiners would look askance at the typically student minor scrapes with the townspeople, most of them instigated by his friend Tyle. No, Johann dared not miss any of the offices until that examination was behind him.

He took a piece of cloth to mark his place and reluctantly closed the book. He went over to the librarian, a rotund little old monk, who was so near-sighted he had to read with his nose practically touching the page. But it was said that he knew every book in the vast library by heart and that he could recognize each book by the color or decorations on its cover. The library at Hildesheim was one of the largest in Germany, boasting over a hundred books and manuscripts, and the old monk was justly proud of his charges.

"Brother Hugo," said Johann, "may I leave the book on my desk until I return from church? I must needs study more in it. And it will save you getting it out for me again."

"Well, I don't know," replied the old monk. "It is a very valuable book. It was copied from the original by the Deacon Guntbald for Bishop Bernward of blessed memory in the year 1011. . . ."

"I'll be back directly after tierce," interrupted Johann, who had heard all that before. "I promise you."

"Oh, very well," sighed Brother Hugo. "Just this once then."

Johann thanked him and hurried from the room, smiling to himself. Brother Hugo had been saying 'just this once then' to students for almost fifty years. Johann almost ran across the wide courtyard separating the school from the church, his gown flapping behind him. The warmth of the beautiful June day struck him forcibly after the coolness of the library, but he knew it would be cooler, even chilly, inside the great church. He bypassed the huge, ornately embossed bronze doors of Bishop Bernward at the main portal, which were only opened on the greatest of feast days, and reached the side entrance just as the bells stopped ringing. Breathless, he slipped into his seat as the priest began the office.

Johann noticed that the seat beside him was empty. Again. Oh, when will Tyle ever take anything seriously? he wondered. He bowed his head and began to pray. He made the responses to the office automatically but his mind was far away, wrapped in his own thoughts, thoughts of his future, and he did not yet know what that was to be.

Johann von Sehnden and Tyle von Eltze had been friends all their lives, although two more opposite young men could scarcely be found. Their families, too, had been friends for generations, an ancestor of each having served Duke Heinrich the Lion of Saxony over a hundred years ago. Yet in their very oppositeness Johann and Tyle seemed to complement each other. Johann was of medium build, strong and stocky, blond and blue-eyed, with a fair rosy-cheeked complexion, typical of his Saxon forebears. He was very intelligent, sincere and deeply religious. Yet his mind worked in a methodical, almost plodding, way and he had to study very hard, but once he learned a thing, he never forgot it. That was why he loved mathematics. Fanciful flights of philosophical debate held no appeal for him.

Tyle, on the other hand, was almost brilliant. He breezed through his studies with little effort, yet Johann suspected he forgot much of it just as quickly. The tall, dark, lean youth revelled in debating the most intricate aspects of Aristotlean theory. His brilliance overwhelmed most of his fellow students and he was a good match for many of the masters. Only his friend Johann knew that the brilliance was a coverup for a shallowness of character and a disregard for religion that was almost blasphemous. He was bored easily and often got into trouble picking fights during drinking bouts. He often displayed an obnoxious arrogance that made him many enemies, yet to his superiors and especially to the female sex he exuded such charm that they quickly overlooked his faults. Tyle usually had three or four beautiful women panting after him, while Johann had to settle for the quiet, mousey types that no one else seemed to want. Yet these suited him just fine. Johann often felt protective toward his friend, although Tyle was probably totally unaware of this and would have rejected it had he known.

Both the von Sehnden and von Eltze families were of the minor nobility of the Duchy of Braunschweig-Lüneburg. Both were more than well-off, but not so wealthy that several years of bad harvests or war would not have wiped out their assets. The tiny village of Sehnde had been a market town for the surrounding farms long before the manor house and demesne had been enfeoffed to his ancestor, the first *von* Sehnden, by Duke Heinrich the Lion. The von Eltze were slightly wealthier and somewhat nobler. They had a real castle on a hilltop and the village of Eltze had grown up around it and was completely dependent upon it. In fact, before Heinrich the Lion had put a stop to it, they had been robber-barons. And therein lay the difference, Johann thought. His family had always worked very hard for everything they had and there was a mutual interdependence between them and their people. The von Eltze took what they wanted and expected it as their due.

And now Johann was praying about his future. Both young men were third sons and their parents expected them to go into the Church. Although both had been knighted two years ago, as a matter of course, in an elaborate ceremony by Duke Otto, that did not preclude their taking orders. In a few days, God and the examiners willing, they would receive their *licencia docendi*, their bachelor's degree, from the prestigious Cathedral school at Hildesheim. This would enable them to teach under the supervision of a Master. In other words, they would be limited to teaching in the monastic schools and would be expected to become monks.

Johann was not at all sure that that was how he wanted to spend the rest of his life. He wouldn't have minded teaching. In fact, he rather enjoyed it. But taking Holy Orders was something else again. He liked

190

women too much, for one thing. Many years ago, priests could marry, but no longer. If he could teach in one of the new secular schools founded by the great merchants that were springing up all over the Hanseatic cities of northern Germany, he would have liked that. But in order to teach wherever he wanted, he would have to study three more years at a *studia generale*, or university, to get his doctoral degree. He would have enjoyed that very much, but he doubted that his father would be willing, or even able, to afford that. There were not yet any such advanced schools in Germany. The nearest and most famous was in Paris and that was a long ways away.

He knew his friend Tyle wanted even less to be a monk or even to teach. He had romantic dreams of being a knight-errant and making a great deal of money in tournaments, which were gradually taking the place of the constant petty feuds among the great lords. Several popes had outlawed these useless local wars, although they never succeeded in stopping them entirely, and tried to inspire the knights with the ideals of chivalry. Tyle would have liked to go on a crusade, but the last Crusade had ended disastrously some twenty years ago and people had lost interest. So Tyle dreamed impractical dreams of seeking the Holy Grail and wooing noble ladies from afar, and from not so far.

About halfway through the office, Johann's thoughts were interrupted by the rustle and rattle of his friend climbing over the kneeling students to slide into the place next to him.

"I thought you were never coming," whispered Johann.

"I almost didn't, but I thought better of it," replied Tyle. "I have wonderful news. Meet me afterwards in the cloister."

Glares and nudges from their fellow students silenced any further conversation.

After the service the students and monks filed silently out of the church and returned to their respective lectures and studies or work.

Johann caught Tyle's sleeve. "I have to go directly back to the library. I promised Brother Hugo. So tell me quickly this news of yours."

Tyle glanced around at the throng of students. "It is not for everyone's ears," he said mysteriously. They were speaking in Latin, as was required of every student for their entire stay at the Cathedral school. "Brother Hugo won't miss you for a few minutes. He has no sense of time at all. Besides, you know all those books inside out, almost as well as he does."

Johann made no reply to that, but his curiosity got the best of him. As he followed Tyle around to the cloister at the back of the church, he wondered what improbable scheme his friend was now cooking up.

191

Although the corridor of the cloister itself was busy with the traffic of monks, some hurrying about their duties, others quietly strolling as they meditated, the lovely garden was a serene island of otherworldliness. The young men went around the famous rosebush climbing up the wall of the apse and now in full bloom until they reached a tombstone on the other side. Here they sat down.

The tomb belonged to one Bruno, a priest who had died in 1192. He was undoubtedly one of the many Brunos descended from the famous Saxon heroes Wittekind and his brother Bruno. It was a favorite meeting place of the students when they wanted privacy. Johann thought about Bruno. Is this the sort of life I want? To spend the rest of my life in a cloister and never leave it even in death? Somehow he didn't think so.

He looked at the beautiful rosebush, now increasingly being called the 500-year rosebush, although many of the old townspeople claimed it was far older than that. There had been a Saxon shrine here long before the people were converted to Christianity, and the rose had been sacred to it. Charlemagne had built a small missionary chapel dedicated to the Virgin here, but had originally intended to found the bishopric at a place a few miles to the west, called Elze. The castle there belonged to a distant branch of Tyle's family. Charlemagne never got around to it, but in 815 his grandson Louis the Pious came to survey the area and on his way to Elze stopped for a brief rest at this spot. He hung his famous reliquary, which he never travelled without, on a branch of the rosebush. When he went to continue his journey, the reliquary was so tangled in the thorns that his strongest knights could not pull it out. He interpreted this to mean that the Virgin wanted him to seat his bishopric here in Hildesheim rather than in Elze. As soon as he promised to build the cathedral here the rosebush released the reliquary easily.

Tyle often joked, "But for a thorn, we would be bishops instead of knights."

Now the young men spoke in Low German, their native tongue, as no one could overhear them.

"So tell me now," said Johann, "what is this wonderful news that must keep me from my studies?"

"I have had a letter from my father," replied Tyle.

"So?"

"He has finally given in to my pleas to let me have a few years of freedom before I decide whether or not I want to take the vows."

"He really said that?" Johann knew his friend's exaggerations and half-truths too well.

"Well, not quite. But he has given me two years to see a bit of the world."

"And then?"

"Well—he still expects me to go into the Church. But don't you see, Johann?" Tyle exclaimed excitedly. "In two years I can certainly prove to him that a knight-errant can make a lot of money. Enough to support myself and certainly a wife, too. And I would make no claim on the inheritance. That's the only reason he wants me to go into the Church anyway. He knows I have no bent for it."

"Tyle, Tyle." Johann shook his head. "Do you really think you could do it? You could be killed as well, you know."

"Not nowadays. These tournaments are only games. They use blunted lances."

"I have heard of many deaths."

"Johann, you worry too much. Just think of all the money to be made. Why, I have heard of an English knight, William Marshall, who won so many tourneys that he was richer than his king. And the women. Can't you picture all those lovely ladies just begging the hero to carry their favors? We shall be in heaven."

"We?"

"Johann, I want you to come with me."

"My father would never allow it."

"Have you asked him?"

"It never occurred to me."

"But you've long wanted to go to University. Haven't you ever asked him about that?"

"I've mentioned it but never got much of a response."

"I'll tell you what," said Tyle, enthusiasm bubbling over. "After graduation, I'll come with you to your home on my way to Eltze. I'll tell your father that mine is allowing me the two years to go to Paris. I'll imply that I'm going on to the University. He'll let you go then. He would never allow the von Sehnden to be outdone by the von Eltze."

"Tyle, my father is not as gullible as that. Tell me true. Does your father know of your real plans for the two years?"

"No, of course not. And I don't intend to tell him. After we've convinced your father, you'll come to Eltze with me and tell him that you're going to the University of Paris and I'll hint that I am going, too. I plan to go to France anyway. That is where the best tournaments are. But this way maybe he'll give me a little more money than he promised me."

"Tyle, Tyle, you are too devious. I don't know what to say."

"But, Johann, you want to go to the University, don't you?"

"I'd give anything if I could."

"Then here is the perfect solution. If we go to your father together, he won't deny you."

Has anyone ever denied Tyle anything? Johann wondered. "I suppose it's worth a try," he said.

Tyle clapped him on the shoulder. "I knew you'd agree. Let's go out this evening and celebrate our two years of freedom."

"Tyle, I have an examination at dawn tomorrow and so do you," Johann reminded him soberly. "I am going back to the library. Brother Hugo is probably furious with me."

"The devil take Brother Hugo."

"Tyle, that's blasphemy."

Tyle only laughed as Johann left to go back to his studies. Johann wondered if his friend would admit all this to his confessor before the Commencement Mass. I doubt it. Would I? he asked himself. Perhaps I wouldn't either, knowing that the confessor would condemn the whole plan. Another doubt as to his true vocation crept into his conscience.

A few weeks later Johann and Tyle rode out of the castle at Eltze at daybreak and headed northwest. They had not only their respective father's blessing and a fat purse each, but student passports issued by the Duke himself. These 'safe conducts', originally authorized over one hundred years ago by the Emperor Friedrich Barbarossa, were worth their weight in gold, for they guaranteed, among other things, protection against unjust arrest, trial by their peers and the right to dwell in security. Moreover, they each had a sturdy servant to act as 'squire' and for additional protection, for the roads were never safe even in the best of times.

Johann still marvelled at how Tyle had glibly convinced his father that he was indeed going to Paris to study. The elder von Sehnden agreed that his son must have the same opportunity, and Johann seriously intended to make the most of it, regardless of what foolish plans his friend had. In fact, he hoped, once there, that he could stretch it to the three years required to earn his doctoral degree. His father did insist on one condition, however. And that was that they spend some weeks at each of several monasteries on the way, in order to become acquainted with the rules of different orders and their way of living. That way, he was sure, his son would find one of the disciplines to suit him. He was willing to give him the two years to find himself, but he refused to countenance any thought of his not entering the Church as either monk or priest.

So it was with high hearts that the young men set out on their journey. Their first lengthy stop was to be at the famous Premonstratensian monastery at Heiligenberg, founded in 1215 by the great St. Norbert himself. In about an hour they arrived at the ford across the Aller River at Celle.

"What is going on here?" asked Johann.

"Haven't you heard?" replied Tyle. "The Duke has decided to enlarge the new watchtower of the toll station into a full-fledged castle, and he's going to move the whole town over here to the island. He claims it is more strategic and more easily defensible than the old one, which is set back too far from the river."

"How interesting. But won't the people object to being uprooted from their homes?"

"Some have, and they can stay in the old town if they want. But most will be moving, for the Duke is offering ample compensation for their land, giving them larger plots and actually building the houses for them."

"And what are all these lines and squares on the ground?"

"That is the layout of the streets. Everything will be straight and square. No crooked, narrow streets. It will be completely preplanned, nothing left to chance. It will be the most modern town in Germany."

"There is your practical application of geometry."

"Leave it to you to say that, Johann. But truly it will be a wonderful town to see when it is finished. Well fortified, too. I understand the wall will enclose both the town and the castle."

Johann would have liked to linger to watch the workmen laying out the streets in precise patterns, but he knew they must press on. They hoped to reach Nienburg by nightfall. But Celle intrigued him. He would have to come back here someday to see it when it was all finished.

They crossed the Fuhse and took the road leading west to Nienburg on the Weser. From here on the countryside was flat and sparsely populated. Not a town, not even a village interrupted their progress. They rode through miles and miles of dense forest teeming with game.

"I wish I could have brought my falcon," sighed Tyle. "She would have caught us dinner in five minutes."

"It would not have been practical," said Johann. "I'm sure the weapons we have will suffice."

195

One of the servants brought down a rabbit with his sling. He quickly skinned it while the other built a fire, and dinner was roasting in minutes.

Towards evening they finally reached the broad, beautiful Weser and spied the town and castle of Nienburg on the other side. Thanks to the long summer days the ferry was still operating. They hailed the ferryman and when he saw that it was four passengers, he quickly rowed across to meet them. The men boarded the boat and the horses were left to swim in its wake.

Nienburg was the second capital of the Count of Hoya. He had taken over the town and surrounding countryside by guile and purchase not long ago, having decided it was safer than his ancestral castle at Hoya farther north, whose proximity to his perpetual enemy the Archbishop of Bremen subjected it to frequent attacks and pillaging. It was probably more comfortable, too, for the old castle was situated on a sandspit almost surrounded by the river and was always damp.

Having crossed the Weser, Johann and Tyle had now left their home Duchy of Braunschweig-Lüneburg, but the Count of Hoya was vassal to their Duke, so that they were still in friendly territory. They did not seek to stay at the castle, however, for Baron von Eltze had warned them that the Count was a little bit crazy and not to be trusted. Johann suspected that the real reason was that his father did not want the impressionable Tyle to come under the dubious influence of the wily and conniving count. Instead, they sought out an inn Tyler's father had recommended.

The inn was typical of the small towns, of inferior quality, but the only one available. That it existed at all was due to the fact that Nienburg lay on the ancient north-south Volksweg that ran along the west bank of the Weser, and merchants and traders had been stopping there since time immemorial.

After supping on a watery stew that contained more cabbage than the few chunks of unidentifiable meat and a tankard of thin beer, they bedded down, the servants with the horses in the stable and the young men in a large bed with two other guests. Johann would have preferred the stables, although that was beneath their dignity, for they got very little sleep between guarding their purses and scratching the fleas that infested the musty straw mattress.

The next morning they headed directly north along the Volksweg. It was beautiful riding along the lazy river. Occasionally they met other travellers and sometimes boats passed them heading downstream on the current to the great port of Bremen on the North Sea. Although there were still heavily forested stretches, villages and farms were more frequent now, all well kept and prosperous. Most were very, very ancient for this was the heartland of old Saxony.

"Think how many people have travelled this road before us," mused Johann.

"Now don't wax philosophical on me," replied Tyle.

"But I thought you enjoyed philosophy," teased Johann.

"Not now that I'm finished with school."

"But truly, they say this road led all the way to Rome even in ancient times."

"Then we're going in the wrong direction," retorted Tyle. "In fact, we should be heading west right now, instead of taking this detour to your monastery."

"It's not *my* monastery. Besides, I promised my father. We'll only stay a few weeks and then I'll have fulfilled that obligation."

"A few days would suit me better," grumbled Tyle.

They rode on in companionable silence and in a few hours reached the lovely little village of Bücken with its very ancient church, monastery and school.

"We must seek directions here," said Johann, "for here is where we must turn off for Heiligenberg, but I understand it is not a direct road."

"Why don't we just stop here?" suggested Tyle. "One monastery is as good as another."

"No, my father specifically mentioned Heiligenberg. Besides, this is exactly the same as Hildesheim, only much smaller. We would learn nothing different from what we have been doing the last five years."

"Lead on then."

They inquired at the monastery and were given directions to Heiligenberg.

"Are ye then so devout that ye seek the strictest rule in all of Hoya?" asked the chubby porter.

"We merely wish to visit them and learn of their rule," replied Johann.

"Have a care that you don't become permanent guests. They are very persuasive," said the monk.

"No fear of that," boasted Tyle. "But tell us, how are they so strict?"

"Well, to my mind they overdo the scourging and flagellation and the hair-shirt bit."

"Really?"

"And they're practically cloistered."

"But I thought they followed the Augustinian rule," put in Johann.

"Officially, yes," said the monk, "but they have been heavily influenced by Bernard and his Cistercians. Only the priests leave and go preaching all over the County. The monks and lay brothers stay put on that hilltop."

"I see," said Johann.

"Already I don't like them," said Tyle, "and you don't seem to either, Brother."

"I should not be Christian if I admitted that," replied the porter, "but they have caused us a great deal of harm."

"How so?"

"They have already taken over the churches at Vilsen and Asendorf and tried to insinuate themselves here, but we put a stop to that. Trouble is the Count and several of the powerful nobles, who seem to have guilty consciences, favor them. They are constantly endowing and enfeoffing them with rich farms and benefices to atone for their sins. It has hurt our living a great deal. We have been here over four hundred years and they less than seventy and already they are ten times richer than we, while we have been reduced to living off our students' fees and the few farms left to us right around Bücken here. Why, when we were founded, that Holy Mountain was still a pagan shrine, and to my way of thinking it hasn't changed much."

The young men were surprised at such vehemence. There was obviously no love lost between the two monasteries. A bell rang somewhere inside.

"We had best be on our way and we thank you, Brother, for the information."

"Wait," said the monk, patting his rotund belly. "We are about to have our midday meal. You had best take it with us, for today is one of their fast days and you won't get anything until tomorrow. They fast completely two or three times a week and never ever eat meat."

"Oh, my God," moaned Tyle.

After a hearty meal with the jolly monks of Bücken, the young men headed once again into the country. They passed several old farms, even neater and more prosperous than before. Then they entered a dense wood. The track diminished to nothing more than a path. Suddenly a clearing opened before them. A tiny but tall house stood next to a sparkling stream. But what was unusual was the huge wheel in the water at the side of the house. It was turning slowly, propelled by the force of the water falling over a dam behind the house. Inside the house they could hear a deep rumbling sound.

"It is one of those new-fangled water mills," exclaimed Johann.

"I believe you are right," agreed Tyle, for once showing some enthusiasm. "I have heard of them, but I've never seen one before."

The principle of the water-driven mill had been known to the Romans in antiquity, only to be reintroduced to northern Europe by the returning Crusaders, who had learned a much improved version from the Arabs. It had been a decisive factor in making the thirteenth century the turning point of the medieval economy.

"Let's stop and look at it before we go on," suggested Johann.

"Yes, let's," said Tyle. "I'm interested in seeing how it works."

They went to the door and knocked, but the sound was drowned out by the noise of the machinery and the rumble of the millstones.

"Halloo! Halloo!" they called out as loudly as they could. "Is anyone there?"

Finally the door opened and the dusty miller-monk, with a flour-covered apron over his habit, peered out.

"Who are you? What do you want?" he growled. "Can't you see I'm very busy?"

"Good afternoon, Brother," said Johann politely. "We are come to visit the abbey and would like to see your mill."

"This is private property and no one may come here except on abbey business," the miller replied.

"But we shall be guests of the abbey and are very interested in learning how such a modern mill works," said Tyle sincerely.

"Then go about your visit. No one comes in here without the Abbot's permission. Good day to you. I have work to do." He slammed the door in their faces.

"Well, I must say that was a warm welcome," said Tyle.

"I, for one, intend to get the Abbot's permission," Johann insisted. "This place fascinates me."

"I certainly hope the Abbot is a little more agreeable," said Tyle. "It will not be a very pleasant stay here if they are all like that."

"We're not coming here for pleasure," Johann reminded him, "but for the good of our souls."

"That's what I'm afraid of."

From the mill the path led up a steep hill for about a half a mile. At the top was a large walled enclosure. There was a gate with a bell but no porter's lodge. Since the gate stood wide open, they saw no need to ring the bell but rode straight in. To their left stood a large but very plain church, beyond that a fine new half-timbered house, which they assumed was the Abbot's. There appeared to be no cloister, but a partially covered passageway led from the church to another plain building that lay behind and stretched beyond the house. Next to that was a very large barn. Farther on lay an extensive orchard, still-green apples and pears hanging heavy on the branches.

The top of the hill was flat and formed a natural circle. To their right the path led to a half-dozen tiny thatched cottages and vegetable gardens. The entire center of the large circle was taken up by fields of ripening grain. Beyond the wall on all sides the forest lay thick and very still. They saw peasants working in the fields. Or at least they seemed to be peasants until Tyle and Johann noticed their habits tucked up between their legs.

"No porter and apparently no guest houses," observed Tyle. "What do we do first—tackle the Abbot in his lair or go into the church and pray for guidance?"

"Let's wait here a moment and see if anyone comes," suggested Johann. He glanced up at the sun. "It should soon be time for nones. Then at least some of them will come to the church."

Just then one of the horses whinnied and several of the workers in the nearest field looked up. One of them dropped his hoe and ran quickly to the Abbot's house. He did not go into the front, however, but around to the rear.

"Now something will happen," said Tyle.

A few minutes later the monk reappeared followed by another garbed in an immaculate white habit. The worker returned to the fields, and the other man approached the waiting party. He raised his hand in blessing.

"The peace of the Lord be with you."

"And with thy spirit," chorused the young men.

"Welcome to the Abbey of the Blessed Virgin Mary of the Holy Mountain. I am Prior Werner. What can I do for you?"

"I am Johann von Sehnden and this is my friend Tyle von Eltze. We are newly licensed clerks from Hildesheim and would like to visit with you for a while to learn something of your Rule, before we make our vows."

"I see," pondered the Prior. "Then you are not sure which rule you choose to follow? Why is that? Were you given no counselling at Hildesheim?"

"Oh, yes, my lord," spoke up Tyle. "They would have wanted us to stay there, but we seek more of a challenge than they had to offer."

"I see. But you are sure of your vocation?"

"Definitely, my lord. We both graduated with honors."

"Very well," said the Prior. "I shall arrange for an interview with Abbot Herman later today. Mind you, we have no guest houses here. We are deliberately located off the roads as we do not cater to itinerants. You shall have to stay in one of the lay brothers' cottages. You shall have to give up your horses. Your servants may take them to the barn. No one rides here except His Lordship. Your other possessions may be left in my keeping. You will have to wear your own clothes until you are accepted as postulants."

"But—but—" Tyle was about to object until Johann kicked him.

Just then the bell for nones sounded.

"Come, it is time for the office. Pray to Our Lady for guidance," said the Prior. "Afterward I shall show you around." He directed the servants to the barn and turned into the church.

"You and your big mouth," hissed Johann.

"I just thought to impress him," whispered Tyle. "I never thought he'd take us so seriously."

"Well, he did. And now we're in for it."

For the first time in his life Tyle looked humble.

They entered the church, which was as austere inside as out. There were no seats except for the choir stalls. They stood through the short service or knelt on the hard stone floor as required. They counted four priests, including the Prior, ten monks and some twenty or so lay brothers.

After the office as they left the church they greeted some of the lay brothers.

Their greeting was returned with nods, a few tentative smiles, but no words.

"Do they observe a rule of silence here?" asked Tyle.

"I didn't think so, but it certainly looks like it," replied Johann.

Outside, their servants met them with long faces. "There are no proper stalls for the horses, my lord," said Tyle's husky man Jacob. "We had to leave them in a meadow behind the barn."

"Not to worry," Tyle reassured him. "I don't think we shall be here very long."

"Where are the saddles and our gear?" asked Johann.

"Just inside the door of the barn, my lord," replied Dierck, the wiry little man who served him. "There was no proper place to hang them either. But we brought the saddlebags with us. We didn't like the look of that man in the barn."

Johann and Tyle exchanged looks as the Prior came out to join them.

"I shall advise Abbot Herman of your arrival. You may wait in the anteroom. The servants can wait here, unless you wish to send them home."

Tyle gasped. Johann quickly said, "I think it best if they remain at least until we have spoken with His Lordship."

"As you wish. Come."

They followed the Prior into the house. The anteroom was small and absolutely bare of any furnishings save a simple crucifix on the wall. They waited and waited. Finally the Prior returned.

"His Lordship is meditating now. He will be able to see you in about one hour. He has given permission for you to bide in one of the lay brothers' cottages until he decides if he will accept you. Come this way and then I shall show you around a bit."

He led them to one of the little cottages. Although sparsely furnished, at least it had a feeling of having been lived in. Stacked against one wall were six straw-filled pallets. On the other side was a bench and a small table. Although there was no fire in the small central hearth and the floor was beaten earth, there was an aura of warmth. Perhaps it was the tiny bouquet of wildflowers carefully placed under the crucifix. It had probably been a peasant's home before the monks came.

"Only three brothers sleep here now," explained the Prior. "The others are off working at some of our outlying farms. Meals are taken in the refectory, not here. However, today is a fast day. The next meal will be tomorrow after nones. Do not tempt your housemates into sin by speaking to them this evening. We observe a partial rule of silence here. Conversation is permitted only for one hour after sext and in the hours between vespers and compline except on fast days. The Abbot will explain the rule further. Come, I shall show you the rest you need to know."

As they filed out of the cottage, Tyle having to duck his head to clear the low door, Dierck whispered to Johann, "Methinks, my lord, to stay here with the saddlebags. Jacob can tell me later what there is to know."

Johann nodded.

The long building behind the Abbot's house contained storerooms and a kitchen on the ground floor and the refectory above.

"We also use the refectory like a chapter house, whenever His Lordship would speak to the entire congregation. The building beyond is the priests' and monks' dorter. There is no need for us to go there now. The barn is used for storage only. You will have no business there, unless the Abbot assigns you to work there later."

"But what if we wish to see to our horses?" asked Tyle.

"For the moment they are in the pasture. If you are accepted, you will no longer have any need for them. They will be given to one of our farms."

"But," sputtered Tyle, "they are not draft horses."

"No matter, they can be trained," said the Prior, dismissing the subject.

Johann, afraid that Tyle would lose his temper, laid a hand on his arm in warning.

"You may go anywhere else within the enclosure except the barn and, of course, the Abbot's house," continued the Prior. He led them around the back of that building. "Here are my rooms. You must never approach His Lordship directly unless he calls you. Any business with him must be directed through me. But rarely does anything arise that I cannot handle. If you are accepted, naturally you will not approach me directly either. You will have a confessor and a novicemaster to turn to for guidance."

Johann and Tyle looked at each other but said nothing.

"Now I shall leave you. Present yourselves at the proper time in the anteroom where you waited before. Meanwhile I suggest you go into the church and prepare yourselves. Pray to Our Lady for guidance in your vocation." He raised his hand as though to bless them, but did not, and turned into his room.

Neither of the young men made any comment until they had casually strolled some distance from any of the buildings, Jacob trailing behind.

"I'm ready to saddle up and leave right now," said Tyle.

"No, wait," said Johann. "Let us at least talk to the Abbot. I am sure he will understand when we say we only want to visit for a while. Besides, it's too late in the day to go anywhere now."

"I suppose you're right. No one could be as insufferable as that pompous Prior."

"He is a little dense, I'll admit," said Johann, "but he did say they are not used to visitors. He just could not conceive of anyone coming here other than as a postulant."

"Or on business," put in Jacob.

"What do you mean?" asked Tyle.

"That kind thinks that servants have neither eyes nor ears, but I can tell you why he doesn't want you going into the barn," replied Jacob.

"How so?" asked Johann.

"Because that barn is stuffed to the rafters with the strangest assortment of things I've ever seen in a barn. There are no stalls for animals except for the Abbot's horse and only enough hay for him. And one little corner where they keep a few farm implements. But the rest looks like a market—nay, like the tinker's, saddler's or cloth merchant's booth at a fair."

"Jacob, tell us what kind of things," asked Tyle.

"There's grain for one thing. But not like they were going to use it for themselves. All kinds—rye, wheat, barley, oats—and it's all measured carefully into baskets. And the pots and pans—iron cauldrons of all sizes, pewter bowls and beakers. There are saddles, harnesses, horse-collars, even boots and shoes, stacks of them, and bolts and bolts of linen cloth and I know not what else. Methinks yon monks are not so poor."

"Amazing!" exclaimed Johann.

"It seems like our friends are running a lucrative business, for all their piety," said Tyle.

"Mayhap the piety has to do with some guilty consciences," commented Jacob in his succinct peasant wisdom.

"Let us keep this knowledge to ourselves for now," cautioned Johann. "Shall we go into the church?"

"I, for one, can sort my thoughts out better in the fresh air," replied Tyle.

"As you wish," said Johann, "but don't be late for our interview." He left his friend and entered the church. He knelt down before a side altar. He was not even sure what saint it was dedicated to.

Father, he prayed, I may end up in a place like this even though it is not my first choice. Help me to look at it objectively. But he could not, as his thoughts whirled around. He said a Paternoster and a couple of Aves, and it helped calm him somewhat. But he still felt lost and confused. He stared up at the giant crucifix and tried to meditate on the wounds of Our Lord and the seven sorrows of His Blessed Mother.

After a while he sensed another presence and looked up to see Tyle kneeling beside him. I am glad he has decided to pray, too, thought Johann.

But his friend did not pray long. "It's almost time," whispered Tyle, even though they were alone in the church.

"I know," acknowledged Johann. "Let us go, although he'll probably keep us waiting. I am glad you decided to pray, too."

"You know what I was praying about?" asked Tyle, then added without waiting for an answer, "I was praying that he doesn't entice you to stay here. I know it's not for me, but I can't bear the thought of making that journey to Paris without you, my dearest friend. Half the fun would be gone."

Johann grinned and embraced his friend. "Don't worry, Tyle, God will guide us."

Once again they waited for a long time in the uncomfortable anteroom. At last a monk came from within and bade them enter. Abbot Herman was a tall, ascetic-looking man with a hawklike face and piercing eyes that seemed to look right into their souls. He stood behind a large table in his white habit, a beautiful jewelled pectoral cross his only adornment. As they knelt before him, he extended his ring for them to kiss, which they did.

"You may rise," he said, his voice deep and sonorous. He sat down on a stool behind the table but did not offer them a seat. "Prior Werner tells me that you seek to become postulants here. Why did you choose us?"

"That is not quite true, my lord," replied Johann. "He assumed more than we intended to convey. May I explain, Your Grace?"

"Please do," replied the Abbot.

"I am Johann von Sehnden and this is Tyle von Eltze. We are newly licensed clerks from Hildesheim. Although we believe we have the vocation, we do not yet know into which order we wish to make our vows."

"Were you given no guidance at Hildesheim?"

"Not really. They would have gladly accepted us, but understandably, they told us very little of all the other fine orders that serve Our Lord." The Abbot nodded. "So my father suggested we spend the summer visiting three or four different monasteries, so that we may learn of their different rules, before we make this important decision. We came here first because the Premonstratensians are so renowned for their piety."

The Abbot nodded again, obviously pleased with the compliment. "And where else do you have in mind to go?"

"Perhaps to Fulda or Corvey, maybe even as far as Cluny. We may also seek out the Franciscans."

The Abbot looked shocked. "Heaven forbid that two such noble young men as yourselves should become wandering, barefoot mendicants."

"But Francis himself was a nobleman, was he not?"

The Abbot shook his head. "The Franciscans are a disgrace. And as for Cluny, they have erred in the opposite direction. They have become so dissolute, so profligate. They are so burdened down under all their wealth, St. Benedict would never recognize his own rule. Stay away from Cluny for the sake of your immortal souls."

Johann was shocked at his vehemence. Even Tyle looked surprised. "Thank you for the advice," said Johann diplomatically. "Tell us then, what we may find here to our souls' edification, for we are woefully ignorant."

"We follow the Rule of St. Augustine with certain modifications laid down by our founder, Norbert of blessed memory. He, too, was a young nobleman gone astray until Our Lady came to him in a dream and showed him the error of his ways. He gathered his first disciples at Prémontré near Laôn in France, but most of his foundations were here in Germany. He ended up as Bishop of Magdeburg. This particular house came about when the Archbishop of Bremen, Gerhardt of blessed memory, wanted to establish a monastery somewhere in this area, being no longer satisfied with the monks at Bücken. Our Lady came to him in a dream also and made it clear to him that this holy mountain which had been sacred to the heathens would be the best place to stamp out the last vestiges of heathenism among the people. So he called us in and gave us the land and several benefices that belonged to it. That was in 1215.

"We are partially a preaching order and partially contemplative. The lay brothers also work on the farms. We are not cloistered, but the monks, who mostly serve by praying for our work and the souls of our people, may not leave unless ordered to accompany a priest and assist him in his work. The ordained priests are out constantly preaching the Gospel to the heathen."

"But I thought all the people hereabouts were Christians," interrupted Johann.

The Abbot shook his head sadly. "Nominally they have been Christians for three or four hundred years, but the old paganism is still rampant among them. Why, this very mountain was a pagan shrine and the people to this day hold it in awe because of that, not because we are here. They still have spring dances when they plant the fields and harvest festivals and bonfires on Midsummer Night."

"But they do that everywhere," said Tyle. "Is it so wrong that they have a little pleasure? Their lives are hard."

"It is paganism and we are here to stamp it out and convert their souls. Why, most of them still believe in elves and fairies. When they are ill they go to witches in the woods instead of praying to Our Lady."

"There are witches?" asked Johann.

"Many of them," replied the Abbot. "But when we catch them, if they don't recant and let us convert them, we burn them, make no mistake. But they are wily and the people protect them, so our work is difficult."

"Where do you preach?" asked Johann. "Do the people come here?"

"No, no. Our priests preach in almost all the village churches hereabouts, except Bücken. We sought to go there, too, for they have fallen into corruption, but they objected to the Archbishop and he forbade us. But we have permanent priests in both Vilsen and Asendorf, where they say Mass as well and tend to the needs of the parish. The rest move about from place to place, preaching, teaching, correcting and guiding the local priests."

"I see," said Johann.

"Then let me tell you briefly of our rule. We observe, of course, the usual vows of poverty, chastity and obedience. In addition, we fast on Wednesdays and Fridays throughout the year and three days a week during Lent. We observe partial silence. We strive to subdue the flesh in order to free the spirit. More of this will be explained to you as you progress. It is almost time for Vespers. Do you have any questions?"

"Yes, my lord. If we must observe the rules of silence, how do we ask questions in order to learn?" asked Johann.

"I shall assign a confessor to each of you. You may speak to him at any time except during the offices, at table or after Compline. How long do you plan on staying? I would suggest a minimum of three months."

"We had thought but a few weeks, Your Grace," replied Johann.

The Abbot scowled. "Hardly enough time to learn anything." Then he seemed to think better of it. "God will guide you, I'm sure."

"I have a question, my lord," said Tyle. "Are *we* bound to remain in the enclosure also, or will we be free to ride out occasionally?"

The Abbot scowled again. "Young man, you seem ready to escape before you even enter. Hardly a proper attitude. But no, you will be *expected* to remain here and seek guidance in your vocation, but since you have made no vows, I cannot bind you to it."

Just then the bell for Vespers started to ring. "We must go now," said the Abbot. "Your confessors will come to you later. I should like to speak with you again before you depart, but meanwhile I shall pray that you decide to remain with us."

They knelt for his blessing and left to go to the church.

Johann and Tyle settled into the regimen of Heiligenberg. For a few days they attended all the offices, rising in the middle of the night for Matins and Lauds, then Prime at dawn. After Mass they worked in the fields until Tierce and again until Sext. Then they were allowed an hour of 'recreation' when they could speak to the monks and lay brothers. In the early afternoon they studied the Bible and other sacred writings in the small library, which was nothing compared to what they had been used to at Hildesheim. After Nones they partook of the one frugal meal of the day, during which a lector read to the assembled company from edifying material. They then conferred with their confessors, who tried to guide them in the contemplative life. Between Vespers and Compline was another so-called recreation period, but they soon learned that only the lay brothers enjoyed this, the priests and monks preferring to read, pray or meditate. Each evening they fell gratefully onto their hard straw pallets for the short night's sleep.

It was not long before Tyle took to sleeping through Matins and Lauds waking barely in time for Prime. His confessor chastened him and gave him penances, but as he remarked to Johann, "A few extra Aves and Paternosters are worth a full night's sleep."

Johann meanwhile had not forgotten his interest in the mill. His confessor could not understand it. "A man with your education would be a miller?" he asked.

"No, no, Father. It is the mechanics of it that interests me. It is an extraordinary feat of engineering to make a small stream of water push those heavy millstones. I would learn how it is accomplished."

The priest shook his head. "That is hardly what you are here to learn."

But Johann kept at him until he finally obtained the Abbot's permission. The very next afternoon during recreation hour the two young men went to visit the mill. This time the miller was exceedingly polite and gladly explained the workings of the mill. Johann was fascinated by how the various wheels fitted within one another, not only to change the vertical thrust of the waterwheel into the horizontal movement of the giant millstones but also to enable the miller to precisely control the pressure needed to grind the grain into flour.

After this the two friends visited the mill frequently and met some of the farmers from the surrounding countryside, who were obliged to bring their grain here, as the lands they farmed were enfeoffed to the monastery.

"God's greetings to you," shouted one big, burly red-faced, brown-haired man over the rumble of the millstones. "I am Willem of the Bruns." He extended a huge calloused hand.

The young men shook it. "I am Johann von Sehnden."

"And I, Tyle von Eltze."

"Don't tell me two fine-looking lads like yourselves are learning to be millers," said the farmer.

Tyle laughed. "Never fear. My friend here is just interested in the workings of the machinery."

"Ach, ja," said Willem, "a damn sight better than we had not a hundred years ago when the women ground the grain by hand in querns."

The miller-monk glared at the farmer's profanity.

Tyle smiled. "Besides, it gives us a chance to get away from the monastery."

The farmer glanced at him in surprise and sneezed, a great bellowing explosion. "Come, let us step outside into the fresh air. The dust in here is too much for me."

The friends followed him out. "I usually prefer to stay in there and watch. No matter how much I sneeze. Never trust a miller, they say. But yon monk's ears are too big. You two are new lay brothers?"

"No."

"Novices, then?"

"No," replied Johann, "we are merely visiting, to become acquainted with their rule. We know not yet which order we seek to follow."

"Speak for yourself, Johann," said Tyle. "I have already decided that monkish ways are not for me."

Willem noticed Johann's embarrassment. "Rest easy, lad. You can trust your secret with me. And if you want my advice, seek elsewhere. The white monks are hard men to deal with. None knows better than we farmers."

"You are a vassal of theirs?" asked Johann.

"Ja, and all the farms hereabouts," sighed Willem. "But it wasn't always that way. We Bruns have lived here for hundreds and hundreds of years. Our forefather was Bruno, the brother of our great Wittekind. We always owned the land and were enfeoffed directly to the Count of Hoya. But no more." He lowered his voice. "The present count is a wild one, a little bit crazy, methinks. In order to atone for his many sins, which I won't

209

mention, he has turned over all the farms from Vilsen to Asendorf and beyond, for all I know, to the white monks. Now we must give them a tithe of all we produce, besides still paying a rent to the Count, out of which he, too, pays them something. And we still owe him our feudal dues of labor and military service in time of war, which happens often in these parts. Then we must also give a tithe to the church, which no one begrudged before, glad to pay it in fact, but now they have taken over the churches in both villages and so most of it goes right back to them. On top of all that, yon miller will take a tenth part of my grain, more if I don't watch him, in payment for grinding the flour."

"That hardly seems fair," commented Johann. "Why, you are paying almost double what you should."

"Ach, ja, don't I know it," said Willem, "but what can a man do but try to beat them at their own game? But they watch us, how they watch us. And always upbraiding us. Why you couldn't ask for better Christians than the good people hereabouts, but they say we're still heathens just because we keep the old hex signs on our barns. Who knows what manner of witches and devils be flying through the night when a man's sleeping? I, for one, trust the old magic more than yon monks' prayers." He looked a bit abashed at having said too much.

But Tyle reassured him. "Don't worry, friend Willem. Your secret's safe with us."

Willem relaxed. "Why, thank ye, lads. I guess I got carried away a bit. But I knew ye were good-hearted men the minute I laid eyes on you. But I tell ye, few hereabouts have any love for the white brothers. And since ye're my friends, I'll tell ye something else. If ever ye've a mind for a good meal on their fast days, go to my brother Hinrik's goodwife Adwilda. He's the cabinetmaker hard by the church in Vilsen."

"And we thank you, Willem," said Johann. "We just might do that, if we can ever get away that long."

"Ye're smart lads. Ye'll find a way. Now I'd best check on yon miller afore he takes double his share of my flour."

Just then the bell rang for Nones.

"Oh, my God," said Johann. "I had no idea it was so late." And he started to run up the steep hill.

"Best hurry, lads," called Willem, "or they'll take the scourge to ye."

But Tyle said, "Tell Adwilda we'll be there." And to Johann he called, "I'll not run up that hill. We're late anyway. What's a few more Aves?"

But the punishment was not just a few more Aves. Their confessors were irate. One of them collared the two young men after the office. "We have tried to be lenient with you when you missed some of the night offices. We understand that you are new and young and not yet postulants, but if your purpose is sincerely to learn of the rule, then you must accept the discipline of it. Today you have gone too far. You not only overstayed the recreation hour but skipped your study hour entirely and then had the gall to arrive after the office had begun. " You," he pointed to Johann, breathless, "and you," he pointed to Tyle, "strolling in as if you didn't care. Hardly a proper attitude. I fear for your souls. Whether you choose to stay or not, you *shall* observe the rule while you are here. For penance you shall remain here in the church on your knees, praying for your souls, until the end of Compline."

"You mean after dinner, Father?" asked Johann.

"I mean from this moment," replied the priest sternly. "You will go without dinner today.

"But Father," objected Tyle, "tomorrow is a fast day. That means two days . . ."

"You are not here to dwell on bodily needs but to learn to subject the flesh to the will of the soul. Perhaps next time you think to break the Rule you will be better disciplined." The priest turned with a swirl of his habit and left them alone in the church.

They knelt down and started to pray.

As soon as he was sure they were entirely alone, Tyle whispered to Johann, "Tomorrow we go to goodwife Adwilda in Vilsen."

Johann hissed back, "Tyle, how can you even think such a thing? We'll get into more trouble. We *were* wrong today, you know."

"According to their lights, mayhap. But I never claimed to have a monkly vocation. I'm just putting up with this to humor you. I hope this will open your eyes."

"Tyle, you know as well as I that he was right. One of the most important things a monk must learn is to subdue the desires of the flesh."

"Do as you wish, Johann, but tomorrow while you are subduing your hunger, I'll be enjoying a good meal with the goodwife Adwilda. She might even have some meat. Ah, I can taste it already."

"Tyle, the Devil is speaking through you to tempt me. I will not hear any more of it. I must give this thing a chance. After all, I promised my father."

"And that's the only reason you're going through this. You're no more cut out to be a monk than I am. Let us take leave of this place tomorrow."

"No, Tyle, not yet. Hush now and pray. Or at least let me pray."

Three hours later the white-robed monks filed in for Vespers and found the two young men still on their knees. No one spoke to them or even acknowledged their presence. After the monks left, Tyle started pacing around the church. This is ridiculous, he thought. Here I want to be a knight-errant and I am wasting my time in this desolate place. Why, we haven't even been able to exercise the horses. We should be on our way to Paris. But I won't go without my dearest friend. Oh God, please make him realize that this is not the life for him. And despite himself he found himself praying again.

Johann meanwhile persevered in his prayers and self-condemnation. He tried to achieve humility, but he did not feel humble. Humiliated was more to the fact. The more he tried to ignore his hunger, the more he thought about the possibility of a good meal in the nearby village of Vilsen. The more he tried to convince himself that he had a vocation as a monk, the more he thought about the university in Paris and someday teaching—or building mills or even laying out whole towns like Celle. It is the Devil trying to tempt me, to confuse me, he thought. But deep within he began to realize that he did not have the vocation, even though he did not yet know what he wanted to do with his life. But it is selfish of me to hold Tyle back. He *knows* what he wants to do. Yet it is equally selfish to renege on my promise to my father and his promise to the Church. Oh God, guide me, show me the way that Thou wouldst have me go.

By the end of Compline his knees were so sore and his back so tired that Tyle had to help him up. Back in their cottage their servants met them with long faces. Dierck pulled two pieces of dry bread out of his shirt and offered it to them.

"Maybe it will help," he said. "It was all I could steal. They watch us very carefully."

"That is wonderful," said Tyle. "Thank you, Dierck."

"How much longer do we stay here, young masters?" asked Jacob. "We can tell that you are not happy here."

"I would leave tomorrow, if I had my way," replied Tyle, "but I have yet to convince my friend Johann here."

Johann thought a bit before he spoke. "I will compromise with you, Tyle. I know I am not being fair to you, but let us stay at least one more week so that I can keep my promise to my father. But then we will not stop at any more monasteries except for overnight lodging. We shall go directly to Paris. Then while you are jousting and courting the ladies, perhaps I shall seek out a teaching order like the Dominicans. I don't know, but I agree that these Premonstratensians are not for me."

"Bravo!" shouted Tyle. "I could ask no more." He lowered his voice when their cottage-mates sighed and rustled their pallets. "And do we go to Adwilda's tomorrow?" he whispered.

"I don't think we should dare," replied Johann. "Let us at least try to discipline ourselves as long as we are here."

"And who might Adwilda be?" asked Jacob slyly, for Johann and Tyle had not seen their servants since they returned from the mill in disgrace.

"Do these holy brothers keep women here that we haven't discovered?" asked Dierck.

"No, no," replied Tyle, laughing. "The goodwife Adwilda is sister-in-law to our farmer friend Willem Bruns. He has offered us a good meal there any time this fasting here becomes too much to bear."

"Then I suggest we all go there tomorrow," said Jacob. "Even on the days we are allowed to eat, these monks begrudge us every morsel. If Dierck here didn't manage to steal us a bit extra, we'd be nigh on fasting every day."

"I didn't realize they were treating you worse than us," said Tyle. "Then tomorrow we go to Vilsen."

Johann shook his head doubtfully. "We'll see," was all he would say.

That night they dutifully arose for the night offices, but by late morning hunger and the lack of sleep were taking their toll. Johann could no longer resist the importuning of his friend and the servants. "But there is no way we can walk all the way to Vilsen, eat, and be back in only one hour," he warned.

"We can if we ride," said Tyle.

"But they will never let us take the horses," said Johann.

"My lord, if I may suggest," put in Jacob, "we have been exercising the horses almost every day, even though we nearly had a fight with the barn keeper the first time. If we were to take them down the hill a ways, until we were out of sight, you could meet us there."

"A capital idea," said Tyle.

"All right," Johann agreed cautiously, "but what if they stop you from leaving the enclosure?"

"We'll take them while you're at Sext. No one will be around," said Dierck. "Even yon miller will be there, but you must hurry out of the church before he does."

Not long after midday the four rode into the charming little village of

213

Vilsen. The very ancient stone church stood on the side of a hill surrounded by neat half-timbered houses and cottages, some large, some small, but all well kept and prosperous looking. Four of the largest boasted red-tiled roofs and real chimneys. The others were thatched. At the top of the hill stood a small, very ancient castle, the Altenburg.

"Now which can be the house of the cabinetmaker?" wondered Tyle.

"He said hard by the church," Johann reminded him.

"But it seems all the houses are hard by the church," replied Tyle.

They stopped in the road where a path led into the churchyard. "Dierck," directed Johann, "inquire at yon great house where we may find Hinrik the cabinetmaker master. This is not it, for I see no signs of a workshop, but surely they can direct us."

They watched as a dour-faced man in a white robe answered the door. Johann and Tyle quickly turned their heads. "Oh, no," said Johann. "Now we're in for it. I should have known that would be the Pastor's house."

Dierck returned. "You picked a good one to ask, my lord, but never fear, I told them we were come from Bücken to order some fine furniture from Master Hinrik. I know they're none too friendly with them at Bücken, and methinks this priest doesn't go up to the Holy Mountain very often, so it's not likely he knows of us."

"Good thinking, Dierck," said Tyle, "and now where do we find Master Hinrik?"

"Directly there across the Pastor's barnyard, but we must go around the cloth merchant's house and up the hill to the next street, called Garden Way, which runs in front of the wall."

The family was already eating dinner when the friends arrived, but Adwilda was not the least nonplussed to have four hearty young men join them. She was short and chubby, with thick blond braids wound around her head and rosy cheeks, only of average looks, but to the women-starved young men she looked beautiful.

"Welcome to our house," she said. "Willem sent word that you might be coming, but I didn't expect you so soon. But no matter, we have plenty. Come, children, move over, so our guests have room to sit."

Hinrik was a taciturn man who said little, but the three squirming children were consumed with curiosity, as was Adwilda herself, but she refrained from asking any questions until she had refilled the bowls on the table from the cauldron simmering over the round hearth.

The meal was simple but hearty, and Johann and Tyle appreciated it

214

more than many a banquet they had enjoyed in the past.

When they finished eating, Adwilda said, "I'm glad to see you enjoying the food. It appears as though you have been starved. What brought you so soon?"

"We very nearly were starved," Tyle replied and told her what had happened.

"Ach, ja," she said. "Those monks up there are strange men, although this Pastor they have given us is not too bad, if one doesn't pay too much attention to his sermons. He scolds us like we were all still heathens, just because we like to bring a little tree into the house and decorate it at Yule. Oh, I'm not supposed to say that," she corrected herself. "At Christmas. And we like to dance around the bonfires at midsummer. What harm in that? There are far worse sins. But he does take good care of the parish, like christenings and weddings and funerals and comforting the sick and the poor. And he teaches the children their letters, even them as can't pay. I suspect he charges the wealthy ones a little more. But what harm in that? I can truthfully say there's hardly a soul in this village that can't read and write and figure. We can thank them for that.

"But those up on the Heiligenberg, that's something else. I've heard they beat themselves raw with whips and scourges just for the pleasure of it. Themselves, mind you, not like they were beating someone else who stole from them or swived their wives, but themselves. Something sick about that, if you ask me. Have you seen aught of it?" She paused for breath.

"Not really," said Johann, "but we haven't been there very long. Besides we're staying in one of the cottages, not in the dorter."

"That's nice," she replied. "Those used to be the farmers' homes, you know, long before the monks came. In those days they worked directly for the Count."

"We suspected as much," remarked Tyle. "Even stripped as they are, they're a shade too comfortable for monks' cells."

"Ja, ja, and before that—well," she whispered, "you know that's always been a holy place, even in the time of the old religion. You want to know why they built the monastery there? Some say it's because the Archbishop had a dream. The monks say it's because it was still a heathen place and that's the only way they could keep the people from following the old ways. But you know the real reason?" She paused dramatically. "Power, that's what. Power. That place has been a holy place as long as there's been a Saxon people. And there is power there from even before that. Powerful

215

magic, I tell you, and when the monks came, they could feel it, too. They sought to take advantage of it and I guess it worked for them. In less than eighty years the white monks have become ten times richer and more powerful than the dear monks at Bücken could in over four hundred."

"That's very interesting and we'd like to hear more about it," said Johann, "but I really think we had better be on our way."

"Yes," agreed Tyle, "we don't want to get into any more trouble."

"Ach, bide a while," coaxed Adwilda. "What more can they do to you? Today's a fast day up there anyway and you've eaten."

"I suppose you're right," said Tyle.

"It's not often we get company from so far away," she said. "Where are you lads from anyway?"

"Braunschweig-Lüneburg," replied Tyle. "Our homes are not too far from Braunschweig."

"Ah, then you're Saxons, too."

"But there's no such thing as Saxony anymore," said Johann. "Not in the old sense anyway, and the new Saxony is far to the east."

"Well, don't argue that with anyone around here. This will always be Saxony as far as we're concerned. And hereabouts is the very oldest part of it, the ancestral lands. All the Bruns, and there are many of them, are descended from the great prince Bruno, brother to our great hero Wittekind."

"Yes, Willem told us that," said Tyle.

Hinrik spoke up for the first time. "And did he tell you that his farm by the Brüne spring was the marriage portion of Bruno's son, the first to become a Christian when Karl the Great was here?"

"No, he didn't. That's very interesting," said Johann. "Now I'm afraid we really must take our leave."

Adwilda ignored him and kept right on talking. "Have you been to the Sacred Spring yet?"

"No," replied Tyle. "Where is that?"

"Right there on the Heiligenberg," she informed him, "just down the hill a ways in a sort of ravine. It's the one holy thing from the old times that the monks haven't destroyed, even though they dammed up the stream to make the mill pond. It has very powerful magic. All our girls go there to bathe before their weddings. The monks don't like it much, but it's outside the enclosure, so they can't stop them. And it cures all sorts of illnesses, too. For some you drink it and for other kinds you bathe in it. You have to know, but there's power there still, I tell, you lots of power."

216

"We'll have to try it sometime," said Tyle.

"Tyle," urged Johann. "We really must go."

This time Tyle agreed. "Yes, I'm afraid we must, but we'll come back before we leave. Thank you, goodwife, for the fine meal."

"Yes, thank you so much," added Johann. "We really appreciated it."

"You are more than welcome," replied Adwilda. "We'll look forward to seeing you again."

The friends rode quickly down the winding lanes of the village and along the narrow track leading to Heiligenberg. They had almost reached the top of the hill when the bell for Nones started to ring.

"Oh, my God!" exclaimed Johann. "I had no idea it was so late. It was so interesting being with—uh—people again, the time just flew by. Now we're in trouble again."

"But we won't be late for the office, thanks to the horses," said Tyle.

"But we overstayed the recreation period," Johann reminded him.

"Mayhap, but it's not as bad as yesterday. Anyway, what can they do to us? We've already eaten."

At the top of the hill the young men left the horses with their servants and hurried to the church. They arrived just as the bell stopped ringing and quietly took their places with the lay brothers.

But for all their care, their escapade had not gone unnoticed. Immediately after the office their confessors once again confronted them.

"Where have you been?" they asked.

"We just took a walk through the woods," said Tyle.

"You lie. You took the horses."

"But they have not been exercised in a long time, Father," said Tyle.

"Besides, the Abbot himself told us we were not restricted to the enclosure, since we have taken no vows as yet," added Johann.

"But you overstayed the recreation period—again," said the priest.

"It is so beautiful here we forgot the time," murmured Tyle.

"Yes, Father, we were meditating in the woods," said Johann. "It is easy to commune with God in nature in such a holy place."

"Heathen talk—and more lies," sputtered the priest. "You have been eating somewhere, on a fast day. Have you no discipline at all?"

"No, Father," denied Tyle, "we just . . ."

"Don't compound your sin with another lie. I can smell onions and beer on your breaths," snapped the priest. "I shall recommend to His Lordship that you be sent away in disgrace as soon as possible, but meanwhile you must be punished for your waywardness. Let me see. Five

217

counts—overstaying the recreation period, eating on a fast day, and worst of all, three lies. It will go hard with you, I'm afraid. You will have the opportunity to confess, before punishment is meted out. Come with me."

The confessor led them to the Prior's rooms. The other priest went over to the monks' dorter. They waited in trepidation in the outer room while the confessor went in to speak with the Prior. They did not know what to expect. Neither one dared say a word.

Very shortly the priest returned with the Prior. The latter looked at them as though they were vermin to be crushed beneath his foot. At last he spoke. "I knew right from the start that you were not meant to be one of us. I doubt that you have the vocation for any order, but mayhap some place like Cluny, where they wallow in luxury, would be suitable for you. However, since you claim you want to learn of our rule, you shall learn of our discipline as well. Here we know how to subdue the wayward flesh to the spirit. We use the scourge and the whip deliberately to free the soul from the desires of our sinful bodies. It is very uplifting. You shall see." He paused for a moment to let that sink in. "You will make your confession before the entire company."

"Father," exclaimed Tyle, falling on his knees. "I wish to make my confession now." The priest sought to stop him, but the words poured out of him. "I admit that I came here under false pretenses. I know I have never had the vocation. I only came because my friend's father insisted we do, and I wanted to be with him."

"You would add cowardice to your sins as well?" sneered the Prior.

"No, no," cried Johann now on his knees as well. "Father, he is right. He only came to accompany me. I am the one who thought I had the vocation, but I admit I am too weak for your Rule. Let Tyle go, Father. I will take his punishment."

"As you wish," said the Prior.

"No, Johann," Tyle argued. "I can't let you."

"Nevertheless, you will," stated the Prior with finality, "and you will pray for his soul as you watch. Enough of this. Come." He led the way to the refectory, the priest holding the arm of each young man as if he were afraid they would run away.

The monks and lay brothers were already assembled. The monks stood in a double row, facing each other, about six feet apart. Each had a scourge or a whip in his hand. The scourges were five-tongued short whips with a knot tied at the end of each tongue. The lay brothers stood in a circle in the background.

"You knew," hissed Tyle to the priest. "You knew before you even spoke to the Prior."

"Naturally. It is customary in these cases," replied the priest sardonically.

"You are not men of God," retorted Tyle. "You are inhuman beasts."

The priest slapped him. "Enough of your insolence. Perhaps we should triple the punishment. On your knees." Two burly lay brothers pushed him down. "See that he does not look away — or cry out," the priest instructed them.

The Prior led Johann to the head of the line of monks. "Now make your confession."

Johann knelt down before him. He began haltingly, "Father, I have sinned. I have overstayed the recreation period. I have eaten on a fast day, but only because yesterday . . . "

"Never mind why," snapped the Prior. "The Devil in the person of your friend lured you. What else?"

"I lied."

"How many times?"

"I only lied once, Father."

"Remember you are taking on your friend's sins — by your own wish."

"We lied thrice, Father, and we are heartily sorry for these our sins and I humbly repent and promise to do better in the future." He paused as though he could not continue.

"Go on," urged the Prior.

"I accept whatever penance you lay upon me, knowing it is for the good of my soul, and I beg for your absolution."

"The penance will be two stripes for each of your sins, and again the same for your friend's sins, plus four more for insolence and lack of humility. I charge you to think of Our Lord's scourging by Pilate, think of His suffering and rejoice that you have the opportunity to share in it. After each stripe, you shall say with the prophet Isaiah, 'By His stripes we are healed and then an Ave. Now strip," he ordered.

Johann thought, twenty-four stripes. Oh, God, give me strength, he prayed silently. He stood up and took off his tunic and hose. A monk handed the Prior a scourge.

"I shall deliver the first four, then walk slowly down the line until the penance has been completed. Kneel."

The Prior raised his arm. Johann gasped as the first blow struck. "By His stripes we are healed," he said. "Ave Maria . . . " Two. Three. Four. "By

219

His stripes we are healed. Ave Maria, gratia plena . . . "

"Now get up and walk—slowly," snarled the Prior.

Johann staggered to his feet. Five, six. "By His stripes we are healed. Ave Maria . . ." Some of the monks struck him lightly, as if they were sorry they had to do it, but others struck with a vengeance as though to punish him for the chastisement they customarily inflicted on themselves. Seven, eight. I will not cry out, Lord, give me strength, he prayed. Nine, ten. I will not faint. Eleven, twelve. The knots bruised his flesh until it felt as though his ribs were going to crack. Thirteen, fourteen. The whips opened the welts from previous blows into bleeding cuts. Fifteen, sixteen. He stumbled and fell, but the monks hauled him to his feet. Seventeen, eighteen. Sweat and tears burned his eyes, he could scarcely breathe. The agony was unbearable. Nineteen, twenty. One of the monks was a vicious master of the whip. He deftly curled the whip around Johann's body until the tip flicked against his bare penis. Twenty-one, twenty-two. Johann screamed, doubled over and fainted.

Tyle broke from his captors and rushed to his friend's side. "You've killed him, you devils."

"Enough," called the Prior. No one was sure if he spoke to Tyle or to the monks.

"But the penance is not complete, Father," complained the last monk, who had been relishing delivering the last blows.

"Then finish it," said the Prior coolly, "but revive him first."

"No! no!" screamed Tyle, trying to shield Johann's torn body with his own. But the lay brothers dragged him away. Someone brought a bucket of water and threw it in Johann's face. He moaned and his eyelids flickered.

"Finish it," ordered the Prior.

The last monk struck his blows and Johann fainted again. "It is finished," said the monk. All Tyle could think was, those were the last words of Jesus before He died. He was sure his dearest friend was dead.

"Thank you, Brothers," said the Prior and blessed the entire company. "You may go now. Pray for his soul." They filed quietly out of the refectory and left Johann in a pool of blood on the cold stone floor.

Tyle's guards released him and he ran to his friend. "Johann, Johann," he wept. "I have done this to you. Oh, God, forgive me, but will *you* ever forgive me?" And as he knelt by the bloody, broken body, he realized that his friend was still breathing. A vein in his neck pulsed. "He lives, he lives."

"Of course, he lives," said the Prior. "What is a little beating like that? If he had not been such a weakling, he would now be in ecstasy. Thank God for lifting his spirit out of the filthy cage of his body."

Tyle ignored this. Instead he reminded the Prior, "You have not yet absolved him."

"He did not complete the penance."

"What!" exclaimed Tyle. "Twenty-four stripes, you said. He lies here half-dead, and you say he did not complete the penance. How can you?"

The Prior smiled. "He did not say the last Ave."

"Oh, God, I shall say it for him," said Tyle and promptly did so. The Prior then pronounced the absolution over both of them.

"I shall send your servants to you. Get that sorry thing out of here immediately." He nudged Johann's prostrate body with his foot. "I shall expect you to leave Heiligenberg before Prime tomorrow." He walked out and left Tyle weeping over his friend.

Tyle had been wondering where the servants were. Surely had they been here we could have prevented this. When they burst into the room a few moments later, the shocked looks on their faces gave him his answer.

Dierck exclaimed, "By all the saints, what has been going on here?" He knelt down by his master.

Jacob explained, "They had us locked in the barn all this while. We knew something was amiss, but we never imagined anything like this. Will he live, do you think?"

"I don't know," moaned Tyle.

"Of course, he will," said Dierck, taking charge. "It is not a pretty sight, but I have seen far worse right in the marketplace at home. Let us cleanse his wounds before we move him. The main thing is to prevent putrefaction. It is better if we do it before he regains consciousness. The pain will be terrible. Jacob, fetch some water."

As Jacob ran to do his bidding, Dierck began to search through the various chests and cupboards in the large room. At last he found what he wanted, several small squares of linen and a large tablecloth.

"Aren't those altar cloths?" asked Tyle.

"I don't care if they are the Devil's diapers," replied Dierck. "They are clean."

Jacob returned with the water. Dierck carefully cleansed Johann's wounds. When he had washed away the copious blood, the back did not look quite so bad. It was covered from top to bottom with bruises and welts, but there were only two or three places where the skin was broken and only one of these was a deep gash that kept bleeding. Then he placed the tablecloth beside Johann.

"Now let us carefully lift him onto this. Don't let him roll over onto his back." They did as they were told. Johann moaned in agony.

Tyle stopped. "We are hurting him," he said.

"No, no, my lord," said Dierck. "Hurry now. We must get him back to the cottage before he wakes up. Jacob, fetch a bucket of clean water." Jacob did so. "Now, my lord, if you don't mind bringing along that bucket and more of those clean cloths, Jacob and I will carry him on the cloth like a stretcher."

Back at the cottage Dierck directed, "Keep the cloth under him. Those pallets are filthy." Gently they laid Johann down. He moaned but remained unconscious. Dierck wet several of the small cloths and laid them across Johann's back. "If we keep them wet until the bleeding stops, it will not stick and tear the wounds open again," he explained. "Also, it will help cool the bruises and welts so they will not swell too badly. If only we had some of my old mother's unguent to put on that one bad cut, it would heal without leaving a scar. She was a skilled healing-woman, God rest her soul. I wish now I had listened more carefully when she tried to teach me, but I was young and wanted no part of womanish things. Well, we'll have to make do as best we can."

"They must have a physicker here," suggested Tyle.

"No, my lord," said Dierck. "I would never let him near my lord Johann. The fool would only bleed him and he has lost too much blood already. Besides, I doubt that he'd come, saying he only tends to the sick and that this man isn't sick but, according to their lights, deserving of his punishment."

The three men sat in silence, watching Johann struggle to breathe, each wrapped in his own thoughts. Suddenly Dierck struck his forehead. "I must go and steal another tablecloth to cover him with."

"But surely the day is very warm," said Tyle, "and he seems to be feverish. Would he not be more comfortable without it?"

"But it grows cool here at night," Dierck reminded him. "But more than that, he may be in shock when he awakes and will shiver violently. Fever or no, we must keep him warm. When is Vespers?"

"It should toll very soon now."

Dierck nodded. "As soon as they are all in the church, I shall fetch it." He pondered for a moment. "You know, my lord, even if he wakes from his swoon during the night, he will be in no condition to ride forth tomorrow."

222

"I was thinking the same thing," said Tyle. "What are we to do? I'll not stay here another day, but I'll not leave him either."

"If I may make a suggestion, my lord," put in the taciturn Jacob, "because I have been worrying about it, too. Could we not take him to the goodwife Adwilda?"

"But how do we get him there?" asked Dierck.

"Didn't you say the farmer Willem had a wagon, my lord?" asked Jacob.

"Of course!" exclaimed Tyle. "I was so anguished, I didn't think of it. Do you think she will mind?"

"I'm sure she won't," replied Dierck, "and I'm willing to bet that she knows a wisewoman, too."

"Then we must make arrangements before nightfall. Thank God it's summertime," said Tyle. "Jacob, as soon as they ring Vespers, take one of the horses and fly."

"The barn will be locked then, my lord, and I won't be able to get a saddle. I'd best go now."

"Then take care, Jacob," said Tyle, "and if that monk at the barn gives you any trouble, give him a taste of their own ecstasy."

"Happily, my lord," replied Jacob and ran out the door.

Not long after, the bell rang for Vespers.

"I should really go and pray for him" said Tyle doubtfully, "but I don't even want to see those men again."

"God will hear your prayers just as well from here, my lord," commented Dierck. "Besides, you must stay with him while I go to fetch another cloth. Bathe his face with a cool cloth every so often. I shall be back quickly." A moment after the bell stopped ringing he left.

Tyle knelt by his friend and placed a wet cloth on his feverish forehead, then took his hand and held it. "Johann, Johann, my dearest friend, I did this to you. I was too cowardly. I thought if I told them I had no vocation, they would let us go. Instead they put it all on you. Will you ever forgive me? Oh, God," he prayed, "heal my friend, in Thy great mercy. Let him not be angry with me." He put his face in his hands and wept.

Johann stirred. "By His stripes . . . " The words drifted off to a mumble.

Tyle quickly wiped his friend's face. "Johann, Johann, are you awake?"

Nothing.

Tyle took his hand again and in a few moments he could feel a slight pressure against his own.

Johann tried to shift his tortured body. "Ave Maria . . . I have sinned . . . I am no longer worthy . . . " His breath came in gasps. He tried to lift his head. Then he screamed and fainted again.

Just then Dierck came back with the second cloth. "What is amiss?" he cried.

"I think he is coming to," said Tyle, "but it seems as though he is reliving the whole thing."

"That often happens. We must be patient. The shock to the body is so great, it sometimes affects the mind."

"You mean—you mean he might be out of his mind? Crazy?" asked Tyle, shocked.

"Not permanently, my lord," Dierck reassured him, and prayed it would not be so, for he knew that it sometimes happened. "But remember, his last memory is of them still scourging him, so the first hour or so after he awakens, he may think he is still in the midst of that. We must be exceedingly kind and gentle with him, and—don't weep, my lord—above all, we must be cheerful."

"Cheerful?" echoed Tyle in disbelief.

After Vespers the three lay brothers whose cottage they shared came in, picked up their pallets and two of them left without so much as a glance at them. The third lingered a moment.

"How fares the young man?" he asked hesitantly.

"Not good. He is still unconscious and in great pain. For a while we feared for his life," replied Dierck when he saw that Tyle was not going to answer the man.

"I am sorry, truly sorry." He glanced down at the pallet under his arm and explained, "We have been ordered not to stay in the same house with sinners."

At this Tyle exploded. "Sinners! How can you say that? The Prior himself absolved us. Both of us."

"The Prior has been known to contradict himself ere this," he replied softly. "If it's any consolation, Abbot Herman is away and knows nothing of this. I don't think he would have let it happen. It shouldn't have happened at all, in my opinion. But," he shrugged his shoulders, "Prior Werner is in charge when His Lordship is away. I wish I could help, but I dare not. I shall pray for your friend—and for you all."

"Thank you, brother," said Tyle and Dierck together as the man hurried out of the cottage.

After a time Dierck said, "I suggest you try to sleep a bit, my lord. One of us will have to watch with him all night. And if Jacob does not return before dark, he may not come back until first light." No man in his right mind would be on the roads at night if he could help it. Not only for fear of highwaymen, but who knew what sort of devils and demons haunted the watches of the night ready to snare a man's very soul from him or turn him into a frog or a werewolf? "I shall sit with him until midnight and then I shall wake you."

Tyle nodded. "I suppose you are right, though I doubt I can sleep. But promise to call me if he wakes."

"Certainly, my lord."

Time passed slowly. Tyle fell asleep despite himself. Dierck watched his master's shallow breathing. Compline came and went and Jacob did not return. Dierck was not surprised. He suspected Jacob had to ride not only into Vilsen to alert Adwilda of their coming but then back several miles in the opposite direction to Willem's farm. Still he prayed for the other servant's safety, as well as for his master's recovery. Johann stirred several times and mumbled disjointed words, most of it incoherent nonsense. Dierck did not disturb Tyle, however, for he knew it was still the delirium of the fever and pain. At last Matins rang and he nudged Tyle awake.

"I shall watch together with you, my lord, for a little while," he said, "for I think he will wake soon, and, as everyone knows, a man's soul is at its most vulnerable in the middle of the night. I would not have the Devil snatch it away when he is so weak. I wish we had a fire on the hearth. It helps keep the demons out, you know."

Tyle nodded and shivered. "I shall unsheathe my sword and stand between him and the door."

Not long after, Johann's eyes flicked open and Dierck could see they were clear.

"Dierck, Dierck, my loyal servant," he murmured. "Am I still alive?"

"Indeed you are, my lord, and God be praised."

Johann tried to raise himself on his elbows and fell back. "Ow, my back! Water. Do you have water?"

Dierck quickly took a dipperful from the bucket and held it to Johann's lips. "Slowly, my lord," he warned as Johann tried to gulp it down.

"My dearest friend," said Tyle as he dropped his sword and knelt by the pallet.

"Tyle," asked Johann, "and how fare you? Did they hurt you, too?"

"No, Johann, I am fine. Only worried about you. Will you ever forgive me, my friend?"

"Tyle, no, don't think such a thing," replied Johann. "There is nothing to forgive on my part, but, tell me, did that—did we receive absolution?"

"Yes, we did, Johann, although he almost wasn't going to do it. I made him."

"Good, then we are in a state of grace. Now see if you can help me up. I fear I shall be terribly stiff. How bad is it, Dierck? It feels as though I were kicked by ten horses and scratched by twenty cats."

"And it looks almost as bad, but really only one cut still bleeds when you move and even that could heal without a scar if we could get some unguent. But it will take time."

"There is certainly no unguent to be found here. They probably revel in counting who has the most scars," said Johann ruefully. He tried once again to get his elbows under him and this time succeeded in keeping his head up, although the pain the effort cost him was obvious in the sweat that poured from his brow. "Anyway, help me to get up. I have to pee."

"Don't roll over on your back, my lord," cautioned Dierck. "Try to get your knees up under you. Then we'll help you to stand."

With tremendous effort they got him to his feet. Everything whirled around him. "Wait," he said. "I am dizzy. I have no wish to swoon again." They held him up until the dizziness passed. "Now help me outside before I burst."

Dierck draped a cloth over his shoulders. "You must not take a chill, my lord," he warned when Johann groaned.

When they returned, Johann sat down gingerly and tried to examine his penis, but it was too dark to see anything. "That finished me, when they tried to cut my prick off. But I feel from the pain that it's still there, thank God. If that's their idea of celibacy, I want no part of it."

Everyone roared with laughter and it broke the terrible tension.

"Tyle, we must leave here, just as soon as I can ride."

"We've already been ordered to do so before Prime," replied Tyle.

"Then ride I will, if it kills me," asserted Johann.

"There'll be no need for that, if our plans go right," said Dierck.

"What plans?" asked Johann. "And, by the way, where is Jacob?"

"We have sent him to the farmer Willem to bid the use of his wagon," explained Tyle. "We hope to go to the goodwife Adwilda and there bide until you are healed and fit to ride again."

"An excellent plan, Tyle, and I shall reward her generously," said Johann.

"It was actually Dierck's idea," admitted Tyle. "I confess I was too distraught to think clearly."

"Well, be distraught no more, my friend," Johann reassured him. "I promised you no more monasteries except as overnight guests, and I mean it more than ever now."

Tyle smiled for the first time.

Shortly after daybreak, at least an hour before Prime, Jacob rode in.

"Ah, my lord, I am happy to see you revived," he said to Johann. "Willem comes with his wagon not far behind me and the goodwife *insists* that we bring you there. What's more, she knows a healing-woman whom she will fetch as soon as you are settled in."

"Wonderful," said Dierck. "Let us go and saddle up the other horses and load on the saddlebags. And then me must help my lord Johann walk to the wagon. I, for one, cannot be quit of this place soon enough."

Johann held up his hand. "Wait, we must speak to the Abbot first."

"The Abbot is not here," Tyle informed him. "He knows naught of what took place. It seems yon Prior grows overzealous in his duties when he is left in charge."

"Then let us away, and right quickly."

Adwilda had made her own and Hinrik's bed ready for Johann when they arrived. It even had that luxury of luxuries, a feather mattress.

Johann objected. "I'll not turn you out of your own bed, goodwife."

"Nonsense," she replied. "For a few days we can easily share the loft with the children. Your back will heal the faster if it is not irritated by straw. The rest of you will have to bed down over the stalls, but there is plenty of room and the straw is fresh and clean." She also had a pot of nourishing broth simmering over the fire. "Here, drink this while it is hot. It will give you strength. Then take your tunic off and let me see what needs to be done for your back."

Johann winced as she pulled the tunic over his head. The blouse had stuck to the congealing blood, and furthermore, he could barely lift his arms. He moaned as she carefully felt each one of his ribs and examined the welts. "Nothing that won't heal in a few days. But I shall go to the wisewoman for some of her unguent. It will keep the skin flexible as it heals and prevent putrification. She will have something for the pain as well."

"Let my servant go with you," said Johann.

"Nay, nay, she doesn't trust strangers." She started looking through her cupboards. "Now what can I take her? Ah, a jar of honey will be fine."

"I insist on paying her," said Johann.

"Nay, she doesn't trust these new-fangled coins either. But I shall be happy to take your money, my lord, for my honey," she hastened to add as she threw her shawl over her back and went out the door.

By the next day Johann was able to walk unaided, although he was stiff in every muscle of his body.

" 'Tis better if you move about, my lord," suggested Adwilda. "Why don't you take a stroll about the churchyard? 'Tis a pleasant day and the sun on your back will help loosen it up."

"Yes. A good idea. Come, Tyle, walk with me."

The two friends wandered about the neat churchyard. A few grazing sheep kept the grass trim. Here and there people had planted flowers on the graves. Butterflies and bees hummed among them. A cuckoo called from the top of a giant linden tree that overshadowed the church. It was very peaceful.

"Come, let us sit a bit," said Johann at last. "I find I am tiring more quickly than I expected." They sat on an ancient tombstone.

"It is very old," remarked Tyle.

"Yes, let's see if we can read it."

"It is too weathered."

"Nay, here is a bit I can make out. It is the date—the something September 1048. That *is* old indeed. I can't make out the name. I wonder who has been lying here all those years."

"A Bruns, no doubt," said Tyle.

Johann laughed. "Very likely. This seems to be their country. I wonder how old the church is."

"Even older, I should guess."

The church was small but solidly built of large fieldstones. It was in the old style which was beginning to be called Roman as opposed to the new style called Gothic. But they could see new stonework around the windows. An attempt had evidently been made to enlarge the small windows of the old style to let in more light and the result bore a slight resemblance to the pointed Gothic. The tower was square with thick walls and a crenellated top, as if it had been a fortified church at one time.

"Shall we go in and offer a prayer of thanksgiving?" suggested Johann. Tyle nodded.

The friends crossed themselves as they entered. The chill struck them immediately. The very thick walls shut out all the day's warmth. But once inside they were caught up in the glow of the most beautiful paintings either had ever seen. There was no stained glass such as proliferated in the new cathedrals and churches springing up all over Christendom, but every available bit of wall space was covered with colorful patriarchs and prophets, saints of every description. As much of Holy Scripture and the lives of saints as could be squeezed into it was there. They approached the altar across the huge flagstones. Above it hung a large, delicately carved crucifix, on either side of which were life-size paintings of the Virgin Mary and the beloved disciple John. All of this looked relatively new, but the altar itself was very old and had strange markings carved onto it.

They knelt on the chancel steps and prayed.

At length Tyle whispered, "It's beautiful, isn't it? This is my idea of a church, not that barren shell up at Heiligenberg."

Johann nodded. "It must be to inspire even you."

They suddenly sensed a presence behind them. They turned to find the white-robed pastor watching them.

"God's blessings on you, my sons," he said. "I am Father Hildebrandt."

"Thank you, Father, and good morning," they replied timidly, wondering if they should tell him who they were. More than likely he already knew.

"I noticed you admiring our lovely church. The building is over three hundred years old, but the paintings were done less than twenty years ago, not long before I was appointed here. The crucifix was carved about a hundred years ago."

Johann, who had expected another lecture, warmed to him. "Yes, it is all very beautiful and inspirational. I suspected the building was about that old. We read one of the tombstones outside."

"You can read then?" asked the priest.

"We are clerks from Hildesheim," said Tyle.

"Then you would be interested in the history of this place, at least what I know of it."

"Yes, indeed we should," replied Johann with more enthusiasm than he really felt.

"This is the third church here. The original was built by Bruno, the nephew of Wittekind, shortly after his conversion. This had been a holy place for the heathens long before that. It was dedicated to the martyrs who died here when Charlemagne tried to convert them, but since they were pagans and not Christian martyrs the Archbishop refused to consecrate it until they changed the name to St. Cyriacus. But the people are stubborn here and the old name Vilsen stuck to both the church and the village. The Church even tried to get them to call the village Aldenburg after the old castle. The Counts of Hoya use that as one of their titles, but the people would not have it, so Vilsen it remains. Not many people remember how it all came about, so the Church no longer bothers to press for the change. The first two churches were wooden and burned. Then they finally built this one. It is so sturdy because it was also a place of refuge in those troubled times."

"That is very interesting," said Johann.

"Yes," agreed Tyle. "Let me ask you Father, a beautifully decorated church like this seems to contradict—uh—what we know of the austerity of your order."

Johann was ready to kick Tyle again, but the priest took no offense at the question. "As I said, it was done before I took office here. Heiligenberg was only granted this benefice by the present Count. He—uh—has many sins on his soul. But while we do not encourage frivolity, we only practice austerity in our own abbey churches. I have no objections to anything that helps the people learn about their religion."

Johann was pleasantly surprised at this. Perhaps this priest was different from his brethren on the Holy Mountain. He said, "We have heard that you teach the children their letters. That is very good of you."

"Yes," replied the priest. "I believe that no man should sit in darkness."

Johann tried to think of something else to say. He felt very awkward. "The altar seems to be very old as well. What are those strange carvings on it?"

"Ah, I can see you are a scholar," said the priest. "Very few people even notice that they are not just decoration, and fewer still can read them. They are runes, the alphabet of the old Saxons. The altar is far older than the original church. It was a pagan altar which the people insisted on keeping for the first church. So the Church reconsecrated it just to keep the peace and carved crosses at the corners, as you can see. I wish I could read it, but if there were anyone who could teach me, I would never hear of it. They would be too afraid to admit to their knowledge. But I doubt that there is. The reading of the runes was a closely kept secret of the pagan priests and unfortunately, very few of them chose to accept Chris-

230

tianity and Charlemagne put them to the sword, so the secret died with them. Most of the people today don't even know that it is writing. They just regard them as magic symbols, and the Church has capitalized on that, so that they now associate them with the power of the Body and Blood of Christ."

"That is indeed interesting," said Johann. "Father, I believe we have learned more ancient history of the Saxon people from you and from the people we are visiting than we ever did at Hildesheim. They just stopped at Charlemagne and then skipped back to the Roman emperors and to the Bible, as if no one even existed here before him."

"I am afraid there are many in the Church who choose to ignore the fact that every land and people, even many in the Bible, were heathen before Our Lord came to lighten the Gentiles."

"And yet you allow a pagan altar in the church when I understand your order is vehement about stamping out paganism," blurted Tyle.

"The Church in her wisdom has had to make many compromises. If the people can better understand their Christianity by means of some of the old ways, then I believe in using them. No one has shown this better than the great Thomas of Aquinas, lately of the University in Paris. He has taught how even the philosophy of the pagan Aristotle can help us better understand our own religion."

"Ah, Paris," signed Johann, "we shall be going there soon. We hope to study there."

"Indeed?" replied the priest somewhat skeptically. "And do you seek a true vocation there? Or do you just seek freedom to drink and wench and brawl?"

"What do you mean?" asked Johann, offended and immediately wary.

"You see," replied the priest gently, "I know who you are and what happened up there on the Heiligenberg. I'll not condemn you again, but if you tell me the truth, perhaps I can advise you. Although it matters not whether you tell me the truth, it is important that you be true to yourselves."

"Thank you, Father," said Johann hesitantly, not sure whether to trust this man or not.

"We did tell the Abbot the truth," insisted Tyle, "or at least part of it. He knew we were only there as visitors to learn about your order. Was it our fault that they have no facilities for guests? But that Prior—that—that . . ."

"I know," said Father Hildebrandt soothingly. "I cannot criticize his

231

actions, even though I am not subject to him but only to the Abbot and the Archbishop, but it is well known that Prior Werner hears only what he wants to hear. I shall say this though, I know it would never have happened had His Lordship not been away."

"So we were told," murmured Johann. His back was beginning to pain him intensely now, and he longed to get away. "I think we have taken enough of your time, Father . . . "

"They nearly killed him, Father," interrupted Tyle vehemently. "They had no right to do that."

"Tyle, Tyle," said Johann, "let it go. It is over and done with. If you'll excuse us, Father, I am suddenly feeling very tired."

"Of course, how thoughtless of me," said the priest. "Has the wise-woman been to see you?"

"We understand she is leery of strangers," said Tyle.

"I'm afraid that's true," said the priest. "I know she will only come into the village when I am away. More's the pity, for she is a very skilled healing-woman. May I come to visit you tomorrow?"

"If you wish."

Out in the bright sunshine once again, Johann shivered and Tyle had to support him on the short walk back to the cabinetmaker's cottage. Exhausted, he sank gratefully into the welcoming featherbed.

Father Hildebrandt came to visit the next day and the next. He made no more mention of what had transpired at Heiligenberg. Johann suspected he was somewhat ashamed of what the Prior had done. But he did learn the truth, that Johann was the scholar and that Tyle was interested only in becoming a knight-errant. He told Johann all that he knew of the University. Although he had not been there himself, he knew many men who had. When the conversations became too intellectual, Tyle grew bored and went off for long rides. Johann wished he could accompany his friend, but he was weaker than he had expected to be. He realized he must be patient and husband his strength until his torn and bruised body was fully healed, for once they left the goodwife's care there would be no more cosseting and few comforts for at least two months of hard travelling. Even when they reached Paris, if what the priest told them was true, they would find little comfort in the student accommodations.

Each day Johann was able to take longer walks and by the fifth day he pronounced himself well enough to take a short ride. The servants happily saddled up their mounts, but in less than two hours he was staggering back into the cottage.

"I grew up in the saddle," he said to Adwilda, "but by God's teeth, I never knew a horse could rattle so many bones and muscles." He groaned as she massaged his back with the unguent.

But the next day he was determined to try again. And it went better. After that he improved rapidly, and soon the friends were making plans for their departure.

"We have taken advantage of goodwife Adwilda's hospitality long enough," said Johann. "I shall reward her handsomely."

"Not too handsomely," warned Tyle. "We have a long journey and two years ahead of us. We may need all we have in both purses and then some, ere that."

"Nonetheless, I shall," replied Johann. "What should I have done without her? Now, let me see if I still have a sword arm."

Thus Father Hildebrandt found them fencing in the yard as he approached the cottage.

"Ah, I see the knights-turned-clerk have turned back into knights again," he said with a twinkle in his eye.

"Aye, Father," replied Johann, panting and wiping the sweat from his brow with the hem of his tunic, "clerk or no, I must be sure I can defend myself on the road ere we leave. I fear I am sadly out of practice."

"You will be leaving soon then?" asked the priest. "I suspected as much."

"In two or three days at most," replied Tyle. "We have already delayed our journey too long."

"Then I am glad I came today. Can you step over to my house for a few minutes? I have some things to show you."

Johann and Tyle gave their swords to the servants and followed the priest wondering what he had in mind.

When they were settled in his parlor the priest said, "Abbot Herman is returned." The young men held their breath. "He is exceedingly wroth—at your erstwhile friend, the Prior." They slowly let out their breath. "He has written to the Archbishop requesting that the Prior be transferred elsewhere. This is, of course, to be kept confidential, but I thought you would be happy to know. He also wishes to make amends as best he can. He sends you these."

He carefully unwrapped a piece of cloth and handed each young man a beautifully inscribed silver medal.

"That is a copy of the great seal of Heiligenberg—Our Lady of the Holy Mountain. It carries a hundred days indulgence for wearing it and a further hundred days each time you pray to her while wearing it."

Johann and Tyle were overwhelmed. Such powerful indulgences were not given out lightly. One usually had to purchase them or donate huge sums to the church or monastery.

"Convey our heartfelt thanks to His Lordship, Father," said Johann. "Such magnificent recompense was hardly necessary."

"He felt that it was," replied the priest. "He begs your forgiveness and asks that you pray for him, as he will for you."

"Certainly, Father," they chorused.

"There is more," said the priest, unrolling two pieces of parchment.

"What more can there be after such a gift as this?" asked Johann.

"He felt that these two letters would help ease your journey to some extent. The first states that with his blessing you are on a pilgrimage to the holy shrine of the Three Magi at Cologne. You have to pass that way anyway, and there are Papal indulgences available for visiting the sacred relics. But more than that, it will afford you protection and open the doors of every monastery and convent en route. Even many hostelries will give you a lower price or better accommodations as pilgrims, for it is to the benefit of their souls as well." The two young men gaped at him in awe, but there was more. "The second letter is to his good friend the Archbishop of Cologne, one of the most powerful prelates in the Empire. He has many excellent connections at the University in Paris. Many of the masters there are graduates of the great cathedral school at Cologne. He can be a great help to you. I suggest you call upon him just as soon as you have completed the pilgrimage."

Johann was tongue-tied at this good fortune.

Tyle answered for them. "That indeed we shall do. And how can we thank you, Father, and His Lordship, for his magnanimity?"

"Just pray for him," replied the priest, "and tell me that you forgive him, that I may carry the message to him. He is soul-sick and anguished over what happened. He is responsible even though the Prior did it without his knowledge or consent."

"Then tell him, Father, that we most heartily forgive him and we shall always pray for him," said Johann, "and, too, that we shall remember him fondly."

Two days later, after attending early Mass at the lovely old church in Vilsen, the two friends and their servants set out on their journey to Paris. Father Hildebrandt gave them a special blessing. Adwilda gave them a huge bag of food.

"Enough for two days' journey," she said and then handed another bag to Dierck.

"What is that?" asked Johann.

"Unguent, medicines, tonics, and whatnot from the wisewoman." he replied. "After this experience, I thought it best to be prepared."

Johann clapped him on the shoulder. "The best servant in the world is my Dierck."

A week later the friends were riding along the south bank of the beautiful Ruhr River. They had taken a slight detour in order to see the famous Wittekind stone at Exeter. To their surprise, they found it to be a huge rock outcropping, riddled with caves, in the topmost of which was a tiny Cistercian chapel. To their further amazement they noticed that the altar had as many pagan carvings as Christian, most notably that of the Irminsul, the pillar that the ancients believed held up the world and led the soul to the gods. The monks, due to their vow of silence, would not answer their questions, but a local shepherd, who had given them shelter for the night, explained that it had been a holy place for thousands of years before Christianity came and, in fact, was the center of the world force, from which led the network of holy lines of earth energy that connected all the holy places of old Saxony. He told them that the people would not let the monks take over the ancient chapel unless they included some symbols of the old religion. He conceded that there were still many people in the area who practiced the old ways, although nominally Christian.

When Tyle asked, "And do you still believe in the old ways?" he shrugged his shoulders.

"There is great power hereabouts." And that was all he would admit.

"Another compromise," commented Johann.

And now as they descended from the mountains, although the forest was still thick, the valley was widening out.

"Look, another mill," cried Johann, pointing. "Have you ever seen so many mills anywhere?" he asked no one in particular. As always he was fascinated by mills, and the proliferation of them in this river valley excited him beyond measure.

"Why in the world would they want so many mills?" asked Tyle. "There are hardly any farms around here to support them, nor even many villages."

"A man told me where we stopped last night that these mountains are rich in iron mines," interjected Dierck.

235

"What has iron got to do with mills?" asked Tyle. "They can't grind it into flour."

"But they do use the power to drive the machinery that crushes the ore and to work the bellows for the forges, even, I have heard, to wield the hammers that shape it," replied Dierck.

"Amazing!" exclaimed Johann. "You mean all these are actually iron mills and not flour mills? I must stop and see one."

"No, no more detours," groaned Tyle. "You promised me after Heiligenberg, and yet I let you talk me into Exeter. It will be winter before we reach Paris at this rate."

"All right, all right," agreed Johann, "but if we pass one on this side, I'm going to take a quick look. You must admit it is an interesting concept and we should keep up with all these modern innovations."

Tyle shrugged.

Johann was to be frustrated in his desire to visit an iron mill, but he soon forgot all about it in the magnificent vista that opened before them.

"It is the Rhein," exclaimed Tyle, excited for once.

"Holy Mother, I never knew a river could be so big," admitted Johann. "And look at all the ships."

"But how do we get across?" asked Tyle. "I don't see anything that looks like a ferry. They all seem to be going up and down."

"Perhaps if we ask . . ."

"There is a bridge at Cologne," interjected Dierck matter-of-factly.

"A bridge?" asked Johann.

"Across that?" added Tyle. "How."

"It was built by the Romans almost a thousand years ago," Dierck informed them.

"And still in use?" asked Tyle unbelieving.

"From what I hear, better engineered than anything built today," replied Dierck.

"Where do you learn all these things?" added Johann.

"I talk to people."

"All right, which way do we go?" urged Tyle, eager to keep moving.

"We turn south and follow this road along the east bank. It should lead us directly to it."

A few hours later they came to the massive span.

"It looks like a castle spread across the river," remarked Tyle.

"It certainly is solidly built. No wonder it has stood a thousand years," said Johann. "I suppose we shall have to pay a toll."

236

Not only did they have to pay a hefty toll, but their safe-conduct letters and other documents were carefully scrutinized.

"You will have to get the archepiscopal seal on these if you intend to go beyond the city," the tollman informed them.

"We have business with the Archbishop anyway," said Tyle importantly. "Would you be so good as to direct us?"

"I don't believe His Grace is in residence at the moment—summer, you know—but any of his clerks at the palace can take care of the seal. Turn right once you pass through the city gate. You will see the new cathedral a building. It is hard by there."

"And where might the Archbishop himself be found?" asked Johann, somewhat disappointed.

"Probably at one of his castles upriver. They can tell you at the palace."

"Thank you, my man."

They clattered across the well-paved road. When they reached the far end of the bridge they were still some distance from the gate in the imposing wall, but along the shoreline on either side of them was what appeared to be a city in itself. Innumerable markets and warehouses of all kinds were densely packed along the riverbank. Ships from all over the world were tied up at long, solidly built quays, for Cologne was one of the stars in the crown of the Hanse. The hustle and bustle of commerce was everywhere apparent.

"Have you ever seen anything so big?" remarked Johann. "It's like a city in itself."

"Never," agreed Tyle, "and we're not even inside the gates yet."

At the gate they had to pay another toll. Once inside the walls they were swept along by the throbbing pulse of the great queen city of the Rheinland.

"These people certainly know how to make money," commented Johann.

"Seems so," said Tyle, a bit bewildered. "They are scrambling about like—like ants. What is their hurry? Where is their chivalry?"

"I have heard that this is the power of the future," replied Johann, "and that the Code is rapidly becoming outmoded in places like this."

"How can that be?" Tyle shook his head. "Without the Code of Chivalry the world would be in chaos. It is the only thing that keeps knights honorable instead of constantly at one another's throats. I do not like what I see here."

237

"But these people are not of the nobility. The Code means little to them."

"No, of course, you are right," admitted Tyle. "They don't know any better. One must be born to it. But what are they then?" he asked, puzzled. "Certainly not peasants. Why, some of them I see here are more richly dressed than many nobles I know."

"I don't know exactly how they fit into the three established estates of men—clergy, noble and peasant," replied Johann. "They seem to be outside all three and it looks as though they couldn't care less."

"You are right, my lord," put in Dierck. "These wealthy merchants and the powerful guilds of artisans don't give a fig for the feudal system. I've been told that just a few years ago they revolted against the Archbishop and now rule the city themselves."

"Woe is me," sighed Tyle. "If that is so, what will become of the world as we know it?"

"I don't know, my lord," replied Dierck, "but Master Johann was right when he said that commerce is the power of the future. We are seeing it here and now."

They soon saw the scaffolding of the new cathedral ahead of them. Although only the choir and apse were so far under construction, it was already huge—and so light and airy that it seemed to float up to heaven. They learned that it had already been forty-four years a-building.

"It will be exquisite when it is finished," said Tyle.

"But when will it ever be done?" asked Johann. "At that rate it will take hundreds of years."

They were directed to the nearby archepiscopal palace. A bored clerk looked at their documents.

"Are you clerks or pilgrims," he glanced up at their clothes, "or just knights-errant?" he asked, making the last category sound synonymous with 'troublemakers'.

Before Tyle could start bragging about being a knight, Johann quickly answered, "We are pilgrims here in Cologne, but we are also students on our way to Paris. We need the Archbishop's seal on our safe-conducts in order to pass through his territory."

"Ambitious, aren't you? Cologne and then Trier, Burgundy, Champagne and then the King of France himself. You'll need seals from them all. Why don't you stay here for a while? The Cathedral School is the best in Germany. Many of the greatest masters at Paris taught here first."

"We are aware of that," countered Johann, "but we are limited in time and funds. Our desire is to study in Paris."

The clerk shrugged. "Make your pilgrimage then and come back tomorrow."

"Can you tell us where we might find His Grace? We have a letter for him from his friend the Abbot of Heiligenberg."

The clerk looked down his nose. "He is not in the city. Summer, you know."

"So we have been told, but if you could just tell us where we might find him."

"Godesburg. But I doubt he can be bothered with so trivial a matter," replied the clerk with disdain.

"Thank you. And could you also suggest where we might spend the night?"

"Ask at the school."

Out in the street once again the two friends looked at each other. "Not very friendly, was he?" commented Tyle.

"An inflated idea of his own importance," agreed Johann. "I'll wager the Archbishop himself is friendlier." And so he was.

They made their pilgrimage to the shrine of the Three Magi, whose bones Friedrich Barbarossa had stolen from Milan over a hundred years ago. They were more impressed by the workmanship of the magnificent gold casket than by the efficacy of the relics contained therein. But they made the proper prayers and donations and received their indulgences.

They wandered around the lovely city on the Rhein like any sight-seers, marvelling at the ancient Roman ruins as well as the opulent new public buildings that bespoke the wealth of its ruling merchants. The next morning they retrieved their safe-conducts from the same bored clerk and rode out the Severinstor, heading south.

"Ah, 'tis good to be out in the open country again," sighed Tyle, breathing deeply.

"What will you ever do in Paris?" teased Johann. "They say it is many times the size of Cologne, one of the largest cities in Christendom."

"I may not stay there too long," retorted Tyle. "I only go to France because there are more tournaments there than anywhere else. There's money to be made there."

"You are very foolish, my friend," chided Johann. "Besides, from what I have just seen, there is a great deal to be seen in town life. There's money to be made there, too—perhaps more, and more easily, too."

" 'Tis said," put in Dierck, "that town air is free air."

239

Tyle became livid. "If you were not my best friend's loyal servant, I would take the rod to you for saying that. 'Tis the very radical type of thing that is making the peasants run away from their obligations."

"Tyle, Tyle," said Johann, trying to smooth things over. "The peasants run away from abject poverty. The world is getting too big and the feudal system simply cannot support them all."

"Then let them have fewer children," snapped Tyle.

"And where would that leave us?" asked Johann. "Don't you realize, my friend, that the majority of those wealthy merchants were originally second and third sons of noble families?"

"Is that true?" asked Tyle, and strangely enough, he looked to Dierck for confirmation.

"I have heard that it is so, my lord," murmured Dierck.

"Hmm," muttered Tyle thoughtfully.

"Gives one something to think on, no?" said Johann. Then changing the subject he asked, "Dierck, have you been able to learn how far is this Godesburg?"

"About two days ride, I believe," he replied. "It is said to lie a few miles south of a little village called Bonn."

"And is this road safe enough?"

"I am told that it is reasonably safe that far," Dierck told them. "Beyond that there are said to be many castles of robber-barons, who prey on unarmed travellers. Apparently the late Emperor tried to wipe out these hornets' nests about twenty years ago, but quite a number of them still flourish unmolested."

"Hah, that is good to know," said Tyle perking, up out of his black mood at this news. "Then I suggest that after Godesburg we don our armor and act like the knights we are, instead of puling clerks."

"Perhaps that would be wise," agreed Johann reluctantly.

They reached the Godesburg, an imposing fortress perched high above the river, late in the afternoon of the second day. They threaded their way up the steep path through lush vineyards that lined the slopes of the mountain. When they reached the top, they found the drawbridge was up and the gates closed. There was a gatehouse on the hither side of the deep moat, but no one seemed to be about.

"Now what?" asked Johann.

"He seems to be in residence," Tyle pointed out. "See his pennant flying from the top of the keep."

"But why is everything shut so early in the day? Do you suppose they're expecting an attack and we've walked right into the midst of it?" asked Johann with some trepidation.

"I didn't see any sign of an army approaching as we came up. And look, you can see far and wide even from here. Perhaps he's just extra cautious. We shall soon see. Jacob!" called Tyle.

"Yes, my lord."

"You shall be our herald. Since we have no trumpet, bellow out in your best hog-calling voice that we come in peace."

"Yes, my lord," replied Jacob. "Halloo!" he called, and again, "Halloo!" As the echo came back to them and over the valley, two heads appeared in the second gate tower above the portcullis.

"Who awaits without?"

"My lord Tyle von Eltze and my lord Johann von Sehnden."

"Do you come in peace?"

"We come in peace."

"How many are you?"

"Only four."

"State your business."

"My lords have a letter for His Grace the Archbishop," yelled Jacob.

"Wait," came the reply.

They waited the better part of a half an hour. Finally two armed guards appeared at the gatehouse where no one had been before. They must have used a secret passage. They held razor-sharp halberds at the ready.

"I see no coat-of-arms," said one. "How are we to know who you are?"

"I am Tyle von Eltze and this is my friend Johann von Sehnden."

"I have only your word."

"Our surcoats are packed in our bags. It seemed too warm to wear them."

"No one travels without identity in these parts," warned the man. "Show me."

The friends bade their servants unpack the garments and displayed the upside-down crescent and star of Sehnde and the black grouse of Eltze.

"I have never seen these before and you are tonsured besides," said the guard doubtfully. "Where are you from?"

"From the Duchy of Braunschweig-Lüneburg."

The man nodded his head as if that explained everything. "And are you knights or clerks?"

"Both," they replied, and the guards looked more puzzled than ever.

"Show me the letter for His Grace."

Johann produced the parchment from inside his tunic and handed it to them. He knew they could not read, but they were shrewd enough to look immediately at the seal.

"Looks authentic enough," said the first man to his companion. They returned the letter to Johann and signalled someone in the gate tower, then went inside the gatehouse and reappeared on the other side to open the first set of gates as the heavy drawbridge rumbled down. The horses clattered across the drawbridge as the second set of gates swung open and a wicked portcullis was raised. A tunnel under the thick walls led them into the bailey of Godesburg.

A man, probably the bailiff, met them as grooms came to take their horses. Once again they stated their business with the Archbishop.

"Wait," he said. "You may refresh yourselves if you wish." He indicated a well with a trough next to it and disappeared up a flight of stairs leading into the main part of the castle.

They washed the dust of the road from their hands and faces and drank deeply of the clear, cold water from the well. Then they looked about them while they waited. There was no doubt that this was the residence of a very wealthy man. The walls were high and wide and manned by a large number of armed retainers. On one side were extensive stables and storehouses for grain and fodder, along with the requisite workshops of blacksmith, farrier, harness- and saddle-makers and armorers. Along the other side ran the palas, the two- and in places, three-story living quarters. The ground floor consisted of more storerooms, as well as working quarters for the domestic staff—laundresses, seamstresses and a buttery. At the far end, slightly off-center from the apex of the triangle, stood the massive round keep. It towered above them and the Archbishop's pennant flew proudly from the top. The stairway up which the bailiff had gone rose where the palas and keep joined.

The man soon returned and beckoned to them to follow him. They ascended the narrow, steep flight which wound around to the right and soon entered the great hall. Although it was still early, a number of knights lounged about. Clerks and servants of various sorts scurried among them. A youngish man—it was hard to tell his age—richly dressed in a brown silk robe approached them. Or rather he glided toward them, a limp hand extended. Tyle wondered if they were supposed to kiss it.

"Good day, strangers. Welcome to the Godesburg. I am Sir Baldwin,

His Grace's secretary. And whom do I have the honor of addressing?" His voice was silky smooth and obviously condescending.

"I am Tyle von Eltze and this is Johann von Sehnden."

"Ah, yes. And what brings you to Godesburg, other than the possibility of shelter for the night?"

Once again Johann explained about the letter as he withdrew it from his tunic. This time he knew the man could read it. A sharp one, this, he thought, one to watch.

"Ah, yes. The Abbot of Heiligenberg. It is amazing, is it not, how all these minor clergy claim His Grace for their friend? Yet they still sit living out their penance in places like Heiligenberg. Where is it, by the way?"

Johann bridled at the sarcasm, but tried to answer civilly. "Near a town called Vilsen in County Hoya."

"Of course," and it was quite apparent that Baldwin had never heard of it. "His Grace is resting now, but he can probably spare you a little time between Vespers and supper. He is a very busy man, as you know. Perhaps he may even invite you to table with him since we have no other guests tonight. I shall show him the Abbot's letter and apprise him of your presence. We are always willing to help aspiring clerics."

"Thank you, my lord," murmured Johann.

"Perhaps you would care for some refreshment after your journey?" He clapped his hands, and a servant was immediately at his elbow. "Some wine for the gentlemen."

"Yes, my lord." And the servant hurried to a huge sideboard and returned with two brimming goblets.

"Return here after Vespers," continued Baldwin, "and I shall advise you when His Grace can see you."

"Thank you again, my lord," said Johann, "and where is the chapel?"

"Continue up the stairs that brought you here. It is in the small tower." Baldwin turned then and left them to their own devices.

"I don't want to go to Vespers," said Tyle, when the secretary was out of earshot. "I've had enough of that."

"Tyle, we are accepting an archbishop's hospitality," chided Johann. "It's the least we can do. Besides, this one is one of the most powerful men in the whole Empire."

Tyle made a moué and grudgingly agreed.

When the bell for Vespers rang they made their way up another flight of the steep winding stairs. The chapel was a little gem set in stone, richly embellished with lacy stone carvings, brightly painted saints and jewel-like stained glass emblazoned by the setting sun. A mere handful of the occupants of the hall accompanied them.

"Not so many here are in awe of His Grace's power," commented Tyle. "Perhaps familiarity breeds contempt."

Johann shrugged.

The service, conducted by a fat, colorless, elderly priest, was very short. When they returned to the hall, the servants were setting up the trestle tables and placing torches in the many wall sconces. Many more people had arrived from wherever they had spent the day. In order to stay out of the way Johann and Tyle strolled around admiring the heavy, richly worked tapestries that lined the walls. All the themes seemed to be warlike. There was St. George slaying the dragon, St. Michel chasing Lucifer from heaven and various other fully armored saints dispatching an assortment of foes — animal, human and demonic.

"Methinks our Archbishop would have liked to have been a warrior rather than a man of God," remarked Tyle.

"Perhaps," said Johann. "I wonder if he was a second or a third son."

Tyle laughed.

Sir Baldwin approached them. "I see you are admiring His Grace's taste in art. He had these made to his own order at the best manufactories in Flanders. He insists on only the finest furnishings for all his castles. These were very costly." Johann and Tyle were duly impressed. "His Grace would like to visit with you for a while before supper is served. If you will come this way, I shall show you to his private rooms."

Johann winked at Tyle. The change in the secretary's attitude was so obvious. While not quite obsequious, he was now being extremely courteous. It seemed the Abbot was a true friend of his lord and not the typical sycophant Baldwin was used to dealing with.

He led them to a large comfortably furnished room with more of the same tapestries on the walls and a real Turkey carpet on the floor. A tall man with the build of a warrior but slightly run to fat from good living rose to greet them. Despite his white hair, his face was that of a much younger man, clean-cut with the ruddy complexion of the outdoor man. His brown eyes were sharp and penetrating, and yet there was a twinkle in them that said he probably enjoyed a good joke. There was nothing pompous about him — he left that to his secretary — but he exuded authority and power. Not a man to be gainsaid. He wore a simple but rich purple cassock and the pectoral cross of gold and amethyst that hung from his neck was probably worth more than all either Johann or Tyle possessed.

Baldwin astonished them by remembering their names. When he had performed the introductions, he discreetly withdrew. The young men knelt and kissed the Archbishop's ring, and when they arose the prelate embraced each in turn.

"Please sit and be comfortable," he said. They did so. "Now tell me of my dear friend Abbot Herman. I have not seen him for years, although we correspond occasionally. We were students together here at Cologne, but then we went our separate ways, I to Paris and he into Holy Orders, but we have remained close friends. Perhaps like opposite sides of a coin, we look in different directions but are an inseparable part of a whole. Did I detect something of the same here with you two young men?"

He is shrewd, thought Johann. He ignored the Archbishop's last question and told him about Abbot Herman. "He seems to be fine, although we only really met him once. But he was kind enough to give us the letter to you because"—he could not tell him the real reason—"because he wanted to help us. We dealt mostly with the Prior the short time we were there."

"Ah, that one. An insufferable fanatic," said the Archbishop. "I wonder that Herman tolerates him at all. I believe he feels that it is a cross he must bear, although I can't imagine what sins he could have. This is a very strict order, those Premonstratensians. Much too ascetic for my taste, but each of us must serve God in his own way."

"As we were leaving, we heard that the Abbot had requested that the Bishop transfer the Prior."

"About time. Herman is too fine a person to be saddled with the likes of him. But something very serious must have happened for him to go to that extreme."

"I—ah—believe—uh—" Johann bit back the words, but too late. The Archbishop jumped right on it.

"You were there when it happened. Tell me."

"No, Your Grace," protested Johann. "What I was about to say is of no importance."

The Archbishop looked him straight in the eye as if willing the truth to come forth. Johann looked down, flustered.

"Tell him," said Tyle suddenly. "If you don't, then I shall." And so the whole sordid story was told.

"Not a pretty tale, but no worse than what I should expect from them. I am sure it has thoroughly discouraged you from the monastic life. Pity."

"Not entirely, Your Grace," replied Johann a bit hesitantly, "but I

245

want to study at Paris for a while and learn something of the other orders."

"It certainly has discouraged me," interrupted Tyle. "I want no part of it."

The Archbishop smiled.

"But we should certainly appreciate your advice and guidance, Your Grace," said Johann.

"Then tell me about yourselves. Everything," said the prelate. "I must get to know you better before my advice would have any worth."

They told him their stories—their hopes, desires and frustrations. Under the prelate's careful probing, Tyle even admitted his longing to become a knight-errant instead of taking orders. They felt at ease with him.

When they finished, he stroked his smooth chin a bit and then leaned forward in his chair. "Yes, I was right—two sides of the same coin, but an entirely different situation than Herman and I. Times have changed a lot in fifty years. I have lived through most of this century that is soon drawing to a close and the changes I have seen are unbelievable. I tell you this has been the most progressive century since the early Roman Empire."

"But, Your Grace," protested Tyle, "I don't understand. It seems as though everything that has represented security and solidarity is falling apart. Even the feudal system itself. Why, when I saw all those people in Cologne, footloose and—and belonging to no one, I feared for the order of the world. Where is their loyalty?"

"To themselves, I'm afraid," replied the Archbishop. "It is called freedom. And, my son, like it or not, it is the wave of the future."

"Your Grace," put in Johann, "I don't necessarily agree with Tyle. This new kind of life in the cities rather appeals to me, but how can you say this has been a progressive century when for twenty-three years there was the Interregnum with no emperor, followed by one more rapacious and self-seeking than the other? And now there is not even a pope!"

"Because you see only *what* is happening, not why. Your philosophy teachers at Paris will show you how to look beneath the surface for the real meaning of things. But look ye, the population is greater than it has ever been, but there is little hunger or unemployment. We no longer have to send them off on crusades to rid ourselves of the problem. New methods of agriculture enable the farmers to grow enough for themselves and their lords and still have plenty to support the multitudes in the towns. Improved machinery, yes, those mills you so admire, Johann, and the looms that wove these tapestries, cut down manufacturing time and increase production, so that the excess products can be traded for the peasants' excess produce. And who provides the capital for these new machines and methods? The very same merchants who profit so tremendously on the trade itself. Their guilds are very powerful. They have almost become a new nobility of the towns. In fact, many are beginning to call themselves patricians. And now new guilds of artisans are springing up all over, which ensure the quality of the work. Yes, the towns are easily absorbing all the excess population — and I mean not just the ten too many sons of the peasants but the younger nobility as well. I tell you, the power of the future lies with the towns and the commerce that supports them. Just look at the Hanse, of which Cologne is one of the most influential members."

The young men were only vaguely aware of the Hanseatic League, so sheltered had their lives been at Hildesheim. In fact, much of what the Archbishop had been saying was beyond their comprehension.

"Interesting," murmured Johann while Tyle looked bewildered.

"Ah, forgive me for going on so," said the prelate, "but I have just recently come to these insights myself and would share them with you. Four years ago the townspeople of Cologne rebelled against my authority. They wanted to govern themselves. It was a short but bitter war. I was too blind to see all this. All I could see was the lost power and revenues. I couldn't admit the power was waning anyway. Now I use my power as an Elector to make sure there is a weak emperor, which enhances the freedom of the towns. As for revenues, the new freedom to conduct their affairs as they wish has increased their profits, which flow back into the Church as bequests and endowments as well as increased tithes given freely. I have even invested some of my own wealth in their enterprises, and it has increased as never before. But enough of this. You came seeking my advice."

They nodded but said nothing.

"Tyle, I shall address you first. You are simpler. I mean that not in a derogatory sense, but you are just as I was before the rebellion opened my eyes. You are looking back to the glory of Chivalry as it was in the last century. But believe me, it was not so glorious except in the songs of the Minnesänger and is less so now. And the so-called Court of Love — bah, foolishness. Call them Courts of License. At least the Church has succeeded in stemming *that* by promoting the cult of the Virgin, although even that is beginning to get out of hand. So many innocent young girls

247

now fear marriage that our convents are being flooded with silly females who have no true vocation at all.

"The knight-errant is fast becoming an anachronism as well. I grant you that there are still a few, hardened in years of battle and natural show-men besides, who make a great deal of money. But they are the lucky few. The vast majority lose everything they have and often their very lives as well. Besides, the armies of the future are becoming more and more mercenary. I'll wager your own father has often paid scutage to avoid going to war." Tyle admitted that he had. "Of course. So my advice to you is by all means learn all you can at Paris. You know they have new courses there now. Not everything is theology, philosophy and rhetoric. They even have studies in mathematics, medicine, agriculture and navigation, that are promoted heavily by the Hanse. But be sure you study some philosophy. That opens the mind like nothing else. Then and only then, if you still wish to make fighting your profession, attend the masters in mathematics and engineering. Learn about the new seige machines and weapons. I saw them in action some twenty years ago when Rudolf of Habsburg swept down the Rhein trying to drive out some of the robber-barons. He destroyed impregnable castles quicker than you could blink an eye. Then get a commission in a crack mercenary troop such as they have in Italy."

Tyle blinked and looked aghast. All his dreams of the flower of knighthood dashed to the ground. It was almost blasphemy. For once he had nothing to say.

The Archbishop paused a moment and then continued. "Now Johann, you are an entirely different case. My advice to learn all you can at Paris also pertains, but I don't think I have to urge you to that. I can see you are eager for it. I think your vocation truly lies in Holy Orders, but not as a monk. No, never. You have too inquiring a mind to stifle it with their discipline. Get your doctoral degree so you can teach if you think that will make you happy. But I suggest you get yourself ordained priest and purchase a good benefice. You can do just as much good and get rich besides."

Johann was shocked. "But Your Grace, that is simony."

"So it is. But what else? It is accepted practice from the Pope and Curia on down. Where do you think all this came from?" He waved his hand around the luxurious room. "This and three other strong castles, fully staffed, plus a palace in the city. Whence think you came the money to invest in the merchants' enterprises and the Hanse ships? Do you think I sway the Electors' votes through their love of me? We despise one another. Only the common desire for a weak emperor unites us. No, money is power and there is as much opportunity for it in the Church as anywhere else. The sale of benefices—I prefer to call that an investment—and indulgences. That is where the money and the power lies. Think you not that the Canons at Cologne were overjoyed when Barbarossa presented them with the Magi relics. Who knows where Milan got them? What does it matter? They are a drawing-card, a moneymaker. They are paying for that magnificent cathedral we are building."

Johann was now as dismayed as Tyle. They looked at each other and down at their hands folded tightly in their laps. Neither wanted the powerful prince of the Church to see their disillusionment. But he knew.

"Do I shock you, my innocents? Know ye this then. The Church is not all bad. She does her best to instruct the children in the precepts Our Lord taught. But when they become adults, she gives them what they want. Our people are still half-heathens at heart, so she gives them all this half-heathenish claptrap and they love her for it. The Pope can dabble in politics all he wants, have ten sons by as many mistresses and give them the richest benefices in Italy, and the people will still worship him because there is magic in the triple crown and the chair of Peter he sits on."

A gong sounded in the hall and reverberated through the castle.

"Come sup at my table," invited the Archbishop. "It is not often I have two charming young men about to set out in life as guests. A welcome relief from the sycophants and politicians who would woo my favor or potential enemies sizing up my weaknesses. I hope I have been some help to you."

"Indeed you have, Your Grace," stammered Johann, "and we thank you."

"Yes, Your Grace, it was very enlightening," added Tyle.

"Good. Then before you leave tomorrow, I shall have Baldwin prepare letters to two of the Masters at Paris who are my very dear friends. Meanwhile pray for guidance and place your lives in Our Lord's hands."

Indeed, thought Johann.

Early the next morning, after Mass and a hearty breakfast, they set out on the next stage of their journey. They hoped to reach Coblenz by nightfall. They were not yet wearing their armor, although the Archbishop had concurred with Dierck's advice.

"Until you reach the Moselle you are in my realm and quite safe. After you cross the river, you will be in Trier's territory, and I am afraid he has very little control over his barons. From there on until you cross into Burgundy, your strong arm and a fast horse are your only protection."

They reached Coblenz in good time and felt safe within its strong walls. It was a charming town situated at the confluence — whence its original Roman name — of the Moselle and Rhein rivers. Although there was an embryonic stirring of commerce, its main source of revenue was still the tolls from the ancient Baldwin bridge across the Moselle, the ferry across the Rhein, and the roads leading south up the Rhein and west up the Moselle.

They left there fully armored and took the west road along the right bank of the Moselle. The river would eventually lead them into the heart of Burgundy and on to France.

"My lords," warned Dierck suddenly, "there are horsemen on the crest of yon hill."

"What can we do?" asked Johann. "There is no castle or other shelter that I can see."

"You are right," agreed Tyle, "but they make me uneasy after all the warnings we have had."

"We have no choice but to keep on. Let us hope they will consider us too poor prey to be worth their while. Perhaps they are merely watching the road."

"I hope so, but we must be prepared to take a stand."

Weapons at the ready, they continued along the road. Around the next bend they lost sight of the riders. Their horses could not carry them as fast as they would have liked, for they were only palfreys and the weight of a fully armored man was considerable. Destriers they were not.

After a while, when nothing happened, they began to relax a bit. The road narrowed and they were forced to ride single file. Tensions increased. And then it happened.

As they rounded the next bend, they were confronted by a single armed horseman. He ambled slowly toward them in the middle of the road as if daring them to shoulder him aside. The riverbank at this point fell away steeply, rocky and treacherous. The densely wooded slope on the other side left little room for maneuvering, but they could have passed if the rider had but hugged the thicket a little. He obviously had no intention of doing so.

Tyle, who was in the lead and saw no danger in a lone man, rode right up to him. "Hail, stranger, the greetings of the road and peace be with you."

250

Instead of the customary answer, the man drew his sword and held it across his saddle in front of him. "You are trespassing."

"But this is a public road," objected Johann. "We paid the toll at the last gate. We have every right to cross this land."

"Hah!" growled the man. "You have no rights at all and you go no farther."

"By whose authority?" asked Tyle

"By my master's, who owns all this land. Dismount, if you value your lives."

"Not without a fight," shouted Tyle as he drew his sword and charged. But his foe was quicker and stronger. In one fell swoop he slashed Tyle's sword arm and knocked him to the ground.

As Johann rushed to Tyle's aid, the bandit laughed. "Fool, you are surrounded." And as he spoke, several men armed with swords and cudgels rushed out of the woods and two others perched in the trees, deadly arrows nocked in their bows.

In a moment one of them whacked Johann's horse in such a way as to make him rear. Strong hands grabbed him from behind and dragged him off. Someone pulled off his helmet and delivered a stunning blow on the side of his head. Before he passed out, he thought he heard hoofbeats and a splash and wondered vaguely if they were being rescued.

"Hah," he heard the leader say, "the cowardly servant takes to the river. Let him go, he won't last till the next bend. The current is swift there."

Dierck, thought Johann in anguish, and then all was blackness.

"Bind them well and let's be off and collect our reward," instructed the bandit. They forced Tyle to remount although he was weak from loss of blood. He gritted his teeth as they bound his arms behind his back and his feet under the horse's belly. They bound Johann first and threw him over the back of his horse. Jacob had to walk, his horse commandeered by one of the underlings. As soon as I am able, he thought, I must tell Sir Johann that Dierck is no coward. He had seen Dierck slap his horse on the rump and send him back the way they had come and then deliberately jump into the river. He knew Dierck could swim and was resourceful. Pray God he would bring succor.

They followed an almost invisible track up the steep hill and soon arrived at a forbidding castle, a voracious bird of prey hovering over the valley. The gate opened for them immediately and they entered the bailey with their captives.

A comely maiden dressed in a plain grey kirtle was crossing the yard and stopped to watch. More hostages! Who can these be? she wondered. O Blessed Virgin, when will Father stop these atrocities? To what purpose? He only earns the undying hatred of every knight in Christendom from the Emperor on down. And mine, too, she thought. She did not fear her cruel, half-demented sire as her poor cringing mother did, but she hated him.

Although close to fainting from pain and weakness, Tyle noticed her and automatically straightened up despite the awkward position enforced by his bonds. He caught her eye and she started to smile hesitantly but then quickly looked around. He noticed the look of fear that crossed her face, but no one else paid any attention to her and he returned the smile. What a beauty she would be, he thought, with proper clothes and that raven hair properly dressed. He continued to watch her as they untied his feet, but although she stood rooted to the spot, she would not again raise her eyes to his face.

With his arms still painfully bound they jerked him from the saddle. His legs, all pins and needles, collapsed beneath him, and unable to break his fall, he rolled in the dirt. They dragged Johann from his horse like a sack of meal and tossed him on the ground next to Tyle. Johann groaned as the jolt brought him partially to. Jacob, arms also bound, was tied by the neck to a ring in the wall, so that he could not move more than a foot or two without choking himself.

"Oh, they are both badly hurt," cried the girl, suddenly coming to life at the sight of the captives' plight. "What have you done this time, Rolf? Who are these young knights?"

"Stay back, my lady." He put up an arm to block her as she tried to approach. "Just carrion we cleaned off the road. Traitors if you must know."

"Traitors? To whom? To what? They hardly look the part," she exclaimed sharply. "Are these more of your trumped-up charges to provide my saintly father with more of his gruesome entertainments?"

"Ssshhh, my lady," warned Rolf, "if he hears you, it will go ill with you."

"What care I if he hears me?" she retorted. "He well knows what I think of his nefarious undertakings. Look to yourself, scoundrel. When you cease to please him, your life won't be worth a wooden penny. What is he paying you for this job?"

"Well enough, chit," he snarled, "and mind your tongue, for I should like nothing better than to remove it from your pretty mouth, but first I would see that it licks my cock."

She turned away from him in disgust, fighting back tears of frustration. The man was not only obscene, he was evil incarnate and her father's favorite minion.

Rolf left the captives where they lay, guarded by two underlings, and entered the hall seeking his lord. As soon as he was out of sight, the girl ran to the well, drew a bucket of water and took it to the strange young men. She knelt down and took Tyle's head in her lap, holding the dipper to his lips.

He drank deeply and looked up into her face. "You are an angel," he whispered hoarsely. She really smiled then and her whole face changed. "Truly an angel," he repeated. "Who are you and where are we?"

She put a warning finger to her lips and whispered, "I am called Chlotilde and this is Castle Rheinfels. Where are you wounded? I see so much blood."

"My arm," he moaned, "but take care of my friend first. He suffered a right fierce blow to the head. I am Tyle and he is Johann, my lady angel."

She moved to Johann and tried to get him to drink, but he was barely conscious and most of the water dribbled down the front of his hauberk. She fetched a cloth and bathed his face. She held the cold water to his temple, and gradually he began to revive. She helped them both to a sitting position. She attempted to cleanse Tyle's wound, but the chain mail was in the way.

"That should be cleaned and cauterized, ere it festers, but there is little I can do with you trussed up like this," she said. Suddenly they could hear voices raised within. She jumped up. "I cannot be caught aiding you, or I shall not be able to help you later." She planted a light kiss on Tyle's forehead, grabbed the bucket and fled. For all his pain, Tyle's heart fluttered with joy.

A very subdued Rolf returned to the courtyard following a short heavy-set, but powerfully built man, dressed only slightly better than the bandit in filthy hose and tunic. His beard and hair were so thick and black that only his sharp nose distinguished him from a beast. His black eyes flashed evilly. Johann, still foggy, thought, I have seen the devil himself.

"But, my lord," Rolf whined, "there *were* four. Ask the gatekeeper. One of the servants jumped in the river."

"You blundering fool," snarled the lord of the castle, "these are not the men I sought. I said four knights, with at least that many squires and

253

perhaps some foot soldiers as well. Think ye I sent so many men with you just to take two babes barely separated from their nursemaids? Meanwhile the ones I wanted have probably gone scot-free. Who are these two anyway?"

"Perhaps they separated from the main party when they saw us on the crest of the hill," suggested Rolf limply.

"They saw you on the hill?" screamed the master. "You idiot. Had those I sought seen you at all, you would never have captured a one. Now who are these two?"

"In that case, I admit I don't know," said Rolf placatingly.

The dark man shook his head at such stupidity. "All right. Let's get them into the hall and I shall question them. Perhaps they can be of some use to us anyway. If not, they can provide us with a little entertainment. But not you." He held up his hand as Rolf was about to kick the young men to their feet. "You get yourself and your henchmen back out on that road and see if you can't find the right ones. If not, you will feel my wrath such as you've never known."

Rolf slunk away, signalling his men to follow him.

The lord instructed a servant to bring the young men to the hall and turned on his heel. Tyle and Johann were hauled roughly to their feet, tied together with Jacob by the same neck halter, and led by the rope across the yard, up the stairs and into the hall.

Unlike the beautiful hall they had visited just two days ago, this one was dark, dingy and smoke-blackened. The moldy rushes underfoot stank from rotten food and dog droppings. The walls were bare and the benches rough-hewn. Mangy mongrels growled and slinked away to cower beneath the stacked boards. The few men idling about were just as ill-kempt as the dogs. Their dark-visaged lord sprawled in what passed for a chair near the cold, ash-laden fireplace, a tankard of beer in his huge paw.

Johann tripped over an old bone buried in the rushes and nearly strangled before the servant jerked him upright.

"What! Drunk so early in the day?" asked the master snidely.

"No, my lord whoever you are," snapped Tyle. "Your rowdies dealt him a mean blow to the head for no reason at all and he is barely conscious. I demand to know who you are and where we are. Why have you taken us prisoners?"

"In due time," he replied. "I am glad to see you at least have some spirit, even though your friend mopes from a little tap on the noggin. We grow them with harder heads around here. You mean you really don't know where you are — or why?"

"No idea," retorted Tyle. "I only know we were peaceably travelling on the road from Coblenz to Trier and have no business with you. I demand that you release us forthwith and let us continue our journey unmolested."

"Hah," laughed Blackbeard. "You are hardly in a position to demand anything. Now tell me who *you* are."

"In due time, my lord," mimicked Tyle.

"Dare you to mock me?" fumed the man. "I have racked men for less than that. Perhaps a gentle stretch of the limbs would cure your bad manners."

Tyle realized his bravado had carried him too far. "I am Tyle von Eltze and this is my friend Johann von Sehnden."

"Where in the world are those benighted places?"

"In the Duchy of Braunschweig-Lüneburg, my lord."

"A long way from home, then. And what were you doing on my road?"

"We paid the toll and sought only to pass through your territory, my lord. We are students on our way to study in Paris."

The mention of Paris triggered a violent reaction. "Fully armed?" he screamed. "Paris?" he screeched. "Students? Bah! A likely story. You have just admitted that you are exactly what I knew you to be. That asshole Emperor's mercenaries going to fight for the French or the English — whichever — he's not fussy, as long as he gets paid."

Tyle was totally bewildered by this tirade and tried to answer calmly in order to avoid provoking another outburst. "We are no one's mercenaries, my lord. I know nothing about the fighting between the French and the English except that it has been going on for centuries and probably always will. We are indeed students, and if you would be so kind as to have my saddlebags brought here, I can show you our safe-conducts issued by our Duke himself. I pray that as a gentleman," he nearly choked over this, "you will honor them."

"Forged, more than likely."

"My lord, if you wish further proof," argued Tyle, "we also carry letters from His Grace the Archbishop of Cologne to some of the Masters at the University."

"That old reprobate," smirked the man. "Didn't he give you letters to his favorite whores as well?" He laughed at his own joke. "But I forget, 'tis said he prefers boys. Did he perhaps share his delights with you?"

Tyle was growing faint from loss of blood and this senseless discussion. Johann, keeping upright through sheer willpower, leaned against Jacob. If he had slid to the floor, he would have strangled them all.

"Tyle," he whispered faintly, "let him do what he will and have done with this. I can no longer stand and will choke you if I fall."

"Jacob," said Tyle quietly, "let us kneel down." Jacob and Tyle, supporting Johann as best they could between their shoulders, knelt and eased Johann into a sitting position on the filthy floor.

"Ah, isn't that sweet," quipped the man. "Three humble supplicants. Perhaps now you will tell the truth."

"My lord," said Tyle in despair, "I have told you the truth. There is nothing more to tell. If you will but fetch our saddlebags, I can show you."

"Like I said, no doubt false." Tyle realized then that he probably could not read. The man stroked his tangled beard for a moment. "Suppose I should take you at your word for the moment, what would you be worth to me?"

"I'm afraid I don't understand," replied Tyle.

"Don't be coy. You can't be that innocent," said the black lord sarcastically. "How much ransom would your noble families pay to get you back? Do I make myself clear?"

Tyle was shocked. "Very clear, my lord. But I am afraid the answer is nothing."

"Nothing?" stormed their captor. "But I have to pay Rolf and his men. I have to live. No one leaves Castle Rheinfels without paying his due. I am Ludolf, the most powerful knight in the Rheinland, and you dare to say 'nothing'?" he raged.

"Sir Ludolf, our families are noble, it is true, but greatly impoverished by bad harvests," explained Tyle, praying that God would forgive the lie. "Furthermore, we are both third sons intended for Holy Orders. They have sent us away because there are many other mouths to feed at home. You will get nothing from them."

Ludolf sputtered and fumed. "That fool Rolf. That stupid idiot." Gradually he calmed down. "Then you must earn your keep."

The man must be mad, thought Tyle. How does one reason with such a beast? "My lord," he ventured, "we wish no keep from you. We have no desire to stay here at all. Return our weapons and horses to us and we shall gladly leave forthwith."

As if he heard not a word of that, Ludolf mused to himself, "Yes, you must earn your keep. And in order to do that you must be fit. Churl, fetch that slut who calls herself my daughter. She is the only one with healing knowledge around this hovel."

As though she had been waiting outside the door, the servant returned almost immediately with Chlotilde.

"You asked for me, Father?" she said demurely, eyes downcast.

"I am saddled with some fools here who claim they can raise no ransom. So we shall save them for our entertainment, but first they must be fit. Heal them, girl. You are good for nothing else."

"Yes, Father. Immediately, Father." Only then did she permit herself to look at the three woebegone captives. "I can do nothing for them tied as they are. Father, order their bonds removed."

Ludolf grimaced every time she so sweetly called him Father, but he commanded the servant, "See to it. And follow whatever orders the Lady Ludolfa gives you. When they are revived, throw them in the dungeon until I decide what to do with them. I am going hawking. This place stinks." He rose and left the hall.

As soon as they were untied, she ordered the servant to fetch buckets of hot and cold water, clean cloths and some brandy.

Jacob chafed his arms to restore the circulation and volunteered, "My lady, I am unhurt. Let me help you, for I fear both my young lords are badly injured."

"I shall be most grateful for your help — uh — how are you called?"

"I am Jacob, my lady, and why did he call you Ludolfa? I thought I heard you tell Master Tyle that your name was Chlotilde."

"And so it is. He calls me that in derision. He hates me because I was not the son he desired and now I fear my poor lady mother can have no other children due to his maltreatment of her. So he hates us both, but I try to ignore it as best I can. Nevertheless, Chlotilde, I was christened."

"The man is mad."

"I daresay he is, but let us be about our business. Help me remove their armor. Be especially careful of Tyle's arm. I fear bits of metal may be in the wound."

Jacob did as he was told, and by that time the servant had returned. The first thing she did was give them each a stiff measure of the brandy. Johann choked and sputtered, but Tyle rather enjoyed the burning sensation as it went down.

"My lady angel, that is not wine. What is it?" asked Tyle.

"It is called brandy. It is a fairly new discovery of some monks in

France. It was long a closely guarded secret, but the method filtered down the Moselle to us in the Rheinland. It is distilled from the spirits of wine and very potent."

"That it is," he agreed, "but tasty, too."

She smiled. "It is not for your pleasure, but for medicinal purposes only." She turned to Johann. "I shall tend to you first, for there is not much I can do but try to reduce the swelling."

She washed his face, especially the ugly bruise at his temple. Then she wiped the spot with a cloth soaked in brandy.

"How strange that it burns your gullet but cools your skin," said Johann, feeling somewhat better already.

Chlotilde then set Jacob to holding cool compresses to Johann's head and turned to Tyle. She cleaned the wound carefully, shaking her head.

"Make a fire," she instructed the servant.

"There is no wood, my lady."

"Then find some, and quickly," she retorted.

"But my lord . . . "

"Never mind my lord. He told you to obey my orders, did he not?" she snapped.

"Yes, my lady." He scurried out and returned shortly with an armful of kindling and small sticks. "That is all cook would give me. He says . . . "

"I care not what he says. That will do."

When the meagre fire was burning brightly she took a sharp dagger from her belt and heated the point in the fire.

"Drink some more brandy, Tyle," she said.

"You would have me drunk, my lady," he replied doubtfully.

"It will dull the pain of what I must do. Jacob, let Johann apply his own compresses now and hold Tyle steady for me."

"What is this?" objected Tyle. "I am no weakling."

She ignored his protest and began probing the open wound with the tip of the knife. Tyle groaned and turned white. She drew out a sliver of steel and probed some more. The third time he fainted in Jacob's arms.

" 'Tis better," she said to Jacob.

When she was satisfied the wound was clean, she soaked it with the brandy. Tyle moaned. Then she returned the knife to the fire and held it with a tongs until it was white hot and quickly held it against his arm. Tyle screamed even in his swoon. The stink of burning flesh made Johann retch, but he knew it was necessary to save the arm from putrefying. "Hold him as he is, Jacob, I must fetch my herbs. If he awakens, give him more brandy."

After a while she returned with two poultices. One she laid along the slash on Tyle's arm and bound it securely. The other she placed on the lump on Johann's head and tied the ends around. Almost immediately he could feel it drawing the pain out.

"Methinks you are indeed an angel of mercy, my lady Chlotilde," he said. Then suddenly something occurred to him. "Jacob, where is Dierck?" He tried to stand. "Is he—is he—?"

"Don't try to stand, Johann," warned Chlotilde and lowered her voice to a whisper. "You must not appear to revive too soon, if you take my meaning."

Johann nodded but glared at Jacob.

"He escaped, my lord," replied Jacob. "At least I hope he did. He jumped into the river."

"Oh, oh," moaned the girl. "He will never survive. Who is he?"

"He is my squire and very dear friend," said Johann. "He is a strong swimmer."

"I hope you are right," said the girl doubtfully. "I shall pray for him—and all of you, too. Now drag out two pallets," she instructed the servant, "if you can find any that are not too filthy."

"But my lord said they are to go into the dungeon when they revive," said the servant.

"Mind your tongue, you surly churl," snapped Chlotilde. "Even a clod like you can see they are hardly revived yet and won't be for some time."

The servant laid out the pallets and helped Jacob carry Tyle to one. Johann felt he could walk by now but, heeding Chlotilde's warning, let himself be helped to the other and lay down gratefully.

"Now take away this mess. Just leave me one bucket of water, and go. I shall stay with them until they revive," she ordered. She sat down on a stool by the pallets, took some embroidery out of her pocket and began to stitch.

When they were surely alone, Johann asked, "What will happen to us now, my lady?"

"I don't know, Johann, I don't know. I shall do all I can to help, but it will take time for I must be very devious and subtle. The kindest thing that could happen, although you may not believe it, is if he left you in the dungeons and forgot all about you. I have helped others escape when that happens. I simply tell him they have died. But if he decides to have one of his 'entertainments', oh!" She put her head in her

259

hands. "I cannot bear to think on it."

Johann thought on that for a while. He had heard tales of the gruesome torture chambers many of these robber-knights maintained. They were a sick, sadistic lot who took pleasure in inflicting pain on others. Fortunately, there were few of them left. In his own Saxony, of which Braunschweig-Lüneburg was a part, the great Duke Heinrich the Lion had eliminated all of them over a hundred years ago. Here in the Rheinland the late Emperor Rudolf of Habsburg had wiped most of them out about twenty years ago. The notorious castle Rheinfels was one of the few that had successfully resisted his every effort. It didn't appear to be that strongly defended now, but the present Emperor was not much better than a robber-knight himself. Why of all of them did they have to be captured by this one? He let himself drift off into a natural sleep, for he knew he must shepherd his strength if they were to stand any chance of escape.

Tyle meanwhile had awakened and heard the last part of Chlotilde's statement. He, too, thought about it, and the prospect was far from pleasant. His arm was very painful, and he knew he would not be able to lift a sword for a long time. He prayed he would not lose the arm, but something told him Chlotilde's poultice would heal it cleanly. He turned to look at her. A tiny ray of sun that had somehow managed to find its way into the dark hall haloed the top of her head.

"My lady angel," he whispered.

She looked up from her work, "Ah, Tyle, you are awake. How do you feel?"

"The arm hurts like all the fiends of hell."

"That will take time, but I think I got all the slivers out. It should heal well."

"With your loving care, I am sure it will. But I heard what you said to Johann. Why does a sweet angel like you stay in a hell-hole like this?"

"It is my home, Tyle. I have no place else to go, nor dare I."

"A man like him must have many enemies. He will not live long."

"And then what? I am dowerless. Who would want me?"

"I might. I think I am falling in love."

"Don't talk foolishness, Tyle, you hardly know me."

"Nonetheless, if we ever escape from here, I vow I shall return and rescue you."

She smiled and shook her head sadly. She knew it was an impossible dream.

Servants entering the hall interrupted their conversation. They began setting up the trestle tables and benches. Their lord would return soon and supper must be ready.

"Why are these two still cluttering up my hall?" he stormed as he came in. "Have I not ordered them to the dungeon."

"Father," protested Chlotilde, "they are still weak and feverish. I pray thee let them first partake of the meal."

"Very well. Baby them a while longer if you must," he growled, "but then they go."

She fed them herself, keeping up the pretense that they were too weak to feed themselves. The soup was tepid and greasy, the meat stringy, the cabbage sour and the bread moldy, but they ate every bit, for they knew it might be their last meal for a long time.

They lay in each other's arms in the darkness and filth, Johann cradling Tyle like a baby. For three days he had raved in the delirium of fever, but now he was quiet, sleeping the sleep of exhaustion. Or was he dying? Johann did not know. He could only pray that God would not abandon them. He had never felt so alone and helpless in his life.

The dungeon was no more than six feet to a side, cut into the native rock. One wall dripped constantly, keeping the whole place damp and slimy. A pile of moldy, flea-ridden straw lay on the drier side, and here they huddled, barely able to stretch out. Some twenty feet above, a manhole covered with an iron grating grudgingly admitted the only light and air. The stench of years of urine, feces and death was almost asphyxiating. Voracious rats were nightly visitors. Besides trying to keep Tyle from hurting himself in his delirium, Johann had constantly to fend off these predators.

So far at least they had been given food of a sort—usually dry bread or a watery gruel—and water, no doubt thanks to Chlotilde. Although one day the man who lowered the food down the manhole had not brought the pitifully small bucket of water. When Johann asked for it, he was spat upon and told that that was his water for the day. He had been using a great part of the water to cool Tyle's fever, but after that he ceased being so lavish. Sometimes the wet cloth was all he had to soothe his own parched mouth.

Tyle finally became coherent after the fever broke, but he claimed to have no feeling in the arm at all. "Perhaps the rats have gnawed it off." "The fleas are driving me crazy. I can't scratch with that arm." "Johann, the walls are closing in, get me out of here," he screamed.

Johann, in misery himself, tried to comfort him as best he could. He could well understand how men could go mad confined in a place like this. He tried to get Tyle to pray with him. He talked about what they would study in Paris. He even spoke of the spectacular tournaments. Anything to ward off the growing hysteria his friend was heading for. He did not know how long he could hold out himself, weakened by hunger and thirst, lying in their own filth, breathing their own excrement, his only consolation that they had not been put to the rack or the iron maiden or any of a dozen other fiendish tortures their captor might think of.

After about two weeks—Johann had lost track of how often he had counted the murky daylight seeping down the shaft, and Tyle, quieter now, often seemed to be in another world—the grate opened and the rope descended. Expecting the usual rancid food, Johann barely looked up until a voice whispered, "It will soon be time. How fare you?"

And there, framed by the manhole, was Tyle's angel. Johann thought at first he was hallucinating, too, and Tyle wept, "I am dreaming."

But she spoke again. "Tyle, Johann. Are you alive?"

Then Johann stood up. "My lady Chlotilde." His voice was rusty from lack of use. "I had never thought to see you again. I am as well as can be expected, but I fear for Tyle."

"His arm?" she asked.

"His arm and I fear his sanity as well," he replied.

"Hope will heal his mind," she promised, "but I fear for his arm. I dared not come sooner. Take off the bandage and tell me if the wound smells rotten, if it is swollen, and if he winces when you touch above the wound. Quickly now."

Johann did as he was told. "With all the foulness around us, I cannot be sure, but it seems to smell clean and there is only a slight swelling."

Tyle finally realized that she was not a dream. "My lady angel," he cried, "help us to get out of here. I fear I shall go mad. I have no feeling in the arm at all. I think the rats have gnawed it off."

"No, your arm is still all there," Johann assured him.

"I shall send a fresh poultice this afternoon. I am also bringing you better food. The best I can find. You must build up your strength while I make plans for freeing you. It should take no more than a week if luck is with us. Meanwhile try to exercise your arms and legs as best you can, especially your arm, Tyle. The feeling will come back if you do. You must be ready to ride. Meanwhile, if anyone comes and I am not with them, pretend you are dying. Groan or weep, but say nothing at all—to anyone but me. Is that clear?"

"Yes, my lady, and thank you," they chorused together. "God bless you, my lady, and have a care for yourself," said Johann. "I love you, my angel," sang Tyle.

When the grating had been replaced with a resounding clang, they turned to the food and found that it was the same as that served in the hall. Poor quality they had considered it when they first arrived here. Today, it was ambrosia—nourishing, and almost too much for their shrunken stomachs.

"Johann," asked Tyle, "was I dreaming, or was it really she?"

"Yes, she was real," Johann reassured him, "and so is this food. The first real food in weeks. Eat slowly or it will make you sick. And look ye, she has sent us an extra bucket of water. Perhaps we dare indulge in washing ourselves."

"Don't tempt me with dreams of such luxuries as a bath. I have almost forgotten such things exist. Do you really think she can free us? I am almost afraid to hope."

"I, too," agreed Johann, "but she seemed confident, although I have no idea how she plans to accomplish it."

"Johann, I must talk her into going with us. This is no place for such a gentle maiden, and besides, I do love her."

"Tyle, Tyle, how can you say that? You barely know her."

"Nonetheless, I know that I love her. I knew it from the first moment I saw her. I have never been so struck by a woman, and you well know I had more than my share back in Hildesheim."

Johann shook his head, "I agree this robbers' nest is no place for her, but while you were swooned in the hall, she told me she had helped others escape. Yet she did not leave. Have you no thought for her feelings? Perhaps she would not forsake her mother."

Tyle pondered this. "Yet I must try to convince her. Not only do I love her, but on my knight's honor I must rescue her from—from this dragon. The Code would not have it otherwise."

"The Code would not condone abducting a maiden from her parents either. No matter how cruel and degenerate, he is still her father and has rights over her until he hands her over to a husband. Any knight you met on the road would be obliged to rescue her from you, by your same precious Code, and send her back here."

"Then she must disguise herself and become my page. Johann, you must help me convince her."

"Tyle, I think this dungeon has truly addled your wits. You know I would help you in just about anything, my friend, but not this. If the lady herself suggests it of her own free will, of course, then I will do all I can to help you both. But I shall never try to coerce her into risking her reputation, and mayhap her very life, in such a hare-brained scheme. We are not even sure of our own escape. Ludolf may yet remember us and decide to have an 'entertainment'. Think on that."

Tyle hung his head. "You are right as usual. I fear I was so fired with hope I got carried away by my own dreams. We may well die here in our own filth."

"I did not mean to take hope away. It is all we have to sustain us. But let us prepare sensibly. Here, let me massage your arm."

In the event, more than a week passed and they were still no wiser as to Chlotilde's plans for their escape. She had sent a new poultice and Tyle's arm was beginning to heal. They exercised diligently and realized how weak they had become. The food was always warm, nourishing and ample, if not the best, and slowly their strength returned. As often as possible she sent an extra bucket of water, once even a cake of soap, a luxury they rejoiced in. She did not come every day, but the servants were definitely kinder than they had been before. When she did come, Tyle ardently pursued his strange courtship from the bottom of the dungeon. She seemed to accept his overtures, no longer chiding him for foolishness or discouraging him, but neither did she encourage him. Johann could not tell if it was just her innate kindness or, worse yet, pity. Perhaps she really was interested in Tyle. It was hard to tell, separated as they were by twenty feet of vertical darkness.

All this time Tyle was so smitten he never once expressed concern for his servant Jacob. Johann had finally asked and was reassured that Jacob had been sent to work in the stables, but it disturbed him that Tyle should be so callous. When Johann finally commented upon it, Tyle said that he had been afraid to ask, fearing Jacob was dead. Johann said nothing.

Then one day Chlotilde whispered, "A friend of yours has come to help."

"Dierck!" exclaimed Johann. "Thank God and all the Saints that he lives."

"He would not give his name, but I am sure it is he."

"Oh, bless him. He will think of something. He is very clever."

"So I have learned," she said. "He has already improved on my plan.

264

In three or four more days I shall tell you our plan. Be ready."

"And what of Jacob?" asked Tyle.

"He is still within, but free to come and go. They have met. He has become well trusted in the stables, if you take my meaning."

"Ah, our horses," said Tyle. "Oh, my lady angel, be sure there are five."

She put her finger to her lips. "I can say no more. Pray." And she was gone.

True to her word, on the fourth afternoon she whispered, "Tonight is the dark of the moon. Do not go to sleep. Be ready."

"Tell us what the plan is, my lady," said Johann, "so we may know what to expect."

She shook her head. "I shall not be here. The two servants I shall send can be trusted implicitly. Do exactly as they say."

"My love," cried Tyle, "please come with us. I beg of you one last time."

Again she put her finger to her lips. "Go with God, Tyle, and trust Him—as I do." Her voice caught. Then she blew him a kiss and left them.

Tyle sat down on the damp straw and put his head in his hands. "That was farewell. I shall never see my love again."

"Perhaps she will be at the gate," suggested Johann. "Just think, Tyle, we are soon out of this putrid hole, if all goes well. That alone should cheer you up."

"Sure it does, but—oh, well," he sighed resignedly. "Let's eat and wash."

"And pray, like she said."

Darkness covered the hole and they waited. It was difficult to stay awake in the fetid air. They could not even see each other. They held hands and were reassured. They took turns praying and guessing just how their escape would be effected. They wondered what day of the week it was, even what month, so disoriented they had become.

About three hours after darkness they heard the scrape of the grate being removed. It was so black they could see nothing, but they sensed there was more than one person up above.

"Shall we call out?" whispered Tyle.

"No, not yet. She said they would give us instructions."

Suddenly something was pushed down the hole and they felt the rungs of a ladder.

"Shall we go up?" asked Tyle.

265

"I suppose," said Johann, but then they realized someone was descending.

They flattened themselves against the wall and waited. They could hear the man's heavy breathing as he negotiated the almost vertical ladder. "Shall we jump him? It might be our only chance," suggested Tyle.

"Don't be foolish. There is another one above," replied Johann. "Besides, don't you trust your lady?"

The man evidently heard them, for the walls of the dungeon amplified even the tiniest sound. "I can be trusted," he said. "I am my lady's faithful servant and follow her instructions." When he reached their level, he asked, "Are you able to climb?" They said they thought they could. "Good, then listen carefully." He turned his head toward the hole and bellowed, "You're right. There's nothing here but two stinking bodies. Must have died a couple of days ago. Lordy, let's get this over with before I puke." Then he whispered, "You understand? You are supposed to be dead. When you reach the top someone will lift you out and lay you down on the floor. Be limp, don't move and breathe shallowly. And you stay dead no matter what happens until you are well outside the castle walls and someone tells you to wake up." He laughed at his little joke. "Now which one is Master Tyle? You first and go very slowly, then Master Johann. And I shall be right behind in case you are weaker than you thought."

Slowly they started the ascent. Tyle's arm soon began to ache from the strain. He bit his lips to keep from moaning and shifted his weight so that the left side bore the brunt of it. Johann wondered that the ladder would bear the weight of all of them. For all their weakness, they were not breathing nearly as loudly as the man who was huffing and puffing behind them. Then Johann realized it was all put on, for he was supposed to be carrying a deadweight body. He almost laughed.

At the top they lay limply while the man pulled up the ladder and closed the grate. The temptation to gulp lungsful of fresh air was overpowering. Then each man slung one of them over his shoulder like a sack of meal and off they went. As they passed the hall, Johann risked a peek through lowered eyelashes. All the men seemed drunk or asleep. They went boldly across the bailey and along the inner wall until they came to a tiny postern gate. The guard there was totally passed out. Johann wondered if Chlotilde had not cast some spell over the men. Perhaps she is a witch. In that case Tyle is well rid of her. And yet . . .

Outside the gate they were met by a priest. Johann risked another glance. In the dark he could not see the man's face, only his vestments.

"Come quickly. Let's get this over with. The graves are already dug." Did that voice sound familiar?

"Aye, Father," said one of the men. "And none too soon for me. They stink."

They set off at a good trot following the priest. After travelling some distance through the woods, they arrived at a small burying-ground. Although it was quite dark, they could see two freshly opened graves. Johann was getting nervous when suddenly they were dumped on their feet.

"Now the resurrection and you will be in heaven," said the jokester.

"Shall I shrive you now or later, my lord?" asked the priest.

"Dierck!" shouted Johann and fell into his arms.

"Quiet, my lord," replied Dierck. "It is too soon for merriment. I must commit the bodies. And you do stink." He held his nose and backed away.

Suddenly a horse nickered in recognition and Tyle looked up to see Jacob stroking the animal's nose and next to him, holding other horses, stood a young page dressed in a shabby, baggy tunic.

"My lady angel," cried Tyle and stumbled over to where she stood. She went into his arms as naturally as if they had been lovers for years. "Ah, my love," he murmured into her ear. "You did not fail me. You are going with us." She nodded. "I love you so."

"I love you, too, Tyle. And I go willingly, at probably more risk to you than to me. I pray Our Lady will guide us and guard us. Now we must make haste."

"There are six horses. Who else?"

"No one," she replied. "It is a packhorse, well laden with all your armor, some of my clothes and plenty of food, so that we need not stop until we are safely in Burgundy. We will travel faster without all that added weight on your own horses. I shall tend this one. Now here are your swords. Buckle them on. And your cloaks."

They were grateful for this for they were already shivering with the nip of fall in the air. It was mid-September and the leaves were beginning to turn.

Dierck removed his vestments and said, "I think I shall keep these. They just may come in handy another time. I make a fair priest, don't you think, my lord?"

Johann cuffed him on the shoulder. "But why the graves? That was a bit too realistic to suit me." He shuddered.

"We have used the same ones many times before," interjected Chlotilde. The men were already starting to fill them in. "They must look freshly turned, just in case anyone should check. Although few come here. It is not the castle burying ground, but unconsecrated ground where he leaves those unfortunates who do not survive his 'entertainments'." She crossed herself and they all followed suit. "Now let us away. We must walk the horses quietly through the woods until we are well past the second toll gate. Then we can use the road, but I suggest for the next few days we ride by night and sleep well hidden by day."

"My lady, tell me one thing," said Johann. "How could you be sure they would all be drunk tonight?"

She smiled. "Your Dierck and I between us concocted a lovely sleeping potion." She took Tyle's hand as she started to lead them down the path. "And I think he worked a potion on me, too, Tyle. He convinced me that you need a good woman."

After they had skirted the second toll gate and were a safe distance from the castle, they mounted and took to the road. They rode westward at a brisk pace until dawn, when Chlotilde led them off the road to find a resting place. The hills were turning into mountains and the forest was very dense. They did not have to go far before they were well sheltered. Johann and Tyle were exhausted. The ride, which would have been long and strenuous under any circumstances, taxed their weakened bodies to the utmost. They could barely stay awake while Chlotilde doled out breakfast. They had many questions, but they could wait. Suffice it that they were free—and breathing fresh air.

They slept most of the day, ate well, and were riding again soon after dark. Both Johann and Tyle were stiff all over but neither complained of it, for they knew the lives of all of them depended on keeping up the pace. The next day they camped beside a sparkling brook that rushed down to the river.

"A bath!" exclaimed Tyle. "By Our Lady, I must have a bath."

"I, too," agreed Johann. "I wonder the rest of you can stand the stink of us."

"You *are* rather ripe," said Dierck.

"And I shall burn these rags," said Tyle.

"No," said Chlotilde. "We do not have that many clothes to spare. I shall wash them for you."

"See what a wonderful wife she will make," said Tyle.

Chlotilde smiled.

268

They gasped with shock at the icy water but afterwards felt better than they had in a long time. Gradually they learned that Chlotilde's mother had died two weeks after their capture. Murdered, she said, by Ludolf's abuse. So she had nothing to hold her and, in fact, was afraid to live in the castle alone with him. Dierck related how he had drifted down the river on the current, whistling to the horse all the while, until he was finally able to come ashore. Chlotilde told them how she had immediately hidden all their weapons, clothes, and papers, leaving only their money in their saddlebags.

"I had to leave that, or he would surely have tortured you to find out where it was."

"Then we are travelling with no funds at all?" asked Johann.

"Never fear," she laughed. "I stole most of it back out of his coffers when he was drunk."

"Bless your brave heart," said Tyle, eyes full of love. "I shall make it all up to you when I win my first tournament."

Dierck said he had considered going back to the Archbishop for help but decided against it when he learned from the local people how poorly defended Castle Rheinfels was under Ludolf. He had planned on drugging the guards and attempting the rescue by himself until Jacob told him that Chlotilde was an ally.

"And oh, yes," she added, "I too brought most of my medicines. And I even succeeded in wheedling my mother's inheritance out of him. Pittance though it is, every bit will help."

A week later they considered it safe enough to ride by day, but they still camped in the woods by night. They bypassed the city of Trier on the other side of the river.

"Not a safe place for us," explained Chlotilde. "Yon archbishop is his lord's overlord. Word of our passing could too easily filter back."

"Yes," Tyle agreed, "we had already heard from the Archbishop of Cologne that he was not to be trusted."

Chlotilde laughed. "None of those high potentates trust one another. Nor do their vassals, for that matter. It is the way of men."

"But it shouldn't be that way. We trusted you and we all trust one another," put in Johann.

Chlotilde just smiled and shook her head at his naïveté.

A few days later they crossed the border from Trier to that part of Lorraine called Brabant and could finally relax from their fear of pursuit, although never their vigilance. The roads were never safe for a small party.

269

Politics being what they were, they were not sure if they were still within the bounds of the Empire or not. Lorraine, with its valuable iron mines, was ever a pawn in the hands of her powerful neighbors, the Holy Roman Emperors and the Dukes of Burgundy, and even the increasingly powerful Kings of France. The territory changed hands with alarming frequency.

They continued to follow the Moselle, which swung to the south above Trier. At Metz they spent their first night at an inn. Not only were the nights growing chillier, but they had run out of food. For the first time the question of sleeping arrangements arose.

"Not to worry," announced Tyle. "I shall cradle my love in my arms, but I swear by the Virgin that I'll not touch her beyond that. Johann, you are my witness."

So they slept, three in the bed, with the servants in the stables, but contrary to custom they kept all their clothes on. Tyle thrilled to Chlotilde's enticing warmth and was hard put to keep his vow. But they were all so weary from the day of hard riding that sleep quickly overtook them.

There they finally left the Moselle behind and followed the ancient Roman road directly westward to Châlons. At an inn there they met some Flemish merchants whose ideas were to change their whole lives.

All the inns were crowded and they were hard put to find a bed. They had ridden a long stretch that day and longed for food and rest. At the third inn at which they were refused, they were debating whether to bed down in the courtyard, if the innkeeper would let them, or to push on. But it was very foolhardy to travel at night especially now that they were in a strange country. Two middle-aged, well-dressed merchants with a long string of packhorses, who had arrived just moments before them, got the last bed. They overheard the young people's dilemma and one of them approached.

"Good morrow, young sirs," he said. "I overheard your conversation and I can see that you are strangers here. I would not advise travelling at night even though the roads are crowded, for there are that many more ruffians abroad. My partner and I are only two in our bed. This is a comfortable inn. We can surely fit four, if you would care to share with us. We are honorable men." His manner was kindly and he spoke to them in heavily accented Low German. Since they spoke no French, they had been thrown back on their Latin since crossing the border of Champagne.

Praise the saints, thought Johann, he sure is a kindly person and speaks our native tongue. "Thank you for your offer, kind sir, for my part I am happy to accept your hospitality. What think you, Tyle?"

"I—uh—I mean, we usually sleep three together," stammered Tyle. The man looked puzzled. "Chlo—uh—my page is accustomed to sleeping with us."

The man frowned. "Well, that would never do. In that case . . . " He started to turn away.

"Wait, sir," said Chlotilde. "My lord Tyle, there is no need to turn down a good bed on my account. I shall be perfectly safe with Dierck and Jacob. Besides, with all these horses here, there can be no stable room either. They will need my help."

Tyle could not argue with her without giving away their secret.

"Then it is settled, sir, and grateful are we," said Johann. "Since you seem to be familiar with the inn, tell me, do they serve a good board?"

"Excellent," was the reply, "but with all these people they may run out. I suggest we eat before we even unload the horses. Will you join us?"

"Most eagerly, sir, for we have been long on the road."

They left the horses in charge of a groom and trooped into the common room of the inn. It was already packed, but they found an empty bench along one wall and all seven of them squeezed onto it. The merchants' servants would eat later, for they dared not trust their valuable merchandise to the care of a stranger.

"I am Hendrik and my friend is Piers," said the merchant who had first spoken to them. "We are cloth merchants from Bruges on our way to the cold fair at Troyes."

"The cold fair?" said Tyle. "What is that?"

"You mean you do not know the Champagne fairs?" asked Piers, indicating by the tone of his voice that they were indeed unworldly boors from some far backwater. "They are the greatest fairs in Christendom and all the world comes here to trade."

"Indeed we must plead ignorance of trade," said Tyle. "But why do you call it the 'cold' fair?"

"There are six fairs throughout the year in four different towns in this area," explained Hendrik patiently. "Troyes has two, the 'hot' fair in summer and the 'cold' fair now in the late fall."

"I see," said Johann. "Then that is why the inns and the roads are so crowded."

"Yes indeed," replied Hendrik. "But where are you from and where are you bound, that you have never heard of these great fairs?"

Johann introduced themselves, calling Chlotilde Ludolf although he knew she hated it. "We are students from Braunschweig-Lüneberg bound for the University in Paris, where we hope to continue our studies."

The merchants' faces fell. Tyle noted it and quickly added, "We are also knights, my good man." He tried not to sound condescending, but it came out that way. The merchants looked at each other. Either way, they should not be sharing the board, much less a bed, with these two young nobles. As merchants, especially because of their wealth, they were several steps above students in the order of things, but still commoners in relation to any nobles.

Suddenly Piers burst out laughing. "And you have set out to seek your fortune?" He could see the irony of the situation and his wit eased the awkward moment.

"I suppose you might say that," said Tyle, still a little put out.

But Johann could see how ridiculously innocent they must seem to these men of the world. "We plan to study first—at least I do—and then seek our fortune."

"And what do you plan to study?" asked Hendrik.

"We're not really sure. Our families intend us for the Church, but Tyle does not want that and even I am beginning to have some doubts, as we see more of the world."

"I want to be a knight-errant and make lots of money at tournaments," burst out Tyle. "That's the real reason I'm going to France."

Piers looked at Tyle's tall, slim, aristocratic frame and began to laugh again. "Forgive me, young sir, but you seem too intelligent for that. Those giant blockheads that make their living at tournaments are all brawn and no brains. How could they have any brains when their heads are constantly being dented every time their helmets are?"

Tyle tried to look insulted but smiled in spite of himself at the man's description. And he had said he was intelligent.

"I take it you are second or third sons," commented Hendrik.

"Third, both of us," replied Johann.

"Well let me tell you there are far better ways to make a fortune than getting your head bashed in and your ribs broken and, yes, than mumbling prayers in some dank monastery while you scratch the fleas in your hair shirt. Trade, that is what you should get into. That's where the money is."

Johann looked at Tyle, who frowned. Dierck smirked knowingly.

"We saw something of it when we passed through Cologne," said

Johann, "but I must admit I had no idea of the wealth of these merchants. Why, some of them were dressed more richly than many nobles."

"And verily they are wealthier than many as well," said Piers. "But surely if you are from Braunschweig-Lüneburg you are familiar with the Hanseatic League. Both Braunschweig and Lüneburg are members, as well as Hamburg and Bremen. The patricians of Lüneburg are extremely wealthy from the sale of her salt."

Tyle looked surprised at this. "Yes, we have heard of the League, but to be honest we have never been to Lüneburg. We were both raised in our parents' castles and then sent to the Cathedral school at Hildesheim."

"An episcopal backwater," commented Piers.

"But they have a growing merchants' colony," said Johann defensively.

"And even their own church, the Jacobikirche," added Tyle.

"But infinitesimal compared to the Hanse cities," said Hendrik.

"To tell you the truth," Johann replied, "we heard more about the Hanse in Cologne than we ever did at home. They say she is queen of the League."

"If she is queen, then Lübeck is king," said Hendrik. "The Lübeck code is law in all the Hanse cities and her money is the standard of exchange throughout northern Europe."

"Really?" exclaimed Johann. "I had no idea."

"But what has the Hanse to do with you and with this fair you speak of?" asked Tyle.

"We are Hanseatic agents. The Hanse controls all the trade in northern Europe—all the land, rivers and especially the sea routes. Her ships can be found in every port from London in the west to Novgorod in the east. They bring lumber, furs, and especially grain from the more backward lands to the east and trade them for Flemish cloth at Bruges, which in turn is made from wool shipped from England. And from each transaction the merchants and the shipowners, who are often one and the same, make huge profits."

Johann and Tyle could not hide the amazement from their faces. Chlotilde said not a word, but her mind was sifting all this fascinating information. Dierck wore a look of 'I told you so'. Jacob took a swig of ale and left these mind-boggling concepts to his betters.

Johann thought a moment and said, "Then if Lübeck and Cologne are the king and queen of the League, Bruges appears to be the center."

"You might say so. We certainly think so."

"Then why do you leave there at all? Why go to a fair at a small town in the middle of nowhere?" asked Johann.

"Hah," chuckled Piers. "You may think it's in the middle of nowhere, but in fact it is the center of the world for us."

The friends looked more puzzled than ever. "How so?" they asked.

Tyle said, "I thought you just said Bruges was."

Added Johann, "I thought Rome was."

"Bah, Rome. A degenerate rabble that plays dangerous politics with the Pope," said Piers vehemently. "There are only two cities in Italy worth counting. They are Genoa and Venice—and possibly Siena and Florence—but Rome is nothing."

"What Piers is trying to say," put in Hendrik, "is that there is another whole network of trade in the southern sea, which they call the Mediterranean. And Genoa and Venice are the king and queen of this. They control all the trade from the Levant to Portugal. And they and we meet and trade at the Champagne fairs."

"By the Virgin's breasts, then you speak right when you say that these fairs are the center of the world," exclaimed Tyle.

"And these trade networks encompass the whole world," added Johann.

"Not quite," replied Hendrik, "but certainly all of Christendom and a good bit of the rest."

"And then there are the Lombard bankers who tie it all together," said Piers.

"The what?" asked Tyle.

"The bankers from northern Italy who act as money–changers, lending agents, and the clearinghouse for the bills of exchange that make all this trade possible."

The friends looked bewildered.

Tyle said, "Good sirs, I can see now why you thought us country bumpkins. I had thought that trade was the pedlar with the sack on his back that sold my mother and sisters needles and ribbons in exchange for some eggs or a chicken. I never would have conceived anything of the magnitude of this commerce you describe. We were taught that it is demeaning, but I see now how these merchants can become so rich. I admit I find it fascinating."

"And bewildering," said Johann. "I have been able to follow all you describe up to this last bit about the bankers. I am not even familiar with the word. But you speak of money–changers. I thought the Church forbade usury and only the Jews could engage in it."

"Bah, don't you believe it," chuckled Piers. "The Church forbids many things, but the Church is so far behind the times, it will never catch up. The Church even forbids making a profit on a sale. Did you know that? She would have the world remain back at the level of your mother's eggs for the pedlar's ribbons. Why should a merchant not make a profit? Why should a shipowner not charge for his services — and his risk?"

"Look ye," said Hendrik, "when a merchant buys tons of grain from the farms of Poland, he pays as little as he can, because they have so much surplus it would only rot or be food for the rats, if he did not take it off their hands, so anything he pays them is a lot to them. But why should he not charge a high price, after transporting it a thousand miles to London, where they are begging for bread?"

"Yes, I can understand that," said Johann, "but you have not answered my question about the bankers."

"I shall explain," said Hendrik patiently. "Time was when a merchant carried his money with him, sometimes in huge chests. With trade the scope of which we are speaking, this can be very cumbersome, let alone unsafe. So the Lombards came up with an innovation that far surpasses the simple usury permitted to the Jews. They call it a bank. Say a merchant in Genoa has a thousand florins for which he has no immediate use. He entrusts it to the bank in Siena, which is the largest. They may lend it out at interest or invest it in shares in a ship or some trading enterprise. If such is profitable they split the profits. Meanwhile the merchant wishes to buy some cloth from a merchant in Bruges. The bank gives him a bill of exchange for that amount, for they have other depositors' money which can cover for it while that is lent out. The merchant's agent comes to Troyes and buys our cloth and *pays* for it with the bill of exchange. We in turn buy some spices, which we know we can sell at a huge profit in London, from a Venetian merchant, and we pay for it with the *same* bill of exchange. The Venetian's agent then takes it back to the bank in Siena and collects his money. That is as simply as I can explain it. In practice it is sometimes a bit more complicated than that, for these bills are often discounted or bear interest and very often pass through a dozen or more hands before they are returned to the bank or to the original merchant, and everyone makes a profit along the way."

"Amazing. Absolutely amazing," said Tyle, shaking his head.

"And all legal?" asked Johann, ever the worrier.

"According to the Lübeck Law and the laws of Venice, Genoa and

Siena, completely legal, and spelled out very carefully in the Codes. According to Mother Church totally illegal, so she must sell her indulgences to pardon our sins," Piers guffawed. "But there is not a prelate alive, even the Pope himself, who has not borrowed from us merchants, and at hefty interest, in order to buy a benefice or to fight their wars. And they are the worst risk of all, let me tell you."

Johann was shocked but fascinated. These men made it all seem so right, and Piers' mirth was contagious.

Even Tyle said, "Good sirs, we have learned more from you this night than ever in all the years at school. But we must soon to bed. We have a long ride on the morrow."

Then Hendrik said, "Why go to Paris at all? You seem to be bright young men. Come with us to Troyes and learn more. Perhaps you can even make a little money."

"Us?" they asked, surprised.

"Why not?" replied the merchant. "It seems a little late to be starting the term at the University."

"It is that," agreed Johann. "We were—uh—delayed. What think you, Tyle? We can always start at the January term."

"I—uh—I must needs give it some thought," said Tyle, glancing at Chlotilde, but Johann could see he was clearly interested in the merchants' offer.

Then Hendrik delivered the parting shot. "We were both third sons, too, I of a noble family whose castle was destroyed in the everlasting wars between England and France, Piers of a freed peasant who fled to Bruges and worked as a skilled woodcarver."

"And now you are partners? And wealthy?" asked Tyle.

"Yes, to both. We were fortunate enough to have been apprenticed to the same merchant in our youth and have been friends ever since. Anyone with brains and initiative can do the same. It is a new world we are part of."

"Good sirs, we shall think carefully on your offer and let you know in the morning," said Johann.

After supper they went out to check on the horses before going to bed. They were eager to discuss the merchants' proposition.

"Do it," urged Chlotilde. "I have never heard anything so exciting. If I were a man, I wouldn't hesitate a minute."

"I don't know," said Tyle, "I admit it sounds fascinating, but not very manly. I was taught that a man either fights if he is a noble, prays if he is a clerk or labors for the other two if he is a peasant—the three classes of society, nothing else. And the idea of an apprenticeship like any common artisan is abhorrent to me. Why, one's master might once have been a peasant. I have to think of my family's name."

"Tyle, you are not only an old-fashioned snob but crazy as well," exclaimed Johann. "I remind you that ever since we crossed the Weser our family names have meant nothing, absolutely nothing, to anyone. And I remind you also that we are third sons of families that are nowhere near as wealthy as the least of these merchants. We are only a burden to them that they want to be rid of. Those are the cold, hard facts."

Tyle looked abashed.

"And furthermore," said Chlotilde, "if you think I am going to go trailing around half of Christendom with the type of uncouth roughnecks that follow the tournaments just to see you wear my kerchief while you get your head bashed in, you don't really know the kind of woman I am at all. I love you, Tyle, but I have no intention of marrying a cripple or—or a drifter. And I had not realized what an insufferable snob you are. Most likely your precious family would look down their noses at the daughter of an infamous robber-baron."

Tyle's look changed from one of shock to one of heartbreak. "You really mean that, don't you?" he asked.

She nodded and turned away to hide her tears.

"Master Tyle," said Dierck quietly, "the times are changing and you must change with them. I know that this new commerce is money and money is power. It's a good opportunity. Think on it."

And even Jacob spoke up. "Master Tyle, I don't understand much of what those gentlemen were talking about, but I know you never were much of a fighter—a scrapper, ja, but not a heavy warrior. You don't have the experience these knight-errants have. I've always been worried about this tournament idea of yours, if you'll forgive my saying so. I think the lady is right. And I'll say this, she is the best thing that's ever happened to you. Made more of a gentleman out of you. And if the lady thinks this is a good thing, then I'm all for it, too. Begging your pardon, my lord."

It was the longest speech bovine Jacob had ever made, and Tyle was astonished. Just a few months ago he would have beaten the servant for his presumptuousness, but now he listened and saw the sense of it. Besides, he could not bear the thought of losing Chlotilde. *I guess she has made me more gentlemanly,* he thought.

Johann could see him wavering. "Come on, Tyle. Let's at least visit Troyes and see what it's all about. What have we got to lose? We are too

277

late for the term at Paris anyway. I'm really curious to see this whole process firsthand."

Even my best friend, thought Tyle. Could it be that they are right and I am wrong? Suddenly he made up his mind, before his courage failed him. "I'll go," he said, "and worry about the family later."

Three days later they rode into Troyes. It was not a large town, even by the standards of the day, but for four months out of the year its population quadrupled. The entire town was given over to the business of the fair. Every space, the few streets of any width, every church porch and the halls of public buildings were filled with booths. Each group of merchants, the cloth dealers, the goldsmiths, the purveyors of spices and so on, had its own exclusive spot. The Flemish cloth merchants had a choice spot inside the great hall of the Hotel-de-Ville.

While their servants unpacked the horses and started setting up the display of their wares, Hendrik and Piers went directly to the Hanse house. There they sought the latest news, picked up mail, received and placed orders and, above all, checked on the current prices of all the commodities that interested them. Johann and Tyle trailed along with them and met several more Hanseatic merchants and agents, one even from Lüneburg. But the press of business was so great that no one had time for them, so they just stood and watched, intrigued by it all but completely bewildered.

After about two hours the merchants found them still standing in almost the same spot they had left them.

"Come, we must check on our goods and be sure our assistants have set everything up to our liking. Then over supper we shall explain to you a bit of what went on here today. Tomorrow we shall show you the rest of the town, for it is our custom for one of us to mind the stall in order to take orders for our own goods and the other will go looking about for those things which we wish to buy."

"But first we must seek a place to sleep," Johann reminded them, "I fear it will be difficult."

"But you are staying with us," said Hendrik. "We have two rooms here."

"Your own rooms?" asked Johann in disbelief.

"Yes, of course," replied Hendrik. "The Bruges Hanse owns the house, but we reserve them far in advance. Always the same ones every fair, so they are just like home. And the service is excellent."

"The service?"

"Why, yes. The Hanse has its own servants who cook and clean for the whole house. The meals are sent up to us. We are too busy to worry about such things during the fair."

Tyle immediately foresaw a problem. He did not want to relegate Chlotilde to the servants' quarters for two months. He longed to hold her in his arms again. What to do? On the way from Châlons he had grown quite friendly with Piers. At first Tyle had detested the man, for no other reason than that he was of peasant stock. But Piers jovially made mock of all the established institutions of the day, especially the Church and even the feudal system itself. Gradually losing his own touchiness, Tyle began to enjoy Piers' reparteé, for he himself was a cynic at heart. By the time they reached Troyes he felt Piers was a friend and decided to trust him.

The streets were too narrow to walk more than two abreast, so Tyle purposely fell in with Piers and let Johann accompany Hendrik.

"I should like to ask your advice on something, Piers," he ventured.

"Do I look like your confessor?" was the rejoinder.

Tyle laughed. "That's the last thing I need, but I feel I can trust you."

"That depends," warned Piers. "I am honest to my toes when it comes to business, but don't trust me with your wife."

"I don't have a wife, but—but I have a dear lady whom I love very much."

"So? We all do, if it comes to that."

"Her name is Chlotilde," stammered Tyle.

"A charming name. A good Low German name."

Piers was making this very difficult.

"She is right here with me," Tyle blurted out.

"Where?" Piers looked about the narrow street.

"The page you know as Ludolf." There, at last it was out.

Piers guffawed loudly and slapped Tyle on the shoulder. "God's teeth! That is good news. And here I was worried for my own virtue. I thought you were a boy-lover."

Tyle blushed. "I—I had to tell you."

"And naturally you want to sleep with her. No problem, we have plenty of room."

"Yes—I mean no—I mean, I haven't touched her yet—that way, I mean."

Piers laughed again at his discomfort. "But you don't want to trust her to the servants' quarters."

"Exactly."

"Can't say as I blame you. That *would* be a problem. They are none too private. Do you intend to wed her?"

"Eventually, yes, but not for a while. I must make some money first."

"I daresay that would help. Wives are expensive, let me tell you. Wait till Hendrik hears this. Hey, Hendrik!" he called out. Johann and Hendrik stopped and turned around. "Now reintroduce me to your lady."

Tyle beckoned to Chlotilde. "I have told him about us," he whispered.

She blushed. "Does he think . . . ?"

"No, sweeting, I told him exactly how it is between us, but I couldn't be separated from you for two whole months."

Piers executed an exaggerated bow. "My lady, it is a pleasure to meet you at last. You have just been promoted from belowstairs to the exalted heights of a Hanse apartment."

Hendrik, witnessing Piers' clowning, was not the least bit surprised when they told him the truth about Chlotilde. His only comment was, "Then we had better introduce you as his wife, my dear, after you get out of those clothes, of course. The servants at a Hanse house can be a bit stuffy. You see, there are so many of the lovely—uh, ladies of the town coming and going at all times, and we wouldn't want them to think you were one of those."

"But suppose he decides to become an apprentice," said Piers, serious for once. "They can't be married, you know."

"We'll worry about that if it ever comes to it," replied Hendrik.

The next day, Johann and Tyle helped out for a while at the merchants' booth, listening avidly to the transactions being made. When Hendrik took an order for cloth he did not have right there, Johann asked, "How can you sell something which you do not have?"

"I have a warehouse full of it in Bruges. As soon as we return I shall deliver it to this man's agent there, who will ship it to him. He could not possibly carry all he ordered on his pack animals anyway. But by his buying a very large quantity we can give him a better price."

"You mean the prices are not fixed?" asked Tyle. "I wondered why you were asking about prices yesterday at the Hanse house."

"They vary from day to day at a fair and even from month to month elsewhere," explained Hendrik. "It is all a case of supply and demand and, to some extent, shipping conditions."

"You mean like bringing grain from the east to London."

"To some extent. But there are even more refinements than that.

This is the best time of year to sell our cloth, for the demand is high. The sheep are shorn in the early spring and the cloth is woven in late spring and early summer, right? But then there is a glut on the market because no one is thinking of woolen clothes then. So we buy it up then, when it is cheap, and hold it in our warehouses until now, when winter is approaching. Also, it is customary for most lords to give their servants and retainers their new robes at Martinmas, and many ladies will want a new gown for Christmas. So you see?" He held out his hands, palms up, to indicate the simplicity of the matter.

"I understand," said Tyle.

"By the same token," went on Hendrik, "it is a good time for us to buy spices from the Venetians, for they have been bringing them from the east all summer when sea conditions are favorable and there is an ample supply, so prices are relatively cheap—although spices are never cheap. But soon, when folks start slaughtering the pigs and preserving food for the winter, the demand will be higher, and then we can sell them at a good profit."

"Fascinating," said Tyle.

Later in the day Piers took them around the town to see the rest of the fair. The grain market alone took up a whole square.

"You mean men are willing to buy on the strength of just those samples?" asked Johann.

"Yes, tons of it, for if the quality is not what the merchant claims, he will not get paid and, worse, no one will buy from him next year."

Johann noted that the spices were sold in much the same way, but from even smaller samples. "Spices are worth more than their weight in gold," explained Piers, "nay, I should say silver, for the merchants of the east will take nothing but silver. It is worth more to them than gold. That is where your city of Goslar profits. She ships almost all the silver she can mine directly over the Alps to Venice."

The friends nodded. Goslar was not far from Hildesheim, and they had heard of her rich mines. But Johann was more interested in the spices. He looked at the tiny, shriveled black and brown particles and wondered how one could tell good from bad. He recognized peppercorns and cloves, but most of the rest were completely foreign to him. He wagered his mother would know more. Perhaps even Chlotilde. He watched Piers dickering and realized the years of experience it must take to be so knowledgeable.

When this deal was completed, the Venetian said suddenly, "Hey,

Piers, have you heard the rumors that the Polos yet live and may be coming home?"

"The Polos?" said Piers blandly.

"You remember the two brothers and a son who left Venice some twenty years ago to travel to the end of the silk road and try to find Cathay."

"God's teeth!" exclaimed Piers. "Why, I was not much older than these two young friends of mine when they left. We all thought they were crazy. I reckoned them long since dead, devoured by beasts or fallen off the edge of the world. You say they live?"

"So 'tis said," replied the Venetian. "Our agent in the Levant had it from his caravan drover, who had it from a ship's captain in India, who had it from God knows whom that they are supposed to be sailing from Cathay around India—sailing, mind you—and heading for Persia on an errand for the Khan of Cathay. Of course, it's only rumor so far, and even if it's true, they might not make it home. But can you imagine what tales they will have to tell? It could open up a whole new world of trade for us."

Piers was so excited he could hardly contain himself. "Amazing. Absolutely amazing. If it's true."

"Yes, if it's true," agreed the Venetian wistfully.

Johann and Tyle did not know what to make of this exchange. They had enough trouble grasping the fact that they were face-to-face with a Venetian from the other side of Europe. Of course, they had a vague notion that spices came from India and silk from Cathay, but these had always been places relegated to the realms of mythology. No European had ever seen them to know they really existed.

"Did you hear that?" asked Piers as they turned away from the spice merchant. "Wait till I tell Hendrik."

"Who are these Polos?" asked Johann.

"Is there really such a place as Cathay?" asked Tyle.

"Where is the silk road?"

"What is a caravan?"

"Whoa!" cried Piers. "One question at a time." And then he told them how one of the Polo brothers on a journey of almost ten years had once followed the silk road as far as Bokhara and there met delegates of the Khan of the Mongols who controlled all of the territory east of there, including the fabled Cathay, which was reportedly the terminus of the silk road. They had requested that he return with a delegation of learned men from the Pope to visit the Khan himself. But when Polo returned, the Pope who was his friend had died. So he and his brother, together with his son, then about the age of Johann and Tyle, decided to make the trip on their own for trade purposes. For since the Saracens had taken control of almost all the Near East, their high tariffs had made the cost of spices, silk and other luxury products from the east prohibitive. "Ah, if they return safely," sighed Piers, "Venice will be the richest city in the world."

"How so?"

"Everyone is seeking new routes to the east to circumvent the Moslem world. He who is first will control it. Even some Swedes once tried to find a northern route, but they never came back."

"They may yet," said Johann. "When did you say these Polos left?"

"Around 1270, I believe."

"God's teeth," exclaimed Tyle. "That's over twenty years ago. What a journey!"

"But the Swedes left almost two hundred years ago," quipped Piers.

"Oh."

The next few days Hendrik and Piers were extremely busy, so Johann and Tyle wandered around the town by themselves. They took Chlotilde and the servants along. Every aspect of the fair interested them, but what impressed them most was that it was almost all strictly business, and very big business at that. There was little of the fun and frolic that accompanied all the small town fairs they were familiar with. The only local trade seemed to be in the tremendous amount of food and drink required by the merchants, their assistants, apprentices and servants.

"What I want to see are these bankers in action," said Tyle. "Where do we find them, Piers?" he asked one day.

"Right now only the money-changers are operating. Wait until the end of the month, when the trading is mostly ended and the accounts are being settled. That is when the big bankers like the Buonsignori of Siena set up their tables. That is the most interesting part. You will find them on the porch of the church of St. Jean de la Marché in the Rue Moyenne just beyond the spice market where we were the other day."

Tyle went there immediately. Even though the big transactions were not yet taking place, he was fascinated by the money-changers. Their only equipment was a cloth-covered table on which stood a scale, a small covered pot and a large sack of coins or ingots. Many of them had women working with them, wives or daughters. And they were heavily guarded.

Johann and Tyle noticed that from every transaction the money changer extracted a coin or two and deposited it in the little covered pot.

"I wonder why they do that," said Johann.

"That must be their percentage of the exchange," Tyle suggested.

"Can that be legal?" wondered Johann. "It certainly smacks of usury."

"Now who is being old-fashioned?" teased Tyle. "If men who deal in money can't make money on it, who can? The coins and ingots are just as much a commodity to them as the cloth and spices are to the other merchants. Remember what Piers said about the Church's outmoded policies."

"You're right, of course," agreed Johann. "I just didn't think of it as being a commodity."

At the end of the month the bankers' agents arrived. Their only additional equipment were huge leather-bound ledger books and plenty of quill pens and ink. Every transaction of the fair that was not a strict cash deal was entered under the accounts of the merchants involved. Bills of exchange were cashed in or credited to an account. All the debits and credits were balanced and new bills of exchange were issued where needed or sometimes requested. Loans were repaid with interest and new ones were issued. Where credit had been extended, it was meticulously recorded.

Occasionally there were heated arguments as to the rate of interest charged or paid or the amount of discount on a bill of exchange, but not one merchant questioned the banker's right to that interest or discount, or to the commission he charged for other work.

Tyle found this the most interesting part of all. "If we ever do get to Paris, I see I shall have to study mathematics. This is the best part of the whole fair."

Johann was pleasantly surprised to hear Tyle talk like this.

One time during a lull, Tyle approached one of the banker's agents and asked him all kinds of questions, particularly regarding an apprenticeship.

The man sounded surprised. "I am afraid that is not possible. You see, all the banks are family-owned and-controlled, and only sons and nephews are taken into the business. And we have many children in Italy. It would never do for a stranger to learn our secrets."

Tyle's face fell. The man seemed to sympathize. "I am sorry, but perhaps in Bruges or London, where we have permanent branches, there may be a chance. I have heard that these offices are expanding so rapidly that we are running out of cousins." He shrugged. "But I still doubt they would hire any but other Italians. Sons of friends, you know. Why don't you apprentice to the Hanse? You are German. They would take a bright young man like yourself in a minute."

Tyle thanked the man and turned away to rejoin Johann and Chlotilde. They had already inquired into the Hanse apprenticeship and had learned it usually lasted as long as ten years, with another possible ten as journeymen. The training usually took place in such godforsaken outposts as Bergen in Norway or Riga at the far end of the Baltic and was very strict. They were forbidden to marry, drink or gamble during the whole time. Although in reality plenty of drinking and wenching went on, there was the constant threat of severe punishment or even expulsion.

No, the Hanse apprenticeship did not appeal to Tyle, nor to Johann for that matter. Chlotilde was as disappointed as Tyle. She had counted on his newfound interest in commerce to draw him away from his dream of being a knight-errant.

"I have an idea," she said suddenly. "Perhaps we can still be a part of all this, at least in a small way. Since we do not need it right at the moment, I should like to invest my inheritance with these bankers. I wonder how much interest they will pay me."

"Chlotilde!" cried Tyle, shocked. "I cannot let you think of such a thing. It would be like I was dependent on you. Besides, I am not sure that I trust them."

"Silly boy," she said. "All these great merchants, who are far more experienced in such matters, trust them."

"Better to invest it in shares in a ship or in a merchant's venture," suggested Johann.

"Too risky," she said. "Besides, I'm afraid that would require a lot more than I have."

"Slow down, all of you, if I may be so bold," put in Dierck. "All commendable ideas, but not to be undertaken without ample investigation. You are all innocent babes compared to these people. I suggest you have a serious talk with Hendrik and Piers and take their advice. They are men I trust."

"You are absolutely right," agreed Johann. "I fear we all got carried away with the excitement of all this. It is so new. Let us talk to them, for they will be leaving soon and we also have some very practical things to consider, like where do we go from here."

They returned to the Hotel-de-Ville to find Piers directing the assistants in the packing of their goods.

Hendrik was busy writing. He looked up as they approached the stall.

"Ah, I was just thinking of you," he greeted them. "Well, what do you think of commerce now? Did you enjoy the fair?"

"Exciting," said Tyle.

"Absolutely fascinating," agreed Johann.

"It has given us a lot of food for thought," chimed in Chlotilde. "We should like to ask your advice on certain matters."

If Hendrik was surprised at Chlotilde's unfeminine interest, he showed no sign of it. "I should be happy to advise you where I can."

"We have to decide what . . . ," began Johann.

"I somehow have to get involved in this banking," interrupted Tyle. "I'm intrigued by it."

"And I want to invest my inheritance," added Chlotilde.

Hendrik laughed. "I see you have all fallen under the magic spell of trade, even my lady here, who is not supposed to have such unmaidenly thoughts, much less understand any of it. Did you hear this, Piers?"

"I heard," he replied. "Quite a change from when we first met them in Châlons. But then, I'm not surprised. How can anyone of intelligence not be fascinated by it? Tell them, Hendrik, that there's more than one way of skinning a cat."

"Ach, ja, that there is," said Henrik. "My first bit of advice is that a merchant or anyone connected with trade must first of all be intensely practical and very patient. That does not mean we don't take risks or are afraid to move fast when an opportunity arises. But we prepare ourselves by constantly studying the market, gathering information of all sorts, keeping up with news from all parts of the world. So forget impossible dreams, but have infinite patience with the achievable dreams.

"My second bit of advice is prepare yourselves thoroughly, gain all the experience you can."

"But how can we, Master Hendrik, when all doors seem to be closed to us?" interrupted Tyle.

"Because you are knocking at the wrong doors," replied Hendrik. "The Lombards have banking business exclusively, but they will not be able to keep their secrets forever. Already in Bruges and London and, I believe, Hamburg, too, some of our Hanse merchants and others are experimenting with their ideas. It won't be long before they break the Lombards' monopoly. As far as the Hanse itself is concerned, I realize that you are too old to start an apprenticeship there. Besides, that, too, is becoming very exclusive. Almost all the new apprentices are sons of the wealthiest members. But remember this, when Piers and I first started, the Hanse was not so powerful nor so well entrenched in Bruges. Our old master joined later and then got us in after we became masters in our own local guild. That is the way I think you should go. But first . . . " He paused and took a long swallow from a tankard of ale at his elbow. "First, go to Paris and study. I don't mean theology and such like. Did you know that they now offer courses in such practical things as agriculture, wool-processing and navigation? Yes, indeed, and most of them endowed by wealthy merchants. Study practical mathematics and geography. Even the so-called 'practical' philosophy includes studies in business and personal ethics. Very important, if you are to be successful."

Tyle's mouth hung open and Johann said, "I had no idea. I knew that Paris was the most prestigious university in all Christendom, which is why I wanted to study there, but I really thought it was just more of the same as we learned at Hildesheim."

"It once was, but things have changed greatly since the days of Peter Abelard and Thomas Aquinas," replied Hendrik. "But now for more immediate concerns. There is no point in going to Paris before Twelfth-night. It is no place to spend Christmas if you know no one. As you now know, one of the four Champagne fair towns is Provins, which lies not quite halfway between here and Paris. There are two fairs there as well as here. In Provins, in the upper town, the German merchants have a permanent settlement, and we have several very dear friends among them, with whom we often stay. When you arrived, I was just now writing a letter to one of them, Herr Kaufmann, who I am sure will welcome you if you care to stay with them. They are a childless couple and very kind. It will also give you a chance to observe the ordinary routine of a merchant's business. It's not all fairs, you know."

"I didn't imagine it was," said Johann, "and you are most thoughtful of us, Hendrik. I can't tell you how grateful we are, for in truth we did not know where to go next."

"You are kinder than we deserve, Hendrik," added Tyle, "and your advice has been most encouraging. I, for one, intend to act on it." Everyone was amazed at this from Tyle. "But, tell me true, will your friends accept Chlotilde?"

"Of course they will, for I have written it in my letter. But don't be surprised if Frau Kaufmann puts a little pressure on you. She has a reputation for being quite a matchmaker. May even find someone for you, Johann."

"Oh, no, I am not ready yet," objected Johann.

"One is never ready for love," laughed Piers, joining them. "If it comes, just grab it with both hands and bed it quick, before you lose it."

They all laughed.

"Then it is settled," said Hendrik. "Let me finish my letter. Come back to Provins at the end of the term. The fair will be through then, and we shall meet you and see if you are still of the same mind. If our business is still thriving when you finish your studies, we may have some need of assistants in Bruges."

Even Johann was surprised at this. "Hendrik, you are more than kind," he exclaimed. "Let us see what happens."

"There is one thing that is not settled," spoke up Chlotilde. "You have not advised me how to invest my money."

"That I haven't," admitted Hendrik. "I thought perhaps Tyle . . ."

"I love Tyle dearly," she snapped, "but he is not my husband yet, or even my betrothed. I am acting entirely on my own."

Hendrik was taken aback by her fierce determination. "Then you can do no better for now than to deposit it with the Siena bankers—but not all of it. Keep some back. Living in Paris is not cheap—or you may want a wedding gown. How much do you have?"

She blushed becomingly and told him.

"Then keep about a hundred back, but change it into deniers, and put the rest at interest. Be sure they pay you a good rate. Piers will go with you. He handles all our dealings with the bankers and sharp he is at it, too. Be sure they give you a bill of exchange collectable at the Provins fair next summer. Then you can decide if you want to invest it further or cash it in."

Chlotilde was all excitement as she turned to leave with Piers. Tyle made to accompany her, but she said, "No, Tyle, please, I want to do this by myself."

"Let her go," advised Hendrik. "She is in good hands with Piers. Times are changing in more ways than one, my young friend."

A few days later they were on the road again, heading northwest. Hendrik and Piers had given them a parting gift of good Flemish cloth, enough to make new gowns for the men and a new kirtle for Chlotilde, all of which she promised to make as soon as they were settled in Provins. They also carried gifts for Frau Kaufmann and ample food for the journey, for the countryside was sparsely populated, although the road was heavily travelled with people leaving the fair. The weather, fortunately, stayed mild although it was almost December. They noticed everywhere the vineyards for which Champagne was famous and, as they neared Provins, numerous rose gardens, obviously cultivated for market.

Provins was a picturesque town in two parts—the upper town on a high butte which dated back to pre-Roman times, and the lower town, which grew up around the monastery of St. Ayoul after the Viking raids of the ninth century. It was divided by the tiny Durteint river and surrounded by massive well-maintained fortifications. After they passed through the gate, the first thing they saw was the extensive monastery, where, they learned later, Peter Abelard took refuge more than a century ago, after he was driven from Paris because of his radical teaching and his verbal defeat at the hands of Bernard of Clairvaux. There were many beautiful new buildings and rich houses in the lower town. After wandering around a bit and losing their way, they inquired how to get up to the upper town and were directed to the only street that led up to the heights, the Rue St. Thibault, named after the great count of Champagne who founded the famous fairs and was born here.

"If you're looking for Germanstown, turn left just beyond Caesar's Tower," advised their informant.

"How did he know we were German?" wondered Chlotilde.

"Because we spoke Latin instead of French," replied Johann.

After leading their horses up the steep hill they readily found the Kaufmann residence. It was a solid half-timbered house with a steep gabled roof, large and comfortable without being ostentatious. When they presented the letter from Hendrik, they were welcomed like long-lost family. Both Kaufmanns were portly and grey-haired, intelligent and hardworking. Motherly Frau Kaufmann immediately took Chlotilde under her wing. There was plenty of room for all, including servants and horses. Before long they were sitting before a cheery fire in the parlor telling their stories while a servant laid the table for supper.

"And so now you would become merchants," said Master Kaufmann when he had heard the whole tale.

"We are very interested," agreed Johann.

"Not much to commend you," remarked the merchant, "a potential cleric and a potential knight-errant, both from isolated fiefs, whose only exposure to urban life was secluded behind the walls of a cathedral school." He shook his head. "Your only assets, that I can see, are your intelligence and quick-wittedness. Your desire is great, but is it strong enough to stand up under adversity and discouragement?"

289

"Master Hendrik told us that we must have lots of patience," said Tyle.

"And be very practical and gain all the experience we can," added Johann.

"All that is necessary," agreed Master Kaufmann," and there are two other requirements—frugality and hard, hard work."

"Hard work we understand, but frugality?" asked Johann.

"Yes. I thought all merchants were rich," said Tyle naïvely.

"Not at first," said their host, "none of them. When one starts out, he must be frugal to the point of denying himself everything but the meagrest necessities of food, shelter and the humblest of clothing. Every bit of profit must be reinvested in the business. For not every venture turns a profit and some are outright disasters. In the beginning everyone makes mistakes, some foolish, some just bad luck. Then with experience come prudence and a sharpened sense of what could be profitable and what is too risky. You think all merchants are rich because you see only the successful ones. The business of commerce and trade is a ruthless mistress. She quickly weeds out the spendthrifts, the fools and the laggards."

"Are you then trying to discourage us?" asked Johann, crestfallen.

Master Kaufmann smiled. "No, not at all, Sir Johann. I only wish you to understand what is involved, so that if you decide this is what you want, you go into it with your eyes wide open."

"I understand and I appreciate your making so clear the pitfalls as well as the advantages," said Tyle, "but how can we go about acquiring some of this experience, so that we can really find out for ourselves if we are suited for it or not?"

"Hah," chuckled the merchant. "I see Hendrik did not tell you all he wrote in the letter to me. He suggested I put you to work immediately. I cannot afford to pay you beyond your keep, but he felt sure that would be more than agreeable to you."

Johann and Tyle were flabbergasted. "It certainly would," said Johann. "Yes," agreed Tyle. "We had thought we would be lucky to be allowed to observe from the sidelines."

"Good. Then you will start tomorrow."

Tyle looked around. "But where do you conduct your business?" he asked. "I don't see a shop."

"Hah!" said the merchant again. "The first thing you must learn is the difference between a merchant and a shopkeeper. I buy, or rather my agent in Bruges buys cloth from the weavers in Flanders and I sell it to the shopkeepers here in Provins, who in turn sell it to the public. Rarely does a merchant deal directly with the ultimate consumer. We handle the big ventures, the long-distance trading."

Once again the young men realized how incredibly little they knew about all this.

"I have an office here," he waved toward the front part of the house, "and some store rooms on the upper floor. I also have a warehouse in the lower town from whence I sell to the shopkeepers. So, I think I shall put you there, Johann, getting to learn the various types of cloth, measuring, cutting, becoming acquainted with the shopkeepers. I have two apprentices and a journeyman there, who may be a little jealous at first, but I shall smooth that over, never fear."

"And I?" asked Tyle.

"You, Tyle, I shall start here in the office working on the books."

"The books?"

"The accounts. The recording of every transaction, every penny, denier, mark or ducat we take in and pay out. You expressed your interest in banking, so I think you will suit very well there. My wife usually does it for me, but now that she has some feminine company I know that she will welcome a chance to spend more time in the kitchen and sewing room preparing for the Christmas festivities."

"Amazing," said Tyle.

"What is amazing?"

"That a woman should be responsible for one of the most important aspects of your business."

"Don't fool yourself," said the merchant. "Women are often far more meticulous at figures than men. Doesn't your mother keep her own household accounts?"

"Yes, of course," mused Tyle. "I just never thought of it that way. She's always scolding Papa about keeping the estate profitable. He just doesn't seem to care. He'd much rather be off hawking or riding to hounds."

"You see."

And so the two young men quickly settled into learning their new duties—and there was a great deal to learn. In the evenings before the cozy fire they discussed each other's phase of the business and Herr Kaufmann tried to relate their newfound knowledge to the vast scope of the Hanseatic network.

Chlotilde made them all new gowns, but when the sewing was done she could find little to occupy her time, as the servants were well trained and very efficient. She soon took to sitting quietly in the office while Tyle

291

worked, partly because she wanted to be with him, but also because the financial aspect of the business fascinated her. She listened carefully while Frau Kaufmann explained the procedures and often understood more quickly than Tyle. The merchant's wife smiled secretly to herself, and before long the two were doing the work together.

As Christmas approached, Frau Kaufmann took Chlotilde aside. "Have any of you sent word to your parents to let them know where you are? This is the time of year when families are the closest, and they may be trying to locate you in Paris and will worry that you are not there."

"No, never. Not my father. I never want to see that man again," cried Chlotilde in anguish. "If he were ever to find me, he would drag me back and let every uncouth brute in the castle have his way with me so that no man would ever want me." She sobbed and clutched at the woman's hands. "Please, Frau Kaufmann, don't ever tell him where I am. I've been happy here for the first time in my life. Let me stay."

Frau Kaufmann, having heard most of the girl's story, was not surprised at this outburst. She replied soothingly, "There, there, child, fret yourself not. We'll never tell him and, of course, you can stay as long as you like. I fear I spoke amiss when I said 'any of you'. I know how unhappy your home was. But I was thinking of the boys. Surely their families deserve some communication at this time of year. I only mention it because I heard my husband say that the last ship of the season is leaving Bruges for Bremen soon and our courier to Bruges is leaving day after tomorrow."

Chlotilde, reassured, calmed down. "Yes, you are quite right. I shall suggest it to them this evening. And, Frau Kaufmann," she hesitated, "they should go to Paris before the Lenten term begins. After all, their fathers did give them the money for the tuition. Tyle wants me to go with him, but I—I mean, he's not permitted to marry while he's studying, and I—I hear it's a very rowdy place and I would be alone much of the time. I'm just a little afraid, but I daren't tell Tyle that or he would not go. But if—if I could stay here."

Frau Kaufmann drew the girl to her ample bosom. "Certainly you may, my dear. Didn't I say you could stay as long as you like? I was hoping you'd suggest it. Paris is no place for a maiden, and the accommodations even for the young men are truly dismal."

That evening Chlotilde conveyed Frau Kaufmann's suggestion to the young men.

Johann threw up his hands. "Ach, I've been so busy trying to sort out greige from beige and fustian from serge and the length of an ell in thirty different cities, I haven't given it a thought."

"And I trying to figure out bills of lading and bills of exchange in thirty different currencies and change it all into Lübecker Thalers," added Tyle. "But to tell the truth, it had crossed my mind that I should like to tell them about my sweet Lady Chlotilde. They may be somewhat upset that it is not someone of their choosing, but I know they'll accept it eventually," he added confidently.

"I am afraid mine will be exceedingly wroth when they learn I have decided not to join the Church, neither as monk nor as teacher," said Johann. "They look not too highly on merchants or even town life. But then," he mused half to himself, "my eldest brother is already a priest, the second will inherit the land, why should they care what I do?"

Tyle was elated at his friend's new turn of mind. "Then let us both write and let them get used to the idea."

Christmas was celebrated joyfully in traditional German fashion. They all attended Midnight Mass at the great church of St. Cyriacus, called by the French St. Quiriace, the site of the Provins fair in May.

"It has the same patron as the little church in Vilsen," remarked Johann. "Could that be significant, I wonder?"

Tyle looked at him, perplexed. "Perhaps. But who was St. Cyriacus?"

Johann shook his head, but Chlotilde answered, "He was a fourth century Bishop of Jerusalem, a Jewish convert, who helped St. Helena find the True Cross."

"How did you learn that?" asked Tyle.

"I, too, was curious," she replied, "so I simply asked."

They all burst into gales of laughter at this.

"See what a brilliant wife she will make," exclaimed Tyle.

"Then let us take him as our patron saint," suggested Johann.

"An excellent idea," agreed Chlotilde and Tyle.

Immediately after Twelfth Night, Herr Kaufmann set out for the fair at Lagny-Sur-Marne. He had urged the young men to accompany him, but his wife and Chlotilde had been urging even more strongly that they prepare to leave for Paris within the fortnight.

"We can still make it in time for the Lenten term if we leave Lagny before the end of the fair," suggested Tyle.

"With what? A sack of dirty linens and no place to stay?" retorted Chlotilde.

293

"She's right," chimed in Frau Kaufmann. "You have no idea how scarce accommodations can be in the Latin Quarter when the classes are in session. I have heard they often squeeze ten to a room fit for four."

"What is the Latin Quarter?" asked Johann.

"Why, that is what folk are beginning to call the area on the Left Bank where the learned doctors and tutors hold forth, because nothing but Latin is heard there. And you must live there. The good citizens of Paris will not have it otherwise."

"Really? Why is that?" asked Tyle.

"Because the great majority of the students are constantly drinking and wenching and brawling. What respectable merchant would subject his family or his business to that? Why, 'tis said the battles sometimes get so violent that they tear up the paving stones and fling them at one another. There are murders every night over such insignificant theological questions as does the devil's tail have two or three prongs." The merchant's wife quickly crossed herself as she said this, just in case the point was not as insignificant as she deemed. "Ah, my innocents, you have much to learn about Paris itself before you begin your formal studies. It is a wicked and sinful city."

The youths were shocked. "But if all this is so," asked Johann, "do they ever learn anything?"

"Strangely enough, they seem to," she replied. "Probably because the tutors will not refund the tuition fees if the students do not attend the classes," she added cynically. "But that is another reason for going early. Only the best tutors have rooms in which to hold their classes, which naturally limits the number of students they can accept. The others lecture in the streets, squares, church porches, taverns, wherever."

"How would you suggest we go about finding accommodations?" asked Tyle.

"Ask around when you get there, is all I can say. But be careful. They will ask outrageous prices for a hovel, and even the best are not much better, especially when they see you are newcomers. Only the very rich and the very poor are lucky."

"The rich I can understand, but how can the poor be lucky?" asked Johann.

"It seems that a very few of the wealthy merchants in Paris have begun to realize that there are some very talented young men among the poorer classes who are deserving of an education. They have set up scholarships for them that include dormitories, at least one meal a day and varying amounts of their tuition. Master Robert Sorbon is said to have been so generous in this respect that many people are beginning to call the University after him."

"Really?" said Tyle. "And what do the merchants expect in return for such largesse?"

"Nothing, as far as I know," replied Frau Kaufmann, "only that they complete their studies and practice their chosen profession. If they become successful, it is to be hoped that they in turn will help other students."

"Amazing," said Tyle. "Peasants actually capable of being educated?"

"Didn't I tell you the times are changing, Tyle?" reminded Johann.

And so the two young men came to Paris and did indeed find it a different world from anything they had known before. Even Cologne paled to insignificance by comparison.

They arrived on a dismal day that could not make up its mind whether to rain or snow, and so did both. They held their cloaks tightly around them against the chill wind that swept down the Seine. At the well on the Right Bank, called La Samaritaine, their horses clattered across the bridge of the same name and onto the isle still called by many by the ancient name of Lutetia. Downriver on their right lay the forbidding fortress of the royal palace and directly ahead rose the majestic towers of the recently completed Cathedral of Notre Dame. They had been directed to go there first, as most of the faculties of the University were under the direction of the monks of Notre Dame, except for a few renegade professors who had recently placed themselves under the jurisdiction of the Abbey of Ste. Genevieve on the Left Bank.

When they entered the narrow street they lost sight of the Cathedral, but at least they were sheltered from the wind. But they were appalled by the filth and the stench. Accustomed though they were to the lack of sanitation of the times, still the German towns of their homeland seemed spotless compared to this. Rotting garbage and animal droppings of all kinds covered the street, making the stones extremely slippery for the horses. Raw sewage filled the gutter that ran down the center of the street and emptied into the river.

Even as they picked their way along carefully avoiding the worst of the debris, a shout from one of the houses overhanging the street brought them to a halt. "Mind the slops!" The contents of a chamberpot landed directly in front of Tyle, splashing his horse and his own shoes.

"Ugh!" he exclaimed. "And this appears to be one of the better parts of town. What must those student hovels be like?"

"We shall soon see," replied Johann, laughing at his friend's discomfort. "After two years your nose will grow used to it. Seriously, though, would it not be wise to seek an inn around here for tonight before we get to the student neighborhoods? Surely it is past nones, for the day is closing in, and we have ridden a far pace this day."

"An excellent idea," agreed Tyle, "and I was hungry before I just now lost my appetite. Perhaps if we get out of this cesspit, I shall find it again."

"I, for one, would rather bed down on yon bridge," grumbled Dierck. "It might be cold but at least the wind blows the stink away and the shit falls down into the river. But the horses need a dry stable and a good rubdown, if they don't slip and break a leg 'fore that. Let me ask about."

"There's an hostelry of some sort in the next street," remarked Jacob matter-of-factly.

"How do you know?" they asked.

"My nose tells me. I smell a roast a-turning." They looked at him in amazement. He shrugged. "When a man spends his life in the stables, he don't even notice the manure, but the smell of supper a-cooking, ah, that comes through."

"Lead on then, Jacob," said Johann. "We will follow your nose."

Jacob led them around a corner and doubled back into an even narrower lane, and there, sure enough, tucked away among the tall, slender houses they saw the sign of the dove. To those who could read it also said 'La Colombe.' It was a small inn with an aura of elegance.

"It looks expensive," said Johann hesitantly.

"We can afford it," replied Tyle. "Besides, it's only for one night."

"But we have to watch every penny from now on."

While they were arguing, Dierck pushed forward. "Let me haggle with them, young masters. Do not tell them you are students. You are journeymen merchants come to check out the markets in Paris for your master, who will not bring a bit of business to this city if his employees are put upon or taken advantage of. You will not be overcharged, my lords." He winked at them broadly.

They rode into the courtyard.

La Colombe was indeed tiny and elegant. It appeared to cater primarily to visiting prelates who had business with the Archbishop of Paris or the Abbot and found the accommodations at the Abbey too austere for their tastes or perhaps wanted to discreetly entertain a woman. At this time, no doubt due to the weather, there were few guests, and Dierck was able to obtain a private room for his masters, stabling for the horses and servants, and a hearty meal for all at a reasonable price. At a well in the courtyard they washed off the grime of the journey, and then in the cozy public room before the fireplace, where a young lad was laboriously turning the spit, they relaxed with a bottle of good French wine.

They were soon joined by two portly priests who introduced themselves as Father Edouard and Father Martin. They appeared to be the only other guests.

After the usual amenities, one of them asked, "Is this your first visit to Paris?"

"Yes," replied Johann politely, "and so far we have been quite impressed by the city."

"Impressed indeed," said Tyle. "We have only just arrived and were welcomed by a pot of slops on our heads."

The priests guffawed. "One of the hazards of this fair city. You will soon learn to watch the top of your head as well as where you set your feet. Do you stay here long?"

"Uh, two or three months, perhaps, depending on business," answered Johann.

"And you intend to stay here at La Colombe that long? Your master must be rich indeed."

"Ah, that he is, but miserly, too," added Tyle, joining the game. "He has only given us a pittance for our expenses. We only stay here for this night because the weather was so bad and we had no heart to look further."

"Then you must find other lodgings, but I advise against this quarter."

"Why is that?"

"Too rich and greedy," replied Father Edouard, "although you will probably do most of your business here. Most of the great merchants live here and the market lies between the Cathedral and the Palais."

"Did you know that the wicked uncle of our beloved Héloïse lived in that large house on the corner?" whispered Father Martin, as though it were a deep secret.

"Really?" replied Johann. "Then Peter Abelard must have come here often."

"Once too often," whispered Father Martin, relishing his story. "The barber who—ah—unmanned him lived in the very house next door to this inn."

"How interesting."

297

"Yes. 'Tis said his very balls were buried in the cellar underneath."

"How awful!" exclaimed Tyle, shuddering.

"Disgraceful," agreed the fat little priest. "To my mind they should build a shrine over them instead of canonizing that cold fish Bernard. I doubt he had any balls," he whispered.

"Father!" chided Father Edouard, shocked.

The young men laughed. "I sense you admire Abelard, Father," said Johann.

"A sensible man," replied Father Martin.

"When we were in Provins we visited the monastery where he spent his exile," Johann told them. "He was much admired there, too, yet Bernard won the debates."

"Politics, my dear boy," spat Father Martin. "Bernard was a silver-tongued politician, nothing more, and a rabble-rouser, and," he lowered his voice to a whisper again, "in the pay of those devil's spawn, the Templars."

"Father, you go too far," warned Father Edouard. "Have a care. The Templars are too powerful for the likes of us."

"Powerful indeed," replied Father Martin. "They rule France, for the king is so deeply in debt to them that he will never be able to repay them."

The young men were aghast at this fascinating information and would like to have heard more, but Father Edouard, knowing that next would come the entire replay of the Bernard-Abelard debate or else the long list of grievances against the Templars, decided it was enough. He did not really trust these young strangers. No one could trust anyone in Paris anymore.

"Father, I think these young men are tired and would rather seek their beds than hear a long theological discussion, however worthy. Let us bid them good night."

Johann held up his hand. "Good fathers, it was a most interesting introduction to Paris and we thank you, but before you go, can you advise us where to seek lodging, if not in this quarter. That was the original question."

"But of course, and I apologize for my friend," replied Father Edouard. "I know the very place, if you do not mind being on the Left Bank. But this is no student hostel, mind you. A very respectable lodging house owned by a very respectable widow, but not too respectable for two young men on their first visit to Paris, if you take my meaning." The boys grinned. "Her name is Mme. Richard, and it is the fourth house to the right from the bridge, directly facing the quay. She also sets a good board and I know her fees are quite reasonable."

The next morning they moved into Mme. Richard's. They were quite pleased with the charming little house facing the river, and the rent she asked seemed to be within their means, although they had no idea as yet what their tuition fees would amount to. The lady herself reminded them of a little gray bird. She fussed over them and fluttered her hands as she spoke, but underneath they detected a strength that would tolerate no nonsense.

"What will happen when she discovers we are students?" worried Johann.

"Don't worry," Tyle reassured him. "We shall be such perfect gentlemen these next few weeks that she will grow to love us like her own sons and will not have the heart to throw us out."

"I hope you're right," said Johann doubtfully, remembering his friend's escapades in Hildesheim, although admittedly he had behaved himself in Provins.

"I am. You'll see. I know how to handle women," boasted Tyle.

Johann was even more doubtful about that, and yet, Tyle seemed to have matured somewhat since the advent of Chlotilde. Time will tell, Johann thought with a shrug.

They left their horses in Mme. Richard's stables under the tender care of the servants and retraced their steps to the magnificent Cathedral. At first they acted like any tourists and oh'ed and ah'ed over the jewel-like rose windows, the colorful statuary, the fantastic gargoyles.

"I suppose it is time we let yon monks know we are here," suggested Johann.

"I guess you're right," sighed Tyle. "We might as well find out what the next few months have in store for us."

They made their way into the great Abbey surrounding the church.

"You must first affiliate yourselves with a nation," explained the monk who interviewed them.

"A nation?" asked Tyle. "I'm afraid I don't understand."

The monk looked at them with an exasperated sigh. "You know, where you were born. *Ubi natus es?*"

"We were both born in the Duchy of Braunschweig-Lüneburg," replied Johann. "That's part of the Holy Roman Empire."

"I have heard of it. We don't have a German nation here. Perhaps you should have gone to Bologna." At their look of perplexity, the monk sighed

299

again and addressed them as if they were little children. "Let me explain. Many years ago when the University was first founded the students formed guilds, just as merchants, artisans and other town folk do. But as the number of students grew, the system became unwieldy. There was no control and many problems arose. They are now divided into four nations—French, Norman, Picard and English—according to the land of their birth. Each has its own professors, and each offers all the courses of the trivium and usually most of the quadrivium. Each is led by a proctor, an upper-class or doctoral student, who is responsible to the dean of the faculty, who in turn is responsible to the Rector, who is the head of the whole University. Now do you understand?"

"Yes, Brother, but where does that leave us?" asked Tyle.

"I don't know. We have several German students here and they seem to have spread themselves among all the nations. So it is up to you to make your own choice and see which one will accept you. I doubt the French will. They consider themselves very elite and are quite reluctant to accept foreigners. The others not so. Since I assume your mother tongue is Low German," (the interview was being conducted in Latin), "you will probably fit in best with the Picards or the English. Your Hanse has united them all to some extent. Anyway, I shall give you the names of all the proctors and where you may find them—if you are lucky—and when you have been accepted by one of them, come back here and let me know, so we may enter it in the register."

"And how do we go about finding the professors and finding out what courses are being offered this term?" asked Johann.

"The proctor will tell you all that. If a professor has room in his class, he will accept you as soon as you pay him his fee. The first year you have no choice. Everyone starts with the trivium."

"But we have already completed the trivium at Hildesheim," objected Tyle. He was referring to the basic course of grammar, rhetoric and logic taught in most schools above the elementary level. "We have even studied some mathematics."

"I have heard that Hildesheim is a very good school, but I don't know of it from my own experience. Now if it were Cologne . . . Nonetheless, the standards of teaching vary so widely among schools that everyone—without exception—must study the trivium the first year. Then if you pass the examination, you may study the quadrivium the second year and in the third year philosophy, where you may study in the field of your choice toward obtaining your doctoral degree."

300

He saw their faces fall—Johann's because he feared he only had enough money for two years and Tyle's because he expected to be bored for a whole year.

The monk decided to offer them some encouragement, although it was against his policy. But he liked these two ingenuous young men who had come so far for an education, although he feared they would not remain innocent for long at the hands of the other students. "You will find that the trivium, as taught here, is greatly expanded from what you have already studied. It delves much more deeply into the subjects. I think you will find it interesting and challenging to your minds. And there is also the possibility," and this was something he *never* told beginning students, "that you may take the examinations for the trivium at the end of the term. If you pass them all, you may start taking courses in the quadrivium next term instead of waiting a whole year. There are also the *considiarii*—sort of student advocates—in each nation. Cultivate their friendship. They can be of more help to you than the proctors."

"That sounds a bit more encouraging," sighed Tyle with relief.

"Yes. Thank you, Brother, for your advice," said Johann. "I hope we can show you how well Hildesheim has taught us."

The monk smiled and stood up, indicating the interview was at an end. "Go and seek out the proctors now. They can also suggest where you may seek lodging. Good luck."

"Now where do we find the Rue de Fouarre?" asked Tyle, as they wandered around the Latin Quarter looking for the proctors.

"I suppose we had best ask again," replied Johann, "although this last fellow's directions indicated it should be about here. It's a pretty derelict neighborhood, isn't it?"

"I haven't seen a really good one on this whole Left Bank," agreed Tyle. "But then I didn't expect the students to be living in luxury after what we've heard."

They asked a passerby. "Why you're standing right on it," he informed them.

"But—but, I thought it was Rue de—de . . . " said Johann.

The man laughed. "You must be newcomers. It has a real name, but everyone calls it Rue de Fouarre because this is where the professors, whose chambers are not large enough, lecture and during terms the street is full of the straw that the students sit upon."

The young men looked at him in disbelief. "Then this must be where the poorest professors and students gather," suggested Tyle.

"Au contraire," said their informant. "It is where some of the most learned and popular hold forth. And some of the richest, because they attract so many students that there are few rooms big enough to hold them and the students will gladly put up with any discomfort to hear their lectures."

"Amazing," said Tyle.

"No, not so amazing," the man replied. "Regardless of what you may have heard, most of the young men studying here are eager students and grateful for the opportunity of being here. May I be of any further help to you? Is there someone in particular you seek here?"

"Why yes," replied Johann. "We are seeking the proctors of the Picard and English nations. We've been told we might find either or both somewhere around here."

"You are students then? Or would-be students?" he asked.

"Would-be. We have only just arrived in Paris."

"Then thank your lucky stars that you have met me before you run into those rowdies who tease and torture newcomers and even run the timid right out of the Quarter. I am Etienne of Ghent, a considerarius of the Picard nation. And where are you from?"

"I am Johann von Sehnden and this is my friend Tyle von Eltze. We are from the Duchy of Braunschweig-Lüneburg."

"No, I meant at what school have you studied?"

"At Hildesheim. It is . . . "

"Ah, excellent school," interrupted Etienne. "Second only to Cologne of the north German schools—in my opinion at least."

"Then you are much more encouraging than the brother Registrar," said Tyle.

"Ah, dear brother Petrus," sighed Etienne. "I'm afraid he mistrusts any school that is more than five miles from Paris, unless it be Chartres perhaps, which is their most bitter rival but highly respected nonetheless by the authorities here. And so you wish to join our nation, or mayhap the Englishmen?"

"To tell you the truth, we have been told to look them all over, since it seems that we are 'men without a nation' here," joked Tyle.

Johann could have kicked his friend, since it was obvious that Etienne did not regard this as a joke at all. "We should be grateful to be accepted by any nation that feels we would be an asset to it, but Brother Petrus did suggest that either of you might be more amenable to accepting Germans."

"Than the French or Normans, who have already discouraged you," finished Etienne.

"Well, not exactly," said Tyle, "but they didn't really make us feel welcome."

"Understandable. We are much freer and more flexible, more proletarian, if you will. And less concerned with politics. The French and the English hate each other, and the Normans hate them both. The English, mind you, are mostly Saxons like yourselves, because the Normans who happen to live in England still consider themselves Norman, but you may find the English theology a bit radical for your tastes. All of them both hate and love us, because Picardy and Flanders are the richest part of northern Europe—and we try to avoid their political factions."

"Interesting," commented Johann, trying to digest all this. "We don't wish to become involved in politics either, for truthfully, we understand little of what these interminable wars between the French and English are all about. We just want to learn everything that Paris has to teach us."

Etienne smiled. "An admirable goal, if a bit ambitious. Good, then let me take you to the Proctor—if we can find him. He is usually at the sign of the Cock and Cat. But first let me warn you of one thing. Here at Paris we forget all pretensions to nobility. The only things that will set you above any others are brilliance in your debates and excellence in your examinations. From now on you will be Johann and Tyle of Hildesheim, nothing more. Understood?"

"Understood," the two friends agreed.

In the event, they found the proctors of both nations at the Cock and Cat, engaged in a friendly but heated theological discussion. Either one would have welcomed them warmly, but they finally chose the Picards, largely because of Etienne's friendship.

They were soon immersed in their studies, attending lectures in the mornings and laboriously copying out texts in the afternoons. For the first few weeks they returned to their lodgings each evening and studied diligently, but it soon became obvious that they were missing a lot by not joining other students in the evening for spirited discussions. Here it was that they learned what other professors were expounding and what their students thought of it. Here their mental capacities were stretched to the limit and their outlook broadened to include the whole world of the thinking of their time.

Tyle quickly renewed his reputation as a brilliant debater and Johann basked in reflected glory. He noticed with thanksgiving that a great deal of

Tyle's former arrogance was gone, but unfortunately, his growing maturity did not yet include control of his temper. If an opponent did not quickly yield a point, Tyle often stalked out in a huff and went on to get miserably drunk.

Johann felt embarrassed on his friend's behalf but would leave with him to keep an eye on him, remembering too well the numerous tight spots he had rescued him from back in Hildesheim. As yet Tyle had not chased after any women, but Johann knew it was only a matter of time. He feared that Tyle was already getting bored. Oh, I wish Chlotilde could be here, he thought.

Then one afternoon Tyle disappeared. At first Johann thought nothing of it, expecting him to turn up that evening at one of the taverns where the discussion groups gathered. When he still did not arrive, Johann went looking around all Tyle's usual haunts, but no one claimed to have seen him, although Johann did notice a few winks and knowing looks that belied some of the denials. At last he gave up his search, having come to the conclusion that Tyle had at last broken his vow to be true to Chlotilde and had gone with a woman, in which case he would hardly welcome his friend's intrusion. Johann returned to Mme. Richard's and went to bed.

But he could not sleep. Something was bothering him. Suddenly he remembered. In all his diligent search he had not seen Rollo or Abro, a pair of particularly obnoxious Normans, who always made their presence felt wherever they were and whom, as luck would have it, Tyle had insulted not two nights ago.

Rollo and Abro typified, to Johann's mind, the two most common types of Normans. Rollo was of medium height, stocky, burly—in short, a warrior, with the mentality to match, always ready to fight rather than think a thing through. Abro was the opposite, tall, thin, ascetic, almost effete, with a devious mind inclined to treachery. They were both supremely arrogant and not well liked by the other students. But they were the leaders of a small group of like bent, malcontents and troublemakers. Johann had not seen any of their cohorts tonight either.

He bolted out of bed and quickly dressed. He took care to buckle on his sword and stuck a dagger in his belt but opted against any armor as being too cumbersome. He quietly let himself out of the house and ran to the stables to wake Dierck and Jacob. Jacob was all for taking the horses, but Johann refused.

"They will wake the dead and warn the living. The last thing we want is the watch on our heads. Stealth is what we need. Besides, they wouldn't even fit into some of the alleys and cul-de-sacs we must search. I wish I knew where to begin."

"If it's the Normans you seek," said Dierck, "most of them lodge hard by Ste.-Genevieve."

"How did you know?" asked Johann.

"While you are busy studying and whatever, we are not sitting here idly talking to the horses," replied Dierck. "We have gotten to know every byway of this quarter better than you, I daresay. And we keep our eyes and ears open. When we heard how Master Tyle tweaked yon unholy pair's balls, we feared something was afoot. Their servants are braggarts, too, you know."

The servants armed themselves with stout staves and daggers, and the three hurried towards the Abbey. The night was black as pitch. The tiny sliver of moon had long since set and at this late hour not even a candle shone through a window to light their way. There was little danger of running into the watch, for once the taverns closed they seemed to avoid the Quarter like the plague. Johann was grateful for his stalwart companions and grateful, too, for Dierck's sharp instincts that led them unerringly through the dark streets and alleys to the precincts of the Abbey.

"Now we must go slowly and listen carefully," whispered Dierck, "for if those buffoons have a victim, they will not be quiet."

"A victim?" asked Johann, horrified at the implication.

"They don't play pretty games," warned Dierck.

"Ja, and the bodies end up in the Seine," added Jacob.

"Holy Mother of God, help us," cried Johann.

"Save your prayers for later," said Dierck. "Let's go."

For at least a quarter-hour they wound up and down streets and alleys, scanning courtyards, listening at doors and windows.

Suddenly Jacob stopped. "I smell smoke."

"And I hear voices," said Dierck.

"There's light shining out of the next alley," Johann reported. "Is it a fire or could it be them? Pray God we're in time."

"Careful now until we see what's what," warned Dierck. "We don't know how many they are, and I'm sure they're all drunk, which will make them extra vicious." He placed a restraining hand on Johann's arm as they rounded the corner into the alley. "Don't do anything foolish, no matter how bad it is."

They crept down the alley, hugging the walls. They could see reflected firelight. It did not seem to be a building burning, but a small bonfire in the courtyard at the end. A number of men were milling about. They could not yet see how many, but there appeared to be at least a half-dozen. They were all looking at something on the ground in the center of the tiny area. Then an unearthly scream rent the night.

"That's Tyle!" exclaimed Johann.

Dierck held onto his arm. "Wait," he hissed. "They are too many for us. You block the exit with your sword. Let Jacob and me do the rest. We know how to fight dirty."

As they drew near, they could see Tyle tied spread-eagled on the ground. His tunic was drawn up, exposing his genitals where his hose separated. Rollo was kneeling on the ground next to him, a wicked-looking dagger in his hand. Abro was dancing around holding a burning faggot with which he would poke Tyle's hands and feet, provoking the screams. The rest of the men were leering drunkenly, so intent on their victim that they did not notice the stealthy approach of the three friends.

At that moment Rollo took hold of Tyle's testicles and pulled them up, brandishing his dagger. "Well, men, what shall it be?" he shouted. "Shall we cut his tongue out so he can't insult us anymore or shall we start with these? I think with these, since he likes Abelard so much, we'll make him just like him. Then he won't bother our girls anymore. What say you?" The men started to murmur, some obviously afraid of going that far.

Just then a shutter flew open in the upper story of the house opposite. The irate householder screamed, "Get out of here, you devil's spawn! Take your victim elsewhere, you goddamned fiends, ere you set the whole quarter on fire."

The Normans started to laugh, but their laughter was cut short when a bucketful of water was flung from the window and the fire sputtered into darkness. At that moment the three rescuers made their move. Big Jacob grabbed two of the Normans and knocked their heads together. At the same moment Dierck jumped over Tyle and landed with both feet in Rollo's face. Johann swung about with his sword and felt it sink into flesh and bone. Someone grabbed his tunic and he sank his dagger into the hand. A fist connected with the side of his head, momentarily stunning him, but he shook his head and drove his sword in that direction. He could barely see the shadowy figures by the fading light of the embers. He knew he must try to free Tyle but was afraid to turn his back on the Normans until they were all subdued or chased away.

Suddenly the last of the embers were extinguished in a shower of sparks as a body landed in them and screamed. Jacob bellowed, "See how you like the hot faggots up your ass, my lord Abro!" Another scream was silenced by a jaw-breaking fist.

Johann noticed Dierck freeing Tyle, who had passed out, and was about to help him cut the bonds, when he noticed Rollo coming to and groping for his dagger. With no compunction he slashed down with his sword and severed the hand from the wrist. With their leaders subdued the remaining Normans, who were still able, fled.

"Help me with my lord Tyle, Jacob. He can't walk on those burned feet," called Dierck, "and let's get out of here."

Jacob picked up Tyle easily and flung him over his shoulder, and the three hurried out of the alley.

They let themselves quietly into Mme. Richard's and laid Tyle gently on the bed. Jacob quickly stripped off Tyle's filthy garments and Dierck carefully examined him all over. Other than the burnt hands and feet nothing seemed amiss, although Tyle remained in a half-faint.

"See if you can find some lard or goose grease in Madame's larder," Dierck instructed Johann, "while I fetch my herbs. God bless once again the wisewoman of Vilsen. I must quickly dress those burns. Jacob, stay here and keep him quiet if he should wake."

"Suppose Madame catches me in her larder," said Johann. "She will surely turn us out."

"Not if you play on her woman's sympathies," replied Dierck. "Tell her some of your rich merchant friends plied him with more drink than he, the poor innocent, could handle and he tripped and fell into their hearth."

Tyle could not attend the lectures for the next several days. At first he was contrite. "Now the score is even, my friend," he said to Johann. "We have each saved the other's life after our own foolishness, and I am grateful to you. And I almost betrayed my dear Chlotilde for no other reason than that I was bored. I think I must quit this place and be by her side."

"No, no," said Johann, "do not give up so quickly. She will be sorely disappointed in you if you quit before even one term is over."

"She will be even more disappointed if I lose my manhood. God's teeth, Johann, they still ache. Do you think I shall be impotent?"

"No, no," Johann reassured him. "You'll be all right after the bruises heal. Thank God we got there in time, though." Johann tried to find out what exactly had precipitated the attack and if his friend had really betrayed Chlotilde, but at first Tyle would say nothing.

After several days Tyle was able to hobble around painfully for short periods. He then became angry and started threatening to seek revenge. Johann began to worry and sought out Etienne, to whom he related the whole incident. The considiarius came to visit Tyle.

"My friend," he said, "you have already been avenged by your friend here and your servants. Rollo almost bled to death and now has a stump at the end of his sword arm. Abro cannot sit or walk, and perhaps his balls were fried, too. I know not. One man is dead, the others all wounded. Honor has been served. Let it be. The authorities will take no action unless you call attention to yourself. But if you stir things up, Johann might even be arrested for murder. Not likely, but possible."

Tyle thought this over for a moment. "You are right, of course. But has honor truly been served? It was a set-up. They deliberately led me into a trap of their own devising. Even I am not such a fool as to deliberately provoke the likes of them. I knew Rollo was angry after I bested him in the debate. I was taking all care to avoid him."

"Tell me what really happened," said Etienne.

"I was bored and edgy, Etienne, I must admit it," Tyle replied hesitantly. Etienne said nothing. "I haven't had a woman in a long time," Tyle went on, avoiding Johann's eyes. "I thought it would help. I went to the street where the whores congregate. I found a willing one almost immediately. Too quickly, I realize now. She took me through back alleys I didn't even know existed to the house she used for her trade. We went up the ladder to a tiny loft which she said she shared with three others. That was why a curtain was hung across the middle of the room, she said. As soon as she divested me of my belt and knife and began her ministrations, they jumped me. There were four of them, none I recognized, but I knew they were Normans. They said something about raping a nun, and that's the last I remember until I woke up bound and gagged on the floor of another room. It was considerably larger than the other and quite well furnished. I knew it was near the Abbey because I could hear the bells. As it was growing dark Rollo and Abro came in and kicked me about and then tried to tell me that the woman was a nun visiting from Normandy, the cousin of someone or other, and that I had raped her and for that I deserved death, but first they described all the tortures they would subject me to before they dispatched me. I couldn't even curse them, much less deny their allegations. But I tell you that woman was no nun. I hadn't even touched her, but she was already fondling me, and expertly, too. She was no nun, but an experienced harlot."

"Yes, she is," agreed Etienne. "She is well-known as their minion.

They use her services often, usually just for blackmail, which is why their chambers are so well furnished, but sometimes for more serious intrigues, such as this. What then?"

"Nothing much. They left me after a while and I lay there in the dark for hours and hours, listening to those damn Abbey bells. Apparently they were afraid to do anything while people were still abroad in the streets. Thank God they didn't take me to some cellar or you'd never have found me. But it seems Abro has this thing about fire. I heard his mother was burned as a witch. I wouldn't doubt it. Anyway, they finally came back with several others. They were all very drunk. That helped delay things, for they had great difficulty in untying me and retying me to the stakes. I struggled, but drunk as they were, there were too many of them. You know the rest." Tyle paused. "And I must offer a special prayer for that man who threw the water. It was probably his whole night's supply. I would thank him myself if I dared go near that neighborhood again."

"Now you are talking more sense." Etienne smiled .

Johann, who had listened to this incredible tale with mounting horror, now asked, "Is there nothing that can be done to stop this sort of thing? Can't the watch . . . ?"

Etienne laughed. "The watch only comes through the main streets once a day at curfew, which no one observes. The civil authorities are not permitted even to enter the Quarter, since the entire University is under the jurisdiction of the ecclesiastical court, which turns a blind eye to all these goings-on. So each nation has its own corps of guards, ostensibly students, to protect and prevent where possible, avenge where necessary. It is the only law there is here, but effective enough. Don't worry, you won't have any more trouble with those particular Normans," he assured them. "Others I can't vouch for."

Tyle returned to his classes, and nothing more was said about his leaving the University. The term ended on St. Peter's Day, 29 June, and they had been highly successful on their examinations for the Trivium and were advised they could begin their studies in the Quadrivium in the St. Remi term, the first of October. They took great pleasure in advising Brother Petrus of this. He grudgingly admitted that perhaps Hildesheim had taught them well after all.

Mme. Richard bid them a tearful farewell. "I know now that you are students," she admitted, "but your behavior has been so exemplary, I'll forgive you your little fib." She had never found out about Tyle's escapade. "In fact, if the room is still available, you may return here in the fall," she surprised them by saying. "And your two delightful squires have been so much help to me. I shall miss them."

With the whole summer before them they quickly set out on the road to Provins and Chlotilde. Three days later, as they approached the town, they came upon another of the famous rose gardens. So rare as yet in the rest of Europe, they seemed to grow in profusion here.

Tyle called a halt. "I know what I would do. I must needs have one of these exquisite red flowers to give to Chlotilde."

"Still feeling guilty after the Norman whore?" Johann teased him.

"No, of course not," denied Tyle testily. "It's just that she has been alone so long, I want to bring her a love gift. Dost think yon peasant will give me one?"

"More likely sell you some," replied Johann. "It looks to be their only cash crop."

Tyle approached the well-kept cottage and called out. After a moment the goodwife came hurrying around the building amongst a flurry of chickens. "Good day to you, messieurs, how can I be of service to you?" She was obviously surprised at her visitors, but not in the least cowed by their rank.

In his broken French Tyle explained how he had been these many months in Paris away from his lady love and wondered if he might have one rose to take to her.

The woman shrewdly sized him up. "They are not mine to give. They belong to our liege lord, who expects a tithe of all we sell. They are very rare, you see, and most are destined to adorn the halls of the great lords, even of the King himself. Fifty years ago they were not even known in this part of the world. One of the Comtes de Champagne brought the first plant back from the Crusades and they have been the flower of royalty ever since. My husband's great-grandfather was the Comte's head gardener, and my lord gave him this land to raise them on." She spread her hands. "So you see how it is."

At Tyle's look of disappointment, she continued. "Only once have we given one away. When the widow of our late Comte Henri le Gros, God rest his soul, married Edmund of Lancaster, brother of the King of England, she plucked one herself to give him for a favor, and do you know, he was so enthralled by its beauty that he incorporated it into his arms. In England they call it the red rose of Lancaster, but it really came from this very garden in Champagne."

"Very interesting," said Tyle, more determined than ever to have one.

"Since the Comte does not have another widow for me to marry, perhaps he would not mind if you sold me some."

His sarcasm was lost on the peasant woman, but she heard his offer of purchase. "For a good penny I would be willing to give you not one, but three," she quickly replied. The deal was quickly consummated and they soon entered the St. Jean Gate of Provins, Tyle gently holding the three roses and inhaling their delicate fragrance.

Chlotilde was delighted with the unusual gift, but the fragile roses were almost crushed in the lovers' fervent embrace. "Oh, Tyle, I have missed you so and have prayed every day for your safety. You must tell me everything you have been doing. Is Paris really as evil as they say? And Johann, how fare you? Come in, come in, we have been expecting you these several days and Frau Kaufmann has a special roast a-basting. You must be famished. There is so much to tell you, too." She never stopped chattering as they entered the merchant's house. "And oh, there are letters for both of you from your families," she added as an afterthought. "We didn't bother to send them on, since we knew you'd be home soon. Hear how I call this home, but truly it is the best home I have ever had. I shall hate so to leave."

Both Kaufmanns welcomed them warmly, but Frau Kaufmann soon put a stop to Chlotilde's exuberance. "Girl, girl, give them a chance to come into the house and wash the dust of the road from themselves. Go and fetch them a draught of beer to quench their thirst, but here, first put these lovely roses in a jar of water."

All during supper and for a long time afterwards Tyle regaled them with stories about Paris and life at the University. Most were greatly embellished and exaggerated, some very far from the truth. But no matter, Johann thought, 'tis better that he appear more enthusiastic than he really is. He noted that Tyle was careful to make no mention of his attack by the Normans, although he acknowledged that such things occasionally did happen to other people.

Johann was anxious for news of his family and so while Tyle was holding forth, he quietly slipped into a corner by the fire and carefully broke the seal on his missive. His father wrote of his disappointment that he was not going to make a career of the Church. He was saddened by Johann's unhappy experience at Heiligenberg and begged him to investigate other orders before finally deciding against it. His eldest brother had been ordained priest and was sure to go far. Meanwhile he had a small parish in some town to the east that Johann never heard of. One of his sisters was

311

betrothed and would probably marry this summer. His second brother, who was the heir to the estate, was suffering from a gripe of the bowels but seemed to be improving with the warm weather. His mother sends her fondest love and prays for him every day. And then his father closed by saying that he still wished Johann would change his mind about his career, "but you have your share of the inheritance. It is not for me to tell you what to do with it."

Johann was saddened but relieved that at least his father had not disowned him. He wondered what Tyle's letter said.

Later that night as they were going to bed, Johann reminded him. "You have not yet read your letter."

"I know," replied Tyle. "I'm afraid of what it will say. I didn't want to spoil our happy homecoming."

"If you think it's that bad, read it and know the worst, so you can sleep on it. Otherwise you will still have it to worry about in the morning."

"I suppose you are right." Tyle lit their one candle and broke the seal on his letter. It was not very long. After reading it through, he tossed it over to Johann. "Read it for yourself. It's about what I expected."

Johann did so. After acknowledging Tyle's letter and saying that all were well, his father went into his tirade. Johann could just envision him. "After being a knight-errant I can think of only one thing worse and that is becoming a common tradesman, or worse, a usurer. As for the robber-knight's slut, have no fear that I shall betray her whereabouts. I should be ashamed to admit that any son of mine consorted with such. You have your share of the inheritance and there is nothing I can do about that, but I tell you if you disgrace this family by either becoming a merchant or marrying that woman, I shall no longer call you son and I forbid you to bear our arms in either peace or war. Your mother continues to pray for you. I know not why."

Johann gently handed the letter back with no comment. Tyle let it fall to the floor and put his head in his hands.

After a time he said, "You were right that I should read it tonight. I am not surprised at the content, only at his vehemence. But I know him well enough. He thinks more of his damned arms than he does of his family." He was silent for a while and Johann thought his friend was praying—or weeping. Then he raised his head and Johann saw a fierce determination in his dark eyes. "I shall not go back to Paris in the fall. I must save what's left of my money to make more money. Perhaps I can buy some shares in Herr Kaufmann's business. And I'm more determined than ever to marry

Chlotilde, but first I must make lots of money so that she will be proud of me. I would not ask her to marry me until I can properly dower her."

"I think it best that you sleep on it, my friend," advised Johann gently. "And on the morrow talk it over with both Herr Kaufmann and Chlotilde."

"Yes, and Frau Kaufmann, too. It was she who has taught me so much about the accounting end of the business," replied Tyle.

The next day the Kaufmanns also had disturbing news to impart. "The great Champagne Fairs are dying. We have seen the signs these last several years ever since the King of France married the daughter of the late Comte, Henri de Gros. She brought him the whole County of Champagne as her dowry, and almost immediately he imposed tariffs and tolls where before there were none. Old Count Thibault, who founded the Fairs, knew that free trade was the only way to make money, and the Fairs grew in importance, the merchants prospered and so did the County. But this fool, whom they call Phillippe the Fair—and, I would not dare to say this outside of these four walls, whom I think should be called Phillippe the Vain and Profligate—has laid on us even more and harsher tariffs, until trade has dried up to a mere trickle. Why should the merchants have to charge and pay higher prices here when they can buy and sell the same goods for much less directly in Bruges? Even Antwerp is benefitting by the failure of the Fairs." The merchant paused indignantly.

"I always wondered how the Fairs came to be here in such relatively small towns," observed Johann.

"Small, but on the direct overland route between north and south," replied Herr Kaufmann. "The old Comte was wise. He could see that trade was the coming thing, so he made his county the only place in Europe free of tariffs and tolls for bona fide merchants. Everyone flocked here to do business, but no more. The Hanse has ordered us to finish up our business and move to Bruges by next year."

"I can scarcely believe it," exclaimed Tyle. "You mean that the Fairs will no longer exist at all?"

"Very soon, I'm afraid. Oh, the Lombard bankers will be around for several more years. All the accounts must be settled up and the bills of exchange satisfied or transferred. But the merchants will be fewer and fewer and finally none at all. Why, that fool king is even going after the Templars, who have been bankers to kings and popes for over a hundred and fifty years. I have no use for them myself, but the truth of the matter is that he is so deeply indebted to them that his only way out is to destroy the

313

order. Instead of being honest about it, he is trying to convince his lackey the Pope that they are heretics."

"We heard something about that in Paris," said Johann.

"Then what will happen to my money I have invested with the bankers?" cried Chlotilde. "Will I lose it all?"

"And what about the hopes I had of learning about banking?" asked Tyle at the same time.

"Have no fear, my dear," the merchant reassured Chlotilde. "Your money is safe. The Lombards are solid and he can't touch them. They already have a huge house in Bruges where they are transferring their assets from here. I understand they are also opening new branches in Antwerp and even in London. And as for your hopes, Tyle, your chances are better than ever. The more branches they have, the more outsiders they will be forced to employ."

"But if they are transferring everything to Bruges, how can I get my money back from them?" worried Chlotilde.

"Didn't I tell you they would be around here for a good many years yet winding up all the settlements of account? At the Troyes cold fair we will go and withdraw your money and then, if you choose, you may reinvest it again against an account in Bruges, where we shall most likely be by the following year. Do you understand now?"

"I guess so," she replied.

"This is all very bewildering," said Johann. "It is hard to believe that a King of France could be so stupid as to destroy the very thing that is making the county rich."

"Incredible, but unfortunately true," agreed Herr Kaufmann. "And mark my words, this act of stupidity will set France back into her feudal ways and mark the end of trade for her except on a local basis. The rest of the world will pass her by. Why, only a few years ago the Genoese braved the Pillars of Hercules and sailed directly to Bruges to link up with our Hanse there. That, too, helped sound the death knell for the Champagne Fairs. Soon no one will bother to brave the arduous overland route with all its tolls and brigands. And have you heard? The Polos are truly back in Venice. They have described two new trade routes to the east, one along the ancient silk road to the north and the other by sea around India. The world gets larger every day. I find it very exciting. And the Venetians are building up the overland trade routes into Germany right through the heart of your homeland. I wouldn't be at all surprised if the Hanse doesn't soon incorporate some of those inland cities like your Braunschweig and

Lüneburg and Goslar with its silver that the Venetians need. Perhaps even the new town you spoke of. Celle, did you not call it? There, in a place like that, to my thinking, would lie your opportunities."

Johann and Tyle thought about this, each in his own way.

Perhaps I could invest in a boat for the river trade on the Weser and Aller, thought Johann.

I have to make a lot of money, first, thought Tyle, and then in a new town like that no one will question my dear bride.

I am confused, thought Chlotilde. I wonder where life will lead me. Will my dear Tyle ever realize that I love him whether he has money or title or not.

The balance of the summer Johann and Tyle spent working for the Kaufmanns learning more and more about the cloth business. One or the other of them occasionally attended the various fairs with the merchant, and everywhere the talk was of two things: the fabulous journey of the Polos and the orders from Lübeck that the Hanse merchants wind up their affairs and leave for more hospitable trading climes.

Tyle was still of two minds whether to return to the University or not. Chlotilde encouraged him to do so. "The more you learn, the better equipped you will be to handle your own business someday," she said. What she didn't say was that she hoped he would mature a little more and rid himself of his feudal bias.

Johann added, "Don't forget—the quadrivium includes a lot of arithmetic, which is your forte."

And Herr Kaufmann reminded Tyle, "I can't pay you or even offer you employment here. The Hanse rules are very strict. But once we get to Bruges I can open a lot of doors for you with the bankers there. Or in Bremen or Hamburg, where the Lombard concept of banking is almost unknown. My wife and I were thinking we might even go back to Bremen if things don't work out in Bruges for us."

To which Frau Kaufmann added, "And don't worry about your dear Chlotilde. She has become like a beloved daughter to us. Wherever we end up, she will have a home with us for as long as she wants."

At last Tyle was convinced and returned with Johann to Paris for the St. Remi term and was glad he did. The new courses of the quadrivium consisted of arithmetic, geometry, music and astronomy, all of which fascinated him. Time flew by for them both and there were no more unruly incidents. There was no time for them to go to Provins for Christmas, but they sent gifts to both Kaufmanns and Chlotilde and received their gifts in

315

return, including a huge basket of food from the ladies. Toward the latter part of Lent they had a few weeks off before the Easter term began and they hurried to Provins, but this time there was no doubt in Tyle's mind that he would return to Paris, so engrossed were they both in the new world of knowledge that had opened up to them.

The only thing that began to preoccupy them now was whether they would have enough money to complete the third year instead of the two they had originally planned on. In the third year they would have a choice of four sets of courses: theoretical, which, strangely enough, lumped together theology, physics and advanced mathematics; practical, consisting of morals and ethics — personal, economic and political — an acknowledgement that many young men were beginning to seek careers in business and government rather than the Church; logical, a very specialized combination of the trivium and literature, designed for future professors; and lastly the mechanical, a concession of the great theological school to the changing times, probably in deference to its mercantile benefactors, which included such specialties as wool processing, navigation, agriculture, medicine and such-like humble but very practical subjects. It was studies in the mechanical course that both young men looked forward to pursuing.

One day toward the end of the term the bells of Paris rang wildly. The Queen of France had finally presented Phillippe the Fair with a second son. The University declared the day a holiday since the students were all out in the streets celebrating anyway, though few except the French nation cared less that the King had another heir.

Just as the term was about to end, word spread that the King had announced that there would be a week of celebrations at Provins, including a great tournament to which were invited all the knights of Christendom.

"Johann, I am going to enter the tournament," announced Tyle with great excitement. "With luck, I'll make a lot of money, at least enough to finish the third year and marry Chlotilde as well."

"You're crazy," replied Johann. "You're completely out of shape, for one thing."

"It won't take me long to get back into shape. There's an excellent tiltyard below the walls at Provins, with a quintain and everything. I'll practice every day from the moment we get back there."

"I still say you're crazy. Your only experience has been in little local tournaments back home. Here you'll be matched against the greatest knights in Christendom, knights that are fighting in tournaments and jousts every few weeks, and that for years. You won't stand a chance."

"Yes, I will," insisted Tyle, "as good a chance as anyone else. I'll pick my opponents very carefully."

"You'll lose everything you have," warned Johann. "And don't ask me to pay your ransom."

"You won't have to because I intend to win."

Johann just shook his head and wondered what Chlotilde would think when she heard about this.

Day after day, whenever she could be spared from her duties with Frau Kaufmann, Chlotilde stood on the high parapets of Provins, looking down on the tiltyard where Tyle was practicing. She saw him hit the quintain and be swiftly battered by it. She watched him joust with blunt-tipped lance against equally young and inexperienced opponents who managed to unseat him more often than not. She did note with pride that he excelled at hand-to-hand sword combat, for here litheness and speed counted for more than brute power. Nonetheless, her fears for him increased with each passing day.

She knew he would be no match for the experienced professional knights who would be coming to the tournament. For one thing, he and his young acquaintances played by the rules. She knew from a lifetime of observing them at her father's castle that most of the knights-errant paid no more than lip-service to the Code of Chivalry, for the benefit of the ladies and the clergy. In reality they were brutal, uncouth animals who flaunted the rules, who practiced and expected treachery, who would fight to the death whenever they could get away with it. No, Chlotilde feared far more than his losing everything he had—she feared for his life.

By the end of the week she could no longer contain her anxiety. She confided her fears to Johann and the Kaufmanns, beseeching them to help her dissuade Tyle from entering the tournament.

"He will not listen to me," she moaned. "Perhaps you can convince him of his foolhardiness."

"It will not be easy," said Herr Kaufmann. "He thinks he will win a lot of money even though he risks his neck for it."

"Ach, ja," agreed Frau Kaufmann, "and he thinks he has to prove himself to his lady love. More male foolishness." She shook her head.

"Oh, doesn't he realize that I would marry him if he didn't have a penny?" cried Chlotilde. "I love him."

"But he wouldn't marry you," sighed Herr Kaufmann. "His pride

317

wouldn't allow it. What worries me is that he will lose all that he has worked so hard for."

"Perhaps," put in Johann, "if we could just convince him to stay out of the melee, a few jousts would be enough to satisfy him. His pride be damned, I think a few lumps would do it some good."

Chlotilde smiled at that. "Perhaps you're right, Johann, but yes, we must keep him out of the melee. That will be deadly."

But Tyle was adamant. He intended to enter every event he possibly could.

The following week the knights began arriving in Provins. Every possible dwelling from the Count's palace and the noble houses down to the meanest hostelry rapidly filled to overflowing. They came from all points of the compass, some alone with only a squire in tow, many riding magnificently caparisoned palfreys, feathers bobbing from the helms and horses' heads, with a half-dozen squires leading as many fierce destriers and trailing hundreds of richly clad retainers. A whole tent city mushroomed outside the walls of Provins.

Soon the visiting knights elbowed the local youths, Tyle included, from the tiltyard. If nothing else, this soon convinced Tyle, at least partially, of his foolhardiness.

"They are so uncouth," he confided to Johann in a shocked whisper. "I can't believe the things they say and do, and this only in practice. I don't trust them. No, not at all." And then with a snort of disgust, he admitted, "Perhaps you are right. I think I shall forgo the melee and shepherd my strength for the single combat where I can choose my opponent."

"I think you are very wise," agreed Johann.

Chlotilde breathed a sign of relief and a quick prayer of thanksgiving to the Virgin but said nothing.

At last King Phillippe and his court arrived and the tourney began. The great melee was ferocious indeed. Hundreds of knights on each team rode against their opposite numbers. Although, for once, no one was killed, dozens were grievously wounded. Many more lost their precious mounts. Still others were eliminated from any further competition, simply because they lost the battle to their opponents, which meant they had to give up armor, weapons and horse if they were unable to ransom them back.

Once the individual jousting began, Tyle enlisted every day, proudly wearing Chlotilde's favor on his sleeve. He still used the von Eltze black grouse on his surcoat, although his father had forbidden him its use, for he had no other. He hoped the heralds, who were sticklers about such things, hadn't news from so far away.

The first day Tyle was quickly unseated, and although he disported himself well on the ground, his opponent was a much heavier man and soon had him down.

"Now, you see," chided Johann. "It has cost you almost all the money you have worked so long for."

But his friend wouldn't be deterred. "I shall win it back tomorrow. You will see. Never fear. I know what I did wrong. I'll do better tomorrow."

And sure enough—whether through sheer luck or fierce determination his friends couldn't guess—Tyle did win the next day.

"Tyle," begged Chlotilde, "you have proven to me what a fine knight you are. Don't go on. Give over while you are even."

"No. I must go on," he insisted. "After tomorrow's eliminations, the King will start awarding prize money as well."

"That's just why you should quit now," urged Johann. "Tomorrow's competition will eliminate all those except the few competing for champion. You don't have the experience and the stakes will be higher."

"I'm gaining experience every day and the winnings will be higher, too."

The festive air of the tournament had turned the town into one grand fair. The glittering court of the King and the gorgeously clad ladies cheering on their favorites all added to the luster. It was easy to distinguish the wealthy knights by their elaborate surcoats matched by their horses' heavy caparison. Many had special tilting helmets bedecked with huge feathers, horns or ribbons, and feathers bobbed from their horses' heads. Armor was highly burnished, some even gilded. The unruly crowd of spectators was in a gay mood. The purveyors of food and drink added their shouts to the clamor.

But underneath it all tensions were running high. Some of the contestants had no fancy caparison for their destriers, no feathers on their helms, only a simple surcoat to identify them, plain old everyday armor much battered, mail ofttimes mended. These were the ones to watch, said the crowd. These were the battle-hardened veterans of many wars and feuds. These were the knights-errant who made their living fighting in tournaments throughout Europe. A few would be offered duty in the King's own guard. Most would refuse the honor, preferring the freedom of their wandering life. Kings were notorious for not paying.

By the third day the greater part of the remaining contestants consisted of these knights, except for a few nobles who had chosen not to

319

waste their time until the "riffraff" were eliminated. As Tyle waited on his side of the field, he could see his assigned opponent across the lists. He was one of these knights, a big, burly man. Tyle did not know who he was. His arms were unfamiliar, and with his visor already down his face could not be seen. A few questions crossed the young man's mind. Was his persistence wisdom or folly? He made himself sit straight in his saddle and forced the fears away. He was committed now. If he left the field, he would forfeit everything anyway.

When the herald blew for him, he spurred his destrier toward the barrier rail, lance set. The stunning blow from his opponent's lance nearly turned him around in his saddle, but his sturdy shield deflected it and he retained his seat. As they turned to charge again, Tyle realized that his lance arm was quivering. The blow must have twisted it somehow. He had no chance but to keep going. Their next encounter was a disaster. Not only did Tyle's lance fly up over his head, but somehow his horse was injured as well. The brave beast stumbled a few more steps carried by the momentum of the charge, and then fell, taking Tyle with him. As he dragged himself out from under the horse, a searing pain shot through his leg. The crowd went wild, the horse was screaming. Tyle's ears were ringing. He thought he heard a woman's voice crying, "Stop it, stop it." Chlotilde. But only the King can do that. Even Tyle's befuddled brain knew that. When he saw his opponent standing over him with drawn sword, he managed to drag himself to his feet, the pain in his leg excruciating. The man was courteous enough to wait until he had drawn his own sword, but Tyle knew he didn't stand a chance against him. His sword arm was weak and the leg hampered his agility. Yet he managed to put in a few good blows before the leg gave way beneath him. As the victor stood over him, foot planted on his heaving chest, sword tip at his throat, he heard the crowd yell, "Finish him, William! Kill the greenhorn that dares to challenge a champion." Then he realized who his opponent was—William of Yarmouth, a famed English knight. Why I have fought a champion, thought Tyle. I have actually fought a champion. And he fainted.

A few days later Tyle lay on a cot set up in the Kaufmanns' parlor. He was totally despondent. The physicker had set and splinted his broken leg and bound the shoulder, warning him not to try walking, even with crutches, for several weeks. But no one could ease his mental anguish. The affects of the laudanum had worn off and he was extremely irritable. Chlotilde tried to reassure him to no avail.

"I am a failure," he moaned, "a complete and total failure. I made a fool of myself at the University, a greater fool of myself in the lists. My father has disinherited me and I can't marry my love because I have lost everything and have no livelihood."

When she saw that sympathy only deepened his despondency, Chlotilde tried to scold him out of it. "Stop talking like that, Tyle. You know that I would marry you if you had nothing. Don't utter such nonsense. Besides, you have been learning a good trade."

"Trade, bah! What is that for the son of a nobleman?"

"A third son," she reminded him.

"Stop fussing over me and leave me alone. Get out of here!" he screamed.

She fled in tears. It was their first real fight.

Sometime later Frau Kaufmann poked her head in the door to announce that he had a visitor.

"Who would want to visit me?" he grumbled.

"I don't know," she replied, "but he is a very large and amiable young man. He says it is quite urgent that he see you today."

Tyle mumbled a reluctant acquiescence.

The big blond man almost filled the doorway as Tyle gaped in astonishment.

"I've come to congratulate the would-be champion," his voice boomed.

"You—you must be William," gasped Tyle.

"That I am and I've had the devil's own time trying to track you down. Here, let me help you," he said as Tyle struggled to sit up. He lifted the invalid like a doll as Tyle winced with pain.

"But what do you mean by congratulate? I am so ashamed," moaned Tyle.

"Of what, my friend? Only one can win. You put on a good show and the ladies loved it. I have fought many men and none brave enough to keep on fighting with a broken leg."

"Brave?" echoed Tyle.

"Why, yes, man, not many a clerk would even enter a tourney, much less last till the third day and fight well to boot."

"Clerk? But I am a knight," objected Tyle weakly.

"Bah, an empty title. But I admit I never expected to find you in the house of a Hanse merchant."

"Well, I—I mean, we're just staying here temporarily." Tyle was thoroughly confused by the conversation, but he was sure he knew why William had sought him out. "I suppose you've come to collect your ransom. If you'll let me know how much—you'd have no use for a dead horse . . ."

"The horse lives and will no doubt mend before his owner. Just a nasty cut across the hindquarters, which my squire took care of. Although he'll never fight again and you should not make him, but for sturdy transportation he'll serve you well enough."

"I don't understand. You speak as though the horse were still mine. It is yours by right of forfeit or until I pay the ransom, which you still haven't named."

"No ransom," replied William. "I've made some good prize money this time round, although I didn't make champion of the tourney. Too much prejudice against an Englishman right now. Understandable. England and France are at war, as usual, you know."

Tyle couldn't believe his good luck. Yet custom demanded that he pay. "But I insist," he said, but not too vigorously.

"No," the blond giant insisted in turn. "I shall return your horse and armor—though what use you'll have for that if you are apprenticing to a Hanse merchant I'll never know—on the condition that you'll take my advice and stay out of the tournament circuit."

"But I've always dreamt about becoming a knight-errant," insisted Tyle. "You said I fought bravely."

"Foolish boyhood dreams," spat William. "It's a hell of a life. Wandering from place to place, no home to call your own. Sleeping in the rain more often than not, with only your saddle for a pillow. Risking your neck for what? A little ransom or prize money that you're just as apt to lose next time round. My father is a merchant in Yarmouth—in fact, he has a good relation with the Hanse, wool, you know—and every day, man, I tell you, I kick myself a hundred times for not staying with him and learning the trade."

"But I thought you were a knight."

"Knighted in the field, in Gascony, followed good King Edward's rally boys, when they came to Yarmouth for ships. But what good is a knighthood without land? Just an excuse to get a higher scutage out of you when you decide you're too tired to fight anymore. Man, I tell you, I'm but four and twenty and I feel older than my father. Take my advice, lad, stick with the Hanse. That's where the money is—and a soft bed to boot."

322

Tyle shook his head in disbelief at the man's bitterness. "I had no idea."

"And let me tell you something else," continued William. "You see yon comely lass out there just dying to be your wife? Don't let her get away. Marry her tomorrow, before something more important than a leg gets broken. How can a man on the road take a wife? Or if you do, what good is she to you locked in a chastity belt hundreds of miles away? Oh, sure, the ladies love you when you win and shower you with kisses, but when you really need to bed a lass, what's left to you but the poxy whores in the taverns?"

"Couldn't you go back to Yarmouth?" suggested Tyle hesitantly.

"Pa thinks I'm a bum. And there's six other sons already in the business. It's too late for me now," he said wistfully.

Tyle lay pondering for a long time after William left.

A few weeks later Tyle was still undecided as to his future. He had reluctantly accepted the wisdom of William's advice and admitted that the life of a knight-errant was not for him. Lack of money precluded his returning to the University. He wondered how long the Kaufmanns would let him work for them. He had found that he really enjoyed the intricacies of keeping the accounts. As the household was in a frenzy of preparation for the imminent move to Brugge, he knew that he would have to make a decision very soon.

He was seated at the table with his leg propped up on a stool helping Frau Kaufmann close the books when Johann came in bearing a letter.

"Ah, news from home?" asked Tyle.

"Yes, but I'm afraid not very good news," replied Johann. "Both my father and my brother have been carried off by the pox. My mother and sisters were very ill, too, but have recovered. It is my older brother, the priest, who writes and says I must come home immediately. I am now the Freiherr von Sehnden."

"My God!" exclaimed his friend. "Holy Mother, pray for their souls. Johann, my dear friend, I am so sorry. But I suppose—I suppose I should congratulate you. The third son now the lord. What strange tricks the fates play on us."

"Cruel tricks," signed Johann. "It was the last thing I wanted, and certainly not this way. But I must go. The demesne cannot be left too long in the hands of the steward, reliable though he is. The peasants need to know who their lord is, and my mother needs protection."

"Travel with us," put in Frau Kaufmann. "You will get there much quicker by taking ship at Brugge for Bremen—and we can certainly use your protection on the road. We shall have many packhorses with goods."

"You are probably right. I shall think on it," replied Johann. "Right now I just want to be alone until I get used to the idea. I have much to pray about." He hurried out as tears threatened to overwhelm him.

"Well, that was certainly shocking news," commented Frau Kaufmann. "But in a way I am glad for him. He is such a hard worker and now his future is assured. And now what will *you* do?"

"I still don't know," said Tyle. "I still haven't fully absorbed the gravity of his news. But I know I have to make a decision soon. I have an idea that I would like to talk over with Herr Kaufmann—and Chlotilde."

"No, we don't need a Mass, high or otherwise," stated Chlotilde firmly. "We simply can't afford it. The hand-holding on the church porch with the priest's blessing will bind our troth just as tightly as any pomp before the altar."

"But I insist on St. Quirace."

"But, of course, my love," she replied. "I know how you and Johann feel about that particular saint. Someday you must take me to Vilsen to see that church. But tell me, why the big hurry now when I've been willing to marry you all these three years? Mind you, I'm overjoyed that you have finally made the big decision, but you're overwhelming me with so many things at once."

"Because the Kaufmanns are leaving in a few days."

"And?"

"And we are going with them. First we will be married tomorrow, here in Provins where we are known, and then . . . "

"What about the banns?" she interrupted.

"I spoke to the priest about that right after William was here. I've made up my mind to marry you no matter what my father said. I wanted to surprise you, but then Johann's news came . . . "

"Oh Tyle, I am so happy. I love you so," she exclaimed. "But what has Johann's news to do with us?"

"Because we, too, are going home," he announced.

"Home? To Eltze?"

"No, never to Eltze," he declared vehemently.

"Tyle, would you please explain yourself?"

"I had a long talk with Herr Kaufmann last eve. Do you remember

324

when we first came here he told us there were many opportunities for bankers and merchants in towns where the Hanse and the Lombards were not yet established?" Chlotilde nodded. "And do you remember my telling you about that brand-new town the Duke is building on the banks of the Aller? It's called Celle." Chlotilde nodded. "My love, I am going to be the first banker in Celle."

Chlotilde threw her arms around him. "Oh, Tyle, I am so proud of you. It sounds very exciting. But how . . . ?"

"Herr Kaufmann may be willing to invest in the enterprise. Of course, it will have to be from his own personal capital. The Hanse must know nothing about it. That depends on what his own circumstances will be when he gets to Brugge. But I have done the accounts these many months. I know how very rich he is—and, what's more, how he is getting richer all the while. I was blind when I looked down my nose at trade. It is the only way to make money. I know that now."

"I love you so much," crooned Chlotilde, "and I'm so happy that I'll be sharing all this with you."

Brugge was a charming and unusual town laced with canals. They crisscrossed it, bisected it, encircled it, so that it seemed there were more canals than streets. Elegant homes faced on them. It was also a very rich and prosperous town, the center of the wool trade. The cloth merchants' guild hall was as richly embellished as the count's palace. The harbor on the River Scheldt teemed with shipping from every seafaring nation in Europe. Each of several Lombard banks owned large buildings on the main square, which were their northern headquarters.

Once arrangements for the passage to Bremen were made, it was Johann and Chlotilde who went about sightseeing. Tyle was busy frequenting the banks. He had to be very circumspect about this as the Lombards were very close-mouthed and jealously guarded the secrets of their operations. But Tyle had enough knowledge of business methods by now to enable him to learn things simply by observing. The day before the sailing the Kaufmanns announced that they, too, would be going home to Bremen and were happy to do so.

The voyage was swift and uneventful. The great Hanse cog was crammed with goods for the north German hinterlands, leaving little room for passenger accommodations. At Bremen they bade the Kaufmanns farewell with promises to keep in touch and boarded a riverboat bound for Celle.

Tyle learned from the boatman that Duke Otto the Strong was in res-

325

idence at Celle overseeing the building of his new castle. So the very first thing Tyle did was seek out an audience with His Grace. They were amazed to see how the town had developed in their absence. Neat, well-built houses, some large, some small, lined the straight, squared-off streets, which themselves were exceptionally clean. Construction was going on everywhere. A large church, which would be dedicated to the Virgin and a small town hall as well as the castle itself were in various stages of completion. They had even laid out a tiltyard right in the middle of town next to the church and perpendicular to the market square. They had diverted the River Fuhse to form a natural moat around town and castle before it flowed into the Aller. And a great wall was a-building that would protect both castle and town, with the front of the castle open to the town, only a narrow moat separating the two, a very advanced concept for the time. Along the Aller waterfront outside the wall, quays were already in place for the receiving or transshipment of goods. Granaries and warehouses of all sorts were springing up where grassy banks had been.

"So you want to found a banking house?" Duke Otto guffawed and slapped his thigh, as if it were the funniest joke he had heard in years.

Tyle felt himself shrinking before the man. Otto had earned his cognomen of 'the Strong' not only because of military prowess, but because he knew what he wanted and made it happen. Hadn't he moved a whole sleepy little village five miles to the northeast to found what promised to be a burgeoning metropolis?

"Well, I thought—perhaps—I mean, with the increase in trade—I thought there would be a need," stammered Tyle.

"We don't even have many merchants yet," said the Duke, "and without merchants there is no need for a bank. Anyway, leave that nonsense to the Lombards. I sometimes wonder where you young men get all these newfangled ideas." The Duke seemed to muse for a moment. "Von Eltze, you say? Didn't I knight you a few years back?"

"Yes, Your Grace, you did," replied Tyle.

"Good family," murmured the Duke, "one of the oldest around here. Maybe I can find some way to help you. Tell me what you've been doing since then."

Tyle told him, carefully omitting some of the details and hoping the Duke hadn't spoken to his father lately.

When he had heard him out, Otto scratched his chin thoughtfully. "Young man," he said, "do you know why I moved Celle to its present location?"

"Because it's more easily defensible," ventured Tyle.

"Only partly," replied Otto. "The real reason is that very trade you're talking about. Do you realize that three major roads meet here? From Lüneburg in the north, Braunschweig in the south and Hannover to the southwest. Here they must all cross the ford or, more importantly, transship to the riverboats. I have decreed that Celle henceforth will have the only toll-collection point on the Aller. You say you have a head for figures?"

"I am fascinated by them," replied Tyle, "and as I told Your Grace, I learned a great deal in Provins."

"Then I have the very job for you if you're interested," said the Duke. "I need a reputable, honest toll–collector. It can be a very lucrative position. You would receive a percentage of every toll collected, and a house goes with it. It's the only thing I can offer you right now. I suggest ye think well on it."

Tyle didn't hesitate a minute. All his past indecisiveness was gone. He could see the tremendous possibilities of the offer—wealth as well as prestige. He tried to sound humble but excitement welled up in him. "I am very grateful, Your Grace, for the offer and I shall endeavor to do my best. I am aware of the tremendous responsibility with which you are entrusting me, but I feel that your faith in my ability will be amply justified."

Chlotilde was overjoyed at the news and Johann a little saddened. He hated to depart from his friends. "I am happy for you, Tyle," he said wistfully. "You are starting a new life in a new town, while I must go back to the same old pigs and peasants."

"But you are Lord of the manor," Tyle reminded him, "while this erstwhile banker has become a toll-collector."

"And you must come and visit us often," added Chlotilde.

"When I get my first boat, I'll come back." Johann waved as he rode down the road to Sehnde.

Intermezzo

In the event, Tyle's descendants held the position of toll-collector in Celle well into the seventeenth century. The von Eltze were considered one of the founding families of the town and certainly became and remained one of the wealthiest—all through trade. They expanded into grain, cloth and shipping, among other things, but never into banking per se. One of them was almost always on the Town Council and several of them were mayors of the town.

They must have maintained their friendship with Johann's descendants, because although none of the von Sehnden were mentioned in Celle records until well over a hundred years later, they seem to have been already well-known and were immediately received into the charmed inner circle.

The Duke needn't have worried about merchants. They appeared almost simultaneously and Celle prospered. The town received its charter in 1301 and the Liebfraukirche was consecrated in 1307. The Castle was added to on and off over many centuries. The town's government was one of the first truly democratic in Europe. It consisted of two mayors and a council first of nine, later twelve, elected by the people from among the wealthy Bürgers. The merchants backed by powerful guilds brooked no interference from the Duke, who was well aware of who held the purse-strings. In fact, so proud was he of his creation that he declared it a *Residenzstadt*, although his official capital was in Lüneburg, and he and his descendants ruled from there most of the time until the beginning of the eighteenth century.

The latter part of the thirteenth century was no doubt the apogee of the Middle Ages. Other than the sporadic skirmishes between the Valois and the Plantagenets, Europe was relatively peaceful, and with peace came prosperity. A little "industrial revolution" was taking place. The Electors, tired of the power and avaraciousness of the Hohenstaufens, chose what they thought was an unknown weakling from a little backwater called Austria. His name was Rudolf Habsburg. The Papacy, too, was at its weakest, with sometimes two popes, sometimes none, and the forced move to Avignon soon to come. Unencumbered by these two factors, trade flourished as never before. The population burgeoned, but the growing towns easily absorbed the excess. The merchants needed artisans to serve their needs, and these, too, soon formed powerful guilds. And both classes needed menials to do their tasks. The farms flourished, as the towns required food and, furthermore, had the ability to ship the excess produce to other population centers. In many cases serfs were fully or at least partially freed. "Town air is free air" became the watchword. What could have resulted from all this prosperity is interesting to speculate upon. A united Europe perhaps?

But before long into this rosy picture came a dark cloud from the east. It was to change the whole world around. It was called the Black Death.

4

AD 1350

Thousands of colored lights. Sparkling, flashing, scintillating, pulsating, swirling, swirling, swirling. Stars? The aurora? The celestial light?

And humming, humming. Throbbing, ringing, crescendoing. The wind? Bees? An angelic choir?

Surely I have died and am approaching heaven. Swirling, humming, swirling, humming. How beautiful.

But it is fading. Don't go away. Don't leave me. It is so beautiful.

"Mama."

And suddenly she awoke.

"Mama."

I am alive. I have survived the Black Death.

She lay drenched in her own sweat, too weak to move. Cautiously she opened her eyes. Yes, she was still in her own bed, the curtains of the cupboard partially drawn. She could see a dim light filtering through the oiled vellum covering the window. But when she tried to turn her head, waves of dizziness overcame her. She felt someone tugging at her arm.

"Mama, Mama, are you finally awake?"

My baby still lives. Oh, thank God. "Ja, kleinchen, I'm awake, but I'm too weak to move yet."

"Oh, Mama, I'm so glad you're awake." She felt her adored five-year-old kiss her cheek, but her arms were too weak to hug him. "I'm hungry."

"Where is Greta?"

"They took her away, just like they took Papa. They wanted to take you, too, but I wouldn't let them. I knew you were just sleeping, but they wouldn't believe me. So I was very brave, just like you told me to be. I stood in front of your bed cupboard and kicked them till they went away." And suddenly all his bravado deserted him and he started to cry. "Oh, Mama, I was really so frightened."

330

With great effort she managed to raise one arm and fold him to her. Greta dead, oh, God have mercy. The devoted servant who had saved her life with her magic potion made from bread mold and Lord knows what else and who wouldn't take any to save herself. Oh, God have mercy on her soul. She held her son to her breast until his sobbing was spent.

"Mama, the men laughed at me and said they would be back in a few days and take us both. They won't do that now, will they?"

"No indeed, they won't dare now, my baby. Your mama was very sick, but I'm going to get better very soon."

Suddenly the sturdy blue-eyed blonde mustered all his five-year-old dignity. "I am not your baby anymore. I am the man of the house now. You told me yourself, when Papa died."

"And indeed you are, but you'll always be my baby. But that will just be between us, all right?"

"I s'pose."

She smiled and her cracking lips reminded her how parched her mouth was.

"Fetch me a drink of water, kleinchen, I can hardly talk anymore."

"Yes, Mama." He ran over to the bucket and returned with the dipper brimming. She managed to spill much of it as she drank, but it didn't seem to matter, she was so wet anyway. She shivered a little as the cold water trickled down her breasts, but it felt good after the burning fever.

"Ah, that was refreshing," she sighed as she fell back against the sodden pillow.

"But, Mama, I'm still hungry," he reminded her.

"Is there no food in the house?" She had always prided herself on her well-stocked larder.

"I ate it all."

"All? How long have I been asleep?"

"Days and days and days. I don't know exactly. It was a long time. I even ate the moldy bread Greta was saving for you. I'm sorry, Mama, but I was so hungry—and I didn't know how to make the potion anyway."

"No matter," she murmured. That saved him, the moldy bread kept him from contracting the plague. Oh, God be thanked for a miracle. "Then you must run to the baker's shop and buy something. Are there any pennies left in my jar or did they steal them?"

"Yes, no. I mean, one of them wanted to, but the other said, 'let be, there's nothing to be bought with them anyway. Save them to put on her eyes when she's dead.'"

"Oh, how barbarous." She shuddered. Then something else occurred to her as she felt down her body for her chatelaine's belt. "My keys. Where are they?"

"Greta hid them when she undressed you and put you to bed."

"Do you know where she hid them?"

"In the back of your oven," he whispered, "and the fire was still burning when the men were here, so they didn't look. But it's out now," he added apologetically, "because I couldn't lift the big logs."

She was suddenly aware of how chilly the room was and shivered in the sodden bedclothes. "I must get some dry warm clothes on," she said as she struggled to put her elbows under her. "You run now to the baker's shop and fetch us two juicy meat pies."

"Mama, I can't reach the jar." He glanced up at his mother's beautiful jar on the mantelpiece, purposely set high out of his reach. She managed to get one elbow in place. "Besides, the baker and his wife are both dead. 'Tis said even their fires are cold and the men who took them away took all the bread, too."

She got the other elbow under her. "How do you know these things?"

But the boy continued, "And besides, they have nailed the door shut."

"They wha-a-t?" She sat bolt upright. Waves of dizziness threatened to overcome her, but she held on until they passed. Gingerly she slid one leg after the other out from under the covers until she was sitting on the edge of the bed, gasping with the effort but at least no longer dizzy. "You say they nailed the door shut? Whyever?" she queried.

"They said the Town Council ordered it so that no one still living with the Plague could go out in the streets and pass it to others."

"I see."

"Otherwise I would have gone out while you were sleeping and stolen some food."

"Never!" She was shocked.

"But everyone is doing it. The dead people don't care. Or I could have begged," he added.

"Never!" she gasped. "Fetch me some more water. Bring the whole bucket over here." This time she drank deeply and then splashed the cold water on her face. How refreshing it felt, although it started her shivering again. The child ran to fetch a towel. When she had dried her face she felt better. "Kleinchen, come here."

As the boy stood before her, she placed both hands on his shoulders.

332

"My son, I want you to remember one thing. You are Johann Wiese, son of Uwe Wiese, master shoemaker and Bürger of the town of Uelzen, and his wife Mistress Elizabeth Wiese. We do not steal, neither from the living nor from the dead. Nor do we beg. Is that clear?"

"Yes, Mama."

"We work for what we have. We pay our taxes and we pay our way. Do you understand?"

"Yes, Mama."

"Good. Then help me change into some clean clothes and lay the fire. Then we shall see about doors nailed shut. Nailed shut indeed."

Little did Elizabeth realize then that she would soon refute her own proud words.

Her knees nearly gave way as she stood, but with each effort she felt her strength returning. She stripped off her sweat-soaked shift and quickly washed off in the icy water. Dry, warm clothes made her feel better and she suddenly realized she, too, was hungry.

"Help me lay the fire, kleinchen. Maybe between us we can get some logs in. I am still so very weak. But first climb in the oven and get my keys." She smiled as she watched the little boy climb into the big brick oven next to the fireplace. He is growing so fast, he won't be able to do that much longer, she thought.

With her key ring once more dangling from her waist she felt more in charge of things. By leaning on the wall, the table, and various other pieces of furniture, she slowly made her way to the fireplace and took down the jar from the mantelpiece. There were ten pennies in it, enough to feed them for several days, even two weeks if she were very careful. The effort of retrieving the jar cost her dearly. She collapsed onto the nearest chair and rested her head on her arms on the table.

"Mama, are you all right?"

"Ja, kleinchen," she sighed, "but not as strong as I thought. I don't think I can lay the fire just yet. Fetch me my shawl and put the water bucket here beside me." When he had done so, she handed him a penny. "I'll be stronger if we can just get something to eat. Take this to the baker . . ."

"But, Mama, the baker . . . "

"I know you said he's dead. But someone must be doing his work. The apprentices perhaps."

"I think they ran away."

"But you don't know. If not there, try somewhere else, even the sweet

333

shop. Someone must have some food that we can buy."

"Yes, Mama," agreed Johann doubtfully. "How am I going to get out of the house?"

"Have they nailed the window shut, too?"

"I don't think so."

"Then there you go," she urged. "I know you've gone that way before." He grinned at her sheepishly. Mamas seemed to know everything. "We'll worry about the door after we've eaten some food."

The little boy dragged a stool over to the window that faced on the street. He climbed up and unlatched the casement and in a twinkling was over the sill.

Elizabeth murmured a prayer that he would find something and sat back to wait. She was so weak. She glanced at her hands and down at her body. Skin and bones. She had lost a tremendous amount of weight. Her armpits were still sore where Greta had lanced the buboes. But they were healing well thanks to the magic ointment. Oh, Greta, she wept, I shall miss you so. You saved my life. Why couldn't you save your own? Oh, I am so weak. She considered going back to bed but was afraid she might not be able to get up again. She put her head down on the table and dozed.

As Johann wandered the streets he was frightened. The usually bustling town was deserted. He felt he was the only person still alive. Windows were shuttered, curtains drawn, he noticed many doors were nailed shut. But some stood wide open and the houses within appeared to have been looted. He came to the baker's shop in the next street.

It, too, was wide open. Cautiously he entered. No one was about. The ovens were indeed very cold. Even the flour bags had been carried away. No hope here. He wandered farther down the street. As he approached the great marketplace the stench hit him. He had noticed it earlier in the narrower streets exuding from the deserted houses, but the cool breeze from the river had diluted it. He remembered happier times coming here with his mother or Greta. The thought of all the crisp, bright vegetables and fruits, of the meat and fish, of the sweets that could be bought or just looked at longingly. He thought of the mouth-watering smells of the past. Surely someone must still be here selling something.

But the putrid odor that engulfed him as he approached the square— really a triangle—was far from mouth-watering. It was nauseating. He had never smelled anything like it before. It was the stench of plague and death. He held his nose and trudged doggedly on. He entered the wide end of the square and found it deserted. Although not unexpected, the prospect dismayed him. So intent was he inspecting the shops on either side of the marketplace to see if any might be open that he didn't notice what was at the end. The square narrowed and ended at a point behind the Holy Ghost Church. And there piled behind and beside the church were the corpses. It seemed to him there were hundreds in varying stages of decay. Maggots crawled over them, a few mangy dogs tore at them and the buzzards were feasting. Beyond the pile near the Lüneburger gate two men in masks fitfully chased the buzzards away as they chucked the decomposing bodies into a cart.

Johann turned and ran as fast as he could back the way he had come. A stitch in his side made him stop. Leaning against a house front, he retched. There was nothing in his stomach to vomit, but he retched and retched. Weakly he sat down on the doorstep and cried. After a bit he thought, I have just told Mama I am no longer a baby. I must stop crying and think what to do and—he added as an afterthought—pray for these people's souls. He got up and slowly made his way to Gudestrasse, the main cross-thoroughfare of the town.

He turned right. This was the street of the luxury merchants—the cloth cutters, the furriers, the goldsmiths. No hope of food here. Then down the block he saw rising before him the great bulk of the town church dedicated to St. Mary. Hope rose in his breast. Surely the Mother of God will help. Surely the good priests will have food they can spare. He entered the church. No one was about. A few flickering candles told him there must still be someone alive in the town. It crossed his mind that he should pray, but there wasn't time. Mama was so weak and needed food. He murmured a quick Ave, crossed himself and left.

He crossed the street to the parish house and rang the bell. He could hear it echoing through the house, but no one came to answer it. He rang it again and again. He was just about to turn away when a gruff voice called from the other side of the door, "Go away. We do not open to anyone."

"I am just a boy, Father, and I am not sick," replied Johann.

"Go away."

"But, Father," pleaded Johann, "I only ask for a bit of food for my mother, who is well again. I can pay," he added.

"We have little enough for ourselves, and none to spare," growled the voice. "Go away." And then as an afterthought, "I am sorry. God bless."

God bless indeed, thought Johann as he turned away in despair. How often have my parents given them money for the poor? why can't they help now? He wandered aimlessly down yet another street. Suddenly from the dark depths of an alley he thought he heard singing. As he drew nigh, singing it was indeed, terribly off key but sounding happy nonetheless. The sound was coming from an ancient tavern as lusty male voices were raised in a dirty song he wasn't even supposed to know. He had learned some of the words from other boys, although he had no idea what most of them meant. Hesitantly he slipped into the open doorway and waited until his eyes adjusted to the dimness.

He started as a huge hand clapped his shoulder. "Hey there, Willi. Look, another live one walking the street. What can we do for you, laddie? Wouldst care to join our celebration?"

The singing had stopped as all eyes turned toward the small boy standing in the doorway. Johann didn't know how to begin. "Wh—what are you celebrating?" he asked.

"Why, the end of the plague, that's what."

"But, but—I saw all those dead people . . . ," he gagged as he pointed vaguely.

"Ah, but that's from weeks and weeks ago. There was no place left to bury 'em. But finally the Council got one of yon priests to go out and consecrate a new burying ground outside the gate. And now the few carters that are left are lugging them out bit by bit and shoveling 'em in a mass grave." Johann turned white and almost gagged again. "Here, Willi, give the lad a small beer."

As the family always had beer for breakfast, Johann had no qualms about accepting, although he really wanted food, but he had been taught to be polite. "Thank you very much," he said, accepting the draught. "How can you be celebrating the end of the plague, when—when . . . ?"

"When there's still bodies lying about?" finished the man. "Because in all of last week there were only ten deaths, instead of forty or fifty a day back in the summer, and *no new cases*. That's the important thing, no new cases. We think the colder weather is clearing out the bad air," he pronounced.

"I see," said Johann as he finished his drink.

"Have another?"

"No, no thank you. What I really need is to buy some food for my mother. They stole all ours when she was sick, but now she's better. But she's still very weak and needs food."

Unconsciously they all moved a few steps away from the boy. "Your mother had the plague and survived?"

"Yes, God be thanked."

"Now that is a miracle indeed."

"Yes."

"Them ain't many that do."

"I know."

"But food I can't help you with," put in Willi, the tavern owner. "We're all in the same boat. The farmers won't come into town. There ain't been a market in nigh on two months. And them's that have any left ain't giving it away for love nor money."

"I see. Well, thanks for the beer anyway," said Johann sadly as he started to turn away.

"Wait, hold a minute laddie," bellowed Willi. "How would your ma like a pail of nice sweet cider? Might refresh her a bit."

"Oh, thank you, sir," replied Johann. "I can pay."

Willi waved the boy away as he drew the cider. "Save your penny for food, lad, if you can find any. It's on the house. These lads here won't drink anything that they can't get drunk on. Take it with my blessing."

"Oh, thank you, sir," said Johann again. Carefully holding the brimming pail of golden cider, he left the tavern thinking that Willi's blessing meant more to him than the priest's.

Johann was about to head for home when it occurred to him there was one more place he might try. Heading into the wealthier part of town, he knocked at the door of a beautiful three-storied house. The shop on the ground floor was shuttered, but he knew that this door to one side of the shop led upstairs to the living quarters. He had visited here a few times with his parents. The second and third floors were beautifully half-timbered and had real glass windows. The whole was topped by an elaborate gable, making a storage attic so large it was almost a full fourth floor. He knew he shouldn't be here but he felt it was his last chance. He was that desperate. He knocked again at the door of the home of the head of the Shoemaker's guild, Master Mestwart.

At last a window on the second floor opened a crack and a woman called out, "What do you want with that racket? Like to raise the dead."

"I seek Master Mestwart," replied Johann politely, although he knew she was a servant. "Is he at home?"

"We don't open to no beggars," she shouted back.

"I am no beggar. Please tell your master that Johann, the son of Uwe

337

Wiese, Master Shoemaker, must speak with him," demanded the boy with all the dignity he could muster.

"Wait," she mumbled.

Johann waited. After some time he heard footsteps descending the stairs. The door opened a crack. It was the master himself, a vinegar-soaked cloth held over his nose and mouth. Johann explained his errand, emphasizing that he was not really asking for charity, but that no food was available for sale anywhere in the town.

"Your mother has recovered!" exclaimed the old man. "Saints be praised. I heard about your father's death. I am so sorry." He crossed himself piously. "Of course, the Guild will do all it can to help the survivors. Unfortunately, money we have aplenty. Food we do not. Perhaps there is something to spare. I sent my family out into the country for safety months ago, so there is only myself and the housekeeper to feed. I think we might have a little to give you. When your mother is fully recovered, ask her to call on me about her membership. Wait here."

He shut the door in Johann's face. He had not really expected to be invited in. Their fear was palpable. But it was a bit demeaning to be left on the stoop when his family had once been so welcome. After a while the door opened a crack. It was the maid this time. She, too, had the vinegary cloth on her face. She handed out a small basket. "This is all we can spare. Don't bother to return the basket." And she quickly slammed the door.

Something smelled delicious under the white linen cloth. Johann couldn't resist peeking. He carefully set down the pail of cider and lifted the cloth. A full loaf of bread, still warm from the oven, a huge chunk of cheese, two slices of some kind of meat, a pear and a bunch of grapes. A veritable feast. He tucked the cloth around it again, picked up the pail of cider and headed for home. This time he, too, felt like singing, but not the bawdy song of the tavern. He lifted his voice in a psalm of praise.

"Mama, Mama, help me!"

Elizabeth woke with a start. For a few minutes she was totally disoriented. Where am I? What am I doing here at my own table? I thought I was dead. No, that's right. I woke up and sent Johann for food. Where can he be? It's taking so long. I hope . . .

"Mama, come quickly. They're trying to steal our food."

That aroused her fully. "Who is trying to steal from you? They'd better not," she called out. She pushed herself up and stood for a moment until a wave of dizziness passed. Laboriously she made her way to the window. Johann was standing there, both hands filled, surrounded by three older boys, ruffians by the looks of them. At her appearance they backed off a bit but kept taunting him.

"Quick, take this," said Johann, handing her first the basket of food and then the pail of cider. Her arms almost gave way with weakness as she lifted it over the sill.

At the same time she scolded the urchins, "Leave him be or I'll call the watch."

They laughed at her. "What watch? Ain't been no watch in months. Where you been, mistress?" Then they noticed the barred door. "There's plague in this house. Let's get out of here." And they ran off as if a thousand demons were after them.

Johann laughed as Elizabeth reached down to help him climb up to the windowsill. "They tried to bully me, but look how scared they are now. That's all right, Mama, I can climb up by myself."

"Then you'd best do it," she replied, shaking her head. "I have so little strength, I almost spilled that lovely cider. But tell me, where did you get all of this? It's a very feast."

The lad jumped down from the window. "I'll tell you in a minute, I have to go out to the privy first. Here is your penny back."

"Kleinchen! You didn't beg?"

"No, Mama, I didn't beg. It's a long story. I'll tell you all about it, but I really have to go bad." He picked up the water bucket as he headed toward the back door. "I might as well get some fresh water while I'm out there." He did have to go, but he really needed time to decide whether to tell her the truth about where the food came from. He knew his mother would be angry that he had gone to Master Mestwart, but after all, he had had no other choice, had he? She didn't want him to beg. There was no one to beg from anyway. He must impress that upon her. And the food looked so good. Better even than their usual fare. And he was lucky, wasn't he, that the Master himself hadn't gone to the country with the rest of the family. He debated back and forth and finally decided to tell his story from the beginning, very slowly, emphasizing his frustration, so that by the time he got to the end, she couldn't possibly be angry. He would dwell on the horror of the corpses, although even that didn't seem so horrible now that he was away from the smell. But he would make the most of it. That and the churlishness of the priests and the kindness of Willi. In the end she would praise him for having had the courage to go to Master Mestwart. Johann didn't realize it, but the horror of the Black Death had thrust him out of babyhood into a street-smart childhood, which in itself would not last long.

When he returned, she was seated once again at the table looking very wan. "I waited until you got back," she said, "but that cider looks so good I was tempted to drink some right out of the pail. Wherever did you get it?"

"Let me fetch some cups," he suggested, sidestepping her question. He pulled a chair over to the cupboard and carefully climbed up to reach the cups.

"You didn't steal it, did you?"

"Of course not, Mama," he replied indignantly. "You know I wouldn't steal, no matter how desperate we were."

"I know. I'm sorry," she apologized. "I shouldn't even have thought such a thing. And we're not that desperate. Just as soon as I can restock the larder, we'll be fine."

He placed the cups on the table and carefully poured some cider, before saying very slowly and deliberately, "You won't be able to restock the larder, Mama. There's nothing to be bought. Absolutely nothing." And he told her the story of his quest for food. He even embroidered a little, telling her that the few survivors were eating dogs and rats, which he had heard but didn't know if it were true. In the end, she wept. She hugged him and kissed him and wept some more.

Through her tears she murmured, "My poor baby. I mean, what a brave young man you are, kleinchen. How awful that one so young should have to see such horrible things."

"Oh, it wasn't that awful." He could afford to be brave now that he was safely back home with the food, but he had really been more frightened of those ruffians than he had been of the dead bodies. They were more desperate than he, and there had been three of them, all twice his age. He squared his shoulders. "Come, Mama, dry your tears and let's eat some of this wonderful food. I'm so hungry."

She smiled then. "Ach, yes, let's. But we must shepherd it carefully. We can't dare ask the old—uh, Master Mestwart for more. The plague must have changed his heart. Let's enjoy it while we can."

She carefully divided one piece of meat and broke off some chunks of bread. They washed it down with a little cider and felt as though they had had a royal feast.

"I think I shall lie down for a while." At his worried look, she added, "Don't worry, I'll not sleep for weeks. I feel stronger already. This evening

340

we shall eat a little bit more of this wonderful food. And by tomorrow I hope I shall be strong enough to see about getting that door open."

The next day she felt strong enough to venture out into her garden. My God, she thought, they even helped themselves out here. What ghouls. They thought I was going to die, too, but I fooled them. She smiled at the thought. Then she shook her head in dismay at how badly her beloved garden had been ransacked. She found a wormy cabbage and a few turnips. How did they miss them? Probably they were still too small back then. Thank God for that. She noticed there were still a few apples on the highest branches of the tree. Johann will have to climb up for them. She couldn't wait until they fell. She chose the cabbage. The turnips would keep better.

Together they dragged in some logs for the fire. Every little effort exhausted her, but she forced herself to keep going. While the child laid the fire, she cut up the cabbage and carefully picked out the worms. Ach, she thought at last, if they're boiled long enough they can't hurt us. She put the cabbage into her big iron pot and threw in the other piece of meat. That will add a little flavor and stretch out the strength that is in the meat a little further. I wonder if they left any of my precious salt. She couldn't find it.

Even that. She shook her head. Salt, a precious commodity in many places at that time, was usually readily available in Uelzen, being so close to the famous salt mines of Lüneburg, but with trade at a standstill she supposed that had become scarce, too.

With the fire taking the chill off and more food in her belly, she felt her strength gradually returning. That afternoon, for the first time since her illness, she went into her husband's workshop. The rich smell of leather, the half-finished shoes, his customers' lasts hanging neatly on the wall, the tools on his workbench, just as he had left them when he was stricken—it all overwhelmed her with sadness. In her struggle to survive his passing had been just one more part of the nightmare. She was already very ill when he died. Greta had taken care of them both. Now it suddenly hit her—the grief, the aloneness, the helplessness. For the first time she realized she was now a widow—a widow at twenty, a widow in a town almost wiped out by the Black Death, a widow with a trade, for she could make shoes as well as her husband and was a full member of the Guild, but with no customers, a widow with a little money saved that could buy nothing, a widow with a child to raise by herself. The enormity of it all was almost more than she could bear. She sat down at Uwe's worktable and wept. Not the gentle weeping of weakness, but great, wrenching sobs of grief, the anguished wails of a woman in travail.

When at last the worst of her tears subsided she found herself fingering a wondrously soft piece of shoe leather, already cut to shape. They were to have been beautiful shoes for Frau Schmied. Tiny, diminutive Frau Schmied, so different from her big, burly husband, the smith. She had loved beautiful things. Elizabeth wondered if they were still alive. How many children did they have? Quite a few, she recalled. Did any still live? She thought about their other clientele. Did any of them still live? She had best find out before she confronted Master Mestwart. And confrontation it would surely be, unless she could prove to him that she had enough loyal customers for her to take over and carry on her husband's business. And what if she didn't?

Thoughts of the future once again overwhelmed her with a feeling of helplessness. Johann must start school next year, and she would start training him as a shoemaker at the same time. It was customary to wait until children were a bit older to start their apprenticeship, but these were unusual times and those rules did not apply to the masters' families anyway.

The Hanse had established excellent schools in most of its towns. The wily, very practical merchants had long ago thrown up their hands in disgust at the vague and usually very impractical curricula of the church schools. They needed their sons—and daughters—to learn more than just reading, writing and theology. Their heirs would eventually have to handle complicated bookkeeping and accounts, bills of lading and letters of credit, ships' manifests and warehouse inventories. They would have to have practical knowledge of geography to sail the ships and figure the length and problems of overland travel, of weather conditions in far-off places, of crop harvests and failures, of the quality of wool on the sheep's back and in the finished cloth, of the price of spices or silk in Venice or of lumber or furs in Novgorod, of the exchange rate of hundreds of foreign currencies. So the merchants set up their own schools in all the larger Hanse towns of northern Germany and the Baltic and North Sea perimeters. At first only their sons and later their daughters were allowed to attend. But as the various artisans' guilds became wealthier and more powerful, the merchants saw the advantage of having an educated middle class as both suppliers and customers. So they opened the schools, for a fee, to the children of master artisans and tradesmen as long as they were citizens of the town.

Elizabeth checked her wandering thoughts. She had always prided

342

herself on being a very practical person. There was no sense worrying until she knew how bad the situation really was. As soon as she was a little stronger, she would find out for herself.

A few days later she made her first foray abroad accompanied by Johann.

"Are we going to visit Master Mestwart?" asked the child.

"Not yet," replied his mother. "First I want to test my strength. And I want you to show me some of the things you saw."

"Not all of them, Mama," objected Johann. "Those dead people will make you sick again."

"Well, maybe not those," she agreed. "But perhaps they've been buried by now. Did you meet any of our friends or neighbors?"

"No, no one. I told you, the streets were empty—or almost. I don't know where those three bad boys came from, but suddenly they were following me. We must be very careful," he said protectively.

"We shall, don't worry. Perhaps they smelled the food. This time we shall have nothing with us that anyone would want to steal."

They strolled up Schuhstrasse and Elizabeth was shocked at the number of doors nailed shut or wide open, the houses looted. At least two or three of the other shoemakers would obviously never be doing business again. So, that much less competition, she thought and was immediately ashamed of the thought. I've become as ghoulish as the rest of them. She said a quick prayer for the repose of their souls.

They crossed Gudestrasse and approached the marketplace.

"Do we really want to go there?" she asked.

"I don't smell anything. Perhaps they're gone," replied her son. "Shall I run ahead and see?"

She took him by the hand. "No, no, we'll stay together." They entered the square. There was no sign of any market stalls. All the shops and houses were still tightly shuttered. And then suddenly the stench hit them. The breeze that had been blowing from behind them had died. The pile of corpses was much lower than when Johann had first seen them, but the decay was far more advanced, and the vultures were far more numerous. Even the dogs and rats had left. "Let's get out of here," she exclaimed, turning quickly. "Let's sit by the river awhile where we can get some fresh air." They hurried back to Gudestrasse and turned toward the river.

The great gate tower on the bridge over the river loomed before them. She noticed that the gate was tightly shut and unmanned. "Are we then prisoners in our own town?" she asked of no one in particular. They climbed the battlements of the wall and sat for a while, looking out over the river and the rich farmland beyond. Here the Ilmenau was shallow and meandering, but there was always enough water for the flat barges that carried grain and goods to and from this normally bustling town. Now it was empty of traffic. Not even a fishing boat was in sight. But there were other things that really turned her stomach. Bloated bodies of horses and cows, dogs and rats, even an occasional human corpse drifted by on the placid stream. At least up here you can't smell them, she thought, but the sight was revolting. She turned her eyes to the countryside beyond. The road leading into the town was deserted. That she had expected, but she could see no sign of any livestock or poultry. The trees were almost bare of their foliage by now but not a living thing moved among them. Hay stood in fields uncut. Even the ubiquitous Heiden sheep were nowhere to be seen. It looks like the end of the world she thought despondently. Where do we go from here? Why, home, her brighter self asserted. At least we are alive.

As they left the walls, she mused, "Are we the only ones left in this pesthole?"

"I'll show you some live people," chirped Johann, taking her hand. "Come, Mama, you must meet Willi."

"Oh, I really couldn't go there," she objected.

"Why not? They were kinder than the priests. Maybe he'll give us some more cider."

"Very well," she agreed reluctantly, allowing her son to lead her. "I really should thank him."

She hesitated when they entered the alley. "Come on, Mama, it's not far. But they're not singing today. I hope they're not closed." But the door of the tavern stood open and, standing a moment as before to let his eyes adjust, he was recognized by the owner.

"Ach, here's my little friend again," bellowed Willi from behind the bar. "Come for more cider? Did your Mama enjoy it?"

"I brought her to thank you," replied Johann as Elizabeth stepped in beside him.

"Ach, Meinfrau," said Willi obsequiously. "Come in, come in. Such a fine lady has never graced this humble tavern before."

"This lady is not so fine that she can't thank you for your great kindness," replied Elizabeth courteously.

" 'Twas nothing," murmured Willi. "Come sit and have some refreshment." He hurried around the bar and dusted off a table and a bench, then hurried back to pour two mugs of cider before she could object.

"How come they're not singing today?" asked Johann, indicating the few morose drinkers across the room.

"Even drunks sober up and face reality sometime," said Willi sadly. "They're mourning the dead or looking for food for them that's left. That's the harder of the two."

Elizabeth looked up from sipping her drink. "Ja, I can see that that is not just our problem. Do you know of any place we can buy food? Anything, any kind?"

"That I don't, Meinfrau. I wish I did. I've heard that there's food aplenty outside—rotting on the ground for lack of picking, dying in the stalls for lack of milking or feed. But they won't open the blasted—your pardon, Meinfrau—they won't open the gates to let us out or anyone in. But I've known of a few who've managed to sneak out and back in again. But the prices they ask!" Willi shook his head and began to philosophize. "Ach, ja, the Black Death has been a great equalizer. Serfs that don't know what freedom is, selling their master's milk and eggs over their dead bodies. Maids wearing their mistresses' fancy gowns. And the wages they ask for a little bit of unskilled labor! And getting it, too, because there's no one left to work. Yet masters and fine ladies like yourself, Meinfrau, go begging because those—those louse-ridden villeins won't bring it into town. But, forgive me, Meinfrau, I go on. Will you have another drink?"

"No, no thank you, Master Willi, we must go home. I've not got my strength back yet. But you've given me some interesting information. Tell me, is there someone I could pay to go outside and get us food?"

"Aye, there is, but I wouldn't risk it, Meinfrau. More'n likely you'll never see your money again nor any food. But even if the man were honest, which is rare these days, he'll have little chance of getting back in. There's only a few who know certain people, if you take my meaning."

Elizabeth pondered this. "Well thank you for the drink, Master Willi. I shall never forget your kindness to us. When I get my business back together again, you must give me your wife's shoe size."

"I ain't got no wife no more. She got took," said Willi sadly.

"Oh, I am so sorry," replied Elizabeth as she and Johann took their leave.

On the way home, she realized that she would be saying that over and over again for weeks to come.

Back home again, she boiled up another turnip into a thin soup. If we ever get some decent food, I'll never eat another turnip again, she promised herself.

With their limited diet her strength returned very slowly, and it was some weeks before she felt able to face the daunting task of resuming Uwe's business. But during her convalescence she had given it a great deal of thought and she knew that her first priority was to see how many, if any, of their clients still lived and then try to build up an additional clientele from the customers of those shoemakers who had perished. She carefully copied out lists of names from her husband's account books.

Meanwhile the weather had turned cold and blustery, promising an early and bitter winter on top of all their other troubles. The plague seemed to have run its course—for this year, at least—and the town gates were finally reopened. But the surrounding countryside had been devastated almost as badly as the town, and what should have been rich harvests lay rotting on the ground. A great deal of livestock had also succumbed to the pestilence and many more had been ruthlessly slaughtered by starving foragers. What little food now reached the reopened but greatly diminished market commanded exorbitant prices. Elizabeth knew her carefully hoarded savings could not last long without some money coming in.

At last, one cold but bright day, she donned her second-best gown— the best was reserved only for church and extra-special Guild affairs— wound her starched wimple around her hair and under her chin, wrapped herself in her warmest shawl and set out, list in hand. What she learned appalled her, frightening her more than the plague itself. More than two-thirds of their former clients were dead. Many others had fled the town, never to be heard from again. The few remaining were sympathetic.

"Mistress Wiese, I understand your problem, but I, too, have no clients. It will take me months, maybe years, to build up my business again. Shoes are the last thing I can afford."

"My shop was looted when I was ill and all my tools taken. I have to start all over from scratch."

"My wife died and her shoes fit my daughter. I'm sorry, but it will be a long while before she'll need new ones."

"My husband died and I am destitute. He never taught me his business. You are so lucky you have your business. The Guild has only given me a pittance to feed four children."

Am I so lucky? thought Elizabeth. Oh, the supreme irony of it. What good is a business with no clients? And the greatest shock of all came when, after she knocked on a friend's door, a simpering housemaid, arrayed in her mistress' best gown, answered.

"Ach, the Master and Mistress be taken and no family to even bury them. The house be ours now and all that's in it." She pirouetted around gleefully. "Sure the old skinflint put all his cash with the Council. But shoes, ach, shoes and clothes and jewelry the old gal left aplenty. I might even sell some o' them myself to buy bread."

Heartsick, Elizabeth turned away in disgust. She did get a few vague promises for future orders, when and if business picked up. But they were very few and very vague. She returned home weary and discouraged.

She knew she could not put off going to see Master Mestwart any longer.

The next day she put on her best gown. The old Master Shoemaker greeted her cordially, but very formally. He had always called her Mistress Lisa at Guild socials. Now he said, "Of course, Mistress Wiese, you know your standing in the Guild remains the same. As a working wife or widow of a Master you are still a full-fledged member of the Guild—provided, that is, that you keep your dues up-to-date and maintain your previous business standards."

"But that is why I have come to seek your advice, Master Mestwart," said Elizabeth with as much dignity as she could muster. "There is no business out there."

"I am afraid we all have the same problem. Just be patient. It will come."

"Meanwhile I have a child to feed and am running out of money."

"Mistress, I sympathize, but you know full well that the Guild cannot extend welfare to Masters in good standing, only to those who have lost all means of livelihood. You will have to work even harder than when your husband lived."

"Master, I am willing to work harder than three people," she said, exasperated, "but shoes are not like loaves of bread that you can throw in the oven and hope someone will come and buy them. Shoes must be made to order, to a specific size and last."

"Mistress Wiese, I do not need you to tell me how shoes are made."

"I am sorry, Master. I am overwrought for, indeed, I trudged the entire town but yesterday, and most of my clients are gone. The rest have also fallen on hard times. What am I to do?"

"Then, Mistress, my best advice would be to marry a shoemaker who has lost his wife and pool your resources."

Elizabeth was aghast. "You can't be serious."

"I am very serious, my dear Mistress Wiese. But be sure you marry inside the town. To go outside would forfeit your Guild membership, as I'm sure you're aware."

"Master Mestwart, how can you suggest such a thing with my dear husband scarcely buried?"

"I not only suggest it but strongly urge it. Forget mourning. Everyone is mourning these days. Hence no one is. Life must go on. As I see it, you have no choice but to remarry as quickly as possible. Think on it. Good day, Mistress."

Shocked, Elizabeth stumbled home blinded by tears. She would not even speak to Johann but flung herself on her bed and wept out her grief, her despair and most of all, her frustration.

A few days later Johann came running in from she knew not where. Overcome by her sorrow, she had paid him little mind lately, and the child had taken to wandering about the town on his own.

"Mama, Mama, a man from the countryside is selling eggs in the market. Fresh eggs! And chickens, too!"

"Really?" She shook herself out of her lethargy. "Then you must run back quickly and buy as many eggs as you can for a penny. I'm sure the chickens are more than we can afford at today's prices." She reached into her jar and handed the child a penny. "Run quickly before they are gone." Her precious supply of pennies was dwindling rapidly. With this one gone there were only three left. If things did not get better soon, she would have to dig into her coffer and start using her silver thalers—Lübeckerthalers, the standard currency of all the Hanseatic towns. Thank God, they did not steal that when I lay ill, she thought. But for Greta's forethought in hiding her keys, she was sure they would have. Their life's savings. She and Uwe had vowed never to touch it except for Johann's education, and perhaps a horse. A horse would have been nice—for going out into the country when the weather was nice or keeping one's feet out of the snow when it wasn't. Uwe had had a dream about one day buying a country home such as many of the rich merchants owned. Not so luxurious, of course, but a little cottage with some land and some chickens and geese and perhaps a cow. Quite a few had been coming on the market recently with so many freemen deserting the land for the towns and the nobles finding they simply could not push their serfs any further. I wonder what that situation is now. She had not thought of their dream for a long time.

The child seemed to be inordinately long in returning. She had begun to worry that he had been set upon by ruffians again when he

348

pushed open the door, a woebegone look on his face.

"Were they all gone?" she asked.

"No, I bought two." He placed them carefully on the table.

"What! Only two eggs for a whole penny?" she exclaimed.

"No, Mama, two eggs for two pennies. I borrowed a penny from Master Willi."

"You did what? I can't believe this!"

Johann started to cry. "Don't be angry with me, Mama, I thought I was doing right. One egg is hard to share."

She took him in her arms. "No, kleinchen, I am not angry with you. Only with that thief in the market who is charging a whole penny for one egg. Not long ago, before—before—ach, we could buy a whole dozen for a penny." She sighed. "And now I am beholden to Master Willi again."

"He said not to worry. Pay him back when you can. He says he trusts you because you are a fine lady."

Elizabeth smiled at that. "Nonetheless, I shall go immediately and repay him. It is my fault. I should have gone with you. I could have haggled with the man. He took advantage of you."

"No, Mama," objected Johann. "Everybody paid the same price. I watched for a while before I put my penny down."

"So be it. Then let us put these golden eggs in the basket before they roll on the floor and we shall enjoy a fine dinner with them as soon as I return."

"But, Mistress, I told the lad there was no hurry to repay," objected Willi when she handed him the penny. "I know you to be an honorable lady."

Elizabeth smiled at the misnomer. Lady, indeed. "Honorable I may be, but I'm rapidly becoming as poor as the meanest serf in the land. Hah, while they become rich selling eggs worth their weight in gold."

"Ja," agreed Willi, "and getting it, too. And five pennies for a quarter o' them scrawny chickens he had."

"Holy Mother, that's highway robbery!"

"That it is."

"It can't be legal. Can't the Town Council do anything?"

"Not a thing, Mistress, as long as folks are willing to pay the price, including the Council. Why, they had their maids down to market in a trice as soon as the word got around. Exceptin' for those lucky few as still have their backyard biddies, ain't a soul in this town as seen a fresh egg these many months."

"I know. I'm one of them. They stole my hens when my husband died and I lay ill."

"It happens. Whyn't you sit a spell, Mistress, and have a cup of cider?" offered Willi, changing the subject. "How's the shoe business?"

"The shoe business isn't," sighed Elizabeth. "And no, thank you, Master Willi, I'd best be going."

"Suit yersel', Mistress, but when you've got more time, I'll tell you what I'd do were I in your shoes." Big Willi suddenly blushed, realizing his gaff. "Pardon my little joke, Mistress."

Elizabeth smiled. "No offense, Master Willi. And maybe I'll have that cider after all. Time is what I have plenty of. I'm interested in hearing what you'd do in my shoes—although I doubt they'd fit you."

Willi laughed uproariously. "That's the gal—I mean my lady—I mean Mistress. Keep your sense of humor and things'll never be as bad as they seem. Here, sit over here close by so I can talk low and keep my eye on the customers. Wouldn't want those fools stealing my ideas."

Elizabeth sat on the bench he indicated and waited until he had set the cup of cider in front of her. "Now tell me, Master Willi."

"Well, you know that churl as selling the eggs? Well, he ain't no farmer, nor villein nor even a serf. I know for a fact he's nothing but a ne'er-do-well wanderer as lives by his wits—or his sticky fingers, more like. Comes in here once in a blue moon when he's got a penny or two and blows it all getting drunk—and then shoots his mouth off, the fool. He'll be in later, mark my word."

"But what has that to do with me?" queried Elizabeth.

"Wait. I'm telling you. Where do you think he got those eggs and fowl?"

"I have no idea."

"Not by the sweat of his back, I'll tell you. Except'n mayhap the effort of lugging them into town. Him as ain't done a stick o' work in his life. Must ha' been quite an effort. Hah!"

Elizabeth was still puzzled. She sipped her cider as Willi went on.

"So where did he get 'em? I'll tell you. He found 'em. Running free as the air. Didn't even have to steal them."

"How can that be?" asked Elizabeth. "I thought the farmers were all being so tight-fisted with what little they have left."

"Them as still are living, that's for sure," replied Willi. "But, Mistress,

350

I hear tell that there are hundreds of small-holdings, ja, even big farms, going begging since the Pest. Whole families died off. None are left to care for what stock might be left. None are left to even claim ownership. And you know, many of the noble families got hit just as hard as their peasants. Them as are left don't half know what they got and ain't got."

It gradually began to dawn on Elizabeth where all this was leading to. "Do you mean not just chickens and eggs, but whole holdings are there for the taking?"

"Ach, you're a quick one, Mistress. That's exactly what I'm saying. Anyone with guts—pardon Mistress—with courage and a little know-how can find himself a nice holding—and plenty of food."

"But wouldn't that be illegal?"

"The dead can't make no claims, and there's as many dead out there as here in town, I hear tell. How many deserted houses did you pass coming here today?"

"Too many."

"Just so. And I hear even the milords on the great demesnes are starving for want of serfs to work the land. They'd be happy as a sow in pig for just any tiddly bit of rent once a farm was in shape again."

"I take your meaning," said Elizabeth thoughtfully.

"Think on it. 'Tis always said 'town air is free air'. Hah, no more. Those few outside as got food to spare are holding us prisoners with their high prices. It's time a few smart townsfolk turned the tables on them. I'd go myself, but I've got a good business here and I'm getting a mite too old to change. But you're young yet and, I take it, nothing to hold you."

"No, nothing to hold me. And I do thank you for your advice and information, Master Willi. I shall, indeed, think on it. It is certainly better than Master Mestwart's suggestion. Ach," she suddenly blushed. "If he ever saw me here, he'd throw me out of the Guild."

Willi laughed. "Never fear, he'll never know it from me. He doesn't speak to the likes of me. And what, may I ask, did Master Mestwart suggest?"

"That I marry another shoemaker."

"There's that."

She shook her head. "You know, Master Willi, you have suddenly made me realize something I couldn't see for myself. Town air isn't free air anymore. And I value my freedom. You're right. There's nothing to hold me."

During the next few weeks Elizabeth made her plans. She took five silver thalers out of the coffer and carefully sewed them into a belt and that onto her sturdiest shift. The rest of her savings she took to the Town Council for safe-keeping.

"Mistress," said the Town Clerk as he started to write the receipt, "you are very wise. It is not good for a woman alone to keep so much money in the house."

"Exactly," she agreed. "Things have changed so much these last months, it is frightening."

"Quite so. Do you simply wish to leave it with us for safekeeping or would you like us to invest it for you?"

"Invest? You mean at interest with the Jews? Isn't that usury? I thought the Church forbade that."

"It does. That is not exactly what I meant. You see, many of our great merchants who deal, for example, with the Merchant Adventurers of England in the wool trade will allow people with small, but substantial, sums such as yours to buy shares in their ventures and thus, when the deal is completed, you share in the profits. The Church frowns on it, but since it is not truly interest, there is nothing they can do. In fact," the clerk warmed to his subject, "the Lombard bankers in the larger towns such as Hamburg and Antwerp automatically invest any monies left with them, so that often the depositors don't even know the source of their profits and call it interest. The Church has tried to stop it, but those Lombards are so powerful they tell the Church to mind its own business. If truth were known, many kings and the Pope himself borrow from them at high rates of interest."

"That is very interesting. But what of the risk? Suppose the deal falls through or the ship sinks or the wool is of poor quality?"

"There is a certain risk, of course," replied the clerk, "but the merchants of Uelzen are about the shrewdest in the whole League. Why else would the great Merchant Adventurers of England choose Uelzen for their headquarters in Germany?"

"Why, indeed," agreed Elizabeth, "but I am not an adventurer of that caliber. For now, I shall just leave it in your safekeeping."

"As you wish, Mistress," replied the clerk as he handed her the receipt.

"However, do I have the privilege of changing my mind in the future?"

"At any time," said the clerk, "as long as there is some venture to invest in, you may do so. If I may suggest, it is the ideal way for a woman alone to make money."

"I shall think on it, and thank you for the information."

Well, thought Elizabeth as she walked home, another bit of advice far superior to Master Mestwart's. I'll bet he has invested plenty of money in these ventures, but would he suggest such a thing to me, a mere woman? No, of course not. Marry another shoemaker. Hah! Master Mestwart, I'll show you yet. The idea of the investments had great appeal, but not now. A nebulous profit months down the road would not put food on the table now. No, she would go on with her plans.

Next she made a new pair of sturdy shoes for her and Johann, two pairs of good winter boots, and two pairs of soft house slippers. I might as well use up the leather that is to hand. As an afterthought she made herself a fancy pair of pointy dress shoes from the beautiful blue leather intended for the late Mistress Schmied. Though, Lord knows when I shall ever wear them. But it made her feel good. Then she made two strong knapsacks from large pieces of uncut leather, a large one for herself and a small one for Johann.

While she was working at this, she had Johann pick all the apples he could reach and the rest of the turnips. Then came the decision as to what to take and what to leave behind. Only one change of the warmest clothes. One cooking pot and two spoons. Cups? Perhaps, if there's room. Their eating knives they always wore attached to their belts. The blanket or the featherbed? The featherbed was warmer and lighter to carry but also bulkier. In the end she took both, making cushions of them under the knapsacks. The bucket? No, many wells had buckets attached. If not, she could use the pot for water. A pot of honey the looters had missed was carefully stowed.

She wrapped her precious bit of salt in a piece of leather. Her flint in another. Tinder? Perhaps I'd better take a little. This time of year it might be hard to find dry tinder. She wrapped it with the flint. Candles? They're so expensive, I hate to leave them. Yes, they'll fit. Her scissors already hung on key ring. She tucked needles and thread into the flap of her knapsack, she checked her husband's workshop and stuck a few of the smaller, more useful tools into her belt. She decided to take another large piece of leather for a ground cloth in case they had to sleep out.

During all these preparations Johann asked endless questions. She cautioned him, "You must not tell anyone that we are leaving. Not your friends. Not the neighbors. No one at all. Promise?"

"I promise, Mama. But where are we going?"

"I'm not sure yet."

"Will you know before we go?"

"I doubt it."

"Will you know when we get there?"

"I expect so."

"When are we leaving?"

"Soon."

"Why are we taking so many things with us?"

"Because no one in the country has anything either."

"Then why are we going?"

"To find food."

"Oh."

Also to find a new home, God willing. But she couldn't tell her son that.

She stood staring at the contents of her large coffer. If I could only take some of my beautiful linens. She pulled out one towel, slammed the lid shut and locked it carefully. Fool, she thought, if you find a place and can claim it as your own, you have enough money to hire a carter to carry furniture and all. Meanwhile, the fewer people who saw them go, the better.

When all was in readiness, she went to say goodbye to Willi. She felt she owed him thanks for planting the idea in her head and she was sure she could trust him.

"So you're really going." said the burly tavernkeeper.

"Ja, Master Willi, you gave me the idea and the courage. I thank you."

"Nay," he protested.

"But I want to ask you one more small favor. Do you know someone very trustworthy who could keep an eye on my house from time to time?"

"But ja, no one more trustworthy than myself. I shall stroll by there early every morning before I open up here. Send word when you are settled somewhere."

"I shall indeed, Master Willi, and thanks again for everything."

"Good luck, Mistress, and God bless."

She went from there to the church—the great church of St. Mary the Virgin—whose building had been interrupted by the plague. She knelt to pray for guidance and strength. Maybe a little luck, too, dear Lord. But her eyes kept straying to the famous golden ship—the church's greatest treasure—given a hundred years ago by the merchants of Uelzen. A perfect model of a Hanse cog wrought in pure gold—given in thanksgiving to

God and His Blessed Mother for the ships that had made them so wealthy. Someday, dear Lord, thought Elizabeth, someday.

The morning they were set to leave, they woke up before dawn to find it snowing. The town was blanketed with it and very quiet. She almost lost her courage and thought about putting their departure off a day or two, but then she thought better of it. Fewer people to see us leave. She had planned on being at the gates when they opened shortly after dawn. There was always a press of people on both sides waiting for the gates to open and she hoped to slip through the crowd unnoticed by anyone she knew.

After breaking their fast with an apple and some water, they put on their new boots and their warmest cloaks. She strapped on Johann's little pack, made sure the fire was out and slipped into her own. The weight of the pack made her painfully aware that she was still somewhat weak from her illness and their meagre diet. But the excitement of their adventure gave her strength and hope. She carefully locked the door behind them and they set off hand in hand through the snow toward the Veersser Gate. There were two other choices she could have made. The road from the Lüneburgertor led north to that town across the desolate heath where there was little chance of finding any dwellings at all, and Lüneburg itself was a much larger town than Uelzen and certain to have double the problems. The Gudestor faced east across the Ilmenau and she had heard that the Plague had been heading east from the south and west and this she wanted to avoid at all costs. Although the Veersser Gate faced south, she knew that the road divided a few miles out of town at the tiny hamlet of Veerssen. She had never been beyond that point, although she had heard that the better farms lay to the west. She would make that decision if and when they got that far.

The crowd at the gate was much thinner than she had counted on, undoubtedly because of the bad weather. But for the same reason the guards were checking them through very quickly, in fact, seemed only to be checking the few inbound farmers' carts and pedlars. Holding Johann's hand tightly, she slipped through and in a few moments she was outside the walls. Before her lay a pristine white wilderness. It was snowing so hard she could barely see the road but for the carters' tracks, which were rapidly filling in. The snow was stinging her face and eyes. She put her head down and trudged forward.

Normally she knew that in good weather the walk to Veerssen could be accomplished in less than two hours. But the snow made walking difficult, and their heavy burdens slowed them down. Moreover, she had to accommodate her stride to little Johann's short steps as he valiantly plowed through the heavy, wet snow. At the end of what she judged to be two hours she still had seen no sign of a group of dwellings that could be the tiny village. She was quite sure she hadn't missed the fork in the road, but she had no idea where she was. She knew they were still on the road because occasional horsemen or carts passed them. No one had offered a ride and she was afraid to ask this close to town. So they plodded on. She was also becoming aware that the little boy was tiring.

"Are you getting tired, kleinchen?"

"Just a little, Mama," he answered bravely, "but don't worry. I'm strong."

"We should be coming to Veerssen soon. We'll rest awhile there," she assured him with more confidence than she felt. In fact, she was beginning to curse her stubborn pride, her foolishness in starting out on a day like this. What difference would another day or two have made? Less food, she told herself. More people looking for places in the country.

Suddenly she became aware that the snow was letting up. The sky was a bit brighter. She raised her head and looked forward and found that she could actually see a short distance down the road. At the limit of her vision were ghostly shadows that seemed to have the shape of houses. Please, God, let it be Veerssen. There was a church there, she knew. We'll seek shelter there for a while.

Gradually the visibility became better and she could see that there were, indeed, a few dwellings off to the left. As they drew closer, she could see that there was also a road going off to the left. Ah, the fork in the road. This must be Veerssen. When they finally reached the intersection, the snow had almost stopped and she could see the sign with the usual tiny shrine beneath it. Soltau to the right, Celle straight ahead. Celle, where the Dukes of Braunschweig-Lüneburg had their favorite residence. Celle, famous for being a planned town. She was not quite sure what a planned town was, but everyone was in awe of its great beauty. She wondered how far it was. Too far, she decided, because she did know that there was another wide and desolate expanse of heath between here and there. And yet most of the carters' tracks seemed to go that way. It's a good thing it stopped snowing or I might have followed them right past the fork.

She turned to the right. Soltau. I wonder how far that is. No matter. I hope we don't have to go that far. The half-dozen or so houses of Veerssen were strung along the Soltau road. She walked slowly into the village. Although most of the houses were shuttered against the snow and cold, none of them appeared to be deserted or neglected. She could smell the smoke coming from the chimneys and longed for a warm place to sit down. There were sheds or stalls behind most of the houses but she didn't see or hear any signs of animals, not even chickens. Is it just because of the snow, or have they taken them all? She wandered slowly studying both sides of the street. In a few places little paths led between the houses but she didn't follow any of them because they didn't seem to lead anywhere except to someone's garden or field. She had almost come to the end of the settled area when she finally spied the church off on a side path almost wide enough to be classified as a street. It was small, but solidly built and looked very old. She almost dragged Johann the last few yards in her eagerness to find shelter.

"Here we shall rest awhile, kleinchen, and then decide what to do."

"Ja, Mama, I'm tired now."

"So am I."

To her dismay, the great oaken doors were locked. Of course, dummi, she thought. They would only be opened on Sundays. There must be a small side door. She was looking about when a woman came out of a nearby house.

"You looking for the Vicar? He's away today. Probably be late getting back with this snow."

"Not really," Elizabeth called back. "We've walked from Uelzen this morning and are just seeking shelter for a little while before we go on. Is there an open door somewhere?"

The woman peered across the white expanse at them. "Why, you're a woman!" she exclaimed. "And you walked all the way from Uelzen in this snow? With a little one besides? Are you crazy?"

"I don't think so," replied Elizabeth, "just tired and cold."

The woman continued to assess the situation. "Where's your man?"

"Dead."

"You got no other man with you?"

"No, just us."

"Crazy, crazy." She continued to scrutinize them and finally seemed to come to a decision. "Wait," she said and ducked back into her house.

"Mama, I've got to do pee-pee bad," wailed Johann.

"Then do it. Here, hide behind my skirts."

"But in the churchyard?"

"Never mind. Just do it. You can't have wet hose in this weather."

The little yellow puddle steamed in the cold air. She carefully kicked

357

snow over it. I have to go myself, she thought, but didn't want the woman to catch her. It's too obvious when you're a female.

At last the woman reappeared wrapped in a shawl and boots, bearing a large wooden shovel. She started to clear a path from her door to the church. "Was going to wait till closer to when the vicar comes," she muttered half to herself. "But I guess it looks as though it's stopped snowing for a while."

"While you're doing that, is there a latrine or privy somewhere I could use?" asked Elizabeth.

"Ja, but you'll have to wait. It ain't shoveled out yet."

"I don't mind," replied Elizabeth.

"Ach, but the vicar does. He don't want no trampling the snow down. Turns to ice, you know."

"Oh, yes, of course." She didn't know what else to say. What kind of fussbudget can this priest be? Oh, well. They wouldn't stay around long enough to find out.

At last the woman reached the place where they were standing on the church porch. She then headed around the far side of the church, muttering the whole way. Finally they reached a small door just before the apse. She produced a large iron key from the sleeve of her gown.

"Can't be too careful these days," she said by way of explanation. "Vicar says keep the church locked when he ain't about. There's knaves wandering about the countryside'd steal anything ain't nailed down."

"Even from a church?" exclaimed Elizabeth.

"Ja, even from the church. It's that bad. But seein's how you're alone with the babe."

"I'm not—"

"Sshh, Johann."

For the first time the woman smiled a little. "Hah, think you're a man grown lugging that big pack, do you?" She patted his head. "Where you heading Meine Frau?"

"Uh, towards Soltau," said Elizabeth quickly. "We—uh—have cousins that way."

"Long ways. And you going to lug that basket of apples all that way?" she asked Johann.

"Why, yes," said Elizabeth. "They have less than we do."

Before she could stop him, Johann piped up, "They're for our supper and breakfast."

"And midday meal, too, I suspect," commented the woman.

Elizabeth blushed at being caught in a lie. "Would you like one?" she offered the woman.

"Nay, nay, I got better in my root cellar yonder. And I suspect those cousins of yours do, too, if they live on the land." She turned to unlock the door, saving Elizabeth having to tell another lie. "There you go." She pushed open the door. "Ain't very warm in here, but at least you're out of the wind and wet for a spell. I see you got blankets. That'll help. Here, let me take that." She took the basket of apples from Johann and set it down. "Poor little mite." His hand was stiff and red from the cold. She began to chafe it between hers.

Elizabeth set her pot of turnips beside the apples and shrugged out of her knapsack. She felt a hundred pounds lighter, but when she tried to straighten up, she grimaced with the pain. Struggling doggedly through the snow, she hadn't realized how tired she was. She removed the small pack from the child's back, spread the leather sheet on the stone floor and then the featherbed.

"Lie down and rest a bit, kleinchen," she bade Johann.

"Well, I'll leave you now," said the woman. "Vicar won't be back afore dark. Comes dark early these days, you know. But he's most always back for Vespers. You'd best be gone by then, or there'll be the Devil to pay with my hide."

"I shall, indeed," Elizabeth assured her, "and I thank you for your kindness. But before you go," the woman turned, "the latrine."

"Ach, ja. Then I'd best keep shoveling the path now's the snow's stopped."

When Elizabeth returned, Johann was curled up in a little ball, fast asleep. She covered him with the blanket and sat down on the edge of the featherbed so as not to disturb him. She wrapped her cloak tightly around her, fully intending to wake him in about one hour, eat a raw turnip, and be on their way. But where she was going from here she had no idea. She hadn't the faintest notion where to look for these supposedly deserted farms. She wished she could talk to someone locally, someone she could trust, someone who knew the lay of the land. As she began to thaw out, her brain began functioning properly again and she realized the solution to that dilemma was right to hand. The very fastidious Vicar, who better? He must be secure enough in his benefice, she reasoned, to have no ax to grind. She had heard there was even a shortage of priests, so many having died giving comfort and last rites to the stricken. Ja, she would wait right here for him, regardless of what she had promised the old woman. She

359

would try to persuade him not to punish her.

Sitting on the stone floor did nothing to rest her back. So, her decision made, she stretched out beside her son on the featherbed, pulled part of the blanket over her and promptly fell asleep.

A cold draft awakened Elizabeth and she sat bolt upright. It was fully dark. The door was open, and she could hear the old woman saying, "I expect they're gone by now, Father, but I just wanted you to know why the door was unlocked. I felt so sorry for the poor little one, but the foolish woman should have known better than to be wandering about in this weather. Still, I expect they were desperate."

"Ach, ja, like so many these days," said a man's voice. "What's this?" Elizabeth caught her breath as she heard him trip over the pot of turnips.

She quickly stood up and straightened her gown and cloak. "Ja, Father, we're still here and I beg your forgiveness, but I should like to talk to you. Perhaps you can help us."

"I have no money and very little food to spare," said the voice in the darkness. "Gertrud, fetch a light." The woman scurried off.

"I need neither money nor food, Father," replied Elizabeth, "just your advice and guidance—when you have time."

"That I can give you and gladly." She could hear the relief in his voice that she was not asking for handouts. "But you will have to wait until after Vespers. It is already late. The snow delayed my return."

Gertrud returned with a torch, which she set in a sconce in the wall. The priest was revealed as a much younger man than Elizabeth had expected. Not more than a few years older than she, and very handsome.

She curtseyed deeply. "I am Elizabeth Wiese, lately of Uelzen, widow of Master Shoemaker Uwe Wiese, and this is my son, Johann."

"And I am Father Borchard Bergmann, Vicar of this parish, St. Margarethe's in Veerssen." He bowed perfunctorily to Elizabeth and glanced beyond her to Johann who, now fully awake, was standing listening to the conversation. He bowed very properly when he was introduced. "And how old are you, my son?"

"Almost six, Father," replied Johann.

"And do you know your Paternoster, Credo and Ave, Johann?" asked the priest.

"Of course, I do," replied the boy, "and the Decalogue, too, and my ABCs, and I can count, and I can write my name."

"Amazing in one so young," commented the Vicar. "He has been

360

well taught, Mistress Wiese."

"Thank you, Father," replied Elizabeth, trying to sound humble, "I have tried my best."

"Well, you must excuse me now. It grows late."

"May we stay to hear the office, Father?" asked Elizabeth.

"By all means, stay if you wish. I doubt there will be any other parishioners in this weather."

"May I serve for you, Father?" asked Johann. "I know all the responses."

"Do you indeed? Then I can see no harm in it. Come along."

On her knees, Elizabeth could not help but swell with pride as Johann made all the responses correctly, his little voice ringing high and clear after the priest's deep bass. When they prayed, "Defend us from all perils and dangers of this night," her prayers were more fervent than theirs.

After Vespers the priest walked back to where Elizabeth was waiting. Johann skipped along beside him.

"You have a very bright young man here, Mistress Wiese. I wish I had even one like him in the parish."

"Thank you, Father," murmured Elizabeth.

"Now what is it that you wanted to ask me?"

"Well," she hesitated, not sure how frank to be with him, "we have just this day come from Uelzen."

"So you said."

"Well—we are not indigent, Father," she hastened to assure him. "We—that is, I own a house and shop. We even have a little money put by with the Council." No way was she about to mention the five silver thalers around her waist. "My husband and I had a very good business before the Plague. But now—now—" she choked up and struggled to go on. "Now all our customers are dead or too poor to need shoes. So there is no business left. And even if one had business and a good income, there is no food to be bought in the town. My baby—my son needs good food and I—I'm afraid I'm still a little weak, although have no fear, Father, I am fully recovered from the illness," she hastened to reassure him.

"Have you tried to seek out new clients for your business?" he asked sternly.

"Of course, I have, Father," she replied indignantly. "I am not lazy. For the past months I have gone from door to door, knocking at every house where anyone was still alive. I even made several pairs of house slippers—which do not have to be made to order—and in all those months I have sold only one pair. Don't you realize, Father, that almost two-thirds of the population of Uelzen died?"

"I am aware of that. It was almost as bad out here in the country. But with so few to share it, there should be more food for each one, I should think."

"Father, the gates were locked for months, and even when the Pest had finally run its course and they reopened them, the country people were afraid to come in for a long time. Now a few are coming but the prices are so high and the quality so poor that only the richest can afford them. Why, just a few weeks ago a man was selling one egg for a penny, whereas we used to get a whole dozen for that."

That seemed to shock him a little. "I truly hadn't realized it was that bad. Food is also very scarce here in the country. Many of the harvests lie rotting on the ground for lack of workers to garner it. Many animals have died of starvation and even of the Plague. But there is food for those still alive and who have been careful. Is that why you came all this way in the worst weather of the year, to buy food?"

"Well, not exactly, Father," she replied. "What point is it to buy as much as we could carry back into town only to have to return in a month or so when things are scarcer and the prices will undoubtedly be higher? That," she pointed to the pot of turnips and basket of apples, "is what we have been living on these past months. It is all we have left. But do you think we would have carried it all the way out here if we were going to return?"

"I shouldn't think so. Then what do you have in mind?" he asked, puzzled. This spunky woman was beginning to interest him.

"Father, may I ask your advice in strictest confidence?"

"Certainly, my daughter."

"I am told that the man with the eggs for sale simply stole them — or, as it was put to me, simply found them where the dead could not object. I do not intend to steal eggs. Father, if I am going to be damned, it will be for something bigger than eggs. I am seeking a new home where we can raise our own food. I have heard that there are many such small holdings, deserted, neglected, the owners all dead and no heirs to be found. I know the reverse is true in town. I have seen it with my own eyes. Servants today own their masters' homes, villeins, freedmen, even escaped serfs coming in from the country and just moving into empty houses without so much as a by-your-leave. Is that also true here? Could we find such a place?"

He hesitated momentarily. "Yes, I'm afraid it is. And yes, I imagine you could. You are not the first and probably won't be the last. But a woman alone?"

"I am not entirely alone. I have my son. Already he is a great help. With good food he will grow fast."

"But you are a town woman. What do you know of farming?"

"I had a large well-tended garden—until they stripped it while I lay ill. A healthy flock of chickens, too. That knowledge is enough to start until I can learn more. And believe me, I'm not afraid of hard work."

"I'm sure you're not. But a woman alone—it could be dangerous in these times."

"I'm willing to chance that. It is as bad, if not worse, in town. No neighbors alive to call on, the watch totally dysfunctional, bands of ruffians looking to steal whatever food you might have. It can't be that bad here."

"Perhaps you're right. At least off of the main roads." He pondered a moment. "I admire your courage, Mistress Wiese. Let me think on this a bit and see what I can find out for you. You may stay here tonight and we shall discuss it further in the morning. I bid you good night and God bless."

"Thank you, Father," said Elizabeth.

As he turned to leave, he almost tripped over the pot of turnips again. "This is truly all you have to eat? You've had nothing hot in this cold weather?"

"Yes, Father. No, Father," she replied.

"There's a pot simmering on the hook. It's more than I need for my supper. I'll send some over. You understand I can't invite you. I have no housekeeper."

"I understand, Father, and thank you very much."

He left them then. Damn these new celibacy rules, he thought as he crossed the snowy churchyard to his house. It's never bothered me before, but this woman intrigues me. She has courage, spirit. He thought wistfully of all the priests still married with families from before the new rules, some even afterward in defiance of them. Don't get carried away, he warned himself. He knew exactly what he was going to do to help her. But he wanted to test her sincerity a bit more. Let's see what the morning brings.

About a half hour later Gertrud came stomping in bearing a steaming bowl and a small bread basket filled with chunks of bread and a little cheese. "I suppose you sweet-talked him into giving up part of his supper," she grumbled.

"No, Frau Gertrud, honestly I didn't," objected Elizabeth vehemently. "He volunteered it and I'm very grateful."

"Ach, such a soft heart he has. But I'll tell you, if it wasn't for the little tyke, I'd not have agreed to carry it over. Volunteered indeed. He might be a priest, but he knows a pretty face when he sees one, just like any other man." She handed Elizabeth the bowl and two spoons and set the basket on the floor. "I'll be back for them things in a bit."

In the bowl was some sort of thick gruel, probably oatmeal, but it was so well laced with cabbage Elizabeth couldn't be sure. An odd mixture, but the best part was that it had been cooked in real meat stock, making it a wonderfully rich and wholesome dish. They settled down to the best meal they'd had since Master Mestwart's donation of food months ago.

"Eat slowly, because your stomach's not used to so much food," warned Elizabeth.

"I know, Mama, but it's so good."

"I know."

They ate in silence then, savoring every mouthful. At the end they mopped up the bowl with small pieces of bread.

"Let us save the rest of the bread and cheese to break our fast in the morning and have an apple for dessert," she suggested. She carefully hid the remainder of the bread and cheese in her knapsack for fear Gertrud would take it away again and they shared an apple.

After a while the old woman came back and wordlessly collected the bowl, spoons and basket. She then took the torch out of the sconce. "Can't leave that burning all night," she mumbled.

"Oh, just one question, Frau Gertrud," Elizabeth called after the departing figure. "Where is the well? I didn't see one when I went to the privy."

The old woman threw her a disgusted look. "It's in the Vicar's private garden, and you can't go in there. You'll just have to drink melted snow." And she departed in a huff.

Of course, she didn't explain how I was to melt snow without a fire, thought Elizabeth, half-laughing to herself at the ludicrous situation. How much more cheerful one feels with a full belly.

Since they had had such a long sleep that afternoon, neither she nor Johann was tired enough to lie down as yet. She sat with her arm around the child, mesmerized by the tiny flame of the candle over the tabernacle on the altar, the only glimmer of light in the church. The wind had died down and it was very still—and cold.

364

"Why does that old woman act so mean to us?" asked Johann.

"I expect it is just her way," replied his mother.

"But the Father is so nice, why can't she be?"

"I imagine she is just being protective of him. She is afraid we might take advantage of his kindness."

"What does that mean, 'take advantage'?"

"It means, well, acting in such a way that he will feel sorry for us and feel he has to help us, even if he doesn't want to."

"But that's what you want, isn't it?"

Elizabeth smiled in the darkness. Children can be so astute. "Of course it is, but I'm not really trying to make him feel sorry for us. I just told him the truth. And besides, I think he really wants to help us. He likes you, you know."

"I tried to remember all the responses up there at the altar. I was a little nervous, but I didn't make any mistakes, did I?"

"No, you did very well. I was very proud of you."

"But I didn't have proper vestments on. Do you suppose he minded?"

"He didn't seem to mind at all. Come now let's say our prayers and get under the blanket. It's getting very cold in here."

Elizabeth woke before dawn and at first was so disoriented she couldn't remember where she was. All she knew was that she was stiff and numb with the cold although she was still fully dressed. Then she saw the tabernacle light and came to with a start. She woke Johann.

"Hurry, kleinchen, we must run to the privy and pick up our things. He'll be coming to say Mass soon, and we can't have him find us still abed in the middle of the church."

Together they ran to the privy and did not linger any longer than necessary. The sky was clear but it had turned very cold. The last quarter of the moon made the snow sparkle.

"Wash your face and hands in the snow," she instructed.

"Ooh, Mama, it's so cold."

"I know, but it will wake you up."

Back inside the church, she carefully folded up their bedding and stacked it with their knapsacks against the side wall. She hid the pot of turnips and basket of apples behind them. It would never do if the priest tripped over them again. Then they knelt to say their prayers and sat back to wait.

"Can we have some of that bread and cheese now?" asked Johann.

"Not till after Mass."

"Oh, I forgot. When will that be?"

"Soon, I should think." The late winter dawn was beginning to crack.

"Do you think he will let me serve the Mass?"

"Perhaps, but I doubt it. He probably has a regular acolyte."

Not long after, their question was answered. A boy of about nine or ten slipped through the side door and was startled to see them.

"Oh, I didn't think anyone was here yet. Is Father here already?" he asked.

"No, he hasn't arrived yet," replied Elizabeth.

"Thank God. I thought I was late," said the boy, obviously relieved. "Who are you?"

"I am Mistress Wiese and this is my son, Johann. What is your name?"

"Arnulf, the shepherd's son. You're not from around here. Where are you from?" he asked.

"We came yesterday from Uelzen. We're just visiting," explained Elizabeth.

"Oo-ee, that's a long way off. I've never been there. I could tell right off you were a proper lady." He touched his forelock. "You must be visiting Milord."

Elizabeth had to smile at this assumption. "No, just the Vicar." She wondered who the lord of this land was. Would she have trouble with him?

Johann piped up. "I served for the Vicar at Vespers last night."

"Did you now?" replied Arnulf, cooling visibly. "It was supposed to be that lazy Rudolf's turn, but I guess he didn't show up. He says he's so busy now his ma and pa's dead, but he's really just lazy. He won't like it, though, when he hears. Well, I'd best get vested and light the candles. Vicar'll be here any minute." He disappeared in the direction of the sacristy.

"Now why was he upset that I served last night?" asked Johann, perturbed.

"Country people often don't like newcomers," explained his mother. "They're afraid someone will take their place. We'll have to be very careful of that wherever we settle."

Johann plainly didn't understand, but any further conversation was cut short by the arrival of the Vicar.

"Good morning, Mistress, Johann. Did you fare well through the night?"

366

"Very well, Father, and I thank you again for letting us stay."

The priest set another basket of bread and cheese near their belongings. "Something to break your fast after Mass."

"Ach, Father, that wasn't necessary," protested Elizabeth.

He waved her protests away. "We'll talk after Mass. I have an idea for you." He hurried off to the sacristy.

Arnulf was lighting the candles. A few other people started drifting in. Some ignored them totally and went about their prayers. Others said good morning and eyed them up and down with obvious curiosity but asked no questions. Gertrud came bustling in and said not a word but joined some of the other peasant women. Elizabeth knew the news of their arrival would soon spread like wildfire. She wondered if that was good or bad.

After Mass the peasant women filed out after Gertrud. A few of them nodded to her and Elizabeth smiled as sweetly as she could. Their curiosity was palpable.

When they were once again alone, the Vicar said, "After you have broken your fast, we'll talk. Meet me outside in about a half an hour. I may have the solution to your problem. It is safe to leave your things here."

They quickly ate their bread and cheese and took a little snow to wash it down. In less than the half hour they were outside waiting. The priest appeared shortly. He locked the church door with the big iron key and hung it on his belt.

Elizabeth looked at him questioningly. "You are going away?" she asked.

"We are going for a walk. I wish to show you something," he replied. He set off briskly through the churchyard and into the street she now knew was Kirchestrasse. The snow crunched under their boots. It was still too cold to have melted, but the sun made the surface slippery. Even Elizabeth found the walking difficult. Little Johann had to struggle to keep up. Suddenly Father Borchard noticed. "I am sorry. I'm so used to rushing from place to place in my duties, I forget that some people have shorter legs than I. Would you like a ride?"

Before the child could answer, he hoisted him up on his shoulders and continued down the street, Elizabeth beside him. What a wonderful father he would have made, she thought. It's too bad.

Soon Kirchestrasse was joined at an angle by another street. "This is Bauerstrasse, the Farmers' Road. It leads to the fields which the people living in the village own or lease. A few people actually live or lived out there as well, but most of them prefer to live in the village. This whole area, the village of Veerssen itself, the farms, and especially the great forests you see all about, is part of the demesne of the Baron von Estorff. The family was once very powerful and wealthy, but even before the Plague there were several years of bad harvests, even famine, as you may know, partly due to unusually bad weather all over Europe. But here it was also due to bad management. The late baron left everything in the hands of incompetent stewards while he was off fighting in tournaments and other countries' wars. Unfortunately, his lady was also a weakling. She could not manage the estate as well as so many other women in similar circumstances can and was no match for the lazy but wily steward. When her lord died, it was given out that he had succumbed to the Plague which was then sweeping France, where he was at the time. But it's well believed hereabouts that he was killed in a tournament or perhaps in the endless wars between the French and the English, because she had to sell off several parcels of land to pay his ransom."

Elizabeth, fairly well educated though she was for a woman of her time, was not even aware that there were wars going on in France and couldn't have cared less. She was aware that the English merchants had been steadily shipping wool into Uelzen and the other Hanse towns, so it obviously hadn't affected trade very much. It was the Plague that had dried that right up. She wondered where all this was leading.

The priest continued, "Be that as it may, the poor woman was at the mercy of this stupid, but not so stupid, steward. Revenues fell off partly because he was lining his own pockets and partly because the peasants refused to work for him because he was charging them extra tithes, far above what they were supposed to be paying. They reasoned the less they produced, the less they would have to pay. Of course, they were hurting themselves as well, but in their anger at the steward they couldn't see that. He meanwhile tried to convince the lady that the land was poor in the hope that she would turn some of it over to him for a pittance. But the peasants got wind of this — it is amazing, this peasant grapevine. News travels faster over it than the fastest post rider."

"I'm sure," agreed Elizabeth. "This is all very interesting. How little we knew, shut behind our walls, of what was going on almost outside of them. Yet we had news of the wool market in England, the cloth market in Bruges, the spice market in Venice — anything that affected trade, trade, trade. But what has this fascinating local history to do with me?"

"You will see very shortly, Mistress." They were well beyond the village now, tramping along a cart path between open fields, dark forests in the far distance. He went on, "Anyway, the peasants sent a delegation to the lady of the manor. They almost came to blows with the steward over this, but somehow he lost his bravado and was afraid to gainsay them. And for once in her life the lady did something sensible. And the peasants, too, for once were smarter than their wont. They forbore saying anything about the steward's extortion and cruelty. They only told her that they heard she was considering selling him the land for a pittance and wouldn't it be fairer to let them who worked it all these years have first choice for the same pittance. You see, these were not serfs, but free tenants. The lady thought that was definitely the fairer thing to do. She did not care who bought the land. She just wanted to be rid of it because the steward had convinced her it was worthless. Most of the villagers had scrupulously saved their market money over the years and were able to buy the land. The steward was furious but there was nothing he could do. And the land was not worthless but excellent bottomland. The new freeholders worked hard and their first harvest was bountiful. It would have been again this year but for the Plague."

"Ach, ja, everything would have been bountiful but for the Plague," sighed Elizabeth. "And I suppose you are telling me that this wonderful, worthless, not so worthless land is now ownerless."

"That is exactly what I am telling you," he replied. "The Plague carried off almost a third of the villagers, fewer on the land, but lots nonetheless. It took the wicked steward and all his family but one son, and unfortunately, it also took the lady and her elder son and daughter. The present Baron von Estorff is a three-year-old babe in the hands of servants, none of whom I trust but one."

"How very sad." she murmured.

"Fortunately, all those freeholdings were legally recorded. I saw to that at the time. I now have all the deeds of the deceased in my safe-keeping."

"There are no heirs?" she asked. Now she was getting excited.

"None that I could find. You must understand most of these people have never been more than a few miles from the place where they were born. These families have lived on this land for hundreds of years."

"But what about escheat?" she asked. "If there are no heirs, won't the land automatically revert to the Baron?"

"Those servants that are left up there are so busy enjoying the mas-

369

ter's wine and their mistress' clothing and jewels that they couldn't care less what's happened here. I doubt they even know. I fear for the poor child. No legal guardian can be found as yet. Although eventually I suppose the Duke will take him as a ward. But in the meantime, as I said, I have all the deeds."

Elizabeth looked at him sidewise. Something wasn't quite right here, but then everything seemed topsy-turvy these days. "I see," she said, but then cast her doubts aside. "Show me," she said eagerly.

They continued walking until a narrow path appeared on the right. The priest turned up this. The hedgerows on either side were so close one could touch them both at the same time. The snow was pristine. Obviously, no one had been this way for some time. They continued some distance along this path until she could see a small but apparently well-built cottage in the distance. She wondered if that was where he was leading her. She began to take more interest in the fields on either side. The snow was not deep enough to cover the bent stalks of wheat, their heads touching the ground, rotting. How sad, she thought, what a waste. She could not see the quality of the soil but the wheat looked as though it had once been healthy enough.

When they reached the house he turned into an even smaller path leading to the front door. The remnants of dead frozen flowers stood on both sides. The house itself was solidly built, half-timbered brick. It looked as though it had recently been rethatched.

The Vicar stopped then, set Johann down and asked, "If you would like it, this could be the new home you are seeking."

"Oh, Father!" she exclaimed. "It looks charming. May I go inside?"

"By all means. No one has lived here for a long time—no human, that is."

She looked at him questioningly.

He laughed. "No, it is not haunted. There is a sow in pig which I've sort of adopted. And a few stray cats. Don't let them frighten you. They've gone a little wild, living off the land."

Cautiously she pushed open the door. It seemed stout enough. The inside consisted of a large kitchen with an ample fireplace. Behind the fireplace was a tiny bedroom with two sleeping cupboards, both double-width. A ladder led to a roomy loft. A rough-hewn table and benches stood in front of the fireplace, and in a corner stood a stool and spinning wheel. There were small cupboards on either side of the chimney piece.

"Just as they left it," she remarked.

"Just about," he replied. "I have tried to protect it as best I could. I know the local people helped themselves to a few things, but it is not visible from the road, so strangers didn't know it even existed. I guess I was waiting for someone like you—" he suddenly became flustered, and she smiled at his discomfort, "er, that is, they were good people and I know they would have wanted to leave it to someone who would appreciate it," he finished lamely.

"I certainly should. It would suit me perfectly," she said in as businesslike a manner as possible. Then she jumped as something soft rubbed against her skirt. She bent down and petted a sleek black cat, who immediately began purring.

"See, he is welcoming you. He's never been that friendly towards me."

"Mama, does a witch live here?" asked Johann.

"No, of course not. Why should you think that?"

"Well, the black cat—don't they belong to witches?"

"Not always. That is a silly old wives' tale. He is just lonely for his family who have all died," she reassured him. "I shall call him Raven, after Wotan's ravens, you know."

The priest looked at her askance.

"No offense, Father," she apologized. "Just the old stories."

He decided to overlook that but was more curious than ever about this strange woman. He still didn't think he was wrong in bringing her here.

"Let me show you the other member of the family," he said.

The wall of the room opposite the fireplace was only a half-wall with a gate leading to the animal stalls. The half-wall served the very practical purpose of allowing the heat from the animals' bodies to warm the house in winter. There were six stalls, three to a side, and they had obviously once been full. Above were neat rows of nests for long-gone chickens. Now all the stalls were empty but the farthest one. The moment the priest opened the gate the lonely sow set up such a squealing to wake the dead. He picked up a pail of mashed turnips and took them to her.

"I wasn't able to come to feed her yesterday. Usually the farmers let them forage in the woods for roots and acorns, but I wouldn't dare do that now. She'd disappear in a twinkling. They had a cow, too, and some chickens, but they either wandered off or were stolen."

Elizabeth peered past him at the huge pink sow, now munching contentedly. She seemed to be in good health and was obviously pregnant.

371

"When will she bear? In the spring?" she asked.

"As near as I can guess."

"What happened to her boar?"

"I let the villagers take him in return for leaving this one for me. Christmas is almost upon us, you know."

"I am painfully aware of that, Father."

"Don't worry. They shared generously with me. If you decide to stay here, I'll see that you have a piece of ham for your Christmas dinner."

"Oh, Father, you are too kind. I wasn't hinting."

"I know, but I should like to do it for you and Johann. That is, if you decide to stay."

"I think I have already decided," she replied, "but I have a lot of questions."

"Ask away."

"Is there a well?"

"Yes, and a very good one, I believe. Come." He led them back into the kitchen and out the back door. What must have been a sizeable kitchen garden was neatly fenced in. At its center stood the well. Elizabeth dipped the bucket in, drew it up and tasted. The water was sweet and cold. She noticed a neat privy at the far end of the garden, piles of steaming manure beyond the fence. There were two small sheds attached to the house on either side of the kitchen door. One was stacked more than half-full of cordwood. The other, empty now, must have been used as a root cellar. It looks better all the time, she thought.

"Tell me about the land," she said.

"It is quite large," he said. "It extends all the way to the woods you see over there and back to the lane in the other direction. The other boundary is that long hedge over there. Perhaps you can't see it with the snow, but it is a good piece of land. And besides this, they owned three fields on the other side of this little road opposite the house. There is no longer a house on it. There was once, but it burned down many years ago and that wicked steward I mentioned refused to rebuild it, so the poor people — they were serfs — simply ran away. When the Lady von Estorff sold off the land, these people bought both that piece and this one. You may have it as well, if you wish."

"Father Borchard, you are too good!" exclaimed Elizabeth, astounded. "I should love to have it as well. But are you sure there will be no problem — legally, I mean?"

"No problem at all," he reassured her. "You are the distant cousin and heir of the Lüdemanns that I have been searching for these many

372

months." He winked at her.

Her mouth fell open. "I take your meaning. I shall have Masses said for their souls."

"That would be most commendable."

"And is there nothing I can do for you in return?" she asked.

"Perhaps there is," he replied. "Two things, in fact. Save me a suckling pig for my Easter dinner."

"Promised," she agreed. "And the other?"

"Let me teach your son."

She hesitated. "I had thought to send him to the Hanse school in Uelzen, but now . . . Is there a school in a village this small?"

"I tried to start one and it was going fairly well, considering. But now since the Plague . . . " He threw up his hands.

"Very well, I owe you that—for this. For a few years at least. But I insist he learn more than theology and rhetoric."

"He shall, I promise," said the priest.

They walked back into the house. Johann was sitting on the floor playing with a fluffy gray tabby. "Mama, wait till you see what I found," he chirped.

"Did the cat change color?" teased Elizabeth. "Maybe it *is* a witch."

"Oh, Mama, you're joking," said Johann. "Katie chased the black one off."

" 'Katie' is it?"

"Ja, I call her Katie for 'little cat'. Come see what she has." He led them into the tiny bedchamber. There, almost buried in the corner of one of the cupboards, the cat had made a nest and in it were five almost newborn kittens, their eyes not even open yet. Katie quickly jumped up to protect them from these intruders, and the kittens started nursing hungrily.

"Well, it seems life goes on, despite plague and snow and—and sorrow." Elizabeth started to choke up. The priest instinctively put an arm around her. "Does that mean there's still hope for the world, Father?" She looked up at him through tear-filled eyes.

His heart filled with pity for her, but then, as if he suddenly realized what was happening, he quickly took his arm away. "Yes, I am sure there is still hope for the world," he reassured her. "In fact, I don't believe that God sent this scourge on us at all. But don't let my Bishop hear me say that."

"That is what the priests in Uelzen are telling everybody. They sit safely behind their cloister wall with food on the table telling everyone to do more penances. How can God require more penances when everyone has already lost almost everything?"

"I agree with you. Sure, we are all sinners, but no worse than men have been for thousands of years. A bit complacent, perhaps, but not deserving of this. I don't know where this terrible pestilence came from, but I am certain it was not from God."

"Some are starting to say that the Jews poisoned the wells."

"Bah," he said vehemently. "That is ridiculous. Some people just have to look for a scapegoat to blame their troubles on. If that were true, how come as many Jews as Christians died? But I am afraid many Jews will be made to suffer doubly for it anyway. No, I am more inclined to agree with some scholars who claim that it was caused by the noxious vapors rising from the filth in the swamps. But we'll probably never know. Anyway, enough of that. So have you definitely decided to become the Lüdemanns' heiress and one of my parishioners as well?"

"Yes, Father, I have. I'm sure we'll be very happy here. What think you, Johann?" she asked.

"Oh, yes, I like it here," replied her son. "May we keep the kittens?"

"Perhaps. We'll see. The first thing we must do is clean it thoroughly and burn the bedding just in case there are any traces of the sickness still about. May we go back to the church now, Father, and fetch our things? I'm anxious to get started."

As they were leaving the church laden with their belongings they met Arnulf.

"You going away again?" he asked.

"No," replied Johann, "we're going to be living here with you. Father gave us a house."

"Father gave—?"

"The Lüdemanns were distant cousins of mine," interjected Elizabeth quickly, surprised at how easily the lie came to her lips. "We only now learned that they had died. We shall be living in their house."

"Oh, I see," said Arnulf rather dubiously.

"Will you be my friend?" asked Johann hopefully.

"I suppose," replied the other boy. "Will you be serving on the altar again?"

"I don't know. I hope Father will let me."

"Oh, my. Rudolf won't like that."

Johann ignored that. "Father's going to teach me, too."

"Teach you, too?" Arnulf sighed. "He was starting to teach me my let-

374

ters, but now since the plague everyone left is too busy. I wish he'd start the school again. I liked it. But Rudolf didn't. He tried to keep the rest of us from going."

"Why does it matter so much what Rudolf thinks?" asked Elizabeth.

"Well, he's the biggest boy in the village and the steward's son." Something seemed slowly to dawn on Arnulf. "But he's not the steward's son anymore, is he? I guess he's not as important as he used to be, but he still wants us to think so."

"Then I wouldn't worry what he thinks," said Elizabeth. "I hope you and Johann can be friends."

"Ja, well—I would help you carry those things, but my father's waiting for me."

"That's quite all right, Arnulf, we'll manage. Thanks for the offer anyway. But before you go, tell me, is there anyone in the village who could sell us a little food until we can grow our own?"

"Ja-a-a," he replied hesitantly. "There are those as has more than enough put by, but I doubt they'll sell to strangers. Maybe when they get to know you better. But my pa," he added quickly, "he might sell you a little mutton."

"Wonderful!" she exclaimed. "Which is your house?" The boy pointed it out. "Tell him I'll stop by to see him in a day or two. Thank you, Arnulf."

Very slowly Elizabeth and Johann made themselves known to the villagers and the few peasants left on the surrounding farms and very gradually were accepted by them. The plague had carried off at least a quarter of the inhabitants, but far fewer than in Uelzen. Elizabeth was able to buy ample food for their needs, plenty of vegetables and fruit, even an occasional piece of meat or some sausages. Only flour was difficult to come by, partly owing to the lack of wheat harvest and also because the local miller had been one of the victims and no one had as yet been found to replace him. But she did manage to get a little flour, and the first loaf of bread she baked seemed like manna from heaven.

Rabbits and the ubiquitous black grouse were everywhere feeding on the fallen wheat.

"If I only had a bow and arrow, I could catch one for you," said Johann.

"Well, you don't, nor traps either," replied his mother. "Let them be."

"There's lots of deer in the woods, too."

375

"Forget them, too. You know very well hunting is forbidden there. The woods belong to the manor. All we're permitted to do there is gather firewood."

"But the boys said the gamekeeper is gone—dead or run away, nobody knows."

"You heard what I said," she replied sternly.

"Yes, Mama."

Johann had made friends with Arnulf and his friend Karl. She was grateful for that but also afraid the older boys were too daring and Johann too young.

Christmas came and went and it was a sad time for her. She missed her loving husband and their former happy Christmases. She was afraid to cut a tree in the forest although she knew most of her neighbors did not hesitate to do so. So she made do with a few greens to decorate the mantel and doorway. They attended Midnight Mass, and as she came to realize that everyone present had suffered the same or worse losses than she, her grief lessened somewhat. They were all very supportive of one another and by now welcomed her into their midst. All the boys served so there was no cause for any jealousy.

They met the infamous Rudolf, who continued to make disparaging remarks behind their backs, which she ignored. In fact she felt sorry for the lad. He had lost his entire family and before that had had no example but his obnoxious father. He still tried to throw his weight around, but even the children no longer paid much attention to him. He still lived in the steward's cottage, but the family had not owned it, so that when and if ever the Baron's guardian appointed a new steward, Rudolf would be homeless.

The Vicar made good his promise of a Christmas ham. And so replete after their first real feast in too many months, warm and cozy in their little cottage, Elizabeth felt for the first time that she could face the new year with hope.

The winter remained cold and blustery with lots of snow. Food supplies began to get scarce, but she and everyone else carefully husbanded what little they had to make it last. The desperate wolves came closer and closer to the village and she forbade Johann to go far from the house, but he was growing fast and it was hard to keep him in.

One day he came home triumphantly bearing a rabbit. "Look what I have for you, Mama."

"Wherever did you get that?" she asked, taking the creature from him. It was still warm, so she knew he had not found a dead carcass somewhere.

He drew a leather sling out of his sleeve. "Arni made me a sling and taught me how to use it. I've been practicing ever so long. Aren't you proud of me?"

"What a great hunter you are!" She embraced him. "I certainly am proud. Now we can have some meat again once in a while—and a nice, warm rabbit skin besides." Suddenly she thought. "You didn't kill it in the woods, did you?"

"No, Mama, right here in our own field. I tried to catch a grouse, too, but they're still too quick for me. I need to practice more."

"A rabbit will do just fine," she assured him.

Some weeks later she thought she heard voices out front when Johann came running in, blood streaming down his face from a cut over his eye.

"Holy Mother, what happened?" she screamed.

"Mama, the boys are throwing rocks at me," he sobbed. "I don't know why."

She flew to the door and saw Rudolf, Arnulf and Karl standing in the little lane shouting imprecations. The eldest boy had a handful of stones. The other two were just standing there looking reluctant.

"She's a witch, I tell you," yelled Rudolf. "Go back to hell where you came from. It was her as brought us the plague that took my pa. It was her as killed old Jake so's she could steal his house. And so's her witch's spawn could pollute the altar in the church." He was working himself up into a frenzy.

"I am no witch and I did no such thing and you know it," she called back. "Get yourselves off to home now where you belong and leave us alone." As luck would have it, Raven chose that moment to rub around her skirts.

"Look there!" screeched Rudolf. "I told you she was a witch. There's her familiar." He lobbed another stone, which struck the doorjamb and ricocheted hitting her in the shoulder. She winced with pain and ducking back into the house, slammed the door. The cat fled.

"Whatever brought this on?" she asked.

"I don't know, Mama. I didn't do anything to them."

"I'm sure you didn't. Go wash the blood off your face and I'll tend to that cut in a minute, but first I've got to get them away from here. That Rudolf is crazy." She went into the stalls and grabbed the pitchfork and

377

was just going back out the front door when she heard a man's voice.

"What's going on here? Why are you kids out here when you should be working?"

There was complete silence. Arnulf's father, the Shepherd, had his son and Rudolf by the scruff of their necks. Karl was edging away as quickly as he could.

Finally Arnulf stammered, "Rudi said she was a witch and that we had to scare her away or the plague would come back."

The Shepherd flung his son to the ground. "You know better than that," he said angrily. "I don't know where the plague came from any more'n you, but it was here and gone long afore this good woman came. She ain't no witch either. I'm ashamed of you, Arni. Now you get yourself and Karl home and don't you dare and leave the house till I get back. I'll take care of your punishment when I get there." Arnulf picked himself up off the ground, and he and Karl slunk off. The Shepherd still held Rudolf. "As for you, you turd." He slapped the boy's face hard back and forth.

"You can't do that to me," gasped the boy. "I'm the steward's son."

"No more you ain't. And I'll do it any time I catch you making trouble for decent folks." He slapped the boy again and threw him to the ground. "If I had my cane, I'd beat you to within an inch of your life right now. No more'n you deserve."

"But I'm—" the boy started to protest.

"You ain't nothing but an orphan that's only still got a roof over your head by the good graces of the village. Keep on with your foolishness and we'll see quick enough what the Manor thinks of you still living in the steward's house. Now get up."

Rudolf sat there in the mud rubbing his burning cheeks.

"I said get up."

The lad slowly got up and then started to run, but the man grabbed him. "Oh, no, you don't. You're going to apologize to this woman first." He led him by the arm to where Elizabeth was standing, pitchfork still in hand. "Say you're sorry you hurt her and the lad."

"No! See she's got the devil's fork in her hand. She's a witch, I tell you."

The Shepherd slapped him again. "She's no more witch than I am." He raised his hand again. "You want more o' that?"

"No," stammered the boy, trying hard to keep from crying.

"Then apologize."

"I'm sorry I hurt Johann. I just wanted to scare him."

"Apologize for calling her a witch."

That was harder. "I—I didn't mean—to call you a witch."

"Good. And what's more, come spring, you owe her a full day's labor, if she'll have you."

"No, I won't work for her," he said, defiant once more.

The Shepherd shook him. "You will if I have to stand over you with a cane the whole day." He gave the boy a shove. "Now off with you, and don't you come near here again without her leave."

The boy fled down the lane.

"Thank you, Master Shepherd," said Elizabeth, visibly shaken by the incident. "Won't you come in? I'm afraid I have to sit down for a minute."

"No Master, just Shepherd," he said as he followed her inside. "'Tis lucky I came by just then. He's a bad 'un, that."

"And yet I feel sorry for him," said Elizabeth as she sat down. "Come here, Johann. Let me see your head." With the blood washed away, she could see the cut was minor and would soon heal.

"Mama, I was scared," said Johann. "I thought Arni and Karl were my friends. Why were they so mean, too?"

"I expect they were just following the leader. I think they will still be your friends."

"You're right," agreed the Shepherd. "That Rudi, being the oldest, is always trying to lead them into mischief and threatening to hurt them if they don't go along. I'll soon disabuse them of that, Mistress, never fear."

"Thank you, Shepherd," said Elizabeth. "Uh—don't you have a name?"

"They call me Alf."

"Ah, Alf. That's better. Like I said, I still feel sorry for the boy."

"That's the trouble—everybody feels sorry for him and him taking it as his due. He don't appreciate one bit what the people been doing for him. Still thinks he's Dom Lord-awmighty, second only to none but the babe up to the Manor, and maybe not even to him. O' course, he's got his pa to thank for putting that idea in his head. Lad's not too bright either. Why, my Arni's two years younger and knows more'n him."

"I wish I could help him," said Elizabeth, "but after today I'm a little afraid. I really wouldn't know how to go about it."

"Work is what he needs. Something to keep him so busy he ain't got time to think up mischief. But he's too lazy to go seeking it until they

379

throw him out of yon cottage. And that'll be a long time comin', I fear, the way things are going up to the Manor."

"Perhaps the Vicar can help," she suggested.

"I was thinking the same, Mistress. I'll talk to him. And you talk to him, too."

"I'll do that," she agreed.

He got up. "And now, you must be wondering why I happened along just then, lucky as it turned out to be." She nodded. She *had* wondered. "Well," he went on, "I heard your sow is in pig. About to throw 'em in a month or so, right?"

"I think so."

"Well, Mistress. Alf be more'n just the shepherd hereabouts. I be the one as cares for the stock when they're ailing or giving birth or acting up or whatever. Thought I'd just come by and take a look at her, see how she's doing, being I had a little spare time."

"Why, thank you, Alf. I'd appreciate that. I didn't know you were a midwife, too."

He laughed. "Name me what you will, Mistress. They all call old Alf when the time's come for the birthin'." He checked the sow. "Looks fine to me. Should have a healthy litter, 'bout a month, five weeks, I'd say. Now you send the lad for me when she starts, even if I be up in the far meadow."

"I shall, Alf, and thank you. I don't know too much about pigs. How many do they usually have?"

"Usual about eight. She could have ten from the looks of her."

"Oh, my goodness."

"Them's barterin' money you got there, Mistress," he said and took his leave.

Elizabeth thought about what he had said for a long while. How different was life in the country. She had only thought of the prospective piglets as future food. Now she realized they represented wealth as well. She would keep some, of course. But ten? She would trade some for seeds, maybe for some chickens as well. Maybe she could even take one or two to market in Uelzen. Wouldn't Master Mestwart be shocked if he saw her selling pigs on market day! She laughed at the thought.

At last some guardians were found for the Baron—an elderly great-aunt and -uncle who were happy to move into the Manor to care for the child but who were totally ineffective in controlling the servants. Their presence did serve to keep the estate from reverting to the Duke, but not much else. In any event, they had too many problems right there in Estorff to worry about Veerssen and the other villages that belonged to the Manor. Rudolf continued to live in the steward's house. Elizabeth had told the Vicar about the stoning incident and he in turn had spoken to the boy on several occasions, trying to make him realize that he should find work before all the available jobs were filled by strangers coming from other manors. And there were many of them. They moved into the empty houses and were more than willing to work for the rent. Elizabeth realized how lucky she was to have left Uelzen on that snowy day, even though she thought she was foolish at the time. She even heard that the next estate down the main road to Celle—a small castle called Holdenstedt—had been taken over in its entirety by a wealthy family from Uelzen. And I worried about the legalities of this little place, she thought.

She knew she would have to hire one or two people to help with the farm until Johann was older, but she hesitated to hire any of these new people. She kept thinking about Rudolf and how she would like to help him. But the lad remained adamant. She couldn't decide whether he was just plain stubborn or too lazy or too stupid. Probably a little of each.

One day she thought she could smell spring in the air. It was still cold and the snow lay heavy on the ground, but there was that indefinable something that told her winter would soon be over. She got thinking about her house in the town and all her good furniture. Now that she was sure she was going to stay here, would it be the time to move it, before spring came and she was frantically busy with the farm? She began to inquire around as to where she might hire a horse and cart.

"The only cart in the village is the steward's," Alf told her. "Actually, it belongs to the Manor, but they always left it here, so's anyone could use it. For the estate's work there was no charge, but anyone else had to pay—just a penny or two, though. It's still there as far as I know. But what happened to the horse, I don't know. Like as not, run off, or mayhap that fool ate him."

"Oh, dear," replied Elizabeth, "that means I would have to deal with Rudolf. Besides, what good is the cart without a horse?"

"He could pull it himself," suggested Alf.

"I doubt it. I'm talking about moving heavy furniture I left behind."

"Oh. In that case, perhaps you'd best buy a horse. Hear they're pretty cheap these days."

"Do you know of any for sale?"

"No, but I'll ask around."

A few days later she heard someone hallooing from the lane. She poked her head out the door. It was Rudolf.

"What do you want?" she asked.

"I don't mean you no harm, Mistress. Alf has told me not to come here except by your leave. I'm asking your leave."

"Yes, you have it. What is it?"

"I hear tell you be looking to hire the cart."

"I might. But it's no good to me without a horse."

"I can get a horse."

"You can? Where?"

"Up to the Manor."

"The Manor! You won't be stealing it?"

"No, Mistress. 'Tis the horse what belong here. I took him up there myself when there weren't no more feed here. I love that horse, Mistress." The boy sounded as though he were going to cry. "I just couldn't see him starving."

Elizabeth was touched. This was the opportunity she had been looking for, the way to the boy's heart. "Very well," she said. "Fetch the horse and have him harnessed and ready to leave at daybreak tomorrow. I'll pay you a penny for the day's hire. Is that fair?"

Rudolf's eyes lit up. "Ja, Mistress, that be fair."

"And Rudolf, I'd like to hire you for the day, too. We'll need help in loading some heavy furniture into the cart. It's another penny just for you."

"A whole penny just for me? Ja, Mistress, I'll be here."

Rudolf was waiting in the lane before dawn even broke. Elizabeth and Johann climbed onto the cart. The horse was old but seemed strong enough, although he was probably out of shape.

"We're going into Uelzen town," Elizabeth told him. "Do you know the way?"

"I know the road, but I ain't never been into the town. You'll have to show me."

"I shall."

"The horse—his name be Ross, after old Wotan's eight-legged horse—never could figure out how a horse can walk with eight legs. Seems as though they'd get all tangled up."

Elizabeth smiled. "I expect you're right, but that was a magic horse. Maybe they're different."

"I s'pose." And Rudolf went on talking about horses almost all the way into Uelzen.

When they arrived at the town gate and were waiting to be admitted,

Rudolf couldn't help but exclaim in awe, "Ain't never seen so many people in a bunch afore. Do they all fit?"

"All them and many more."

After they entered the town he was agog again over the cobbled streets and the tall houses jam-packed together. "Don't they fall down? Mother Maria, how can people breathe?"

Elizabeth smiled.

When they pulled up at her house, she readied her keys. It was the first time she had worn them since they left. There was no need for them in the country. The house felt cold and damp, but everything appeared to be exactly as she had left it. Willi has done a good job, she thought, I shall have to thank him before we leave. There was little packing to be done. Clothes and linen were already in their coffers. Pots and pans and dishes she simply stacked in the cart, wrapped up in bedding. The empty knapsacks which she had brought she filled with utensils and Uwe's tools—not that she intended to make shoes anymore except for themselves, but tools were expensive and they had other uses. She took her loom. That she intended to use again someday, if she could trade pigs for sheep.

While they were going back and forth to the cart, one of her neighbors popped her head out the door. "Ach, Mistress Wiese," she said. "I see you're back. We didn't know what happened to you."

"I'm back only to fetch my things. Then I'm leaving again."

"What are you going to do with the house?" inquired the woman.

"I don't know yet. Nothing right now, but eventually I'll probably sell it."

"Ach, it's too bad we didn't know where you were. There was a man here just two weeks ago looking to rent it. Doesn't pay to leave it empty. There were others just wanting to take it, but we ran them off."

"I appreciate that," replied Elizabeth. "Do you know if that man is still in town?"

"I have no idea. But if any others are interested, tell me where they can find you."

"I'm living in Veerssen. It's not far. Anyone there can direct them to my house. It's just outside the village."

"I'll remember that. Do you have food there? It's still so bad here. It was the worst winter I can remember."

"We don't have much, but at least we're not starving. I intend to start growing my own. Maybe come summer I'll see you in the market."

"Hah! Good luck to you, Mistress."

When Elizabeth and Rudolf had finished loading the cart, she carefully locked the house again. Now that people knew she was really gone, there was no sense tempting vagrants. But the neighbor had given her an idea. Why leave it empty until she was ready to sell it? And there was no sense thinking about that now with all the empty houses. She would get nothing for it. But renting might be a good idea.

"I have to see Willi before we leave and tell him where we are living. Now you boys mind the cart and I'll be back in a few minutes," she told them. Maybe he even could find a tenant for me. She made her way through silent streets, almost as empty as they were during the plague. It was as if the somnolent town could not shake off the lethargy left behind from the terrible blow the epidemic had dealt it.

She thanked Willi for watching the house and he was happy to hear that she had found a place. He also had heard there were families looking to rent. He would keep his ears open. He pressed more cider on her, but she insisted on carrying it back to the boys rather than drinking it there. She was happy when they passed through the gate once more and out into the country. The town had depressed her.

The old horse plodded slowly under the heavy load. It would take them quite a bit longer to get home. Rudolf, who had said very little while they were loading the furnishings, was now apparently at ease again.

"Mistress, why would you want to go and leave a big fancy house like that for a little farmer's cottage?" he asked.

"Because there was no food in the town and no work," she replied.

He thought about that for a moment. "You like to work, don't you?"

"Yes, if it's satisfying work."

"I don't know that I quite understand what you mean by 'satisfying' work," he said. "Work is work. Nobody wants to work if a body don't have to."

"You like driving the cart and caring for the horse, don't you?"

"Ach, ja, I love old Ross."

"That is satisfying work because you like doing it," she explained. "So is planting a garden so you can have food in your belly or raising sheep or pigs or chickens so you can sell the wool or meat or eggs and buy things you want; so is cleaning or repairing your house so you can be more comfortable. All that is satisfying work."

She let him think about it a bit. Then she asked, "Would you like to work for me, Rudolf?"

"I don't know. Maybe," he replied. "My pa didn't look at it like that."

"I'm sure he didn't."

"Vicar says I should look for work. I don't know what to do." He was silent for a while as the horse plodded on. "My friends call me Rudi."

"Am I your friend, Rudi?" she asked.

"I s'pose. What kind of work would I have to do?"

"Help me plow the land and plant and later, if we're lucky, harvest."

"That's the kind of work my pa said only the serfs do."

She was going to retort angrily but then thought better of it. She took a different tack. "Would you like to raise horses, Rudi?"

He looked at her eagerly. "Ach, ja, Mistress, that is what I'd love to do. I know a lot about horses."

"But there's no market for horses right now. And no feed either, for that matter," she warned.

His face fell. "I expect you're right."

"But I'll tell you what, Rudi. You work hard for me for one year. You won't be a serf. I'll pay you in real money plus your bed and board. And you save every bit of it, and if we have a good harvest, I'll save mine, too, and at the end of the year maybe we can buy a couple of horses between us. And the market should be better by then, too. You see, sometimes you have to do work you don't particularly like in order to save for something you really want."

"You mean that, Mistress?"

"Every word." She mentally crossed her fingers that she could keep her promise.

"I'll think on it," was all he would say, but she felt she had won him over.

It was almost dark by the time they arrived at the cottage. "Let us hurry and get these things unloaded while we can still see," she urged. "Do you have to take the horse back tonight, Rudi?"

"I ain't taking him back. He belongs here," replied Rudi. "Besides, they'll never miss him."

"I thought you had no feed for him."

"Spring's comin'. Snow's meltin'. I'll find enough forage for him till the grass gets green," said Rudi defiantly, as if he dared her to challenge that.

Two days later Rudi was back with the horse. Ross was heavily laden with two side baskets and other things piled on his back. Elizabeth stared. "What's this?"

"I been thinking about what you said, Mistress. Talked to the Vicar, too. He says you're a good woman, be fair with a body. I've come to work for you," he said and quickly added, "just for one year, mind, till I can buy me a horse."

"Why that's wonderful, Rudi. I'm so glad you decided," she exclaimed delighted.

"You don't have to pay me the first day. I owe you that," he said, a bit shamefaced.

So he remembered, she thought. Well, she wasn't going to let him off. "Agreed," she said. "And now, what's all this on Ross' back?"

"I brung what food was left in the house. No sense leaving it for somebody else. And a few thing o' my ma's I sort of wanted to keep, if you don't mind."

"I don't mind at all. There's plenty of room in the loft for them and you, too."

"Thank 'ee, Mistress. Vicar says I'll like earning my own money. I hope so, as long as I can buy a horse one day with it. Besides, I felt creepy all by myself in that old house after my ma and brother died."

Elizabeth noticed he did not include his pa. "I'm sure you did," she sympathized. "I hope you'll be happier here with us. Now what about the horse?"

"Well, Mistress, I was hoping—ah, that is—would you mind very much if I pastured him in one o' them fields across the way?"

Elizabeth thought a moment. She didn't want any trouble with the manor. "In that case I'll have to charge *them* rent for him."

"Oo-ee, Mistress, you're a smart one, but I doubt they'd pay it. They'll have a fit."

"Let's do this then," she said. "They can pasture him there as long as I get the free use of him whenever I need it. How does that sound?"

"Ach, Mistress, Vicar said you would be fair, can't be fairer 'n that."

Rudi was duly ensconced in the loft. She put him to work immediately collecting firewood. He could drag in much bigger logs than Johann and cut them up twice as fast. Meanwhile she went about the village and neighboring farms trying to find someone to do the plowing as soon as the ground was dry.

The lad proved to be much more knowledgeable than she had suspected, and he was not lazy at all. Evidently she had hit on the right incentive.

He reamed out the sow's stall and laid in clean straw. "Can't have ol' Suzie a-birthin' them piglets in that muck." He had insisted on naming her. "Just cause they ain't sprinkled with holy water don't mean an animal shouldn't have a name. How you goin' to tell 'em apart?"

He cleaned the weeds and dead plants out of the kitchen garden, carefully taking off what seeds he could find. With this and some of the manure he made a compost pile next to the privy. "That manure ought to ha' been spread on the fields long ere this." And he promptly did so. He even took seeds off the dead flowers by the front door. "Ma, she always liked flowers, even though Pa said they were useless."

Spring was definitely starting to break. Although it remained cold, there was that certain delicious smell in the air of the earth coming back to life, of grass greening, of bulbs pushing flowers through the frosty ground. They woke one morning to find Suzie in labor.

"You know anything about birthing pigs?" Elizabeth asked Rudi.

"Not much," he admitted, "but it can't be too different from horses, only not so far to drop and more of 'em."

She sent Johann running for Alf. By the time he arrived, the sow had already borne five. Soon there were ten. They waited. Suzie was still straining. "Afterbirth should be coming," said Alf. "If she don't throw it soon, I'll have to reach in and help her." Instead out came two more piglets. "Holy Mary!" exclaimed Alf. "You got any more in there, old gal?" Sure enough, she did. A few minutes later the thirteenth was born and shortly thereafter she threw the afterbirth. "God almighty—you got enough there to be a very rich lady, Mistress Wiese, providing they all survive." He gave the afterbirth to Rudi to bury. "But we're going to have to take one away. She ain't got enough teats and the runt'll suffer. Thirteen's unlucky anyway. Give her plenty of water now and let her rest. She'll clean 'em up. Watch 'em for a couple of days and see which one gets shoved aside by the bigger ones once they start nursing. Then I'll take that one and see if I can sell it for you."

"Alf," said Elizabeth, "would you trade it for a lamb?"

He looked at her as though she were daft. "You want to raise sheep, too? They take a lot of pasture."

"Just one or two," she said. "I'd like to have a little wool of my own."

He shook his head. "Woman, you got a lot of courage. Very well. Lambing be starting soon. As soon as I get one weaned, I'll bring it to you."

After that, things seemed to happen almost faster than she could handle them. The awful waiting was over. A glorious spring arrived with green grass and buds on the trees, flowers blooming and birds singing as if the land was making a supreme effort to erase the scars left by the plague. She was busy day and night. A man turned up to do the plowing. She had been able to purchase oat and barley seeds, but wheat was still impossible to find. So she decided to leave the wheat field alone and see if by chance the fallen heads would have seeded themselves. Arni and Karl came to help when they could, but since their parents needed them as well, she had to have another man part-time. Even the Vicar came to help a few times. Several women in the village gave her vegetable seeds for her kitchen garden, which she dug up and planted herself. She had onions and leek, peas and beans, cabbage and turnips. Laughing to herself at the irony, she planted a whole field of turnips, because Alf told her if she intended to raise pigs that was good food to fatten them.

Easter was approaching and she was thinking she would have to go into Uelzen to withdraw some of her savings to pay the workers. Laborers of all sorts were customarily paid four times a year—at Easter, on St. John's Day at midsummer, at Michaelmas and at Martinmas. She was debating whether to take one of the piglets with her to sell at market, although they were a bit small yet and would fetch a much better price when they were bigger, when word came from Willi that he had found a tenant for her house. She dropped everything and rode old Ross into town.

The prospective tenants were a young journeyman cabinetmaker and his wife, heavily pregnant. They had come from somewhere far away where there was no work in his trade, but apparently in Uelzen the carpenters' guild had been more greatly decimated by the plague than the shoemakers' guild and they were willing to accept him. They seemed like an honest and industrious young couple and were delighted with the house and especially with the workshop, which could easily be converted to his needs. He paid Elizabeth a quarter's rent in advance and she gave him the key. Now she did not have to touch her savings. She had enough to pay the workers and then some.

By Holy Week everything was planted and they could all relax a bit. She and Johann and Rudi went to church every day to observe the Passion of Our Lord. Father Borchard told them of strange doings in Uelzen. A strange sect called Flagellants was parading around the town calling the people to repentance to avoid the Plague. Elizabeth was revolted by their form of penance, which consisted of lashing their bare backs with nail-studded whips as they paraded. They refused to enter the churches but, rather, held outdoor services of penance in the squares in front of the churches. Most people ignored them but as with any appeal to the baser emotions of the mob, they stirred some people up against the Church and enticed converts to follow them to the next town. Unfortunately, instead of preventing the Plague, they seemed to have brought it with them, and with the warm weather a new outbreak hit the town. Although it was far less severe and with fewer cases than the previous year, the poor townsfolk had not yet recovered emotionally or economically from the last onslaught and went into a panic. Fortunately, the area around Veerssen was spared any new cases.

On Good Friday, Elizabeth chose one of the little pigs and took it to the Vicar.

"So you remembered," he said.

"I never forget my obligations," she replied. "I owe everything to your kindness."

"But surely you and Johann must share it with me," he insisted.

"Thank you, Father, but no, I . . . "

"It will taste so much better if you cook it," he said coaxingly.

"But what will the neighbors say?"

"I'm sure the neighbors know you well enough by now to trust that you will not lead me astray," he joked. "Besides, Johann will be there to chaperone."

She smiled and thought, But how do they know that you will not lead me astray? She was well aware that he was falling in love with her. But she enjoyed his company and some intelligent conversation would be a welcome change from the constant work on the farm. Why not do it? What harm can come of it?

"Very well," she agreed. "You gut it and clean it tomorrow and I'll be here at dawn before first Mass on Sunday to dress it and put in on the spit."

Some weeks later she had another surprise. She knew it was soon time for Alf to bring her the lamb. But when she saw him coming up the lane with the lamb over his shoulder and leading a cow, she couldn't believe her eyes.

"Wherever did she come from?" she asked.

Alf laughed. "I don't rightly know, Mistress, but ole Bossie here was one of Jake Lüdemann's cows. T'other morning there she was big as life grazing in the meadow amongst the sheep. She's yours if you want her."

Elizabeth looked at the poor beast. She was in a sorry state. "I don't really know, Alf. She doesn't look too strong or healthy."

"Nor would you, had you spent the winter in the woods without proper food or shelter. I figure when no one came to milk her, she just wandered off. Must ha' been in terrible pains for a while 'till her milk dried up, 'cause I know for a fact she was always a good milker. She might look a bit scrawny now, but she'll come back with proper food and care. She gotta ha' been strong to survive. Beats me how the wolves didn't get her. They were right fearsome the winter past."

"I know." She still hesitated, because it would be an additional expense without any return for a long, long while.

Meanwhile Rudi and Johann had joined them in time to hear the end of the conversation. Rudi was carefully inspecting the cow. "She got to be mighty brave, too," he said. "I bet she just kicked the shit out o' them old wolves. I don't see a mark on her. Mistress, we can keep her in the same pasture with ol' Ross. He won't mind. There's enough for both."

"Oh, yes, Mama," chimed in Johann. "Please, can't we keep her? We haven't had any milk in ever so long."

"And it will be longer still," said Elizabeth. "She has to have a calf first and we don't have any bull."

"If you've a mind to keep her," said Alf, "I know of a bull as can service her once she comes into heat. It's up to you, Mistress, but I'd keep her, was I you. Good cows are mighty scarce hereabouts these days. Most as was wandering free without living owners got et up by hungry folks or got took by the plague themselves."

"I suppose you're right, but . . . "

"Ja, sure and he's right, Mistress," said Rudi. "I don't know of any cows left around here at all but one or two half-dead old things up to the Manor that even the old bull won't look at. She ain't as old as she looks. Just needs a little weight on her."

"You're both very persuasive."

"Please, Mama," pleaded Johann.

"Very well," she relented with a sigh, "but you boys take care of her, and if she doesn't come into heat soon we'll sell her for beef."

"She will, and soon," said Alf, nodding sagely. "Starvin' often prevents it. Good pasture will bring her around soon. And here's your little lambkin."

"Ach, that is what I was looking forward to," she said as she cuddled the wooly little creature in her arms. It started to squirm and bleat at the strange touch and smell. "Now she's going to have to share the pasture with a horse *and* a cow. Good heavens, what a menagerie I'm accumulating. And I'm just about to buy some laying hens a farmer down the road is willing to sell me. All we need to complete the picture is a dog."

Alf roared. "If that's what you're looking for, one o' my bitches is about to whelp in a couple of weeks. Nothing like a good sheepdog to help you keep them animals in line."

"Could we, Mama?" pleaded Johann.

"No!" she said vehemently. But in the end she relented, and in due time they acquired the puppy.

The first year had been the hardest, Elizabeth reflected twenty years later, partly because she had been reluctant to touch her savings to hire people. The wheat had indeed seeded itself and, although it was not of the best quality, they had ample flour for their own needs. The pigs had provided a steady income. Eventually Rudi had urged her to build a smoke house and they smoked their own hams, bacon and sausages. The cow had recovered and freshened and in due time gave them enough milk, cream and butter to take some to market along with the eggs. She and Rudi had travelled several times to the annual horse fair at faraway Verden and each time had bought some good breeding stock, so that as the economy gradually recovered, both noblemen and farmers came from all over to buy palfreys for their ladies or draft animals for farm work. The little lamb had grown into a herd and Elizabeth had wool and mutton to sell, as well as her own cloth. The dog had proven invaluable with the animals, and the cats kept the rats away.

She considered herself singularly lucky, but almost everyone round about Veerssen knew that it was her own hard work and business acumen that had made her so wealthy and they admired her for it. Naturally, however, there were the jealous few who resented her success, more especially because she was a woman.

Of course, she could not have accommodated all this on the original little farm. Gradually she had acquired or bought seven other farms in the nearby countryside, some from the Manor itself, which had fallen on hard times through mismanagement or no management at all. In some cases the tenants came with the farms and by fair treatment she assured that they would stay. She bought Alf's freedom from the Manor and set him, Arni and the sheep up on one. Rudi eventually married, built himself a little house across the way and remained her right-hand man. And on one of the farms she raised flax, which she and the women wove into exquisite linen—everything from heavy damask altar cloths to the sheerest for shifts for fine ladies.

The second year Johann had started his formal schooling with Father Borchard. The boy was a born student and loved it, which pleased Eliza-

391

beth very much. She had insisted that Rudi go with him, at least until he learned his letters and numbers. By this time the boy wanted to please her and so went willingly, although he fretted over who would do his work while he attended school. She did most of it herself. She even persuaded Arni's and Karl's parents to let them return to their studies, at least part-time. Eventually the young baron from the Manor joined them. There had been a bit of a wrangle over this. The elderly guardians had first insisted that Father Borchard come to the Manor to tutor him privately. They didn't want him to have to associate with the riffraff. But the Vicar had insisted the experience would do him good. And since priests were at a premium, so many having died in the fulfillment of their duties during the Plague, they didn't want to lose him, especially since his benefice was not too regularly paid. So they gave in. The boy and Johann became fast friends, although the heir to the estate was nowhere near the student that Johann was. He had dreams of becoming a knight, but sadly, there was no one left to teach him.

All this brought the Vicar and Elizabeth closer, until in private they were calling each other Borch and Lisa. Their love for each other grew and the inevitable happened. It blossomed into a sweet and poignant love affair. He knew it was wrong, but times being what they were, he went with the flow. He was not alone. After the horror and devastation of the Plague, people seemed to grasp at anything that would give them the feeling that life was still worth living. On Eliza-beth's part, although she knew there was no future in it, she had been without a man so long, she desperately needed the comfort of a man's arms about her, the consolation of a man's strength to lean on. They were sure the whole village, even the whole demesne, knew what was going on, but so well liked were they both that not one soul so much as hinted that he thought anything was amiss. After about five years, the initial passion spent, they voluntarily ended the sexual part of the affair, but they remained dearest friends for the rest of their lives. He absolved her, and he made his confession to a wandering Franciscan friar, an un-derstanding old-timer, one of those who had been so fearless and kind to the people during the Plague.

After a few years, Johann decided he wanted to become a priest. Although Elizabeth had wanted him to go to the Hanse school in town and she recognized Father Borchard's persuasive influence, the child did seem to have a natural bent for helping people and teaching others. So, after only token objections, she let him have his way. And one day—how quickly time passed—an excited teenager went off to the new and only German university in far-off Heidelberg. Father Borchard had insisted on paying a part of Johann's tuition, although she had long since invested the money she had left with the Council and with the interest from that, plus her farm income, she was a relatively rich woman. Johann had since returned from Heidelberg a grown man and an ordained deacon. The Bishop of Verden had insisted Johann serve his diaconate in the great Marienkirche in Uelzen and, once he was ordained priest, to serve in one of the small parishes of which there were many without priests, in order to broaden his experience. But since the Bishop and Father Borchard were close friends, the former had agreed to let Johann return to Veerssen after four or five years to assist the Vicar.

Meanwhile, once Johann reached his majority, Father Borchard had insisted that Elizabeth put all her property in her son's name. Times were still unsettled and one heard too many horror stories of widows and other single women being robbed of their property by quasi-legal means or even brute force.

And so, Elizabeth reflected as she sat before the fire embroidering a piece of fine linen, life has been good to me and she thanked God for all her blessings. She still had her health, despite her terrible illness and the fact that she was getting older. She was a wealthy property owner. She had a man she could depend on, who would probably give his life for her, if it ever came to that, she was intensely proud of her son, and now she watched with contentment her little two-year-old grandson playing with a cat before the hearth.

That was another of the many strange coincidences in her life.

One day about three years ago a bedraggled and terrified girl of about sixteen had wandered up the lane.

Elizabeth watched her for a while, as strangers were rare and the girl had a furtive look about her. At length she asked, "Are you lost?"

"No, Mistress. Ah, I mean, I don't know—," replied the girl.

Elizabeth immediately became suspicious. "What do you mean, you don't know? Where are you coming from and where are you going? This track doesn't lead anywhere except into the woods."

"I guess that's where I was heading," stammered the girl uncertainly. "I—I thought to bide there awhile. Do you think I would be safe?" She suddenly started to cry. "Oh, Mistress, I'm so frightened."

"Where are you running from? From whom are you hiding?" asked Elizabeth sharply.

"I can't tell you that, Mistress. I didn't mean to bother you. I just thought to spend the night there and go on." She started to head along the lane.

"Well, I doubt you'll be very safe in those woods. There are wolves and wild boars and hunters."

"Oh," said the girl and stopped. She looked more frightened than ever.

"Have you committed a crime?" asked Elizabeth, although she hardly expected her to admit that.

"No, Mistress, I have not," replied the girl indignantly.

"Are you a runaway serf?" Elizabeth knew the answer to that already. The girl was too well-spoken.

"No, Mistress, I am not."

Elizabeth was beginning to be intrigued. Well-bred girls simply did not wander about the countryside in disarray. "Have you eaten today?" she asked.

"Eh, not really," she replied, "but I'm not begging," she hastened to add.

"I'm aware that you are not, but perhaps you're not too proud to join me for a little bread and cheese. Perhaps things won't look so bad with a little food in your belly."

The girl hesitated. "You're very kind, Mistress." She was obviously hungry, yet she debated. "Yes, it's not right to be proud. They—I mean it's a sin, isn't it? I guess I would like a little bread and cheese, but I'll eat it out here. I'm so dirty."

"The well is right back here," said Elizabeth, leading the way, "and there's soap."

"Real soap?"

"Yes. I make it myself. We have sheep."

"How wonderful!" exclaimed the girl, showing the first bit of enthusiasm.

After she had washed, a little bloom came into her pale face. Why, with clean clothes and her hair dressed properly she could almost be pretty, thought Elizabeth. "Now you must join me at table," she insisted. "I don't make a habit of eating second breakfast out-of-doors, except during plowing or haying time, which it is neither."

"I don't want to make trouble for you."

"A few minutes won't be any trouble," said Elizabeth, deliberately misconstruing the girl's meaning. She sensed there was a story here and was determined to find out what it was, but first she had to get the girl to relax. She hoped she could help her.

The girl perched on the edge of the bench as if she were a little bird ready to fly away at any moment while Elizabeth put bread, cheese and a cup of milk on the table.

Elizabeth sat down opposite her and said, "Now we can't very well share a meal without knowing one another's names, can we? I am Mistress Wiese. What is yours?"

"I—I am called Christine," she whispered shyly.

Elizabeth felt sure she was lying but it didn't matter. "And where is your home?"

"I don't have a home."

"But you must come from somewhere."

"I used to live—uh, well,—far away. It doesn't matter. I won't go back," she sighed.

"No family?"

"Not anymore. My parents are dead."

"Surely not of the plague? No, you are too young for that."

"My mother had the plague and survived."

"So did I," said Elizabeth.

"You did? But you look so healthy. My mother never recovered her strength and when I came along it was too much for her. She died soon after I was born. I lost brothers I never knew to the plague. My father never got over it. He tried to do his best for me. He saw that I had a good education and had my mother's jewels and some money set aside for my dowry."

"I knew you were no peasant girl," commented Elizabeth.

"I sometimes wish I were. They seem so jolly. Papa never stopped mourning. Sometimes he didn't even know I was there. In the end he died, I guess, of a broken heart."

"You poor child," said Elizabeth with genuine sympathy. "But surely you still had a home and that dowry. What are you running from? Why are you so frightened?"

"Mistress Wiese, it is better if you don't know. You are so kind. I don't want to make trouble for you."

"How can you make trouble for me if you've done nothing wrong?"

"I said I didn't commit a crime, Mistress, but I have done something terribly wrong," sobbed Christine.

"Are you pregnant?"

"No, no, not that," she half-smiled through her tears. "I guess that would be worse, wouldn't it?"

"I can't know if you don't tell me what's troubling you, child."

"No, it's better you don't know."

"Would you tell a priest?" asked Elizabeth.

The girl jumped up. "No! No priest! Don't tell any priest you've ever seen me. I'd best be on my way."

"Sit down," commanded Elizabeth. "All right, no priest. But you can't keep wandering aimlessly around the countryside like this, or you will be pregnant or worse before you know it."

Christine sat down again. "Nothing's happened to me so far."

"You're just lucky. How long have you been on the way?"

"Four, five days. I don't know."

"And where do you plan on going?"

"I don't know." She raised her hands. "Just away."

Elizabeth shook her head. "Would you like to stay here for a while until you get your bearings?"

Christine looked around. "You live alone?"

"All alone. I have a son, but he's away studying at the University in Heidelberg."

"Ah, Heidelberg," Christine sighed. "I've heard of it. How I wish girls could study at a university."

"You haven't answered my question. Would you like to stay here? You can earn your keep."

"What could I do? I don't know anything about farms." She was obviously considering the offer as she looked about the room. She spied Elizabeth's embroidery frame. "I can sew and embroider."

"Then that's what you shall do. And you can learn other things, too, if you have a mind. Then it's settled? You'll stay?"

"You won't tell anyone I'm here?"

"Not if you don't want me to, but in return you must be honest with me. I want the truth, the whole truth."

"You are too kind, Mistress Wiese. I believe I can trust you."

"That you can," Elizabeth assured her, and waited.

Christine sat for a moment thinking and then began slowly, hesitantly. "After my father died, I stayed in our house alone for a while. He was not wealthy but we had been quite comfortable. I was not starving and the neighbors were kind. And I had my books." She paused for so long, Elizabeth thought she was not going to continue, but she did. "They all urged

396

me to marry, but I was not betrothed and there was no one among our friends' sons whom I wanted to marry. I did not intend to be forced into a loveless marriage like some I knew," she said indignantly.

"It happens often, but I can understand how you felt," agreed Elizabeth. "Then what happened?"

"Then, then, this uncle, the only relative I had—not a blood relative really, he was married to my mother's sister—and he was a cruel and terrible man. Oh, Mistress, I can't bear to think of it," she sobbed.

"Tell me anyway," urged Elizabeth. "'Tis best to have it out or it will be in your heart like a festering wound." She already suspected what was coming. It was an all too common occurrence.

"He came to—to my home and took all my dowry and the money Papa had left me and made me go to live with them in his castle. Oh, it was a horrid place. Cold and drafty and filthy dirty. It was far away from any place civilized, way out on the Eastern Marks—a military post really—they were always fighting to keep the Slavs from crossing the border. They lived like animals. Oh, Mistress, it was horrible." Elizabeth nodded understandingly. "Oh, the knights and men-at-arms got fed well enough, but my aunt and her daughters got nothing but the leftovers. And I was treated like an orphan. Of course, I was, but I mean he treated me like the meanest serf's by-blow. He resented me because he had three daughters and no sons and not enough to dower them with. And my poor aunt couldn't do anything. She was so down-beaten, I don't think she cared about anything anymore."

"Did he have his way with you?" asked Elizabeth. It was all too common in situations like this.

"He tried, more than once, but I fought him. I kicked and bit him till he gave up. But I was severely beaten for it every time. I finally had the courage to say to him if I was such a burden, why wouldn't he let me go back to my home? But he had already sold Papa's house, so there was nowhere for me to go. I finally ran away."

"And that is what you are running from now?"

"No, no, that was over a year ago. He sent men after me and they caught me and he locked me in the tower room on bread and water for weeks. At last he announced he was sending me to a nunnery and good riddance. I was glad because I thought at least the nuns would be kind. And they were at first. You see, I mistakenly thought I was just staying there as a lay sister until I could one day leave to marry. Like the rich old ladies who retire there. But I found out he had only given them a tiny part

397

of my dowry. So they started training me as a novice. Mistress, I didn't want to be a nun. I know they do a lot of good and there are those who are happy with that kind of life. But all the prayers and fasting and penance, that's not for me. I want to sing and dance and read romans and be happy. I want a husband and babies. Is that too much to ask?"

"So you ran away again?"

"Yes, Mistress. That is the terrible thing I've done. I know it's a sin, but . . ."

"Had you made your vows?"

"No. That was to be in two weeks, when the Bishop was to come."

"Then you have committed no sin that I can see."

"But won't they send after me?"

"I doubt it. They have your dowry for their trouble."

"But suppose they tell my uncle?"

"They probably have, but I don't imagine he would care at all." Except for the waste of the dowry, thought Elizabeth. "I'm sorry to say it, my dear Christine, but I doubt that there is anyone at all who is the least bit concerned about you. Your fears are unfounded."

"Do you really think so?" she asked timidly but hopefully.

"I am quite certain of it, provided you have told me the whole truth."

"Oh, I have, Mistress. I have."

"Was it Kloster Lüne?"

"How did you know?" exclaimed Christine, aghast.

"Just a shrewd guess, from the distance you'd come. Then you are running from nothing. They are too uppity to bother about any but the most richly endowed," said Elizabeth with a touch of sarcasm. Kloster Lüne was better known as a comfortable place of retirement for wealthy, elderly widows than for its piety.

"Do you really think so?" Christine sounded relieved. "But Papa used to give them—I mean . . ."

"Your home was in Lüneburg?"

"Yes, it was."

"Then you are safely out of the diocese. Veerssen is beneficed from the Bishop of Verden."

The girl sighed. "Oh, Mistress Wiese, you are so kind. How can I thank you?"

"You can earn your keep here until you decide what you want to do. I can use your help," said Elizabeth. "And is your name really Christine?"

"Yes, it is."

"A very pretty and pious name. And what was your father's name?"

"Werner von—just Werner, that's enough, isn't it?"

"It will do. So, to all and sundry you will be known as Christine Wernering," announced Elizabeth.

And so Christine settled in as Elizabeth's helper. And a great help she was. She cleaned and washed and baked and her embroidery was exquisite, although Elizabeth insisted that she first make herself a new gown. She fed the hens and gathered the eggs, but she didn't much like the pigs. For all her adventures, she was still very much the innocent, as only a well-brought-up girl without a mother would have been. And so Elizabeth tried to be that mother to her and teach her womanly knowledge as well. The girl was a dreamer, though, and even overcame her fear of priests when she learned that the Vicar had books she could borrow.

And that was how it came to be, that when Johann came home from the University for the summer vacation he found a kindred soul. At first their common interest was books. Then high-flown philosophical discussions. And before either one was aware of it, they fell in love.

Elizabeth tried to warn Johann. "You can't marry her, you know."

"Then I won't be a priest. I'll be a farmer," he retorted defiantly.

In her heart his mother knew he was not cut out to be a farmer, nor a businessman either. He would never be happy unless he was a priest. Oh, Holy Mother, why did she even take the girl in? She tried another tack. "And all your hard-won education? Will it go to waste? Will you throw it all away for a girl we know very little about?"

"I know all I need to know about Christine, and I know that I love her. I don't want to live without her."

"Then live with her, but don't marry her," said Elizabeth angrily, regretting the words the minute they were out of her mouth.

"Mother, how can you?" exclaimed her son, shocked.

"Please, Johann," she said in a softer tone, "don't give up everything you've striven so hard for."

"You're asking me to give up the one thing I love the most, and I won't." With that he slammed out of the house.

His cold reserve frightened her more than his defiant anger. Although she knew he was growing away from her, they had never been estranged before. Yet she couldn't really fault the girl. She knew Christine hadn't led him on. It had just happened. The most natural thing in the world between two young people of like mind. She would have been overjoyed had it not put his chosen career as a priest in jeopardy. Oh, God, what should she do? She sought solace in prayer and found none.

In the end it was Father Borchard who at least temporarily solved the problem. What passed between them Elizabeth never knew, but several days later Johann returned from visiting him and announced, "I am going to finish my last year of studies at the University before I make a decision." It was as close to an apology as he ever came. "Christine will wait right here. Mother, please don't blame her or treat her badly."

"Of course, I won't. You know better than that," replied Elizabeth. Although she had secretly been thinking of ways to get rid of the girl, she was so overjoyed at this respite, she added, "I love her, too. Under any other circumstances . . . "

"Mother, I don't wish to discuss it any further."

After harvest, Johann returned to Heidelberg and Elizabeth tried to figure out the kindest way of moving the girl as far away as possible. But fate had other plans. Christine discovered she was pregnant.

I can't put her out now, thought Elizabeth, but she was furious. For the longest time she blamed the girl and could barely bring herself to be civil to her. But she noticed that as her pregnancy advanced, Christine forgot her books and high-flown ideas and devoted herself to preparing for the baby. Whenever she had time from her duties, she was sewing baby clothes. Rudi made her a cradle. She seemed unusually—nay unnaturally—meek.

That is born of guilt, which I have forced on her, Elizabeth admitted. And gradually she reconciled herself to the fact. After all, it is my grandchild, she told herself. A dream she had never expected to be fulfilled.

The Vicar had long talks with them both, together and individually.

"You can give out that she was already with child when she arrived here," he suggested.

"That would be an abnormally long pregnancy," scoffed Elizabeth. "We figure about April."

"Not many people are aware of just when she came. Remember, you were very secretive about it for a long time."

"True, but than I shall never be able to acknowledge my grandchild," sighed Elizabeth.

"You can't have it both ways. Then you might as well let them marry, for acknowledging the child will destroy his career just as effectively. This is not Rome or Avignon. Popes and cardinals may get away with it, but never a simple parish priest, especially one just starting out," he said sternly. "And besides that, I have heard that the Inquisition is starting to work in this part of Germany."

"Oh, no, no!" cried Elizabeth. "Whatever for?"

"Apparently the Dominicans have convinced His Holiness that the Plague was a direct result of unrepentant heretics, which in their way of thinking includes everything from lepers and Jews to people of low moral standards. There have already been burnings in Magdeburg and Braunschweig. They're bound to come to Uelzen eventually, especially since the town admitted the Flagellants."

"How frightening! And after all this time. Can't the Bishop do anything?"

"Can't and won't. He's bound to obey the Pope's orders, and the Holy Office has his blessing. But the Town Council is at least trying to make it difficult for them. My Franciscan friend told me the Dominicans requested a house in the town ostensibly for a rest stop for travelling brothers, but the Franciscans, who you know are powerful and well liked here in Uelzen, opposed it, saying they were well able to take care of the spiritual welfare of the town without any interference from the Dominicans. But the Council didn't dare thwart the Inquisition entirely, so they made them build a little house outside the gates."

"That is unbelievable. I have heard no one trusts the Dominicans."

"And with good reason. Fear of the Inquisition has set brother against brother, husband against wife; even priests aren't safe from their insidious power. This is why I tell you, Lisa, you and your son must do nothing to attract their attention. Nothing whatsoever. Do you understand?"

"I understand, Borch," she replied meekly.

"My dearest, I love you both too much to let anything happen to you. I have spoken of this to Christine. She understands."

"You told her about us?"

"Not in so many words. But I explained that if you truly loved a person, you would be willing to give up everything for the welfare of that person's soul. I believe she loves Johann enough to do this. You have to give her strength, not make her feel guilty. You are a strong person, my dear. Look at all you have accomplished almost single-handedly. Use that strength to good effect, not evil. It matters not that you cannot acknowledge your grandson or granddaughter to the world. *You* will know who he or she is, and the two most important people in the child's life will know. And above all, God will know. That is all that matters."

"As always, you are right, Borch," acknowledged Elizabeth with a sigh. "I shall make amends starting right now. I know the child has suffered great guilt because of my—my coolness toward her. I was selfishly thinking only of Johann's best interest. But who is to convince him of the rightness of all this? He can be very stubborn."

"She will. Trust her."

A few days after this conversation, Christine came to Elizabeth almost as a supplicant. "Mistress Wiese, I know you must hate me . . . ," she began.

"No, no, never," objected Elizabeth.

The girl held up her hand. "I don't want you to think I am ungrateful for all you have done for me. You have been the mother I have never known, but I know I have hurt you and disappointed you with . . . with . . . " she patted her swelling belly.

"No, it's just that . . . "

Christine interrupted. "I promise you I shall never marry Johann. I love him too much to destroy his life. I shall always have this part of him." She held her belly again as if she were already embracing the child. "That is more than enough. I shall go far away and have the child, and no one will ever know."

Elizabeth was shocked. "No, no, never. Don't even think that way. This is your home now and always will be. Here you shall have the child. After all, he is my grandson, too, and I want to be around to welcome him."

"Do you really mean that?"

"With all my heart."

"And do you believe me when I say I will not marry Johann or upset his life in any way?"

"Yes, I do, my dear."

"Then do you, perhaps, forgive me, Mistress?"

"There is nothing to forgive and the fault is as much mine. Don't you think you should start calling me 'Mother'?" She held out her arms. Christine fell into them and they wept together.

On Holy Thursday Christine was delivered of a healthy boy. They named him Christian after his mother and because he was born on such a holy day. It was given out that Christine had been raped and left to die by highwaymen on the way to Veerssen, and since no one knew who the father was, the child was known as Christian Wernering. Johann didn't even know of his existence until he arrived home at the end of June.

And now Elizabeth sat before the fire watching Christian play with

402

the cat and she was content. I must be getting old that I reflect on the past so much. But the future lies with him. Johann had been ordained and assigned to a parish some distance away. He came home infrequently, as it was a poor parish that kept him very busy. But she had good reports of his work from Father Borchard, who had it from the Bishop himself. Christine kept busy teaching the baby and making her exquisite embroidery which she now sold when they took the farm produce to market. Elizabeth knew Christine was saving every penny of it for the boy's education. Elizabeth and Christine had grown as close as any natural mother and daughter. Ach, God has been so good to us, Elizabeth thought, and so forgiving, too. She didn't know it then, but it was the last time she would be happy for many years.

All worries about the Inquisition had been forgotten. True, in the first year they had heard numerous horror stories of torture and burning. In the beginning the victims had been mostly the poorer Jews. The rich ones usually were able to buy their freedom. But later, because certain powerful people were so deeply indebted to them, they were arrested as well. Most of them, however, had ample warning and packed up their valuables and fled to the east, to Poland especially, where the king protected them for the sake of his Jewish wife. But the Jews were not the only victims. Many elderly widows, and even younger women, were accused of witchcraft, suffered and died. Everyone knew these people were innocent, but no one dared to intercede for them. A miasma of fear permeated the town. The most feared and hated man in all of north Germany was the Archinquisitor, a Dominican named Walter Kerlinger. He seemed to delight in the fear and took great pleasure in inflicting pain. He personally supervised the unspeakable tortures and often lit the flames himself.

Elizabeth refused to go to market or anywhere near the town if she knew there was to be a burning, even though it cost her lost income. In fact, the Town Council would not permit them to set up the stakes in the marketplace, as so many towns did, but rather on a flat piece of land across the river where the town gallows stood. Even so, when the wind was just right, the stench of burning flesh often drifted as far as Veerssen, making everyone ill. After about two years the horror lessened somewhat. Perhaps they had run out of victims. Everyone prayed that it was so, prayed to God and the Virgin that they would go away.

For a few months everything was quiet. It was reported that Kerlinger had gone to Lüneburg. God have mercy on their souls, prayed everyone, but please God, let him stay there. And people began to relax.

Thus it came as a complete surprise when, a few months later, two armed horsemen rode up the lane. Elizabeth, who had been conferring with Rudi's wife, spied them through the open door.

"Stay here with the babe," she said. "I do not like their looks, but perhaps they are just lost. If they make trouble, run for your husband."

The girl nodded.

They were definitely not knights, but uncouth ruffians. A shiver of fear went through Elizabeth, but she knew that Christine was alone in the front yard planting flowers. She stepped out the door, closing it behind her. The men rode up and stopped.

"Which of you is known as Christine Wernering?" shouted one.

Christine stood up from her planting and shook out her skirts. "Who wants to know?" she asked.

"Ah, my pretty," he leered, "Dominus Walter of the Holy Office would like the honor of your company."

Both women gasped. Christine turned to flee, but he was faster. In one leap he was off his horse and upon her, wrestling her to the ground. When Elizabeth tried to go to her aid, the other horseman rode up behind her and grabbed her wimple, almost strangling her. Rudi's wife, peeping through the window, had heard enough. She swooped up the child and ran out the back door to seek her husband.

"On what charge?" choked out Elizabeth.

"That's for him to say, but there's talk about broken vows."

"I never . . . ," sobbed Christine.

The man slapped her across the mouth.

"Stop that," cried Elizabeth. She tried to free herself from the other man's grasp. "Unhand me, you beast."

The man just laughed and tightened his grip. "Methinks the Inquisition would enjoy your company, too, Mistress Witch."

"How dare you?" screamed Elizabeth. "I am no witch and you know it."

"There's been talk," said the man in a monotone. "Anyway, harboring a runaway nun is crime enough."

Meanwhile the first man was already tying a stunned Christine's hands behind her back. "Enough of this dilly-dallying. We've got to get these two in custody afore Dom Walter gets back from Lüneburg. Then you can do all the talking you want, my ladies," he said sarcastically. He threw Christine astride the horse and mounted in front of her. The other man did the same with Elizabeth. Then they tied a line from each woman's ankle to the pommel of the opposite horse. Any thoughts of escape fled from their minds, as they would be dragged head-down by the other horse.

They set off at a brisk pace, which jolted the women cruelly since they could not brace themselves. Once Elizabeth called out to a farmer, "Help us!"

The captor murmured through his teeth, "Don't do that again or you'll be dragged by your ankles the rest of the way." She believed him. "Besides," he added, "they wouldn't dare interfere." He was right. People along the way recognized the woman's captors and turned away as though they were invisible.

Meanwhile Rudi took his fastest horse and rode bareback across the fields to the Vicar's house, hoping to head them off. But he was too late. They were already well down the road to Uelzen. He helped the priest saddle his own horse, a gift from Elizabeth.

"I will go after them alone. It is better," said Borchard. "You would only get yourself into trouble, too. She needs you here. Meanwhile round up as many trustworthy men—by that I mean men courageous enough to stand by her—as you can and await word from me."

"I will, Father."

"And tell the women to care for the child."

"I will, Father. And have a care yourself, Father."

"And, Rudi, not a word of this must reach Johann."

"I understand, Father. You can count on me."

The priest rode off toward Uelzen as fast as he could. But the men had almost reached the town gate before he caught up with them. He cut them off and brought them to a halt.

"How dare you molest these innocent women?" he charged. "By whose orders have you arrested them?"

"Why, Father," said the first man sweetly, "surely you recognize the badge of the Holy Office." He turned his sleeve toward him.

"Well, I say you have no right. They are innocent. I demand you release them."

"You demand nothing, priest. Only the Pope gives orders to the Holy Office. Have a care, Father, lest you yourself run afoul of the Inquisition."

This frightened Elizabeth into speaking. "Let them be, Father. God will protect us."

"Right," said the man. "If they are innocent, they will be released.

Now, out of our way, country bumpkin." He urged his horse forward, almost unseating the Vicar.

Father Borchard stood aside and followed them through the gate. He was filled with shame that he could not rescue them. For the first time in his life, he who preached peace wished he had a sword to run the men through. He was terrified for Elizabeth. He knew how very few were ever released by the Inquisition, and most of them were by then hopelessly crippled or blathering idiots.

He followed discreetly at a distance because he wanted to see where the women would be held. Uelzen having no castle, the only dungeon was beneath the Gudestor and was rarely used except briefly for petty offenders. This was where they were taken. He waited for a while to see if the men left. The gatekeepers themselves were local people employed by the Town Council. He hoped he could bribe them. But the women's captors never left.

Inside the dark stinking dungeon Elizabeth was chained to the wall with leg and arm shackles. But the men had other plans for Christine. They threw her down on the filthy stones. While one held her, the other already had his codpiece loose and his swollen member in his hand. He knelt and thrust it into her savagely. Christine screamed. Elizabeth strained helplessly at her chains but could do nothing but watch. So she cursed them.

"You filthy son-of-a-bitch. You plague-ridden bastards." She shocked herself at some of the language she knew.

The ruffian who had been holding Christine came over to her and thrust his erect penis in front of her face. "You shut your mouth, witch, or I'll shut it for you. You want a taste of this?" He tried to force his penis into her mouth, but she turned her head as far to the side against the slimy wall as she could. "Ach," he said, "we can't be bothered with old witches. We like young meat," and took his turn raping Christine. When they had their fill, they chained her to the wall as well, warning them, "We'll be back later. Dom Walter let's us have all we want before he takes over. Once he gets ahold of these lovely bodies, they ain't good for nothing. Maybe we'll even give you a little next time, old witch." Elizabeth shuddered but held her tongue.

When Borchard heard the screams, forgetting all caution, he charged like a raging bull at the door of the prison. The gatekeepers held him back.

"You can't go in there, Father. There's nothing you can do."

"I'll kill them, the beasts."

"No, you won't, Father. We won't let you. It's their due, and we're under strict orders to see nothing and hear nothing of what goes on in there."

"But I've got to help them. They're innocent."

"That's as may be. Most are, but you won't be any help to them if you get yourself arrested, too. A little rape never hurt a woman. They're built for it. But I'd hate to tell you what they do to the men they get ahold of."

Borchard slumped in their hold. "Oh, God, what can I do?"

"Pray for them, is all. And you'd best get yourself gone afore they come out." The gatekeepers released him, for all the fight had gone out of him. Then one whispered more kindly, "Go to the higher-ups, if you know anybody with enough influence or money. Kerlinger ain't back yet. There's some have gotten out with the right kind of payment."

"I understand. Thanks for the advice," murmured the Vicar and turned away so they wouldn't see the tears in his eyes. Then he ran as fast as he could to the Franciscans at the Marienkirche. He knew they hated the Dominicans.

The Franciscans welcomed him kindly and listened sympathetically to his story. Then they shook their heads.

"We have tried long ere this, but you know their authority comes directly from the Holy Father himself. There is nothing we can do, but there is hope. Our Provincial and many others have written to Rome about the atrocities. There is no doubt that Kerlinger's zeal in seeking out heretics has gone far beyond the bounds of his authority. He is a fanatic. But it will take time to recall him. As you know, Franciscans in Rome are not too influential in Avignon. We are sorry, but at least we shall add our prayers to yours for their souls."

Dejected, the priest stood in the street outside the church. So much for influence. Money, he thought. Who? He remembered Elizabeth mentioning a Master Mestwart. Did he dare? It was worth trying.

The old master shoemaker greeted the priest coolly. In fact, the Vicar felt that, had he not been a priest, he would have been left standing on the doorstep.

"Mistress Wiese? Of course I remember her. Husband was a fine shoemaker. Too bad he died. Far too many died back then. But she is no longer a member of the Guild. Hasn't paid her dues in years. Not that we could have kept her on the rolls anyway. Left town under rather mysterious circumstances." The coolness became frigid.

"There was nothing mysterious about it, unless wanting food and a better life is mysterious," replied the Vicar. "I know her well, Master Mestwart. She is a member of my parish, a good woman."

"Cowardly. Others had the courage to stay at their work."

"She had no work at the time, if you recall, and a young son to provide for. Anyway, that matters not now. You are a wealthy man and very powerful in the affairs of the town. Is there any way that you could help her?"

"If you mean bribery, I am ashamed to hear a man of God suggest such a thing. Besides, I don't mix with the Inquisition. They have their reasons for doing what they do. How do I know what this woman may have been doing these last—how long is it? At least twenty years. I suggest you go to an ecclesiastical advocate. If she is as innocent as you say, they will be able to get her acquitted of the charges. I bid you good day, Father." He called a servant and Borchard was unceremoniously ushered out of the house.

Ecclesiastical advocate indeed. The old fart knew very well there was no such thing in Uelzen. The few there were dwelt in the diocesan see towns, where they served at the Bishops' courts. And it was well-known that only a Dominican advocate had even a slim chance of getting an acquittal from the Inquisition and that they rarely would step in until the victim was a mangled cripple. Besides, there was not a Dominican within a thousand miles that he would trust.

I am too overwrought to think clearly and this requires my best ability. He sought his horse and slowly rode back to Veerssen.

Several days passed and Kerlinger had still not returned. Every day Borchard rode into Uelzen for news. He was neglecting his own flock, he knew, but they understood. Rudi told him the two flunkies had been out several times searching for the child, but everyone professed ignorance. The women were passing him from household to household, and sometimes two or three of them would spend a whole day and night hiding him in the woods.

Meanwhile, Elizabeth and Christine sat in the damp straw praying and trying to console each other. At least twice a day the two beasts and several others came and had their way with Christine. She no longer fought them off or even screamed. She just lay on the cold stone and let them do what they would. Sometimes one forced his swollen penis in her mouth while the other rode her hips at the same time. Elizabeth could hear her gagging and choking, but Christine had lost the will to resist. Elizabeth feared for her sanity.

Once a day they were brought water and a thin, tasteless gruel. They began to get weak from lack of food and mobility. There was only enough slack in the chains that bound them to move to one side and relieve themselves in the same filthy straw they sat and slept on. But the worst part was the waiting and not knowing.

Christine began having nightmares. "I dreamed the flames were already consuming me. Oh, God, let them hurry and get it over with. Death will be a blessed release."

God have mercy, prayed Elizabeth. It has come to this. I'm sure that is their intention. So far they had not touched her, but they threatened her every day.

One day Borchard succeeded in bribing one of the gatekeepers to take a note to Elizabeth. Although the Vicar knew the man could not read, it was worded very noncommittally, simply assuring her of the prayers and love of everyone in the parish. He did not sign it. She would understand.

It was a ray of hope. "Father Borchard will help us," she said with more confidence than she felt. "I know he will."

"It is too late for me," Christine muttered resignedly.

As he was leaving the gate tower, the priest felt someone jostle him. He clutched his cassock tightly about him, fearing it was a cutpurse. "Willi wants to see you," whispered a voice in his ear.

He turned to face the man, a vagrant and obviously intoxicated. "Who is Willi?" he asked.

"Friend." The man jerked his head toward the gate tower.

The priest was puzzled at first, and then came a vague recollection of Elizabeth mentioning someone named Willi years ago. "Oh," he said. "Where do I find him?"

"Leave your horse in the market square and I'll show you." The man disappeared into the crowd.

Borchard did as he was told and stood in the square looking about for the man. The voice behind him startled him. He had not seen the man at all. "Follow me at a distance."

When they reached the tavern, the messenger seemed to disappear. Willi signalled the priest to come close to his side at the bar. He carefully looked over his patrons before he spoke in a discreet whisper. "Mayhap we can save her, if you want us to try."

The priest was flabbergasted. For a moment he could not answer. Then the questions rushed out of him. "Which one? How? Why not both? Who are 'us'? Are you sure?"

Willi answered the last question first. "No, I'm not sure. It's very chancy trying to trick the Inquisition. But we've managed it a few times before. Can't try it too often or they'll wise up. Kerlinger's not back yet, so we've a little time to plan. As to the how and who, it's best you don't know anything about it, for your own safety, Father."

"I understand," replied the priest. "But why just one? Can't you try to save them both? And which one would you save?"

"Why, the Mistress of course," replied Willi. "Her and me been friends these many years. A fine woman."

"I agree. But it seems if you could help one, you could help both."

"Too chancy. We'll be lucky if we get one. Try for both and we end up with neither and a pack o' trouble for ourselves. Besides, the girl is too far gone. She's half out of her mind already. Must be carrying the seed of at least a dozen of them louts by now."

Borchard was shocked. "How do you know this?"

"I got ways," was all Willi would say. "Besides that's their standard routine. Weaken one to the point where she'll admit to anything. Then the other is so terrified when it comes to the questioning, they usually fold right under. Anyway, do you want us to try?"

"Absolutely. You know I do. You've given me the first bit of hope since they were arrested. Is there anything I can do to help?"

"Money, for one thing. Men don't risk their lives for strangers for nothing."

"I don't have much," replied Borchard, "but I'll give you all I can."

"It will be enough to start. Mistress still have some invested with the Council?"

"As far as I know, but I can't touch that."

"I know, but she can. We'll get her to sign a note. They'll think it's for bribery money. Happens all the time, usually to no avail. But we do it different."

"I see," but he didn't see at all. "Is there anything else I can do?"

"Are there two men you can trust and three fast horses?"

"Yes, indeed."

"Put them on alert to ride a long distance at a moment's notice. And pack up a few of her clothes and one of your cassocks and keep them in readiness at your church."

"One of my cassocks?" he asked, puzzled. Then it dawned on him. "Oh, I see. No one will bother a priest and his servants on an errand of mercy."

410

"Exactly, Father."

"Willi, I don't know how to thank you."

"Bring me the money tomorrow and save your thanks till she's safe. And pray."

"That I shall do."

"And, Father, be very, very dumb."

The priest nodded and took his leave.

The next day the Inquisitor arrived and went immediately to the Dominicans' little house across the river. The women were brought fresh water and were told to wash their hands and faces.

"Drink some of it first, Christine. It will refresh you," urged Elizabeth. No one had been in to molest the poor girl that day, and she seemed relatively calm. But Elizabeth couldn't look at her eyes. They were blank and staring, as if her soul had already left her body.

"Wash," ordered the guard. "Dom Walter is waiting and he doesn't like to see filth."

"Then it will take more water than this to wash the filth of this place from us," snapped Elizabeth.

The guard made as if to slap her face but thought better of it and simply repeated, "Wash."

They washed as best they could.

Their shackles were unlocked from the rings in the wall and they were ordered to stand. Neither one could. More guards came in and, two each, hauled the women to their feet. After the pins and needles left her feet, Elizabeth was able to stand and even walk a little, albeit with great difficulty due to the chains around her ankles. But Christine could not. The guards ended up dragging her most of the way.

In one room of the little house Dom Walter sat like a king upon his throne. At his side sat his clerk, quill pen and parchment ready. Elizabeth gasped when she saw the various instruments of torture. Christine showed no emotion whatsoever. The older woman was stood against the far wall of the room, a guard on either side of her. The younger was led in front of the Inquisitor. He began the inquisition.

"Your name?"

"Christine Wernering."

"You lie. Your real name?"

"That is my real name." The guard twisted her arm. She gasped with the pain and gritted her teeth.

"Your full name?"

411

"I'll not tell you." The guards twisted both arms. She sobbed.

"Are you not the daughter of Werner von Leiden?"

"If you know, then why do you ask?" she replied. The guards twisted harder. She screamed and turned white.

Kerlinger smiled evilly. "Because I want to show you are a liar before witnesses. Enough." He signalled the guards to release her arms. She would have fallen had they not held her up.

"Do you believe in God, the Father, Son and Holy Ghost?"

"I do."

"Say the Credo."

"I believe in God the Father Almighty . . ." The guards twisted her arms brutally. She screamed again.

"Go on."

"Creator of . . . I can't remember." The guards released her again.

"Of course you can't, because the Devil is in your heart. Did you not abjure your vows because Satan told you to?"

"I never made any vows."

"I see it is time to purge the Devil from your heart before we can redeem your soul. Rack her!" Christine fainted.

Elizabeth screamed, "No! No!"

"I am going to eat my dinner," he said calmly. "Do a good job and let me know when she has confessed her sins. And take this one back to the dungeon." He indicated Elizabeth. "I'll not have a witch coaching her in her answers." He left.

They threw water in Christine's face to revive her and were already stretching her onto the rack when the other guards hauled Elizabeth out.

Back in the dungeon, Elizabeth could hear Christine's screams all the way across the river. And then there was silence for what seemed like hours. The cold sweat ran down Elizabeth's back as she prayed fervently but almost incoherently. And then came the most blood-curdling scream of all. Oh, God, have mercy on her soul. She must surely be dead, thought Elizabeth.

Then just before twilight, they brought Christine back and dumped her on the filthy straw. They didn't bother to reattach her chains. She was unconscious.

"Tomorrow she goes to the stake," said one guard. "And then, my lady, we'll have some fun with you."

Elizabeth stared in horror at the arms pulled out of the shoulder joints, the legs twisted out of the hip sockets, and she could smell the seared flesh where Christine's womanhood had been. She retched and retched until she could vomit no more. She lay back against the damp wall, exhausted. What fiends are these that could do this in the name of God? Surely the Devil himself could do no worse.

The girl's eyelids flickered. "Mother," she whispered hoarsely.

Elizabeth took the rag they had washed with earlier and wiped her forehead. "I am here, sweeting."

"Take care of my baby. I—I didn't tell them."

"Brave girl. I will if I can, but I . . . "

"I am going to Jesus soon, but you will live." Elizabeth could barely hear Christine's faint whisper. "Our Lady came to me . . . " Elizabeth thought she had fainted again, but in a few minutes she continued, "It's all right. I don't feel any pain anymore. Our Lady—told me—the angels will guard you. You will—raise my babe—like your own."

"If she told you, then it must be true. You have my promise," Elizabeth assured her, wondering how this could possibly be, yet she believed in miracles. If Our Lady said so, it must be true.

"And, Mother— tell Johann—I'll always love him."

"I shall, sweeting. Now rest and I shall pray for you." But her last words went unheard. Christine had fainted again.

Elizabeth could not sleep listening to Christine's labored breathing. She tried praying, but she had prayed so much these dreadful days and nights, it seemed she had run out of prayers. She dozed fitfully but heard every hour the watch called out. The town quieted down for the night. The bells for Compline rang and she wondered if she would ever see the inside of a church again. She thought about Borch. She hoped he wouldn't get into trouble trying to help them. She hadn't heard any more from him since his little note two days ago. Does he know what they did to Christine today? And what is to happen tomorrow? She couldn't bear to think about it, yet the horror remained foremost in her mind. Now that Kerlinger was back, she had lost all hope. How could anyone, let alone a priest, commit such atrocities on an innocent child? She shuddered to think what they would do to her. Charges of witchcraft were far more serious than forswearing monastic vows. She almost retched again but tried to control it with prayers.

Before she knew it, Lauds rang out. Why, it is tomorrow already. She heard the gatekeepers change their watch. Strangely, their voices seemed louder or closer than usual. Probably because I can't sleep.

But she wasn't mistaken. A few minutes later one of the gatekeeps

413

came in carrying a dimly lit lantern. He put his finger to his lips and handed her a piece of paper.

"I ain't supposed to come in here," he whispered, "but I'm willing to help out a friend. Master Willi wants you to make your mark on this here paper. Seems as you owe him some money he wants to collect before it's too late."

"I don't owe—oh, I see," she whispered as she read the paper. Across the top, which could easily be torn off, it said: "Trust me, Willi." Beneath that was a formal order to the Town Council to release ten Lübecker thalers from her savings to Willi for services owed. It was an exorbitant amount, but their lives were worth far more than that, if she was understanding the message correctly. "What can I write with?" she asked the gatekeep.

He produced a piece of charred wood. "The best I got," he apologized. "Town don't supply us with fancy quill pens and ink pots."

Elizabeth willingly signed her name. The gatekeep left and she was in darkness once more. Her heart beat wildly with anticipation. Willi will do something. She knew he would. Then she looked at Christine and wept with guilt. It's too late for her. She will never walk again, never use her arms again and she's terribly burned inside. It's a wonder she's still alive. Listening to the girl's stentorian breathing, Elizabeth doubted she would live until morning. Why couldn't this have come before Kerlinger came back?

Elizabeth spent the rest of the night tormenting herself with guilt and agonizing with hope. Exhausted with emotion, she finally dozed off just before dawn.

Sometime later she was awakened by the guard who brought her gruel. She noticed it was only half the usual meagre portion.

"None for her," sneered the guard. "She's got an appointment with the fire today. Don't need it where she's goin'."

Elizabeth was about to push the bowl away but then realized she might need what little strength it would give her. She managed to choke down some of the vile stuff before she gagged and could eat no more. Christine was still asleep or, more likely, unconscious. Her breathing was hardly perceptible.

In a while the guard returned with three more of his ilk. "Time to go." He threw a pail of water in Christine's face. "Wake up, my beauty. Can't have you sleeping through all the fun." Christine sputtered and screamed with pain when she inadvertently tried to move her arms to

414

shield her face. Two of them lifted her up by the tortured shoulders and half-carried, half-dragged her out.

Elizabeth didn't know if Christine could hear or not but called after her anyway. "Go with God, sweeting. I'll pray for you."

"Hah," laughed the guard, "fat lot of good the prayers of a witch will do her." He disconnected Elizabeth's shackles from the wall rings and they hauled her to her feet.

"Why me?" she cried. "Why do I have to go, too? I don't want to see it."

"Oh, don't you? Well, you're going to. Dom Walter's orders. *Everyone* watches the burnings. Even the town folk. It's good for their souls." They prodded her out the door.

By the time they arrived at the gallows place Christine had already been bound to the stake and they were piling very dry fagots around her feet and almost up to her waist. The guards were right. There already was a good crowd of people there, and more kept coming. Of course, there were always the ghouls that relished gruesome and sensational happenings, but Elizabeth noticed quite a few of the Bürgers and even three or four town councilmen trying to look pious, but she could see the disgust—and yes, fear—in their eyes. She kept her own eyes down, but she needn't have. Even people she knew well ignored her as if she didn't exist. The guards parked her in the forefront of the crowd, where she would have a good view of the stake. But eventually more eager spectators pushed forward until she was surrounded by a tightly packed throng. The tension grew.

At last Dom Walter stepped forward and signalled for silence. The crowd stopped murmuring and eagerly stretched necks forward to hear and see.

"In the name of the Father, Son and Holy Ghost."

"Amen," replied the people.

"Christine von Leiden, I give you one last chance for absolution and to save your soul. Do you repent of abjuring your sacred vows?"

Elizabeth was watching carefully and did not see the girl's head or even her lips move. She doubted Christine was even conscious, but Kerlinger evidently assumed her answer to be negative.

"Then I commit you to the flames!" he shouted almost gleefully as he thrust the first torch into the dry wood. "May God have mercy on your soul." He stepped back and his flunkies threw more torches onto the pile. The flames leapt up. Elizabeth saw Christine's body arch once against the

415

stake and then could see no more. The flames had enveloped her.

Several people screamed. A few fainted. Elizabeth felt the guard's grip on her relax, but so numb with pity and horror was she that she did not realize why. A voice whispered close to her ear, "Say nothing. Pretend to faint." She didn't have to pretend. She collapsed. Two men wrapped her in a blanket, chains and all, and carried her away. Her two guards were lying on the ground. The people assumed they, too, had fainted and stepped over them, and the crowd closed the gap.

When they reached Willi's, he hustled them into the back room where he lived. The tavern was noticeably empty. An armorer was waiting to strike her chains off. Willi himself washed her face while the man did so. The man was paid and left. Not a word was spoken. Willi chafed her wrists and ankles and put unguent on the raw skin. Then he placed a cup of hot chicken broth in front of her.

"Oh, Willi," she sobbed then. "How can I thank you?" She put her head on the table and wept.

"Thank me later when you are safe. Now drink up. You need the strength, and time is short. We must get you out of here while the crowd is busy across the river. And don't send any messages to me direct. Send it through your Vicar, if you must."

She drank the broth as quickly as she could. How good it tasted. Her stomach almost rebelled, but she held her breath and fought for control. They wrapped her in a shroud, leaving only her nose and mouth free, and bade her climb into a coffin. She shuddered.

"'Tis the only way, Mistress. There's still plague about here and there," he said and then reassured her, "There's airholes drilled in the cover. Now in you go. 'Tis only for a short ride."

She would have laughed if she hadn't been so frightened. She knew she was near hysteria. Again she fought for control. Slowly she climbed in and lay down in the coffin.

"You don't mind if we throw in a few sprigs o' garlic, do you? Wards off the plague, you know. They smell that and no one'll want to look in." He shut the lid.

Four men hoisted the coffin on their shoulders and hustled through the half-empty streets to the Veerssen Gate. When the gatekeepers went to stop them, one of the bearers shouted, "Plague! Stand back. Him wantin' to be buried in his ol' hometown." The keepers let them pass. Outside they loaded her onto a cart that was waiting and returned into town to Willi's, where they could each attest that all of them had been drinking all

416

morning. They had been well paid for a few minutes' work.

The cart had already reached Veerssen, delivered its burden and was on its way back to Uelzen when, hours later, the hue and cry went up that two of the Holy Office's guards had been stabbed in the back. Later the story went around that the witch herself had been seen flying away the moment the flames engulfed Christine.

Inside the coffin Elizabeth had nearly fainted from claustrophobia. The strong scent of the garlic in such an enclosed space almost made her ill, but later she was grateful for it. It kept her awake. Her eyes were watering fiercely and she could not move to wipe the tears away. She knew she was in a cart but had no idea where they were taking her. The ride seemed interminable.

At last they arrived at the Veerssen church and Father Borchard was waiting. There was a freshly dug grave in the churchyard, obviously for the carter's benefit. He had been hired by Willi but knew nothing about the rescue. He honestly believed he had carried a plague victim to his final resting place. Rudi, Arni, Karl and Johann himself carried the coffin into the church.

The Vicar carefully locked the church doors before he opened the lid of the coffin. When Elizabeth looked up into his face through tear-filled eyes, she couldn't believe it.

"Oh, Borch, is it really you?" she cried.

"Yes, it is, my dear Lisa." He helped her up out of the coffin and she fell into his arms.

"Oh, Borch, Borch. I can't really believe I'm safely home again. It was so horrible." He held her for a while, while she wept out her grief, and then warned, "Home again, but not safe yet, my dear. You can't stay here or in your house for some time. It is the first place they will look."

She backed away from him, wiping the tears from her eyes with her filthy sleeve. "I suppose you are right." She looked puzzled. "But where . . . ?" She looked around for the first time and saw her son. She ran the few steps to him and he embraced her tightly. "Oh, Johann, Johann." She started sobbing again against his chest.

"Mama, Mama, it's all right now," he said as he held her. "The whole village has been praying for you and—and—Christine." His own voice broke. "They would not let me go."

"He was like a caged tiger when he found out what happened," said Borchard.

"I'm sure he was," said Elizabeth, calmer now, "but I'm glad you

417

held him back." She turned again to her son. "You would only have forfeited your own life, to no avail. They are like beasts. It was horrible, horrible." She paused for a moment, fighting back the tears. "She died bravely, Johann. She never told them about you or the babe, for all the — what they did to her." She vowed he would never know the true details of that. "The last thing she said to me was to tell you she will always love you."

Johann was crying now. He held his mother again. "And I loved her, too."

After giving them a moment or two, the Vicar interrupted. "Come now, Elizabeth, you are far from safe yet. We must get you away from here, and that quickly. Do you have the strength to ride?"

"Probably," she replied, "but I'm not sure how far. Where am I going?"

"Willi has made all the arrangements. He has friends in Celle, where you will be safe for as long as necessary."

"Celle!" she exclaimed. "That's a long way away. I've never been there. They say it is a lovely town."

"Yes. It normally is a full day's ride, but in your condition it may take two or three, and you will have to be very careful."

"What about the babe?" she asked. "I promised Christine I would mother him like my own."

"He is fine and being well cared for by Rudi's wife and the other women. He is too young to understand and is better left where he is. He will be safe until you can return," the priest assured her.

Elizabeth nodded. "Have I time to wash and change these filthy clothes? I can't stand the stink anymore."

Arni spoke up. "Ach, ja, Mistress, we's goin' to put 'em in the coffin and bury 'em in yon hole waiting for the plague victim."

Elizabeth laughed despite her grief.

"There is water for washing in the sacristy and a hooded monk's cassock," instructed the Vicar. "Tie your hair up and don the cassock when you have washed. Some of your own clothes are already packed along with food for the journey. Rudi and Johann are going with you. You will be the old priest they are taking back to his family. Let them do all the talking. You must pretend to be a little deaf and senile. Now hurry, my dear."

In a very few minutes Elizabeth was ready. She looked for all the world like the decrepit old monk she was supposed to be. They had to help her mount, but once in the saddle she felt better. Arni and Karl were already filling in the grave over the coffin. The priest gave her last-minute instructions.

"When you get to Celle, seek out one Cordt von Eltze. I understand his is a very prominent and influential family there, above suspicion but not above hoodwinking the Inquisition on occasion. In fact, one sister is reportedly a Beguine. Don't communicate with any of us here unless it is absolutely necessary. If you write, don't sign your name. One or the other of us will come to you as often as we can, but don't expect anyone for a while, until things quiet down and we see how the wind blows. Before he leaves you, sign over to Johann all your investment with the Town Council and date it a month ago, or they will confiscate it all. Von Eltze will help you arrange it. They say he is a financial wizard. It's fortunate we put all your other property in Johann's name long ago or it would all be forfeit. Now ride as fast as you can when no one's on the road, but slow down when you meet people or they will become suspicious. Have a care, my dearest, and God bless you." He made the sign of the cross as they rode off.

As soon as they left the village environs, they rode like the wind until they came to the next little village of Holdenstedt. Here they rode at a sedate pace simply waving when people greeted them. The little castle there was the one some rich Bürger had taken over at the same time she had moved to her farm. It looked prosperous enough but apparently was not lived in too much.

After that they were out on the open heath—the great moor that extended from Lüneburg to Celle. Although this was the main highway between Uelzen and Celle they met few travellers. The countryside was desolate, mostly wide open moor, some swamps and a few small forests. The few isolated farms all seemed to raise nothing but the famous Heiden sheep. There were no other villages at all.

Several miles down the road Elizabeth began to tire badly. At first the excitement and urgency of the escape had kept her going, but now she was flagging. She was still too weak from her ordeal to sustain such effort.

"I—I shall have to stop and rest soon," she gasped, "or I shall fall off the horse."

The men closed in beside her, ready to grab her in case that should happen. "We can't stop here in the open," said Rudi. "There is a small wood up ahead. Can you make it that far?"

She nodded. But they slowed their pace for her sake.

When they reached the wood, Rudi dismounted and, leading his horse, gingerly tested for bogginess or quicksand. The moss-covered ground seemed solid enough. He signalled them to follow and led them well off the road into the woods. He stopped and listened. It was very quiet but he had heard what he hoped to find. A little further on they came upon a little spring gurgling merrily. "Perfect," he pronounced.

Johann dismounted and helped Elizabeth down. Her legs nearly gave way as she plopped down on the greensward. Rudi let the horses drink first and then filled a cup for Elizabeth. The water was icy cold and clear. It refreshed her.

"I don't know how much farther I can go," she said. "I am so weak."

"A little food will help," said Rudi as he dug in his saddlebag for bread, cheese and some ripe plums. "We'll rest here as long as you need to, but I would like to get a little further on before nightfall. But not too far or we shall come into the demesne of Eschede. That's a famous monastery," he explained, "well endowed by the Bürgers of Celle and renowned for its hospitality. But I think we do not want their hospitality this time."

After they ate, Elizabeth lay down on the soft moss and fell into an exhausted sleep.

The moor ended sharply as they rode down a slope to the Aller River. Celle lay before them on the opposite bank. They crossed the bridge and received directions from the gatekeep. The name of von Eltze held some magic here obviously, for immediately upon hearing it the man became extraordinarily polite, bowing as if they were nobility. They rode slowly into the town, through the market square, and found that Zöllnerstrasse was the main intersecting street of Celle. The von Eltze house was very large and colorfully painted on the half-timbered facade, a mansion almost, except that like all the houses, it was more tall than spread out. They must be very wealthy, thought Elizabeth. I hope they don't send us to the servants' entrance.

But word of their impending arrival had evidently been sent. An elderly housekeeper answered the door and quickly ushered them in. She instructed Rudi where to find the stalls for the horses in the back. Then she showed them into an elegant parlor. "Please wait. I shall tell the Mistress you are here."

Moments later a tall, not unattractive woman swept into the room. She was wearing the most beautiful gown Elizabeth had ever seen. Like a princess, she thought, although, never having seen royalty, she had no idea what a princess would wear, but it was a far cry from the dowdy, frumpy attire of even the richest Bürgers' wives in Uelzen. Inadvertently she curtsied.

The woman held out her hands. "Welcome to Celle. I am Geseke von Eltze."

Elizabeth did not know what name she was supposed to give, so she simply said, "Thank you, my lady."

Geseke smiled. "You must be Mistress Wiese. Oh, yes, I know the whole horrid story, or most of it anyway. Have no fear. You will be safe here in Celle. My husband Cordt is the toll-collector, a position that has been in the family ever since the town was founded almost eighty years ago. He is also the Duke's closest advisor. And the Duke will have no truck with the Inquisition, in fact, forbade them to come within three miles of the town walls. And Cordt's father is Bürgermeister. He and the Council back the Duke one hundred percent in this. So I assure you, you will be quite safe."

"Thank you, my lady," murmured Elizabeth, "it's comforting to know that."

"I am no lady, just a Bürger's wife. This branch of the family is not nobility—or not quite—despite the name. But that is a long story. So since you are going to be living with us for a while, you must call me Geseke."

Elizabeth smiled for the first time. The woman was so warm and welcoming. No insecurity here. "Then I am Elizabeth," she replied, "and this is my son, Johann."

"Again, welcome to Celle. But enough of this chatter. You must be exhausted, my dear. Let us get you out of those outlandish clothes and into a nice warm bath. Then we can get to know each other better over a little refreshment—unless you would prefer to rest awhile first."

"Well, both, I guess," said Elizabeth shyly. She was still overawed by all this splendor.

Geseke rang a bell and a maid appeared almost immediately. "Show Mistress Wiese to the room she will be using and pour her a bath. We'll let you nap for about an hour and then have the refreshments." As Elizabeth followed the maid upstairs, the lady of the house turned to Johann. "And now, young man, would you also care for a bath? I assume you and your servant will be staying the night?"

"Yes, to both," replied Johann. "A hot bath is a luxury I haven't enjoyed in a long time. And, my lady—I mean, Mistress von Eltze—I can't begin to thank you enough for sheltering my dear mother. I just hope it won't make any trouble for you."

421

"Pah! No trouble at all. The Bürgers of this town will do almost anything to tweak the nose of the Pope. We have no use for a puppet in the pay of the King of France. As for the so-called Holy Office, Dominicans are *persona non grata* in Celle. We have a very powerful Franciscan monastery—Holy Cross, right here at the other end of this street—which is richly endowed by the Duke himself. Need I say more?"

Johann laughed. "I guess not."

"Good. Now get you off to that bath. I assume your servant has already made himself comfortable in the kitchen. I must check." She swept out of the room and a manservant came to lead Johann upstairs.

Elizabeth stayed in Celle for almost three years. She finally began to relax, and bit by little bit the horror faded from her mind. She enjoyed the cosmopolitan aura of the town. Celle was the Duke's favorite Residence town, although not his capital—that was Lüneburg—and fully one-third of its citizens were employed in one capacity or another by or as suppliers to the Court. Geseke took Elizabeth to the castle and presented her when the Duke was in residence, on the theory that knowing him personally would provide even more protection. They attended grand balls at the Castle and all sorts of social functions held by the powerful Cloth Merchants' Guild, of which Cordt was the head and Geseke a full member. How different from old Master Mestwart and his staid Shoemakers' Guild, reflected Elizabeth. These people were wealthier by far and worked just as hard, but they knew how to enjoy their wealth and power. They even had the Duke eating out of their hands, because their taxes—and loans—supported his Court, his wars and his pleasures.

Elizabeth enjoyed wandering about the clean, well laid out town. She soon shed her fear and made many good acquaintances. Although Geseke was much younger, they became close friends and confidantes. Elizabeth even told her about her little grandson, Christian, whom she missed terribly. She kept busy with sewing and embroidering, but she missed her farm and her own home, despite all the luxury and social whirl.

Either Johann or Rudi tried to come every month or so. Father Borchard came a few times but was cautiously formal and reserved even when they were alone. Even Willi came about once a year. But the news was not good. It was still not safe for her to come home. Kerlinger had left Uelzen and apparently Lüneburg as well, but he was still exercising his evil fanaticism in Bremen, Lübeck, Rostock and elsewhere—towns too close for comfort.

422

Willi had managed to scotch the story about the witch flying away. His cronies—for a small fee—gladly spread the word that they had seen the Blessed Virgin and a host of angels rescue Elizabeth and lift her to heaven with their own eyes. The same superstitious fools who had believed the witch story now avidly swore that they had witnessed this one. Soon it was whispered that Elizabeth might be a saint, just like her namesake the Queen of Hungary, for hadn't she survived the plague and didn't she help the poor farmers, and so on?

"They will be expecting me to do miracles next," she said.

"That will come when we resurrect you from the dead," joked Willi. "But not yet."

"Soon, I hope. They've been terribly kind to me here, but I'm homesick, Willi."

"Keep the faith, Mistress. It might not be too much longer. I hear tell Kerlinger's ailing. Maybe someone'll help him on his way to hell ere long."

And the activities of the Holy Office were not the only bad news. War had broken out over the succession to the Duchy. This was no simple feud where a greedy lord and a small company of armored knights attacked the castle of a weaker lord in the typical land grabs that were all too common in the lawless days after the Great Plague. The common people were seldom affected by such, merely exchanging one master for another with a resigned shrug of the shoulders and going about their work as usual. This was a major civil war within the Duchy, with full-scale battles engaging hundreds of knights and armed foot soldiers, burning castles and whole villages, devastating the countryside, foraging off the land, waylaying travellers and robbing the peasants.

Geseke tried to explain the intricacies of what had caused it. In 1369 Duke Wilhelm, the last Welf in direct line of descent from Heinrich der Löwe died childless. A distant cousin of Welf descent, Magnus Torquatus claimed the Ducal throne and was enthusiastically backed by most of the nobles and towns of the Duchy. But the Emperor thought differently and appointed two brothers, the Dukes of Saxony-Wittenberg, to the fief. Magnus raised an army and enlisted the aid of other Dukes outside of Braunschweig-Lüneburg who were sympathetic to the Welf cause. Much of the fighting centered around Uelzen and Lüneburg. Although the battles were mostly to the east of both towns, Elizabeth feared for her farms, her flocks and her tenants, and above all for Christian. Uelzen's old wooden stockade and part of the town itself had fallen to the flames and the Saxon

423

dukes forbade the town from building a new wall and fortification. On the other hand, the town was often the site of negotiations between the warring parties and even of an armed truce that lasted several months in 1372, all to no avail. Magnus Torquatus was a hothead fighting desperately for his rights and wanted no part of a negotiated peace in which he could only be the loser.

In 1373, in a fierce battle near Leveste, Magnus was killed, and the ducal brothers from upper Saxony took over the Duchy. Elizabeth was saddened to hear of the death of the dashing young duke to whom she had been presented at the Castle. He had left two young sons, approximately the same age as her own grandson, who were carefully guarded by the good Bürgers of Celle. His supporters continued the fight sporadically for many years on behalf of these two, whom everyone except the Emperor and his two vassals regarded as the rightful heirs. But without their fiery leader, all the starch had gone out of the cause. Celle had been spared completely because the new dukes loved the town as well and actually moved their capital there from Lüneburg.

Shortly after they heard the sad news of Duke Magnus' death came the welcome news of Walter Kerlinger's death. The Inquisition, already losing its power due to the war as well as the constant pressure of the Franciscans, disappeared from that part of Germany.

Elizabeth decided it was time to go home. Due to the unsettled conditions, especially the danger from marauding bands of soldiers, temporarily unemployed, both Rudi and Arni came to fetch her and Cordt von Eltze insisted on sending some armed men along to escort her. She and Geseke had a part-tearful, part-joyous farewell, promising to visit one another often.

Upon arriving home she found her cottage almost exactly as she had left it. Only two of her properties had been burned and the flocks stolen. A few of her horses had been commandeered by imperious knights who had lost theirs in battle and considered it beneath their dignity to pay for them. But Rudi had hidden the best of the breeding stock. The most worrisome problem was that of the men who had voluntarily left to join the fighting and never returned, leaving widows and orphans for her to provide for.

But all this paled to insignificance when faced with the joyous reunion with her little grandson. Christian was six years old now and did not recognize her, although Rudi's wife had done everything possible to keep Elizabeth's memory in the forefront of the child's mind. But patience and love soon overcame that obstacle and they became first fast friends and then as close as she had been with Johann at that same age. In fact, the resemblance between father and son was so startling, she often marvelled at it.

Another slight problem arose when word of her return got around and the sightseers and gawkers came to see this would-be saint. She quickly explained that she was no saint at all, just an ordinary innocent woman who had trusted in and prayed very hard to the Blessed Virgin, and that the Holy Mother had come to her in a dream assuring her that she would not die just then. And that when she had fainted, a whole troop of angels came and struck off her chains and bore her to safety in Celle, where she had been biding these many years with kind people. And that when Kerlinger had been struck dead for his crimes, the Blessed Virgin had come again to her in a dream and told her it was safe to come home. The credulously ignorant believed every word of the "miracle", and the more intelligent, better-educated did not gainsay her. For who knew? 'Twas better to believe than be sorry, for this woman was obviously blessed by God.

Elizabeth worked very hard to restore the farms and flocks devastated by the war to profitability. The losses had cut her income considerably, but she still had her investment with the Town Council, which had been growing steadily during her absence. That year two things happened that made it grow even more quickly. The Franciscans finally convinced the Pope to issue a bull curbing the activities and ferociousness of the Inquisition. And Uelzen, though long associated, became a full-fledged member of the Hanse. Both of these things stimulated trade to an unprecedented degree, even though the War of Succession dragged on.

Christian started his schooling with Father Borchard, and when a few years later the boy announced that he had no desire whatever to be a priest like his father, nor a farmer like his grandma, but intended to become a great merchant, she pulled strings to get him into the Hanse school in Uelzen. Although it was against all the strict Hanse rules, since she was no longer a member of any guild, she was still legally a citizen of the town and because of the "miracle" the Bürgers were still a little in awe of her possible influence with the Almighty. So a place was made for him in the prestigious school and he boarded with a family in town, surprisingly another generation of the Mestwart family, who had left shoemaking to become very successful cloth merchants. When he completed his schooling, they took him on as an apprentice to their business.

425

Meanwhile, whenever she had the opportunity Elizabeth went to visit her friend Geseke in Celle and as often as possible took Christian with her. He became friends with the von Eltze children and, more importantly, with the two young heirs-presumptive of the Duchy, Magnus' sons Berndt and Hinrik.

"Did you hear what Master Lembeke, the Bürgermeister of Uelzen, has done?" asked Elizabeth.

"He has done many good things, and some not so good," replied Father Borchard. "If you mean endowing a new Vicarage for the Holy Apostles Altar in the Marienkirche, yes, I heard. It's one way of guaranteeing his nephew Dietrich a job."

"Don't be sarcastic, Borch, it doesn't become you," chided Elizabeth. "Besides, there's a lot more to it than that. After their deaths most of the income is to go into a student stipendium. I think that's a fantastic idea. You know how much it cost to send Johann to Heidelberg and I'm sure it's a lot higher now. With new universities starting up all over the land, there will be many ambitious young men wanting to study at them who might not be able to afford it."

"Then they should not be so ambitious but be satisfied with their lot."

"Borch, I'm ashamed of you," she exclaimed. "That is old-fashioned thinking. Everyone who wants to learn should have an opportunity to go, be they noble, Bürger or even peasant. Even young women, for that matter."

"Women? No, never. Now you're going too far."

"And why not? I don't have much education. Oh, yes, I can read and write and do my accounts, which is more than some noble ladies can do, but I would loved to have learned about other things. Dear Christine — God rest her soul — would have been a natural. We talked about the most interesting things that she read in her books, and you know she read everything she could get ahold of, a lot more than just your books."

"Elizabeth, I don't think you'll ever see that come to pass. Why, it's less than a hundred years since higher education became available for young men and only a few years since they have been able to take studies other than those leading to the priesthood. I personally think it's not necessary to spend two or three years at a university to study medicine or geometry or astronomy. Whatever for?"

Elizabeth shook her head. "Anyway, I think the idea of endowing a student stipendium is a marvelous idea. I'd like to do something like that myself. I have more money than I'll ever need."

"Don't forget all your property is still in Johann's name."

"I'm very much aware of that. Do you think he would agree?"

"I doubt it." The Vicar thought for a moment. "If you want to spend your hard-earned money foolishly—or perhaps that's not the right word— recklessly, I guess—there is something you could do. You know I've been after the Bishop for years to appoint Johann as my assistant. He agrees there is a need. I'm getting old and the parish is growing, but he says there is just not enough money for a new benefice. As you know, mine is paid by the von Estorff family, as the village is part of their demesne, but there were some years it was not paid at all or only in part and the Bishop had to help out. So there's no hope there, but if you wanted to endow an additional vicarage right here in Veerssen, you'd be helping both Johann and me, as well as the parish. Just as old Lembeke has done for his nephew. And think of the indulgences the Bishop will grant you for your own immortal soul."

Elizabeth smiled. "I'll do it. That's just what I shall do. And not for the sake of the indulgences either."

"Don't forget," he reminded her, "all your property is still in Johann's name. He can't very well endow himself."

"I know. I'll use part of the investment with the Town Council. He'd be willing to transfer that back to me. I know he would. He deserves to have a decent post after all these years in tiny, poor churches. And I'm going to talk to him about a student stipendium, regardless of what you think."

"As you like."

In due course the endowment was set up to establish a new vicarage at the altar of the church in Veerssen, and Johann took over a great part of Father Borchard's duties. His mother was happy to have him nearby home again.

The town of Uelzen began building a new wall. Never again were they going to be overrun or burned out by warring parties whose quarrel was not their own, or so the Bürgers thought. More than five years in the building, it was of heavy stone and fill, almost a mile long and fourteen feet high. It had nine large towers and eleven small ones. The Ilmenau was diverted to form a triple moat around the whole. Huge fortresslike keeps were built at each of the three gates, the largest at the Gudestor. The old dungeon where Elizabeth had been imprisoned was gone, but she hated to think what must be under those impenetrable bastions.

In fact, she did not even enjoy going to market during those years, as the dust and mess of the construction permeated the whole town. She could easily have sent Rudi's or Arni's wife, and sometimes did, but she usually went herself anyway, because she did not want to miss any opportunity for a brief visit with Christian.

The lad was more than halfway through his apprenticeship and fast turning into a young man. Reports of his work from Master Mestwart were always good.

"His grasp of figures and accounting, weights and measures, is uncanny," he told Elizabeth, "faster than my own Heineke sometimes. He's learning to judge the quality of cloth now. It won't take him long."

"I'm so happy to hear you say that, Master Mestwart," replied Elizabeth. "Christian has told me that he loves the work, but I wasn't quite sure if it was the right choice for him."

"He couldn't have made a better one. He's a natural. I wouldn't let the boy hear me say this," he lowered his voice conspiratorially, "but I predict his journey years will be short—provided, of course, he has the right financial backing." He looked straight at Elizabeth.

She ignored the implication. "I see. And he gets along well with your son?"

"Like brothers."

"I'm so glad of that. You see," she confided, "I was beginning to be a little worried that he might be unduly influenced by the two princes. They've been good friends for years, and I've heard that now that they are almost adults they intend to raise another army and prolong this foolish war."

"I've heard that, too, and I'm sure they will. They are the rightful heirs after all and should have the title. But this time Uelzen will be safe. These new walls and fortifications that have cost us Bürgers so dearly will protect us."

"I'm sure they will, but that's not what I meant," she replied. "I am afraid those two will talk him into fighting with them. He is totally untrained for war. He could lose his life. But I don't dare let him know I'm concerned."

"I understand your concern, Mistress Wiese, but I am sure your fears are unfounded. Christian has already seen how soldiering and trading are at the opposite end of the scale. He knows war and commerce don't mix. And he is already highly involved in commerce. And if it will ease your mind any, I'll tell you something that I don't want the boys to know yet. If

428

all goes well, I am planning on taking both boys with me to Brugge next year. Now that our beloved town is a full Hanse member, all doors are open to us. There they will see the heart and soul of the cloth trade. And, incidentally, be out of the way of any wars."

"Oh, Master Mestwart, that is fantastic," she exclaimed. "You have indeed put my mind at ease. You are a generous master."

"But a very demanding one, too. They'll have to earn the privilege. And mayhap I might just take them to England the following year." Elizabeth gasped, almost as excited as she knew Christian would be when he heard. "But mind you," warned Master Mestwart, "not a word to anyone until I'm of a mind to tell them myself."

"I promise," she assured him. "My lips are sealed. And now I must bid farewell to my dear grandson—" The Master looked at her askance. "—I call him that, you know," she quickly covered her gaff. "His dear mother, Christine was like a daughter to me—God rest her soul. And I'll have to promise to bring him more of my almond cakes next market day."

The Master smiled, "Ja, we tend to forget that they are still boys."

And so Christian was safely away in Brugge, the great cloth center and financial metropolis of Flanders and the whole of northern Europe, when in 1388 the two ducal heirs finally won their war. The peace treaty was actually concluded in Uelzen. They immediately reconfirmed the town's privileges, and in July the Bürgers hailed them as their new Dukes. They promptly divided the Duchy in half, with Berndt ruling the northern Lüneburg from Celle and Hinrik ruling Braunschweig.

The following year Christian completed his apprenticeship to Master Mestwart's satisfaction. The merchant kept him on as a journeyman. At first he handled the accounts and later he was placed in the sales end of the cloth business. He enjoyed every phase of it. He had inherited a good head for business from his grandmother. At last Master Mestwart announced that Christian would soon begin the real journeying part of his training, as he must become familiar with every branch of the far-flung trading company and with every product they handled.

Elizabeth received a letter from Novgorod.

These Russians are a wild sort of people. They will be singing and dancing and hugging one another one minute and fighting the next. And they constantly partake of very strong drink. I suppose I can't blame them. It is very cold here. They all wear furs, even the meanest peasant, which is, of course, why we can buy them so cheap. I have had a fur-lined cloak and a fur hat made for me. It is no luxury here, I assure you. I've never been so cold in my life.

From England:

It is certainly much more civilized here than in Novgorod. London is a very large town, but also very dirty and evil-smelling. Fortunately, we have our own enclave here called the Stahlyard, which is kept relatively clean and doesn't smell too bad except when the tide is low on the Thames. The English people are very friendly, although very shrewd traders all the same, but—thanks be to God—we can understand one another, their language being very similar to ours. All the nobility and their silly young king speak French, but I think that will change soon. I have made the acquaintance of a very astute and interesting man, Master Chaucer by name. He is a wine merchant, politician, diplomat, and Lord knows what else. He also dabbles in poetry. The interesting thing is that he writes all his poems in the English tongue—no Latin for him—and it really sounds delightful. I have learned a lot about how the English people think from his book, *The Canterbury Tales*. I wish someone would do that for us in Low German.

How his mother would have delighted in hearing that, thought Elizabeth. From Flanders he wrote:

Brugge has got to be one of the most beautiful towns in the world. It has almost as many canals as streets, all clean and neat. It's like a breath of spring after London. But it is also very sophisticated and cosmopolitan. I have met people from all over the world. I didn't know there were so many places and so many different kinds of people. The Venetians and Genoese send whole fleets of ships twice a year, laden with all sorts of luxury goods they trade with the local merchants as well as with the Hanse. The Venetians get spices from some islands far beyond India, while the Genoese have a trading post on the Black Sea (at the other end of Russia) at the end of the Silk Road where they buy the precious cloth from merchants from far-off Cathay. The Lombards and Florentines have banks here, very closely held and secretive, but everyone trusts them to settle the accounts. From what I can see of it, their system is far superior to ours, but the Hanse merchants say ours is quite efficient enough for our needs. I tried to talk Master Mestwart's factor into buying some bolts of silk—it is truly beautiful—but he says it is too expensive for there to be much demand for it among our clients. But I shall bring you a length so you can have the most beautiful gown ever, my dearest Grandmama.

Elizabeth held the letter to her breast and almost cried. She could just picture herself feeding the pigs in a silken gown. The dear boy. But no, I mustn't think of him as a boy. He is a man full-grown now and a grandson of whom I am very proud. In between each of these trips he had been home for a month or two reporting to Master Mestwart and planning the next journey. She had seen him briefly each time and was amazed at how mature he had become, and how knowledgeable. Don't worry, Master Mestwart, I shall see that he has enough capital to set up his own business as soon as he feels he's ready. And it's time and enough that he had a wife. I shall have to start looking around for an eligible girl.

When Christian returned from his last trip, Master Mestwart announced that he would like to take him into the business as a junior partner provided he could raise the capital to invest. It was the supreme honor.

"I have the capital and I want you to have it," said Elizabeth, "but why not your own business? Why a partner, and a junior one at that, where you will only get a small share of the profits?"

"Grandma, do you really have any idea what's involved?" replied Christian. "This is no little shoemaker's shop, where you buy the leather, add in a charge for your labor and perhaps a little profit, and sell it to a pre-arranged customer. This is a huge trading empire. I once thought like you, too. I had no idea of the extent of the business or what was involved. I do now, and I'm still learning. These men don't just buy and sell cloth. They own shares in ships, warehouses and offices all over the world. There are factors, agents and bankers who must be paid commissions. They have a vast network of information on which to base decisions. For example, how cold the winter is in Russia would affect the quality of the fur but could also put a glut on the market. Political unrest in England could affect the quantity of wool. A shipwreck or pirates thousands of miles away could create a shortage of spices. Do you begin to see what I'm saying?"

"I think so," she replied. It was as if he were describing another world.

"If you were to invest every penny you had in me, I couldn't begin to compete with that. One small disaster or bad decision and we could lose everything."

"But you could lose your investment in the partnership, too," she argued.

"True, but only a tiny portion of it, because of the great variety of enterprises Master Mestwart is involved in. One thing balances the other.

And even his loss would be slight because it would be shared by the whole Hanse. This is why the League was formed in the first place. And the opportunity for profit is tremendous. Do you have any idea, Grandma, what my share of the profits would amount to?"

She shook her head. It was all mind-boggling.

"From just one successful venture I could earn three or four times a whole year's income from your shoemaking."

Elizabeth's mouth fell open.

"And Master Mestwart alone has several ventures a year, most of them very successful. You see, even a small loss would not cut into the profits very much."

"It is almost beyond my comprehension," she said. "But I had so wanted you to have your own business, be independent."

"Not yet, Grandma, maybe never. I am grateful for your faith in me, but in truth that would not make me more independent. It would severely limit my opportunities. The trend nowadays is more and more toward partnerships, even larger groups they call companies and, of course, the League itself."

"I see," she said, although she was not quite sure if she did or not. "Then how can I help you?"

"I shall ask Master Mestwart how much he wants for this junior partnership and I'll let you know. You can make it part of my inheritance."

"Foolish boy," she chided. "I'll make it an investment in your future."

Christian hugged her. "Oh, dear Grandma, what would I do without you?" Elizabeth said nothing but hugged and kissed him and loved him dearly.

A few days later Christian rode out to her cottage in Veerssen on a borrowed horse. She welcomed him joyfully, knowing that only something of the utmost importance would bring him out there when he could just as well have waited until she came in to market the following week.

"I see the first thing I must do," she said, "is see that you have a horse of your own. With all the fine horses Rudi has here, it's shameful that you have to borrow a horse."

"Ach, Grandma, I haven't needed one until now. Yes, I really would like to have a horse of my own. I know just the one I want, if Rudi will let me have him. And I sincerely thank you for the offer."

"Pick which one you want and it's yours."

"Fine. Later. Now I have more important things to talk about." He produced from his tunic a sheaf of papers. "Master Mestwart has drawn up the partnership contract. I've already stopped at the village and had Father Borchard—and, er, my father—look them over. Father Borchard says as far as he can see everything is in order. He's really much more knowledgeable about those things than Father Johann, isn't he?"

"I daresay he is. He has given me legal advice from the first day I came here. I wouldn't have this farm but for him. Did I ever tell you that?"

"You probably did, but I was too little to understand then. He also said he thinks you have ample money to pay for it. Do you, Grandma? I was almost afraid to come out here when I saw how much Master Mestwart wanted me to invest."

Elizabeth spread the papers out before her on the kitchen table. She had already done some checking the last time she was in town. The Clerk of the Council had told her the exact amount her investment was worth. It had increased more than tenfold since she originally put the money with them. She also verified Christian's description of Master Mestwart's business, and it was even more extensive and successful than her grandson was aware. She had also been given some reliable figures on about how much Master Mestwart would expect Christian to invest for the junior partnership. It was a large amount, but she had more than enough, so she was not too surprised when she saw the exact figures.

"Ja, I have it, and more besides," she said without hesitation.

Christian was flabbergasted. "Then you are a very rich woman, Grandma, and with all these farms and flocks and things besides." He shook his head. "I had no idea. And yet you live so simply."

"That's the way I choose to live," she replied. "I started out by investing a very small amount wisely and by lots and lots of hard work. You must do the same."

"Oh, I shall, Grandma. I shall."

"I'm sure you will. Now there is something else I learned from my inquiries. As you convinced me, a junior partnership is well and good enough for now, probably all you can handle at the moment. But if you ever hope to become a full partner and Hanse member in your own right, you must become a Bürger of Uelzen, and in order to do that you must be a property owner."

"I'm aware of that, but there's plenty of time for that. Master Mestwart has already said I can continue living with them as long as need be."

She held up her hand. "I am going to give you my house in Uelzen."

Christian was dumbfounded. "Oh, Grandma, I don't know what to say. It isn't necessary yet, you know."

"I know, but I want to do it. I'm getting old, Christian, and with our somewhat questionable legal relationship it's better if I transfer as much as possible while I'm still alive."

They talked for a while longer about the partnership contract and it was agreed they would go together to the Town Council next market day. The Clerk had explained to Elizabeth that she did not even have to withdraw the cash. All she had to do was sign something called a bill of exchange in Master Mestwart's favor and he could withdraw the money as needed.

"That's just the way the Lombard bankers do it, only they can draw on banks all over Europe. Now, dearest Grandma, I have another surprise for you. Wait right here." He hurried out to get something from his saddlebag and returned bearing a large bundle wrapped in leather. He opened it and spread out the contents on the table. Shimmering before her eyes lay the most gorgeous piece of cloth she had ever seen. Real silk, it looked blue, but when one moved it a little it seemed to turn green. Christian could see the tears of joy glistening in her eyes. "You see, Grandma," he said, "I didn't forget. I promised you a length of silk, and there it is."

"Oh, my dearest boy," she said, "I am overwhelmed. It is simply beautiful, but where in the world am I going to wear it? Certainly not for feeding the pigs." She laughed through her tears.

"Why, to my wedding, of course," he replied with a big grin. "That is my other surprise."

"To your wedding?" she exclaimed. "To your wedding? What in the world has been going on behind my back?"

"Nothing at all, Grandma. Some years ago I fell in love with the sweetest girl, but naturally we couldn't do anything about it until I was of age and financially stable. I am now."

"Who is she? Do I know her?"

"I don't know. Her name is Dorike Brasche."

"Brasche. Holy Mother, that is one of the most prominent families in Uelzen. Far richer than Master Mestwart, I'm sure. What makes you think they would even consider someone of — of your background?"

"I think they will. I have met her parents and they seem to like me."

"Hah, liking you means nothing. Those people think only of money and power when it comes to marrying off their daughters."

"Not necessarily. They don't think like nobility. They consider brains, ambition and potential just as important. In fact, Master Mestwart confided in me that Master Brasche speaks so highly of me that he is afraid he will steal me away. This is one reason whey he wants this partnership contract signed quickly."

"I see," said Elizabeth thoughtfully. "And does Master Mestwart know of your—ah, feelings toward this Dorike?"

"He may suspect, but you are the first one I have told. Since you are my legal guardian, you are the one who will have to speak to Master Brasche on my behalf and arrange the marriage contract."

"Oh, my dear God, I don't know if I can."

"Of course you can, Grandma. You are an astute businesswoman. You don't give yourself half enough credit. Everyone in Uelzen admires you for what you've accomplished. Just think of it as another business contract like this one." He indicated the papers on the table.

"What of your father?" she asked.

"I'll tell him, of course, but for now I think it's better that they don't know that my father is—my father."

"All right, Christian, I'll do it. I'll consult with Father Borchard on the marriage contract. But I hope you won't be too disheartened if they turn us down."

"They won't. Dorike is well loved by her father and she assures me that he wants nothing but her happiness. I think she may already have spoken to him, since he volunteered to be one of my sponsors for the Bürger oath when I become a man of property."

Elizabeth hugged him. "Oh, you scheming little devil."

A few minutes later she watched with pride as he rode off on the borrowed horse.

The partnership with Master Mestwart was duly consummated. Heinike Mestwart became the other junior partner in the firm. Elizabeth deeded the house in Uelzen over to Christian along with a fine horse of his choice. A few months later both Masters Mestwart and Brasche sponsored Christian for the Bürger oath which made him a full citizen of the town of Uelzen. The betrothal ceremony took place and several months later the wedding.

It was the social event of the year. Almost all the wealthy Bürgers of Uelzen and their wives attended which therefore included the entire Town Council and the Bürgermeister. Elizabeth had insisted that Rudi and all her peasants from Veerssen be invited and made sure that their wives were all presentably dressed. She even arranged that they be allowed to stand at the back of the church to witness the ceremony, which was far from customary, the lower classes usually being obliged to hear what they could from outside. And, not to be outdone by the splendor surrounding the bride, Elizabeth invited her friends the von Eltze and others from Celle, who willingly made the journey to share in her happiness.

The marriage took place before the high altar of the great Marienkirche. Father Borchard assisted the officiating priest and Father Johann attended his son, although not one of the distinguished guests knew of their relationship. The bride was dressed in a sumptuous gown of the yellow silk that Christian had brought her from Brugge. It was low-necked, high-waisted and gold-trimmed and flowed beautifully beneath a wine-red velvet, fur-lined houppelande. Her heart-shaped headress was covered with gossamer lace, also from Brugge, into which tiny pink rosebuds had been worked. Her long blond hair hung down her back in a simple thick braid interwoven with yellow and red ribbons. It was the last time anyone but her husband would see her hair. Christian, too, was resplendent in a mustard-colored fur-trimmed, pleated tunic over tight yellow hose. A wide golden girdle circled his waist and over it all an elaborately scalloped green velvet fur-lined houppelande. Elizabeth herself felt as beautiful as the bride in her new silk gown, which seemed to change colors from blue to green as she moved. Like a peacock's tail, she thought irreverently.

As they were leaving the church, her eye caught the famous Golden Ship. Yes, she thought, today my dreams have come true. I can ask for no more. The wedding celebrations went on for three days, and everyone agreed it was an excellent match.

A little over a year later Elizabeth's first great-grandchild, Christian, Jr., was born, followed the next year by a daughter Dorike. After a few years along came another daughter, whom they named Bedeke, a feminine diminutive of Berndt, her grandfather's name.

"You each have one for yourselves," remarked Elizabeth. "This one will be mine, regardless of her name."

"All right, Grandma," agreed Christian, "but just don't spoil her."

"Not much chance of that in the few years I have left."

"Oh, Grandma, don't say that. Sometimes it seems as though you'll live forever."

"I hope not," she laughed, "but I may just outlive your father. His health has been failing lately. Which reminds me, we must talk to him again about setting up that student stipendium."

"Yes, I think that is an excellent idea and a worthy cause," agreed Christian. "I have spoken to him and he seems to think it a good idea. Even Father Borch doesn't object so strenuously anymore. Yet he does nothing. Why won't he?"

"It isn't that he won't. He is just so other-worldly that money and property mean nothing to him. And so just as soon as either of us leave him, he forgets all about it."

Christian shook his head. "I hope he's not getting senile like Father Borch."

"Now don't you say that. Borch is only a few years older than I, and I'm certainly not senile. He's just a little forgetful is all."

"Of course, Grandma. I meant no offense," he apologized. "But what can we do to get Father moving?"

"We're going to have to point out to him very forcefully that if he passes on without a will, all that property—my property that I worked so hard for—will escheat to the Church and to the Dukes. And those two wild dukes are the last ones I should want to have it."

"You're right. I never stopped to think of that. I've always thought of it as your property, which, of course, it is. But legally it's still all in his name, isn't it?"

"Every bit of it, and as it stands now, he has no heir whatever. He loves you dearly, I know. We must impress upon him that if he does nothing, you and your children will be left destitute."

"Well, hardly that, Grandma."

"But he doesn't know that. He's never had any interest in business or finance. He has no real idea of how well you have done for yourself. And until this matter of a will is settled, we're not going to tell him. We must count on the shock value of your being disinherited to wake him up."

"I suppose you're right. Very well. I'll help you pressure him as best I can."

At last, thought Elizabeth as she spread out the lengthy document before her. All the excitement was over. She sat alone at her kitchen table looking at her copy of the—what did they call it?—the foundation. The heavy parchment was covered with beautifully written Latin. Although Father Borchard had translated it for her and assured her it was all in order, she wanted to read it for herself. She only had a little Latin, but enough for her to get the gist of it.

It had all been a lot more complicated than anyone expected. They

437

had had to travel to Lüneburg to meet there with the Bishop of Verden, Johann's superior. Father Borchard had sponsored them to the Bishop— Johann as founder, Christian as petitioner, although she was named as the first heir. Then Christian and his heirs, both masculine and feminine (that had pleased her), and after their deaths all heirs in direct line of descent from Christian, both masculine and feminine equally (that had pleased her even more), were entitled to twelve marks per year as long as they maintained good character, and so forth. Then it went on to explain that the income to support this foundation was to come from her house and farms in Veerssen and all her other properties, explicitly listed. It ended with a warning under pain of excommunication, to anyone who should be tempted to misrepresent himself as an heir. And there it was: "Datum Lüneburg Anno Domini 1406 in Vigilia B. Apostolorum Simonis et Judae," and the Bishop's seal was hanging on it.

She sighed with pleasure. Her final dream had come true.

Intermezzo

The Black Death was the turning point of the Middle Ages in many ways—politically, spiritually, socially, economically. The old feudal system began to crumble and in its place throughout Europe chaos and lawlessness was the norm for almost the next hundred years.

England and France fought the Hundred Years' War, which devastated France and bankrupted England. The Italian city-states feuded more fiercely than ever amongst themselves and against the Pope, France and the Emperor. In Germany a series of arrogant and dissolute emperors from the House of Luxembourg, unable to control Italy or the popes, turned their greedy eyes toward Bohemia and Hungary, and neglected Germany almost entirely. This led, inevitably, from disrespect to disobedience among the Electors and Princes, and their power increased proportionately. When they tried to reassert their lost feudal privileges, however, the newly wealthy towns and cities, although expressly forbidden to do so under the famous Golden Bull of 1356, banded together into several leagues to defend their rights. Most of these battles ended in draws, with no one trusting anyone else, least of all the Emperor. The lesser local nobility, already on the brink of economic disaster due to the loss of manpower from the Plague, were crushed between these two powerful forces and often reverted to highway robbery, although in a few cases they swallowed their noble pride and followed their serfs into the towns to become ordinary citizens. The serfs themselves, after surviving the initial disruption of their lives by the Plague, benefited perhaps the most. Newfound freedom, taken or reluctantly granted, enabled them to wander freely about the country seeking better masters or profitable freeholds, demand higher wages and more privileges, and in many cases flee to the "free air" of the towns, there to form a new and growing artisan class.

The Papacy, too, lost the respect of everyone. The popes finally left Avignon and the control of the French king and moved back to Rome but immediately fell into the Great Schism, during which there were two and

439

sometimes three popes until the confusion was finally ended by the Council of Constance in 1414. More seriously, on a local level people began to question the Church. If the Plague was an Act of God as punishment for their sins, why were good and bad, rich and poor, Christian and Jew, young and old equally stricken? Why could the Church do nothing? And worse, why did the good priests and friars who tried to help and comfort the people die when the wealthy and dissolute bishops were spared? Moreover, more people were learning to read—and question. Wycliffe in England, Hus in Bohemia, the Waldensians in France tried to reform the Church within the old bounds. Although they were unsuccessful in their efforts, the seeds of the Reformation had been planted. From the Low Countries a low-key reform movement among lay people of the growing middle and wealthy merchant class spread rapidly across northern Germany. Pious, sincere, calling themselves Beghards and Beguines, they grouped themselves together in order to bring the Church back to the basics of Christianity—helping the poor, sick and unfortunate, educating the children, doing good works as needed. They were similar to the Third Order of St. Francis, with which some groups later merged.

The economic forces already in motion at the beginning of the fourteenth century were given tremendous impetus by the social changes left in the wake of the Plague. No longer were there the three stagnant feudal classes of people that had been the norm ever since the fall of Rome. The Church ("we pray for you"), the Knights ("we fight for you"), and the Serfs ("we work for you") were being rapidly superseded by a fourth class, the towns and their wealthy merchants. Trade and its sister Capitalism became the dominant factors in the phenomenal growth of Northern Europe.

The Duchy of Braunschweig-Lüneburg suffered in microcosm all the pangs of the dying feudal monster, but also enjoyed all the pleasures of a growing capitalistic society. The two ducal brothers, still following the ancient Salic law, divided the Duchy between them, although it was never recognized as more than one unit by the Emperors. Sometime after the successful conclusion of their War of Succession, they decided to 'punish' Lüneburg for taking the part of their enemies in the war. At the same time they held Uelzen to an exorbitant 'ransom' as the price of withdrawing their troops. Both towns suffered financially and the loss of trade dealt Uelzen a severe blow from which it never fully recovered, although it remained a power in the Hanse for another century and a half.

Celle, on the other hand, became the crown jewel of the Duchy.

Duke Berndt moved the seat of government there, although Lüneburg officially remained the capital. He favored the town and its merchants with all sorts of special privileges, most important among them the right to be the only toll station between Braunschweig and Bremen on the Aller and Weser river system. The Celle Bürgers capitalized on every one of these and soon became more powerful than the Dukes.

5

AD 1430

The hot July sun beat down on Lüdeke's back as he rode proudly beside his father, Hans von Sehnden. Lüdeke's new doublet was soaked through with sweat, but he would not have taken it off for anything. It was the first time he had ever had anything so fine — soft leather with green velvet trim. His black and yellow hose were new as well.

And the horse was new, too. New for him. The first he could call his very own. No matter that his feet did not quite reach the stirrups. They soon would. He was growing fast, so his mother said. Not fast enough for him. But it was difficult gripping the horse with one's knees. He was very tired although he would never have admitted that to his father. The journey from Sehnde had been long.

But now a new excitement took over and Lüdeke forgot all about being tired, hot and thirsty. He could see the walls of Celle in the distance. They would soon be there. And there he would begin a new kind of life altogether. He was ten years old and his parents were taking him to be fostered by the Duke of Lüneburg himself. Lüdeke considered himself very lucky that the Duchy of Braunschweig-Lüneburg had been divided in half many years ago by this man and his brother, so that now there were two Dukes, or else he would never have had this opportunity. An old family tradition, said to go back to the days of Heinrich der Löwe, had it that the von Sehnden heir was always fostered by the reigning Duke. The other boys were parcelled out amongst lesser nobility, who in turn sent their sons to Sehnde.

But Lüdeke was not the heir. He was the third son. His eldest brother, according to old Saxon custom, was promised to the Church. The second brother, the heir, had been sent to the Duke at Braunschweig two years ago. Ordinarily Lüdeke would have been sent to some other noble family for fostering, but instead he was going to the other Duke. That was why he was glad there were two dukes, although he had no concept whatever of the strange political situation this created.

Before them rode his father's herald and standard-bearer, the great banner fluttering fitfully in the slight breeze. Lüdeke wished the wind would blow it out straighter. It was very important that they be recognized. He was very proud of their arms, a star over a reversed crescent on a red field, with the ancient Saxon bison horns crowning it. He could hardly wait for the day when he was eligible to wear it on his surcoat and shield.

Immediately behind on his father's right flank rode his squire. In a few years, I'll be a squire, too, Lüdeke thought. I wonder whose. Maybe the Duke himself.

Next in line came his mother and a few of her ladies, all looking very pretty on their handsome palfreys, veils fluttering from their tall steeple headdresses. Behind them rode a troop of about twenty-five armored knights and then the servants with the baggage wagons. Very little of the baggage belonged to Lüdeke. Just his winter clothes and a few books his mother had insisted he take, since he would have to continue his studies, although from now on his primary education would be in arms, learning to be a knight. He could hardly wait to start.

Although the von Sehnden were Old Nobility, that is, of the very best blood, they were no longer very wealthy. Plagues, famines, wars and social unrest of the last century had cut into their revenues considerably. But his mother had insisted they look their very best, and to that end she and her ladies had been working for weeks sewing them all new clothes. The company might be small, but they *looked* wealthy, and that was all that counted. The von Sehnden were a proud family. And it showed as they rode up to the gates of Celle.

The herald blew on his trumpet and announced them. The bearer raised his standard so that it was clearly visible. They were acknowledged from the watchtower and the gates immediately swung open to welcome them.

To his left Lüdeke noticed some knights practicing in a large tilting yard. His excitement grew. And then they were inside the town. His eyes opened wide at the sight of the tall, richly decorated houses, at the number of well-dressed people, at the wide cobbled streets and above all he noticed how clean and neat everything was. He had never seen anything like it. Sehnde was a tiny village where more pigs than people wandered up the main street.

Ahead was the Market Square with the Rathaus on one side, looking

443

like a piece of an old keep. Although there was no market that day, the square was still filled with bustling people, for there were many shops on the ground floors of the houses. Instead of entering the square, they turned left into a large open field known as the Stechbahn. It was here that the Duke held his many tournaments. Lüdeke's imagination went wild. He hardly noticed the great Liebfrau church on its north side. In a few moments they were in the plaza facing the castle.

The great gothic hall lay on the north side of a large park surrounded by a wide moat, created by diverting the River Fuhse around it. The drawbridge lay open for it was peacetime, but they dared not cross it without permission. Their herald blew his trumpet and announced them to the watchtower. The bearer once again raised their standard.

They waited until an understeward from the castle came to welcome them and lead them across the park to the courtyard of the castle itself. How wide open and unprotected, was Lüdeke's first thought, until he realized that the great town walls enclosed both the castle and town with the same mighty fortifications and double moat. The Duke must really trust the town's people, he thought. What an innovative idea.

"You may refresh yourselves here if you wish," said the understeward curtly, indicating the well in the courtyard. But he did not pause to let them do so. He continued on into the Great Hall. "You may rest here. His Grace will hold audience after Vespers. I shall fetch you at the proper time. Then you may join him for supper afterwards."

Lüdeke's mother looked around in dismay. The hall was packed with people of all sorts—knights drinking before the fire, which was burning despite the heat outside, servants dicing in a corner, squires polishing armor and weapons, pages running to and fro or napping wherever they could find space, dogs quarreling, playing, scratching.

"Is there not a solar?" she asked as the man was about to leave them.

He turned to her in surprise. "But, of course, my lady. I did not know you were acquainted with Her Grace." She chose not to comment on this remark but glared down her nose at him. "I shall send a maid servant to take you there," he mumbled and backed off.

"What a rude man!" she exclaimed. "If he were my servant, I'd have him whipped for insolence. I hope you will learn better manners than that here, Lude."

"I'll try, Momma," he replied.

At the audience Lüdeke was disappointed to learn that he was only one of six new boys joining the ducal household, soon to become anonymous among the dozen or so other pages already there. The von Sehnden name had lost its magic, no longer a key to automatic preferment. In fact, except for the usual formalities and courtesies, Duke Berndt paid no more attention to Lüdeke's parents than to any of the other proud elders present. He was already an old man and Hans remarked later, he thought he was getting a little senile.

The von Sehndens stayed for a week of festivities, including a small tournament on the Stechbahn, which featured some very minor and incompetent knights. At the end of that time they bid their son a fond farewell, his mother openly tearful. Lüdeke tried to be brave, but he knew he would not see them again for many years, unless the Duke specifically invited them, which looked doubtful. Lüdeke would be almost a grown man before he would be permitted to leave.

At first the time sped by for Lüdeke. There were so many new things to learn. His major duties consisted of waiting on table and running errands for anyone and everyone who so demanded it of him, but mostly for the squires, some of whom were kind and tried to teach him things, and many of whom were churlish and delighted in teasing and making things difficult for him. The knights rarely spoke to him except to scold. Woe betide him if he spilled so much as a drop at table, but let one of them drunkenly vomit on him and he had to clean up the whole mess, the knight, the floor and himself. The boys slept in the hall on thin straw pallets wherever they could find space, often two to a pallet, and sometimes on the cold stone floor, if there happened to be guests with a large number of knights and their squires, who commandeered all the pallets available.

In the mornings the new pages were taught riding, in which Lüdeke already excelled, and swordplay at which he did not. He was a strong, husky boy, but he did not have the reach of some of the taller, lankier boys.

"Ach, son, you will do better when you have the weight and height of a destrier under you and a lance at your shoulder," said the armsmaster.

"Or a mace," sighed Lüdeke. The man looked at him strangely and shook his head.

In the afternoons they had lessons with the castle chaplain. Several of the boys could not even read and write. So the priest had to start with the basics, and it soon became apparent that he had no intention, or perhaps was not capable, of teaching much more than that. As a result, Lüdeke and the few other boys who already had their letters soon became bored and often skipped the classes entirely. No one seemed to notice or care. Lüdeke was glad he had brought the books his mother had insisted on and soon realized how well she had taught him.

In the good weather he would often take a book and wander out into the park, where he could read undisturbed. The only trick of not attending the lessons was not to be noticed by a squire or knight, who would then promptly find work for him to do. Sometimes he would climb up to one of the towers, where he could watch the shipping on the Aller. This fascinated him and it pleased him to let himself dream about how it would be to travel far on one of those boats. In winter it was more difficult as the great hall was crowded, noisy and stuffy.

After a few years he realized that he was nothing more than a servant. He finally admitted to himself, if no one else, that this was not the kind of life he wanted. The tournament circuit had lost its glamour. What was a knight, he asked himself, but a mindless hulk encased in a shell of steel like a turtle, trained to bash another's brains in or be bashed in turn. But his whole upbringing had led him to believe that this was the only avenue open to the son of a noble family. This, or the Church, and he wanted no part of that. He felt stifled, frustrated and, as he entered his teens, at times despondent. And there was no one to whom he could turn.

At times out of sheer boredom he would leave the castle park and wander about the town. He was not supposed to, but he soon learned that as long as he did not neglect his duties, no one cared or even missed him. He liked to look at the elaborate facades and gables of the Bürger houses. He tried to read the words carved into the beams, usually verses from the Bible but also ancient folk proverbs. He tried to imagine what the insides were like and what kinds of people lived in them. He even played guessing games with himself, assigning characters to the imaginary inhabitants based on the carved sayings. This one was extra pious, that one a jokester, this one kind and thoughtful, that one querulous and mean.

The market drew him like a magnet, as it did all children. But since he had no money, he was more interested in watching the activity, the methods of buying, selling, haggling. When a vendor was not busy, Lüdeke was sure to be there asking questions. Most of them were happy to tell him about their products, how they were raised or made, whether they were local or from far-off lands. He learned more from the vendors than from the fusty old priest at the castle, more, that is, that interested him. He became a familiar figure to the market people and many of them felt sorry for him. Because he never told them his name, they started calling him, amongst themselves, 'the little waif from the Castle'.

His favorite excursion, and this was riskier, as he had to go outside the walls of castle and town, was to an area of the Aller River bank called 'in dem Vischern'. Here were the huge granaries and warehouses of the wealthy grain merchants. Here all the goods that passed through Celle were transshipped, tolls and fees collected on each shipment. It was always a very busy place. When he could see they were not occupied, he asked questions of boatmen and longshoremen, warehousemen and wagon drivers. And he learned even more fascinating things.

There were a number of other boys there, most working, some obviously apprentices to the great merchants, others idling or merely watching the activities just as he did. Two in particular interested him, as he had occasionally seen one or the other of them in the castle courtyard. Yet he knew they were not members of the castle household. Here in dem Vischern he could not quite figure out what they were doing. They did not appear to be working, yet they studiously followed a man carrying a great tally board and did not pay attention to any of the other boys. Lüdeke longed to speak to them, yet something held him back. He felt it was beneath him. It was one thing to address obvious inferiors, such as the market people or the boatmen, but these boys had an air about them that told him that they would expect to be addressed as equals, and he was not quite ready for that.

When Lüdeke was fourteen, the old Duke fell very ill. The word was that he was dying. There had been no tournaments or other festivities at the castle for a long time. Now even their practice at arms and all other noisy activities were suspended. The knights and squires were permitted to continue their practice in the tilting field outside the town walls, but the pages were in a sort of limbo. There was very little for them to do. Servants tiptoed about and spoke in whispers. It was as if the whole castle were holding its breath until Duke Berndt passed on to his Maker.

At age fourteen the pages' formal school lessons ended and they were supposed to be appointed squires to the new knights. However, all those little ceremonies had been postponed, perhaps even forgotten, in the air of near-mourning pervading the castle. Nevertheless, one of the pages had somehow seen the list of assignments and shared the information with his fellows. When Lüdeke learned of the soon-to-be-knighted squire to whom he was to be assigned, he almost cried. The man was one of the most incompetent, least liked of the group, a surly lout. Lüdeke was appalled. Had the von Sehnden name and influence sunk that far? Obviously it had. If he had had doubts before about the knightly way of life, he was now firmly convinced it was not for him.

But what to do? He could not go home. His father would no doubt send him right back, unless he could convince him that he had prospects of another career. But what? He knew nothing but his knightly training. And his lady mother would be shocked. She was so proud. Nor could he just run away. He longed to sail away down the river on one of those boats he so loved to watch, but he knew if he ever left the castle without the ducal permission, which was obviously impossible to obtain in the present circumstances, he would be disgraced throughout the entire Duchy, if not the whole world. What to do?

The old Duke's end seemed to be drawing near. His two sons arrived from wherever they had been and remained closeted with various advisors. Or at least the elder did. He was called Otto the Lame, because he had one leg cruelly twisted by some childhood disease. But he rode a horse well despite his infirmity and seemed intelligent enough. The younger, Friedrich, seemed to confer more with priests and monks than with secular advisors.

But Lüdeke could not care less. He knew it was sinful, but he hoped the old Duke would hurry up and die so the castle would come to life again. But on the other hand, then Lüdeke would become squire to that obnoxious boor. And he dreaded that. He became more despondent than ever. And he was bored, so bored.

Then one day as he was ambling across the courtyard with a book under his arm that he had already read at least ten times, he saw a boy lounging by the well who did not belong there. At least, he was not one of the castle inhabitants. Lüdeke knew that certain prominent Bürgers often came to the castle on business and even that their wives occasionally accompanied them to social events, but the town children were rarely ever seen in the castle precincts. As he drew closer, he recognized the younger of the two boys he had observed following the man with the tally board in dem Vischern.

Inadvertently he smiled in recognition.

The boy smiled back. "Good morning."

Surprised, Lüdeke replied, "Good morning. What are you doing here?"

"I am waiting for my father. He is conferring with the heir-presumptive, Lord Otto."

"Oh. But your father is a Bürger is he not?"

"Of course. He is one of the leading Bürgers in Celle, the toll-collector."

"Oh. And he has business with the Lord-heir at a time like this?" Lüdeke tried to make his voice sound nobly arrogant at such presumptuousness on the part of a mere Bürger, but it came out sounding merely curious, which, in fact, he was.

"Of course," replied the other boy. "My father is Duke Berndt's leading advisor and is here to see that the transfer of power is as smooth as possible."

Lüdeke's mouth hung open at this revelation. "But I thought the nobles . . ."

The other boy frowned. "I know you are training to be a knight, but the truth of it is the knights know nothing but how to fight or hunt or write silly poems to silly ladies. They haven't the slightest idea how to govern wisely or do business. But my father and his friends are experts in these matters."

Lüdeke was shocked. The boy's remarks turned everything he had been taught upside down. Yet he had no reason to doubt the truth of his words. And of the whole statement, the part that cut most deeply was that he was being equated with those stupid knights and their silly ladies. It confirmed everything that had been bothering him these many months. His whole emotional turmoil boiled to the surface. Unwittingly he blurted out his denial. "I don't want to be a knight. I hate everything about it." He fought back the unmanly tears that were threatening to fill his eyes. "I would rather be, uh, just about anything else."

It was the other lad's turn to be shocked. "Really? Then what are you doing here? Why *don't* you do something else?"

Lüdeke sighed. "I have no choice. I don't know anything else."

The boy pondered this for a moment. He suddenly felt very sorry for this lad. No wonder the market people called him the little waif from the castle. He held out his hand. "I am Eggeling von Eltze. Would you like to be my friend?"

Lüdeke was so surprised, he reacted without thinking of the arbitrary line between them. He shook Eggeling's hand and replied, "Lüdeke von Sehnden. Ja, ja. I would like very much to be your friend. I—I haven't made any real friends since I've been here. They all seem so—so . . ."

"Stupid," finished Eggeling.

Lüdeke smiled. "You're right, you know."

Eggeling nodded. "Von Sehnden. That name sounds so familiar. I think my grandfather used to correspond with a family by that name, but I haven't heard it in a long time."

"And you say that yours is von Eltze. Isn't that noble?"

"The family is, but one of my ancestors, the first one to come to Celle, was disinherited because he married someone beneath him and also because he chose to work. He was the first toll-collector here for the Duke. And the funny part of it," he laughed, "is that now we are far wealthier than the other branch of the family that still lives in the old castle at Eltze. They are too proud to ask, but sometimes my father has to help them out."

"Really? And your father became so wealthy just by being the toll-collector?"

"Certainly. That is a very important position. He is also a merchant and a Bürgermeister of Celle."

"I see," said Lüdeke, but he did not really see at all. Bürgers—mere townspeople—wealthier than ancient, landed nobility? Advisors to the Duke, instead of the noble knights, however stupid, that surrounded him? And granted, most of them were stupid, trained only to fight and kill, and happy to do so. This Eggeling did seem more intelligent than any of the boys he had met at the castle. "How old are you, Eggeling?"

"Fourteen. And you?"

"The same. Can you read and write?" Here surely he could show some superiority.

"Of course, and figure, too. I have just completed my studies at the Hanse school, and in a few weeks I begin my apprenticeship in my father's business. He's already taught me a lot. I know how to write bills of lading and bills of exchange and all kinds of other things. Have you finished your schooling yet?"

Lüdeke had not the vaguest notion what these things were, but he tried to put on a brave front. "Certainly, just recently, but I found it a big waste of time. I don't think I learned any more than I knew when I first came here. My lady mother taught me well and gave me some books, but yon monk had to start with the basics, for so many of them did not even know their letters at all, and we never seemed to get beyond that."

"How sad," commiserated his new friend. "I really enjoyed learning interesting things like geography and astronomy and how cloth is made, but I'll be honest, I'm glad school is done, because I can't wait to get into the real business. My brother—his name is Lüdeke, too—is even now in there with Lord Otto and my father, so that he can learn about advising the Duke. My elder brother Tilo is already my father's factor in Bremen, and, of course, the eldest, Hildebrand, has gone into the Church, as is our Saxon custom."

"Of course. My eldest brother is studying to be a priest as well, and my second brother will be the heir to the estate, and I—I . . . " Suddenly the tears threatened to overwhelm him again. "Ach, Eggeling, how I envy you your enthusiasm for what your life will be, while I—I hate the very thought of what I must be."

Eggeling pondered this comment. "You don't really have to be a knight, you know. Many younger sons of noble families are breaking the old traditions and coming into the towns to go into trade and banking and even crafts. What would you really like to do if you had a choice? Have you ever thought about it?"

Lüdeke did not hesitate a moment. "I'd love to sail on one of those boats down the river and see what's at the end of it."

"Bremen is at the end of it and then the sea beyond that," answered Eggeling practically. "If that's what you really want to do, maybe my father could arrange it."

"Oh, I wouldn't dare. My father would be very angry. Well, maybe not my father so much, but my lady mother."

"So? You said you are not the heir. Therefore, you have no responsibility to the estate, only to yourself. Your life is your own to do with as you choose."

Lüdeke thought about this for a moment. "I suppose you are right. You know, I have been so imbued with the old traditions, I never thought to question them. Do you really think I could? Go on one of the boats, I mean?"

"I don't see why not." Eggeling was not at all sure he should have committed himself that far, but he liked this boy and felt sorry for him. Eggling promised himself to do what he could to help him. "Here come my father and brother. I don't dare ask him now. He will have many things on his mind after talking with Lord Otto—but next time I see you down in dem Vischern, I'll introduce you to him."

Lüdeke watched as Eggeling joined his father and brother, noticing they were more richly, though more soberly, dressed than any at the castle except for the mightiest nobles and the Duke himself. For the first time since the excitement—and disappointment—of his arrival four years ago, he felt himself experiencing little flashes of happiness, but he was afraid to indulge in the feeling too much for fear of more disappointment. Nevertheless, the conversation with Eggeling had revealed a whole new world to

451

him and had engendered the hope that there could be a more interesting life for him beyond the stultifying walls of the castle. For the first time he voluntarily went to the castle chapel and prayed.

A few days later a message arrived inviting him to partake of the midday meal with the von Eltze family the following Sunday.

Long before the day he carefully brushed and cleaned his only 'good' hose and doublet. He had one new blouse that his mother had sent him for the previous Christmas, which he had never worn. This was certainly the occasion for it.

At the last minute he almost got caught. One of the knights called to him, "Hey there, page. Go find my squire, wherever he is hiding, and send him to me immediately."

Lüdeke had no idea where the squire might be. It might take an hour or more to find him and he did not want to be late for the dinner. He quickly turned the errand over to a younger page and almost ran across the drawbridge. He might be in trouble when he returned, but right now he did not care. On the streets of the town he felt safe and stopped a moment to catch his breath. Then he walked briskly to the von Eltze house on Zöllnerstrasse. Now at last he would see the interior of one of these tall houses that had so stirred his imagination.

When he arrived opposite the house, he stopped for a moment to read the carving on the main beam. The beam itself was painted dark green and the incised letters were gold. It was a Bible quotation, the first verse of the first Psalm.

"Blessed is the man that walketh not in the counsel of the ungodly nor standeth in the way of sinners."

How appropriate for the toll-collector, he thought. Perhaps I was right and these carvings do reflect the people that live in the houses. He was full of excitement as he mounted the steps to the door and rang the bell that hung beside it.

A maid servant promptly answered and led him through a dark hallway toward the back of the house. "The family is enjoying the garden until dinner is ready," she informed him. "It is cooler there."

To his right he could see a larger room brightly lit by many windows facing the street. Then they passed the kitchen off to one side with a huge fireplace from which emanated mouth-watering smells. At the end of the hall a stairway with tile risers and beautifully carved balustrade led to the upper storeys. And then they were in another bright room, longer but narrower than the first, which ran across the back of the house and had windows opening on to the courtyard. It was obviously a room where the family played and relaxed. The maid opened the back door and indicated a large grape arbor under the shade of which the family was seated on various wooden benches and stools.

Eggeling ran to meet his friend. "Come, Lüdeke, you must meet my family."

Eggeling first introduced Lüdeke to his parents, then to an older woman, his grandmother, then to an ancient old lady who apparently was his father's grandmother, and lastly to his brother Lüdeke and four younger sisters, whose names he could not yet keep straight.

"We are happy to have you with us, Lüdeke," said Master von Eltze. "You know, ever since Eggeling told us about you, we have been trying to remember the old family stories. It seems the von Eltze and von Sehnden were close friends long ago, but they seem to have drifted apart in the last few generations."

"Really?" said Lüdeke. "I've never heard my father mention any von Eltze. How long ago was it?"

"Oh, at least three or four generations ago, I should guess."

"Over a hundred years ago," said Grandma.

"Much more than that," chimed in the old one they called Oma.

"No, I meant when they were last in touch with one another," said Master von Eltze.

"That's as may be," replied Grandma. "Your father handled all the correspondence, so I don't rightly know. He used to speak of them, but I don't think they ever came here. I meant it was over a hundred years ago that they were close friends."

"Yes," continued her son. "They apparently were schoolmates together and came here not long after our new Celle was founded. Our ancestor stayed to become the Duke's toll-collector, but his friend von Sehnden—I don't recall his first name—was the heir and had to return to his home. After that, I guess, they drifted apart."

"That's more or less the right of it, but there was much more to the story," said Grandma. "I had it from your grandpa. They studied together at Hildesheim and then went off to seek their fortunes, because they were both third sons. Then our Tyle fell in love with this girl in some foreign place, maybe Paris or Brugge, I don't know, and married her, and as we all know, the old people out at Eltze disinherited him and so that's why he took the Duke's offer."

"Was she French, Grandma?" asked one of the little girls.

453

"No, no. She was German through and through — good stock, as you can see by us — but not Saxon. From some place in the Rheinland, I think. I don't know what they had against her."

"And what happened to my ancestor?" asked Lüdeke, his curiosity whetted by this fascinating story.

"When they arrived here in Celle, he got word that his elder brother had died and he was the heir. So he had to go home. The two friends never intended to separate, but that was the way of it."

"That is so interesting," said Lüdeke. "I shall have to ask my father if he has heard the story."

"And that's just the end of the story," chirped Oma, caught up in the tale. "The beginning goes way, way back. I had it from my husband's great-grandfather who was our Tyle's son, so he should know."

"Then you tell it, Oma," said Eggeling's father. "I myself had never heard any more of it than that."

"Then I had best tell it, so it won't die with me. It should be passed on if you two are to be friends again." She nodded to Eggeling and Lüdeke. The old lady had lost all her teeth, so it was difficult to understand her, but everyone listened attentively. "It goes back all the way to the time of Heinrich der Löwe."

"That far?"

"Ja, ja. Maybe further, but that's all I know. It was the time of the Crusades. The von Eltze of the time was a knight at Heinrich's court and the von Sehnden — but he wasn't a von Sehnden then, I don't know what his name was — was his squire. They all went to the Holy Land together and for some act of bravery or other, Duke Heinrich knighted the squire on the field with the von Eltze as his sponsor. When they all returned safely, Heinrich awarded him the demesne of Sehnde. And they vowed then and there to be friends forever." She paused a moment to catch her breath, sure of her awed audience. "And what's more, the Duke promised them both that if ever either family needed a favor, it was theirs but to ask. And that is why, dear child," she looked pointedly at Grandma, "Duke Otto offered our Tyle the position of toll-collector, which has been our family's privilege ever since. I don't know if the von Sehnden ever sought any ducal favor or not."

Eggeling clapped his hands. "Then it was meant that we should be friends again."

"Perhaps," mumbled Oma.

"It is strange hearing my family's story for the first time from people I

454

have just met," said Lüdeke. "I thank you Meinfrau, for telling me. I really believe it is God's will that has brought us together."

Eggeling's mother smiled at his father, who merely shrugged.

Just then the maid put her head out the door. "We are about to serve dinner, Master."

The family trooped into the front parlor, which also served as a dining room. It was a large area with an ornate fireplace at one end, around which were several comfortable chairs. The real glass windows facing the street were hung with exquisite heavy lace curtains and were decorated with colorful flower boxes on the outside. On the side of the room opposite the fireplace was a small table laden with books and papers. Behind it on the wall hung shelves divided into numerous pigeonholes, which were crammed with all sorts of documents. It was obviously the Master's workplace. The dining table itself surprised Lüdeke the most, for it was a real table, not the trestle boards they put up and took down after each meal at the castle. And wonder of wonders, it was set with individual plates of pewter, not the wooden platters or hollowed out trenchers shared by every two people in more common use. And beside each plate was a spoon and one of the newfangled forks that Lüdeke had heard of but had never seen in use. He had his own eating knife at his belt, but he wondered if he was supposed to use one of these things and if so, how. Well, he would watch and see what the others did.

A succulent smoked ham was brought in, but instead of being placed in the center where everyone could hack off what they wanted, it was set before the Master, who neatly carved it into generous slices. And then he first asked the Lord's blessing before passing it around the table. Similarly a large bowl of vegetables was at the other end and Lüdeke noticed no one dove into it with their hands, but used the large spoon provided to fill their plates. Goodness, he thought to himself, no noble family I know of has such elegant manners as these.

After they enjoyed the meal, the conversation got around to Lüdeke's desire to travel on one of the riverboats.

"I can arrange for you to sail down to Bremen and back if you just want to take the trip, provided you can be excused from your duties at the castle for a few weeks," offered Master von Eltze. "However, if you're interested in an apprenticeship, you must have your father's permission."

Lüdeke looked doubtful. "I am not sure that he would give it. Not that he wouldn't want me to be happy," he hastened to add, "but he simply would not understand. And my lady mother—she would be aghast. They are so set in the old ways. It would never occur to them that knighthood is not for everyone. Nor even very honorable anymore." He sighed.

The Master shrugged. "Then there is not much I can do to help you, but the offer still stands."

"I thank you, Master von Eltze, and I shall think on it—seriously."

"You could at least ask. It wouldn't hurt," put in Eggeling. "I would."

"But . . . " Lüdeke hesitated.

"But our father is not noble," said Lüdeke von Eltze. "He is a free Bürger, not bound by all the foolish rules and regulations that bind the nobility, and the Church, too, for that matter. He is a man of the future, part of the changing times. Most of the nobility are stifled by the past but cling to the old ways because they are afraid to let go."

"Lüdeke, that is enough," chided his father Brandt sternly.

"But he is right, Master," protested Lüdeke von Sehnden. "That is just how I feel—stifled. But I should not be afraid to let go of the old ways. It's just that I'm not sure how to go about it without hurting my parents. I shall pray on it."

"An honorable attitude," agreed Master Brandt.

A few days later Lüdeke approached the Bürgermeister. "I think I should like to accept your offer of a trip on one of your boats," he said. "With His Grace so ill, no one at the castle will miss me for a week or two. They are all so bored with the waiting, they do nothing but fight and get drunk. Besides, I should like to see Bremen. I've never seen a great seaport. Then, if I like it, I shall have a strong argument for my father."

Brandt smiled and nodded. A sensible lad, he thought. "I shall arrange it."

When, after a few weeks the von Sehnden lad did not return, no one was overly concerned.

"He is enjoying Bremen," said Lüdeke von Eltze.

"But he is all alone with very little money," replied Eggeling.

"Not to worry," his brother reassured him. "He is having a great adventure, I promise you."

Their elder, Master Brandt, kept his counsel and only hoped that the von Sehnden parents would not hold him responsible had anything untoward happened to their son. At length one of his captains brought him a note. "To the estimable Master von Eltze from his humble servant Lüdeke von Sehnden. Thank you for the most enjoyable and interesting trip to Bremen. I have gone to visit my parents and shall not be back to Celle for some time."

456

But Lüdeke was doing nothing of the sort.

Lüdeke Mestwart had no qualms about leaving Uelzen. He had no regrets whatsoever. Although the town had been home to his family for untold generations and they were among its wealthiest, most powerful citizens, he hated it. His father and grandfather were eminently successful merchants and both were town councilmen. Another branch of the family had headed the powerful Shoemakers' Guild since its inception over a hundred years ago. He had been trained for and could easily have stepped into his father's business, following his older brothers, but he did not want to. He felt stifled. Perhaps that was part of the problem. There were just too many Mestwarts in Uelzen. He wanted to be himself, not just part of a huge, albeit prominent, clan.

He had always leaned toward his mother's side of the family, the Wernering. They seemed kinder, gentler, real Christians. Not like the merchants who paid ostentatious lip service to the Church and then cut one another's throats financially. She, too, had inherited wealth, but the family's origins were lost in the nebulous time of the Black Death. The wealth itself stemmed from farms and stock, and the income therefrom was tied up in a student stipendium, which he himself and his brothers had studied under. Each generation was expected to work for its own living and never touch the capital. If family history was to be believed, the wealth had originated with a woman, his great-great-grandmother Elizabeth Wiese. He vaguely remembered the old lady. She was still alive when he was a little boy, still active on her farm in the suburb of Veerssen. One thing she had told him stood out clearly in his mind: "Take care of the land and the people, and you will always have wealth."

When he had announced his decision to leave Uelzen and seek his fortune elsewhere, his mother had entrusted him with a copy of the stipendium. "Your brothers are not interested, but I know you will take care of these properties no matter where you are. This is the wealth of all the future generations."

And that was another reason Lüdeke wanted to leave Uelzen. He felt it was a bad luck town. Throughout its history it had been plagued by plagues, devastated by fire, floods and other natural disasters, and always seemed to be in the path of whatever war was currently being fought in the Duchy. And on a personal level, he thought ironically, what future generations? His dear young wife, Alhuyt, had already had two miscarriages and a stillborn child, and her health seemed to be failing. He attributed it to all

457

the illnesses brought on by the bad air in the town that lay along the swampy Ilmenau.

His grandfather Christian Wernering gave him a letter to a prominent family in Celle, the von Eltze. "I doubt there's any alive that still remember me, but I lived with them for a few years when I was very small. My grandmother, Mistress Elizabeth, took me there to escape from the plague. You'll find the air is healthier there, and I remember them as being very kind to me." He did not mention to his grandson stories of accusations of witchcraft and miraculous intercession by the Virgin because he simply did not believe them.

And so Lüdeke Mestwart packed all his belongings onto a wagon and together with two servants he and Alhuyt on fine horses set out across the vast Lüneburger Heide towards Celle.

As they crossed the magnificent bridge over the Aller and approached the Hehlentor, the northern gate of Celle, Lüdeke began to worry. Had he made the right decision coming to a strange town where he knew no one? Suppose these von Eltze no longer existed. His grandfather had not even known where they lived. Although Lüdeke carried a letter from the Cloth Merchants' Guild in Uelzen attesting to his good standing, suppose they would not admit him. He knew many towns were extremely protective of their own and would admit no strangers no matter how skilled or wealthy. And where would they sleep this night? He was leery of inns, if there even was one, and a monastery might not admit his dear wife even in their guesthouse. Lüdeke Mestwart was a born worrier.

And his wife knew it. For all her physical frailty, Alhuyt had a cheerful disposition and always tried to look on the bright side. She sometimes felt she spent half her days trying to keep her husband from worrying.

"Look, Lude," she pointed ahead. "See how pretty the town is and how clean."

"But what if . . ."

"No 'what if'," she replied. "I have a feeling we shall be very happy here."

"How can you say that when we are not even inside the gates yet? We don't even know . . ."

"Then let us ask," she interrupted. "See those two men over there. They look like some sort of officials."

Lüdeke had not even noticed the two young men standing on the quay where one of the grain boats was tied up. One had a tablet in hand and the other seemed to be inspecting the cargo. The boat's crew appeared ready to cast off as the captain waited impatiently in the stern.

"They look like they're busy," said Lüdeke hesitantly.

"Certainly not too busy to answer one question," replied his wife. "If you won't ask them, I shall."

"Very well." He bade the servants wait outside the gate with the wagon and they rode together along the quay towards the two men. As they approached, the captain handed the elder what appeared to be a bag of money and ordered his crew to cast off.

"At least you charge an honest toll," the captain called to the men on shore. "If we're lucky, we'll slip by the old Bishop in the dark of night."

"Good luck then!" The two men waved.

"Good afternoon to you, good sirs," said Lüdeke. "I can see you are busy, but we are strangers newly arrived and would ask just one question of you."

"But of course, my good man. Glad to be of help if we can."

"We seek to know if a family named von Eltze still lives here and, if so, where we might find them."

"Von Eltze. That's us," exclaimed the younger man.

Alhuyt smiled as though she already had known that this would be the case. Lüdeke looked perplexed. "But—but," he stammered, "you are too young to be those whom we seek."

"Then perhaps you seek our elder brother Hildebrand who is a priest in the Marienkirche," suggested Lüdeke von Eltze.

"No, no, not really. Not a priest. That is, I . . . "

"Then it is our father Brandt you want," stated the ever-practical Eggeling. "He is presently the Bürgermeister of Celle."

"Well, I guess, perhaps. You see . . . "

"Lude," interrupted Alhuyt, "the von Eltze that Grandpa knew would have had children and grandchildren. You cannot expect to find the very same ones."

"Yes, of course. How stupid of me. Thank you, my dear. I am afraid I am not thinking clearly. Perhaps a bit overtired from our journey."

"We are all one family," confirmed Lüdeke von Eltze. "The von Eltze have been here since Celle was founded in 1292. I am Lüdeke von Eltze and this is my brother Eggeling. And who, may I ask, seeks the von Eltze? And on what business?"

"Forgive me, my lord. I am Master Lüdeke Mestwart lately of Uelzen and this is my goodwife Mistress Alhuyt."

"No 'my lord' is necessary, Master Mestwart," corrected Lüdeke. "We

459

no longer have claim to the title, only the name. And what brings you here to Celle, business or pleasure?"

"Both, I hope. The foul air in Uelzen has been very detrimental to my wife's health, so we decided to come here and make a new start. I am a fully accredited member of the Cloth Merchants' Guild, but, of course, I would need to be accepted here."

"Then my father is the man you want to see. He is head of the Guild as well as Bürgermeister. And I believe you mentioned something about your grandfather knowing one of us?"

"Yes, I have a letter from him to the present head of the von Eltze family, who I presume is your father. He stayed with someone of your family for a short time when he was a small child, but I am sure it was too long ago for anyone to remember."

Lüdeke von Eltze laughed. "You may be surprised. Papa may be head of the family, but we have two old grandmothers who remember *everything* for hundreds of years back. So you and your goodwife must come and meet the whole family. That was our last ship of the day, so if you can wait but a few moments while we finish our business, we shall be going home directly. I am the toll-collector, you see, and Eggeling is the assistant, so who better to be the first to welcome you to Celle? Now please excuse us." He headed off to the little tollhouse standing back on the quay, while Eggeling went to fetch their horses.

Alhuyt smiled knowingly at her husband. "You see," she said, "my good feelings never betray me."

Lude shook his head. "What good luck! I can't believe it. The very family we seek, and obviously one of the most prominent in town. What will they think of us coming like beggars . . . ?"

"Oh, stop it, Lude. We are not beggars and your family is just as prominent in Uelzen. I am sure we shall be welcomed just as warmly as these two young men have done."

The von Eltze brothers returned, Lüdeke carrying three heavy money bags. He handed two up to Eggeling and mounted his own horse.

"Come follow us," he directed. "We must first stop at the Rathaus and deposit the day's tolls with the Treasurer of the Council. If Papa is still there, you shall meet him first and then we shall see if Oma remembers your grandfather."

"You are too kind," protested Lüdeke Mestwart.

"Nonsense. Celle is proud of its hospitality and we are proud of Celle. I have travelled all over the world on our family's business, and there is no place I'd rather live. I hope you will like it here, too. We only do not welcome beggars, vagabonds or thieves."

Mestwart winced and Alhuyt could scarcely keep from laughing.

At the Rathaus they learned that the Bürgermeister had left and was somewhere in town about his business.

"No matter," said Lüdeke. "He will be home soon. It is getting near suppertime."

"Then you must direct us to a guesthouse or tavern. We can meet him on the morrow. We cannot inconvenience you anymore."

"Why, we won't hear of any such thing," exclaimed Eggeling. "You are our guests for supper, and I'm sure Mama can find an extra featherbed somewhere. We have a very large house."

"But, but . . . "

"That is very kind and gracious of you," said Alhuyt, "for we are truly weary from our journey."

When they arrived at the von Eltze residence in Zöllnerstrasse, Eggeling directed the servants with the wagon to the stables in the rear while Lüdeke led their guests into the spacious home.

"Mama! Mama!" he called. "We have guests. I hope you have more than bread and cheese for supper."

"What are you talking about?" came a voice from the depths of the kitchen. "It's not Lent. Of course, we have more than bread and cheese. Which of your gluttonous friends have you dragged home with you this time? Don't their own mothers ever feed them?"

Lüdeke Mestwart and Alhuyt looked at each other, not sure whether to be embarrassed or to smile. They were not used to such frivolity between the generations.

A tall, handsome, dark-haired woman appeared in the hall. Wiping her hands on her apron, she looked for all the world like one of the servants.

"Oh!" she cried. "Oh! I beg your pardon, Master, Mistress." She drew herself up to her full height, and the annoyed expression on her face changed to one of graciousness and dignity. There was no doubt she was the chatelaine of the house. "I thought my sons had invited some of their wayward friends. I do apologize." She extended her hands in welcome.

"Mama, this is Master and Mistress Mestwart lately of Uelzen. They have decided to move here to Celle. They don't like Uelzen anymore. The air is healthier here."

"Indeed?"

"Ja," said Eggeling, who now joined them, "and their grandpa knew

461

our grandpa—or somebody anyway—and he sent them to us."

"Indeed? Then I bid you welcome to our home, Master and Mistress Mestwart. Uh, have you no baggage?"

"Oh, yes, Mama," Eggeling informed her. "A whole wagonload of household goods, trunks and whatnot, and four horses and two servants."

"I see," said Mistress von Eltze, secretly relieved that their new acquaintances were not paupers. "And have you seen to the horses and servants?"

"Of course, Mama."

"Then come. I'm sure our guests will want to refresh themselves before supper." She led the way to the cheerful room at the back of the house. Then, as a woman, she noticed what none of the men had. "Eggeling, fetch Mistress Mestwart a cup of cold water." Alhuyt, for all her cheerfulness, was near to fainting. Mistress von Eltze put her arm around the young woman to steady her. "I think a short rest before supper would not be amiss. You can lie on my daughters' bed. And perhaps a bath as well?" she suggested.

Alhuyt could only nod as she sipped the refreshing water. "I don't wish to impose. It is not seemly, since you hardly know us. And please, my name is Alhuyt and my husband is Lüdeke."

"Fie. No imposition at all. My dear girl, I trow you could not walk another step. Lüdeke! Carry Mistress Mestwart up to the girls' room. Eggeling, tell Ule to fetch up some bathwater."

Both Lüdekes jumped at her command. Lüdeke Mestwart gathered his wife in his arms and followed the mistress of the house up the stairs.

"I am sorry, my dear, I didn't realize," he whispered in her ear. "I was so nervous."

"I know," she replied. "Don't be. They are good, kind people."

After a warm bath, Alhuyt snuggled into the featherbed. She felt she had come home. Her last thought before she fell asleep was of the extraordinary family amongst whom they had found themselves. She was sure they would be very happy in Celle.

Later the Mestwarts met the rest of the von Eltze family, and after a generous repast, they settled down to get better acquainted. Brandt immediately wanted to talk business, to know how things were in Uelzen, and Lüdeke Mestwart would gladly have accommodated him, but the rest of the family would have none of it.

"Tell us about when your grandpa was here, Lüdeke," urged Eggeling. "Let's see if Grandma remembers him."

462

"I don't really know the whole of it," replied Lüdeke. "It was back in the last century when he was a little boy, probably at the time of the Black Death—I'm not sure."

"It couldn't have been that far back," said Alhuyt. "That's almost ninety years ago. No one is still alive from that time, and he's about seventy, isn't he?"

"Yes, you're right. It was probably later, but in any event, they were escaping from something, maybe one of the wars. And *his* grandmother brought him here and they lived with your family for several years until it was safe to go back to Uelzen. He has always had fond memories of your family's kindness, and that was why he was so sure you would welcome us, as you so graciously have."

"How old was he at the time?" asked Grandma.

"About five, I think."

"Gracious, no. I was just a little girl myself at that time and not yet married to a von Eltze. Oma, what say you? Does the story ring a bell?"

The old lady cackled. "Every time they want the family history, they turn to old Oma. Why doesn't someone write this all down?"

"Maybe someone will someday, but, Oma, do you remember aught of a little boy and his grandma from Uelzen?" asked her daughter-in-law. "My Cordt would have been about five then, too."

"Ja, ja, I might, but the name was not Mestwart."

"No, no," replied Lüdeke. "He is my mother's father, Christian Wernering."

"Of course, of course," chuckled Oma, as if she had known all along. "And his grandma was my dear friend Elizabeth Wiese, with whom I kept in touch until she died not long ago."

"That's right," said Lüdeke, amazed. Elizabeth had been dead over fifteen years. "So you do remember them?"

"They were from Veerssen, not Uelzen itself."

"That's right. I own that farm now—that is, as part of a family stipendium."

"Ah, so. She was a remarkable woman, Elizabeth. I was a little afraid at first when a man my husband's father had dealings with in Uelzen asked us to take them in for a while. I remember little Christian. He was such a sweet child. I didn't know he was called Wernering. I thought he was called Wiese. But my memory's not so good anymore."

"Your memory's fantastic, Oma," said Eggeling. "But tell us, Oma, why were you afraid?"

The old lady shook her head for a moment. Then she whispered, "They were not fleeing the Plague. That was long past. But you must remember the whole world was in a turmoil for many years after that terrible time. They were fleeing one of the most horrible aftermaths of the Plague." Everyone leaned forward as she dropped her voice even lower. "They were fleeing the Inquisition!" Mouths dropped open and eyes widened. "There were charges of witchcraft."

Alhuyt gasped and Lüdeke turned white. "Oh, no!" he cried. That can't be."

"Of course, it was not true," continued Oma in her normal quaky voice, now thoroughly enjoying the hold she had on her audience. "Not true at all. I told you Mistress Elizabeth was a remarkable woman. Her husband died of the Black Death, and she built that farm up from nothing into a very well paying enterprise *all by herself*. And naturally there were those that were jealous, especially because she was a woman alone. Jealousy is a terrible thing at any time, but when there exists such a nefarious thing as the Inquisition to do one's dirty work, everything runs out of control. I thank God every day that our Duke of blessed memory and my dear father-in-law and the good council of the time would not let the Inquisition come any where near Celle."

"Then what happened, Oma?"

"Oh, there were stories of a miraculous intervention by the Blessed Virgin." She laughed. "But the truth of it is that she was rescued by a band of ruffians hired by old Brandt's friend. She arrived here hooded like a monk, half-starved and scared out of her wits. I myself nursed her back to health. They brought the boy later. They lived with us three or four years, until it was safe to go back. Then she started all over again. I grew to love her dearly even though she was much older than I. A remarkable woman."

"What a fantastic story!" exclaimed Alhuyt. "Did Grandpa ever tell you any of that, Lude?"

"Not a word," he replied. "Perhaps he was too young to understand what was going on."

"And what do you know of Christian's parents, Oma?" asked Alhuyt. "That has always been somewhat of a mystery to us as well."

"Very little," replied the old dame. "I fear it was too late to save his mother from the Inquisition by the time they effected the rescue. I believe she was already dead, although the charges were equally false. That is why Elizabeth brought the boy up as her own."

"And what of his father?" asked Lüdeke.

"I know nothing, not even his name. Only that he was Elizabeth's son and he may have died young." Old Oma was astute enough to realize that Lüdeke Mestwart was a very sensitive young man, and fearing she had already told too much, no way was she going to add the stigma of illegitimacy and a priestly father to his burden.

"Then who was the Johann Wiese who wrote the Stipendium?" asked Alhuyt.

"An uncle, I believe," answered Lüdeke matter-of-factly.

"So enough of history," said Oma. "It seems as though every time you children bring a new acquaintance into the house I must delve into the old stories. Whatever happened to that young lad you brought home not long ago? Another Lüdeke, wasn't it?"

"Ja, ja, Lüdeke von Sehnden," answered Eggeling. "And it was all of four years ago, at the time of the old Duke's death. May he rest in peace." They all crossed themselves. "I remember because he and I were both fourteen at the time and now I'm eighteen."

"He went back to Sehnde, didn't he?" put in Brandt. "At any rate, we never heard any more from him."

"Well, not exactly, it seems," said Lüdeke von Eltze. "There were stories along the river."

"Oh? What kind of stories?" asked his father. "I never heard any of them."

"It was rumored that he was working the riverboats along the Weser."

"Indeed? And why not ours? If you recall, I offered him a job if his father would give permission."

"I don't know, but I suspect that he was afraid that his father would not give him permission and that you would send him back to the castle without it."

"Which I should have been obliged to do," agreed Brandt. "Is he still working there?"

"I don't think so. That was long ago."

"Then we heard that he was mixed up with that crazy Count of Hoya for a while. The one that is always feuding with the Bishop of Bremen," added Eggeling.

"Good heavens," sighed Brandt. "I'm sure his father would never have blessed that. How sad, if true, that he became an adventurer. Is he still alive, do you know?"

Eggeling did not think it was sad at all but rather envied his lost friend, but he dared not let his father know that. "I would imagine so," he

465

replied. "We did not hear any more for a couple of years, but then a few months ago—you tell it, Lüdeke."

"When I was last in Hamburg on our business," continued his brother, "the bankers there told me that he has set up a courier business from Hamburg to Milan, just like the Lombards have out of Brugge, and has made quite a success of it."

"God's holy eyeballs!" exclaimed Brandt, revising his earlier opinion. "That takes courage. A most hazardous occupation, but very lucrative, too, if one can stay alive. And he's only eighteen?"

"Yes, Father," replied Lüdeke, "and I heard that he now has two employees and two horses and has extended his route into a triangle— Milan, Brugge and back to Hamburg through Bremen."

"Unbelievable, and even more dangerous. The Lombards will not look kindly on that. Such an enterprising young man is to be admired— and cultivated. Did you meet him?"

"No, Papa, he was away on a trip when I was there, but I knew you would think that. So I left word that he should contact us."

"Quite right. We have a great need for such a service. We must convince him to include Celle in his route." Brandt shook his head. "I can't believe it. That poor little lad seemed so unsure of himself."

"He wasn't really, Papa," put in Eggeling. "I knew him best. He just needed the right opportunity."

Inadvertently Alhuyt yawned.

"Come now," said Mistress von Eltze, standing up and shaking out her skirts. "Here you are going on and on about something which couldn't interest our guests in the least, and they so tired from their journey. I, for one, am going to make up their bed and see them in it right quickly. Look ye. Oma's asleep in her chair already."

"You are right, my dear," agreed Brandt. "I apologize, Lüdeke and Alhuyt, for being so thoughtless. It's just that the young man we were discussing had interested me. I was surprised to learn my sons knew so much about him that had escaped my ears. When one is confined to the rarefied air of the Rathaus, one misses the gossip along the river and at the gates. I hope we hear from him."

"Don't count on it," said his wife. "I doubt you ever will."

"Perhaps. In any event, Lüdeke, come to my office tomorrow after you've rested well and we'll talk business. I must see you properly introduced to the Guild. And perhaps, my dear, you can find time to take Alhuyt around to look at houses. There are a number for rent until you

466

decide what to do. I have one in particular in mind . . ."

"Brandt! Tomorrow!"

"Yes, my dear."

Lüdeke and Alhuyt settled into life in Celle readily. Lüdeke was accepted into the Cloth Merchants' Guild, although not without some reluctance on the part of older members. While they were relieved that no one would have to hire him, since he was obviously not a pauper and had a goodly sum to invest in his own business, still they were leery of the potential competition. But Brandt was not head of the Guild and their own elected Bürgermeister for nothing. His smooth, statesmanlike talk soon overcame their objections. And Lüdeke himself, once he forgot his initial nervousness, convinced them that he was indeed a Master in his field and an astute businessman. They soon grew to like and trust him for he was both honest and pious, as well as shrewd, qualities they greatly admired.

The couple rented a modest but comfortable house until they could afford to build their own. It was owned as an investment in the growing town by one Anton von Wintheim, a patrician from Hannover, who came but once a year, sometimes bringing his young daughter, and the rest of the time never bothered them. Alhuyt was impressed by the great amount of open land still to be found within the walls. It was so pleasant after the crowded streets and alleys of Uelzen. Sponsored by Mistress von Eltze, Alhuyt quickly joined the social whirl. The Guild held numerous dances and parties, the Church had all kinds of festivals, and the women themselves had sewing circles and various charitable endeavors. She loved every minute of it and was very happy. Lüdeke had come out of his shell and matured, and she was happy for that, too. Now if she could only bear a living child. But it was not to be. Not yet, anyway.

Some two years later on a day in early spring, Eggeling von Eltze was standing on the quay admittedly daydreaming. It was that kind of a day. Fluffy clouds drifted across the pale blue sky carried by a warm south wind. The ice on the river had broken up a few days ago and all that remained were some clumps of gray slush rushing downstream on the swollen current. The buds on the trees were swelling, in fact the early willows on the opposite bank were already green.

His brother Lüdeke joined him. "What are you doing here staring into space when you should have been helping me at the tollhouse by the Altenceller Gate?"

467

"I didn't know you had any business today."

"We certainly did. A whole wagonload of goods came in from Braunschweig."

"Forgive me. I'll come right away."

"Never mind. I handled it myself. There was no rush really. They were so anxious to catch the first boat out. Instead they'll end up paying a week or two of storage before any of the boats are ready to leave."

"Well, you can't blame them for trying. First to market gets the best prices, while goods are still scarce. Papa's impressed that on us often enough."

The brothers stood silent for some moments savoring the sweet air, the first pleasant day of the year.

Then Eggeling asked, "Lude, what's it like to be in love?"

His brother smiled and thought for a moment. "Kind of like this spring day. A warm feeling, a refreshing feeling, a happy feeling. Why do you ask?"

"Well, you're going to wed Geseke come Easter, and I don't even have a girl. It just seemed like the kind of a day to be in love. Do you think I'll ever find someone?"

"Of course you will—and if you don't, Papa will."

"Oh, no, never that! I'll do my own choosing, and I want to marry for love, like you are."

Lüdeke put his arm around him. "Dear little brother, I hope you do. Although you're not so little anymore, are you? God's balls, I can hardly get my arm around those broad shoulders anymore. Come on, the air is starting to chill. Let's go home. These early spring days are still too short."

Arm in arm, they started along the quay, heading back into town, when Eggeling caught something out of the corner of his eye. He turned to face downriver.

"Look, Lude, is that a boat or am I seeing things?"

His brother turned. "You're right. It *is* a boat. Now what fools would be taking a chance plowing through the ice this early in the season?"

"I don't know. It's no boat I recognize."

"Nor I. Let's wait and see."

As the boat labored upstream against the current, they spied a dandified figure standing in the prow. They could see his tight, vivid parti-colored hose, a short bright green cloak over one shoulder, a square hat in the very latest fashion sporting a preposterous feather, but he was still too far away for them to see his face clearly.

"I bet the points of his shoes curl up to his knees," remarked Lüdeke.

Eggeling laughed. "And a codpiece of ermine." They both laughed. "Must be some fop heading to court, certainly not a river man."

As the boat drew nearer, it started heading into the quay. "Hi-ho," said Lüdeke, "he's waving to us. Do we know him?"

"I don't think—wait a minute." Eggeling stared hard into the fading light. "No, it can't be. Yes, I think it might be. Though he'd be a man grown now and I'm not sure I'd recognize him."

"Who in the world are you talking about?"

"I just think our old friend Lüdeke von Sehnden has finally returned."

"You're joking. Are you sure?"

"No, I'm not at all, but we'll soon find out. Let's go help them make fast since there are no dock men around."

The brothers ran to the quayside and grabbed the lines thrown to them. "Von Sehnden, is that you?" called Eggeling.

"So you *do* remember me," said the dandy as he stepped from the ship. "It is the von Eltze brothers, is it not? Eggeling and Lüdeke. I was hoping you'd be on hand when we arrived."

"Welcome back to Celle, von Sehnden," said Lüdeke, although the tone of his voice belied his words.

"I was hoping you would say 'welcome home'."

"Indeed?"

"Yes. I have decided to make my home here from now on. That is, if I am still welcome on that basis."

"Certainly you are, Lüdeke," said Eggeling. "We've often thought of you."

"You'd have been even more welcome a few years ago when my father wanted to talk business with you," said Lüdeke, unable to resist a touch of sarcasm. "Didn't you receive my message?"

"I did, and I apologize for not answering, but I wanted to prove myself first. I wanted to be able to say to him, 'I am just as able a merchant as you, and now I have the wealth to prove it'. I wanted to be able to talk to him as an equal, not as a beggar."

"You were never that, Lüdeke," Eggeling reassured him, "and you certainly seem to have done quite well for yourself, judging by your splendid clothes. But come, you must join us for supper. The rest of the family will be delighted to see you again."

"Eggeling, we must check the cargo first. Friend or no, we are still the toll-collectors."

"Of course, of course," Eggeling winked at his friend. "With my brother duty always comes before pleasure."

"Who is the owner and the captain of the ship? Do you know?" asked Lüdeke von Eltze.

"I am he," replied Lüdeke von Sehnden.

"You?" The toll-collector was obviously shocked. "And the cargo?"

"Mine as well. All of it."

"Then you have done well for yourself. Forgive me, Lüdeke, if I doubted you. I thought you were just a passenger. And the first ship in, too?" He shook his head in amazement.

"You may have heard, my friend, that I spent a great deal of time among the Lombards and in their home territory, too. I kept my ears and eyes open and was not too proud to learn from the masters of commerce. I well know the rules for making money. First to market with the best."

"And what does your cargo consist of and from where comes it?"

"Furs from Russia, silk from Cathay . . ."

"From Cathay?"

"By way of Venice and Brugge. English wool woven into superb cloth by the Flemish weavers, a few hogsheads of spices — pepper and cloves, again by way of Venice — and two tuns of the finest wine of Burgundy. If I can't sell the latter, I'll keep it for my own cellar. I know not many people's tastes here run to wine."

The von Eltze brothers' mouths hung open. "But you can't sell any of it in the market," Lüdeke informed him. "The Guild rules are very strict. No foreigners can have a stall."

"I am aware of that. This first load I intend to sell in its entirety right here on the quay to your father. He will have to be my factor until I can join the Guild."

"But that won't be so easy. You have to be a Bürger of Celle first and have sponsors."

"I intend to see to that forthwith. I'm sure it won't take very long."

"And what makes you think my father will buy your goods?"

"He will."

"Oh, Lude," put in Eggeling, "furs from Russia, silks from Cathay, spices. How can he resist?"

"It's all or nothing," said von Sehnden. "But you're right, friend

Eggeling, he won't be able to resist, because the price will be right and we'll both make money."

Amazed at the self-assuredness of this man, Lüdeke von Eltze could scarcely believe it was the same shy, insecure little boy they had once known. "You'll have to discuss that with Father," he said. "Now I'll check this magnificent cargo for toll purposes and we can be on our way. Come Eggeling."

"The horse is not part of the cargo," said von Sehnden. "She was the only passenger. I'll take her ashore now, if I may, and walk her a bit. Her legs must be pretty shaky. And I have a few personal belongings."

The personal belongings consisted of two large, heavily laden saddle-bags and a huge coffer.

"That will have to wait until you can hire a cart. Can you trust your men to guard it, and the cargo, overnight?"

"Absolutely," von Sehnden assured him.

"Then let's check the cargo right now, before — er — any of it walks ashore on its own accord."

"I told you they can be trusted."

The elder von Eltze shrugged.

While the toll-collectors were inspecting and evaluating the cargo, Lüdeke von Sehnden walked his horse, a beautiful dapple-gray mare, slowly up and down the riverside. As he was doing so, a smartly dressed young woman rode out of the town gate and onto the quay, followed at a discreet distance by a groom. Lüdeke ogled her unabashedly. Her riding gown was of the finest velvet, her cloak fur-trimmed, her wimple crisply white, and from her fashionable steeple headdress floated a veil of sheerest gauze. She kept well to the far side of the quay, but as she drew closer, he could see her face was very attractive — not quite beautiful, but very attractive indeed. He tried to catch her eye. He knew she had seen him. But she turned her horse aside and lifted her chin just a fraction.

Why you haughty bitch, he thought to himself. One day very soon you will not turn your nose up at Lüdeke von Sehnden. I'll see to that. He wondered who she was.

As if she could read his thoughts, she turned her horse around and said very audibly, "Come, Heinz, I've had enough for today. I thought the quay would be empty today, but it seems there is no escaping commerce anywhere in this town."

Lüdeke smiled to himself. Oh, I'd love to put you in your place, my beauty.

As she was leaving the quay, the von Eltze brothers came ashore. Von Sehnden was still staring after the young woman.

"That is indeed a luxury cargo you have there," commented the toll-collector. "You should do well with it, provided, that is, that my father will buy it from you."

"He will, I assure you. And if not, I am certain there are others who will gladly vie for it. And who, may I ask, is that delightful piece?" asked von Sehnden, indicating the rider who was just then approaching the town gate.

Eggeling laughed. "You mean Miss High-and-Mighty?"

"The toll will be considerable," said Lüdeke von Eltze, ignoring this exchange. "I shall figure it for you exactly in the morning. I assume you're prepared to pay."

"Of course, I am. I know about how much to expect," he replied and turned to Eggeling. "Is that her name, High-and-Mighty?"

Eggeling laughed again. "No, but we call her that because she is so — so uppity. Considers all us mortal men way beneath her. Her name is Adelheit Bünsel, only daughter of one of the wealthiest men in town. Owns more ships than anyone else. Descended on her mother's side from one of the original families of Old Celle before the new town was founded. In her opinion, that makes her better than nobility."

"Aha," said von Sehnden thoughtfully. "Just the kind I'd like to sink my teeth into."

Lüdeke von Eltze looked shocked, but Eggeling chuckled. "Go to it, man, but have a care you don't lose a few teeth in the bargain."

"Is she betrothed?"

"No, there's those that would love a piece of her father's money, but not enough to risk being stuck with her."

Von Sehnden in turn chuckled. "The sort of challenge I love. How can I meet her?"

"Not easy," replied Eggeling. "She . . ."

"Enough of this," interrupted his brother. "It's time we were on our way or we'll be late for supper. Eggeling, fetch the horses while I close up the toll house." He turned abruptly and left them. Eggeling winked at his friend and went to do as he was bid.

"We have to stop at the town hall first and leave the keys. If Papa's still in his office, you could talk to him, but it's so late I doubt he will be. Anyway, Mama will be sure to want you to stay to supper."

The three rode off into the town.

As expected, Brandt von Eltze snapped up Lüdeke's entire cargo. On top of that success, the merchants from Braunschweig offered him a premium to take their goods to Bremen, so happy were they not to have to pay a week or two storage. The local merchants were furious that he had beaten them at their own game.

Brandt smoothed the way for Lüdeke to take the Bürger oath making him a citizen of the town, but being accepted by the Cloth Merchants' Guild was another matter. The Gewandschneider, as they called themselves, were the most powerful guild in Celle. Only the Goldsmiths came anywhere near rivalling them in wealth, but in local politics they had no peers. Ever since the town received its charter from the Duke in 1301, they were prominent among the mayors and councilmen, but in the past hundred years, while the other guilds occasionally succeeded in electing some of their members to the Town Council, it was simply understood that the two Bürgermeisters were always members of the Gewandschneider. As such they became trusted advisors as well as money lenders to the Dukes. And they were not merely "cloth cutters". Among them they owned all the shipping on the Aller and Weser Rivers as well as extensive real estate in both the town and the surrounding countryside. Some years ago they had convinced the Duke to grant them exclusive rights to market or export all the produce from a three-mile radius around the town. This included not only grain and other staples, hogs and sheep, wool and flax but also a lucrative bee industry that produced the finest honey and beeswax, as well as a famous stud farm for horses. They also controlled the rich hinterland beyond Braunschweig indirectly, in that all grain and other goods coming by wagon had to be transshipped into their boats at Celle for a hefty fee, on top of which the shipper had to pay the town a toll, from which the von Eltze, in an almost hereditary privilege, received a commission. They maintained a vast trading network, overland through Augsburg to Milan, Genoa and Venice, and through their membership in the Hanse, by river and sea to all of northern Europe especially the great financial and trading center of Brugge.

Belatedly Lüdeke realized that perhaps he was not so smart after all bringing in such a rich cargo before their boats were even in the water for the season. His little coup had antagonized many of the associates, and they had no intention of rewarding what they considered his unconscionable act with membership in the Guild. Although Brandt used his best diplomacy, too many were afraid of a potential partnership between the two that might undermine their own businesses. Hinrik Bünsel was

473

one of the most vehement opponents to his membership.

Help came from an unexpected quarter. Lüdeke had been introduced to Lüdeke Mestwart at the von Eltze home, but as yet he had not gotten to know him very well. The other merchants had come to respect Mestwart's shrewd business acumen, but few of them knew him well personally, as he was usually very quiet and unassuming, rarely speaking up at all at the Guild meetings. If anything, he was more renowned for his extreme piety and generous donations to the church.

Thus they were surprised when Mestwart spoke up in von Sehnden's behalf. "I feel that von Sehnden would be an asset to our Guild. He may not be a Master or even have journeyman status in any Guild as yet, but he has certainly proven he is capable of being so called. You should be ashamed of yourselves for being jealous that his was the first boat in. Sure, we should all like to be first, but only one can be. That it happened to be a stranger this year is to his credit, not our detriment." He paused for a moment to let that sink in, but before anyone could comment he continued. "Moreover, he has established an excellent courier network that Celle has long wanted to be a part of. Do you think the Lombards would ever bother with a small town like Celle when they don't even include Hamburg and Bremen in theirs?" He held up his hand when some of them would have objected. "Yes, say what you will. Celle might be one of the wealthiest towns in the Duchy, second only to Lüneburg, and the favored Residence of the Duke, but it is still a small town. You have all been to Brugge and you know as well as I that without the sheltering wings of the Hanse, the Lombards would leave us standing out in the street." He saw heads nodding and knew he had them. "The contacts he has made can be invaluable to us, to say nothing of the courier service itself. Think how it could expedite our orders, bills of exchange and so on. And do you think for one minute that if we refuse him membership in the Guild, he will not take his business elsewhere? Of all the great cities and towns he could have settled in, he chose to become a Bürger of Celle. I, for one, say we should admit him to the Gewandschneider. If we do not, Masters and associates, we stand to lose an opportunity that may never come again. We have everything to gain." He sat down amongst the hubbub of voices vying to be heard. He had never made such a long speech in his life, but he felt strongly that they were letting their own greed cloud the case. He wiped his face with the sleeve of his gown.

He had obviously convinced a number of them because there were vehement arguments back and forth. But one voice rose above the others.

"I don't trust him," shouted Hinrik Bünsel.

"And why is that, Master Bünsel? Have you evidence of untrustworthiness?" asked Lüdeke Mestwart very quietly.

"The very day he arrived, he looked—uh—he looked lasciviously at my daughter."

The silence in the room was palpable.

"And who told you that, Master Bünsel? Were you there?" asked Mestwart.

"Why, Adelheit herself," declared Bünsel indignantly.

A great guffaw sounded from the other side of the room.

"Hinrik," said Peter Stratheman, "until your daughter starts acting like the twelve-year old child she is and stops pretending to be a sixteen-year-old young woman she is not, she will invite those kind of looks."

"Why—why . . . " sputtered Bünsel.

"We all know her," continued Stratheman, "but a stranger could easily be fooled by her airs."

Bünsel turned purple. "I have never been so insulted in my life."

Almost everyone was laughing, the younger men slapping one another on the shoulders.

"Masters! Masters!" shouted Brandt von Eltze above the uproar. "The meeting will come to order. Hinrik, I am sure no insult was intended, but if you feel so, then I apologize on behalf of the members. However, your daughter's problems are not the subject of this meeting and I believe we can answer the question of what happened quite quickly. Both my sons were with von Sehnden from the moment he set foot on the quay. Lüdeke, were any untoward looks directed toward Fräulein Bünsel?"

"None whatsoever. Of course, we all noticed her. There was no one else on the quay. But no one gave her more than the slightest glance."

"Least of all von Sehnden," added Eggeling. "He was too concerned with what toll we were going to charge on his cargo."

"Then that is settled," said Brandt. "Hinrik, I suggest your goodwife remind your child of the Ten Commandments. Slanderous exaggeration is as bad as bearing false witness."

"Hrumph," mumbled Bünsel. But he remained quiet.

"Now," continued Brandt, "is there any further discussion on the subject at hand? I believe Master Mestwart has made some very valid points, and I, for one, am ready to accept Lüdeke von Sehnden into the Gewandschneider."

There was a great deal of discussion back and forth. Mestwart had obviously convinced a number of them, but there were still several who objected.

"He has not even served an apprenticeship."

"That hardly matters when he is so obviously a successful merchant already."

"It's not fair to our own sons. He's not even the son of a merchant."

"What difference does that make?"

"Who knows anything about his background or where he comes from? We only have his word."

"He comes from a fine old family, ennobled by Heinrich der Löwe." This from Eggeling.

"Well, we certainly can't admit him as a Master."

"Granted. But as an associate."

"I say no more than a journeyman."

"Why, that's insulting to a man over twenty years old, who has already journeyed on business far more than almost any one of us. Think of the courier service."

"Yes, there's that. Couldn't we just hire him and defer membership until we see how that works out?"

"He'd never go for it. You heard Master Mestwart. We need him more than he needs us."

"Yes, I suppose you're right."

"I still don't trust him," mumbled Master Bünsel.

"Masters, Masters," said Brandt, "it is time we took a vote."

"Master Brandt, may I speak once more before we do?" asked Lüdeke Mestwart. "Masters and associates, I realize that some of your objections are valid if we were to go strictly by the rules. And those rules do serve a definite purpose in the case of seven-year-olds or fourteen-year-olds fresh out of school with no knowledge of business or the world. But I assure you Lüdeke von Sehnden has served a far more arduous and exacting apprenticeship and journey years than we expect of any of our sons—*and made a success of it*. Rules have been bent and exceptions have been made. How many of your sons have served their six months in that fish-stinking Hanse outpost at Bergen? No, you buy them out of it. I served my time there and I can't say that I blame you, but the Hanse rule is very strict and buy you did. How many of you have been to Milan or Venice and treated with the Lombards on their home ground? Von Sehnden has, and I assure you there is far more to be learned there pertinent to our type of commerce than in Bergen.

"I should like to propose this to you: Instead of sponsoring him for full membership, to which I can see too many of you still object, I ask you to bend the rules a bit and allow him probationary associate membership. I am willing to take him into my own business as an associate and be fully responsible for all his actions, personal," he glared at Bünsel, "as well as business. And at the end of one year, when he has proven himself, I shall again sponsor him for full membership, which you will then accept, or you may eject us both from the Guild." He sat down and once again wiped his brow with his sleeve.

"A most unusual and interesting proposition, Lüdeke," said Brandt. "Masters, I propose we accept Master Mestwart's offer. We have nothing to lose. He is willing to take full responsibility for this man, while those of you who still have doubts will have ample time to get to know von Sehnden better. May I see a vote?"

The vote was unanimous in favor of Mestwart's proposition, except for Hinrik Bünsel, who abstained.

Outside, Brandt and his sons together with Lüdeke Mestwart informed von Sehnden of the Guild's decision.

"I am not surprised at their objections," he sighed. "I expected it. After all, I am a stranger to most of them. They fear the competition—fear the unknown is perhaps more to the point. What they don't realize is that with my connections I can bring more new business into Celle than all of us together can handle. And, Lüdeke," he turned to Mestwart, "I am deeply honored at your confidence in me. You won't regret throwing your lot in with me. I promise you that."

"It is my pleasure," replied Mestwart. "Not to seem presumptuous, but I believe I am more far-seeing than most of them, except, of course, for Master Brandt here. I expect we shall do well together."

"I expect we shall. Thank you, Lüdeke."

"There is just one other consideration that you should be aware of," continued Mestwart. "I also accepted responsibility for your personal life. I think I don't have to say more."

Von Sehnden looked at him somewhat puzzled.

"He means stay away from Adelheit Bünsel," enjoined Eggeling.

"What! Whatever brought that into it?"

"She told her father that you looked at her in a 'lascivious' manner."

"God's balls! The scheming bitch. I'll fix her. Lascivious, indeed."

"Easy, Lüdeke, easy," warned Eggeling. "I don't think you realize that she is only twelve years old."

"What?! I don't believe it. She looks sixteen, if a day."

"She'd like to have everyone think that," replied Eggeling, "but she is nothing more than a precocious spoiled child. With a very rich father, I might add."

"Best forget her. She's nothing but trouble, which you don't need right now," said his brother.

"Agreed," said von Sehnden. "I shall keep my distance—from both her and her father. Now let's talk business."

"Lüdeke and Lüdeke," said Eggeling, "my brother and I should like to work with you. We feel that by combining our talents and know-how, as well as our resources, we can make Celle the richest town in the Duchy, and ourselves the richest Bürgers in Celle. My father agrees. What say you?"

"Great. I like it," agreed von Sehnden. "Better than cutting one another's throats. What say you, partner?"

Ever cautious, Mestwart thought for a moment. "A capital idea. Yes, I can see its merits, but we shall have to work out the details."

"Then let us retire to our house and do so," suggested Eggeling. "Perhaps Mama will have some dinner ready to sustain us."

Brandt smiled his blessing on the four young men and went back to the Rathaus.

They soon became known as the Three Lüdekes and Eggeling. And the Bürgers soon envied their success. Everyone wondered at how well they worked together, for four more disparate young men could not be found.

Lüdeke von Sehnden was the most outgoing, brash, some said, adventurous, daring, willing to take risks, but well-considered, never foolish, risks. Of somewhat more than medium height and broad-shouldered, he was very blond but not especially good-looking. Yet there was something about his blue eyes that made people think he was handsomer than he actually was. They were very expressive eyes reflecting his moods—sky blue in feigned innocence, twinkling like the river at some deviltry, or ice blue in anger. He had lost his youthful awkwardness through the years on the boats and in the saddle. As quick with the sword as with verbal reparteé, he tried hard to curb his temper during the year of probation but was not always as forgiving as he might have been. He introduced his courier service to Celle and for the first few years did most of the travelling for the group, often acting as courier himself, maintaining his valuable contacts in Italy and Flanders. Although they were all well-educated for the times, his education was perhaps the broadest, due to his extensive travels. He was always receptive to new ideas and never lost his love of books. He was the most outspoken of the group, too much so, thought some, and although paying lip service to the Church as a matter of good business and citizenship, he felt free to criticize the abuses that had crept in during the last century and was often heard discoursing on the teachings of reformers such as Wycliffe in England and Hus in Bohemia, much to the chagrin of those who still feared the Inquisition, although Celle had never, ever allowed that infamous office to function within its walls.

Lüdeke Mestwart was the most conservative of the four, extremely devout, some said excessively pious, due in part to his family background and his fear for his wife's health, but there was no doubt that he was sincerely religious. Outside of his business he devoted almost all his time, money and energy to the Church, setting up new vicaries, doing what he could to ease the lot of the poor and helpless. Of average height and slightly built, he, too, was blond, blue-eyed and the best-looking of the lot, but he paled in comparison with his more flamboyant partner. Although the warm welcome he had received in Celle had mitigated his initial shyness somewhat, he was still a very private person and still a worrier. But he never let it interfere with his business acumen, which was very shrewd. Yet he never made hasty decisions, carefully weighing all aspects of a situation before making a move. He acted as a leash, so to speak, on his more reckless partners. Still they got along very well, each complementing the other, more successful than either could have been alone. Meanwhile he bore his personal cross, praying God daily to grant him a living child.

Lüdeke von Eltze was the most serious. To the others he seemed overly concerned with rules and regulations, overly conscientious in the execution of his duties as toll-collector, and he seemed to lack a sense of humor. He considered his younger brother frivolous; Eggeling in turn considered him dour and strait-laced. He was looking forward to his impending marriage with Geseke (poor Geseke, thought Eggeling) and had hopes of becoming his father's factor in Bremen or Lüneburg. Therefore, from the beginning he took a less active role in the partnership, being more concerned with his father's business, and eventually he was to drop out entirely. In fact, the main reason he entered into it at all was because he did not feel confident that Eggeling was mature enough to handle it. Lüdeke was soon proven wrong.

Eggeling was the most enthusiastic. He was tall, dark and thin, though well built, and his piercing black eyes darted everywhere, missing nothing. His long, sallow face was not handsome but arresting. His black hair was sure to stand out among any crowd of blond Saxons. Eggeling was fascinated by politics and fully intended to follow in his father's footsteps in the local government. As a member of one of the first families of "new" Celle, Eggeling was the only native of the three and took great delight in regaling them with stories about various members of the other leading families, past and present, often ribald, sometimes sad, but always entertaining. And this knowledge was usually helpful in their business dealings with others, because outside of their little group he presented ever the aspect of the dutiful and pious son of the Bürgermeister. The family donated heavily to the Church, setting up numerous endowments and stipends over the years. His eldest brother, Hildebrand, was already a priest, but privately, Eggeling did not take his religion too seriously, often deriding or making fun of the many abuses that had crept into the Church. He was much more interested in the new "Renaissance" of art and literature, which was slowly spreading from Italy to Flanders.

During the first several years von Sehnden was away from Celle much of the time, letting Mestwart handle the local end of the business. His courier service was his first concern and soon became a boon to the other Celle merchants, who quickly realized that it gave them an edge over their competitors in placing orders and collecting their due bills. The merchants of Braunschweig, their fiercest rivals, at first refused him entrance into the town but soon realized they had more to gain by using his services. The work was not without its perils, however. The overland route through the Alps was often impassable in winter and although the times were generally peaceful, highwaymen abounded and there were still some robber-barons and unscrupulous bishops, relics of darker days, who on the pretense of collecting toll would throw a man into their dungeons, never to be heard from again.

Von Sehnden's partners were always glad to see him safely returned. Once when he arrived far later than expected, Eggeling, embracing him, said, "Where have you been? We were so worried."

"We have been offering prayers to Our Lady for your safe return," added Mestwart.

"The city of Augsburg does not like me," replied von Sehnden nonchalantly.

"Augsburg!" exclaimed Eggeling. "What happened there?"

"They arrested me by order of the Town Council, instigated, I learned later, by the Lombards."

"Whatever for? What did you do?"

"Absolutely nothing. Just passing through. I was not even soliciting new business." He wiped his brow with his sleeve. "I thought never to see the light of day again."

"But why? I don't understand."

"They feared the competition."

"But that is no crime. In fact, it makes for good business," declared Mestwart.

"Augsburg is a Hanse town," put in Lüdeke von Eltze. "There are rules . . ."

"But he already said it was the Lombards," interrupted his brother, "not the Hanse merchants. But what sort of charges could they possibly have brought against you, Lüdeke?"

"Oh, they trumped up some charges based on an obscure and ancient town ordinance about bringing a horse into town if you were not a member of the nobility—which, of course, is so much shit of the same animal," replied von Sehnden. "Thank the Good Lord and His Blessed Mother that I can talk well. Fortunately, some of the councilmen are some of our own business connections, and I pointed out to them that very few of the nobility came into town anymore, but that every merchant and most of their wives had two or three horses stabled in their very own backyards. The whole thing was ridiculous, but I had to do some fast thinking to talk my way out of it. But in the end it gave me the opportunity to point out to them the advantages of having our direct connection to northern Germany instead of the roundabout way through Burgundy to Bruges and then by sea to Bremen. I also threatened to bypass Augsburg in the future. That really shook them up. It all ended with them making profuse apologies and may have done us some good. Augsburg is one of the richest towns in Germany, and now they are well aware of us. Of course, I had to smooth some ruffled feathers when I got to Milan and promise I would not solicit any new business along their routes. They are so used to having monopolies, even the *thought* of competition scares them. Witness how they hate the Florentines."

"But won't that promise hurt us?" asked Mestwart.

"Not really, because I don't intend to keep it."

"Lüdeke!"

He snapped his fingers. "Promises to the Italians, outside of their own families, mean nothing. I know, Lüdeke. I've dealt with them for years. I shall be very circumspect. I shall not solicit, but just you see if they don't come to us of their own accord. There is nothing an Italian loves better than intrigue."

"I hope you're right."

"I am. You'll see. But enough of my adventures." He put his arm around Mestwart's shoulders. "What news of here?"

"Well, my Alhuyt is expecting another child—and I'm so worried."

"Worried? Whatever for? That is a cause for rejoicing."

"But she is so frail. If anything happened to her, ..."

"Oh, come now. They say the frailest ones are often the strongest in childbed. When is the babe to arrive?"

"Not for five or six months yet."

"God's balls, man, then get hold of yourself. If you're to worry yourself to death for six months, the poor babe will end up with no father."

Mestwart smiled. "You're a good friend, Lüdeke. You're right as usual. I've missed your blunt humor."

The year passed quickly and once again Lüdeke von Sehnden's name was put forth for full membership in the Gewandschneider Guild. This time there were no objections. The vote was unanimous in his favor, except for Hinrik Bünsel, again abstaining. Von Sehnden was duly sworn in with all the attendant solemn ceremony.

"What ails Bünsel?" asked Eggeling afterward.

"He cannot ever admit that he might be wrong," replied his brother.

"Never mind him," advised Mestwart. "This is a cause for celebration. Now we can be full partners, and, Lüdeke, there's no one I'd rather have." He put his arm around von Sehnden's shoulders. "Our association is working out well and the business has grown beyond belief."

"Thank you, Lüdeke," replied von Sehnden, "and shall I tell you how I'm going to celebrate? I am going to buy another boat. I've already placed the order at the Bremen shipyard."

"Wonderful!" exclaimed Eggeling. "Bünsel will see green."

"Good. I hope he does, because let me tell you, I fully intend to catch up to him. Give me a few years and I'll surpass him. I'll have more fully laden boats on the river than he ever dreamed of."

Mestwart looked skeptical but held his tongue. He had learned to expect the impossible from his partner. Changing the subject, Mestwart said, "Now that you are a sworn member of the Guild, you must join the Kalands' brotherhood. Our next feast will be in about two months."

"The Kalands?" replied von Sehnden. "I've heard of it but I'm not exactly sure what it is. I thought it was a religious brotherhood and you know I'm not too keen on that sort of thing."

"Not anymore it isn't," Eggeling assured him. "It's a great feast twice a year. The whole court and even the Bürgers' wives come and we have a lot of fun."

"But we still celebrate the Mass for the Dead," put in Mestwart.

"And I'm not sure I approve of the way things have changed," said Lüdeke von Eltze.

"I'm confused," enjoined von Sehnden. "How can the Mass for the Dead be fun? Enlighten me."

"Let me explain," replied the elder von Eltze. "It started some hundred or more years ago when the priests and canons of our Liebfraukirche invited the priests of all the outlying parishes to come into town—Old Celle, actually—to celebrate a Requiem Mass for the late Duke and his family. They gave them a nice meal afterwards, which most of them probably rarely had, and formed this brotherhood so that they wouldn't feel so isolated. It was a welcome break and good fellowship for them. The current Duke and later his family, always attended. They met on the first of every month, hence the name. After a while the nobles from the outlying areas felt they should be included, as it was a Mass for their liege lord and they more or less invited themselves. In response to that the Duke felt that since the Bürgers were paying for it anyway, they, too, should be invited. Gradually they did not meet so frequently, as it was a hardship for some to come so far, and eventually they moved it into the Marienkirche in town. After the Bürgers got into it, the feasts became more and more elaborate and overshadowed the Mass in importance, although I am sure there are still some devout souls who adhere to the original purpose." He glanced around the group. "Now we only meet twice a year. The Mass is still held in the church, but we have our own house in the Kalandgasse for the banquet."

"Thank you for the explanation, Lüdeke," said von Sehnden. "I'll think on it."

"Oh, you must join," urged Eggeling. "Everybody who is anybody belongs."

"And we also do many good works, such as the schools," added Mestwart.

Lüdeke von Sehnden was finally persuaded to join the Kalands' brotherhood. True to Eggeling's word, von Sehnden met many more of the important people of the town, whom he had not known before due to his frequent travelling. He became especially interested in the school, which had had its start early in the previous century as a choir school for the church in the Franciscan monastery of the Holy Cross. Under the sponsorship of and heavily endowed by the Kalands' brotherhood, it had been moved to its own building in the Kalandgasse and the curriculum broadened to meet the strict and more practical standards of the Hanse schools.

In the event, the long-anticipated banquet was not as much fun for the partners as they had hoped, although Eggeling was determined to enjoy himself no matter what the circumstances. Alhuyt had miscarried a few days before and her husband fell into a deep despair. Von Sehnden worried about him.

"Take heart, Lüdeke," he advised. "It's not the end of the world. It happens often."

"But suppose she had died. I love her so, I couldn't bear it."

"But she didn't, and she'll recover her health in no time."

"I don't know. She is so depressed. She wanted the child so badly, as much for my sake as for her own."

"There will be others. You're both very young yet."

"That's just it. I'll be afraid to go near her. I can't subject her to that again."

"That's foolishness. It's up to you to cheer her up, and what better way to show your love? Mark my words, women want children. As soon as she's able, she'll want to try again just to prove to herself that she can do it."

Mestwart looked aghast. "How do you know so much about women? You're not even married."

"No, but I know women. Anyway, if you insist on staying celibate until she's well again, I have an idea. It's time you came to came to Brugge with me for this year's settlements of accounts. You haven't been there in years and never since we've been partners."

"No, no, I couldn't, not now. I couldn't leave her."

"Ask Frau Symberg to stay with her. She'll probably heal faster without your gloomy countenance hovering about."

Mestwart smiled. "Lüdeke, you are so unsympathetic. Just wait until you are married."

"Not much chance of that for a while. I'm waiting till I'm really rich. So will you come to Brugge with me?"

"What about the business? Who will look after things if we're both away?"

"We have two other partners you know."

Mestwart shook his head. "Ja, one of them is more interested in furthering himself in his father's business than ours. And Eggeling, I don't know. He just doesn't have the experience yet."

"What about your brother Radeke? You have been training him since he arrived from Uelzen, and he had plenty of experience there."

"Perhaps. I'll think on it."

"Lüdeke, you worry too much."

"That's what Alhuyt always says, but that's just the way I am."

In the end it was Alhuyt herself who persuaded Mestwart to make the journey to Brugge with von Sehnden. She convinced him it was important for the Hanse merchants as well as the Venetians and Lombards to know that von Sehnden really had another partner.

Then Eggeling surprised them by asking to go along. "I've never been, you know, and I don't really feel like a full partner until I've learned firsthand how the settlements are handled and all that. I'm sure I have a lot to learn."

"That you will. It won't be a lark, you know," warned von Sehnden. "We work harder there than we ever do here and amid such hustle and bustle that you've never seen the likes of."

"Yes. Brugge is a fascinating city," added Mestwart. "I'm sure it has grown a lot since I was last there. It is the financial center of the world."

"I understand," replied Eggeling, "and I'll work as hard as either of you, I promise. I can't wait to see it."

"And have you heard," said von Sehnden, "that a group of merchants there have formed a stock exchange? That is something I intend to look into while we're there."

"What is that?" asked Eggeling.

"It is the buying, selling and trading of shares in other companies, ships or goods, and sharing equally in the profits."

"Hopefully," said Mestwart.

"You mean some men actually sell parts of their business to others?" asked Eggeling. "Isn't that a bit foolish?"

"Not when you need the capital," replied von Sehnden. "It's the only way to expand, to build bigger ships, to buy larger consignments of good, to have ready cash for some unique opportunity. And it spreads the risk around."

"I see," said Eggeling, although he was not sure if he did or not.

On a balmy September morning the three partners set off on their journey in von Sehnden's boat. They wanted to be in Brugge before

485

Michaelmas, an important settlement date and probably the latest the fleets from Venice and Genoa would arrive before the autumn and winter storms made the treacherous Bay of Biscay too perilous for their Mediterranean-type ships to cross. The Hanse cogs were built entirely differently to withstand the rigors of the uncertain North Sea and were more capacious as well.

The river was as calm as glass, reflecting the cerulean sky, as they drifted downstream with the current. They rarely used the sail except on the upstream trip, the crew alert with poles to fend them off of sandbars, as the water was low after the summer. On either bank prosperous peasants were cutting the last hay and already harvesting some vegetables. Apple trees hung heavy with fruit waiting only a touch of frost to ripen. Healthy-looking cattle, sheep and horses grazed in the meadows.

"Ach, it's all so peaceful," sighed Mestwart, relaxing at last.

"Ja" agreed von Sehnden, "and peace means prosperity. All that you see there is wealth, one reason why Braunschweig-Lüneburg is one of the richest duchies in Germany—and all without beating our peasants to death."

"Let us hope it stays that way," said Eggeling. "With so many wars going on around us, I often worry. How long is it now that the French and the English have been fighting? Nigh on a hundred years, methinks."

"Ja," said von Sehnden, "and our Emperor and the Pope ever at odds and the Italian states constantly fighting them both and each other as well."

"It's the Turks that worry me," put in Mestwart. "They've already conquered part of Byzantium. What will happen if no one can stop them?"

"Then we'll deal with them," replied von Sehnden cynically, "just as Venice and Genoa already do."

"But I mean what will happen for Christendom? It's frightening. The Pope wants another crusade."

"The Popes always want a crusade, but no one will go. How long has it been since Duke Philip of Burgundy and his famous Order of the Golden Fleece took their 'oath upon the pheasant'? I don't see any of them going to fight the Turks. Never mind Jason and the Argonauts. If you ask me, their Golden Fleece is the wool from England that they turn into gold."

"Lüdeke," said Mestwart shocked, "you are being sarcastic."

"No, I'm being truthful. Don't we do the same?"

"Of course, but we didn't take an oath."

Von Sehnden laughed.

"That brings a question to my mind," said Eggeling. "How does Brugge get ever wealthier and remain peaceful when the French and English war has been going on around them for so long?"

"Because the merchants won't let anything interfere with trade," replied von Sehnden. "The Duke knows who supports the most luxurious court in Europe, not his nobles of the Golden Fleece but the merchants. He has been playing one side against the other for years. He ostensibly sides with England yet refuses to let English wool be shipped to the weavers of Brugge. He is descended from the French royal house, yet he captured Jehan d'Arc and turned her over to the English to be burned. Both of these events happened about the same time—around twenty years ago—and I understand there were fierce, bloody riots in Brugge, Ghent and other Flemish towns. He almost lost everything, but he is a consummate politician and somehow talked his way out of it, and pacified the people. He has been quite circumspect since then. He knows that his 'Golden Fleece' is really trade. Except for the ban on English wool. That is why I'm carrying a load of wool, among other things."

"Wool? To Brugge?" exclaimed Mestwart. "Lüdeke, you're crazy. Why—why, that's like—like carrying herring to Bergen."

"No, it isn't. The weavers of Brugge are crying for good wool. Their own Flemish wool is quite inferior to the English, whereas what our 'Heidenschnucke' produce is every bit as good. The only reason I don't take more is that we don't have the quantity. Most of ours goes for home consumption. And remember, too, that the ban does not extend to other towns such as Antwerp, so both the merchants and weavers of Brugge are losing money."

Mestwart shook his head. "Perhaps you are right, but I still think it is a foolish gamble. What else are we carrying, may I ask?"

"Oh, the usual—mostly grain and quite a bit of our fine beeswax. The Italians will fight over that to see who can get the highest price out of the Pope. And some silver ingots from Goslar."

"Silver!" exclaimed Eggeling, surprised. "I don't understand that."

"The Venetians or Genoese will grab that," explained von Sehnden. "They ship it to their trading posts in the Levant, where silver is rare and gold is cheap. They trade the silver for gold with which to make their famous ducats, with which they will pay us a nice profit."

Eggeling nodded. "There *is* much to learn, isn't there?"

Soon they arrived at Ahlden, a small castle where they had to pay a toll.

"That doesn't seem fair," commented Eggeling. "We do all the work and they collect the money. My father and the other leaders of the Gewandschneider are trying to convince the Duke to have Celle be the only toll-station on the Aller."

Von Sehnden laughed. "You are a toll-collector and you don't think it's fair?" he chided. "For some of these little places it's their main source of income. And most of them are reasonably honest and use most of the money to maintain the bridges and roads. The main objection I have is that it slows us down."

In less than two hours they had to pay another toll at Rethem.

"Here we shall stop for supper and some sleep," announced von Sehnden.

"But it is nowhere near dark," objected Mestwart. "Why should we stop so early? At this rate we'll never get to Bremen by tomorrow evening."

"Oh, yes, we shall. By about noon, in fact."

The other two looked puzzled. "What tricks are you up to now, Lüdeke?" asked Mestwart.

"Only the same trick that almost all the Aller and Weser boatmen use," he replied. "Let me explain. A while ago we were discussing the fairness—and usefulness—of tolls. Well, there is one toll that I and most of the others refuse to pay. At Verden where the Aller joins the Weser. The Bishop there is so greedy, he is no better than the old robber-barons. Worse, I think. He not only charges a toll far higher than the agreed upon limits set by The Concurrence—of course, he is not subject to the Duke and can do as he pleases—but if anyone objects, he holds boat, cargo and boatmen prisoners."

"That's terrible," said Eggeling, "but why?"

"They say he is jealous of Celle because the Duke favors us, so he bears down even harder on Celle boats. He has announced that he will charge Celle boats double his already outrageous tolls. He is even threatening to put a chain across the river!"

"So how do you propose to avoid this avaricious bishop?" asked Mestwart.

"We have an early supper here at Rethem. The innkeeper, as well as the one at Hoya on the Weser, is quite cooperative. Then immediately to bed. We arise at midnight and under cover of darkness drift very quietly down the river past Verden. We shall be in Bremen by noon if all goes well."

"But isn't that dangerous, travelling at night?" asked Mestwart. "Suppose we hit a shoal or get stuck in one of the water meadows that line the banks in that area?"

"Fear not," von Sehnden reassured him. "My lads have done it many times. They know these rivers better than the Bishop knows his Paternoster. They could do it with their eyes closed."

The innkeeper duly woke them at midnight. The crew, who had slept on the boat, already had the steering oar muffled with rags. Silently they drifted down the river. No one spoke. As they neared Verden, they hugged the east bank closely in order to be as far as possible from any watchmen on the town walls opposite, thankful that there was no moon. Quietly, carefully, they edged past the town. Suddenly the steersman swung the boat toward the middle of the river.

Mestwart looked a question at von Sehnden, who whispered, "We are nearing the confluence of the Weser. He can feel the pull of the current. If we stayed too close to the bank, the stronger current of the larger river would push us right into it. There are also whirlpools."

As von Sehnden had predicted, they arrived in Bremen well before noon. The bustling seaport was alive with boats and ships from dozens of Hanse towns and cities.

They tied up at a quay already crowded with riverboats. Farther down the riverfront towered several of the fat, round-bottomed Hanse cogs, whose holds could carry almost twice the cargo that any Mediterranean ship was capable of.

Von Sehnden jumped ashore. "Come, Lüdeke, Eggeling, let us find our ship, meet the captain, and see about loading our cargo."

They strode down the waterfront to find their factor at the Hanse office. This worthy informed them that cargo space was booked for them aboard the 'Maria Himmelfahrt.'

"But I did not know you were bringing your two partners with you, Lüdeke," he said. "That could be a problem. As you know, passenger space is very limited."

"'Maria Himmelfahrt'," mused von Sehnden, "I know the ship well. Captain Süring, is it not?"

"Right."

"Then there's no problem at all. He is a good friend of mine and a Celle man as well." He turned to his partners. "Hans Süring is a cousin of the Sürings of Celle, by way of Lübeck, I believe. Come, let us see when we can transfer our cargo."

They found the 'Maria Himmelfahrt' tied up to the big quay. The captain was not on board, but the mate remembered Lüdeke and assured him that the captain would welcome them in his own cabin. He also told them to bring their boat alongside in about two hours to have their cargo transferred to the larger ship. As they left the ship, von Sehnden said, "Now to the market for victuals. You know, each man must bring his own food on these voyages. They only supply water, and not much of that. If we are lucky the captain may have some wine." This done they returned to their own boat and brought her alongside the 'Maria Himmelfahrt.' The unloading and loading were done by both their own men and ruffians from the town hired by the captain for just this purpose. Von Sehnden carefully supervised every step of the transfer, especially seeing that the precious beeswax and silver, which was cleverly disguised, were stowed in safe places in the hold. He double-checked the already meticulous manifest of the mate against his own.

This done and their personal gear stowed in the captain's cabin, the only cabin on the ship, von Sehnden announced, "Come now, my friends, we shall now seek out my friends here in Bremen who were so kind to me when I first ran away from Celle as a lad. On your father's very own boat, Eggeling."

Eggeling smiled. He had heard the story many times before and was, therefore, quite interested in meeting these people.

"If we are lucky they will give us a fine supper—the last *real* meal we'll have until we get to Brugge."

"Don't let those girls of the town keep you too busy tonight, lads," the mate called after them as they left the ship. "We sail right after dawn on the morning tide."

Mestwart frowned. Eggeling giggled. Von Sehnden waved back at him. "Never fear, Mate, not tonight. We have other plans. Very sober ones. We'll be back long before dawn."

When they returned to the ship later that evening, the captain was still ashore, spending his last night before sailing with his family in Bremen. They lay down on pallets in the stern cabin and were soon dead asleep, having had so little the night before. They awoke to the sounds of the ship getting under way—orders being shouted, rigging rattling, sails unfurling, hawsers being tossed ashore. Before they even got themselves together to go on deck, they could hear the water rushing past the hull, could feel the swell as the river carried them to the sea.

"A tight ship," remarked von Sehnden, "a fine captain."

When they appeared on deck, the captain, although busy giving orders to the helm and to the mate as they made their way through the heavy river traffic toward the North Sea, took time to greet them.

"Good morning and welcome aboard, Lüdeke. I hear you have brought the whole company along this time."

Von Sehnden introduced his two partners. Then they left the big, burly, red-bearded captain to his duties and strolled about the deck.

"He looks like a Viking," whispered Eggeling.

Von Sehnden laughed. "Perhaps he is. He sometimes acts like one. But what better seaman could you ask for than a Viking?"

Mestwart was more interested in the construction of the ship. "This is one of the new ones with the stern-mounted rudder. I had heard about them and was anxious to see one."

"Yes," said von Sehnden, "it is a great improvement over the old steering oar. Can you imagine how large an oar would be needed on a ship this size? And the strength it would take to maneuver it? With the rudder center-mounted one man can steer the ship very easily and far more accurately."

"But where is the helmsman?" asked Mestwart. "I don't see him."

"He is under the stern castle. A big tiller attached to the rudder comes through the hull."

"But how can he see where he's going?"

"He can't. That is why the captain or mate must give him constant orders from the poop deck."

There was only limited space for them to walk around the deck, which was piled high not only with cargo but also with cages of live chickens and even two sheep.

"It looks as though we shall eat better than I expected this trip," commented von Sehnden.

The voyage was uneventful and once they were well at sea Captain Süring occasionally had time to visit with them. One day he said, "You know, don't you, that Brugge will soon no longer be the commercial capital of the world?"

"How so?" asked von Sehnden. "Because of the ban on English wool? I feared as much."

"Only partly that," answered Süring. "The Zwin is silting up."

The three men looked at him questioningly.

"Every time we go in to that harbor," continued the Captain, "we have to be increasingly careful. We have to feel our way with *two* leadsmen on the bow. The channels are in a different place every time, what

491

channels there are left. They are trying desperately to keep it open, but it is a losing battle. I give it ten years, maybe a little more, before Brugge ceases to be a seaport."

"You're joking, surely!" exclaimed von Sehnden.

"How can that be?" asked Mestwart, worried.

"Why, that's impossible," added Eggeling. "Brugge has been the most important port in Flanders for hundreds of years."

"It is possible and it is happening," replied Süring. "We see it every trip. They don't call them the Low Countries for nothing. The sea and the rivers are more powerful than the land. The coastline is constantly changing despite all their dikes and windmills."

"Then what will happen?"

"I don't know, but my advice is go to Antwerp. Many of the foreign merchants already have. Move your office or your factor there soon, before the general exodus. The Hanse already has a house there, although they still maintain the huge one in Brugge. And I understand that some of the Italian banks have already moved there. Although the Medici stubbornly insist they will remain in Brugge. Do what you want, but I tell you Antwerp is the up-and-coming place. The Scheldt is a faster-moving river and they have a good harbor which seems to stay clear. It won't be too many more years before I, too, will refuse to even try to get into the Zwin."

"That is amazing," said von Sehnden. "We must investigate very carefully what is going on. Not that I doubt your word, Hans, but is there any possibility that the process may reverse itself and the sea clean it out again as I understand it has done before?"

"That is always a remote possibility, but such a storm that could dredge out that harbor again would be so violent it would destroy all the port facilities as well. I think it is irreversible."

"Dear Mother Mary, that is worrisome," said Mestwart. "We shall have to inquire very discreetly what the other merchants plan to do."

"God's teeth," complained Eggeling, "just when I finally get to see Brugge, it appears to be in its death throes. What luck!"

Süring clapped him on the shoulder with a huge paw. "Don't worry, lad, she's a beautiful city and she's still got a lot of life left in her. She's not Duke Philip's favorite residence for nothing. And wait till you see all the lovely ladies just eager to entertain you."

As they eased their way into the Zwin, von Sehnden could notice a slight difference from when he was last there, but Mestwart, who had not been to Brugge for several years, saw a vast difference. "Why, there is already land in what used to be part of the harbor," he exclaimed. "Unbelievable!"

It took them so long to get in, even with the aid of a local pilot, that by the time they tied up at the quay in Sluis, the actual port of Brugge, word of their arrival had spread and the quay was crowded with merchants waiting to bid on their cargo. There were also two Genoese ships and a Venetian galley as well as a Portuguese carrack in port. Each of these was also interested to see what cargo from Bremen they could load onto their own ships.

Von Sehnden and Mestwart were right in the thick of it while Eggeling carefully listened to each transaction. Factors from other Hanse merchants who had cargo on the 'Maria Himmelfahrt' also added to the hubbub.

They traded the grain for Flemish cloth, silk from the Genoese, sugar and ivory from the Portuguese and spices from everyone and the precious beeswax to the Genoese for more expensive spices. When the furor died down somewhat, von Sehnden had only left the wool and the silver ingots.

"I thought you were so sure of selling the silver to the Venetians," said Mestwart.

"I already have," he replied, "but we must go to the Medici bank to have it assayed. Can't blame them for that. They are going to pay me in gold and pearls."

"Pearls?"

"Yes indeed. Can't you just see our goodwives of Celle outbidding one another for those? I may even make a small gift to Her Grace the Duchess—that is, if my profit is good enough to warrant it."

"And the wool?"

"We sell right here in Brugge, directly to the weavers. I know we could get a higher price if we went through a middleman, but I feel sorry for these poor people. They are so desperate for work."

"So you have a heart after all," commented Mestwart succinctly.

"Ja, ja, Lüdeke, sometimes I do."

When they were at the Medici bank, they asked many astute questions about the probability of their moving to Antwerp. The Italians were equally cagey in their answers. "Our master, the great Cosimo, feels there is no problem in Bruges. We intend to stay."

But one man let slip, "We have the means to hang on till the end. Some of the others cannot afford to. That way when we are the only bank left here, we shall reap even greater profits."

"So that is the way the wind blows," said von Sehnden when they were back out on the street. "What think you, Lüdeke?"

"It seems to me," answered Mestwart, "that we should at least look into the possibility of Antwerp. But I should want to hear the opinions of the merchants as well as the bankers."

"When we were on the wharf, I did some inquiring amongst the Italians," said Eggeling.

"And what think they?"

"They all—or mostly all—think that Antwerp will soon lead Brugge as trade center of the world. Not for ten years or so, mind you. But they say it is already growing fast."

"Very interesting."

"And have you heard this," continued Eggeling, "that the Portuguese are seeking a way around Africa? Their Prince Henry supports every new exploration. That would put the Italians right out of business."

"I had heard," replied von Sehnden, "but have they found it yet?"

"Not yet, but they discover new lands and islands every year. Look at that ivory you bought. You would have had to pay twice that to the Arabs, who have to trek it across the great Sahara by caravan. From the Portuguese it comes direct from the source. And the sugar—they are already growing it themselves on the islands they have discovered."

"You are right," said Mestwart, "and I wish them every luck. I do not like having to deal with the Turks, however indirectly. But suppose there is no way around Africa. I prefer to deal with reality. Let them have the dreams. Those kinds of dreams cost a great deal of money and show no profit—at least not for many years."

"Well said, Lüdeke," agreed von Sehnden, "but it is interesting to contemplate, is it not? Spices direct from the Indies, silk from China."

They arrived at the great beautiful Cloth Hall with its massive tower indicative of the fabulous wealth of the town. It stood on one side of the large Market Square, the center of bourgeois life. On the left side of the square was the famous Wasserhalle. After they had sold their wool to the eager weavers, von Sehnden said to them, "Come, you must see this. It is unique." He led them to the Wasserhalle.

When they entered the building they could see that it was built directly over one of the many canals that laced the city. The entire ground level consisted of quays along the canal, and goods were being unloaded from the boats straight into the building.

"Amazing!" exclaimed Eggeling.

"Ja," agreed Mestwart. "I have seen it before but it always fascinates me. Your goods are protected from the weather. No cartage to a warehouse, and the market right here."

"Just so," said von Sehnden. "These Flemish have many clever ideas. They are shrewd but honest businessmen, yet also very merry and fun-loving people. I enjoy doing business with them. It will indeed be a sad day if Brugge ceases to be the wonderful city it is. Come now, I want you to meet my friends Mynherr and Mevrouw von Ruysbeck. He is one of the leading merchants and also well connected at the ducal court. If anyone can tell us what the true situation is, it is he."

"That will be good," commented Mestwart.

"And," continued von Sehnden, "he is also a good friend of the court painter, Jan van Eyck, a truly great artist. Perhaps, Eggeling, you should have your portrait painted in miniature, so in case you meet a girl that takes your fancy, you can give it to her."

Eggeling laughed. "Not yet, my friend, not yet. Let me find a girl first, then I'll think about portraits. In fact, I'll probably wait for such luxuries until I, too, am as rich as you say you're going to be."

Back in Celle, their business grew more and more prosperous, so much so that they each ran their own part of it, almost as a separate enterprise, although they still worked together.

The only shadow was that Mestwart's Alhuyt continued to miscarry. Although outwardly she remained cheerful and optimistic, it was obvious to everyone that her health was failing both from the constant physical effort as well as from the stress of the continued disappointments. He himself became morose and spent more time at his prayers and devotions, donating even more heavily to the church, although he never for a moment neglected his business.

One time while visiting Mestwart, Eggeling met a vision. At least, so he thought. She was not the most beautiful girl he had ever seen, but her cheerfulness in that house of sadness outweighed any lack of beauty. She was obviously very intelligent, which to Eggeling was very important, and decidedly straightforward and outspoken, which appealed immensely to him. Metke was there to help her mother, Frau Symberg, another merchant's wife and a skilled midwife. Eggeling fell in love and immediately started to court her.

In the New Year of 1444 both Eggeling and his brother Lüdeke von Eltze were elected to the Town Council. The local government of

Celle was far ahead of its time, almost a true democracy. Originally when the town was founded in 1292 the sole governor was a powerful vassal called a *Vogt*, or steward, appointed by the Duke and responsible only to him. In less than ten years, by 1301, the Bürgers grew strong enough to convince the Duke to grant the town a charter, which provided for, among other things, limited self-government and the right to hold various markets. It was not long before the powerful Bürgers achieved total self-government with the right to assess and collect taxes to be used solely for the town's benefit, with only a token payment to the Duke. Every Bürger, that is, every native-born male, when he reached a certain age, usually twenty-one, although there were exceptions, who could prove good character and financial responsibility, was entitled to vote. But first he must take the Bürger Oath, a sort of coming-of-age ceremony, involving in-depth questioning before the Council. Once the Oath was sworn, his name was listed in the *Bürgerbuch* for that year and he earned all the rights, privileges and responsibilities of full citizenship. Men from other towns, such as Mestwart and von Sehnden, could apply to the Council to take the Bürger Oath, but in addition to proving good character and financial responsibility, they had to be sponsored by one of the leading Bürgers and had to convince the Council that they would be assets to the town.

The government consisted of the Town Council of twelve and two Bürgermeisters, each elected for a term of one year, but eligible for reelection ad infinitum. The Council was elected by all the voting Bürgers, but the Bürgermeisters were elected by the Council. In time the powerful Gewandschneider Guild controlled most of the Council. Although members of other guilds, especially the Goldsmiths and Lace-Makers, were often members of the Council, the two Bürgermeisters could only be chosen from the sworn members of the Gewandschneider. Thus the Guild literally controlled the government of the town and, in the Bürgermeister's capacity as advisors to the Duke, also had a large say in the affairs of the entire Duchy. As prime money lenders to the Duke, as well as to other towns, counties, duchies and bishoprics, even to the Emperor, they became very powerful. As members of the Hanse, they were part of a commercial network that literally ruled northern Europe.

The election, as well as the New Year, was an occasion for celebration and the Bürgers always held a great ball in the Town Hall. Eggeling had double cause for joy—not only his election to the Council, but he and Metke had decided to become betrothed very soon and

Brandt was going to announce it at the ball.

Wünneke Bünsel and her daughter were getting dressed for the ball. Hinrik was grumpy as usual, having no desire to go dancing but knowing it was expected of him. He was a hard man to live with, but Wünneke, who was his second wife, never let him forget that it was *her* dowry that had made him one of the richest men in Celle and the owner of more boats than anyone else. She also would not let him forget that her family, the von Feuerschütten, had been nobility and more important, among the first founders of 'Old' Celle centuries before the 'New' town was laid out in 1292 by Duke Otto. To give Hinrik credit, tight-fisted though he was in his dealings with others, he was very generous with his wife and daughter—Wünneke saw to that—and Adelheit had become quite spoiled.

Until one day some four years ago when Hinrik came storming home from a Guild meeting and called Wünneke to task for letting her daughter act like a wanton instead of the child she was, for leaving him open to ridicule, for being too snobbish to bring her daughter up properly, and on and on. Wünneke suddenly realized that she had been remiss in her daughter's upbringing, having been too involved in her social activities to be aware that the child was growing up. Although Wünneke would never admit guilt, she agreed to take the matter in hand. And so she did, very firmly.

She discovered that the girl had been borrowing her fancy headdresses and other clothes in order to look more grown-up when she rode out on the town and put an immediate stop to that. When she learned that the townspeople called her 'Miss High-and-Mighty' behind her back, she was livid.

"If you wish to be worthy of your noble ancestors," she lectured, "you must first learn to act like a lady instead of a spoiled brat or, worse, a tramp."

Adelheit at first resisted the new restrictions placed upon her but soon realized that it was fun learning the graces of a true 'lady', even though the family was now mere bourgeois. It made her feel that she was truly growing up instead of just-pretend. Moreover, she had been a lonely child. Although she had several brothers, she was the only girl and had been totally ignored by her father and partially neglected by her mother. Now she gloried in the lavish attention being showered upon her and delighted in the new closeness with her mother.

"Mother, I have decided to let my hair hang loose tonight. I believe it

497

would be more attractive. What think you?" Wünneke was delighted and agreed that it would. At sixteen her daughter was of marriageable age but as yet had no suitors, in great part because of her 'high-and-mighty' reputation. Although she was not unattractive, her shimmering blond tresses were her best feature and if left loose would make her appear more the demure miss she was meant to be. Now if only she will curb her sharp tongue, thought Wünneke, and act like a gracious lady, perhaps she will meet someone tonight.

As though reading her mother's thoughts, Adelheit said, "I wonder if that Meinherr von Sehnden will be there tonight."

"Adelheit," exclaimed Wünneke, "that is one name you must not mention in this house. Do you want the roof to fall in?"

"Oh come, Mother, that was years ago, and I realize now how stupid it was of me to even mention it to Papa. I never meant to cause the man trouble. I am sure Papa realizes by now that it was just a childish thing."

Wünneke replied, "I am sure he has forgotten the source of his hatred, but hate him he does. It would be best not to speak his name around your father. If you want the truth, I think he is jealous—of his success and growing wealth."

"Jealous?" exclaimed Adelheit. "But why should he be jealous when he is already one of the richest men in Celle."

Wünneke sighed. "You do not know your father as I do. Come, let us forget this and choose our jewels for tonight."

Escorted by her parents and elder brother, Adelheit walked the short distance from her home to the Town Hall. A light but wet snow had begun to fall but she was warmly wrapped in a cloak of fine wool lined with sable. It was her first ball and she was very excited but tried not to show it.

"Why do we have to wear these old klompen to a ball? It's disgusting. We look like peasants and sound like horses," she complained as the wooden shoes rattled against the cobbled street.

"One more complaint out of you, child, and you can go back home," growled Hinrik.

"Everyone will be wearing them tonight," added Wünneke. "You wouldn't want to ruin your new silk dancing slippers in this weather. We'll change as soon as we get there. You did remember to bring them, did you not?"

"Yes, Mother, right here under my cloak."

Somewhat mollified that his wife had agreed with him in something, Hinrik said more gently, "Those silk slippers cost a pretty penny. Not many will look as pretty as you two."

As they approached the Town Hall they saw the Market Square was crowded with the more humble folk of Celle, come to watch their first families arrive in all their finery. Some had even climbed up on the house next door to peer through the windows. Before the night was over, they, too, would be dancing in the snow in the square.

The upper floor of the Town Hall on which normally the Gewandschneider displayed their wares, doubled as a ballroom or banquet hall as needed. It was brightly lit by deer horn chandeliers. A great fire was roaring in the huge fireplace. The musicians in the far corner had already struck up a lively tune and several of the young people were dancing holding hands in a circle.

Adelheit did not quite know what to do.

"Your father does not dance these fast dances," remarked Wünneke. "Come, we shall sit over here and watch what is going on for a while."

Adelheit looked crestfallen. Not with those old people, she thought.

Her mother caught the look and understood. "Well, you may wander around a bit and greet your friends. But remember, you are a lady."

"Yes, Mother. Thank you, Momma." She moved off into the crowd and suddenly realized how few friends she really had. She knew many people, of course, and nodded politely to this one and that, stopping to chat here and there with her better acquaintances. But then she thought, What do I do now?

Lüdeke von Sehnden stood near the fireplace and watched her progress through the hall. He thought he recognized her, but he wasn't sure. She looked so different from what he remembered of her. Much more attractive, he thought, with her silvery tresses falling over her green velvet gown, and decidedly unsure of herself. Could it be the same girl? he wondered. Whoever she was, he felt drawn to her, wanted to meet her.

When the round dance was over, the Mestwarts and Eggeling and Metke rejoined him. Alhuyt was obviously out of breath and had to sit down. Mestwart hovered over her solicitously.

"Are you all right, my dear?" he asked.

"I'm fine — just getting a little old, I'm afraid," she sighed wistfully.

"We can go home if you wish," he said.

"No, no, I wouldn't think of it. I'll be just fine as soon as I rest a bit," she assured him.

On the other hand, Metke's eyes were glowing. She looked as though she could dance all night and still be fresh and cheerful. Eggeling held

499

her hand tightly as if he were afraid she would fly away.

Von Sehnden regarded the two couples, his best friends, whom he loved dearly. The two faces of marriage, he thought. On the one hand so much sadness and frailty, on the other such robust happiness. I don't think I have the courage for it yet. But then he remembered the girl with the silvery gold hair. His eyes found her wandering throughout the crowd.

"By the way," he asked his friends, "who is that girl over there in the green velvet gown with the long blond hair? Is it who I think it is?"

"Why, that is Adelheit Bünsel," exclaimed Alhuyt. "Don't you remember all the trouble she caused you when she was but a child?"

"I certainly do," replied von Sehnden, "but she looks so different, I scarcely recognized her."

"Well, she has grown up finally," rejoined Alhuyt. "After that incident, her mother took her in hand, and I mean strictly. She is quite a changed person from that snippety child."

"I would meet her. Do you know her?"

"Slightly, but not well."

"I know her," interjected Metke. "We were friends in school, that is, sort of friends. She was not easy to get along with then, but I know she has changed."

"One could easily feel sorry for her," said von Sehnden. "She looks so lonely and well kind of lost."

"Now don't start going soft," warned Eggeling. "Remember, she's still Hinrik Bünsel's daughter."

"All the more of a challenge," replied von Sehnden, grinning.

"Come along, I'll introduce you," said Metke, sensing a bit of intrigue. She pulled Eggeling by the hand and von Sehnden followed to where Adelheit was standing.

"Adelheit, how lovely you look," gushed Metke. "Your gown is magnificent. I wish my father could afford such fine velvet."

"Why, thank you, Metke." Adelheit had the grace to blush, which von Sehnden found quite charming. "You look quite fine yourself. Or is it that being in love makes your eyes sparkle so?"

Metke giggled. "Perhaps. Have you no partner for this evening, Adelheit?"

"Well, no, not exactly," she stammered. "That is, just my brother." She glanced around the room and could not spy her parents, for which she was grateful. "But he doesn't seem to be about."

"Then you must meet our friend Lüdeke von Sehnden. He, too, is alone tonight, and I know he just loves to dance. Perhaps you would consent to join him in the next dance."

Adelheit was overwhelmed. Not only was she meeting him but she was being asked to dance with him. But she must remember she was a lady.

"I should be happy to accompany Meinherr von Sehnden in the next dance," she replied with as much sophistication as she could muster. "That is, if he wishes me to do so."

"By all means," replied von Sehnden, matching her tone. "I shall be delighted, although I'm afraid I'm a bit out of practice."

"Uh, so am I," she murmured.

The musicians were starting to play again, this time a slow, stately measure.

"Then this one should be just right for us." He held out his arm and she lightly placed her fingertips on his sleeve and they moved out in time to the music.

She could hardly contain her excitement. Be gracious, she could hear her mother saying.

"Why, you dance very well, Meinherr von Sehnden."

"As do you, Fraülein Bünsel. But, please, you must call me Lüdeke."

"I—uh, oh—but, Meinherr, we hardly know each other."

"I hope we shall amend that in due time. Come now, I insist."

"Very well, Mei—uh—Lüdeke." After a moment she continued in a whisper, "I should like you to call me Adelheit as well, but I'm afraid my father would not approve."

He laughed. "Then all the more reason to address you by your Christian name."

She smiled. How daring he is and, I warrant, courageous, too. How foolish I was as a child. Best not to bring that up now.

He was saying, "It is a fine name. It means 'nobility', you know."

"Yes," she acknowledged. "My mother's family was noble back—I don't know, a long time ago."

"So was—is mine, but that doesn't mean much anymore. Most of us merchants are richer than any of the nobles hereabouts, barring His Grace the Duke, and do you know it is mostly our money that supports him?"

She was shocked to hear him being so outspoken but liked his forthrightness. "Mein—Lüdeke, you must be careful when you say things like that. My father says the same thing, but he only whispers it to his closest friends."

501

"I fear no man," he said. Nor do I trust any of them, he thought. "Adelheit, someday I shall be richer than your father. Count on it."

After that they told each other about themselves. He learned that she enjoyed riding, preferred reading to sewing, and loved to help her mother with the accounts when she had the chance. This interested him.

"A woman who enjoys ciphering is a rare thing," he remarked. "Most do it only because they feel they must to be true Hanse goodwives."

She laughed. "I'm afraid you're right. My mother is very good at it, but she hates it. It takes too much time from her social life. That is why I often help her."

The dance ended then and he led her back to his friends, while the musicians gratefully quaffed their tankards of beer. He noticed her glancing about the room, almost as though she were afraid.

"Why so apprehensive, little one?" he asked.

"I—I'm not," she stammered. "It's just—just that I wouldn't want my father to see me with you. He—he . . ."

"Why ever not?" interrupted Metke. "You're a woman grown, are you not?"

"And in good company," added Alhuyt.

"Indeed, I am," replied Adelheit. "It's just that he's not very understanding."

"But you're enjoying yourself, are you not?" put in von Sehnden.

"Oh, yes!" she exclaimed. "More than I have in a long, long time."

"Then we'll not let him spoil it for you," said von Sehnden firmly, taking her hand to lead her out for the next dance.

"Not to worry," said Eggeling. "I saw your mother urging him downstairs some time ago to where they're playing chess and cards. She'll keep him there for a while."

"Yes, we women have to stick together," giggled Metke. "She'll know what to do."

Adelheit smiled her thanks and began the next dance with von Sehnden.

Toward the end of the evening, but long before most of the guests were ready to leave, Otte, Adelheit's brother, came hurrying across the ballroom. He interrupted their dance with a breathless, "Papa is coming, Adi. He wants to go home. Momma delayed him as long as she could, but he's getting cranky."

"I'm sorry," she apologized to von Sehnden.

"No problem, little one," he replied as he quickly led her back to their friends. "I'm glad we were able to enjoy as much time as we did. May I see you again?"

"I'd like to very much," she replied hesitantly, "but I don't know how . . ."

"Ride out with me. It's the New Year. Not many will be about."

"But you don't dare come to the house," she protested.

"Of course not. Meet me on the quay, where we—uh—first met," he chuckled.

She smiled. "I'd like that. At about what hour will you be there?"

"Is prime too early?"

"Oh, yes. If I don't go to Mass, Papa will surely suspect something. Tierce would be better."

"Tierce it is then. Until tomorrow." He patted her arm lightly and moved off among the crowd.

"And I'd like to invite you to dinner next Sunday," suggested Alhuyt Mestwart. "Lüdeke will be there, as always." She grinned connivingly.

"Thank you very much," replied Adelheit. "If Momma has no other plans, I'd like very much to join you."

Not to be outdone, Metke chimed in, "And you must come shopping with me next market day. It's such fun, especially if there's a boat in."

"I'd really enjoy that. I've never been allowed alone, only with Momma."

"I'm sure she'll let you now that you have friends," replied Metke cheerfully, brooking no argument.

Adelheit's happiness in her newfound friends was short-lived, however. She felt someone grab her arm. "What are you doing here?" growled Hinrik.

"Why, Papa, these are my friends," she tried to introduce them.

"Friends, hah! I know who they are. Trash, more like. And I saw that rogue touch you."

"What rogue, Papa?"

"That—that whoremonger, that reprobate—," he sputtered.

"Hinrik!" exclaimed Wünneke. "Keep a civil tongue in your head."

"And I'll thank you, goodwife, to keep a respectful tongue in yours. Come now, we're leaving. We'll discuss this at home." Whereupon he took his daughter roughly by the arm and led her toward the stairs, leaving Wünneke to follow shaking her head.

The next morning Lüdeke von Sehnden rode up and down the quay

503

hugging his warmest cloak to him. The day was cold and blustery, a sharp north wind blowing up the river, a wan sun trying to peep through the clouds to melt the night's snowfall with little success. It was long past the hour of tierce and no Adelheit. He was not too surprised. Mestwart had told him of her father's tirade the night before, but Lüdeke had hoped she might find some way of escaping his watchful eye. His disappointment gradually turned to anger. I'll best him yet, the miserable old tyrant, he said to himself. One day I'll have his daughter to wife as well as beating him in trade. It was a promise he was determined to keep.

Finally he gave up waiting and took a furious ride out into the snowy countryside, returning only in time for Alhuyt's New Year's dinner.

No one saw Adelheit for weeks. She did not come to Mestwart's for dinner. She did not go shopping with Metke. They could only surmise that her father was keeping her prisoner in her own home. This fired Lüdeke's determination to court her even more, but business was business and he must soon leave town again.

"Oyez! Oyez!" shouted the town crier as he strode through the marketplace. "Hear the horrible news. Constantinople has fallen to the Turks. Byzantium is no more. And the devil's horde is sweeping westward towards Hungary. Oyez! Oyez!"

Lüdeke von Sehnden had already heard the dire news, having brought it himself to Celle. But he mingled with the crowd, anxious to hear their reactions. The year was 1453 and all Christendom had feared the onslaught of the Turks for centuries, but this was no occupation of rural villages or wild mountain tribes that no one had ever heard of. This was the bastion of Eastern Christianity, the stronghold that everyone had thought was impregnable. And it had fallen. The city of Constantine, founder of Christianity in Europe, was in the hands of the infidel. It was cause for panic. And some did.

"Holy Mother of God, pray for us."

"What will become of us if they come here?"

"They will rape our wives and put our daughters in harems and make eunuchs of all of us."

"Oh God forbid!"

"St. Vitus, St. Gertrude, St. Elizabeth, St. Anna, pray for us, pray for us, pray for us."

Many ran into the great church to pray and light candles.

But by and large the stolid Bürgers of Celle remained calm — worried, yes, but outwardly calm as they tried to stem any panic with logic.

"They'll not get here. The Emperor is already mustering troops."

"And the Pope has called for a crusade."

"Much good that will do."

"You're no doubt right there, but I hear that the King of Hungary and even the King of Poland are already fighting them."

"Good. Let the Slavs take care of them. Save us the trouble."

"And, you know, there is good news, too. The French and English have finally ended their foolish Hundred Years' War."

"So what good is that? Now they will compete with us."

"Nay, the French never. Their king's too set against trade. Why, he taxes everything beyond reason, so that the poor people scarcely have bread on the table. And salt! Forget it."

"And England is so bankrupt from the cost of the wars, it will be a long time before they are any threat."

"Ja, but the English will come back long before the French. They are shrewd traders. And they have their wool."

"Ah, ja, their wool. Flanders needs their wool and we need the Flemish cloth. Did you hear that the English are importing some of the Flemish weavers in order to make their own cloth?"

"I did hear that, but I doubt the quality will be the same."

"Well, I, for one, am more interested in matters closer to home. Do you know that our noble Duke Friedrich the Pious is promulgating yet another set of rules to reform the Kalands? He'll soon make us all so pious that all the fun will be gone."

"Perhaps he thinks it will stop the Turks."

"I doubt it. He is too wrapped up in his own little world. Look at the new cloister he is building for the Franciscans. Holy Cross, he calls it. And inviting the Dominicans to preach in our church."

"Yes indeed, that worries me. The 'Barefoots' I can take. They do do some good. But the 'Preachers' I don't trust. They're synonymous with the Inquisition. No Duke of Lüneburg has ever allowed the Inquisition into Celle. I hope our Friedrich doesn't intend to change that policy."

"I don't think he would dare. He's more concerned with his own soul. I even heard that as soon as the new cloister is finished he plans on retiring there and letting his son Bernhard rule."

"You don't say! Maybe that will brighten things up a little."

Lüdeke von Sehnden left the Market Square, reassured that the Bürgers of Celle still had things under control. He was more elated with his own good news, which he could hardly wait to share with his partners and friends. Hinrik Bünsel had finally relented and was, no doubt reluctantly, going to allow Lüdeke to court his daughter Adelheit, if he still so desired. Did he ever so desire! During the intervening years he had seen her often, but always at public functions and strictly chaperoned by her mother or brothers. The forbidden fruit enticed him even more, but recently he was beginning to think he was a fool for ever thinking she might one day be his. He knew that she had stubbornly refused to consider any other potential suitors. She was already of spinster age, almost too late for childbearing. Which of those factors succeeded in changing her father's mind Lüdeke did not know. One day he would find out. Now all that mattered was that he was going to court her, properly and quickly.

When he had returned from his latest journey, he had received a message from Wünneke asking him to call on her. It was she who gave him the welcome news during their brief meeting. No explanations. Hinrik was not present, nor was Adelheit, but Wünneke assured him that she had her husband's permission to tell him and that her daughter still favored him.

"Should there eventually be a formal betrothal, of course, Hinrik will draw up the marriage contract with you. Meanwhile he has asked me to handle things."

"Of course."

Wünneke softened a little. "Are you still interested in her, Lüdeke? She's no longer a child, in fact, she is almost past marriageable age. But she is still my daughter and I'll not see her heart broken after pining for you all these years."

"Fear not, meine Frau, I am still interested in her. I have grown very fond of her over all these years, but forgive me if I was beginning to fear her father would never accept me."

"Well, he has, but ask me no questions. Off with you now. We'll talk again."

"May I ask her to Sunday dinner at my friends the Mestwarts'?"

"You may and I'm sure she will want to go, but I'll let her accept for herself."

Lüdeke realized he should have asked Alhuyt's permission before extending such an invitation, but he was so sure she would be as happy about his news as he was that she would not mind.

Alhuyt Mestwart was seemingly more and more frail, yet an iron will inside that tiny body apparently kept her going. But she was pregnant

506

again and this time even her friends as well as her husband were worried. Lüdeke Mestwart had done well in politics as well as business and had been serving on the Town Council for a number of years, and many expected that he would soon be elected one of the Bürgermeisters. Eggeling von Eltze had also been on and off the Council several times. He and Metke had long since married and already had three children.

Von Sehnden need not have worried about his presumptuous invitation. The Mestwarts were overjoyed at his news, as were all his friends.

"Maybe now you will join the land of the living," said Metke slyly.

"Now you must find a proper house," suggested Lüdeke Mestwart. "Not that you're not always welcome here, but . . . "

"I understand, my dear friend. In time, in time. Let me get used to the idea that I can court her openly."

Adelheit had sent him a note accepting his invitation to dinner and even suggested that they ride out together that morning. He felt as though he were flying up in the clouds.

"Come down to earth, Lude," warned Eggeling. "If old Bünsel sees how eager you are, you won't get a good marriage settlement."

"How practical you've become, Eggeling," teased von Sehnden.

"Let me tell you, my friend. Marriage and children force a man to become very practical. You'll see."

Lüdeke von Sehnden threw himself into his courtship with the same enthusiasm he had for everything else. Adelheit had matured over the years, but there was still an innocence about her that delighted him. They rode together, they danced together, they attended church together. His friends entertained them frequently. She seemed to blossom like a flower in the sun.

"You have no idea what it's like living with Papa," she once remarked.

"No, but I can imagine. But we're going to change all that," he replied. "I want to make you happy, my dear. Let us get betrothed ere long."

"Oh, Lude, do you mean it?"

"Of course, I mean it."

"Do you truly love me?"

"More than you know, my darling."

She fell into his arms and they kissed long and hungrily. He felt himself become aroused. He could not wait to have her. He just sensed that she would be good in bed, virgin though he was sure she still was.

She backed off. "Lude, you'll have to talk to Papa now, if we're to be truly betrothed."

"I'm aware of that. Don't worry, little one, it won't be as terrifying as you think. I'm sure I can handle him now."

When von Sehnden called upon her father to ask for Adelheit's hand in marriage, Hinrik was all prepared, no doubt at Wünneke's prompting. Although his manner was cool and formal, he greeted Lüdeke as cordially as was possible for that irascible man.

"Now let's get down to business. You've been wondering, no doubt, why I've finally decided to permit your courtship of my daughter."

Lüdeke agreed that he had.

"No hearts and flowers. A purely practical matter. She could have pined her heart out for you forever, for all I care. Or gone into the Beguines, as she sometimes threatened. Though what a waste that would have been. Women, bah! I don't pretend to understand them."

He paused, but Lüdeke said nothing.

"As you know, I have three sons," continued Bünsel. "One has gone into the church, as is to be expected. The second has left home—disappeared. I have no idea where he is. Even his mother does not hear from him. The third is only somewhat interested in the business, and I'm not at all sure how well he will do. Too soft. No gumption. None of them like me. I don't know where I fell short in raising them, but there it is."

Lüdeke could sense the man's perplexity at this turn of events but still made no comment, wondering where all this was leading.

"Adelheit is the only one to show any spirit, although I've tried to break her of it. Not very becoming in a female. What good is a girl child anyway, but to make a good marriage? And who would have her with that temperament? You seem to be the only one who could handle her. And I've watched you. Don't think I haven't. I didn't think you would succeed. To be perfectly honest, I didn't trust you. Your ideas are too modern, too brash. I personally prefer a conservative approach to business—and to life itself, for that matter."

Lüdeke only nodded at appropriate places during this statement, appalled at the man's old-fashioned attitude, aware nonetheless that it was the prevailing attitude of men toward women at the time.

"But you have succeeded," continued Bünsel, "and very handily, I must admit. I am convinced that you are the only one who can handle my daughter. I wish you well of her."

"My deepest thanks, Meinherr. I assure you that I love her very much."

"Love, bah! I said no hearts and flowers. Don't talk to me of love or

508

I'll think I have misjudged you. I warned you this is a purely practical matter. The question is, can you handle her?"

"I'm certain I can, Meinherr, and with ease." Annoyed though he was at the man's attitude, Lüdeke realized he had to follow his lead.

"That's better. Then that is settled. The other, more important matter is that I shall expect you to take an active part in my business, at least until my son shows some aptitude."

Lüdeke was surprised at this, not sure if it was the blessing it purported to be or not. "I thank you very kindly, Meinherr Bünsel, for your confidence in me. I shall do the best I can, but don't forget I have two other partners and a very heavy work schedule myself."

"I am aware of all that, but I am sure you can find the time. That is part of the deal of giving you my daughter. It's both or nothing."

Lüdeke bridled under this threat but resolved to remain cool. "In that case, Meinherr, I most certainly shall find the time to help you in your business and to train your son. I must ask, however, that you give me freedom to make any innovations I deem necessary."

"I appreciate your offering to train my son. As to innovations, we'll discuss those as they come along. I'm not dead yet. Whether I leave the business to you when I go or to my son, or part and part, remains to be seen. Don't count on it."

"I wouldn't think of it, Meinherr."

"All right. Now that we have all that settled, I have had a marriage contract drawn up." He drew a parchment out of his sleeve. "I hope there won't be too much haggling over this. She is my only daughter and I had always planned on dowering her generously, but in view of what we have just agreed upon, I am adding a little more to my original intentions."

Lüdeke wondered what the man's idea of generosity was. Probably a goat or maybe a cow, if he was lucky.

Hinrik read from the parchment. "'I, Hinrik Bünsel, Bürger of Celle, etc., etc., do settle upon my daughter, Adelheit, upon the occasion of her marriage to Lüdeke von Sehnden the following. Item: All the jewelry she now possesses plus a pair of gold earrings and an especially fine pearl necklace.' That latter," he interspersed, "will be generously donated by my goodwife, which she had from the girl's von Feuerschütten grandmother."

Lüdeke nodded.

"'Item: Fifty Lübecker Thalers, which I have invested with the Lüneburger Council, the income of which she is to have for life for her own personal use'."

Lüdeke's eyes opened wider. Better than he expected.

"'Item: The fine mare, which she is now accustomed to ride, together with its saddle and bridle. Item: One milch cow in calf.'"

Lüdeke smiled.

Hinrik now cracked his stern face in what Lüdeke supposed was a smile. "That was to have been her original dowry. I have now added the following: 'Item: Two of my riverboats, namely the St. Anna,' named for her, of course, 'and the Holy Spirit, on the condition that her betrothed provides captain and crew, and on the further condition that all income therefrom be equally divided between husband and wife'."

Lüdeke gasped. "You are more than generous, Meinherr. I never expected such largesse."

The older man actually chuckled. "Surprised you, didn't I? As I said, she is my only daughter. I can't have my future son-in-law be poorer than I. Wouldn't look good."

"I don't know what to say."

"Say nothing. If you can handle her, you deserve it. Glad to get the chit off my hands, if you want the truth." He consulted the parchment again. "This, then, goes on with the usual obligations on your part. You must provide her with bed and board, a household income sufficient to continue her present lifestyle, children if God wills it, etc., etc. Nothing out of the ordinary here. So, if you are agreeable to all the provisions of this contract, I shall call in witnesses in a few days and we shall sign and have done with it."

"I certainly am agreeable and again thank you for your generosity. Is Adelheit aware of all this?"

"She will be advised as soon as we sign and the betrothal takes place. And you had better purchase a suitable house as soon as possible."

"I intend to start looking forthwith, Meinherr. And when may we have the betrothal?"

"The sooner the better, I say. But you know these women. Both my goodwife and my daughter would have me drawn and quartered if we did not give them time to do all their sewing and other things they deem necessary for such an occasion. And I am sure I must provide a wedding feast."

"I'm sure, and it must be lavish, as befits our station."

Hinrik smiled again. "I see you understand. Fine then. I shall consult with Wünneke as to the most propitious date, and you have my permission to consult with Adelheit. When those two are agreed, we shall proceed with all the arrangements."

Lüdeke could scarcely believe his good fortune. To have the woman he craved and a munificent dowry besides was more than he deserved. No, that was not true. He certainly deserved it after all the years of frustration, but it was definitely more than he expected. He even felt more charitable towards Hinrik Bünsel, in fact, felt a little sorry for the man. He would never understand his high-spirited daughter, who preferred to read than sew and who loved to do accounts. She should have been the son. Lüdeke was grateful, indeed, that she was not.

He knew that she would be dying to know what had transpired at his meeting with her father, but he was not due to meet her until the morrow. He returned to the Mestwarts' home and told his dear friends the good news. They both embraced him heartily.

Lüdeke was sitting in the garden after dinner discussing all that must be done with Mestwart. He knew he should be attending to business, but his happiness and excitement at his forthcoming marriage was so great, he could not keep his mind on anything else. Suddenly the maid came into the garden with the announcement, "There is a young lady come to see you, Master von Sehnden—all alone," she added with obvious disapproval.

And directly behind her Adelheit burst from the house and flew into his waiting arms.

"What are you doing here?" he asked as he embraced her fondly.

"Oh, dearest Lude, I know I shouldn't be here uninvited and alone, but I couldn't wait to hear what transpired at your meeting with Papa. Forgive me."

"Of course I forgive you, my dear one. And everything went very well. I cannot tell you all the details until everything is signed and witnessed, but he was very cordial to me. And I shall tell you this much—the settlement will be far, far more generous than I ever expected."

"Oh, tell me, Lude," she pleaded.

"I can't. Not yet."

"Not even a little hint?"

"No, not even a little hint. You'll know soon enough. But for now there will be lots to keep you occupied. He has decided to let you and your mother set the date for the betrothal—and the wedding, too, if you wish."

She clapped her hands, "Oh, as soon as possible."

"Then you had best put aside your reading and accounts and get busy with your sewing, like it or not."

"Oh, I shall, I shall. I know exactly what my gown is going to look like. I've planned it for years. I even have a bolt of the most beautiful cloth hidden away. Papa doesn't even know. But I'll not tell you what it will be like. That will be my secret."

He laughed and gently slapped her bottom. "You presumptuous little minx. Now be off with you before your papa finds out you are here alone and cancels the whole thing. I have to start looking for a suitable house for us."

"Lude, I already know exactly the house I want."

He blinked at her. "You do?"

"Yes. It's on Zöllnerstrasse. The second house in from the corner of Poststrasse. An old widow lady owns it and she is too old to live alone and she is going to go to live with her children as soon as she sells it. It is big enough for you to use the top floor for your warehouse. It has a huge garden, stables and everything."

"Zöllnerstrasse. That's a pretty upscale neighborhood."

"Of course, it is," she replied. "Anybody who is anybody in this town lives either there or on Ritterstrasse. And I'm sure Papa made you promise to keep me in the style to which I am accustomed."

"That he did," Lüdeke agreed.

"Then let me tell you something, Master von Sehnden," she said very formally, but with a twinkle in her eye. "In a few years' time you are going to be one of the richest men in Celle. I promise you that. So we start right now with a suitable house."

Von Sehnden guffawed. "Minx," he said again. "I'll go look at it this very afternoon. Now go!"

She went.

Lüdeke Mestwart could hardly contain his laughter. "Lude, my friend, you'll have your hands full with that one."

"I hope so," replied von Sehnden.

In the event, the betrothal and wedding took place simultaneously. When von Sehnden agreed that he did not want a long betrothal, Adelheit took him at his word. She appealed to her grandfather, old Arndt von Feuerschütten, who was a crony of old Father 'what's-his-name'—she could never remember—one of the elder priests at the Marienkirche, to speak to him on her behalf.

"Most unusual," mumbled the old priest, "but not unheard of. She waited long enough for him to speak his piece, I know. I guess she deserves it. Poor child, almost a spinster, wasn't she?"

"Never mind all that," said Arndt. "Just get them married."

The betrothal ceremony was very solemn and very elaborate, with three priests officiating and most of the elite of Celle in attendance. After plighting their troth and receiving the blessing, the betrothed couple and the whole congregation trooped out onto the church porch and there were wed, as was the custom, before almost the entire populace of Celle.

The wedding feast was one of the most sumptuous ever seen in Celle. They had hired the Kalands' meeting hall for the purpose. All their friends and every member of the Gewandschneider Guild, together with their wives, were invited. Also included were many prominent members of the other guilds, notably the Goldsmiths, as well as a number of lesser Bürgers of the town. A less elaborate feast was also provided in the Market Square for the captains and crews of their boats, Lüdeke's couriers, and everyone's servants, apprentices and journeymen. The entire Town Council attended together with their wives, and the crowning glory was the brief appearance of Duke Bernhardt and his Duchess as well as his brother Otto with his wife Anna von Nassau, herself a new bride. They did not know it then, but this gracious lady was to feature prominently in all their lives for many years to come.

The ladies' gowns scintillated in every color of the rainbow and every known luxury material—silks and satins, taffetas and velvets. But Adelheit outshone them all. Her gown was of sheerest off-white velvet with an overkirtle of cloth of gold. The waist was high and the bodice cut daringly low, barely covering her nipples. The sleeves, fashionably full, hung to the floor. She shimmered as she moved. Her jewels were of gold set with topazes, which perfectly matched her gown. Even her headdress was unusual. Most of the ladies sported the popular steeple style draped with a dazzling array of veils, but hers was a huge heart-shaped affair, her silver-gold hair wound around the wire frame and interwoven with more jewels. Lüdeke wondered how she could hold her head up but never tired of watching her delectable body as she moved through the crowd in the flowing and seductive gown.

The men, too, were like peacocks in their colorful broad-shouldered, narrow-waisted doublets whose short peplums disguised nothing. Their brilliantly hued hose, many parti-colored, were so skin-tight that none of them dared have a lascivious or even a loving thought toward any of the women, as it was immediately apparent. Although some of them don't seem to care, thought Lüdeke, as he noted some of the obvious bulges among the company. All the men wore fancy caps of various styles, most with ribbons or tassels hanging down and some with feathers so long they

513

would tickle one's nose if one were to venture anywhere near them. And they seemed to be trying to outdo one another in the length of their pointy shoes. Some were so ridiculously long that they curled up and had to be tied to the owner's knees to avoid his tripping over them.

The older generation to be sure still generally wore the traditional gowns they had worn for many centuries, which hardly differentiated between men and women. Nothing perhaps was more indicative of the changing times than this outburst of color, luxury and even frivolity in clothing styles. The world was changing rapidly, culturally as well as geographically. It was an exciting century to be alive.

Lüdeke, however, did not intend to wax philosophical. He was too busy enjoying himself, eating and drinking of the lavish feast, dancing with his beautiful bride, noting with pleasure the adoration in her eyes, wondering how soon they could tactfully leave the festivities and he could bed her down in their new home. Obviously not for a while yet. He mingled with the crowd as the Duke himself led Adelheit in the dance. No one could leave while the ducal party was still in attendance.

There was only one niggling disappointment which Lüdeke had shared with no one. He tried to put it to the back of his mind but it would not stay there. He had sent an invitation to his family at Sehnde in the hopes that his father had finally forgiven his defection. But he had heard not a word, not even a blunt refusal. So be it, he told himself. If that's the way they want it, so be it.

"Why so glum? You are supposed to be the radiant bridegroom." Anna von Nassau took his arm. "Come dance with me. My husband seems to be otherwise occupied with a charming but very pregnant lady."

He looked beyond her. "Alhuyt. That is Mistress Mestwart. My partner and dearest friend's wife. A charming lady indeed."

"Then he is perfectly safe," she joked.

"Quite safe." He laughed and led her into the dance.

"Now tell me what was troubling you a moment ago," she asked.

"Nothing really, Your Grace."

"Oh, come now. I could see it cross your face in an unguarded moment when you thought no one was watching you. Something like that is best shared so it won't spoil your happiness. I won't tell a soul."

"Well," he said hesitantly, "it's just that I have been estranged from my family for many years. They are noble and have never forgiven me for choosing to become a merchant. I sent them an invitation, hoping—but I guess it was not to be."

"A very common story," she sighed. " 'Town air is free air' not only for the peasants, but for many, many a noble younger son. Unfortunately, all too many of the older families cannot understand that their way of life is becoming antiquated, is losing its importance in the scheme of things. But look around you, look at all the wonderful friends you have all sharing your joy on this happiest of days. They are worth more than gold — or long-lost families, nay?"

"You are absolutely right, Your Grace, and I apologize . . . "

"No apologies necessary. I have a good ear and I hope I shall always be ready to listen when someone needs that ear. In fact, I see a great need for that sort of thing in this town. After you and your bride have had a chance to enjoy one another and have settled down, perhaps you and Master Mest-wart would like to hear some of my ideas. I have a great many of them."

"I should be happy to do so, Your Grace."

The dance had just ended and he was leading her back to her husband when she stopped and looked toward the entrance. "If I am not mistaken, Master von Sehnden, your wish is about to be granted. A strange gentleman has just arrived who looks suspiciously like you."

He followed her glance. The man was obviously a gentleman, although his old-fashioned clothes had seen better days. And he looked very much like Lüdeke. He dropped her arm.

"Franz! Excuse me, Your Grace. It *is* my brother."

"I told you. Now go. I can find my husband by myself."

He rushed over to the man who was standing by the door looking a bit bewildered.

"Franz!" He embraced his brother. "So you came after all."

"Lude!" Franz hugged him in turn. "Ja, I came. I had to. It wouldn't have been right without someone from the family here. But I almost didn't. Father is still adamant. But I arose in the middle of the night and have been riding ever since. That is why I am so late. I'm sorry I missed the wedding. I should like to have witnessed it. You *are* married, aren't you?"

"Yes indeed, about two hours ago. Come, you must meet my bride. She is the most wonderful woman I could ever hope to find."

Franz was duly impressed by Adelheit, who turned on all her considerable charm. "I am so glad you were able to come," she cooed. "Lüdeke was so disappointed when he heard nothing from his family."

I never mentioned a word about it to her, thought Lüdeke. Perhaps she is even more discerning than I realized. Ah, my wonderful wife.

Together they introduced Franz to her family and all their friends

515

and finally, when an opportune moment arose, to the Duke and Duchess.

"Ah, yes, von Sehnden. I knew there had to be a fief somewhere. Lüdeke wouldn't have made the name up," bumbled the Duke, obviously caught unaware. "It's in the Braunschweig part of the Duchy, is it not?" Lüdeke could see the hurt in his brother's face.

"Yes, Your Grace, it is," replied Franz. "My father was once a very prominent knight in your father's entourage."

"You must mean my grandfather's," corrected the Duke, totally unaware of the distress he was causing. "My father is Friedrich the *Pious* and he would have very few active knights about him. Well, enjoy yourselves," he concluded, dismissing them. "We are very happy for your brother. He is one of our leading Bürgers, a man of which this town can be very proud."

Lüdeke put his arm around his brother. "Don't take it to heart, Franz. His Grace meant no insult. It's just that times—and priorities—are changing."

"I can see that." Franz glanced about the room. "This is a whole new world to me. I shall have to visit you more often, no matter what Father says. He clings so to the old feudal ways, I don't think he even knows what goes on in the world outside the demesne. And just look at you." He held his brother at arm's length. "Those clothes bespeak wealth. You look more the prince than yon duke."

Lüdeke laughed. "In a way you are right. We merchants are His Grace's main support. He could never survive nor carry out his projects on the tithes he gets from his vassals. But believe me, it has taken years of hard, hard work to get where I am. But tell me, how are things," he almost said 'down on the farm', "at home?"

"The same as ever. Nothing much changes. Father complains and the peasants complain. Yet all are well fed and reasonably happy. Yet they complain. I suppose it relieves the boredom. Mother sends her love and congratulations."

"Thank her for me. I *do* miss *her*. But come now, you must be famished after so long in the saddle. Partake of this wondrous feast, while my bride and I see to our other guests."

As they moved off, Adelheit whispered, "How sad. He is nothing like you at all, is he? But I am glad for your sake that he was able to come."

"We were once quite close, but he is the heir and he took his obligations very seriously. You see what living under Father's thumb all these years has done to him. I just had to escape."

516

"I am sure all this is a revelation to him."

"I know it is and I'm also sure that defying Father and coming to our wedding feast is probably the most daring thing he has ever done in his life."

Eventually the ducal party left and the celebration livened up even more. Not that it had been very quiet before. The musicians played faster and louder. The jongleurs and acrobats went through their paces yet again, although by this time not too many of the guests were paying much attention to them. Men were getting drunk and women flirtatious.

"It's time for us to go, too, my love," whispered Lüdeke. "I have eaten my fill and I have no intention of getting drunk tonight."

"Do you think we can sneak out of here without anyone knowing?" replied Adelheit. "I just don't think I want to go through that public bedding ceremony."

"You are not going to go shy on me now?" teased her husband.

"On you, no," she replied. "But why does the whole world have to make sure we are bedded together?"

"It's the custom, sweet. The women would be terribly disappointed if they did not see that you were properly prepared for—for my attentions. And the men, well, they have to have their fun, too. I promise you I'll keep them under control. Just close your ears to some of their remarks. It's all in fun."

"If you promise . . ."

"I promise. And we'll only tell a few of our closest friends. The rest of these people won't even know we're gone."

They approached Alhuyt and Lüdeke Mestwart. "We are leaving now," von Sehnden informed them. "We don't want any big crowd accompanying us to the house. We prefer to go alone."

"Oh, but you must at least let us accompany you," objected Alhuyt. "Adi may need help getting out of her gown. And that magnificent headdress. You wouldn't have the slightest idea how to undo that without pulling every hair out of her head."

Both bride and groom could see the wisdom of that.

"And I'll keep the truly raucous and ribald out of the house so they won't be up to any tricks," promised Mestwart.

"And we're coming, too," exclaimed Eggeling and Metke together. "You can't keep us away. Besides," continued Metke, "Alhuyt can't do it all alone—in her condition. Adi needs my help, too."

"Not only that," chimed in Eggeling, "but since you are the last of us

517

partners to be wed, we won't have an opportunity to see this for a long, long time. Don't deny us our fun."

"Oh, very well," conceded von Sehnden reluctantly, "but only just you two."

But then, of course, they had to include Wünneke, the mother of the bride, and her brothers and Lüdeke's brother. And pretty soon there was a whole troop of well-wishers accompanying them down Kalandgasse, past the great church, through the Market Square, where the crowd of underlings gave a great cheer for them, and so to their new house in Zöllnerstrasse.

Lüdeke had been able to purchase the old widow's house at a very good price, but due to the short notice, Master Tischler had not been able to complete any of the elaborate furniture they had ordered.

"Fine pieces such as you want cannot be completed overnight," the old master had warned them. "And I'll not stint on the work."

"As long as we have a bed," Lüdeke had pleaded.

The old man smiled. "A bed you shall have, but you'll have to make do with a straw mattress and a woolen cover. Even my most accomplished women cannot stuff featherbeds that quickly."

"We'll put up with the straw for now. It's better than sleeping on the floor."

"Ja," agreed Tischler. "Many a poor peasant would consider it a luxury. And I'll even loan you a table and a couple of rough benches, so you won't have to eat standing up, until yours are ready."

So the bridal party arrived at their large, but nearly empty house. True to his word, Lüdeke Mestwart stood guard at the door and kept all but his wife, the von Eltzes and the family out in the street. There was a great uproar, but he stood his ground. Then the remarks started—some merely risqué, others downright crude.

"We may have to show him what to do with that prick of his."

"How do we even know he has one?"

"How can we be sure she's a virgin?" That from a woman.

"What difference does it make to you, old hen? You'll never see that day again."

And so it went.

Inside the house the three women hustled Adelheit up the stairs to the big bedroom, while Lüdeke waited below with the men, pouring them cider but drinking very little himself.

"Ach, this room is practically bare," complained Metke. "Where

518

shall we put your beautiful gown?"

"Throw it on the floor," replied the bride. "Papa will be sending over a chest of my clothes in the morning. I'll pick it up then."

"And I'll lend you Hanni to help out until you can hire your own servant," offered her mother.

"Why, thank you, Momma. I'll appreciate that. There just wasn't time, you know. Ouch!"

"Be careful, Metke. Those jewels are wired to the frame," cautioned Alhuyt.

"I see that now. I guess I'll never make a ladies' maid," said Metke. "Sorry, Adi."

"Maybe I should send for Hanni right now," suggested Wünneke.

"No, no, we'll manage," said Alhuyt. "See, it's coming apart right now."

"No, Momma. I don't want her tonight. Besides, it would take too long," sighed Adelheit.

"Aha," teased Metke. "Our bride is getting anxious for her groom."

"I am not!"

"Well, you'd better be. He'll be very disappointed if you're not."

"Stop teasing, Metke, I'm getting nervous."

Alhuyt put her arm around her. "Don't be nervous, Adi. It is truly a wondrous experience. I am sure your Lüdeke will be as kind and considerate a lover as mine is."

"And I'll wager he's hot and passionate, too. I'd love to have tried him."

"Metke! Shame on you. You're as bad as the men outside."

"All right, girls," said Wünneke. "Enough of this nonsense. If we keep him waiting too long, her husband will be neither hot nor considerate. Let's get her into bed." They passed a diaphanous white gown over her head, brushed her lustrous hair until it shone, propped the pillows behind her, and pulled the cover up to her neck. Wünneke sat beside her on the edge of the bed. "Now, girls, leave us. I wish to have a few minutes with my daughter—alone."

Adelheit threw her arms around her mother. "Oh, Momma, how can it be that I am so happy and so scared at the same time?"

"A normal reaction," Wünneke answered her. "I've already told you what to expect. Just be your usual flirtatious self, and the moment his arms are around you, you will forget all your fears. I'm sure both your friends are right. I have a feeling he will be a fine lover. There may be a moment of quick pain, then—ah, heaven. Just remember one thing. A woman can

519

get as much pleasure out of it as a man, maybe more, if she wants to. Just don't lie there like a lump of ice. Be an active partner."

"I'll try."

"And one thing more. If you ever need me for anything whatsoever—even years from now—come."

"Thank you, Momma."

"Now I'll send him up. God bless you with happiness, my child."

When Wünneke appeared at the top of the stairs, Lüdeke almost raced up them in his eagerness to be with his bride. The other men followed. At the door of the chamber he turned and stopped them.

"You are not going to see me climb into bed with her," he snapped.

"Ach, Lude, don't spoil the fun," said Eggeling. "We have to be sure."

"Of what?"

"That—that—"

"That she's really there? Peep over my shoulder, and that is all you're going to see of her. This is no royal wedding where we have to be sure the heir is really mine. As to her virginity, I'll attest to that without any viewing of bloody sheets in the morning. And now, masters, I bid you 'Auf Wiedersehen'. I've waited long enough." With that he slammed the door in their faces and slid the heavy bolt.

He strode over to the bed and held her in his arms.

"Dearest Lude," she whispered. "Thank you for keeping them out. I should have been so embarrassed."

"I promised, didn't I?" He stroked her hair and kissed her hungrily. "I'll always try to keep my promises to you, my love." He stood up and tore off his doublet. "Let me get these fancy clothes out of the way so I can hold you properly." He removed his shirt.

"Oh, Lude, must you?"

"Must I what? Take off my clothes or love you?"

"Oh, I mean—I know you have to take off your clothes, but couldn't you just sort of—what I mean is—I've never seen a grown man naked before—I—oh—I'm so confused."

He sat down on the edge of the bed and took her in his arms again. "There's nothing to be confused about, you silly goose. I'll very gently lead you every step of the way and in a little while I'll make you happier than you ever could have dreamed possible. We're going to remove this pretty little nightgown soon, too, because I want to see all of your beauty from head to toe."

"Oh, Lude, not yet." She clutched the cover to her breast.

520

"No, not yet. I'll let you tell me. And while my body may not be as beautiful as yours, you'll have to get used to it right from the start. There's no other way."

"Yes, Lude," she replied meekly, and suddenly she realized she was curious. Instead of turning her eyes away as she had intended, she watched, fascinated, as he removed first his shoes, then his chausses and hose, finally his small clothes and stood before her in all his superb maleness. She gasped as the thing between his legs seemed to have a life of its own and rose and rose. She simply stared at it.

He smiled at her consternation. "That, little one, is what will give you this great happiness, but not until you're ready." He pulled down the cover and climbed in beside her.

For a while he just held her in his arms, kissing her lips, her eyes, her ears, her neck. She could feel the thing, hard as a rock, poking into her side. Soon she felt herself respond to his kisses. After all, they had kissed many times and she had always been avid for more, although not really understanding what more meant. She remembered her mother's words and turned toward him, putting her own arms around him. She could feel the thing slip between her legs and started a moment, but he held her even more closely. Then he began caressing her breasts, and thrills ran up and down her body. When he kissed them, her body began writhing of its own accord. Stop, no, don't stop, she thought. When his fingers found the secret place between her thighs, all thought ceased and only a glorious feeling took over. He slid down her body and began kissing that secret place; her body responded with a frenzied rhythm she could not control. Nor did she want to. She thought she would go out of her mind with pleasure. It can't be better than this, she thought.

"I think you're ready for me, my love." He slid on top of her and gently raised her knees. He slowly entered her to a point, then thrust hard. She gasped with the momentary pain, but then he was inside her, thrusting deeper and deeper, and her body demanded more and more. He moved slowly at first, then faster and faster and deeper and deeper until she picked up the rhythm. Suddenly stars burst from heaven, bells were ringing, and she was floating with the angels high above them. When again she thought it couldn't be better than this, it happened again and again. Then he moved faster and faster until she couldn't keep up with him, carrying her to new heights, and suddenly he tensed and exploded within her with a deep groan. He collapsed on top of her and was still.

521

She lay panting beneath him, drenched with sweat, but now his weight was too much for her.

"Lude, I can't breathe."

"Sorry, love." He raised himself on to his elbows. "I forgot for the moment."

"You groaned. Was that good or bad?"

"Very, very good, little one. And you screamed."

"Did I? I don't remember. I felt like I was flying into the blue like a bird or an angel."

"You are an angel, sweet."

"No wonder Momma said it was like heaven. May we do it again?"

He laughed. "In a little while, love. I just knew you would be a sensuous one. Let us rest a bit until my little man recovers." He reached down to pull the cover over them, but not before she had a glimpse of his shrunken penis.

She laughed. "That—that is the same thing? Did I do that to it?"

He joined her laughter. "You sure did, little one, and you can do it any time you want to."

Before long he was hard again, and this time he took her more slowly and very eloquently.

Thus began a dynasty.

A few months later Alhuyt Mestwart was in her huge kitchen carefully adding ingredients—a little of this, a little of that—as she stirred the contents of the iron pot hanging over the fire. Her maid of-all-work, Roswithe, was chopping vegetables at the table to be added later.

"Meine Frau," she said, "you shouldn't be doing that. It's too close to your time. I'll do it as soon as I've finished here."

"No, no. It's all right. Just stirring a pot can't hurt me. Besides, I want this to be real special today. You know Her Grace Anna von Nassau is coming to dinner with us. She wants to talk to Lüdeke about building a hospital for the poor. Imagine her coming to us instead of commanding us to the Castle. She is such a kind and charitable person."

Suddenly the broth started boiling furiously and instinctively Alhuyt tried to lift it to a higher notch in the great hook that hung from the fireplace. She screamed as a pain shot through her.

Roswithe rushed to her side. "What happened, meine Frau? Did you burn yourself? Here, let me do that." She hefted the heavy pot to a higher notch.

"Oh, no, Roswithe. It was just a pain. Oh, I hope it's not going to be today of all days," she moaned.

"Sit down, sit down," urged Roswithe. "You know you can't be too careful. You've carried this one to full term, and we know it still lives. You *must* be careful. Shall I send for Frau Symberg?"

"No, not yet. It could be a false alarm." But it was not. Five minutes later another sharp pain tore through her. She clutched her distended belly. Then another.

"Help me upstairs, Roswithe. Perhaps if I lie down a bit, it will subside before dinner is ready."

Roswithe did so. She took off Alhuyt's shoes and gown and helped her into bed in just her shift.

"Thank you, Roswithe. Ah, that feels good." She sank back against the feather pillows. "I'm sure a little rest is all I need. I've been too excited about this dinner. I'll call you if I need you. Now watch that pot."

"Ja, ja, meine Frau. Everything will be fine. Don't worry." But Roswithe was worried. Orders or no, she sent the stable lad for Frau Symberg.

That worthy lady came very quickly, for she knew how precarious Alhuyt's situation was. As she mounted the stairs, with her servant carrying the birthing chair, she murmured a prayer. "O Holy Mother, let this one live. The poor child is worn out with so much futile childbearing. O dear God in Heaven, have mercy on her and guide my hands." But when she entered the chamber, she presented a cheerful face.

"Ach, Frau Symberg. I told Roswithe not to bother you. I think I just strained myself trying to lift a pot. I don't think it's time yet."

"Better to bother me too early than too late. As long as I'm here, let me take a look at you." She pulled up Alhuyt's shift and felt her belly. "When did the babe drop?"

"About two weeks ago."

"So long and you didn't tell me," she chided.

"Well, you always said it could be a month or more after it drops."

"And so it could, but with you, I want to know everything. The babe seems to be in a good position. God willing, Alhuyt, this should be an easy one for you at last. Your water hasn't broken yet, has it?"

"No. That's why I think it's just a false alarm. But I do have to use the chamber pot. Let me get up."

Frau Symberg smiled knowingly and helped Alhuyt up. As she stood she felt the trickle down her legs and screamed as it gushed all over her and the floor.

523

The midwife called for Roswithe and ordered, "Now back into bed. It is not a false alarm, but it will be a while yet. No sense struggling in that uncomfortable old chair until it is necessary."

Roswithe appeared with mop and pail. Frau Symberg ordered her to put water to boil and have clean cloths ready. "I know what to do, Mistress," she grumbled. "It's not like it was the first time."

No, thought Frau Symberg, not the first time. How many times had it been over these years? Ten, at least. I've lost count myself. And not a living babe to show for it. God grant this time . . .

"And I've sent word to Master Mestwart as well," Roswithe continued.

"A little too soon for that. I don't want to alarm him."

"As you yourself often said, 'better too early than too late'," snapped Roswithe as she left with the bucket and mop. She had also taken it upon herself to send a message to the castle so that their distinguished guest would not arrive in the middle of all this.

A few minutes later Lüdeke Mestwart rushed in, thoroughly distraught.

"Calm yourself, Master," advised Frau Symberg. "It is early times yet. There is nothing you can do."

"Let me at least hold her hand and comfort her," he begged, knowing full well that the midwife reigned supreme in the birthing chamber.

"All right, hold her hand for a while, but don't upset her. And when I say it's time to leave, out you go."

Immediately following him came Metke. "I've come to help you, Mother, although I see it's early yet. But Alhuyt is my best friend. I just have to be here."

"Very well, but I should have sent for you in time. Meanwhile, make yourself useful. You know what needs to be done."

About two hours later Anna von Nassau herself arrived with her personal physician in tow.

"Oh, my lady," moaned a surprised Alhuyt from the bed, "I regret I shall not be able to attend the dinner I had planned in your honor. I apologize for not sending a message, but you can still dine with my husband, if you wish, and discuss your plans with him. I am so sorry."

"Don't be sorry, my dear," crooned Anna. "After all, we cannot stop the will of God. And I *did* receive a message. I haven't come to dine but have brought you Master Jakob, the finest physician in Celle. I have told him how often you have—er—had problems. He will take charge here and see that all goes well."

"Thank you, Your Grace," murmured Alhuyt.

"I don't think that will be necessary," said Frau Symberg a bit testily. "Everything is under control. She is doing as well as can be expected — in fact, better than several other times. The babe's head is well positioned. It should be a relatively easy birth."

"I shall examine her."

"If you wish, Master." She noted with horror his filthy gown and the dirt under his fingernails. "Wash your hands!" she exclaimed.

"Mistress," he replied haughtily, "I have just come from the Castle, where we take baths once a week, which is probably more than I can say for you."

Frau Symberg sputtered as he walked over to the bed, raised Alhuyt's shift, and reached inside her none too gently. She screamed.

He turned back to the midwife. "The head, as you say, seems to be well positioned, but it will be a while. I foresee no problem. Why is she not in the birthing chair?"

"Because she is more comfortable in the bed until closer to the time. She is very weak."

"All the more reason to hasten things along. Put her in the birthing chair."

"Yes, Master, whatever you say."

"I can't see as there's any need for me to wait around here. It'll be several hours yet. Send for me when it starts to come and I'll deliver it."

In a pig's ass, I'll send for you, thought Frau Symberg as she ushered him out the door.

In less than an hour, Alhuyt's pains were coming hard and fast. The midwife chased everybody out of the room except Metke, her trained assistant, and Roswithe, who was bringing pails of hot water and had attended all of Alhuyt's other lyings-in.

"Push with me," Frau Symberg said as she pushed down on Alhuyt's belly and Metke, kneeling on the floor, watched for the infant's head to appear.

"I'm trying, but I have no strength left," murmured Alhuyt.

"Yes, you do. I'll help." She pushed again. "And scream all you want. It'll help."

"It's coming, Mother," said Metke.

"All right, then, one more big push and it'll be over with." She and Alhuyt pushed together, and then she felt the girl go limp under her hands. She had fainted, but the baby's head was out. Frau Symberg pushed her daughter aside and gently took the tiny head in her hands, manipulating it carefully until the shoulders were out; then the rest came easily.

"Ah, a fine boy and a healthy one from the looks of him." She quickly cut the cord and tied the knot. She put her finger in his mouth to remove any phlegm, then turned him upside down and slapped his little buttocks. He howled.

"Ah, and a lusty one, too. I'll leave you to the afterbirth," she said to Metke, "while we wash and dress the little fellow for his father. Come, Roswithe, help me."

"Is that my baby?" asked Alhuyt. His cry had brought her out of her faint.

"Yes, it is, dear Alhuyt, and a fine healthy boy for you at last."

"Saints and God's Holy Mother be praised," whispered Alhuyt weakly. Then she screamed again. "What is happening to me? Isn't it over yet?"

"Just the afterbirth. Have to get rid of that." She threw it into a pail at hand for the purpose, which the maid would bury later. "Metke, hand me some of those clean linens. I have to pack her. She seems to be bleeding a bit too much. Then let's get her cleaned up and back into bed."

"I want to see my baby," whispered Alhuyt.

"Just in a moment, my dear. We've got to get both you and him cleaned up a bit. Birthing is a messy job, you know."

"I know. I don't envy you your job, Frau Symberg, but I don't know what I'd have done without you. I didn't like that dirty man."

"Nor did I. Baths once a week, humph! His pigs are probably cleaner than he. Now carefully, back into bed with you."

"And here is your beautiful son, Mistress," said Roswithe as she placed him in Alhuyt's arms.

"Oh, he is beautiful, isn't he?" exclaimed Alhuyt. "Are you sure he's healthy?"

"He certainly seems to be. Now have a smile for your poor husband, who has no doubt chewed his fingers to the bone by now." She called from the top of the stairs, "Master Mestwart, you may come up now. You have a fine, healthy son and your dear wife is very happy."

Lüdeke rushed up the stairs, but Frau Symberg detained him for a moment at the door.

"She is very weak. Don't stay too long and tire her."

"I'll not," he replied, "but I must see her. And the child lives?"

526

"Ja, ja. Not only lives, but looks to be a strong and healthy one."

Lüdeke entered the room and at first was more concerned with Alhuyt than with the babe. He kissed her and held her hand.

"Lude," she said. "don't you want to see our son? Look, isn't he beautiful? The first strong one I've given you. Oh, Lude, I'm so happy."

"And so am I my dearest." He looked at the red, wrinkled bundle she held to her breast. There was nothing beautiful about him, but he was alive. In fact, he was already hungrily sucking on her nipple, although there was no milk to be had as yet.

"He is beautiful, and healthy, too," Lüdeke agreed.

"Isn't he, though? Just look at those little hands kneading my breast already. I can feel the strength in him. What shall we call him, Lude? I was afraid to pick out a name after so many failures."

"I know. I, too. I think I should like to call him Johann after that great ancestor of mine who left us the stipendium."

"What a lovely thought. Ja, ja, then Johann it is," she agreed. "Hello, little Johann." She patted the baby's damp head. "You'd better call Father Josef and have him arrange for the baptism right away."

"If he's as healthy as Frau Symberg seem to think, there's no hurry."

"Oh, Lude, don't argue. I want him baptized before the week is out. I just don't want anything to go wrong. I have a strange feeling about that."

"No, my dear." He put his arm around her comfortingly. "Don't have any strange feelings. It's just that you are very tired, worn out."

"I know. I would rest now. But know that I want Lüdeke von Sehnden and Eggeling von Eltze for godparents. And do you think Her Grace Anna von Nassau would consent to stand godmother to him?"

"I don't know. I think she might. I'll ask."

"Yes, see to it, my dearest husband. And call Roswithe to take the baby. I'm exhausted."

"Sleep well, my love." He kissed her and left to tell his friends the wonderful news.

Two days later Anna von Nassau herself carried the baby to the great Marienkirche, proudly accompanied by his father Lüdeke Mestwart. Their friends were there waiting for him. Father Josef christened him Johann before the chapel altar that Lüdeke himself had donated some years before. Alhuyt, even had she been strong enough, could not have attended, for the Church strictly forbade women from entering the church after childbirth until the ritual cleansing ceremony called the

Churching of Women took place forty days after the birth. After the baptism, they all accompanied Lüdeke back to the house to partake of a celebratory meal and to congratulate Alhuyt.

Roswithe met them at the door with a long face. "She's hot and feverish, Master. I'm worried."

Lüdeke dashed up the stairs, shouting over his shoulder, "Call Frau Symberg."

"I already have."

The next day the fever was raging and Alhuyt didn't know anyone.

"The milk won't come in. The child will starve," moaned Roswithe.

"I'll arrange for a wet nurse immediately," said Frau Symberg. "We must at least save him. There's not much we can do for her except try to break the fever."

"Perhaps Her Grace's physician," suggested Roswithe hesitantly.

"That pig," snapped Frau Symberg. "Never. He's the cause of all this, putting his dirty hands on her. I've seen it happen before. Oh, when will they learn?"

The next day Father Josef came to give Alhuyt the last rites. She couldn't confess. She was not even aware of him.

By the end of the week Alhuyt was dead — of the dreaded childbed fever.

Lüdeke knelt by her bed. "It was the will of God," he said and wept.

By the time Johann reached the toddling stage he was spending more time in the von Sehnden and von Eltze homes than in his own. So much so that he considered them all his homes, even though Roswithe cared for him as well as his own mother would have done. Each family now had three sons, the youngest of which, each named after their fathers, Lüdeke and Eggeling respectively, were close to Johann's age. Adelheit and Metke loved him as their own and felt so sorry for him. He enjoyed playing with their little sons so much that often he did not want to go to his own home at bedtime. His father seemed so cold and distant to him.

The adults realized that Lüdeke Mestwart was still carrying a heavy burden of guilt and grief. Always pious, he had more than doubled his gifts to the Church and charity, but his former warmth and kindness seemed to be lacking. The hospital planned by Anna von Nassau, St. Elizabeth's, had been taken over by another wealthy merchant during Lüdeke's period of deep mourning, but he was already planning another on his own. He threw himself almost blindly into his business, and it was growing beyond all expectations, so much so that he had to sell some of his property in Veerssen near Uelzen in order to pay his taxes to the Duke. But he had no satisfaction in it. He was elected Bürgermeister and so able, fair and just an administrator was he that it looked as though he would be reelected for many years to come. Again, he did his job meticulously, often more than was required of him, but his old warmth was lacking.

"He needs another wife," said Metke to Adelheit.

"I agree with you," she replied, "but he won't look at another woman while he still mourns Alhuyt, and so deeply. And the guilt. He blames himself, so I doubt he could even get it up."

Metke giggled. "I don't think it's that bad that the right woman couldn't cure that. But who? There must be something we can do."

"There should be, but I don't know what—or who. He needs to be shaken out of that stupor he's let himself sink into. I'll talk to Lüdeke when he comes home."

"And I with Eggeling. Together maybe we can come up with something."

Adelheit's talk with her husband had perforce to be delayed a bit, because when he came home from his most recent trip he had exciting news.

"I have decided to sell the courier business."

"Lude, how could you?" she exclaimed. "It was your first business and is still a very lucrative one."

"Now, my dear, you of all people should know that one cannot be sentimental in business. For one thing, it takes me away too much. I want to spend more time at home. I have three growing sons who barely know me and a lovely wife who is running my main business almost single-handedly."

"I don't mind that at all," she objected. "In fact, I enjoy it immensely."

"I know you do, my dear, but there is really a far more important reason for selling out right now. There is this man—I'm not sure if he's a gentleman yet or not—named Franciscus Tassi, I don't know where he's from originally, who has been operating a rival courier service out of Milan for some years now. Somehow or other—I don't know the whole story—he ran afoul of the Duke of Milan and he and his brothers had to flee for their lives. They took refuge in a castle over the border in the mountains and appealed to the Emperor himself. Apparently, they are excellent salesmen—although it's well known how Friedrich hates the Sforzas. Anyway,

529

they convinced him to consolidate all the courier routes into one single Imperial Postal Service stretching all the way from the toe of Italy to northernmost Netherlands, with themselves as sole operators. Of course the Emperor will get a nice percentage of the revenues, so everybody benefits, except us. So you can see the wisdom of selling while it is still a money-maker, before they drive us into the ground. They are quite ruthless, methinks."

"Yes, I can see your point," she agreed, "but why couldn't you have approached His Majesty yourself?"

"Had I known he was so receptive to the idea, I might have. But by the time I heard about it, it was an accomplished fact. Besides, it would have kept me from home even more and I honestly don't think I have the resources to do it. It would have taken a huge outlay of money. So as soon as I heard about it I went to speak to this Franciscus. He made me an excellent offer. We shall not lose by it, my dear."

"I can see the wisdom in that, but it still seems a shame."

"It was inevitable — in fact, badly needed. One uniform postal service serving almost all of Europe will expedite things tremendously. They're even going to set it up so that private people as well as businesses can use it to send letters by paying a small fee at their post offices, which will be located in every major town. It's even rumored that the King of France is interested in joining the network, so that *all* of Europe will be served by the same postal service."

"How interesting."

"And this should make you smile, my dear. The deal is this. He will pay me a sizeable sum in cash and the rest in stock in the new company, so that we shall still have an excellent income from it without doing a stitch of work."

She did smile. "Now I see what a clever husband I have. And it *will* be good to have you home more often. Will the cash part be enough to buy another boat?"

"Indeed it will. Possibly two."

She fell into his arms. "Oh, Lude, that's wonderful. That calls for a celebration."

"There's just one thing that might make you a little jealous," he warned, but with mockery in his tone.

"What's that?"

"Friedrich has decided that no lowborn person could possibly run the Imperial Post, so he is giving him a title — Germanized, of course. He is to be known as Count Franz von Turn und Thaxis."

"Who cares?" said Adelheit. "He can have it. Let's celebrate." In her haste to lead him to their bedroom, she forgot all about Lüdeke Mestwart and his problems.

The next day Metke reminded her. "Did you speak to Lüdeke?"

"Oh, I forgot," she apologized. "Lude had such exciting news, we talked about it half the night, and poor Lüdeke Mestwart completely slipped my mind."

"Well, Eggeling had nothing much to offer. He said leave him alone. But I have an idea."

"Tell me."

"Well, you know that I was to their house many times, at every one of dear Alhuyt's miscarriages and stillbirths. I mean the old house they used to rent from Meinherr von Wintheim from Hannover."

"So?"

"So you probably never knew him, but he used to come here quite often to collect the rent and see to repairs and so on."

"So what are you getting at?"

"So he often brought his daughter with him. She was just a young maid then—a child really—but quite fetching."

"And?"

"And during those many times when Lüdeke swore he would never put Alhuyt through this again and so on and so forth, he seemed quite interested in her, quite taken with her."

"You jest! Not Lüdeke Mestwart!"

"I am very serious. Underneath all that piety and quiet demeanor, he is a man just as avid for a woman as any other."

"Aha! So you think we might . . . But she may be wed by now."

"No, she is not. Her father still comes to Celle—he owns several houses here—and very often she comes with him. I met and spoke with her but a fortnight ago. That is why I know she is still unwed and no prospects in sight that she mentioned. I don't know why. She is fair to look upon and seems quite pleasant."

"So you are suggesting we bring them together. A little private dinner might work, but how, since I don't know them?"

"The next time they come to town, I shall bring her to meet you. She is often bored with her father's business and at loose ends."

"A capital idea. I shall look forward to it. My, Metke, I knew you were a conniver, but this beats all."

531

Metke laughed. "But it is in a good cause."

"Indeed it is, if it works," agreed Adelheit.

The next time the von Wintheims came to Celle, Metke prevailed upon Catherine to come with her to visit her friend Adelheit, who set out fancy little cakes and served her finest wine. The three women chatted for some time about nothing in particular. Then the three little boys, Lüdeke, Eggeling and Johann escaped from the maid and came into the parlor begging for cakes.

Adelheit introduced them. "This is my youngest and Metke's youngest."

"And who is this?" asked Catherine.

"That is Lüdeke Mestwart's son Johann. He stays here quite often as he is so lonely at home. You must remember Lüdeke, do you not?"

"I do indeed," replied Catherine. "I was so sorry to hear his wife died. But it is a few years now, is it not? And he has not remarried? What a shame. He is such a nice man." Metke's and Adelheit's eyes met over her head in a conspiratorial look as Catherine bent to hug Johann.

When it came time for Catherine to leave, Adelheit suggested, "Perhaps next time you come to Celle you and your father would like to partake of dinner with us."

"I should like that very much," replied Catherine. "And I'm sure Papa would, too. We get so tired of eating at the inn. It's so—so boisterous and the food is only just passable. Thank you very much."

"You shall be most welcome. And when would that be?"

"In about a month. I shall let Metke know in ample time."

After Catherine left, Adelheit said to Metke, "I like her. She is not too clever, but that very simplicity should appeal to him. He won't feel overwhelmed."

"I agree," replied Metke, "and she's so sweet. Look how she took to the child."

Thus was the trap set for an unsuspecting Lüdeke Mestwart.

The dinner was a great success, although Mestwart attended very reluctantly and only after the strongest urging by his friends. But after that they noticed the change in him. He seemed to brighten up and some of his old warmth returned, although the shadow of sadness that hung over him was with him until the day he died. He took a more active part in the social life of the town, escorting Catherine whenever she was in Celle. They even attended the Kalands' semiannual dinner, which he had shunned for some years. Suddenly he was making 'business' trips to Hannover quite frequently.

"Although whatever business he has in that little town I can't imagine," remarked Lüdeke von Sehnden.

"And nothing shows on the books for it," said Eggeling. "Very strange."

Adelheit and Metke were overjoyed that their plan seemed to be working and merely smiled at the obtuseness of their menfolk.

Before year end Lüdeke and Catherine were married, and before the following year was out she presented him with a lovely baby daughter. They immediately named her Anna and Her Grace Anna von Nassau, now Duchess, her brother-in-law having died, proudly stood Godmother for her. Catherine never became pregnant again and no one knew why, whether she could not or was using some means to prevent conception. But no one cared, as she and Lüdeke seemed to be quite content and she doted on his two children.

In 1471 Mestwart's new hospital, which he named St. Anna's after both the Duchess and his daughter, was finally ready to be dedicated. It included a chapel and places for six sick people. It stood near the Aller bridge right next to St. Elizabeth's, which had its own chapel, and took in sick, poor and needy strangers. Eventually the Duchess felt there was something lacking here and conditioned a heavy endowment on combining the two foundations into one, St. Anna's Hospital, with the appropriate building additions, and, most importantly, that twenty women, especially the poorest, be taken in, as well as the sick and strangers. Anna von Nassau was regarded as almost a saint by the people of Celle. She continued many of the worthy projects her father-in-law, Friedrich der Fromme, had begun. With the blessing of her husband Duke Otto and all the bishops, she instituted a reform movement in all the monasteries and convents throughout the Duchy. To this end she engaged one Johannes Busch, prior of a reformed cloister in Hildesheim, to return especially the convents, which had grown lax and slovenly, to a strict observance of their Order's rule. In Celle itself she ordered the so-called Beguines, a large sisterhood of unmarried young women and widows, to conform to the Rule of the Third Order of St. Francis. Friedrich had given them a sister house adjacent to the Kalands house, but she noticed some abuses had crept in and she ordered 'one table and one cooking-pot for all, and that the younger ones take care of the elder, not rule over them'. She also established a house for unmarried and widowed pregnant women, and while they were awaiting the birth of their babies they partially earned their keep by serving as laying-out, or death, women.

She also laid out new ground roles for the very ancient hospital of St. George near the Braunschweiger gate. This had originally been the town's only hospital, before the other two were founded. Although it had been founded by some of the noble families in the area, by this time its only income was from the church's poor box. As a result, most of the inmates resorted to begging and those who were too old or infirm to do so received little or no share of the proceeds. Anna again heavily endowed St. George's on the condition that begging was to be limited to one day a week, that those who were able to work do so, and that all received equal and compassionate care.

Perhaps Anna's greatest contribution was to change the thinking and attitude of the entire populace toward these unfortunates. Previously the males, if they were lucky, were dumped in these hospitals and forgotten. The females were totally neglected unless they had enough money or influence to join the Beguines or enter a convent. What support they received was a mere pittance from the church and an occasional contribution from a charitably minded Bürger. Anna insisted that they were the responsibility of the government—from the Dukes to the Bürgermeisters and Town Council right down to every tax-paying citizen of Celle. And she made it stick. Thus were sown the first seeds of the Reformation and Renaissance in Celle. St. Anna's and St. George's exist to this day as homes for aged women and men, respectively.

Then tragedy struck.

The crowds, many dressed in their Sunday best, gathered early. It was a merry crowd, for Duke Otto had declared a holiday. Later in the day there was to be a great tournament, to which he had invited famous knights from far and near. An accomplished and experienced knight himself, Otto loved nothing better than a tournament. He enjoyed testing his skills against those of the greatest knights of Europe and usually won. He can be forgiven if a little egotism entered into it as well, for he sincerely wanted to show his people how well they would be protected in the event of real war.

The lists were already set up in the Stechbahn, a large rectangular open space in the heart of town opposite the Castle, regularly used as a tilting yard. It was bounded on its north side by the great church and adjoined the marketplace at its east end. Here was where most of the crowd of common people were gathered, their excitement mounting

534

although not a horse or a knight was yet in sight. Those who were lucky enough to have friends or relatives in the houses along the south side were already hanging out of every window and even sitting on the roofs. Vendors of food, drink and baubles circulated among them, hawking their wares. Although gambling was strictly forbidden, many a wager was made and taken among friends. The pennants of both local and visiting knights fluttered in the gentle breeze at either end. It promised to be a perfect day.

Alongside the church temporary stands had been set up for the ducal family and court, the Bürgermeisters and Council and other of the prominent families, as well as for visiting dignitaries. These were beginning to fill up. The von Sehnden and von Eltze families were already there. Adelheit and Metke sat for the moment with their husbands and the rest of the Town Council, although they knew that when the Duchess arrived they would probably be invited to sit with her, as they were all best friends. The Mestwarts had not yet put in an appearance, as Lüdeke was now one of the Bürgermeisters and it was not seemly for them to show up too early. The Duchess herself would be the last to come, but many members of the Court were already in their seats.

At last the Mestwarts arrived, slowly making their way to their places, as they had to stop and greet everyone along the way. The crowd cheered them.

Catherine leaned over to the other women. "Isn't it exciting?" she gushed. "I just love tournaments. I never got to go to many in Hannover."

Adelheit and Metke couldn't decide whether it was the tournament Catherine loved or the adulation of the crowd.

Adelheit replied, "And I have seen so many of them, I don't really get very excited anymore."

"How can you say that?" said Catherine. "These brave men take their life in their hands."

"Oh, come now," chimed in Metke. "It's not as dangerous as all that. They have blunted tips on their lances and their swords and special tilting helmets. The worst they can suffer are some heavy bruises. But they have fun and so does the crowd."

"Oh, dear," sighed Catherine, shaking her head.

Adelheit patted her shoulder. "Don't worry, you'll have your excitement. At first it may be a little boring with the younger, new knights. But when some of the more experienced knights start to fight there will be plenty of heart-stopping drama. I hear there are even one or two from France and I think England, too, as well as from all over Germany."

"Ja, I heard that, too," agreed Metke. "And I'll say one thing for our beloved Duke Otto. He goes strictly by the rules. He is not one of these royalty, like so many, who insist that their opponents let them win just because they are royal. Oh, no. He fights fair and, if his opponent should be superior, takes his loss gracefully. Although it doesn't happen too often, because he really is a fine knight."

Just then the first trumpets blew from the Castle. Although it was only a short way, the Duchess rode her magnificent white palfrey into the lists up to her seat, where she dismounted and took her place to the wild cheering of the crowd. Indeed, they loved her very much. As the groom led her horse away, along came a little pony cart with a nursemaid and Anna's infant son and heir Heinrich. The nurse held him up and the people cheered again. Then she took her place behind the Duchess.

As soon as the crowd's attention was elsewhere, for they knew that the knights would soon appear, Anna beckoned to Adelheit and Metke to join her.

"Don't you two look lovely today," she said. "I apologize for taking you from your husbands. I hope they don't mind, but I just wanted to have my best friends near me today."

"Thank you, Your Grace," they replied, and Metke continued, "No apologies necessary. We spend enough time with them. They're so busy talking business, they probably won't even notice we're gone."

"I wish I could say the same," sighed Anna. "I always have to sit alone and keep smiling for the crowd, no matter what I feel inside. Truth of it is, I hate these tournaments, but don't ever tell my husband that."

Adelheit smiled. "I agree, but they're just games that the men enjoy, and so do the people."

"Ja," agreed Metke, "and they do have to keep their skills honed in case of real war. We can be thankful the Duchy has been at peace for so many years."

"Ach, ja," said the Duchess, "that would be much worse. Just the thought of war frightens me. I'm sorry to be so glum, but I woke up this morning with this strange, frightened feeling for no reason I can think of. And I can't seem to shake it, even on such a beautiful day as this."

"Perhaps you just had a bad night."

"As a matter of fact, I did. Heinrich was fretful for hours. I think he is cutting another tooth."

"That could do it."

And the two women fussed over the child for a bit.

"My, isn't he growing!" exclaimed Adelheit. "It looks as though he'll be walking soon."

"He's already trying," replied Anna. "He has a stubborn streak in him just like his father. And chatters like a magpie, although no one can understand a word he's saying."

Her friends smiled. Metke said, "You can be thankful he's such a healthy, active child. I wish you the joy of several more like him, Your Grace."

"Why, thank you, Metke. That will be according to God's will."

Adelheit patted her arm. "Now forget about being glum. I think the knights are coming, and I'm sure His Grace, your dear husband, will win as usual."

Anna smiled at her wanly as the trumpets blew from the Castle.

Duke Otto led the procession. The knights had not yet donned their armor. On a day like this the sun would cook them like roast pigs if they wore it too long. But they wore their long surcoats, beautifully embroidered with their arms so everyone would know who they were. Their great destriers were covered with matching caparisons. At the Castle end of the Stechbahn a number of brightly colored tents had been set up. The sweating squires lugging the heavy suits of armor stopped here, where the knights would change into armor as their turn to joust came. The procession wound down the far side of the lists, then turned up the other side until the Duke stopped in front of his Duchess. All the knights turned their horses and bowed to her. Anna gave him her favor, a green silken scarf. At that signal the knights broke ranks and each rode up to his lady to receive his favor—a scarf, a handkerchief, a broach to pin on his sleeve, a flower. The Duke then led the procession off the field to the tents, to which the first contestants retired to don their armor with the help of their squires. The rest stood watching as the Master of Ceremonies announced that the tournament was about to begin.

As Adelheit predicted, the first few jousts were boring, even a bit comical. These were the younger, less experienced knights.

The first pair thundered down the lists and seemed to be aiming their great lances properly, but both missed. The crowd hooted and hollered as they rode to the end of the field and turned to try again. On the second attempt they both missed again and the audience burst into laughter. The third time round they did manage to brush each other with the lances, but it seemed at though they were really afraid to do any real damage.

The onlookers yelled, "Give it up!" "Send them back to the

quintain!" "Fight or get off the field!"

The Master of Ceremonies signalled to the bailiffs at either end to stop them. "Can't have them riding up and down all day," he mumbled to his associates and announced the next pair.

These two were somewhat better. On the second attempt one did manage to unseat the other. Their squires rushed in to help the one to his feet and the other to dismount, as there were very few knights who could accomplish this on their own in the cumbersome suits of armor. But these two were so inept at swordplay on the ground that the bailiffs finally stopped them as well.

And so it went, the third and fourth pair proving only somewhat more competent than their predecessors. The crowd was growing restless. This was not what they came to see.

"Send them back to the nursery!" "Bring on the champions!" "Let our beloved Otto show them how to fight!"

So the Master of Ceremonies acceded to their wishes—which was more or less what had been planned anyway. A French knight-errant was matched with a local knight from the Court.

The great destriers thundered down the lists. The long lances smashed into shields, but both remained seated. On the second run the Frenchman unseated the local and splintered his lance in the process. The squires rushed in and got them on their feet. Once again they were evenly matched, and the sword cuts and thrusts were fast and brutal. The crowd went wild. The Celle man seemed to be tiring. It took tremendous strength and stamina to wield those heavy swords in a full suit of equally heavy armor. Suddenly the man was down and the Frenchman stood with one foot on his chest and the sword's tip at his throat. The bailiffs rushed in and declared the visitor the winner.

The jousters were not there to kill, only to win, for the loser had to forfeit weapons, armor and horse to the winner. They could ransom them back by paying whatever sum the winner demanded. Many knights-errant accumulated vast fortunes riding the tournament circuit. But they were the champions. Many others lost everything they owned and never recovered.

Next a pair of German knights, both strangers from somewhere in the south, competed. A big, burly fellow was the winner. Two more jousts followed and then Duke Otto entered the lists. The crowd cheered wildly before the joust even began. They knew he would only fight against the best, the champions. This was what they had come to see, to know that their Duke was a champion.

He won his first match handily, and then the winners of some of the previous contest were paired off against each other. The Frenchman was still winning every match when Otto decided to take him on. It was a difficult fight, for they were well matched. Hoofs thundered and the dust made it hard to see. Both lances splintered against the other's shield. They then had the choice of new lances or fighting on the ground. They chose lances. Twice more they clashed until Otto finally unseated the Frenchman. On the ground the Frenchman at first seemed to have the advantage for he was a fine swordsman, but he could not compete against the finely honed skills of the Duke. Finally Otto got him down and was declared the winner.

Almost immediately Otto decided to challenge the big burly southern German whom no one knew but whose arms were strangely reminiscent of the Imperial arms.

"Oh, no!" cried Anna, although no one heard her but Adelheit and Metke. "Why does he do that? He is too tired. Rest a bit, my love."

Her friends tried to reassure her. "He is doing what he loves doing," said Metke. "He'll be all right."

"I am sure if he were too tired he would wait," said Adelheit.

"That's the trouble," declared Anna. "He doesn't know enough to wait. He doesn't even realize he's tired. He gets so carried away with the heat of the battle, he loses all his sense."

"Well, he's still winning," said Metke. "You can't blame him for wanting to keep on."

"He'll win, I'm sure," agreed Adelheit.

But as the horse started down the list, Anna put her head in her hands and wept. "Oh, Otto, you fool."

The other women were so surprised to hear her speak like this of her husband and their Duke, that they almost did not see what was happening on the field.

It was apparent to many that Otto was indeed tiring. When the two knights clashed, his lance dealt the southerner's shield only a glancing blow, whereas his opponent's hit his squarely. It was a devastating blow, but Otto remained seated, and the crowd cheered. On the rebound, however, the big man succeeded in unseating the Duke and he fell to the ground. It was not the first time, and everyone fully expected that Otto's superior swordsmanship would still win the day. The squires rushed in as usual to help both knights, but then everyone realized that something was not right. A hush fell over the crowd. Anna screamed. Her friends held her hands as the squires beckoned to the bailiffs, who came running. His opponent stood back as the squire gingerly removed Otto's helmet.

When a litter was called for, Anna could no longer hold back. Decorum be damned, she dashed down onto the field, her friends with her.

"Otto! Otto!" she cried as she knelt by his side.

He weakly took her hand in his still-gauntleted own. "It's all right, my love," he barely whispered. "An unlucky fall is all."

The squires struggled to remove as much of his armor as possible. When the litter arrived, they rushed him to the Castle, the women following. His physician and priest were waiting for them, but he had no time to make his confession. As Anna held his hand, he managed to say quite clearly, "You shall be Regent, my dearest wife," and died.

Otto had broken his neck, and Anna suddenly found herself Regent for her infant son, Duke Heinrich.

Anna knelt by the bed, weeping and praying. The priest tried to comfort her, but she shrugged him off. Realizing that she wished to be alone in her grief, Adelheit beckoned to priest, physician and the courtiers who crowded the room.

"Let us leave her to her grief for a while," she said, choking back a sob. "It was too sudden for anyone to bear nobly."

Metke agreed tearfully. "Ja, she wishes to be alone with him, but you'll see. She will recover soon. She is a very noble lady."

The courtiers, all weeping, wiping tears on their sleeves, blowing their noses, seemed relieved to have someone tell them what to do.

"We shall wait right here outside the chamber door until she is ready," said Adelheit. "If she has need of any of you, we'll call you immediately. Meanwhile some of you had better see to the nurse and our new Duke."

At this most of them, sniffling and snuffling, went about their business, although a few of the ladies-in-waiting continued to hover nearby and Anna's personal maid insisted on waiting with her friends.

"She will want to change her clothes," she said practically, "and I have sent for water so she may wash away the tears. I know Her Grace too well. She will never appear before the public disheveled. I have served her since she was a child in Nassau."

"You are quite right, of course, Lise," agreed Adelheit. "I hadn't meant to send everyone away, only to leave her alone for a bit. She will need the support of all her faithful servants, like yourself—and us, too."

This seemed to appease the old woman, who was trying to maintain her dignity despite her tears, but her hands wringing her crisp apron gave away the extent of her grief.

Finally they heard a stirring in the bedchamber and all three were alert.

"Lise," called Anna. As she came to the door she spied Adelheit and Metke. "Oh, thank God you are here. What would I do without my dearest friends?"

"We are here for as long as you need us, Your Grace," said Adelheit while Metke rushed in and embraced the Duchess. They wept together in each other's arms for a moment.

"Oh, why, why?" moaned Anna. "He was so young and full of life." She sobbed uncontrollably for a few minutes while Metke held her. "I told you this morning, didn't I? I had this terrible frightening premonition, but I never expected anything this bad."

"It is God's will," said Adelheit.

"And you will be strong," added Metke. "We are here to help you."

Anna nodded. "I must be," she sighed. "You heard what he said. Regent. It is an awesome responsibility, and Heinrich only a babe. How many years must I be strong?" she cried in anguish. "Oh, dear God, give me that strength!"

"He will, Your Grace. He will," Adelheit assured her.

"You don't think . . ." Anna almost broke down again, but with an obvious effort regained control. "You don't think anyone will challenge it, do you?"

"Not if the Bürgers of Celle have anything to say about it," declared Metke. "You are well beloved, Your Grace, and they know you are capable." Perhaps more so than your husband, she added to herself.

"There are so many cousins," sighed Anna, "and the Duchy is already so fragmented from what it was in the first Heinrich's time. I couldn't bear to be the cause of more trouble."

"You won't, Your Grace, don't even think it," said Adelheit. "His Grace stated his last will very clearly. We all heard him. There were many witnesses. No one would be such a fool as to challenge that."

"I hope you're right. And I suppose the Emperor will have to confirm it."

"Probably. But don't worry about that now," advised the ever-practical Adelheit. "Come now. Change your clothes and freshen up a bit. I'm sure the people are awaiting some word from you."

"Holy Mary, Mother of God, forgive me," she exclaimed. "Here I am

541

worrying about myself and the people haven't even been told that Otto is . . . is dead."

"I'm sure the Chancellor has already told them that," suggested Adelheit, "but they will need some reassurance from you that there *will be no challenge* to the succession."

Anna resumed her dignity and once more became the proud, noble Duchess of Lüneburg.

"Lise, fetch my mourning clothes," she commanded.

"They are already laid out, Your Grace," replied the maid. "I was just waiting until you were ready."

"Dear Lise, I am ready. Help me now." In a few moments she had changed into deep mourning and sent for the nursemaid to bring Heinrich. He arrived bawling at all this untoward excitement but calmed somewhat when Momma took him in her arms. But where was Papa?

With the baby in her arms, she mustered all her dignity and went out onto the balcony of the oldest tower of the Castle. The silent crowd stirred and waited.

"My dearest people," she said, with a catch in her throat that she quickly controlled, "you already know that our beloved Duke is dead. God rest his noble soul." She held up the baby. "Long live Duke Heinrich." The citizens of Celle cheered even as they wept.

She assured them that everything would be as before, that she would carry on all her late husband's good works as well as her own, that with God's guidance she would try to be a good regent until her son reached his majority. The crowd cheered her every statement. She could feel their love coming across the distance that separated them and was comforted.

When she returned to the great hall a young blond giant of a knight was waiting for her.

He knelt before her. "My lady," he said, "I cannot tell you how sorry I am to have been the cause of your noble Duke's death. May God strike me dead if I do not do humble penance for my act."

"Why, it was no fault of yours, young sir," insisted Anna, shocked that he should feel so. "It was an unlucky fall. *You* did not break his neck. It was God's will. Rest assured that my beloved husband died doing what he most loved to do. No penance is called for." She raised him up. "And whom do I have the honor of addressing?" she asked.

"Your humble servant Rudolf of Habsburg, Your Grace," he replied.

"Habsburg? His Majesty's . . . ?"

"Very distant cousin, my Lady."

"Indeed," she replied graciously. "Then be so kind as to convey our good wishes to your cousin. And be assured, Rudolf of Habsburg, that we bear no animosity toward you. You will always be welcome at our Court."

"Thank you, my lady," he murmured. "You are indeed gracious, Your Grace."

Eggeling von Eltze and Lüdeke Mestwart had been joint Bürgermeisters for many years and would be for several years to come. Lüdeke von Sehnden had long been on the Town Council. Together they formed the governing triumvirate of Celle, which would usher in the Reformation and the Renaissance and a heretofore unheard of prosperity to the town—the Golden Century of Celle—which their descendants would bring to fruition.

Book II
Merchants and Mayors

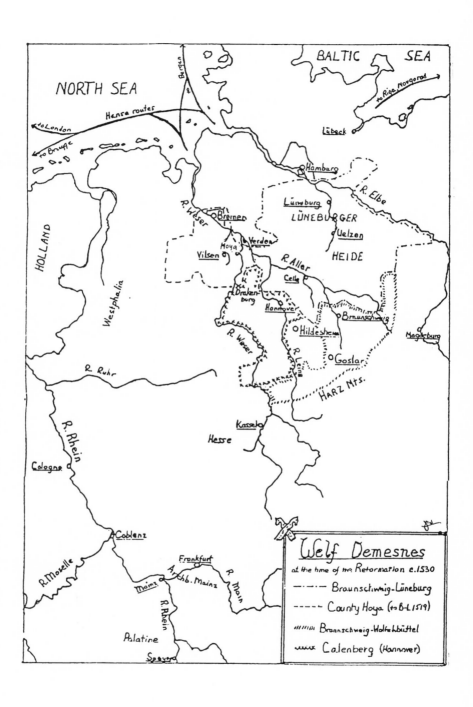

NORTH SEA

BALTIC SEA

Hansa routes

to London

to Bruges

to Riga, Novgorod

Lübeck

Hamburg

HOLLAND

Westphalia

R. Weser

Bremen

Hoya

Verden

Vilsen

R. Aller

Celle

Drakenburg

Hannover

R. Weser

Hildesheim

R. Leine

R. Ruhr

R. Rhein

Cologne

Coblenz

R. Moselle

Frankfurt

Mainz

Archb. Mainz

R. Main

R. Rhein

Palatine

Speyer

Lüneburg

LÜNEBURGER

Uelzen

HEIDE

R. Elbe

Braunschweig

Magdeburg

Goslar

HARZ Mts.

Kassel

Hesse

Welf Demesnes
at the time of the Reformation c.1530
— · — Braunschweig-Lüneburg
— — — County Hoya (to B-L 1519)
///////// Braunschweig-Wolfenbüttel
⌇⌇⌇ Calenberg (Hannover)

6

AD 1485

Anna Mestwart trudged through the wet, slippery snow as she left St. Anna's Hospital and crossed the Vischern. A sharp northwest wind blew up the river and she hugged her fur-lined cloak more tightly about her. She loved her work at the hospital and wished she could have stayed longer, but it got dark so early this time of year. Not that she had to work there at all. She was not even officially administrator—the Duchess was that— but she felt she owed it to her dear father of blessed memory who had founded the hospital. Besides, she really enjoyed helping those unfortunate people who took shelter there. She was thankful they had a place to stay on a night such as this.

As she approached the Aller bridge, which led to the heavily fortified town gate, the wind grew sharper and the snow came down thicker. She pulled her hood down and hugged the cloak closer. With eyes thus downcast on the path before her, she almost did not see the rider coming towards her across the bridge. Only the clip-clopping of the horse's hoofs alerted her. She stopped just in time to avoid being run over by the huge destrier bearing a knight in full armor, his cloak swirling about him in the wind.

He stopped also and asked, "What fair maiden goeth abroad alone on such a foul night? May I be of assistance?"

As she looked up at him, the snowflakes stuck to her eyelashes and she could not see his face clearly. Although his helm was perched on the pommel before him, he, too, was hooded and with the wind swirling his cloak, she could not identify what arms he bore.

"And what brave knight comes fully armed for war to a town that knows only peace?" she asked with a touch of sarcasm. Who did he think he was anyway, nearly running her down in the dark?

But when she raised her face to him, he apparently recognized her.

547

"By all the saints, if it isn't little Anna Mestwart, now fully grown to a ravishing young lady."

"Good sir knight," she replied, "you obviously know me,—and I am hardly ravishing in this awful weather—but if I'm supposed to know you I'm afraid my memory fails me."

"Anna, Anna," he said more gently, "we used to play together as children. We were even betrothed after a fashion. I suppose we still are."

At this the dawn broke. "Lüdeke—Lüdeke von Sehnden!" she exclaimed. "Holy Mother Mary, forgive me. I truly did not recognize you. It's been so many years."

"Too many," he agreed. "Now may I be of assistance? Come, I'll give you a ride home."

"No, no, that's quite all right," she objected. "Thank you anyway, but I'll walk. It isn't far."

"Far enough in this weather," he urged. "I do know exactly where you live, you know. And this is no place to be having a conversation."

"I agree," she said and started to turn away. Suddenly she felt herself gripped under the armpits and lifted up onto the saddle before him. "Lüdeke, put me down."

He laughed and she suddenly remembered what a tease he had always been. "I certainly shall," he replied, "right at your front doorstep. Besides, we have to continue our conversation."

She knew better than to argue or make a fuss before the guards at the gate. It would have been too embarrassing. And his grip was too strong. But inwardly she seethed. How dare he catch her up like some—some damsel in distress? Besides, the ice-cold joints of his armor were poking into her ribs, which did nothing to improve her mood.

After they passed through the gate, she asked, for want of something better to say, "Why fully armed and armored? Are you on your way to war again?"

"No, mein Fraülein. I lost my squire."

"Oh, I am sorry."

"And my palfrey and almost everything else I own but what I have on my back. The only way I could carry the armor was to wear it."

She didn't know what to say to this revelation. "Isn't it cold?" The moment she said it, she realized how stupid that must have sounded.

But he answered her seriously. "A bit, yes, I must admit, but I have my good quilted hauberk underneath. I've been colder. And I expect there will be a good fire awaiting me at home—if I'm welcome there, that is."

Again she was at a loss for words. This was not the daredevil Lüdeke she remembered. "Are you coming home, then, for good or just passing through?" she asked.

"For good, I hope. As I say, depending on my welcome. Would that make you happy, dear Anna?"

"Lüdeke, I honestly don't know what to say. It's been so long. I don't feel as though I know you anymore."

"Well, we'll have to remedy that, won't we?"

She was saved from answering that, as they had arrived at her house. "I would ask you in, but I'm sure you want to get home as quickly as possible."

"I expect so," he said as he set her down. "May I call on you tomorrow?"

"Perhaps," she replied. "Thank you for the ride." And she ran into the house.

Catherine was waiting in the best parlor, where there was no fire.

"Mama, why here in the parlor where it is so cold?" asked Anna.

"I thought I heard a horse, but I guess I was mistaken. It must have been your klompen on the cobbles."

Anna let this pass. She was in no mood to discuss Lüdeke von Sehnden. She knew Catherine would gush and want to know everything. And what was there really to tell her? That he was back from wherever he had been all these years and apparently impoverished. Anna hadn't wanted to ask any details. She really didn't care to know. Furthermore, she was sure the whole town would know his story within two or three days. The von Sehnden were not known for their reticence.

Only Adelheit, there was a noble lady, if ever. Anna knew how disappointed she was in her sons and how especially worried she was about Lüdeke. But she kept her counsel and seldom spoke of it.

"I am going into the kitchen to get warmed up before the fire. It's a nasty night out there."

"Of course, my dear. I wasn't thinking. And how was your day? Any new people in the hospital?"

"Quite a few, but that's to be expected in this weather. Nothing unusual, though."

Anna really didn't want to talk to her mother. As she warmed herself by the fire and then ate her supper, she reflected on how limited Catherine's world was. She had no interest in the hospital; in fact, she dreaded the sight of the poor, the crippled, the sick. Yet she loved to hear the stories of the more lurid cases. Even her social life, which she claimed to adore, was very limited, more so since the death of her husband. Her intellect simply could not cope with the upper echelons of the Gewandschneider, so she took refuge in looking down her nose at them because few had noble blood. Quite sad, thought her daughter, pitiful even.

And on this evening Anna wanted nothing more than to retire to her own room and reflect on Lüdeke von Sehnden. She suddenly realized that his return had affected her more than she had first admitted. She would have to do some serious thinking about him. And she did not want her mother's idle chatter to interrupt those thoughts.

Lüdeke meanwhile rode the few doors down the street to his own home. He turned the horse directly to the stables in the large yard at the back of the house. The groom was already at his supper in the stable loft. No one was expecting him.

"Halloo," he called out. "Halloo there, Fritz."

The poor man came tumbling down the ladder, half scared out of his wits. "Who is it? Who is there?"

"It is I, Fritz, home from the wars."

"Why, Master Lüdeke, I would scarcely have recognized you," exclaimed the surprised Fritz. He looked beyond Lüdeke. "Where is your squire?"

"Lost," replied Lüdeke gruffly. "Here help me down and get me out of this armor, would you?"

"Certainly, Master, right away," said Fritz, bewildered. Since he was just a groom, though a fine one, and not a squire, he had a great deal of difficulty in extricating his young master from all the buckles and straps of the armor, but finally it was done.

Lüdeke apologized. "I am sorry to put you to so much trouble, old friend, but I have ridden for many a day in that pile of metal and it is a great relief to get it off. I must stink like a fishwife and probably have more fleas than yon old hound. Just leave it here in the stable for now. I'll have no need of it for a while."

"Very well, Master, and it was no trouble," replied the groom. "I am just happy you are home again, and I'm sure your Lady Mother will be, too. She has great need of you."

"Oh?" Lüdeke looked at him questioningly.

"I do not mean to speak out of turn, Master," Fritz went on, "but your Papa does not do well. She needs a man to help her, if I may be so bold."

"That's all right, Fritz. I'm glad you warned me. Take good care of my poor horse." And he hurried to the house.

He entered the great kitchen quietly for fear of startling everyone, but their old cook-housekeeper, Helga, was there alone cleaning up after supper. And he did startle her. But she had known him since he was a babe and nothing much he did ever surprised her.

"Why, Master Lüdeke, I would scarcely have recognized you," she exclaimed.

He hugged her and bussed her soundly. Then he held her at arm's length. "Dearest Helga, old Fritz said the very same thing. Have I changed that much?"

She studied his face for a moment. Thin, too thin, and gaunt, the blond hair dulled to a dirty brown. And his eyes, beautiful blue they always were and sparkling. They were shining now with the old light even as he embraced her, but for a few minutes when he first came in they looked haunted. They have seen terrible things I don't want to hear about, she thought. And older, too, older than his years warranted.

"Not really," she said. "You've matured, but that's to be expected, these many years. And you've lost weight, but a few of old Helga's good meals should remedy that. And I suspect a hot bath would be in order."

"That it would, dear Helga. When you have time would you send some water up to my room. That is, if I still have a room."

"Of course you do, silly boy, and kept just as you and your brothers left it."

"But first I must greet my parents. Where are they?" he asked with some trepidation.

"Your Lady Mother works on her accounts day and night. I fear she will ruin her eyes." Helga shook her head. "But she tries so hard to keep the business going."

"And my father? Is the business not going well?"

"Oh, very well indeed, as far as an ignorant woman such as I can see. But he has been ailing. Not sick really, just tired and lackluster so much of the time. I truly think he has lost heart with all of you gone. Perhaps you can cheer him — both of them — up. But are you home for good, or are you going to break his heart again?"

"Someone else asked me that very question. Home for good, Helga, if he'll have me."

The old housekeeper smiled. "Then go to them quickly, while I fix you some supper."

"The bath first."

"Very well, but go, while the water heats."

If his mother was working on the books, he knew she would be in the front parlor, half of which was allocated to their 'office'. He tiptoed in. Adelheit was there alone hunched over the big desk, straining to see by the light of two candles, a luxury indeed. A pile of bills and invoices lay at her left hand, while her quill pen scratched busily in the great ledger that lay before her. She was concentrating so, she did not hear him. He stood watching her for a moment, wondering where his father was.

"Mother," he said quietly.

She started and then very slowly put down her pen and turned around.

"Lude," she cried and jumped up to embrace him. "Lude, Lude, where did you come from?"

"Everywhere and nowhere," he answered cryptically. "It is a long story that I'll tell you sometime, but not now. I have been almost two weeks coming home and am right glad to be here at last."

"And how long do you stay before you leave us again?" she asked, not without a touch of bitterness.

"Forever, if you and Father will have me."

The look she gave him was incredulous, full of doubt. "Do you really mean that, Lude?"

"From the bottom of my heart. Truly, Mama. I have finally realized that the life of soldiering is not for me. The glories of knighthood are no glories at all. Chivalry no longer exists. And the tournament circuit is totally ridiculous. I guess I've grown up."

She hugged him again, fiercely. "Thank God, thank God and His Holy Mother. Oh, how I've prayed for this. Lude, Lude, welcome home, my dearest son." She could not help the tears streaming down her face.

"I am ready to take my place in the business, if you and Papa will have me. I can already see that you need help." He gestured toward the ledger. "I know I have a lot to learn, but I promise I'll learn fast. I have not used my brain much these past years. I'm sure it will be grateful for the exercise."

Adelheit smiled through her tears. "Your Papa will be happy to hear that."

"Do you really think so?" he asked. "I have been worrying about that all the way home. I was not sure if he would even allow me in the house."

"You did well to worry," she agreed. "If you had been about to depart again, I'm sure he would have said, 'I have no sons at all, ungrateful curs'.

It has reached that point, Lude. He fares not well."

"So Helga told me. What is really wrong? Is he ill or just — just brokenhearted?"

"Tired and discouraged and, yes, brokenhearted. Oh, Lude, if you truly mean what you say, I'm sure it will go a long way to curing his malaise. He was always a fighter and such a hard worker, but I'm afraid he feels there is nothing left to fight for."

"Mama dearest, I truly mean what I say." Now Lüdeke was almost in tears himself. "I shall try very hard to restore his fighting spirit. He wouldn't be Papa without that. I can't imagine him giving up, but I guess I can understand it."

She made to hug him again, but he held her off. "Don't embrace me again, Mama, until I've shed these filthy rags and had a bath. I am afraid fleas are not fussy where they jump."

"Oh, heavens, yes!" she exclaimed. "Go have your bath while I prepare him for your coming and your good news. He lies above but I am sure he's not sleeping. It is better if I go first. I should not want the sudden shock to stop his heart."

"Then it *is* serious," he said, concerned.

She shook her head. "I think not. Nothing that your promises won't cure."

He followed her up the stairs but turned to go to his old room while she continued to the parental chamber. He looked about the room. It was, as Helga had said, just as he had left it. There was the big bed that the three brothers had slept in, piled high with featherbeds. How inviting it looked. And the big chest that they used to fight over for clothes room. He looked out the window. He could just make out in the dark the outline of the big old apple tree, bare now, that they used to climb to get in and out of the window, until they got caught. The comfortable old rocking chair where they had all been nursed was still there and beside it someone had lit a candle. It cast a soft glow over the room. Home, he thought, I'm really home.

The big brass tub was already in place, and now Helga and a maid brought steaming pots of water.

"Have a care, Master Lüdeke," Helga warned. "It's very hot."

"I shall. Thank you, Helga, my weary bones will welcome it."

After his bath and some supper he returned to the parlor to await his parents. What is taking them so long, he wondered. Mama must really be having a hard time convincing him of my good intentions. And he began to get nervous again. After a while he turned to the big ledger book. I might as well try to learn something while I'm waiting. But he could make very little sense out of what was written therein. Finally he heard footsteps on the stairs and his parents entered the room.

He fell on his knees before his father, but not before he noticed how the man had aged. He is an old man. Have I done this? But not I alone. I have two elder brothers who contributed to it, too.

"Father, your prodigal son has come home. Can you find it in your heart to forgive me?"

"What is this?" demanded Lüdeke von Sehnden gruffly. "Get up off your knees and grasp my arm like a man. I am not some saint to genuflect to. As to forgiveness, we shall see if what your mother tells me is true."

Lüdeke rose and took his father's arm and then embraced him, overcome with emotions, happy that the older man's voice still sounded like that of the father he remembered. "Papa, I do sincerely mean everything I told Mama. I am home for good. I do want to learn the business and take part in it, if you'll have me."

"A little late for an apprenticeship," growled his father, "but I suppose better late than never." He grasped the back of a chair, obviously overcome with emotion, but trying to hide it beneath his gruff exterior. "I have to sit down. Not as young as I used to be." Whereupon he sat and Lüdeke and Adelheit took chairs opposite him, thankful that the first hurdle had been crossed. "I don't know how many years I have left. You'll have to learn fast," he continued.

"Oh, Papa, don't talk like that. You have many good years left. And I shall strive diligently to learn very fast. I promise you that."

The elder shook his head. "We'll see, we'll see." After a pregnant pause, he went on. "You know, the business is three times as large—and many times as profitable, I might add—as when you left. It has grown beyond belief. Besides that, my dearest friend and partner Lüdeke Mestwart died three years ago and we have taken over his entire share. That silly, shallow wife of his couldn't add two and two if her life depended on it."

"Yes, I know. Mama wrote me."

"She wrote you? I didn't know. Wherever to?"

"It took months and months to catch up with me, but I did receive it at long last."

"I wrote several over the years," put in Adelheit, "but I imagine some never found you."

"I guess not. I only received two in all these years."

The elder Lüdeke went on as if this exchange had never occurred. "Anyway, we pay them a substantial income. They live very comfortably."

"They? You mean Catherine and Anna?"

"Ja, ja. And Johann got his fair share, too, but that went right into the Church. He was ordained priest in '81, just a year before his father died."

"I expected that."

"Ja, ja, in that religious family what else would you expect? Of course, it's only right that the eldest son go into the Church. That is our old Saxon custom. Eggeling's eldest has, too. Only mine has not." He broke off for a moment. "And the girl is just like him."

"You mean Anna?" He was losing his father's rambling train of thought.

"Ja, ja, she wanted to go into the Beguines, but Lüdeke made her promise not to—because of the Stipendium, you know."

Lüdeke was not quite sure if he did know, but he wanted to get off the subject of Anna. "And what of the von Eltze?" he asked.

"Eggeling has been Bürgermeister for many years. I guess you know that." His son nodded. "When Lüdeke Mestwart died, he got his son Cord elected as the second Bürgermeister, and the two of them literally run Celle—and the Duke, too—and very well, I might add. We are no longer partners but still best of friends. He still has a very profitable business, but he prefers politics. The whole family does. Every one of them has some sort of political job—toll-collector, councilman, whatever."

"Ja," acknowledged Lüdeke. "I can remember his son Eggeling, my friend, telling me—bragging, in fact—that they have been toll-collectors and Bürgermeisters since the very founding of Celle. It seems almost hereditary in that family."

"Ja, it does," agreed his father, "but we wouldn't keep reelecting them if they weren't capable."

"That's true. Now tell me of the business. I want to start learning immediately."

"Grain, primarily, as it always has been, and cloth, of course. Your mother inherited most of your grandfather Bünsel's boats, so we now have the largest fleet of riverboats on the Aller and the Weser. Your uncle Hinrik Bünsel got his share, but he stumbles and bumbles, so we have to help out there occasionally. Your grandmother Wünneke does what she can to guide him, but she is tired of the business, although one smart woman in other ways. Everything basically is about the same, only so much more of it that we can barely handle it. Ach, we have any number of clerks and assistants and apprentices to do the actual physical work. Your mother works night and day, but I am afraid I am not doing my fair share. We need management, Lude, management, and I just haven't found it in my heart to appoint anyone outside the family." He looked at his son with piercing eyes.

"I understand, Papa. I want to learn."

"We'll see, we'll see." The older man hesitated as if gathering up his courage to continue. "Your brothers, bah! I am disappointed — nay, disgusted with them. Paulus, the one who should have gone into the church — well, if he didn't want to I can understand that. The Church is not what it used to be. Rotten to the core. But what does he do? Dabble in politics in Lieffland, in some little village not even on the map. He didn't have the patience to earn his way here, where it would have been worthwhile. And Hans, marrying some girl from Lübeck and setting up as a shopkeeper there because she didn't want to leave home. What a comedown! We are *merchants*, not shopkeepers!" he shouted.

"Lüdeke, calm yourself," warned Adelheit.

"You are right, my dear, I must not get myself upset." He shook his head and said quietly, " 'How low the mighty have fallen'." He looked at his son. "And then you."

Lord, have mercy, thought Lüdeke. Here it comes. But his father surprised him.

"You, I could almost understand. Almost, I say, because my route was just the opposite from yours. I, too, left home at fourteen. They wanted me to be a knight, fostered me with the Duke and all, and I hated it. But I was fascinated by commerce from the start, especially after I met the von Eltze. Oh, I, too, did some fighting along the way, for the Graf of Hoya and others, to earn my bread. But that was not for me. Now tell me why *you* have decided that war is not your profession."

Lüdeke thought carefully for a moment. "The futility of it all, for one thing. One day a man is your enemy, the next your companion-at-arms, but if you have already killed him, what is the point? One day you fight for the Emperor, the next for the Pope, another day for some petty lord who has nothing better to do than pick boundary disputes with his neighbor, the next against a real enemy like the Turks with a host of thousands. And the atrocities! Holy God, what I have seen. I dare not describe them before my lady mother."

"I am no innocent virgin," interjected Adelheit. "I have heard of them. Tell it, if it will ease your mind."

He nodded. "The infamous galley slaves were the least of what they did to their captives. Prisoners of war, who, by all the rules we were taught, should be ransomed or exchanged. The Turks do not go by our rules. I fought against them at Otranto and was captured. Fortunately, as the tide of battle changed a group of us escaped, or I should not be here today to tell of it."

His mother gasped and his father looked aghast.

Lüdeke went on. "The floggings, brandings, maiming. To cut a man's tongue out because he was suspected of being a spy, to cut off the right hand of a brave archer so he could never draw a bow again, to castrate an innocent man so he could be a slave in their harem . . . And it's not just the Turks. I have seen things almost as bad among Christians. Papa, have you ever witnessed an auto-da-fé?"

His father nodded grimly.

Lüdeke continued. "Because an old dame keeps a cat or a midwife helps a poor woman, who already has twelve children she cannot feed, abort an unwanted babe or a goodwife nurses a dying person back to health, they call them witches and burn them. And those who, even inadvertently, complain of the corruptness of Pope or the Church are labeled heretics and fare even worse. The Pope is a filthy lecher. He who is supposed to be celibate, he's just married off his son to one of the Medici in order to get his hands in their money bags. He has stepped up the sale in indulgences to gullible people to an unprecedented degree in order to finance his wars. Wars! He shouldn't even have an army."

"I agree wholeheartedly," said the elder Lüdeke, "but be careful to whom you say such things, although more and more people are beginning to think that way. They're simply fed up. Thank God the Dukes have never permitted the Inquisition to set foot in Celle and the sale of indulgences is more or less controlled. Lüdeke Mestwart could have told you a story of an ancestor of his who was almost burned as a witch."

"Really? Here?"

"No, in Uelzen, but that's not far."

"Anyway, I didn't mean to get so far off the track, but I'll finish telling you the rest of my reasons. Chivalry is dead. There is no more glory in knighthood; no one fights by the rules anymore. It is all brutality, and one doesn't need a brain for that. Better if you don't have one sometimes."

"I'm glad you can see that at last."

"And those powerful new cannon. Not only are they terrifying to man

557

and horse alike, but the finest suit of armor or the strongest castle wall is no protection from them."

His father nodded. "Instruments of the devil in the hands of unscrupulous men," he commented.

"So I thought I would try the tournaments to try to recoup my finances. What a joke. Men playing at children's games because they do not have a real war to fight at the moment. But a real soldier doesn't stand a chance against the professionals. They have their own tricks, and not always very nice ones. I was in Provence when I lost almost everything and decided to quit that foolishness. When I announced I was leaving for home, my squire left me, took my beautiful palfrey, most of my clothes and money, the rogue, said he would seek a *man* to serve, not a ninny. That was the final blow to my self-esteem, or so I thought. I shall never forget the tournament in which our Duke Otto was killed, though I was but a small child clinging tightly to Paulus' hand. I dreamed of being a great knight like that, but now I see how foolhardy that was, endangering his life and jeopardizing the whole Duchy. How fares the Duchess these days?"

"Well enough," answered Adelheit. "She remarried, you know, the Count of Katzenellenbogen, but she remains here as Regent, overworked and worried about her son. He, too, dreams dreams of knighthood and wars and worst of all, revenge. She put him for a while with his grandfather, who still bided with the Franciscans, in the hopes that he would learn compassion and clemency, but the old man was too far gone in his spiritual world to do much good. He learned nothing from the good brothers but his letters, and that not as well as he would have in our good Hanse school. He is almost illiterate and surly. He wants to take over the government already, but so far Anna and the Chancellor as well as the von Eltze and all of us have held him in check. But not for long, I fear. He speaks of nothing but war and revenge."

"Revenge?" asked Lüdeke. "Against whom?"

"Against the Emperor and the whole house of Habsburg, all because of that unfortunate young man—a distant cousin, I believe—who knocked his father off his horse."

"God's balls! Sorry, Mama. That's madness. He could lose the whole Duchy."

"We try to tell him that, but he is adamant. Perhaps you could talk to him, disillusion him. You've been there. It might carry some weight. The Duchess would certainly appreciate it," she suggested.

"I could try, but I doubt he would listen. Holy Mother, what a soup he could get us into. The whole feudal system is dying and he acts like it was two—nay, three hundred years ago. I spent last night with Uncle Franz."

"Oh," said his father, "and how fares he?"

"Well enough, and sends his regards. They received me with utmost kindness, but I can see why you left. What a narrow existence they live. Those little demesnes are soon a thing of the past. If I have learned one thing, it's as you have always said, Papa, that commerce is the lifeblood of the world and brings peace among strangers and divers peoples, but by the same token it must have peace in which to thrive."

His father's smile gradually broadened into a big, happy grin. "Welcome home, my son," he said. "Welcome home." And they embraced once again, while Adelheit wept for joy. "And now I must to bed. This excitement is too much for an old man. But tomorrow morning, at sunrise, mind you, and for the next six months, perhaps even a year, you will follow me around like a puppy dog, and I shall endeavor to teach you how to be a prosperous merchant."

"Thank you, dearest Papa."

As exhausted as he was, Lüdeke was too excited to fall immediately to sleep. He snuggled under the featherbed, the whole big bed to himself, the first decent bed he'd lain in for many months, and he let his mind wander. The snow fell silently outside. A benediction. That's what it was. His father's acceptance of him was the best part—essential to any dreams of the future. He kept hearing the elder Lüdeke say, "We'll see, we'll see." Well, he would show him how fast he could learn, how soon he could be of help. And he had management capabilities, hadn't he? After all, he had commanded troops. Although the moment he thought this, he dismissed it. He knew the situation would be entirely different. He thought about the boatloads of grain. God's teeth, the biggest fleet on the river from the one little boat in which his father had arrived in Celle! And the ells and ells of cloth, which justified their membership in the Gewandschneider and his parents among the most powerful people in that Guild. And the spices, jewels and precious metals and whatever else they traded in. How could they do it all by themselves? The thought was mind-boggling. It suddenly came to him that his father was a genius. And Mother is brilliant, too. With some dismay he remembered that big ledger. But I'll learn what it's all about. And she is a good teacher. I know that.

He let his mind drift to the various Hanse cities his father would probably take him to. He had never been to any of them. All his fighting years had been spent in the east or the south, mostly in the south. And frankly, he was fed up with the dullness and stupidity of the east and the decadence and duplicity of the south. He thought of Antwerp, financial queen of the north, where east and west, north and south, met to trade the whole world's goods and settle their accounts. She had long ago super-seded Brugge, when that harbor had silted up. He had always wanted to go to Antwerp. Now perhaps — no — probably, he would. He dreamed of Lon-don and Novgorod and, closer to home the great seaports of Bremen, Hamburg and Lübeck. There he would meet good, solid, hardworking Germans — maybe even a girl . . .

And his thoughts turned to Anna Mestwart. He hadn't really wanted to discuss her with his parents. Not yet, anyway. He wondered if the betrothal was still valid. Well, those things could always be set aside. His father seemed to think she was too religious; his mother had offered no comment. Anna hadn't struck him as being overly pious during their brief meeting. A little cold and haughty, perhaps. But then he had taken her so by surprise and after so many years, it was no more than he could expect of any decent girl. He would try to avoid her for the next few weeks until he could get some inkling of what other people thought of her, although that might be difficult. They were bound to meet in church or even on the street, living so close by. On the other hand, maybe he should pursue her, get to know her better and form his own opinion. Well, there was time enough for that. It was best left in the hands of the Almighty for now. He had more important things to think of.

With that he drifted off to sleep.

Anna, too, was lying in her bed, watching the snow drift down, and thinking of him. What a shock to have him appear out of the night like that. Like someone out of the old fairy tales. But he was real. A man grown, and so different from the laughing, teasing playmate she re-membered. But maybe not so different. He obviously had enjoyed teas-ing her when he lifted her up onto the horse. But adult teasing was not the same. There was a note of seriousness running through it. She was not sure if she could cope with that. In fact, she was ambivalent about his return. She was glad, naturally, for his sake, that he had come home. She hoped he was serious about it and that his father would ac-cept him. She rather thought he would, but not without giving him a rough time of it. He would have to settle in quickly and toe the line. Master von Sehnden made his own rules and permitted no deviation from them. He was especially intolerant of what he considered foolishness or frivolity. Yes, Lüdeke would not have it easy.

From her own point of view, she was not at all sure how she felt about his return. It would certainly upset her quiet, carefully structured life if he insisted on the terms of the betrothal. She, too, wondered if it was really valid. They had both been very young children. She barely remembered it. And many such had been set aside. Although she had promised her father, shortly before his death, that she would not join the Beguines or enter a convent, she had not promised to marry just anyone, only Lüdeke, and when he disappeared for so many years she felt relieved of that obligation. She never thought he would return to claim her. And if she were really honest with herself she knew what her father had had in mind when he extracted that promise from her. The Stipendium. That generous foundation from her ancestor Johann Wiese that provided for a university education for two descendants every generation. Somehow her father had wrested it from his uncles and elder brothers. She had heard that there was another such from the Mestwart in Uelzen, so perhaps they hadn't cared. No one knew back then that she would be the only descendant of her father capable of continuing it. Her brother, Johann, had studied under it, and the other scholarship had been reinvested. But he, being a priest, could not marry. So it was up to her to marry and have children to pass it on to. If she did not, it would revert to the Duchy or the town of Uelzen or perhaps Celle. She wasn't sure. But it would be lost. What a terrible obligation for one young maiden, who did not want to marry at all. If she could not live the life of a sister, at least she was doing their work. She was happy helping the poor and unfortunate and especially serving in St. Anna's Hospital. She wanted nothing more out of life.

And now Lüdeke had returned to stir up all sorts of uncertainties. If only there was someone she could talk to. Her mother would be useless. Catherine could not understand her daughter at all. Adelheit would, of course, favor the marriage to her son. Besides, Anna knew the von Sehndens' attitude toward the church. They only paid lip service to it for business reasons, always criticizing the Pope and quick to point out all the corruption that had crept in. Metke von Eltze the same, but for political reasons. Not that they were entirely wrong, but there were a lot of good people in the church, too. Like her brother. But she couldn't talk to him, either, or any of the priests at the Marienkirche. Not about this. They would tell her to follow her conscience, but with an eye on the money. And what did her conscience tell her anyway? She knew she couldn't betray her father's wishes. Then she thought, the Duchess. She has successfully combined marriage—twice over—with all her good works. Of course, she had reams of servants to help her, but then, too, her works were on such a grandiose scale that Anna's seemed a pittance by comparison. I shall seek her advice the next time she comes to the hospital. She of all people will understand how I feel. And there is no hurry. I may not even have to make that decision if Lüdeke should change his mind about me. She laughed at herself. I may be worrying over nothing. With that settled, she, too, fell asleep.

The next morning as Lüdeke followed the elder von Sehnden from the office in the house to his several warehouses, to the granaries and boats on the quay, to the Rathaus, to wherever else his business took him, he noticed the changes that had taken place in Celle. New half-timbered houses with tile roofs had replaced many of the older wooden, thatched dwellings. Even new streets were being laid out, and at one end of the church a flurry of building activity was going on.

"What is happening there?" he asked.

"Ah, thanks to the Duchess, we are finally going to have a new bell tower to replace the one the von Eltze built that fell down in a tornado many years ago."

"I remember that. It was frightening."

"Just poorly built," said his father. "Let us hope this one stands longer. But if the fools do too much in this weather, the mortar will freeze and it will go the same way. A useless frivolity, I say, but the people like to hear the bells."

"So do I, I must admit."

His father grimaced but ignored that remark. "Not only that," he continued, "but Her Grace intends to start construction this year on a new west wing to the Castle, thereby enclosing the entire bailey. Part of her plans include building a brand-new chapel in the southeast tower to replace the old one."

"My, she certainly is an ambitious woman. Who pays for all this?"

"The castle building out of their own income. The Welfs, you know, are just about the wealthiest royalty in Germany, more so even than the Emperor. But, of course, their income comes directly from their vassalage fees and indirectly from our taxes. But I say, if they have to spend it, better that way than on useless wars."

"I agree completely. And the bell tower?"

"That, I am afraid, we are paying for directly through our tithes and a

562

special assessment to the church as well as through our taxes. The town is paying a good share of it and the Council approved, so what can I say?"

For the next several months Lüdeke did indeed follow the elder von Sehnden like a puppy dog and learned and learned. He asked intelligent questions and eventually contributed some ideas of his own, which seemed to please his father greatly. The late afternoons and then evenings, as the days grew longer, he spent with Adelheit learning the books. She explained how the new double-entry bookkeeping made their records so much more accurate. Soon the big ledger was no longer a mystery to him.

One evening when they had finished their work, she laid down her quill and sat back in her chair with a sigh. "Have you given any thought to marriage, Lude?" she asked.

He was so taken by surprise, all he could say was, "Not really."

"If you truly intend to take over the business from your father one day, you must needs have a family of your own to pass it on to."

"I'm aware of that, Mama, but I don't feel quite ready for that yet," he objected lamely.

"It's high time," she replied. "More than high time." She shut the ledger with a bang and left him alone in the room.

Now the pressure will start, he thought. God's teeth, I don't want to be tied down yet. He was grateful she had not mentioned Anna Mestwart specifically. He had seen Anna in church and about the town and had always greeted her cordially but as yet had made no effort to cultivate her friendship. Besides I'm just too busy. Papa is giving me more and more responsibility and that's all I can handle for now. With that self-justification, he decided to put the matter out of his mind.

But it was not to be for long. Before the week was out his father asked, out of the blue, "Are you paying court to Anna Mestwart yet?"

"Why, no. I haven't given it a thought," he replied.

"You had better. You are betrothed, you know."

"We were but children. Can such a betrothal be valid?" he objected.

"It is valid, all right. Lüdeke Mestwart and I promised each other that our families would be united, just as our businesses were."

"I thought arranged marriages only took place in the families of royalty."

"Not anymore. Many of the great merchant families are doing it more and more. It's simply good business."

"So now it's a business proposition. Another part of the business I must learn, right?"

"Don't get sarcastic with me."

"I don't mean to, Father, but I hardly know the girl. Can't I have some say in the matter?"

"No. And it's time you got to know her. It's insulting to her that you've let it go so long. She's a good girl and perfect for you, in my opinion. She would temper your wild streak."

"I thought you considered her too pious."

"All the more for you to brighten her life, give her other interests besides that hospital, worthy though that is."

"I don't feel ready for marriage yet."

"Well, it's high time you did. More than high time. Let's get back to work."

Lüdeke gave it no more thought until he was alone at the end of the busy day. And then it was all he could think of. *I suppose I might as well get to know the girl or they will give me no peace. It will be something to do in my time off. And frankly, I have looked around a bit and I must admit I haven't seen anything else that interests me as yet. At least she's an old friend. And just maybe she's no more interested in marriage than I. I do know for sure that the Church's stand on these childhood betrothals is that if both parties, when they reach the age of consent, agree to have it set aside, it can be done. I'll call on her on Sunday. That will keep Mama and Papa quiet for a while and at the same time I can find out how she feels. But I shall have to be very discreet. She's an intelligent woman. I'll ask her after Mass.*

That Sunday he fell in with Anna as both families were leaving the church.

"Good morning, Fräulein Mestwart."

"Good morning, Lüdeke. And why so formal? You always called me Anna when we were children."

Suddenly Lüdeke was tongue-tied. "Well, I mean—that is—er—we're both adults," he stammered, "and it's been a long time. We're practically strangers."

"And whose fault is that?" she asked sharply.

"Mine, I guess," he replied rather meekly. *God's balls,* he thought, *this is not the shy little Anna I used to tease unmercifully.* "I should like to amend that, if I may," he added.

"Oh?" she said. "It seems to me it was snowing hard the last we spoke and here it is sunny and beautiful, nigh on midsummer. That adds up to six months on my calendar."

"I have been working very hard learning the business," he pleaded. "Papa has kept me on a tight leash."

"So tight that you must needs work even on Sundays and Holy Days? Even serfs make merry then."

He cringed at the well-deserved chiding, but then she smiled. A broad, bright smile that changed her whole face.

"Why, you're teasing me, Anna." He suddenly relaxed and smiled back. "I guess that repays me for all the tricks I played on you long ago."

"Perhaps." She laughed.

"Then may I call on you this afternoon? We could take a walk. It's such a lovely day."

"Very well. Come after dinner, that is, if you remember where the house is."

"Stop teasing me, woman, or I shall have to think up some of my old tricks."

"No tricks, Lüdeke—we're adults now, as you chose to remind me. Auf Wiedersehen." With that she rejoined Catherine and they went on their way.

That wasn't so bad, thought Lüdeke as he watched them go. We've broken the ice. At least we're still friends. She seems as though she is an interesting woman—and a challenge, too, methinks. She is sure not the shrinking violet I remember. A twinge of excitement went through him as he headed home to dinner.

After that they met frequently and their meetings were always enjoyable, interesting and to Lüdeke, sometimes educational. She was a very fount of all sorts of unusual facts—and fantasies.

"Where did you learn all these things?" he asked her.

"I read."

"Books?"

"No, dummy," she teased. "I find them in the stars in the sky."

He looked at her, amazed. "You mean you actually read whole books?"

"Why, yes. Don't you?"

"No. I don't think I'd have the patience—or even the ability—to read a whole book. My reading consists of bills of lading, bills of exchange, inventories, that sort of thing."

"You should try it sometime. It can open up a whole new world for you."

"I have seen enough of the world."

565

"But you have only seen war and devastation. I have recently read Master Polo's book about his journey to Cathay. It is amazing to learn that there is another huge kingdom on the other side of the world from us."

"I heard that that was mostly fantasy."

"No indeed. Several friars have followed in his footsteps and written about it as well. It is all true. And where do you think the spices come from that you merchants so covet? Why are the Portuguese so diligently seeking a sea route around Africa, if they didn't believe it exists?"

"Possibly so, but they haven't found it yet."

"No, but they will. And what about history? One of the first books we purchased was our own Bible. Mother and I read a bit of it every day."

"She reads, too?"

"Not too well. She has trouble with the Latin. But I read it to her. And do you know that many of the things the Church teaches us are not in the Bible at all?"

"I'm not surprised at that."

"I think Master Gutenberg's invention is the greatest thing that has ever happened to mankind."

"But I heard his partners cheated him and he died a pauper. That was not good business."

"Oh, don't always look at things from a business point of view. Think what a gift he gave to the world. He should be made a saint. Now everyone who wants to can read the truth for himself."

"And the Church does not look kindly on that."

"I am afraid you are right. I have heard that in some places—Italy and Spain, I think—the Inquisition has banned and even seized and burned precious books. And why? Because they don't want people to know that not everything the Church teaches is true."

"My goodness!" exclaimed Lüdeke. "Don't get so vehement. You sound like one of the reformers preaching in the marketplace."

Anna laughed. "Sorry. I don't mean to get carried away, but I feel so strongly about these things."

"Just don't let the wrong people hear you. We wouldn't want the Holy Office to come to Celle."

"Don't worry. I think I'm safe from that abomination. Duchess Anna feels much as I do, and she has quietly carried out many, many reforms of her own."

"I know and Celle can consider herself very fortunate that we have her."

What an intelligent woman she is, thought Lüdeke, after this conversation and many others in a similar vein. She stimulated his intellect, his imagination and his curiosity. He even investigated the little printing press and bookshop that had been set up in Celle, similar to hundreds springing up all over Germany and spreading from there to all parts of Europe. He even tried to interest his father in it from an investment point of view.

"Bah! Artisans and shopkeepers. We are merchants," was the usual answer. "It is just a fad that will soon pass. Not enough people outside of the towns can read to make it viable."

"But it will encourage them to learn," Lüdeke objected.

"I doubt it, especially when the Church discourages it. Why, half the noble families out on the land can't read or write. They keep clerks to do it for them. But everyone, rich and poor, needs the food and cloth which we supply, as well as the spices and jewels their wives covet. But books? Never."

Lüdeke didn't argue, but he knew his father was wrong.

One of the things Lüdeke enjoyed most about his conversations with Anna was how she presented an argument on a given subject but rarely argued, merely led the discussion. He realized, as he had once admitted, that his brain needed the exercise, and he revelled in the many new worlds she opened up to him. Their friendship deepened and, for now at least, the intellectual stimulation was enough. Occasionally he missed having a woman to cater to his needs, but when he was with her the lack of a physical aspect to their relationship never occurred to him. Not that she was objectionable. She had a good figure and her face, while not beautiful, was comely enough. He was beginning to think that perhaps she might make a good wife, if he ever reached the point of wanting one. For the moment, he was grateful that not once in any of their conversations had the subject of betrothal or marriage ever come up.

Also, for the moment the fact that he was visiting her frequently seemed to satisfy his parents. They never asked what Lüdeke and Anna did during their visits, probably assuming that the courtship was progressing. Catherine, Anna's mother, was always all a-twitter when he came, but because their conversations were so often beyond her intellectual capacity, she usually relinquished her duty as chaperone and left them alone in parlor, kitchen or garden. But then a third party decided to take a hand in things. One day old Wünneke Bünsel, Lüdeke's grandmother, called on Anna.

"Why, Mistress Bünsel, how nice of you to call," said Anna, surprised when the maid ushered the woman into the front parlor, for she had never been part of Catherine's social circle, although they were well acquainted. "I am sorry my mother is not at home right now. Perhaps . . . "

"No, it is you I came to see," interrupted Wünneke.

"I?" said Anna.

"Yes, you, my dear. At my age I don't stand on social amenities, so I shall come right to the point. I came to talk about you and my grandson Lüdeke von Sehnden."

"I and Lüdeke? But whatever have we done to displease you, Mistress?" queried Anna.

"It's what you have *not* done. When are you going to publish the banns?"

"But—but he has not asked me. We have not spoken of marriage," she objected.

"You are betrothed, are you not?"

"I suppose so, but that was long ago when we were but children. We are just good friends now."

"And how long do you think that will last? I understand you dissert like the learned doctors at the University, instead of the flirtatious exchange normal between a man and a woman."

"How do you know of what we speak?" asked Anna, immediately on the defensive.

"Your mother talks. My daughter talks. Soon the whole town will be talking. People think it is not natural. So I took it upon myself to take things in hand."

"But we both enjoy it. At least he seems to and I know I do. We have done nothing untoward, nothing to be ashamed of. How can people say it is not natural?" Anna demanded. "It is none of their business anyway."

"True, but people would rather see a bit of what you call untoward behavior. To most that would be more natural between a man and a woman."

"I don't think I follow you," demurred Anna.

"I mean you should be a little more flirtatious, a little coy."

"But only silly, empty-headed women do that. I take pride in my brain. And Lüdeke appreciates that."

"Holy Mother Mary, girl, do you really believe that?" exclaimed Wünneke. "I warn you. The first silly, empty-headed woman who makes a fuss over his broad chest and strong arms and lets him pet her a little will steal him away from you."

"If that's what he really wants, she may have him," replied Anna, but in her heart she knew she did not really mean that. Close to tears, she fervently wished this woman would leave her alone but had to be polite. Aside from the fact that Wünneke was Lüdeke's grandmother, one had to respect the wisdom of the aged.

"Girl, girl," sighed Wünneke, "you know you don't really mean that. I never thought I'd have to teach any female to be more coquettish. I had to counsel my own daughter to be *less* flirtatious. In her innocence she did not realize to what it could lead."

Anna tried to imagine the dignified, ladylike Adelheit as being too flirtatious and could not. Yet she had childhood memories of her and Lüdeke's father holding hands, touching each other, eyes sparkling, and suddenly realized that they had been in love and no doubt still were. She thought of Metke von Eltze, still flirtatious toward Eggeling, yet she had a good brain. And then Anna realized she had never known love in her own family, did not really know what it was. Her own father, although she was sure he had cared for her deeply, had been too reserved to express it. She suddenly understood that he had been so much in love with his first wife and so devastated by her death that he refused to leave himself vulnerable to hurt again. As for Catherine, what she called love was really a reflection of her own self-centeredness.

"I—I am just not that sort of person," Anna replied. "I should not know how to go about it. Anyone, Lüdeke especially, would know it was false, and I'd feel like a fool."

"No, you won't," Wünneke assured her. "It will be very easy if you love him, and I think you do and don't even know it."

"But, Mistress Bünsel, I don't feel ready yet for marriage. I don't know that I ever shall."

As Wünneke stood up to take her leave, she put her arm around Anna. "Anna, dearest child, you are more ready than you think. I didn't mean to upset you, but someone had to wake you up before you lose him. Think about what I have said. Try it out. You may be surprised." And she departed.

Anna did think about it for a long while, and she still came to the conclusion that she simply was not that sort of person. She had no way of knowing if Lüdeke was of the same mind as his grandmother or if he was even aware that she had been to see her. She decided the best thing to do would be to avoid a confrontation for the time being. Besides she was becoming remiss in her duties at the hospital. Lüdeke's visits had grown more and more frequent, cutting into the time she should have spent with the sick and the needy.

The next time Lüdeke called at the Mestwart home, the maid told him that Anna was at the hospital. And the next, and the next. At first he merely thought that his timing was bad, but it finally dawned on him that she was deliberately avoiding him. Why? he pondered. What had he done to offend her? He could think of nothing. She had seemed to enjoy his company as much as he did hers. He missed her. He grew morose and despondent. Ofttimes his father had to call his attention back to the business at hand.

Once when Wünneke was visiting the von Sehndens for a Sunday dinner, she put the same question to him as she had to Anna. "When are you going to publish the banns?"

"What banns, Grandmama?"

"Between you and Anna Mestwart, that's what," she stated.

"Grandmama, we have not even spoken of marriage and now she seems to be avoiding me, so I guess we never shall."

"Fiddle faddle," snorted Wünneke, "you are as foolish as she."

"Mother Wünneke," put in the elder Lüdeke, "you gave my Adelheit some good advice before we were wed. Can you not talk some sense into this boy? He moons around like a lovesick calf, instead of grabbing her by the hair and dragging her to the altar. Some brave knight!"

"Father, how can you say such things?" demanded his son.

"Hold your tongue, Lüdeke," she admonished her son-in-law. "That is no way to treat this particular maid." And to her grandson she said, "My best advice would be to go away for a while. If the girl truly misses you, she will be at home for you when you return."

Lüdeke pondered this for some time and finally decided old Wünneke was right. Who did Anna think she was, making him sit on her stoop like a beggar? If she really missed him, she would be eagerly awaiting his return. Yet he still shied away from thoughts of marriage. He merely wanted to resume their old relationship. He did miss that—and her, if he were truthful.

Lüdeke made several business trips to Bremen, Hamburg and Lübeck for his father and then a long one to Antwerp with him. After more than two months Lüdeke returned and once again called upon Anna only to be told once more that she was busy at the hospital.

He stormed away from the house. "Enough," he said aloud. "I shall seek her out among her invalids, and duties be damned. I must know why she is avoiding me. Doesn't she know I love her?" He stopped dead in his tracks, so that passersby looked at him strangely. Love? he thought. Do I really love her? God's balls, I guess I do. And he headed swiftly down the street and across the Vischern to St. Anna's.

He found Anna there ministering to the invalids, the plainest of wimples covering her hair and a huge white apron protecting her gown. She was serving the watery gruel that sufficed for these poor unfortunates' dinner. He paused momentarily. The stench was overpowering, although the place looked clean enough. How could she stand it? He gathered his courage and approached her.

"Lüdeke!" she exclaimed and almost spilled the gruel.

He took the bowl from her and handed it to the patient.

"Here is your dinner, my good man," he said. "Your nurse has other duties."

Whereupon he swept her into his arms and kissed her soundly. She turned six shades of red. Her patients applauded.

As she recovered from the kiss, she gasped, "Lüdeke, whatever are you doing? Not here!"

"Why not?" he asked brusquely. "These are your friends, are they not? Hear how they applaud." And he kissed her again.

With her body molded to his, she felt it tingling all the way to her toes, a pleasant sensation she had never before experienced.

"Bravo!" shouted one old fellow. "It's about time."

"She needs a good man," agreed another.

"Love her well, son," croaked a third. "She is a fine lady."

With his arms still around her, Lüdeke turned to the patients. Without even thinking he announced, "I want you, her friends, to be the first to know that Fräulein Mestwart and I are to be wed, and that right soon."

The applause and cheers from those who could drowned out Anna's surprised, "Lüdeke, how dare you? You never even asked me!"

One old man, too weak to either cheer or applaud, lying on a pallet in the corner, beckoned to them feebly with one finger. Anna led Lüdeke over to him.

"God bless you, Mistress Anna," he whispered hoarsely. "He will be a good man to you. I can see how he loves you." He paused for a moment to catch his breath while she held his hand and waited, since he clearly had more to say. "If you treat him half as well as you care for us, he will be very happy."

"I'll try, Hans, and thank you for your blessing," she replied gently.

571

The old man turned his eyes to Lüdeke. "You have an angel here, young sir. Handle her with care." And he closed his eyes, exhausted by the effort.

Lüdeke took his other hand. "I'll try, Old Hans," he sighed, "and God bless you, too."

Anna led him out of the infirmary and into the chapel, where they could be alone.

"How dare you?" she hissed. "I am so embarrassed."

He laughed. "It seemed the only way I could catch up with you was to come here, where you spend all your time. Once I decided I loved you, I had to tell you. What better place than here?"

"Oh, Lüdeke, I have missed you, I truly have. Do you really mean that, that you love me?"

"I do indeed," he replied and kissed her again. This time she did not feel embarrassed.

"I think," she said hesitantly, "I know, nay, I am sure I love you, too, Lüdeke."

They kissed again, deeply and passionately, while St. Anna, Mother of Mary, looked down from her pedestal in silent blessing.

They were wed in due course with all the splendor the leading Bürgers had come to expect. Anna von Nassau attended, sincerely expressing great joy at her young protégée's happiness, and she even coerced her reluctant son, Duke Heinrich, to join her in wishing them well. "They are *your* contemporaries," she advised him privately. "*They* will be paying your bills. It is not wise to offend them."

That night Lüdeke had ample reason to give thanks for his precipitous proposal. His tender lovemaking elicited in Anna a passionate response that even he had not suspected she was capable of. As for Anna herself, she never ever thought that the supreme act of marriage could be so pleasurable, so exciting, so—so exquisite.

The next morning when he looked into her radiant face, he knew she was as happy as he.

"Why did we wait so long?" he asked.

"I don't know," she replied. "We were very foolish, weren't we?"

He reached over to take something from the candle stand by the bed. He handed her a piece of chamois in which was wrapped a small but perfect ruby set in an intricate gold ring.

"A small token of my love for you, dearest Anna," he said.

If she was disappointed at the size of her 'morning gift', she did not show it. "Oh, Lude, it is exquisite." She slipped it on her finger. "The workmanship is very fine."

"Made by the most talented goldsmith in the world, especially for you."

"Oh? Not here in Celle?"

"No. This is not my morning gift to you, dearest wife, but only a token of it. My morning gift is so big and wonderful it would not fit in this chamber, nor in this house, nor even in all of Celle. So I had to give you a symbol of it until I can give you the real thing."

"Lude, you are teasing me," she declared, intrigued. "Stop talking in riddles."

He laughed. "I am going to take you on a trip to the most beautiful city in Italy, where all of your wonderful intellect can feast on the greatest art and music and philosophy of our time."

"Italy?" she queried a bit doubtfully. "But aren't they fighting there all the time?"

"Only in a few places, and I know the best routes to bypass that, and where we are going there is peace. You have heard of Florence?" She nodded. "And the Medici?"

"Yes, to both, but—"

"We may have to combine a little business with our pleasure, but only a little."

"You would," she remarked caustically.

He smiled. "You will have to learn something of it if you are to be my helpmate," he said, only half-teasing. "First lesson: We are going to transfer most of our financial dealings in Italy and Antwerp to the Medici bank. The Lombards—Milan, that is—are becoming less and less trustworthy and Milan itself is in constant danger of being conquered by France. But for our purposes Lorenzo de'Medici, whom Papa knows well, is the key that will open the doors to all the finest art and literature in the world. I thought it would please you to see firsthand so much of what you have read about. I hope I'm not wrong."

"Dearest Lude, it will please me no end. If I sounded doubtful, it's simply that I cannot yet comprehend the magnificence of this gift. And I have heard of Lorenzo de Medici. He is the one who is having all the old Greek philosophers translated into Latin and the classical Roman poets printed into books. It will be very exciting to meet him."

"Yes, that and more. He is not only a banker and an excellent civic leader and a patron of the arts, he is probably the greatest all-around scholar of our time. And he has surrounded himself with other scholars, each one an expert in his field. He is not called 'Il Magnifico' for nothing. I hope to learn much from him myself."

"Oh, Lude, I am getting so excited. When do we go?" she asked.

"Very soon. Papa is failing and once I take over the business myself it will be a long time before we can take another pleasure trip."

Anna threw herself wholeheartedly into preparations for the journey.

"What clothes shall I take? I fear I do not have gowns appropriate to meeting 'Il Magnifico'."

"Take your warmest riding habit and also your summer one. We'll be spending many days in the saddle."

"The warmest? But it is spring here now and I have heard that Italy is always like summer."

"True enough, but we must first cross the mountains and there it will still be like midwinter. Take your warmest habit as well as your fur-lined hooded cloak. You will be glad you did."

"And gowns?"

"Only one or two of your plainest."

"But, Lude," she objected. "I can't possibly be seen in them in Florence."

"Don't worry, dearest wife," he replied. "When we get to Florence, I shall buy you the finest silk you have ever seen. They make their own there now. It is no longer necessary to import it from far Cathay."

Their trip to Italy, though long and tedious—it took them four weeks—was without incident. Lüdeke knew the best routes to avoid any fighting, especially France's almost constant attempt to conquer Milan. He took great pleasure in pointing out to Anna the changing beauties of the countryside, the highlights of each town through which they passed, and was rewarded by her delighted reaction to it all.

"Ah, dearest Lude," she remarked, "you are right. No book can compare with seeing these things firsthand."

"I told you so," he replied, "yet books can describe these wonders to those who cannot afford to make such a journey."

"That is supposed to be my argument," she said, and they laughed together.

When they arrived at Florence, they found the city in a frenzy of celebration.

"Whatever is going on?" Lüdeke asked the watch at the gate.

"Ah, signore, I thought the whole world knew." He shook his head at the ignorance of these Tedeschi. "These six weeks past the very illustrious son of Il Papa Innocent has wed the most beautiful and pious daughter of Il Magnifico."

"Son! . . . pious! . . . ," sputtered Anna.

Lüdeke poked her with his elbow to shut her up and asked, "Six weeks and they are still celebrating?"

"Si, signore, it is a very great fiesta, one of the most elaborate la Bella Firenze has ever seen. And the festivities will go on for another month or so."

"I think perhaps we have come at a bad time," said Lüdeke.

"No, no, signore," objected the guard "You see Florence at her best. We Florentines are happiest when we are singing and dancing, when wine flows from the fountains." Lüdeke looked at him questioningly. "Ah, si," he went on, "we revel when the Patrici spend their money. The butchers, the bakers, the tailors and dressmakers, especially the artists and musicians, even down to the merest peasant bringing his vegetables from the countryside, all benefit. Even we here at the gate receive munificent gratuities for helping a gentleman who—uh—who perhaps has imbibed too much, to control his horse. It is indeed a great fiesta."

"I can understand that. It is the same in our town, only perhaps not so," he was going to say 'wild', but quickly changed it to "elaborate." What I meant about coming at a bad time," he added, "is that we have come on business with the House of Medici. I am afraid they are too taken up with the wedding celebration to have much time for the likes of us."

"Oh, no, no, signore," declared the man. "Il Magnifico is always ready to do business. Is not his most important business to govern Florence, although he holds no official office? And to govern the Florentines, one must keep them happy." He spread his arms about, indicating the crowds of revellers. "Is that not so? You should have been here a few weeks ago, when the press of the throngs was so great you could not get near the Palace. But now, pouf!" He snapped his fingers. "The ways are open. You will have no problem. Shall I send a lad to direct you?"

"No, no, thank you. I know the way. I have been here before," replied Lüdeke, handing the man a coin. "Thank you my good man, for the information."

As they went their way, Anna asked, "Why did you give him money when he did nothing?"

"Because we deprived him of the services of the lad, which is probably his son. In Italy everyone expects to be paid even for nothing," he

575

explained. "Another thing, my dearest wife, in Italy never criticize the Pope or the leading families, in this case the Medici, by so much as one word or even a look unless they do so first and then be extremely careful never to reveal your true feelings in the matter, because they change their loyalties — or I should say alliances — like the wind. The Italian temperament is very volatile."

Anna shook her head. "But, Lüdeke, the Pope's son! When he is supposed to be celibate, nay, an example of celibacy to all priests. And to call the girl pious!"

"I know it is shocking to you, my dear, but that is the way of things here. They think nothing of it."

As they approached the Palace, Lüdeke said, "I hope we can stay here. I should hate to subject you to an inn under these circumstances. They know we are coming, but I couldn't say exactly when."

"That is a Palace?" commented Anna. "Big, yes, but so plain and boxy-looking."

Lüdeke laughed. "Just wait until you see the inside. Your mouth will hang agape when you see all the treasures therein."

He need not have worried about staying there. The majordomo welcomed them effusively. "Ah, Signore and Signora von Sehnden. We have been expecting you. A suite has been held in readiness ever since Il Magnifico received your letter. I trust your journey went well. Please come with me."

"A suite?" whispered Anna.

Lüdeke smiled. "Just wait and see."

Anna's mouth did, indeed, fall open as the servant led them through reception rooms filled with art treasures — paintings, sculpture, tapestries, beautifully wrought furniture — and then upstairs and down what seemed like miles of exquisitely decorated corridors. The suite, when they finally reached it, was almost as large as a whole floor of their home in Celle. It consisted of sitting room, bedroom, dressing room and even a separate room for bathing and other sanitary necessities.

"Please make yourselves comfortable. I shall have water for your baths sent up forthwith and the footman will be bringing your baggage shortly. He can show you later where your horses are stabled. A maid and a valet have been assigned to you. If you have any needs, just let them know. And now I shall leave you to rest while I announce your arrival to Il Magnifico. He is presently closeted in his study with the Platonic Academy as he is every afternoon. He most probably will want to meet with you

576

for an hour or so before supper. He is a very gracious host."

"I know," agreed Lüdeke. "Thank you, my man." And he handed him a coin as Anna glared.

"Grazie, Signore." He kissed the coin and bowed before tucking it in his sleeve. "I am at your service."

"This really is a palace," declared Anna with awe when they were alone. "Never in my life could I have imagined anything so grandiose. I am sure many a king has nothing so fine. Why, the Castle at Celle looks like a, what shall I say, like a hovel compared to this."

Lüdeke laughed. "I warned you, did I not? But don't ever let your dear friend the Duchess hear you say that."

"No, of course not. But you were so right. No book could have prepared me for this. And I thought we were rich."

"We are, my dear, but no, nowhere near like this. And all wealth is relative. In Celle we and the von Eltze are just as powerful as the Medici are in Florence. And we German Bürgers are not so ostentatious as the Italians. Our wealth lies in our ships and granaries and warehouses. And in various banks. I have heard rumors that Lorenzo spends more time and money with his scholars and artists, to the neglect of the bank. That is one thing I came here to check on."

Anna ignored the implication of this. "And to think these scholars are right here with him now. Oh, Lude, how I should love to meet them, perhaps talk with them."

"Possibly it can be arranged."

"Do you really think so? Me, a mere woman?"

"Very possibly. He is known to be very liberal in his thinking."

The maid and valet arrived with the footman who brought their baggage. After Lüdeke and Anna had bathed and rested and the servants had helped them to dress, Lorenzo's secretary sent word that they were to attend him in his study. Another footman came to show them the way.

Their host rose from behind a huge desk to greet them. "Buon giorno, Messer Ludovico," he said as he embraced him, "and Madonna — Anna, is it?" he asked as he kissed her hand while she curtsied.

"Si," replied Lüdeke.

"I know you speak Italian from all your years of fighting here, but does Madonna Anna?"

"I'm afraid not. It is her first time to your beautiful country."

"Then we shall speak Latin like civilized people," said Lorenzo.

During this exchange Anna was observing their host. Not a handsome man, almost ugly in fact, with a long, thin face and a prominent hooked nose, but striking nonetheless because of the eyes. Eagle's or hawk's—definitely a raptor's eyes. She would not want to be his enemy, she decided.

"I am happy to see that you arrived safely," continued their host, "but we must have no business talk today. Perhaps after you have rested a few days. Besides, I understand this is a wedding trip. Therefore, first of all, let me offer my felicitations and those of the whole House of Medici."

"Thank you, Messer Lorenzo," they replied.

"We have just had a wedding here ourselves as I'm sure you're aware. A very felicitous arrangement, on both sides I must say. Do you know that fool Innocent was so obsessed with outdoing all his predecessors and contemporaries in the richness of the festivities that he mortgaged the triple crown and all the better papal regalia? To us, naturally. Whether we'll ever get our money back is questionable, but I can always withhold my daughter's dowry. So either way it is a good deal. Madonna Anna, don't look so aghast! Business is business, and here in Italy much of it revolves around His Holiness. One either loves him or hates him. We are either buying him off or fighting bitterly against him. And believe me, he is always open to the highest bidder. So in this case, it was strictly a good business deal. He needs our money and backing; we need his power to be on our side, for the moment at least."

Anna's mouth hung open. She could not say a word. Lüdeke merely smiled knowingly.

De'Medici seemed to delight in shocking her. "The arrangement will suffice for a few years, until someone makes a higher bid and he excommunicates us all."

"Oh, no, I don't believe this," exclaimed Anna, despite her intention to say nothing.

"Ah, Madonna Anna, I do not mean to distress you, but you must realize that the Pope is only a man, greedy for power, whether it be Innocent or another. He is a pawn in the hands of the great rival families of Rome and of Florence. But enough of this. I said we should talk no business today. You must enjoy your stay in our beautiful city. Florence is *the* city of art. Ludovico, you must show her everything—the Duomo, Santa Croce, everything. I hope you are as interested in art as I am, Madonna."

Lüdeke answered for her, while she recovered from her shock and the abrupt change of subject, "Yes, indeed, she is, and I shall show her everything. And my beautiful and *intelligent* bride has a special request, if I may be so bold."

"And that is?"

"She would like to meet the scholars of your Platonic Academy, perhaps listen to their discussions. I guarantee she will understand more of their disputations than I."

"Ah, an intellectual woman as well as a lovely bride. A rare combination," commented Lorenzo. "By all means, you must meet them. It shall be arranged, whether they like it or not." He laughed. "You are fortunate that they are all here in the city for the festivities. Usually they meet out on one of my country estates. But perhaps you could go there, too." He thought for a moment. "Yes, you must go out to the Castello and see the two most beautiful paintings of my favorite artist, Sandro Botticelli. One is called *Primavera*, the other *The Birth of Venus*. Exquisite." He kissed his fingertips. "Unfortunately, the artist himself has been called to Rome together with Ghirlandaio and others to paint the new chapel of Sixtus. And speaking of Ghirlandaio, there is a new young artist I have stolen from him that I want you to meet. No, not really stolen—I must not shock Madonna Anna again—I have bought up his apprenticeship. He is a very competent painter, but his real love is sculpture and he could not learn that there. I have placed him in my school under Maestro Bertoldo di Giovanni, my court sculptor, and already he has proven that my instincts are never wrong. It is as if by magic that his hands can draw such beauty out of the rough marble. He will be famous one day if his irascible temper does not get in his way. But then artists must be allowed their little flares of temperament, no? His name is Michelangelo Buonarroti. Remember it well. In ten years or so you can be proud to say you met him."

As Lorenzo waxed eloquent about art and his artists, Anna changed her opinion of him. How can a man who loves art so and donates so much of his fortune to the artists' support be bad? She wondered. A very strange and complex man, their host.

Lüdeke and Anna spent over a month in Florence, most of the time as typical tourists. They visited all the important churches—Santa Croce, where they twisted their necks viewing Giotto's famous frescos, now almost one hundred years old, and the newer ones, not yet complete in the Duomo by Ghirlandaio and his school, in which Michelangelo had taken part. They met this very ugly and morose young man and were not particularly impressed. They also met another strange man named Leonardo da Vinci, said to be an artist, but also a very skilled engineer, who was advising Florence on improving her defenses. They journeyed out to Castello to see the Botticelli paintings, which they thought were truly lovely, light and airy, such a welcome change from the usual religious art. They viewed his *Adoration of the Magi* in which three of the Medici were prominently portrayed—old Cosimo, a much younger Lorenzo and his brother Guiliano.

"Such conceit," commented Anna.

"It is not unusual for donors to be included in a work of art. Consider even the windows of our own Marienkirche. It is quite clear which guilds donated them."

"But whole guilds, not individual people," argued Anna, "or if there are, they are tucked inobtrusively in a corner, not the most prominent figures of the piece."

Lüdeke shrugged. "I guess if you spend the amount of money on art that these people do, you are entitled to have your portrait included."

Anna got her wish to meet the members of the Platonic Academy, or at least some of them. There was Angelo Poliziano, a poet and Lorenzo's dearest friend, of whom his wife Clarice was insanely jealous, for no other reason than that he taught their son Latin from ancient Roman texts rather than from Scripture. There was another amusing poet they called Gigi, another learned writer Marsilio Ficino. There were three scholars from Greece who were working on a translation of Homer's epics. There was the great musician Squarcialupi, the Cathedral organist and choir director, other writers, and always several of the leading artists of Florence. Anna revelled in listening to their serious discussions as well as their lighthearted conversation. She could not understand why Clarice hated them all so until she realized that Clarice had not the vaguest notion what they were talking about.

Meanwhile Lüdeke was reassessing the decision to transfer their assets to the Medici bank. Observing Il Magnifico on his homeground, it was quite obvious that he had very little interest in the bank itself, leaving most of the decisions to managers. His patronage of the arts, while commendable, did not come entirely from his personal fortune but drained the bank as well, faster than its income. Bad loans also were commonplace. He knew that the Brugge branch had gone bankrupt some years ago, but he had believed that it was due to the harbor silting up and the city losing its status as financial center of the north. He was appalled to learn that it was primarily due to impecunious loans to the late Duke Charles the Bold of Burgundy. The closing of the London office, too, had been brought on by disastrous loans to both sides in the English Wars of the Roses. And witness this latest frivolity—lending money to Pope Innocent for his son's wedding. Did Lorenzo really think it would ever be repaid, tiara or no?

Lüdeke came to a decision and hoped his father would agree. In order not to offend their host, who had indeed been gracious to them, he would transfer some of their Italian business to the Medici bank. Some, but not all. And Antwerp he would not even mention. It was time the merchants of northern Germany set up their own bank in Hamburg or perhaps Bremen. To date the only German banker of any consequence was Jakob Fugger of Augsburg, and Lüdeke did not trust him. Fugger was already loaning vast amounts to the Habsburgs. Lüdeke did not hold with lending money to emperors, kings or dukes, since chances of repayment were almost nil. This trip had certainly been an eye-opener. He would have much to discuss with his fellow Gewandschneider when he returned to Celle.

Time passed swiftly and the world around them changed even more rapidly. The gossip in the marketplace centered on international trade:

"Have you heard that the Portuguese have finally reached the end of Africa?"

"Ja, some fellow by the name of Dias."

"I wonder how much farther they have to sail to reach the Indies?"

"A long ways, I'm sure, but at least we know there is a way to circumvent the Turks."

"And Venice, the traitors."

"Ja, imagine them paying tribute to the Infidels to maintain their trading rights."

"But the Turks are still pushing further into Europe. If you were as close to them as they are, you might think differently."

"Maybe so, but I doubt it. And I hear that there is another fellow—a Genoese—trying to get funding to sail west. West, can you believe it? But the Portuguese turned him down."

"Why shouldn't they? They've found the way."

"And now he's trying to convince Isabella of Spain."

"I wish him luck, but she's too busy fighting the Moors."

"And promoting the Inquisition."

And on the growing power of the Habsburgs:

"The Emperor's son Maximilian has married Mary of Burgundy. So

581

they will now add that to their domains."

"That's not good for trade. We needed an independent buffer between the Empire and France. The Flemish towns have already revolted."

"Much to their grief. What good did it do them? Louis has already destroyed Arras."

"Ja, it saddens me that we shall never see those beautiful tapestries again."

"What worries me more is that Emperor Friedrich treats Max like a crown prince. They would like to make it a hereditary monarchy."

"They still have the Electors to deal with."

"But most of them are knuckling under to them."

"I'm afraid you're right. Except for our own foolish Duke Heinrich, who is not even an Elector. He still vows vengeance on them for his father's death."

"Foolish is right. Now that he has reached his majority, his gracious mother has no more control over him. He still dreams dreams of the days of chivalry and picks petty quarrels with all his cousins in the neighboring duchies. Friedrich is getting old and right now doesn't pay too much attention to him, but one day I'm afraid he will be like the gnat in the elephant's ear. He will become so annoying they will smash him. And that will hurt us all."

Lüdeke's father, the elder von Sehnden, passed away quietly in his sleep, but the business continued to flourish. Lüdeke was elected Master of the Gewandschneider and then to the Town Council. And Anna despaired of ever having children.

The year 1492 was even more momentous. On the second of January, Ferdinand and Isabella conquered Granada and drove the Moors from their last stronghold in Spain. Innocent III died, and after much wrangling a new Pope from the Spanish family of Borgia was elected. Everyone hoped that he would be better than the not so innocent Innocent, but Alexander VI turned out to be the worst Pope in the history of the Papacy. Later that year Isabella of Spain was finally persuaded to fund the voyage of the Genoese mariner, Christopher Columbus, who returned after many months claiming he had found the westward route to the Indies. And Lorenzo de'Medici, Il Magnifico, died. The Medici bank fell apart, to the consternation of most of the merchants of Europe, and his son Piero was so incompetent and so hated that the family, whose forebears had done so much for Florence, was driven from the city.

And Anna found she was finally pregnant.

Old Emperor Friedrich was ailing and died in 1493. As everyone expected, his son Maximilian was elected Emperor and he immediately began to consolidate his power in many ways. The Pope shocked everyone by naming his scheming, treacherous warrior son Caesar a Cardinal.

Late that year Lüdeke and Anna's first son was born. They named him Heinrich after the Duke, whom they secretly despised, although they were still close friends with his mother, the gracious Anna von Nassau, and after Lüdeke's grandfather and uncle Hinrik Bünsel, whom they also held in low esteem, but did so to please old Wünneke, still a hale and hearty dowager.

In 1494 the Pope, mediating a dispute between Spain and Portugal, arbitrarily divided the world in half between the forty-eighth and forty-ninth meridians by the Treaty of Tordesillas, which allowed Spain to claim all new discoveries west of the meridian and Portugal all those east of it. (A few years later a Portuguese captain, John Cabot, sailing for Henry VII of England—the English had never paid much attention to the Pope anyway—rediscovered the northern route to the western continent and claimed vast territories for his employer.)

The same year a rabid monk named Savonarola took Florence by storm preaching reform. But his approach was a twisted one, blaming the sins of the luxury- and art-loving Florentines for the corruption in the Church. He preached fiery sermons in the Duomo against all the new learning and art, converting hundreds of people to his puritanical asceticism. Sumptuous clothing and jewels, thousands of books, hundreds of precious works of art were consigned to his bonfires. Even the gentle Botticelli became one of his devoted followers and became so morose that he painted no more. In 1497 a terrible famine struck Florence and the people said, 'Enough'. They blamed Savonarola and wished they had the Medici back, but it was too late. The Pope excommunicated the monk, and in 1498 he, too, was consigned to the flames.

Anna and Lüdeke discussed it sadly.

"There is no doubt reform is needed," she said, "but that is no way to go about it, destroying beautiful things, when it is the very heart of the Church that is rotten."

"Ja," agreed Lüdeke. "The fool played right into the hands of the Church. They were both against the new learning, but they are not going to stop it now that people are used to it, nay, want it. They have only succeeded in destroying Florence."

"You are right. When you take away beauty, it destroys men's souls. And by destroying books, they seek to set men's minds back hundreds of years. But people have a taste for reading now, and they will hunger for it all the more. Why couldn't they have quietly reformed the Church from within, reordered the monasteries and convents as our beloved Duchess Anna did here?"

"Because the Pope does not want reform and because the Italians never do anything quietly. But Florence's loss is our gain here in the north. The new learning is spreading everywhere in Germany, and Flanders and Holland are becoming the new art centers. Why, every time I go to Antwerp I hear of new painters, and I have seen some of their work. And it's much more to my taste, I'll admit, depicting everyday people as they really are in everyday life."

"Oh, Lüdeke, I should love to see them."

"Then come with me next time I go. Heinrich will be fine with old Helga."

"Not this time, dearest husband," she said with a smile. "I have conceived again."

Anna had had a miscarriage and a stillbirth since their son was born, and she lived in constant fear that she would take after her father's first wife, although she was no blood relation. But Anna was strong and healthy and even gave up her hospital work for this pregnancy. In due time a healthy boy was born to them, whom they named Franz.

Meanwhile Duke Heinrich had married and began producing heirs—a son Otto, then Ernst, born in Uelzen in 1497, followed by Franz. Everyone hoped that marriage and children would help settle him down and for a while it did, but not for long.

The turn of the century—the end of the first half of the second millennium—1500 saw relative peace in much of Europe except for France's stubborn attempt to invade Italy and the relentless assault of the Turks in the east. Columbus' exploration had proven disappointing—no spices, although they did bring back a number of new and unusual foods and a strange substance called tobacco—and no jewels, but there were well-founded rumors of gold and the Spaniards were determined to find the source.

In Germany trade prospered as never before, but there were restless undercurrents, not only disgust with a corrupt Pope and a Church rotten to the core, but a seeking for freedom from the unrealistic and anachronistic restrictions of a religion that heretofore had regulated every moment of their lives. The new learning promulgated much of this. Books proliferated by the thousands on every conceivable subject, many openly critical of the old ways. People hungered after knowledge. True scientists appeared everywhere.

Lüdeke returned from a trip to Flanders and for once his first conversation was not of business.

"Remember that fellow Michelangelo we met in Florence?" he said to Anna. "The one Lorenzo said would one day be famous?"

"Vaguely," she replied. "I was not particularly impressed."

"You would be now. Lorenzo was right. The merchants of Brugge commissioned a *Madonna* from him and, Anna, it is the most exquisite thing I have ever seen."

Anna laughed. "It must be to engender such enthusiasm in you. I promise I shall make the next trip with you. Now my news is not so earth-shaking. We have a new family at St. Anna's, and I should like to help them."

"A family?"

"Yes, a woman with two small sons and a third on the way. She is destitute. Apparently her husband was killed in some sort of accident—I don't know all the details—and she wandered into Celle seeking refuge."

"A likely story," commented Lüdeke. "How do you know she ever had a husband?"

"She's not that type of woman. I have been working with the inmates there for lo, these many years, and I think I have become quite a good judge of character. I am sure she is telling the truth. She is too refined and gentle a person to have been a whore. She can read and write as well. I am convinced that some great tragedy befell her. Something so horrible that she cannot speak of it. Give me time and I'll find out once I gain her trust."

"So what more can you do for her than the care you are already giving there?" asked Lüdeke.

"Lüdeke, St. Anna's, as fine an establishment as it is, is no place for them, especially the children, with all those vagrants and crippled, sick old people and, yes, whores. I have already spoken to Her Grace about placing the woman in the house for expectant widows on Ritterstrasse. I understand it is full, but I think our dear Duchess will make room for her as a special favor to me."

"Then what is the problem?"

"Oh, Lude dear, sometimes you can be so dense," exclaimed Anna, exasperated. "What of the children? They can't stay there with her." She paused for a moment to let that sink in. "Could we not take them in for a while? At least until the new babe is born and the mother is on her feet again. They are just the right ages to be companions for our boys. And, Lude, to be honest, I despair of ever getting pregnant again. I seem to have such trouble conceiving. It is so long between each one, and I wanted to give you lots of children." She was almost in tears as she finished speaking.

"No, no, my dearest wife, don't fret yourself over what must be God's will. You'll conceive again, of that I feel sure. Anyway, even if you don't, we have two healthy sons to be proud of. Just look at my best friend Eggeling von Eltze—married before I was and only one daughter to show for it in all these years."

"I know. You are right. I'm being selfish instead of thankful for what we have. But you haven't answered my question."

"About these children?" She nodded. "I understand your desire to want to help them," he said, "but frankly, I think it is asking too much of Helga. She is getting very old. After all, she was my mother's nursemaid."

"This woman claims she wants to seek work as soon as possible after the babe is born. We could hire her and let Helga retire. And that would keep the family together."

"You've thought it all out, haven't you, you little minx?" said Lüdeke, only half joking.

She smiled. "Well, you taught me to be logical and efficient before undertaking anything of importance."

His heart melted. He wanted so much to please her, but he was still very hesitant. "All right," he said at last. "I won't say 'yes' or 'no' at the moment, but I'll consider it. Meantime find out all you can about her. I don't want any irate husband or father or master coming down on my head."

"Oh, thank you, dearest Lüdeke. I can't ask any more than that. I'll learn everything about her there is to know. I hope we can work it out. She is so sweet and they're such dear children."

"What is her name, by the way?"

"Catherina Stockman and the boys are Franz and Berndt," she replied.

Every day that Anna went to the hospital, while she never neglected any of the patients, she spent an inordinate amount of time with Catherina trying to gain her confidence.

"Where are you from?" Anna asked.

586

"Oh, just a tiny village you would never have heard of, not far from Hannover," she answered vaguely.

"And what made you decide to come to Celle?"

"I wanted to get out of Calenberg, and you know what they say: 'Look over the walls of Hannover and you see Celle'. It was the closest large town to lose myself in."

Anna looked at her askance. "You are not in any sort of trouble in Calenberg, are you?" she asked.

"No, no, Mistress von Sehnden, I assure you I am not," replied Catherina vehemently. "I just had to get away from there, that is all. And I have always heard that the people of Celle are very kind to strangers in need."

This pleased Anna, although she was quite well aware that the flattery, however sincere, was intended to get her off the subject of the woman's background.

One day, over Helga's objections, Anna took her two boys with her to play with the children while she visited with their mother. She had cautioned her sons to be kind to the strangers since they were poor and had no home of their own. For a while they played nicely in the garden of the hospital, but then, as boys that age will, Heinrich started to brag.

"I have been in school for almost a year now," he boasted.

"So what?" replied Franz Stockman.

"I can read and write and you haven't even started school," needled Heinrich.

"Well, I will, just as soon as — as soon as the new babe is born and my mother finds work."

"Oh, no, you won't."

"I will, too."

"Not here you won't. You have to be a Bürger's son."

Franz pondered this a moment. "Well, I will anyway," he retorted. "My mother says so."

"Hah," derided Heinrich. "Your mother doesn't know anything."

At this Franz started to cry and ran in to where the two women were conversing. He clung to Catherina's skirt. "Mama," he sobbed, "that nasty boy said you don't know anything."

"Heinrich," scolded Anna, "have you been teasing Franz? I'll have your father take the rod to you."

"No, Mama, no," replied a chastened Heinrich. "I just told him he couldn't go to school here because he's not a Bürger's son."

587

From the safety of Catherina's skirts Franz retorted, "But he said Mama didn't know anything. She knows how to find food in the woods and build a shelter from branches to hide us when the evil men were seeking us. I bet you don't learn that in school."

The two women looked at each other and the silence hung between them. There is far more to this than meets the eye, thought Anna. I wonder if she'll ever tell me.

Catherina, so adept at changing the subject, was the first to break the silence. She sighed, "I wish he *could* go to school. He is so intelligent. But I fear that is not possible."

Anna agreed. "What Heinrich has said about the school is correct, but," she turned to address her son, "you had no right to say Mistress Stockman knows nothing. Apologize to her at once."

An abashed Heinrich mumbled, "I am sorry, Mistress Stockman."

"Very well," said Catherina. "now go and play with your little brothers."

"But their games are too childish for us," objected Heinrich.

Franz said nothing, but the women could see he agreed.

"Wait a moment," said Anna. "I have an idea. Why don't you and I teach Franz his letters? I have many books at home, and Heinrich could help by telling him what he has learned in school each week. Would you like to do that, Heinrich?"

"I suppose," replied Heinrich sullenly.

"Mistress, you are too kind," objected Catherina, "but I am afraid it would take too much of your time. You do so many good works here as it is. But if you have books, could I read some of them? I have not read anything but the Bible and that not since—er, for many years. I hunger for reading and I could teach Franz myself."

"But I shall find the time," said Anna. "In fact, I should enjoy teaching him, and it will be good for Heinrich. As for the books, you're welcome to read as many as you like, but I hesitate to bring them here. They are still quite precious even though the printing press has made them a lot less expensive."

"I understand," said Catherina, obviously disappointed. "It was just a thought."

"But perhaps you can come to visit me and read them in my home," suggested Anna.

"Do you think they would let me? Leave here, I mean?"

"I'm sure it can be arranged. Let me see what can be done," replied Anna.

That evening Anna put the pressure on Lüdeke.

"Can't we take them in for a little while?" she pleaded.

"But you still know nothing more about her than you knew before, except that they spent some nights in the woods fleeing from someone or something."

"Her son said they were evil men. Doesn't that prove she is innocent?"

"Anna, my dearest, it is you who are innocent. Any little boy whose mother is threatened will call the threat evil. She could be a runaway serf."

"She is not a serf," replied Anna indignantly. "I told you she can read and write."

"And now she wants to borrow your books. Perhaps to steal them."

"Oh, you are being ridiculous."

"What says the Duchess about taking her into the expectant widows' home?"

Anna hung her head in defeat. "The same as you," she replied softly. "We must know more about who she is."

"Then find out. Verifiable facts, though, not a lot of vagaries about evil men."

"I'll try my best."

"Since it means so much to you, I'll promise you this much. If the Duchess will take her in, I'll let you keep the children. But for a short time only. And if she won't tell you the true facts, then she doesn't deserve to be helped."

"Oh, dear Lüdeke, I know I could count on you. I'll find out if I have to—to put her on the rack."

Lüdeke laughed. "I wouldn't go quite that far."

Several days later Anna arrived at St. Anna's to find Catherina very upset, angry and close to tears.

"Whatever is wrong, my dear?" Anna asked.

"Oh, Mistress von Sehnden I know you have been very kind to me and I don't mean to seem ungrateful, but I must leave here. I don't know where I'll go, but I must get out of this place."

"Come out into the garden where we can talk." She took her by the hand. When they were seated under a tree with the children nearby, she said, "Now calm yourself and tell me what has happened to upset you so."

"Oh, Mistress," she blurted, "I caught one of the old men molesting my little Berndt. I know he is old and simple-minded and the child didn't understand what he was about, but I can't risk that again. I just can't."

"Did anything actually happen?" asked Anna.

"No, Holy Mother be praised. Franz saw it and came running to tell me. I am afraid I cracked the old man in the balls," she said with half a smile.

"I'm sure he deserved it." Anna was hard put to keep from laughing, envisioning this.

"But now the little one is frightened and he doesn't know why. Oh, Mistress, what can I do? Where can I go?"

Anna knew this was her opportunity. She took Catherina's hand. "Now hear me well," she said, "I could have found you a better place to stay while you await your time long ere this." She silently prayed that the Duchess would forgive a slight exaggeration. "But you have been so reticent to tell me or anyone who you really are, where you're really from and from what you are fleeing, that no one trusts you. To everyone but me you are just a vagrant beggar, some even say a whore." Let that sink in, she thought. "But the Duchess has promised as a favor to me to make a place for you in the home for expectant widows, even though you are not a Bürger's or nobleman's widow or daughter, if only we knew who you are. I promise if you tell me your story, the whole truth, with verifiable facts," she echoed Lüdeke, "it shall be a secret between us. I shall tell no one except those directly concerned—my husband and the Duchess—and them only as much as they need to know. The choice is yours. If not, there is nothing I can do for you."

As she spoke, she watched Catherina's face change from fear, to indignation, to surprise, to hope.

"I am not a whore," she stated.

"I never thought you were," replied Anna and waited.

"You will not send me back if I tell you?" Catherina queried timidly.

"I cannot promise that. That depends on what you tell me." Anna could see the indecision, the anguish, the fear with which Catherina was wrestling.

"I am—was—a nobleman's daughter," she began hesitantly, "the fifth daughter of a very minor, impoverished knight, with a tiny demesne called Engelhart. It lies south of Hannover. My father was a very old-fashioned man, clinging blindly to the old feudal ways, unable to see that the feudal system is fast becoming obsolete. He preferred the hunt to the neglect of the farm, if you know the type."

Anna nodded. "My father-in-law ran away from just such a place, but that was seventy some years ago. Had he no sons?"

"No, and he hated all of us—just for being female. He still owned all his serfs—refused to give them their freedom, until things got so bad that he tried to sell them their little plots of land in return for their freedom. A few of the more enterprising ones were able to do this, but most could not. There was great resentment on their part, and many ran away seeking better masters or even to the towns. He only made half-hearted attempts to recover them, reasoning that there were then fewer mouths to feed and clothe, not realizing that there were also fewer to work the farm. Those that remained became even more resentful and worked sullenly and carelessly, so that the farm suffered even more.

"Then came the time when my older sisters reached marriageable age and he had nothing with which to dower them—no money, no jewels, only the land. He gave a piece to each of the three eldest, but the prospective sons-in-law, seeing what a poor manager he was, refused to enfeoff themselves to him and claimed they needed all the income for themselves. Which was true enough. The shares of land were so small that many of the more ambitious freedmen were wealthier than they. By this time nothing was left to him but the house itself, one pasture and a small garden, which my mother tended. All but two of the serfs had gone with the land to my brothers-in-law.

"Then came the turns of my fourth sister and me, and there was nothing left for dowries. He became more cruel and resentful of us. He hated us just for being. He wanted us to go into convents, but we both refused. Although I had a love of learning, I knew it was no life for me, especially with the conditions that exist in most of the nunneries nowadays. And we knew he could not force us, because all of them require dowries as well—and they don't want poor, unproductive land. They need money to support their frivolities."

"How sadly true," commented Anna. "But what of your mother?"

"She is a true gentle lady but very timid. When we were younger she had the courage to teach us to read and write, unbeknownst to him. She may have loved him at one time, but as things grew worse fear displaced whatever else she may have felt for him and she became reclusive, retired to her solar with her embroidery, whenever she could get the precious silks for that. She had very little to say about our fates."

Anna nodded. So far there was nothing unusual about Catherina's story, but she sensed the worst was yet to come.

Catherina took a deep breath, as if gathering up courage to continue. "My sister ran away from home. In retrospect, I think he was incestuously

591

molesting her, but I was still a little too young to understand these things. I do know that my mother rallied herself enough to protect us somewhat, and I believe she connived to help my sister get away. Where she is I have no idea.

"Then, then a year later," she swallowed hard, "a year later, without any warning, he sold me to an itinerant blacksmith. Sold me, Mistress, like the meanest serf!"

Anna patted her arm. "It is nothing to be ashamed of," she commiserated. "It happens."

"Manfred was kind enough to me in his own rough way. Big and burly though he was, he was basically a weak man, except when he was drunk. Then he became belligerent, but rarely to me. Though totally unlettered, he was a skilled armorer as well as a smith, but he could never save enough money to have his own forge and shop because of the drink. And so we wandered from place to place. He took me to the castle where he was then working, and immediately the lord claimed the first night rights. Manfred accepted it meekly, as though he expected it. It was a horrible experience for me, a thirteen-year-old virgin, but fortunately, I did not get pregnant from it. Each of our children was born at a different castle. You wondered why I have been so vague as to where I'm from. I have never had a real home, Mistress, except where I was born, and you can understand why I have no wish to return there."

Anna's heart went out to her. How safe my life has been, she thought thankfully. How seldom do we realize what others have suffered. "And then what happened?" she urged.

"About six months ago we came to a place called Verdammteburg, not far from Burgwedel, which as you know is just over the border. All seemed well. They needed a great deal of armor, so it seemed as though we would stay there for a while. I became pregnant again, and Manfred was so busy he was drinking less. Then the younger son of the lord took a fancy to me. I rejected his advances. And that is not easy, Mistress. They think because they are lords they own you, even though we were not serfs. Since I was already with child, I had no desire to be flirtatious, and Manfred was a very jealous man. I could easily have lain with him and claimed the child was his bastard. There are many who do that hoping for a rich settlement, but I am not like that, Mistress. I took Christian vows to be faithful to one man, whether they were forced upon me or not, and I intended to keep them. But this young nobleman was very persistent, would not leave me alone, followed me every chance he had, waylaid me in unexpected places, even on my way to the latrine. So far it had been only hugging and kissing, squeezing my breasts or pinching my bottom, but I knew it was only a matter of time before he would want more. I avoided him as much as I could.

"Then one day Manfred had to go to Burgwedel to get some supplies. I was alone in our hut with the children, seated at the loom, weaving some cloth for the lord's lady. She did not permit any idle hands. It was raining very hard and no one else was about. Suddenly—suddenly this man burst through the door. 'Now, now I shall have you', he said. 'I am tired of . . .'" She began to sob.

"Go on," prompted Anna. "It is better for your soul if you tell it."

"He—he threw me on the floor and began to rape me. I screamed and fought like a lioness. The children ran out the door screaming for help. Just then Manfred returned. He had been drinking. He pulled the man off me, threw him out the door and with one blow broke his neck."

Catherina put her hands to her face as if trying to shut out the sight of it and wept uncontrollably.

Anna put her arm around her and held her to her, letting her cry.

At last the distraught woman calmed down somewhat to great shuddering sobs, wiped her eyes and blew her nose on her sleeve and continued. "The next part is the worst. Manfred was too drunk to know what to do next. 'Manfred, we must flee', I urged, but he just stood there in a daze. 'Manfred, come away quickly. You have killed him', I kept saying, but he just stood there and said, as he kicked the dead man, 'I shall tell the lord what a devil's spawn this scum is and demand reparation for you'. 'No, Manfred', I pleaded, but it was too late. People were coming from all over the bailey to see what the ruckus was all about. The guards grabbed him, and I knew there was nothing else I could do. I took the children by the hand and ran for the gate. It was seldom shut and everyone was too busy watching Manfred and the dead man to pay us much mind. I wouldn't go too far, in case he lived, but I knew there was not much chance of that. I hid the children in the woods and bade them be very quiet no matter what happened. Then I climbed a tree near the edge of the woods where I could see without being seen. Oh, Mistress, I can barely tell the rest. It is so horrible, what they did to him." She shook herself like a wet dog and continued, "But I shall tell you because you've been so kind to hear my tale. First they whipped him to within an inch of his life; then they cut off his balls. He screamed terribly but still would not faint. This angered them and drove them to a frenzy. The lord looked on the whole while. He seemed to enjoy it, what they were doing. Only his lady knelt by their dead son. Then they cut off his right hand so he could never work again even if he survived. I prayed he wouldn't. He finally fainted from loss of blood. I thanked Our Lady for that. But they left him hanging there tied to the whipping post. I couldn't leave because he was still alive. I vomited and was afraid they would find me because of it, but they weren't looking for us yet. Finally they threw water in his face to revive him and dragged him to the battlements and hung him from the castle wall."

She hung her head, sobbing again, and barely whispered, "Then I found the children where I had hidden them and fled through the woods. Eventually I heard them crashing around looking for us, but it was still raining and we were well hidden. Saints be praised, they had brought no dogs. And I don't think their heart was in it, whether they were sorry for me — some of them hated that son — or whether their bloodlust had been sated I don't know, but they soon gave up. We were still very careful. Three nights we spent hiding in the woods, in soaking wet clothes — I didn't dare make a fire — until we finally came here."

Anna held her close and let her weep again. "And you are safe here," she assured her. "I shall see to that. I am so glad you told me all. Now I can help you."

"I have nightmares about it," sighed Catherina.

"I am sure you do, but that will pass now that you have shared your burden. I shall tell the Duchess, and soon you will be in a more comfortable place."

"But what about the children?" asked Catherina. "I can't leave them here."

"No, no, certainly not. I have plans for them, too. Don't worry. They will be nearby you."

Catherina was obviously exhausted from the emotional strain.

Anna said, "Lie down now and get some rest and keep the children near you. It grows late and I must leave, but I shall return as soon as I speak to the Duchess." And to my husband, she added to herself. He can't turn me down now.

Anna von Nassau was immediately sympathetic. "You and I shall take her there together, but apprise her first of the rules: 'Everyone is to be treated alike and everyone gets an equal share, the young must help the older women, and all must participate in the laying out of the dead as required'. Warn her to expect some jealousy at first, until they get to know

her, but I shall soon put a stop to that. Our story will be this: She is a nobleman's daughter, which is true enough, and a very distant cousin of your
mother's, since she is from Hannover. Do you think she will go along with
that?"

"I'm not sure," replied Anna. "I don't think Mother is capable of
lying convincingly if anyone were to question her directly. Better a cousin
of my husband's. Sehnde is more or less in that direction. I'll prompt him."

"All right then. Whatever. She is a widow, but no one need know who
her husband was. Advise her not to tell of the manner of his death. He was
thrown from a horse and broke his neck, or some such accident."

"I shall tell her."

"Now, what of the children?"

"I am going to take them in for a while. At least until after the babe is
born. Lüdeke has said I may, if you accept the mother."

The Duchess nodded. "And what then?"

"I hope to hire her as a maid and gradually retire Helga. Or Lüdeke
might place her in one of the weavers' cottages. We'll have to see where
best her talents lie."

"Very well. As long as she won't become a beggar again. I'll not abide
that."

"She won't, I assure you, Your Grace. She wants to work. She is a very
independent type person."

The next day, accompanied by Anna and the Duchess, Catherina
was ensconced in the home on Ritterstrasse. The first thing they made her
do was take a bath and burn her filthy, flea-ridden gown.

"But what shall I wear?" she asked. "I have no other."

"Hold your head high no matter what," advised Anna. "I'll get some
clothes to you, but you may have to alter them considerably." Anna was a
tiny woman, Catherina taller and quite buxom, besides being over six
months pregnant.

Anna took the children home with her and did the same thing. But
their clothes were no problem. She had plenty of things her own sons had
outgrown.

Lüdeke was not quite so soft-hearted as the Duchess. Although he
took to the little boys immediately, he preferred to remain cautious. He
sent one of his most trusted messengers, disguised as an itinerant pedlar, to
investigate Catherina's story. At Verdammteburg he easily confirmed that
a drunken armorer named Manfred had indeed killed the lord's youngest
son, that the death penalty hung over the wife's head, if they ever found

her, for seducing the poor unfortunate boy, but also that no serious attempt was being made to seek her. Good riddance was the attitude.

At Engelhart it was a bit more difficult. Her father refused to talk to him, as expected. His wares appealed more to the female members of the household. Her mother wanted to see his pretty ribbons and silken threads but apologized that she had no money to buy any. When he questioned her, she was very vague, so much so that he feared she was losing her mind.

"Ja," she sighed. "I once had a daughter named Catherina, my baby, but she is lost to me now."

He was unable to ascertain whether she was lost as a baby or as an adult.

"But you must go to see my daughter Isolde on the next farm. She may have a penny to spare for a new ribbon. Even if she doesn't, she would like to see them. Tell her," said the old woman craftily, "that if she has a second penny to spare I need some of that red embroidery silk." She fingered the thread longingly.

The pedlar pretended to think carefully for a moment. "Let me make you a gift of the thread, my lady," he said. "I should hate for you not to be able to finish your beautiful embroidery for lack of a little red silk," for he could see her dire poverty.

She accepted it like a happy child. "Why, thank you, Sir Pedlar. You are very kind," she chirped. "I hope Isolde has a penny to buy something from you. I have two other daughters, a bit further afield."

"So that is all you have, just the three?" he asked, as he packed up his wares.

"Ja, just the three," she replied.

When he reached Isolde's farmhouse—it was hardly more than a large hut—she welcomed him cordially. They were so isolated that few pedlars came their way, and it was well-known that pedlars were the most important bearers of news and gossip for the far-flung farms and tiny villages. She was ready to chat awhile, so it came as no surprise to her when he asked about Catherina.

"Yes, I have—or had—a younger sister by that name. Do you bring news of her?" she asked eagerly.

"Well, not news exactly," he hedged. "Just that she is happily married and living in Hannover." He had been specifically warned to say nothing of Celle. "She asked if I ever came this way to convey her regards. Your lady mother, however, seemed a little vague about her."

"Yes, she would. She has never gotten over the loss of my two younger sisters. They were forced—but a moment, you said happily married? Then that wouldn't be the drunken smith."

"I know nothing of any smith. As I say, she *appears* to be happily married." He had all the information he needed and was ready to leave, but Isolde was not ready to let him go.

"Did she mention her husband's trade?"

"No, my lady, but I should suspect he is a successful artisan of some sort. She appeared quite prosperous. She bought several ribbons, threads and needles from me." He hoped he had not fabricated too much, but the better to put them off the track. Hannover was a large town. Let them seek in vain.

"Then that is surely not the smith. He must have died. I am so glad she is happy and well-off." He could see the greed in her eyes. "Do you know her husband's name?"

"I have no idea, my lady."

He finally made his escape without selling Isolde a thing and high-tailed it back to Celle to report his findings to Lüdeke.

Lüdeke shared the information with his wife. "Probably the warning is unnecessary, but tell her never to go near any of those places or be in touch with any of those people, ever. The family is ready to take every penny she may have, and the other doesn't even bear thinking about."

In the interim Catherina came every day her duties permitted to the von Sehnden home to help with her own children and with whatever tasks she could. She spent many enjoyable hours reading Anna's books. At first Anna had to help her, as she was so out of practice, but soon she was devouring everything that came to hand. Then she began teaching her own children, until she became too ungainly to drag herself around.

Soon thereafter she gave birth to a darling baby boy whom she promptly named Hinrik—after the Duke, in gratitude for all the Duchess' help. She was strong and healthy and recovered quickly except for a persistent cough, which Anna attributed to those nights in the woods in wet clothing. She moved into the von Sehnden home and unobtrusively began helping Helga.

At first the old housekeeper seemed to resent this, but she finally admitted, "Well, perhaps she can churn the butter. I can't seem to make it come quickly anymore."

And then, "Perhaps she could carry the hot water upstairs. My old legs are not what they used to be."

597

And finally Catherina was accepted as part of the household. Her children became as brothers to Anna's two.

Lüdeke meanwhile was becoming more and more involved in the politics of the town. The members of the Gewandschneider pleaded with him to become Bürgermeister, but he kept refusing.

"But you are the most successful merchant in Celle," they reasoned.

"And that is why I have no time to be Bürgermeister," he replied. "What about you, Eggeling?" he suggested to his friend von Eltze.

"I am already toll-collector and that is enough for me," said Eggeling. "My brother Cord has been a Bürgermeister for years, and my father and several grandfathers before him. It is time for a change. We need new blood and there is no one else with your intelligence and strength of character to do the job in these turbulent times. Can't you just see the likes of Heinrich Bünsel or some of the others standing up to our capricious Duke? Celle needs you, Lüdeke."

Finally Lüdeke allowed himself to be persuaded. He knew he could do a good job and he agreed with Eggeling that the times would be more turbulent as the century progressed, although even he could not have foreseen what was to happen in the next few years to turn their world upside down. He agreed to one term.

In 1505 Lüdeke von Sehnden was elected Bürgermeister and Anna at last became pregnant again.

"So we have two things to celebrate," he said, hugging her as she congratulated him.

Later that year she presented him with a healthy boy whom she wanted to call Lüdeke.

"I don't want anybody named after me," said her husband.

"Then let's say he is named after your father and my father," she insisted. "You had your choice on the first two. Let me have my way on this one."

"Very well, if you insist," he replied. "I don't care what he's called, as long as he's bright and healthy."

And bright he was. Young Hinrik Stockman, not quite four, took to him immediately. He begged to be allowed to take care of him. Each of his elder brothers had his counterpart in a von Sehnden son, but he had no one. They became playmates, companions and later fast friends for the rest of their long lives.

Meanwhile Pope Alexander had died and the new Pope, Julius II, another libertine, whose many foibles were to some extent forgiven because he was an ardent patron of the arts, immediately began plans for rebuilding St. Peter's. The ancient basilica built by Constantine was falling into disrepair. In order to finance this tremendous undertaking, Julius stepped up the sale of indulgences to an unprecedented degree, as well as simony and heavy fines for 'priestly concubinage'. Architects and artists such as Bramante and Michelangelo went to Rome to work for him.

A Polish scientist named Copernicus received his doctorate in Canon Law at Ferrara and promulgated his theory that the earth and other planets revolved around the sun—a theory considered heresy by the Church but long believed by mariners.

In 1502 Friedrich, Elector of (Upper) Saxony, founded a new university at Wittenberg. He commissioned an altarpiece for the castle church from the popular painter and engraver Albrecht Dürer, who there met a young law student named Martin Luther, who after having nearly been struck by lightning and having prayed to St. Anna for guidance, decided to become a monk. He entered the Augustinian monastery there and in 1507 was ordained a priest.

A few years later Catherina Stockman very meekly asked to speak to Anna, who was immediately suspicious, for Catherina was not a meek person. I hope she is not going to leave us, thought Anna. I need her more than ever now that old Helga is fully retired to her own little cottage that Lüdeke provided for her. Or, worse yet, I hope she is not in any sort of trouble. Catherina had fitted very well into the von Sehnden household and her children were no trouble, although the two older boys should long since have been apprenticed somewhere, but Catherina could never make up her mind as to what trades she wanted for them. "Anything but a smith," she would say and let the matter slide. Of late Lüdeke had been growing a little impatient over this.

"Mistress," she said, "would you be very upset if I were to remarry?"

This was the last thing Anna expected, although it should have come as no surprise. Catherina was a lusty wench. But somehow Anna thought that after her disastrous first marriage she would not want to take on another man. "Why, no," she said after a moment, "I should be very happy for you, but . . ."

"Have no fear, Mistress, I'll not leave you. I shall continue to work for you. He has said I may. But it would be nice to have my own home."

"Of course," replied Anna, relieved. "You deserve it. And who is the man who has offered for you?"

"He is called Balthasar Murmester."

"Ah, the Master Mason. I have heard of him, although I do not know him personally. I believe he is of good repute."

"Ja, Mistress, I have heard that he is. And I think he is a very kind man. He has already offered to apprentice my two older boys."

"How wonderful for you. You deserve a kind man after all your troubles. Tell me, is he widowed or never married?"

"Widowed, Mistress, and he has no children of his own."

"Good, then he will bring up yours as his own."

"I hope so."

"You realize, of course, that he should have spoken to my husband first."

"I know, Mistress, and he will, but I wanted to see how you felt about it first."

Anna smiled. "I am very happy for you, as long as you don't leave me. And what of little Hinrik?"

"He is too young to be apprenticed yet. I shall bring him with me every day because I want him to keep learning his letters, if that's all right with you."

"Fine, for little Lude would surely miss him. Now tell me how you met this man. You seem to have so little time for yourself."

"Every day that I have time I take the children for a walk about the town, sometimes when I do the marketing or sometimes just for fun. They love to watch the new bell tower of the church being built. Many times we will stand there an hour or more. Balthasar—that is, Master Murmester— noticed this and began talking to them and then to me. He would explain many interesting things to them. Eventually, when he had a few minutes, he would walk with us a bit, so we've gotten to know each other quite well."

"Interesting. And when had you thought of marrying—that is, if my husband approves?"

"Soon, I hope, Mistress," replied Catherina. "We had thought about Michaelmas. He is due a large payment from the Duchess then."

"That is not too far off. Have him speak to Master von Sehnden immediately."

"I shall, Mistress, and God bless you for your kindness."

A master mason in the great days of cathedral and castle building was no mere artisan but one of the most highly skilled of all the craftsmen. He was architect, planner, and engineer, master of the works, talented stonecutter and often sculptor as well. It took years to reach that status and it was a very responsible position. The best of them were highly sought all over Europe. He was completely in charge of a project from start to finish and had large teams of various skilled and unskilled workers under him. Most of them, though still considered craftsmen by the great merchant guilds, became very wealthy. Anna had heard that such was the case with Balthasar Murmester. She knew that, provided Lüdeke approved and she was sure he would, it would be several steps up in status for Catherina. While Anna was happy for her, she wondered how much longer she would have a housekeeper.

A few days later Balthasar called upon Lüdeke.

He was a large heavyset man, all muscle, no fat on him. A gleam of astute intelligence shone from his eyes. He was dressed in a gown rather than hose and doublet, whether because he was old-fashioned or because he felt the occasion warranted it, Lüdeke could not tell. He appeared to be very clean. He addressed Lüdeke humbly, which seemed out of character. Lüdeke sought to put him at ease.

"I know why you have come, Master Murmester. Would you share a mug of beer with me?"

"That would be very nice, Master von Sehnden. I'm afraid I'm not very good at these formal occasions. You say you already know why I am here?"

"Yes, Catherina has already spoken to my wife. That's not how things should be done, but you know how women are."

"I have not had too much experience with women, Master. My first wife died of the pox less than a year after we were wed. I've been alone for a long time."

"I'm sorry to hear that," said Lüdeke. "Now relax, man, and tell me a little about yourself."

"I have been a Master Mason for over ten years. I have directed most of the work on the Castle, and now the bell tower. I was born and raised right here in Celle and have taken the Bürger oath. I own a house in the Blomlage. It is not very large, but adequate. Mistress Stockman has seen it and feels she can be quite comfortable there. I have worked hard all my life and saved my money. In fact, Master, I have even invested some of it in various of your enterprises."

Lüdeke raised his eyebrows at this. It was most unusual for a man from the artisan class. He already felt he liked the man and this surprise was greatly in his favor.

"Then you feel you can provide well for Catherina, keep her happy?"

601

he asked. "She has not had an easy life."

"Very well, Master, better, I think than either her father or first husband did. She has told me a little of her background, but I judge a person by what they are, not where they come from. She is a good woman, Master, and I am more than a little fond of her. She suits me very well, and I hope I can keep her happy. She seems to think so."

Lüdeke smiled. "That sounds like a good beginning. It is not easy to keep a woman happy. Blessed is the man who does. Now what of her children?"

"I have agreed to apprentice the two older boys. The eldest will be starting much too late, but they both seem bright and I hope he can learn quickly. Otherwise there may be some resentment among my other workers. We shall have to see, but I am willing to take the chance. For Catherina's sake."

"That is commendable. I am sure Catherina will appreciate that. I know I do. The eldest should have been apprenticed some years ago and it has been a growing concern with me. I am relieved to know you have a place for him. And what of the youngest?"

"He will live with us, of course, but at the moment I cannot take on more than two apprentices. But he is young yet. When the time comes, perhaps we can find some other trade for him. You may even know someone who can take him."

"I may," replied Lüdeke, "for he seems to me the brightest of them all."

"Bright, yes, but a different type altogether, if you take my meaning. The other two are rough and ready, ideally suited to my trade, but the little one—what can I say?—seems more the scholarly type, so serious for one so young, but that may change."

"Possibly, and as you say, he is young yet. I hope you will let little Hinrik come to visit us often. He has become fast friends with my youngest, Lüdeke."

"Certainly, Master. I have no objections to that, as long as you will permit it. I wouldn't want him to become a nuisance."

"No chance of that. I am quite fond of the boy myself," replied Lüdeke. "Now one last detail. You realize, I'm sure, that Catherina has no dowry. She may have saved a little from her wages here, but it can't be much."

"I am well aware of that, Master. I have no need of any dowry. In fact, I am prepared to make a generous marriage settlement for her, so that she will have her own income no matter what happens to me. You know that I am much older than she."

"I had thought of that, and it relieves my mind that you will provide for her. One last thing, then. She has promised my goodwife that she will continue to keep house for her. Does that meet with your approval?"

"I have no objections if that is what she wants to do. We have discussed the matter. She is no longer a young virgin that I would have to keep an eye on."

Lüdeke laughed. "Then, Master Murmester, you have my consent to the marriage. And I wish you the best of luck. Also, you may count on a goodly wedding gift."

"Thank you, Master von Sehnden. You are very generous. I shall do right by her, you may count on that."

After Balthasar left, Lüdeke sat and pondered awhile and came to a decision. I am fonder of young Hinrik Stockman than even I myself was aware. I shall apprentice him myself when the time comes. I can see his potential already. Scholarly, indeed. Hah! He will make a better merchant than either of my elder sons. They are the scholars. He and little Lüdeke working together. I can just see it. But I shall say nothing to anyone until he is of the proper age.

7

AD 1520

Hinrik Stockman sat alone in Lüdeke von Sehnden's countinghouse. He was in an introspective mood. Slight of stature, although strong and wiry, he was a very private person, even somewhat shy among strangers. He had finished his work for the day and as yet had no desire to leave the quiet premises for the hustle-bustle of the street. It was Saturday afternoon, market day. He began to reflect on his life so far and was well satisfied. He had completed his journeyman years and was now a fully trusted associate of Master von Sehnden. (Among the family he was allowed, encouraged, to called them Uncle Lüdeke and Aunt Anna, but in public and the business it was strictly Master.) Hinrik had not yet been accepted into the Gewandschneider, nor would he be entitled to be called Master until he had his own business, but that would come in time. Of that he was convinced. Of the 'when', or more importantly, the 'how' he was not sure, but happen it would, of that he was positive.

He attributed his small build to the hardships his mother had endured while carrying him. He was totally different from his brothers. They were big and burly like the father he never knew. They were earthy, gregarious men, he the quiet intellectual, who preferred his own company to drinking beer in the taverns. He loved to read everything that came to hand. He was much like Aunt Anna in that respect. His mother had also claimed a love of reading, but after they left the von Sehnden household, he had seldom seen her crack a book except her Bible, and that only sporadically.

He thought about his mother. She had been devoted to and evidently quite happy with his stepfather, Balthasar Murmester. She was a hard worker and threw herself wholeheartedly into everything she did, as long as she was able. But the cough she had contracted when she fled from Verdammteburg grew steadily worse until she became so weak she could do nothing at all. The bell tower had been completed that same year, and

Balthasar refused to take on any new work but sat by her side day and night nursing her. She died in 1516, the same year Hinrik completed his apprenticeship, and was quietly buried in the old Bürger cemetery up on the hill across the river.

He remembered the exact date, the eighth of April, the same day their beloved Duchess Anna von Nassau had died in St. Anna's Hospital, her favorite charity, two years before. He remembered that funeral very well. What pomp and panoply! The great Marienkirche packed with Welfs, Nassovians and Katzenellenbogens from all over Germany as well as all the leading Bürger families of Celle. Hundreds and hundreds of common people mobbed the square and Stechbahn outside the church. The liturgy was long and complicated. The choir boys, joined by the Franciscan monks from Holy Cross, sang beautifully. Old Pastor Cord Lüdeke preached a lengthy eulogy, although there were some who said afterward that much of it was tongue-in-cheek, as he had always been opposed to her reforms. Everyone commiserated with Duke Heinrich, but, there again, the cynical Bürgers of Celle knew that his grief was far from sincere. He could now conduct his feuds and battles without any interference from his mother. At the end she was laid to rest in the large crypt beneath the high altar, all her good works never forgotten.

He thought about his brothers. Franz was already a master stone cutter and under Master Murmester's tutelage could well become a Master Mason one day. He was about to marry and was saving to rent his own home. Berndt was another matter. He was still a journeyman and chafing under the restraint put on him, but his devil-may-care attitude, while fine in the taverns, worried Murmester in a job as precarious and dangerous as theirs. Hinrik thanked God he had not had to follow that trade, admirable though it was. He would be forever grateful to Lüdeke von Sehnden for seeing that he was very different from his brothers.

Throughout his journey years and now he lived in the house in the Blomlage with his stepfather. He had not wanted to leave the old man alone after his mother's death, and since he had reached adulthood they had grown quite close. He was really very fond of Balthasar, the only father he had ever known, and he was quite sure the feeling was mutual. But the happiest times and fondest memories of his childhood and all the apprentice years had been in the household where he had lived since his birth. Uncle Lüdeke had been very strict, but understanding, and Aunt Anna had been very kind, teaching him his letters and the love of books, until somehow, he never knew quite how,

605

Lüdeke had managed to get him into the Latin school.

Their oldest son, Heinrich, who should have been the one to go into the Church, had refused and chose to study law instead and was now an advocate in Bardowick. The second son, Franz, had followed in his footsteps and was now close to completing his studies at Wittenberg. Both had studied under the famous—or infamous, depending how you looked at it—Dr. Martin Luther, the monk-priest who had startled all of northern Germany and most of Europe by having the courage to point out ninety-five items of abuses and false teachings that had crept into the Church. This happened on 31 October 1517, but some years prior to that all the honest, respectable merchants of Germany had been shocked when Jakob Fugger, the Augsburg financier to whom the Emperors were greatly in debt, had been awarded a contract to sell indulgences in Germany. The Dominicans did the actual selling in just about every town square in the land, but a Fugger representative stood by to collect the money. The bit of doggerel:

> "When the coin in the coffer rings,
> The soul from purgatory springs,"

typified for many the egregious depths to which the Church had sunk. There had been a new Pope since 1513, Leo X, a Medici this time, Giovanni, Lorenzo's son. As seemed to be the case in the last fifty years or more, each one was more corrupt than his predecessor. Ostensibly, the sale of indulgences was to pay for the new St. Peter's, but in actual fact, after a hefty commission to the Fuggers, more than half went to the Archbishop of Mainz, who was heavily in debt to the Fuggers, and only a trickle ever reached Rome.

In one such town, Jüterbog, Martin Luther happened to be in the crowd when the Dominican Johann Tetzel uttered his pious mouthings coupled with some high-pressure salesmanship and the Fugger representative stood by to collect. To Luther the whole performance was an obscenity. When he returned to Wittenberg, Franz von Sehnden told Hinrik, he was livid and vowed then and there to devote his life to cleaning up the corruption in the church even if he was martyred for it. Six months later he wrote a letter to his Archbishop, Albert of Mainz, listing ninety-five theses describing abuses in the Church.

Some said that Luther nailed them to the door of the castle church in Wittenberg. But Franz told Hinrik that this was not entirely true. Luther followed correct procedure in writing first to his Archbishop, but most of his friends and students, especially Philip Melanchthon, fearing that in that prelate's hands, the letter would never see the light of day, had many copies printed, and one of them did the nailing to the door. Whatever the truth of the matter, copies were soon circulating all over northern Germany. Since the advent of the printing press, more people than ever before could read and there soon arose a furor of emotional response, both pro and con. An irate Leo called Luther to Rome, but fearing that he, too, would never again see the light of day, he refused to go. He stayed at Wittenberg under the protection of his patron, Elector Friedrich of Saxony, and continued to have debates with local clerics. Just this year he had circulated a letter titled "An Address to the German Nobility" demanding a conference to address Papal abuses. It was written in German rather than Latin, so no one could have the excuse of not being able to read it.

Celle had not been bothered too much by the indiscriminate sale of indulgences since the Dominicans had long been forbidden to operate within the town. They represented to everyone the dreaded Inquisition. Nevertheless, it was the talk of the marketplace, the countinghouses, the homes. Hinrik himself leaned toward the reformer, although he considered himself a devout man and attended Mass regularly. But he asked himself, could buying an indulgence have helped his mother or his father on their way to heaven? He doubted it. In fact, was there even such a thing as Purgatory? There was no mention of it in his Bible. The Bürgers of Celle were divided in their opinions. He knew the von Sehnden were strongly in favor of reform. But their best friends, the von Eltze, were against it. Why? Because for centuries their family had been supporting the church by paying for memorial services for their ancestors—the so-called Totenglocke, the Bells for the Dead. In Hinrik's opinion, although he would never say so, these Masses, some of them quite elaborate, were Celle's own peculiar form of indulgences. Outside the towns the landed nobility in general were against reform. Didn't most of them receive considerable income from the churches and monasteries in their fiefs? The common people, on the other hand, welcomed it with rejoicing and fervor. Hinrik was quite sure which way the Duchy would eventually go. Even now Ernst, Duke Heinrich's son, was studying with Luther at Wittenberg.

Duke Heinrich was one of the few who could not care less. He was too involved in his petty feuds. And this concerned the long-suffering Bürgermeisters and Council of Celle more than any church reform. He

607

had nearly depleted the Ducal Treasury. Lüdeke von Sehnden was still Bürgermeister, having been reelected innumerable times. He had grown tougher over the years, especially where money and the good of the town were concerned. He and the Council were now on the verge of refusing Heinrich any more money. His present feud was concerned with whether the Bishopric of Hildesheim belonged to him, that is, to the Duchy of Lüneburg, or to either of his cousins, the Dukes of Calenberg and Wolfen-büttel. It was a bitter internecine strife that only ended when Heinrich won a resounding victory in 1519 near Soltau. It was the last battle in Germany fought in the old-fashioned feudal way, with fully armored mounted knights. Then suddenly, to everyone's surprise, the new Emperor, Charles V, grandson of Maximilian, stepped into the fray. Whether he just wanted to rid himself of Heinrich's nonsense on trumped-up charges or whether there was any validity to the accusations no one knew. Charles accused Heinrich of being a partisan of François I of France, the Empire's most bitter enemy, and declared the victory at Soltau no victory at all, divided Hildesheim between Calenberg and Wolfenbüttel and, worst of all, placed Heinrich under the Ban of the Empire. This was disaster for the nearly bankrupt Duchy. It meant that Heinrich personally lost all civil and legal rights and would be treated as a common criminal or traitor. For the Duchy itself, there was the dire possibility of its being placed under the jurisdiction of one of the Welf cousins or any other prince, temporal or spiritual, who asked for it, or it could be retained as an Imperial fief. Either way would be a disaster. Lüdeke von Sehnden and the independent-minded Bürgers of Celle were agreed on one thing. Something must be done, and quickly. It was time they took things into their own hands.

But what can I do? thought Hinrik. In all these things, for now at least, I must go the way the wind blows. It was a worrisome situation, but worry never solved anything. Lüdeke von Sehnden was a brilliant and powerful administrator and a very clever man. He will come up with a solution, never fear.

Hinrik shut the ledger book with a bang. What am I doing pondering all these troublesome affairs that I can do nothing about? I shall go home and share a simple supper with old Balthasar and my brother Berndt, if he is not off in a tavern somewhere (another worry), and then perhaps a game of chess before the fire. He put the ledger away, carefully checked the money chest to be sure it was double-locked, and left the countinghouse, securely locking the door behind him.

When he stepped into the street, he changed his mind about going directly home. It was a beautiful fall day, sunny but crisp and cool. The leaves were beginning to turn to red and gold. He could smell the earthy, invigorating smells of autumn, leaves burning and the wood smoke from the town's many hearths. He decided to take a stroll through the town before going home. Without paying much attention to where he was going, he found himself at the Hehlentor, the northern gate of the town leading to the Aller bridge. He decided against crossing to the other side. I am too lazy today to go that far. To the right were the grounds of St. Anna's Hospital. No, too depressing. A brisk wind blew up the river, dispersing the wood smoke and bringing its own fresh river smells. He took a deep breath of the invigorating air and turned left.

This was the long quay where the boats drew up, where the great granaries of the Gewandschneider were located. They looked like top-heavy towers, almost like giant chessmen, he thought. He liked walking along the river, with its singular beauty and its promise of faraway places, but even more he loved seeing the outward and visible signs of the wealth of the town. Some day some of this will be mine, he dreamed.

He meandered along the quay meeting few people. On a Saturday afternoon most housewives had finished their marketing and were busy baking, readying baths for the once-a-week ritual, refurbishing clothes, and otherwise preparing for the Sabbath. Many of the men would be at their barber's for the same reason or tending their gardens, which they had no time to look after during the week. He strolled as far as the Ratsmühle, the town mill, for which a special narrow sluice had been built to lead the water over the great mill wheel.

Suddenly he heard someone singing, a sweet, plaintive song, although he could not make out the words. At first he could see no one, but as he drew closer he saw a girl sitting all by herself on the great stones that formed the edge of the sluice. Apparently she did not hear his approach. Then suddenly she turned, saw him, and stopped singing.

With more courage than he thought he possessed, he said, "I thought it was the Lorelei. Your song is lovely. Please do not stop singing."

She gave him a puzzled look, and he could see she was more than a girl, a young woman, but tiny as a fairy. He expected her to fly away any minute. "I do not sing in front of other people," she said.

"Then pretend I am not here," he suggested as he sat down on another stone close by, but not near enough to frighten her. "You have a lovely voice. I should like to hear your song again. Methinks it is a very old one."

She turned her back to him and said nothing for a while as she stared out over the river. Then she started to sing. It was a simple song of unrequited love:

"He has gone away on the breast of the river
To the sea, to the sea
The Goddess has taken him from my heart
Send him back, Lady, to me."

"Beautiful," he said when she finished. "It *is* a song from the old times, isn't it? Do you know any more?"

"Lots of them," she replied. "My grandmother taught me."

"I knew I was not mistaken about the Lorelei." She blushed becomingly but said nothing. "But you are a Christian, are you not?" he asked.

"Of course I am a Christian," she replied indignantly, "but she taught me all about the old religion, the old stories, the old songs. There is a lot of truth in them, you know."

"I suppose. I wish I had had a grandmother like that," he sighed nostalgically. "I never knew my grandparents. I am an orphan."

"So am I," she said brightly, "but at least I had Grandmama until she died. I shall always thank Our Lady for that."

"I had my mother and she remarried before she died. So I do have a stepfather. Of whom I am quite fond. But it is not the same."

"No, it's not," she agreed.

He was amazed at himself that he could confide so much in her. He did not feel shy at all. Maybe because she was equally shy.

"How are you called?" he asked.

"I am Ilsebe," she replied, but did not ask his name.

"And I am Hinrik," he volunteered. He wanted to keep the conversation going but could think of nothing else to say. Then he thought of her song. "That song you were singing—do you really have a love who has gone away to sea?"

"Nay," she replied with a sigh. "It is only a song. I have not yet had a lover."

"Nor I," he replied. There was another lull in the conversation. He wanted to know more about her. "Do you work?" he asked. "Or are you a lady of leisure?" The moment he asked, he knew it was the wrong thing to say.

"Of course I work," she snapped. "We poor people have to work to eat, you know. Not like young lords who stroll about in their finery."

He looked at his clothes. They did not seem that fine to him. He could not ignore the sarcasm but was at a loss to know how to answer. "I have been very poor, too," he said almost apologetically. "But I guess I was very lucky. I have recently finished my journey years and am now an associate of Gewandschneider and Bürgermeister von Sehnden."

"Bürgermeister von Sehnden!" she exclaimed. "Then you are many cuts, several ells, above me, a poor lacemaker."

"But lacemaking takes a lot of skill and talent. It is an art. Do not belittle it," he chided.

"Maybe so, but I have yet to earn my living at it. I, too, have finished my apprenticeship and must work for the Mistress for seven years to pay for it. There was no money to pay her when I started."

"It will go by fast," he assured her, but he knew how she felt.

The sun was rapidly sinking behind the town at their backs. Balthasar would be wondering where he was. "May I walk with you back to your house?" he asked hopefully.

"No, thank you," she replied. "I should like to sit here for a while and sing to the river and then to the stars when they come out."

"Very well, but be careful. It is not safe after dark."

"Don't worry. I shall not fall into the sluice."

That was not what he meant, but he realized she was being deliberately dense. "May I see you again, Ilsebe?" he asked.

"I come here often," she replied, "to commune with the Goddess," and would say no more.

He decided she really wanted to be alone. So he left her and headed home. Unwittingly he found himself whistling the song she had sung.

The next morning at Mass he looked for her but did not see her. However, the church was very crowded, it being the feast of St. Luke and the St. Remi market about to open, which brought many strangers to town. He dared not be too obvious in his search.

The following day all thoughts of Ilsebe fled his mind when Lüdeke von Sehnden stormed into the countinghouse and broke his news.

"We have decided how best to handle the Duke. We must save the Duchy—and Celle," he said.

"And that is?" asked Hinrik.

"I don't want to tell you the details yet, but I want you to be present at the meeting."

"I?" queried Hinrik. "But I am not a member of the Council. I

611

haven't even taken the Bürger oath as yet."

"That is just why I want you. I need someone I can trust absolutely to be my personal secretary and witness and take down everything that is said. It cannot be anyone even remotely connected to the Court or to the town government."

"I appreciate your trust, Master Lüdeke. I shall be there. When is this meeting?"

"Tomorrow, one hour after tierce, in the Ratskeller, the meeting room of the Council. Bring plenty of sharp quills and paper. You can transfer it to parchment later."

On Tuesday Lüdeke and the Council waited and waited, but Duke Heinrich did not show up. After sext rang, they sent out to the baker's shop for food for their dinner, fearing to leave in case the Duke should come.

"That irresponsible pup," said one man. "He is deliberately flaunting us."

"It doesn't surprise me," said another. "I never really expected him to come."

"Would to God his blessed mother were still alive. She'd make him come."

"If she were, he wouldn't be in this mess in the first place. But she's not, so it's up to us to pull his chestnuts out of the fire."

"Would to God they were only chestnuts. I fear for the whole Duchy and all of us."

"What happens if he never comes?"

"Then we must go to him."

"Do you think he would see us?"

"Who knows?"

After nones rang, they sent a messenger to the Castle to inquire of the Duke's intentions. The man returned very shortly with the information that the Duke was out hunting and no one had any idea when he would return.

"God's balls," swore Lüdeke, pounding his fist on the table. "Tomorrow then, my friends. Tomorrow we shall beard the lion in his own den."

"Weasel, more like," commented someone.

"Slippery as an eel," said another.

"Tomorrow," continued Lüdeke, "before prime has rung, nay, let us make it before dawn, we shall catch him still abed, before he even has a chance to use the chamber pot."

"Do you think they will even let us in the Castle?"

"I think they will," replied Lüdeke. "Feeling against Heinrich is running high even among the courtiers. They do not want to lose their comfortable life of leisure. And don't forget, we hold the purse strings. I have recently spoken to the Chancellor about this, and he agrees something must be done—and that urgently. Why, if we were to call all the debts at once we, my friends, would own the Castle and everything in it. No one would dare deny us entry into our own Castle. But just in case some overzealous, unenlightened Castle guard should say us 'nay', I intend to bring several of the Town Watch, fully armed, with us. I shall keep them carefully in the background, of course, so he won't feel threatened, but I think the matter of the money will be enough to bring him to heel."

The Council applauded this with, "Hear, hear," and, "Bravo, Lüdeke."

"Then let us adjourn to our homes, and early to bed, so that we have our wits about us in the morning."

Hinrik sat through all of this silently, amazed at the daring step they were planning. He had never before quite realized what a great leader Lüdeke was. He would put courage in any heart, he was so sure of himself, Hinrik thought.

The next morning the Bürgermeisters and Council met at the Rathaus before dawn. They were each dressed in their most formal gowns. Only Hinrik felt out of place in his doublet and hose. Each of them, without having been told, had with him an accounting of all the debts the Duke owed him. In addition, the Town Clerk had given Lüdeke a concise list of all the monies loaned to the Duke by the town itself. With eight armed men, two from each quarter, behind them, they set off for the Castle.

Dawn was just breaking, pink and delicate, over the river when they crossed the drawbridge over the moat. The sleepy guards at the gate, anxious for their beds, did not even challenge them. They entered the second gate to the inner courtyard, where servants were just beginning to stir. They were approaching the new wing that Heinrich and his mother had recently built when a maid finally noticed them.

"You can't go in there, Master," she cried. "His Grace has not yet arisen."

"Fine, that's just what we want," said Lüdeke and kept on walking.

"No! No!" she cried. "Guard!"

Her cry brought guards, footmen, and other servants who tried to block their way.

At a signal from Lüdeke, the Town Watch formed a wedge in front of them and started to force their way through the crowd.

"Stand aside!" shouted Lüdeke. "We have more right to enter here than you have to prevent us. Stand aside, and no one will be hurt."

They were beginning to make headway again when someone must have called the Chancellor, Johann Förster. This worthy came hurrying out the door, shrugging on his gown over his nightshirt as he ran.

"What is going on here?" he demanded.

"Good morning, Master Förster," said Lüdeke suavely. "We are merely keeping an appointment we have with His Grace."

"Oh, Master von Sehnden, Master Oelmann, Master von Eltze, Master Schulte, uh . . . uh . . . I did not see you behind these—these soldiers. But so early?"

"So late, Master Förster," replied Lüdeke. "The appointment was for yesterday morning, but His Grace decided that the hunt was more important than the fate of the Duchy."

"Ah, yes, I heard about that," said Förster. "Unfortunate."

"We are here to make sure that disaster does not overtake the Duchy," continued Lüdeke. "You can understand the urgency. So if you would step aside . . ."

"Yes, yes, of course," replied Förster. "Perhaps you would like to come into the hall and discuss this, but could you leave your—your guards outside?"

"Certainly, Master Förster. It was just a precaution against interfering maids and footmen." Lüdeke glared at the crowd, which began melting away once they saw the Chancellor was welcoming them.

They entered the hall. The Chancellor, wringing his hands obsequiously, said, "Now, if you'll tell me what you wish to see His Grace about, I'll be happy to see if he has arisen and can see you."

"Nay, Johann," said Lüdeke, dropping all formalities now that they were well out of earshot of the servants. "We do not wish to be announced. We cannot have him flying out the window before we get there. There will be no discussion. We have come to *tell* him how we propose to save the Duchy. If he does not agree, we are prepared to call in all our debts immediately—all of them."

Förster was aghast. "But, Lüdeke, you know there is no money left in the treasury. You and I have discussed that often enough."

"Ja, Johann, we have discussed it often enough. And we have also discussed how we might save the Duchy from being dissolved by Charles, but apparently nothing of what we have said has penetrated the ducal skull. There is but one alternative left, and we are here to see that he does it. It is a matter of last resort."

"Can you not tell me what you have in mind, so that I can prepare him?" asked Förster meekly. "You know how irascible he can be."

"Exactly. Which is why there will be no preparation, no warning. You may come with us if you wish, but we do the talking. Come, Masters, let us mount to the ducal chamber!"

Lüdeke strode purposefully toward the stairs, the rest following, with the Chancellor, still wringing his hands, trailing behind them. At the door of the ducal apartment they were met by a footman, who feebly protested but, after one look at Lüdeke's face and signal from Förster, stepped aside and let them pass. After crossing an anteroom, Lüdeke flung open the door of the bedchamber and entered. The rest crowded around him. Hinrik, with his quills, ink pot, and paper, slipped off to one side. Lacking a table to use, he found a prie-dieu and turned it around to use as a desk.

Heinrich sat on the edge of the bed, stark naked, rubbing the sleep from his eyes.

"Hans," he mumbled sleepily, "see what that commotion is all about. I'll have the knaves who woke me so early flogged within an inch of their lives. But first fetch me the chamber pot."

"The pot is right beside you, my lord, and there will be no floggings today," said Lüdeke.

Heinrich's eyes flew open and he stared, mouth agape, at the group of men standing before him. "What—what are you doing here? Who gave you permission to enter my presence? Where is Hans?" Then he remembered something. "I believe it is customary for villeins to kneel in my presence until I grant you leave to speak," he said haughtily.

Lüdeke ignored the insult. "And we know, my lord, that you have been placed under the Imperial Ban, by which you have lost all civil and legal rights, including our obligation to do homage."

Heinrich spotted Förster in the background. "Johann, get these louts out of here. They are lying. Can't you do something?" he screamed hysterically.

The Chancellor took a tentative step forward. "I am afraid not, Your Grace. They are absolutely right. Your Grace has been aware of the Ban—and its possible consequences—for some time now and has chosen to ignore it. As far as the Emperor is concerned, you have no Ducal rights, no legal rights, you do not even exist as a person."

"You lawyers, you think you know it all," flared Heinrich. "You are dismissed. I'll find me a new Chancellor."

"I think not, Your Grace," replied Förster calmly. "I would suggest that you hear what these eminent Bürgers have to propose. I do not know what it is, but if you do not agree, they have threatened to call in all your debts to them."

"Hah! Much luck to them. There is no money in the treasury."

"Quite so, Your Grace, but there is this castle, which you have fraudulently used for security many times over, all its furnishings, your stables, your arms, Her Grace's jewels."

Heinrich put his head in his hands. "Even you, Johann. Even you are against me."

"Not against you, Your Grace, but *for* the good of the Duchy. It behooves you to listen to these men. I beg you hear them." Förster stepped back again behind the others.

Heinrich signed. "I have to pee," he said forlornly.

"We'll wait while you do that," replied Lüdeke. "We would not want anything to divert your full attention from what we have to say."

Heinrich peed noisily into the pot and put it aside with distaste.

"My clothes," he said.

"The sheet will do," said Lüdeke.

Heinrich pulled the corner of the sheet across his lap, but remained seated on the edge of the bed. "Now, what is this miracle you have concocted that will save the Duchy from that devil of Habsburg whose cousin murdered my father?" he asked sarcastically.

"After much serious deliberation, we have decided that the only thing that will save the Duchy and appease the Emperor is to ask for your abdication."

"Abdication!" screamed Heinrich. "*You* have decided! Hah! And if I refuse?"

"Then we shall *demand* that you abdicate in favor of your sons. We shall take possession of the castle and all your goods and chattels and leave you to the tender mercies of the Emperor," declared Lüdeke.

Heinrich turned white and they thought he was going to faint. For a long time he said nothing. Then very quietly he asked Förster, "Johann, do you agree with this?"

Förster replied, "I believe, Your Grace, that it is the only way to solve our problems."

Heinrich sat quietly for a long time. Some thought he was praying, but Lüdeke doubted it. At last Heinrich murmured, "What must I do?"

Lüdeke stepped forward. "We have here a parchment already prepared, written in the proper legal terms. All you have to do is fill in the name of which son you are abdicating in favor of and sign it. You may have Chancellor Föster read it first, if you wish, to be sure everything is in order."

The Chancellor took the parchment from Lüdeke and studied it carefully. "I find it to be in order," he said finally. "The legal verbiage is quite precise. I urge you to sign it forthwith."

Heinrich took the document from Förster. He could not read too well but made a pretense of understanding what was written. "Where do I write the name of my son?" he asked. Förster pointed out the place. And Heinrich, in a last gesture of spite, wrote in the names of all three sons—Otto, Ernst, and Franz—thereby effectively dividing the Duchy once again into three smaller segments. Then he signed it with a flourish. "Fetch my seal, Johann. It should be in that chest somewhere."

As Förster rummaged through the chest, he thought, he doesn't even take proper care of that, the most important symbol of his office. Finally, amid old hose, hats, jewelry, playing cards, dice, and whatnot he found the box containing the seal. The wax was duly melted over a candle and the seal impressed upon it under Heinrich's signature. Johann Förster, Lüdeke von Sehnden, the other Bürgermeister, two of the Councilman, and Hinrik Stockman witnessed it. Each of them had brought his own seal.

"Thank you, Master von Welf," said Lüdeke. "You may rest assured that we shall find other means of collecting the monies owed to us and shall leave the Castle intact for your sons."

Heinrich ignored him. "Johann, you will see to it that my sons know about this. Ernst is still at Wittenberg with that renegade monk. The others could be anywhere. You'll have to find them. I can't keep track of their comings and goings. Now leave me alone."

When they were back in the hall, Förster grabbed Lüdeke's arm. "Brilliant! Brilliant!" he declared. "I should never have dared. But it is by far the best solution. My congratulations."

"Withhold your congratulations, my friend, until we see whether Imperial Karl will accept this," warned Lüdeke.

"I don't see why he would not," replied Förster. "It should satisfy him."

"He won't like the further division with three Duchies," put in Eggeling.

617

"Nor do I," said Lüdeke, "but he can override that in a trice if he really wants to make us an Imperial fief."

"I don't like it either," said Dietrich Schulte. "Heinrich played us an underhanded trick with that one, but look at it this way: three small, weak duchies are far less of a threat to Karl than one big one. It may be enough for him to leave us alone."

"Perhaps you are right. Let us hope so," replied Lüdeke. "Now, Johann, send for those heirs forthwith and do us this favor, if you can: in the division, see that Ernst gets what is left of Lüneburg and Celle. He is the only one with any brains and common sense. The only one I trust."

"I agree with you wholeheartedly," said Förster. "Otto is crazy like his father, and Franz is a weakling like his mother. Ernst is a good man, much like the old Duchess, and we can hope that his time spent with Doctor Luther will have made him a more devout man than his father as well."

"Amen to that," enjoined several of the Councilmen.

"I am sure I can arrange things as you wish, my friends. I suppose, technically speaking, that I am now unofficial regent until the heirs are installed."

"I suppose that you are," agreed Lüdeke. "Just remember who put you in that position."

"I'll not forget," replied Förster. "I'll see to it that Earnst is the next Duke of Lüneburg. The others we can foist off on a couple of insignificant border towns and call them duchies."

"Well spoken, Johann. Then see to it," said Lüdeke. "Meanwhile we'll send this parchment by fast courier to the Emperor, and let us hope that he is so preoccupied with Doctor Luther and his fellow reformers that he will thank us for removing this one thorn from his side."

Ilsebe woke long before dawn as was her wont, but this day she could lie abed, if she chose. It was a holiday. Usually she had to be washed and dressed, her fast broken, long before daybreak so that she could start work promptly at prime. The Mistress was very strict about that. But today the new Duke, Ernst, was being crowned in the great Marienkirche. Lately some people were beginning to call it the Stadtkirche. She wasn't quite sure why. Something to do with the new religion. She didn't understand too much about that either. Neither did anyone else, as far as she could tell, although everyone talked about it. She knew that the Popes and many bishops had set bad examples for the people, that there were too many silly "Do-as-I-say, not-as-I-do" strictures. People *should* be able to worship God (or Goddesses) as they wished, but why change the beautiful name of a beautiful church? Silly.

Should I go and watch, or should I not? she debated. I care not a fig for all their pomp and ceremony. She knew there would be no room for common people such as she in the church. It will be packed with courtiers and the Bürgers and their families. People from far off, too, no doubt. She had never witnessed a coronation in her life. Even the procession from the Castle to the church and the attendant festivities would be exciting. Yes, if you had someone to share it with. No, I won't go. I can't be bothered. But all Celle will be there, she argued with herself. Maybe I'll see that nice young man.

Unwittingly her thoughts drifted to Hinrik Stockman. He had met her two or three times at the millrace. Sometimes they would talk about all sorts of interesting things. At others he would just sit quietly with her. He seemed to understand her need to commune with the river goddess, although he never expressed it in quite that way. Lately, though, Ilsebe had been avoiding him. She wasn't sure why. Maybe she was growing just a little too fond of him and she did not want that. She did not want to get involved with any man, not for quite a while yet anyway. But he was not just any man. He was so different from most of the men she came up against—either loutish boors or snobbish Bürgers' sons. And they all wanted just one thing, and that she was not yet prepared to give. Hinrik had never even so much as hinted about anything like that. He was so kind and gentle and, yes, understanding. Maybe because he was an orphan, too. Although he was far better educated than she, he never talked down to her. In fact, he treated her like—like a lady.

Hah! Enough of this foolish daydreaming. Let me be up and dressed. She would go to see this wonderful coronation. She had nothing better to do. She thoroughly brushed and then donned her only gown. She brushed her blond hair until it shone, then carefully braided it and wound the braids around her head. She took a clean, freshly starched wimple and arranged it over her braids. Usually she only changed to a clean one on Sunday, but this was an occasion, wasn't it? She was grateful that the old style of wearing it tight under one's chin had gone out of fashion. They were more like head kerchiefs now. No apron today. She pulled on her heavy woolen stockings and slipped her feet into the old klompen. She did not own a pair of real shoes. Someday. Then she decided to indulge in her one luxury. She took out of her chest a heavily starched lace ruff that she had made herself in her spare time. She had never worn it before. She

619

admired it for a moment before carefully arranging it over her gown. It was beautiful work, if she did say so herself. She did not have a mirror, but she knew it changed her whole appearance, made her look like a fine lady.

She went down to the kitchen to break her fast. No one was about, but at least it was warm here. She held out her rough red hands to the meagre fire. She would like to have built it up a little, but far be it from her to be accused of wasting wood when the house would be empty most of the day. She helped herself to a small beer and a large crust of stale bread smeared with goose grease.

Then she took her cloak and carefully arranged it over her shoulders but under the ruff so as not to crush it. She hating wearing the cloak, it was so ratty and threadbare, but it was the only one she had and it was very cold outside, although the sun was shining. It was just after the New Year. She hoped that the beautiful lace collar would distract people's eyes so they would not notice the cloak. She stepped out into the street.

Everyone was hurrying to the Stechbahn through which the procession would wend as it made its way from the Castle to the church. When she arrived there, it was already packed. She wondered if she would be able to see anything at all. She wormed her way through the press of humanity as only very small people can do, until she was near the west gate of the town. Here the tide of people was against her and she felt herself being pushed to one side, but fortunately it was in the right direction and she ended up on the corner where the procession would have to turn to enter the Stechbahn as it approached from the Castle. She decided it was as good a spot as any and held her ground.

"Here they come!" cried several people at once.

"Hush, hush," cautioned others.

Just then one of the guards employed to keep the crowds back moved in front of her. She stood on her tiptoes but could not see over him. She moved to one side in order to peep between him and the next person and bumped into someone. She felt an arm snake around her waist.

"Well, look who's here," said a gruff voice. "If it isn't the little lace-maker." It was Hans, the butcher's apprentice, who sometimes delivered meat to the back door of the Mistress' house.

"Unhand me, you boor," she hissed.

"And don't we look like a proper little lady today." he started fingering the ruff. "Look here, Heinz," he said to his equally boorish companion, "see the fancy ruff she probably stole from her mistress."

"I didn't steal it. I made it," she retorted, "and leave me alone." The press of the crowd pushed them together, and she felt his hand slip down to her buttocks. "Get your filthy hands off of me," she cried. She tried to twist away, but he was holding onto the ruff and she feared he would tear it. Finally she screamed again, "Leave me alone, you filthy lout!"

Several people turned around and some scolded her, "Hush, now, His Grace is coming."

But one young man pushed his way through the onlookers and made his way to her side. It was Hinrik. She was so embarrassed, she turned six shades of red as if it were her fault.

"What is going on here?" he demanded. "Why are you molesting this young maid?"

Hans quickly dropped his hand. "Uh—uh—just admiring her ruff, Master."

"Unhand her then and admire from a distance," said Hinrik angrily.

"Hah! So you can have her for yourself, fine young master?" replied Hans, growing bold again. "She's nothing but a serving wrench. Just your kind." His friend was tugging at his sleeve.

Hinrik grew livid but kept his temper. "To me she is a fine lady. And if you ever speak like that again, I'll see that the watch claps you in the pillory. Now get thee hence."

"Come on, Hans," said Heinz. "Your big mouth will get you in trouble yet."

Hans started to retort but, seeing Hinrik's face, though better of it. The two kerls faded back into the crowd.

"Oh, Hinrik. Thank you so much," said Ilsebe. "I am so embarrassed."

"Why should you be so embarrassed? They were the loutish boors."

"That you would think I were of their ilk."

"You know I never thought that. I meant what I said, that to me you are a fine lady. Now let me fix your elegant ruff. It is truly a work of art. Did you make it?" She nodded. "Now come up front where you can see better. My friends are saving my place. The front of the procession is already here." He took her hand and eased through the crowd to the very front row, right next to the guards. They seemed to know him. He stood her in front of him, hands gently resting on her shoulders so that no one could push her out of the way.

First came a troop of cavalry, knights of the ducal household, their armor so highly burnished it shone like silver in the bright sunlight. The great destriers were draped with colorful, richly embroidered caparisons, each one emblazoned with its owner's coat-of-arms. Most had colored feathers waving from their heads. Some even sported bells attached to the bridle. Then came a band of musicians beating drums and blowing trumpets vigorously as if to keep themselves warm, while their breath floated above them in the frosty air. Following came the contingent of guilds, twenty of them, each bearing the banner of their trade. At the end of this group marched the Kalands brotherhood, that elite corps of Bürgers, nobles, and clericals.

Next came the clergy—several brown-robed, open-sandalled brothers from the Franciscan Monastery of the Holy Cross, then the canons, priests, and vicars of the Marienkirche and its local chapels, led by the head pastor, old Cord Lüdeke, all resplendent in their finest vestments. Then came the Bishop of Hildesheim and his court, glittering in cloth of gold and jewels, acolytes carrying his golden crozier and other accoutrements of his office. Behind him came the boys from the Choir School, their sweet, angelic voices soaring on high with joyous hymns but totally out of cadence with the band that preceded them. No one cared. Everyone was enjoying the show, even singing along with them.

The civilian courtiers followed, clerks of the court and other officials, led by Chancellor Johann Förster. They, too, were most gaily dressed and bedecked with jewels. Then at last came His Grace of Lüneburg, the new Duke Ernst himself. He rode in a new, shining, most modern carriage drawn by four coal-black horses. He himself was somberly dressed all in black velvet only relieved by his crisp white stock and a great jewel that hung on his chest. He was a handsome man with dark hair and beard and flashing brown eyes. Although he could ride well, it was said that he purposely chose the carriage because he was not a knight, but a humble clerk. His Duchess sat beside him. She wore a fine, but very unostentatious, gown of blue velvet.

Behind the ducal equipage walked her very dignified ladies-in-waiting, followed by an excited group of little girls who tossed flowers to the crowd and sang old Saxon folk songs. Where they got the flowers in midwinter no one knew, but the crowd loved it. The procession ended with another mounted troop, this time of the Castle guards, some of whom looked decidedly uncomfortable on a horse.

By the time they passed, the front of the procession was already inside the church and the Duke was handing his lady down from the carriage at the great west door. The crowd cheered and cheered as the great bells started ringing. Many of them fell in behind the end of the procession although they knew there was not a chance of squeezing any more people inside the church. It was already packed with the leading Bürgers and their families, Welf relatives from all over Germany, royalty and bishops from all over the Empire. Even Emperor Charles had sent a representative.

"Well," said Ilsebe, "that was nice. I'm glad I came after all. I wasn't going to."

Hinrik was still holding her shoulders. He leaned down and brushed the tip of her ear with a quick kiss. "I'm glad you came, too," he whispered. "I've missed you."

Before she could answer him, someone said, "Why, Hinrik, you old fox, where have you been hiding this delectable little maid?" She turned around and this time she saw Hinrik blush.

He ignored the question and said, "Ilsebe, let me introduce you to my three best friends. Peter Stratheman, Eggeling von Eltze, and Lüdeke von Sehnden."

"I am very happy to meet you," she said demurely as she curtsied. She recognized the names, all sons of the leading families. Eggeling of the long, dark, typical von Eltze countenance, obviously three or four years older than Hinrik; Peter, about his same age and by far the handsomest of the lot; and Lüdeke, still in his teens, a bit homely but with piercing blue eyes that looked far more knowledgeable than his age. What an odd assorted lot, she thought. But if they were Hinrik's friends, she was prepared to like them. She felt she could trust his judgment.

"Hinrik, you never told us you had a girl," said Lüdeke.

"She's not exactly my girl," replied Hinrik, "just a very good friend."

Lüdeke looked dubious, and Eggeling smiled knowingly.

Peter said, "But you haven't answered my question. Where have you been hiding her?"

Hinrik smiled mysteriously. "I don't hide her. She hides herself. She is a river sprite. Like a fairy princess, she appears and disappears as she wills."

"Hinrik, you're joshing," said Lüdeke.

"Nay, 's God's truth," he swore.

Ilsebe laughed in spite of herself at the perplexed faces. They did not know whether to believe Hinrik or not. But she thought it better to change the subject. It could be dangerous falling on the wrong ears.

"And why are you young masters not inside the church taking part in the great coronation?" she asked.

623

"We could have, but it's much more fun out here," replied Peter.

"It's boring," moaned Lüdeke, "and it will go on for hours."

"We much preferred to be with Hinrik, who was not invited," said Eggeling. "And just think—then we should not have learned his secret. I should much rather meet a river sprite than watch a Duke being crowned."

Ilsebe smiled again. Hinrik took her hand. "Come," he said. "I have heard they are serving hot soup at the Ratskeller for those of us unfortunate enough not to be partaking in the ceremony. It will taste good on a cold day like this. Let's go before it's all gone."

"But I alone with four men?" objected Ilsebe. "It's not seemly."

"You are alone with me," corrected Hinrik. "They are just trailing behind."

She noticed that the three friends had left the couple to walk alone. What decent young men they are, she thought, so unlike the boors that molested me. She smiled and said, "Then in that case I won't disappear. Not today anyway."

"A holiday from being a river sprite?" She nodded. He wished there were some way he could find out where she lived. She always avoided a direct question. Perhaps today she would let him walk home with her.

They slurped their soups from wooden bowls as they stood in the marketplace outside the Rathaus. The soup was a bit thin and watery but very hot, and it warmed their innards in the brisk air.

Hinrik pulled an apple from his pocket. "Will you share dessert with me?" he asked.

"I'd like that," she replied. Even common fruit was a rarity at the Mistress' house.

"Then you take a bite and I'll take a bite," he suggested. "It will be like kissing your lips."

She laughed and blushed at the same time. "Hinrik, you are such a romantic," she teased, but the thought pleased her nonetheless.

Ilsebe did not say much as she listened to the friends' conversation. None of it was the frivolous, often off-color inanities she expected from young men of that age. They spoke of many things, and all of it interesting.

"Are your brothers here today for the coronation?" asked Eggeling of Lüdeke.

"But, of course," replied Lüdeke. "They wouldn't have missed it for anything. Franz especially. He has become a very close friend of Ernst."

"Lüdeke's brothers, Heinrich and Franz, have both studied at Wit-

624

tenberg with Doctor Luther," explained Hinrik for Ilsebe's enlightenment. "Franz at the same time as Duke Ernst. They became best friends as students."

"And it didn't cost him a penny," put in Peter.

Ilsebe looked surprised. "How so?" she asked. "I thought it was very costly to attend university."

"It is," explained Eggeling, "but their family has a stipendium from their mother's, the Mestwarts', side. A distant ancestor provided it, and it pays their entire tuition."

"But only for two per generation," added Lüdeke. "I should have to pay were I of a mind to go. But I don't care. With those two as clerks, it leaves me as heir to the business. The only trouble is that Hinrik is doing the work that the heir should be doing."

"Do I detect a note of jealousy, Lüdeke?" asked Eggeling.

"Nay, nay," he objected, none too forcefully. "It's just that Father is so strict, insisting that I complete all the journey years like any common apprentice."

"Which is as it should be," agreed Eggeling. "My father did the same. You will be the better merchant for it."

"I suppose so," said Lüdeke grudgingly. "But it takes so long, and I admit I am impatient to be doing Hinrik's job."

"And then what of Hinrik?" asked Peter.

"I hope by that time to strike out on my own," replied Hinrik. "I know it takes a tremendous amount of capital, but I'll find it somehow. Meanwhile I am eager to learn everything Master von Sehnden has to teach me. Not like some young pups who think they already know it all," he joked as he clapped Lüdeke on the shoulder.

Lüdeke grimaced but took it in good humor. Hinrik was still his idol.

Ilsebe was fascinated by the stipendium. "Tell me more about this stipendium," she asked. "How does it work?"

"An ancestor left a large sum of money, well invested, and several rent-bearing properties to the Mestwart," explained Eggeling. "The descendants were not to touch the capital, and the income was to be used only to pay the university tuition for two sons every—how often, Lüdeke?"

"Only once each generation," he replied, "and each applicant has to prove his direct lineal descent from this ancestor. Johann Wiese was his name. It goes back over a hundred years."

"But only for sons?" asked Ilsebe. "Nothing for the daughters?"

"Not in this case," replied Eggeling. "Remember, women were not considered educable in those days. Still aren't in most cases. Although I've heard that there are a few universities beginning to admit them."

"That doesn't seem fair," said Ilsebe. "I should loved to have gone to university. I know I could have done the work. There are many women, you know, who have more brains than some men."

They all laughed. "Agreed," said Peter, "but by and large the rest of the world doesn't think so."

Ilsebe was adamant. "Someday it will. There will be women leaders everywhere," she predicted. "Look at Isabella of Spain."

"She may have pawned her jewels to send Columbus to the New World, but she wasn't too wise to use the Inquisition to chase the Jews out of Spain. They have all come to Germany and are making more money than most Christians," said Eggeling.

"Be that as it may," said Hinrik, "if I ever get wealthy enough, I, too, should like to set up such a stipendium, and I shall include something for the daughters, Ilsebe, never fear."

"Bravely spoken," applauded Peter.

"Well and good," agreed Eggeling, "but you must get your business first."

"I shall—one day," Hinrik assured them.

"That he will," agreed Lüdeke. "I've known Hinrik all my life. Whatever he sets his mind to, that he will do."

One of the first things Duke Ernst did was to continue and enlarge upon a building project initiated by his father Heinrich der Mittler. The original plan had been to extend the new castle wall until it joined the town wall, making it all one secure entity. However, in recent years the town had grown considerably, overflowing the walls on the south side to include a large suburb known as the Blomlage. Ernst wisely foresaw that in these troubled times of religious differences that were erupting into violence in some places, and with fear of possible retribution for his father's follies, the town needed a new higher and stronger wall throughout its circumference and that the people of the Blomlage deserved protection as well. His grandiose plans included all this as well as a moat contrived by rechanneling a part of the Fuhse around the walls. Balthasar Murmester was appointed Master Mason of the project.

The house where Hinrik Stockman lived with his stepfather lay in the Blomlage directly in the path of the proposed wall. This house and those of many of their neighbors would have to be torn down to make way for the construction and the people relocated.

"That doesn't seem fair," commented Hinrik. "Why can't the wall be run a little farther out and include everyone?"

"Because of the lay of the land," explained Balthasar, pointing to a plan, "it would not be practical. The only feasible place to run the moat is through here. Beyond that the land is soft and swampy and could not bear the weight of the wall."

"I see," said Hinrik. "You are the one who is knowledgeable about these things. But what are we to do?"

"We'll buy another house. With all of us working, we can well afford it. It's time we moved to a better home anyway."

"But what of the others?" asked Hinrik. "Many are quite poor."

"I don't know. Perhaps the Duke will do something for them. It's not my problem. Besides, I suspect that the large Jewish community that lives here will not be allowed to stay within the town. That would leave a lot of houses available for those who will lose theirs."

"That isn't right. The Jews are hardworking people. They have contributed a lot to this town. A number of them have only recently fled persecution in Spain. Why should they be put upon here?"

"I agree. But that's the way things are, what the Church dictates."

"But the Church is changing, if Doctor Luther has his way," protested Hinrik.

"I doubt it will change to that extent," said Balthasar.

Work on the wall progressed rapidly considering the laborious, tedious toil involved. As the masons and stonecutters laid course upon double course of stone, hundreds of day laborers dug out the wide moat and trundled the earth up great ramps to fill the inside of the wall. Before one section was completed, the next was already under way. As the condemned houses in the Blomlage were torn down, one or two at a time, this rubble was also dumped into the wall as fill. The old wall had had four gates, one for each quarter of the town. The new plans called for only three, eliminating the Blomläger Gate on the south side. Those remaining were the West Gate, just south of the Castle, the Hehlentor on the north side facing the Aller Bridge, and the Braunschweiger Gate on the southeast corner. Each of the gates would have new, stronger fortifications in the wall itself, a new bridge across the moat, and an additional fortified gate on the far side of the moat. Across the Aller bridge was another strong gate leading in zigzag fashion to the great Hehlentor. Aside from the fortified towers of the Castle itself, there were to be six watch towers along the south and east sides of the new wall. The planners evidently considered the two rivers protection enough on the other two sides.

One day as Hinrik was heading home from midday dinner, he stopped for a moment to watch the great crane work. This was a wooden machine designed to lift the heaviest stones to the upper courses of the wall. Its rear was counterweighted with huge boulders so that the weight of the stone being raised would not tip it over. A system of ropes, pulleys, and gears ran up the length of it powered by a large treadmill in which three or four men walked all day long. As the great stone was raised, men at the bottom, midway, and upper levels guided the stone, finally pushing it over to the men on top of the wall who carefully eased it into place and loosened the ropes. At this point, the treadmill was reversed and the rope lowered to the ground for the next one. It was very dangerous work.

As he watched, he spied a group of boys, some of them old enough to know better, throwing stones at the big stone as it was being raised, presumably to see who could throw the highest. Among them he saw with dismay was someone he knew, who certainly should have known better.

"Lüdeke," he shouted above the din, "what in the world are you doing?"

Lüdeke looked a little embarrassed, but he brazened it out, saying, "I just happened by and I was showing the little fellows how to lob the stones higher."

"What wrong with you?" asked Hinrik sternly. "Suppose they hit one of the men?"

"But we aren't throwing them at the men, just at the big stone," piped up a little boy.

"Don't you realize that when and if you hit the big stone, the small stones will bounce off in some direction and could easily hit a man in the eye blinding him or in the head and kill him?"

The boys looked at him, perplexed. "We didn't think of that, Master," said one. "We were just having fun." Lüdeke just looked shamefaced and said nothing.

"Even if you just hit a man on the hand or back, he could slip and lose his grip on the big stone," continued Hinrik. "And if that came crashing down, several men could be killed." The boys gaped at him. "My father works on this wall, and every man up there is someone's father or brother. How would you like it if your father or brother were killed or blinded?"

"I wouldn't", "That would be terrible." The boys mumbled in chorus.

"Then get out of here and find your fun somewhere else," said Hinrik angrily, "and if I ever see you doing that again, I'll have the watch put you in the stocks."

The boys slunk off. Some made faces behind Hinrik's back, and he knew they would return, but at least he had averted a potential disaster for the moment. "As for you, Lüdeke, I am ashamed of you, acting like a thoughtless child instead of the man you claim to be. I won't say anything to your father this time, but it's time you grew up."

"I'm sorry, Hinrik," Lüdeke apologized. "They were having such fun. I just didn't think."

Hinrik went home to dinner, shaking his head. He wondered if Lüdeke would ever be capable of taking over the great von Sehnden business empire.

As the demolition crews moved closer to their home in the Blomlage, Hinrik began to get a little nervous. When would Balthasar find them a new house? He had not as yet made any move to do so as far as Hinrik knew. What was he waiting for? They would be put out in the street before much longer. Hinrik was tempted to start looking for one himself, but he did not want to usurp his stepfather's prerogatives.

At last as Hinrik arrived home from work one evening, Balthasar greeted him with a big grin. "We have a new house," he declared triumphantly. "Much, much bigger than this one and in a very nice neighborhood."

"Not Zöllnerstrasse?" joked Hinrik.

"Nay, nay, we're not that wealthy yet," laughed his stepfather. "One must be a Bürgermeister or Councilman or, at the very least, a Master in the Gewandschneider to live there. This is on Schuhstrasse. It's almost brand-new and it hasn't cost us a penny."

"What?" exclaimed Hinrik. "How did you manage that?"

"The Council decided that as even I, the Master of the Works, was losing my home to the wall, they owed it to me as part of my compensation. I suspect your master, Bürgermeister von Sehnden, greatly influenced their decision."

"I expect so," agreed Hinrik. "Why, you old fox," he teased, "so that is what you were waiting for? I was afraid we would all end up in St. Anna's."

Balthasar laughed again. "No fear of that. I have been—er—negotiating this deal for quite some time. I was quite sure they would agree, but I did not want to say anything to you lads until it was for sure. Just wait until you see it. On Sunday I'll take all of you over there. Then next week we'll hire a carter to move our things." The old man was obviously quite pleased with himself. Hinrik was happy for him. He deserved a better home after putting up with him and his brothers in the tiny crowded house in the Blomlage for so many years.

On Sunday after Mass Hinrik and his brothers accompanied their stepfather to the new house. Schuhstrasse was a long street running east to west on the north side of the town. It began at the grounds of the Holy Cross monastery and ended at the Market Square. Beyond that, it changed names to Ritterstrasse (Knight's Street), where the most palatial homes in Celle were located. But Schuhstrasse itself consisted mostly of better-class artisans' homes. A disastrous fire some years ago had destroyed a large part of one side of the street, and there it was that many new houses were being built. Balthasar's house was one of these. It was a four-storey half-timbered house with beautifully decorated carvings along the main beam.

"There you see it," he said proudly as he pulled a large key from his sleeve and unlocked the door. He led them in. "Down here where the shop is, I shall make me an office." Behind that on the ground floor was a large dining room and beyond a well-equipped kitchen with a huge fireplace. Out back they could see a sizable garden with fruit trees and stables. On the first floor were two parlors, the front one with real glass windows facing the street, and another smaller room. He led them up the next flight of stairs. "This should make you happy—four sleeping chambers! One for each of us. No more sleeping three abed."

The brothers looked at each other. What luxury! Each had his own plans for this unexpected bit of privacy. Franz could only think of it as a secure place to keep his growing hoard of savings—safe from Berndt, that is. Hinrik never asked to borrow a penny. Berndt's first thought was, Now I can bring in a wench if I want. Hinrik was delighted with the peace and quiet it would give him—freedom from Franz's constant worrying and Berndt's stumbling in drunk at all hours. Here he could read to his heart's content and dream his dreams.

"Upstairs are rooms for servants and above that a loft," explained Balthasar.

"But we have no servants," said Franz.

"We are going to need at least a housekeeper for a house this size," commented Hinrik. "Have you thought of that, Father?"

"I have thought of it, and I suppose you are right," replied Balthasar. "Always did for myself. Not used to servants. But, yes, you're right. We'd better look for someone. It is a big house," he admitted.

"We'll all ask around," suggested Hinrik.

"But not one of your tavern wenches," said Franz to Berndt.

Berndt glared at his brother. It was exactly what he had in mind.

Balthasar led them back downstairs. "And wait till I show you the best part. It even has its own well in the garden. No more traipsing to the public fountain for water."

"Hallelujah," stated Berndt.

"Wonderful," agreed Hinrik.

"That alone makes it worth every penny you paid for it," added Franz.

Hinrik wondered if his brother was joking or if Balthasar had really not confided in him about the arrangement with the Town Council. He decided to say nothing until he was sure.

"We'll need to have Master Tischler make us some new furniture for the dining room and parlors, but beds first. I've already ordered them," said their stepfather. "I'll leave you to fight over which chamber each of you want, but I lay claim to one of those facing the street."

"I, too," said Berndt. "I like to see what's going on."

"That's fine," agreed Hinrik, "because I prefer one at the back where it's quieter and I can look out on the garden."

"I agree with that," said Franz, "only I'll be watching the horses."

"Fine," said Balthasar. "Then that settles that. I always said you were all sensible lads. Next week I'll hire the carter to move us. Start packing your chests this afternoon, for I won't know until I speak to him what day he can come."

As they left the house Hinrik saw a familiar figure emerge from a house two doors down across the street. It was Ilsebe. She turned the other way and did not see him. Something held him back from calling out to her. Somehow he did not feel ready yet to introduce her to his brothers. He knew it was a sin to be snobbish, but they were just not cut from the same cloth as his friends, whom he had been proud to have her meet. He really wanted to know her better and then prepare her for them. But at least now he knew where she lived. As they passed the house, he saw the sign of the lacemakers' guild over the shuttered shop. We shall be neighbors, he thought. He was overjoyed.

They moved in the following week, and not long after their old home in the Blomlage was torn down as the great wall progressed. Hinrik felt a little pang of nostalgia when it happened, but not too much. He was too excited about living so close to Ilsebe. Every day as he walked to and from Master von Sehnden's countinghouse, he peeped as unobtrusively as possible into the lace shop, but he never saw anyone save the Mistress presiding over her wares and occasionally another very young apprentice. Never Ilsebe. She probably worked in some other room way at the back. Several times he was tempted to approach the Mistress and ask for Ilsebe, but then he would have to formally seek permission to call upon her and he was not quite ready for that as yet. Or rather, he wanted to let the girl know his intentions first and find out how she felt about him before taking such a drastic step. He hoped she would welcome them, but he was not at all sure. She seemed to enjoy his company when they were together. Yet the way she often avoided him made him wonder if he were just wishful thinking.

He finally gave up hoping for a chance meeting in the street and went as often as he could back to her favorite haunt on the river by the millrace. But she did not show up there either. After some weeks of disappointment he began to panic. Could she have left town? Run away? No, not that. She was too honest to cheat her employer that way, much as she disliked her. Could the woman be keeping Ilsebe locked in, a prisoner? No, why ever for? She was a good girl, never in any trouble, and the Mistress did not know about Hinrik. At least he did not think so. Then she must be sick. That had to be it. O Holy Mother, let it not be anything serious. He vowed to make special prayers for her.

Then one day she came. He was sitting there staring out at the river, thinking his black thoughts, wishing he could commune with her Goddess. He did not see her, did not hear her, but something made him look up and there she was. He stood up and opened his arms, and she ran into them. He hugged her to him and showered her face with kisses, her forehead, her eyes, her cheeks, her nose, and finally her lips. He kissed her long and deeply, and she did not object or pull away.

"Ilsebe, Ilse, my dearest, I have missed you so," he whispered into her hair.

"And I you, Hinrik," she murmured. "I could not stay away any longer."

He held her close and kissed her again. Her admission thrilled him. He could feel his passion rising—and hoped she did not. It was too soon for that. He did not want to frighten her away again.

Finally they broke apart. He took her hand and led her to her favorite stone at the edge of the sluice. There they sat down close together. He was still holding her hand.

"Tell me, then, why you have been avoiding me," he asked plaintively.

"I have tried not to let myself grow too fond of you," she replied sadly. "Hinrik, I am not the woman for you."

"Why do you say that?" he asked. "I think you are perfect."

"Nay, nay," she replied. "I am poor, uneducated, and, most importantly, I have over four years left of my indenture. It would not be fair to ask any man to wait that long, least of all you."

"Ilse, my love, and I do love you," he declared, "I am poor, too. Nothing but a clerk in Master von Sehnden's countinghouse."

"But at least you get to keep your pay," she objected. "I get nothing but bed and board. I never see a penny of what I earn for the Mistress. And you have a chance for advancement."

"Not much, especially now that Lüdeke has finished his journey years. I may be out looking for other work soon, but I'm not going to worry. Something will turn up. As for education, you are quite intelligent. I could teach you a lot. It was only sheer luck that I have any learning at all. If Mistress von Sehnden had not taken a liking to my mother before I was born, I should be totally illiterate. And even then I had to learn from her. They would not let me go to the school for many years, until Master arranged it. I do not know to this day how he managed that, but I am very grateful, especially to Mistress. And that gives me an idea. You say you like to read. She has many wonderful books. Would you like me to borrow some for you?"

She shook her head. "I do not read very well. I fear they would be too difficult. But aside from that, when I have worked on the lace from dawn till dusk, I am half-blind, and Mistress will not allow any candles except to go quickly to bed. By the time Sunday comes, I am just happy to rest my eyes and get a little fresh air. Thank you anyway," she sighed wistfully.

"No matter. It was just a thought." Then he addressed her most important concern. "As far as your indenture is concerned, I can wait. I want to, my love. I, too, do not feel ready for—for any serious commitment, but I would like to see you more often. I so enjoy being with you, really I do. And I feel so low, so sad, when I don't meet you for a long time. I hope you feel the same. Could I not at least see you on Sundays? I know where you live now."

"You do?" she gasped, surprised. "How did you find that out? You haven't followed me, have you?"

"No, no, nothing like that." He explained about losing their home on the Blomlage to the wall and his stepfather acquiring—he did not say how—the new house in Schuhstrasse. "We are now neighbors. It's right across the street from you. The day my stepfather first showed it to us, I saw you come out the lacemaker's door. You were already too far away or I should have called to you."

Ilsebe said nothing for a few moments. Then she said resignedly, "Well, that is interesting. So my secret is out. I can no longer hide from you. That is both good and bad."

"How so?"

"Good that we shall be neighbors and that I can't hide from you. I didn't really want to, you know. I just thought it best. And bad because I fear the Mistress will be wroth if you ask to call on me."

"Why should she be?" he countered. "I shall explain to her very clearly that I understand about the indenture. Don't you want to see me more often, Ilsebe?"

She laughed. "Of course I do, you big fool. So now it seems as though I have no choice. You insist on making the decision for me. Well, so be it." Suddenly she kicked her feet out from under her skirt and dabbled her toes in the water. "Enough of all this serious talk. Let us just be happy."

"Ilse," he exclaimed, "you have no shoes on."

"I have no shoes," she replied, "and it was too hot today for the klompen. That's how I was able to sneak up on you so quietly."

"Like the river sprite."

"Like the river sprite."

He kissed her soundly then and vowed to do something about the shoes. Oh, how he loved her.

They saw each other every Sunday now, and if for any reason she could not she told him so he would not worry. Usually they met at their usual spot by the river, but sometimes, as long as the weather was fine, they took long walks out into the countryside. They visited the beekeepers and watched as the men extracted the honey and precious wax without being stung. He took her to a sheep farm, and she grew ecstatic over the little black lambs of the Heidenschnucken, whose coats would gradually turn white as they grew older. They went to where the flax grew and saw how the women pounded the wet fibers to make them strong yet pliable enough for spinning. They saw the famous stud farm where the great destriers and gentle palfreys were bred.

"All this is Celle's wealth," he explained. "Do you know that long ago the Gewandschneider had a law passed that everything raised, grown, or made within a three-mile circumference of the town must be traded in or through Celle?"

"That doesn't seem fair," she replied. "You mean the peasants can't take their products to another market if they choose?"

"No, they can't. That's the way business is done," he replied. "But on the other hand, it guarantees them a market even when there is a glut."

"I suppose so," but she was still puzzled. "The Gewandschneider are very powerful, aren't they? They really run Celle, don't they?"

"They certainly do. And one day I shall be one of them," he boasted.

"I'm sure you will." Her puzzlement gave way to pride in her dearest friend.

As the days grew shorter and the damp chill of late autumn set in, it was no longer pleasant by the river. Hinrik racked his brain trying to think of another place for them to meet. Then he heard from his friends of a new type of tavern that catered strictly to a high-class clientele. They served no beer or wine but a couple of exotic new beverages along with little rolls or fine cakes. It sounded like the ideal meeting place.

One blustery November afternoon when a fine icy drizzle enveloped them like fog, he invited her to accompany him there.

"A tavern? No," she objected, "a decent woman does not go into taverns. I may be poor, but I'm not a whore."

"Ilse, my dear, I meant no offense. This is totally different from a regular tavern," he tried to explain. "It is not a rowdy place. Very decorous, in fact. They do not sell any beer or wine, only this interesting new beverage imported from Araby. It's not even called a tavern. They call it a coffeehouse."

"A coffeehouse? What in the world is that?" she queried.

"It is — well, sort of like the common room of a fine inn, only smaller and more intimate. All the merchants go there at midmorning to talk business while they enjoy cups of this delightful drink with little rolls. It is a hot drink — just what we need on a day like this." She still looked doubtful, so he went on. "Then in the afternoon their wives and daughters, and mothers, too, go there and do the same, except with little cakes. I mean they drink the coffee. Instead of business they have their gossip." He noticed her shivering in her threadbare cloak and took her arm. "Come on, Ilse, a hot drink is just what we both need in this weather. They are sure to have a good fire. It will be warm and dry and we can sit and talk to our heart's content."

Reluctantly she allowed herself to be persuaded. They could not stand on this cold corner all afternoon.

"All right," she agreed. "If the Bürgers' wives go there, my reputation can't suffer too much. It will be a new experience. Let us go and drink this—what did you call it?—coffee."

"Yes, you will like it. It's very different."

They entered the coffeehouse and immediately she was struck by the intimacy, the coziness. It was panelled in dark wood, and there was indeed a cheery fire on the hearth. Instead of trestles and benches, there were tiny tables with two or four individual chairs. They were covered with snowy linen clothes, and each had its own candle. She automatically toted up the cost of that. No wonder only wealthy people come here. She could see no bar. Evidently service was from a kitchen beyond a door at the rear. The place was crowded and that surprised her as well.

They found a tiny table off to one side and sat down. All the best tables near the hearth were taken, but they felt warm enough. The room was so small. Immediately a wench came to them, but this was no common tavern wench. She was immaculate, for one thing, with a crisply starched apron and cap. For another, she was polite and soft-spoken.

"Good afternoon, mein Herr, mein Fräulein, will you have coffee? Or perhaps the young lady would like to try our newest beverage, chocolate."

"What is that?" asked Ilsebe.

"It is a delicious new drink imported from America by way of Spain. A bit sweeter than coffee."

Ilsebe looked at Hinrik. "We'll have coffee," he said.

"Will you have it plain or with a little cream?" asked the girl.

"Plain," said Hinrik.

"I think with a little cream," said Ilsebe.

Within moments the girl returned bearing a pewter pot and two delicate cups, a tiny pitcher of cream, and a plate of little cakes, the likes of which Ilsebe had never seen before.

"Oh, aren't they pretty. They look delicious," remarked Ilsebe.

"They are, mein Fräulein," replied the maid, "made with lots of butter and real sugar."

"Real sugar? They must be very—" She bit her tongue. She did not want the girl to think that expensive sugar was a luxury she never enjoyed.

The serving wench gracefully poured a steaming brown liquid into

636

each of the cups and left them.

"What an unusual aroma," commented Ilsebe. "Does it taste as good as it smells?"

"Try it and see," said Hinrik. "Be careful, though, it is very hot."

She took a small sip and made a face. "Oh, it is terribly bitter," she said.

"You have to get used to it. It takes a little while," said Hinrik. "Try it with the cream. You might like it better."

She poured a good dollop of the rich cream into the cup. It lightened the color considerably. Perhaps it would cut some of the bitterness. She took another sip. It helped, but not very much. She still did not care for it. She looked around the room. Everyone seemed to be enjoying it, some pouring second or third cups from the pewter pots. If this is the drink of the elite, she thought, I had better learn to like it. I'll force myself. Hinrik was obviously enjoying himself. She took another sip. It did not seem quite as bad. She helped herself to a little cake. It was so delicate it almost crumbled in her hands. The rich sweetness helped counteract the bitterness of the coffee to some extent.

Hinrik was watching her reactions. Her face was so expressive. "Well, what do you think now?" he asked.

"This place is so charming," she replied. "I agree it will be an ideal locale for our Sunday afternoons. If only I could learn to like the coffee as well." She took another sip. "I shall make myself, just so we can come here."

He laughed. "You will. It takes a little time."

Just then in walked his friend Peter Stratheman. He looked around the room and spied them.

"I see the little river sprite prefers a cozy fire today," he joked.

"November is not a congenial month for river sprites," she replied coyly.

"May I join you?" asked Peter.

"Please do," invited Hinrik. "There is plenty of coffee left in the pot. Help yourself."

Peter took a chair from an empty table and signalled the serving maid for another cup. "And how do you like this newest innovation on the social scene?" he asked them.

"I find it very charming, but . . . ," said Ilsebe.

"Ilsebe is tasting her very first cup of coffee," interrupted Hinrik, "and I'm not at all sure that she cares for it."

Peter laughed. "I think we all felt the same at first. A bit bitter, isn't it? But wait until you see how it makes you feel."

"What do you mean?" she asked.

"It will perk you up, pep you up, make you feel more wide awake than you ever have before," replied Peter.

She looked at him askance.

"He's right," agreed Hinrik. "It will. There's none of the dulling effect that beer or wine has after a while. You'll see."

She still looked incredulous but said, "Then it would seem to be a good thing to drink first thing in the morning."

"I agree," said Peter. "And I predict it won't be long before we can have it in our homes. You can see how popular it is already." He waved his arm around the room.

"It is still too expensive," said Hinrik, "but if we could import it wholesale in large quantities or, better yet, find a source to bypass the Venetians . . ." She could see him pondering the possibilities.

"There speaks the merchant," she teased. "Why don't you suggest that to Master von Sehnden?"

"My father has already considered it," said Peter. "We're hoping the Portuguese will find a way."

And then it happened.

"Oh, Hinrik," she exclaimed. "Suddenly I feel so wide awake, I would sing or dance—like—like—the little lambs in springtime."

Both men laughed. They forbore from saying 'I told you so.'

Duke Ernst had wholeheartedly embraced the new reforms while a student of Luther and immediately upon his accession encouraged the people of the Duchy to do so as well. But he did not use force, as happened in some other places. After some initial hesitation, the majority of his subjects of both high and low degree followed his lead, most joyfully, a few reluctantly, but there was little outright opposition except in a few quarters. One of these, as might be expected, was in the Marienkirche itself. While many of the canons, vicars, and lesser clergy were willing to try the new liturgy as revised by Doctor Luther, the Head Pastor, old Cord Lüdeke, was adamant in his refusal to do so. One of the biggest stumbling blocks was the requirement to administer the Holy Communion to all the people in both kinds—that is, the congregation was given both the consecrated bread and wine, instead of only the bread while the priest alone drank the wine as heretofore. "Blasphemous," declared old Pastor Cord.

There were a few more objections after Luther translated the liturgy into German, but most of them came around eventually when they realized how much more meaningful it was to the people to have the Mass celebrated in their native tongue rather than Latin, which was by now only understood by a small handful of the most highly educated parishioners. Then Pastor Cord nearly had apoplexy when a few of the priests decided to marry with Luther's and the Duke's blessing. The pastor threatened to excommunicate them, but since many of the bishops in the area were also converts to the reform, he had nowhere to turn except to Rome, already swamped with thousands of such requests. So nothing was done and the situation eventually accepted.

Meanwhile Luther, already excommunicated and under indictment of heresy, remained in hiding under the protection of the Duke of Saxony. Luther's work and teaching in Wittenberg were continued by his friend and disciple Philip Melanchthon and Andreas Carlstadt. But soon there was a falling-out between them. Carlstadt wanted to go too far. He advocated smashing the images, dispensing with all music, second baptisms, and other fanaticisms. Luther was asked to return to Wittenberg to mediate. He did so at the risk of his life, but things had gone too far. He told Carlstad to leave. The latter promptly joined a far more radical group led by Thomas Münzer of Zwickau, a town in southern Saxony. They called themselves the 'Zwickauer Prophets' and advocated the 'slaughter of the unfaithful' and in doing so stirred up the disastrous Peasants' Revolt of 1524–25, which was summarily put down by Heinrich, Duke of Wolfenbüttel, but not without extensive loss of life. Thomas Münzer was caught and executed.

Shortly before Easter of 1524, one of the Zwickauer Prophets by the name of Wolf Cyclop came to Celle, preaching his fiery message. Up to this point the reformation in Celle and the Duchy of Lüneburg had proceeded quietly but steadily under the intelligent guidance of Duke Ernst. Now this fanatic, who was not even a priest, but a physician, tried to stir up the people. Since most of the reforms were already in force in the Stadkirche itself, his main target was the Franciscans of the Holy Cross monastery. These mild, gentle monks, while letting it be known that they were vehemently against the Reform, did nothing to interfere with it or undermine its progress in the town. Now this fanatic was trying to incite hatred and violence toward them.

Everyone went to hear him, including Hinrik and his friends, most out of just plain curiosity. It was hard to avoid Cyclop. Since he was not ordained clergy, he was forbidden to preach in the church. So he spewed forth his invective in the Stechbahn next to the church, at the town and castle gates, in the marketplace, anywhere he could gather a crowd.

"Why, that's terrible," said Ilsebe. "I thought the Reform was all about going back to Our Lord's teaching of 'love thy neighbor'."

"It is," said Hinrik. "Even Doctor Luther will have nothing to do with these so-called prophets."

"I doubt many people will pay much attention to him," said Lüdeke. "It's just the ignorant who choose force because they have no brains."

"That's just what I fear," agreed Hinrik, "that the ignorant will follow him into violence."

"And he forgets that another thing the Reform is all about is freedom of religion," said Peter. "Let the Franciscans worship the way they want as long as the rest of us can worship the way *we* want. So far they have done us no harm. Let them alone, I say."

"I think the Duke should use a little force of his own," advocated Eggeling, "and drive this maniac out of town before he commits irreparable harm."

"Well, I for one have heard enough of his radical nonsense," said Hinrik, taking Ilsebe's arm. "Let's go and have our coffee."

"This time I think I'll try the chocolate," she said.

They all laughed and went to the coffeehouse.

Shortly after Easter the Duke himself had enough and told Cyclop to leave Celle. He fled towards Zwickau but on the way stopped for several months at Magdeburg. His few converts drifted away. But from there he continued his fight against the Franciscans with a constant barrage of printed letters, which the Abbot of the monastery finally felt compelled to answer.

Hinrik and Ilsebe had fallen deeply in love. He treasured the Sunday afternoons and occasional Saturday evening as the days grew longer. They moved their rendezvous back to the river but still spent rainy afternoons at the coffeehouse. But it was not enough. He wanted marriage, a home and family of his own. He had not approached her Mistress about officially courting Ilsebe, partly because he already was seeing her as often as was possible anyway, but mostly because he did not know what to do about the indenture. Nothing but wait, he supposed. His friends knew nothing about it, and they all assumed that they would be wed soon. They even had started teasing him about posting the banns. The other reason he was hesitant about broaching the subject of marriage was his job insecurity. Lüdeke was now very capably doing the same work as he, and at times he felt superfluous.

Hinrik finally decided that he needed some advice, and what better person to turn to than Tante Anna, Bürgermeister von Sehnden's wife, the woman who had been both mentor and surrogate mother throughout his childhood. He knew her to be a very practical, extremely intelligent, and perspicacious person. He knew she would not pass judgment without carefully investigating a matter, as she had in his mother's case so long ago. And he trusted her judgment.

One evening after work he approached her. "Tante Anna, if you're not too busy, may I have a word with you?"

"But, of course, Hinrik, come in, come in. I haven't seen you in so long, and it's always a pleasure visiting with you."

"Tante Anna, I need some advice."

"Oh? Then come into my library. Master von Sehnden is not at home yet. We shall be undisturbed." She ushered him into the wonderful room lined with books. It was a room he loved. She indicated a comfortable chair next to the hearth and took the one opposite. "Now, tell me. I can tell from the look on your face that it involves a girl."

"Tante Anna, you are too astute. How did you know?"

She laughed. "Young men in love always have a certain look about them. But I do not have the second sight. I have heard rumors. The coffeehouse is quite a public place after all. And young Lüdeke has brought home tales of your magical young—what did he call her?"

"River sprite, probably," replied Hinrik, starting to relax. She always put him at ease.

"Yes, that's it. Now start from the beginning. I want to hear all of it. What is her name?"

"Ilsebe Cuzzens."

"Hmm, not a name I'm familiar with."

"I doubt you would be. She is an orphan like myself."

"How did you meet her?"

"By the millrace, quite by accident, almost two years ago." Hinrik hesitated, not sure if he should go on, but he trusted her. "She claims she likes to commune with the river goddess. Hence I teased her about being a river sprite."

Anna looked at him strangely. "One of the old ones. Hinrik, be careful," she warned.

641

"She is not a witch, Tante, nothing like that," protested Hinrik. "She is a good Christian. She told me her Grannie, who raised her, was a wise-woman, but I'm sure even she was not a witch. She just taught her something of the old ways. Anyway, she is long dead and Ilsebe is just a kind, gentle, very sweet, and loving person—a bit timid, too—who takes great delight in nature—the river, animals, flowers, everything like that."

"The old ways, which should be preserved," mused Anna, "but not worshipped," she warned.

"No, no, she doesn't do that. I told you she is a good Christian and very much in favor of the new teaching, the Reform, as am I."

"Yes, she would be. But two years. That is a long courtship for a young man of your age. Have you not spoken to her of marriage? Is she perhaps not as fond of you as you seem to be enamored of her?" asked Anna.

"Oh, yes, she is. Of that I am sure. But of marriage I have said nothing yet, although I crave it. There is a problem. Two, in fact."

Ah, so, thought Anna. Now I shall learn why he came to me. "Tell me," she urged.

"She is a lacemaker, very skilled and hardworking."

"An admirable trade, and difficult, too," agreed Anna. And a bit beneath him, she thought. But then he did not know the plans her husband had for him.

"She has long since completed her apprenticeship," continued Hinrik. "The problem is that they were so poor and then her Grannie died, that there was not enough money to pay for her apprenticeship and so she had to indenture herself to her Mistress for seven years. She has four yet to go."

"I see. That is indeed a problem, one not easily solved. Have you spoken to her Mistress at all?"

"No, I have been afraid."

"You, Hinrik, afraid?"

"I mean afraid that she might forbid me to see her at all."

"There is that possibility. Then you are not courting her legally?"

"Not really, Tante, but . . . "

"No matter. Things are so different in this day and age than they used to be. I was not supposed to go out anywhere without a chaperone. But I did," she said slyly. Her eyes grew misty with reminiscence. "Lüdeke caught me alone one time at St. Anna's and forced me to marry him."

"Forced?" said Hinrik, surprised.

"Yes," she laughed, "with hugs and kisses. I did not even realize until then that I loved him."

Hinrik laughed with her. The things you don't know about people, he thought. He could not quite picture his Master, Bürgermeister von Sehnden, as a dashing young lover, or the staid Anna either, for that matter.

"So there is always a solution to every problem," she went on. "We'll find one. Let me think on it. And the other?"

"This perhaps I should not burden you with. I don't want you to think I'm not satisfied," he said hesitantly.

"Out with it," she commanded. "You've already laid one on me. Let me hear it all."

"Before I can consider marriage, I have to be sure I can support a wife and the children that I hope will come. I know that Master von Sehnden pays me well, for which I am grateful. But now that young Lüdeke is also doing the same work as I, I fear I may no longer be needed." He rushed on before she could answer. "I would like to have my own business, but I have nowhere near enough capital to even consider such a thing. I fear to offer for Ilsebe while I feel so insecure financially even if it were not for the other problem. It would not be fair."

He expected her to utter such platitudes as, 'Poor people are being wed all the time,' or, 'If you are really in love, it doesn't matter,' and so on. She surprised him by saying, "Well, you can lay that fear to rest. Your job with Master von Sehnden is secure. You can count on that. We have discussed this very thing quite often. You must know that his business is so extensive that he has need of both you and Lüdeke, perhaps even a third helper. Besides, I know that he has plans for you. I cannot tell you what they are, because I honestly don't know. And please don't mention that I even so much as hinted to you about this. But you can feel very secure financially and go ahead with your plans. You may have your own business sooner than you think."

"Oh, thank you, Tante Anna. You have taken a great weight off my mind, and I'll not breathe a word of what you have told me. I promise. Now, if I could only solve the other problem as easily . . ."

"As I said, let me think on it for a bit. Meanwhile I should like to meet your river sprite, Ilsebe. Bring her here this Sunday. No, wait, I am busy this Sunday. I am meeting with some of the Gewandschneider wives to try to show them how they can help their husbands, really to teach them their own worth. It is amazing how old-fashioned and even semiliterate some of them are. Don't you let your Ilsebe fall into that rut. But I doubt you will. You are a modern man."

"Thanks to you, Tante Anna."

"Then bring her here next Sunday. I look forward to meeting her."

"I shall, and God bless you, Tante."

About a week later Lüdeke von Sehnden the Elder came into his countinghouse. "I am sending you to Antwerp this time," he announced. Hinrik and Lüdeke the Younger looked up from their work. "Both of you," continued the Elder, "for the Michaelmas settlement."

"But, Papa," objected the Younger, "you've always done that before."

"Then don't you think it's high time you took over that responsibility?" replied his father. "I have simply too much to do here to be away that long. What with being Celle's leading merchant, Master of the Gewandschneider, and Bürgermeister besides, it's getting to be too much. Your Papa is getting old, Lüdeke. I want you two increasingly to take over the business end of it. Being Bürgermeister is no longer just governing the town. It now involves keeping peace among the adherents of that fanatic Cyclop, the Franciscans, and the Duke. I never thought the simple, obvious reforms proposed by Doctor Luther would create such unrest here in Celle. Be that as it may, the business must not suffer. In that you two must be my right arm."

Hinrik noted the word *two* and was delighted to be given such responsibility but said nothing. He sensed there was more to come.

"Lüdeke," he addressed his son, "you will handle the settlements, but Hinrik will be by your side to see that you make no glaring errors. Hold out for the highest price possible on the grain and wax I'll be sending with you. You know that, of course. But you may be able to get a better price than usual for the grain because we had the forethought to store a great quantity in our granaries before that disastrous Peasants' Revolt broke out in upper Saxony. That certainly has affected the harvests. There may be some shortages, so don't sell to the first bidder. The wax may be another story. The Pope is mad at us in northern Germany, and with so many churches going over to the new beliefs and using fewer candles, the price may be down. Do the best you can."

"Now, Hinrik, I have a special task for you. We need another factor in Antwerp."

Hinrik was surprised. "Is Master Hillenbrandt no long satisfactory?" he asked.

"He most certainly is, the best. But we need another. The business is

644

growing so fast, the poor man has scarcely time to breathe. And I don't want just a help for him, but someone who can work with him and yet be experienced enough to act independently as well. I shall give you the names of three men I have been considering, but I want you to make the choice as if you were engaging him for your own business. And don't feel you are limited to these three. I prefer a Hanse man, but if you find another with sufficient experience to suit you, and he is trustworthy—I cannot emphasize that enough—then hire him."

"That is quite a responsibility," replied Hinrik, "and I am honored that you have so much confidence in me, Master von Sehnden. I shall do my best." Hinrik had picked up on the words *as if*... for *your own business*. He wondered if this were a part of the 'plans' Tante Anna had hinted at and, if so, what they were. Master von Sehnden certainly knew how to give one an incentive. He would surely make a better job of his assignment even if he were only to pretend that it was for his own business.

There was only one thing troubling him, and at the first opportunity he went to see Mistress von Sehnden.

"Tante Anna, have you said anything to Onkel Lüdeke yet about Ilsebe?" he burst out. "Could it be he is sending me away to separate us?"

She laughed and laughed, but Hinrik could see nothing funny at all.

"Forgive me, Hinrik," she said, "but it seems as though history is repeating itself, although that is definitely not the case here." He looked at her, greatly puzzled. "I have told you how my husband proposed to me," she went on, "but before that he was acting like such a lovesick calf because of my feigned indifference, his father sent him to Antwerp, too—in fact, it was his grandmother who suggested it—on the theory that I would fall into his arms when he returned. It didn't work out quite that way, but it worked. But this is entirely different. He really wants you and Lüdeke to become more independent of him. He needs your help badly." Hinrik nodded, somewhat reassured. "And no, I have not yet mentioned Ilsebe to him. But don't fret yourself. Now that I have met your charming little river sprite, I shall take her under my wing so she won't be too lonely while you are gone. I enjoy the coffeehouse myself, and sometimes I shall invite her here. I think she would like that. I noticed her eyes almost pop out of her head when she looked about this room."

"Tante, I thank you. You have set my mind at rest," said Hinrik. "And I'm sure Ilsebe will like coming here. She wants to learn to read better."

"Yes," replied Anna. "If she is to be your wife, I see that I shall have to undertake her education as I did yours. Don't worry, we shall get along famously."

"Oh, Tante Anna," exclaimed Hinrik, "what should I ever do without you?"

She smiled and kissed him on the forehead. "Just do a good job in Antwerp and I shall pray for your safe return."

Anna was, indeed, charmed by Ilsebe, even though she found her a bit naïve, and tried to think of ways to sophisticate her a little without losing that delightful innocence. They went often to the coffeehouse together and there indulged in good old-fashioned 'woman talk.' Anna invited Ilsebe to her library and helped her to improve her reading ability. She started her on a book on herbs, potions, and simples that was sure to appeal to her 'old ways.' It did. She taught her how to cipher and was amazed at how quickly and accurately she took to it, proving the old saw that even the most illiterate peasant is shrewd when it comes to counting his money. She was careful to give no indication that all this was to prepare her for becoming Hinrik's wife. She let her set her own pace and choose what subjects interested her, which proved to be almost anything. The girl was avid for knowledge and quick to learn.

"Mistress von Sehnden, how can I ever thank you?" asked Ilsebe one day. "You have opened up a whole new world to me. I never dreamed there were so many things to learn."

"No thanks are necessary," replied Anna. "My pleasure is in seeing how eager you are for knowledge. And now that we are friends, why don't you call me Tante Anna? Hinrik does."

"Oh, I couldn't," she objected and then thought again. "Well, it would be nice. I never had an aunt, or a mother either."

"I know. Hinrik told me," said Anna. "And he has been like a son to me, too."

Ilsebe looked at her with a flicker of alarm. "Mistress—I mean Tante Anna, are you doing all this for me because you think Hinrik and I will be wed? We can't, you know."

"Hinrik told me about your indenture. Is there any other reason?"

"No. No."

"Then somehow we'll find a solution to that problem. The important thing is do you truly love him, enough to wed him if you could? As I said, he is like my son. I couldn't bear to see him hurt. He is a very sensitive person."

"Oh, I do. I do, Tante Anna," she started to sob. "I love him with all my heart. I would be overjoyed to be his wife, but it is impossible."

"There, there," said Anna consolingly. She put her arm around the weeping maid. "I promised Hinrik I would try to seek a solution to your dilemma, and I make you the same promise. It may take a little time, but as the old saying goes, 'there are more ways than one to skin a cat'."

Ilsebe looked up at her and tried to smile. "I hope you're right. Thank you, Tante Anna. I shall try to be brave and—and patient. I trust you."

Anna visited the lacemaker's shop. She had no intention of discussing Ilsebe with her as yet. She first wanted to see what sort of woman she was. Anna pretended to be interested in buying some lace. She noticed immediately that the workmanship on some pieces was far superior to that of others. She suspected they were Ilsebe's.

"Do you make all the lace yourself?" she asked.

"Of course," snapped the woman. She was perhaps Anna's same age, but her dour expression made her seem much older.

A difficult nut to crack, thought Anna. "But I notice a great difference in the quality," she remarked.

"They're all made here in my workshop. I can't be bothered to differentiate as to who makes what. They're all the same quality."

So, she will not give credit where credit is due. Another problem.

"Then the price must be the same for all similar pieces," said Anna.

"Oh, no, Mistress, the finer pieces are a bit more."

"But you just said they were all the same." Anna delighted in catching the woman in her own lie.

"Well, I mean—that is, some are more elaborate. Therefore, they would cost more."

"I was speaking of quality, not elaborateness. Do you pay your journey workers according to the quality of their work?"

"Who are you?" The woman grew excited. "Are you a spy for the guild?"

"No, Mistress, just a simple goodwife looking for a new collar," replied Anna calmly. "But if you are suffering from pangs of conscience, I would suggest you abide by the rules of your guild. The next customer might just be one of their inspectors."

The woman was highly indignant. She huffed as though she were about to explode but did not retort as she would like to have for fear of driving away a potential customer.

"Now what are you asking for this piece?" asked Anna innocently, as if nothing else had been said.

The woman named a price. They haggled back and forth, Anna as only a successful merchant's wife could. She obtained the beautiful lace collar, which she did not need, at a ridiculously low price.

Later she checked with Ilsebe and ascertained that the piece was indeed her work. Anna decided it was time to talk to Lüdeke.

She approached him one evening when he was sated with a good supper and comfortably ensconced by the fire in their second parlor. She told him the whole story of the young couple's love and frustration at not being able to wed.

"Aha! I suspected there might be a girl. He shows all the signs. And young Lüdeke has dropped a few hints as well. Are you sure they are serious about marriage?"

"Very serious," replied Anna. "Very much in love and in my opinion well suited."

"Well suited? But she comes from the lowest class," remarked Lüdeke.

"But highly intelligent, a sweet, loving personality, and eminently trainable," countered Anna. "She is also a very diligent worker and avid to learn. I find no fault in her."

"Perhaps, but Hinrik has at least a streak of noble blood in him," he objected.

"And much good it did him. I have only a tiny streak and you married me," she declared.

"That was different. Your father was my father's partner."

"No different at all," she retorted. "If anything, it will help him appreciate her qualities all the more."

"All right. All right." He held up his hand. "You've convinced me you are intent on matchmaking. You remind me of my grandmother, old Wünneke, God rest her."

Anna laughed. "Yes, God rest her and bless her. Now what do you think can be done about this indenture?"

"We'll buy it out, that's all," he suggested.

"That may not be so easy. The price will high. Ilsebe is her best worker, and the old woman is greedy."

"I'll find the contract on the indenture. That's public record and we'll argue from there."

"I also learned where she is most vulnerable."

"Oh?"

"She is not abiding by the guild's rules for compensating journeymen."

"Are you sure?"

"Just a shrewd guess, but reasonably sure."

"I know the Master of the Lacemakers' Guild, Paul Henning, very well. But we'll not use that weapon unless it becomes necessary. Ilsebe may want to keep working at her trade for a while, at least until the children come, and we would not want to make it difficult for her. But I'll keep it in mind."

"I knew you would come up with a solution, dearest Lüdeke," said Anna, "but there is one other thing. Hinrik may object to *you* buying out the indenture. You know, young male pride."

"We'll call it a wedding present,' said Lüdeke. "And I'll now tell you this in strictest confidence. If he is successful in Antwerp, I have in mind to make him a partner."

"Oh, how wonderful," she said. "And Lüdeke, too?"

"Not yet. He is four years younger. He can wait four years. By that time Hinrik should have saved enough to go on his own—with my help, of course."

"Oh, Lüdeke," she cried. "I love you so. I'm so glad I married you. Let's go to bed."

They made love that night as though they were newlyweds themselves.

One day when Ilsebe was reading in their library, Lüdeke made a point of meeting her. After some desultory conversation to put her at ease, he said, "Tell me about your indenture."

If she was surprised at the question, she did not show it. "It is for seven years, Master. I have yet four years and some months to go."

"What was the agreed upon price?" he asked.

She quoted a figure precisely the same as on her contract. After a moment's thought she stated the exact amount to the penny left to be paid. He secretly marvelled at her ability to do complex calculations in her head so readily. Hinrik will have an excellent bookkeeper, he thought.

"I see," he said.

"But I know the Mistress would say I owed more," she added.

He looked alert. "Why do you say that?"

"I don't wish to make any outright accusations, Master, because I am not exactly sure. But I firmly believe she is not crediting me for all the work I have done, or not enough anyway."

"But that does not make sense," he replied. "An indenture is based on time served, no matter how good or bad one's work is, not on piecework. Of course, one could be beaten if her work is shoddy, but as long as one puts in the time, the indenture is served. A true journeyman, on the other hand, could do piecework, especially if he were an independent outworker. Most of those that work in the shops receive bed and board and a token wage, always the same, although there may be a minimum amount of work required."

"Thank you for explaining that, Master," said Ilsebe. "That is the way I understood it to be, but I know that is not the way my Mistress does it."

"Then she is not only breaking the Guild rules but cheating you illegally as well."

"Oh, Master, I am aware of it, but please, please do not say anything of what I have told you," cried Ilsebe, distraught. "She would make my life unbearable and perhaps cheat me even more. Then I should never be free of her."

"Don't worry, my dear," Lüdeke reassured her. "What we have discussed here will go no farther than my ears. You can trust me."

"I am sure I can," she said, somewhat mollified. "And I shall tell you something else." A spark of indignation and pride lit her eyes. "My work is the finest of any in that shop, yet she complains constantly. Sometimes even complains that it is too fine, that she dare not ask the price it is worth. Can you imagine such a thing? I know she is lying."

"Yes, my goodwife told me as much."

Ilsebe looked surprised and then she remembered. "Ah, ja, she showed me the collar she bought."

Lüdeke rose. "Well, I am sure you would much rather be back to your books, so I shall leave you to them." He patted her on the shoulder. "Don't worry, my dear. Things will work out." And he left her alone.

Ilsebe could not concentrate on her book. Her mind kept going over and over this conversation. Why was he so interested in her indenture? If it were Hinrik, she could understand. But Master von Sehnden? It didn't make sense.

Hinrik and Lüdeke returned from Antwerp puffed up with pride in their success. And Lüdeke the Elder was well pleased. They had sold the grain at inflationary prices and the beeswax at a better profit than he expected. They brought back with them English wool, Flemish cloth, Russian furs, and spices—a great variety of spices, not only from the Venetians, but now from the Portuguese as well. Also included in their cargo were bags of the new coffee and chocolate beans plus the beans of a new flavoring called vanilla. Above all he was pleased with their acquisition of a quantity of precious sugar.

Hinrik was pleased with the new factor he had hired and hoped Onkel Lüdeke would be, too.

"I did not engage any of the three you suggested, Master," he explained. "Two had already moved to new employment with other merchants."

"I'm not surprised. They were good men and ambitious," commented Lüdeke. "And the third?"

"I did not trust him. I had a strong suspicion that he was taking bribes from the Genoese. But I found another who I think will be quite satisfactory. His name is Werner Titze."

"I know of the family, but not him. However, since you will be working with him personally more than I, I will accept your judgment."

"Thank you, Master. I think you'll be pleased."

"Now, Lüdeke," he said to his son, "If you will run home and find out what time your mother will be serving dinner, I have some other things I wish to discuss with Hinrik alone." Lüdeke the Younger realized it was a command, not a request, and left reluctantly.

"Hinrik," continued the Elder without preamble, "I have decided to make you a partner in the business."

Hinrik was stunned, absolutely flabbergasted. He did not know what to say. "Master von Sehnden," he exclaimed. "I—I . . ." Then the enormity of it struck him. "Master, I do not have the wherewithal."

"Perhaps not in money," replied Lüdeke. "I do not need that at the moment anyway. You will easily earn that for me—for us. But you have other qualities—experience for one, dependability and trustworthiness, good judgment, and above all good business sense. What shall I call it? A feel for what it takes to be a great merchant."

"Oh, Master. I am overwhelmed. You do me great honor."

"Bah! No more than you deserve. Be aware that you shall have to work harder than ever before."

"I am fully aware of that, and I shall. Master, I shall."

"And starting right now let us go back to calling me Onkel Lüdeke. No more 'Master.' We shall be equal partners. Except, of course, at the Gewandschneider meetings." Hinrik smiled. "As soon as we have signed all the necessary legal documents, I shall submit your name for associate membership."

651

Hinrik's mouth hung open. He could hardly grasp what was happening to him.

"I know you have dreams of having your own business one day, so consider this a step in that direction."

Hinrik finally found his tongue. "But what of Lüdeke?" he asked.

"He has four years less experience and maturity than you," replied the Elder. "He can wait four years and learn while he is waiting. And another thing to start you on your way toward that goal, I am giving you one boat complete with crew. It will be your total responsibility and, I hope, your own profit. You can do what you want with it—fill it with cargo or let it sink to the bottom."

Hinrik gasped. "Onkel Lüdeke, no! A partnership is one thing. That I'll accept and fully, but this is too much."

"I want no argument. Aside from the fact that it has become a tradition in our family, it is part of the responsibility I am putting on you. I insist on it."

"Put that way, I understand your point and I'll accept," said Hinrik, "but I am not family."

"You are to me and my goodwife. And I intend to do the same for Lüdeke when the time comes, if that's what's worrying you."

Hinrik could not believe his good fortune. He could hardly wait to tell Ilsebe. He wondered how she was faring. He had not yet had time to see her or even go home to change his clothes.

As if they both had the same thought, Lüdeke said, "Now one other thing."

Hinrik blinked. "There's more?"

"This is personal, not business. I have met your little river sprite. Your Tante Anna is quite charmed by her. I understand you wish to wed. Is that so?"

"You have?" Hinrik wondered a bit stupidly what had been going on while he was away. "Yes, yes, I want so much to wed her. She is so sweet, so gentle . . . "

"I am aware of her virtues."

"But it is impossible. At least for quite a while. But I am willing to wait."

"You won't have to wait. I am buying out her indenture."

"Onkel! But no! That I cannot accept. That is my responsibility."

"I insist. Call it a wedding present, if you will. But I cannot have my partner washing his own clothes, doing marketing, being hot in his breeches, when he should be attending to business. You need a goodwife, and since you have already chosen the maid, let it be soon."

Lüdeke von Sehnden had not been Bürgermeister of Celle and Head Master of the Gewandschneider for many years for nothing. He was a stern commander. He made decisions, gave orders, and expected them to be obeyed without question.

Hinrik humbly acquiesced. He could hardly wait to tell Ilsebe. He wanted to run and skip and jump like a little child.

Sensing his mood, Lüdeke held up a hand of warning. "You may tell your Ilsebe about the partnership and all the business news, but please say nothing to her about the indenture. I do not want her to indicate, even inadvertently, anything to make her Mistress suspect that we plan to do. It will make our task that much more difficult."

Hinrik reflected, "Ja, I can see the sense in that. But that means I can't ask her to marry me yet."

Lüdeke smiled. "No, not yet, but I hope very soon. Just think of it this way: a few more weeks is better than waiting over four years."

And perforce Hinrik had to agree with that. He went home to see if there might be any dinner on the table, since no one was expecting him. When he passed the lace shop he peered in, but there was no sign of Ilsebe. As it was only Thursday, he knew he would have to be patient until Sunday. If there were only some way he could send her a note, but he did not dare. When he entered the house, Balthasar and his brothers were just finishing.

"Hinrik, welcome home," said the old man. "I heard your boat was in. So we saved something for you. Come, sit down and eat. I trust you had a good trip?"

"Very successful, Papa, and wait until I tell you the news." Excitedly he told them all about the partnership. "And I am to have a boat of my own as well."

"My, my," said Berndt. "Pretty soon you'll be too grand to associate with us."

"Now, now, lads, it's time you got back to work," said Balthasar, sensing a bit of jealousy. "Go on, I'll be along in a few minutes. I want to hear more of this. We can be very proud of our Hinrik." The brothers left. "Now, tell me more."

"I don't know too many of the details yet," said Hinrik. "He just now told me about it, but he is going to propose me for associate membership in the Gewandschneider."

"Excellent," said Balthasar. "That is the road to wealth and power in this town."

"Of course, I can't be a Master until I have my own business, but as Onkel Lüdeke said, it is the first step in that direction. And I mean to get there somehow. All I need to do is prove myself and save my money."

"You'll get there. I know you will. I always said you were cut from a different cloth than your brothers."

"Different perhaps," agreed Hinrik. "But they are fine men, too."

"Franz, yes, he is doing very well. But Berndt, I don't know. I'm still having problems with him, drinking and wenching too much. I doubt he'll ever settle down. But never mind them. I want to ask you if there's truth in those rumors we've heard, that you are courting a young maid and have not even brought her here to meet us. Are we not good enough, Hinrik?"

"No, no, Papa, it's nothing like that. It's impossible because it's not official yet." And Hinrik explained about Ilsebe's indenture, being careful not to breathe a word about Master von Sehnden's plans with regard to it. "So you see, Papa, it's not that I wanted to keep anything secret from you, but with her living and working just across the street, if I were to bring her here, her old Mistress would surely get wind of it. And that would not be good. Besides, with my not yet having permission to court her I wasn't sure what your reaction would be. Franz would be shocked, and Berndt would treat her like a whore."

"And I? Didn't you think I would be sympathetic?"

"I hoped you would, Papa, but I just didn't want to say anything to anybody until I could proudly announce it to the world."

"I see," said Balthasar. He looked thoughtful for a moment. "We could try to buy out the indenture."

Hinrik looked surprised. "Onkel Lüdeke offered to do the same thing. I wasn't supposed to say anything about it, but I shouldn't want you two working at cross-purposes. Two bidders would surely drive the price up."

Balthasar laughed. "You're right about that. Your poor Ilsebe. It sounds like we're bidding on a prize horse. But good for Master von Sehnden. He can afford it better than I, and I'm sure he is far more adept at this sort of thing. Nonetheless, I think I shall pay our Bürgermeister a visit."

A few days later Balthasar went to see Lüdeke in his office in the Rathaus.

"Welcome, Master Balthasar," Lüdeke greeted him carefully. "How goes the wall? Any problems?"

"None that can't be solved," replied the Master Mason. "The wall goes as well as can be expected. We're about halfway around the town."

"I know. My guess is about four more years to completion."

"That's about right, if we don't run into any major problems. But I have not come to see you on official business. Rather on personal."

"Ah, so?"

"About Hinrik. I am very grateful to you for offering him the partnership with you. Your business is far more to his taste and inclinations than mine. I am very proud of him, and I hope he will make you so, too."

"I already am," replied Lüdeke, "or I should not have made the offer."

"But now I want to see him settled as well," said Balthasar. "He has told me something about this young maid he is secretly—or not so secretly—courting. It seems there is a problem of a long indenture." He held up his hand at the scowl on Lüdeke's face. "I know he promised to say nothing about your intention of buying it out, but all unknowingly, I made the same offer. He had to confess, so that we should not be working at cross-purposes. That is what I have come to see you about. I do not have the means that you do, but I should like to pay a part of the cost."

Lüdeke's scowl changed to a soft smile. "That is very generous of you, Master Balthasar, but I am going to refuse your offer and suggest something else in its stead. First I shall tell you the reasons. I have already begun the negotiations, through a third party, of course. The old termagant is a tough nut to crack. I tell you this in confidence. I am working through a good friend of mine in her own guild. There have been some, shall we say, irregularities in her dealings with the girl. We are using these to—uh—pressure her a bit. I feel by that means we shall get a just price, probably less than the original contract. The negotiations are in a very delicate stage right now, and I do not wish to do anything that will upset them or make it difficult for the young lass. Furthermore, it makes a lot more sense for a cloth merchant to want a lacemaker to complement his business than a master mason. You could obviously want her solely for purposes of marriage to someone, if not yourself, and we do not want the old Mistress to know that as yet."

"Ja, ja, I can see the sense of that," said Balthasar slowly.

"Have you met her yet?"

"Nay, not yet, and I was a little hurt by that, but now I can understand a little of Hinrik's reasons for keeping her a secret, at least in part."

"A charming young maid. My goodwife is quite taken with her.

Although she is a peasant, she is highly intelligent and quite biddable. I think it will be a good match, or I should not have gotten involved. You know Hinrik has been like a son to me."

"I know. You said you had another suggestion."

"Yes. Not for now, but a few years down the road. You know Hinrik dreams of having his own business. I believe he will be quite capable of it after a few years as my partner. But he will need capital. Lots of it. Save your money for that, Master. It will serve a far better purpose than this."

"Ja, ja, you are right," said the old man, quite happy again. "That's just what I'll do. Thank you, Master Lüdeke, for putting the idea in my head."

A few weeks later Ilsebe's Mistress called her into her private parlor that also served as an office of sorts. Ilsebe entered with some trepidation. What fault will she find with me now? she wondered. She stood with hands folded demurely until the woman indicated that she should sit.

"I have news," she said.

Ilsebe said nothing but sat with eyes downcast.

"Someone has taken over your indenture. One of the Gewand-schneider," said the Mistress.

Ilsebe's face fell. "Oh, no!" she murmured. Not a new Master. As bad as the old Mistress was, at least Ilsebe was used to her ways. What would happen now? She could even be sent away to another town and never see Hinrik again.

The woman ignored her exclamation and continued. "For the time being you are to continue working here, until he can make a place for you in his own workshop." At least a little respite, thought Ilsebe. "He will pay you a small wage as well as your bed and board, and all your work is to go to him, with a commission for me, of course."

Ilsebe brightened a little. A small wage and still be indentured? That did not make sense, but far be it from her to question it. "Can you tell me who it is?" she whispered.

"I don't honestly know," replied the Mistress. "All the negotiations were conducted through Master Henning of our guild. I have my suspicions who it might be, but I don't want to say in case I am wrong. You can be sure it is someone high up in the Gewandschneider, though, and someone right here in Celle." Ilsebe felt relieved at that. "All I know is I have my money and am glad I won't be dead and buried before I get it from your work. Let him have the pleasure of you."

Why, that callous old bitch, thought Ilsebe as she went back to work, her mind spinning with a thousand questions. She wondered when she would know who her new Master was. Perhaps Mistress von Sehnden could find out for her. Or even Hinrik. He was going to be a member of the Gewandschneider soon. She was so proud of him. He was doing so well, and she seemed to be sinking further and further into debt. Was there ever any hope that they could wed? She doubted it. She was tempted to run right across the street this evening to tell him, although he had never invited her to his home and it would certainly be a serious breech of good manners to do so. But no, she thought. He has been so happy lately. Why plunge him back into the depths with her news?

When they met on Sunday, he announced, "Today we are going to have afternoon coffee with Mistress von Sehnden."

"Oh, I thought we were going to the coffeehouse," Ilsebe replied.

"We were, but something important has come up."

She ignored what he said, too sunken in her own dark thoughts. "Then there is something I must tell you before we get there." And half in tears, she spilled forth the whole story of her new indenture.

"I know," was all he said. He did not seem perturbed in the least at her news.

She began to panic. He has finally give up on me, perhaps even found another woman, she thought despondently. She struggled to stem her tears and control her emotions as they walked through the deserted marketplace to Zöllnerstrasse and the von Sehnden home.

When they arrived there she was surprised to find not only Mistress Anna but also Master von Sehnden himself and their son Lüdeke in attendance. The table was already set with several luscious looking cakes and, obviously, their best pewter and cutlery. There was a snowy linen cloth and even a bouquet of late fall flowers. It looks like a celebration, she thought. I wonder what the occasion is.

The Bürgermeister himself welcomed them and bade her sit next to him at the head of the table with Hinrik on his other side. Mistress Anna sat at the other end and young Lüdeke next to Hinrik.

"Now, my dear," said the elder Lüdeke when they were all settled and Anna had started pouring the coffee, "I have several announcements to make." They all looked at him expectantly. She looked around the table and saw their varying expressions. Anna with her lovely, comforting smile, young Lüdeke as though it were a big joke. Hinrik was radiant, but Master von Sehnden was very serious.

"The first thing I must tell you," continued Lüdeke, "is that I am now your new Master, for a few minutes anyway."

Ilsebe gasped and stared at him. "I wondered who . . . ," she started to say, when the latter part of his announcement sunk in. "What do you mean, Master, 'for a few minutes'?" Was he going to turn her over to yet another person?

He laughed. "Because I have here your indenture papers plus another document stating that you have completed your indenture to my satisfaction and are now a free woman."

Ilsebe gasped. She could not speak. Finally, she stuttered, "Master, Master . . . ," and burst into tears.

"Ilsebe, don't cry," said Hinrik. "You should be happy."

But Anna knew better. She came around the table, sat next to Ilsebe, took her in her arms, and held her close to her breast while the girl sobbed.

At last Anna said, "Hinrik, you have a lot to learn about women, and one thing is that they always cry when they are extremely happy."

Hinrik looked puzzled but nodded. Tante Anna always knew best.

Onkel Lüdeke also nodded and smiled. "Ja, Hinrik," he said, "women are strange creatures, God love them. We can't live without them, but we'll never understand them."

When Ilsebe's tears subsided, Anna wiped her face but remained where she was anticipating the next announcement.

Ilsebe finally found her tongue. "Oh, Master von Sehnden, how can I ever thank you?"

"Just make me fine lace," he teased. "Now, before I turn these papers over to you, there is one more thing while I am still your Master." Ilsebe could not imagine what else. Hadn't he already done enough for her? "Since you have no family," he went on, "Hinrik has asked me, as your Master, for your hand in marriage. I have agreed to a formal betrothal and have here a tentative marriage settlement."

Once again Ilsebe gasped, but this time she was quick to reply. "But he hasn't even asked me!"

"Ask her, you dolt," said young Lüdeke.

Everyone laughed.

Hinrik turned red as a beet. "Ilsebe, beloved, will you marry me?" he finally stammered.

"Yes, yes, yes," she replied eagerly while the von Sehnden family cheered.

"Then here are your papers making you a free woman," said Lüdeke the Elder, "and a suitably betrothed one as well." He handed her the papers and kissed her lightly on the forehead. "From now on you shall call us Onkel Lüdeke and Tante Anna, for Hinrik is like family to us."

"Yes, Onkel," said Ilsebe shyly.

Young Lüdeke could not help but comment, "That has got to be the strangest marriage proposal ever. Not one shred of privacy for them."

His father laughed uproariously. "For once my son is right. I am afraid it has been too much all at once for poor Ilsebe. After we indulge ourselves with this wonderful kuchen, Hinrik, I give you two permission to retire to the privacy of the library to make your plans."

"Thank you, Onkel Lüdeke," said Hinrik.

Suddenly Ilsebe surprised them all by exclaiming, "Hinrik, you devil, you knew it all along and didn't tell me. Let me worry. I hate you."

Hinrik hung his head. "Onkel Lüdeke made me promise not to tell. He wanted to be the one to surprise you."

"So the little river sprite has some spirit after all," said young Lüdeke. "Watch out, Hinrik, or she'll drown you in the river."

"Oh, I wouldn't do that," said Ilsebe. "I only hated him for a little minute. I really love him very much." Then she added, "And you just watch out yourself, Lüdeke, or I might drown you. Wait till you are betrothed. Hah!"

Ilsebe was so excited she cold hardly eat, although the cakes were delicious. Hinrik was so relieved he more than made up for her lack.

"Ilsebe," he said, "you must ask Tante for these recipes."

"Isn't that just like a man?" she commented. "We're not even married yet and he wants me to start collecting recipes."

When at least they retired to the library, he hugged her and kissed her as if he could not get enough. "We must wed soon, don't you think? I don't want to wait any longer."

"Nor I," she agreed, "but it is close on Advent. We can't marry then. Besides, I need time to make some clothes. I refused to be wed in these old rags and klompen. I think during the Christmas season would be nice."

"Christmas sounds lovely. I'll talk to Pastor Cord about the banns right away."

"No, not Pastor Cord," she said. "I want to be wed simply, in the new way. Talk to one of the younger priests who espouses Dr. Luther's liturgy."

"Very well, I'll do that."

"But, Hinrik, what am I going to do about clothes? I have no money for cloth until Master—I mean Onkel Lüdeke pays me the wage that was promised."

"Talk to Tante Anna," suggested Hinrik. "After all, you are marrying into the Gewandschneider. If they can't supply cloth, I don't know who can. And don't worry about shoes. I've long wanted to buy you some, and now I am going to get you the finest pair I can have made."

"Hinrik, you are so sweet."

He kissed her again deeply and then said, "Come now, let us bid 'Auf Wiedersehen' to the von Sehnden, for I have another treat for you."

"Yet another?" she exclaimed. "I don't know if I can stand any more. I'll never sleep tonight. What is it?"

"It won't be long before you'll be sleeping in my arms," he said, "but tonight we shall have supper at my house. My stepfather has long wanted to meet you. He is expecting us, but my brothers don't yet know you are coming."

"I shall look forward to that," she replied, "but I don't promise to eat very much. All this excitement is too much for one day."

He laughed and kissed her again.

On the way to his house Hinrik tried to describe his family to her. "Balthasar is probably the kindest man you ever met. There isn't a mean bone in his body. Yet he can be very tough with his laborers because he is a perfectionist where his work is concerned. Franz is very serious and a hard worker without a shred of imagination, but a good man nonetheless. Berndt is something else again. You may find him a bit uncouth, but pay no attention to any of his lewd remarks. Just ignore them."

"That sounds like an interesting assortment of relatives. I shall look forward to meeting them all," she replied politely.

Balthasar himself met them at the door. "Welcome! Welcome!" he boomed. "At last we meet Hinrik's secret love." He took Ilsebe by the hand and had led her into the front parlor, where a cheery fire was burning. That in itself was evidence of her welcome, as they rarely used the room at all. Hinrik was pleased.

"Papa, this is Ilsebe. Ilsebe, my stepfather, Balthasar," Hinrik introduced them.

"So, so," said Balthasar, leading her to a chair near the fire. "We shall sit here and talk a bit before supper. It's nothing much. Our housekeeper does not work on Sundays, so we always have a cold repast on Sunday evening. Unless you're very hungry, that is?"

660

"No, no," Ilsebe assured him. "I enjoy sitting by the fire. It is getting chilly outside." She glanced about the room. Strictly a male domain, lacking a woman's touch. Well, she would soon put that to rights.

"Now tell me all about yourself," said Balthasar. "I want to get to know you, since I understand you are soon to be my daughter."

They talked for almost an hour. Ilsebe found herself relaxing after all the excitement of the afternoon. She liked the old man very much. His kind heart shone forth in his eyes, just as Hinrik had described him. While she had great respect for the von Sehnden and was especially fond of Mistress—Tante Anna, this was her kind of people and she felt far more at ease. They even talked a little of the old ways when she told him of her Grannie. She chattered on gaily when she told him how proud she was of Hinrik. And she could see this pleased his stepfather very much.

When they entered the dining room she saw the table was laden with a lavish assortment of cold meats—ham, beef and chicken legs—lots of rich cheese, and the good old-fashioned brown peasant bread that she loved. She suddenly found she was ravenous, as she had only picked at the delectable cakes at the von Sehnden's coffee hour because she was so nervous. Here she was relaxed.

She met Hinrik's two brothers, and they were exactly as he had said— Franz ultra serious and a little stodgy, Berndt already a little tipsy. It was hard to believe her Hinrik came from the same parents. She was ever so grateful for the difference. She took his advice and largely ignored his brothers except for the requisite courtesies. She continued conversing with Balthasar and grew to like him even more.

Hinrik and Ilsebe were formally betrothed the following Sunday before the altar of the Stadtkirche, and the banns were read for the next three weeks. He gave her a beautiful ring, a lustrous pearl surrounded by garnets, and, shortly before they went to church, her first pair of shoes. They hurt her feet a little because she was not used to them, but they were so soft and beautiful that she was determined to walk like a lady to that most important ceremony of her life.

They were wed on the Sunday between Christmas and Epiphany. It was a simple ceremony conducted by Father Gebhardt, a young priest who avidly espoused Dr. Luther's new beliefs. Just a solemn exchange of vows and a blessing of the newlyweds, no Mass at all. Lüdeke von Sehnden gave her away, and Anna stood as her matron of honor. Balthasar was Hinrik's groomsman. Ilsebe's gown was a rich dark red velvet, hurriedly put together by Tante Anna's seamstress and graced by one of her own lace ruffs. It had the wide side overskirts of matching brocade that were just beginning to come into style.

Afterwards, the von Sehnden gave a small but lavish party for the newlyweds at their home. There she met many of the Gewandschneider the leading Bürgers of Celle, and she vowed right from the start not to be in awe of these people. It was hard to believe that she was now one of them, and she determined to act the part until it came to her naturally. She was surprised to find that they were just ordinary people like herself despite their great wealth. These solid German Bürgers had no pretensions to nobility, as was the case in some other countries. She was sure she would fit in with them very well.

That night when Hinrik led her home to the house on Schuhstrasse, these two shy people each wondered how they would face the next few hours. But when they cuddled together under the featherbed in his own room their sheer happiness in each other took over and no one would have believed them shy, had there been anyone to observe them. But no one did.

Later that very same year the former monk Dr. Martin Luther took to wife a former nun, Catherine von Bora, and they eventually produced six children.

The year 1526 was to prove an eventful year—for Hinrik and Ilsebe personally, for Celle, for the Duchy, for Germany and for the world.

Eggeling von Eltze was ambivalent about the new religion. Eggeling von Eltze was ambivalent about many things. Just recently a Portuguese sailing for Spain, Juan del Cano, lieutenant of Fernando Magellan, had returned to Spain, proving without any doubt what most mariners had long believed, that the world was indeed round, but far, far larger than any man's wildest imaginings. So the world was round. Well and good. Did that make the sea route to the Spice Islands, in order to circumvent the Turks, any easier? The Fuggers of Augsburg evidently thought so, having quickly grabbed up that monopoly. And from the newly discovered lands to the west Spain was pouring gold into Europe, lowering the standards until now German silver Thalers or Groschen were worth more than Venetian ducats or Florentine florins, which was fine within Germany but which made trade with the cities using gold currency more and more difficult. The exchange fluctuated wildly from day to day. But, so what? Pretty soon all of Christian Europe would have to take to the sea. The Christian armies had just suffered a terrible defeat at a place in Hungary called Mohacs, and the Turks had captured the capital city of Buda. New art, literature, and music were pouring into northern Germany from Italy, new—almost ridiculous—fashions from the decadent Valois court of France, a new and ruthless type of politics, mixed with religion, from as far away as England. Even Antwerp, that bastion of free and easy trade for all the merchants of Europe, was suffering under more new rules and regulations as the Emperor tried to dip his greedy fingers into the pie.

Eggeling von Eltze was even ambivalent about his name. He had been christened Cordt Eggeling after his grandfather Eggeling and great-uncle Cordt, many times Bürgermeister, but the last of the family to hold that office now that the elder Lüdeke von Sehnden seemed to be monopolizing the position. Even the Celle branch of the family seemed to be dwindling down. His eldest great-uncle Johann was a priest, therefore had no descendants. Uncle Cordt's only daughter Ilsebe had joined the Beguines, therefore no descendants. Another great-uncle had left Celle for parts unknown. His mother, Adelheit, was Eggeling's only daughter. When she had married his father Lüdern von Geiss, much to the disapproval of his family, who looked down on him as a very minor and insignificant noble not worthy of the daughter of a great merchant family, indulgent old Eggeling insisted on but one condition—that the groom take the bride's family name, von Eltze, instead of vice versa. Adelheit, being a very proud young lady, readily agreed. Cordt had never even been able to ascertain his father's true feelings in the matter. Although he too was intensely proud of the family name, he somehow felt it had been demeaning to his father. In any event, his mother, who called him Kuno, the ancient Low German version of his name, at home insisted that he be called Cordt Eggeling von Eltze. Gradually, as he reached adulthood, people forgot that his first name was Cordt and called him simply Eggeling von Eltze.

But Eggeling was especially ambivalent about the new religion. He did not deny for one minute that the Church needed reform. Almost all the educated and serious-minded north Germans agreed to that. But he was more inclined to follow the promulgations of the great Erasmus, reform from within. Admittedly, Eggeling understood that had been Luther's original intent as well, but the mistake, he felt, was encouraging the new teachings among the ignorant common people. Luther himself was even now fighting against the radical element of reformer-anarchists who had stirred up the terrible Peasants' Revolution.

The von Eltze had been the most generous and consistent supporters of the great Marienkirche—he still refused to call it the Stadtkirche—since its founding over two hundred years ago. They had endowed altars, chapels and vicaries and had donated innumerable windows, statues, vestments, candles, bells, and other appurtenances. Aside from the great Duchess Anna von Nassau of blessed memory, their name appeared more times than that of any other Celle family in the great Memorial Book of the church—commonly called the Läuterbuch, after the bells that were rung on the occasion of each Requiem Mass. They were considered one of the most pious families in Celle. It was very difficult to gainsay that heritage.

Yet now Duke Ernst was asking him—and a Ducal request equalled a command—to accompany him to a special meeting of reform-minded princess in Speyer. Johann, Elector of Saxony, and Philip, Landgraf of

Hesse, had formed the League of Gotha and Torgau to protect and extend Lutheranism, but it was Duke Ernst who urged that all the Lutheran princes meet at Speyer to repudiate the Edict of Worms. Most of the imperial Free Cities were expected to send representatives as well. The von Eltze had always been the leading advisors to the Duke since the founding of Celle, although recently that coveted role had been taken over by Bürgermeister von Sehnden the Elder. But the Duke was a young man and an avid disciple of Luther, having studied under him at Wittenburg, and wanted to surround himself with equally dedicated young men. He had also asked Lüdeke von Sehnden the Younger and Hinrik Stockman to accompany him to Speyer.

Eggeling knew that the von Sehnden, both father and son, had immediately followed the Duke's lead in openly embracing the new learning—probably more for business than religious reasons, he thought sardonically. Never once had *their* name ever appeared in the Läuterbuch. I must not think like that, he chided himself. They have done a lot of good for the town. Their bent was more civic-minded than church-oriented. Hinrik Stockman was more conservative. While he obviously leaned toward the Lutheran teaching, he kept his own counsel and rarely joined in the heated arguments among the friends. And because the three were best friends, the Duke had simply assumed that he, Eggeling, was likeminded. And that was what was tearing him apart. Ernst expected his support and advice. Yet can I in good conscience be unbiased? he asked himself.

The Duke had taken his advice last year, he reminded himself, in the matter of Wolf Cyclop. Ernst had brought in the radical preacher to encourage the people in the new learning, but the man had turned out to be too extreme, even for the most dedicated Lutheran Bürgers. Instead of educating the people, he had turned his vitriolic sermons against the benevolent Franciscans, the only order to have a cloister and church within the town walls. They were well beloved by all the townspeople, whether Catholic or Lutheran, because of their humility and good works. Therefore, the Duke had left them alone. But this Wolf Cyclop, who was not even a priest but a physician and for that reason was only permitted to preach on street corners, had turned out to be a violent rabble-rouser who stirred the people up against the monks.

Although the Duke had soon realized that the man's acerbic preaching was not to his taste at all and on Eggeling's advice had ordered him out of Celle, he had planted the seeds of hatred and prejudice against the

Franciscans among the common people. Already there had been numerous incidents of name-calling and harassment, even occasional refuse and stone throwing, against the monks. Even the nickname Barefoots, which had once been a gentle euphemism, had become a term of disparagement. Duke Ernst, hoping to calm things down, had suggested, first kindly, then strongly, that the problem would easily be solved if the monks would simply convert to Luther's teachings. It was not as though there were no precedents. Hundreds of monks and nuns all over Germany were voluntarily converting en masse. At first the monks ignored these 'suggestions,' but when the pressure became too great Brother Bernhardin preached a fiery sermon shortly after Christmas of 1525 firmly rejecting any possibility of their converting. The die was cast.

Bernhardin not only spoke scathingly of Luther's teachings but also chastised most of the clergy of the Marienkirche. There, too, was division. Almost all the younger priests had willingly, eagerly, embraced Luther's precepts. These were supplemented by several converted monks and priests from other parts of Germany brought in from time to time by Duke Ernst to preach and teach. But old Cordt Lüdeke, the head pastor of the church, stubbornly refused to change. He claimed that at his advanced age he was too old to comprehend these newfangled ideas. But old or not, his mind was still sharp. He was an eloquent preacher and a dedicated pastor, a power to be reckoned with.

No wonder I am confused, thought Eggeling. For practical reasons he knew the Lutheran way made more sense. It gave the merchants freedom to do business as it should be done. But for personal and family reasons he just could not bring himself to break completely with the old Catholicism. He was even now on his way to meet with his friends Lüdeke and Hinrik at the coffeehouse. Eggeling knew he had to make a decision about Speyer soon. His friends were not even aware of his quandary, and the Duke was growing impatient.

"Oh, there you are," said Lüdeke as Eggeling entered the coffeehouse. "We were beginning to think you weren't coming."

"Sorry to be late," replied Eggeling. "I ran into a—a small problem at the tollhouse."

"I didn't know there were any boats or wagons in," said Lüdeke.

"There aren't," said Eggeling. "It was just—just a minor thing, easily solved."

Hinrik, more perceptive than young Lüdeke, noticed his friend's hesitancy. "Eggeling," he asked, "is something troubling you?"

"No, not really." But, yes, there is, he thought to himself. Suddenly the need to talk about it was overwhelming. These are my best friends. Whom else can I confide in? "I can't go to Speyer," he blurted out.

"But whyever not?" exclaimed Lüdeke. "The Duke is counting on you."

"Perhaps I don't feel I can give him the support he needs or expects," suggested Eggeling.

"But your family has always been advisors to the dukes since—since, almost forever," objected Lüdeke. "You have to go."

"Lüdeke," sighed Eggeling. "You simply don't understand. It's personal."

"I think I can understand how you feel," interjected Hinrik.

"Can you? Can you really?"

"Yes, I can," replied Hinrik. "My dear little goodwife has made me understand how the people of the Old Religion felt when Karl der Grosse forced them to become Christian. There are many out in the countryside still who only pay lip service to the Church."

"But that—that's blasphemy," exclaimed Eggeling.

"No different, really, than what the Pope and Dr. Luther are accusing one another of."

Eggeling thought about that for a moment. "Put that way, it makes some sense. But those were two entirely different religions. This is division within the same Church. It is very tragic."

"But you admit that the Church needed cleansing," put in Lüdeke.

"I'll readily admit that. But if only they could have cleansed it and yet left the old ways alone."

"Dr. Luther tried just that," explained Hinrik patiently, "but the Pope and men like old Archbishop Albrecht are too greedy and avaricious to even consider changing their luxurious and wanton lifestyles."

"Perhaps so, but some have gone too far. What is wrong with the Mass in Latin? What is wrong with an occasional prayer to our Blessed Mother? The biggest mistake these reformers made was putting those new ideas into the hands of the common people. I say hands, not minds, for I doubt most of them have any notion what it's all about."

"But they are learning, Eggeling, they are learning, and that right rapidly," said Hinrik. "Putting the Mass into German was the best thing that could have happened. Do you realize how many of your country people were drifting away from the Church and back into the old religion—the old, old religion, mind you—because they had no idea what was going on up at the altar?"

"You would say that because of your river sprite."

At this Peter, who had been silently listening to the give-and-take, spoke up. "Eggeling, that was uncalled for. We all know that Hinrik's goodwife is a sincere, practicing Christian. And, furthermore, what Hinrik says is true. I travel a lot throughout the countryside buying for my father, and I have seen the Sachsenross at the gable peaks, the hex signs on the barns, the wisewomen in their tiny cottages, ja, even the sacred groves. It was not Dr. Luther per se who put the new teaching in their heads, but the printing press. They are becoming increasingly literate, eager to learn. More so than many a noble who clings to his ancient feudal ways and turns his nose up at learning to read and write as being clerkly and effeminate."

"That may be so," agreed Eggeling reluctantly. "I don't really know. My duties at the tollhouse don't allow me to get out into the countryside very often. Perhaps it is a good thing. But I still prefer the Mass in Latin."

"But Latin is becoming less and less the lingua franca of Europe," said Lüdeke. "Throughout the north our Hanse Low German is the language of trade. It is well understood in Antwerp, even as far away as London and Novgorod. And French is rapidly becoming the language of diplomacy in the west, also in England and Italy."

"Yes, and Italian the language of art and music," added Peter. "Latin is quite limited to the universities and the lawyers — and many of them are changing."

Eggeling shook his head. "I guess I am truly way behind the times, although I still can't say I like it. But what, pray tell, is wrong with an occasional prayer to Our Lady?"

"The same thing," said Hinrik.

"What do you mean?"

"That the people in their ignorance merely substituted her for one of the goddesses of the old religion. A prayer asking for her intercession is one thing, but they were praying directly to her alone instead of to God," replied Hinrik.

"But that is blasphemy!"

"Precisely. But no one took the time to explain that to them. Too many priests were — and are — as ignorant as the people they served."

Eggeling took a sip of his coffee and put his head in his hands. His friends respected his silence. They knew he was wrestling with a difficult decision. At last he raised his head. "All of what you say makes sense to me.

And some of it has been a revelation. But I still don't think I should go to Speyer."

"Eggeling, you must go," exclaimed Hinrik.

"It is an honor, and besides, the Duke is counting on you," added Lüdeke.

Eggeling shook his head.

"Look at it this way," said Peter, ever the mediator. "There are hotheads on both sides. Someone is needed to cool them down. Even Ernst himself and the other princes could go too far in their enthusiasm for the new learning because they are so vehemently opposed to the Edict of Worms. And rightly so. It is a terrible piece of legislation. But if Charles and the Diet see that there is someone of a conservative bent advising them, perhaps there can still be a reconciliation. It is still not too late."

Eggeling looked at him admiringly. "Peter, you are so wise. You should be the one going, not I. What can I alone do?"

"You continually stress the fact that your family has been a staunch supporter of the Church for centuries," continued Peter, "but they have been equally wise advisors to the Dukes since the founding of Celle. Don't forget that. It is your obligation to carry on that tradition."

Peter had finally struck a note of pride in Eggeling. "You are right," he said slowly and thoughtfully. "It is my obligation, no matter how I feel personally. Very well. I shall go to Speyer. But I shall have to have a lot more of these discussions with you three so that I can carefully weigh both sides of the matter."

"Well spoken, my friend, you shall have them," said Hinrik. "There speaks an intelligent man."

"Bravo, Eggeling. You are a true von Eltze," added Lüdeke.

"A true Bürger of Celle," concluded Peter.

As soon as the roads became passable in the spring, Duke Ernst made preparations for the journey to Speyer. It would take them three weeks if they were extremely lucky, most probably twice that, if they were forced to take huge detours due to bridges washed out by spring floods or fords too deep to cross. Horses could become mired in mud, and although messengers were being sent ahead to ensure them a welcome at various castles and towns on the way, there was always the possibility that they might not reach their goal on any given night and they would have to stop early so that the huntsmen could shoot game for their supper. A heavily armed troop was to accompany them, not only as protection against the ever-present brigands but also as a strong deterrent should they have to pass through hostile—meaning Catholic—territory. The planned route led mostly through neighboring Hesse, already staunchly Lutheran, into the Imperial Free City of Frankfurt, which had also declared for the reform. Beyond that, however, was the territory of the despised Archbishop of Mainz and several minor ecclesiastical lords that could give them trouble. In any event, Ernst intended to be well prepared. The three friends were permitted one servant and packhorse each in addition to their own horses, Hinrik's servant and packhorse having been loaned him by the von Sehnden.

During the weeks since Hinrik had learned he was to accompany the Duke, Ilsebe had been busy sewing him new clothes.

"We can't have you looking like a poor cousin. You must be a worthy representative of Celle," she said. "I am sure Lüdeke will be dressed like a bright popinjay."

Hinrik smiled. Clothes were the least of his worries, although he was a cloth merchant. But he was so proud of his sweet little bride and touched by her concern. With all that, she was still working diligently at her lacemaking, which Lüdeke von Sehnden readily sold for her. His brother Franz had since married and had moved to his new home in Neustrasse. Ilsebe had turned the vacated bedchamber into her workroom.

A few days before they were to leave she presented him with a new suit of clothes. Fancy puffed and slashed hose, brand-new soft stockings, a dark blue velvet doublet beautifully embroidered with silver, even a warm cloak.

Hinrik kissed her soundly and thanked her profusely. "I shall outshine the Duke himself in this fine raiment. Now promise me you will rest your eyes and not do any more for a while."

"Oh, but I have lots more I have to do," she objected.

"Whatever for? This is more than enough for me."

"Not for you, silly," she laughed and pirouetted around. "For our son or daughter who is on the way."

"Ilse! Why didn't you tell me?" he exclaimed. "I can't go to Speyer now."

"I wanted to be very sure," she replied, "but I wanted you to know before you left. And of course you can go to Speyer. Whyever not? Do you think I want you around while I lie sick abed of a morning? You will be back months before the babe is born."

"But I can't leave you alone at a time like this," argued Hinrik.

"I'll not be alone. I'm sure Tante Anna will be more help, should I need it, than any man. I am strong and healthy. It's not as though it were something unusual. Women have babies every day. And I'm also sure that Papa Balthasar would not let a fly harm me."

"But it is your first—our first."

"So? One has to start somewhere."

He kissed her then and held her close. "Oh, my little one, I am so happy," he whispered into her hair. "So proud of you."

"Well, you had something to do with it, too."

Hinrik was still capable of blushing. "I suppose I did," he chuckled. Then more seriously, "But do be careful, sweeting. No heavy lifting, no strenuous work. I could not bear if anything happened to you or the babe."

"I know. I know. I don't intend to work on the wall," she teased. "Now get to your packing and set your mind on convincing the Emperor that Dr. Luther is right."

The Ducal party rode out of Celle with much fanfare on a cool bright May morning. All about them fruit trees were in luxuriant bloom, wildflowers covered the meadows and newborn black lambs gamboled in the pastures. The whole countryside seemed to encourage fun and frolic, but few of the men noticed their surroundings, so intent were they on the seriousness of their mission. They headed southwest to Hannover, where they intended to spend their first night. They were welcomed at the Leine castle by Erich, Duke of Calenberg, Ernst's much older cousin.

At first the party from Celle cautiously refrained from any discussions of religious matters, although this was uppermost in their minds, for this was a house—and duchy—divided. Old Duke Erich, almost on the point of senility, remained adamantly Catholic, but his much younger second wife Elisabeth of Brandenburg staunchly espoused the new faith. Similarly the Town Council of Hannover sided with the Duke in remaining true to the old religion, but the majority of Bürgers and common people were increasingly embracing Luther's teaching.

After a hearty supper, Duchess Elisabeth herself introduced the subject of religion and cleverly led the discussion that followed. She was already full of radical plans, among them, to turn the cloisters into schools and cultural centers for all the people. Duke Ernst listened to her ideas with great interest, as did most of the men from Celle. The old Duke Erich hardly contributed a word and was soon nodding in his cups.

When they finally bedded down for the night in the great hall, Lüdeke said to Eggeling, "So, you see, there is an example of how both sides can live together in harmony."

"Hardly an equal battle, I should say," replied Eggeling, "he on the verge of senility and she a vibrant, highly intelligent young woman. I hope he is not representative of everyone on the Catholic side."

"Of course not, although the Pope and many bishops are of a similar age. But it is the Church itself that has become senile and corrupt. It is we younger men who can push the reforms," said Lüdeke.

Eggeling gave him a look of disdain that clearly said, "Speak for yourself, Lüdeke."

Hinrik, hoping to steer them away from a fruitless argument, said, "The Duchess does have some interesting ideas, don't you think?"

"Some of them too radical for my taste," replied Eggeling. "I have to admit that most of the monasteries have strayed far from their founders' intentions and many convents are nothing more than rest homes for wealthy widows. But to have the state take over—that is going too far, in my opinion."

"Our own Ernst seemed quite taken with her proposals."

"Perhaps, but I am quite certain even he would not condone that. But come now, my young friends, let us get some sleep. Today was the easiest part of our whole trip. Tomorrow we head into the mountains and we shall need all our strength."

The next morning they continued in a southwest direction until they reached the upper Weser. They crossed the river at Hameln, the lovely old town of Pied Piper fame. From there they continued due south along the left bank of the river. Here the Weser was not the broad, placid stream lined with water meadows that these lowlanders were used to but a wide, swift current that wound hither and yon around the mountains. It curved this way and that, almost doubling back on itself at times. In some places the gorge was so narrow that the road ran almost in the water and they had to go single file.

"Have a care," warned one of the knights. "At this time of year the river often overflows the road and the horse can easily slip or become mired."

"Ja, and keep a sharp eye out and your weapons at the ready," declared another. "Brigands love this sort of terrain because you can't see what's around the next curve."

"Ja, ja," enjoined a third, "and let your horses set the pace. Don't push them too hard up these steep inclines or they will tire too soon."

The three friends took these warnings to heart.

Hinrik said, "I have never seen this part of Germany before. All my travels have been to the north by boat."

"Nor I," agreed Lüdeke. "It is very beautiful, is it not? But who would want to live here?"

"Truthfully, I don't see anyone," said Hinrik.

Eggeling laughed at this. "They are there, but they don't have the broad farms, pastures, and meadows that we are used to. They are mostly miners and woodsmen. These mountains are rich in all kinds of valuable ore. I have travelled through here several times many years ago. Nothing seems to have changed. But if you think these are mountains, just wait until we get south of Frankfurt. They get higher, steeper and more rugged until, beyond where we are going, they are snowcapped all year round."

At Münden the Weser split—or more correctly, the Werre flowing from the southeast and the Fulda from the south joined to form the Weser. A half-day's ride from Münden brought them to the border of Hesse. The border guards welcomed them but checked all their passports nonetheless.

"You should reach Kassel ere nightfall," said the chief guard. "The road is not too bad considering the time of year. My Lord Philip is expecting you."

Duke Ernst thanked him and they continued on their way following the Fulda, a stream even more convoluted than the Weser, until at last they came to Kassel, capital of Hesse.

They rode directly to the castle and there were heartily welcomed by Philip, Landgraf of Hesse.

Two more disparate men than the Duke and the Count could not be imagined. Whereas Ernst was quiet, unassuming and very serious, Philip was loud, boisterous and reputed to have a fiery temper. In many ways he still had the mentality of the old feudal robber-barons, who would rather fight than mediate. But he also had greater political vision than most of his contemporaries and there was no doubt that his enthusiasm for the new religion was genuine. He was also very young, younger than both Eggeling and Hinrik at twenty-two.

They were treated royally by the Hessians. The food was sumptuous and plentiful. After supper Ernst and Philip sat by the fire in the great hall and began to discuss plans for the upcoming Diet. The three friends sat nearby their Duke, listening carefully but ready to offer comments only if asked to do so.

"Bide with us for a couple of days until all my men come in," invited Philip. "Then we can travel together."

"'All your men', my lord?" queried Ernst. "How many do you plan on taking with you?"

"Oh, just a few hundred," replied Philip. "They'll all be here within the next day or two."

"But, my lord, that is an army!" exclaimed Ernst. "We have but thirty armed retainers with us. Why so many?"

"Your Grace, I believe in a show of force," said Philip. "I trust neither the Emperor nor the Archbishop of Mainz, whose territory we must cross, nor any of the others. I don't intend to use the men, but I want those in power as well as the other Catholic princes to know that we are prepared to fight for our rights and for our faith—if need be."

Ernst shook his head. "I think it is the wrong approach. We have to negotiate."

"Naturally, Your Grace, we intend to negotiate. Our purpose is to rescind the Edict of Worms, is it not? And they are not about to do that willingly or easily. A strong force at one's back never hurt negotiations. Johann, Elector of Saxony, agrees with me."

"Does he now?"

"Yes, because even Dr. Luther warned that this could lead to either revolt or war."

"I know he said that, but look what happened with the disastrous Peasants' Revolt."

"A misguided, undisciplined effort stirred up by a few radicals. I have a dream, Your Grace, that this is the opportunity for a united Germany— or at least a united northern Germany—to throw off the yoke of Pope, yes, even of Emperor."

"My lord, you speak treason," said Ernst aghast.

"Perhaps now, Your Grace, but if we all stick together in a show of strength and demand the rights to rule our states and worship our God as we choose, who can gainsay us? The Pope, who even now is fighting with Charles again? The Emperor, who has not set foot in Germany these many years because he is so busy fighting foreign wars that do not concern us and who pays more attention to Italy, Spain, and the Netherlands than he ever does to us?"

"You may be right in that, my lord, but I recall my ancestor Heinrich der Löwe tried, almost successfully, to unite northern Germany, opposed the Emperor, and was betrayed and sent into exile for his pain. As a result, my Duchy of Braunschweig-Lüneburg is all that is left of his once vast realm. We should not mix politics and religion."

"Theoretically true, Your Grace, but impossible in Germany—or anywhere else in Christendom, for that matter. And who is at fault? The Popes and their bishops with their vast secular territories have been playing politics for centuries. The Church has its finger in every pie, political as well as social."

"Yes, that has to change. But remember, we are going to Speyer to discuss the Edict and our religious rights under the Reform."

"Agreed, Your Grace. But isn't the Reform at least partly about getting the Church out of politics and the secular life of our people?"

"Out of politics, surely. But who then would be responsible for the schools, the hospitals, my lord?"

"The States, of course. The Hanse has already shown, for example, that they can operate far more successful schools than the Church. Your own grandmother, Anna von Nassau, of blessed memory, did much to induce the Bürgers of Celle to be responsible for the hospitals if I am not mistaken."

"Yes, that she did, and you are right about the schools. Perhaps we have been so fortunate in Celle not to have the Dominicans breathing down our necks that we are unaware of the plight of others. But how would one pay for all this?"

"Taxes, of course, but the people would pay no more. The only difference would be that the revenues would stay in your own treasury instead of being sent to Rome to further enrich the Pope and build a new St. Peter's."

Ernst grew thoughtful. "My cousin by marriage, Elisabeth of Brandenburg, had some interesting suggestions about closing the monasteries and using the revenue for education."

"A capital idea, Your Grace. I have considered it myself," said Philip.

Although Duke Ernst was anxious to move on, he realized it would be pointless to arrive in Speyer before Philip, who was one of the acknowledged leaders of the Reform-minded princes. So the party from Celle had a welcome respite from their journey and thoroughly enjoyed the rough-and-ready hospitality of the Hessians.

After a few days Philip had assembled his 'army' and once again they set out, on the winding mountain roads that led south to Frankfurt. This Imperial Free city was one of the fastest growing towns in Germany. Its book fairs were already famous, and it was rapidly becoming a financial center to rival Augsburg. The three merchants would have liked to spend more time there, but Ernst and Philip hurried them on. Frankfurt was also the last Lutheran town on their itinerary. Thereafter they crossed into the extensive domains of the Archbishop of Mainz. Immediately they noticed the difference. No longer were they made to feel welcome. The enmity of the border guards, and even of some of the people, was palpable.

At last they came to the great river Rhein, which they followed to Worms and thence to Speyer. Many of the delegates to the Diet had already arrived from all parts of Germany. Speyer was not a large town and space was at a premium. The princes, of course, were provided for, and their armed escorts were required to camp outside the town walls. But the in-between people such as Hinrik, Eggeling and Lüdeke were left to fend for themselves. Most of the inns were already full, but fortunately, Lüdeke's father had foreseen this problem and had given them a letter of introduction to one of the leading merchants of the town. The merchant's family opened their home to them, and their servants and horses found ample room in the stable, so they were luckier than most.

Most of the delegates were in high and hopeful spirits. At this point no one, even the most adamant followers of Luther, wanted a complete break with the Mother Church, but even the most conservative Catholics realized there could be no going back to the status quo. The mood was for reconciliation, but with freedom. Everyone felt that Charles would be in a receptive mood after his resounding victory at Pavia, during which he made the French king his prisoner. But before the opening of the Diet François I was back in France. The slippery Pope Clement VII did an about-face and, together with several Italian princes, made an alliance with François against the Emperor. So once again Charles was at war in Italy. To make matters worse, the Turks were overrunning Hungary on his eastern front.

Their first disappointment came when the Emperor's brother Archduke Ferdinand opened the Diet and announced that Charles would not be attending. The second, though not unexpected, was the betrayal of the Pope. Charles sent a message via his brother that the delegates were not to discuss certain reforms, especially those urging the separation of the secular from the religious, and that only a Church council called by the Pope could decide on these matters. Since the Emperor and the Pope were now bitter enemies, this was obviously impossible. This greatly strengthened the Lutheran cause, and even many of the Catholic princes became disgusted. The Diet concluded by passing a unanimous resolution that the

676

Edict of Worms could not be enforced and the princes "with their subjects would live, govern, and act in such a way as everyone trusted to justify before God and the Imperial Majesty". It was intended as a stopgap measure until such a council could be called, but it was to have powerful repercussions throughout the rest of the century.

On their way home Duke Ernst said to Landgraf Philip, "So you did not need your 'army' after all."

"Perhaps," replied Philip, "but it didn't hurt to show them our strength. I, for one, intend to call a council of my own in Hesse. This resolution has given us the right."

And Hinrik said to Eggeling, "See, my friend, you needn't have worried so. Both sides agreed that we may worship as justified before God."

"I am glad there was a compromise, but, my dear Hinrik, I think you are interpreting the Resolution too loosely. The choice is not ours but our Duke's."

"I am sure he will carry it out wisely," added Lüdeke.

But Eggeling shook his head doubtfully.

They arrived home to find that tragedy had struck Celle. Hinrik returned to a house in mourning.

He was greeted by a tearful Ilsebe. He hugged her to him as though he would never let her go. He was grateful that at least she appeared to be safe and well. "There, there, sweeting," he comforted. "I am home now. Dry your tears. Did you miss me so?"

"No—I mean yes," she sobbed. "Hinrik, Hinrik, your brother Berndt has been killed!"

"What? Killed?" he exclaimed. In a way Hinrik was not surprised. He had long feared that one of this brother's frequent tavern brawls would end in his death, but the truth was far worse than that. He led his wife into the big cozy kitchen and sat her before the fire.

"Now tell me what has happened. Can I fetch you a warm drink?"

She shook her head. "It happened about a month ago. We could not wait until your return to bury him."

"I understand. Go on."

"There was a riot against the Franciscans. Some of those ignorant boors who had listened to that rabble-rouser Wolf Cyclop started stirring up the common people. Onkel Lüdeke called out the Watch, but they couldn't control them. There were too many, and more and more kept joining them. They were throwing rocks and garbage and offal and shout-

677

ing obscenities at those poor innocent monks, who were doing nothing but going about their business. Oh, it was awful, Hinrik, shameful." She put her hands in his hands.

"And Berndt was among them?" he asked.

"No, no. You probably didn't notice since you came into town from the West Gate, but they are now working on the section of the east wall where it runs behind the garden of the cloister. Berndt was up on the wall, about halfway I should guess, tipsy as usual but definitely not drunk. O God, have mercy on his soul." She buried her face again.

Hinrik waited until she had control of herself again. "And he fell?" he asked.

"No, worse than that. One of the rocks that the rioters were throwing at the monks hit the man above him who was just steadying the huge stone to move it into place. The rock hit the man in the eye, and inadvertently he pushed back against the stone. It came tumbling down, taking the crane with it, and it crushed Berndt and the man below him."

"Oh, my God!" Hinrik turned white. "Dear God, have mercy. Holy Mother, pray for him."

"Oh, Hinrik, it was so horrible. I barely recognized his poor mangled body when they brought him home. I could not bring myself to lay him out although it was my duty. Thank God for Tante Anna, who called the laying-out ladies from Duchess Anna's home. They took care of everything for which I was grateful."

Hinrik held her tight within his arms for a long time. "Let your grief out, my love. I am here now to share the burden with you. I just hope no harm has come to you or the babe from this."

"To me none," she replied. "I thought I had myself all cried out, but the telling of it has brought it back so vividly. As for the babe, I have prayed constantly to our Blessed Mother and made an offering to the Goddess that there be no mark on him. But he seems to be normal and is kicking quite vigorously now." She took his hand and laid it on her now quite distended belly. "Say hello to your son, my dearest husband." After a moment he could feel the baby move within her. His eyes glowed with wonderment.

"My son," he breathed prayerfully.

"Would you be disappointed if it were a daughter?"

"I'll take whatever you and the good Lord give me, as long as it's healthy."

He sat down again. "Now tell me," he asked, "what of Balthasar? How is he taking it?"

"Very hard, very badly," she replied sadly. "He is my greatest worry. He has changed so you won't know him, Hinrik. He curses the mob, he curses the Barefoots, he even curses God at times, but most of all he blames himself."

"But why? Because he let Berndt work when he was tipsy?"

"Partly, but mostly because he feels he should have stopped all the work and called the men off the wall when the riot started. But who could have known it would get so violent or even reach that area? They've thrown stones before. Even the children do."

"I know. Was anyone else killed?"

"Not immediately, but the man who was blinded lived about a week and then died. The physicker said he was bleeding inside his brain, and although they bled him profusely, they couldn't save him. The four men inside the crane were badly hurt but live."

"Did they arrest the man who threw the rock? That is murder, you know."

She shook her head. "No, the rioters ran for their lives when the stone fell. And then another crowd of people trying to help gathered. So no one knows who it was. But, Hinrik, you must talk to Balthasar. He grows more despondent every day. He hardly eats. I doubt he sleeps much. He just sits here and stares into the fire for hours. You must convince him it was not his fault."

"I shall try. Where is he now?"

"Out on the wall, of course. He goes to his work every day, but his heart isn't in it. He has lost all his enthusiasm. Franz actually is doing most of the master work, and Balthasar simply watches. He is a broken man."

"Let us hope things quiet down now that the Duke is back."

"I'm not so sure," she replied. "Feelings are running too high in some quarters, and these people feel the Duke is being too lenient with the Franciscans. Even many intelligent people agree. Onkel Lüdeke and the Town Council are all for throwing them out of Celle, but the decision is up to His Grace. He must take a firm stand on the matter of the Barefoots or this will happen again, and next time it could be worse."

Hinrik shook his head in disbelief. "To think such a thing could happen in our beloved Celle. It has always been one of the most civilized and sophisticated towns in Germany."

"I hear it is happening everywhere. It is a sign of the times. People are confused and when ignorant people are confused they turn to violence."

"You must be very careful when you go out. I could not bear it should anything untoward happen to you or the babe."

"I am careful and I don't go out any more than I have to. And believe me, I stay far away from the vicinity of the Holy Cross. And anyway, pretty soon I'll not be able to go out at all. You and Mädl shall have to do all my errands." She laughed for the first time. "Here I am babbling on and on and I have not given you a proper welcome after being away almost three months. Would you like something to eat? And then tell me about Speyer."

"I think I can wait until suppertime, but I am a bit saddle weary. I think I should prefer a nap, and if you want to give me a proper welcome, you may join me upstairs. Speyer can wait." She eagerly followed him up to their bedchamber.

As the summer waned, the situation in Celle grew quieter, although there were still occasional sporadic outbreaks of violence against the Franciscans. With the Duke once again in residence, people hoped the worst was over. Yet many, including most of the leading citizens, strongly kept urging him to take a definite stand in the matter of the Barefoots.

Hinrik and Lüdeke were back at work in the von Sehnden counting-house and warehouses, so busy trying to catch up on all that had happened in their absence that Hinrik was scarcely aware of what was happening in the political and religious arena. He was very much aware, however, of what was happening at home. Balthasar continued to grow more despondent. Although he had brightened somewhat at Hinrik's return, the mood did not last. And now Hinrik seriously feared for his health—and even his sanity.

Toward the end of summer the Duke had the Resolution of Speyer read from the Stadtkirche's pulpit, from the steps of the Town Hall, and in all the public places of Celle, adding his own resolution that from hence-forth the official religion of the town would be the teachings of Dr. Martin Luther, with the entire Duchy soon to follow.

"What about the Barefoots?" shouted someone in the crowd.

"Ja, doesn't that apply to them, too?" yelled another.

Small outbreaks of violence began again. The Duke tried to negotiate civilly with the Franciscans, urging them to convert, as had so many monasteries throughout Germany, but the Abbot firmly refused and eventually ceased all discussion with the secular authorities.

One day there came an urgent pounding on the countinghouse door. When the clerk opened it, one of Balthasar's laborers rushed in. "Master

Stockman," he gasped, out of breath, "come quick. Your Papa. He has fallen down."

Hinrik threw down his pen. "Take me to him." He followed the man, his gown flapping behind. "Is he bad hurt?" he asked.

"Not hurt, Master, but I fear very sick."

They ran through the town as though demons were after them to the spot below the wall where Balthasar lay. Someone had fetched a blanket and they had laid him on it. Someone else had stuffed an old tunic under his head. Franz was kneeling beside him holding his hand. Balthasar's other hand was pressed to his chest, and he was breathing with great difficulty.

Hinrik knelt on his other side. "Papa, Papa," he cried, "what has happened?"

"Ah, thank God you are here, my son," whispered Balthasar. "I am dying, Hinrik. My old heart . . ." He gasped for breath. Hinrik held his other hand tightly. "No, no, Papa, you will be all right. Try to rest now, and don't talk." And to his brother, "Has the doctor been sent for?"

"Ja, ja," Franz assured him, "and the priest, too."

But Balthasar persisted. "My old heart is tired. I am leaving you soon to go to my beloved Catherina." Hinrik began to weep at this, and he noticed his brother choking up, too. "Hear me now," continued the old man with great difficulty. "My will . . . is in . . . the—the great chest in—in . . ."

"In your bedchamber?"

He nodded. "And Master von—von . . ."

"Von Sehnden?"

He nodded again but could speak no more.

"Has a copy?"

His nod was barely discernible.

Someone brought a cup of water, which Hinrik placed to his lips, but he could not drink.

The doctor and the priest arrived together. The doctor put his ear to his chest, listening intently, and rose shaking his head. "He has had a heart attack. If he lives through the night until this time tomorrow, he may recover. There is nothing we can do but pray."

The priest was about to take over when someone cried, "Give way, give way." Ilsebe lumbered through the crowd of onlookers as fast as her bulk would permit. She was due in a few weeks.

"Give him air," she cried as she knelt clumsily beside Balthasar.

681

Hinrik was shocked. "Goodwife," he exclaimed, "what are you doing here? You shouldn't be abroad."

"How could I stay away?" she snapped back. "Convention be damned." She took the cup of water and wet a rag to cool Balthasar's forehead. She squeezed a few drops through his parched lips. The old man's eyes brightened a bit. He seemed to be trying to say something but could not. She leaned over and kissed his forehead. "Papa, I love you. Go with God," she whispered and then beckoned to the priest.

The priest gave Balthasar the last rites in the old way, and no one seemed to notice the difference. Dr. Luther had not yet clarified some of those things. The words seemed to comfort the old man, and soon Hinrik felt the hand he was holding weaken in his grip. A terrible rasping sound came from Balthasar's throat and he was gone.

Hinrik and Franz wept unashamedly where they knelt on the cobblestones. Many of the workmen did as well. The priest tried to comfort them, but Ilsebe indicated no, let them cry it out, they would be the better for it. Someone started an Ave and was quickly shushed. The priest recited the Twenty-third Psalm instead.

Hinrik felt his wife's gentle touch on his shoulder. "Come we must take him home," she said.

Hinrik arose stiffly and six of the stonecutters and laborers lifted the blanket and bore their Master to the house. Ilsebe sent for the laying-out ladies and took Hinrik upstairs to bed.

Hinrik and Franz took turns for the day-long and all-night vigils. Work was temporarily suspended on the wall, and all of the workers and many other townspeople came to pay their last respects, for Balthasar had been well loved by his men and highly respected in the town as well. The elder von Sehnden came immediately, and Tante Anna took over the feeding of the many guests to spare Ilsebe, who was exhausted both physically and emotionally. Many of the workers' wives sent food as well.

On the second day the Duke himself visited briefly, and the family felt greatly honored. "He did well by me," said Ernst, "and by my grandmother also. See that you do as well," he said to Franz and officially appointed him the new Master Mason of the wall.

After His Grace left, the Bürgermeister called Hinrik aside. "Have you read his will as yet?"

"Nay, Onkel Lüdeke," replied Hinrik, "my grief is so great, I haven't given it a thought. He was a real father to me, though not my own. I shall miss him terribly."

"So shall we all," agreed Lüdeke, "but take a look at it first chance you get. It may cheer you up a bit, for he loved you dearly. After the burial we'll talk."

He left quickly and Hinrik's curiosity was piqued. As soon as he could get away from the visitors during Franz's turn to sit with the dead, he went up to Balthasar's chambers and opened the great chest at the foot of the bed. There were many mementos of his mother, and these brought fresh tears to Hinrik's eyes and he almost dreaded looking further. But close to the top was the last testament of Balthasar Murmester.

Hinrik slowly unrolled the parchment. He recognized the fine hand of the Bürgermeister's chief town clerk. So, thought Hinrik, Onkel Lüdeke has had a hand in this. He sat down to read.

It was very brief. After the usual preamble asking for God's mercy on his soul Balthasar said: "To my son Franz Stockman, who has helped me so much, I bequeath my whole business and all my tools and clothes. To my son Hinrik Stockman I bequeath all my savings and investments which are in the care of Master von Sehnden, in order that he may have his own business, as well as the dwelling house on Schuhstrasse. To my beloved daughter, Ilsebe Stockman, I bequeath all my late wife's jewelry."

Hinrik sat with his mouth open and quickly breathed a fervent prayer for Balthasar's soul. Then he rushed to tell Ilsebe.

"I wonder how much it is," she said.

"I can't imagine," replied Hinrik, "but at the time he had this written, he must have thought it was enough for me to start my own business."

"With Onkel Lüdeke advising him, it must be," she agreed.

"And that is why Onkel Lüdeke wishes to speak to me after the funeral. He said it would cheer me up, and for all my grief, I must admit that it has. Oh, Ilsebe, I can't wait." He patted her belly. "Mayhap it won't be long before this little one can call his Papa Master Stockman!"

Ilsebe smiled. "And this beautiful, big house, too, all our very own. God willing, we shall fill it with children."

"Just have this one safely, my little river sprite, and we shall see about that." He leaned over and kissed her. Hugging was almost impossible now. "I must go and tell Franz."

"I hope he won't be disappointed."

"I think not. He lives the business just as Balthasar did. He will be quite satisfied."

The day of the funeral was raining and miserable as late September

683

often could be. A sharp wind blew off the river. Hinrik forbade Ilsebe to attend. Although originally she had been insistent on doing so, this morning she readily agreed.

"I don't feel too well," she admitted. "It's this awful weather. I think I shall bide the whole day in my bed."

Hinrik heaved a sigh of relief. She could be very stubborn at times.

The bearers arrived very early and carried Balthasar's body to the church. After a brief service—no Mass—the procession wound through the town to the Hehlentor, across the Aller bridge to the old Bürger cemetery on the hillside opposite. There the eulogies were long and sonorous as the company stood shivering in the rain. Finally, they laid Balthasar to rest.

Ilsebe lay on the big bed listening to the rain, myriad thoughts running through her head. She hoped Hinrik would not take a chill, although she had insisted he don his heavy cloak. She could not imagine why she felt so listless. The babe was not due for at least two more weeks. It had to be exhaustion from all the emotional strain of the past few days. She was alone in the house. Even Mädl, the housekeeper, had gone to the funeral. The house creaked and groaned as Ilsebe watched the rain stream down the window. She started to doze as her thoughts turned to Balthasar's will. I hope it will be enough. I shall help Hinrik every way I can.

Suddenly a sharp pain knifed through her dreams. Oh, no, it can't be. Not yet. The midwife was not due to move in for another week and there was no one to send for her. It must be a false alarm. It has to be. The pain subsided and she decided to ignore it. Then she felt an urgent need to relieve her bladder. She struggled up groggily to use the chamber pot. She sat for a moment on the edge of the bed until she got her bearings. She tried to stand, but her legs wouldn't seem to work. Suddenly she felt the rush of water. For a moment she stared stupidly at the puddle on the floor. She could feel her sodden shift. Oh, no, it can't be. Not yet, she convinced herself. Oh, yes, it is, said her common sense. What do I do now?

Another pain shot through her. She lay back on the bed. They say it takes hours and hours, especially for a first one. I shall just wait. Someone will be here soon. If not, I shall simply birth it myself, she told herself with more bravado than she really felt. She tried to make herself more comfortable, tried to force herself to sleep, but this time she could not.

The pains were coming at regular intervals now, although still not too close together. She knew there was time. Someone must come soon. What was keeping them? How long does it take to bury a body? Oh, forgive me, dear Lord. Balthasar was a good man, the only father both Hinrik and I have known. They have to take time to do him honor.

She thought to call to a passerby in the street, but with the rain few were abroad. She doubted she could get to the window anyhow. There, at last, she thought she heard the front door open.

She called out, "Hinrik, Hinrik, help me!"

No answer. It must have been the wind.

Mädl, in fact, had come in, but she had gone straight back to the warm kitchen to shed her wet clothes and did not hear Ilsebe.

She must have dozed between the pains, because suddenly she woke up screaming and Hinrik was there beside her.

"What is wrong, sweeting?"

"Oh, Hinrik," she cried, "you're here at last. The baby is coming. Send for Frau Lindemann."

"Oh, Blessed Mother! Are you sure?"

"Of course, I'm sure," she snapped and clutched her belly as another pain hither.

"I'll be right back. You stay right there," he said and fled.

Foolish man, she almost laughed despite her discomfort. Does he think I am going anywhere?

Hinrik rushed to the kitchen but did not have the heart to send Mädl out into the weather again. "See to your mistress. The babe is a-borning. Do what needs be while I fetch the midwife." He ran out of the house.

Frau Lindemann arrived with her assistant carrying the birthing chair as calmly as if she were going to Saturday market. Instead of going straight upstairs, she first went into the kitchen to instruct Mädl, who was already heating water and collecting clean cloths. Frau Lindemann asked for a cup of coffee and sat down at the kitchen table as Mädl served her.

"Hurry! Hurry!" urged Hinrik.

"My good master, calm yourself," said Frau Lindemann deliberately. "Think you not that I know my own business. Do I tell you how to sell cloth? It will be hours yet, mayhap days."

"Oh, no," said Hinrik.

"Oh yes. Go take a walk, visit your friends, seek solace in a tavern, whatever, but stay out from underfoot. Better yet out of the house," she instructed firmly.

Hinrik went back up to Ilsebe.

"Frau Lindemann is here. She will be up shortly," he told her.

"Oh, thank God's Blessed Mother."

685

"How do you feel?"

"Terrible."

"She said it will be hours yet."

"I know, but I'm beginning to be a little afraid." She took Hinrik's hand. "Stay with me, my love."

"I don't think she will let me. She told me to get out of the house."

"Oh, my." Ilsebe smiled. "Then I suppose you had better. My friends tell me she can be an old termagant if her orders are not followed, but she is said to be the best midwife in Celle."

"That is why I engaged her, but I didn't expect to be thrown out of my own house."

Another pain grabbed Ilsebe and Hinrik held her hand until it subsided. "I suppose you'd better obey her," said Ilsebe. "Go to see Tante Anna. She will calm you, and she should be told anyway."

"I suppose so, but I hate to leave you at a time like this."

At this point the midwife entered the room. "At a time like this we don't need nervous husbands in the way." She pointed to the door. "Out!"

Hinrik quickly kissed his wife and fled.

He found Anna von Sehnden in her library with a cheery fire burning on the hearth. It was a welcome haven on a dismal day.

"Tante Anna," he exclaimed, "the babe is coming!"

"Ah, so," she said calmly. "A little early, but I'm not surprised with all the strain of the past days. Sit down, Hinrik, and have a cup of coffee."

"But, Tante," he began as he paced back and forth. "I—I am too nervous."

"Hinrik, sit down and have a cup of coffee," she repeated.

"Oh, you women! You act as though—as though . . . "

"As though it were a perfectly natural, everyday happening, which it is. Now sit down," she ordered sternly.

Hinrik sat.

She poured a cup for him from an ornate pewter coffeepot. "I was just about to have a cup myself. Would you care for one of these little cakes? They're quite delicious."

"No, no thank you, Tante. I'm too—too nervous."

She laughed. "Calm yourself down, my son. You know, one of the things my Lüdeke has always admired about you is your calmness in the face of any business or financial crisis. You always keep a cool head and think things out carefully rather than panic as some would."

Hinrik stared at her. "But—but this is entirely different," he blurted.

"Only in that it's not a crisis. And it is your own personal creation. I'm sure you had fun when you put that babe in her belly."

"Tante Anna!" Hinrik turned beet red. Then he agreed almost ashamedly, "I suppose I did."

"Then think of the joy this little one will bring you."

"Oh, yes. We've been so happy about it, but now I worry about Ilsebe."

"She is very young, strong and healthy. She should have no problem."

"And I do hope it is not an evil omen for it to be born the very day we have buried Balthasar."

"Nay, nay, never that. In fact, I should say it is a good omen. A life for a life. The good Lord takes one and immediately gives one back. Think of it that way."

"Tante Anna, you are so wise."

"And what will you name this precious child?"

"Ilsebe wants to name him after me, but perhaps in view of what you have said we should call him Balthasar."

"No, no, never that. Hinrik is better. After all, it is your firstborn."

"Yes, I suppose you're right."

"And what if it is a girl?"

"We hadn't really thought."

"Then may I suggest you name her after her mother?"

Anna kept Hinrik talking about this and that for as long as she could, but finally he could contain his anxiety no longer. He stood up.

"I must go back and see what is happening. Thank you, Tante. I feel calmer now."

Anna doubted that this was so but only said, "I shall go with you to see if I can be of any help. Just let me fetch my cloak."

When they arrived at the house, they went immediately upstairs.

Frau Lindemann opened the door. "I thought I told you . . . Ah, Mistress von Sehnden, how nice to see you. Everything is going well. It should not be more than another hour or two. We'll put her in the birthing chair soon."

"Another hour . . ." Hinrik started to exclaim, but shut his mouth when Anna laid her hand on his arm.

"Can I be of any help?" she asked the midwife.

"Not right now, Mistress, thank you. Perhaps later. For now just keep this young man out of our way."

687

Anna led Hinrik back downstairs and into the kitchen. Mädl was busy heating huge kettles of water over the fire.

"I'm afraid it will be a cold supper tonight, Master Hinrik," she said.

"I couldn't eat anyway. Don't worry about it."

Both women laughed. "You will, you will, once the babe is born," said the housekeeper. "She's doing very nicely for a first one. It shouldn't be too much longer." She picked up a stack of clean linen and left them.

Time dragged for Hinrik. He fidgeted and fussed. Anna tried to keep him talking, but the conversation lagged. He seemed hardly aware of what she was saying, so she finally gave up. They sat in companionable silence, and he seemed to be praying. She added a few of her own.

It grew dark early because of the rain.

"Candles," he murmured. "We need a light. And I don't even know where she keeps them," he admitted shamefacedly. He got up and started rummaging through the cupboards.

Just then Mädl returned. "Get out of my cupboards before you mess everything up." She fetched a candle and lit it for them, then took two more and went back upstairs.

"You see, I am not even master in my own home," sighed Hinrik.

Anna laughed. "Lüdeke is the same. He can tell you the whereabouts of every ell of cloth in his warehouse, yea, every quill in the counting-house, but he is lost in the kitchen. 'Tis better so. We women have to have someplace to call our own."

"I guess so," said Hinrik and sat down again.

Just then a chilling scream came from above. Hinrik jumped up, but Anna laid a restraining hand on his arm. "Not yet," she said. "It is the worst possible time for you to be underfoot. It is almost over. Close your ears." Another scream pierced the silence. And then another.

Mädl came scurrying down for a kettle of water. "The head is almost out," she said, and Anna followed her up.

"Stay here till we call you," she warned Hinrik.

Hinrik found himself breaking out in a sweat although his hands were like ice. He paced back and forth, but he obeyed. Another scream, then silence. And suddenly he heard a faint, mewling cry, such as he had never heard before. My son, my son is born, he said to himself. He wanted to rush up but dared not. He sat down again and thought he would faint.

It seemed forever until he heard Anna calling his name. "Hinrik, you may come up now."

He mounted the stairs slowly. He felt weak in the knees. Imagine how Ilsebe must feel, he thought contritely. Anna was standing in the doorway of the bedchamber holding a tiny bundle.

"Hinrik, you have a lovely daughter," she said.

"Daughter?" he said vaguely. "But how is my dear wife?"

"Tired, but fine."

He barely glanced at the infant as he rushed to Ilsebe's side. Mädl and the midwife's assistant were gathering up bloody sheets and cloths. Mädl carried a pail of what looked like bloody fish guts out the door. He tried not to look as his eyes sought his wife. She had on a clean shift and was covered to the chin, with a huge feather pillow under her head. She looked exhausted but radiant.

He took her hand and leaned over to kiss her. "How are you, my dearest love?"

"I am fine," she replied. "A little tired, a little sore, but fine. Frau Lindemann said I did very well for a first time. It wasn't a long labor at all."

"Not long? It seemed like eons."

"Not long at all," said the midwife. "Some go on for as much as two days. She is well built for bearing children."

Anna came over then and placed the little bundle in Ilsebe's arms. "Hinrik, meet your daughter, little Ilsebe," she said.

He looked at the funny little wrinkled face, and his heart melted. My very own, he thought, and immediately loved her. He put a finger out and the tiny hand clutched it.

"Tante Anna said you wanted to name her after me," said his wife. "That makes me so proud. I'm sorry I couldn't give you a son, but, God willing, maybe next time."

He choked up. "I shall cherish her all the same," he said wonderingly. "A baby river sprite."

Ilsebe smiled and the midwife looked puzzled. "Let her rest now, Master, and in a couple of hours see that she gets some rich nourishing broth." She and her assistant packed up their gear and left.

Anna took Hinrik by the arm and led him downstairs.

The next day he went to see Lüdeke von Sehnden.

"I hear congratulations are in order," said the Bürgermeister.

"Thank you," replied Hinrik. "With all this excitement, I haven't given Balthasar's legacy a thought, but now that I am a father, I must needs know the details."

"I think you will be pleasantly surprised. There is more than enough

689

to set yourself up nicely in business, enough to purchase a good supply of cloth when next you go to Antwerp, perhaps even another boat, if you're so minded."

Hinrik gasped. "I had no idea Balthasar was so rich."

"Not rich, really, but a very thrifty man who saved every penny he could over a long lifetime. A frugal man who rarely, if ever, indulged himself in any luxuries. And don't forget, once you and Franz were grown, you supported the household so he could save even more, and the house was given to him free and clear. There were times that you probably did not know about when the Duke, and before him the late Duchess Anna, rewarded Balthasar handsomely above his normal compensation. She especially was greatly pleased with the church tower, which they are now talking about tearing down. I am glad neither of them lived to hear that."

"I, too," agreed Hinrik. "But how much in actual cash money, Onkel Lüdeke?"

Lüdeke named a figure that far surpassed Hinrik's wildest imaginings, even after the buildup. "And all in good silver Lübeckerthalers. It rests in a strong coffer at my house. I did not want to leave it here at the Rathaus or in my countinghouse for fear it would inadvertently get mixed with town monies or my own business. Besides, if it had been at the countinghouse, you would have wondered what it was." He laughed.

Hinrik laughed with him. "I expect I would have. Oh, Onkel Lüdeke, I can't believe my good fortune."

"There is more. In addition to the silver, he also invested some, on my advice, mostly in Hamburg. You are free to draw on it should the need arise. Otherwise let it earn interest."

"I shall need your help and advice to get started!"

"Freely given, but for one year only. You have been well trained. You should not need much. Moreover, I shall rent you one of my small warehouses for one year, until you can buy your own. Also, if you're of a mind to buy another boat, you may rent some space in one of my granaries. But all for one year only. After that we become competitors. Or, more likely, you shall compete with young Lüdeke, as I'm getting old and have a mind to step down in a few years."

Hinrik laughed. "You, I would fear. With young Lüdeke I think I can compete fairly, perhaps even best him."

"That would not surprise me. But he is coming along nicely and beginning to settle down. Next we must find a wife for him."

Hinrik smiled at that. If he knew his friend, Lüdeke would want to find his own wife. So all he said was, "Onkel Lüdeke, you can't imagine how much I appreciate all your help and advice. I am sure one year will be ample time, perhaps less. I can't wait to get started."

"There is one thing more, and this is a gift of sorts," said the Bürgermeister. "When next you go to Antwerp, advise Master Titze that he is now in your employ, your factor there."

"I had a suspicion you might say that. Thank you again. He is a good man."

"And in one year I promise you shall be a full-fledged member of the Gewandschneider. I shall sponsor you for associate membership immediately."

This to Hinrik was the crowning glory.

Hinrik prospered and Ilsebe bore babies—girls, that is. The second a year later they named Katharina after his mother. Two years later a third was named Anna after Anna von Sehnden. The von Sehnden and Franz's wife stood godparents for all of them.

Meanwhile the situation with the Franciscans worsened. In October the preachers of the Stadkirche offered to have an open discussion and, hopefully, a peaceful reconciliation of their differences with the monks before the Duke and the Town Council. In a fiery letter to the Duke, the Abbot rejected their suggestion out of hand. Thereafter the Duke had no choice but to order the cloister vacated, which he did on the day after Epiphany 1527. Still in the Christian spirit, however, he offered to care for the elderly monks under the auspices of the Church and Town. Those who wished to become preachers in the church could do so, and the others would be taught a trade so that they might earn their living in the world. The monks stubbornly turned down the offer. At last, in 1528, Ernst lost all patience and ordered the cloister torn down and the monks were left to fend for themselves.

Encouraged by this example, Chancellor Johann Förster, still struggling to make ends meet after the horrific indebtedness of the Duke's wayward father, suggested to Ernst that all the monasteries and convents in the Duchy be secularized. Already partial to the idea through the influence of his cousin-in-law Elisabeth and Philip of Hesse, Ernst readily agreed. With the Reformation rapidly being accepted throughout the Duchy, it should have been easily carried out. The churches were given three years to make financial arrangements with the Duchy treasury, with their income-producing properties coming under State administration.

691

The cloisters were to be adequately provided for by the State, and their surplus assets were to be distributed to poor and needy churches. Förster, however, ran into some unexpected opposition from a number of the nobility who derived a great part of their income from these monasterial properties under the old feudal system. Some of them, in fact, chose to remain Catholic for this reason alone. And in all, it took ten years to accomplish this, and by that time the Reformation was well established in all of northern Germany.

In 1529 another Imperial Diet was called at Speyer. Charles promised his imminent arrival in Germany, but once again the Emperor's message was delivered by Ferdinand. In it Charles declared that since his reconciliation with the Pope a Church council was a possibility, the Resolution of 1526 was null and void, and no religious 'irregularities' were to be permitted until such council met. The Catholic majority went along with the proposal, but the Lutheran minority wrote a formal protestation, which stated that under the laws of the Empire a unanimous decision could not be abrogated by a simple majority. From this came the first use of the term Protestant. Duke Ernst was one of the signatories.

In 1530 Charles called another Diet, this time at Augsburg, a very Lutheran city, and actually presided over the meeting. And this time the Lutheran Electors and Princes were better prepared. Although Luther himself was still under the Ban of the Empire and attendance could have cost him his life, he had Melanchton draw up a document consisting of twenty-one articles of faith and seven on rights, called the Augustana, better known as the Augsburg Confession. Luther encouraged the delegates with a torrent of letters from Castle Coburg. Duke Ernst was the main sponsor and a prime signatory of the Augustana, which earned him the sobriquet Ernst der Bekenner—or Ernst the Confessor.

The Catholic theologians wrote a Confutatio, which advocated nothing more than a return to the old ways, and when Charles presented it to the Diet he said it cancelled all intermediate Diets and returned to the despised Edict of Worms. Philip of Hesse rode off in disgust without even taking leave of the Emperor. The other princes remained for a month in order not to offend and tried to negotiate, but Charles would not listen and the princes remained firm in their support of the Confession. Great pressure was brought on the scattered cities and towns to recant, but they, too, all held firm. Even Augsburg, with the Emperor within its walls and surrounded by Catholic Bavaria, remained staunchly Lutheran. Nothing was accomplished however, and after the Protestants departed, the remaining Catholic delegates voted to return to the Edict of Worms. When Charles asked them for their monetary and military help in enforcing it, however, no such aid was forthcoming. Charles realized the weakness of his position and gave the Lutherans a year in which to conform.

Rather than conformation, the Lutheran princes and cities, none of whom trusted Charles not to take up arms against them, on 27 February 1531, entered into a defense alliance called the League of Schmalkalden. Again Ernst and Philip were among the leaders. Six princes and ten cities signed the original charter, with four more important towns joining in the next few months. Over the next several years almost all the Protestant estates in Germany became members. Most importantly, they overcame Luther's personal aversion to opposing the Imperial authority. Thus were religion and politics joined to set the scene in Germany for more than a century.

Hinrik Stockman did not attend any of these Diets. He was too busy organizing and building up his new business. The Duke respected that and thankfully did not ask him.

He did, however, ask Eggeling von Eltze, who very tactfully refused. When Duke Ernst returned from Augsburg full of enthusiasm for the Confession and the solidarity of the Lutherans, he called Eggeling to attend him.

"Eggeling, it appears to me that you are not happy," he said.

Eggeling was still ambivalent about the religious conflict, although less so since Speyer. He regularly attended church, although he was not too pleased with the new rites. He was very upset about the brusque treatment accorded the Franciscans, but he could not tell the Duke that.

"Thank you for your concern, Your Grace," he replied. "I am well and enjoy my work. Happiness does not enter into it."

"You need a wife," said the Duke.

Eggeling permitted himself a faint smile. "Perhaps, Your Grace, but I have not as yet found anyone to my liking. If it is to be, God will provide, I am sure."

"I am sure," agreed Ernst. "Perhaps a change of scene, then?"

Eggeling looked at him with raised eyebrows. What did he have in mind? "Your Grace is not satisfied with my work?" he asked.

"Eminently satisfied, but collecting tolls cannot be very stimulating to one of your intelligence. You have great talents I should like to use."

"Thank you for the compliment, Your Grace, but how so?"

"I have a small fief for which I need a steward. It is a little village called Bissendorf, not far from Lüneburg. Would you be interested in the office?"

Eggeling hesitated. "I don't know, Your Grace. Tell me more about it."

"As my personal representative you would be totally in charge. They have no Bürgermeister or council. You would be the sole administrator, responsible for keeping the peace and making legal decisions. You would collect all taxes and fees due me and see that the monies are safely sent to the treasury in Lüneburg. Much of the fees would be in kind, and this would have to be sold at market, although you may keep a certain percentage for your own use. It is basically a little farming community, although there may be a few craftsmen now. I don't really know. The peasants have always been well behaved and very loyal to me, so you should have no trouble there."

Eggeling thought about this as the Duke spoke. Would he be satisfied in a tiny rural backwater, he who was town-born and -bred? Yet the work seemed challenging. He would be totally on his own, responsible only to the Duke. Perhaps it might be good to get away for a while from the hustle and busyness of Celle—and the conflict. And, yes, he had to admit, it might even be good to get away from his domineering mother. He quickly put that disloyal thought from his head.

"It sounds interesting, Your Grace," he said, "but I should like some little time to think about it, if I may."

"That you may, but not too long, for if you're not interested I must needs find someone else."

"Of course, Your Grace. What about housing?"

"There is a small manor house with servants to care for it and you. Nothing so luxurious as your mother's grand house, I'm afraid, but more than adequate."

"And I shall need time to set my business in order."

"A fortnight should be enough for that. From what I hear, your business is so well organized it can run by itself."

Eggeling laughed. "It took a lot of hard work to get it that way. Thank you, Your Grace. I shall give you my decision in a fortnight or less."

The Duke gave Eggeling permission to retire.

Eggeling decided to accept the appointment. His friends received his news with mixed emotions.

"We shall miss you, Eggeling," said Hinrik. "Our little group will not

694

be the same without you. We have been so close."

"I'm not leaving forever, you know," replied Eggeling. "Four or five years is probably all I can take. I'll be back, never fear."

"And think of the great experience," said Lüdeke. "When you return, we'll elect you Bürgermeister."

Eggeling laughed. "I hardly think administering a tiny village like Bissendorf will qualify me for governing a great town like Celle."

"And try to get into Lüneburg often," added Peter. "It is a charming town, very cultural. Perhaps you'll meet someone."

Eggeling laughed again. "That would be an added benefit, but I'm not counting on it."

Lüdeke von Sehnden the Younger was thoroughly engrossed in the family business. With his best friend, Hinrik, now in competition and a fellow member of the prestigious Gewandschneider he had to devote all his time to it. And as he gained more experience, his father gave him more and more responsibility. But one fine late spring Saturday afternoon he was at loose ends. Eggeling was gone, Hinrik in Antwerp at the moment, Peter off somewhere. Lüdeke didn't want to go to the coffeehouse alone. His mother's library held no appeal on such a beautiful day. Anyway, though highly intelligent, he admitted he was not the intellectual that Hinrik was. What to do? Should I saddle up my horse and ride out into the countryside? But I don't really feel like going alone.

He stood at his bedroom window looking down at his mother's lovely garden. The apple and pear trees were in luxuriant bloom. Bright daffodils and tulips made splotches of color all over. His gaze wandered to the yard behind. It actually belonged to a house around the corner on Poststrasse. He wondered if he would see the girl. Yes, there she was seated on a swing someone had hung from a branch of the great linden tree. She looked so charming and carefree as she glided gently back and forth. He had been watching her for some weeks now and longed to meet her. If only the fence between were not so high, he would go down right now and say something. But he might frighten her. He knew who she was—Margarete Rüschers—but he had never met her. Her father was a goldsmith. Although the goldsmiths' guild was the second-most prestigious and powerful in Celle, they were far below the Gewandschneider on the social scale. They simply did not move in the same circles as the close-knit Gewandschneider. His family would probably look down on hers. Yet he just had to meet her. But how?

695

He went downstairs and out the back door. No one else was at home. He strolled along the fence to see if perhaps he could catch a glimpse of her from here. Ah, there was a loose board. He wiggled the board until it came off. There, now he could see her. She had left the swing and was picking a bouquet of flowers. Suddenly brash Lüdeke was tongue-tied.

Gathering up all his courage, he called, "Good afternoon, Fräulein."

She was so startled she almost dropped her flowers. "Who is that?" she managed to get out.

"Over here by the fence," he said. "Your neighbor Lüdeke von Sehnden."

"Oh, my goodness," she said, "you gave me a fright. I thought it was a spirit out of the tree. What are you doing there?" She turned to face him but did not approach the fence.

"Talking to you, I hope."

"Well, Lüdeke von Sehnden," she said, somewhat indignantly, "that is hardly a proper way to meet a young maid."

I hope she's not going to be stuffy, he thought. "I am sorry if I startled you. I—I saw you from the upstairs window. I mean I wasn't spying on you. I mean, I just happened to see you." Inwardly he cursed himself for being so tongue-tied. What was wrong with him? "You were swinging and you looked so happy, I just wanted to—I mean, it's such a beautiful day."

"Just what do you mean, Master von Sehnden?" she asked, but her tone was somewhat gentler.

I am certainly making a mess of this, thought Lüdeke, but she's not running away, at least. "Perhaps you would like me to push you," he suggested. "It's ever so much more fun than swinging by yourself."

"I agree, but I hardly see how you can push me from the other side of the fence." She laughed, and her face seemed even lovelier.

"You could invite me over," he suggested.

She laughed again. "Aside from the fact that it would be highly improper, I fail to believe you could squeeze yourself through that tiny crack in the fence."

"Well, I . . ." Lüdeke blushed.

She held up a hand. "Don't even think about tearing down your mother's fence. I fear she would be quite upset."

Lüdeke felt like a fool. "Well, I—I've been wanting to meet you for a long time," he stammered.

"Have you now?" she teased. "Then I would suggest that there are more appropriate ways to become acquainted with a proper young maid."

He realized she was giving him an opening, but his brain refused to function logically. "I suppose you are right, and I apologize for frightening you. It was just an impulse." He was about to turn away in embarrassment, but she sweetly rescued him.

"No need to apologize," she said. "I am complimented by your impulsiveness. But, Master Gewandschneider, do you run your business on impulse?"

Lüdeke blushed again, "No, of course not. My father would disown me."

"Then mayhap I must think for both of us. That is, if you really want to become acquainted with me."

"Oh, but I do, I do," he protested. "What do you suggest?"

"Do you go to church?" she asked.

"Most Sundays," he admitted.

"Then it should not be difficult to strike up a conversation on the church porch tomorrow, and since we are neighbors, no one would think it amiss if you were to walk home with me."

"A brilliant idea. Why didn't I think of that?"

"Because methinks you attend church rather reluctantly and cannot wait to rush off afterwards to the coffeehouse with your friends."

Lüdeke was amazed. "Why, you know more about me than I do of you."

She laughed again. "Perhaps now you will open your eyes. I must go in now. Until tomorrow."

"I'll be there," he said joyfully.

The next morning Lüdeke was up early and dressed in his best. Anna was amazed because lately she had often to drag him to Sunday worship. Since his father was Bürgermeister, the von Sehnden pew was perforce at the very front of the church, which made it difficult for Lüdeke to see whether Margarete was in attendance. He could not obviously turn around and look for her, although before the service began he did manage a few quick glances over his shoulder in either direction, but he did not see her. They stood for the opening hymn, and he sang lustily, if a bit off-key. Several rows behind him he could hear a light but very sweet voice. I wonder if that is she, he thought. The sermon was long and repetitive, and he tried not to fidget. At last the choir left, singing a glorious Rogation Day hymn about planting and seed growing and all the blessings of spring. After the closing prayers he wanted to run down the aisle to be the first one out so as not to miss her, but his mother stopped to chat with someone and he could not squeeze past. At last he managed to edge around her and push his way through the crowd. People glared at him, but he did not care.

Margarete, however, was prepared for this. When Lüdeke reached the church porch, he saw her gossiping with another young girl, but she was very obviously watching for him. He slowed himself down and nonchalantly strolled up to her.

"Good morning, Fräulein Rüschers."

She pretended surprise. "Why, good morning, Master von Sehnden. How are you today?"

"Very well. And isn't it a beautiful spring day?"

"Quite delightful," she replied,

At that moment her father, Hans, called to her, "Come, Gretchen, we are going home now. It appears your mother has finally finished her gossip."

"Yes, Papa, coming."

"Since we are going in the same direction," suggested Lüdeke, "may I accompany you?"

"I should be charmed to have you," she replied.

Just then Lüdeke the Elder and Anna emerged from the church. "Where is Lüdeke?" asked his father.

"Probably off to the coffeehouse," said Anna. "Oh, no, there he is."

"Isn't that Hans Rüschers' girl with him? Don't tell me he's involved with her."

"He can hardly be, since it appears they have just met," replied Anna. "And so what if he is? It's time he settled down."

"But she is not a Gewandschneider daughter."

"Oh, Lüdeke," chided Anna. "Don't be such a snob."

Although it was but a short walk from the church to their homes, the young couple dragged their feet as slowly as possible to make it last. When they finally reached her doorstep, Lüdeke asked, "May I walk out with you this afternoon after dinner?"

"You shall have to ask Papa," she said. Hans was just entering the house when she called after him, "Papa!" He turned to look at them and seemed to see Lüdeke for the first time. "This is Lüdeke von Sehnden."

"I know," Hans replied gruffly.

"Papa, he craves your permission to walk out with me this afternoon."

"Cannot he speak for himself?" asked Hans.

Lüdeke was about to reply when her mother immediately sized up the situation. "Oh, I think that would be lovely," she chirped. She knew a

698

good catch when she saw one. "It is such a fine day for a walk. We shall be done with dinner in about two hours."

"Oh, very well," grumbled Hans.

"Thank you, Master, Mistress," said Lüdeke, and to Margarete, "I shall call on you then."

She smiled and waved to him as she followed her parents into the house. Her father mumbled, "Women!"

In 1535 Lüdeke and Margarete were wed, much to Lüdeke the Elder's disgust, Anna's gratification, Margarete's mother's delight, and her father's reluctant admiration for he had finally grown to like Lüdeke and realized what a step up the social ladder this marriage represented for his daughter.

9

 The same year, to the west in Grafschaft Hoya across the Weser, Jacob Bruns drove his wagon up to the Cloister Mill at Heiligenberg. As he off-loaded his bags of grain, the miller came out to greet him. The monk had grown much friendlier in the past few months.

"Ho, there, Brother Paulus," shouted Jacob above the noise of the millrace. "What news?"

"Just more of the same," replied the miller. "Some are leaving; some are staying. Some are converting to the new learning, some are holding firm to the old."

Jacob nodded. "Ja, I can see where it would be a wrench for them. But I hear that they are luckier than most. 'Tis said that in most monasteries and convents in Braunschweig-Lüneburg they have been forced to convert in a body or be thrown out without a by-your-leave. At least Graf Jobst is giving you fellows time to think about it and make your own decisions."

"Ja, that's true for now," sighed Paulus, "but I fear not for long. Now that Jobst is the last Graf of the Hoya line and the takeover by Welf Duke Ernst is imminent, that may change soon. Already all our revenues go to the Count and thence to the Duke. They barely leave us enough to live on."

"You must admit the cloister has been very wealthy for centuries," said Jacob. "A lot of folk around here were a mite envious."

"Mayhap, but we've done a lot of good, too."

"But you still can. I know for a fact that that Antwerper monk Adrian Buxschoten, sent by Duke Ernst into Hoya, has already converted all the monks at Bücken en masse, and they still go about their work among the people as before. He was trained by Luther himself and is now teaching others."

"Bücken never had as strict a rule as we. They were weaklings."

"But good people just the same and well loved by their neighbors,

700

most of whom favor the new learning. I say it takes more courage to stand up against the old church than to do nothing."

Paulus looked at him as though wondering whether to admit to his own feelings in the matter but only said, "We have just elected a new abbot, Rudolf Koch. We'll see what he decides. Come, let's get your grain inside the mill. It grows late."

Jacob usually stayed to watch his grain ground into flour. It went without saying that you could never trust a miller not to take more than his share. But this day he could see Paulus did not want to talk anymore and he himself was tired of the oft-discussed subject of religion.

"I'll be back in a few hours," he said and headed his team towards the village of Vilsen, where one of his brothers was a cabinetmaker. The Bruns were an ancient and extensive family in the district claiming descent from the great Saxon prince Wittekind. Jacob had not visited this particular brother in a long time, what with being so busy with the early wheat harvest, and his wife made the most delicious plum cake. His mouth watered at the thought as he drove along the road to Vilsen.

His brother's home was hard by the church, and as Jacob approached he heard such a hammering and clattering and crashing of stones that he thought they were tearing down the church.

"Ho, there, Willem," he called out as he drew up to the house. "What is going on here?"

Willem came out of his workshop, which was attached to the house, wiping the sawdust off his hands onto his apron. "Ach, Jacob," he greeted him. "Good to see you. It's been a long time. Haven't you heard? We are enlarging the church and tearing out all the old medieval idolatry. Already a new transept has been built. See the date over the side door—1534. Now they are opening and raising the old Roman windows to a new shape—the tall, pointed arch style. It will let in more of God's light as He meant us to worship. But how long since you've been here that you didn't know about this?"

"Quite a while," admitted Jacob, "what with the harvest and all. And betimes my goodwife likes to go to the Asendorf church or even to Bücken. It is nice now to have a choice and not be limited to one parish."

"That it is. But come in, come in. Dorothea has baked a plum cake, and we were just about to have afternoon coffee."

Jacob just knew he had been right about the plum cake, but he said, "Coffee? You drink that stuff, too?"

"Oh, ja, almost everyone in town does now. Have you never tried it?"

"No, not really."

"Then you must. It gives you a lift when the afternoon grows weary."

Dorothea welcomed Jacob and set the cake and a steaming mug of the coffee before him. Jacob did not much care for the coffee, but the sweet, delicious cake took some of the bitterness away.

Dorothea chattered on about the remodeling of the church. "Ach, the noise is deafening and it makes so much dust in the house, but it will be beautiful when it's done. And did you hear we are to get a new pastor?"

"What happened to the old one?" asked Jacob.

"He refused to change his ways, so they sent him packing."

"Who did?"

"Why, Superintendent Buxschoten, on the orders of Graf Jobst and Duke Ernst. And do you know what he did?" Jacob shook his head. "He fled straight to that wicked Bishop Christof of Verden and is helping him to burn Lutherans at the stake. Isn't that horrible?"

Jacob agreed that it was.

"That Christof is the only one in all this area who hasn't turned to Luther," she went on. "Even the Archbishop of Bremen has converted along with the whole town and diocese. But then, Verden has always been a den of iniquity." Jacob nodded. "Anyway, the man they are considering for the new pastor is one of the last monks of Heiligenberg, one Jobst Busse. He is even now being trained by Superintendent Buxschoten."

"One of the last?" queried Jacob. "But Miller Paulus just told me there are several left."

"Only a few and they are soon to leave," she replied.

"Why, then, have they elected a new abbot?"

She shrugged. "Who knows? Just to keep up appearances, I guess."

"Well, I must be on my way to collect my flour. Thank you for the kuchen. As always, it was delicious."

"My pleasure," she said. "Give my love to your goodwife and bring her to see us once in a while."

"I shall, when it's not so busy."

Back at the Cloister Mill, he loaded his bags of flour on the wagon, paid the miller his tenth part and was about to leave when curiosity overcame him.

"Brother Paulus," he said. "I have just heard that almost all the monks have left. Why, then, go through the farce of electing a new abbot?"

Paulus looked a little indignant, then shamefacedly admitted, "By orders of the Duke. We were told not to say anything, but all those who would not convert have left and those that would are scattered about studying under various of Dr. Luther's disciples. Only the Abbot and Prior Bernhard remain to care for the place. They are making an inventory for the Duke."

"And you?" asked Jacob.

"I have been allowed to remain because I am an honest miller and the mill brings in revenue. I am thinking of switching myself."

"Good," said Jacob. "It is no doubt the wise thing to do."

Paulus hesitated. "Can I entrust you with a secret, my friend?"

Jacob nodded. "Most assuredly, Brother Paulus."

"I truthfully care not much for the new learning, but I shall convert if I can stay here at the mill. I love the old mill and I enjoy my work. I hope they need me enough to allow me to stay."

"I'll not betray your trust, Paulus, and I wish you luck."

Several weeks after this exchange, a von Sehnden boat sailed leisurely down the Aller from Celle. It passed Verden and as it reached the confluence with the Weser, instead of continuing on its usual route down to Bremen, the crew brought the boat about, picked up a freshening northwesterly breeze and sailed up the broad Weser. The boat carried no grain or other produce but a group of passengers, men personally selected by the Duke and Chancellor Förster to perform a special task. Under the leadership of one Henning Behr, the group included the younger Lüdeke von Sehnden and a brilliant clerk by the name of Markus Lindemann among others. As the boat rounded a broad bend in the river, it headed in to a quay that lay just below the ancient castle of the Graf of Hoya. Beyond lay an equally ancient bridge, one of the few crossing the northern reaches of the Weser and hence heavily travelled. Its tolls had once been a steady source of revenue for the counts, until an earlier duke had abolished them. Men were waiting on the quay to help them tie up. After disembarking they were welcomed, if somewhat coolly, by some representatives of Graf Jobst. While they waited for their horses to be brought ashore, they looked up at the castle. Seen from close up it was really quite decrepit.

Markus, who was an avid student of history, had told them that it had been reduced to ashes several times in its long history. Many of the old counts from earlier centuries had been very warlike robber-baron types constantly attacking their neighbors to the north and west, at places such as Bremen, Delmenhorst and others. Seldom did they emerge the winners, yet they persisted in trying to enlarge their territory, much to the chagrin of their people. Now the ancient line had died out, the present Graf Jobst being a distant cousin appointed by Duke Ernst and nothing more than a figurehead. By right of the heritage from Heinrich der Löwe, the Welf Dukes of Braunschweig-Lüneburg fell heirs to the entire county of Hoya.

The group from Celle was here on a twofold mission. They were to oversee the peaceful transition of authority from the Counts of Hoya to the Dukes of Braunschweig-Lüneburg. They did not expect any trouble from Graf Jobst, who was by and large a puppet and quite inept. But there was another possible source of contention. Countess Katharina, widow of the Count of the direct line, was claiming the right to inherit for her sons. With the appointment of Jobst and the imminent arrival of the Celle delegation, she had fled with her five children to the fortress of Nienburg in the southern part of the county, where she sought refuge still loudly proclaiming her rights. Henning Behr had been instructed by the Duke as to how to treat her fairly, but now these decisions were to be made for her *in absentia*, whether she liked it or not. Still she was a force to be reckoned with.

The Celle group's other task was to see to the dissolution of the monastery at Heiligenberg. The Abbot himself as well as Graf Jobst were supposed to be taking an inventory, but Duke Ernst trusted neither one to give a true accounting. The men from Celle were to make their own much more detailed inventory of everything from widely scattered revenue properties to buildings and treasure down to the last horse, cow and peasant hovel belonging to the monastery. It was a formidable task.

Once the horses had regained their land legs, the Graf's representative led the Celle men to the adjacent castle. It was situated on a low mound directly on the riverbank. Since this was very flat country with no natural hills, it could be assumed that this was the ancient motte from the original wood and earthwork fortress. They entered through a long wooden palisade, many of the boards rotted and crumbling. Here and there along its length and from the tower of the small keep colorful pennants bravely fluttered.

"No wonder they could never defend this thing," whispered Lüdeke to Markus. "One well-placed torch here and the whole thing would go except for the keep."

"Which is probably exactly what happened," replied Markus, "and yet they kept rebuilding it in the same old way. How foolish."

"I notice also that Jobst could not condescend to meet us," remarked Lüdeke.

"Yes. I have heard that he thinks of himself as a king in his little domain," said Markus.

"That could portend trouble."

"Possibly, but I doubt it. But I have also heard that there is one person he is afraid of—the Countess Katharina."

Lüdeke laughed. "Mayhap we should be dealing with her."

"Thank God we are not," said Markus. "He will be easier."

They entered the great hall. Immediately the musty smell assaulted their nostrils. The damp was all-pervasive. The river itself seemed to be seeping through the stone walls. A huge fire roared in the fireplace, necessary here even though it was quite warm outside. Graf Jobst sat on a dais. He was elaborately clad, although on closer inspection one could see the filth and tatter.

A herald announced them. "Master Henning Behr representing His Grace Duke Ernst of Braunschweig-Lüneburg and others."

"How very polite," muttered Markus sarcastically.

"Probably too stupid to remember all our names," agreed Lüdeke.

"Welcome to Hoya, Masters and—er—clerks," said Jobst in squeaky voice that totally belied his bulky frame. "Come, sit by the fire. Wulf," he commanded a servant hovering in the background, "fetch my guests some mead or beer or whatever we have to assuage their thirst."

Lüdeke and Markus simply looked at each other in disgust.

"We can offer you supper in due time," continued the Graf, "but I'm afraid it will not be an elaborate repast. We—er—don't have much."

"Ever crying the poor-mouth," commented Markus.

"He's been doing that in all his correspondence with Ernst. That is one reason why His Grace did not trust him to do an honest inventory," explained Lüdeke.

"I can see that," replied Markus, "but this is rich farm country. I don't understand."

"Too much spent on futile wars and profligacy."

Markus nodded.

Henning said to the Count, "We shall be most happy to share your humble repast, my lord."

"Why don't we seek out an inn?" whispered Markus.

Lüdeke shook his head. "His Grace instructed us to force him to accommodate us."

"I see."

Henning continued, "And I assume you can offer us sleeping accommodations as well, my lord."

Jobst cleared his throat, but his voice still squeaked. "Well—er—ja." He waved his fat bejewelled hand. "Here in the hall is ample room for your men. There should be a few extra pallets around. And there are one or two empty rooms up in the Palas for you and a few others, but I am afraid the furnishings will be rather Spartan. You see, the Dowager Countess took most of it with her when she—er—departed for Nienburg."

"Fled, more likely," commented Markus.

"She obviously didn't trust him either," said Lüdeke.

"We shall manage, my lord," Henning assured him. "Don't fret yourself."

"It's just that I was totally unprepared for your visit," mumbled Jobst. "I really don't think it is necessary."

"His Grace thought otherwise," replied Henning. "He understands your financial straits and thought to help you by sending his own expert clerks."

"I am much obliged, but—but it just isn't necessary," repeated Jobst lamely.

"He is livid but afraid to show it," said Markus. "He knows he will be caught out."

"Of course," agreed Lüdeke, "that is why we are here. Methinks, my friend, you will have your work cut out for you."

Markus nodded. "And I understand now why we must stay the night here, no matter how primitive, or by morning his treasure or whatever else he has will have disappeared."

"Exactly."

Henning continued. "I really don't want to get into a lengthy discussion until after we have inspected the castle and property, my lord. We shall begin on the morrow. My men are travel-weary. Right now we should appreciate a bath and then some supper."

"Bath?" hooted Jobst. He laughed uproariously. "There is the horse trough."

Henning was one of Ernst's finest diplomats, but his patience was wearing thin. He said sternly, "My lord, kindly have your servants bring some ewers of *warm* water up to the rooms in the Palas that we shall be using. With your leave we shall retire there now."

Jobst could see that his joke was unappreciated. He snapped his fin-

706

gers at the servant. "Wulf, you heard the man. See to it."

Upstairs, the Palas, or living quarters, was constructed entirely of wood on top of the much older stone walls. Although in better condition than the palisade, it was indeed spartan. There was an ample solar, almost bare of furniture, and they could see where tapestries had been removed from the walls. But the sleeping chambers were tiny cells. Each had two small windows covered with oiled parchment. No glass. They barely let in enough light to see by. There appeared to be three or four unoccupied, but they were only offered two. One had a large bed with a straw mattress but no coverings. The other was totally empty.

"God's teeth," cursed Lüdeke, "even the monks sleep better than this!"

Henning immediately ordered pallets to be brought. "Clean ones," he said to the servant, "and what is taking so long with the warm water?"

"It takes time to heat, Master," replied the man.

"Heat it? Don't you keep a cauldron a-boiling over the fire at all times?"

"I'm afraid not, Master. My Lord Jobst seldom—uh—requires it."

Henning had to bite his tongue to refrain from commenting on this. "Very well," he said. "Bring it as soon as you can." The man turned to leave. "And candles, too," he called after him.

The man looked surprised. "But this is the wrong time of year for candles." Henning looked exasperated, so the man quickly added, "Perhaps I can find some rush lights for you." He went down the stairs shaking his head.

"God's teeth!" exclaimed Lüdeke again. "Our meanest peasants live better than this!"

Henning agreed. "There is absolutely no reason for this penury. The Graf is deliberately trying to make us feel unwelcome. I can't believe they really live like this."

"I believe they do," said Markus. "You saw what a pig he is, and a poor manager as well, I know. We shall soon see tomorrow when we look at his accounts, if any."

"I don't envy you that job," said Henning.

Henning and two of the older leaders of their group took the chamber with the bed. They could easily sleep three in it. Lüdeke, Markus and another young man took the other. The junior members, clerks and their servants would have to put up in the hall, the men-at-arms in the stables with their horses. The boat crew would take the boat back to Celle on the

707

morrow and return for them in a few weeks. Lüdeke the Elder would not let it remain idle for that long.

A servant brought the pallets. They looked reasonably clean, if somewhat tattered, bits of straw sticking out of holes in the ticking. At last the water came, two small pitchers barely lukewarm.

"But where are the basins?" asked Lüdeke.

"Basins?" asked the man. "I don't believe we have any. You can just pour it over your heads. It won't hurt this stone floor, and eventually it will run down the stairs."

Lüdeke glared at him. "And meanwhile soak these miserable pallets and all our other possessions."

"Well, perhaps you could use the chamber pot," he indicated a much-dented old pot in the corner that they had not noticed, "before, that is, you use it for—uh—other things."

Meanwhile Lüdeke's own servant Gundrig brought up their saddlebags. He was shocked at the conditions his master would have to endure. "They are doing it deliberately," Gundrig declared.

"I agree," said Lüdeke, "but they act like a bunch of imbeciles. Even Master Behr can't seem to get anything out of them."

"I shall investigate. Just let me get you settled first."

Lüdeke waved his hand. "Don't unpack anything. There is no place to put it except on this filthy floor. See what you can do."

"Leave it to me," said Gundrig. "I shall explore this pile of stones down to the dungeons, if need be. Don't worry. Master Lüdeke, I shall set things to right ere long."

Lüdeke smiled. "Just don't get lost in the dungeons. I have a great desire to wash at least my face and hands before this luxurious supper we have been promised." After Gundrig left, Lüdeke said to Markus, "He will set things to right. Count on it. He has a nose for chicanery."

It was not long before Gundrig returned bearing not only a battered old basin but also a small piece of soap and a scrap of ragged linen for a towel.

"Wonderful!" exclaimed Lüdeke. "I knew we could count on you. Such luxury."

"It was the best I could find on short notice. It is the cook's bread bowl. You can be sure he will find something better for you so that he can have it back in the morning."

Lüdeke laughed. "It will serve admirably for now."

"The supper you will be served is meagre indeed," Gundrig told them. "As is often the case with a harsh master, the servants eat better than he, but at best it is poor fare. If you are still hungry afterward, mayhap I can steal a morsel or two for you."

"Thank you, Gundrig, but I hope it won't be necessary."

"Another thing," the servant went on. "There is not a woman in the place. Evidently the Countess Katharina took them all with her. That would account for the shoddy condition of everything and the poor food."

"In part, at least," agreed Lüdeke. "You are an excellent spy, Gundrig. Tomorrow when you explore further you must report everything you learn to Master Behr or me, for I am sure they will try to hide a great deal from us."

"I'll do that, Master. And how long will we be staying here?"

"I don't know. A few days at least, mayhap a week or more. It depends on what we see on the morrow."

Early the next morning Markus and the other clerks began examining the accounts, while Henning, Lüdeke and others took stock of the castle itself and all its appurtenances. Jobst chose to go hunting, leaving his steward behind to answer any questions. Henning sent some of their own men-at-arms out hunting as well to be sure they had some decent food on the table for the next few days.

Gundrig did his own prowling. He spent some time in the kitchen trying to make friends with the servants, but they were a surly lot and he soon gave up. He wandered into the ground floor of the keep, the oldest part of the castle, where something caught his attention. He noticed that the trapdoor leading down to the ancient dungeon was in better condition than just about anything else he had seen in the castle. He knelt down to get a closer look. The hinges were well oiled and the hasp looked new. He tried to open it but it was extremely heavy. Gradually he succeeded in raising it a crack and noticed that the rope hanging beneath it was brand-new. So engrossed was he in his task that he failed to hear stealthy footsteps behind him. Suddenly a severe blow to his head sent him crashing down on top of the heavy door, almost catching his fingers beneath it. He tried to cry out but could not. Nor would his limbs respond when he tried to move. Hovering on the verge of unconsciousness, he could barely discern voices above him.

"Shall I hit him again?"

"No, no, we mustn't kill him." Gundrig held his breath to keep from groaning as the man kicked him in the ribs. "He'll be out for a while."

"But we can't leave him here."

"No, of course not. We'll drag him out to the stables—they're all away—and pour some beer over him, so they'll think he's drunk."

"Good idea. Then no one will believe him. But should we not move the chest to another place?"

"I don't dare until my lord returns. Besides, I don't think he saw anything."

Gundrig was rapidly waking up as he listened to this conversation, but he continued to feign unconsciousness as they dragged him out to the stables and threw him on a pile of hay in a dark corner.

"Now go and fetch the beer while I watch him," ordered the first man.

As soon as the other left, Gundrig gathered all his strength. He knew that in his dazed condition he would have only one chance. In one swift motion he was on his knees and butted the man in the belly with his head. He saw stars for a moment and his wound throbbed intensely, but he had knocked the wind out of the man. Quickly rising, Gundrig clenched his fists and gave the man two brutal blows to the jaw and to the solar plexus. The man passed out. Gundrig found some rope and tied the churl's hands behind him and his ankles together and dragged him into the corner where he had been left. None too soon, for in a moment the other man returned, but Gundrig was waiting for him, pitchfork in hand. He struck him on the back of the neck with the stout handle and then prodded him in the belly with the tines of the fork—not enough to kill him but enough to wound him badly. Then he trussed this one up in similar fashion and tied the two together. The beer had spilt all over the second man, but there was still enough remaining in the pitcher to pour over the first.

"Tit for tat," said Gundrig and strolled nonchalantly out of the stable. He stopped at the horse trough to bathe his wound. Some blood had trickled onto his shirt, but the bleeding had apparently stopped. He could feel a sizable lump rising. The cold water made it feel a little better, but he was still light-headed. He wanted nothing more but to lie down and sleep somewhere, but he knew it was urgent that he find Master Lüdeke or Master Behr immediately, before the Graf returned.

Gundrig found them on the uppermost floor of the keep in the private chambers of Graf Jobst. Here indeed was luxury, in startling contrast to the rest of the castle. A cheery fire burned in the only fireplace in the keep. The bed hangings were rich and full, the rushes on the floor reasonably clean. Beautifully carved chests stood about the walls. Although there were no windows, only the arrow slits from the old days when the keep was the last line of defense, the walls were hung with heavy tapestries to keep out the draft. The other room contained a heavy oaken table, some chairs and benches and a prie-dieu.

"That must be from the old times," remarked Lüdeke.

"But even Lutherans still pray," said Henning, "although I doubt our friend Jobst does much of that."

"Quite a contrast from the rest of the place."

"Quite," agreed Henning, "and I'm sure he had no intentions of letting us come up here, but since he is away and we were not expressly forbidden . . ." Henning let the words trail away as he spread his hands and shrugged his shoulders.

The heavy oak door at the head of the stairs stood open and suddenly Gundrig burst through.

"Ah, Masters, there you are at last. I am sorry to interrupt you, but I must tell you what I have discovered."

"Gundrig, what's amiss?" asked Lüdeke. "You are bleeding."

"Ach, just a knock on the head," he tried to dismiss it lightly. "But I have a thick skull."

"And how came you by that?" asked Henning, concerned.

"Well, I was exploring down in the bottommost part of this here keep and I came upon something that I don't think they wanted me to see. So they tried to take me out, but like I say, I have a thick skull."

"Who did this to you?" asked Lüdeke.

Gundrig shrugged. "A couple of his servants. I don't know their names, but I have them all nicely trussed up in the stable for you."

"They shall be punished," said Henning.

Just then the Graf's steward came in. "What are you doing here? You have no right to be here," he exclaimed excitedly. "This is my lord's private apartment."

"We have every right," replied Henning coolly. "The entire castle, ja, the entire county, is now enfeoffed to Braunschweig-Lüneburg, and we are His Grace's duly authorized representatives."

"But—but these are Graf Jobst's personal possessions," objected the steward.

"We shall be the judge of what is personal and what belongs to the castle. We have not touched a thing, and shall not until he is with us. But we could not help but notice the contrast between this luxury and the rest of the run-down castle. How do you account for that?"

"I—I don't really know," mumbled the steward. "I am rarely permitted to come up here."

711

Henning gave him a look of disgust. "Well, we have urgent business elsewhere. If you would kindly step aside." Henning pushed past him and started down the stairs, Lüdeke and Gundrig following. "You have my permission to enter there," he called over his shoulder. "I'm sure you will find nothing disturbed."

The steward stood there unable to decide what to do.

When they were out of earshot, Gundrig whispered to Lüdeke, "We sure don't want him trailing along."

"I don't think we need worry for a little while anyway," replied Lüdeke. "If what he says is true, I'm sure he will welcome the opportunity to do his own nosing about."

"And I would also suggest, Master, that we have a couple of our own men-at-arms with us to guard our backs. I wouldn't want the same thing to happen to you." He gently touched the throbbing lump on his head.

"Did you hear that, Henning?" asked Lüdeke. "Are all our men out hunting, or are there still a few here?"

"Ja, I heard," he replied. "I think only four or five are out. I made sure we were not left defenseless in just such an event as this. But you'll have to find them. Gundrig, will you see to it?"

"Ja, certainly, Master Behr."

"We shall pretend to be looking about the kitchen. But don't bring our men there. Send them directly to the keep and then come and fetch us by yourself."

Henning and Lüdeke wandered into the huge kitchen. Before they entered, they overheard a scrap of conversation that convinced them that the kitchen help knew nothing of what had transpired.

"Where have those two oafs got themselves off to now?" bellowed the cook. "I need some firewood in here."

"I don't know," replied his assistant, "probably off drunk again."

"This early in the morning?"

"Well, you can be sure they are not chasing chambermaids as was their wont."

"They are nothing but trouble. I don't know why my lord keeps them."

"They are his strong-arm boys. They do his dirty work."

"Hush. Don't let the steward hear you say that."

When Henning and Lüdeke entered, the servants all fell silent and made a great show of kneading bread dough and preparing vegetables for the noon meal.

"Good morning," said Henning. No one answered. He walked directly up to the cook. "Good morning," he said again.

The cook glared but decided he had better return the greeting. "And to you, Master."

"I see victuals aplenty here," said Henning, looking about. "I am curious then as to why we were half-starved yestere'en."

"We, er, were ill prepared on such short notice."

"But your master knew several weeks ago exactly when we were coming."

The cook shrugged. "I only follow orders. I was told nothing until you arrived. But things will be better today with my lord out hunting. He will bring in something, I'm sure."

"And all these vegetables and fruit. Do not the peasants tithe regularly or sell them to the castle?"

"They're supposed to, but—well, you know how it is. They're getting very uppity these days, and oftentimes my lord cannot afford the prices they ask, so they take their produce elsewhere. It was different when my Lady Countess was here."

Henning nodded. "I'm sure."

Just then Gundrig signalled to them from the doorway.

"My servant tells me we have other business to see to," said Henning, "but I have enjoyed having this conversation with you, Master Cook. Perhaps we can continue it later when you are not so busy."

"Hrumph," growled the cook.

Henning and Lüdeke followed Gundrig back to the keep, where two of their men were waiting.

"No one is about," Gundrig assured them. "Our men have already checked carefully. We shall be undisturbed." He led them to the trapdoor leading to the ancient dungeons and pointed to the new hardware. "Now I shall need some help lifting this thing. It is exceptionally heavy."

Lüdeke called one of their men over and added his own weight to their efforts. It took the combined strength of all three of them to lift the heavy door and fold it back. But it opened without a squeak or a groan. The new rope that Gundrig had noticed earlier was tied to the door and came taut when the door was fully open as if there were a great weight at the bottom.

"A light. We need a light," said the guard.

"No, we don't dare," said Henning. "We shall just have to feel our way. Is there a ladder?"

"There appears to be," replied Gundrig, peering down into the hole.

"Then down you go and see if you can feel what it is before we pull on the rope."

Gundrig turned white. Without thinking, he crossed himself. "Holy Mother, I hope there are no bodies down there."

Lüdeke laughed. "I wouldn't be surprised if there were. But they would be so old as to do you no harm. This doesn't look like it's been used for an actual prison for a long, long time."

Gundrig still hesitated but he was not one to have his courage called into question. He reached down and tested the first two rungs with his hand. They seemed solid enough. He swung himself over the side and started down the ladder. His head was about a foot below the opening when they heard a sickening crack.

"Holy Mother, I'm falling!" he screamed.

"Grab the rope, Gundrig!" shouted Lüdeke.

He did so and they could see him swinging between his last hand-hold on the ladder and the rope. "I can't hold on very long," he gasped. "My arms are still weak from the blow."

"Can you shinny up the rope?" suggested Lüdeke.

"No way. It would bring the whole trapdoor crashing down on my head."

"We'll try to pull you up." But with the combined weight of Gundrig and whatever was at the bottom the rope wouldn't budge.

"Swing your feet over to the wall," said the guard, "and try to walk up sidewards until you can reach a higher handhold. About another rung up and we can reach you."

Gundrig did as he was told and inched his way up. When he was almost doubled over, he held tightly to the rope and made a mighty lunge with his other hand for the next higher rung. It held.

"One more and we can reach you," encouraged the guard.

After a moment to catch his breath, Gundrig repeated the maneuver and succeeded. Two mighty pairs of arms of the guards grasped him under the armpits and hauled him up.

During all this excitement the door to the keep had been left unguarded, and now in rushed the steward sputtering, "What are you doing here?"

"I don't know," said Henning calmly. "Perhaps you can tell us?"

"There is nothing down there but old bones and rats for all I know," snarled the steward.

"Ah, so. Then you won't mind if we pull on this rope to see what it is stuck on."

"No, no, you must not touch that," cried the steward in near-panic.

"If there is nothing but old bones, what difference does it make? But if it is a recently deceased corpse, perhaps we have a case of murder on our hands."

The steward was genuinely shocked. "No, no, never that!" He turned obsequious. "Masters, I truly do not know what is down there. My Lord Jobst has forbidden me to come here. He comes often late at night with no one but his two, er, servants. But I am sure that no—uh—crime has been committed."

"That we shall soon see," said Henning. "Stand back."

Lüdeke went and stood close by the steward just in case he should try any tricks, but the man was visibly shaken. The two guards went to help Gundrig pull on the rope. At first the rope would not budge. Then gradually they got a little slack and whatever was at the bottom began to move. Several times it crashed against the side of the shaft.

"Whatever it is, it's not a body," remarked Gundrig.

"Not unless he is in full armor," said Lüdeke. The steward began to shake and sniffle. Lüdeke laid a firm hand on his arm so that he would not bolt and alert others.

Very gradually the heavy object came into sight.

"It is a coffer or chest of some sort," said Gundrig.

"Aha!" said Henning.

At last they manhandled it out of the shaft and slid it across the trap-door and onto the solid stone floor. It was a large oaken coffer bound with iron straps and securely locked.

The steward gasped. "So that's where it was. Masters, you can't open that until my Lord Jobst is present!"

"We don't intend to," replied Henning, "but we shall take it into safe-keeping up in the solar where our clerks are checking the accounts. We shall want several unbiased witnesses on hand when His Lordship does open it. Now what does it contain? You seem to recognize it."

"I don't know what it might contain now, but it belonged to the Dowager Countess and when she—er—left rather hurriedly, it was missing. She claimed it contained some of her jewels and the deeds to her various properties, among other things. I don't honestly know if it actually contained those things. I only had her word for it. But she was very upset about its loss."

715

"If it does contain those things, I can well understand her being upset. And how came it to the bottom of the dungeon? I'm sure she didn't put it there," asked Henning.

"No. My Lord Jobst," stammered the steward, "I mean—uh—I have no idea how it came to be there."

"You lie," said Henning indignantly, "but no mind. We shall get the truth from Jobst himself. Come now, accompany us to the solar with it so that you can be sure no one will tamper with it."

Gundrig and one of the guards lifted the heavy coffer to their shoulders, while the other guard kept a firm hand on the steward. When they arrived at the solar, Markus was awaiting them anxiously.

"Ah, Master Behr," he said, "I am so glad you have come. There are things I must discuss with you. There are several rather strange discrepancies in these accounts. I see you have brought the steward with you. Perhaps he can answer some of our questions."

"Don't even ask," growled Henning. "He lies so much, he can't even keep his own stories straight. Meanwhile, guard this with your life." Gundrig and the guard set the coffer down on the floor.

"What is that?" asked Markus.

"We don't know yet, but I suspect it may solve at least some of your discrepancies. We shall open it when Graf Jobst returns, but until then let no one, not even Jobst himself, near it until we are all assembled here."

"I understand," replied Markus.

"Now I believe we have some prisoners in the barn to attend to." Henning swept out the door with the other men following, leaving Markus and his clerks staring bewildered after them.

In the stable the two assailants could be heard calling for help, but as yet no one had heeded their pleas. It was obvious none of the other castle servants had any use for them either. They were trying desperately to untie each other's bonds.

"Are these the two—what did you call them?" Henning asked the steward.

"Yes, Master," replied the man. "My lord's personal—er—body servants."

"Common ruffians, more like," said Lüdeke.

"Why are they trussed up like this?" asked the steward. "My lord will be wroth."

"Not so wroth as we," snarled Henning. "They tried to kill our servant Gundrig."

"Oh, no, they wouldn't do such a thing!" exclaimed the steward. "Perhaps he picked a fight with them."

Gundrig was fuming and Lüdeke placed a restraining hand on him ere he throttled the steward.

Henning said as calmly as he could, "I think we have no further need for you at the moment, Steward. Go, leave us now, but be available."

"But I shall have to report . . . " objected the steward.

"Report all you want," said Henning. "Methinks your master will also have a great deal of explaining to do ere we are finished here."

The steward slunk out the stable door.

Henning turned his attention to the two culprits. "Separate them, Gundrig, but leave their hands and feet tied." Gundrig did so, perhaps a bit more roughly than necessary, but no one objected. He hauled them to their feet and stood them before Henning and Lüdeke.

"Now, why did you attack Gundrig so brutally?" asked Henning.

Both men started to speak at once.

"We did not. He fell. We tried to help him."

But at the same time the other blurted, "Our master told us to."

"Hush, you fool," said the first.

Henning looked from one to the other. "And what were you doing in the keep when you should have been out gathering firewood for the cook?"

"We were just passing by when we heard a strange sound."

"We were told to guard the treasure."

"Ah, treasure it is? And you were just passing by?" said Henning sarcastically. "Well, rest assured you won't have to guard it any longer. It is in safekeeping." The men looked at each other, perplexed. Henning turned to Lüdeke. "Have you noticed whether there are stocks or a pillory out in the bailey?"

Gundrig answered for him. "A pillory and a whipping post, Master. I did not see any stocks."

"Good. Then let us dispose of them there, until their master can mete out his own rough justice." For the first time the two ruffians looked frightened.

While Gundrig and the two guards saw to securing the two assailants, Henning and Lüdeke returned to the solar to confer with Markus.

"You see, up until about a year ago," explained Markus, "the accounts were kept fairly neatly and accurately." He pointed out the carefully written columns of income and expenditures. "But then they dwindle down to a few scattered entries and then in the past few months nothing at all."

"Very strange," agreed Henning.

"Either someone totally incompetent took over the bookkeeping or he was deliberately ordered to leave no record," said Markus.

"Probably both. What else?"

"About the same time when the County secularized the monastery at Heiligenberg, we were given to understand that the income, or most of it, from their vast holdings was to go to the Dowager Countess Katharina for her lifetime. There are a few haphazard entries of income therefrom but not one-tenth of what it should be, and nothing was paid to her, as far as we can see."

"Passing strange," said Lüdeke.

"Not so strange when you consider the man with whom we are dealing," replied Henning. "I would not doubt that he would cheat his own mother. And we know there was no love lost between him and the Dowager Countess."

"True enough," agreed Lüdeke, "but if he kept all that income from her, where has it been spent? Certainly not on this castle."

Henning glanced at the coffer. "I suspect we shall find some of it there. The rest, no doubt, thrown away on his useless feuds and futile bribes that did him no good. Fetch that steward up here, Gundrig. Perhaps he can answer some of our questions, although I fear we shall have to wait until Jobst himself returns."

"And that, I trow, will be a harder nut to crack," remarked Lüdeke.

Gundrig returned with the cowering steward in short order. Henning let him stand there and sweat for a few moments. The man obviously thought he was going to be questioned again about the contents of the coffer.

"Masters," he whined, "I've told you all I know about that—that box."

"It isn't the box that interests us now, but you."

"Me?"

"How long have you been steward here?" asked Henning.

"A bit less than a year, Master."

"And what happened to the former steward?"

"I—I believe he accompanied the Countess to Nienburg."

"But you're not sure?"

"So I was told."

"I see. And did he train you in the keeping of accounts and the managing of the estate before he left?"

"Not really, Master. There was not time."

"Because he did not know he would be leaving? Because the Countess had to flee for her life in the middle of the night?"

"Yes. No. I mean—er—something like that."

"And what did you before you were appointed steward?"

"I was but a footman, Master."

"Quite a promotion," put in Lüdeke.

"And no one taught you even the rudiments of bookkeeping?" continued Henning.

"Well, my lord Jobst did show me the book and told me what to write in it."

Henning shook his head in exasperation. "Can you even read and write, Steward?"

"A little," he admitted. "But I can cipher pretty well."

Henning pointed to the huge book. It was very obvious where the handwriting had changed. "And these entries of income—did you actually count the monies or weigh the produce? Did you even see it?"

"Well—er—no, not really. Like I said, my lord told me what to write."

"And there were no expenses at all in the past several months? I find that hard to believe. Surely you must have bought food or beer or horseshoes."

"Not very often, Master. My lord Jobst felt he could just take what he wanted when we needed it from the peasants hereabouts. They owed it to him."

Henning hit his forehead with the flat of his hand. "You may go now, Steward. We have no further questions for you, but when your lord Jobst returns send him to us immediately."

"Yes, Master." And the steward crept out of the solar.

Henning sighed. "Do you realize what this means?"

"That we'll have to interview every peasant in the area, perhaps the whole county, as to what they owe and what they have paid," said Lüdeke, "and hope they aren't lying, too."

"God's teeth! That will take months," exclaimed Henning.

"May I suggest an easier way?" said Markus. "That is, if Chancellor Förster and His Grace will permit it."

"Go on."

"That we simply grant a general amnesty and start all over again from scratch. Michaelmas is coming soon. That would be a good time to start."

"That sounds sensible to me," agreed Henning. "I shall send a messenger to the Chancellor at once. And we shall need to appoint our own steward. But what of the Countess Katharina?"

"We shall have to set up a separate book for her," replied Markus. "No doubt if the old steward is with her, he can keep it up."

Just then they heard the clatter of horses entering the bailey. They went to the window to see who it was. But it was only their own men returning from the hunt.

"I see they have a nice buck and some birds as well," commented Lüdeke. "So at least we shall eat well today and tomorrow."

"Thank God for that," said Henning. "But I wish my lord Jobst would get back here soon."

"I am willing to wager," said Markus, "that he will stay away until dark. He knows very well what we are doing and that we shall have innumerable questions."

"I am afraid you are right," agreed Henning.

True to Markus' prediction, Jobst and his men rode into the bailey just as it was growing dark. Jobst had missed both dinner and supper, which seemed unusual for a man of his appetites. In addition, he had no game at all to show for a full day's hunting. The men from Celle immediately became suspicious.

"He was not hunting at all, methinks," said Lüdeke.

"More like up to some deviltry," agreed Henning, "but what?"

"Hiding things or threatening peasants or—who knows?" added Markus.

They saw the steward rush out of the hall to greet Jobst. "My lord, the Masters from Celle wish to see you the moment you arrive."

Jobst waved him away. "Not now. I am tired. I am going straight to my chamber. Bring me a tankard of beer and then don't disturb me."

"Yes, my lord. And will my lord be wanting supper?"

"No, we ate on the way."

"My lord, I have to tell you . . . "

Jobst waved him away again. "Tomorrow. Now leave me."

"But, my lord, they have found the treasure from the dungeon," blurted the man.

"What?!" At last Jobst gave the man his attention.

"Yes, my lord, even now they have it up in the solar, but they said they would not open it until you were present."

"God have mercy!" exclaimed Jobst. He swung himself off his horse, handed it over to the waiting groom and headed for the stairs. It was then he noticed the two culprits.

"Master, have mercy. We have done no wrong," cried the one in the pillory weakly.

"We were only following your orders, my lord," whined the one tied to the whipping post.

"What is with these two?" Jobst asked the steward.

"They, er, tried to prevent one of their servants from finding it," replied the steward.

"And no doubt gave the secret away. I'll deal with them later." Ignoring the men's pleas, he strode toward the staircase, ranting, "Why is it I can't leave for a moment without some fool's bungling things?"

No one answered him.

When he reached the solar, Henning, Lüdeke and Markus were awaiting him. The other clerks had gone to their pallets in the great hall, but Henning had taken the precaution of having four of their own armed retainers with them. Two of them stood guard over the coffer.

"What are you doing with that?" stormed Jobst.

"Merely awaiting your return, my lord, so that you can open it," said Henning politely. "We rescued it from that dark dungeon, where it would surely rust away in time."

"It is mine, all mine!" shouted Jobst. "You have no right . . ."

"We were told it belonged to the Dowager Countess," put in Lüdeke.

"That goddamned, shitless steward!" raved Jobst. "And what other fairy tales did he tell you? I'll hang him by the thumbs."

"It was not the steward gave your secret away," said Henning calmly, "but your own inept henchmen yonder." He pointed to the bailey.

"Those fools. I knew I couldn't trust them. I'll—I'll . . ."

"What you do with them is not our concern," said Henning. "Our concern is with the contents and ownership of this coffer. Also, we would ask you some questions about the accounts."

"What accounts? There are none. I told him . . ." Jobst suddenly realized he said too much.

"Perhaps you had better sit down, my lord," suggested Lüdeke.

Jobst dropped his bulk onto a bench and wiped his brow with his sleeve. He just then seemed to notice that the room was brightly lit with several candles and rush lights.

"Why so many candles? Do you think I am a rich man? It is not meant for men to work after dark. Only the devil's work takes place at night!"

They ignored his ranting, although Lüdeke was on the verge of commenting about the devil's work, but thought better of it. The silence grew heavy.

At last Jobst sighed, "What do you want of me?"

"The key to the coffer, if you please, my lord," requested Henning.

"I shall have to go and get it," said Jobst.

"We shall send someone after it, if you but tell us where it is," said Henning. They were not about to let him leave the room.

Jobst sighed again. He threw back his doublet and began opening his shirt. Hanging about his neck on a chain was a large iron key. He did not pull it over his head, however. "I shall want some witnesses of my own," he said.

"Certainly. Guard, fetch the steward."

"Not that fool," objected Jobst. "My two body servants."

"Have you forgotten, my lord? Your two henchmen are prisoners."

Jobst wiped his brow again. "Very well then, that fool steward will have to do."

The steward must have been hovering nearby, for the guard returned with him almost immediately. "My lord, I . . . ," he began.

"Shut your mouth," snarled Jobst.

"Yes, my lord."

"Now, my lord, if you would kindly open the box," said Henning quietly.

Jobst took the key from around his neck and stumbled over to the coffer as the rest crowded around him, the guards alert. The lock opened easily. He opened the lid. Inside appeared to be many leather bags and purses, some finely wrought, others rough. But the first thing that caught their attention was the coat-of-arms painted inside the lid.

"Are these not the arms of the Dowager Countess?" asked Henning.

"Well, yes," replied Jobst, "but it's mine. She—er—gave it to me. She was going to throw it away."

"Oh, really. Then let us see what those purses contain. I seem to hear a jingle of coins."

Jobst seemed incapable of touching the contents. He remained on his knees and simply stared at it.

"Steward, start removing those bags and place them on the table. We

722

don't have all night," ordered Henning sternly.

"I—I don't—I mean it would—er—be better if you did it."

"Very well. Then keep careful count. Markus, start removing the contents."

Markus lifted two of the heavy bags. They definitely heard the jingle of coins. He laid them out on the table but did not open them. Two more, and then finally a total of eight of the poor quality bags, such as a peasant might make. Then he came to an exquisite purse of soft leather and rich silk, beautifully embroidered with gold and silver thread. It was large but nowhere near as heavy as the others.

The steward gasped, "That is . . . " Jobst growled and the steward shut his mouth.

Henning smiled. "Let me guess. Surely the great Graf of Hoya would not have such a feminine-looking purse. It must belong to the Countess."

The steward nodded imperceptibly behind Jobst's back. Markus placed the purse on the table. At the bottom of the chest were several rolls of parchment, some of the older ones cracked and crushed by the weight of the bags.

Henning took one out and opened it. "Aha, the deed to some of her properties," he remarked. "I should think she would be sorely missing these." Jobst groaned but said nothing. Henning replaced the parchment in the chest. "We can tend to those later. Let us see what we have in these bags." He sat down on one of the benches at the table and indicated that Markus and Lüdeke sit on either side of him. "Now, my lord, if you and your steward would kindly sit on the opposite bench so you can witness what we find here."

Jobst mumbled an obscenity, heaved himself to his feet and stumbled to the bench, the steward following. They noticed the steward sat himself as far away from his lord as the bench permitted. Henning opened the first bag and slowly poured its contents on the table. The glitter of gold covered the table—Florentine florins, Venetian ducats and other coins from farther away.

"Count it, Markus," Henning ordered. "Well, my lord, it appears you are richer than His Grace the Duke himself, mayhap richer than the Pope. How came you by this? I don't believe your peasants pay their tithes in this kind of coin."

"Uh—uh, from the tolls on the bridge and on the river," replied Jobst brazenly.

"His Grace abolished all the tolls years ago. Have you been collecting them illegally?"

"Nay, nay," objected Jobst. "They are from years ago, before the County fell to Braunschweig-Lüneburg."

"Indeed?" said Lüdeke, picking up one of the coins. "This appears to be newly minted. See the portrait of Alessandro de'Medici. Methinks it smells of highway robbery."

"Nay! Nay!" exclaimed Jobst again. "I—I don't know where some of them came from."

Henning looked skeptical as he opened the next bag. It was stuffed with French ecus. "Now this is interesting," he said. "The Venetians, Florentines, I can understand. They trade with us all the time. But French merchants rarely come this way. In fact, they rarely leave France. How do you explain this hoard?"

"I don't know. That was before my time. Perhaps it belongs to the Dowager Countess."

"More likely a bribe from François, as he has done with so many petty German nobles, in order to enlist their help against the Emperor."

Jobst turned white. The steward's mouth hung open.

"And that, my lord," continued Henning, "is treason."

No one said anything. Henning and Lüdeke stared at Jobst until he put his head in his hands and wept. It was a pitiful sight. Markus kept counting.

Henning quickly looked into the remaining bags. They contained coins from a variety of German states, but mostly good silver Lübeck-erthalers. "We shall have to lock this up again and put it under guard for the night. Poor Markus can hardly count it all tonight. And I shall keep the key. But first I would inspect this lovely lady's purse." He opened it carefully and drew out an assortment of rings, a necklace, some earrings, all finely wrought and studded with precious gemstones and pearls. He glanced up. Jobst was still weeping. "Steward," he said, "I can see by your face that you recognize this." He held up the necklace.

"I—I have seen the Countess wearing it," he replied.

"As I thought. I shall have to report all this to His Grace and let him decide what to do with it—and you. You can be sure that justice will be done."

Early the next morning, Henning dispatched two swift messengers, the first to the Duke and the Chancellor to apprise them of the situation at Hoya, the second to the Dowager Countess at Nienburg asking her to identify which of the contents of the coffer belonged to her.

"There is nothing more we can do here until we have instructions from His Grace," he said, "so I propose we ride out to Heiligenberg and see what the situation is there. It will also give us a chance to survey some of the countryside hereabouts."

The young men welcomed the suggestion after being cooped up in the dark, unwelcoming castle for the past few days. So as soon as they had broken their fast, Henning, Lüdeke, Markus, and one of his assistant clerks, armed with ample quills and paper, had their horses saddled and rode out. Aside from the servants and grooms, they took only a few armed men with them. Henning had taken the precaution of leaving several armed men behind to guard the coffer and the solar itself day and night. It was a beautiful day with the kiss of summer still in the air.

At first they rode through a dense oak forest teeming with game that lay right outside the village of Hoya. The huge ancient trees formed a canopy over the road. It was as though they rode through a green tunnel dappled with sunlight. Several times deer sprang out of the woods and dashed across the road directly in front of them.

"There is no reason why they could not have meat on the table every day," remarked Lüdeke.

"Unless you're too fat and lazy to bestir yourself," said Markus.

"Or too busy making mischief," added Henning.

Gradually the forest thinned and they came to land that had been cleared. The soil looked rich, the pastures lush, the standing crops on the verge of harvest appeared to be abundant. Placid cows grazed contentedly. The farmhouses themselves, most of brick and half-timbered, were built around a courtyard, house, barn and storage buildings all attached, forming three sides of the square, and often a brick wall with a gate closed the fourth side. They were all heavily thatched with no sign of rot or mildew. And without fail, the crossed Saxon horses stood at the gable peak.

"Did you know," said Markus, "that that pattern of building dates back centuries and centuries, to the time when the Norsemen raided up all these rivers? Each farm had to be its own little fortress."

"Ever our historian," teased Lüdeke.

"But that is interesting nonetheless," said Henning.

They came then to a tiny settlement call Bruchhausen, too small to be called a village. The few houses huddled together were strung out between the road and a sparkling brook called the Eyter.

As they were approaching, Markus looked off to the left and exclaimed, "Why, there is a mill. I didn't know there was a mill here. I

725

thought the only one in the vicinity belonged to the monastery."

"According to what we were told, there are, or were, three mills owned by the monks. This could be one of them."

"But so far away?" questioned Markus.

"It could be on the same brook, however," explained Lüdeke. "Very often these ancient charters granted them water rights far beyond their own land."

"You're right, of course. And look at the farm around it. Rich land, but totally neglected. If this is indeed monastery property, I wonder if I could buy it from the Graf."

"Markus, you're crazy," exclaimed Lüdeke. "you're not a farmer — or a miller either, for that matter."

"I know, but I've always dreamed about living in the country and just having a garden big enough to supply my own needs. And mills have always fascinated me."

Henning laughed and shook his head. "Markus, Markus, you'd best stick to clerking."

Markus merely smiled.

Soon they arrived at the thriving market town of Vilsen and encountered the first hill in that otherwise flat country. They rode up the hill to the ancient church. They could see where some recent additions and remodeling had taken place. The roads beyond the church ran to the right and to the left with a smaller path leading on up the hill.

"We had better stop here and ask directions," announced Henning. "I am not sure which way to go."

They knocked at the large house next to the church. A young man wearing white vestments opened the door.

"Good morning, Father — I mean Pastor, or is it Brother?" said Henning, a bit nonplussed.

The young man smiled. "Understandable confusion," he said. "I am Jobst Busse, newly appointed pastor of this church, but I am afraid I must continue to wear my old monk's robes while I am having a suit of civilian clothes made and new vestments, too. How may I help you?"

Henning introduced himself and his companions. "We go to Heiligenberg to take an inventory there for His Grace Duke Ernst, but we are not quite sure which road to take from here."

"Then you have asked at the right place. I am the last monk to have left Heiligenberg. I could see the light in Dr. Luther's teachings and am now the first independent pastor here. Won't you come in and partake of a little refreshment before you go on?"

Henning was about to refuse, pleading lack of time, when it occurred to him that here was a ready fount of information they could use, and probably unbiased at that.

"Thank you, Pastor. We'd be happy to partake of your hospitality, but for a short while only. We wish to be there before noon."

They entered the house and were led to a spacious parlor that ran across the entire front of it. The furnishings were very plain but plentiful and of good quality.

"Please make yourselves comfortable," said Pastor Busse. "I shall be right back." He returned momentarily and informed them, "I think I have just the guide you need. Heiligenberg is not far but the path leading to it is so insignificant you could easily miss it and be wandering about the woods for hours. My neighbor's brother seems to be visiting, and he goes right by there on his way home. I shall send and find out when he is leaving."

"Much obliged," said Henning, "but if he is staying there for dinner, we should not wish to wait that long."

"Naturally. In that case I'll take you part way myself."

Just then a young woman came in bearing mugs, a flagon of beer, a flagon of wine and some bread and cheese.

"Masters," said the Pastor, "this is my betrothed, Mistress Elizabeth. Unfortunately, we have no servants as yet, so she kindly helps me around the house. We shall be wed very soon."

"Congratulations, Pastor," said Henning.

Lüdeke and Markus looked at each other, trying to keep a straight face. As soon as the girl left the room, Lüdeke blurted out, "Methinks, Pastor, that that is one of Dr. Luther's teachings with which you are in full agreement."

The poor man blushed to the roots of his hair. He obviously was not used to such ribald remarks. "Why—er—yes—er—that is," he stammered. Making an effort to control himself, he cleared his throat and began again. "I agree that celibacy is an unnatural state for a man, or for a woman, too, for that matter. But you must not think that that was my sole reason for turning to Dr. Luther's teachings. Heaven forbid."

"Of course we don't," Henning assured him. "You mustn't mind Lüdeke. Sometimes his mouth opens before his brain is functioning." This seemed to appease the man, because he smiled, and Henning, not wishing to get into a lengthy theological discussion, asked, "What can you tell us of the dissolution of the monastery, Pastor? How is it going?

727

I hope there has been no violence."

"No, no outright violence against the monks personally, although some of them became quite irate at their being forced to leave. Those that did not wish to see the light, that is. The rest have been studying under Dr. Luther's disciples, as did I, and are serving as pastors in various parishes around the county. They are all gone, but before they left the Graf had them go through the motions of electing a new abbot, one favorable to Dr. Luther's cause."

"But what was the point of that if there are no monks left to govern?" asked Henning.

"That's what we all asked." The Pastor shrugged. "To guard the property, I should assume. Graf Jobst already has removed the treasure to the castle for safekeeping." Lüdeke and Markus nodded to each other. "But there was much of value in the barn and in the church. There has already been some looting by the peasants."

"I'm not surprised," said Henning. "What can one man alone do?"

"There are two—the Abbot and the Prior—three, actually, if you count the miller, but he is not up on the hill."

"Even so." Henning shook his head. "That is why we are here—to take an inventory and see that nothing else is stolen. His Grace has ordered that the wealth be distributed to needy churches and only the excess is to go into the Ducal treasury."

"I don't believe that is how Graf Jobst has understood it."

"We are already aware of that. Tell me, this so-called abbot—what is his name and do you feel that he is trustworthy?"

"Oh, yes," replied Busse. "His name is Rudolf Koch, and he is definitely the Graf's man and a willing convert to Dr. Luther's teachings as well. Just between us, I think he is only biding his time until he can achieve a high position in the new church."

"Interesting," commented Henning.

Just then there was a commotion out in the street and much shouting.

"That will be Jacob Bruns, your guide," explained the Pastor. "He can be a bit ebullient, but a good, solid man nonetheless."

The Celle men got up to leave, thanked their host, and were heading out the door when the Pastor called out to them, "I doubt you will be going back to Hoya tonight! If the monks' cells are not to your liking, you are welcome to stay the night here. It is a big house and it will be a while until I can fill it with children." He winked broadly at Lüdeke.

Jacob Bruns turned out to be an atypical peasant. Not only did he appear to be clean, but he was intelligent as well. He had a cheerful demeanor and they liked him immediately.

"Come, my hearties," he shouted. "Mount your nags and follow this luxurious coach drawn by two superb geldings and we shall lead you to the Holy Mountain." They all laughed and fell into line behind the old farm wagon.

Lüdeke thought this could be another opportunity to get information about the monastery. He rode up beside the wagon and started a conversation with Jacob, who was eager to impart what he knew.

"The first thing that happened was Graf Jobst took all the treasure, or at least all he could lay hands on, but I suspect there is more. It was a very wealthy monastery, and the monks rarely parted with a penny. They had some peculiar practices, but what did we care what they did to each other? They were generally good to the people. Why, every child in Vilsen and any who wanted to come in from the countryside were taught their letters and some ciphering."

Lüdeke was amazed. "You can read and write?"

"Oh, ja, not as good I'd like to because I always had to work on the farm, but better than most I know."

"So the monks did do some good?"

"Oh, lots. They only thing they hated were our May dances and harvest festivals—pagan, they said—and they were always hunting down the poor old wisewomen in the woods who knew more about healing than any ten monks. They were greedy in some ways, too."

"How do you mean?"

"Take the mill, for instance. Every one of us farmers in this vicinity has to bring his grain to be made into flour to the Cloister Mill only, nowhere else. We were given no choice even though there might be other millers who charged less."

"I see. But I thought there were three mills belonging to the monastery."

"There are, but each of us has been assigned to one mill in particular and no other. This has been so for over three hundred years. But the miller himself, Brother Paulus, is not a bad sort—as millers go. Everyone knows you can never trust a miller. He says he has switched to the new religion in order to keep his job. Can't say I blame him."

"Perhaps he will charge less now that he doesn't have to turn it over to the monastery."

"Hah, I doubt it. Graf Jobst is even greedier than the monks, and a spendthrift to boot. The monks hoarded it all, rarely spent a penny. And this new abbot-without-an-abbey, Rudolf, is his toadie. If you don't mind my saying so, don't trust him."

"I was wondering about that. Thank you for the warning. Is that why the Graf was able to take the treasure so easily?"

"Nay. He just rode in with a company of his knights and took it. Wanted to get his hands on it before you people came, I would imagine."

"I see."

"But to give him credit, yon Rudolf did stand up to the Graf on another matter. Seems he wants to tear the church and some other build-ings down in order to build a new castle. Claims the old one is too damp."

Lüdeke laughed. "I can vouch for that. But why destroy the church? Why not imply quarry new stones?"

"That would be very costly. You may not have noticed, but we have almost no stone hereabouts. All the substantial buildings are made out of brick, the rest half-timbered or just plain wood. That we have aplenty."

"I did notice that but never realized the reason why. What about the looting? We've heard there has already been some."

"Looting? I wouldn't call it that. Just a few poor farmers helping themselves to what they feel is rightfully theirs. I never did myself, mind you. I am better off than most. Our farm is not monastery property. It has belonged outright to the Bruns for over seven hundred years. We do not even pay a tithe to the Graf, only the military duty to keep from having to fight in his senseless feuds."

"That is a long time."

"Ja. But with the monks continually demanding a tithe for this and a tithe for that, many small holders became impoverished. What is an iron pot here and there? Or a horse harness or a plowshare? Or some fruit to carry home in the pot? It was going to rot anyway. There are no monks left to eat it or preserve it or even harvest it. And that barn is so full of things the monks could never have used in a hundred years. I have seen it myself. What need did they have for a hundred pots? There were only twenty of them. Or fifty horse harnesses? They had only one old nag for the Abbot's use."

"That's amazing," said Lüdeke. "Why would they have saved so many things of that sort?"

Jacob shrugged. "Who knows? Greed, probably. Maybe they were going to set up a booth at the next fair," he joked. "Anyway, don't be too hard on those few who walked off with things. No one will tell you who they are anyway. And 'tis well known that the monks helped themselves to quite a bit before they left."

"I'll bear that in mind," said Lüdeke. "Now I had best drop back and share what you have told me with my companions. How much further have we to go?"

Jacob pointed with his whip. "See yon wayfarer's chapel up ahead? The road to the Holy Mountain is just before that. It is very narrow, warn your friends."

"And is that the Cloister Mill beyond it?"

"No. That is Bruchmühlen, the second mill. The monk who ran that is one of the ones who left, so it is not operating at all at the moment. The Cloister Mill lies right at the very foot of the mountain. You shall soon see it."

Lüdeke reined in his horse and waited for Henning and Markus to catch up. He told them much of what Jacob had said. "So perhaps we have accused Graf Jobst unjustly. The contents of that coffer could be the monastery treasure," he suggested.

"It's possible, but I doubt it," said Markus. "Monastery treasures usually consist of plate—crucifixes, chalices, patens, that sort of thing—rather than coins."

"That's true," agreed Henning. "And why did he act so guilty instead of protesting that it came from here? In any event, he has no right to but a small part of it. Let us question the Abbot carefully as to what it consisted of."

"This must be the turning," said Lüdeke as they saw Jacob's wagon turn to the right. "God teeth, it is narrow and overgrown, too. Watch yourself for these branches. We cannot ride more than two abreast, if that."

"Thank God we found Jacob. We should surely have missed it," agreed Henning. And that put an end to any further conversation.

Very shortly they arrived at a small clearing where the path made a sharp right-angle turn to the left. Directly in front of them lay the famous Klostermühle. Jacob had stopped the wagon and waited for them to ride up to him.

"Do you want to stop here at the mill first or later?" he asked.

"We might as well see what's here," said Henning. They dismounted and turned their horses over to the groom.

Jacob climbed down from the wagon. His horses stood perfectly still. "I'll go fetch him," he said. "He can't always hear when the mill wheel is turning. He's a good man, but be forewarned, he can be a little testy if he's interrupted in the midst of a grinding job." He disappeared through a tiny door at the side of the mill.

While they were waiting, Markus walked over to the millrace. The great waterwheel was turning slowly as the brook flowed over a dam that held back a large pond above the mill.

"Everything looks to be well maintained," he commented.

"Probably the only part that still is," remarked Henning.

"I shall have to ask our friend Jacob about that other mill," said Markus.

"I'm sure he'll be able to tell you. He claims his family has been here hundreds of years, before the monastery was ever founded," Lüdeke replied.

At last the thundering noise inside the mill stopped and Jacob returned with the burly miller in tow and introduced him to the men from Celle. Henning explained to the miller why they were there.

"Masters," said Paulus, "I can tell you, you will find everything in order here. This is still a working mill, and vital to the people hereabouts. The only part of the old cloister that is, I might add. Come in, come in and see for yourselves."

They followed him through the little door and up a few steps that led to a sort of catwalk alongside the huge millstones. "I am in the middle of a job, but my friend Jacob said you people were in a hurry to get up the hill. So, I thought, what better opportunity to show you how the mill works. Stand back now." He thrust his weight against a gigantic lever and the heavy millstone began to turn. The noise prevented any conversation, but they could see that all the cogs, gears and other machinery were well oiled and cared for. The lofty room filled with flour dust and Lüdeke sneezed. The miller laughed. After a few moments of the demonstration, he pulled the lever back and the stone came to a halt. He moved another lever and the upper stone gradually rose from its mate, revealing the unground grain. He clapped Lüdeke on the back and said, "Gets a bit dusty, what? But you get used to it." He turned to Henning. "This is one of the best designed mills in the whole of County Hoya, maybe even in all of Germany. And would you believe this is all the original equipment from the year 1215? Not a thing has been changed. Those old monks sure knew what they were doing. I am told it was the first thing they built here, even before the church. Now come over here, I'll show you something else." He led them down a few steps to the lower floor. In the corner was another lever, which he pushed down. "That opens the water gate." They could hear the great waterwheel slow down and finally come to a stop. "Now the water is running through the sluice instead of over the wheel. Clever, huh? Saves the machinery. Also handy in time of flood."

Henning thanked him for the demonstration and said, "You can be sure we shall tell His Grace what a good job you are doing here and how well you've cared for the property. I don't think you have anything to worry about."

"Thank you, Master."

Henning looked about. "Do you live here as well, Brother Paulus?"

"You can drop the 'Brother'. It's just plain Paul now. See I've even dropped the Latin ending, although I still wear my monk's robes. More practical. Everything gets white here anyway." The men looked down at their own clothing and saw they were covered with the fine dust. "But no," Paul went on. "I still sleep up on the hill in my old cell in the dorter, but Graf Jobst has promised to build me a little house alongside the mill. I hope he keeps that promise, because if he tears down the dorter, I'll have to sleep with the Abbot." He slapped his leg. "Ha, ha, wouldn't that be fun!"

Henning smiled. "I'll do all I can to make sure the Graf keeps that promise."

"Thank you again, Master."

As they left the mill, Henning turned and asked him, "Is there anything you feel we should know about conditions up on the hill before we go there, Paul?"

The miller pondered a moment. "Not really. You shall see for yourself. In just this one year it is falling to rack and ruin. In my opinion the Graf's biggest mistake—but I really shouldn't say. After all, I am his vassal now."

Henning urged him on. "We shall respect your confidence. Go on— in your opinion . . ."

"Ja, well, like I said, he took all the treasure and wants to tear the buildings down, but he has sent no workers to replace the monks. I don't mean in a religious sense, but the home farm up there is a very rich one. He seems only interested in the income from the outlying properties and seems bent on destroying this one. That does not seem very practical to me. There is many a poor peasant hereabouts who would rejoice at the opportunity of working there in exchange for one of the little huts and a share in the bounty." He paused for a moment as if hesitating to go on.

"And this has always been a sacred place to the people around here since the beginning of time. It was their holy mountain long before the monks came. You see this brook here. The source of it is a wondrous clear spring in a deep ravine next to the hill. It was a sacred spring to the old pagan Saxons. Karl der Grosse destroyed their shrine. And now this. It seems as though every time there is a change in religion they seek to destroy instead of build up. But they never can take away how the people feel about this place. It is their Holy Mountain. They have a deep, almost superstitious, respect for the place, if not always for its occupants." He paused for breath. "Perhaps I have said too much, but it is important that you understand this."

Henning pondered this a moment, "Very interesting," he said. "I agree that it is important."

"Fascinating," agreed Markus. "I should like to talk with you more later, Paul. I am very interested in history." The miller nodded. "What can you tell me of the other mill over in Bruchhausen?"

"The Wehlenmühle," replied Paul. "Ja, that belongs to the monastery, but even they abandoned it some years ago."

"Why was that?"

"Two reasons. The stream flow, by the time it gets down there, was just not strong enough to do a good job, and the farms over there were just too few and poor to support it. Too much swamp and moorland."

"I see. And what will Graf Jobst do with it?" asked Markus.

Paul shrugged. "Who knows? Probably just let it fall down."

"And would you care to give us your opinion of this new Abbot?" asked Henning.

Again Paul hesitated. "I can only say he would never have been elected Abbot in the old days. Too soft, for one thing. And with his nose up the Graf's—you know what. And the Prior is an absolute nincompoop. They make a good pair. But there was no one else. All the others, on either side of—of the fence, so to speak, had more ambition. If the Graf ever pushes these two out as he did the others, they will be totally lost out in the world."

"I see," said Henning thoughtfully. "Thank you, Paul, you've been a great help. Now we must be on our way."

Jacob was waiting for them as they returned to their horses. "Now we go straight up the Holy Mount," he shouted as he started his team up the hill. At the top he turned right and stopped at an open spot where the path divided. "That is the church on the left. Big but very plain. They did not go in for fancy decorations. That path to the right leads to the huts where the lay brothers used to live and runs all around the perimeter. Directly ahead is the Abbot's house and behind it the monks' dorter. Beyond lies the barn."

They could see that the top of the mount leveled off like a huge round table. There were orchards heavy with fruit, fields with ripening grain, and lush pastures, but no animals that they could see.

"Let me roust out His Grace-lessness from his morning nap," said Jacob, "although he may be awake. It's almost dinnertime." He glanced at the sun. "No more bells to tell them when to eat and when to sleep. They seem helpless without them." He got down from the wagon and pounded on the door of the large house. Waited and pounded again. "Ho, Brother Rudolf," he called. "Wake up. You have visitors." At last the door opened and a tall, gaunt man came out. He was still tying the cincture of his robe.

"Oh, Jacob, what do you here?" he asked, blinking in the sunlight.

"These goodmen of the Duke's have come to visit with you for a bit."

The monk seemed to see them for the first time. "Oh, Masters, welcome to the Holy Mountain of the Blessed Virgin Mary. I mean to Heiligenberg. Can't get used to the new ways. My lord Jobst sent word that you would be coming, but I did not expect you quite so soon. I would offer you some refreshment, but I am not quite prepared. Been so busy, you know."

To keep him from going on and on, Henning said, "No matter. We have brought our own victuals for our noon repast. If you could just tell us where our grooms can water and rest the horses."

"Yes, yes, of course. How thoughtless of me. We're not used to horses, you know. Over there by the barn is a trough with running water and across from it is the pasture where the cows used to graze."

"Used to?" snapped Henning. "Where are they now?"

"Well—uh—they seem to have wandered off. No one to milk them, you know."

Henning shook his head as if to clear the cobwebs. "You don't know how to milk a cow?"

"Well, er—no, not really. The lay brothers did all that. We prayed for them."

"I see. Then if you can show us where we may eat our meal . . . or are we to picnic here on the grass?"

"Oh, no, no. Of course, how thoughtless of me. There is a large table and benches in the refectory. I shall call the Prior to show you."

Henning was exasperated. "Don't bother. Just point us in the right direction and we shall find our way."

Lüdeke thought, is he really such a blathering idiot or is he craftily pretending to be stupid?

At this point Jacob guffawed loudly. "They never did know the first rules of hospitality. They are not used to guests. Never were." He pointed with his whip. "The refectory is beneath the dorter. Just go behind the Abbot's house and you will see a big door. And now I must be on my way. My goodwife will be wondering where I've got to. If I can be of any more help to you, just let me know. Will you be able to find your way back to Vilsen?"

"I'm sure we can, Jacob," said Henning, "and thank you for everything."

"I should like to visit with you some more if time permits," said Markus. "Where do I find you?"

Jacob gave him directions to his farm and then leaned down and whispered to Lüdeke and Markus, "He is not the clown he pretends to be. As the saying goes, watch your back." They nodded, and Jacob turned his team around and waved as he headed back down the hill.

Henning addressed the Abbot. "Now we shall quickly eat and then get down to business."

The monk looked nervous. "Business?" he echoed. "Of course, of course."

Henning led the way to the refectory, the others following. When they were out of earshot, he murmured to himself, "If he says 'of course, of course' once more he'll find that rope around his middle wrapped around his neck." Lüdeke and Markus merely smiled.

After a quick meal they pounded on the door of the Abbot's house. There was no answer. Henning did not wait but walked in. Next to the hall was an almost bare waiting room and beyond it the Abbot's study. This was richly furnished with every comfort. But no one seemed to be about.

"What an opportunity to go through his papers," remarked Lüdeke.

"But we won't," cautioned Henning. "It could be just what he expects us to do, and it may be a trap. Check the rest of the house."

Lüdeke searched the rest of the first floor and Markus ran upstairs. On the opposite side of the hall was a spacious parlor and a private dining room. Above were three bedchambers. They found no one.

"Where can that knave have got to?" asked Henning. "He knows we want to talk with him."

"Probably praying for courage," said Lüdeke. "Let's check the church."

The church was large, solidly built of stone, but with small old-fashioned windows and no exterior decoration. They entered and immediately felt the chill. It was just as plain and austere inside. They heard chanting and there upon the chancel were the Abbot and another monk singing the office of Sext. Although Henning was furious, he was too polite to interrupt. There were no pews, so they wandered around looking at empty niches where there must have been statues at one time. They were all gone except for the ancient seated figure of Mary behind the high altar. She was holding a Christ child partially covered with her drapery. Both wore golden crowns. Above her head was an eight-pointed star and in her right hand a branch of some sort, to her right what appeared to be an oak tree.

At last the office was over and the Abbot came hurrying down to them. "How nice to have a congregation for a change," he said cheerily.

Henning frowned. "I thought you had forsaken the old religion and were now an adherent of the new learning."

"Of course, of course. Although, actually, I am still a bit ambivalent about that," he admitted. "After all, we are still monks." Henning glared. "Oh, this is Brother Bernhard, our Prior."

"Our?"

"Well, I mean *the* Prior. He can probably help you more with what you want to know than I. He was elected Prior under the former Abbot Johann von dem Busche."

"And still a Catholic?"

"Well, sort of. . . ."

"Why not let him speak for himself?" suggested Henning.

"With Your Grace's permission." Bernhard bowed to the Abbot and then faced Henning. "I am still a believer in the one and only true faith, the Holy Catholic Church. I am a Praemonstratensian. We follow the Augustinian rule—the same as your heretic Luther, I might add—but we follow the Cistercian ideals of austerity as well. I only stayed at the request of His Grace Abbot Rudolf, and of Graf Jobst, to see that the desanctification of this holy place does not become desecration. Sadly, some of that has already taken place, which I was powerless to prevent. As soon as I am given permission, I shall happily leave this—this godforsaken place and go to France, where I know I shall be welcome. Until then I must abide by the Rule. Does that answer your question, Masters?"

"It does," replied Henning, "and I admire your forthrightness and commend you for your honesty, Brother Bernhard." The monk nodded.

"Now if we may ask you both a few questions. Write everything down from here on," he instructed the clerk. "We have been told that Graf Jobst has already removed the treasure. What exactly did it consist of?"

"Not all of it," objected Rudolf. "He didn't take all of it. Our former Abbot Johann . . ."

"Took nothing," interrupted Bernhard. "I tell you again, His Grace took nothing. You have only Graf Jobst's word on that."

"But I saw him pack his gold-embroidered, gem-encrusted mitre and cope," argued Rudolf. "The great crozier, too."

"Those were not part of the treasure, merely the symbols of his office," snapped back Bernhard.

"But he was supposed to leave them for me," moaned Rudolf.

"And what use would you have for them if you are going to become a—a heretic?"

"Brothers, brothers, enough!" Henning had to raise his voice. "You are acting like two spoiled children. For the moment let us not argue about who took what. Our question is what *exactly* did the treasure consist of? Brother Rudolf?"

"Nothing much, really," he stammered. "Some bags of money. The Communion sets, some of which are still here. You see, honestly, I don't know. I was never privy to that before—before I became Abbot, and by then some of it was already gone. At least, I believe so," he added quickly.

"Can you be more specific, Brother Bernhard? Or were you not privy to this either?"

"I was, to some extent. I kept the accounts of the monies. The cellarer kept the accounts of all the grain, produce, livestock and other things we were tithed. That was our real wealth. As for the plate, crucifixes, vestments and so on, an inventory was required every time the election of a new abbot took place, but that was not done this last time because of all the—er—turmoil. The last proper inventory was taken in 1522. There should be a record of that somewhere, but whether it would have been applicable to last year I cannot say."

"Very well," said Henning. "Then since the monies were your field of expertise, tell us how much there was and of what type of monies it consisted."

"For the exact amount there was—or should have been—I should have to check my ledgers. It consisted of four or five large purses of everything from pennies to Lübeckerthalers. We customarily gave most of the pennies to the poor, but when too many accumulated we took them to the

Archdiocesan Chancellor at Bremen and changed them for thalers."

"Were there any from other lands outside of Germany?"

"Yes. It was supposed to be kept secret, but it doesn't matter now. Our motherhouse at Prémontré near Laôn sent us a purse of French ecus to provide travelling expenses for the brothers who wished to go there. It had not all been distributed ere Graf Jobst and his men came. Some of the brothers fled for their lives with nothing," he said sadly. "I, too, was to have had a portion of it, but . . . " He spread his hands in a gesture of resignation.

"Aha! That explains something at least," said Henning. Markus and Lüdeke nodded.

"Is there something further amiss?" asked Bernard.

"No, no," said Henning, "just a private joke among us. Were there any, say, gold florins or ducats?"

"Not that I recall seeing," replied Bernhard, "and I certainly would remember gold coins."

"And you, Brother Rudolf?"

"No, no," denied the Abbot quickly. "I've never seen any like that."

"All right. We'll have the clerks check your ledger later," said Henning. "Now the plate. Where was it kept?"

"Here in the sacristy," replied Rudolf.

"Locked?"

"Of course, of course, but there were several who had keys."

"And where are all those keys now?"

"I have mine and Prior Bernhard his, but the others have—well—disappeared," said Rudolf and then quickly added, "But it doesn't matter now because one of Graf Jobst's—er—followers broke the lock, when we denied them entry."

"I'm not surprised. Is there anything left?'

Both monks shook their heads, "Not much," said Rudolf sadly. "They left us no but a battered old pewter Communion set that we used to use to take the Eucharist to the sick and shut-ins."

"And what did they take?"

"Two silver Communion sets, one plain for everyday and one beautifully chased and engraved for feast days, the processional cross of oak and ivory, the crystal reliquary with St. Cyriacus' finger, and all the vestments and altar linens. They pulled all the saints from the niches and smashed them down into the ravine." Rudolf was almost in tears at the end of this recitation.

"Anything else?"

"Not that I remember, but there could have been," he wept.

"No gold? If there were these gold-embroidered vestments you spoke of, surely there must have been some gold plate."

"Not that I know of," said Rudolf.

Bernhard spoke up. "I remember an exquisite set long ago, but it was only used once in a great while, when a bishop or our provincial paid a pastoral visit. I have not seen it since, er, in many years."

"You started to say 'since,'" queried Henning. "Since when?"

"Since—since, er, soon after the heresy started," said Bernhard hesitantly. "Yes, right after the Edict of Worms was promulgated."

Henning looked askance at him. "And was it kept here in the sacristy as well?"

"No, it was locked in a special chest in Abbot Johann's private chamber."

This seemed to surprise Rudolf. "I have never seen it," he murmured.

"Then it could have wandered off with the former Abbot and his vestments?" suggested Henning.

"Possibly. That's it."

"Never!" cried Bernhard. "His Grace was an honest man."

"But the times are strange and unsettled," commented Henning and let it go. He did not want to endure another argument between the two monks. "We have seen and heard enough here. Brother Bernhard, if you would kindly make your ledgers and any other records available to Master Lindemann here and his clerk, Master von Sehnden and I shall look in the barn and other buildings."

As they left the church, Rudolf was still weeping, or pretending to. Henning asked him, "Did Graf Jobst order this desecration or did his men do it on their own?"

"I don't know," sobbed Rudolf, "but he was right here and did nothing to stop them. He even laughed when one of them hung a precious Lenten alb—purple, you know—around his shoulders and said what a handsome cloak it would make and another took altar linens and said his goodwife needed a tablecloth and a new shift."

Henning shook his head. "I only know that is not what His Grace Duke Ernst had in mind when he ordered the dissolution of the monasteries. He hoped to turn them into schools or homes for the indigent so that you could go right on serving the people. You can be sure we shall make him aware of what has happened here."

Henning and Lüdeke entered the barn and stood amazed. Jacob had not exaggerated when he spoke of hundreds of pots, horse harnesses and such-like. They were stacked to the rafters. Tools of every kind imaginable lay in piles or leaned against the walls. They even filled most of the stalls. Many were very old-fashioned, some so ancient they were rusting away. Only three of the stalls showed any sign of having been occupied by animals.

"What in the world were they doing with all these things? What did they need it for?" exclaimed Lüdeke, bewildered.

"And more to the point, where did they get it?" asked Henning. "Surely not all their vassals and villeins were blacksmiths and harness makers. I shall be curious to hear Rudolf's story on this."

"He will only say he doesn't know."

"No doubt," agreed Henning. "There is no point in attempting to count all of this. I shall urge His Grace to appoint a steward to sell it or give it away. Let us check the refectory and cellars." In the refectory they found most of the linens and utensil chests empty, rifled, no doubt, by Jobst's men. The cavernous cellar beneath the dorter was likewise almost bare, a few torn sacks of flour all that remained of what must have been plentiful stores. "This is a waste of time," he said disgustedly. "Let us see how Markus is faring."

When they returned to the Abbot's house they noticed two men, obviously peasants, seated on the bench in the waiting room. Henning paid them no mind but walked directly into the study without knocking. Markus and his clerk were seated at the Abbot's desk poring over a huge and very ancient ledger. Brother Bernhard sat in the guest's chair looking suitably humble but alert.

"Well?" asked Henning.

"Everything seems to be in order here," said Markus. "The German money tallies almost exactly with the contents of those five purses in Jobst's coffer. He can't have spent much of it. Probably only enough to bribe his two roughnecks."

"And the French?"

"That is all noted in a separate secret ledger." Markus indicated a small book to one side. "It was originally a sizeable amount, but more than half, almost two-thirds, has already been paid out to those monks who left, according to their rank, with Abbot Johann helping himself to the lion's share even though he is believed not to have gone to France . . ."

"He did not 'help himself'," interrupted Bernhard. "That was his fair

741

share. After all, he held the highest rank here, and no one knows that he may not eventually go to Prémontré. We also paid several who later became — er — apostate. We tried to be fair and had to take their word for their intentions. If they lied — well, that's on their consciences."

"Can't say as I can blame them," said Henning. "And the balance tallies with what you found in that purse?"

"Exactly," said Markus. "He was probably afraid to go to a money changer, which is the only way he could have spent any of it."

"Quite so. And no mention of any Italian money, even from pilgrims?"

"None whatsoever."

"Then we shall have to find the answer to that back at the castle. Now, Brother Bernhard, what is the purpose of that collection of junk in the barn?"

The Prior shook his head and wrung his hands. "Junk it is not. I tried to convince Abbot Johann years ago that it was foolishness to keep collecting those things, but he was a stickler for obeying the rules."

"That was part of your Rule?" queried Henning.

Bernhard smiled, "Not *Rule* with a capital *R*, but back in the thirteenth century when this cloister was founded it was written into our original charter that all excess money over and above what was needed for our support and the maintenance of the churches under our jurisdiction, what was sent to Prémontré and the Archbishop and what was given to the poor, was to be spent on plowshares and other farm equipment so that none of our properties would lack for those things. As you may know, we have, or had, enfeoffed to us over eighty farms, some of them far beyond the borders of County Hoya. It was customary over those three hundred years for many people to will them to us or give them to us to absolve their sins or for various other reasons. In recent years this has not happened very often, but every quarter Abbot Johann and his predecessors bought plowshares and other tools that were no longer needed."

Henning shook his head. "Typical of the poor management and waste in so many of these monasteries. And the convents were only slightly better. We are going to urge His Grace the Duke to appoint a steward to sell all that junk and run the farm. It seems to me a worse sin to let all that fruit and grain rot."

"I agree, but all the lay brothers have left and Graf Jobst took what money we might have used to hire men."

"The steward will hire them and Graf Jobst will have to pay them," Henning assured him, "and that reminds me. Are you aware there are two men waiting outside?"

"Yes. They are two former lay brothers. They asked to talk to Abbot Rudolf."

"And where is he gone off to?"

"I don't know."

"Then let us talk to them." Henning opened the door and explained to the two men that they represented the Duke and could they help them?

"I am—or was—Brother Diedrich and this was Brother Niklaus. We cannot find work. There are too many unemployed monks wandering the countryside, and yet we see here the fruit and grain going to rot for lack of harvesters. We want to come back, but *not* as lay brothers. We know every tree, every blade of grass on this farm and can do a good job, but we want to be paid a proper wage. We want a share of the produce as well and each a cottage of his own."

It was probably the longest speech the man had ever made and his face turned redder by the minute as he twisted his cap in his hands.

Henning turned to Bernhard. "This seems to be the answer to your problem."

"But two are not enough," said Bernhard.

"If two are paid a decent wage, more will come. As Diedrich here just said, there are many men at loose ends out there."

"How can we trust Graf Jobst to pay them?"

"I shall personally see to it that he returns enough of your funds for you to do so."

"And why a cottage for each? They slept four to a hut before. Isn't that good enough?" asked Bernhard.

"We have taken wives, my lord," said Diedrich, and Niklaus nodded.

"Wives!" exclaimed Bernhard. "Women on the Holy Mount! Never!"

Henning laughed at his dismay. "I beg to remind you, Brother Bernhard, that the Blessed Mother herself who resides above your high altar is a woman. And this is no longer a Catholic monastery. Even priests and monks are permitted to wed under the new learning."

Bernhard looked as though he were about to suffer a fit of apoplexy. When he finally got control of himself, he replied, "Very well. We need them. If you can guarantee their wages . . ."

"I shall see to it," Henning assured him and then turned to Diedrich

743

and Niklaus. "From now on Graf Jobst, or possibly the Dowager Countess Katharina, will be your liege lord, and very soon His Grace Duke Ernst will send a steward to be your immediate overseer."

"But what of Abbot Rudolf?" asked Diedrich.

"He, too, is a vassal of the Graf and shall see only to your immediate needs, such as plowshares and pruning hooks, until the steward arrives."

Lüdeke and Markus almost burst out laughing at this, but of course the two laborers were not aware of the joke.

"Very well, Master," said Diedrich, "we shall move in and start work at dawn tomorrow. Thank you, Master."

"Ja, thank you, Masters." Niklaus spoke for the first time. "And I fear our wives will have their hands full cleaning up those rat-infested hovels. But they'll make them into homes, you can be sure."

Back at Castle Hoya two messengers were awaiting Henning. Each handed him a thick letter. One was obviously instructions from Duke Ernst. Henning did not immediately recognize the seal on the other but assumed it to be from the Dowager Countess. At the same time, Jobst was begging in his squeaky voice for a private word with him. He waved him away.

"Later, my lord. First let me read what His Grace has to say."

"Have a care when you open it, Master Behr," warned the Ducal messenger. "His Grace told me to tell you there is a small letter for Master von Sehnden enclosed."

"Aha! Then, Lüdeke, you had best come with me. Must be your new bride misses you," he teased. "And, Markus, come, too." They retired to the locked solar with the missives.

Henning broke open the Ducal seal. The smaller letter fell out. He picked it up and handed it to Lüdeke and began to read the Duke's lengthy missive. "'Ernst, by the Grace of God, Duke, etc., etc., etc., to Master Henning Behr greetings . . .'" The Duke went on to give them permission to clear the books as Markus had suggested and start anew at Michaelmas. That would give the new steward time to advise all the vassal peasants of their just and proper dues. He had appointed one Ulrich von Broitzen to be the steward for County Hoya, and this worthy should be arriving in a few days. Graf Jobst was to cooperate with him unconditionally and could not dismiss him for any reason without first consulting with the Duke. As to the money that was found, he trusted Master Behr to discover the rightful owners and return to them their share less any amount due the Duke. As for Heiligenberg, he reiterated that upon the accession of Graf Jobst all parties had agreed that upon the secularization of the monastery all income from its properties was to be paid to the Dowager Countess Katharina less the dues to her liege lord in order that she not be left destitute, but only for her lifetime. Her children were not to inherit. Upon her death the properties would revert to the Duke, not the Graf of Hoya. The Duke admitted that some of this income might be difficult to collect since some properties lay in the territory of the Bishop of Verden, a vehement Catholic, but the Duke would do his best to assure that these tithes would not be withheld or confiscated by said Bishop. He also appointed one Friedrich von Gladebeck as steward for Heiligenberg, who was entitled to a small share of the income in return for his services. He would be responsible directly to Chancellor Förster, and Graf Jobst was to cooperate with him in all things.

When he had finished reading the Duke's missive to them, Henning was about to turn to the other letter, but Lüdeke jumped up with ill-concealed impatience and, waving his letter before him, shouted gleefully, "I am to be a father! Would you believe it—a father. I must go home."

Henning laughed. "Yes, I would believe it. And when is this miraculous event to take place?"

"Oh, not for months and months," admitted Lüdeke a little sheepishly, "but I must be with her. It is her first."

"Then a few more days will not matter. You will get there soon enough," Henning assured him. "Master von Broitzen will be arriving on one of your boats, and we shall return on the same. Meanwhile we have a lot of work to do here, not the least of which is straightening out Jobst's attitude. Let us see what the Lady Katharina has to say."

The letter was written by her steward. Most probably the lady could not read or write. After a lengthy diatribe describing her cousin-in-law as a thieving rascal, a drunken wastrel, and other choice epithets, she identified the coffer as her own "not given to him as he claimed, but stolen from me." She accurately described all the various deeds and pieces of jewelry. Then she said: "My dower returned to me on his deathbed by my beloved late husband, the last *legitimate* Graf von Hoya, was stolen from me by this upstart who threatened to torture my children if I did not yield it to him. It consisted of a large amount of gold coins which I obtained from the money changers during two journeys to Antwerp, because they advised me that because of the unrest in all of Germany, gold would be more stable than silver. Your Grace, it was all I owned to my name and I am now destitute. If you find it among the things in that coffer, I beg you to return whatever is left to me ere my children starve." The steward had added a note as to the approximate amount, which, allowing for some exaggeration, came to just about what Markus had counted out.

"Well," said Henning, with a sigh of relief, "that solves the last mystery. Now let us confront our friend Jobst with all this information."

"When we left him in the hall just now he seemed to be in a conciliatory mood," said Markus.

"I should think that having been absolved of a charge of treason, he would agree to anything," suggested Lüdeke.

"Perhaps," said Henning, "but he is brazen. I don't envy Master von Broitzen his job of having to watch over Jobst's finances. He is slippery as an eel. Call him up here, Markus."

In the end Jobst agreed to everything, but not without multiple excuses and objections.

"I really thought she was giving it into my safekeeping. I would have returned it to her had she asked."

"I hardly think a lone woman would willingly turn over all she possessed to that person who threatened her children," said Henning. Jobst wilted a little. "And the Heiligenberg treasure?"

"I was afraid they would hide it or bury it somewhere and try to cheat His Grace."

"Yet you saw fit to lie to us, His Grace's representatives." Jobst wilted a little more. "We can still charge you with theft."

Jobst pulled his weeping act again. "No, no," he moaned, "that was not my intention. Anyway, you have it all now. And I don't like the idea of this new steward. Who is he anyhow? It is an insult to my honor."

"You have no honor, my lord," said Henning disgustedly. "He is a competent man chosen by His Grace and Chancellor Förster to see that you remain honest, if not honorable."

"You insult me, Master, but then what can I expect from a mere clerk? At least Friedrich von Gladebeck is a man I can deal with. He is a local man whom I know well."

Lüdeke and Markus exchanged glances at this. Would he intimidate von Gladebeck? they both wondered. But Henning only said, "I remind you, my lord, that my lord von Gladebeck is responsible directly to His Grace, not to you."

Markus never did get the opportunity to inquire about the Wehlenmühle and its adjoining farm, but he kept the dream alive and eventually was to tell it to his children and grandchildren in the hopes that one of them might one day achieve it.

10

Ilsebe Stockman sat at her friend Gretchen von Sehn-den's kitchen table munching on a raw kohlrabi. She was heavily pregnant. Why, oh why, do I always have these cravings for strawberries when it is long past the season? she thought. These endless pregnancies, when will it end? Probably not until I'm dead, she thought morosely. She loved her Hinrik dearly and could deny him nothing, but nine times in fourteen years, six of them living so far, and all girls. Maybe this time it would be the son Hinrik so yearned for. Ilsebe was no longer the demure little river sprite. She had grown fat and her health was no longer good. Not that she ever had much time between carryings to know what her real figure would have looked like. She chewed on the tender green vegetable to take her mind off of luscious berries and barely heard what her friend, also pregnant with her third, was saying.

"Ilsebe, where are you?" asked Gretchen. "I was saying I am worried about Papa Lüdeke."

"He misses Tante Anna," replied Ilsebe. "We all do. She was the only mother I ever knew. Oh, why did she have to go so soon, and so quickly too?" she sobbed.

"She was over seventy," said Gretchen. "That's very, very old, and he is even older. I doubt he'll last long without her."

"Ja, they were very close," agreed Ilsebe, "but aside from his grief, which I can understand, he's not really ill, is he?"

"Not that I can tell, just tired, he claims," said Gretchen. "He says he intends to retire as Bürgermeister very soon. After all, he has been governing Celle for more than thirty-five years. He says it is time some of the younger ones took over."

"I suppose he's right but that doesn't sound like him. I can see why you would worry. He was always so vigorous. The best Bürgermeister Celle has ever had. That's what most people say."

748

"And that's true, but a lot of his success was due to Mama Anna in the background. She tempered his—uh—temper." Gretchen laughed at her own pun.

"Without a doubt," agreed Ilsebe. "She was so highly educated. Did you know she taught me to read and write? Back then girls of my class were not permitted to go to school. All that changed under Onkel Lüdeke due to her influence. When I first saw her library, I was awestricken. I couldn't believe there were so many books in the whole world. And she was every bit the lady, more than most noblewomen I've since met."

"She had some noble blood in her veins, as does Papa Lüdeke."

"True, but Tante Anna never flaunted it," said Ilsebe. "She was always content, proud, in fact, to be a simple Bürger's goodwife. Not like some people I could mention."

Gretchen laughed. "Ja, Mama Anna was the one person who could cut her down to size and be as sweet as honey in the process. I suppose when our guest arrives we shall have to retire to the parlor. It would never do for her to see us sitting in the kitchen nibbling on raw vegetables like a couple of rabbits." Just then the bell hanging outside the front door jangled. Gretchen got up. "Go, settle yourself in the parlor, Ilsebe, and leave that kohlrabi here. I'll be serving coffee and cakes very soon. She'll be shocked enough when I answer the door myself."

Three years ago Eggeling von Eltze had returned from his tour of duty in Bissendorf bringing with him, to everyone's surprise and delight, a wife and two children, with a third on the way. His wife stemmed from a very patrician Lüneburger family, and she never let anyone forget it. Her name had been Ilsebe Buwang in Low German, but ever since Dr. Luther's translation of the Bible had made High German the language of choice for educated people she had let it be known that her name was Ilse Bauman. In addition, there had always been an unspoken rivalry between Lüneburg and Celle. Lüneburg was officially the capital of the Duchy, but Celle was the Residence Town—that is, the Dukes' preferred dwelling place—and for this reason Lüneburgers were slightly jealous of Celle. Lüneburg was also a far more cultural town and many Lüneburgers looked down their noses at Cellenses as they would at country cousins. This did not bother the industrious merchants and Bürgers of Celle one bit. They were too busy making money. And they had the Duke.

Much of this was reflected in Ilse von Eltze's attitude toward her new friends. To give her her due, she tried to be friendly in her own way, but there was always that condescending touch of snobbishness that made

749

people uncomfortable in her presence. The one thing, however, that made them forgive a lot of this was that she was an ardent follower of Luther and being in love seemed to have settled Eggeling's ambivalence in regard to religion and he was now an enthusiastic convert to the new learning. For this alone all his old friends were grateful to her.

Gretchen opened the door. There stood Ilse in all her finery, with a farthingale so wide she could barely fit through the door and an elaborate ruff almost as wide that stood up in back of her head like a picture frame. Her mouth dropped open when she saw Gretchen, but she retained her poise and said to her footman, who was helping her up the steps, "Be back for me in one and a half hours."

"Ja, Mistress," he said and backed off when she seemed to be safely up the three steps to the stoop.

Ilse turned to Gretchen who was still holding the door. "My dear Margarete," she gushed, "how nice to see you. I didn't expect you to open the door yourself."

"It's the housekeeper's afternoon off," said Gretchen. "Do come into the parlor, Ilse."

Ilsebe was sprawled in the most comfortable chair in the room and filled most of it. Although there were other similar chairs scattered about, Ilse had perforce to sit on the straight-backed, armless one because of the width of her skirt. She perched on it as if she were about to fly away any minute.

"Make yourself comfortable, Ilse, while I set the coffee a-boil," said Gretchen.

Ilse tut-tutted, "You have only one servant?"

"Only one housekeeper. The nursemaid is busy abovestairs with the little ones. And we have a groom to tend to the horses and the garden, but he has enough to do. I should hardly expect a man to work in the house."

Ilse shook her head. "I don't know how you manage, and it's not that you can't afford it. Why, I have six and couldn't do with less. In fact, I'd like two more but I haven't yet found any to suit."

"I find three to be ample," replied Gretchen. "I'm not exactly crippled myself. Now if you will excuse me just a moment." She headed for the kitchen gritting her teeth. I'll not let her get under my skin, she told herself.

After she left, Ilse seemed to notice Ilsebe for the first time. "Ah, my dear Ilsebe," she chirped, "how *do* you do? My word, you seem to be getting bigger every time I see you."

750

"That is the nature of babies," replied Ilsebe. "They do grow, you know. And I am doing quite well, thank you." She, too, determined not to be annoyed.

"Of course." Ilse smiled sweetly. "And you do look to be due soon, are you not?"

"Not really. Two more months, in fact, but as you say, I get bigger every time."

"And how many times does this make? You have so many, forgive me if I forget."

"My ninth pregnancy. Six living, all girls—Ilsebe, Katharina, Anna, Margarethe, Sophie and Apollonia. All in good health, God be thanked, except for baby Apollonia, who is suffering from nothing more than a little summer colic."

"Good heavens! Of course, you can be thankful they're all healthy, but did you really want so many?"

It's none of your business, bitch, what I wanted, thought Ilsebe, unwilling to bare her private feelings. Instead she said, "Hinrik wants a son. I shall keep trying until the good Lord sees fit to give us one."

Or die in the attempt, thought Ilse. "An admirable attitude," she commented, not meaning it at all. "And do you do nothing to prevent—I mean the pregnancy?"

At this point Gretchen returned. "Prevent what?" she asked.

"Why, these endless pregnancies, of course," stated Ilse. "Our poor dear Ilsebe looks worn out. And look at you, my dearest Margarete, already on your third and scarcely married five years. Do you intend to have nine, too?"

"What I'll have is my business—and Lüdeke's," replied Gretchen sharply. "And it seems to me you have three sons yourself."

"Of course, and grateful I am for them. All healthy boys, and here is poor Ilsebe still trying for the first one. But no more, I tell you," smirked Ilse. "I have finished with that nonsense. And you may have noticed mine are each two years apart. There are ways to control it, you know."

Gretchen and Ilsebe looked askance at her. "There are?" asked Ilsebe, bewildered.

Gretchen, ever the bolder of the two, asked, "And how, if I may be so rude, does Eggeling take it when you turn him away from your bed?"

"Oh, but I don't turn him away at all. Have you never heard of the sheep's intestine?" The two women shook their heads, puzzled. "We in Lüneburg," continued Ilse, "have more uses for our Heidenschnucken

751

than just for wool and mutton. Our midwives take the intestines and treat them somehow, cut them into lengths and then very carefully sew up one end. When your husband wishes to—er—come to you, he simply slips this sheath over his—er—ah—thing, and lo and behold, it catches baby and all. No problem." Ilse looked smugly satisfied with her superior knowledge.

The other two women looked aghast. Then Ilsebe burst out laughing. "Sheep's guts! I can just see Hinrik putting that over his prick." She laughed so hard she had to hold her sides.

Then Gretchen chimed in, tongue in cheek, "Maybe Lüdeke should go into a new line of business. You mean the midwives actually sell these things?"

"By the dozens," said Ilse, "and quite profitably, too, I understand."

The other wives doubled over in laughter, because Ilse was quite serious.

"But I did not come her to discuss babies and sheep's intestines," she said. "I have good news."

"Let me fetch the coffee and kuchen before you tell it," said Gretchen. "This has been an interesting conversation so far."

When she returned and had served both her guests, she said, "Now tell us."

"The Duke has finally learned to trust Eggeling again," Ilse bubbled, "and about time, I say. Eggeling has finally convinced him that he is sincere in his belief in the new learning. And His Grace has asked him to accompany him to Regensburg."

"I don't think the Duke ever distrusted him," objected Ilsebe. "I knew him for many years before he met you. It was Eggeling himself who had doubt."

"Well, he has none now," said Ilse, "and best of all, I shall be going with him."

"Another Diet?" asked Gretchen. "You will be bored to death. And do you really think they will accomplish any more than all the others?"

"Of course, they will. And I am to have a whole new wardrobe. Eggeling promised me."

"You won't have much social life there," said Gretchen.

"Oh, yes. This time several women are coming. There could be balls and fetes. I'll have a chance to meet duchesses and countesses. I can't wait to see Phillip of Hesse's new wife."

"You won't meet her there. The Emperor has charged him with

bigamy," put in Ilsebe, "and the most you'll see of the others is when you sit behind them in church."

"Lüdeke doesn't trust Charles," said Gretchen. "He says he's using this charge against Phillip to force him out of the Schmalkaldic League."

"Nor does Hinrik trust the Emperor," agreed Ilsebe. "He thinks Charles is preparing for war against the League, and with Phillip immobilized they will have lost their strongest leader. Our dear Ernst simply doesn't have the charisma to hold it together."

"Well, whatever, I've never been to Regensburg," said Ilse sulkily. "Have either of you?" They shook their heads. "They say it is a beautiful city on the Danube surrounded by mountains. I'm so excited. I can't wait."

At the same time their three husbands were in the coffeehouse with their other friend Peter Stratheman, discussing the very same thing.

"So our Ernst has decided to take you back into the fold," said Lüdeke.

"I don't think I was ever out of the fold," replied Eggeling, "but he was right to be unsure of me. I had doubts myself, if you remember. But my dearest Ilse helped me to see the light. I don't see how I could have been so stubborn. I guess it was all the changes coming at us so suddenly. I have always been ultraconservative."

"All of Germany is still trying to contend with these changes," said Hinrik. "We are fortunate here in the north to have a leader like Ernst."

"Which is fine for us," agreed Peter, "but Charles is trying his best to break up the League, and I honestly don't believe our Ernst is strong enough by himself to hold it together."

"I agree," said Lüdeke. "He has imprisoned our two strongest leaders and no one trusts this young Duke Moritz of Saxony. He is trying to turn the whole situation into a political game."

"Yes," agreed Hinrik. "He is too young to remember what we went through at the very beginning of the Reformation. Instead of defending our faith, he is after that Electoral vote."

"Do you really think this Diet will accomplish any more than the previous ones?" asked Peter.

"No, I don't," replied Eggeling. "In fact, probably less. Charles is leaning more and more to the old tenets of Catholicism and less and less toward reconciliation. He is frustrated and that is why he is now openly talking about armed conflict to stamp out what he calls heresy. It will take a while, for France and the Turks are still a threat and even his wise sister Mary, Regent of the Netherlands, advises against it, but he is heading that way. He will, of course, have to import troops from Spain, but now that Pope Paul has publicly offered him troops and money it is only a matter of time. Meanwhile the League is growing weaker because they can't agree amongst themselves."

"Not a pretty prospect. It will tear Germany apart," said Hinrik, "but I for one will not abrogate my faith no matter what happens."

"Nor I," agreed Eggeling, "but we must prepare for the worst."

"And that means lending our money once again," said Lüdeke.

"How true," Peter added. "What would the princes do without us? And speaking of which, what do you think of the Emperor's new edict that we merchants may bear coats-of-arms?"

"Just a ploy to get us on his side," said Lüdeke. "The Fuggers of Augsburg were responsible for that. They say his debt to them runs into the millions."

"True," said Eggeling. "This coat-of-arms thing is just a sop to their dignity, for I fear they'll never see a penny of that money repaid with Charles' constant wars."

"I'm sure you are right," said Hinrik, "and I often wonder how much we'll get back from the Welfs. Where would they be without us? It's time we got a little recognition, even if it is a meaningless right to have a coat-of-arms. I, for one, am going to take advantage of it."

"I, too," said Peter. "Have you thought yet of what you're going to use?"

"There has been talk among the other merchants and the Town Council, too, to use the old runic hausmarks," said Eggeling. "They would certainly be ancient enough and typically Saxon, too."

"I heard that, too," commented Hinrik. "It's an intriguing idea, but I thought your family had one, Eggeling. If not, wherefor the *von?*"

"When the first von Eltze came to Celle, he was in disgrace and disinherited, forbidden to bear the arms. He kept the name, whether with permission or in defiance we don't know."

"So you will need a new one, too," said Hinrik

"I shall, indeed, and I am going to take the old hausmark that the earliest von Eltze Bürgermeisters used."

"But they are so plain and—well—colorless," put in Lüdeke.

"But you already have one," said Peter, "and very colorful and elaborate at that. Yet I'm sure you have never been anywhere near the family demesne."

Lüdeke laughed. "No, I admit I haven't. No one has since my grandfather. But at least we were never disinherited. We still have the right to it. What was yours like, Eggeling? Could you not try to get it back?"

"It was a black grouse," replied Eggeling. "Nowhere near as colorful as yours. But, no, I can't be bothered. I'll stick with the hausmark."

"Well, it's time to be getting back to work," said Hinrik. "Business goes on with or without a coat-of-arms. How Tante Anna would have enjoyed this little farce."

"Indeed she would have," agreed Lüdeke. "Mama loved to make fun of the nobility in her very subtle and noble way."

"Yes, she did," agreed Hinrik, "and yet she was more of a lady than many noble dames."

"That she was," said Lüdeke, "and yet do you know what was one of the last things on her mind ere she died? Our family stipendium. It meant so much to her. She made me promise to have copies made for each of my children as soon as possible. It's been four months now and I haven't done it yet, nor even registered them at Uelzen. I feel so guilty," he said with a catch in his voice, so unlike Lüdeke.

Hinrik patted him on the shoulder. "She would understand. It takes a while to get used to the fact that she's no longer here. We all loved her and miss her. She was my second mother. But go talk to Markus Lindemann. He is a scholar who can read the Latin and writes a fine hand as well. I'm sure he would be happy to make the copies for you."

Hinrik went home from his countinghouse that evening full of thoughts about hausmarks and stipendia. It had long been a dream to set up such a stipendium as the von Sehnden-Mestwart one for his descendants. Now he could well afford to do so. If only he had a son. But he wouldn't say that to his dear Ilsebe. Instead, over supper he asked her views on the hausmark.

"My first question," she replied, "would be: If both your mother and your real father were noble, there must be a real coat-of-arms to which you would be entitled?"

"For one thing, she would never tell me who they were," he replied. "She claimed to be noble but I don't think my father was. She hated and feared him so much, she would never even speak of him nor let us ask. I wasn't even born yet, but my brother Franz remembers nothing but terror, although I often think it was a tiny child's fear of sleeping in the dark woods more than fear of what they were fleeing. And my mother hated her own family almost as much. She often claimed they sold her into slavery when they forced her as a very young maid to marry my father. Also, they refused to help her when she finally escaped. So to answer your question, no. I should want nothing from either of them, even if I knew where to search. I have a suspicion that Onkel Lüdeke knows, but I would not ask him either, as I respect her wishes."

"Then we shall have to think of one that would be appropriate," said Ilsebe. "I wish my old granny were still alive. She could read the old runes, and though she taught me a little of it, I don't remember too much. Could we not use the one from the old house on Schuhstrasse?"

Some years ago Hinrik had moved his growing family to a larger and more modern house on Dorstrasse, the short street leading to the Hehlentor. Ilsebe loved the house, although she thought the street too noisy and busy.

"No, I don't think so," replied Hinrik. "Technically I believe they belong to the house itself, or at least to the family who originally lived there."

"Then we'll just have to design our own. Let me rack my brain and see how much I remember of the old runes." She thought a moment. "You always start with an upright shaft."

"That I know. Then what?"

"A crosspiece just below the top to indicate you are head of the family."

"But actually Franz is the elder."

"You are the head of *this* family, and anyway, he's not a merchant. He can use the shield of the masons' guild, if he chooses."

"Granted. And then?"

"A small steplike line on the right side just above the foot to indicate you are the first of the line."

"Very well. So far, so good, but it's still a little plain."

"Then let's fancy it up a bit. Let me think." After a brief pause, she continued. "How about a forty-five-degree angle coming up from the foot on the left side to indicate you are striving to reach the top? But it must be on the left side since you are not sure of your ancestry."

"I like the striving part, but I'm not sure I care for the ancestor part."

She laughed. "But it's true, isn't it? You just said so."

"I suppose."

"Then let's add one more thing. A short crosspiece perpendicular to that angle line to indicate that the world acknowledges your striving and is proud of you despite the left-hand angle."

This made Hinrik laugh. "My dear love, you are so clever. Now tell

756

me true, is this really what the runes mean or are you making this all up?"

"A little of both," she admitted smiling. "But there are so few people left who can still read the old runes, and even they disagree on their meaning, who's to dispute it?"

"You're quite right as usual. Then that's it," said Hinrik. "That will be our hausmark."

"And one more thing," Ilsebe added. "When you have a son, he will be entitled to add a small vertical line on the right side of the top cross bar, indicating he is the eldest."

"A son?" said Hinrik, suddenly serious. "Don't tease me, sweeting. You know how I feel about that."

"I'm not teasing, Hinrik." She patted her belly. "This one will be a son. My old grannie came to me in a dream and told me so."

Hinrik kept his skepticism to himself and was truly surprised when less than two months later Ilsebe presented him with his first son, a strong, healthy boy they named Franz after his uncle. Ilsebe was triumphant. "See, I told you so. Grannie was never wrong." But although it had been an easy labor, she was exhausted. "From now on we shall use the sheep's gut for a while."

Hinrik had no idea what she was talking about.

The year 1546 began in sorrow and ended in disaster.

Early in January their beloved Duke Ernst of Lüneburg died. In February Martin Luther followed him to the grave. In early spring Hinrik Stockman's dearest Ilsebe met her Maker. And in June after two more fruitless Diets at Worms and at Regensburg, the Emperor decided to declare war on the Protestants.

Although Ernst had willed that each of his four sons were to succeed him one after the other in order not to further divide the Duchy, a Diet was immediately held at Uelzen to determine a regency, as the eldest Franz Otto was still a minor, although just a few months short of age twenty-one. Ernst's sister Apollonia, who had been a nun at Wienhausen but left the cloister five years ago to care for Ernst's eight children, fought for the post, and the Diet very reluctantly agreed, but only on the condition that the very able Jürgen von der Wense, the Ducal governor, be co-regent.

Martin Luther shortly before his death had finally reversed his opinion that regardless of religious beliefs, Germany should remain loyal to the Emperor. In Luther's last days, instead of 'our beloved Emperor,' he called Charles 'that Spaniard' who wants to reduce Germany 'to the cattle-like servitude of Spain.' Melanchthon, Luther's staunchest lieutenant, however, was backing down on some of his firm stands. Seeing war on the horizon, he said that by virtue of military might the Evangelicals should win, but the stars said they would not, thereby reinjecting medieval superstition into hearts just beginning to emerge from it.

Hinrik Stockman paid very little attention to any of this. His beloved river sprite had been very ill since she had finally borne him another son, named Balthasar after his stepfather, the previous year. After the birth she had bled for a long time and everyone despaired for her life. Miraculously she had seemed to recover, but month by month she had lost a great deal of the weight she had gained over the years. Instead of this enhancing her appearance, she became wraith-like, pale and wan. It soon became obvious that she was very ill indeed. Although she fought valiantly, the best doctors shook their heads. They did not know what was wrong and could not help her. As the worst of the winter weather struck, she began to cough and, too weak to go on, took to her bed. Markus' mother, the elderly Frau Lindemann, came in to look after the children with the help of the eldest daughters. Hinrik himself insisted on nursing Ilsebe, almost to the detriment of his own health. He began to neglect his very lucrative business until his loyal friends Lüdeke, Eggeling and Peter, although competitors, stepped in to help him in that area.

Hinrik sat by her bed every day and held her in his arms by night. One day in early spring as the last snow was melting, she murmured, "Hinrik love, help me to the window that I may see the first crocuses blooming in my garden."

"It will be too much for you, sweeting," he objected.

"I want to see flowers once more before I go," she insisted. "Help me, Hinrik. I haven't much time."

"No, no, don't say that."

But she was adamant, so he gently lifted her and carried her to the window. The bright purple, yellow and white blooms were just thrusting through the last of the snow. The sight seemed to cheer her. Then she started to gasp for breath and he could almost feel the fever rising in her frail body. He carried her back to the bed. The noise had alerted the older girls and Frau Lindemann, who came rushing in.

"Papa, what are you doing?" cried Ilsebe the younger.

"Your Mama wanted to see the crocuses," he replied.

"I am happy now," whispered Ilsebe. "Thank you, my love." And to the girls, "I am going to my river goddess very soon. Fetch the little ones." Frau Lindemann rushed to do Ilsebe's bidding. After gasping for breath again, she added, "Bury me as close to the river as you can, dearest Hinrik."

"No, no, you're not going, love."

"Promise me."

"Very well, I promise."

"Mama, Mama, don't leave us," cried young Ilsebe and Katharina in unison.

A few moments later Frau Lindemann ushered in the rest of the children, carrying the baby in her arms. The two teenagers Anna and Margarethe were very subdued. The two younger girls Sophie and Apollonia were weeping. Little five-year old Franz tried to put on a brave face.

"Mama is going to the river goddess," he stated.

"No, she's not," objected Anna. "She's going to Jesus."

"But she told me so yesterday," declared Franz, choking back a sob.

"Now, children, don't argue," said Hinrik. "Not now."

Ilsebe raised her arm weakly and everyone subsided. "Let me hold my baby one last time," she whispered. She could not sit up, so Frau Lindemann gently placed the little one in the crook of her arm. "Ah, my little Baltke, I shall never see you grow up." She kissed him and when her breathing became labored again, the midwife took the baby away. Then after a moment Ilsebe said, "Dearest Franzele, you must be a brave man and help your Papa in every way."

"I will, Mama, I will," he sobbed.

"Ilsebe and Käthchen, my dearest daughters, I know you are both betrothed and will wed soon, but until then, please be mothers to the little ones."

"We shall, Mama," they said.

"And Anna and Gretchen, you are growing up fast. When your sisters leave home, you must be little mothers too."

"Oh, Mama," gulped Anna through her tears, and Margarethe simply nodded, unable to speak.

And to Sophie and Apollonia, "You must be very good girls and obey your sisters. I shall be watching over you. And don't worry. Jesus is coming for me, but He will let me live with the river goddess." Neither of the youngest girls seemed to understand what was happening, but little Franz brightened at this statement. However, the effort was too much for Ilsebe and she lay back gasping, her breath becoming shallower every minute. At last she was able to murmur, "I love you all, my sweetings. Auf Wiederse-hen and God bless you. Now leave me alone with Papa."

Frau Lindemann ushered them all out of the room as Hinrik held Ilsebe's hand tightly as though by doing so he could keep her from leaving him. She made one more effort to speak, but so faint was her voice, he had to lay his head near hers to hear. "Hinrik, I love you. You have made my life a wondrous thing." She shuddered and tried to continue. He strained to hear. "But now let me go and try—try to find another—another mother for them." She shuddered again and closed her eyes.

He held her hand tighter and wailed, "Ilse, sweeting, don't leave me." But she was gone. Still holding her hand, he threw his head on her breast and wept uncontrollably.

After a long time Frau Lindemann tiptoed in and found him in the same position. She gently tapped him on the shoulder. "Master Stock-man, she is gone," she said consolingly. "Know that she loved you, but your children need you now. You must be strong for them." He slowly raised his head and looked at her dully, the pain in his eyes terrible to see. He stood up stiffly, like a man twice his age, and nodded. "Don't worry here," she said. "I shall see to the laying out. Now go to them."

After the funeral Hinrik went back to work. At first his heart was not in it, but soon he realized that it took his mind off his loss and he buried himself in it to such an extent that he was seldom at home. Ilsebe and Katharina had perforce to postpone their nuptials until after the year of mourning was past.

Ilsebe had inherited her mother's sweet voice and her love of music. She was also a dreamer. Now that women were permitted to sing in church choirs and composers, including Luther himself, were writing hymns in four-part, she was in her element. She had been singing in the choir for some years when a young man fresh out of seminary at Witten-berg was appointed one of the junior clergy. He also sang in the choir when he was not needed to assist at the service. He played the organ quite capably as well. His name was Heinrich Freye, and it was not long before their common interest in music and church work drew them together. Her father tried to discourage the match because the boy looked sickly to him, but Ilsebe in her quiet way was just as stubborn as her mother had been, and the betrothal took place.

Katharina was the more practical of the two. She had inherited her father's head for business and during her mother's illness and after her death ran the Stockman household as a stern but kind martinet. She often wished she were a man and frequently helped out in Hinrik's counting-house, not because she had to, but because she loved working with figures, loved the tension of wholesale buying and selling. Hinrik even allowed her to travel to Antwerp with him occasionally because it gave him pleasure to watch her keen mind at work. It was through the business that she met her future betrothed Hinrich Schrader. Though by no means of Gewandschneider status, the young man came from a solid Bürger family and was already making his mark as a buyer and seller of real estate. He and Katharina were perfectly matched.

Of the four older girls, fifteen-year-old Anna was the most serious. She only grudgingly learned the running of the household and other feminine attributes, much preferring scholarly pursuits. Once she could read well, she haunted the von Sehnden library, frequently shutting herself away there for hours on end. She enjoyed talking to old Lüdeke von Sehnden, who had finally retired as Bürgermeister in 1542. He regaled her with stories of the history of Celle and enjoyed her company more than that of his own grandchildren. She also spent time visiting Frau Lindemann's husband, a classical scholar who had given all of his children Latin names. Hinrik despaired that Anna would ever marry but thought perhaps she would grow out of it.

Margarethe at thirteen was the fun-loving one. Ever cheerful, she joked and teased the others unmercifully but never in a mean way. Too frivolous to settle down, her attempts at cooking and sewing were disasters, although she sincerely tried. Katharina often said she doubted Margarethe had a serious bone in her body. But Hinrik considered her his little river sprite and was sure she would grow into a fine woman. And she was a marvel with the younger children. She dried their tears and cuddled them. She taught them games by day and entertained them with an endless supply of fairy tales at bedtime, and they adored her.

In June of 1546 the Emperor finally declared war on the Protestant princes of the Schmalkaldic League. It was a poorly organized war on both sides but the Protestants had superior military forces and could easily have been triumphant had they attacked immediately while Charles was waiting for his troops to arrive from Spain. But they believed the Emperor when he stated that it was a purely political war to punish a few recalcitrant princes. However, the Pope openly announced that it was a crusade to stamp out the Lutheran heresy and sent him both money and troops to back it up. This infuriated the German people, who were more than willing to fight for both religion and homeland had they but had the leaders to lead them. But their strongest leaders were gone, either dead or prisoners of the Emperor. There was little agreement among the others, and they timidly decided on defensive action only and sat back and waited to see what Charles would do. Their composure was further shattered by the defection of young Moritz of Upper Saxony, a lifelong Lutheran, to the Emperor's fold for strictly political reasons. The Emperor had promised him the Electoral vote that belonged to his cousin, now Charles' prisoner. The Emperor promised the same thing to the Duke of Bavaria, who, though Catholic, hated the Habsburgs with a passion and wanted no part of the war. They both believed the Emperor, but in the end neither promise was kept.

Most of the fighting was in the south where Charles tried to wipe out those brave pockets of Protestantism scattered amongst the Catholic territories. But there were also many battles along the borders of the Lutheran north and the Catholic south. In addition many Catholic rulers encouraged by all this started to persecute the Lutherans living within their lands. Among these were the Duchy of Lüneburg's two nearest neighbors, Wolfenbüttel and Calenberg, both cousins and offshoots of the ancient division of the Welf lands. Heinrich der Jünge of Wolfenbüttel had remained Catholic, partly because of two powerful brothers, the Archbishop of Bremen and the Bishop of Minden, and partly because he was a true Machiavellian type, totally untrustworthy, who lived openly with his mistress. (Even though poor Phillip of Hesse had been arrested by Charles for the very same sin simply because he was a Lutheran.) And all this despite the fact that der Jünge's capital city, Braunschweig and almost all his people were Lutheran. Erich II of Calenberg had been brought up a Lutheran by his mother Elizabeth, the same one who had once convinced Duke Ernst of the wisdom of secularizing the monasteries. For political reasons only, presumably in order to be on the winning side, Erich reverted to Catholicism and even held his former teacher and mentor Anton Corvinus prisoner for many years. And this, too, despite the fact that his capital city, Hannover and his entire Duchy were staunch Lutherans.

Celle, fortunately, was spared any of the fighting, but it was to her that many of the refugees from these neighboring duchies fled.

One Sunday Ilsebe came home from church, always a little later than the rest of the family, as she had to put away her vestments and music, accompanied by two strangers. The young woman appeared to be a year

762

or two older than she, the young man perhaps a bit more. They were both very plainly dressed and quite shy and retiring. They seemed overawed by the richness of the Stockman parlor.

"Papa," cried Ilsebe with much excitement, "we have two new singers in the choir."

Hinrik looked up from the book he was reading. "Indeed? I really hadn't noticed."

"I wonder if I might invite them to dinner," queried Ilsebe.

It was only then that he noticed the forlorn pair standing behind her. "Er—ah—" he hemmed. "You'll have to ask cook if there be enough. Who are they?"

"Oh, Papa, you know there is always more than enough," Ilsebe said. "But I'm sorry. This is Margarethe von der Ohe and her brother Martin. They have only just arrived here in Celle from a little place nearby Peine. They have fled from the persecutions."

At this point Katherina entered the room and on hearing this last remembered how Ilsebe as a child was always dragging home stray kittens. Now, she thought, she's dragging home stray people. What next?

"Indeed?" said Hinrik. "I wasn't aware that it was that bad."

"Oh, Papa," replied Ilsebe. "Both Wolfenbüttel and Calenberg are trying to put all the Lutherans in prison, even torturing some of them."

Hinrik looked askance. "I fail to see how they can put the entire populations of two duchies in prison."

Katharina thought it was time to interrupt. "I came to tell you, Papa, that dinner is on the table," she said.

"Are neither of your young men coming today?" asked Hinrik.

"My Hinrich is dining with his parents today," replied Katharina. "We shall be going out walking later. I don't know about Ilsebe's."

"He won't be here either," said Ilsebe. "So you see, Papa, there will be more than enough."

"Very well," replied Hinrik. "As Christians we can hardly turn away refugees from persecution."

Katharina raised her eyebrows at his sarcasm, which went right over her sister's head. "I shall tell Mädl to set two more places," Katharina said and left the room.

Hinrik put aside his book and his newfangled spectacles. He stood up. and donned his doublet, which had been hanging over the back of the chair, and followed her. All this time the two young people had said not a word.

763

"Come into the dining room, Margarethe, Martin," invited Ilsebe. "I'm sure you have not had a good meal since you left home. And we have a very good cook. And you must meet the rest of the family." The couple followed her in silence.

When they were all seated at the table, Ilsebe announced to all, "These are my friends Margarethe von der Ohe and her brother Martin from Peine. This is my sister Katharina, whom you have already met." Katharina blinked but nodded graciously. "And Anna." Anna thought, a pair of illiterate imbeciles, and turned away as soon as it was polite to do so. "And Margarethe." Margarethe smiled a welcome. "And Sophie, Apollonia and Franz. On Sundays we let the little ones join us. We also have a baby up in the nursery."

At last Margarethe von der Ohe found her tongue. In a tiny voice she murmured, "Thank you so much for inviting us," and blushed becomingly.

Her brother echoed, "Ja, thank you," and looked about to dive into the food before Hinrik could say the grace.

As they all began eating Hinrik tried to draw them out. "And why did you choose to come to Celle, Mistress von der Ohe?" he asked.

"We heard it was safe for—uh—people like us," she replied. "And please do call me Geske, Master Stockman."

"Do you have family or friends here?"

"No, no one."

There is more to this than meets the eye, he thought. "Where do you plan on living?" he asked.

"We don't know yet."

As I thought. He turned to Martin, who was shoveling food into his mouth as if he had not eaten in a week. "And what do you do for a living?"

"He is a journeyman butcher," his sister answered for him.

"Did you bring transfer papers from your guild?" he asked, still addressing Martin.

"I don't know," she said. "Martin, do you have papers?" Martin shook his head.

"Papa, I'm sure you can help him find work," interrupted Ilsebe. "You know just everybody."

Hinrik could have killed her. He hated to be placed in an awkward position. "I don't know," he said hesitantly. "The guilds are very strict here in Celle. I have only a passing acquaintance with the Head Master of the Butcher's guild, hardly enough to ask him a favor. Without proper papers, it will be very difficult. The butchers are not exactly my line of business."

"I'm sure you'll think of something," said Ilsebe. "And would you mind if they stayed with us for a little while until Martin gets work and they can find a place of their own?"

Katharina sputtered, "Ilsebe!" but bit her tongue. It was up to her father, who looked decidedly uncomfortable.

Geske could see this was not going well at all. "I would be happy to help around the house," she said timidly. "And I'm very good with babies."

Hinrik thought a moment. Ignorant though they seemed to be, they were smart enough to go first to the church and latch onto someone as gullible as his daughter. He suspected their motives and wondered what their real story was. At last he reluctantly agreed. "Very well. In all Christian charity we cannot turn away folks in need. But only for a few days, mind you. Then they shall have to go to St. Anna's until Martin finds work. I shall inquire for him, but I will promise you nothing."

"Oh, Papa, thank you," cried Ilsebe. "I knew we could count on you."

"There is only one spare room available, in the servants' attic," he said. "They will have to share it. Extra pallets are up in the second attic. Show them where, Ilsebe, and Martin can carry them down. There is a well for washing out in the garden. After today they may share the servants' meals in the kitchen." Hinrik was determined not to let them feel too much at home. "Where are your clothes and things?" he asked.

Geske spread her hands. "We left in such haste we did not have time to pack anything, Master."

Ho! It gets worse and worse, thought Hinrik and Katharina at the same time. I fear we have here a pair of montebanks pretending innocence, thought Hinrik. And Katharina thought, she is looking for a rich husband. Thank God our Franz is too young for her.

After dinner, when Ilsebe had taken the von der Ohes up to the attic to show them their room, Hinrik rose from the table and said, "Have a care for your purses and jewels, my girls, for I trust them not."

Katharina and Anna agreed, but Margarethe said, "I feel sorry for them. She is so sweet and shy."

"Just heed what your father has said," warned Katharina sharply.

Although Hinrik made a few token inquiries on Martin's behalf, just to get them out of the house, he made no serious effort to find work for the young man. In the end it was Martin himself, no doubt with his sister's help, who found a job. Not as a butcher or even butcher's helper, to be sure, but as a menial laborer at a tannery outside the town walls by the river. Part of the work consisted of cleaning up the entrails and odure after the tanners left for the day and part as a sort of night watchman. To this end the compensation included a minuscule airless sleeping hut, one sparse meal a day and a penny a week. Because of the stink, tanneries always lay downwind outside the walls and their denizens were rarely welcomed inside the town.

Since there was no possibility of Geske's moving in with her brother, Hinrik permitted her to stay on at the Stockmans' for a while. With Martin's departure a burden seemed to have lifted from her and she brightened a bit and became less shy. Nevertheless, she flitted about the house as unobtrusively as a shadow. She willingly helped wherever needed. She did scullery work in the kitchen and uncomplainingly washed the heaviest laundry; she polished furniture and silver under the watchful eye of the maid, and she was especially helpful with baby Balthasar, of which the nursery maid took full advantage. For all Geske's help, none of the servants really liked her, for no obvious reason than a reflection of their master's distrust.

Ilsebe was enthralled with her new friend, which made for an awkward situation, since one was the Master's daughter and officially, though not in fact, the mistress of the house and the other a servant on largesse. Ilsebe solved this partially by acting Geske's equal at choir rehearsals and church and other activities away from home and ignoring her almost completely within the house. Ilsebe did talk her father into giving Geske a length of cloth for a second gown, but Hinrik made sure it was the plainest, coarsest brown fustian. Yet Geske was embarrassingly grateful for it.

Katharina, who was the actual mistress of the household, and Anna, who had trouble hiding her disgust, both ignored Geske. But Margarethe seemed to like her, primarily because of her kindness to the younger children, and soon they were sharing the games and bedtime stories.

Soon both Ilsebe and Katharina became immersed in plans for their weddings. It was Ilsebe who realized that if they waited for a full year of mourning for their mother to pass, they would be in the middle of Lent when no weddings could take place or, if they did, were considered unlucky. She pointed this out to her sister, and for once Katharina agreed with her that they should convince Papa to let them marry before Lent since they both had postponed their nuptials for many months already.

Hinrik could see the sense in it. "I am sure your dear Mama would have agreed," he said. "She did not want us to mourn excessively. She always wanted this to be a happy household." Although he would miss

766

Katharina's efficiency, he did not think it fair to hold her back from her own happiness. As for his eldest daughter, it was time a husband took Ilsebe in hand and weaned her away from what he considered her unhealthy attachment to Geske. "But we must keep it simple. No elaborate festivities, because officially we shall still be in mourning and there are those who would regard too much hilarity as disrespectful to the dead."

The girls were so relieved at obtaining his permission that both readily agreed to this restriction. Together they planned a double wedding for the Sunday after the Epiphany.

The Christmas festivities were necessarily subdued but happy nonetheless. Everyone enjoyed baby Balthasar's delight at the sight of his first Christmas tree. Now walking, albeit unsteadily, he had to be constantly restrained from burning his hands on the brightly lit candles as he tried to pull off marzipan apples and other decorations strung on the tree. It seemed by common consent Geske's lot to watch over him. On Christmas Eve the servants were permitted to join the family celebration and they all went to church together. Ilsebe gave Geske an expensive jewel for Christmas, which annoyed Hinrik no end. And again on Twelfthnight when the servants took over the household, they elected a stable hand Lord of Misrule and, to everyone's surprise, he chose Geske as his Queen. She acted as regal a princess as any real queen but blushed endlessly at the ribald jokes. Her forfeits for the most part were milder than the groom's and just plain fun except for one. Of Hinrik she demanded a kiss from the Master. Everyone's mouth fell open, but Hinrik took it in the spirit of the season, stepping up to her throne and giving her a slight buss on the cheek. Immediately she turned beet-red, but he noticed that her complexion was as soft and smooth as any lady's.

After Ilsebe and Katharina left home, he turned the management of the household over to Anna and Margarethe. Anna, though very efficient, hated it. Margarethe, however, revelled in her newly acquired authority and turned increasingly to Geske for guidance in domestic matters. Under Geske's tutelage even Margarethe's cooking and sewing improved considerably. Now that the girls were sixteen and fourteen, Hinrik also realized it was time he started seeking suitable husbands for them. He also could not forget his dearest Ilsebe's last words to him, that he find another mother for the little ones. The smoothness of Geske's skin kept haunting him and he avoided her all the more studiously.

He turned his mind to possible prospects for his next two daughters. He would dearly have loved an alliance with his best friends Lüdeke von

767

Sehnden and Eggeling von Eltze, but both their eldest sons were too young for Anna. Perhaps for Margarethe when the time came. He would have to hint about it. But Anna would be a difficult one to find a mate for. Not many men would put up with her bookishness and lack of interest in household matters. Well, there was time yet. Perhaps she would change now that she had more responsibilities.

One particularly bitter February evening he was seated at his desk in the second parlor, which he used as a home office. Although there was a bright fire in the hearth, he still felt the chill. The wind whistled about the house and the snow came down heavily outside the window. It had been an exceedingly frustrating day. The river had frozen solid earlier than expected and a shipment of cloth had failed to arrive. By the feeble light of a single candle he was poring over some documents when he heard quiet footsteps behind him.

It was Geske bearing a steaming cup of chocolate. She placed it at his elbow. "I thought you might enjoy this," she said quietly. "It will take the chill off and mayhap help you sleep."

"Why thank you, Geske," he replied. "That is very thoughtful of you."

The next night she came again bearing the chocolate. And again on the third. She appeared to be making a routine of it, and although he was still leery of her motives, over the months that she had become part of the household she had given him no reason whatever to doubt her sincerity or her honesty. And he really appreciated the gesture. Anna would never have thought of it, and Margarethe was long abed.

On the third night he invited Geske to join him. Not the least bit flustered, she went to fetch another cup. When she returned, he indicated she should sit opposite him by the fire. He said, "I can't seem to concentrate on my work tonight. Perhaps a little conversation would help."

She replied, "Methinks you work too hard, Master Stockman. Day and night is too much."

"One must when one has one's own business, but I should rather talk about you. In all the months you have been here I confess I know very little about you. And I do apologize for not thanking you for all you do around here without any remuneration."

She waved his words aside. "I am just grateful to have a roof over my head with a kind family. That is re—remun —," she stumbled over the strange word, "reward enough."

He smiled. "So tell me about yourself."

"What is there to tell?"

"Your name, for a beginning. It suggests nobility. Yet you arrive here with no but the clothes on your back and work as a servant." He was remembering his mother's story and wondered if hers was similar.

"We have noble blood in us, although very minor penniless Landsknecht. But I am afraid most of it is on the wrong side of the blanket—or of the left hand, as my grandmama used to say."

"I see," he said. "And you and your brother were younger children of younger children and so on."

"Something like that," She hesitated and he sensed there was more to come. She finally decided she could trust him. It would be good to tell someone at last. "Nay, nay, Master, it was worse than that. Ja, we were the youngest of the youngest living on the sufferance of the eldest, who was impoverished himself, but landless though we were, we had the run of the hall, other children and dogs to play with, and enough food to keep from starving. But then the troubles began. I wasn't lying when I said we fled from persecution, but I wasn't telling the whole truth either," she admitted, and whatever she was about to say brought the blush to her cheeks again. "True, we were devout Lutherans and Duke Heinrich had his men riding to and fro through the Duchy seeking out heretics,—or so he claimed. In reality—I'm sure you have heard of his reputation as a womanizer, Master." Hinrik nodded. "In reality," she went on, "he was seeking out young maidens to tickle his old man's fancy." This time Hinrik blushed. That makes me an old man, too, in her eyes, since he is my contemporary. But Geske did not notice and continued, "He mostly picked on the poorer ones who could not defend either their land or their daughters. He dared not offend the more important lords, as he needed their support and their troops. When his men found a likely maiden, he would ride out himself and claim 'dvadasen . . .'", she struggled over the French term.

"You mean *droit-de-seigneur*," clarified Hinrik. "But that went out of practice a hundred or more years ago."

"That's the word he used," she said, "and for someone like Heinrich it never went out of practice. And it helped salve his conscience, if he had any, if one was Lutheran besides." She hesitated, and tears came to her eyes.

"Go on," Hinrik urged gently. All he could think of was his mother. "Tell me all of it."

She brushed away the tears with the corner of her apron. "My elder sister Ursala was one of the ones picked out for him. He rode in one day and simply raped her. Martin was a teenager then and tried—foolishly as it turned out—to protect her virtue. He was hit on the head by the duke's men for his trouble, and left for dead. He has been a little—a little simple—ever since. Ursala became pregnant, but she did not want his child. Many women did, you know, thinking they could get money and position from the Duke—the more fools they. He already had enough and more bastards around the countryside. So she went to our local wisewoman to rid herself of the child. She did, but she died as well. But before she died, she made the old woman promise to send the—the mess—I can't call it a baby—to the Duke." She was openly weeping now.

"My poor child," sympathized Hinrik.

"There is not much more to tell. Heinrich, of course, believed it was the family that sent him the—the corpse. He was furious and came and threatened to burn the house around our heads. But then he saw me. 'I'll take this one instead,' he said and raped me in front of the family."

Brutal though the times were, even Hinrik was shocked at this.

Geske choked and then continued. "He spared the house but burned the barn and pigsty and killed our best milker. He said, 'Let that be a lesson to you in case I've filled this one's belly'."

"Oh, my poor child," exclaimed Hinrik again. "And how old were you then?"

"No but thirteen," she replied, "but I was lucky. At least I did not get pregnant."

"And how old are you now, Geske?" he asked.

"I am three and twenty."

"And for ten years you have been fleeing?" he inquired in disbelief.

"Nay, nay," she replied, "We were home. The Duke left us alone after that. But last year when the troubles with the Emperor started, he sent his men all over the Duchy taking all the young men for his army whether they wanted to go or not. I knew Martin could not possibly serve as a footsoldier, and truthfully, I was afraid again for myself. Also, by then our grandparents were dead and the eldest cousin let it be known that we were just two extra mouths to feed which he didn't need. So we went first to Hannover and that was where Martin started his butcher's apprenticeship. I am sorry I lied about that, but we were so desperate. He was not a journeyman at all, just a beginning apprentice, and the only reason the butcher even took him in was because his wife needed a maid. Forgive me for that."

"No matter now," said Hinrik, secretly glad he had not pursued the matter of Martin's employment. It could have been terribly embarrassing, even damaging to his own reputation. "Then how came you to Celle?"

"When the Duke of Calenberg, Erich, decided to turn back to being a Catholic again—and I simply cannot understand that—he was worse in his persecutions than Heinrich ever thought of being. Just to prove himself to the Emperor, I suppose. Anyway, it was the butcher's wife who warned us, 'He will pick on strangers first, and since you have not lived in the town yet a year, you are in danger.' It was she who suggested we would be safe in Celle. It was she who told us to go first to the church. And you know the rest." She spread her hands and sighed.

Hinrik nodded, unable to comment on her story. All he could think of was how Anna Mestwart—his beloved Tante Anna von Sehnden—had taken in his mother and brothers under similar circumstances. His daughter Ilsebe had done the same. He must apologize to her when the time was right.

A bit frightened by his silence, Geske pleaded, "I hope you will not turn me out, now that you know the story."

"No, never. Never fear that, dear child," he reassured her. "Someday I shall tell you a similar story. But now it grows late."

She did not come the next evening. Nor the next, though he waited in vain. It had been pleasant to end the day in her company. Although he felt fatherly toward her, he also had to admit to himself that he missed a woman's company. The following evening he went out to the kitchen, the servants' domain, where he seldom ventured. She was helping the others clean up after supper.

In order not to seem too familiar in front of the other servants, he ordered, "Geske, I should like a cup of chocolate later on, when you are finished here."

"Yes, Master," she replied formally. "I shall be there in about a half hour, if that is convenient."

"Quite," he agreed and went back to the second parlor. He found he could not concentrate on his work, such was his impatience for her company.

When at last she arrived bearing just one cup of steaming chocolate, he asked, "Why did you not come last eve? I have missed you."

She looked surprised. "But, Master, I feared you could not stand the sight of me after what I told you of myself."

"Foolish girl," he chided. "It was not your fault, and you were no but

771

a lass. Now fetch yourself a cup of this delicious brew and come sit with me a bit."

When she returned, he bade her sit. "Now I shall tell you a story." And he told her as much as he knew of his mother's saga. It was a long story, and she sat demurely with hands folded on her lap but listening intently throughout. When at last he finished, he said, "So you see, were it not for blessed Tante Anna and later for my dearest stepfather Balthasar, I, too, would be wandering penniless throughout the countryside, instead of sharing chocolate with you in an opulent parlor."

She shook her head in amazement. "The things you don't know about people. I just assumed that you had always been rich."

He shook his head. "Very few of the Bürgers of Celle started out rich, although not all became so as recently as I. For example, my friend Lüdeke von Sehnden, it was his grandfather who came here as an impoverished knight. And Eggeling von Eltze, his ancestors go back several hundred years to the founding of Celle, but the first one was disinherited and banned from the family castle. We all made our way through hard work. So, you see, you were wise to choose Celle. Of all towns it most exemplifies the old saying that 'town air is free air'."

"I understand what you are saying," she murmured, although she was not quite sure that she did. Yet somehow she now felt a sort of kinship with him.

The beautiful clock on the mantel, which she had always admired, although she could not read it, chimed ten.

"Oh, my dear," exclaimed Hinrik, surprised that it was so late. "I fear I have kept you from your bed. I know you must arise before dawn or cook will be furious. I do apologize."

"But it has been very interesting, Master Stockman," she demurred. "But yes, I must run now." She gathered up the cups.

"Will you come tomorrow evening?" he asked.

"If you would like me to."

"I most certainly would."

Although Celle itself suffered from no battles in the Schmalkaldic war, the rest of the Duchy of Lüneburg did not fare so well. Bordered as it was by the only two territories of any size in the north ruled by Catholic princes, it suffered several punitive incursions because it was one of the strongest Lutheran lands in all of Germany. Ironically, almost all the people and towns of these two neighboring duchies, Wolfenbüttel and Calenberg, were staunchly Evangelical, so that their armies consisted mostly of mercenaries supplied by the Emperor. On the other hand, the late Duke Ernst of Lüneburg had consistently maintained a force of knights and men intent on defending their homeland against Catholicism and the Emperor. In addition, every single city, town and village had a well-trained and enthusiastic militia, which grew out of the original town watches. After the demise of Duke Ernst, his cousin Erich of Calenberg, who had reverted to Catholicism for purely political reasons, decided that with a weak regency on the ducal throne, the time was ripe to increase the frequency and ferocity of these attacks and under the cover of religion turned it into an internecine strife.

The new Graf of Hoya, as peace-loving as his predecessor Jobst had been warlike, nevertheless knew that the broad Weser valley had ever since time immemorial been a high road for armies and invaders. He saw that his town and village militias were well trained and well armed with swords, pikes and halberds as well as many of the expensive new muskets as he could afford. Moreover, the major cities and towns of the north, Bremen, Hamburg, Lüneburg, and Celle, among many others, had become fed up with these incessant harassments and decided it was time to take the offensive. Despite the regency, the core of the ducal army was still intact, and every city, town and village sent as many contingents as they were able to join it. It was organized under the able command of Graf Albrecht von Mansfeld.

One bright Sunday afternoon at the beginning of May Jacob Bruns' two eldest sons Erich and Christian were exercising with the local militia in an open meadow in Vilsen.

"See how quickly I can reload this musket," bragged Erich.

"Not as quickly as I can touch off this pistol," said Christian. He rammed the powder home, inserted the ball, took a step forward with his arm extended supported by his other hand and while his brother was still trying to get his smoldering wick to ignite the powder in his musket, pulled the trigger, which set a little wheel spinning against a flint, thereby releasing a shower of sparks that set off the gunpowder. His ball hit the target pretty close to where he intended.

Several of their friends gathered round to examine this unusual new weapon.

"What is that strange weapon you have there, Christian?" asked one man.

"It's called a pistol and it's much faster than a musket," he explained.

"But it doesn't have the range," said another. "I saw you step forward to hit the target."

"Admittedly it doesn't," he agreed. "But think how useful it will be in hand-to-hand fighting. And you don't need a tripod to rest it on."

The man shook his head. "I don't know," he said doubtfully. "Like to blow your own arm off instead. I'd rather trust a sword any day."

"And what of the power?" asked another. "A quarl from a crossbow can pierce armor. The ball from that thing would just bounce off."

"Not if you aim for the neck or the groin where the armor doesn't cover," said Christian. "And it's so fast to reload I could get off three shots while you're still winding that cumbersome thing."

"And where came you by that?" asked this first friend.

"My father got them in Bremen," replied Erich. "A merchant's widow was selling them. No use to her. Said her husband bought them in Antwerp from an Italian merchant. Some Italian gunsmith name of Pistoia, or something like that, invented it, called it a pistol. They were a pair, so we each have one, but I'm not as good at it as Chris. It might be slower, but I feel safer with the musket."

Some of the men agreed and others were fascinated by the workings of the new gun. At last their sergeant called them to attention, "Come my hearties, you won't kill any Papists blathering about a new toy. On with your practice."

Those with muskets fired at the target, a man-shaped bag of straw hanging from a branch. The swordsmen fought each other, the halberdiers swung at imaginary heads, the pikemen rushed to drive their pikes in the ground to impale make-believe horses, while the crossbowmen wound up their heavy machines again and again. After a strenuous hour the sergeant called a halt.

"All right, me hearties, enough for today," the sergeant shouted above the din. When it quieted down enough for him to be heard, he said, "Now I have the news you have been waiting for. In a week or two, at the most, we are going into battle. The real thing."

The men greeted this news with a boisterous cheer.

"As most of you know, Calenberg is once again troubling Bremen with his attacks. The Duke has finally ordered the army under General Graf Albrecht von Mansfeld to go against him. And about time I say."

The men cheered again.

"Now the plan is this. Mansfeld is coming over from Lüneburg, pick-

774

ing up troops from Uelzen and Celle on the way. He intends to take a stand near Drakenburg, which is very close to the border of Calenberg. Our Graf has ordered all us men from Hoya to join him there." Another cheer. "We don't know on which side of the river Duke Erich will be returning, but it is there that he must cross the river in order to return to Calenberg. Now pay me close mind. We are under strict orders not to attack him or even let it be known that we are under arms, should he pass this way. Mansfeld wants the entire army together before we fight. Only in that way will we have the strength to best him and his mercenaries. Is that very clear?" The men nodded or mumbled assent. "Hopefully we shall be gone from here and already with Mansfeld before he comes by."

"But what of our homes?" asked one man. "Who is to defend them?"

"The General feels that once Erich hears of the size of our host waiting to do battle with him he will not stop for anything. I trust his judgment." Some of the men looked doubtful at this, but no one argued with him. "Now, one thing more. We have been ordered to bring wagons—one for every twenty men. Those families who have two *must* contribute one. We need them not only for supplies, but especially to carry the big cannon from Hoya Castle and elsewhere. So," and he paused significantly, "unless you hear from me otherwise, report here next Sunday fully armed and armored, with enough food and water for three or four days, and don't forget a blanket or warm cloak and your flint and tinder."

The men disbursed to their homes. When Erich and Christian told Jacob the news, his first reaction was, "War! I hate to see it, but I suppose it was inevitable. Have a care, my sons, I don't want to lose either of you." His second reaction was more practical. "A wagon!" he exclaimed. "We need both here on the farm."

"But, Papa," pleaded Erich, "it's just on loan. We'll bring it back."

Jacob knew that was not too likely. Then Christian added, "But, Papa, with neither of us here, there would be no one to drive it anyway."

Jacob had to agree with that, so very reluctantly he said, "Very well, but take our second-best one. And I hope the Duke or someone will reimburse us, should it be lost." Although he knew in his heart that this would never happen.

On the following Sunday, joined by a small group from Bruchhausen, the little troop bravely set off, banners flying. Those who had armor glistened in the sunshine. Most did not, but their stout leather cuirasses were well oiled and almost as bright. At Bücken they were joined by that local group as well as a large troop from the castle and village of

Hoya to the north and another small band from Asendorf to the west. The knights from the castle were mounted on gaily caparisoned destriers, but they rode slowly enough to let the foot soldiers keep up. At their head rode the Graf himself, and at the rear followed the creaking wagons, some already laden with guns from the castle. Together they headed south on the road that ran along the bank of the Weser.

Late in the afternoon they arrived at a point opposite the tiny village of Drakenburg. Here they were joined by a large well-armed force of knights and foot soldiers from the castle and town of Nienburg and several smaller groups from numerous towns and villages in the southern part of the county. The Nienburg contingent also brought some cannon with them and specially trained men who knew how to shoot them. Ahead lay the bridge. Obviously they were in time, as no one had seen any sign of Erich of Calenberg. Together they numbered over two thousand men and knights. On the other side Mansfeld's army awaited them, although partially hidden by a hill that ran along the river. In the distance could be seen some of the colorful tents flying a wide variety of pennants.

The Graf bid them rest here while he and his lieutenant from Nienburg, his second capital, rode across to receive Mansfeld's orders for their deployment. While they waited, Erich and Christian, who had been lucky enough to have driven their own wagon, climbed down to stretch their legs and check out the lay of the land. At this point the Weser flowed in two parts. From frequent floods over thousands of years the river occasionally changed its channel. At this time the so-called old channel flowed sluggishly on the west side. A marshy low-lying island separated it from the broader, swifter, more easterly new channel. The ancient bridge spanned the whole. Beyond, the road turned to the left to avoid the steep hill and ran through the village of Drakenburg along the river before turning east through gentle fields and thick forests. The ruins of an early medieval robber-baron's castle—the Dragon's Fortress—could be glimpsed on the top of the cliff-like hill, commanding a fine view up and down the river. And unbeknownst to the Bruns brothers, their most ancient forebears' earthwork and palisade fort, Brunsburg, lay but a few miles to the east.

When Hoya and Nienburg returned they ordered the majority of their force to cross the river and join up with Mansfeld. Only two cannon and their crews plus a small task force to guard the bridgehead were to remain on the west side. Erich and Christian were among them. The word spread rapidly from Mansfeld's troops that Calenberg's General Wrisberg with his main army was moving south along the east bank of the

Weser, a more difficult way that involved crossing the Aller but affording them a measure of safety, as that crossing was within the territory of the very fanatical Catholic Bishop of Verden. They were expected to arrive within a day or two. The word also had it that Duke Erich himself with a small contingent was not with his general, although they had agreed to stay together. And no one knew where he was or if he would appear at all.

The men settled down for the night, the knights in tents, but the majority on the ground wrapped in cloaks or blankets beside meagre campfires, for although it was late May, the temperature still dropped sharply at night. The Bruns brothers were lucky in that they could still sleep on their wagon for this night at least. Most of the wagons had been commandeered by Mansfeld, but they had been ordered to turn theirs over in the morning to one of the gun crews from Nienburg that remained on the west bank.

"We are lucky tonight," said Erich. "Tomorrow we have to sleep on the ground."

"Maybe the battle will be joined tomorrow and we can go home tomorrow night," said Christian optimistically.

"Hah! Don't be too sure of that. We could wait for days," replied Erich as he snuggled down in the straw brought along for the horses that cushioned them somewhat from the hard boards of the wagon bed.

Christian lay awake for a long time staring up at the brilliant stars in the cold night sky. For all his optimism, he found himself wondering if they would even be alive tomorrow night. For reassurance he patted the pistol wrapped securely in his cloak to keep it and the powder dry from the heavy dew. At last he drifted off into a restless sleep.

Before dawn he was startled awake by the pounding of hoofs. He shook his brother awake. "A rider comes. What do we do?" he whispered.

Erich sat up groggily and listened. "Nothing yet. It is but a lone rider, probably a messenger."

As the man drew closer, they could see it was one of Mansfeld's scouts. When the man saw them, he waved and shouted, "Calenberg comes with all haste down this side—and not far behind me. Where is Mansfeld?"

Erich waved across the river. "Over yonder," he replied.

The rider pounded across the bridge and was gone. Within minutes they could see and hear all sorts of activity on the other side, campfires being doused, the clank of armor being donned.

They climbed down from the wagon and hastily splashed some cold

777

river water in their faces, then peed in the same river. Erich rounded up the horse, which had been grazing nearby, and hitched him to the wagon while Christian gathered up their weapons and other belongings from it.

"We must get the wagon to the gunners quickly," said Erich, "They will soon have need of it."

"Will we have time to break our fast?" asked Christian, frightened yet elated at the same time.

"Probably lots of time, but the wagon first."

"Erich, we can't defend this bridge against an army all by ourselves with this small force," declared Christian."

"Of course not. But don't worry, Chris. Mansfeld will send help."

They hitched up the horse and drove the wagon over to the gunners who were waiting for it. With boards brought along for the purpose they helped those men trundle the heavy cannon up onto the bed of the wagon so that it could be conveyed into whatever position was needed. Then they loaded on cannonballs and bags of gunpowder. When they finished, they were panting and sweating. Dawn was just breaking.

Within the hour Mansfeld sent a company of about two hundred men to their succor—musketeers, archers, halberdiers and pikemen, but no mounted knights. The captain had orders for the Vilsen men and Nienburg cannoneers. First he apologized, "He can spare no more lest Wrisberg come down upon him. But here is the plan. The main body will stay well hidden in yon wood, the guns in front, but hidden as well. The Vilsen militia will also be hidden, but in the tall marsh grass and scrub on the island, even under the bridge if need be. We are to let Erich, his knights and most of the foot soldiers pass onto the bridge without firing a shot. Absolute silence is necessary so that they will think our entire army is across the river. When their rear guard approaches the bridge, the two cannon will rake them, cutting off any retreat. Then we shall attack them from all sides. Our main force here will follow and push them right into Mansfeld's arms, the men on the island will attack from both sides, but have a care that you don't shoot each other. Is that all clear?" The men nodded. "Remember now, not a shot or even a whisper until you hear the two cannon fire. Then do as you have been instructed. There will be no further orders until we are victorious. To your positions now." He saluted them with his sword.

The bridge at Drakenburg was really in three parts. A low arch spanned the old channel and the section across the island was nothing more than a raised causeway about a man's height above the land. The third section was a high, almost semicircular arch across the mainstream. Its medieval engineers obviously considered accommodating the masts of the riverboats of more importance than the welfare of weary horses dragging laden wagons up its deep slope. This would slow Calenberg's troops down, creating a bottleneck where the Vilsen men hoped to catch them.

Erich and Christian appreciated the cleverness of Mansfeld's strategy but did not relish crouching in the scratchy marsh grass under the causeway. The ground underfoot was very damp, and anyone foolish enough to kneel or sit was soon soaked to the skin. Nor did anyone dare lay his weapon or powder horns in the wet.

"I hope we don't have to wait too long," whispered Christian.

"I doubt we will," replied Erich. "My leg is starting to cramp."

Very soon they heard the pounding of horses' hoofs. "They come," whispered someone near the end of the bridge and then all was silence, every man alert and seeing to his priming. Within minutes the horses were treading directly over their heads, followed by the troop of men marching at the double. Erich and Christian glanced at each other. Soon, their eyes said. Suddenly they were all startled by the boom of the big gun as it raked the enemy's rear guard. Then the second roar and they were up and aiming their muskets at the men on the causeway. After the first shot the men in front stepped back to reload and the second line shot. The men on the bridge milled about in confusion, not quite sure where their opponents were coming from. While the musketeers reloaded, the pikemen and halberdiers clambered up on the bridge, the one to impale the horses, the other to behead their riders if possible. The screams of horses and men filled the air. Some actually jumped or were pushed into the river, where the weight of their armor soon dragged them down to a watery grave.

Christian soon became impatient with the slow musket. He wanted to try out his pistols. He had both of them, fully primed and loaded, since his brother did not trust them. Besides, Christian longed to be in the midst of the fray. He climbed up on the causeway. He ducked a swinging battle-axe, an old-fashioned but deadly weapon if a strong arm wielded it. With great satisfaction he shot its owner in the neck. The man fell at his feet. He kept shooting and reloading until the pistols became very hot, but in the wild exhilaration of killing the hated enemy he disregarded the warning. Suddenly a nearby horse with its rider tumbled over the side of the causeway. At first he paid it no mind, until he heard a bone-chilling scream. He glanced over the side to see that the horse had pinned Erich down and its rider, apparently unhurt but still disentangling himself from the stirrups, was on the verge of running his brother through with his sword.

Christian jumped down and shot the man with his first pistol, then took careful aim before the thrashing hoofs could do more damage. He shot the horse, but at the same time the overheated gun blew up in his hand sending burning shards of metal up along his face to his eye. At first he felt no pain, just so stunned he could see nothing at all. All he could think of was that he must find the strength to pull his brother out from under the crushing weight of that horse.

"Erich! Erich!" he cried. "Hold on. I'm coming." Through the dense fog in his head he could hear his brother screaming. Christian thought it was a cry for help, and he repeated, "I'm coming, Erich, but, God have mercy, I can't see." As his head began to clear, the excruciating pain set in. He realized it was the blood from his wound that was blinding him. He tried to wipe it away with his sleeve. Gradually the vision in his left eye cleared but the right would not. He tried to concentrate on getting to his brother, but then as the ringing in his ears let up he was able to distinguish Erich's words.

"Chris, my God, Chris," screamed Erich, "what happened to your face?"

"The damned thing blew up," croaked Christian and realized that his jaw was not working too well either. He summoned all his strength and crawled over to where his brother lay pinned under the dead horse and took his hand. "Don't worry Erich, I'll pull you out from under. Can you help at all?"

"No, Chris, don't. You'll bleed to death from the strain. I think my legs are broken, at least one anyway. Just wait. Someone will help us." But no one came. The fight on the bridge still raged furiously. Erich looked at his brother again, closely, and nearly gagged. "Chris, my God, your eye. It is gone!" He closed his eyes to shut back the tears. His handsome little brother, and so young, too, oh, God, let him live, he prayed, through his own pain.

After a few minutes Christian seemed to revive a little and tried to push the horse off his brother's legs. He managed to budge it a few inches. "Can you pull your legs out if I lift it a bit, so?"

Erich braced himself with his arms and tried to push back with all his might. "I can move the one leg a bit, but the other seems dead." Together they pushed and pulled until finally he was able to extricate his left leg from under the horse, but the right one gave him excruciating pain and would not move. The effort proved too much for Christian. He fainted across his brother's chest, his blood soaking into Erich's tunic.

After what seemed like an eternity to Erich, though it was less than an hour, the fighting on the bridge ceased and their victorious men rounded up the stragglers and drove them across where Mansfeld's men took them prisoner. This done, the general then sent details out to seek the wounded. The dead would have to wait until after the approaching major battle with Wrisberg.

"Here, here," cried Erich weakly as a party searched the island. At last help came. "Take care of my brother first," Erich moaned. "He lives yet but is sore wounded. His eye, oh God, his eye." The men gingerly lifted Christian off him and turned him over. He could see by the shock in their faces that the sight almost nauseated them.

"He can't live long like that," said one man.

"Yes, he will live. He will live," insisted Erich. "Take him to the chirurgeon quickly that he may cleanse and bind the wound. Blinded he may be, but he will live with the proper care."

"And you? By all the saints, man, you're covered with blood, too."

"It's his, not mine. If you can just get this damned horse off me, I'll be all right. Although I fear my leg might not be."

The men dragged the horse away and Erich screamed with the sudden torsion on his leg. When he tried to sit up, he could see that it was twisted at not one but two very odd angles. At one place a glistening white bone stuck out of his calf.

"Man, you're not all right either. Lord Christ, the chirurgeon will never be able to set that."

"Just help me up," insisted Erich. But try as he may, there was no way he could stand even on the uninjured leg, the pain was so great. He finally fainted in the man's arms and they loaded both him and his brother none too gently onto the waiting wagon, already half-full of other casualties.

While the wounded were waiting their turn outside the chirurgeon's tent, Erich came to and tried to look about him. Christian was unconscious but still breathing. Better so, thought Erich. He looked beyond the confines of the wagon and at a distance could see the Lutheran army lined up in battle formation. But they were kneeling. How strange, he thought. Then they rose and knelt again, and again. Suddenly he realized they were praying. He raised himself on one elbow, the better to see, although the pain in his leg nearly defeated him. In the far distance he could see that the Catholic army had arrived and was also in battle formation. But Wrisberg's men were exhausted from their long forced march, whereas

Manfeld's were well rested. That should give us some advantage, he thought.

Then he heard the sound of rousing music as the men lifted their voices in Luther's greatest hymn, "A Mighty Fortress Is Our God." The men sang at the top of their lungs, " 'The prince of darkness grim, we trouble not for him; his rage we can endure, for lo! his doom is sure, one little word shall fell him.' " Erich choked up with emotion as the tears streamed down his face. We shall surely win now for God is with us. How he wished he could be fighting with these brave men instead of being laid up here on this wagon.

When the final 'Amen' was sung, the trumpets sounded and the battle for their homeland began.

Just then the chirurgeon's mates came out of his tent for more of the wounded. "We've got to hurry along here, my friends," said one, "for soon the next batch will be coming in from yon field." They could barely hear him, the noise from the battle was so deafening. It was Christian's and Erich's turn next. The brawny mates carried them into the tent and laid them on pallets to wait. They were met with a scene from hell—blood and gore everywhere, pails full of severed limbs. The stench was overpowering. Erich choked back the vomit and tried to turn his eyes and nose away, but there was nowhere to look. The chirurgeon was working on a man laid on a makeshift table. The man screamed as the saw bit into his arm and then all was silent except for the hacking of the saw. Blood spattered everywhere, the arm was thrown into a pail, and then came the sickening stench of burning flesh as the cauterizing iron sealed the stump. The chirurgeon quickly stitched a flap of skin over the wound and the man was carried out to another tent. They lifted Christian onto the table.

"Can you save his eye, Master?" asked Erich weakly.

"A friend of yours?"

"My brother."

"Let's wash the blood away and we'll see." They washed Christian's wound with none-too-clean water. "Sorry, friend, the eye is blown away. Best we can do is try to pick out all those slivers of metal so it doesn't fester. He's lucky it didn't go into his brain. Then we'll pack it with unguent and stitch him up. If it doesn't putrefy in a week or so, he'll make it."

Erich didn't really want to watch, yet he was fascinated by the careful way the rough chirurgeon probed the wound for splinters of metal. How different from when he hacked off limbs. Christian moaned but mercifully did not regain consciousness. Erich began to wonder about his own leg. Would he lose it, too? Every time they had moved him the pain had been excruciating. Now the man was stitching Chris' face. How would he react when he learned he had lost an eye? They moved him out to the other tent and now it was Erich's turn.

They manhandled him onto the table while the chirurgeon wiped his hands on his blood-soaked apron. The man took one look at Erich's leg and shook his head. No, Erich thought, no.

"It's got to come off, my friend," said the chirurgeon brusquely.

"No," cried Erich. "No. I'm a farmer, I need my legs."

"It's the leg or your life. The bones are splintered every which way. There is no way we can set that."

They tied Erich's hands down and forced some wine between his lips. He almost choked on it. When the first knife bit into his flesh, he screamed and almost fainted. When the man approached with the saw, Erich screamed again and the last thing he remembered was that his scream sounded louder than the battle cries going on outside.

Erich woke up late at night. All was silent except for the moans and snoring of the wounded men around him. Christian was still unconscious—or perhaps sleeping. His breathing seemed more regular. Erich's leg pained horribly. He tried to move his foot, which he could still feel, until he realized there was no more foot. Oh God, I wish I had died in the battle. No, he checked his thoughts, I must not think like that. He wondered how the battle had gone.

Sometime later a man came in bearing a bucket of water and a dipper. He went around giving welcome drinks to those who were awake and could drink. When he came to him, Erich asked, "How went the battle?"

"A victory, my friend, a resounding victory," said the man enthusiastically. "Mansfeld carried the day and Wrisberg slunk back to Calenberg with his tail between his legs."

"How long did it last?"

"All of the morning and until almost three of the afternoon."

"A right long time. Were many of ours—uh—hurt?"

"Over twenty-five hundred dead on both sides and as many taken prisoner. Many, many wounded, more than we have tents for. You're one of the lucky ones."

"That's dreadful." Erich did not consider himself lucky at all.

"Maybe so, but we won, man, we won. Never again will Lüneburg be threatened by the Papist fiends." Erich wondered, but the man continued.

"There was one problem, though. The mercenaries won't get paid."

"How so?"

"When Wrisberg called retreat, his left flank came around our side trying to flee towards Calenberg. They came across our wagons and stole every one of them, supplies, everything, including the treasure chest meant to pay the men. Well, I must move on. A lot of thirsty knaves tonight."

Erich watched the man go and thought about his father's wagon on the other side of the river. He wondered if it was still there, and their dear old horse, too.

Erich dozed on and off for the remainder of the night as the pain permitted. Sometimes the leg went numb, there was no pain at all, and he could sleep. Then it would shoot up his whole right side as if the chirurgeon were still attacking it with the saw. He was watching the first gray light of dawn seep through the tent, when he heard his brother stir.

"Erich?"

He reached over and took his hand. "I'm here, Chris."

"Where are we? What happened?"

"We are both wounded, Chris, crippled," Erich replied bitterly. "Don't you remember?"

"Not much." His head ached abominably as he tried to think. "I remember shooting the man who was about to kill you. But then my whole head seemed to explode." He reached up and gingerly touched the wrapping that covered half his face. It was soaked with blood.

"Dear Chris, you saved my life, but at what cost."

"Did he shoot me?"

"Nay, Chris, your pistol blew up in your face. You have lost one eye."

"Oh, God, no," moaned Christian and turned away. Erich held his hand tightly and prayed for his soul. After a while Christian said, "But if I saved you, why are you here lying next to me?"

"That damned horse crushed my leg into splinters. They have lopped it off."

"Oh, no." Christian sat bolt upright and his head swam with dizziness, pain and nausea. He forced himself to wait until the spasm passed. "Oh, God, Erich, for a moment I thought I could not see out of the other eye either. But now I can see—oh, Erich, how awful. And it's all my fault. If I had stayed with you, instead of climbing up on the bridge . . . "

"Stop it, Chris. You didn't push the horse on me."

"No, but . . . " Then Christian's natural sense of humor took over.

784

"What a fine pair of soldiers we make, hey? You be my eyes and I'll be your legs."

Erich smiled wanly.

"And I suppose we missed the main battle," said Christian.

"Ja, but we won," and Erich told him what the water carrier had told him.

"So Hoya is free from the Papist threat?" asked Christian.

"For now, at least."

When morning fully broke, another man brought them some thin gruel. "Not much," he apologized, "but it will give you a little strength."

About an hour later a man poked his head inside the tent flap. "Anyone for Bücken? We have a wagon and room for three or four more, if any want to go home."

For the first time Erich began wondering how indeed would they get home. But Christian was quicker. Despite his injured head, his brain was working. "Ho, friend," he called out. "We live but a half hour beyond Bücken. Get us that far and we'll manage the rest of the way."

"Good enough. How far beyond?"

"Toward Heiligenberg."

"Ah, so. Then climb aboard. Can you walk?"

Christian stood up, swayed and would have fallen had the man not caught him around the shoulders. When the dizziness passed, he said, "I can—I think—but my brother can't. They took his leg."

"Then we'll carry him, but let me help you first." The man guided Christian to the wagon and helped him mount. Then he and two others went back for Erich. They picked up the corners of the pallet and used it as a stretcher. He gasped with the pain as they jarred his leg but he was determined not to scream.

When they finally got him settled on the wagon bed, he murmured, "Thanks, friend, for your help. You know, we brought a wagon, too. It was left on the other side of the river. Perhaps it was not stolen and we can find it."

"We'll take a look. Ours was over there, too. That's the only reason we have one now."

After picking up two more wounded men, they started off with a jerk. Almost every man screamed or groaned in pain. The wagon was so crowded the men were falling all over each other, causing more cries, and the poor horse could hardly pull it. The axles, too, screeched and groaned. After a tense and agonizing haul over the bridge, Erich insisted that Christian and another man help him to sit up, ostensibly to give some others more room but in truth because he feared sliding off. At last they reached the other side and the horse was able to pull more easily. They stopped near the woods and Christian climbed down with the three able men who were driving. They found the Bruns wagon readily enough but it was broken beyond repair. The weight and recoil of the heavy gun had caused it to collapse.

"Oh, my father will be sore wroth," said Christian, "but it was worth a try." Then he heard a rustling in the bushes and a faint whicker. "A horse," he exclaimed. "I think it might be ours." He tried to whistle but could not. "Blitzen! Blitzen!" he called. One of the other men whistled.

Very cautiously a horse poked his head through the bushes. "It *is* our horse. Blitzen, old fellow, don't be afraid. It's me, Chris." He walked toward the animal holding out his hand. When the horse caught the scent, he whinnied and nuzzled his shoulder, nearly knocking him over. "Maybe I can ride him," suggested Christian, taking the bridle.

"You're crazy, man," said the other. "You can hardly walk. Look, your head is bleeding again." And, in fact, they had to help Christian back to the wagon. "We'll tie him behind and he can spell our horse if he gets too tired. But he don't look like no lightning to me," the man joked.

"He used to be, but he's getting old now," replied Christian. "His friend Donner is still home."

Slowly they made their way north. Every jolt over the rough road was bone-crushing and agonizing for the wounded passengers. Some fainted. Gradually they dropped one and then another off at their homes along the way, which helped lighten the load. Late in the afternoon they finally reached Bücken. There they off-loaded all but Erich and Christian.

"We'll take you the rest of the way," said the driver.

"No, that won't be necessary," protested Erich, "You've been too kind already."

"Yes," said Christian, "if you could just send a message to our father, he will come and fetch us."

"No, we'll take you. It is our duty." At their perplexed look, the man explained. "We are from the monastery. Lutheran monks now," he added proudly.

When they arrived at the Bruns farm, their mother Hanne came running out. When she saw them she put her apron to her mouth to stifle a scream. "My sons, my sons, my dearest sons, what has happened to you?" The younger children came crowding around mouths agape.

786

One of the monks helped Christian down from the wagon. He embraced his mother. "Ach, Mutti, we are a trifle the worse for wear," he joked feebly.

"Ach, Du Lieber Gott, have mercy," she said. "Jacob, Jacob, come here," she cried. "Ach, he is still out in the fields and does not hear me. Heinzi, run and fetch your Papa."

"We'll help them into the house," said the driver, and they promptly did so. "They will need a lot of care," he said. "Can you cope?"

After she got over the initial shock of seeing her two eldest sons so sorely wounded, her natural efficiency took over. Yes, she would cope. "I have bound their wounds since they were babes. I know what to do. And I shall send for the wisewoman, if I need help."

"These are far worse than childhood bruises," warned the man. "We are from the Cloister at Bücken and have many medicines and simples should you need them."

"Thank you for your offer, kind brother, I shall keep it in mind," she replied. "And bless you, too, for bringing them home."

"Our Lord said 'what you do for the least of these . . .'" he quoted and shrugged. He knew these independent farm wives. "And where do you want the horse?"

"Oh, put him in the barnyard for now. The children can tend to him."

He nodded. "Then, Mistress, we shall be on our way. We shall come to visit your sons in a few days, if we may. We have become friends through this battle."

She in turn shrugged. "If you wish."

A few moments later Jacob rushed into the house. Although forewarned by Heinzi, he was still shocked when he saw his sons but tried to put on a brave face. Christian was seated at the table head in hands. Erich still lay on the pallet they had fetched him on from Drakenburg. Hanne had set water to boil and was in her still room selecting the herbs and medicines she would need. Their young sister was fashioning bandages out of old sheets and petticoats. Another child had been sent for the wisewoman.

Jacob tried to lighten the mood. "Well, I see the brave soldiers are back from the war, though minus a few pieces."

"Papa, don't joke," moaned Erich. "How can I ever help you on the farm again with only one leg?"

Jacob immediately became serious. "Of course you can. Just as soon

787

as your stump has healed, we'll have your Onkel Willem fashion you a wooden leg. He must be good for something besides making fancy furniture for fine ladies." At last Erich smiled. "And meanwhile," Jacob promised, "I'll make you a pair of crutches myself. At least the spring plowing and planting are done. There's not a lot to do until the first haying. So don't worry."

"And what can I do if I can't see?" wept Christian.

"I thought you still had sight in your left eye."

"It comes and goes," replied Christian. "When the pain is great, I can't see at all. Then it gradually comes back. Oh God, what if I lose that eye, too?"

"You won't. It's just the shock," his father assured him and hoped he was right. "What you need right now is plenty of rest and some good food. Now tell me of the battle. I don't even know if we won or lost."

"Jacob get out of here," ordered Hanne sternly. "Time enough for battle talk later. Can't you see how filthy they are? If I don't clean and dress those wounds immediately, they will putrefy. If you want to help, fetch me more water and then see if you can get Erich's breeches off without disturbing his leg too much."

Jacob went meekly out. And the wisewoman arrived.

"Oh, my, my," was all she said and immediately went to work with Hanne, cleansing and dressing the wounds. After she left, both men felt more comfortable.

But only after Hanne fed them some good nourishing food did she say to her husband, "Now, Jacob, if they are not too tired, you may ask them about the battle."

Christian answered with a bit of doggerel one of their wagon mates had sung:

> "Wir han das Feld! Wrisberg das Geld!
> Wir han das Land! Wrisberg die Schand!"*

No one in the Bruns family would ever forget the Battle of Drakenburg on 23 May 1547. And no one anywhere realized it was but the forerunner of a century of horror for Germany.

---

*"[We have the field! Wrisberg the money!
We have the land! Wrisberg the shame!]"

AD 1549

Gretchen von Sehnden poured coffee for her friend Ilse von Eltze. In recent years she had changed her attitude toward Ilse. She still sorely missed her dearest friend Ilsebe Stockman and without her Ilse was one of the few of their wealth and status to whom she could turn for uninhibited companionship. At the same time Ilse had lost some of her haughtiness and had made a sincere effort to blend in with the Bürger wives of Celle. They settled down for an hour of good gossip.

"I see congratulations are in order on Lüdeke's having been elected to the Council."

"Why, thank you, Ilse. We're very happy and I'm very proud of him."

"I wish Eggeling would take more interest in the town government. He should have been on the Council long ago."

"Perhaps because the von Eltze have long been courtly advisors to the Duke, whereas Lüdeke has always been under his father's tutelage and longs to follow in his footsteps."

"You're probably right," agreed Ilse. "And what of Hinrik Stockman? He, of all people, should be on the Council.

"He claims he had no interest in politics," replied Gretchen, "and now with this new wife of his, I doubt he'll ever be asked."

"Yes, how sad. Whyever did he marry her?"

Gretchen shook her head. "We all wonder. He was lonely and she no doubt took advantage of that fact. You know men—put a warm body in bed with them and their brains cease to function."

Ilse laughed. "True enough. But she is totally unlettered and not even intelligent enough to learn."

"Yes, the complete opposite from dear Ilsebe. But she must have something he likes. She's already given him another son, and I understand she's breeding again. But I shouldn't talk. Here am I carrying my sixth."

Ilse smiled knowingly. "I'm satisfied with my four. That is enough for me." She fondly patted her youngest Kunigunde on the head. Ilse had only consented to have another after three boys because Eggeling had wanted a girl so badly. Now she was proud that she had. The little four-year-old sat at her feet playing with the two youngest von Sehnden children, Joachim and Diderich. Perhaps someday there will be a match here, she thought, but not that Joachim—he's not quite like the others and Diderich is too young to tell what his character will be. "At least with only

789

one girl, there's only one dowry to think about," she said.

Gretchen agreed. "You're right, although I haven't given it much thought. I suppose I should. My Clara is thirteen and Lüdeke has already mentioned trying to find someone to betroth her to, but she doesn't seem interested yet. Well, there's time."

"Of course. She's young yet. But I do feel sorry for Hinrik Stockman with all those girls, although he is certainly wealthy enough to provide well for all of them. What do you think of young Ilsebe's second marriage? How did that come about anyway?"

"It is a rather strange situation. After young Kreye died—he never was very strong—she and her baby daughter moved back in with Hinrik. She was the one who introduced Geske into the house in the first place and the only one really friendly with her. Be that as it may, one day there came this so-called merchant from Hannover, Johann Fockrell by name—at least he calls himself a merchant, but he is a member of the Butcher's Guild, which doesn't make sense at all, shopkeeper perhaps, but merchants such as we, never. In any event, he came looking for that idiot brother Martin, and Hinrik, being the kindly man he is, asked him to stay with them the while. He said he wanted Martin to come back to work for him, that it was now safe in Hannover. Of course he met Ilsebe and within weeks, just like that," she snapped her fingers, "they were wed. She moved to Hannover with him but comes back often. In fact, just between us, methinks it is not too happy a marriage, as she spends almost as much time here in Celle as in Hannover."

"Strange indeed," agreed Ilse. "I have never seen such a variety of personalities as among those children. Katharina seems to be the only one with any common sense, yet they all seem intelligent enough."

"Oh, very. Anna perhaps most of all, but she is so serious. Margarethe is so gay and lively and gregarious. I predict she will be the next to wed, before her sister. The two younger girls have been so influenced by Geske, it is hard to say how they will turn out, and little Balthasar, too. Young Franz is every bit his father's son, with a good dollop of Ilsebe's compassion thrown in. But it is Anna whom I worry about. She hates her stepmother to an unhealthy degree and stays away from home as much as she can. She still spends hours in our library and chooses to talk endlessly with Papa Lüdeke instead of with young men her own age. It is unseemly, in my opinion."

Ilse nodded. She was already bored with hearing about the Stockman children. "And how is your dear father-in-law these days?" she asked.

"Well enough for his age," replied Gretchen, "although he takes to his bed more and more. He has been at such loose ends since he retired from being Bürgermeister. I suppose I should be grateful to young Anna for that. At least she keeps him from underfoot. Although Lüdeke's election to the Council has sparked a little interest in him again. He is full of all kinds of advice."

"That's understandable. Well, I must be off. It's time for Kunigunde's nap."

Hinrik Stockman was a little late as he entered the crowded coffeehouse and looked about for his friends.

"Over here, Hinrik," called out Peter. "We've been waiting for you. Come, help us celebrate Lüdeke's election to the Council."

"Indeed I shall," replied Hinrik. He embraced his best friend. "Congratulations, brother. I knew you could do it. It's time some of our generation took a hand in things."

"Agreed," replied Peter, who also had ambitions of being a councilman. "Our Eggeling should be next."

"Not I," demurred Eggeling. "My cousin is Bürgermeister now. One politician in the family is enough."

"Not necessarily," put in Lüdeke, "although the Gewandschneider obviously agree with you. They would not even consider nominating me until after Papa retired."

"There, you see," agreed Hinrik. "And how fares dear Onkel Lüdeke?"

"Not well at all," replied Lüdeke. "Although the physickers say nothing is wrong with him but old age. I fear his time is nigh. However, my election has given him a bit of a spark."

"No doubt it has," said Eggeling. "And I'm sure he's full of advice for you."

"That he is."

"Is he pushing you for Bürgermeister already?" teased Peter.

"Actually, no." replied Lüdeke. "He says a couple of years on the council are necessary first and also he warns me to keep my mouth shut and just listen for the first few months."

"Aha," chuckled Eggeling. "He knows his son. And what grandiose ideas are you planning to effect?"

"Nothing yet, but one thing I'd like to bring about someday is a new Rathaus."

791

"What's wrong with the old one?" asked Hinrik. "It has the Rathskeller where the Council meets, the Bürgermeister's office on the first floor and the armory in the attic. What more do we need?"

"Lots more," said Lüdeke. "There should be a place for the council to eat, so they don't have to leave their meetings. Every time we hold a major social event, we have to clear the Bürgermeister out of his room. We Gewandschneider have no single place under a roof where we can all display our cloth. And in these unsettled times the armory is far too small and inconvenient."

"Those *are* grandiose plans," said Eggeling. "Leave it to our Lüdeke to think big."

Lüdeke smiled. "And it needs modernizing, too. There is a new style of architecture called Weser Renaissance. Lüneburg, Wolfenbüttel, Hameln and several other towns have already started using it, or at least are talking about it. It is quite light and decorative compared to that ancient fortresslike building we have now."

Peter laughed. "And leave it to our Lüdeke, the moment we elect him, to put his fingers in our purses."

"Speaking of these unsettled times," put in Hinrik, "there is still widespread opposition to the 'Interim'. And I mistrust these shifting alliances. Think you we'll have peace for a while?"

"Here in the north we should," replied Eggeling. "Drakenburg settled that. And our major cities Bremen, Hamburg and Lübeck, stand firm."

"As long as Charles is Emperor there will always be unrest, especially since he now refuses to compromise at all," said Lüdeke.

Peter added, "There are rumors that he is tired of the whole thing and is thinking of abdicating in favor of his son Phillip of Spain."

"That would be the worst possible thing that could happen," said Hinrik. "That Spanish fanatic would destroy Germany. They say even Ferdinand is upset about that."

"True," agreed Lüdeke. "Why, even now, every time one goes to Antwerp one never knows what to expect."

"I predict there will be revolt in the Netherlands before long," said Eggeling. "But if the unrest here in Germany can just be contained in the south, it shouldn't hurt our business too much. It might even help us."

"I hope you're right," commented Hinrik, "but enough of politics. I have news. I have just bought a new house. I shall soon be your neighbor, Eggeling."

792

"Indeed? Where? On Ritterstrasse?"

"Yes. That large, beautiful house at number 17 at the opposite end from you."

"That is a fine house," agreed Eggeling. "It should give you a lot more room for your—er—ever-growing family."

"And right around the corner from us," said Peter. "I believe the property runs all the way down to the river, does it not?"

"Yes, it does," replied Hinrik. "It has a large garden with its own well. Fine, sweet water. Stables and even a vineyard backing on the Duke's own. In addition, there are two small cottages on the side near your house that I can use for additional warehouse space."

"Well, that is good news," said Eggeling.

"You men will make me feel lonely all by myself over on Zöllnerstrasse," joked Lüdeke.

"Why don't you move, then?" teased Peter. "Now that the old nobility are moving out, Ritterstrasse is becoming *the* address in Celle."

"Papa would never allow it. Nor would my wife," replied Lüdeke. "Besides, Zöllnerstrasse is the traditional home of Celle's Bürgermeisters."

"Aha! So you do plan on being Bürgermeister," said Peter.

"Who knows?" replied Lüdeke. "Perhaps one day, and at least I'll be living on the right street."

They all laughed at that.

"And how fares young Franz with his apprenticeship?" Eggeling asked Hinrik.

"Very well," answered Hinrik. "As young as he is, he loves it. Takes to it like a fish to water. I'm quite proud of him."

"You're very lucky and you certainly had to wait long enough, with all those girls," said Lüdeke. "I wish I could say the same for mine. The two eldest hate it and are already talking about going to University under our family stipendium. And what will they be? Pastors or lawyers or some such. With all my boys, I hope at least one of them aspires to be a good, honest, hardworking merchant," he added somewhat sadly.

In 1550 Lüdeke von Sehnden the Elder passed away quietly in his sleep. All of Celle mourned. He had been the greatest Bürgermeister in Celle's history, well loved by all. He had guided the town wisely and safely through all the upheavals of the Reformation, and the town was far wealthier for it. Even the ducal family donned mourning on his behalf. But no one mourned him as much as Anna Stockman.

793

"Oh, I miss him so," she sobbed to Gretchen. "He was like the grand-father I never had."

Gretchen held her close. "We all miss him terribly. It seemed as though he would live on and on, but we all must go sometime, as the Lord wills."

"I know. But whom can I talk to now?"

"I'm sure there must be some young man about who shares your interests. I only wish some of my sons were old enough for you. What are you now, almost twenty?"

"Nineteen."

"And still no beau?"

"Oh, young men," she said in exasperation, "they don't want to talk. All they want is to get their hands up your petticoat."

Gretchen laughed despite her mourning. "Well, there's truth in that, but they do grow up. And believe it or not, a few of them have brains and enjoy intelligent conversation."

"I have yet to find any. Even Papa has changed. I used to be able to talk to him, but now, now he's so—so obsessed with that woman. I hate her, oh, I hate her so."

"Hush, child, you mustn't talk like that."

"But it's true. She's stupid and childish and—and—just plain uncouth. If I could only leave home, I would go in a minute."

"Then you must find yourself a husband."

"Back to that again. Why can't a woman just live by herself?"

"It just isn't done. Years ago the answer to that was a convent, but now . . . ?" Gretchen spread her hands.

"Mistress von Sehnden, may I still continue to read in your library, even though Onkel Lüdeke is—is no longer here?" asked Anna.

"Certainly you may, my dear, any time you wish."

In 1551 Lüdeke von Sehnden was elected Bürgermeister. Almost immediately he began consulting with a leading architect, Jacob Riess, about his plans for enlarging the Rathaus. But it would be many years before they came to fruition. Many Bürgers could not see any purpose to it and most of the leading Gewandschneider were still smarting under the debts owed to them by the Duke for the losses of the Schmalkaldic War to be interested in laying out money for such a project. Lüdeke slowly under-took a subtle campaign to get his friends and allies elected to the Council. Eggeling finally acquiesced to his pleas and was elected in 1552.

11

Margarethe Stockman was dressing for a ball. It was the social event of the winter season of 1553, the Twelfthnight ball given by the Duke at the Castle. Of the Bürgers, only the upper echelon families were invited. The other guests would be all nobility and courtiers. Although she had often frequented the Castle grounds and had been attending Bürger balls at the Rathaus for some years, it was her first ball at the Castle, and for this reason she was very excited.

Since it was Twelfthnight it was to be a masked costume ball, and she had decided to go as Cleopatra. Anna had helped Margarethe design her costume after much consultation with the elder Master Lindemann, although she never told the old man why she was interested in ancient Egyptian clothing for fear of shocking him. Geske fluttered around being totally useless. She had not the vaguest notion who Cleopatra was. Anna wished she would leave them alone.

"Isn't it a bit risqué?" asked Hinrik.

"Oh, Papa," sighed Margarethe, "don't be stuffy." He had insisted she at least cover her breasts, and she had to go along with that or he would not have permitted her to accompany them. "He should be thankful I'm not going as Venus," she had said to her sister later. "Then I should be really naked."

At last he urged Geske out of the room. "Come, my dear, we must start dressing ourselves." They were going as Hansel and Gretel, at which Margarethe had rolled her eyes heavenward. "And, Anna," he asked, "what of you? Who will you be?"

"I am going as myself," she replied succinctly.

"What, no costume?"

"So few people have ever seen me in a ball gown," she said, "that will be disguise enough." Although Anna had learned to dance well, she did not care for balls and all the social chit-chat that was required.

Hinrik worried about her. And Geske thought Anna was decidedly strange.

When they arrived, the Castle courtyard was brightly lit with torches flaring everywhere, and the ballroom was a sparkling fairyland. Thousands of candles in huge chandeliers and wall sconces lit every corner. Greenery hung from the beams and walls. The place was already crowded, and the musicians were starting to tune up their instruments, although more and more guests continued to arrive.

The costumes were as varied as the people in them, some quite imaginative, others hard to guess who or what they represented. There were several Wittekinds and Heinrich der Löwes and other characters from German history, fierce Vikings and knights in armor. How they must be sweating, thought Margarethe. One couple came as a Roman Senator and his wife, both duly swathed in yards of toga. That must be the Lindemanns, she guessed, but she could not be sure. But because the people in this part of the country so loved the old fairy tales, the great majority were dressed as characters out of the ancient stories. There were a number of quite wide-awake Sleeping Beauties and their Princes, a bedraggled Cinderella and her Prince, several wolves with either Red Ridinghood or kids or pigs, a Goldilocks with one of the bears. One of the most enterprising was a group of young men garbed as the *Bremer Stadtmusikanten*. Their only problem was that when it came time to dance, the hind end of the ass had to separate himself from his front-end partner in order to stand up straight. Their antics sent waves of hilarity through the crowd.

But Margarethe was the only Cleopatra, and although she had long outgrown her teenage giddiness, she was still the most ebullient member of the family. And when every eye was drawn to her scanty costume she basked in the adulation. Her blond hair was covered with a black Egyptian wig secured by a brassy uraeus crown, so that she was sure no one would recognize her, although in a way she hoped they would. Just wait until the unmasking at midnight, she thought mischievously.

She danced the first dance with a knight who she thought was one of the von Eltze brothers, but his scratchy armor poked uncomfortably through her diaphanous gown, so she begged off the next dance and looked about the huge room for another conquest. Before she could decide, Hanswurst—the Joker—came up to her.

"May I?" he asked.

"Why not?" She extended her hand to him.

796

The next dance was a slow, stately one and they had a chance to talk.

"Your costume is quite unique." He had a deep resonant voice that thrilled her. "Methinks not too many here are aware of whom you represent."

"But you are."

He nodded. "I wish now I had come as Julius Caesar or Mark Anthony."

She blushed at that and he realized she well knew the exploits of the Egyptian queen. But she caught herself in time. "I like Hanswurst quite well," she said. "He suits my mood. I am a fun-loving person."

"I could tell you were, and so am I, when I have the chance."

"It seems as though you don't get the chance too often."

"Not as often as I'd like."

"What do you do?" she asked.

He laughed. "But that would be telling you who I am." And she could get no more out of him.

He danced well and she felt quite comfortable with him. The next dance was a wild fast round dance in which an even number of eight or ten people holding hands performed a rapidly gyrating jig around the odd person in the middle. The odd one chose a partner from the circle, danced a few measures, and then separated to return to the circle. The new odd person would then choose another partner in turn, and so on. When the music stopped the one left in the middle was considered the dunce. The music got faster and faster towards the end as the dancers in the middle rushed to complete their turn and rejoin the circle so as not to be the last one left.

When the music ended, Margarethe-Cleopatra was left in the middle. The rest of the dancers howled and clapped and laughed, "A forfeit, a forfeit," they cried.

"A kiss for everyone," suggested Hanswurst. They all agreed and he let everyone in the circle buss her, waiting until last to claim her. When his turn came the sweat was pouring down her face. He kissed her gently but soundly and she could feel the thrill of it down to her toes. He held her at arm's length and laughed.

"Your wig and crown are slightly askew. I can see your blond hair peeping out."

"Oh, my," she gasped, out of breath. She reached up to adjust things.

"Here, let me do that," he said. He gently straightened the wig and tucked a few errant tendrils of blond hair back under it. She thrilled again

797

to his touch, and then unexpectedly he kissed her again.

"Oh my," she said again, "that was not part of the forfeit."

"Did you mind?"

"No, not really," she admitted. "I liked it."

He smiled. "I think it is time we find something to quench our thirst. That was a hectic dance." And she knew it was more than the dance that made them both so warm. He took her hand and led her off to where the refreshments were being served.

Although Margarethe danced with a few other people, Hanswurst always seemed to be by her side. She was dying with curiosity as to who he was. She could hardly wait until midnight.

Shortly before that fatal hour the Duke, dressed as a Prince, naturally, and his Duchess, Snow White, called a halt to the dancing and announced that it was time to choose the King of Misrule and his Queen. Several suggestions were made, but the overwhelming majority chose Hanswurst for King and Cleopatra for Queen. He took her hand and led her regally to the throne. The Duke knelt before them in mock homage and kissed Cleopatra's hand.

Then everyone heard the great bells of the church start to ring the hour. Within seconds several ornate clocks around the ballroom added their chimes. Masks were pulled off amid shouts of joy—and an occasional groan of dismay—at learning who their partners of the moment were. Margarethe removed hers slowly. She wanted to see Hanswurst first.

"I know you," she said hesitantly. "That is, I've seen you around, but I'm still not sure who you are."

"And you must be one of the Stockman girls, but I'm not sure which one."

"I am Margarethe, the fun-loving one," she replied. "And you?"

"Hermann Kregel, Rector of the Choir School."

"A minister!" she exclaimed amazed. "And you masqueraded as Hanswurst?"

"Why not?" he laughed. "I often have to act like the Joker just to get those boys to sing."

She laughed, too. "You are such fun and you dance so well, too. I never thought . . . I mean ministers are usually so serious."

"The Bible doesn't say we can't have fun," he rejoined, "nor does it prohibit us from courting a lovely young maid either."

And before Lent of 1553 began Margarethe and Hermann were wed.

The Duke, though long since of age, was still firmly under the control of his Aunt Apollonia, because although well-liked, he was a weak and indecisive individual. For this reason, although he held firm to the Lutheran cause, Lüneburg lost the preeminence among the Protestant leaders that it had held under his father. This lot fell to Moritz of Saxony, who had once again switched sides. The Emperor had kept none of his promises to anyone, least of all Moritz, and was again threatening to use force against the so-called heretics. The greatest fear of all the Germans was that Charles would turn Germany over to his fanatical son, Philip of Spain. The Protestants formed another league, and to everyone's surprise, even Ferdinand, the Emperor's brother, though remaining a Catholic, supported them for strictly political reasons. He, too, was aghast at the thought of Philip ruling Germany.

Late in 1552 Moritz took the initiative and led his troops into the Tyrol in pursuit of Charles. He would have captured him at Innsbruck had not one of his regiments mutinied for lack of pay. The Emperor fled for his life into Italy and was never seen in Germany again.

Meanwhile a strange nobleman with the odd name of Albert Alcibiades, Margraf of Bayreuth, entered the scene. A member of the Hohenzollern family, he was one of the most vicious and ruthless characters in a ruthless age. 'An enormous, insane wild beast', one of his contemporaries called him. He declared Moritz a traitor to the Protestant cause and swore to war against "all Roman priests and the treacherous merchants of the cities." This latter threat frightened everyone. He rampaged across south central Germany in the area of Nürnberg and Bamberg, burning and pillaging hundreds of villages, monasteries and castles, regardless of whether they were Catholic or Protestant. He extracted huge payments from the terrified cities in order to pay his troops.

Then he turned his attention to the upper Rhein hoping to gain the support of the French king. But Henri II wanted no part of him. Instead Charles took this madman into his service in the hope of recapturing Metz from the French. This act of the Emperor caused a furor of indignation throughout Germany. When the attempt on Metz failed Charles left for the Netherlands, leaving Albert Alcibiades loose again to continue his depredations against Germany. He turned to the north.

But this time the Princes were ready for him. They had formed two defensive leagues irrespective of religion, the Heidelberg League in the south and the Northern League, led by Moritz of Saxony. The Northern League also included King Ferdinand and several Catholic bishops. They met Albert Alcibiades at a little place called Sievershausen, near Peine.

This was too close to home for the Celle merchants, and they gladly contributed money, arms and men to their own Duke's army, which joined the League in the battle. It was a hot July day in 1553 and the ensuing battle was a long and horribly bloody one, but in the end Albert Alcibiades was soundly defeated. He fled south, where the southerners stripped him of estates and possessions, and he went into exile to France. Sadly, Moritz of Saxony was fatally wounded at Sievershausen. But peace at last seemed assured.

The Duke's younger brother Friedrich was also killed at Sievershausen, leaving the succession to the third brother, Heinrich, and, if the Duke should outlive him, then to Wilhelm, the youngest.

The German princes had proven that they could work together in unity, but there was still the religious question to be settled. In February 1555 Ferdinand called a Diet at Augsburg to discuss matters between 'members of the old faith' and 'members of the Augsburg Confession', as they were called. The delegates debated for almost half a year and finally came up with what they considered an equitable agreement. The next generation would call it *cuius regio, eius religio*, meaning that whatever the ruling prince's religion, that would be the religion of his territory. There were three problems with the Peace of Augsburg. The common people themselves were guaranteed no freedom of choice. The agreement was strictly between the Catholics and the Lutherans. Other Protestants, such as Calvinists, were not taken into account at all. And there was the 'Ecclesiastical Reservation' which stated that if bishops, abbots and other prelates should choose to embrace Lutheranism, they would lose their entire secular estates and incomes.

These three omissions were bound to lead to other problems in the future, but for now the Peace of Augsburg was a momentous step towards peace, in that the 'heretics' were no longer heretics but had achieved full legal and political protection within the Empire. And the best news of all was when Charles turned his greedy eyes toward England and married his son Philip to Mary Tudor, ushering in a nightmare for England but causing a sigh of relief throughout Germany.

The same year, Sophie Stockman was wed. And after a respite of several years, Gretchen von Sehnden unexpectedly became pregnant again.

"I can't believe it," she said to her friend Ilse. "After eight I thought I was finished. Why, I have already started going through the change, I think."

"That's the most dangerous time, when you have to be the most careful," said Ilse. "I wouldn't be without my sheep's gut, especially not now."

"I just didn't think. Well, it's God's will," said Gretchen resignedly. "I hope it's a girl. I'm tired of boys. And look at Geske Stockman. She's still bearing."

"But she is young yet. It's Hinrik I worry about. He is getting old. If he should pass on, those children will be still young. She certainly is not capable of caring for them."

"He's not that old yet, but I know what you mean," agreed Gretchen. "And I don't think he's too happy with her any longer. Although he never says anything, I can sort of sense it."

Hinrik Stockman was sitting in his countinghouse thinking the same thing. Not that he regretted taking her to wife. He had needed a woman—still did, even at his age—and she was giving him more sons, which he had felt he needed. Now he was not so sure. Of course, they were very young yet. It was hard to tell how they would turn out, but he could not see any of the Stockman intelligence or drive. She spoiled them so, and always scheming, scheming. Why did she have to scheme so? He was wealthy and gave her every comfort, almost everything she wanted, yet she seemed to be trying to drive a wedge between him and his elder children.

Hinrik thought about his children from Ilsebe, all different, yet all intelligent and with character. Not one spoiled and—well—bland like Geske's, with the possible exception of young Balthasar, who had known no other mother but her. Selfish though it was, Hinrik was glad Anna was still at home. She managed the household efficiently and was interesting to talk to. That is, when she was home, which was seldom. She tended to spend more time with the von Sehnden, with the Lindemanns and even with Margarethe and her husband than with him. Why wasn't she wed yet? She had so much to offer, but she was already considered an old maid by most of their friends. Even poor little Apollonia had a frail, sprite-like beauty that was attracting several beaus. Katharina should have been a boy. She and her husband were so interested in the business. But then there was Franz. Ah, now there was a son to be proud of. At fifteen he had completed his apprenticeship and now in the journeyman stage of his training, was already taking part in the business and making some very astute decisions.

Franz was also being tutored from the bottom up under the able guidance of Ciliax Kothman, Hinrik's general factotum, manager and chief accountant. Hinrik had taken Ciliax on as an apprentice years ago, when he had despaired of ever having a son. At one point Hinrik had even seriously considered marrying him to one of his elder daughters and making him heir to the business. But the birth of Franz and then Balthasar had changed all that and Ciliax had never known of Hinrik's thoughts. Like most apprentices, he had been treated as a member of the family and, now married himself with one child, they all had been taken under Hinrik's wing. Ciliax, now in his early thirties, was a serious, hard-working man much like Hinrik himself. He lived for the business, and Hinrik felt free to leave him totally in charge when he made his frequent trips to Antwerp, Bremen, Hamburg and elsewhere.

Ciliax was worried. One day at an opportune time he said, "Master Stockman, you must make a will."

Hinrik looked at him in surprise. "Why, Ciliax, whatever for? I may be well-off, but I'm not that rich yet. Everyone knows the business will go to Franz, as long as he keeps doing as well as he is right now. And all the others will be well provided for. Why? Has anyone complained about that? Katharina?"

"Nay, nay. Never that fine lady. It's—well, I mean no offense, Master," Ciliax replied hesitantly, "but your goodwife thinks otherwise."

"Indeed? And what thinks she?"

"Well, er, I mean—that is . . ." stumbled the usually fluent Ciliax.

"Out with it, man. What scheme is she concocting now?"

That gave Ciliax the courage to speak. "You know, Master, how often she comes in asking for money and you have forbidden me to give her any. And the cloth—always she needs a new gown or suit for one of her little boys—and you have told us only to give it with your permission." Hinrik nodded. "Recently, when my back is turned, she has grabbed the shears herself and then tries to blame Franz."

"What!" exclaimed Hinrik. "I shall put a stop to that immediately. That explains some of the recent shortages."

"All of them, Master. But there is more. Lately she loses her temper and says that when her sons inherit the business she will get rid of me and Franz both."

Hinrik was dismayed but not surprised. "Losing her temper may be due to her condition, but she knows very well that the business is going to Franz and it will be a long time before her sons enter the business, if they ever show any aptitude for it at all." Which I doubt, he thought to himself. "I shall take care she understands that. And don't worry, Ciliax, your position is secure. She'll not threaten you again."

Sometime later Hinrik was having coffee with Lüdeke. "Hinrik, you should make a will."

"What! You, too?" exclaimed Hinrik. "I am not that old yet, nor rich enough to bother."

"You certainly are. Listen, my friend, I have learned a lot about the law since becoming Head Master of the Gewandschneider and Bürgermeister. I've had to judge a lot of these cases. Even many of the more educated peasants make wills so that their sons will not carve up the only horse or their daughters fight over a warm cloak."

"But why this sudden interest in *my* will? Why, but a few weeks ago Ciliax was on me about the very same thing." And he told Lüdeke about the conversation with his factotum—or at least most of it.

"I'm afraid I bring it up for the very same reason," said Lüdeke somewhat apologetically. "Gretchen actually urged me to it. It seems that your Geske brags to anyone in the marketplace who will listen to her that her sons, and hers only, will be your heirs, because *she* is giving you sons and not all girls as Ilsebe of blessed memory did. She seems to ignore Franz's very existence."

"God's teeth, Lüdeke, I've spoken to her. I thought I made it very clear. What more can I do?"

"Make a will and make it even clearer. If you should die without one, she gets the half-portion and the rest is divided amongst the children. That is the law. And I've even heard of some cases where the married daughters of a first marriage are ignored entirely, their dowries being considered sufficient. If it ever came before me, I would never let that happen, but I am limited by the law. And I know that's not the way you want it."

Hinrik was shocked. "No, certainly not. Everyone knows I want Franz to have the business."

"Everyone but the law—and Geske."

"Thanks, my friend, for the advice. I shall think on it." He left without finishing his coffee.

Some weeks later on a Sunday Pastor Ondermarck of the Stadtkirche greeted Hinrik after service. "Hinrik, are you in a hurry? There is something I'd like to discuss with you if you have a few moments."

"Certainly, Pastor. I'm in no hurry." The Pastor often consulted with Hinrik and the other Gewandschneider regarding investments for the church, and Hinrik thought this was another such occasion.

When they were seated in his office, the Pastor said, "Hinrik, I know you have always given generously to the church as well as to St. Anna's and St. George's, and I don't mean to pry into your private affairs, but have you made a will?"

Hinrik was flabbergasted. "Pastor," he said, "as you say, I have always given generously to the church and shall continue to do so, God willing, and I am sure that my children shall see that you are not forgotten when the Lord sees fit to take me. Why is everyone so concerned about my making a will?"

"Everyone?"

"Ja, first my manager, then the Bürgermeister, now you."

"Your charming daughter Anna is worried, and she has spoken to me about it, else I should not have been aware—"

"Anna! But she will get her dowry whether she weds or not. And it looks like she never will. Why is she worried?"

"Not for herself, but for you. Or rather, what your goodwife will do with your hard-earned fortune once you are gone."

Hinrik put his head in his hands. At last he said, "Pastor, everyone seems to know more about my goodwife's intentions than I. Perhaps I should never have married her, but I'll not put her aside. I still have some love for her, although perhaps it is more like pity now. She is so helpless." At the Pastor's look of surprise at this, Hinrik continued, "No, Geske is no Ilsebe, may God rest her soul. No one is more painfully aware of that than I. She claimed to have noble blood, but I doubt it. Her ignorance is that of the meanest peasant who must always scheme to gain his ends. I have tried to show her that this is not necessary, but the older she gets, the worse it gets. She could never make her way out in the world—our world. That is what I mean by helpless. Fear not, I shall see that she is well provided for, but no way will I let her get her hands on the business or my elder children's portion."

"Ilsebe was a saint," said the Pastor. "But Geske I hardly know as well as I'd like. She doesn't come to church as often as she should."

"I know, and you're probably right. Left to her, very little would come to the church. And I worry about Balthasar. He never knew his own mother and Geske has corrupted—no, that's too strong a word—has coddled him so, that he seems to have lost whatever strength of character he may have had. He is every bit as intelligent as Franz, but he is lazy, uncooperative and has no interest in the business whatsoever."

804

At this moment Martin Ondermarck pitied Hinrik Stockman, one of the wealthiest men in Celle. An orphan, under the sponsorship of the powerful von Sehnden, he had built from the tiny inheritance of his stepfather a highly successful, far-reaching financial empire—and was still building. A member of the prestigious Gewandschneider, he seemed to have everything, one of the most beautiful houses in Celle, ten children and the family still growing, and was a singularly devout man, pillar of the church. And yet here he was baring his soul, a very unhappy man. How strange are the ways of the Almighty, thought the Pastor.

He said, "Send young Balthasar to me. Perhaps I can learn where his interests lie. Maybe he is not cut out for your business, but for something else."

"Thank you, Pastor, I shall do that," said Hinrik.

"And make that will. I cannot stress how important it is, especially in view of what you have told me."

"Ja, Pastor. I shall think on it."

And Hinrik did think about it. He even jotted some things down on scraps of paper. But all was forgotten when in 1558 the free Hanse city of Hamburg announced the opening of its own stock exchange. Hinrik's excitement knew no bounds. He was determined to be one of the first to invest.

"Come with me, Lüdeke. There's bound to be money made there," said Hinrik.

"I'm sure there is. And I'd like to go, but I'm not sure I can right at this moment," replied Lüdeke. "It's past time we had our own exchange here in north Germany."

"High time indeed, with what's happening in Antwerp. I was so glad when Charles abdicated that he divided the Empire between Philip of Spain and his brother Ferdinand."

"Good Lord, yes. The only sensible thing he ever did. And now he's dead and Ferdinand to be crowned Emperor. Catholic though he is, at least he is a German. I shudder to think what Philip will do in the Spanish Netherlands. He's already trying to destroy Antwerp."

"That is why it is good we are to have our own exchange here in Hamburg. But we still have to trade through Antwerp. I hate all the uncertainty. It is not good for business."

"True. But while the Hanse may not be as strong as it was a hundred years ago, it is still a power to contend with. They will stand up to Philip. I don't think we have to worry about that for a while yet."

Hinrik shook his head doubtfully. "I wish I were as certain of that as you. Philip cares nothing for trade or commerce, only his fanatical religion. And those Dutch Calvinists are stubborn. They won't let him ride roughshod over them. I predict an armed rebellion before long. And if they can free themselves from Spain's grip, those up-and-coming Dutch merchants will be our Hanse's greatest rivals. Mark my words."

"Perhaps. But speaking of uncertainty," Lüdeke changed the subject, "I worry about our young Duke's poor health. That is one reason I hesitate to go off to Hamburg just now."

"Oh, Lüdeke, that will be a smooth transition. Who comes next—Heinrich, then Wilhelm. Either one will be a stronger Duke than our present one. Ducal affairs can take care of themselves. They won't miss you for a week or so. Think of the investment opportunities."

Lüdeke laughed. "I am thinking. And I shouldn't want you to beat me out. Very well, I'll go."

Lüdeke and Hinrik went to Hamburg accompanied by young Franz Stockman, now eighteen, on his first major business trip outside of Celle. They bought heavily of shares of all sorts of lucrative ventures, and Franz had his first taste of the excitement of the world of high finance.

Not long after the New Year the young Duke died and was succeeded by his next brother, Heinrich, a much stronger and abler ruler. The following year Apollonia was married and Anna was still not wed. Nor had Hinrik as yet made a will.

Early in 1561 Lüdeke was very excited. "Hinrik," he said to his friend, "at last we are going to have the new Rathaus."

"Wonderful," Hinrik replied. Over the ten years of Lüdeke's term as Bürgermeister Celle had grown rapidly in both size and prosperity. It was now one of the wealthiest of the medium-sized towns in all of Germany. So Hinrik had gradually come to see the need for a larger Rathaus. "How did you finally accomplish that?"

"Two things," replied Lüdeke. "Now that Eggeling, Peter," and he named some of his other cronies, "are all on the Council, I have a majority. So it was easier to convince the rest. But more than that, I have come up with an idea that will save a lot of money."

"Oh? How so?"

"You know those three large Bürger houses that front on the Market Square adjacent to the south end of the present Rathaus?"

"Ja, ja. I thought you planned on tearing one or two of them down."

"Now we're not."

"You're not? Then where will you put the addition to the Rathaus?"

"In them!" Hinrik looked perplexed and Lüdeke continued. "We are going to connect them all together with a single roof and a new facade and break through the walls. I consulted with Master Riess, and he says architecturally it is sound; it can be done. In fact, he thinks it is a capital idea. And the Council thinks so, too. It will save so much money, they didn't hesitate to vote for it. Some were even enthusiastic at last."

"I'm so glad for you," said Hinrik. "You've certainly fought for it long enough. When do you plan to start the work?"

"As soon as the weather breaks. It will take several years. We can only do so much at a time."

"I certainly wish you luck. It will be nice to have a new and modern public building in Celle."

"Nice!" exclaimed Lüdeke. "It will be beautiful."

"As beautiful as Hamburg's or Bremen's?" teased Hinrik.

Lüdeke laughed. "Not quite. One of those would fill half of our town. But don't tease. You'll see, you'll see."

"I look forward to seeing it. And are we Gewandschneider really to have a place under a dry roof to show our goods on market days?"

"That's an integral part of the plan."

"Then I hope I live long enough to see it to completion."

"So do I," replied the Bürgermeister.

Later that year Anna Stockman was in her usual favorite hideaway, the von Sehnden library. They had some new books she was anxious to read. Recently she had taken to visiting with Gretchen a lot more than she used to. With Lüdeke's new project of the Rathaus, in addition to his heavy duties as Bürgermeister and the requirements of his far-flung business interests, he was seldom home. And she felt that Gretchen was lonely, in addition to going through that difficult time in a woman's life when one was often depressed. Besides, Anna adored her little 'afterthought child', as Gretchen often called him. Not quite four, little Hans was thoroughly spoiled, as his elder brothers had not been. But not mean-spoiled as Geske's brats were. He was a good child, bright and jolly, and very fat. And Anna enjoyed trying to teach him his letters and numbers. When he got bored or tired, she played with him or told him the old stories.

This day none of the family was at home at the von Sehnden house, only the servants. So Anna settled down to a good read. It was late fall, rainy and dreary, a perfect day for it. Later she thought she heard someone come home, but so engrossed was she in her book that she paid no attention.

Suddenly little Hans burst into the library. "Anna, Anna," he cried. "We have a guest."

Anna looked up from her book. "That's nice," she said, not really interested.

"But he's a very special guest," insisted Hans. "You must come and meet him."

"I'm sure if your Mama wants me to meet him, she will say so." Not another one, she thought. Although Gretchen had been singularly considerate in not calling Anna's attention to every eligible young man, others of their friends were constantly thrusting boring males at her. She hated it and had yet to meet one who interested her. And now that she was thirty, the field had narrowed considerably, and everyone, herself included, felt it was too late. Let them say, 'Poor Anna.' She didn't care.

Hans, rebuffed, went skipping out of the room. A few minutes later he returned with his mother in tow, accompanied by a gentleman. Anna could tell he was a gentleman simply by the cut of his elegant clothes and his manner. He was a mature man, too, no young stripling, probably closer to forty than thirty, if she was any judge. And he was the handsomest man she had ever seen.

"Anna," said Gretchen enthusiastically, "Hans would like you to meet our cousin Franz von Windheim. Franz, this is Anna Stockman, daughter of one of our best friends."

Franz made an elegant leg and gracefully took her hand and kissed it. Anna's heart fluttered. "Mistress Stockman, I am charmed." His voice was rich and cultured.

"And I," replied Anna.

"Franz is visiting us from Hannover. He is our cousin on Lüdeke's grandmother's side," explained Gretchen. "And he is especially interested in seeing our library, and I decided there was no one more qualified to show it to him than you. Anna is our scholar," she said to Franz, "just as her namesake, Lüdeke's mother, was."

"I see we have a common interest," said Franz. "Thank you, Gretchen, for letting me take up so much of your time. I'm sure Mistress Stockman will be an excellent guide through all these volumes."

"Then I shall leave you two to your books," said Gretchen. "I must go and see what the servants have been up to while we were gone." She ushered Hans out the door.

"What is that you are reading?" asked Franz.

"The latest by Jörg Wickram, *Das Rollwagen büchlein*," replied Anna. "I find it quite enjoyable."

"So did I," said Franz. "Hilarious, in fact."

"Yes, if people could only see themselves as he sees them, perhaps there would not be so much unhappiness in the world."

"Ah, so you're a philosopher, too."

She laughed. "Not really. But his farces poke fun at so many pompous types we see every day, it tends to make one philosophical."

"Have you read his novel *Der Goldfade?*" he asked.

"It's right here under my hand, but I haven't started it yet."

"You'll like it, I think. Quite different from the farces."

"And Herr von Windheim, look at this. A German translation of Marguerite of Navarre's *Heptameron*."

"Oooh, Mistress Stockman, you will truly be shocked at those. I don't know but that they are too risqué for a lady."

He called me a lady, she thought. But she said frostily, "And whyever should I be shocked? They are written by a woman, are they not? And a very lady of ladies, a queen, no less."

He laughed. "Indeed, and a very entertaining woman she must be. I'd like to meet her. Won't you call me Franz?"

"If you will call me Anna—and be not a prude."

He laughed again. "Anna it is. And why would I want to meet the far-off Queen of Navarre when such an entertaining woman is right here?"

"Ah, Franz, you are quite the gallant. But don't stop. I like it. A simple merchant's daughter doesn't hear much of that."

They spent the next two hours talking of books and all sorts of things. He was amazed that she was not only intelligent but intellectual as well, with a sharp wit that he enjoyed. And she was astonished that any man her own age could share her interests and make her laugh, too. So engrossed were they in their conversation and each other that they never heard Gretchen tiptoe in.

"Franz," she said, "I am sorry to disturb you both, but supper will be ready just as soon as Lüdeke comes home. Perhaps you would like to walk Anna home."

Franz von Windheim prolonged his visit to Celle as long as he dared and hardly saw any of his other relatives. After that he came to Celle as often as he could. And Anna was floating on air. She was in love. And even Geske didn't bother her.

In the spring of 1562 Franz and Anna were married and she moved to Hannover with him.

Jacob Bruns was getting old. Not that he felt old. No, never that. He still did a full day's work on the farm, although he had to admit on some of these cold, damp winter mornings the old bones did creak and protest when he tried to rise. But he had stalwart sons to do the early-morning chores and now a growing flock of grandchildren, some of whom were already old enough to do a man's work. That alone would make a man aware of his age, but proud, too.

Only his two eldest sons were not working on the farm, they who were wounded at Drakenburg. Wounded, he realized now, not only in body but in mind and spirit as well. To give them credit, they had both tried. Erich, once he got used to it, was quite pleased with the wooden leg his Uncle Hinrik had carved for him, but it made him slow and clumsy and he was painfully aware of that. It also introduced him to the wondrous things that could be made from wood, and as soon as Heinzi was of an age to do a man's work, Erich apprenticed himself to his Onkel Hinrik, and he was now a full partner in the cabinetmaking shop in Vilsen.

Christian had trouble right from the start with his good eye when out in the glare of the sun, although he could see and read perfectly well indoors by the softer light of a candle. At the same time he had become very friendly with Markus Lindemann, who came to visit them frequently. Now there is an interesting young man, thought Jacob. Young man, God above, he corrected himself, he's but a few years younger than I and must have grandchildren of his own by now. Well placed high up in the Chancellor's office, he had used his influence to get a clerical job for Chris there and so his second son had moved to Celle. Chris had discovered another branch of the Bruns family living there. Simple artisans now, they were nonetheless descended from that branch of the Brunonen who had once been German royalty.

All of this fascinated Markus, who never lost his love of history and who still held onto his dream of one day buying the property on the Maidam on which stood the now-derelict Wehlenmühle. An impossible dream now, thought Jacob. The Graf had turned a large portion of Bruchhausen, including all of the Maidam, into a hunting preserve and his ducal overlords of Lüneburg were frequent guests.

810

Another thing that made Jacob feel old was the passing of yet another Graf of Hoya, and it looked as though the demise of the final remnants of their beloved Heiligenberg was soon to follow. Old Graf Jobst had died in 1545 without ever having achieved his heart's desire of tearing down the cloister church in order to build himself a new castle. And now on 18 March in this year of 1563 Graf Albrecht, a son of that Dowager Countess Katherina, whom Jobst had driven from Hoya, had gone to his Maker. A couple of years before his death, he had gotten his brother Otto and Erich to agree that Heiligenberg and its properties would be the inheritance of his wife, another Katherina, daughter of the Count of Oldenburg and Delmenhorst. And now Katherina was about to bring that old dream to fruition. No dark, drafty dower house at Hoya for her, but a bright new Renaissance palace at Bruchhausen erected out of the ancient stones of the monk's church.

Even now Jacob was on his way to Heiligenberg to assist in the undertaking. All the farmers in the neighborhood who owned wagons had been ordered to help transport the huge stones to Bruchhausen. Jacob headed his team of oxen up the hill. He had chosen to use the oxen instead of horses, because although slower, they were much stronger and had greater endurance. Therefore, he could haul more stones on each trip. The Countess had indicated she would pay by the stone. How this was going to work out Jacob was not quite sure, but he already had in mind how he was going to dicker. Although the few remaining cloister buildings were all falling into ruins, the lush orchards of Heiligenberg were still a source of great wealth. Jacob intended to haggle for a piece of that property.

At the top of the hill he turned into the cloister proper. The old gatehouse still stood, forlorn and deserted. He had not been here in a long time. He thought about the time he had brought the men from Celle here, when he had first met Markus. Except for the destruction of the images by the Graf's men, everything had still been neat and orderly as in the monk's time. If only the old abbots had not been so stubborn about changing their religion, everything could have been as it was. There were many prosperous Lutheran cloisters around the Duchy. The abbot's house was long gone, but strangely enough, the old wooden clocktower still stood, although the clock no longer worked. The monks' dorter had been stripped, but two of the vaulted bays of the cellar remained, and at the far end the little bakehouse, still loaded with peat, that ignorant peasants who had never known the monastery in its glory days, called the Angelhouse, because over its portal still stood the guardian angel, the only image the

Graf's men had failed to destroy. The barn had fallen down of its own accord, but weirdly ten horse stalls, which the monks had never used, still stood. And now the church was being demolished.

Jacob parked his wagon near where a group of men were working. "Ho, Otto," he called to the man who seemed to be in charge. "Are you ready to load stones or am I too early? I don't see any other wagons."

"You're the first, Jacob," replied Otto, "but the others should be along soon, I hope. We need all the help we can get. There's a lot of stone to be moved. I figure it will take the best part of a month, maybe more. Not everyone can work every day. They have their own farms to tend to."

"As do I," replied Jacob, "and the beasts must rest. Hauling stone is exhausting work for them."

"Ja. I see you have oxen. That is wise. Those with horses won't be able to do as much."

"I'm lucky I have them. Not everyone is so fortunate. I intend to earn a good reward from my lady Countess."

Otto laughed. "And she can afford to pay, too."

"So when do we start?"

"Just as soon as that last beam is down, we'll start removing the stone. See, the masons have already chipped away the mortar from several at this end. We'll push them down this slide we've built and away you go. Would you want to park your wagon right under the slide? It would save lifting them again."

"And smash my wagon to smithereens? No thank you. I lost one at Drakenburg to those foolish cannon. Not another one here."

"You still remember that after all these years? Why, I was but a lad then."

"I have two sons who remember."

"Oh, forgive me, Jacob, I had forgotten. Anyway, we'll use the block and tackles, never fear. How many can you carry?"

"Let's try two. If the beasts don't strain too much, maybe a third."

At that moment the last great beam crashed down into the nave of the church. As soon as the dust settled, men scrambled to lay it neatly with the others. He noticed several stacks of unbroken roof tiles off to one side. He wondered if they were going to rip up the great flagstones of the floor and whether the ghosts of the abbots buried thereunder would rise up in protest. It was an eerie thought, this demolishing of a church. But then his practical side took over. It was probably just as well that the Countess was doing this now before it, too, disappeared, like most of the other buildings, stolen in bits and pieces by the peasants over the years.

Now the masons atop the wall were laboriously manhandling the first stone towards the top of the slide. Jacob prudently moved his wagon and team well out of the way. The men tugged and pulled and rocked the great stone and finally succeeded in getting it onto the slide. They had placed ropes around it in an attempt to control it, but so rapid was its descent it almost pulled the men with it and the ropes proved useless. The monolith crashed to the ground in a cloud of dust and flying chips of mortar.

Jacob sneezed and thanked God he had not been so foolish as to park under the slide. The mortar dust smelled ancient and he prayed there was nothing contagious in it. He had heard that there had been some outbreaks of plague in some of the seaports. He wasn't sure just where.

"So, are you ready to load the first one?" called Otto.

"They're not going to drop the next one on my head, are they?" asked Jacob.

"No, fear not," Otto assured him. "We have to clear this one out of the way before they send another down. If they crashed together, it could split both stones into pieces."

And my wagon, too, thought Jacob. He cautiously drove the wagon over to where a huge block and tackle had been set up. The men tightened the ropes and attached the great hook. Then three of them, using all their strength, turned the windlass and gradually inched the stone up to the level of the wagon, then carefully guided it over the wagon bed and slowly lowered it onto it. The wagon groaned but held.

"I'll need wedges and plenty of rope to secure this monster," said Jacob. "I'll not have it sliding into my back when I go down yon hill."

"Go over there," said Otto. "Those men will help you."

Jacob drove over to where Otto had indicated, while the men on the wall negotiated the next stone. When the second stone had been loaded and secured, Jacob decided that was enough.

"Methinks the oxen could probably haul another, but I fear me that the brakes on the wagon are not strong enough to slow the descent down the hill." And that did, indeed, prove to be the most precarious part of the journey. Once on the level ground the team plodded slowly along through Vilsen to Bruchhausen.

So two people eventually got their heart's desires—the Dowager Countess her charming little palace at Bruchhausen and Jacob, who had hauled more stones than any of the others, two precious plots at Heiligenberg. The smaller was a garden plot outside the perimeter path that encircled the hilltop, just beyond the last of the workers' huts. It was big enough for both a cottage and a garden if he so chose to build one. The larger plot inside the circle consisted of a hayfield as well as a goodly section of apple orchards. Jacob was well pleased. One day one of his descendants would get it as a bride-gift.

Meanwhile the plague once again spread through Europe. It was the worst in London, where over twenty thousand were said to have died. The Hanse ships refused to call there, but it had already spread to many of its own seaports. Celle shut its gates and prayed. Trade came to a standstill. The pestilence came as close as Uelzen, which had often been decimated by it in the past due to its low-lying location, but Celle was spared.

While Lüdeke von Sehnden deplored the cessation of trade, he was kept busy with his plans for the new Rathaus. He conferred with Jakob Riess daily.

"The north gable must be the most beautiful, the most eye-catching," said Master Riess.

"Why do you say that?" asked Lüdeke.

"Because it is through the Hehlentor that the great merchants and small traders from the north, from Hamburg and Lübeck, from Bremen and Lüneburg, come with their freight wagons. It is the first thing they will see when they enter the Market Square. It will remind them of the splendor and wealth of Celle."

"Ja, I can see your point," replied Lüdeke. "Then do what you want, as long as it doesn't cost too much."

"It won't, I assure you, but it will look as though it cost thousands of thalers," said Jakob. Lüdeke nodded. He was becoming familiar with the elaborate tricks of his master builder. "And I should like to suggest another thing," said Jakob. "It will dress it up and honor you at the same time."

"Honor me?"

"Ja, ja. We have already discussed putting the coats-of-arms of the Duke and Duchess and the Emperor and Empress on the facade on either side of the doorway when it is finished. Would it not be a nice touch to include your coat-of-arms somewhere? Perhaps on the north gable itself."

Lüdeke thought about this for a moment. "Hah, you old fox," he exclaimed. "Are you seeking to honor me or to butter me up for something?"

"Nay, nay, Master von Sehnden," protested Jakob. "My only thought was to honor you. After all, you have been the prime mover of the new

Rathaus. It has been your project from the start. It is only right to honor you. Besides, your arms is such a beautiful and unusual one."

Lüdeke laughed. "The better to dress up your elegant north gable, hey?"

Jakob looked abashed. "That was part of my intention," he admitted.

"And all who arrive by the Hehlentor will see my arms before those of His Grace and His Majesty," chuckled Lüdeke. "I like the idea. Go ahead, do it. But be sure you get a skilled artist, no amateur."

"I have already conferred with a master from Antwerp for the other two. I shall commission him to design yours, too. You will have plenty of time to approve his sketches. It will be years before we reach that point, but I wanted to be able to include a place for it in my plans."

"As I said before, do what you want, as long as it doesn't cost too much."

Jakob shook his head. How typical of the Bürgermeister, he reflected. Nothing but the best would do, yet he kept a tight grip on the purse strings.

Hinrik Stockman decided it was time his son Franz got married. Long past time. But the young man did not seem inclined to do so. This upset Hinrik. After all, Franz was his eldest son and designated heir to the business—although Hinrik had not yet made a will. So far he had done nothing beyond hinting broadly and had received no response. He must have a serious talk with Franz. He wanted his son settled and producing heirs before he himself died. He already had numerous grandchildren from his various daughters, some of whom were nearing marriageable age themselves.

Hinrik had dearly hoped for a union between his family and those of his dearest friends, but it did not look as though it could be. Lüdeke von Sehnden's sons had all been too young for his daughters, and his only daughter was much too old for Franz. The same went for Eggeling von Eltze's sons but there was the little daughter—he could never remember her name—who would be just about the right age. But unfortunately, Eggeling's wife Ilse had more or less cut them off socially because of Geske.

Hinrik was no longer sleeping with Geske, or at least very rarely. He only visited her bed on those few occasions when his need became painful, and he refused to go to a brothel. She had given him five sons, and truthfully, he wanted no more by her if he could help it. The boys seemed to grow more arrogant and undisciplined the older they got, no matter how much he beat them or tried to instill Christian virtues. It was

815

almost as if they were not his children, so different were they from his eight elder by Ilsebe. And Geske herself, more and more uncouth and ignorant, had become unbearably shrewish as the years went by. Too often her sharp tongue drove him from the house.

Suddenly Hinrik noticed a change in Franz. The lad couldn't be in love. His father had never seen him walking out with a lass nor heard of him visiting one. Hinrik had not noticed any clandestine glances at anyone in church. Yet Franz showed all the signs—of, perhaps, unrequited love. Or maybe it was a secret affair, such as Hinrik and Ilsebe had had for years. He hoped it was not an undesirable girl, although at this point almost anyone would be satisfactory. Almost, but not quite. It was time he had that talk with his son.

The opportunity came soon. Although trade was picking up again in the aftermath of the plague, it was doing so very slowly. One rainy afternoon father and son were alone in the countinghouse. It was so dark and dreary that they had to light candles in order to see. Hinrik caught Franz staring at the tiny flame as though mesmerized.

"Franz, are you in love?" asked Hinrik bluntly.

Franz started out of his reverie. "Papa, why should you think that?"

Hinrik smiled kindly and, he hoped, encouragingly. "Because you show all the signs of that illness so common to young men in the springtime, although it is fall and I see no evidence of any girl."

"It is so obvious then? But I am not in love. How could I be when, as you say, there is no girl?"

"Then 'Minneliebe'. Is the lady so far beyond you that you can only dream? Come, you can tell me. Don't forget I was young once and very much in love with your mother for years before we dared let anyone know."

"It's not quite like that. I wish it was. It's only—I guess it's only a dream."

"Tell me anyway. Perhaps I can help."

Franz hesitated. "You think, Papa, that I have not been listening when you drop hints about it's time I was wed. I have listened and I agree. But I want no arranged marriage as is so common amongst our leading Bürger families," he hastened to say. "I want to choose my own wife."

"And whom have you chosen—or would like to choose?"

"I told you it's only a dream, an impossible dream, I fear."

"Nothing is impossible, if you really want it."

"There is only one girl with whom I feel I could fall in love."

"You are already in love, so stop moaning like a sick calf and tell me who it is," demanded Hinrik impatiently.

Franz hesitated again. Finally he blurted, "It is Kunigunde von Eltze."

"Hah!" exclaimed Hinrik, relieved and delighted. "The very one I should have chosen for you, had I been so inclined to arrange a marriage, which I am not. Although I barely know the girl. Have you even met her?"

"Oh, yes. We've met a few times at the dances at the Rathaus and at the Bible study meetings at Pastor Ondermarck's house. We've even walked twice by the river quite alone."

"Your mother's and my favorite meeting place," reminisced Hinrik. "I called her my river sprite."

"I know."

"Then why in the world are you not courting this Kunigunde?" asked Hinrik, so sharply that Franz jumped. "You do not have the obstacles that we had. Is the girl not willing?"

"She is willing enough, and I think—I hope—she has some liking for me," replied Franz, "but her mother considers us way beneath her because of—of our stepmother. And Kuni is afraid of her mother. And so am I a little, to tell the truth."

"That bitch," growled Hinrik, who seldom swore. "I shall speak to Eggeling."

"No, Papa, please don't. I should be so ashamed."

"Don't be stupid, my son. Do you think your mother and I could ever have wed had Onkel Lüdeke von Sehnden not stepped in, unbeknownst to me, and manipulated things? And we had far more obstacles in our path than Mistress Ilse von Eltze. Moreover, Tante Anna, who was a real lady, not a pretend like that one, launched us socially as if we had always been a part of the patriciate. It's time someone took that woman down a peg or two. Lüdeke's goodwife has done it a few times in the past. Now it's our turn to do so."

Franz looked aghast at his father's outburst but did not know what to say.

"So," continued Hinrik, "get off your crying stool and act like the man I know you to be. You go after the girl and I'll go after her father."

Eggeling was delighted when he heard Hinrik's proposal. He had no idea what was going on. In the end the two friends presented it to Ilse as if it were an arranged betrothal when, in fact, it was just the opposite. A year later Franz Stockman and Kunigunde von Eltze were wed in one of the

817

most elaborate celebrations Celle had seen since the wedding of Prince Wilhelm der Jüngere to a Danish princess in 1561. And Ilse bragged that at last it was the union of two of the great Gewandschneider dynasties, as if she had engineered the whole thing herself. Now if only one of their children could marry into the von Sehnden.

In March of 1568 Hinrik Stockman finally made his will. He had been sick much of the previous winter with an intermittent fever that even the most skilled physickers could not diagnose. It had not seemed especially serious, but it lasted so long and left him so weak and depressed that he finally had to admit that he was a very old man and had best get his affairs in order. His friends and Pastor breathed a sigh of relief. Geske was furious.

"What do we need with all those guardians?" she screamed. "Am I not capable of managing my own affairs? Of raising my own children?"

"No, my dear, you are not," replied Hinrik quietly. "It is customary to appoint guardians for a widow, especially one with minor children. After all, they are not strangers. They are the boys' godfathers. They will be true fathers to them after I'm gone."

"Five maybe," she agreed reluctantly, "but why seven?"

"They are all older men. Any one of them could die before the boys reach their majority."

"Hrumph," she grumbled, "overseers, more like."

"Call them what you will," he sighed, "they will share legal custody of my children until they are grown and will guide you in your financial affairs."

"Financial affairs! What financial affairs?" she snapped.

"Geske, I shall leave you a goodly sum in cash and an even larger amount will be invested so that you will have an income for life. You need never want for anything."

"Goodly sum indeed. You're leaving the same amount to me and my *five* children as you're giving to *each* of your other children. That's simply not fair."

"But the investment . . . " he started to say, then shook his head. She would never understand. "Furthermore," he went on, "your income is yours to spend as you please on all the clothes and baubles you so crave. I have left a separate sum with the elder children for the maintenance of the two cottages." He didn't say it was because he couldn't trust her to do so.

"Cottages! Those two run-down hovels. You expect me to live there with those five wild young ones?"

It was on the tip of his tongue to ask who had let them run wild. But he refrained and said, "Geske, they are in excellent condition. And I remind you that I also provided that in case you can't get along there with your children, you may have the other cottage over next to Bartholdt Becker's house to your own use."

"What! And leave those lads to fend for themselves?"

"Whatever you wish. It's your choice after I'm gone. And don't forget the brewery and stables adjacent to those cottages are your portion as well. I had Jürgen in mind there. The lad seems interested in learning the brewer's trade."

She ignored this. "Why can't I just stay here in this house?" she wailed. "It's big enough."

"This house goes to Franz. He will be head of the family then. His wife will be mistress of this house. No house is big enough for two mistresses."

"We'll see about that!" she threatened. "That little mouse will be no mistress to me." Before Hinrik could comment on that, she went off on another tangent. "And all this money you are taking out of—of our inheritance to give to the church and the poor and this—this foundation, whatever that is. All right, leave a token amount to the church, that's expected. But to the poor? Whoever did anything for me when I was poor?"

I did, thought Hinrik. But he said, "I was once very poor and would not be the wealthy man I am today without the help of others—several others. 'Tis the least I can do in gratitude."

"Hrumph," she grumbled.

"And as for the Foundation, I mean to see that none of my descendants suffer for lack of a marriage portion."

"Foolishness. All of your other children—except mine—are already rich. With what you leave them, they'll have more than enough to leave to their children. Let them take care of their own grandchildren."

"Geske, you don't understand. This is not meant for one or two generations, but forever and ever." And she really did not understand.

Hinrik was tired of the discussion. For the first time in months he was feeling better and longed to be out in the fresh spring air. He would take a walk by the river and try to commune with the river goddess. Maybe he would find a little peace. Before he left, however, he could not resist a parting shot. "May I also remind you, goodwife, that I have also included a clause in the testament to the effect that should any one of my children—all thirteen of them—not be satisfied with the terms of my will, he or she will forfeit their portion in its entirety? That goes for you, too, Geske."

The following year a strange thing happened. Or perhaps not so strange considering the frequent subdividing, reuniting and rearranging of their territories that the Welf dukes constantly underwent in following the ancient Salic law. The line of Dannenberg became vacant and the inheritance fell to Duke Heinrich der Jüngere, whether from personal choice or political astuteness is not known, but Heinrich decided to rule there only and turned the governance of Lüneburg over to his younger brother Wilhelm der Jüngere. Whatever the reason for the decision, it was a good one for the Duchy. The youngest son of Ernst der Bekenner was much like his father, quiet, serious, very pious, and one of the ablest rulers in a long time. He and his Danish princess Dorothea were much beloved by the people, who called him 'The Praying Prince'. He immediately undertook the redecorating of the medieval castle chapel in the new Renaissance style. He commissioned a Flemish painter, Marten de Vos, to do the artwork, prominent among which was a huge triptych over the altar consisting of large portraits of himself and his wife, praying, on either side of an inspiring crucifixion. Later he even had de Vos do a painting of himself reading the Bible with all eight of his children, which was placed in a niche along the north wall.

The same year was an exciting and gratifying one for Hinrik Stockman. During his illness Franz had taken over most of the day-to-day operation of the business, but he could never command the honor and respect due to a Master Merchant until he became a full-fledged member of the Guild. This day was about to dawn. Lüdeke von Sehnden and Eggeling von Eltze nominated him and he was duly sworn into the prestigious Gewandschneider. The ceremony was solemn, elaborate and very secret. Hinrik felt as honored, perhaps more so, as when he himself had been received into their midst so many long years ago. Geske had refused to attend, and no one cared. But Kunigunde was there, radiant and proud as a peacock of her handsome husband. She was also pregnant with their first child.

Another thing that made Hinrik happy was that Balthasar was preparing to leave home to begin his studies at Wittenberg in the fall term. Thank God that dear Pastor Ondermarck had gotten Balthasar out of Geske's clutches those many years ago and had turned him into a serious and considerate young man who sincerely wanted to become a Pastor and dedicate his life to preaching, teaching and helping his fellow men. At first

Hinrik was a little disappointed that Balthasar had no interest in the business, but later he realized that it was just as well. This way Franz would have the entire control and there would be no friction. Later Hinrik intended to divide the entire inventory of cloth up among all his children so that Franz would have to start from scratch just as he had.

Hinrik laughed to himself. Well, hardly from scratch. Granted he would have to restock the cloth, although his own share would be more than enough to start with. But he would be inheriting an extensive and smooth-running network of factors, bankers, and other business contacts as well as customers, to say nothing of a huge amount of capital to back him. Hinrik did business in every town in the Duchy and well beyond, including most of the Hanse seaports and as far as Antwerp and London. And now Franz was already sworn into the Gewandschneider. He chuckled to himself. Hardly from scratch.

And there was nothing Geske could do to upset that. Her sons were not interested anyway. Only envious, because she had planted the seeds of jealousy in them. And this led Hinrik's thoughts to another concern — Geske's veiled threats about the house. Now that Franz was almost running the business, sworn into the Guild, suitably wed, and even starting his own family, Hinrik decided to anticipate one more provision of the will.

"I'm so proud and pleased that the Gewandschneider have already accepted you," he said one day, "that I'd like to give you a little gift to celebrate it."

"Papa, you know that's not necessary," replied Franz. "The honor is enough."

"But it *is* necessary," objected Hinrik.

Franz knew better than to argue. He and all his sisters were well familiar with their father's 'little gifts', and how he loved to give them. What's it to be this time? he wondered, a purse of money or an exquisite jewel? So he said, "All right, if you say it is. Then don't keep me in suspense. Shall I close my eyes and hold out my hands?" he joked.

His father laughed. "I don't think you could hold this in your hands. I have decided to give you half the house. In other words, put your name on a joint deed with my own."

Franz was so surprised, at first he did not know what to say. "But, Papa," he objected at last, "you've already left it to me in your will. It doesn't have to be done now, although I appreciate your kindness."

"I think it does," insisted Hinrik. "If not, I foresee problems after I am gone, regardless of what my will says. She could go to the court and claim widow's rights. I wouldn't put it past her. And I'll not have that. This way you'll have no trouble. It will automatically be yours."

Franz was thoughtful for a moment. "Put like that, I can see your point. Very well, I agree."

"Good. Of course you'll have to pay your share of the taxes."

Franz laughed. "I think I can manage that. Although I imagine on this street with a house this size they are quite high."

"They are indeed, but I always believe in paying my fair share. We are wealthy because Celle has been good to us. The least we can do is give some back to her. So come now. The Town Clerk, Steffan Knorr, has drawn up all the papers and a new deed, and it only awaits our signatures."

They walked together to the Town Hall where they had to dodge flying chips of stone and wade through clouds of mortar dust and sawdust to gain entry. The door to the clerk's office was tightly shut, although by law it was to remain open to all comers during daylight hours. Hinrik pushed against the door and found to his relief that it was not locked.

"Master Knorr," he called out, "I feared me you had gone home for the day. What's this with the door shut?"

"Ah, Master Stockman, do come in. I am sorry about the door, but if you had to work all day breathing this dust and listening to this noise, you would soon be as crazy as I have become." Whereupon he pulled a large handkerchief out of his sleeve and sneezed mightily into it.

"Gesundheit," wished both father and son.

"Thank you. I have your deed all prepared. It needs but your signatures and seals. Now if I can just find it in this mess." He shuffled through papers and parchments that covered his desk, fussily dusting off each one as he laid it aside. "Ah, here it is. Now if you will read it over and sign and seal it, I'll enter it in the Town Book myself right while you are here, so you can be sure it is duly registered."

Hinrik put on his spectacles and read the document through. "Everything seems to be in order. Here read it, Franz." He handed it to his son. "Note that I added that the property is to remain in the Stockman family forever."

Franz smiled at this. Lately his father seemed to be more concerned with the future than with the present. The clerk handed them quills and an ink pot, and they both signed, then Hinrik impressed his seal into the the blob of warm wax. Franz did not yet have one.

"That reminds me," said Hinrik. "It's now time we added that little tick to the crossarm of the hausmark, so that you can have your own seal."

They waited while Master Knorr dragged the huge leather-bound Town Book for 1569 from the shelf behind him and duly registered the transfer of deed. Hinrik paid Knorr his fee and they were about to leave when the clerk asked, "When are you going to want me to write up that foundation or stipendium or whatever it is you were talking about a while ago?"

"Soon. Very soon," replied Hinrik. "I just have to decide how I want it divided and distributed. I'll let you know. Now Franz, we go to the tax collector's office." They ascended the broad new staircase to the next floor. Of beautiful oak, highly polished with beeswax, it, too, was already covered with dust. After they registered the change of ownership at the tax office, Hinrik said, "Let me just say 'hello' to Lüdeke."

He stuck his head into the Bürgermeister's room and found his friend staring out the window. "Don't you ever do anything but watch the work in progress?" he teased.

"Ah, Hinrik and Franz. Good morning. Ja, sometimes a bit of town business crosses my desk," he joked, "but what more important town work is there than this Rathaus project? It goes well, but I hope I live long enough to see it to completion."

Hinrik made his standard reply. "Of course you will. You're younger than I."

But this time Lüdeke said seriously, "I don't know. This rheumatism is beginning to discourage me. There are some days when I can hardly write my name, especially when the weather is damp." He held out his twisted, knotted fingers to show them. "My goodwife makes me soak them in warm water. That helps some. But did you hear that we hope to elect Diedrich Schulte as my co-Bürgermeister next year? He will be a great help. He's as enthusiastic about the Rathaus as I and should be able to carry on the work should I become too crippled to do so."

"Ach, Lüdeke, don't talk like that," chided Hinrik. "You'll see it finished yet."

"Perhaps. And what brings you here anyway?"

"We took care of the house today."

"Oh, very good. A wise move," agreed Lüdeke. "So, Franz, now you are not only a sworn member but a property owner as well. I say that calls for a small celebration. Let us repair to the coffeehouse. Even I have to get out of this dust once in a while."

Later that year all Celle was thrown into deep mourning. Their beloved Pastor and friend of almost forty years, Martin Ondermarck, passed away quietly in his sleep. Born in Ghent in Flanders, he had been an early student of both Luther and Melanchthon at Wittenberg. In fact, for a time Ondermarck had actually lived with Luther. As a young man he had been appointed court chaplain by Duke Ernst in 1527. In 1532 he became head Pastor of the Stadtkirche and in 1541 at the death of Urbanus Rhegius he assumed the duties of General Superintendent as well. He was one of the most stabilizing influences of the Reformation throughout the Duchy and beyond. For all his arduous duties he never lost the personal touch, visiting even the tiniest churches of the area regularly. He was close friend and advisor of everyone in Celle from the Duke and leading Bürgers on down to the poorest day laborer. It was largely for this reason that the Duchy remained so staunchly Lutheran throughout all the terrors and hardships of the next century. He left behind a large body of theological writings that became the nucleus of the famous Church Ministerial Library in Celle.

In 1571 another sadness overtook the Duchy, although perhaps not as deeply or widely felt as the Pastor's death. But it struck closer to the heart of Hinrik Stockman. On 31 August Duke Ernst's younger sister Apollonia died at the age of seventy-two. She, who had left the peace of the cloister to mother the Duke's children after his wife died and had helped guide the young princes during the Regency after his death, had never returned to Wienhausen. After the accession of Wilhelm der Jüngere she had retired quietly to the palace at Uelzen, where she and her brothers had been born. And through it all she had never put aside her nun's habit.

Hinrik felt especially sad since she had been godmother to his youngest daughter Apollonia. She had been particularly close to this god-child because of the crippling illness she had suffered as a child. Yet the frail Apollonia had grown up, married and borne two sons. She persuaded her father to allow her to accompany him to the funeral in Uelzen. Her husband Henning Hake reluctantly agreed.

Because she could not ride, Hinrik hired a special coach for the day's journey.

"She's too tired to be making a trip like this," grumbled Henning.

"She insisted," replied Hinrik as they jounced along the hard-baked, rutted road. "And I agree. It's only right. The Princess was very good to her, especially after her own mother died."

"Will you two stop talking over my head as if I weren't here?" said Apollonia. "Yes, I insisted, and no, I'm not too tired. Tante Loni would be very disappointed if I didn't come and I could never forgive myself."

"How can she be disappointed?" asked Henning. "She's dead."

"She would know," his wife replied with certainty, and that was the end of the matter.

Hinrik said nothing, but he, too, was worried about Apollonia's frail health. But he dared not gainsay her. What she lacked in physical strength she more than made up for in a determined character. And he didn't doubt for a minute that she would be in contact with her dead godmother. He had often seen evidence that she had the second sight—both a blessing and a curse. He never let it be known outside the family, because too many ignorant people might interpret it as witchcraft.

After a few hours Apollonia herself began to regret her bravura. Although the seats of the coach were luxuriously padded, the ride was bone-rattling indeed. Her back and her legs began to ache but she refused to complain. She felt sorry for her father, too. She could see that he was really getting old. He must be extremely uncomfortable. She regretted that she could not ride. This journey would take almost twice as long than if they had gone on horseback, and it was all due to her.

They stopped in the late morning at the tiny village of Eschede for a brief rest and repast. And then on again for several more grueling hours. As the sun started slanting toward the west, they arrived at the little castle of Holdenstedt, only a few short miles from Uelzen. The castle was the ancestral seat of Jürgen von der Wense, Ducal Governor of Celle, who had been Chief Regent after the untimely death of Duke Ernst der Bekenner.

"We shall stop here for supper," announced Hinrik.

"But surely if we press on we can be in Uelzen in less than an hour," objected Henning, anxious to get the trip over with.

"He is expecting us. He has invited us," said Hinrik.

"I remember Herr von der Wense," put in Apollonia. "He was Regent when we used to play with the boys at the castle."

"The very same," said Hinrik.

"He impressed me as being a nice man, and so patient, too," she added. "He must be very old by now."

"That he is, and quite sick, too, so I have heard," said Hinrik. "This may be my last chance to see him."

The coach pulled into the outer bailey, nothing more than a wooden palisade with stables and several other outbuildings. There they stepped down to walk the rest of the way for the drawbridge leading to the inner bailey was too narrow for the coach. Immediately grooms came to help the coachman water the horses while one ran ahead to announce their arrival. Apollonia's legs nearly gave way under her as she left the coach and she had to be supported by her husband and father. But after a while the feeling came back. She ignored the pain and insisted on walking unaided. By the time they crossed the small inner courtyard an old man was waiting for them at the door of the castle. He leaned heavily on a cane while a footman hovered nearby.

"Ho, Hinrik, forgive me if I don't come down to greet you. These old legs can't handle the steps anymore."

"Nothing to forgive, Jürgen," replied Hinrik "We are all getting old. But here, I'm being remiss. You may remember my youngest daughter Apollonia and this is her husband Henning Hake."

"Of course I remember little Apollonia. How she used to tease our present Duke when they were children, but when he teased her back she would take refuge behind dear Loni's habit. And now she is gone," he almost sobbed. "It's hard to believe so much time has passed." Then he got hold of himself and smiled. "And what a lovely young woman she has become. Welcome to Schloss Holdenstedt, my dear, and Master Hake, too. Come take an old man's arm and let us go into the hall."

Apollonia blushed and slowly ascended the steps and took the arm that was not holding the cane. Together they entered the castle with Hinrik and Henning following.

Once supper had been served, Jürgen suggested, "Why don't you stay here for the days of the funeral? I am quite alone and there is plenty of room, although some others will be arriving in the next day or two, I expect."

Apollonia was exhausted and would have welcomed ending this journey here in this lovely spot, but she left the decision up to her father.

"Well, I don't know," Hinrik hesitated. "I appreciate your offer, Jürgen, but we had planned to stay with some Mestwart cousins of Lüdeke von Sehnden. They will be expecting us. And I fear the trip back and forth in the coach every day will be more tiring for my daughter than walking a few steps to the church."

"Then just stay for tonight. We can send a servant to the Mestwarts with the message. I can see the little one is already very tired."

Apollonia looked at him gratefully.

"Ja, Papa," added Henning, "the sun is already setting. If we don't hurry on this very minute, the gates will be closing and they won't let us in anyway. I think we should accept Meinherr's offer just for tonight."

Henrik could see Apollonia fading, and to tell the truth, his own old bones were aching. "Very well," he said, "just for tonight. I thank you, Jürgen, and if you could send that message before dark."

"Immediately," replied Meinherr and dispatched a footman to do so. "And what else can I do for your comfort? Would you like to go straight to bed, little one?"

Apollonia wished he would stop calling her 'little one', but she realized he still thought of her as the child who played with the young princes under Tante Loni's watchful eye. "Not yet, but very soon," she replied. "And dare I ask for a warm bath? It helps so much to ease the pain."

"Certainly you may dare," said Jürgen and sent another servant to the kitchen to heat water.

After a bit, she realized that the two old men were dying to reminisce and she did not feel up to that. "I think I shall go up now, if someone will show us to our chamber," she said. "Come, Hen, help me up the stairs."

Early next morning they continued on their way to Uelzen. After a brief rest Apollonia went immediately to the great Marienkirche, where the Princess lay in state before the high altar. The church was crowded with people coming and going to pay their respects. Several of the ducal family nodded to Apollonia as she approached, and a few moved over to let her squeeze onto the kneeler before the bier. There she gave way to her grief. When her first tears were spent, she began to pray unceasingly for the soul of the dear departed. After a time she overheard two Bürger wives behind her grumbling at her forwardness. Who did she think she was, pushing in amongst the royal family?

She turned around and snapped in a harsh whisper, "She is my Godmother, that's who, and more mother to me than my own."

"Oh, my dear, forgive us. We didn't know," apologized one woman.

The other looked stunned for a moment, then said, "May Our Lord and His Blessed Mother comfort you then." And they moved away.

Apollonia wondered at the invocation of the Blessed Mother, staunch Lutherans though she was sure they were. And here they still called it the Marienkirche. They had not changed the name as in Celle. And here before her lay a blessed nun, who had started out as a Catholic and died as a Lutheran, but still a nun, still wearing her snow white habit. It's all the same God. What difference does it make how we worship Him? And in the midst of her prayers for the dead her mind drifted to the stories her own mother used to tell of the old religion before even the Catholic

Church. Yes, what difference did it make?

The Princess Apollonia lay in state for a full seven days, and her god-daughter Apollonia kept the vigil every day and sometimes far into the night, until both Hinrik and Henning had to scold her for making herself overtired.

"It's the least I can do for all she did for me," she would reply and stubbornly continued her vigil.

On the fourth day Duke Wilhelm der Jüngere arrived with his family and took his place among the mourners before the bier, but they always made room for Apollonia. On the evening before the funeral, Lüdeke von Sehnden arrived at his cousin's house, breathless as usual.

"We thought you'd never get here in time," chided Henrik. "People were beginning to talk."

"Let them," replied Lüdeke. "Someone had to run the government with everyone else here."

And indeed, on the day of the funeral it seemed as though the great church was packed with everyone of note in the entire Duchy, as well as ducal in-laws from Mecklenburg, Denmark and elsewhere. After a long but very beautiful service led by a choir of nuns from Wienhausen, the Princess Apollonia was laid to rest in the crypt beneath the high altar of the great Marienkirche in Uelzen. The next day Hinrik, Apollonia and Henning made their weary way home to Celle. Hinrik could see his daughter was on the verge of collapse, but she insisted that the experience had been gratifying and rewarding, so he made no comment.

Several weeks later Apollonia's younger son, six-year-old Henning, came dashing breathlessly into Hinrik's countinghouse. "Opa, Opa," he cried. "Come quick. Mama is very sick and Papa says, 'Come quick'."

Hinrik knew that Apollonia had taken to her bed for about a week after returning from Uelzen, but the last he spoke to her, but a day or two ago, she had been up and about and claimed her strength had fully returned. He could not imagine what sudden illness had struck her. The little boy was tugging at his arm. "I'm coming. I'm coming," he said. "And what are you doing running about the streets all by yourself? Where is your brother?" he asked as he threw on his doublet.

"He went for the Pastor," replied Henning as he led Hinrik down the street.

"Oh," said Hinrik. It must then be serious indeed. "And what happened to your Mama?"

"She tripped down the stoop and fell down and now she can't walk anymore," explained the lad.

Ach, God, thought Hinrik. It was what he had always feared. After her terrible childhood illness, Apollonia had to use crutches for several years, but by exercise and sheer determination she had strengthened her legs to the point where she could walk unaided. She could never run like other children, but aside from the constant fatigue, she seemed well enough as she grew into adulthood. Yet her father had feared those weak legs would one day betray her.

When they arrived at the house, the physicker had just finished bleeding her. Apollonia lay on the bed white as a ghost and unable to move.

"What has happened?" asked Hinrik

"She fell and broke her back," replied the physicker as he put away his bloody instruments.

"But if she broke her back and is not ill, why are you bleeding her?"

"Because she is paralyzed. With a simple break, although extremely painful, a person should still be able to move. She has no feeling at all. Therefore, we must drain off the evil humors that have caused the paralysis before she can heal," explained the physicker.

Hinrik shook his head. It did not make sense to him, but these learned doctors were supposed to know about such things, so he said nothing. As the physicker was leaving, the minister arrived with young Cord, her eight-year-old.

"Ah, thank God you are here," exclaimed Henning, relieved. "Cord, now go and fetch all your aunts. Take Henni with you." When the children had left, Henning said, "Pastor, I want you to exorcise her. I fear she has been bewitched."

"What!" exclaimed Hinrik and the Pastor together.

"Ja, someone at that funeral put a spell on her. I just know it. Maybe even the old Princess herself."

At that Apollonia stirred and said weakly in a voice barely recognizable as her own, "Nay, nay. Papa, don't let them. It is no sorcery. It is just — just that I am tired — so tired — and I'm going home. Tante Loni is waiting for me."

"You see. You see," insisted Henning. "She is communicating with the dead. If that isn't witchcraft, I don't know what is."

"Not necessarily," said the Pastor, not quite sure whom he should listen to. "It could very well be that Jesus is calling her home, but because of her recent grief over her godmother, she is confused."

829

"I tell you, she is bewitched. I want the devil driven out of her," demanded Henning. "Why else would she be perfectly fine one day and totally paralyzed the next?"

"Henning," said Hinrik sharply, "methinks the only bewitchment is in your head. Pastor, hear me. She was crippled as a child. You are new and didn't know her then. Her legs have always been weak. They gave way as she was going down the steps. She fell and struck her back on the stoop. As simple as that. I have seen perfectly healthy men fall like that and immediately become paralyzed. There is no witchcraft there. Just something about the angle of the fall."

The Pastor seemed relieved at this explanation. "Perhaps first we should just pray for her recovery. The Lord has been known to work many miracles through prayer alone. I truthfully see no signs of sorcery here. Your goodwife has always been a very devout, yea, even saintly person."

"But weak," Henning made one last attempt to convince them. "The kind the devil attacks so stealthily."

"Perhaps," said the Pastor, "but to be honest, we don't do exorcisms anymore in the Protestant church. If you insist, I suppose I could look it up in one of the old books. I don't know that we even have the proper equipment."

"Bell, book and candle. That's all you need," said Henning. And the Pastor looked at him, wondering if they were harboring a secret Catholic.

"Nonsense," Hinrik insisted.

At that moment Apollonia's sisters Katharina, Margarethe and Sophie arrived. Sophie immediately rushed to her sister's side and began hugging and kissing her. Margarethe, after kissing both her sister and her father, took the children into another room.

Katharina, ever the practical one, asked, "What is all this talk about exorcisms and witchcraft? Utter foolishness. She fell. She's badly hurt. She needs our help and our prayers, not a lot of superstitious hocus-pocus." She had always thought Henning a little simple-minded, but she put up with him because, after all, he had wed her little sister.

"But—but," stammered Henning. He had always been a little afraid of Katharina.

"No buts. If you are not going to pray with us, get out of here and stop upsetting her. Witchcraft indeed!"

The Pastor decided it was time to take things in hand. "Let us then gather round and pray for our injured sister."

Margarethe came back with the children. They all knelt around the bed, Sophie holding Apollonia's one hand, Katharina the other. Hinrik stroked her hair. Henning stood off in a corner, but he folded his hands and bowed his head as the Pastor prayed. He prayed for Apollonia's swift recovery, but in the event the Lord saw fit to take her at this time he prayed that Jesus would enfold her in His arms and ease her passing.

After he left, Katharina asked, "Loni, would you like me to exercise your legs like I used to do when you were little?"

"If you wish, Katinka, but I'm so tired, I don't think it will do any good." Katharina tried nonetheless, but the limbs were lifeless. "You see," murmured Apollonia, "I am already dead from the neck down. Tante Loni is calling me. She's just waiting for my head to join my dead body."

"Stop this foolish talk about Tante Loni," said Katharina. "We'll help you to get better again."

"I don't think so. Not this time. Sophie and Gretchen, take care of my little boys when I go."

"Of course, we shall," replied Margarethe, "but you're not going yet. They still need their mother."

"Oh, Loni, Loni," sobbed Sophie, "don't leave us. Not yet. Please, dear God."

Hinrik was the only one who believed his daughter. He had seen too many go not to recognize approaching death. And her resignation frightened him. It was not like his Loni not to fight. He could almost smell death hovering over her bed waiting to take her soul. He leaned over and whispered to her, "Shall I send to Hannover for Anna and Ilsebe, if they can come?"

"Ja, Papa. I would like to bid them farewell before I go. But there might not be time. Tante Loni is calling me."

Before her sisters Anna and Ilsebe could arrive from Hannover, Apollonia was gone. She left quietly in her sleep and it was to be hoped that her godmother, the Princess Apollonia, was truly waiting to welcome her.

12

Hinrik grieved for a long time for his youngest daughter. He was an old man. He knew he did not have many more years left to him. But that was in the order of things. Why did the good Lord have to take a young mother in the prime of life? It just was not fair.

But Apollonia's passing made him more cognizant than ever that if he intended to set up that foundation for his descendants, he had better do so very soon. He had already set aside the capital—1020 thalers—back in 1567 with the Council at Hamburg, who held a number of his other investments. It generated five percent interest, or fifty-one thalers yearly. He had a fairly good idea of how he wanted to set it up but he wanted it to be foolproof, to truly last forever.

He conferred with his best friend Lüdeke von Sehnden, who had knowledge of such things from the Mestwart Stipendium and with the other Bürgermeister, Diderick Schulte. Hinrik conferred with his friends on the Council, Peter Stratheman, Jürgen Sieken and Helmeke Harbers. He conferred with Eggeling von Eltze who was very knowledgeable in legal matters. But Eggeling himself was very ill and could not spend much time with him. And above all he consulted with the Pastor of the Stadtkirche and his three canons. He also got some good advice from Johann Zigenmeier, the town treasurer. And last but far from least, he spent many hours discussing the details with his son Franz.

"I want it to benefit both the boys and the girls equally, without prejudice," he said to Franz.

"But how many girls will go to the university?" asked Franz. "None. That alone will favor the boys."

"I predict that sometime in the not too distant future girls will be permitted to study at a university. But I want this to be better, more inclusive, than the Mestwart Stipendium. Therefore, I have decided to make it a wedding stipendium."

832

"But that then will favor the girls since they are the ones who require dowries."

"That's why I'm not calling it a dowry, but a wedding settlement for both the men and the women to be paid only after they have submitted proof that they are honorably wed *and* that at least one of the pair is my direct descendant."

"Hmm. An interesting and unusual idea," said Franz thoughtfully. "But what if no one is wed in a given year?"

"Then I shall allow it to be given for a student's tuition at Wittenberg."

"Only Wittenberg? Suppose they do not wish to study theology or law?"

"A good point. Very well. Then let us say at any approved university."

"Better," agreed Franz. "And what if there are two or more weddings in any year?"

"Ah, my astute son. You think of everything," said Hinrik, and was thoughtful for a few minutes. "I shall have to make provision for that because we can only pay one per year. Suppose we pay the first one who applies—and apply they must, it will not be automatic—and then pay the second the following year. There are bound to be some years with no marriages. It will even out."

Franz was not so sure. "Possibly," he said, "but simple arithmetic tells me that by the third or fourth generation there will be problems."

Hinrik looked puzzled. "How so?"

"Papa, you have thirteen children. If each of us had thirteen, and each of them . . . "

"But you didn't," interrupted Hinrik. "Ilsebe had only one and it doesn't look as though she will ever have any by this husband. The same for Anna. Apollonia is dead, God rest her soul, and she had only two. You have only one, well, almost two."

"So far. But Margarethe has nine. Even nine times nine times nine . . . "

"Ach, you make my head swim," sighed Hinrik. "Then we'll make a list. They'll all get paid eventually. This is why I shall appoint trustworthy administrators."

"Whom did you have in mind?"

"You, for a certainty, and one or two others. I haven't decided yet."

"I?"

"Who better? You are my eldest son, and you will be head of the family when I'm gone. You are a capable businessman and a devout soul. You are intelligent and honest. Who better could I trust to administer this great foundation?"

"I am greatly honored, Papa," replied Franz. "But then perhaps I should have more details. For example, do you intend the whole fifty-one thalers to be paid as this wedding stipend or only part?"

"Only part, about half. I had in mind perhaps twenty thalers, the rest to go to the church and the poor. But I haven't decided on all that part yet."

All this planning took months and months. The Stockmans, father and son, still had a business to run, frequent trips to Antwerp, Hamburg and elsewhere, social, church and guild activities to attend, families to care for. It was not something to be completed overnight.

Each time he went to Hamburg he conferred with the Council Treasurer, who assured him there would be no problem transferring the money safely to the administrators in Celle.

One fine spring day he went to see Pastor Johann Storch, who had succeeded Pastor Ondermarck at the Stadtkirche. Hinrik felt so good he hated the thought of discussing his demise, but he knew that was the very time to do it. It would be tragic if he died before it was all set up.

"I want to leave some to the church and some to the poor, but I'm not sure how to divide it up. Give me your thoughts on the matter."

The Pastor considered this for a moment. "First of all, there should be some for the upkeep of the church building as well as for the clergy." Hinrik nodded. "And then some to both St. Anna's and St. George's. That would take care of the poor. Unless you want to give some to other indigents who are not staying at either of the houses."

"I had thought of that. So often people fall on hard times, but there is no room at either house, or they do not wish to go there. I should like to help some of those, too."

"I agree. The Church usually knows who they are. We can help choose the most needy."

"Ja. I had hoped you would say that. But to these people I don't want to just hand out cash. In most cases they are poor because they cannot handle money."

"True," agreed Storch. "But you are a cloth merchant. Why not think in terms of providing them with warm clothing for the winter?"

"Ah! A very good idea," said Hinrik. "That way they won't spend it in the taverns."

Hinrik then took all of his ideas, as well as the suggestions of Franz and the Pastor and several others, to the Town Treasurer Johann Zigenmeier. "What do you think?" he asked.

"Very good so far," replied the Treasurer, "but let me advise you to be very specific on how you want the money used or spent, especially that which you leave to the church and St. Anna's and St. George's."

"Johann, do I detect a bit of cynicism?" asked Hinrik. "Do you not trust them to use it wisely?"

Zigenmeier laughed. "Perhaps I am a little cynical. What I see every day in my office would make anyone so. But what I really meant was look at all the drastic changes in religion that have come about just in your lifetime. I don't remember it, but you do. Just a little over fifty years ago everyone was Catholic. Now we have not only Lutherans but Calvinists and all sorts of other religions. Who knows what may happen in another fifty or a hundred years?"

"I see what you are saying. So you think that I should specify in each case how it is to be used?"

"I definitely do. And another thing, it's going to cost a little bit to bring the money from Hamburg to Celle and your administrators should not have to pay that. In fact, they should be given a small fee for their time and effort. Your son might be willing to do it for nothing but your grandsons might not."

"A good point. I shall make provision for that. Anything else?"

"Ja, if you will forgive a bit more cynicism. If the money is to be deposited with the Council here in Celle until the administrators pay it out, the Council should have a fee for that responsibility. Also, it would be a good idea to have the entire stipendium read to the Council yearly. That way new young councilmen who have never heard of you will know exactly what is required of them and what your intentions were. You might also consider making the Council earn part of its fee by letting them choose the administrators if the time ever comes that no one from your immediate family is still residing in Celle. You have already seen some of your children and grandchildren move to other towns. Why, in a hundred years they could be scattered all over the Duchy, mayhap all over Germany."

"Ach, Johann, you bring up so many things that I never even thought of. And all good points, too." said Hinrik. "I intend to include them all in the final document."

"Glad I could be of help, Master Stockman. And if I can help more, don't hesitate to call on me. I find the whole concept of this foundation immensely interesting. It is a fine thing you are doing. I like to imagine that some poor soldier or miller's daughter two or three hundred years from now will say, 'My ancestor Hinrik Stockman was a good man'."

"Ach, Johann, that is my dream exactly. But soldiers and millers' daughters? Well, I suppose it could happen. And you have given me another idea. Johann, would you be willing to serve along with Franz as one of the first administrators?"

The Treasurer did not need a minute to think about it. "I most certainly would be willing, and I am greatly honored, Master Stockman. It will be a privilege and a pleasure."

Hinrik went back to his countinghouse greatly pleased, his head full of new ideas on how to divide up the thirty-one thalers.

By September Hinrik had decided on the final form of all the provisions of the Stipendium. He took it to the town clerk, Steffan Knorr, to have it written in his scholarly hand on the best available parchment. Hinrik also had him make fine copies for each of his adult sons and sons-in-law. Geske's sons were not mentioned.

The first and most important provision was the twenty thalers yearly marriage stipend. Each heir, whether male or female, would have to apply for it, would have to submit proof that he or she was legally wed and, above all would have to prove that he or she was a direct descendant of the founder. If accepted by the administrators, the applicant would receive his or her payment at Easter. If there were more than one wedding in any given year, the other(s) would receive their payment the following year(s). If there were no weddings in any year, the money could be paid for a student stipend of up to two years.

The remaining thirty-one thalers of interest were to be divided up as follows: three thalers yearly for the maintenance of the church building; two thalers yearly to each of St. George's and St. Anna's; in addition to this, three thalers yearly to each of the above 'Houses of God', to be paid quarterly at Easter, St. John's, St. Michael's and Christmas, so that each poor person would have a pallet. If any remained, it was to be given directly to the poor of each house. Then the administrators were to take eleven thalers to buy thirty ells of good black Hildesheimer or Braunschweiger cloth and have made therefrom coats or cloaks for five poor men or women. (He made a special note that they were not to buy cloth from Soltau or Walsrode.) In addition, each of these five people was to be given a pair of good shoes. This clothing was to be awarded on the Friday after

St. Martin's in the parish church. Hinrik also noted that if any friends of either of his wives should be in need, these persons were to receive this clothing before any others.

He also designated one thaler each to the church's Pastor and three chaplains; three thalers to the Administrators "for their trouble and to bring the money from Hamburg"; two thalers to the Town Council for reading the Foundation yearly and one thaler to the Town Clerk for the reading thereof. If any of the above were not paid or desired, it was to go to the poor.

He appointed Johann Zigenmeier and Franz as executors and trusted that they would administer the Foundation in good will exactly as he had directed. He also provided that if no one from his immediate family or friends should remain, the Council should appoint two honest and upright Bürgers to the position.

And at last it was 'done on the 26 September in the year after Christ Our Lord's birth one thousand five hundred and two and seventy'. Hinrik was so proud and pleased, he signed it in his bold and scholarly hand, 'Ick, Hinrick Stockman, myn Hand'. Then his good friends the two Bürgermeisters and three of the councilmen signed as witnesses. Hinrik observed that Lüdeke's arthritis must be bothering him badly today. He could almost see the pain in the cramped signature 'Lutke von Szehnde, min Hant'. Then Diderick Schulte signed as usual. Crotchety old Helmeke Harber's signature seemed to match his personality, but cranky as he could be at times, Hinrik knew him to be a good man. Peter Stratheman's was the neatest after his own, as precise as everything Peter did, and last to sign was Jürgen Sieken. After the signing each of them affixed his seal or hausmark attached to silk ribbons at the bottom of the document.

Hinrik instructed that the original was to be kept in a locked box with the Town Council and that each administrator and witness was to have a key. He personally took copies to each of his daughters who were living in Celle. He gave the rest to Franz for safekeeping until Ilsebe, Anna and Balthasar should next come for a visit. And lastly he took his own copy to show his friend Eggeling.

Hinrik had hoped that Eggeling could have been one of the witnesses, but his friend was too sick. He had suffered a stroke a few months ago and then another and now he lay paralyzed and dying. He could hardly speak. When Hinrik entered Eggeling's bedchamber, his eyes lit up with recognition, but his words came out mostly garbled.

Hinrik tried to be cheerful. "Well, it's done and I'm very pleased with it."

"Tash goo —"

"I thought you might want to see it."

"Mmm . . ."

He held the document in front of Eggeling. "Can you see it? Or should I read it to you?"

"Nnnn . . . " And Eggeling's attention faded. He seemed to drift off to a faraway place.

After a few more attempts, Hinrik gave up. Tears came to his eyes as he murmured a prayer. He kissed his friend and went down the stairs. Kunigunde came in just as he was leaving. As they embraced, she noticed his tears.

"I'm afraid he's dying," she said, barely able to control her own.

"I know. I know. The first of our little group to go. It makes me realize how old I am. I'll probably be next."

"Oh, Grandpa, don't talk like that," she objected. "You're still hale and hearty. You'll be around for a good many years yet."

He shook his head. "I just hope I don't go like that. It's pitiful to see him, isn't it?"

She agreed. "Yes, it is. I try to come every day, if I can. But there's not much anyone can do except keep him comfortable. I pray the Lord takes him soon. It would be a blessing."

"It would that. Over fifty years we've been friends," he reminisced. "Did I ever tell you how we all met? It was at Duke Ernst's coronation."

"Ja, Grandpa, you've told me many times. Now I must go see to him. Mama is so helpless."

"Ja, ja," he nodded. "You're a good girl, Kuni. I'm so glad my Franz married you." She smiled as he took his leave.

As he strolled slowly home he thought about his three friends. Ja, it would be a blessing if Eggeling went. That was a terrible way to live. It was as if he were gone already. His son Heinrich, just three years older than Franz, had long since taken over his father's toll-collector's duties and was already a favorite of the Duke, as that family always seemed to be. Hinrik's thoughts turned to Lüdeke, the youngest of them all, yet so crippled with arthritis it seemed he had not long to go either. But no, Lüdeke was a fighter and a stubborn old man. He would not succumb until his beloved Rathaus was finished. Hinrik chuckled at that in spite of himself. And Peter? Peter appeared to be in such good health, he did not even look his age. He'll outlive us all. I'm sure of that. No, I'll probably be next, but not quite yet, dear Lord. Aside from the usual aches and pains of old age, Hinrik felt quite good. I think the Lord will grant me a few more years. I'm not ready to go yet, but is anyone ever? Just don't let me go like Eggeling, he prayed. It's so sad.

When he reached home his morose mood was quickly thrust aside. Balthasar was home from Wittenberg, but the excitement Hinrik sensed in the household certainly stemmed from more than just a normal home-coming.

Hinrik embraced his youngest son from Ilsebe, the one she had barely known. "Welcome home, Baltke. You look well and happy."

"Thank you, Papa. I am glad to see you are looking well, too, and happy, I hope."

"Ja, ja. We signed the parchment setting up the Foundation today. So I am very happy. But more about that later. Tell me your news. How goes it at Wittenberg?"

"Papa, I graduated 'magna cum laude'."

"Wonderful! Wonderful! I'm very proud of you. That calls for a little celebration."

"And there's more to tell you."

"More? And it must be good, judging by the light in your eyes. Come, let us sit in the parlor while you tell me. My old legs are a bit weary. Geske, fetch us some beer."

When they had settled themselves in comfortable chairs, Balthasar could no longer hold back. "Guess what. I have received an appointment as Pastor in Steinhorst."

"What! Already? And as full Pastor, not an assistant?" exclaimed Hinrik.

"Yes, already. And as full Pastor. Actually, the only Pastor. Steinhorst doesn't have an assistant. It's a very small village. And I must admit I was lucky."

"Indeed you are, but how so?"

"The list of unfilled appointments they had at Wittenberg all went to the 'summa cums', but then as luck would have it, the very day before our commencement they received word that the old pastor at Steinhorst had died, and I was next on the list."

"Luck indeed," said Hinrik. "It was God's will."

"So it was and I'm very grateful. I only wish dear Pastor Ondermarck was still alive to share my good fortune."

"God rest his soul. I'm sure he said a few prayers for you up there. And Steinhorst isn't so very far away. You'll be able to come home for a visit from time to time."

"I doubt very often. I'll probably be very busy, being the only pastor."

"Then I'll come to see you."

"Good. And I'll need to hire a carter, if you don't mind loaning me a few pieces of furniture. There is a house, but they tell me it's very sparsely furnished."

"Loan? Don't be foolish," said Hinrik. "Take what you want. With our family shrinking so, we don't need half what we have here. And when do you begin your ministry at Steinhorst?"

"In a bit over a month. At Martinmas."

"Six weeks. Then we have time for a good, long visit before you go. Come, let us tell the rest of the family. It must be nigh on dinnertime."

"Wait, Papa, there's more."

"More? More news?"

Balthasar grinned broadly. "As soon as I was certain of the appointment and knew I would not have to sit home waiting for months and months until the Superintendent called me, I became betrothed."

"You what?" exclaimed Hinrik. "Oh, dear God in heaven, my son, you'll give me a heart attack yet. And how can this be when I knew nothing about it?"

"Well, it's not exactly official yet," admitted Balthasar. "In fact, she and her parents are coming to Celle next week to meet you and—and—to meet you," he finished lamely.

"So at least you are doing things properly, even if it is a bit of getting the cart before the horse. I shall be happy to meet with her father and—er—discuss things. And by what name, may I ask, is this lovely maiden called? I assume she is still a maiden," teased Hinrik.

Balthasar blushed. "Oh, Papa, of course she is. How could you think otherwise?" he asked indignantly.

"It's just, as I said, you do seem to be getting the cart before the horse."

Balthasar finally realized he was being teased. "Papa, you will have your little joke. Her name is Ilse Schwabach."

"Bavarian?"

"No, I don't think so. Well, maybe. Actually, I don't really know. So many Lutherans fled north when Baravia—the Duke, that is—decided to remain Catholic. So it's possible. But she was born in a tiny hamlet called Essel. It's not even a village. It's so small, I'm sure you've never heard of it."

"Truthfully, I haven't. So then, how did you meet her?"

"Part of our training in the last year at Wittenberg was to accompany the traveling pastors who serve those tiny parishes once a month or so. That's how I met her. Then I found out that she and her family frequently came to Wittenberg to visit relatives there. So we were able to see each other quite often. And then we just—er—sort of fell in love. She's a wonderful girl, Papa."

"I'm sure she is. I shall look forward to meeting her. Now I'm sure dinner is on the table. Unless you have any more news . . . ?"

Balthasar laughed. "No, that's all for now. Isn't that enough?"

"More than enough for one day," agreed his father.

As they left the parlor Franz came in the front door—he always came home for the noontime meal—followed a few minutes later by Kunigunde. "Papa, a boat is just in from Bremen. Two ships arrived with all kinds of news. Ach, Baltke!" he exclaimed as he noticed his brother. "I didn't know you were here. Welcome home." The brothers warmly embraced.

"You're all late," grumbled Geske. "How long am I supposed to keep this dinner hot? It'll all be burnt and then you'll complain. And as for you, Mistress," she turned on Kunigunde, "where have you been traipsing again when I need your help?"

Kunigunde gritted her teeth to keep her temper in check. "Geske, that is what we have servants for. And you know very well I have been visiting my Papa, who is dying."

"Ja, and you'll mark that babe you're carrying if you let that sick old man gaze on him too long. Mark my words."

"Geske! Enough," said Hinrik sternly. Then trying to regain his happy mood, he added, "Let us not keep the dinner waiting any longer. It seems this is a very day for news. We'll hear it all while we eat."

"Well, she better tend to her little Willi first. He's been fretful ever since she left," said Geske.

Kunigunde immediately ran up the stairs as fast as her bulk would permit. "Don't wait for me," she called back, as the others took their seats at the table. Moments later she slipped into the seat next to Franz as Hinrik was saying the grace. As soon as they began eating, she whispered to her husband, "There is absolutely nothing wrong with him. He's fast asleep. The nurse put him down early because he had a few tumbles. That upset him because he's trying so hard to walk. Besides, he's cutting a new tooth." She glared at Geske.

841

"Well, since that's no problem," said Hinrik, "let's hear all the news. Franz, yours and mine will have to wait. You must hear Baltke's first."

When Balthasar told of his graduation with honors and his appointment to Steinhorst, Franz and Kunigunde went into accolades of pride and joy. "That's just wonderful, Baltke," she said, and hFranz added, "Little brother, I'm quite proud of you." Even phlegmatic Jürgen offered congratulations and young Michel clapped his hands. Geske's other three sons sat there looking glum and said nothing.

Michel piped up, saying, "I'd like to go to Wittenberg and study, too, like Baltke."

"You'll do nothing of the sort," his mother retorted. "I'll not have you turn into a mealy-mouthed preacher. A good trade is what you'll learn."

"Geske," said Hinrik, "the lad is young yet. Let him be. But if he is still of a mind to study at Wittenberg when the time comes, then he shall go. I'll see to it." Hinrik thought of all Geske's sons only Michel, the youngest, showed promise. Jürgen was next best. Now a journeyman brewer, he was at least decent and hardworking, if not too bright. The other three — he mentally shook his head.

At the same time Balthasar was thinking, thank God Pastor Ondermarck rescued me from her clutches or I should have turned out just like them. Although she was the only mother he had ever known and he respected her for that, now that he was older he could see her for what she was — a grasping, ignorant shrew. Poor Papa.

Hinrik was saying, "But you must hear the rest of Baltke's news. We're to have another wedding soon!"

"A wedding! Ooh, when?" asked Kunigunde.

"Why, you little sneak, keeping it a secret from us," chided Franz.

"Well, it's not exactly official yet," replied Balthasar and told them all about Ilse Schwabach.

"Does she have a sister?" asked Jürgen.

Balthasar laughed. "As a matter of fact, she does, but she's a little young yet and I'm not sure if she's coming with them or not."

"And when is all this to take place?" asked Kunigunde.

"The betrothal just as soon as Papa and her father settle all the details. I had a mind to get married in Steinhorst before my new congregation, but I think she would prefer being wed here in the big church, so that we can go to Steinhorst together as man and wife. In any event, the banns have to be called, so it will be just about the time I have to leave, I should think."

"Martini. Mid-November. Oh, Lord, that's just about when I'm due," said Kunigunde, patting her belly.

Franz laughed. "Then it will be either a race to the altar or a race to the midwife," he joked. "I wonder who will win."

"And I'll be stuck with a houseful of guests, just when it's so busy," moaned Geske.

"What have you to be so busy about?" asked Franz impatiently. "I thought you liked guests."

"Well, it's preserving time and—and so on. And it's always someone else's guests, never mine," replied Geske.

"Geske," snapped Hinrik, "as Kunigunde said but a while ago, that's what servants are for. I hope that you will act like the lady you're always pretending to be when our guests are here. And if you need more help, we can always get a day girl or two from St. Anna's. Now I want to hear all the world news that came by the boat. I can see Franz is dying to tell us."

"Yes," said Franz, "because some of it will affect our business. Most important, the seven northern provinces of the Netherlands have declared their independence from Spain. They're calling themselves the United Provinces and have called William of Nassau to lead them."

"Oooh, that *is* news," Kunigunde put in.

"And I'm not at all surprised," added Hinrik. "They are so firmly Calvinists, it was inevitable. Is there any indication that the south will follow them?"

"They may try," replied Franz, "but Flanders is so tightly controlled by Alba, they're not likely to succeed."

"Either way it will hurt Antwerp. Any war is not good for commerce. And already the Dutch sea captains are competing with the Portuguese in the East Indies and with Spain in the West Indies. If they succeed in gaining their independence, I predict the financial capital will move to Amsterdam and leave Antwerp high and dry. I may not see it in my lifetime, but you may well in yours."

"You may well be right," agreed Franz. "Spain is already on the verge of bankruptcy. Win or lose, it will hurt her badly. May even push her over the brink."

"And the Fuggers with her," said Hinrik. "Hah, it would serve them right for selling indulgences."

"Oh, Papa! Don't be vindictive. You know they were gambling on getting their share of all that gold."

"And instead Spain put it all in her churches and never repaid her debts to them, not even a penny of the interest."

"And if the Dutch revolt doesn't finish Spain, the word is that this English sea rover or pirate or whatever you want to call him, Drake, has been attacking many of the important gold ports of the Spanish Main and stealing tons of bullion right from under their noses."

"Ach, that will hurt them. That Queen Elizabeth is no fool, even if she is a woman. What other news from England?"

"You know that law we heard about that their Parliament passed last year forbidding the export of wool? They are strictly enforcing it. And what's more, they're importing Flemish weavers — Protestants, of course — to teach the English how to weave good Flemish cloth."

"Oh, my," said Hinrik. "Then we shall have to import English cloth instead of just the wool. I expect it will cost a great deal more than the Flemish."

"Considerably more," agreed Franz. "It is going to hurt us."

"What's the matter with our own local cloth made from the wool of our own Heidenschnucken?" asked Kunigunde.

"The quality, my dear," explained Hinrik. "The quality. The English wool is the finest obtainable and the Flemish weavers the most skilled in the world. Our own is rough compared to it and fit only for the lower classes. Why, there is not a noble lady, nor a Bürger wife, for that matter, who would buy it for anyone but her servants. This will indeed make things difficult for us."

"Then if the ladies want the English cloth, let them pay the higher price," commented Kunigunde.

"It's not as simple as that, my dear," replied her husband, "and there's another thing, Papa. You've heard about these English Companies of Merchant Adventurers that are popping up all over?"

"Ach, ja. There's one already established in Uelzen. But we'll never let them into Celle."

"That may be easier said than done. This Queen is challenging the Hanse itself. If the Hanse towns don't let them in, she is threatening to close the Stahlyard in London."

"Ach, dear God in heaven!" exclaimed Henrik. "That is terrible. Imagine a mere woman challenging the mighty Hanse. What is the world coming to?"

"I'm afraid, Papa, the whole world trade structure is changing. Shifting from the Mediterranean and the North Sea to the Atlantic. England may yet become a world power, and what's more, she is backing the Dutch."

Hinrik shook his head. "I'm not surprised. And pray, what other earthshaking news do you bring?"

"Only one bit more. Horrible news from France, although it won't affect us directly. No but a month ago, on St. Bartholomew's Day, thousands of Huguenots were massacred in the streets of Paris, including Coligny himself, murdered in his own home."

"No! That's that Medici woman. I understand even the French call her 'Madame Serpent.'"

"True, the only good thing is that Henri of Navarre, the Huguenots' other leader, escaped with his life, but he is being held prisoner at the palace. And that only because he recently wed the Valois princess Marguerite. He is a good man and may well one day be King of France."

"They would never accept a Huguenot," said Hinrik.

"They may have no choice. It is doubtful the last three Valois brothers will produce any heirs. Charles is mad and an idiot, the second is a pederast, and the last a rebel who keeps changing sides and whose life is not worth one of their worthless sous."

"This stuff is boring," spoke up Otto, Geske's next to youngest son. "Mama, may I leave the table?"

"You will remain seated until we have all finished eating," admonished Hinrik sternly.

"Why should we?" said Hans, the middle one. "It doesn't concern us."

"It would concern you quick enough if it took the food off our table and you had to worry about empty bellies," snapped Hinrik. "Now mind your manners."

"As long as we're sharing all this wonderful news," said Heinrich, the oldest, very sarcastically, "let us tell you ours. Hans and I are moving to Hannover right after Christmas. Onkel Martin, who is now high up in the butchers' guild, has promised us work."

"And I'm going with them as soon as I'm old enough," added Otto.

"What!" exclaimed Hinrik. "You'll do no such thing."

"Heinrich," shrieked Geske at the same time. "You promised you wouldn't tell until it was time."

"Shut up, Mama," said Heinrich. "What difference does it make when I tell? No one is going to stop us. Give the old man time to get used to the idea that we're not interested in his friggin' business nor in his stupid old Foundation either. We'll never benefit from it. He always favors the others. We're going to do men's work, not sit in some musty old counting-house with a bunch of moth-eaten rags, counting pennies all day."

Even Geske was shocked at his language. "Heinrich, don't talk to your Papa like that."

"I'll talk however I like," he retorted. "And what has he ever done for you?"

Hinrik wanted to say, 'I married her and gave her a home, when she had none, and five strapping boys who are acting like imbeciles'. But he'd been over all that before and knew it was no use. It was the vehemence of the tirade that shocked him. He took a deep breath to calm himself and said tersely, "I think you had best leave the table—the three of you—and go to your rooms."

"Gladly," said Heinrich. "But I'm going out." And Hans got up to follow him.

Franz was so furious he could hardly hold back his temper. He worried that his father would have apoplexy. He rose at the same time and, pointing a finger at Heinrich, said, "If you—any of you—ever, ever speak to my father in such a manner again, I'll lay you out on that floor so fast you won't know what hit you. Then you'll see who's a man, brother." Kunigunde placed a restraining hand on his arm.

"Let them go," whispered Hinrik in a strangled voice.

Otto looked from his brothers to his mother, then to his father, not sure what to do.

"Go to your room, Otto," ordered Geske. "I'll talk to you later." Otto left in a sulk.

When they had left, Jürgen said, "I'm sorry, Papa. I tried to talk them out of it, but you know how mean Heinrich can be."

"It's not your fault, Jürg," said Hinrik. "It's mine."

Balthasar could see how close his father was to tears. Fearing a breakdown, he suggested, "Why don't we go into the parlor and try to relax over some nice mulled wine?"

"Good idea," said Kunigunde. "I'll see to it." She leaned over and kissed her father-in-law. "We love you, Papa." And she flounced out to the kitchen bypassing Geske, still seated at the table, perplexed and, for once, with nothing to say.

Franz helped Hinrik to his feet. "Come, Papa, let's go into the parlor where it's quiet. And I say, 'Good riddance to them'."

Hinrik let his dearest son lead him into the other room. He felt shaken and suddenly very old. And that day he never did get a chance to tell them all *his* news about the Stipendium, of which he was so proud.

Balthasar resolved then and there to take Michel under his wing. He was forever grateful that Pastor Ondermarck had salvaged him from turning out like Heinrich and Hans. So if there was any hope at all of Michel continuing his education, Balthasar was determined to be his mentor until the lad was old enough to see if he had a vocation or not. He told him anecdotes about life at the university, encouraged him in Bible study and enthused about the joys of being a Pastor, preaching God's word and helping his people. And Michel took it all in avidly.

Even when the Schwabach family arrived the following week, although he wanted to spend as much time as possible with his betrothed, and did, he kept the boy close to him. When he explained to her why, without telling her anything of the terrible scene of the previous week, Ilse was very understanding, as he knew she would be. He was tempted to take the lad to Steinhorst with them but knew it would not be fair to impose a confused twelve-year-old on a new bride. But he intended to encourage Michel to come and visit them as often as possible.

Hinrik was quite pleased with his prospective daughter-in-law. She was quiet and unassuming, as befitted a pastor's wife, yet very intelligent and quite practical, necessary traits for a woman who would have to work beside her husband in a small parish. He felt his son had chosen well.

At first Geske was cool and even occasionally abrupt with the guests. But then when she noticed that Jürgen was quite taken with Ilse's sister Catharina, she did a prompt about-face and put on her favorite pretense of being the gracious lady, for which Hinrik was grateful. She even found herself hoping that Heinrich and Hans, who were increasingly away from home, would stay away. She was sure they were out drinking with some of their disreputable companions and prayed they would do nothing to upset things. She found herself being stricter with Otto, who resented it but somehow managed to keep his mouth shut for her sake.

Since the Schwabachs knew no one in Celle, the wedding was necessarily small and quiet, although their relatives in Wittenberg did make the journey for the occasion. Balthasar and Ilse said they preferred it that way. As it was, the Stockman clan with their spouses and all the grandchildren, as well as their numerous friends, half filled the great old church.

And Kunigunde managed to hold off until after the festivities. A few days after Balthasar and his bride left for Steinhorst, she was delivered of another boy, whom they named Joachim, after no one at all.

Hinrik never really got over his younger sons' defection. It threw a pall over the Christmas festivities, and when they actually left, right after the Epiphany, he fell into a mood of self-recrimination. Perhaps he should never have married Geske, a girl his daughters' age. By the time she gave him sons, they were more like grandchildren and he, at the peak of his business career, had little time for them. He had left their upbringing entirely to her and that was a mistake. He should have known better. He had realized right from the beginning that she was totally incapable of instilling in them any sense of ethics, morals or culture since she herself had none of these inborn traits. He blamed himself for not taking a firmer hand with them, but at the time he had been too busy making money. Hindsight never solved anything, he tried to convince himself, but it rankled just the same that he should have failed in this important area when he was so successful in everything else.

Franz noticed his father's depression and worried. Although they had agreed some years back that he would gradually take over the business and his father would gradually retire, Hinrik had always maintained an active interest in every phase of it. Now he seemed to have sunken into apathy.

"Papa, don't keep blaming yourself. It was bound to happen sooner of later. Just be thankful that your first eight children turned out so well."

"I am. I am. But your blessed mother, my dearest Ilsebe, was a totally different kind of woman."

"Ja, and therein lies the answer. They have inherited bad blood from Geske, a wild streak and not too many brains."

"I'm afraid you're right. Although they're not all bad. Jürgen has turned out well."

"As well as can be expected, but you must admit even he is no intellectual and has not half the intelligence the rest of us have."

Hinrik shook his head. "I have hopes for Michel now that Baltke has taken notice of him. Maybe he can redeem at least one of them."

"I hope so, for your sake as well as his," said Franz.

"That is why I was so happy about the Foundation, so that none of my descendants would fall into that situation. But I see now that money isn't everything."

"No, Papa, it isn't, but it sure helps when handled right." He also felt like saying, 'Papa, you just had too many children, even for a rich man'. But he refrained from hurting the old man even further. Instead he said, "Your Foundation is a wonderful thing and you have every right to be proud of it. And I promise you I'll do my best to administer it wisely."

This cheered Hinrik some as he tried to imagine what his descendants fifty or a hundred years from now would be like.

Then another sadness fell upon him. His dear friend Eggeling von Eltze died. It had been long expected and everyone agreed it was a blessing, but it was a blow nonetheless.

After the funeral he sat with Lüdeke in the Bürgermeister's office mourning their friend when Peter joined them. "So now we are three," he said.

"Ja," said Hinrik, "and I wonder who will be next."

"It'll be I," said Lüdeke.

"No," said Hinrik. "I'm sure I'll go before you. I feel it in my bones."

"Your bones can't possibly ache as bad as mine do with this rheumatism," moaned Lüdeke.

"Oh, stop it, you two," said Peter. "You both—we all," he corrected himself, "still have a lot of life left in us and a lot to give to this town. How progresses your Rathaus, Lüdeke?"

Lüdeke quickly shook off his grief and took up his favorite subject. "I have hired the stonemason Frederic Soltesborg to do the three medallions and the fancy work on the north gable. Have you noticed some of it already? I am quite pleased."

"Yes I have," said Peter. "Quite elegant—luxurious, in fact."

"I thought so," agreed Lüdeke. "And that is only the beginning. Each step of the gable will have a different design or arrangement of those—those curlicues, I call them. The architects have a special name for them that I can never remember. And then at the peak will be a sort of Roman temple—symbolizing the law—and in that will be the three Bürgermeisters' coats-of-arms. And at the very top a lovely weather vane."

"My goodness. That sounds ambitious and very unusual," said Hinrik, "but why three? There are only you and Diderick."

"I've already resigned myself to the fact that I'll never live long enough to see it to completion. Do you realize it's been over ten years already? Everything takes so much longer than I had hoped. And then there is the question of money. Some years the Council has stopped all the work and made me wait until the new tax money came in. Oh, don't mistake my meaning." He held up his hands as both Hinrik and Peter were about to object. "I know you and Eggeling, too, have donated a great deal over and above your taxes. But there have been times when the Council has had to, er, " he laughed, "curb my ambition. Anyway, to answer your question, I think Henning Behr will be the one to complete my project after I am gone. Provided, of course, that he is elected Bürgermeister to succeed me."

Hinrik and Peter looked at each other. "At least you have planned well for the future," said Peter.

"I've had to," replied Lüdeke. "I am only being realistic, but Hen is as enthusiastic about it as I. I've been sharing my plans with him for a while now. And he has promised to carry them out exactly as I wished after I — I'm gone. So it's only right and fair that his arms be included, that is, if he's elected. My prayer now is that I just see the north gable completed. See, here is the architect's sketch of what it will look like." He pulled a large paper from a pile on his desk and showed them.

Good Lord, thought Hinrik, Lüdeke will run this town even from the grave, and admired his friend all the more for it. "That is indeed elegant," he said as he looked at the drawing. "Your gable will be the centerpiece of this town."

"And what of these other medallions you speak of?" asked Peter. "I didn't know you were going to include the Emperor, too."

"I hadn't planned on it at all," replied Lüdeke, "but Duke Wilhelm suggested it, rather forcefully I might add, as he is the overlord of us all."

"And where will you put them?"

Lüdeke laughed. "Up on a couple of the dormers. One for the Emperor Maximilian and one for the Empress Maria. But the place of honor, on the facade right alongside the entrance, will be for our Duke and his Duchess Dorothea."

"Amen to that."

"And see here," pointed out Lüdeke, returning to the sketch. "This is the motto I have chosen to be inscribed under the Roman temple with our arms. It's from Psalm 127. Appropriate, don't you think?"

"It's in Latin," said Peter.

"Of course," replied Lüdeke. "Latin is still the universal language of the law even though the Church has dropped it. Don't tell me you've forgotten all you learned in school."

"I'm sure he has," teased Hinrik and clapped his friend on the arm. "Peter was never a great classicist. He didn't have your blessed mother, Tante Anna, on his back as we did. I'm surprised that even you remember so much."

"Well, I have to admit I had to look it up," said Lüdeke shamefacedly.

"I'll translate it for you, Peter," offered Hinrik and rendered the verse into High German. "'Where the Lord does not protect the city, so watch the watchmen in vain'."

"Very good," said Peter, "but it would sound better in good old Hanse Low German."

"Peter, how you tease poor Lüdeke," chided Henrik. "I think it's a wonderful saying and most appropriate for Celle's Rathaus."

"Peter, you always were way behind the times," said Lüdeke.

"And you're even further behind with your Latin," retorted Peter.

And they all laughed.

"Who is going to do the carving?" asked Hinrik. "It must be someone very skilled."

"Jacob is already discussing it with Master Hans Gudehus. He's just a young man, but he's already the Duke's Master Carpenter. A fine artist as well as a skilled artisan."

"The very best," said Peter. "I have seen some of his work at the Castle. Superb."

"As have I. An excellent choice," agreed Hinrik.

And so the work went on and the north gable gradually rose in all its splendor.

Sometimes Hinrik wished he had a project to occupy his mind and his time, as did Lüdeke. Now that Franz was running the business, he sometimes even felt superfluous in his own countinghouse. Not that his son ever indicated in any way that he was, and, in fact, Franz always consulted him in any matter of great importance. Although officially he was still heading the operation, he had very little to do these days. Franz made all the major buying and selling decisions and dear Ciliax handled all the day-to-day details. Hinrik's Foundation had been his dearest project for many years, but now that that was all signed and sealed, he felt lost.

He had taken to spending a lot of time in the afternoons in Tante Anna's, Lüdeke's mother's, library. He might be getting old, but his mind was still sharp. Lüdeke's goodwife Gretchen had added some to it over the years, but nowhere near the quantity or quality Tante Anna had amassed. Many of the newer books were too modern for Hinrik's taste, but he read them all. Soon he took to re-reading many of the old ones that he and Ilsebe had enjoyed together in their youth. Often without realizing it, he found himself daydreaming of those long-ago days when the von Sehnden had conspired to let him meet his betrothed there and when Ilsebe was learning her letters from dear Tante Anna. Almost half a century ago. My

851

God, could it really be that long?

Often on bright, warm days he could be seen strolling along the quay as far as the millrace. Most people thought he was just inspecting all the new granaries and warehouses that had arisen in the past several years. Few, if any, realized that he was dreaming of his little river sprite, trying to recapture her presence at the place where they had so often met. At times he was even tempted to pull off his shoes and stockings and dangle his feet in the water as they used to do. But he checked himself with a stern reminder. Why you foolish old man, where is your dignity? You, who are one of the leading merchants and richest men in Celle. People will think you are in your second childhood. And sometimes he wondered if he weren't.

He visited his daughters frequently, those who were still in Celle, and delighted in all his grandchildren. The two who lived in Hannover came to see him often, as it was increasingly difficult for him to make even that short trip. And he was always welcome in their homes, especially since they well understood his unhappiness with their stepmother. But they had their own lives to live, and too soon they would run out of conversation, and even some of the grandchildren were becoming too old to play with. Some of the older girls were already preparing to marry. He could hardly believe it. How time flies!

He realized that a great deal of his torpor and apathy was a result of loneliness and aimlessness, but he could not for the life of him decide what to do about it. He, who had devoted his whole life, and intensely so, to his vast business, was now at loose ends. He appreciated Franz's concern that he not do too much, not overtax himself, not worry about the business. But what his dear son did not realize was that the inactivity was killing him. The lack of busyness was draining the life out of him.

Such was his state of mind that he did not become unduly upset, in fact, did not even care, when Otto ran away from home, presumably to join his wayward brothers in Hannover. He was sure that Geske had known of Otto's plans and most probably knew where he was but he did not make an issue of it. He no longer had the strength. Let him go, if that's what he wants. At least Michel was still at home and travelling frequently to Steinhorst to visit Balthasar, under whose guidance he seemed to be growing into a fairly sensible young man, unlike his brothers. Thank God for that.

Christmas of 1574 was very cold and snowy. Hinrik felt as though he were coming down with a cold or something equally annoying. He was so tired there were times when he could hardly stay awake, much less move. But he said nothing as he did not want to dampen the festivities. He was so happy to be surrounded by his multitudinous family on this most wondrous of nights, Christmas Eve. When he entered the front parlor the candles on the huge, gaily decorated tree twinkled more brightly than ever. His eyes blurred, whether from tears or weakness he was not sure, so that a thousand sparkles of light seemed to pierce his brain. The heat from the roaring fire and the candles themselves brought out the heady scent of the balsam and almost made his head swim. He quickly sat down in his accustomed place so no one would notice and gazed about him.

Besides Franz and Kunigunde, all his daughters were there with their families. Anna and Ilsebe had come from Hannover, each with only one child and a second husband. Katharina had six children, one of whom was already wed. Sophie had several and Margarethe a whole flock. Hinrik missed his dear Apollonia, but her husband and two sons were present. Only Balthasar and his wife were not there, as he must needs celebrate the feast day in his own church, but they had promised to come the day after Christmas and stay until the day before Twelfthnight. Of his other sons, Geske's Jürgen and Michel were there, but the other three had not shown up and no one missed them.

As was their custom, they exchanged their gifts on Christmas Eve. As usual, Hinrik gave each of his daughters, Kunigunde and Geske exquisite jewels, the finest necklaces, broaches, bracelets and rings that the renowned goldsmiths of Celle could produce. To the older grandchildren he gave finely sewn gowns or shirts heavy with silk embroidery and gold thread. To the younger children, lifelike dolls for the girls and for the boys toys that were masterpieces of the woodcarver's art.

To his sons and sons-in-law Hinrik announced that he was going to divide up his entire inventory of cloth within the next few months so that there would be no squabbling after his death. Each portion would be worth several hundred thalers.

Some of the gifts his children gave him brought on gales of hilarity. Franz, thinking that it would give his father something to do, gave him one of the new meerschaum pipes from Holland and a goodly quantity of the new thing called tobacco to go with it. But aromatic though it was, Hinrik was not too sure he wanted to set himself on fire like a chimney full of green wood.

The cook outdid herself serving fine little cakes and cookies, some of which were decorated with the new use someone had invented for chocolate. By melting it with milk, butter and precious sugar, one formed an icing to cover the cake. Soon the little ones had sticky fingers and were being scolded by mothers anxious to keep their best clothes clean for church. Ilsebe's only daughter Katrina had apparently inherited both her parents' talent for music and she sang sweetly for them as she played the virginals. Then they all joined in singing Christmas carols and it was great fun.

Shortly before midnight they all bundled up against the cold and trooped down the Kalandgasse to the great Stadtkirche. Hinrik willingly let Franz and Hinrich Schrader help him along the short way. He leaned heavily on them, but they were unaware that anything was amiss except for old age and perhaps tiredness from all the excitement. The church was banked with evergreens and candles glowed on every altar. All except the little ones received Communion and Hinrik had the unsettling feeling that it might be his last. At the end of the service the great bells pealed forth the good news of the Savior's birth. When they returned home, Franz and Kunigunde helped Hinrik into bed, for which he was grateful, or else he might have fallen asleep with all his clothes on.

The next morning he felt somewhat better, but when the servants laid the great board for Christmas dinner with four fat roast geese and every imaginable side dish, he found he had no appetite. His chest felt as though there were a great weight upon it and his stomach felt no desire for food. But everyone was so engrossed in enjoying the sumptuous feast that no one noticed that he merely picked at the delicious food. After dinner it was customary to have singing and dancing and games. Hinrik sat in his favorite chair and watched the two younger generations enjoy themselves. But after a while he was overcome by such extreme weariness that he asked Kunigunde to help him to his bed.

The next day Balthasar, Ilse and their baby daughter Anna arrived. Ilse's younger sister Catherina accompanied them, much to Jürgen's delight. Another great feast was served since they had missed the great Christmas dinner, and the festivities continued. Hinrik enjoyed watching the young people but took little part. He still felt the need for a long nap every afternoon. His appetite had disappeared and the heaviness in his chest came and went. All of this annoyed him greatly for he was used to being active all day. But it did not seem to be any specific illness that was dragging him down, so he still said nothing. He had no desire to have a gloomy physicker fussing over him during this festive season.

On Twelfthnight came the servants' party, when they and the

854

employees and apprentices of the business received their gifts from the family.

"Franz, you'll have to take over for me this year. I don't feel I am up to it," whispered Hinrik.

"Certainly, Papa, I am glad to," replied Franz. "You just sit here and watch the fun."

"I'll try, but I don't know how long I can last. I'm just so tired."

"I wonder whom they will elect Lord of Misrule this year."

"Anyone but dear Ciliax." Hinrik tried to smile. "He thinks up the most clever forfeits."

"Here they come. We'll soon see," said Franz. "You relax and enjoy, Papa. I'll take care of everything."

But Hinrik could not sit long before his head was nodding. The weight on his chest seemed to be stifling his breathing. Afraid that he would fall over, he signalled Kunigunde as unobtrusively as possible. She was at his side immediately. "Help me up to bed, dear daughter, I feel faint."

When she had settled him in bed, she asked, "Would you like a little wine, Papa? It may help."

He nodded weakly.

She brought the wine full strength, not mixed with water as they usually drank it. He could feel the warmth of it spread through his body. The weight on his chest seemed to lift a little, and he relaxed.

"Ah, that was good, my dear," he sighed. "Please convey my apologies to everyone."

"I shall, Papa. Now you rest," she replied. And he fell into a deep sleep.

At first everyone was having such fun that few noticed Hinrik was gone. As soon as she had a chance, Kunigunde took Franz aside and told him.

"Do you think we should call a doctor?" he asked.

"No. He says absolutely not. He is just tired," she replied, "but I'm worried just the same."

"I, too." Franz thought a moment. "But if you say he is sleeping, it's probably just as well not to disturb him. Let's not spoil the servants' party."

"I agree," she said, but she went quickly about and told all of Hinrik's daughters. They all agreed to do or say nothing for the moment, but they were all worried. Nevertheless, the feeling of unease soon spread to the servants. All of them, except for the very youngest apprentices and scullery maids, were faithful retainers of many years' standing and knew their beloved Master well. Never in their memory had he missed a Twelfthnight party. It was one of his greatest pleasures to give them their annual gifts and encourage their fun. He never even minded the wildest forfeits put on him by their chosen Lord of Misrule. And so they, too, began to worry.

As soon as the gifts were given out, Balthasar and his family had to leave so as not to be overtaken by the early winter darkness on their way back to Steinhorst.

"Wait! Before you go, I have an announcement," said Jürgen above the hubbub. They all turned to look at him, some of them wondering if he, too, was going to desert his father. He held Catharina Schwabach's hand tightly as he said to the entire company, "Catharina and I have decided we wish to become betrothed, provided Papa and her father agree."

Everyone hooted and applauded. Ilse rushed up to kiss her sister and Franz embraced his half brother.

"Well!" said Geske indignantly. "No one consulted me. How could you, Jürgen?"

"Mama, I am a man grown," replied Jürgen, trying to hold back his temper. "I am in the last of my journey years and furthermore, as you know very well, Papa has promised me our brewery to start me in my own business."

"Which was to have been part of my inheritance," sulked Geske.

Kunigunde could have slapped her. She said quite sarcastically, "I can't imagine what you would have done with it, Geske." Then she ignored her stepmother-in-law and turned to the young couple. "Congratulations, Jürg. I'm sure both Papas will heartily approve." Then she embraced Catharina and whispered in her ear, "Don't worry, we'll keep her under control." Catharina smiled at her gratefully.

"And when are the nuptials to be?" asked Franz.

"We'd like to be wed before Lent, if we can," replied Jürgen.

"And if there should be any delay, you know the Church is not so fussy about that anymore," put in Balthasar. "You could always be married on a Sunday, even in Lent."

"And we want you to marry us at Steinhorst, even though we'll be living here," insisted Catharina. "No big wedding," she said to the rest of the family.

"I shall be honored to do so," replied Balthasar. "And I'm sure you'll enjoy helping your dear sister make plans—and clothes, won't you, my dear?" He patted his wife's arm.

"Oh, I shall. I'm excited already," said Ilse.

"And now we had best be on our way," said Balthasar. "It grows late."

"What about Papa?" asked Jürgen. "Shouldn't we tell him before you leave?"

Kunigunde shook her head. "We'll tell him when he awakes, Jürg. I don't think we should disturb him now. And they really should go. It looks like more snow."

Balthasar agreed. "We have the sleigh, so we'll make good time. But even so, I shouldn't want to get caught in a blizzard. We'll see that Catharina accompanies her Papa when he comes to talk to Papa. Perhaps in a week or two. She still has to break the news to him, you know."

And Jürgen had to be satisfied with that.

By the end of the following week Hinrik felt considerably better. The heaviness in his chest had gone away and aside from a little weakness he felt almost like his old self. He decided that all the rest had cured whatever ailed him. He was happy to learn of Jürgen's proposed betrothal, and when he met with Master Schwabach to discuss the marriage settlement, he was as sharp as ever.

At this point Jürgen took him aside and said, "Papa, I know you intend to divide up the cloth soon. But what need have I, a brewer, of it? Give my share to Michel, except perhaps for a little to Catharina in the marriage settlement."

"That is very generous of you, Jürg, and quite sensible, too," Hinrik agreed. How glad I am, he thought, that he is not greedy like his mother. At least one of them has a little of me in him.

And so the betrothal was accomplished and an early February date set for the wedding in Steinhorst. And Hinrik saw to it that Catharina had ample rich cloth for her wedding gown, as well as enough for everything from the daintiest shift to the sturdiest cloak.

Late in January a week of thaw arrived. The snow began to melt and the bitter wind turned into a mild breeze. Hinrik decided that he was well enough and strong enough to resume his perambulations. He showed up several times at his countinghouse and joked with Ciliax about checking on his accounts. Everyone was happy to see him in such fine fettle. Once again he frequented Tante Anna's library and even visited Lüdeke at the Rathaus.

"Well," said his friend, "I am glad to see you up and about again. I thought you had left us already."

"Not yet, Lude, not yet," replied Hinrik. "Soon maybe, but not yet. How is your gable progressing?"

"Nothing much happened over Christmas. You know no one wants to work then anyway. Besides most of the stonemasons from Hameln went home for the feast days, which is just as well for it was really too cold for them to work. Saved me a few days' room and board with no work to show for it."

"I'm glad to hear I haven't missed anything then," said Hinrik.

One bright mild day he was walking along the quay by the river, the melting snow had turned to slush and he picked his way carefully. No one was about as the frozen river had brought all traffic to a standstill. It was the first time he had been here in months and for some reason he felt Ilsebe's presence stronger than he ever had before. Suddenly a sharp pain shot through his chest and down his left arm. The heaviness returned and next thing he knew he was lying face down in the slush. He turned his head so he could breathe and the stentorian sound of his gasping made his head ache. "Ilsebe, help me," he croaked. Warmly dressed though he was, he soon felt the wet snow soaking through his clothes. Dear Lord, don't let me die here, he prayed.

Luckily, a couple of urchins who had been trying to fish through the ice with no success ambled by. "Lookee," said one, "An old drunk passed out in the snow."

"He ain't drunk. He's an old duffer slipped on the ice. Hist, he be calling for help."

"Ilsebe, help me," called Hinrik a little more strongly.

The boys looked around but could see no lady or anyone else for that matter.

"We'd best see if we can help." The boys approached him warily. They could see by his clothes that he was no drunk or derelict. Immediately the first one began calculating what their help would be worth. "Be ye hurt, Master?" he asked.

"I don't know, but I can't seem to get up. Can you help me?"

"I bain't strong enough to lift ye, but I can run for help," said the first boy.

"Do you know the Stockman countinghouse in the alley behind the market?" asked Hinrik.

"That I do, Master."

"A penny for you if you run fast and fetch my son Franz or anyone else who is there."

"I'm on my way as fast as my legs can carry me," replied the lad and flew down the quay.

"What about me, Master?" asked the other urchin. "I be stronger'n Karl. Me pa's the blacksmith. Mayhap I can help you up."

"I know him well," replied Hinrik. The pain in his chest had subsided to a dull presence and the feeling was returning to his arm. But I'll surely catch a chill if I lie here much longer, he thought. "Then a penny for you, too, if you can help me to a dry place."

"I can't lift ye," said the boy, "but I got a strong back. Mayhap if ye lean on me, you can pull yourself up."

"I'll try." Hinrik managed to crawl to his knees. Then he placed his hands on the lad's shoulders and gradually pulled himself erect. He was amazed at the sinewy strength he could feel in the little fellow's body.

"There you go, Master. I knew you could," said the boy. "Now where to? You can't stand here for long."

Hinrik looked around. "How about the steps of yon granary? They look dry."

"Good enough. Careful now you don't fall again. You just lean on me. I'll hold you up."

Hinrik leaned heavily on the lad's shoulder while the boy held his arm with both hands and slowly guided him to the steps. He sank down gratefully on a step, glad to be out of the wet, and the boy sat on the one below. Hinrik felt himself shiver.

"What is your name, lad?" he asked.

"I be Harm, son of Master Schmidt."

"Then I thank you, Harm, for your kindness to an old man. You shall have your penny just as soon as my son arrives."

"Then ye be Master Stockman, the rich Gewandschneider?"

"I am he," acknowledged Hinrik.

"I thought rich men only rode horses. What bein' you doin' out here in the wet all by yoursel'?"

Hinrik couldn't tell him he was looking for his river sprite. The lad would really think him balmy. "Even rich men like to be alone sometimes," he said, "and even rich men get sick, when they least expect it."

"'Tis that a fact?" asked Harm, looking puzzled, as if that could not possibly be.

A few moments later Franz and Ciliax came rushing along the quay led by Karl, who was trundling a wheelbarrow.

"Papa, Papa, are you all right?" exclaimed Franz anxiously.

859

"Better than I was before these lads helped me. But I'm afraid I can't get home by myself," said Hinrik. "Franz, give each of these boys a penny for their kindness."

"I shall give them two. It was young Karl here who suggested we might need the wheelbarrow. A bit undignified, I'm afraid, but all that was at hand in a hurry." Franz gave each of the boys two pennies. And Hinrik, watching their faces as they stared at the shiny copper pieces in their hands, could tell it was more money than either had seen at one time in his whole short life. He resolved to do more for them if he could.

The two men helped him to sit in the wheelbarrow. Then Ciliax took up the handles and pushed while Franz steadied him. Undignified it might have been, but Hinrik was grateful for the boy's forethought in suggesting some sort of transportation. He could never have walked even the short distance to his home. When they arrived Kunigunde immediately dispatched a servant for the doctor and bundled him out of his wet clothes and into his warm bed. She piled featherbeds over him and built up the fire herself.

Geske fell into a fit of near hysterical weeping. "What has happened to him? Is he going to die? Oh, what will become of me?"

"Stop that and make yourself useful," scolded Kunigunde.

"What can I do?"

"Let him rest and don't upset him with your caterwauling. Go and tell cook to fix him a nice hot drink. Can't you see he's chilled to the bone?"

Geske left, still sobbing. Kunigunde gently felt Hinrik's brow. She could feel no sign of fever yet.

"Tell me what happened, Papa, if you can," she said.

This time Hinrik truthfully described the pain and heaviness in his chest that caused him to fall.

It sounds like his heart, she thought. Oh Lord, don't let it be. She said, "The doctor will be here soon."

"I feel better already just to be warm," he replied.

The doctor arrived shortly. "Tell me true, Physicker, am I on my way?" Hinrik greeted him. "Or are you going to tell me I have lots of years left, when I know better?"

The physicker said nothing as he carefully examined Hinrik. He laid his ear to his chest and listened intently to his heart, then arose nodding his head. "You have had a heart attack, Master Stockman, but a mild one. The heart is already beating again."

"I know it's beating or I should already be dead," said Hinrik impatiently, "but is it beating as it should?"

"A little weak and straining," the doctor admitted, "but if you make it through the next three days, you should be well on the way to recovery." Hinrik could hear the echo of the physicker's words when his stepfather died so long ago and he was afraid. "I shall have to bleed you, but just a little bit to take some of the strain off the heart."

"Do what you must," signed Hinrik resignedly.

The doctor prepared his cups and scalpels, made a quick incision in Hinrik's arm and held the cup to it. When it was full, he bound the wound with clean linen. Then he produced a tiny bottle of medicine from his bag. He instructed Kunigunde carefully, as though Hinrik were incompetent. "This is a powerful medicine to stimulate the heart, but it must be administered with great care. One or two drops, no more, on the tongue when the pain is bad, and only then. And not more than two or three times a day."

"Why can't I take it by myself? I am not senile yet," complained Hinrik.

"Master Stockman, it is an infusion of foxglove," explained the doctor, "a deadly poison in large quantities, but of great benefit with a drop or two. If your hand should shake with weakness or you should faint, it could kill you instantly." Then he turned to Kunigunde. "Give him plenty of rich, warm broth, unwatered wine, things that will stimulate the heart. Nothing heavy or fatty or cold. And see that he stays in bed. Don't let him get up for anything. Several weeks of complete rest is the only cure for this. I shall come again tomorrow."

"Thank you, Doctor," said Kunigunde and showed him out.

Hinrik merely grunted. He would not admit it, but he was thankful to be in bed and warm, and, to be truthful, alive. The physicker came every day and bled him and listened to his heart. Hinrik could not tell if he was surprised to see him still alive or simply pleased that his cure was effective. I'll outfox you yet, you old fool, he thought. He had only had to take the medicine twice and was amazed at how quickly it relieved the pain in his chest.

By the fourth day the physicker apparently had decided that Henrik would live for a while yet and instructed Kunigunde, "He may now eat some solid food, but only very light meals for another week. And be sure he stays in bed. And see that nothing upsets him. I shall be back in a few days, but be sure to call me if he should turn worse."

861

Cook fixed him all his favorite foods, but by the end of the week Hinrik was chafing at the bit. "Peeing in the chamber pot is one thing, but when I have to take a shit, it is damned difficult. Move that commode over here next to the bed so I can sit on it."

At first Kunigunde objected, but Hinrik was adamant and the doctor had said not to upset him, so she gave in and placed the commode next to the bed. She gave him a bell.

"Ring that so someone can come and help you. Don't try to get up by yourself," she said. But Hinrik never rang the bell, at least not for that purpose. He did find it convenient for other requests.

"Bring me my spectacles and something to read before I go raving mad."

Lüdeke came to see him often, sometimes twice a day, and brought him all the news of the town, of commerce, and of the cloth trade in particular. "You old fox," he teased, "you're determined to prove me wrong."

"You know I am," riposted Hinrik. "I am four years older than you, you know."

"That's got nothing to do with it," insisted Lüdeke, but tough old cummudgeon that he was, he almost broke down, seeing his dearest friend lying there so pale and wan. "Hinrik, you've always been brother to me, closer than my own brothers. Whatever would I do without you?" And he fought back the tears.

"You'll manage," said Hinrik. "Don't forget your gable."

"Ah, yes, the gable," said Lüdeke, grateful for the change of subject. "How is it coming along?"

"Almost nothing is happening right now with this weather, but as soon as spring breaks, things will get moving again."

Peter came frequently and played chess with Hinrik, but the long hours of concentration tired him, so they switched to simple card games. Many of his other friends and business associates came to call, and at times the room was so crowded Kunigunde worried that it might be too much for him, but Hinrik relished it and perversely enjoyed playing the invalid for their benefit. Secretly, he was amazed at how many people were genuinely concerned for his welfare. Pastor Storch came often and assured him that the entire congregation was praying for his recovery.

And soon came time for Jürgen's wedding. Hinrik sent for his son. "You know, Jürg, that I am truly grieved at not being able to attend your wedding, but I simply cannot make the trip to Steinhorst. They won't even let me out of bed."

"I understand, Papa. And Catharina will understand, too. It's foolish to even think of it. But everyone else will be there and we'll know that you're there in spirit."

"That I shall. And bring your bride to me as soon as you return home so that I may bless you."

"Thank you, Papa. I shall."

"It's too bad the river is frozen. You could take her on a little wedding trip to Bremen. Has she ever been there?"

"I don't know. I doubt it."

"She would enjoy the shops. We'll see about arranging it come spring."

"Thank you, Papa," replied Jürgen, surprised. "That's very generous of you."

So the whole family went to Steinhorst for the day to witness Jürgen and Catharina make their vows. Kunigunde was a little anxious about leaving Hinrik alone, but he assured her that the servants were quite capable of looking after him for one day and promised to behave himself.

As it turned out, that was the one day none of his friends came to visit, so he had plenty of time to read and think. After a while he laid his book aside and his thoughts turned to the two little boys who had rescued him. He had vowed to do something for them and had done nothing yet. He would have to remedy that forthwith. He always had a soft spot in his heart for children because of his own childhood experience. Now what would be best? There was no sense in giving money—that would only go toward the family's victuals, and the individual boys would derive little benefit. He reviewed the whole incident in his mind including the brief conversations with each of them. Then it came to him. Their grammar was atrocious. I am sure neither one has ever seen the inside of a school, much less a book. He made up his mind. That is what I shall do. They both seemed intelligent enough to justify the investment. He could hardly wait for Franz to return home.

There was no room at Steinhorst for such a large family to stay over, so they must needs return the same day, but it was very late in the evening when they arrived back at Celle. In fact, were it not for Franz's prominence and influence, the watchmen might not have opened the town gates for them. They were very tired and longed for their beds, so it was with great perturbation that the moment they entered the house they heard Hinrik's bell ringing furiously.

"Oh, dear God," exclaimed Kunigunde, "something has happened

863

to Papa." She threw off her cloak and flew up the stairs, only to find him sitting up in bed with a huge grin on his face. "Papa, what is wrong?"

"Nothing. Nothing at all. I feel quite well."

She almost collapsed, because she was pregnant again but as yet had told no one. "Oh, Papa, you gave me such a fright. What is it, then?"

"I'm sorry. I didn't mean to frighten you. I wouldn't want to harm that babe in your belly for the world. But I've had this most wonderful idea I must discuss with Franz."

All she heard was the first part of his statement. "How did you know I was carrying? No one else knows yet, even Franz."

"Do you think I've had thirteen children and not know the signs? Are you going to give me a girl this time?"

"I hope so, Papa, but the Lord will decide," she replied.

At that point Franz entered the room. "What's this? What is happening? Did I hear you say you are breeding again and didn't tell me?"

"I was going to in due time, but your Papa guessed."

"And what is your problem, Papa? I don't see anything wrong," said Franz.

"I think he's just feeling a little sorry for himself, having been alone all day," said his wife.

"No, no, it's not that," Hinrik declared. "I have the most wonderful idea that I must discuss with you tonight, Franz."

"Can't it wait till morning, Papa?" suggested Kunigunde. "He's very tired."

"No, it can't. There are things he must do for me in the morning," insisted Hinrik. "You go to your bed, my dear. I'll not keep him long."

Franz knew his father from way back. When he had one of his ideas, it must be acted on immediately, because it would have been well thought out before he presented it. "Yes, you go to bed, Kuni. I'll not be long. I know our Papa. He won't sleep if he doesn't tell me tonight." Kunigunde left, shaking her head. Franz sat on the edge of the bed and took Hinrik's hand. "Now tell me what brilliant thing you have invented now. It can't be about the business. You haven't been there in weeks."

"No, it's about those two little boys."

"What two little boys?" Franz had almost forgotten them.

"The two that rescued me when I fell on the quay."

"Oh, those two urchins. What of them?"

"They are only urchins because they have no education. I intend to

864

pay for their schooling."

"What?" exclaimed Franz. "They might not even want it."

"The one called Harm, the smith's son, will. He struck me as being quite bright. And the other can be convinced. He struck me as being too clever by far, but that cleverness has to be properly guided."

"But, Papa, most poor families need the children to help with the work. Their parents may object."

"And thus each generation becomes poorer than the previous. Don't forget I was desperately poor, too. And Tante Anna taught me my letters and Onkel Lüdeke enabled me to go to the Hanse school. Without that you would not have a thriving business and a fine home to inherit."

"I know all that, Papa, but you can't help every waif in Celle."

Hinrik laughed. He knew he had won. "No, just these two."

Franz gave in. "Very well, Papa. Tell me what you want of me."

"Tomorrow find out everything you can about these two lads and their families and tell me all. Then I'll decide what you're to do next. But don't reveal my intentions yet."

"All right, Papa. I'll do that. Now may I go to bed? And by the way, don't you want to hear about the wedding?"

"Tell me tomorrow. I'm tired now," said Hinrik.

"Good night then." And Franz marvelled at how, even from the sickbed, his father's astute mind kept right on planning things.

The next day when Franz came home for the noon meal, he had the information Hinrik had requested. "The boy Harm is the smith's only child. He is needed to work the bellows for his father, but he is not yet actually apprenticed. The mother is sickly and ineffectual, will probably never have any more children."

"What a waste of a good brain," said Hinrik. "I'll see that there is enough extra for the smith to hire another lad more suited mentally to that monotonous chore. And the other?"

"Karl is the eighth child of ten, with more to come, of a rather mediocre baker named Backstein. They live in a hovel over in the poorer section of town, the ovens taking up most of the building. The father is a gruff type, the mother worn out with childbearing, overwork and poverty. The boy has already been in trouble as a cutpurse. Caught by the watch, but they let him off, as the parents returned the money and pleaded that his work was needed to help the family."

"I'm not surprised," said Hinrik. "I suspected something like that. I could see him calculating what his help would be worth to me. As I said, too clever by far, but that cleverness can be channelled. I don't think it's too late. And I can't help the one without the other. But this will be the more difficult case. I leave it up to your ingenuity."

"Mine?"

"Yes. Tomorrow I want you to go to both sets of parents and tell them that I shall pay for each boy's schooling until he is fourteen, provided that they stay in school, stay out of trouble, and study hard. They can work before and after classes for the parents as long as it does not interfere with their studies. The smith should be easy to convince. I know him. He shoes our horses. He seems like a responsible man who will want the best for his son. The other will not be so easy. Perhaps you might make the offer first to the boy himself. He seems more likely to convince his parents than you would. I leave that up to you."

Franz shook his head. "Papa, Papa, the tasks you put on me. I should rather try to sell a thousand ells of fustian to a Venetian lady than this."

"But you'll do it?"

Franz smiled. "You know I will, Papa."

So the plan went forward. Harm was overjoyed at the prospect of learning to read and write and all sorts of other wonderful things. Karl not so. It was Harm himself who gave Franz the clue to convincing Karl and the baker.

"Ye've got to make him jealous, Master. Tell him when I get done with the school I'm going to be a rich man just like you, Master, and he'll still be a poor oaf, covered with flour. He'll do anything for money, even study."

Franz used that approach and eventually, not without difficulty, convinced father and son of the benefits of schooling and what a great gift Hinrik's offer was.

"We-e-ell, I suppose I can spare him since I got more on the way," agreed Backstein at last. "But he's got to do his share of the work in the morning before he goes."

"As long as it doesn't interfere with his lessons," said Franz.

"It won't," Karl assured him. "Papa, someday Harm and me, we're gonna be rich, just like he says. Then I can help you and Ma. So don't worry."

When Franz reported his success to his father, Hinrik said, "I knew they would come around. Now I'll pay the whole seven years' tuition directly to the school, but you demand an accounting from them every year. Tell Herman Kregel what we are doing. Even though he's no longer Rector of the school, he has a lot of influence and can keep an eye on things. We'll pay the smith for a helper just one year at a time. Mayhap when he sees Harm doing well he'll take on an apprentice and we won't have to pay that any longer."

About a week later a maid came into Hinrik's bedchamber. "Sorry to disturb you, Master, but there are two young lads—scruffy-looking lads, I might add—at the front door asking to see you. I told them to go around back to the kitchen, but they said no, they weren't beggars but had gifts for you. I was afraid to let them in."

Hinrik smiled. "Were their names Harm and Karl by any chance?"

"I think that's what they said, Master."

"Then they have come to see me. Find my daughter-in-law and have Kunigunde bring them up. And fetch Michel, too, if he's home."

The two boys entered the room hesitantly. They looked about them in awe. Finally Harm said shyly, "We wanted to see how you was, Master Stockman. When we hear'd you was still sick-abed, we kinda—a—worried mayhap you caught a chill that day."

"Ja, we worried," echoed Karl.

"That's kind of you to worry about an old man," said Hinrik while Kunigunde smiled at him over their heads.

"Ja, and me Ma says we got to thank you for that we're goin' to go to the school," said Harm.

"Ja, thank ye," said Karl.

"And do you think you're going to enjoy school?" asked Hinrik.

"Ach, I can't wait, I'm that happy," said Harm. "We're startin' at the Easter term."

Karl said nothing.

"And what about you?" Hinrik prompted him.

"Ja, me, too," said Karl, and then he brightened. "Lookee, Master, we brung some presents for ye, to make ye feel better." He lifted a cloth that covered something in a little basket. "Me Ma's very specialest honey cakes, just fer ye." He offered the basket. "Here, try one. They're real good."

Hinrik took one and bit into it. It was hard and tasteless, but he said, "Mmm, very good, but I think I'll save the rest for later. I can't eat too much, you know. But thank your Ma kindly."

"I got to have the basket and napkin back, or Ma'll have me hide," said Karl.

Kunigunde stepped up. "Here, let us put the cakes on this plate. And there is your basket."

"I brung a little gift fer ye, too, Master Stockman," said Harm then.

867

He drew something wrapped in a piece of leather from behind his back, carefully unwrapped it and handed it to Hinrik. It was a crudely but delicately wrought iron angel.

"It's an angel," exclaimed Hinrik. "How thoughtful of you."

"Ja," said Harm. "When you fell, I heard you callin' fer somebody, sounded like 'Ilsebe.' I thought mayhap she was your guardian angel. And I made it all by myself."

"She is my guardian angel," said Hinrik wistfully. "That's wonderful. You are very artistic. I shall treasure it all my life. Thank you, Harm."

Michel stuck his head in the door. What in the world are these unkempt children doing here? he wondered. "Did you send for me, Papa?"

"Yes, Michel, come in. I want you to meet my little friends Harm and Karl. It is they who rescued me when I fell on the quay."

"I see," said Michel.

Of the boys, Hinrik asked, "Do you go to church?"

They looked at each other. "Sometimes," said Harm, and Karl shook his head.

"But not often, heh?" said Hinrik.

"Not often," said Harm, and Karl again shook his head.

"Well, if you want to thank me properly for sending you to school, here is what I want you to do," instructed Hinrik. "Pastor Storch has started a children's Bible school. You will find it much more interesting than regular church. And my son Michel here is going to be one of the teachers." Michel looked startled. It was the first he had heard of this. "And I want you to promise me to go every Sunday. Michel will call for you and take you there for the first few weeks. Will you promise me to go with him every Sunday?"

The boys looked as startled as Michel. "Ooee, more school!" said Karl.

"I'd like that," added Harm.

"Do you promise?" asked Hinrik again.

"Oh, yes," replied Harm and nudged his friend.

"Ja, ja," said Karl reluctantly.

"Good. Now I must rest. But I want you to visit me again after school has started and tell me all about it. Michel will show you out."

When they had left, Kunigunde almost burst out laughing. "You *are* an old fox, just as Onkel Lüdeke always says. Did you see the look on Michel's face? That was brilliant, but tell me true—does Pastor Storch even know about this children's Bible school?"

Hinrik laughed. "Ja, ja, we've discussed it often, but he doesn't know it's starting this Sunday or that Michel will be one of the teachers. You'd better tell him to come see me in the next day or two."

"I shall. Now you had better rest." She leaned over and kissed him. "No wonder my husband is so brilliant, with a father like you. That will keep Michel on the right track and help those boys, too. And wasn't that sweet—about the angel, I mean?"

Hinrik nodded as tears came to his eyes.

By the end of the week Hinrik declared he felt well enough to get out of bed and for once, the doctor agreed with him. "But mind you, you will be very weak at first. So for the first two days just walk about your chamber. Do not attempt to go downstairs until your legs regain their strength. And even then, be sure someone is always with you on the stairs, and no running up and down, up and down. Once you are down, stay there until it is time to come up for bed. And be very sure you keep your medicine to hand at all times."

"But, Doctor," he objected, "I have not needed it for over two weeks now."

"True, but your heart has been resting. Moving about the house, especially the stairs, will put it under strain again. Heed what I tell you."

"All right, all right."

"And by no means go out-of-doors until the weather is warm again and it is dry underfoot."

"Very well, Doctor. Thank you."

Hinrik had told no one that he had already been walking around the room when no one was about to see him. Now he confessed this to Kunigunde and asked her to help him downstairs. At first she was reluctant, but he insisted. "I'm tired of being isolated. I want to eat dinner with the family. I want to sit in my chair by the fire in the parlor. I want to work at my desk. See, I'll show you how well I can walk." He got out of bed and took two brisk turns around the room, his nightshirt flapping about his skinny legs.

"I give in," she relented. "I'll send your manservant to help you get dressed."

Hinrik was overjoyed to be up and about, back in the world again, as he put it. He had no desire whatever to go outside. When he looked out the parlor window and saw the snow swirling around the courtyard, he was content to sit by the fire and just watch it. He had Franz bring him all sorts of accounts and correspondence from the countinghouse and caught up on all the business transactions he had missed. Now he could sit the long hours required over the chessboard with Lüdeke or Peter. Even the food seemed to taste better at the dining room table with the family.

February finally ended and March roared in. The first crocuses and snowdrops started to push up through the snow, but the weather remained inclement and blustery. Often he went out to the kitchen, from where he could better see the garden struggling out of its winter sleep. The servants did not mind. In fact, they welcomed him and complimented him on his rapid recovery. Yet one day, totally unbidden, the recollection came to his mind of how Ilsebe had wanted to see the first spring flowers as she lay dying. I'll be with you soon, my dearest river sprite, perhaps sooner than anyone realizes. He tried to dismiss the thought. He felt so well. But it kept returning—almost as if she were calling him.

One day he was playing chess with Peter by the roaring fire in the parlor. He was winning. He could clearly see his way through two or three moves to a checkmate. Suddenly the most fearsome pain he had ever felt struck his chest like a bolt of lightning. He slumped over the board, scattering the pieces in every direction.

"Hinrik, Hinrik," cried Peter, "what has happened? Can I help?"

"My medicine," gasped Hinrik.

"Where is it?"

Hinrik managed to point a finger upward.

Peter rushed from the room calling, "Kunigunde! Someone! Come help! Hinrik has had another attack." Kunigunde and two servants answered his summons. "Where is his medicine?"

"Upstairs. The tiny bottle by his bed," Kunigunde replied. "You can run faster than I. I'll see to him."

Peter sped up the stairs. Kunigunde quickly dispatched a servant for the doctor and went to Hinrik. She helped him sit back in the chair and chafed his wrists. He put a hand to his chest as if trying to stem the pain. His breathing was labored and harsh. Peter came back with the medicine. She carefully placed two drops on his tongue.

"Pour some of that wine," she instructed Peter. He did so and she carefully held the goblet to Hinrik's lips. "Try to drink some, Papa." With a great effort he managed to take a few sips. He lay back in the chair gasping. Soon the powerful medicine took hold and his breathing eased. His pulse became more regular. But his face was as gray as ashes. He seemed to have aged ten years.

Finally the doctor arrived. "Well, well, a bit too frisky, heh, Hinrik?" he said heartily.

"Never mind that," snapped Kunigunde. "We've got to get him to bed. I'll call his manservant to help."

Together the three men carried Hinrik up the stairs and laid him on the bed. His servant undressed him and Kunigunde made him as comfortable as possible.

"I'll have to bleed him," said the physicker.

"No, no," whispered Hinrik feebly.

"Never mind that now. He doesn't want it," said Kunigunde. "It will only weaken him further."

The doctor was about to argue but then he saw the determined look on Kunigunde's face. "As you wish, Meine Frau, but I cannot accept responsibility . . ."

"I'll take that responsibility," she said. "You'll get your fee, never fear." And she ushered him out.

Hinrik had never felt so sick in his whole life. He had to take the medicine the maximum of three times a day and wished he could take more. It controlled the sharp pains but the heavy weight on his chest would not go away. They fed him rich broths and soups, but he could not swallow solid food. The next day he called Franz to him.

"Franz, the cloth. I said I would divide it up at Christmas, and I never have."

"Don't worry about it, Papa. I'll take care of it," replied Franz.

"No, there are some others I wish to give some to besides the children. I must do it myself before I die."

"You're not going to die yet, Papa."

"Yes, I am. This time I know it. Fetch pen and paper and take down my instructions."

"Very well, Papa. I'll be right back." When Franz went downstairs to get the paper and pen, he quickly said to Kunigunde, "Send for the girls. He says he's dying. And I'm afraid this time I believe him."

"You really think so?" she asked. He nodded. "Oh, Franz," she sobbed. "I'll send a groom on the fastest horse we have to Hannover for Anna and Ilsebe, and another for Balthasar. I'll go for Katrina, Gretchen and Sophie myself."

"No, you'd best stay here in case I need you. Send a maid. Now I must get back to him. He's insisting on dividing the cloth right this very minute."

Kunigunde smiled through her tears.

Franz set himself up at a small table close to Hinrik's bed. He placed the ink pot and several sharp quills on it and spread a large piece of paper before him. "Now tell me how you want to do it, Papa."

"I am going to divide it up into eleven equal portions regardless of how many children or grandchildren they have. Is that clear?"

Franz nodded. "But eleven?"

"Ja, you'll see. But first write: 'I Hinrik Stockman, because I am old and sick and cannot write this by myself, do here authorize my son Franz Stockman to write this and to distribute the cloth for me'." He waited while Franz wrote. "That way no one can claim you made it up. I shall sign it when we're done."

"All right. Go ahead."

"Number one, my daughter Ilsebe in Hannover, my son Johann Fockrell, Ilsebe's daughter Katrina; number two, my daughter Katrina in Celle (you fill in the rest); three, Anna; four, Margarethe; five, Sophie; six, Henning Hake and Apollonia's two sons; seven, my son Franz and so on: eight, my son Balthasar." He paused for breath. Franz expected him to deal with Geske's sons next and wondered how he was going to handle it. So he was very surprised when his father continued, "Number nine, Ciliax Kothman, his wife and children, number ten, Dorthia Stockman, my late brother's daughter in Frankfurt, and number eleven, my son Michel, who is still a minor."

Franz stared at him in amazement. "What about Jürgen?" he asked hesitantly.

"Jürg has already told me he has no use for it and to give his share to Michel," replied Hinrik.

Franz nodded. He had not known of this. "And the others?"

Hinrik shook his head. "Geske's other children are no longer my sons, except as provided for in my will, which is to share her inheritance. She can do as she likes with her portion, but knowing her, I doubt if they'll see any of it," he said bitterly. "Serves them right." He lay back on the pillows and closed his eyes for a few minutes, trying to calm himself. "Now let me read it and sign it quickly."

No sooner had he signed the document than Margarethe burst into the room—she lived the closest—followed shortly by her sisters Katharina and Sophie. "Papa, Papa," Margarethe cried. "I came at once. How are you?"

"Quietly, quietly," urged Franz. "He's very tired. He has just finished dividing the cloth."

"Oh, Papa," said Margarethe. "And Kuni said you were—I mean

872

were very sick."

"He is," said Franz, "but he insisted."

"That wasn't necessary," said Katharina. "Franz or any of us could have done that, Papa."

"Not the way he wanted it," said Franz. "Here, look at this." He handed her the paper.

While she read it, the other two hugged and kissed Hinrik. "We'll all take care of you," said Sophie.

"Yes, we will, and you'll soon be better again," said Margarethe.

Katharina handed the paper back to Franz and bent to kiss her father. "Papa, you were right to do this now. I didn't mean to criticize. None of us would have thought of Cousin Dorthia, so alone and poor in Frankfurt. And Ciliax certainly deserves a share after all the long years of faithful service he has given you. And to be honest, I doubt any of us would have had the courage to cut out some of our dear half brothers. I can imagine Geske's wrath when she hears of this."

Hinrik merely smiled dreamily. "Ah, my sweet little girls," he murmured. "How good that you are here by me. Will Anna and Ilsebe be coming, too?"

"They should be here tomorrow," said Franz. "A fast messenger has already been sent to Hannover."

"Then I shall be happy," whispered Hinrik. "Now I am tired. Let me rest a bit."

Anna and Ilsebe arrived the next day. The five sisters made sure that at least one of them was with Hinrik at all times in order to take some of the burden off Kunigunde. The two from Hannover took turns sleeping on a cot in his room so that those who lived in town could go home to their families. When he was awake Anna read to him and Ilsebe played music or sang to him. Katharina kept him up-to-date on commercial affairs, Margarethe on social news and Sophie on the doings of the numerous grandchildren. Balthasar came when he could, but the demands of his own congregation limited the time he could spend with his father. In actuality, none of them had much to do except pray, as Hinrik seemed to be sleeping most of the time and even when he was awake his attention wandered off.

His friends returned in droves until finally Kunigunde had to forbid the sickroom to all except Lüdeke. She could see that their visits tired him too much and even Lüdeke she begged to stay no more than ten or fifteen minutes. Lüdeke finally figured out that Hinrik was at his best while eating breakfast or supper, although he often slept through dinner. So he tried to come at those times.

On one of the better days Hinrik said to his friend, "You know, Lude, I have had a good life, God be praised, but I have one regret."

"And what is that?"

"That our families were never united in wedlock."

"Ja, I have often thought the same thing, but it just didn't seem to work out. All of your girls were too old for my boys."

"Ja, well, maybe the next generation. But I won't be here to see it," sighed Hinrik wistfully.

"I doubt that I shall either," replied Lüdeke. "If there even is a next generation. I seem to have begotten a brood of clerks, only two of the lot married and, of course, Clara. And only one grandchild so far. You at least are blessed in that. I still have Hans at home. He's growing into a fine young man. A little too fat and lazy perhaps, but a good mind. And at least he's interested in the business and the government. So maybe there's hope there."

"I hope so for your sake. Perhaps if he were to wed and have a daughter," Hinrik mused. "There are Franz's two sons. Hmm. It's a possibility. I'll have to mention it to Franz." Hinrik seemed to drift off into a dream world of his own and fell asleep right before Lüdeke's eyes. Lüdeke offered a prayer for his friend and brother and tiptoed out of the room.

Everyone knew that Hinrik was dying. It was just a matter of when. Several times when they thought the end was at hand he would rally, demand food, and actually be a semblance of his old self for a few hours. But then he would sink again, each time a little lower than before.

The weather turned beautiful as March gave way to April. It was Palm Sunday and most of the family had gone to church. Anna alone sat with Hinrik. He seemed half-asleep and half-awake. She could hear the singing as the Palm Sunday procession left the church and started down the Kalandgasse. They would turn into Ritterstrasse and go right past the house, turn again through the Market Square and return to the church via the Stechbahn.

"Do you hear them, Papa? The procession is coming. They are singing Psalms," she said.

"Ja, I hear them."

"How many times have you walked in that procession? Do you remember when I was little you used to hold my hand so I wouldn't stumble on the cobbles?"

"Ja, I remember. So many times."

874

"They are singing the 'Benedictus qui venit' now."

"'Blessed is He that cometh in the name of the Lord. Hosanna in the highest'," he quoted. Lord Jesus, are you coming to me soon? he thought. And suddenly he was walking in that procession surrounded by all his children, gaily waving their palms. How could they all be so little at the same time? he wondered. But the effort to figure that out was too much, and the dream faded.

And he was alone walking down the quay. And there in the distance — was it really she? He called out her name, "Ilsebe." She opened her arms in welcome and he rushed toward her. "Ilsebe." She enfolded him in an embrace. "Hinrik dearest, let us go home. I've been waiting for you so long." She led him to the river. He held back hesitantly. She said, "Come, sweeting. We're going home to the river goddess." She stepped into the river holding his hand and he followed. For a moment he felt a choking sensation, afraid he would drown. But she held him tightly, and soon he was floating as lightly as a feather, drifting down into the green shimmering depths.

The date was the second of April 1575.

Epilogue

Lüdeke von Sehnden sat in his library and wept unrestrainedly. Let Diderick take care of the town business today. He had no desire to see anyone or go anywhere, even to his beloved Rathaus. He just wanted to be alone with his grief and reminisce. One of his earliest memories was of his mother teaching Hinrik his letters in this very room. And Lüdeke had been jealous. And when he was about twelve or thirteen and his father had promoted Hinrik to journeyman status. Again he had been jealous. He was ashamed even after all these years. His father and grandfather may have taught him to be a great cloth and grain merchant and to be a powerful governor, but Hinrik had taught him to be a man. Oh, how he missed him already, dearest friend and brother.

Lüdeke and Peter had been honorary pallbearers at Hinrik's funeral, but they and all Hinrik's closest friends had been too old and crippled to lift the heavy casket. This had been left to their younger and stronger sons and even grandsons, while the elders hobbled along behind it from the church, across the river to the old Bürger Cemetery on the other side. There they laid him next to his dearest Ilsebe, gone these thirty years.

Late in the summer after Hinrik's death Kunigunde presented Franz with their first daughter, a peaches-and-cream little doll, whom they named Dorothea after the Duchess and also Cousin Dorthia, both of whom stood godmother on behalf of the child.

"There is the link," said Lüdeke, when he heard about it. "She is the one for my Hans. So what if he is almost twenty years older? Many a dynastic marriage has been such-like and worked out well." However, he thought he had better consult with his son before he said anything to the Stockmans.

"I don't mind waiting," said Hans. "I am certainly not going to be ready for marriage for several years What's a few more? I am too busy learning the business right now. And if, as seems likely, none of my brothers care about it, I shall one day have the burden of the whole vast von Sehnden commercial empire on my own shoulders. I really don't need any of the Stockman interests added to it just yet."

"I'm glad to hear you think that way," said Lüdeke. "By the time the girl is of marriageable age, you will be mature enough to handle it."

"I hope so," replied placid Hans.

"Good. Then as soon as it appears that the child has safely survived infancy, I shall broach Franz about a betrothal."

Lüdeke soon recovered from his deepest grief as work progressed on the Rathaus. Although it went slowly, he was pleased with what he saw. A great deal of the interior work in the old section was nearing completion under the able guidance of Masters Riess and Gudehus. Nothing at all had been started in the new part except to break through the walls of the three houses, but outside, the roof, dormers and facade had joined the disparate pieces into the appearance of one building, although the facade had not yet reached its final form. At last, in 1579, the beautiful north gable was finished.

When the final weathervane was mounted at the peak, Lüdeke breathed a sigh of relief. "Thank you, dear God. At least I have lived to see this much done." He knew he would not live long enough to see the whole project to completion. But Henning will carry on, he assured himself. Meanwhile, he was very pleased. But in the midst of his joy, another blow struck.

That same year Peter Stratheman died. Now I am truly the last one left, thought Lüdeke. And there is so much left to do. I know I don't have much time left, but, please God, a few more years, he prayed.

In 1580 when Dorothea Stockman was five years old, Franz, who had once been vehemently opposed to arranged marriages, agreed to a formal betrothal with Lüdeke's son, Hans von Sehnden. The little girl was somewhat perplexed as to what was taking place, but she had promised to be on her best behavior when Papa and Mama took her to the great Stadkirche. When Papa walked all the way down the long aisle with her, she knew something momentous was happening because all the people, Papa's and Onkel Lüdeke's friends, were smiling at her. When they stood before the altar, Papa explained that she must repeat everything Pastor Storch said to her. Then he placed her hand in that of this nice, fat, jolly man whom she was told to call Hans, even though Mama had always taught her to address adults as Master or Mistress. After the ceremony was over Papa explained to her that Hans would be her husband in about ten or twelve years' time.

Since it was more years than she had yet lived, such a span of time into the future was a bit beyond her comprehension. But she was a good girl and always obeyed Papa and Mama, so she believed him.

Soon after the betrothal took place, Lüdeke, ever the consummate politician, saw to it that Franz Stockman was elected to the Town Council. And beyond that, Lüdeke promised in strictest confidence that after his death Franz would be the next Head Master of the Gewandschneider, an even more prestigious and powerful office. Lüdeke also kept a long-neglected promise to himself. He finally had copies made of the Mestwart Stipendium, the so-called Veerssische Lehn, that had come down through his mother from distant ancestor Johann Wiese. He gave the first copy to Hans at Christmas and then others to his other married sons and daughter, but only to them. The beautifully hand-written document ran to several pages and was too expensive to have copied to waste on those with no prospects of descendants.

By 1581 Lüdeke was so crippled and in such pain that he could hardly rise from his bed. After much prayerful deliberation and much urging by Gretchen, he finally decided it was time to retire from the active life. It was a heart-wrenching decision. Between him and his father, the von Sehnden had ruled Celle for the better part of the entire sixteenth century. With great misgiving and sadness he resigned as Bürgermeister and saw to it that Henning Behr was elected in his place.

In 1582 Lüdeke left this earth to join his three friends, and with his passing so ended the glory days of Celle.

Historical Notes

This is a work of fiction. However, I shall not make the usual disclaimer about 'any resemblance to persons living or dead.' Most of the main characters were real people. I have long wanted to tell their story but soon discovered that a genealogy is a mere skeleton, often nothing more than a list of names. Who were these people? What were their lives like? What were their joys and sorrows? Placing them in the context of the history of their period might suggest general things that could have affected their lives, thus fleshing out the skeleton a bit. But I decided that fiction was the only medium that could bring them to life, that could describe their successes and failures, their hopes and dreams, their loves and losses, their souls and bodies.

But for those historical purists among my readers, I hope the following notes will help sort out fact from fiction.

Book I: The Opportunists

Chapter 1

Wittekind and his brother Bruno were renowned Saxon heroes. They each had a son and, at least Wittekind, a grandson named Bruno from whence traditionally the Bruns (Brunos-son) family is descended. The ancient Saxons kept no written records, although there is a rich and extensive oral tradition. Unfortunately, the only written record of the events in the story is by the Carolingian Chronicler and necessarily prejudiced. I have tried to choose those events that were either confirmed by the chronicles or so thoroughly imbued in the folk history that there must be some truth to them. The other characters, other than Charlemagne (Karl der Grosse) himself, are all fictitious.

The remains of the earthwork fortress of Brunsburg may be seen to this day outside the hamlet of Heemsen. All other place names are real.

Chapter 2

Duke Heinrich der Löwe (the Lion), his wife Mathilde and the Emperor Friedrich Barbarossa are real. Heinrich did make a pilgrimage to the Holy Land between the Crusades, but Mathilde was left behind as Regent. I have chosen to have her accompany him in order to describe places and events important to the period and especially to invent an explanation of the unusual von Sehnden coat-of-arms. That there were von Sehnden and von Eltze living at the time in the area there is no doubt, but there is no record of them. There was a monk-priest Theodorich who made a pilgrimage to the Holy Land circa 1172 and wrote an excellent travel guide. That he was part of the Saxon group is doubtful, but I have chosen to borrow his name. All others are fictitious.

Chapter 3

This chapter is totally fictitious, its main purpose to describe the cultural, religious, economic, and industrial 'revolution' that was occurring at this high point of the Middle Ages, along with the gradual demise of the feudal system, as seen through the adventures of the two main characters. One Johann von Sehnde is mentioned several times during the thirteenth century in the records of the Hildesheim Cathedral. One Tyle von Eltze was one of the earliest mayors of Celle. I have tried to describe as accurately as possible circumstances that could have prevailed in each of the locales the two young men visited.

Chapter 4

Johann Wiese, his mother Elizabeth and Christian Wernering are all real, all mentioned in Johann's Foundation. The relationship between Johann and Christian is quite unclear. The obscure Latin of the testament states only 'a blood relative on the maternal side.' Borchardus de Monte (German: Bergmann) is mentioned as Johann's sponsor. The farm in Veerssen existed and along with other properties is mentioned in a late (1580) note at the end of a copy of the original as having been sold by Master Mestwart. All events are fictional but are typical of the period.

Chapter 5

All the main characters are real. However, we know almost nothing about them. Brandt von Eltze was mayor of Celle from 1421 on and off until 1444. Both his sons were elected to the Town Council in 1444, and Lüdeke was mayor in 1451, Eggeling from 1470 to 1482. How or why Lüdeke von Sehnden and Lüdeke Mestwart came to Celle is a total mystery. Only one phrase in each case hints. Lüdeke von Sehnden, "Jahrknecht bey I.F. Gnaden toh Zelle von dem Dörpe Sehnden ut dem Frien" (A year-knight [i.e., squire] by [the Duke's] grace to Celle from the village of Sehnde, unmarried). Of Lüdeke Mestwart, the source states merely that he was "filius [son] of Heinecke Mestwart Senator Uelcensis (councilman of Uelzen), whose wife Bedecke Wernering [was] Christian Wernering's daughter."

Lüdeke Mestwart was elected to the Council in 1447 and mayor from 1456 to 1479. His founding of St. Anna's and his many gifts to the church are well documented. Ludeke von Sehnden was councilman from 1464 on, but never mayor. Heinrich Bünsel did own the most boats in Celle at the time, but sources differ widely as to how many.

Von Sehnden's courier service is totally imaginary, and here I must plead to one anachronism. Franz von Thurn und Taxis was awarded the Imperial Post by Emperor Friedrich III's son Maximilian, but the family was already operator of a successful postal service throughout northern Italy from the 1440's on and could well have been interested in such routes in Germany to solidify their bid for the post.

Rudolf von Habsburg is fictitious. Duke Otto did, indeed, die from a broken neck after a fall from his horse in a tourney in the Stechbahn in 1471, but we have no idea who his final opponent was. I have used this as an excuse for Duke Heinrich's later most unreasonable hatred for the Habsburgs.

Book II: Merchants and Mayors

Chapter 6

All of the main characters except Catherine Stockman are real people, but again, we know very little about them. That St. Anna's was Anna Mestwart's favorite charity there is no doubt, since her father founded it and the family was known for its piety. Lüdeke von Sehnden was mayor from 1505 to 1542. He was known as 'der Ältere' (the Elder)—as opposed to his son, later known as 'der Jüngere' (the Younger)—and because his father was never mayor. This has confused some historians into thinking there were only two Lüdekes, but in fact there were three—grandfather, father and son. Events are mostly imaginary. The story of Hinrik Stockman's origins is pure fantasy. A strong tradition has it that he was an impoverished orphan. Only one record mentions Balthasar Murmester as his stepfather, but whether Hinrik was a total orphan or whether Balthasar married his mother is not known.

Chapter 7

All main characters are real, but of Ilsebe's origins we know nothing. In the only document I could find even her last name is so illegible I had to guess at it. Even their marriage year is an educated guess, based on the later dates of the children. During the turmoil of the Reformation the church records disappear for almost a century. The Memorial Book ends at the beginning, of the 1500's and the Churcn Books do not start until the early part of the seventeenth century. Sketchy but more reliable are the civil records, such as Lüdeke von Sehnden's tax register (curiously bound with a piece of music parchment from the huge choir books formerly used in the church or perhaps from the monastery). From this we know when Balthasar acquired the house on Schuhstrasse, because he had lost his house in the Blomlage due to the wall. Most other personal events in the lives of the two families are imaginary but could well have happened.

Wolf Cyclop came to Celle as the Duke's physician but was quickly thrown out of town when Ernst found his rabble-rousing too radical for his tastes.

Chapter 8

There is no indication that any of the three friends accompanied Duke Ernst to Speyer, but it is entirely possible that one or more did so, particularly Eggeling, as the von Eltze had been advisors to the Dukes for centuries. The riots against the Franciscans and subsequent closure of the monastery are well recorded, but there is nothing to indicate that either

Balthasar's or Berndt's death had anything to do with it. We only know that in 1526 the house in Schuhstrasse was in Hinrik Stockman's name alone and the same year Berndt disappears from the records.

Chapter 9

The monks at Heiligenberg kept fairly accurate records up until the time of the Reformation, but unfortunately, few are extant. How the dissolution took place or why it was so utterly destroyed we do not know, since this was rarely the case in the rest of the Duchy. Only a few brief notations in the records of Ulrich von Broitzen point to the obstinacy of the monks and to the despicable character of Graf Jobst. Von Broitzen does note that Jobst Busse, the last monk from Heiligenberg, was the first Pastor at Vilsen.

These particular Bruns characters are fictitious, but the family has lived in the area since time immemorial and still does today. They do not enter into the written records, since there were none, until well over a century later.

Henning Behr is real, as is Lüdeke von Sehnden, but whether such an expedition took place is hypothetical. Markus Lindemann is fictional, but there was a family of that name living in Celle at the time, which over 150 years later became prominent in Bruchhausen.

Chapter 10

All of the main characters are real except for the Bruns for reasons cited previously, but the events in their personal lives are as I have chosen to believe they might have happened. All historical events, such as the battle at Drakenburg, actually took place, but my description of the details is purely imaginary.

Chapter 11

Same note as above. The circumstances of the Stockman children's marriages are fictitious, but at least we know their spouses' names and, in some cases, their occupations. Hinrik's will and testament is in the Stadtarchiv at Celle. Reading between the lines, his disenchantment with his second wife Geske and his children by her becomes painfully obvious. That Appolonia was the Duchess' godchild is quite probable, but that she attended the funeral in Uelzen is only my guess.

She did die several years before her father Hinrik.

The description of what remained of the monastery at Heiligenberg is taken from the inventory of the Dowager Countess Katharine of 8 May 1563, done shortly after the death of her husband Graf Albrecht. What part, if any, the Bruns played in the church's demolition is not known, but they did acquire a piece of the property around this same time.

Chapter 12

Hinrik Stockman's Stipendium is the first thing to greet the visitor to the Celle Stadtarchiv, where it is exhibited with pride. The distribution of the cloth, from which I have quoted precisely, is also among their collection. Franz was an able executor until his death in 1622, and his quaint and meticulous entries recording the distribution each Easter make interesting reading. The first person to receive the award was Jürgen Stockman, on the occasion of his marriage. This must have been paid only a week or so after Hinrik's death and reflects the painstaking care with which Franz carried out his father's instructions. After that, several grandchildren received wedding payments. In 1581–2 the first student stipend was paid to Heinrich Kregel, Margarethe's eldest son, and then in 1583–4 another to Hinrik's son Michel so that he could study at Wittenberg. After that it was all wedding payments and, as Franz predicted, they soon were far behind. The list of 'Exspectanten' grew longer and longer until by the end of the nineteenth century people were being paid as much as sixty or seventy years after their wedding, if they were still alive! But through thick and thin it was paid regularly until the end of World War I. Then, sadly, the terrible inflation of the early 1920's wiped out the capital itself. The last list of Exspectanten drawn up in 1912, had been projected to 1950.

I have figured out, quite imprecisely, that if the twenty Thalers were still being paid today, it would represent approximately $30,000 in purchasing power. Even back in the sixteenth century the twenty Thalers was at least five to ten times the annual income of the average poor to middle-class family!

Epilogue

Although Celle remained the ducal Residenzstadt for another hundred years and the great merchant fortunes survived another fifty years or so, the preeminence of north Germany in the world of commerce was giving way to Holland and England, and the once mighty Hanse was fading into history. Many historians cite the shift of trade from the North Sea to the Atlantic as the deciding factor in its demise, but there were two other important causes. In the fall and sack of Antwerp by the Spanish in 1585 the Hanse merchants suffered tremendous losses. The financial center moved to Amsterdam and the newly independent Dutch turned from being merely shippers to becoming traders. The Dutch sea captains' demands for *mare librum*—freedom of the seas—clashed head-on with the Hanse's rigid policy of monopolistic rights and privileges. Moreover, increasingly na tionalistic policies in the countries outside Germany formerly dominated by the Hanse led to the loss of most of their overseas posts. St . Peter's Court, the Hanse settlement in Novgorod, had long since been closed by Ivan III of Russia. Sweden imposed crippling tolls and duties in an attempt to control all Baltic trade. Denmark-Norway waited a little longer but with the shift of the herring shoals to the North Sea and the increasing trade with the Dutch in 1560 took over Bergen.

The final blow came when Elizabeth I closed tne Stahlyard in London in August 1589 in retaliation against Charles V's edict refusing to allow the English Merchant Adventurers to trade in Germany. An interesting sidelight—the famous Golden Ship of Uelzen (see chapter 4) had somehow over the centuries made its way to London. The last merchant to leave the Stahlyard, one Valentin von Horn, brought the Golden Ship back with him, and it may be seen today in the Marienkirche at Uelzen.

The other reason for the demise of the Hanse was the very lack of this nationalistic backing from a unified German state. After the Peace of Augsburg the princes were too busy consolidating their political power. Religious reasons for opposing the Emperor took second place to constitutional ones. The Imperial Free Cities, who belonged to no one, without the powerful unity of the Hanse were left to fend for themselves. Some, such as Hamburg, defied the Imperial Edict, trading openly with the English and Dutch and prospered. Hamburg finally got its own bank in 1619. Others, including the two Queens of the Hanse, Lübeck and Cologne, faded into provincial backwaters, as did Celle.

Furthermore with the new religious freedom the second and third generations of the wealthy Bürger families seemed to be spending more money on civic projects, such as Lüdeke's Rathaus, rather than laboring diligently to earn it as their fathers had. The interior of the Celle Rathaus was completed by Hans Gudehus and others by 1588. The new part was called the *Hochzeitshaus* because the upper floor was used for weddings and other Bürger festivities. The ground floor was a large dance hall, which also served as a theater and, at long last, a dry place under one roof where the Gewandschneider could set up their cloth displays on market days.

Franz Stockman did indeed become Head Master of the Gewand-schneider and was so highly regarded that the records of the proceedings often refer to him as 'our beloved father' or cousin or whatever. He was elected to the Council in 1580 and served as Bürgermeister from 1594 to 1619. The next volume entitled *The Heirs* begins with Dorothea's story.

Acknowledgments

My greatest debt is to my grandmother Marie Anna Campsheide, born Bruns, who first told me about the orphaned ancestor who became a great merchant and left the Stipendium. So many people in Germany were helpful, I cannot list them all, but I must single out a few extra-special ones. Heinrich Schlake of Bruchhausen, the Churchbook Custodian of Vilsen, was infinitely patient on several trips there and very interested in my research. He taught me many valuable things about genealogical research in Germany. Hermann Bornbusch, retired archivist of Bruchhausen, pointed me to Hinrik Stockman and turned out to be a seventh cousin! Dr. Guenter, director of the Stadtarchiv in Celle, allowed me to photograph and copy the Stockman Stipendium and gave me free access to all their files. Dr. Egge, Stadtarchivist in Uelzen, discovered for me the 1580 copy of the Veerssische Lehn (von Sehnden-Mestwart Stipendium).